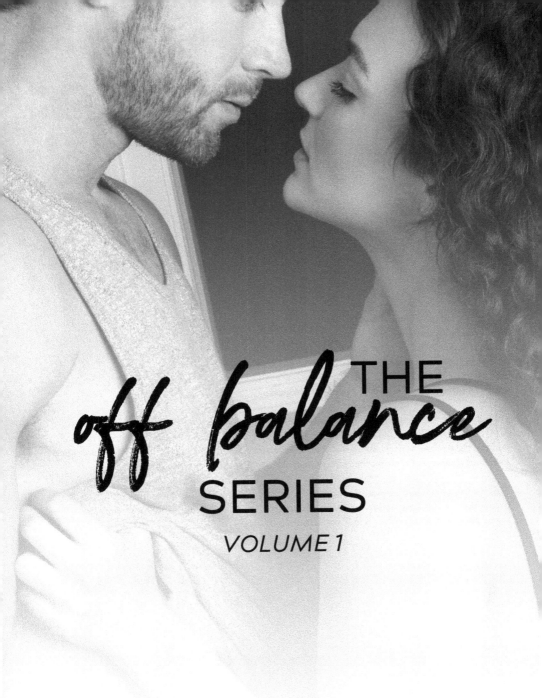

THE off balance SERIES

VOLUME 1

LUCIA FRANCO

Edited by Nadine Winningham
Proofread by Amber Hodge
Cover Design by Okay Creations
Formatted by Champagne Book Design
Photography by Lindee Robinson
Cover Models Shelby Smith and Andrew Kruczynski

MORE NOVELS BY LUCIA FRANCO

Standalone Titles

You'll Think of Me
Hold On to Me

Hush, Hush Duet

Hush, Hush
Say Yes

Off Balance series

Balance
Execution
Release
Twist
Dismount
Out of Bounds

The Off Balance series is a continuation series. The novels must be read in order to follow the story.

This story is purely fictional and does not reflect on real-life events.

Each novel in this five-part series follows a heavy May-December romance between a gymnast and a coach. If you consider this subject and any related content disturbing, then the Off Balance series is not for you.

Gymnastics is a hands-on sport that involves hours of close contact with a coach. My goal was to focus on the beauty of the sport in detail, show the emotional aspect of the dedication an athlete makes, and show how two people are able to cross forbidden boundaries and evolve together.

This story will push you, question you, and take you outside of your comfort zone.

The Off Balance series is intended only for readers 18 years of age and older. Reader discretion is advised.

—Lucia

GLOSSARY

All-Around A category of gymnastics that includes all the events. The all-around champion of an event earns the highest total score from all events combined.

Amanar A Yurchenko-style vault, meaning the gymnast performs a round-off onto the board, a back handspring onto the vault with a two-and-a-half twisting layout backflip.

Cast A push off the bar with hips and lifts the body to straighten the shoulders and finish in handstand.

Deduction Points taken off a gymnast's score for errors. Most deductions are pre-determined, such as a 0.5 deduction for a fall from an apparatus or a 0.1 deduction for stepping out of bounds on the floor exercise.

Dismount The last skill in a gymnastics routine. For most events the method used to get off the event apparatus.

Elite International Elite, the highest level of gymnastics.

Execution The performance of a routine. Form, style, and technique used to complete the skills constitute the level of execution of an exercise. Bent knees, poor toe point and an arched or loose held body position are all examples of poor execution.

Giant Performed on bars, a swing in which the body is fully extended and moving through a 360-degree rotation around the bar.

Full-In A full-twisting double back tuck, with the twist happening in the first backflip. It can be done in a tucked, piked, or layout position and is used in both men's and women's gymnastics.

Free Hip Circle Performed on the uneven bars or high bar, the body circles around the bar without the body touching the bar. There are both front hip circles and back hip circles.

Handspring Springing off the hands by putting the weight on the arms and using a strong push from the shoulders. Can be done either forward or backward, and is usually a connecting movement. This skill can be performed on floor, vault, and beam.

Heel Drive A termed used by coaches to inform the gymnasts they want them to drive their heels harder up and over on the front side of a handspring vault or front handspring on floor. Stronger heel drives create more rotation and potential for block and power.

Hecht Mount A mount where the gymnast jumps off a spring board while keeping their arms straight, pushes off the low bar, and catches the high bar.

Hop Full A giant to handstand. Once toes are above the bar, a full 360-degree turn in a handstand on the high bar.

Inverted Cross Performed by men on the rings. It is an upside down cross.

Iron Cross A strength move performed by men on the rings. The gymnast holds the rings straight out on either side of their body while holding themselves up. Arms are perpendicular to the body.

Jaeger Performed on bars, a gymnast swings from a front giant and lets go of the bar, completes a front flip and catches the bar again. Jaeger can be done in the straddle, pike, and layout position, and is occasionally performed in a tucked position.

Kip The most commonly used mount for bars, the gymnast glides forward, pulls their feet to the bar, then pushes up to front support, resting their hips on the bar.

L-Grip One hand is in the reverse grip position. This is an awkward grip and difficult to use.

Layout A stretched body position.

Layout Timers A drill that simulates the feel of a skill, or the set for a skill without the risk of completing the skill.

Lines Straight, perfect lines of the body.

Overshoot, also known as Bail A transition from the high bar facing the low bar. The gymnast swings up and over the low bar with a half-turn to catch the low bar ending in a handstand.

Pike The body bent forward at the waist with the legs kept straight; an L position.

Pirouette Used in both gymnastics and dance to refer to a turn around the body's longitudinal axis. It is used to refer to a handstand turning moves on bars.

Rips In gymnastics, a rip occurs when a gymnast works so hard on the bars or rings that they tear off a flap of skin from their hand. The injury is like a blister that breaks open.

Release Leaving the bar to perform a skill before re-grasping it.

Relevé This is a dance term that is often used in gymnastics. In a relevé, the gymnast is standing on toes and has straight legs.

Reverse Grip A swing around the bar back-first with arms rotated inwards and hands facing upwards.

Round-off A turning movement, with a push-off on one leg, while swinging the legs upward in a fast cartwheel motion into a 90-degree turn where legs come together before landing on both feet. The lead-off to a number of skills used to perform on vault, beam, and floor.

Salto Flip or somersault, with the feet coming up over the head and the body rotating around the axis of the waist.

Sequence Two or more skills performed together, creating a different skill or activity.

Shaposhnikva A clear hip circle on the low bar then flying backward to the high bar.

Stalder Starts in handstand with the gymnast moving backward and circling the bar with legs straddled on either side of their arms or inside their arms.

Stick To land and remain standing without requiring a step. A proper stick position is with legs bent, shoulders above hips, arms forward.

Straddle Back An uneven bar transition done from a swing backwards on the high bar over low bar, while catching the low bar in a handstand.

Switch Ring Performed on floor and the balance beam. The gymnast jumps with both feet, lifting their legs into a 180-degree split with the back leg coming up to touch their head.

Tap Swing Performed on bars, an aggressive tap toward the ceiling in a swinging motion. This gives the gymnast the necessary momentum to swing around the bar to perform a giant or to go into a release move.

Toe On Swing around the bar with body piked so much the feet are on the bar.

Tour Jeté A dance leap where the dancer leaps on one foot, makes a full turn in the air, and lands on the other foot.

Tsavdaridou Performed on beam, a round-off back handspring with full twist to swing down.

Tuck The knees and hips are bent and drawn into the chest. The body is folded at the waist.

Twist The gymnast rotates around the body's longitudinal axis, defined by the spine. Performed on all apparatuses.

Yurchenko Round-off entry onto the board, back handspring onto the vaulting table and Salto off the vault table. The gymnast may twist on the way off.

balance

BOOK 1 IN THE OFF BALANCE SERIES

"Any coach who has been coaching for ten years and says he never fell in love with an athlete or vice versa is lying."

chapter 1

"**A**BSOLUTELY NOT!"

My father's harsh voice boomed around his home office.

"You haven't even heard what I have to say," I argued my point, not settling for anything less than his full attention.

"I don't care what you have to say. You can talk until you're blue in the face. You are not moving to New Hampshire. End of discussion."

"Dad, just listen. Gymnastics—"

"I've made my decision and it's not changing." He picked up his pen and focused on the papers in front of him. "Now, please, I have work to do."

Devastation sucker punched me in the gut. I was surprised by how unreasonable he was being in not letting me speak. New Hampshire was home to one of the best gymnastics facilities in the country and I'd prove it to him. My weeks of research wouldn't be wasted. I would not give up, I just had to try harder.

"It's renowned for its coaching and athletes," I pressed on.

"No." He gave me his infamous look, the one capable of making a grown man flinch.

My future was at stake and I had to fight for it. As much as I would miss my current gym, it was no longer useful to me. There were only so many extra hours of conditioning and private classes I could take. Advancement in this sport required the proper training, and I couldn't get it at my old gym.

"Transferring to another gym isn't unheard of. A lot of families send their gymnasts to train at better facilities." I stood my ground.

"Adrianna Francesca Rossi!" His tone and anger bled into my frustration, but it didn't stop me.

"Just hear me out! Please," I pleaded, on the verge of tears. My mother would no doubt sniff them in the air and be on me like a bloodhound within seconds. Tears showed weakness, and a Rossi was never weak—at least according to her.

Dad didn't respond. Instead, he stared right through me.

Blowing out a loud, aggravated breath, I stood up and peered through the large window in his office which overlooked the expansive, lush lawn in our backyard. My gaze drifted over to the right, catching the beautiful colors of the late afternoon sun reflecting off the pool. We lived in one of the most elite neighborhoods on the prestigious Amelia Island. We had everything money could buy. Everything except a great one-of-a-kind gymnastics coach that could help push me closer to achieving my dream.

Turning back to my dad, I took in the flare of his nostrils and stiff jaw. He had become eerily still. The room grew cold and goose bumps broke out on my skin. I knew this side of him, and it wasn't pretty. This was a side nobody dared to test.

I had pushed too far.

"Go," he said. "Now." His voice was quiet and calm, dismissing me to return to his work.

I fled his office and retreated to my bedroom, slamming the door just as the tears started to fall.

Gymnastics was everything to me—it was my heart and soul, the air I breathed. It was the one thing that allowed me to be me. To express myself creatively in the way I chose, not how someone else decided for me. I'd rotated between eating, sleeping, and flipping for as long as I could remember. The competitiveness, the challenge of mastering a new skill. The way I defied gravity—my heart soaring, the sound of applause, the gasp from the audience—made the sacrifice worth every bit of pain and manipulation my body went through. Nothing could take that feeling away.

It was the one place I could be free from the restraints my family's name had on me.

My name is Adrianna Rossi and I'm a competitive gymnast. Elite gymnast, to be exact. Or I would be, as soon as I had the right coach.

I had completed all levels required according to USA gymnastics in order to move forward and test for elite. It was only a matter of time before I held the coveted rank. I trained day in and day out for this. My days consisted of four-hour training sessions in the gym, a tutor to homeschool me, and a private chef to prepare my calculated caloric meals.

As I fell onto my bed, devastation hit me hard. The rejection crushed my heart and it felt like my dreams were slowly being ripped away.

Like most hungry gymnasts, my ultimate goal was the Olympics.

If I graphed the training along with my age, I could possibly compete in my first Olympic Games by the time I was twenty. *Possibly*, being the key word. While twenty was still considered youthful by normal standards, it was ancient in the gymnastics world. Though, it wasn't unheard of to compete in The Games at that age. One of my favorites, Svetlana Khorkina, competed in three Olympics by the age of twenty-five, her first at seventeen. Oksana Chusovitina, who competed in six Olympic Games, also started at seventeen. So my goal wasn't completely farfetched, I just needed the proper training. I was good, but I wanted to be great. And the only way to be great was to train with the best.

Though I was young, I wasn't naive. I knew what kind of mental and physical abuse my body would go through in order to reach the professional level. I needed a drill sergeant with a sharp eye.

Needed it, and wanted it.

I didn't fully understand why my dad objected to me leaving. I knew he thought of gymnastics as a hobby, but he'd always done anything to placate me. He never told me no and usually threw money at whatever my heart desired. It wasn't as if he spent much time at home anyway. Frank Rossi was too occupied with expanding and maintaining his real estate empire. Rossi Enterprises was one of the top developers, with properties worldwide. He left my mom in charge of raising my brother and me, which was a joke.

When I first began gymnastics at three years old, my mother used to sit at my practices and attend my meets. It was all about appearances back then, but I was young so she really didn't have much of a choice. However, the older I got, the less of an effort she made. I think the last meet she came to I was twelve years old. Mom was usually too busy with her charity work or trying to keep my older brother, Xavier, out of the media.

At first their lack of interest bothered me. I wanted them to *want* to be there, to watch me tumble and flip and balance on the beam. To see me move up to another level or stick a dismount without wobbling. I craved my parents' attention like all children do, but after years of begging, I eventually gave up and learned to adapt to their indifference. Nowadays, Mom rarely came to practice, and neither of my parents attended many competitions.

Their actions forced me to be independent, something I quickly learned to value. That being said, I refused to give up. I wouldn't let anything, or anyone, take my end goal away from me.

I wasn't sure how much time had passed when I heard a faint knock on my door. I cracked my eyes open and was surprised by the darkness surrounding me. Another, louder knock sounded, and I prayed it wasn't my mom.

"Yeah?"

"Ana?" Relief coursed through me at the sound of my dad's voice. "Can I come in?"

A fatigued sigh rolled off my lips as I sat up on the edge of my bed. "Come in."

Dad opened the door, flipping on the light switch as he walked in. A quick glance at my reflection in the mirror on the adjacent wall had me pulling back in shock. My face was blotchy and swollen from crying. Hair lay stuck and matted to my face. I was a hot mess.

I squinted at my dad, trying to adjust to the light. The sorrow in his heavy eyes showed. It was clear he was remorseful over his decision and the way he reacted. The last time I'd seen him, he'd been dressed in a clean, crisp shirt and tie. Now the tie was gone, a few buttons were undone and his sleeves were rolled up. He was disheveled and worn out, and I knew I was the reason. I'd acted like a spoiled brat and argued with him, something I always tried to refrain from. Usually it was my older brother who caused so much turmoil for my parents, not me.

"Yes, Dad?" I tried to lighten the tension. A soft smile charmed his face. I was a daddy's girl through and through, and he knew it.

"May I sit with you?"

I nodded, and he sat next to me, the mattress dipping a little. He moved the tangled hair from my cheeks and eyed me carefully.

"You look like you've been crying, which can only mean I'm at fault."

I flattened my lips and cast my eyes down. "I may have been."

"I apologize, sweetheart." He ran a tired hand down his face. "About the gymnastics…"

"Yeah?"

"Listen, it's not that I don't want you to do it, it's that I don't want you moving so far away on your own. You're still young and the world is a dangerous place. What if something happened to you? I wouldn't be able to get to you fast enough."

My voice softened over his concern. "Dad, you're always traveling for work." My words caused him to wince, and I instantly felt terrible for stating the fact. But it was the truth, and I had to get my point across. "What would be the difference?"

He ran a hand through his salt and pepper hair. "You're right. I do travel a lot for work, and I'm sorry I'm not around enough, but the difference is I'm an experienced adult and you're not."

I slouched in defeat. "I know. I was just hoping you'd give it some thought. It's not like I'd be completely alone. I'd live in a shared apartment with a den mom and other gymnasts."

"Not *your* mom, though. I don't even know those women, Adrianna. You're my daughter. I can't trust them with you."

I gave him a serious look. "Dad, we both know Mom isn't the kind of mother to do something like that for me." The kind of mother who gives and does anything for her children to see them thrive. Joy Rossi had more important things on her agenda.

My dad sighed. "You've put up a good argument and I've thought about it." I perked up. "I might have a compromise. I have a business associate in Cape Coral who happens to coach gymnastics. Let me give him a call and see what he says."

My eyes widened. "Where's that?"

"South. About two hours or so from here. It's right outside of Florida near the water."

I paused, pursing my lips together. "You have a friend who's a coach? How did I not know this?"

"You met him when you were younger, though you probably don't remember. He bought some real estate from me many years ago and we've stayed in touch. Every so often we'll flip a house together, or he'll ask for advice on property. His name is Konstantin."

The name didn't ring any bells. "What level does he coach?"

"That I don't know. I only know he's a former Russian Olympian and is good at what he does."

Hope sprouted inside of me to the point I couldn't contain my smile. Russians were crazy, their gymnastics training even crazier, which caused my stomach to flutter with anxiety. I wouldn't complain, I'd take what I could.

Beggars couldn't be choosers.

"I can't believe you didn't tell me this sooner."

"His past doesn't come up in our real estate transactions. I didn't know you weren't happy at your current gym," he countered. "If you'd told me your coaches weren't cutting it, Konstantin could've stepped in sooner."

Touché.

"When are you going to call him? Can you call now? Please?" Enthusiastically, I shook his arm and jumped, bobbing on my knees. "Dad!"

He chuckled at my eagerness, the light in his eyes returning. My dad and I had the same exact shade of green eyes. I resembled him the most. From my dark hair, thin straight nose, and skin tone, we were very similar. And just like my dad, when I got excited about something, my eyes turned a brilliant jade color. Although, I wasn't sure where the deep crimson tones in my hair or freckles came from.

He faked a sigh, restraining a smile. "Come into my office and I'll give him a call."

"Really?" I shrieked. When he nodded, I threw my arms around his shoulders and hugged him tightly. "Oh, thank you, Dad! Thank you! Thank you! Thank you!"

He patted my back lovingly. I jumped from my bed and trailed closely behind. Once we were back in his office, I plopped down into a studded leather chair in front of his desk. I placed my hands under my thighs so I didn't fidget while my father got situated.

And by situated, I mean pouring himself a glass of bourbon.

"All right, remind me again what level you are. What's the goal you want to achieve?"

Sadness crept inside me. I wish he knew without me having to remind him. The man could spout off twenty different business transactions from the top of his head, but he couldn't retain a few facts about his daughter.

"I'm a level ten, but I want to test for elite. Find out if he coaches elite first and if he has an elite program."

He nodded and dialed a number, enabling the speakerphone. The phone rang a few times until a deep voice picked up.

"Allo?"

My brows creased together. *A-low?*

"Konstantin, my friend, Frank Rossi here. How are you doing?"

"Frank, it is good to hear your voice. You are just the man I wanted to speak with actually." Dad mentioned he was Russian, and his heavy accent confirmed it.

"Is that so? Perfect timing, then. Did you happen to get my Christmas gift? I sent a bottle of my favorite vodka to you and that pretty girlfriend of yours."

Konstantin paused, laughing lightly. "I will have to ask Katja when I get home. Her appetite for vodka is just as voracious as mine. I hope she did not drink it all without me." He chuckled, as did my dad. "Thank you in advance. That was very kind of you."

"How is Katja doing? Have you guys decided to settle down yet?" Dad asked, swirling his glass tumbler of bourbon. As much as I liked hearing him catch up with his friend, I was anxious for him to get to the point.

"Ah, not yet," he responded with a deep sigh. "It is not for her lack of trying. All in good time."

Dad chuckled and my heart started to beat faster over his next set of words. "I have a question for you. Are you still coaching gymnastics?"

"Funny you should ask. I am, and I just happened to buy World Cup from the previous owners about a year ago. I was thinking about expanding it, but I wanted your expertise on whether it is worth it or not."

"Ah… " Dad's brows lifted, a sparkle twinkling in his eyes. I knew that look. It was his chance to dabble in something. "How perfect the timing is, then. Do you recall telling me when my precious daughter was ready to switch to give you a call?"

He paused. Silence filled the air. My heart stopped. "I do."

"She came to me earlier asking to transfer to some gym in New Hampshire. Do you know of any gym over there?"

"Not one worth remembering."

Dad's eyes bore into mine. He raised a pointed brow. "Well, she said it's one of the best gyms on the East Coast." He let out a huff. "I can't imagine anyone being better than you."

Konstantin chuckled. "You flatter me. I had no idea your daughter was still training. Tell me, what level is she."

I held up two hands to remind him.

"She's a level ten, but she said her gym doesn't have an—"

"Elite coach," I whispered.

"Elite coach, which is what she's telling me she needs," Dad said. "Are you elite?" I cringed at my dad's question. *He* wouldn't be elite, he would coach elite.

"I do have an elite program and team of elite girls." The line goes silent and I hold my breath. "Correct me if I am wrong, but is your daughter in high school now?"

"She is indeed. She'll be graduating soon," he added, proudly.

"Hmm. That is quite old for an elite. Is she training for college now?"

"To be honest, I'm not sure what she plans to do, or can do. I just know she wants to train at an exclusive gym."

That hurt my heart, like a knife to the chest. I'd just told him a few hours earlier what my plans for the future were.

"All right." He cleared his throat. "I have a dinner meeting I need to get to, so can I give you a call in the morning and we can go over this?"

"Perfect, sounds like a plan. I look forward to hearing from you. While we're at it, we can also discuss your expansion idea on your new gym."

"Even better."

When Dad hung up the phone, I didn't feel any better. I frowned. It didn't sound like a sure thing once he heard my age. I almost wished he hadn't been on speakerphone.

"Don't worry, sweetheart. There isn't anything I can't make happen now."

chapter 2

STARING OUT THE WINDOW, I COULDN'T SEE BEYOND MY TRANSPARENT REFLECTION as we passed another mile marker.

My heart fluttered and a small smile curved my lips thinking about how long I'd waited for this moment. In fact, I couldn't remember a time I'd been this happy… or impatient, edgy, and restless. I was a wheel of emotions. The knots in my stomach pulled tighter as anxiety swirled through me at breakneck speed.

I took a deep breath and rested against the cold leather seat, praying it wasn't much farther.

Two months ago, Dad had come through and gotten me into World Cup Academy of Gymnastics, which happened to be one of the top rated gymnastic training centers in Georgia. With my heart set on finding the best gym, I had tunnel vision after a teammate had mentioned the one in New Hampshire. It never dawned on me to look anywhere else. From what I gathered, Dad made a generous donation to World Cup, therefore allowing me the opportunity to train at the facility. Being a struggling athlete, I was desperate to reach the next level. I didn't want to rely on my dad and his business relations, but if it helped get me closer to my dream, then so be it.

As my dad had always said, "You use your connections." I was ready to do whatever it took. This was the one—and only time—I was truly happy about coming from an affluent family.

I'd done some research and found out World Cup wasn't just any gym. Previously owned by former top ranking coaches around the world, it was renowned for its training and ability to take athletes to a new level. The coaches were very particular, elite gymnasts were handpicked, and it took natural-born talent and dedication to be one of its members. Some of the best gymnasts had come out of this gym, trained by a group of intense coaches who pushed their limits with their level of training.

It seemed like hours had passed by the time we veered to the right, finally exiting the highway. Curving around and following the snake-like bend down the street, we pulled up to a gray building with dark tinted windows a couple of minutes later.

"So this is what you want?" my father asked as he made his way around the Escalade. He placed his hands into the pockets of his expensive, tailored pants and surveyed the place as the wind billowed against him.

"More than anything," I replied, unable to hide the smile on my face. I'd been rendered speechless while I stared at the large structure before me. This was what I'd wanted for the past year, and now it was mine. Happiness surged through me fast and my smile grew larger.

My mother stepped out wearing bright red high heels with a matching red dress. Leave it to Joy Rossi to dress like the First Lady. She pulled her stark white jacket tight around her waist, her eyes skittering around, not a blonde hair out of place despite the wind's effort. Judging by the scowl on her face, you'd think we were in the dingiest place on earth.

"This is probably where muggers hide at night and bums come to sleep. Of all the gyms, I can't believe Konstantin picked this place. It looks… disgusting."

I couldn't tell if her shudder was from the breeze or the fact that she thought I had purposely picked some remote serial killer town with no running water or electricity.

"Joy," my father warned.

I shook my head, not agreeing with her judgmental attitude. How she came to that conclusion in a matter of two minutes was beyond me. Deep down, I knew Dad would never have agreed to this had he not done his own research and thought it was unsafe.

Glancing around, all I could see were commercial buildings nearby and hunter green dumpsters placed sporadically outside. Obviously, it was a part of town where industrial businesses were located—a commercial area—not fancy, five-star restaurants where my mother was used to dining, or ritzy boutiques where they didn't sell anything that wasn't couture or in season. Unfortunately, she didn't see things my way. What she saw were dim colors with no life, and most importantly, a place where she would gain nothing.

I saw my future. I saw my dream staring at me from behind the concrete walls, daring me to get my ass moving.

Dad held his arm out, gesturing for me to lead the way, and I headed up the walkway toward the entrance. Grabbing the cold door handle, I pulled it open and stepped inside World Cup with my parents following closely behind.

The smell of chalk permeated the air and my stomach quivered at the first intake of the aroma into my lungs. It was a distinct scent, and taste, to a gymnast, practically part of our food groups, difficult to explain to anyone not involved in the sport. Similar to baby powder, but chalkier smelling. Muffled music blaring through the speakers, a spring board rebounding, and the sound of uneven bars ricocheting as they're released, grabbed my attention. It was music to my ears. The kind of sound that got my adrenaline moving and my pulse thumping, beckoning me to drop everything and wrap my hands around the bars or feel the spring floor beneath my bare feet.

Taking another deep breath, I exhaled, unable to hide my splitting grin. My heart was ready to explode. Finally, I was where I was supposed to be.

Glancing around the empty lobby, I wasn't sure where to go, but the window to my right showed a view of the huge facility. It was completely deceiving from the outside… cue the anxiety. Intimidation definitely hit hard in that moment.

Gymnasts, both male and female, were scattered about, white chalk dusting their skin. I could see not just one, but two floors, three sets of uneven bars, and seven balance beams, along with two vaults. There was also a tumble track, various equipment for men, and a high bar with a foam pit and resi-mat, a huge mat on top of a foam pit used for practicing softer landings. Farther back were a bunch of doors. I had no idea what they were for, but I was curious to what they led to.

Even my parents seemed to be in awe of the gym, if their wide eyes were any indication. A shiver shot down my spine and goose bumps coated my arms in enthusiasm, as a rush of adrenaline began beating through my veins at the sight before me.

The sound of a slamming door from behind me shook me out of my trance, compelling me to look over my shoulder. My parents followed the sound and I spotted a tall, fit man. With his hands on his hips, his eyes surveyed the lobby and connected with my parents' before trailing down and locking with mine, his narrowing gaze holding me in place. All the air left my lungs. His powerful presence demanded attention, and without a doubt, he had all of mine.

Never in my life had I seen someone so unbelievably gorgeous. There was no other word

I could use to describe him. His commanding eyes made me think it was possible he could be a coach, but no coach I'd ever seen had been so attractive. Come to think of it, none of them had ever been under the age of forty without a potbelly and receding hairline. This man was solidly built and full of muscle.

A silent breath escaped my lips as he stalked toward us with power and poise. My heart nearly hurdled into my throat as I stared like he was some sort of Adonis. Dark stubble dusted his square jaw, full lips that begged for attention, straight as an arrow nose. Combined with inky black hair and olive skin with golden undertones, sweet baby Jesus, the man was perfection.

Crossing the room, he extended a hand.

"Frank, it is good to see you again." His forearm flexed, the veins signifying the muscular strength he wielded. It was incredibly difficult to tear my eyes away as he gave my father a firm handshake. He was absolutely, drop-dead gorgeous. Avery would call him fucking hot. My best friend loved to add "fucking" to the beginning of everything.

"Kova."

This was my dad's friend, and he owned this place. Interesting. He looked like he was fresh out of college, no more than twenty-five max. Dad didn't have very many young friends I was aware of—I could count on one hand the friends I had met who were younger than him. They typically had graying hair, crow's feet, and overworked, aging skin. The complete opposite of what was standing right in front of me.

So Kova was Konstantin. Where the nickname came from was beyond me, but the more talking they did, and the camaraderie I witnessed, the more I realized this was indeed the man my dad had told me about.

I remembered hearing the name Konstantin years ago in the gymnastics circle. He was one of the most decorated gymnasts to date, bringing home more medals to Russia than any other male athlete ever had. He'd competed in two Olympics and dominated each of them. He was supposed to try for a third Olympics but pulled out at the last minute due to unforeseen circumstances. Rumors circulated, some even saying steroid use was the reason he didn't compete, but to my knowledge he never publicly gave a reason for his absence.

"Welcome to World Cup Academy of Gymnastics."

That accent was most definitely Russian. For a gymnast, Kova was tall. At least six feet. Paired with his profoundly muscular shoulders and firm chest, evidenced by how tight his shirt stretched, he looked like the perfect package, if there ever was one.

My eyes drifted down, and my cheeks bloomed with heat. Oh, my God. Now, I was checking out his package!

"You remember my wife, Joy, and our daughter, Adrianna. Or Ana as we call her."

I internally rolled my eyes. My name was Adrianna, not Ana. I always hated the nickname. It made me feel like a child being reprimanded, yet they continued using it, knowing how much I detested it. Grin and bear it, I told myself. Grin… and bear it.

As Konstantin shook my mother's hand, I chuckled on the inside. Her hand was enveloped in his and I would bet she worried he'd chip her nail polish. It was a damn handshake for Christ's sake, yet she acted like she was so fragile. There was nothing more annoying than when my mom acted like she was made of porcelain. I guarantee her dainty, cold fingers rested in his hand like they were dead, which only seemed to match her icy demeanor.

"Hello again, Kova. You have a nice… facility." She tried to say with sophistication, but I could see right through her bleached teeth and her pretentious personality. An air of money surrounded her and she wore it like a second skin. My mother and I couldn't be more opposite.

Konstantin turned my way and I nearly lost all common sense. His emerald eyes were encircled by a thick black ring with faint web like lines in the irises. Mesmerizing. They re-minded me of a rainforest—beautifully alluring, uncharted territory with no true knowledge of what lurked all around. Framed between thick lashes, his gaze was penetrating, like he could read my deepest, darkest secrets.

"Ana, it is a pleasure to see you again. Last time I saw you, you barely reached my knees and were running around with pigtails. You have grown so much," he said.

Pigtails? I think I stopped with the pigtails around five. If that was the case, he was clearly over twenty-five.

"Adrianna." I emphasized my full name. The ends of his lips curved upward just a hint and my stomach tightened. I tucked a lock of hair behind my ear demurely and returned the smile.

"Are you sure you are ready for this? The elite program is completely different than level ten. Much more intense. I have already explained this to your father, but I want to assure you this is going to be nothing like your old gym. You are going to be exhausted, and probably bruised and sore until your body adjusts to the training. Just because your dad and I go way back, do not think for one minute I will be easy. I hope you are ready for that kind of conditioning."

The overwhelming urge to repeat his thick accent hit me with a vengeance. I wanted to throw my hands in the air and speak extra loud like a boisterous Italian and repeat every word Konstantin had just said. The way he spoke was so sexy, and that whole intense demeanor thing he had going on worked in his favor.

"I am," I responded confidently.

Glancing back at my parents, Kova said, "How about we head into my office and go over some paperwork before taking a tour of the gym, yeah?"

chapter 3

THE NEXT THIRTY MINUTES WERE SPENT GOING OVER ALL THE FINE PRINT AND signing medical release forms.

My mother appeared as if she suffered from constipation no matter how hard she tried to look composed. Gymnastics, along with legal documents, were so out of her element. Pretending to be a concerned mother was not in her comfort zone. Charity fundraisers were more her thing, where she could dress up, plaster on a phony smile, and act like she gave a shit about something. It was hard to blame her as my own thoughts drifted around the room, taking in the various medals and trophies, quickly losing interest in the topic myself.

The paperwork didn't interest me. All I wanted to do was get on the floor and feel the carpet beneath my feet. Floor was my absolute favorite event, though I excelled at vault. It was where I felt free and could let go, flying through the air at my heart's desire. I loved tumbling, loved defying gravity, and secretly prayed to God I wouldn't land on my ass each time.

I despised beam with pure hatred. But that was another story entirely.

I looked over at my dad in deep conversation with Konstantin. He was interested in knowing more about my training, but then again, he liked reading the small print and knowing exactly what he was paying for. It was why he'd done so well with his own company. No one could nickel and dime him. He loved money and made sure he knew where every penny he made went. And it didn't matter this was a friend he should probably be able to trust, he'd still cover his bases. However, I wasn't stupid. I knew this was more about the business side of things for him than giving me something I loved and was passionate about. This was just another deal for him to analyze and negotiate over, rather than my future.

In the midst of explaining the forms and going over my strict training regimen, I heard the words 'dance class' and my attention snapped back to the conversation.

"Dance class?" I butted in.

Konstantin lifted a perfectly arched brow, his eyes narrowing as if just realizing I was in the room.

"I was mentioning to Frank that you will be taking ballet class, along with jazz."

My mouth gaped open. "Ballet?" I asked, annoyance thick in my tone. Please tell me this was a joke. There was no way in hell I'd take ballet. I hated ballet.

"Yes, Adrianna. Ballet. It helps with posture and grace on the floor. Not to mention, flexibility and core strengthening."

"I have grace and fluidity on the floor already. I don't need extra dance classes."

I never had to take ballet back home, so I was certain I didn't need to take it here. All these extra classes would take away from the one thing I came here to do, and I refused to let that happen.

Konstantin slowly placed his expensive looking, shiny pen down. It was unnerving how he stared at me and I wanted to look away, but I held strong. I kept my eyes trained on him, focusing on the black flecks glittering in his eyes, showing him I wasn't weak.

"I am going to make it easy for you. You play by my rules here. You either take the classes or you will not train at World Cup."

Easy. As if I was some moron who didn't comprehend complex words. My parents hadn't spent thousands of dollars a year on a private tutor for nothing. I'd had straight A's since the fifth grade. I was already taking Pre-Cal and college level courses, and he was treating me like I couldn't spell D-I-C-K.

Slapping on a fake smile, I said in a sugary voice, "Ballet really isn't necessary. It'd be a complete waste of time. I've never needed it before and I don't need it now." I finished with a few rapid blinks and waited for his response. This was what I liked to call my "social event face", a skill my mom taught me. Sweet, innocent, and full of shit, and if you lived in Palm Bay, it was considered a standard fashion accessory.

Konstantin paused and simply stared at me for a few heartbeats. Just when I thought I'd won, he pulled back the papers my dad had in his grip. Looking to my dad, he said, "I can see *Ana* is not ready for this kind of commitment, Frank. It takes dedication, hard work, and most importantly, *listening* skills. And until she understands it is my way—"

My chest heaved, blood pumping rapidly through my heart. He was rejecting me, saying I couldn't train here, but I refused to let that be an option. So I cut in before he could speak another word in that stupid Russian accent of his I loved only moments earlier.

"How many of these classes do I have to take?"

He looked back at me. "As many as you need."

I clenched my teeth and dipped my head slowly in surrender. Despite his good looks, he acted like a total ass, and that was something I wasn't used to.

Konstantin slid the papers back to Dad, but his gaze never wavered from mine. "I spoke with your old coach and asked about your current training, where you could use improvement. He said you lacked flexibility, which is where ballet comes into play—it helps open your hips, stretch your legs, and gives long lean body lines gymnastics often hardens. Contrary to what you believe, he also mentioned you could use more grace. Dance is an important element to have for balance beam and floor. We want you to flow, not come across as a robot. With that being said, an evaluation will determine what your specific needs are."

My blood pressure climbed and it took everything in me not to refute his statement. Just when I thought I was moving forward, I really took ten steps back. I was not a stiff robot on the floor like he insinuated. I knew how to move for fuck's sake.

"And all these extra dance classes—ballet and jazz—are included in her new gym schedule?" My dad piped in, and thank God he did. I was ready to blow a fuse. "She'll be doing two-a-day, along with training for a total of forty hours a week?"

Konstantin turned back to my dad. "Yes, she will have two days off. What she chooses to do with those days is up to her, but when she is here, she is under my supervision and the control of World Cup, along with the other coaches. As much as I want to put gymnastics first, school is more important, so we work around a schedule for all the gymnasts. Once it is set, she will have to take responsibility and balance it. Typically, there will be practice in the morning where we focus on strength and conditioning, break for school, then gymnastics in the afternoon. Dance will be on rotation." He took a breath and continued. "Most gymnasts here are in public school, so their hours are always consistent. A few girls share an apartment to help keep their expenses low. I understand you have rented an apartment for her?"

Dad cleared his throat. "I've gone ahead and secured one of the top floor units at Cape

Harbor for her. It's a two-bedroom condo across town in one of my gated communities. I also purchased an SUV as her own to drive when the time comes."

Now I wish I hadn't skipped out on getting my license when I turned sixteen like everyone else did.

"As you know, being a Rossi brings a lot of publicity, and I need to make sure Ana is safe. She appears much older than she is and has a strong head on her shoulders, unlike most girls her age. I know you'll be nearby if anything should happen, but I still worry about her being so far away. I took the necessary precautions before allowing her to move here. Ana doesn't want for anything, and anything she does need, she'll have so she can focus on gymnastics. My wife has even gone the distance to have her meals delivered to her condo and a tutor in place."

Stifling a groan of embarrassment, I chewed the inside of my lip instead.

Dad always managed to find a way to mention money and how much of it he had. It was humiliating and I detested the pompous manner he spoke about it, friend or not. It was mortifying, especially sharing the fact he ordered meals for me. He knew I was responsible enough to make wise decisions, unlike my brother who reveled in the Rossi name and money.

I stared at Konstantin, trying to gauge his reaction at the unnecessary shit my father elaborated on, but his face gave nothing away. His cold stare—the resting dick face—could rival my mother's. I stifled a chuckle. The way his presence demanded attention caused my heart to hammer against my ribs. As long as he didn't open his mouth to spew more ridiculous ballet suggestions, I couldn't help being drawn to him.

"All right, Adrianna, not only do your parents have to sign, but so do you." Another form? Enough already. Sell me to China, they have good gymnastics coaches over there. So what if they lie about their ages.

Konstantin handed me a stack of papers.

"The first is your commitment to the gym, your oath to train hard and give one hundred and fifty percent, and to not quit, not that I expect you to. However, should you decide to end your time here at World Cup before the year is over, there will be a hefty fee charged to your parents, just like I do with every teammate. I am sure you know this is not an easy gym to get into, hence the need for this obligation. This agreement is renewed every year."

Just as I was about to press the pen down to sign my name, naturally Mom had to get her two cents in.

"Ana, this is a very expensive endeavor. I'm sure more than most parents would be willing to spend. We know you're responsible and trust you to do the right thing, but your father and I would be very upset if we had to pay an unnecessary fee on top of it all," she warned with glaring eyes. "Are you sure you're committed to this?"

"More than anything in the world," I mumbled under my breath. If she wanted to test my resolve at the eleventh hour, she could throw any doubts out the window. I was looking my dream straight in the face, and a few more documents to sign would not get between my goals and me.

"Anything?" Her voice heightened her question. She had no idea how much this meant to me, or how dedicated I was to gymnastics.

"She gets it, Joy," Dad said, and then gave me a satisfied smile.

For whatever reason, my mom pushed me hard on just about everything. It was disconcerting and I wished she'd back off and encourage me instead.

Dad understood my dedication because he was the same way. Once we found something to pour all our sweat and blood into, there was no going back. Our devotion drove us.

"All right, the next document states you will not date anyone while you are under my authority and training," Konstantin said, eyeing me as he slid it across his desk. He couldn't be serious. I'd never heard of a coach doing this before.

"I know it sounds juvenile, but this is actually a very important piece of paper you will have to sign. I do not need you losing your focus. You will end up skipping practices and pissing me off. It could ruin your career and it will only waste my time. My time is precious. I expect, and deserve, your focus and determination, not anyone else's."

"I understand."

I scribbled my name without reading and pushed it back. Konstantin held my gaze. "You should always read the fine print before you sign anything," he said quietly, sounding disappointed.

He peered down at my signature, his eyes moving as he read. "Right here states," he said, pointing, "you will be under my supervision during gym time." Konstantin handed a paper to my father and said, "This is basically the same agreement I gave your daughter. Since there is no parental supervision, she will be under the supervision of World Cup while training in the facility. Anything she does after she steps out of the gym is not my responsibility; therefore, neither I, nor World Cup will be held accountable for her actions. All the gymnasts living on their own while training here must sign it."

Dad read over it silently then looked at me and said, in an unyielding voice, "I hope you realize how much faith and trust we're putting in you to be responsible, young lady. This is no joke."

Wide eyed, I nodded. "I understand completely, Dad."

Dad signed the agreement and Konstantin stacked the papers together, bound them with a paper clip and set them aside. Kova crossed his arms firmly across his chest, leaned back in his leather chair, and looked directly at me.

"My training is unconventional, it is tough and brutal. There will be days when you will not be able to stand the sight of me. It is intense and exhausting. I am not here to be your friend, I am not here to pat your back when times get rough, I am not here to coddle you. I am here to be your coach and help get you to the next level. I come from Russia with some of the strictest coaching around. I have learned from the best, and just because you are your father's daughter does not mean I will go easy on you. You will forget everything you were taught in the past and relearn through me. I will give you all the possible means you need, but it is up to you to dig deep and be the athlete you want to become. You must have the drive and the passion in order to go places. I am just here to guide you down that path and show you your capability." He paused. "This, Adrianna, is your chance to leave. I can rip up these papers and you all can go home."

I looked at Konstantin and realized two things: I was about to get my ass handed to me, and he didn't use contractions.

chapter 4

OKAY, SO I WAS STILL A LITTLE OBSESSED WITH WHAT CAME OUT OF HIS MOUTH. I couldn't help it. That accent was sexy as hell.

I stared at Konstantin with confidence. He met my gaze. With all the passion and drive that breathed through my veins for my love of gymnastics, I poured it into my next sentence.

"I'm not leaving."

The wicked smile that slid across his face nearly knocked the wind out of me.

"Well, that wraps up all the necessary formalities. If you would like, I can show you around the gym now."

Konstantin opened the door leading into the impressive gym.

We followed close behind, taking in every square inch around us. I couldn't stop the unsteady leaps in my stomach from the adrenaline pumping through my blood.

It reminded me of walking into home period on the first day of school. I hadn't had this feeling in quite some time since I'd been homeschooled for the past year, but I remembered it like it was yesterday. Everyone hated the first day.

Gymnasts on the nearby apparatus glanced up, surveying us from head to toe. Mom didn't miss a beat in her three-inch Christian Louboutin heels while my dad strutted around like he owned the place. And here I was in dark denim shorts, a baby doll shirt and sandals, feeling every bit as relaxed as I was.

Konstantin showed us all the parts of the gym, including the rooms in the back that I was curious about. I assumed they were for strength training, but they were actually used for various dance classes and stretching techniques.

"Holly, watch yourself on that dismount. Remember, even the smallest step is a tenth of a deduction. Girls, I would like you to meet Adrianna. She is a level ten, but plans to test for elite. She will be your new teammate here."

He made his way over to the uneven bars and introduced the girls. "This is Reagan." He nodded his head at her, arms crossed firmly against his chest. "She is a senior gymnast and has been training in the elite program for a couple of years. If you have any questions about what goes on here, I am sure she will be more than happy to help." Motioning to another girl, he said, "This is Holly. She has been with World Cup since she was a child, and her twin brother is also training here."

"She'll be training with us?" Reagan scoffed.

"That is what I said," he said sternly.

The ugly glower on Reagan's pinched face fueled a fire inside of me. It was hard not to stare at her. Her features bunched together, giving her an overly dramatic expression. Just because I wasn't in the elite program yet didn't mean I couldn't train with them. Gyms all over the world had mixed classes, and most gymnasts benefited by watching the technique of their teammates while on an apparatus.

I could see her definitely being a problem. Living amongst the wealthy had shown me how to view the true colors of people quickly, no one could pull off bitchy better than blue bloods, and I had been conditioned by some of the best.

"Coach, why isn't she training with her level then?"

Coach? Coach!

"You're the coach! *My* coach?"

"Adrianna!" my mother gasped, mortified over my outburst.

"Last time I checked. Who did you think I was?"

The girls on the team snickered. Warmth climbed my chest and hit my cheeks and ears over my outburst.

"You mean you didn't know, Adrianna," Mom said, adding fuel to the fire. How convenient of her to pay attention now.

Lifting one shoulder, I said candidly, "He's dressed for a business meeting, not prepared to be covered full of chalk for the next eight hours. How's he going to spot in those clothes and dress shoes? I assumed…" I trailed off, biting my bottom lip. My shoulders dropped. "I don't know what I assumed, honestly. I just thought he owned the gym and didn't coach. A lot of owners don't coach."

My cheeks blossomed with heat when I glanced at my *new* coach. The veiled smirk he donned matched the glimmer in his eyes. I'd never had a young coach before, much less someone as attractive as Kova. Intimidating was an understatement. How the hell was I supposed to concentrate when he was the *coach* for fuck's sake?

"As for the rest of you, I decide who you all train with, and as of right now, she is with us." Kova turned toward me and gave a pointed look. "Is this going to be a problem for you?"

"Not at all," I lied.

Yeah… This was definitely going to be a big problem. Like when your gynecologist is hot kind of problem.

"Good, let us carry on and finish the tour so your parents can get you settled. I expect you here early Monday morning."

I nodded and we walked over to the men's team, where they were sharpening their skills to perfection. Just when I thought gymnastics couldn't get any tougher, I observed the brute strength it took for a male gymnast to balance himself on the rings while keeping them steady with very little movement. It was quite impressive to watch their arms slowly extend out to the sides, perpendicular to their bodies while their legs were straight and together to perform an Iron Cross. The control along with the upper body muscle it took was utterly astounding and probably why females were unable to do it.

"Gentlemen, this is Adrianna Rossi. She is a level ten but will be joining the senior girls to train."

There were three senior gymnasts Coach introduced. Solid bodies with flawlessly sculpted, vascular arms. Their shoulders were carved and contoured, the silky smooth skin curved around the tissue and hugged the muscle underneath beautifully. And the best part was it was all natural muscle from years of training, not the steroid-induced kind of shit.

There was something about a male gymnast's body that just did it for me. They yielded so much power and control. It was beauty hiding in plain sight.

I waved. "Hi," I said shyly, and they gave a few polite smiles.

Basketball shorts hung low with form fitted shirts that stuck to their bodies from exertion.

One guy, I think his name was Hayden, was shirtless and had that boy-next-door charm written all over him. Washboard abs, dimples on both cheeks, and perfectly straight, white teeth. He had it all. This guy could cut steel on his abs, which were covered in powdery white chalk. And the V all girls went crazy for—sharp as a knife and pointed right down to his groin. I couldn't help but admire it. But the best part of him, by far, were his arms. From his broad shoulders to his wrists, his honey colored skin glowed with vitality.

I knew my main focus was to train with the best, but they were going to make focusing more difficult. They were definitely not bred like this back home. At least not at my old gym that was for sure. That whole no boyfriend thing no longer sounded as easy as I'd originally thought.

"I usually have the men's and women's senior teams train at the same time in the early morning," *Coach* said.

My coach. I still couldn't get over the fact he was the coach. Or that my mouth got me into trouble once again. I never knew when to keep it shut.

"They will take a lunch break or go to school and then the younger ones come around mid-afternoon for practice. After that, the seniors come back and train for another couple of hours."

Konstantin led us down the hallway and back to the lobby. His shoulders were massively wide, the dress shirt he wore stretched across his back. He was rolled tight, and it was apparent now he was once a gymnast. At first glance, he looked like any regular guy in casual business attire.

I kid. That was such a lie. He definitely didn't look like *any other guy*—other guys weren't built like him. No gymnast's body could ever be considered *regular*.

Turning around, Konstantin's chin slowly dipped, giving us a solid stare. "Now that we have cleared everything up, I will let you guys go. My gymnasts need me," he said to my parents before turning to me. "Adrianna, it has been a pleasure. I look forward to our first workout where you will be evaluated to see what you are suitable for."

My jaw dropped for the thousandth time since entering World Cup. I hoped this wasn't a precursor for what was to come. My heart pounded, prickly heat coated my arms, and I was sure my blood pressure was steadily rising. This had to be a fucking joke.

"What do you mean evaluate me? I am suitable for elite. With my age alone, you have to train me for senior elite. I can't be in any other level. I'm supposed to start the program so I can test this season. That's why I'm here." I had to be with elite by the rules set forth by USA Gymnastics. Not what he wanted.

He raised a brow, his green eyes scolding me once again. With the amount of staring he had done since I stepped through the door, I felt like I needed to decipher his thoughts through his eyes as if he was too lazy to open his mouth to speak his mind.

"I am well aware what the guidelines are. However, I am your coach now, so I will be making the decision to see which level *I* think you are fit for, which skills you will learn and master," he stated. "You will train with the seniors and do your previous routines for now until I do my assessment, along with the other coaches. We will decide if, and when, you can practice for senior elite."

"Ana," my father said, demanding my attention. Dad read the expression on my face and knew I was ready to contest his comment.

Pursing my lips together, I grinded my teeth. I wasn't sure what he thought he could do. It wasn't as if he could just change the rules everyone who trained in the United States had to follow just to suit him. The sole reason I came to World Cup was to be in the elite program, and I'd make damn sure I did.

I hadn't even officially started training and I was already frustrated with my new coach.

chapter 5

LIKE MOST NIGHTS, DINNER WAS STIFF AND UNCOMFORTABLE.
Mother eyed my plate as she shifted her food, trying to appear as if she was eating, which she hardly did. She had an image to maintain, which meant I did as well. I had to be careful with consumption when she was around. I was cautious in general due to gymnastics, but she just made it much more stressful.

"So you have everything you need, Ana?" Dad stated more than asked the question. He washed his steak down with a glass of bourbon. They were getting ready to drive back home.

My parents had been doing better with letting a little rope go the past few years with less and less restrictions. I had three rules I had to follow: don't get arrested, don't do drugs, and be home by curfew. I was still a teenager, but living the Palm Bay lifestyle was like growing up in Hollywood—you matured much faster and fended for yourself. So those rules were not always easy to abide by for my brother. You were thirteen going on eighteen. Parents were hardly present and money was thrown around left and right for anything their kids wanted. Old money, new money. The upper crust with Gucci squad kids. To the outside youth, it was what every teenager dreamed of having—money, fame, and fortune. But it all came with a price.

"I do."

"Use your Centurion Card for anything you need."

Confused, I asked, "My what?"

"The black American Express Card. I gave it to you last week."

Oh. I didn't know it had a special name. "I will."

"Come on, Frank, our driver is waiting." Mom's distant eyes looked around the unknown.

Leaning down, my father kissed the top of my head and said, "Keep me updated with everything, okay?"

I nodded, squeezing him in a hug as tight as I could. "Thanks, Dad."

"Of course, sweetheart."

"Behave, Ana. Focus," Mom added. I tightened my jaw. I wanted to snapback, *I've always focused and behaved.* But I didn't. "I will, Mom."

"You'll let us know when your first meet is?"

Bewilderment with slivers of hope wedged through me. "You want to know?"

Joy jutted out her hip and propped her hand. "Of course I do."

This was news to me. Mom hadn't been to one of my meets in years, and not for lack of trying on my part, either.

"Ana, we're paying a lot of money for this ridiculous hobby of yours. Don't make us regret it."

My shoulders dropped. I should've known. "I'll let you know once I find out."

Her patronizing tone over my "ridiculous hobby" was heartbreaking. For a split second, I thought she actually wanted to watch me do what I love. How foolish of me to think otherwise.

Then she did something surprising. "Please, be safe. I know you're self-sufficient, but I—we—still worry." She leaned down and kissed my cheek. I wasn't sure how to react. I forced a smooth smile and took joy in it.

Mom pulled back, and I saw the love in her eyes she so rarely showed. I had yet to figure out why she rode me the way she did. I hated it, but I'd take what little bits of affection I could from her. She was still my mother after all, and I loved her.

When Sunday rolled around, I tried to get settled as quickly as I could. I didn't have a ton of things to unpack since my condo was fully furnished before we arrived, but I did want everything to be just right. Dealing with the chaos of unpacked boxes and shuffling through them to find things was not something I wanted to deal with. I was used to structure and needed it in all aspects of my life. Monday was the first day of my new workout schedule and I knew I wouldn't have much time for anything once it started. I woke up early and began emptying boxes, finding places for framed pictures of Avery and me, my family, and of good times back home. I even hung some of my most prized medals.

My nerves steadily climbed as the day went on, anxious for tomorrow to come. I was eager to rub my hands through the chalk bowl, feel the springboard beneath my feet as I flipped backwards onto the vault. I couldn't wait to learn more about my teammates, and bond with them.

Into the afternoon, I took a break and pulled out a meal from my mom's favorite fresh food delivery company. My cell phone rang and I smiled at the name on the screen.

"Hey, girl!"

"Hey!" Avery responded. "How's it going? I miss you already."

"Ave—I haven't even been gone a week."

"I know," she whined. "But you're my bestie and you moved thousands of miles away!"

I chuckled at her exaggeration. "You act like I moved to China. It's not thousands of miles away. I didn't move across the world, I'm literally three hours away… max."

"True, but who am I going to people-watch and gossip with now on Ocean Boulevard? I need my girl."

A smile spread across my face, reminiscing about fun times with Avery. Ocean Boulevard was equivalent to New York's 5th Avenue, it had all the top designer stores and restaurants. Tall palm trees lined the streets, flower bushes with the most vibrant colors I've ever seen bloomed beneath the high sun climbing the buildings. Ocean Boulevard was a picturesque little spot.

Avery and I had been best friends since we were infants. Our parents were extremely close—her dad was a partner at Rossi Enterprises, so we were pretty much inseparable. Leaving her was more difficult than I expected. I knew it wouldn't be anything for us to drive to see each other for a quick visit, our parents wouldn't bat an eye, but that wasn't the point. I left behind my one true best friend. She was the closest thing I had to a sister—my confidante and my lifeline.

"Stop being so dramatic. We can still do that on the phone. Plus, I'll be home for holidays and stuff."

"Whatever, so what are you doing now?"

"Taking out all the meals my lovely mother ordered for me," I said sarcastically. After all these years, Avery knew how my mom loved to micromanage certain aspects of my life. "I don't even know what half this stuff is."

"You've got to be kidding me. She's still controlling you from three hours away?"

"Sure is. She had that delivery diet food service set up for me—the same one your mom uses. It's all naturally prepared meals. Though, I've never taken the time to actually look at the food, have you?"

"Nope, never ate the crap either."

"Ugh. Lucky." I picked up one tray and inspected it. "This one looks like…" I trailed off, looking at the name, unable to make out what it was. "You have got to be kidding me. Tofu? She's making me eat tofu? With gluten free croutons?" I scrambled around to look at the rest of the meals in the vibrant green mesh bag. "Oh, my God, they're all gluten free meals! Why the fuck is she ordering me gluten free? I'm not allergic to anything!" My stomach churned as I sorted through the rest of the contents. This stuff would taste horrible.

Chuckling, Avery said, "Gluten causes belly fat and she wants you fit and trim, dumbass."

"Thanks, Captain Obvious. I know that, but I have no belly fat left to lose. She acts like I'm fucking overweight."

"I can only imagine what she thinks of me."

"I'm not eating this shit," I said, dumping one of the trays into the garbage.

"Last time I checked, there's a lot of salt and sugar in gluten free diets. Sugar turns to fat and salt is going to bloat you. What else is in there?"

"Let me see… There's a whole week of terrible looking meals and snacks." I grimaced at the appalling food choices. "Lamb meatballs? How do people eat this stuff? This looks like mystery meat patted together. I can't believe she's expecting me to eat this shit. It doesn't look appetizing at all, it looks disgusting."

"Take a picture and send it to me right now. I have to see this."

I pulled another tray out and mumbled to myself, "What the hell did she order me?" I turned it to the side to examine it. "Well, this doesn't look too bad. It's turkey and green beans in a gluten free wrap." I opened the plastic container and took a bite. "The wrap tastes like cardboard, but I'll take it over the tofu," I said with a full mouth. Before I knew it, the small snack size wrap was gone and I was still hungry.

Avery moved to another topic and began chatting about the sport she loved, talking a hundred miles a minute about her tryouts.

"You'll make the cheer team for sure. I'd be shocked if you didn't."

"I hope so! I mean, I want to make the All-Star competition team. I should be able to after all the private lessons I've had."

"I have no doubt you will. I've seen those girls, and you're so much better. Oh shit, you're never going to believe this. I met my coach."

"Yeah?" she said, unimpressed. "And?"

I sipped my water and told her how I made a fool of myself. "He's really young, a former Olympian, but I just can't picture him training us. It's weird."

"How young?"

"I have no clue, I didn't ask, but I would say around twenty-five? Thirty? I have no idea." I puckered my lips, my forehead bunching together. "That seems kind of young for my dad to be friends with."

"I didn't know you had to be a certain age to be friends with someone."

"You don't, obviously. I just wasn't expecting it."

"Is he hot?"

My cheeks flushed. "Avery! He's my coach!"

"And?"

"And what?"

"Is he hot?"

Hot was an understatement. His jet black hair complemented his stunning green eyes perfectly. A square jaw with hollow cheeks but profound cheek bones. I loved that he was tall and had broad shoulders. All my other coaches had been short and stumpy.

"Well... I mean, yeah, he's hot, but I can't think of him like that. I'm going to be working closely with him for like forty hours a week."

"Send me a picture."

I burst out laughing. "Avery! And how the hell am I supposed to do that? I can't just bring my phone in there and be all 'Hey, Coach, let me take a picture of you.'"

"Fine. I'll Google him. He's an Olympian so there's bound to be a picture of him out there. Hang tight, what's his name?"

I paused for a moment, my brows pinching together. "Well, he addressed himself as Konstantin, but search Konstantin Kournakov. I mean, Kournakova. Or Kova. My dad called him Kova. I think he changed his last name, though."

"Okay. Let's do one name at a time because you just threw like thirty at me. Core... ne—"

"Konstantin Kournakova," I said in a terribly fake Russian accent.

"How do you spell that? There are too many vowels and corn in it."

Rolling my eyes, I laughed under my breath from her exaggeration then spelled it out. Dead silence for a good ten seconds, then...

"Fuuuuccckkk, Adrianna, seriously."

I chuckled into the phone. "What?" I said blandly. I knew what she was getting at.

"Fish lips and all, he's smoking hot!"

"Fish lips? You did not just say that. He most definitely does not have fish lips."

"So you admit to checking him out," she replied swiftly.

"No!"

"Admit it!"

"So what? I already said he's hot."

Avery laughed again. "Okay—I won't call them fish lips, but they are nice and full. Kissable." She paused, then shouted, "Oh, my God! Coach Kissable!"

I groaned loudly. The last thing I wanted to think about was my coach's *full, kissable* lips.

"And it appears he is... actually thirty-two years old."

"Wow. If you saw him in person, you'd never guess."

"Seriously, though. He's fucking gorgeous. Have fun with that. I wouldn't mind having a cheerleading coach who looked like him. Shit, I wouldn't mind having a damn co-ed team in general. All those strong guys to lift me and then cradle me to their chests with their huge ass arms? And have you noticed how hot the guys are? What the hell are they eating to bulk up the way they do?"

"You're crazy, Ave," I laughed, cutting her off. Avery lusted after every boy who crossed her path. She took boy crazy to a whole new level.

Sighing, I looked around at the boxes that still needed to be unpacked.

"I need to finish getting things unpacked and hit the sack early. I have practice at 6:30 a.m., which means I need to be awake by 5:30 to get ready and be there on time."

"Oy. Why so early?"

"Practice, lunch, school, practice again. I won't end until close to six-ish, I think? I'm not really sure."

"Wow. Well, try and call me tomorrow if you can."

"Will do."

"Have fun! And remember—snap a picture for me."

"I'll do my best."

"Later, girl."

The smile I heard in her voice made me miss my best friend dearly. Moving to Georgia's South Coast was my choice and something I desperately wanted. I'd prepared for it, and was ready the day it finally came, but I hadn't anticipated missing my friend so much so soon.

I needed to stay focused on my goal, all these sacrifices would be worth it in the end.

chapter 6

THE SUN HADN'T EVEN BEGUN TO PEEK ABOVE THE HORIZON AS GRAY CLOUDS drifted across the charcoal sky when we pulled up to World Cup.

Thomas, my driver, knew exactly where to go.

My eyes were swollen and puffy from the restless night of sleep I had. I'd been so anxious for the following morning, I tossed and turned all night in bed, thinking about how my first day would go. I was finally going to begin the next phase in my gymnastics career, and it was all I could think about. Just as I was about to fall back asleep, my alarm clock went off, jolting me upright. If I had to guess, I'd say I had about three hours total of sleep.

Stepping outside with my duffle bag, the humidity in the air smacked my face. "Bye, Alfred. I'm not sure how many hours I'll be here, so I'll text you when I get out." Alfred was a personal nickname I used for Thomas. He wasn't crazy about it, judging by his expression every time it rolled off my tongue. In fact, I think he loathed it, but went along with it to appease me.

"I'll be on standby, Miss Rossi."

An exasperated sigh escaped my throat. "Alfred. How many times do I have to tell you to call me Adrianna?" I had been reminding him more lately. I hated the Miss crap.

"How many times have I told you my name is Thomas?" he retorted.

My eyes narrowed, trying to appear mean, but I knew it was a piss poor job.

"Old habits."

"I'll try harder," he said with a wink.

Shutting the door, the sound of fallen leaves fluttering in the wind caught my attention. I glanced over my shoulder, but I couldn't see anything in the dark and continued on.

Stepping onto the sidewalk, I walked in front of the SUV. Thanks to the headlights shining through the window, I got a glimpse inside World Cup. When we arrived the first day, I hadn't been able to see through the tinted glass, but the early morning hours along with the bright lights illuminated a large portion of the gym.

My eyes zoomed in on a gymnast throwing a tumbling pass. She must've been warming up since all she did was a round-off, back handspring, one and a half twist, and then walked off like it was nothing. It really wasn't much on our level, but she made it look effortless. Like a ribbon floating in the wind. Beautiful, really. I could only pray I had that kind of grace. Coach Kova clapped his hands, his lips moving and head nodding in approval. I took in his attire and noticed he wasn't wearing dress pants.

I shuffled my duffle bag around and opened the door. As I did, another hand reached above me and pushed back the metal frame. I looked over my shoulder and came face to face with muscular arms. Stepping inside, I locked eyes with the cutest boy next door smile I'd ever seen. He hardly had any clothes on—shorts, flip flops, and a loose tank top with huge arm holes. Typical southern beach attire.

"I got it."

I gripped my strap tighter. "Thank you."

"I'm Hayden," he said, walking in closely behind.

"Adrianna."

He smiled, and a dimple appeared in the center of his chin. "I know, we met the other day. I'm Holly's twin."

"Huh." I stared at him. "I wouldn't have guessed."

His smile grew larger. "That's good to know. The last thing I want is to hear I look like a chick."

Chuckling at his comment, I followed him down the hall into a small room that had two walls of lockers, one each for the boys' and girls' teams. He stuffed his bag into a metal cage. His movements were comfortable and natural as if he'd been doing this for ages, and maybe he had.

Hayden looked over his shoulder. "Are you nervous about today?"

I bit my lip and shuffled my feet. "Yeah, is it obvious?"

"Not really—but I just remember my first day being able to train at a new level. It's exciting but more nerve-racking than anything."

Hayden reached behind his head and pulled off his shirt. He rolled it into a ball and chucked it in with the rest of his stuff. It took everything in me to keep my jaw from dropping to the floor, but that didn't mean I didn't give him a good once over, openly gawking at his body.

"I'll be honest… I'm petrified."

"That's totally normal. You'll get past it in a couple of weeks once you're comfortable." He slapped his door shut. "Want a tip?"

"Of course."

"Don't talk back. Do what your coaches tell you. Don't show them you're scared. Don't hesitate. They don't want to hear excuses. Show them you're confident and want to be here, that you can handle what they give you and have what it takes. Basically, just agree and nod and that will take you far. They know what they're talking about. I've been through a handful of coaches at this gym, and these are by far the best." He paused, then said something I needed to remember. "And most importantly, there will be days when you'll want to quit because you can't take any more. Those days will come and they'll come often. Just don't give up, because the reward will be worth it in the end."

I took in Hayden's words with a serious nod. He cupped my shoulder with compassion and said, "Good luck," then pulled the door to the gym open and stepped inside.

Looking through the window, there was only one girl out there, and I thought it was Reagan, but I wasn't sure since I met her for only a split second the other day. I watched as she landed a front handspring double twisting front layout into a punch front tuck, her arms out in a T landing to balance herself, but she pulled to the right and took a large step.

"What are you waiting for?"

A deep, baritone voice startled me from behind. I jumped, looking over my shoulder as my heart raced. My hand flew to my neck. Where had he come from?

"What?" I stammered.

Konstantin tilted his head to the side, his face expressionless. "I thought you were a gymnast, not a spectator. My time is valuable. Get in the gym now or leave."

I pulled back, my mind reeling from his unexpected nasty tone. My jaw hung open, silently moving up and down. I struggled with words, trying to find the right response. The way his eyes bore into mine made him unapproachable… And intimidating.

"Where… Where do I put my things?"

He gave me a look that said I should know where my stuff went. He hadn't assigned me a locker, but I had a feeling mentioning that wouldn't be good, so I didn't bring it up.

"Okay," I responded quietly. "Where to after that?"

"This is just like any other gym, Adrianna," he said with a bite, rolling the R in my name. "Let this be a lesson learned after today. After you come in, you place your things in a locker, and you get your ass into the gym quickly. I do not care where you start, as long as your feet are on the blue floor every morning by six thirty and you are coming to me. Yeah?"

With wide eyes and parted lips, I nodded at his dick attitude. Coach marched off and I quickly did as he said as my knees shook. Jesus. He acted as if I was late, which I wasn't, he just hadn't explained what to do once I arrived.

I stripped out of my hot pink, Juicy Couture two-piece zip-up and pants set and rolled it up, shoving it into a metal locker. I'd stick it in my bag later, the last thing I wanted to do was make him wait any longer. I threw my long burgundy hair into a messy ponytail and made my way toward the gym.

Swallowing back the lump in my throat, I pushed my shoulders back, stepped into the gym and walked over to where the women's team was. Coach stared me down, tracking my every footstep. His gaze made me feel two inches tall and insecure.

I chewed the inside of my lip as our eyes locked. His black short-sleeved shirt hugged his muscular biceps. His arms were firmly crossed in front of his chest, muscles perfectly rounded, and his stance spoke of authority. He tracked me all the way across the gym. Heads turned my way in the middle of their stretching, so I quickly tiptoed to the floor. I'd have to let Alfred know we needed to get here a little earlier tomorrow to avoid these uncomfortable stares, just in case. No one liked being the center of attention, so I needed to make sure I'd slip in quieter and unseen.

Legs spread out, I leaned forward and lay on the floor, my arms and legs parallel to each other. I expelled a breath and closed my eyes, rejoicing in what my body was doing. I loved the way my muscles pulled tight and then loosened like they were just waking up. It hurt and felt good all at the same time. Flexing and pointing helped my shins, and I pushed my legs as wide as they could go by scooting up to stretch out my groin.

I was lost in the feeling when I felt the spring floor dip as someone came up next to me and grabbed my ankle, lifting my leg.

"What the…" I mumbled under my breath. I sat up and looked over my shoulder. I almost said fuck, but I caught myself. Coach knelt so close to my face I noticed how incredible his eyes really were. A brilliant green, the color of fresh basil and lime interwoven with each other pulled me in. Mesmerizingly beautiful, and when his hand moved to the crease of my hip and thigh, I drew in a breath.

His fingers dug into my skin where my leotard met my bikini line and he carefully rotated my leg so my knee faced up.

"Back down," Coach ordered. I had no idea what he planned, so I listened and laid my chest flat on the floor, which ended up being a good thing. I didn't want to get caught staring into his eyes.

Or think about where his hand currently was.

Slowly, he lifted my leg and pressed down on my back so I couldn't move. A little grunt left my lips as he stretched out my hips.

"Toes pointed, knees up, Adrianna," he said, like I was an idiot. Maybe the arrogance in his tone was a Russian thing.

Coach slowly pulled my foot up so it was slightly higher than my back. I felt the burning stretch in my groin grow as he raised it. Unwillingly, my body tried to sit up at this tense position to ease the strain, but Coach just pressed harder on my back, not allowing me to move. I held my breath, my fingers spreading wide on the carpet and my stomach flexed. His forearm dug into my back as he leaned over and pressed me down. This shit hurt. I thought my groin was about to be ripped to shreds, and even my butt felt like the muscles were being pulled to their max.

"Breathe," he whispered.

I groaned in the back of my throat as he lowered my foot to the floor, where I began to melt and release the tension in my muscles. It felt so good, but not for long because he switched to my other side and applied the same amount of force. This took stretching and flexibility to a whole new level for me.

"Girls, sit across from the low beam, put your toes on it, and wait for me."

Opening my eyes, I was faced with two large knees just inches from my nose. He may have been wearing workout shorts, but I could see the width of his thighs and the muscles surrounding his knees. They were huge and his legs were free of hair.

Not to mention, he smelled really good. *Too good.*

Twenty years later, Konstantin lowered my leg but I was stuck and stiff. Slowly, I sat up by walking my hands toward me.

"Partner up and take turns stretching out your knees. Bounce lightly, girls. We don't need any broken knee caps."

That accent... I was quickly realizing I liked his accent a helluva lot. It demanded attention every time he opened his mouth. Maybe it was an American thing to like someone else's enunciation, but then I wondered if foreigners liked American accents too. Probably not. There was nothing exotic about an American dialect. We didn't roll our R's the way Russians did. It would come off as a speech impediment if anything.

Moving behind me, Coach's fingers grazed delicately down my forearm. He grasped my wrist, then reached for the other one. He carefully extended both wrists back, stretching my arms out behind me.

"Do not drop your chest. Shoulders back, back straight."

chapter 7

"WHAT ARE THEY DOING?" I FOUND MYSELF ASKING AS MY EYES DRIFTED over to the girls on the low balance beam just a couple of feet away.

"It is a stretching technique that overextends your knees. It helps with jumps so your legs are bowed. You have never done them before?"

"No." I watched the girls lightly bounce on their teammates' kneecaps. This had to be something he picked up in Russia. I could actually see their knees bending backwards as they sat like soldiers taking it. Never in my life had I seen this and I began to worry my knees would pop out.

"What happened to using two mats and putting our feet on them in splits?"

"We do that too, but I change things up and like to use my background. It is things a lot of other coaches do not do. It is a little intense, but it gets the job done."

He let go of my arms and said, "Shake your legs out." I bounced them lightly to a closed position so I could stand. My legs were stiff and now I had to overextend my knees even more?

A hand appeared in my vision and I reached for it. Coach helped me up, and I automatically fixed my leotard from the slight reposition.

Gymnasts picked wedgies out left and right without a second thought and kept walking, myself included. Hey—it came with the territory. Sometimes it got stuck up in there, so it was either fix it or let your ass hang out.

"Reagan, please work with Adrianna, yeah?"

Reagan glared at me for some bizarre reason as I got into the same position as the other girls, my toes elevated on the low beam. I ignored her. When she sat down, she didn't hold back and bounced on my kneecaps like she was bouncing on a giant yoga ball.

It took everything in me not to scream at her and call her a bitch. I didn't see the other girls jumping this hard, but I knew better than to complain. So I rolled both my lips between my teeth and took the newfound pain being delivered to my body.

We switched places, but I didn't go as hard as she did. Honestly, I didn't want to injure her.

"Harder," Reagan demanded. "You won't hurt me."

I stopped and looked at her, because I was really worried I would. "You sure?"

"Yup. Just do it." I followed her command, all the while smiling internally and taking way too much delight in inflicting a fraction of the pain she just handed to me.

After group stretching, we split up amongst the different apparatuses: vault, balance beam, floor, and the uneven bars. Coach walked over to the bars.

"Do a few warm-ups and when you are ready, let me know so I can see your routine."

"Okay," I said, tightening my grips. Then he walked to another part of the gym.

Taking a deep breath, I watched as one of the girls warmed up on bars, doing light release moves where she flowed freely from bar to bar, giant after giant, an overshoot that involved a half-twist mid-air to the low bar, clear hip circles, where the gymnast circles backward without touching the bar to her hips, and then an easy dismount, like a back tuck. The other two girls went and then I was up. We all pretty much did the same warm ups, some adding pirouettes and other elements, but the real fun was about to begin.

A straddle back was one of my favorite skills to do on bars. It wasn't used as often since most did the half twist mid-air to the low bar, but I loved it. There was something powerful in releasing the high bar to straddle the low bar mid-air into a handstand. It took me a while to master this move. My ankles kept hitting the bar, not to mention, initially it scared the shit out of me. Until I figured out the trick to tackling this skill was getting your hips to rise as high as you could manage by flicking them up and back, *not* your feet. Lifting your feet in a straddle back was a hard habit to break, but it didn't actually pull you in the air the way your hips did like you'd think it would. Basically, I lifted my ass, stuck it up and out, and I was golden.

My bars routine wasn't as intense as the other three girls who went before me. I guess it wasn't supposed to be since I was a lower level, however, I became consciously aware I was behind. I didn't have an early start in the sport like most did who were elite. Although I was young when I began recreational gymnastics, I was almost ten years old when I joined the girl's team and officially began rigorous training.

There was a difference between recreational classes and team classes. Both were taught the same skills, but team trained more hours a week and focused on the smallest of details. In the end, those details could make or break you. There was commitment and motivation involved, too. Not just from the gymnasts, but from the parents as well. The financing, traveling, and attitude were brutal. Team was much more grueling but also very rewarding.

I performed my routine a handful of times more before I mustered the nerve to ask Coach to watch. It wasn't my best practice—I could tell by my jittery movements and racing heart, that had nothing to do with my actual routine and everything to do with the intimidating Russian and three hours of sleep. I felt like I was competing for a spot on the US World team and everything relied heavily on this moment.

This was my chance to prove I was ready for elite.

Konstantin stood there near the side of the bars, his eyes trained solely on me, and showing no emotion at all. I thought for sure I was about to be sick. It was a blank stare, and honestly, I wasn't sure if I'd rather that or to see his face fall. My heart was in my throat and all the noise faded away.

Shit. I was so nervous.

A bars routine can last anywhere from thirty to forty-five seconds, mine was thirty-six, and that was simply because of my level and what I was capable of doing. A great deal of training and conditioning went into a bar routine. Most people never realized how short they actually were. After being captivated by jaw dropping release skills and eye-popping combination sequences, it was easy to forget it wasn't even one-minute long.

As I performed my routine, it felt like an eternity of wishing and praying I'd catch the bar, hit my handstands, legs together, and didn't wobble or bend my arms. I mentally chanted to myself, *I got this*, repeatedly with every little element before the dismount happened.

"Once more," he ordered before I could catch my breath. After I chalked up my grips and did my routine again, he dipped his chin and said, "When you get to vault, follow the same instructions," and then walked off. I had no idea if I did well or not, and there was no gauging his thoughts either. He was like a slab of concrete.

"Don't stress—he's always like that." I looked over at the voice beside me. "You'll never know what he's thinking no matter how hard you try. I swear, it's his goal to make you feel like you suck at life." I breathed a sigh of relief knowing it wasn't just me. "I'm Holly, by the way."

I smiled politely at Hayden's twin. "Adrianna. And thanks for the heads up. It doesn't help that I'm nervous as it is, but the way he acts puts me on edge."

"Oh, that's how he normally is. You'll get used to it. We all have."

Note to self: His default personality is dick. Got it.

"Hopefully it doesn't take long. He made me feel like it was the sloppiest routine ever."

Holly laughed. "We all went through it and had the same sentiments. Kova has a keen eye, so while there were probably things you did mess up on, he can spot talent through it."

"Why do you call him Kova? I thought his name was Konstantin."

She shrugged. "It's just what he goes by. None of us call him by his real name."

Interesting.

"Are you from here?" I asked curiously.

She nodded. "I've been with World Cup for years. My family used to live here, but my dad was offered a job in Ohio he couldn't refuse. He moved there while my mom, Hayden, and I stayed back so we could train with Kova. My mom left once we hit sixteen though, because she missed him a lot. She was nervous to leave us, but luckily we have friends and family nearby if we need anything."

I knew in the general public it was absurd for parents to allow their children to train alone at such a young age. It wasn't uncommon for us to go to summer training camp in Texas for three months alone, or to train long hours in the gym without any parental supervision. The gym became our second home. The coaches were extremely close to the parents, which put them at ease when it came time to leave their kids. Plus, we were never completely alone, there was always an adult around, a friend or a mom to help out. While we thought nothing of it, to the outside world, I was sure it looked like neglect.

"How old are you?"

She tightened her wristband, her eyes focused on the movement of her fingers. "Almost seventeen."

"Oh—" My voice heightened. "Wow. So you've been here for almost a year on your own?"

An innocent smile spread across her baby face as she looked back up at me. "I know it's crazy being away from family, and hard at times, but you get used to it. Luckily, they understand our love of the sport and allowed us to stay. But it doesn't come easy. My parents took out a second mortgage so we can continue to train and compete here.

"Last year we had a girl here—Sage. She was incredible, better than all of us and had future Olympian written all over her. Her form was impeccable and she was only nine years old. We used to watch her in awe, but unfortunately, her parents couldn't afford to live in two different places anymore. She has an older brother and it wasn't fair to him, so they packed up and went home to Washington. She cried, we all did. Seeing that made me realize how fortunate I am to be here. I don't know if she's training anymore though... hopefully she is. She was too good not to."

"Holly. You are up," Coach announced.

Holly smiled brightly. "See you later... and good luck."

While Holly geared up, I stripped the grips from my wrists and made my way to vault where a pair of brown eyes stood watching.

"Hey, Reagan," I said, being friendly. I was looking forward to making team friends.

She turned to me, paused, then said, "Hey."

I wasn't sure why, but I got the impression she wasn't a fan of me being here, which kind of bothered me. Team girls were just that—a unified team. We worked together, were like sisters, and usually had an unbreakable bond. I had a good team of girls back home who supported each other to the end, so I expected to have the same here.

"How long have you been on the team?"

"I've been with World Cup since I could walk," she responded hastily without picking her head up from the chalk bowl. "My family is actually from Cape Coral. I'm not a transfer."

chapter 8

SHE GAVE ME HER BACK AND GEARED UP TO TAKE HER VAULT.
I watched as Reagan performed an Amanar, landing almost perfectly without the slightest movement, not even a balance check. My eyebrows hit my hairline over her nearly perfect vault. Knowing I was next, I looked around for Kova to see where he was and noticed his eyes trained on her. Holy hell… there was a smile on his face. I mean, there should've been with that vault, but he didn't seem like the type to ever crack a grin. Reagan beamed at him and walked to the end of the vault runway with confidence in her stride.

I'd been practicing a double-twisting Yurchenko. Unfortunately, I almost always took a step once I landed, which earned me deductions. Most gymnasts took a step or a hop. It was hard not to with all the power and momentum forcefully flying out of us.

My best bet would be to work on my alternate vault, but I wasn't crazy about anything requiring front flipping, so I avoided them as much as possible. I wasn't a lazy gymnast, they just made me uneasy turning in the air in that direction. Not to mention, a blind landing was risky because I didn't want to hyperextend my knees.

But with that bizarre conditioning of bouncing on your knees Coach had us doing earlier, I was almost positive I was training my knees for hyperextension anyway.

"That was incredible!" I said to her excitedly. While it was becoming more popular, an Amanar was one of the hardest vaults in the world for women to get right. It required blocking really hard by pushing off the vault table with your shoulders and keeping your arms straight.

"I know."

My mom would've slapped my face if that had been my response.

"How long have you been practicing it?" Even with her nasty attitude, I was genuinely curious.

She shrugged, not making eye contact. "Not very long. It was easy for me, actually. None of the other girls can stick it like I can," she said smugly. "Kova said my vault will help my all-around and boost my score."

Wow. I didn't want to know if she was capable of becoming any more pretentious.

"Well, that's fabulous for the team. I'm sure the girls are grateful for your capability, seeing as you think they're lacking." I couldn't help it, I had to get in a little jab. Growing up on an island with some of the richest people in the world, I really disliked snotty girls, and I could tell Reagan was just that. So I knew how to get in and get out with a plastic smile.

I made my way to the runway and performed a one and a half Yurchenko, instead of a double. I wanted to impress and went with a clean landing, so I played it safe. The key was to start with a high-tall hurdle with my chest up, then round-off, and drive my arms back into the vault to execute a big, powerful block. Then kick my legs together and scoop my toes, squeezing my butt and using my abs to drive momentum to follow with a tight twist. Spotting my landing, I drove my heels into the ground.

Once I landed with a hop, Kova swirled his finger around for me to do it again. This time, I landed with a huge hop from too much power and I grimaced, squeezing my eyes shut. I knew I screwed up and he caught it.

Opening my eyes, I looked at Kova who stared me down without any emotion on his face. He said nothing, so I opted to speak.

"Shall I do it again?"

"Can you do any other vault?"

I bit the inside of my lip. "I can do a double Yurchenko. It needs a little work, but I can try it."

"Are you going to injure yourself trying it?"

"No." I could do a double, but I was too nervous to so I did the one and a half.

"It is something you have done before?"

"Yes."

"Then do it. Reagan!" he yelled. "Let Adrianna go again real quick."

Reagan made an audible grunting sound, so I apologized to her. The quickest way to make friends was not having the coach ordering me to cut in rotation.

I chalked up my feet and then took a deep breath, shaking out my hands.

I could do this... I could do this...

I snuck a quick glance at Kova, who stood with his arms crossed in front of his wide chest across from the vault. Rising up on my tiptoes, I leaned in and took off running, pumping my legs as fast and as hard as I could to gain speed.

Just before I reached the vault, I did a round off onto the springboard, flipping backward so my hands would land on the leather vault to complete my Yurchenko. Blocking as hard as I could by pushing off with my shoulders, I pulled my twist around and spotted the ground. I landed it perfectly—with a smile—and no hop. Not too much power or rotation.

Finishing, I looked for the same smile Kova gave Reagan. My stomach dropped when I saw the disdain in his eyes.

He cocked his head to the side and said more than asked, "You can do a double? Yes?"

I swallowed hard. "Yes."

"What about a two and a half?"

"Yes, well, not really. I'm working on it."

"So, why didn't you do it?"

"Do what? The two and a half? It's not great." I shrugged helplessly. It wasn't the best way to start off, but I was nervous.

I could feel another set of eyes glued to me, but I couldn't break his gaze to see who they belonged to. And truthfully, I was embarrassed and didn't want to see the stares. Luckily, I was slightly hot so the flush on my cheeks would be brushed off as nothing more than exertion.

One brow arched to a point. Fury radiated off him. "Did you really think I would not know? That landing was too perfect—the whole vault was too good for it to be your alternate. If you want to succeed, you have to try harder elements. Take a risk, trust your body, drop the fear.

"Now get over there and do it with the two and a half so I can see where you need work. I do not have time for games. I need to know what you are capable of right now, today, not next month. What good will that do if I am training you for a two and a half and you have already been working on it?"

I wanted to correct his stiff pronunciation, but I refrained. He sounded like a robot talking at times. So instead I nodded vehemently, and took a stand behind the line. Reagan wore a smirk that deserved to be slapped off her face.

A low groan escaped my throat, irritated by both Kova and Reagan's faces. But more importantly, I was angry with myself for not giving my all in the one moment I truly needed to.

I didn't waste any time before I got behind the line and started running toward the stationary object. Gymnasts had to be a little crazy in the head to come up with the idea of doing back flips over objects such as this one.

Once I hit the vault, I blocked hard, taking flight, and pulled a double twist—adding a half turn. I cranked as hard as I could on my rotation but I knew it wasn't enough. It was risky and I was sloppy in the air. Gymnasts instinctively knew their bodies, but I took the chance and threw it anyway.

Landing, I stumbled to the side, but I caught myself before my knees went down, which was huge. Knees were never to touch the floor on a landing.

Standing, I finished and looked at Kova.

"Same thing with the floor and beam. Do *not* hold back," he stated before he turned his back to me and carried on.

It was going to be a long day.

It was nearly nightfall and I was exhausted. Without looking in the mirror, I knew I was a hot mess. Chalk coated my body and leotard, strands of hair fell from my ponytail and surrounded my face, and my eyes were puffy and swollen, heavy with fatigue. I sat with my legs spread in my little shorts in the middle of the gymnastics' lobby while scrolling on my phone. It was unladylike and my mom would've killed me for it, but I didn't give a shit. I got my ass handed to me today and I was damn tired.

All I wanted to do was go home, take a shower, pop some Motrin, and go to bed. Motrin, the real breakfast, lunch, and dinner of champions. Screw eating a fresh cooked meal.

Unfortunately, I couldn't do that just yet. I had to wait for Coach to finish up before I could leave. Judging by the first real training session I had today, I could tell the next couple of weeks were going to be rough in more ways than one.

After I did the other two events earlier like Coach had asked, I'd gone and met with my private tutors. They went over my syllabus for each class and what would be expected of me, along with my gym hours. Mr. Landry would teach Chemistry and American History, and Mrs. Taylor would teach Pre-Cal and English. I tried to focus on everything they both said, but my mind kept reverting back to the routines I performed and wondering how I did. If my wobbly turn on beam impacted my ability, if the step out of bounds on the floor hurt me, or the fact I held back on vault in the beginning made a difference.

I sighed loudly. I didn't know who I was kidding.

After school, Alfred took me home for lunch, which ended up being small and short since my stomach was in knots. I couldn't eat, my nerves were shot. Plus, I hated training on a full stomach. Once I returned to the gym, Kova had me repeat the same things as this morning so other coaches could judge my routines, which I was sure were shit by that point.

Maybe I was just being hard on myself.

The door slammed shut, taking my attention away from my friends' fun updates on social media. Kova snapped his fingers as he brusquely walked past me. "Let us go."

Dick mode—activated!

Following him into his office, he waited for me to walk in then shut the door. He took a seat behind his desk and I sat in front. I tightened my ponytail and braced myself.

Looking me directly in the eyes, he got right to the point. "Today was a test, an evaluation to see where you currently are." He sighed tiredly. "I am going to be blunt. You do not come close to my standards, Adrianna, and that worries me. You are not ready for the senior team. Not even close. Definitely nowhere near prepared to test this season. You are setting yourself up for failure if you do."

My mouth dropped open and tears formed in the back of my eyes. I would not cry, I wouldn't allow it. Shit, I'd been schooled not to cry. But fuck, that hurt.

Being told you're not good enough in gymnastics was like being kicked while you're down. It was heartbreakingly devastating. Aside from sustaining an injury that forces you to rest, it's probably the worst thing you could possibly hear. You're already hard on yourself as it is trying to be the best. You give your all, you silently deal with the pain and aches, the gnawing hunger, the exhaustion, when you know there will always be someone who will come along that is better than you. It's a double-edged sword. And this shit runs through your head on replay.

"I spoke with Madeline, the other elite coach who evaluated you, and she agreed with me, you need work. You have a lot of bad habits we need to break, which is going to be a tedious task. Little details matter in this sport. Had I evaluated you before you came, without a doubt, I would have turned you away from the elite program. But your father made a generous donation to have our café funded, which allows you to be here." He folded his hands in front of him, looking jaded. "So here you are."

"I'm not even a level ten in your eyes, am I?"

He shook his head, his lips a thin flat line. No Coach Kissable here.

"My standards are high, but that is what wins. Doing safe, mediocre gymnastics is not going to get you on the podium. I think you will agree with me. You were scared today and held back. That concerns me."

I tried hard not to cry, but I couldn't stop the tears from resting on my eyelids. I looked up at the ceiling, willing them to disappear so they wouldn't fall down my cheeks. I was mad at myself for letting my emotions get to me. I wanted to appear strong, but this was equally as frustrating as it was hurtful. The clawing inside my gut to be better was being tackled by a larger beast.

"The worst part is," he continued, "I agreed to train you. Once you test and you do qualify, you must train at the senior level because of your age. You are too old for any other level."

Konstantin Kournakova was a cold man. I wondered if he had kids and prayed that if he didn't, he was sterile.

I knew he wasn't going to go easy on me, but Jesus Christ. His words were as upsetting as a career-ending injury.

chapter 9

"SEEING HOW IT IS MARCH AND YOU ARRIVED IN THE MIDDLE OF ELITE SEASON, did you plan on competing the rest of the regular meet season as practice and then test next season?"

"Since we have until June, I thought I could test elite since a lot of the skills are the same."

His eyes were empathetic. "I do not think that is a wise decision. You are just not ready."

The last thing my heart wanted was to sit a season out, but if it furthered my career then so be it. I lowered my voice and said, "I'd rather hold off on competing and use this time as practice so I could be prepared next season to test."

Kova sat back in his leather chair. His head tilted to the side and his eyes narrowed to thin slits. He cupped his jaw and ran a hand over his mouth. "Do you want this, Adrianna? Really want this deep down? Because it is going to take many more hours of gym time for you to be where I need you. I am talking private lessons after practice and possibly longer hours. Pushing your body past the brink of sanity to not only master the elite level skills, but master them perfectly. And even with that, I do not know if you will get to where you need to be by the time you want. This is going to be complex to manage. A challenge. I am not sure I am capable of moving mountains."

My jaw moved, but I was utterly speechless, trying desperately to form words but nothing came out. Kova's green eyes stared harder, waiting for me to respond.

"I am not getting any younger, Adrianna."

Sucking up my stupid emotions, I needed to be positive, because despite his hurtful words, I was a strong, confident person.

"I want it more than anything. Gymnastics is my life. My dream. Let me prove it, please. Give me one chance to show you. I won't give up and I'll work harder than everyone else in the gym, and you'll never hear me complain."

He stayed quiet, assessing my answer and said, "Bring me your schedule tomorrow, I will see where I can fit extra time in for you. You may have to come in on your day off, maybe do a half-day just for conditioning. I will go over it with Madeline, then call your father and tell him the joyous news."

Ignoring his jab, I responded eagerly. "I'll do whatever it takes."

I quickly learned Kova was a difficult man to read with his prolonged silence, but agreeing to whatever he said got me the approval I sought in his eyes.

"What is it that you are going for?"

Confused, I asked, "What do you mean?"

"Do you plan to compete in college? Retire before or after college… I need to know what I am working with."

I had one goal, and that was my only focus.

"I want to go to the Olympics."

Kova was a deer in headlights. It was the only reference that came to mind as he stared at me, unblinking. He didn't think I could do it. It was obvious.

Snapping his head to the side sharply, Kova cracked his neck. The sound echoed throughout the room, and I cringed. "You do realize how many young girls have the same ambition, right? How difficult it is to achieve?"

"I do."

"And you are aware only five girls in the entire country will make the women's team? That alternates hardly ever get called up?"

"Of course."

"And they are normally making the U.S. Team around fifteen years old?"

I knew where Kova was going with this, and truthfully, I didn't want to hear it. I'd had enough kicks to the gut for the night.

"I'm well aware I'm older than normal to begin the elite path and that my chances are low because of my age, but I have the fight and drive to make it happen. I have passion and determination. I don't care what anyone else thinks. If I don't push for it, I'll regret it. Everything I need is at my fingertips. I can do it… I know I can. I will practice until I can't get it wrong, until my hands are bleeding and my feet are raw. I'll go to the Olympics, and *nothing* is going to stop me. Especially not my age."

Seemingly impressed, Kova nodded slowly, taking in my words. "Go home. I will see you tomorrow, Adrianna."

∞

The moment I stepped out of the shower and dressed in my pajamas, I called Avery to vent.

The entire meeting with Coach Kova replayed in my head, making me sick to my stomach. Even though I should've been heading to bed for tomorrow's early practice, I knew my best friend would still be up. I gave her a play-by-play of my day and the results of my shitty evaluation, feeling bad for myself the entire time.

"Give up, that's basically what he told me," I complained. "I'm shit, Avery. A joke. I can't believe it. And here I thought I was good enough to be on a senior team. He clearly doesn't want me testing for elite, doesn't think I'm good enough, yet he has no choice to."

"What do you mean he has no choice? So he gave you all that shit for nothing, but at the end of the day, he has to train you?"

"Yes. There are junior elite and senior elite gymnasts. It's all based on age and you have to qualify by testing elite through national competitions with a minimum score. I need an elite coach who knows how to train higher level gymnasts and create routines that work with the elite scoring system. There's a certain level of difficulty, artistry, and execution where by combining skills, it gives me a higher start value. I continued training the way I did back home because a lot of the senior and junior elite skills are similar, but I couldn't advance, so technically I can't be deemed elite just yet."

"Just shut up and stop with the pity party. If he has no choice, which it sounds like he doesn't, it's obvious he's saying that shit on purpose to motivate you. You know you don't suck."

"Motivate me? Telling your new athlete they aren't up to your ridiculous standards and may never be is motivation to you? And seriously, Avery, if you'd seen these girls and what they're capable of doing, you'd feel worthless too."

"He's purposely messing with your head and you're allowing it to happen. Brush that shit off and go in tomorrow and act like he never said any of it. Hold your head high and show him what you're made of. I bet Fish Lips tells all the new girls that."

I giggled at her fish lips comment with her. "Why do you keep calling him Fish Lips?"

"Excuse me, Coach Kissable." She chuckled. "He reminds me of Tom Hardy, and Tommy has Fish Lips."

Oh, my God. "You know, when you put it that way it's kind of hot. Now I won't think of a blow fish every time you say fish lips, I'll think of Tom."

"See?" She laughed. "I told you."

I sighed, bringing me back to the moment. "I really hope I can prove him wrong."

"You can and you will. It's just like when your mom talks down to you."

I paused, thinking about what she just said. "You're right, but I really don't want to hate my coach. Not that I hate my mom, but you know what I mean."

"How can you hate a face like that? He reminds me of a brooding, mysterious guy with a dark side to him. I bet his body is even better."

I rolled my eyes, smiling at her comment. I wondered where the hell she came up with this stuff. "I can say with all honesty that I haven't even given his body a thought. I was too stressed about performing today to look." I lied. Of course I had.

"Yeah, okay," she responded sarcastically. "Whatever you say, but maybe you should take a Xanax before you go in tomorrow, you clearly need it."

"No way. That'll only make me tired and I can't have that. I need to be on my A game, re-member? Speaking of pills, I need to take some Motrin before I forget. I'm going to be sore as shit tomorrow." I reached under the bathroom sink and grabbed the white bottle that housed my favorite little orange pills.

"I was only joking with you."

"Ha." I shook two orange pills into my hand and filled the glass I kept by my bathroom sink with water. Swallowing back the pills, I said, "Thanks, Avery, for talking to me. This wasn't how I expected today to go at all. Not even close. I feel like a fool for thinking it would go any other way."

"You mean, listening to you bitch? Anytime!" Her smile seeped into her words, making me grin in return. I wasn't sure what I'd do without this girl.

Shaking my head, I said, "I'm gonna go. I have to be up at 5:30."

"Ugh. Good luck with that. Later, babe."

"Later."

Five minutes. I was pretty sure that was how long I slept before my obnoxious alarm clock went off. I had to do a double take to make sure I read the clock correctly.

Dear God, save me.

Sitting up, my legs dangled over my bed as I rubbed my blurry eyes. My back was tight, as were my shoulders and thighs. It wasn't too bad though, but maybe that was due to the Motrin I had taken before bed. Only time would tell.

Alfred would be here in forty-five minutes to pick me up, so I quickly brewed a cup of coffee from my Keurig and began to get ready.

About a year ago, my mother started giving me coffee to drink to replace meals. To shut her up, I told her it helped curb my appetite, but it never really did. Maybe an hour at most. I worked out hard, and I was hungry often.

In the end, I just developed a taste for Starbucks.

I packed my bag quickly, making sure I had two of those tasteless meals my mom loved so much, along with some protein bars and water bottles. And just in case, I grabbed the bottle of Motrin. Today would be another long day and I wasn't sure how I would fare.

Like clockwork, Alfred texted me saying he was outside. That man was perpetually on time, something I appreciated. Locking up my condo, I took the elevator down and jumped into the SUV.

"Miss—"

I gave him the look. "Thomas." I only used Thomas when I was serious.

He smirked. "How are you this morning?"

"Eh. A little sore, but not as bad as I thought I'd be," I said, fastening my seatbelt.

He dipped his chin. "That's good to hear. Do you know what time you'll be done today?"

"Not really, and after what I learned yesterday, who knows. I don't have school today, so I guess whenever Coach says I'm done. I'll text you when I get out and just wait for you to get there."

"How about you just send me a text during lunch and give me a roundabout idea?"

"I can do that."

Changing the subject, he said, "I hope you're paying attention to where we're going. From what your father says, when you get your license, you're on your own."

"Do you really think my parents will let you leave me alone in this city all by myself? It's one thing being alone on the Island, it's another thing in a town they aren't familiar with. I just don't see it happening anytime soon, especially when the media gets a hold of the fact I'm not there anymore."

Rossi Enterprises was a well-known real estate developer. They were responsible for many residential and commercial buildings in Atlanta. The company had been in my family for many years, beginning with my grandfather Angelo, who founded it. He started small with money he was given by his father, who had been a successful real estate agent at the time. Angelo took a chance against his father's advice and built a hotel with the money, then bought land from that income and built more commercial real estate and eventually residential properties. He did very well, but it was my dad who partnered with Avery's father, Michael Heron, years before either of us were born and created an empire, building high-end properties in major cities around the world. The name grew quickly, as did fame and fortune, and with that came unwanted press. Rossi Enterprises was now responsible for more than twenty-five hundred properties worldwide, coming in as one of the top developers in the world.

But leave it to my brother and his wild friends to attract bad publicity from their drunken crusades at the nightclubs and private parties, not to mention public arrests. It didn't help that Avery had twin brothers around the same age as Xavier. It was an ongoing joke between both families that both pregnancies were planned. My brother and Avery's were thick as thieves and only fueled the press. I lost track of the amount of times Dad had to bail them out of jail for things like drugs, crazy parties, and reckless driving. The band of brothers, as the media called them, were a force that couldn't be stopped. They flaunted whatever they could and took advantage of everything at their disposal. If outsiders only knew what went on behind closed doors.

The Rossi name was soon on everyone's lips. Anything we or the Herons did spread like wildfire, therefore making the boys a magnet for the paparazzi. My parents paid a lot of money to keep things out of the media, but some still made the front page.

Pursing his lips, Alfred snuck a glance at me. "Honey, when it comes to your parents, I have no idea what they'll do. I just want you to be prepared. Personally, I'd like it if you got used to your surroundings and the street names before I leave."

I nodded, agreeing with him as we pulled into World Cup. My stomach was immediately in knots, anxious for what was to come. I was running on five minutes of sleep, Starbucks, and a prayer.

"You're right… I'll pay attention starting tomorrow."

"Have a good training sesh," Alfred said as I stepped out of the Escalade, causing me to pause and look over my shoulder.

"Did you just say sesh? Tell me you did not just say that." Sesh was the slang everyone was using for session back home.

"What? Isn't that what everyone is saying these days? I'm just trying to keep up with the times."

"Alfred," I said, shaking my head with a big smile. "See you later."

chapter 10

LUGGING MY DUFFLE BAG OVER MY SHOULDER, I WALKED INTO THE GYM, FEELING slightly more comfortable than yesterday.

Even though I'd been on time the day before, I was much earlier this morning and had time to put my belongings away, therefore preventing any awkward stares from my teammates… or reprimands from Coach Kova. After last night, I planned to prove I was worthy of being here. I'd shut up and do everything he said I needed to. I wanted this, and I refused to let a few unconstructive comments bring me down.

I undressed down to my leo and was in the middle of sipping water when Kova emerged at my side, scaring the shit out of me. He was like a fucking ninja, always appearing out of thin air without a sound.

I sputtered and water dripped down my chin. I wiped it away with the back of my hand and looked at him, capping the container.

Kova eyed me with anything but concern. "Are you okay?"

"Fine." I coughed.

"Good. Let us go into my office."

I threw my hair into a messy bun, worried about what he wanted to talk about. He shut the door behind me and I took a seat, waiting for him to kill my hopes and dreams once again. It seemed to be his main goal every time I stepped foot into his office. My stomach twisted as our eyes locked, nervousness rippled through my veins as he stared at me for a long, hard moment. This couldn't be good.

"I spoke with Madeline and we devised a new schedule for you. Until you can reach the level where we need you to be, you will be here six days a week with lunch and tutoring in between. Of those six days, two of the days will be dedicated to your favorite ballet class in the morning." A sardonic half-grin tipped his lips. My belly fluttered at the way his eyes flickered when he said that. "Since you do not do tutoring every day, you will be here. Those will be about ten-hour days, coming in at just under fifty hours a week. You will get only one day to yourself for now to do whatever you need."

He had to have been out of his ever loving mind. But knowing better than to argue, I curtly responded. "Okay."

Looking down at his notes, his eyes scanned a few sentences before looking back at me. "You are going to also take some strengthening classes. We need you to improve your flexibility, and I think a couple of private sessions with me before practice will do it. So long as you continue with the drills."

My last coach used to say my hips were tight, but I didn't have a good understanding of what that meant. I guess I'd find out when the private session begun.

"There will be lots of conditioning in between, and every day before you start and when you finish, you will run two miles on the track outside."

"There's a track outside?" I hadn't seen one.

"Yes, just a couple of blocks over there is a high school. You will use their track. Four laps equals one mile, so you will run eight in the morning and eight in the evening."

I fucking hated running. "Whatever you say."

"This schedule is extreme and not something we do for everyone. If you cannot handle it, or even think for a minute you are not capable of it, you should tell us. My time, as well as all the coaches in this gym, is precious. I do not want you wasting it."

That pissed me off. Since I had no one to speak for me, I had to stand up for myself. "You haven't even given me a chance. Not even twenty-four hours have passed. What makes you think I can't do it? Yesterday I made mistakes, I know I did and I'll own up to it, but I was nervous. Give me another chance."

"There are no second chances in gymnastics. You should know this."

"I'm well aware."

"So no excuses."

"I won't make any." He remained silent, so I continued. "World Cup produces champions. I came here to be coached by the best so I can be the best. I'm not leaving."

"It is not about being the best, it is about how hard you work and how much you give without expecting anything in return. How much you train, how much you push when no one is looking. It is about how deep you dig within, knowing you did all you could possibly do and have no regrets at all. Even then, there is a chance it is still not enough." Kova exhaled a heavy breath. "I cannot make you the best, only you can do that. Your body can endure just about anything—it is your mind you have to convince."

Determined, I looked directly in his eyes. "I'll prove I can handle it."

Kova nodded slowly, a devious smile gracing his handsome face. I swallowed hard.

"What doesn't kill you only makes you stronger. Right, Coach?"

"In your case, only time will tell."

"Let us get started."

Following behind Kova, he led the way down the hall to one of the rooms in the back. He walked like he was on a mission. His shoulders were rigid and I found the way he marched when he walked intimidating. It was like he had a one track mind—an assignment needed to be tackled and dealt with. I guess I shouldn't complain since he'd taken time out to help me personally, but he reminded me of a drill sergeant. He was all listen, look, and don't talk.

The "don't talk" part was my biggest weakness.

World Cup was much larger than I ever imagined when we first showed up. Aside from the remarkable gym and dance rooms, there was a muscle therapy room, showers—which I would never use—and a cafe equipped with a kitchen and tables scattered throughout. Thanks to my dad, the cafe was built as part of the agreement for me to train here.

Pushing the door open, Kova flipped on the lights. He didn't waste time starting the private sessions. It'd been three weeks since we had our little chat and he implemented the new schedule.

The room held two exam style tables with navy blue, cushioned tops. There was a tall storage cabinet on the other side of the wall and various exercise equipment. Black folded mats, large yoga balls that were fun to bounce on, and elastic ropes used for restraint training hung from the walls. I knew he was concerned about my lack of flexibility—or so he said—but I was pretty sure he was delusional.

"Get undressed."

My leo was already on, so I took off my shoes, pants, and shirt, and stuffed them into my bag. I always wore loose fitted comfy pants and a regular tee to practice. Easy on, easy off. I took out a pair of black spandex mini shorts and slipped those on and waited.

"So, what are we going to do?" I asked curiously.

"*We*, are not going to do anything—you are." I fought the urge to roll my eyes.

I tracked Kova as he moved around the room. "You are going to stretch without stretching. A lot of athletes believe the more you do will help with flexibility. That is not always the case. Sometimes stretching aggressively backfires. It is short lived and can cause injuries." He paused. "Every athlete is different, so what works for one may not work for the other. It is all trial and error, but I have found this helps with flexibility the best."

I nodded, listening to him. I'd never heard this, but then again, I'd never seen anyone bounce on kneecaps either.

"Your former coach was concerned about your range of motion." Kova patted one of the tables, motioning me over. I closed the distance and jumped up. "I have been watching you the past few weeks, your shoulders and hips are tight. I have noticed you cannot go straight into a split, how it takes time for your hips to loosen until you hit the floor. Your leaps could use work and so could your angles. You are careful and it is obvious. Being cautious is not a bad thing, but it will hold you back. It is almost like your brain is subconsciously protecting you from over doing it, which will hinder your advancement in this sport."

I eased into conversation. "Yes, it does take me a little time to loosen up, but I thought that was normal before a workout for anyone."

He shook his head. "Lie back. Scoot forward so your legs are dangling off the table." I did as he instructed. "Good. Now lift your knee and bring it to your chest. It should be flat to your chest without your other leg coming up."

It wasn't flat, and my knee did come up. Kova gave me a knowing look. "See?"

"Don't you think it's because I just walked in and haven't stretched at all?"

"No, this is a simple thing that you should be able to do. Do it again."

This time when I did it, Kova laid a hand high up on my thigh to hold my leg down. When I couldn't bring my knee to my chest, he stepped in closer and helped widen my range of motion by pressing my knee to my chest, pushing on my shin, and holding down my other leg. His hands were large and capable of covering a vast amount of my skin. I grimaced inwardly so he wouldn't hear me complain about the strain on my muscles.

"You feel it, yes?" he asked, looking into my eyes.

I didn't want to give him the satisfaction, but I also had a feeling he'd be able to tell I was lying. "I do," I grunted when he pressed harder, "but I also think it's because I haven't warmed up yet."

Kova let go and stepped back. "Now, scoot up, bend your knees, and put both feet at the end of the table. Place your hands flat by your sides and then lift your hips."

I wasn't sure where he was going with this, but I did as he asked.

"How does that feel?"

I shrugged my shoulders. "I don't know. Good?"

Kova's eyes slowly grazed the length of my torso to my thighs and a shiver ran through me. "Can you not feel that your hips are not elevated all the way?" My brows cinched together and he stepped closer again. "Lift higher," he ordered, placing his hand to my butt and holding it there. Warmth surged through me from his searing touch. I finally felt it and I couldn't hide the tight pinch in my hips as he lifted me higher.

"I still think this is just because I haven't done any warm ups this morning yet, Coach," I grumbled. Apparently, I needed to remind him the sun was still rising, too.

Ignoring me, he said, "We are going to do various stretching techniques and breathing drills to help you. It is really all a mental thing, so we will train your brain to accept it."

"Train my brain to accept it?" I paused, trying to find the right words because this was the most ridiculous thing I'd ever heard. "I'm sorry, Coach, but I don't understand how basically manipulating myself is going to help with tight hips and shoulders."

He stared at me for a long moment before he said, "It is like relearning a skill you already know how to do and learning it correctly. Like breaking a bad habit. But in order to break a bad habit, you have to think differently. In your mind, if you keep stretching and over stretching, it will help, yeah? It will give you the range of motion you need?"

"Well, yes."

"So you are over doing it, and pushing and straining harder because you *think* it will make a difference when it clearly has not. Over stretching does not necessarily work. It is bad for your muscles. The stretching techniques I am about to teach you do in fact help. There will not be any strain on your body and they are safer for you. At your level, you should have a wide range of motion, but you do not. We can correct that. It is not uncommon, and this is not the first time I have seen this happen, but typically it comes with injury."

This was, by far, the most idiotic thing I'd ever heard. Somehow lying to myself would fix my tightness. Oh, how about I just lie to myself and *think* I could do a triple front tuck on the floor when, in reality, I couldn't. Training myself to think I could do it would only give me a broken neck and a wheel chair for the rest of my life, not the actual ability.

chapter 11

KOVA PROPPED HIS HANDS ON HIS HIPS. "YOU ARE SKEPTICAL."
Sometimes, just sometimes, I wished he'd use contractions.
"I am," I said honestly.

"So we will do a little test. Today, we warm up my way and then you start your workout. Tomorrow, and the next couple of weeks, you do it your way and see how it goes."

I smiled. "I like the sound of that."

Kova ushered me up and took me to the floor, where I did a split that didn't quite reach the ground, and a squat where my hips were parallel to my knees, but I couldn't go any farther. It actually hurt to squat this low without stretching the way I normally did. "Now, remember where you started this morning, yeah?"

I nodded and he took me back to the table. I decided not to question him. Regardless of his unusual training habits, I knew I was limited with my range.

Kova had me lie down, face up, and place my foot on my thigh. My back bowed just a bit and my knee didn't fall to the side, which meant my hips weren't open just yet. I did this with both legs. Then brought my knee to my chest again, and this time he stepped up to my side to help, catching me off guard. Kova placed his hand on the back of my bare thigh and my heart did a little somersault in response. He pressed my knee to my chest and used his other hand to hold down the opposite thigh.

The silence was odd. Really, really odd. Kova fixated his gaze on the white wall behind my head. I was curious to know what went through his mind since his eyes hardly moved. He was focused and in the zone. His body was so close I could see a hint of his facial hair growing in, but he smelled amazing. So good I inhaled a little too loud to get a better sniff.

He looked down and instructed, "No. Breathe with your stomach, not your chest and shoulders. Your stomach should come out when you inhale and your ribs will expand. We will work on breathing too, just not today."

With my eyes locked with Kova's, I drew in a measured breath. My heartbeat picked up in the silence and I took note of where he placed his hand—way up on my leg near my mini shorts. Okay, maybe it wasn't way, way up. It wasn't like I had these long super model legs or anything, he just had large hands that took up a lot of space on my thigh.

I exhaled leisurely and he gave a slight nod of approval. Kova let go and walked around to the other side of the table where he applied the same technique to my opposite leg. He watched me, as I did him, and I wasn't sure what to think of the dense silence between us. I couldn't tell if his focus was on making sure I breathed correctly, or to count the freckles on the bridge of my nose.

His hand moved to the back of my thigh and pressed inwardly, deeply massaging my hamstring with his fingers. My stomach clenched, the sensation shot straight to my core, causing a burst of heat to strike through me. I had a notion it wasn't supposed to feel this good.

"Your hamstrings feel a little too tight. Even with muscle, you should feel soft here, not hard like a rock. Loose and pliable," he said, voice low, and continued to feel around. "This is probably due to over stretching and overuse. Stiff muscles are not healthy and can cause lack of flexibility in both your hips and legs, which then could result in an injury. Stretching your hips consistently is key and should be done daily."

The pull inside my leg was tight and the urge to bend my knee was strong. Kova sensed the lift in my leg and firmly said, "No."

His callused hand leisurely drifted down my leg and gripped my knee. "Breathe. Feel what your body is doing, what position you are in, what it will help you accomplish. Focus on the movement and what it will do for you." His hand continued to my calf and he clucked his tongue in disapproval when he prodded the toned muscle.

I closed my eyes and followed his instructions. My body began to relax as I imagined the position I was in, the new way of stretching that would help me in the future. Opening my hips, I counted to ten and then reopened my eyes, only to find Kova immersed in me.

He was close, so close his breath hit my cheek. I knew his eyes were a pretty shade of green, similar to mine, but where I had wide, doe eyes, Kova's were more prominent and forward. Demanding. The lime green encased by the black circle was remarkable.

"Your eyes…" I whispered, "they're beautiful."

The corners of his mouth curled up, his full lips twisting into a grin. My cheeks glowed with warmth and I became innately aware of my surroundings, Kova's close proximity, and where his hands were, how his fingers pressed into my skin. A flush of heat surged through me and I wondered if he could feel my skin warming. He leaned in just a bit more to press on my leg. The strain was more acute and I fought against a grimace.

Just before backing away, Kova's mouth opened as if he was going to say something. Only, his eyes hardened and a crease formed between his wide brows. Nothing came out.

Me and my stupid mouth.

The weighty silence was too much for me to handle. "You guys should get a radio," I suggested, anything to bridge the weirdness between us. Kova looked perplexed, at a loss for words over my idea. As if a radio was such an appalling suggestion.

"We do not need a radio in this room, only in the gym for floor routines and the dance room. You will lose focus with music. Do eight counts in your head."

This had to be his idea of a joke. A really lame joke. He wanted me to do eight counts, counting to eight over and over to myself… a million times!

My eyes scanned around the room. "I don't see how that's possible with you nearly lying on my leg."

Fuck. Avery would have a field day with me once I told her the stupid shit that came out of my mouth.

"I am not going to acknowledge that sarcastic little comment of yours." Kova stepped back and took my ankle into his hand. "Put your leg down," he said. I did, and he placed my ankle over my thigh to lie flat, in a half butterfly position. Standing in front of me with one hand on my knee and the other on my ankle, he applied pressure.

Jesus Lord, did I ever feel the strain in my hips now. This was a different pull compared to the times I stretched, and I was beginning to see what he meant earlier. My chest pushed out and my head angled back. I squeezed my eyes shut to deal with the burn. "Uh-uh." He lightly slapped my thigh, bringing my attention to him. "Lie flat and breathe correctly. I will let up a little bit."

Focusing on his eyes, I did as he instructed. He kept his word and eased up, but not as much as I would've liked.

"Inhale, exhale, Adrianna. Stop breathing like you are running for the first time in your life. You are not a fish out of water. It is not that bad."

A burst of laughter came out of me. My eyes widened and I flattened my lips between my teeth so I wouldn't laugh again, or smile, which only made it worse. Between his odd comments and heavy Russian accent, I couldn't help but want to imitate him. Not to be mean, but because it sounded funny.

"I'm sorry for laughing," I said, covering my mouth. "I don't know why I found that funny."

Just when I thought he was going to scold me for my outburst, Kova's face relaxed and a flash of humor settled in his eyes. Shaking his head, there was a faint grin on his face.

"If you keep that kind of breathing up, it will only work against you in the future."

"How do you feel now?"

Standing, I lifted my knee and pulled my leg up in a half circle in front of my hips. "I don't know, I think I can tell my range is broader. My hips feel more open, if that makes sense." And they did feel a bit looser, which was nice.

He nodded. "Good. That is what I want you to feel. Now go get ready for practice, I will see you over there."

Kova patted my shoulder and then left. I quickly gathered my things and made my way to the locker room, where I found Hayden.

"How'd it go?" he asked from the other side of the room.

"As good as it could possibly go. His methods are a little strange. "

"What do you mean?"

"With his drills and stretches. He does things I've never seen or heard of in my life."

Hayden smiled, his dimples showing as he looked in his duffle bag. "But he knows his shit." Shutting his locker, he walked over to my side. "You want to go to Starbucks after practice? Grab a coffee?"

I pursed my lips together. "My, Hayden Moore, I hardly know you. Are you asking me on a date?" I said in a heightened, sarcastic, southern belle voice. "'Cause you know Mr. World Cup himself says that's not allowed."

Hayden cracked his knuckles as a smile slid across his face. He was pretty cute. "How about you buy your own coffee. That way it won't come off as a date, because believe me, it's not."

I shut my locker door and turned toward him. "Sounds like a plan."

"Is World Cup everything you thought it'd be?" Hayden asked. It was early, only five in the afternoon, and we were finished with practice.

We grabbed our coffees, plus a sandwich for him, and made our way outside to one of the tables. I'd called Alfred and let him know I was going to get coffee with my new friend and that he would give me a ride home.

I chuckled, unsure how to answer his question. "Hard to say, it's only been a few weeks. Ask me again in six months."

Sitting down, he unwrapped his food and I could smell the delectable scent. My stomach grumbled. I was starving, but I also needed to watch my weight.

"Want half?" he asked.

I gave him a droll stare. "You know I can't have that."

"Sucks to be you," he said playfully, popping a piece into his mouth.

Cupping my venti coffee, I took a sip of the dark roast I'd come to love. With just a splash of coconut milk, I was good to go.

"I'm curious," he said swallowing. "How did you find out about World Cup?"

My eyes shot to the table. "My dad's friends with Coach and gave him a call. They do business together sometimes."

"Ah, that makes sense. So, honestly, what'd you think of Kova?"

I was glad he didn't prod. "He's… interesting. And different than any other coach I've ever had. I'm open to anything that's going to help me, but at the same time, I don't know what to think. You know what he told me this morning? That I have to basically manipulate myself. He didn't say manipulate, he said train my brain, but I'm ninety-nine percent positive it's what he meant. Train my brain to do what exactly? Things I know I'm not ready for so I can break a bone and be out for the season? Who encourages that?"

Hayden laughed and I felt myself loosening up. "I don't think he means it in that sense. I think he just wants you to change your way of thinking to a safer route that will have a lasting effect. Think outside the box. He said similar things to Reagan from what I'm told. And I only know this because my sister told me one night. I've seen what he's capable of, and it's big things."

I nodded, taking in what he said. Interesting that he worked with Reagan. A light breeze blew the unruly strands of hair that had fallen loose from my ponytail across my face and I pushed them aside.

Hayden grew serious. "Don't be afraid to question things, but also trust your coach would never do anything to put you at risk. He can be Captain Dickhead when he wants to be, but have a little faith in what he's capable of doing. You wouldn't be here if he didn't think you could do it."

I sighed and took another sip of my coffee. His encouraging words helped. So much was up in the air, I wasn't sure what to think. I wanted so much in so little time. "You're right."

He ate the last bite of his sandwich and rubbed his hands together. "When do you work with him again?"

I shrugged, looking around. "I have no idea. I guess when he has time. But God, Hayden. The silence was so strange. He was up close and stretching me and shit." Hayden smiled, his blue eyes twinkling, and I found myself smiling in return. Oddly, his presence unruffled my feathers. "I didn't know what to do, what to say. Do I say anything? What did Holly do when she did this?"

"Holly didn't have to do any extra conditioning." My shoulders dropped, along with my self-confidence. Hayden sat up taller. "She didn't have to do what you're doing because we've been at this gym for many years, since we were kids, so she's already accustomed to its ways."

I pursed my lips together. He had a point.

"Why don't you ask Reagan how her sessions went? She worked with him for a while."

"I have a sinking suspicion she doesn't like me, so no."

Hayden looked toward the sky as if he was lost in thought. "Listen," he said, leaning forward and looking me square in the eyes. "Don't stress about the small shit. It won't mean anything in the end. Focus on what's important, the big picture. Your love of gymnastics. Just do you and you'll be okay."

Taking a deep breath, I expelled it and smiled. "I think that's exactly what I need to do."

chapter 12

KOVA SIGHED, DRAGGING A TIRED HAND DOWN HIS FACE.
Doubling my hours and adapting to a new coach proved to be much more daunting than I expected. I'd been to hell since starting this new journey.

And stayed there.

No matter how much I tried, no matter how much effort I put into training, it was never enough for Kova. He could at least give me a little credit so I knew he saw my effort.

"Adrianna," he said, curling the R again. "Why are you holding the bar like that? What the hell did they teach you at that damn gym?" He mumbled to himself in what sounded almost like disgust. My brows bunched together. Every day he had something negative to say. At first I tried to ignore his little comments, but the more he said them, the more aggravated I became. My old gym wasn't shit. It was good, I just outgrew it.

Kova jumped off the blue spotting box and grabbed my wrist, pulling me to the lower bar. "Hang on here."

Confused, I looked at him. "I don't understand."

One brow arched perfectly. I hated when he did that. "What do you not get? Hang on to the bar and pick your feet up. Now."

Shaking my head, I obliged, as always, and looked past my arm up at him. My knees were bent, scraping the mat while I waited for him to speak. Coach shook his head, looking dumbfounded at my hands.

I was beyond puzzled.

"Are you not gripping the bar correctly?" he questioned.

"What?"

Kova touched my fingers to answer my question. "You are resting your fingers on your grips, not gripping the actual bar correctly. It is incredible you can even hang on. Do your wrists hurt?"

I stood and let go of the bar, rubbing my wrists. I learned to block out the pain long ago.

"All the time." In fact, I could use some Motrin right now.

"You are barely holding the bar."

Mystified, he took my wrist into his hands and began removing my dowel grip by unwinding the Velcro. The grips helped execute high velocity maneuvers during swings that were followed by releasing and catching the bar.

Kova held the slightly tattered grip in front of his face. "This is dangerous. You need new grips. I trust you have more?"

"Yes." Of course I had more grips. I just liked this pair because they were worn in.

"Good. You should know better than to use this." He dropped it to the floor, along with the worn out wrist guards before moving onto the tape.

"There is no need for so much tape," he said, more to himself than to me. "No one even does this anymore. Then again, if you were doing it right, you would not need this."

As much I loved removing the tape after a long, rigorous bar training, I wasn't very happy about it coming off since I still had practice time left on this apparatus. It took time to cut the holes and place my fingers through them properly. There were layers upon layers of athletic tape to protect my hands from rips and tears. He pulled off each strand until my hand was bare.

Turning my wrist over to inspect it, Kova hissed at the sight before him. His fingers gently ran over my tender flesh, like feathers dancing erotically over me. Even though I used pre-wrap to prevent the adhesive from sticking to me, my skin was still as bright as a tomato with indentations and outlines. I wrapped it tightly every time, and once my wristbands were on, I wrapped more around them. I used an insane amount, but it got the job done. It helped to keep my wrists straight and locked to give me support. It's what I'd always done in the past and no one had ever said anything.

Kova held my wrist in his hand while he laced his long fingers through mine with his other hand. His palm kissed mine, his long fingers draping over my knuckles. Our hands locked together for a moment before he tenderly pulled on my knuckles, squeezing them as he did. He repeated the gesture and my heart skipped a beat at his skilled touch. *God, it felt good.* Incredibly good. My hands were overworked and dried out, they ached on a daily basis, but the feel of him massaging my fingers was heavenly and I almost sighed out loud. My entire body relaxed and I almost prayed he wouldn't stop.

There wasn't a part on my body that wasn't sore on a continual basis since I started at World Cup. I ached in places I didn't even know possible. A full body massage was something I needed to consider after this.

Glancing up from our entwined fingers, I found Kova observing me. I couldn't decipher what he was thinking as he stared down through thick lashes, his eyes unwavering. I focused on his lips, the fullness that begged me to wonder how soft they would feel pressed to mine. Heat rose to my cheeks and I flushed before him. His hand was much larger than mine, his fingers showing dexterity. He knew exactly how to manipulate my wrist and how to stretch my hand out gently, but with force, pulling on my fingers and then rotating my wrist, making it feel damn near euphoric.

Carefully, he bent my palm back, working it out in circles, flexing it. I stepped closer to him and my fingers curled around his fisted knuckles, lightly holding on to him. His presence dominated the air surrounding us. Why that made my heart race faster, I wasn't sure. Taking a chance, I naturally added a little more weight to my fingers so I could feel him move under my touch.

There was a slight pop and I swallowed, hiding the twinge of pain.

"Did that hurt?" he asked.

"A little bit, but it's nothing I'm not used to."

"Pushing through the pain is a sure fire way to sustain an injury."

Kova moved my hand to the side, but this time, he held my elbow so I couldn't bend my arm. His fingers pressed into my skin. I dipped to ease some of the pressure, but he shook his head.

"You are straining your wrists hanging the way you do. Since you are not gripping the bar properly, all your weight is balancing here." He shook my wrist with his thumb and forefinger. "It makes complete sense now why you use so much tape, you are trying to avoid excess movement. If we do not train you the correct way to hold the bar, you will retire much sooner than you want. Just another bad habit I need to break you of."

"Of course I'm gripping the bar properly. How else would I hold on?"

He shook his head. "You do not understand. You are holding on, but not completely. It is like a lazy hold, you are resting your fingers on the dowel instead of gripping it. When you swing and pivot around the bar, you are pulling and tugging on the ligaments inside your wrists, and the bones are under a lot more stress than needed. We need to rectify this fast."

Coach removed my other grip and tape and worked out my left wrist just as he did with my right. He was gentle with me, his face softening to concern as he worked.

After a few more minutes of tending to my sore muscles, Coach said, "Get back up there."

I reached down for my grips but he stepped on them.

"I need my grips."

"You will do it without them."

My mouth popped open in shock. "But, I'll get rips."

He shrugged like it was nothing. "Then you will learn real fast how to grip the bar correctly. Trust me, you will perform better in the long run."

"You've got to be kidding me."

Never, had I ever, heard of a coach training like this. No one took away a gymnast's protective gear.

No one except Coach Kova.

His mesmerizing eyes bore into mine, his features turning hard, showing me just how little he was kidding. I got the impression he was going to enjoy the pain he knew I was about to endure. The only thing I could figure was he learned it from his previous coaches in Russia.

I was starting to understand just how unconventional Russian coaching could be.

"Look at my face, Adrianna. Does it look like I am kidding? I do not care if it takes you hours and your hands are bleeding. You will grip that bar the *right* way," he emphasized the word with a sneer.

In that moment, I'd come to the conclusion Coach Kova was a closet lunatic. It was the only plausible explanation for his ridiculous training techniques. My hands were about to take a serious beating.

I shook my head in utter disbelief and walked to the chalk bowl. "Am I allowed to use chalk, Coach?" I asked in a heightened voice. He was being such a dick.

When he dipped his chin, I picked up a bottle of honey laying at my feet and squeezed a pile onto my palm, then smashed my hands together to help spread the sticky substance. Honey would create friction and a rough grip on the bars. Since Kova was already under my skin and I was sweating, I applied a hefty amount of powdered chalk next. A sweaty bar could cause me to slip and seeing as I wasn't allowed to use my grips, I didn't want to take a chance. I even used a chunky broken piece of chalk and ran it roughly across the back of my knuckles where the honey clumped together and then said a little prayer.

Clenching my jaw, I stood in front of the bar locking eyes with Kova. I stared hard, letting him see my irritation, not giving two fucks whether he liked it or not.

He pointed to me. "That look in your eyes? That is what I want to see. That is the kind of digging deep and pulling from within I was talking about when you first came here," he added, building a fire within me. "That is what I want to see!" As much as I hated him at the moment, I knew he was right. He was only trying to show me the correct way.

I swung into a kip then used my feet to stand on the low bar, jumping to the high bar. Chalk dust floated in the air, and I closed my eyes for a brief second and held my breath. The amount of chalk I inhaled on a daily basis couldn't be good for my health.

"Legs together!" he yelled as I did a pike kip and moved into a handstand. They fucking were together!

Of course, I didn't actually say that.

A free hip circle into a handstand, I took a deep breath and swung down to do a Gienger, a release with a half twist flying over the bar in a slight pike position, my legs bent at my hips so I was in an L position. Coming back to a handstand, I swung again, this time into a blind change right before moving into a straddle back. I grasped the bar harder than I normally did out of fear of falling, the burn began to resonate through my skin with all the twisting and releasing I'd already done. Kind of like when you wore a pair of high heels for the first time and the back of your feet weren't used to the friction. It was that kind of burn.

The tips of my fingers weren't used to holding and sliding against the bar this way. I'd have blisters by the end of this ludicrous form of training for sure.

A toe shoot to high bar, to a handstand pirouette. Giant to another pirouette and I reversed my grip. My Jaeger was coming up next, and from the corner of my eye, I saw Coach move to spot me. Even though it was normal for coaches to step in, fear streamed through my belly for a split second because there was always a chance anything could happen. My heart jumped into my throat as I mentally prepared for the fast paced bar release. It was now or never. And as much as I loved doing it, it terrified me each time.

Releasing the bar, it ricocheted loudly as I flipped up and forward into a pike position, the muscles in my hamstrings pulled tight while I reached for the high bar. This move would've been easier if I did it in a straddle position, but I liked the challenge of the pike.

You know, to make my life harder than it already was.

At least I'd get a bonus point for added difficulty.

Coming down, I gripped the bar as tight as possible, my palms began to really burn. I clutched it so forcefully the chalk had worn off and I wished for my grips, cursing Kova to hell at the same time. My bare skin rolled and pulled against the bar, but it hadn't ripped yet. It'd blister first before it actually tore open. The pain was like road rash, your hands grinding down on asphalt as you slid across the ground. All I had left were a few more releases and then the dismount. I was good to go.

Once I landed, I looked back at Coach, unable to stop the smug grin on my face. Bars was all about hitting handstands and perfect lines, and it felt like mine were on point. Surprisingly, the routine was actually really good. I had more control than usual. I did my release moves well and landed my full-in dismount, a full-twisting double back tuck.

My smile faltered after mood-killer Coach looked at me. He stood there stone-faced and expressionless.

"I think I actually perform better without my grips," I said confidently, and rubbed my hands roughly together, trying to ease the sting.

He shrugged, unimpressed. "We will see how you feel about that after you do it ten, fifteen more times."

I was stunned into silence.

He pointed with his head. "Back up. And Adrianna?"

I looked up in the middle of coating my hands with more chalk. "Yes?"

"Straighten your knees in your Jaeger. They were slightly bent when you reached for the bar. That is a deduction. You need to extend yourself, elongate your torso, and do not bend your arms." He stepped to me and pressed my shoulders back, and used his hand as an example to lengthen my torso. "Everything you need is already inside here." He tapped his temple. "Prove to me you want it."

Tight lipped, I nodded. I had dug deep, and really did try. I'd worked my ass off to prove myself worthy.

"And point your toes. Flexed feet are ugly."

I have ugly feet. Got it.

"Your elbows were bent in numerous places, it was sloppy looking. Tighten it up."

There went my confidence. And here I thought I did well. Nevertheless, I sucked it up and didn't say a word. Not like I could do or say much else anyway.

"Did you even spot?"

Of course I did.

"Hit your handstands in your cast."

I swallowed back the climbing tears.

"You need to hold that handstand perfectly straight before swinging down in the over-shoot. I have some drills you can do to get those lines. You want to test elite..." He muttered to himself before switching over to Russian.

I seriously hated the sight of Coach Kova right now.

chapter 13

WITH CHALK COVERING MY THIGHS AND HANDS, I PERFORMED MY ROUTINE more than a dozen times before practicing the skills individually.

I asked for my grips—only for Kova to deny me. My eyes widened and my jaw dropped when he said no. I couldn't believe he wouldn't let me use them. He was beyond delusional. Surely he realized inflicting this kind of torture on my hands would render them useless tomorrow.

Unless he just didn't care and expected me to train just as much.

Dear God, I prayed he wouldn't.

I moved onto my dismount with Kova spotting to give me a tad bit more height.

"Tighten up."

"Wrong!"

"Do it again."

"No, no, no, stop doing that."

"Just go for it! What are you waiting for?"

And when he was really fired up, he spat in Russian.

There was always something for him to gripe about. Kova was hardly satisfied, but today he acted like he was the one who slammed his shins on the bars. I was pretty sure there'd be a handful of black and blues blooming beneath my skin by morning. His entire focus had been on me at one point, perfecting my every move. He'd shown me numerous ways to correct my positions, his hands lingering a little longer each time, which I couldn't help but notice. He had the rest of the team do conditioning in between working with Madeline. While I appreciated his keen eye and wouldn't change a thing since he was making me better, in this moment, I despised it.

My hands hurt to make a fist. My skin was searing hot and tight, and I knew if I did any more practicing there was a good chance they'd bleed next.

When you held onto a bar for dear life, like I did, the skin on your palms bunched up and created either a blister or a pocket of blood. Of course I didn't get lucky with just a blister. And now little red bubbles of blood were ready to pop any minute.

Bloody bars were just nasty.

"Take a five minute break and get some water. We will start again."

Coach turned to walk away before I could say anything.

"He's really doing a number on you." Hayden appeared by my side.

"Tell me about it. He's refusing to let me wear grips since I apparently hold the bar incorrectly."

I turned my hands over and Hayden inhaled a sharp breath. "Is that all from today?"

"No, my wrists are usually beaten up pretty badly, but the blisters are new." There was never a time when a gymnast didn't have some type of rough or beaten palms.

"Do you have any Prep H with you?"

I looked at him in confusion. "Prep H? Like the stuff for hemorrhoids?"

"Yeah, it's supposed to help with rips. It will help reduce swelling and numb the rip."

I smiled shyly. "I've never heard of that."

"I bet you never heard of using Bag Balm either, then."

"Can't say I have."

"It's used on cow udders since they tend to crack and split often."

I stood with my mouth agape. I pictured the poor cows with the metal clamps, hyped up on steroids and growth hormones, forced to produce more milk than naturally occurring. Hayden chuckled at my expression. "That's disgusting."

I knew of all kinds of treatments, like using Vitamin E Gel, or a Band-Aid. Some believed in using warm tea bags on the rips with a sock to hold it in place overnight. A gymnast would do just about anything to heal a rip as swiftly as possible so they didn't tear their skin any further. Some even went as far as using a pumice stone to scrub around a rip, removing any calluses and dead skin. Just the thought made me cringe. Hopefully I wouldn't reach that stage. But hemorrhoid cream and the cow balm were new ones for me.

"My mom came up with a secret trick… I don't share it with anyone, but I can stop by your place sometime with it and show you if that's okay. I have a feeling you're going to need it. But you have to promise not to laugh. Or tell anyone."

I met his gaze. We hadn't known each other very long, but I was willing to take my chances. "Thanks, Hayden. I promise not to say a word."

"Social hour is over, girls." Kova's sarcastic tone did not go unnoticed. He clapped his hands and said, "Get back to work."

Hayden nodded, his lips flattened to a thin line. "Make sure to give me your number before you leave."

Back on the bars and my hands were raw, I'd never been in such pain before in my life. They were on fire, like burning flames of heat rolling across my palms.

Coach became relentless, forcing me to keep moving without a second to catch my breath or give my hands a break. He just kept yelling out orders until he was blue in the face and I mastered them to his imaginary level of perfection. My arms ached, the muscles strained and I was exhausted. But at least I had conquered the skills for the day. I was seriously contemplating calling in sick tomorrow.

But I couldn't. There was no excuse to miss a practice. Ever.

With another two release moves and dismount coming up before I was done for the night, Kova moved in to spot me. I was capable of doing them alone, but having a spotter was always comforting. It was a built-in trust that came with the territory, one I knew he'd never break. He'd catch me before he'd ever let me fall.

After I landed my full-twisting double back tuck dismount, Kova patted the side of my ass the way coaches do with football players. I glanced up and he gave me a deep nod. We stood inches apart with our eyes on each other, but I couldn't get a beat on his thoughts. I'd say he was pleased with me, but then again I just wasn't sure.

The team parted ways and prepared to leave. I said goodbye to the girls and gathered my things from the locker room. Food was the only thing on my mind and it wasn't one of those plastic prepared meals either. I was famished. Maybe I would have Alfred hit up a drive-thru on our way home for once.

As I was leaving the locker room, I pulled the door closed behind me and stepped into the narrow hallway as Kova came out of his office. He strode down the hall, eyes on me.

My skin prickled in awareness and I raked my gaze down the length of his body. Navy blue basketball shorts displayed the power and muscle in his legs, and a seemingly tight heather gray T-shirt clung to his chest, showing off his pecs. He was a man who took charge and one you didn't argue with. How someone could be so incredibly good looking and a complete jerk at the same time was beyond me. I bet he knew it too.

Tilting my head to the side, I noticed a look on his face I hadn't seen since arriving here. Contentment.

He stopped in front of me and peered down. "You did well today, Adrianna. Very well. You are coming along just fine, surprisingly." He took a swig of his bottled water.

It was almost too good to be true. I looked into his darkening eyes bound by thick eyelashes and saw he truly meant his words. I wasn't sure how to handle his appraisal without grinning like a fool. He caught me by surprise. Every day I wished he'd say something positive, and not once had he until now.

"Thank you, Coach."

"I will see you tomorrow," he said before continuing his walk down the hall.

"Ah, Coach?"

Kova paused, looking over his shoulder.

"Will I be able to use my grips next practice?"

"Not a chance. I know there is no way *you* learned after one day how to hold the bar correctly."

My jaw dropped in disbelief. *You.* As if I was an idiot. "But my hands are raw, it hurts to even wash them with soap. I'll bleed tomorrow and be completely useless."

Kova turned around to face me, his broad shoulders pulled back, one hand clenched around his water bottle. "Do you think you are the first gymnast to show wear and tear on their hands from bars, *malysh?*"

Kova visibly tensed, stopping short from his last word. Since I didn't speak a word of Russian, I had no idea what he said. But judging by the alarmed look on his face and the thick air between us, whatever he said couldn't have been good.

Snapping his head to the side, he cracked his neck. "I am not going to go light on you. Get used to it. Nobody said it was going to be easy, it only gets harder from here on out. You need to learn to toughen up and take it. Remember what I said earlier? Prove it to me. Every time you step foot into that gym—make it count. I do not care if your hands hurt or your back is sore or you are running on an hour of sleep. Prove it. Champions are not made by complaining. They are made by the endless pursuit of their dream despite the obstacles they are faced with. Push through it and do it."

I took a minute to let the weight of his words sink in. While an outsider would think they were laced with malice, I knew they weren't. That was the furthest thing from the truth. I knew he was pushing me to be better. Not only to prove it to him, but myself as well. Without a doubt, Konstantin Kournakova was a hundred percent right.

Slowly nodding, I looked into his eyes and said, "You're completely right, but I never expected you to go light on me. That's not what I wanted. That's not why I came here. I want the challenge. I want to be better. It's why I pour every ounce of blood and sweat into a sport that gives me so little in return. The truth is, I've never been challenged by a coach the way I have by you, so I'm learning to adjust to it." I held up my hands and showed him the bloody blisters threatening to pop under my palms. "You won't hear a complaint come from me again."

Kova's shoulders loosened and he blew out a ragged breath. His gaze openly traveled the length of my body, taking in every inch. The way his eyes pierced mine, like he was pleased with my response, made my heart rush against my chest with satisfaction.

I took more verbal beatings than any of the girls on the team. Constructive criticism at its finest. The only explanation I could think of was he was frustrated over having to break a seasoned athlete of old habits. He was always on me for something I was doing—grilling me, yelling at me.

"Good. That is what I want to hear." He gave me a lengthy gaze. Stepping closer, he gently brushed his thumb across my cheek. "Chalk," he said in a softer tone, and walked away.

I couldn't explain why, but my gut said there was more than meets the eye with him, I always trusted my gut. And him calling me whatever he just said in Russian, and the speech that followed, cemented it.

That being said, he was out of his ever-loving mind if he thought I was going through another day without using my grips.

chapter 14

STEPPING INTO WORLD CUP THIS MORNING, I FELT FRESH AND READY FOR PRACTICE. Dropping my duffle bag to the floor, the fabric of the strap scrapped along my sore palms and I sucked in a pain filled breath. Looking down, my hands were tattered, the skin pulled tight, aching from working bars. Pressing down on one of the blood blisters with my thumb, I watched the fluid shift under the skin in morbid fascination.

Grimacing, I shook my head and removed my pants and top, shoving them into my bag along with my flip flops. Today, I went with a faded, light blue sports bra and black mini shorts instead of the leo. This wasn't something I typically wore, but I'd seen the other girls do it and decided to. I pulled my hair into a messy bun and then placed my things into my locker and made my way into the therapy room.

Of course Kova was already there. His back was to me and I took the time to study him for a long moment before I made myself known. There were so many things I was curious to know about him. Like how he got started in gymnastics, what drove him toward the sport. How long he'd been a gymnast, how he ended up in the States. How he and my dad became friends. I was oddly intrigued by him. I tried to picture what he'd look like competing at the Olympics. Large, muscular arms. Broad shoulders and a fit waist. Overworked hands and tight buns. Focus pouring out of his eyes. For male gymnasts, their workout consisted mostly of bodybuilding exercises, unlike ours. They couldn't get too big and hefty, strength and balance went hand in hand for them. The rings were commonly used for straight arm work. They'd hold an Iron Cross position with weights tacked on to their feet or waist. This built an incredibly large and tight top half. Not to mention, high levels of strength. I sure as hell couldn't hold a T position, even without the weights dangling on me.

Kova wasn't ripped anymore like I'm sure he once was, but he was still quite built and trim. Sinuous was the perfect way to describe his body. He was definitely easy on the eyes. The muscles in his forearms rippled with strength, and if you watched closely, like I was doing at the moment, you'd see his back flex under his white shirt, along with two round mounds of steel that shifted with each step he took. I could stare at him all day long.

"Ah, Adrianna, you are here," he said pleasantly, taking me out of my daze. I stepped into the room, the cold tile zipping through my bare feet and I shivered.

"I'm here." I walked up to him. "What's on the menu for today?"

Kova turned toward me. "We will work on proper breathing and more of the same stretching we did the last time." He motioned toward the large square blue mat on the floor. "Go lie on your back, legs straight and together."

Walking over, I got into position as Kova followed closely behind. He kneeled on my left side and looked down at me. He spread his hand out and placed it on my stomach just below my ribs.

"Along with brain manipulation, as you so lovingly called it during our last session, you have to breathe correctly, or this extra work will all be a complete waste. It works much like a jigsaw puzzle. One wrong piece and nothing will connect how it is meant to. Proper breathing gives you back and core control. You will have more stamina and won't get tired so fast." He tapped on his temple. "It is all a mental game of tug-of-war. You want more belly breathing, more of using your diaphragm. It will lessen your chance of spinal injury as well. Remember, no fish out of water gasping like last time either. Now, take a deep breath."

I nodded and inhaled. He pinched my sides. "No, wrong. See how your stomach went toward your head and your chest popped up? We do not want that. We want your ribs to expand and your shoulders relaxed, not in your neck. Do it again."

I did it again. "No, keep your hips down," he ordered, and placed his other hand flat on my pelvis. "Again."

I focused on his words as Kova focused on my stomach. His brows furrowed. Breathing shouldn't be this complicated.

His hands stayed in place and pressed into me. "Good. Perfect," he said. "Let us do a set of ten."

I wanted to ask Kova how he knew to breathe like this, who taught him, but thought better of it and decided to wait until stretching came. I didn't think he'd like me to talk while I was learning to breathe properly anyway. So instead I focused on his hand resting on my lower belly. Wondered at the warmth surging through me from the feel of his fingertips on my skin.

"Beautiful," he said softly. "Yes, just like that." He looked into my eyes, almost as if trying to make me believe his words. "It is all about training yourself and remembering it. Doing it a thousand times until it actually sticks. Like muscle memory. Think of it like this—when you flex your abs and breathe at the same time, you are using your diaphragm. It is what gives you a strong core, which is key in so many aspects of gymnastics. The last thing you want is to overexert yourself."

Twenty minutes or so of instructional breathing skills passed, when I said, "I didn't know how important this was. How it can hinder me in this sport. It's very interesting."

He clucked his tongue on the side of his cheek and winked. "Stick with me."

Kova stood up and placed his hand out. I grabbed it and he helped me up. My belly fluttered in response and I averted my gaze. He pointed to the exam like table and said, "Go lie on your back."

I did as he ordered and pulled my knee to my chest and winced, feeling a slight tightness in my hips at first.

"Now, when you do these stretching techniques, remember to breathe properly. It all goes hand in hand, Adrianna."

Kova placed one hand on my leg and the other hand on my hip to steady me, pressing my knee deeper to my chest. I grunted. "All you need to do is hold this position, along with the others, for twenty to thirty seconds every time you stretch. I promise you it will make all the difference."

"Kova? How did you learn all of this?" I asked.

He peered down at me like it was common sense. "I learned most from my coach back in Russia. He was an extraordinary man and taught me well. I also took classes on it to further my comprehension. I wanted the upper hand when it came to coaching, and by applying both methods, I feel like I have that extra something the majority of coaches do not."

A small smile tugged at my lips. He was cocky and I liked that. I liked how he wanted to be a step above other coaches. It's what set them apart. We shifted to my other leg in the quiet room. The heat from Kova's hand danced across my pelvis and my belly dipped in return when he clutched my leg.

"Did you always want to go to the Olympics?" I asked curiously.

He gave a blasé shrug. "That is a tough question. Gymnastics for me was an escape from the life I was born into." A shadow formed in his eyes but it quickly disappeared before I could ask what he meant. "I looked forward to practice every day, but I never saw it as anything other than a hobby that would soon come to an end. My love for the sport definitely ran deeper compared to my teammates that is for sure. I was always trying to do more and I never cut on conditioning. I showed up early and I did not play around. I was devoted. My coach saw something in me and he spoke with my mother. He devised a plan, much like how Madeline and I did for you, and we stuck to it." He took a deep breath and angled my leg to the other side. "It was not until we changed my training and I had a new goal, that I realized just how much gymnastics meant to me, what security it brought me each exhausting day. It is why I went straight into coaching."

Something shifted inside of me and my heart constricted. His fingers dug into my skin as he focused on what he was doing. I felt his words, felt his love for the sport filter the air around us. He spoke from his heart. It was overwhelmingly obvious and I relished it. I didn't have friends who felt this way about sports the way I did, it was just fun and games to them. But watching Kova's eye color change, and hearing his heartfelt words really struck a chord with me. Gymnastics wasn't just a job for him, it was his lifeline. His salvation. And I respected him so much for it. I wanted to know more, like how it brought him security. I suddenly was very interested in my coach.

"In a way, you sound like me."

His brows furrowed as he moved me into another position. I winched when I felt the pinch in my hips and the heat of my hamstrings stretch.

"What do you mean?" he asked.

"Like you, I used gymnastics as an escapism from my life, from my family. I don't have a hard life, and I'm aware of how fortunate I am, but people don't see what goes on behind closed doors that shape us. This may sound terrible of me to say, but I don't look up to my mom as a role model. My dad, a little bit because of his drive, but not my mom. She wants me to be so much like her, but she's everything I don't aspire to be. I don't want to be anything other than me. I'm a gymnast with a craving to take it to the next level. So I decided the only way I could make that happen was to put every waking minute I could into the sport. When I think of gymnastics, I have peace of mind. I see me, and I think that's the most important thing as a person. To be who you want, not how others want you to be. It was how I decided I wanted to go all the way." I paused at the strained look in his eyes. "I'm sorry for rambling."

Kova's eyes tightened at the corners and his forehead scrunched together. He lessened the pressure on my legs but his hands stayed in place. I exhaled lightly. His voice dropped low, but the sincerity in his eyes showed strong when he said, "Even at a young age, taking the road I was offered was eventually a choice my mom left up to me. She did not push me, but coming from someone who has been down that path, listen to me when I say it is not easy at all. It is extremely hard. It was so much more than what I expected. Adrianna, I do not think you have any idea what training for the Olympics entails, or what you have to give up. I lost out on school dances, parties, hanging out with friends, everything a young adult is supposed to do and have a memory of. I missed out on my adolescent years. Maybe your mother does not want you to miss out on that. Yes, it was my choice, and I would not change a thing, but you really have to decide if it is something you want."

I didn't hesitate. "I want it more than anything."

"But why?" he asked, curiously. "What is the driving force?"

"Isn't it obvious? I just told you I love gymnastics and what it means to me."

He scoffed and it annoyed me. "A lot of people love the sport, it does not mean they give up everything and make a career out of it. So few make it that far. You can compete in college and still have a life. Collegiate gymnasts are only allowed to practice half the hours of what you are doing now."

My brows furrowed and my heart began to speed up. I didn't like the direction this conversation was going in.

"I feel like you're against me."

Kova pulled back, his nose flared. "I am not against you, I just want you to be aware of what is required of you. What you stand to lose. I am telling you what your other options are."

"I'm not going to lose anything, Kova, I'm going to gain. I don't need dances or parties, I need to be in the gym. If I don't take a shot at my dream, I'll live with regret, what-if questions that will plague me for the rest of my life. I need to try and see if I can do it. I have all the means to succeed at my fingertips to accomplish what I want." My voice rose and I became heated. I sat up and pulled my shoulders back, his palm rested high on my thigh. "I don't know what kind of life *you* were born into, but others would kill for mine. I'm going to use it to my advantage," I said firmly. "I want this. I want to be elite. I want to make the National Team, and one day, I want to go to the Olympics. I thought by coming here and telling you my aspirations you'd understand."

Kova's posture became rigid, his fingers pressed into my skin.

I was pushing his buttons.

chapter 15

"**I** UNDERSTAND MORE SO THAN ANY COACH HERE," HE RETORTED.

"Then what's the problem? Isn't this what every coach wants to hear?"

We faced off in a battle of wills, both of us determined to make the other one understand. Thing was, I was stubborn and hardheaded. There was no way I was going to back down. Then again, I didn't think he would either.

I placed my hand on his forearm, hoping he'd understand how strongly I felt about this. He flexed under my touch and his grip tightened, but his eyes didn't waver and he didn't pull away. His palm warmed my skin and my cheeks flushed from the reaction.

"You're either with me or you're against me, Kova," I nearly pleaded, just inches from his face.

Silence thickened between us. Kova's jaw flexed and he looked straight at me. "I will be completely honest, no other gymnast I have trained has wanted it as badly as you do. It is rare. You have no idea how refreshing this is to hear." He sighed heavily, his green eyes burned with newfound desire, and I liked it. Being this close to him and having this conversation caused my heart to patter against my ribs.

"If this is what you want, what you truly want, I will do my best to help get you there. But you need to have a good understanding there is a chance you still will not make it all the way. There will be many obstacles in your quest that could eventually halt you instead of finding ways to overcome them. Are you ready for that?"

I absorbed his words deep into my soul and took in the compassion in his eyes. My pulse was racing. A small smile tipped my lips, one I had to refrain from splitting across my face.

"Do you mean that?"

He nodded slowly. The side of his mouth tugged up in challenge. "If that is what you want, but there is no going back once you decide. It is not fair to me, or you."

"This is my dream, and I'm going to show you. I'll prove it. Actions speak louder than words."

He was silent for a moment, then I saw a flash of hunger enter his eyes. I loved it. "I am going to hold you to that."

"I hope you do." I raised a brow. "It wouldn't be in your nature not to."

The room stilled as Kova tilted his head to the side. Pensive eyes stared down at me, and I felt myself falling into a bottomless pit. He had my full attention, I couldn't look away. He was sucking me dry, feeding off my emotion. And truthfully, I didn't want to look any other way but his. I wanted him to see I wasn't kidding about my future.

"You are not what I expected you to be."

That caused me to grin and I laid back down on the table. "Good… Exactly what I wanted." I grew quiet, then asked, "What did you expect?"

"Not someone as determined as you that is for sure. You are strong-minded."

A little laugh rolled off my lips. "I'll take that as a compliment."

Kova ran his tongue along his bottom lip and I tracked the movement. Something clicked between us, an understanding only someone as ambitious as us could identify with. It was there. I felt it, and the look his emerald eyes penetrated me with told me he did too. I hadn't realized it, and I didn't think he did either, but at some point in time during our conversation, Kova had stopped stretching me. One hand was now half on my waist, half on the table. His other hand cupped the back of my leg, nearly holding onto the crease of my ass. I didn't remember him moving them, but I liked it. The tips of his fingers pressed into my inner thigh and caused a rush of heat to sear me. They were dangerously close to my sex and I swallowed as a throb resonated in my core.

I breathed in deeply, the way Kova taught me. One small move and he'd touch me where no one had ever touched me before. I didn't know which was worse, wanting to feel his fingers there or the fact that I didn't find the action repulsive.

I parted my leg slightly and looked in the direction of his hand. Kova followed my gaze, and swiftly pulled away, clenching his eyes shut.

He cleared his throat. "All right. Where were we," he said more to himself than me. He guided me to my stomach and into position. He placed a flat hand on my hamstring, prodding the muscle for tightness and grabbed my knee, pulling it backward.

"Ah, not as hard as last time I see," he said. "This is good."

I watched his movements from the side, my right cheek to the cushioned mat. A tightness developed in my pelvis and a little grunt escaped my throat. I grabbed the edge of the table. Kova glanced at me when I winced and gave a knowing look to breathe. He tapped the side of my butt twice with the back of his knuckles, and I exhaled slowly, then drew in a breath with my stomach. He nodded in approval.

"You know, I was a scrawny thing when I started gymnastics. I could barely hold the bar for more than a couple of seconds."

My eyes widened playfully and I bit down on my lip. I eyed his strong arms. "You're kidding me."

He shook his head. "I wish I was." Then he went into a story about when he first started gymnastics and it lightened the private session, leaving me with a slight smile and a blooming heart, wanting to know everything I could about my coach.

After a full day of training, I was exhausted, and the blisters on my palms were getting progressively worse.

Kova didn't go any easier on me today, if anything, since agreeing to help me with my goal, his dick factor increased. The blisters were tender to the touch and filled with fluid that needed draining. I tried not to pick at them so they could be treated properly at home, but something had to give. My hands were on fire and throbbed from irritation.

As much as I wanted Hayden to help me heal my impending rips, I didn't want him to go out of his way and make him stay up later than usual. It was almost ten o'clock at night, and I imagined he was just as tired as I was.

Before I could give it any more thought, my doorbell rang. I quickly got up from the couch and peeped through the hole.

After unbolting the lock, I opened the door to Hayden standing on the other side in gray sweatpants and hoodie, a pharmacy bag hanging from his hand.

"Hey, come in."

With perfectly white, straight teeth, Hayden smiled and walked in.

"Are you sure it's not too late for you? I kind of feel bad."

I decided the lightning in my kitchen would be best for him to doctor my hands. With the condo's open floor plan, it was parallel to the living room, and the pathway to the two bedrooms was in view. Hayden's nose scrunched up as he took in the view, a grin working across his face. "It's like 9, Aid."

I shot a glance at the clock. "It's 10:15… and I know you have to get up early."

He dropped the plastic bag on the countertop. "I'm a big boy, I think I can handle it. But since you're so concerned about my bedtime," he chuckled playfully, "let's see what you got here so I can get home for my beauty sleep. Show me your hands."

I jumped up and planted my ass on the cold granite countertop, sending goose bumps down my body from the contact. I wore a loose fitting white T-shirt and a pair of cutoff denim shorts. Holding my hands out for him to view, I placed them face up on my thighs and waited while Hayden unzipped his hoodie, revealing nothing underneath except for extremely low sitting sweats.

My jaw went slack and my eyes widened. Hayden draped his jacket over the back of one of the high back chairs I used to have breakfast and began rummaging through his bag. I swallowed hard at the sight of him so close, wanting to reach out and run my fingers down his solid chest. Every inch of his body was honed to perfection, every muscle ripped, curled, and dipped.

This wasn't the first time I'd seen Hayden shirtless, but it also wasn't something I paid attention to at the gym very often. He was just a guy doing the same sport I loved. In fact, I rarely noticed. I had a tendency to get tunnel vision, and lately, it had been nothing but Kova and gymnastics, shutting out everything else around me.

Maybe I should have taken notice though, because his body was a work of art.

"Ah, do you always go out dressed like that?" I asked hoarsely.

Hayden paused, then looked down at his body before meeting my gaze. He cleared his throat and said, "I didn't even realize it. I came from practice and didn't feel like slipping on a shirt since I was hot and sticky. I can put my jacket—"

"No!" I yelled, blinking rapidly. "You're fine, I just wasn't expecting… it."

A half smile tugged on the side of his mouth. "You see me like this every day."

I shrugged, trying to avoid his impish gaze. "Guess I never noticed before." He was right. I did see him like that all the time, just never secluded like we were in my condo. Or so close…

"You guess you never noticed," he deadpanned.

I tried not to smile by flattening my lips, but my cheeks gave me away. They were flaming hot. "What! What do you want me to say?"

He smiled and my gaze drifted to his hair. It was chalky and messy, and I had the sudden desire to know what it felt like against my skin. Feel the softness.

I shook my head, erasing the thoughts.

"All right," he said, stopping to look in my eyes. "Promise not to laugh?"

"Promise."

"My mom is a labor and delivery nurse. When my rips were getting bad and nothing was working," he said, shuffling through the bag and pulling out a purple box but keeping it out of view, "she came home with this stuff."

"What is it?"

Hayden opened his palm and showed me what was laying in it. "It's, ah, ointment," he said sheepishly.

"Let me see," I said, taking the purple box. Flipping it over, I read it out loud. "Lanolin. Soothes and protects cracked…" I trailed off. "Nipples?" Nipples came out high pitched and I looked up at him, bemused.

A rosy hue filled his cheeks and I couldn't help but grin.

"Yeah, it's nipple cream. My mom says mothers who breastfeed use it on their boobs to, ah," he avoided my gaze, "help with cracking and bleeding."

"Bleeding?" A frown formed on my face. "Bleeding nipples? And cracked?" My nipples ached at the thought.

"Yeah, well it works. Take my word for it. At least I didn't bring over nipple cream for cows."

"You mean to tell me you use nipple cream? Hayden Moore uses nipple cream on his hands."

I tried hard to hold it in, but a fit of hysterical laughter over the situation escaped.

"Oh, my God! Do you bring this to practice? Do you share it with your teammates? Do you buy this, or does your mom?"

Hayden didn't seem impressed with my questions, or the fact I that couldn't stop laughing. He leaned over, coming close to my face, and placed his hands on the counter next to each side of my legs, effectively putting his body directly between my thighs. He lifted a brow and waited for me to calm down. I tried to stop humiliating him by pursing my lips together, but I burst out again the moment I looked at his face.

"I'm sorry! I don't know why I find this so funny, I just do!" My head rolled back, tears coated my eyes as I imagined Hayden buying nipple cream and trying to hide it. He pressed a hand to my bare thigh in an effort to gain my attention.

"Laugh it up. By the end of the week you'll be kissing my feet and thanking me."

I grimaced. I hated feet. No way in hell would that happen, no matter how thankful I was.

"Done?" he asked, trying to hide his smirk. I flattened my lips and gave a hasty nod. It was the only way I wouldn't laugh.

Hayden's thumb grazed my skin in circles and it was then I realized he hadn't moved his hand from my thigh.

Our gazes grew deeper.

My breathing slowed as his head tilted just slightly to the side to take me in. I hadn't noticed before, but up close Hayden had the most stunning cobalt blue eyes.

Dark and elusive with shadows of slate gray hidden in between, he was pulling me into him and he didn't even know it.

chapter 16

MY BREATHING DEEPENED.

Hayden stood to his full height, stepping in closer between my legs so his waist was pressed to the countertop. My lips parted, a breath rolling off as he stared deeply into my eyes. His hand carefully cupped my cheek, his fingers holding my jaw steady. I swallowed when his eyes traveled to my mouth, his head dipping down just inches away from closing the distance.

"You're so pretty when you laugh, Aid," he whispered, his nose rubbing mine. Goose bumps broke out across my skin. "Your whole face lights up," he added, this time against my lips as his hand slipped into the back of my hair, kneading my head. "You can make fun of me all you want if it makes you laugh the way you just did."

He closed the short distance and pressed his lips to mine, soft and gentle. My heart pounded, unsure what to think of this moment.

Tenderly, he pulled my bottom lip into his mouth and nibbled on it. I gave in with only a slight hesitation. A simmering heat washed over me when his warm tongue slipped inside and met mine.

I moaned, liking Hayden's kiss. It was completely unexpected and I wasn't sure what to think. Not that I could—or wanted to. Leaning into him, I pressed my chest to his, my back arched and my hands came up to his firm shoulders before sliding into his chalky hair. Even with the fabric of my shirt between us, the heat of his bare skin against mine was heavenly.

Hayden deepened the kiss as I tugged on his hair, and my thighs squeezed his hips, feeling pleasure streaming through my body. Our mouths mimicked each other's, our tongues dancing perfectly as a sweet bliss hit both of us.

Hayden was a damn fine kisser.

And I had a pretty good idea he knew when he pulled me closer. He took control and set the pace, and I allowed it. There was no space between us, my legs wrapped around his back, and my heels pressed into him, wanting to feel him closer to me.

Hayden's mouth became aggressive. Pleasure flowed through my body, starting from my head down to the tips of my toes. A blaze of warmth steadily grew between us and we both drew from it. I'd kissed a couple boys before, but Hayden's kiss belonged in another league.

My hands moved from his hair down his neck and onto his firm pecks, skimming over his honey colored skin. He exuded strength beneath my touch, and I wanted to feel every inch of his body. Moving to his hips, the back of my knuckles danced over the V that dipped into his sweatpants. His stomach twitched, and he squeezed me just a little tighter. Sliding around to his back, I cupped his round ass. This time it was his turn to groan into my mouth, and I liked the sound of it. I gave his ass a little squeeze and he tensed.

"Hayden," I whispered against his lips, but he didn't process my words. His hands didn't stop caressing and kneading my waist, my back, or my thighs. He was everywhere.

"Aid," he mumbled on my lips, palming my cheeks.

"Hmm?"

"I want to feel you all over me." Then he slammed his mouth to mine. His hands roamed my body, as if he couldn't touch me fast enough. My panties dampened at his touch. Hayden moved my hand to the front of his pants to cup his hardness. I held back a grimace, my palms pulsated from my rips, but I sucked it up because curiosity got the best of me. The urge to dip my hand inside his pants was strong. I wasn't a prude, but I didn't have a ton of experience either. I'd had a boyfriend back home who I'd fooled around with, but nothing serious. When he realized gymnastics was more important to me than having sex with him, he dropped me like a bad habit. I was fine with that.

My chest rose and fell, my breathing deepened at the contemplation of my hand exploring him.

The heat of his breath tickled my cheek. "What are you thinking?" he asked roughly.

I had a feeling the look in his eyes mimicked mine. Heavy and glossy, drowning in the intense air enveloping us.

Unable to find the right words, I showed him. My nails grazed the lip of his low sitting sweatpants ever so slowly. Hayden drew in a shaky breath and his hands tightened on my nape, my head tilted back. His jaw flexed as the tips of my fingers dipped inside and brushed his pubic hair. I swallowed hard.

"I think we should stop," he said gutturally.

I paused, insecurity consuming me. "Oh, okay. Am I doing something wrong?" Maybe this was another reason my ex-boyfriend dropped me.

"No," he murmured. "You're not doing anything wrong, it feels good, but if you keep touching me like—"

He cut himself off, clutching my wrist tightly. My fingers were about to slide deeper when he stopped them.

"Adrianna. Do you know how good this feels?"

"No," I answered quietly when he released my wrist.

A brow lifted and he placed his hand on my hip. "Have you ever had a boyfriend?"

"Yes."

His other hand stayed in my hair. "And?"

"We didn't do much, just played around."

"You're a virgin," he stated more than asked. I nodded, inhaling. "I don't think this is such a good idea," he said.

Just as I thought he was about to pull away, Hayden dove in for another kiss, claiming my mouth. For me, that was the green light to dive into him.

Hayden held my face between his hands as he devoured my kiss, my hands slid around his hips. His hands quickly shifted to my chest and I released a little sigh. My stomach tightened and my heart jumped into my throat at the thought of what he—we—would do next. His fingers ran over the sides of my breasts, and my fingertips plunged into the waistband of his sweats and pushed them down just a bit so I could feel how low the V dipped.

He broke the kiss and stepped back.

"No, no more," he panted. My lips were swollen and my breath heavy when he pulled away. "I don't know what I was thinking. This is a big no for our gym. If any coach found out, we could get in a whole lot of trouble. We don't need that."

Overwhelmed with lust, I didn't take a moment to stop and think about how this could affect us down the line. Looking at the ground, I apologized.

"Hey, there's nothing to be sorry about, okay? I liked kissing you and, under different circumstances, maybe we would've kissed longer, but we have bigger things to focus on." He ran a hand through his hair and blew out a ragged breath. "Let's get those hands fixed for you."

Turning my hands over, I chuckled remorsefully at the blisters. "You know, I forgot my hands hurt. You took the pain away for a bit."

The dimples in his cheeks appeared and his eyes glistened. My stomach was full of butterflies and my heart pounded in my chest.

Hayden was so damn cute.

Opening the package, he took out the ointment and uncapped it. He squeezed a small amount on his fingers. "I'm just going to apply this to your wrists right now. Before bed, you'll need to apply a generous amount to your palms and put socks over your hands. Otherwise, it'll get everywhere."

Hayden clutched my wrist and turned my hand over. "Luckily you don't have rips on your wrists too from grips and tape, so this will help heal them nicely."

He began applying the balm, rubbing it into my skin and making sure it got absorbed. "You know we're going to need to pull those off, right?"

I groaned. "Do we have to?"

"I think you know the answer to that."

I did.

His skillful fingers did wonders to my aching muscles and I almost groaned from the sheer delight of the massage. Maybe I needed to hire a masseuse. "You have no idea how good this feels. My wrists are always in pain."

"I overheard what Kova said, how you hang on the bar and all. To be honest, it's amazing you've lasted this long. Between the grip on bars and the bizarre way you wrap your wrists, I'm surprised you haven't quit."

Never. There wasn't a chance in hell I'd ever quit gymnastics.

He grabbed my other wrist and changed his tone. "I'll be honest. I like you, Adrianna. I have since the moment I met you." He shook his head and then met my eyes. "There's a light in your eyes, a will I don't see often from the other girls at World Cup. I see the way Coach grates on you, pushes you down, picks at every little thing, but you never give up. Sometimes I wonder if he has it out for you. You don't cry, you don't want empathy, you don't walk around with a chip on your shoulder—"

"Like Reagan."

He smiled softly, and my heart melted. "Like Reagan. You're determined."

I bit the inside of my lip. "I feel like that's how all the girls are though."

"Yeah, but I don't know." He shrugged. "You're just different."

Reaching into his bag, Hayden pulled out a package of needles and a lighter.

"No," I whined, knowing what those were used for.

He paused. "You have to, Aid. You know this."

I did know this. It didn't mean I wanted to do it.

"This can't be worse than straddling the beam."

I pursed my lips together. "You may have a point, but this is going to make tomorrow even more painful and you know it."

"No, *not* popping them will make it worse. You have to drain them. At least get the fluid to release a little. I won't do to you what I do to my hands, I'll just pop at the corners."

Curious, I asked, "What do you do for your hands?"

"I pop the blisters and then cut the skin off all in one shot. I don't wait for the skin to tear back and die."

I grimaced. I wasn't going that far tonight. Hayden began lighting the needle to sterilize it and prevent an infection, after which he planned to use it to pop my blisters. I'd had rips and blisters before, but never to this extent. I was always given time to heal my hands, so I never really had to treat my skin to this degree before.

"Do you have any other ointment in your bag of tricks? Like some antibacterial kind? I can use that." My heart began to pound. I really didn't want to do this.

"Yeah, but you know none of that will help."

Hayden stepped back and I jumped down off the counter and reached for the filmy, plastic bag and began rummaging through it. Chap Stick, tape, scissors, socks, honey, a pumice stone, antibacterial ointment, all things used for rips.

No…

I pulled the stone out of the bag, but Hayden yanked it out of my hand and held it above his head.

"Give it back to me."

"No."

I jumped, trying to reach it, but it was useless. I was too short.

"Hayden, it's one thing to pop my blisters and cut off the dead skin. It's another thing entirely to scrub my hand. Just please give that to me. You're not doing it." I knew what would happen after.

The dreaded pumice stone. Fuck that. I'd never had to go that far with the stone, mainly because I never had a psychotic coach before like Kova, or gym hours like I did now, but I'd heard war stories, and it wasn't something I wanted to test out.

Plus, they didn't look terribly bad. I may have overreacted with how they looked.

"You know I'll just be back here tomorrow, right?"

"Please," I begged, my forehead bunching together. "Please, Hayden, I'll take my chances. You can drain the blisters, but no stone."

Hayden's eyes softened, pitying me. "Are you sure that's what you want to do? I'm obviously not going to scrub the blisters, just around them to get the calluses off, but you need to start using it every night in the shower to toughen the skin."

I shrugged helplessly, sighing. "I know, and I will after these heal."

"Fine." He cocked his head to the side with a know-it-all look. "Are you a religious person?" he asked out of the blue.

Puzzled, I said, "I mean, we go to church on major holidays, but we're not devout Catholics or anything. Why?"

"Because you're going to need the grace of God on your side tomorrow. I'll be praying for mercy and that Kova will go light on you. Now give me your hand and let's work on those rips."

chapter 17

YESTERDAY MORNING WHEN MY ALARM WENT OFF, THE FIRST THING I DID WAS remove the socks.

The swelling on my hands had gone down tremendously, and the redness on my wrists looked almost healed. The nipple cream was like a magic potion. After practice, I had Alfred take me to the nearest pharmacy to buy every tube I could get my abused hands on.

Much to my surprise, Kova took mercy on me and gave me a day off from bars. It didn't follow into the next day though, because when I walked into the gym this morning, he insisted we work on bars again first thing. He wasn't confident I had learned my lesson.

"You should have popped those," he said arrogantly in a thick Russian accent, eyeing my blistered hands. I swear, because I hadn't popped them entirely, he'd do anything he possible could to make me suffer.

I was certain Kova was a sadist.

Reaching inside my bag, I pulled out a string of tape Hayden had prepared for me. He cut some pieces and showed me how I should apply them to cover my blisters since I wouldn't be allowed to use my grips. "Can I at least use this?"

Kova stepped over the cables and looked down. "Go ahead, it won't help though."

I ignored his flippant tone. Anything would help at this point. I looked at the rest of the team girls, envying the grips they had covering their hands. Placing the strip over the blisters, I ripped a piece of tape from the roll with my teeth and layered it. I was tempted to tape my entire hand, but I wasn't that ballsy to take the chance of getting yelled at and being forced to remove all of it and go bare skinned. I repeated the same method on my other hand and then applied chalk. Lots and lots of chalk.

"Did you stretch out this morning?"

I nodded.

"My way or yours?"

"My way."

He gave me a pointed look. "I did not see you stretch."

"Uh, when… when you were in the back," I stammered. "I warmed up with the girls."

"Did you run?"

Shit. "No, I didn't."

He glowered. "Before you break for lunch, you will run, and you will do three miles." Fuck my life. I hated cardio. "Have you been using any of the drills I showed you?"

Jesus Christ. This felt an awful lot like an interrogation. Like I was under the spotlight. The urge to lie was stronger than ever, but for some reason, I just couldn't. Call it intuition, but I had a feeling he'd know I was being dishonest. "No, I haven't. I mean I have, just not every time."

"You are not proving anything to me this morning, Ria. When I am not around, you must still use these exercises on your own. You are only hurting yourself in the long run." He clucked his tongue in disappointment. "Tonight, after practice, we will work together again before you leave."

Ria? The way he said it gave me butterflies. That was a new one, and I liked it a million times more than Ana.

"All right, let us go." He clapped his hands enthusiastically and stood near the low bar, watching me closely. That was it. No yelling, scowling, or glaring at me? His cheerful mood caught me off guard, and I wasn't sure what to think of it.

Swinging into a kip, I cast to a handstand, free hip circle cast to another handstand, then I piked down and used my core and hips to release and fly to the high bar. Coach watched my posture closely, probably analyzing every little thing I did wrong so he could berate me later. All I wanted to do was please him and prove I was trying, but it never came off that way.

Kova was hard and honest to a fault, which is what I'd wanted when I transitioned to World Cup. It was something every coach should be, regardless of our feelings, but some days we needed a break. Some days it was too much. Some days it could break our spirit.

I found myself making more mistakes than normal when his eyes were trained this closely on me, or when his hands touched me when he spotted. He didn't miss a beat and if I messed up, he caught it and corrected me immediately. He had eagle eyes, and that was both a blessing and a curse for a gymnast.

When my hands gripped the high bar, chalk dust sprinkled in my eyes and I winced. There was a slight burn but I ignored it and continued. I'd use that mind over matter logic and push through the pain.

I could do it. I knew I could.

A simple back tuck for my dismount and I felt more confident with my feet on the soft, blue landing mat. The pain in my hands wasn't nearly as bad as I anticipated, however, I felt a pull in the back of my calf I wasn't used to. Bending down, I rubbed the twinge of heat and walked away wiggling my leg with each step.

Chalking up, Kova moved the spring board to the front of the low bar. "We are going to start with your mount," he said, his eyes raking over my body from head to toe. "We are going to change it up."

"What? Why?"

He expelled an annoyed sigh. "Adrianna, it is too early for your questions this morning. Just do as I ask and do not question everything I say. It is exhausting. Think you can handle that and just keep quiet?" When I didn't move, he voiced, "It will help with your score. Now please just do as I say."

Well *excuse* the fuck out of me. "Sure."

"You are going to do a hecht mount. I will adjust the low bar so you can get used to it. We are going to do this until we nail it. The key to this mount is to pop off with your shoulders without bending your elbows. Arch your back just a tad once you release the low bar and keep those legs tight and together."

Tight lipped, I nodded. I actually knew how to do this, but I wasn't going to tell him. He told me to keep quiet, after all. I grinned to myself when I turned around and walked to the end of the mat, gearing up.

"The bar is low enough that you should have no issue getting over it. I will spot just in case," he said, and I nodded.

Call me crazy, but I wanted to fuck with his head. It seemed he had little faith in me as it was, so why not?

Wiping the excess chalk from my hands onto my legs, I shook my hands out. Sprinting toward the apparatus, I jumped off the springboard, pushed off the low bar and reached for the high bar. In doing so, Coach wasn't prepared for me to actually reach the bar the first time, so when he stepped in to spot and catch me, I plowed right into him. He stumbled, tripping over his feet and fell to the ground, his eyes going wide. I missed the bar and landed partially on his hard body, trying not to laugh. My cheeks burned and I rolled my lips into my mouth when we locked eyes.

Coach moved me off him and stood slowly, towering over me. "I am glad you find humor in this. Why did you not tell me you knew how to do the hecht mount?" he said gravely.

"You told me to just keep quiet." I stifled a laugh, returning his words once I stood.

Rubbing a hand down his face, his jaw flexed. He looked like he was struggling between the pros and cons of strangling me.

"I have never, in all my years of training, had a smart-mouthed one like you. You think this is all fun and games." Lowering his voice, he steadily said, "Get back over there and do it again."

"Yes, sir!" I joked, trying to lighten the mood. Holly snickered from the side, while Reagan gave me a death stare.

I wasn't sure why, but I was in a playful mood this morning. However, when I turned to Coach right before going again, he most definitely was not.

Just another prime example of my mouth getting me in trouble, even when it was closed.

It was the end of the day, and I was dead exhausted. After a long session on bars, I worked beam, which was a blessing in disguise considering how much I hated it. Hardly any abuse was done to my hands. It was a nice little break until I got to vault. The pain had subsided since this morning, but I wasn't stupid. I'd have to take care of the rips properly.

Everyone had gone home for the evening and here I was, stuck in the gym after hours, waiting on Coach for one of his "not stretching, but stretching" drills. I rolled my eyes hearing his voice inside my head saying it.

"I hope that eye roll was not for me," Kova stated, swiftly walking past me. I had no idea where the hell he came from. The man loved to appear out of thin air.

Keeping up with his long stride, I nearly had to power walk to keep up with him. "Uh, nope. I just have some chalk in my eye."

"Right," he responded, drawing out the word. He knew I was lying.

When we made it into the therapy room, he flipped on the lights and got right to it.

"I think an hour in here will do, but Adrianna, I do not teach you these drills for fun. I expect to see and hear that you have been doing them. You have to trust it will help down the line."

Hayden's voice drifted through my mind about trusting my coach. I nodded and decided to go with the truth. "To be honest with you, I don't feel I get the same effect doing it myself. You applied a lot of pressure and held me in the position. I can't do that myself in the same manner you can."

Folding his arms across his chest, Coach studied me. I hoped he saw the conviction in my eyes. While I could do the drills, what I confessed was the truth. I didn't get the same result from doing them myself.

Kova strode over to where I was standing. He captured my gaze and stood inches from me, placing his hands on my biceps.

Affection laced his voice as he said, "If you need me, all you have to do is say something. That is what I am here for, Ria."

Heat rose to my cheeks as the intensity of his gaze thickened. Truth was, I did need him, and he clearly knew it.

His hands slowly slid down my arms to just above my elbows. My heartbeat quickened and I inhaled through my nose to steady my breathing. He gave me a gentle squeeze before releasing me, and ushered me over to the therapy table.

Even after hours of training gymnasts, I could still smell the faint scent of his spicy cologne.

"You will only set yourself back if you do not use what is readily available to you. *Me.*"

Him?

"That is what I am here for." He cleared his throat. "What Madeline is here for. Use us, ask questions."

I bit the inside of my lip. He was right. "I just try not to ask too many questions, you know? I like to show I can do things on my own."

He raised a brow and countered me. "You?" A sexy grin slowly appeared on his face and my cheeks grew hot. "You love to talk back. Is it not almost the same thing as asking questions?"

I lowered my face, trying to hide my growing smile. I bobbed my head, agreeing with him. Kova slipped two fingers under my chin and raised my head so our eyes met again. His touch was thrilling and caused a rush of heat to stream through my body. My heartbeat picked up and the energy in the room grew thicker.

My lips parted as we stared into each other's eyes, unsure what to think. This man was beyond confusing, and his touch left me with questions. Questions I had about myself and my reaction to him. Thing was, I began to like the attention he showed me, liked the touch of his hands and the way they seemed to linger on me.

"Remember to use your resources, Ria. I am sure your dad would agree with me on that."

Yeah, I was pretty sure he didn't want me to use my resources in the way my body wanted to at the moment. Especially not with the way I stared at my coach's mouth.

"Why do you call me Ria and not Ana like my parents?"

He paused. "It suits you better. Ana sounds like a child's name, *Ria*." His thumb caressed the side of my face. "And you are no child, not to me at least."

Kova dropped his hand and walked to the side of the table, murmuring under his breath in Russian. My heart was nearly in my throat and my eyes were huge. Never once had Kova touched me so… so… I wasn't even sure what to call it. Adoringly. Affectionately.

"Okay, we are going to do the same drills as last time, but add in a few more that will be helpful to you. Get on your back and bring one leg to your chest. Hold it for me."

"Yes, sir!" I replied sarcastically, which earned me a smile from him. "I'm sorry, sometimes I can't help it."

Kova shook his head and laughed lightly. "Never had a gymnast quite like you before," he said. "Never a dull moment."

My face lit up. "Why, thank you!" My reply came out in more of a grunt when he leaned in with his body. Kova used one hand to press my knee to my chest, the other on my thigh to hold me down. While I'd been joking only seconds before, the fun was over and I had to focus. Only, it was difficult to focus when all I could think about was how his fingers had been on me and the reason why he called me Ria. Not to mention, where his hands were at the present moment. Well, one hand.

On the crease of my hip and covering most of the mini shorts I had on. His large hand dug into my skin, his fingers pressing down. I wasn't sure why, but I liked his hold on me more than I knew I should.

His touch was hot and my body responded to it.

My hips began to slowly open up as Kova got close to my face.

"You feel that? How your body is relaxing and releasing?"

I think he meant opening up, but I didn't correct his English. Instead, I nodded with my lips pressed together.

"I actually feel it this time."

"Good." He pushed a little more. "This is what we want." Kova held the position a few more seconds and then moved over to my right side. I switched legs and got into position.

"My left side is more flexible than my right." Just about every gymnast had one side that was more flexible than the other.

He dismissed it. "Not a problem for me."

When he pressed into my right leg, even after hours of training, my hip was still so tight I grunted.

"Let me guess, you forgot to breathe how I taught you," he stated more than asked, just inches from my face.

I pursed my lips. "Maybe… "

Kova shook his head, closing his eyes. "What am I going to do with you?" he asked jokingly.

I liked this side of him. He was playful and easy to be around. Not edgy and tense like he was in the mornings. Maybe our time should be restricted to the evening, but I doubted I could make that happen.

Just when I thought we were going to move into another position, Kova applied a heavy amount of pressure that caused my back to bow and my knee to lift in response. My knee was nearly past my shoulder now.

A grumble escaped me and I grabbed Kova for support. My small hand couldn't wrap around his wrist and he twitched under my touch.

"Adrianna, focus on breathing." When I didn't answer, he said, "Look into my eyes and focus. It does not hurt, I am not hurting you. Your muscles are just tight." His Russian accent was strong.

I nodded fast, locking eyes with him. "Breathe in through your nose and release it slowly," he guided me.

Kova's thumb drew small, little circles on my inner thigh, making my stomach flutter. The touch was light, but enough for me to notice. I didn't speak up in spite of knowing he probably shouldn't be doing this, especially considering how close he was to my sex. He was inches, literally just inches away, and I was okay with it.

I liked it.

I wanted to push myself closer to make him touch me.

He created a perfect storm of tension and heat around us. I held my breath as his hand skimmed higher up my thigh, slowly, almost seductively, and held it there. My stomach fluttered and I didn't know what to do other than to allow it.

I couldn't imagine my former coach being this close and touching me. The thought of it repulsed me, but with Kova, it was the complete opposite.

The small therapy room began to feel like a furnace, and I knew I needed to switch the focus to something else or else I was going to do something we both wanted.

chapter 18

"K ova?"

"Hmmm?"

"How come there's an A in your name now? Why not Kov?" I wasn't sure why I asked all of a sudden.

Kova stiffened, taking a moment to answer. "My mother always called me Kova since I was a young boy, even though it was not my given name. I never questioned why she did, but now I wish I had. She used to say it like it was an endearment and I loved it. In Russia, female last names end in—"

"Ova."

He tilted his head to the side, interested. "You know Russian?"

"No, but I know about the language through my family's friends."

He nodded. "So then you know males end with Ov."

"I do."

Kova leaned back, his hand dancing down to my knee and gave me a very tender squeeze. "Turn onto your stomach and scoot over."

Without questioning him, I did as he asked. He brought my hands to the side of my head and flattened them, then he climbed onto the table.

Grabbing my ankle, he made a fist and pushed it into my glute. When he lifted my ankle and pressed down, I grunted. My fingers pressed into the table and my nails turned white from the tightness in my hip. I peeked over my shoulder, trying to see his face.

"So my mother had me out of wedlock. I took her last name, but was given the male version. It is why you see my awards and titles with Kournakov instead of Kournakova. I added an A in honor of her the first chance I got."

"Out of wedlock? Kova, no one says that." I laughed lightly, trying to lighten the mood. "Where is your father?"

Embarrassment clouded his eyes. "I do not know. I have never met him." Shame laced his quiet tone and I felt bad for asking.

"Oh," was all I could say. I wasn't sure how to respond to his admission, but I was curious to know more about the story now. I wanted to know if he was the result of a one-night stand or a boyfriend who took off after he was born, not wanting to be a dad. Or maybe he passed away when Kova was younger. My brows furrowed, my mind playing out so many alternatives as I wondered about all the different ways this story could go, but I never expected his next words.

"She was raped," he confessed quietly, completely avoiding eye contact now.

"What?" I gasped, trying to sit up, only he pressed down harder and lifted my leg higher.

"She was raped," he repeated, and my heart broke at his forlorn voice. I wish I could see his face. I couldn't imagine any child would want to know they were born from such a vicious crime, but he knew.

"Your mom told you she was raped?" I asked, astonished.

"Not at first. Only when I pressed her enough about my father did she open up. When I got older, she finally told me the truth."

I'd never known anyone who was raped, or had been the product of one. "What did you think when she told you?"

He snarled, jumping down and moving to the other side of the table. "That I wanted to kill him. You see, my mother was my hero. Unlike for you, my mom was my role model. She did anything and everything she could for me, to give me what I needed to succeed because she did not have the support she needed when she was growing up. She was alone. It was not her fault she got pregnant with me, and she did not have to keep me. It was a brave choice she made. So when I found out about the rape, pure hatred ran through me."

He applied the same method to my other leg. "So you have no idea who he is then." I couldn't imagine what that would feel like. While my dad wasn't around a lot due to his business, he was still there.

"Oh, I have an idea who he is."

"What? How? I don't understand."

"He is my cousin."

What. In. The. Ever. Loving. Fuck.

"How can that be? That's... but that's incest..." I tried to turn around again, but he put a stop to it. Now I wish I had waited to change the subject so I could read his facial expressions.

"She said growing up he had always touched her in places no one ever had. But she was scared to go to her parents because she was not sure if it was really wrong. It was her family."

"How come your mom didn't go to the police after it happened? Tell her parents? What do they think now?"

Kova tapped the back of my thigh and I turned back over. He guided me to the yoga mat on the floor near the wall.

"Kneel with your back to the wall, about two feet away. Arms up." I did as he asked, and looked up at him expectantly for him to answer my questions.

He got on his knees to the left of me and looked at me sadly, shaking his head. "She did, but no one believed her. Shortly after she found out about the pregnancy, she was thrown out with nowhere to go. She went to some church that housed pregnant teenagers but then moved out after I was born. Soon after she left, she realized she could not afford to live on her own and ran into an old friend from the church she had met. She was working in a gentleman's club and offered my mom quick cash and a babysitter on hand. So she took it. It was the only way she could support us."

I looked into Kova's tortured eyes and my heart bled for him, but my ears were eager for more. He placed a flat hand to my shoulder blade and angled me back so my arms were straight and my hands were flat on the wall. I grunted at this odd position of a half back bend.

"Why didn't she leave once she had enough money saved up?"

"Because she could never make the money she did while working behind the counter as a cashier. When I asked her, she said she did not want to struggle and wanted me to have everything she did not have."

He moved to the front of my body and placed both hands low on my hips. Gently and carefully, he pulled them forward with a squeeze. His thumbs pressed daringly into my hip bones and a shot of heat jolted through me. My chest burned and my heart raced. Even after all the hours of practice today, I felt the burn from the stretch, but more outrageously, I could feel heat radiating off him. The cloth of his shorts danced against my bare legs. I took a deep breath and exhaled. He relaxed his hold, allowing me to breathe. My hips shifted back for a moment, but he never removed his hands.

"Once I got into gymnastics at a competitive level, I am sure you can understand how expensive it was for her, there was no way she was stopping. She said she saw potential in me," he huffed sadly as he drew my hips toward him again. Breathe, I told myself. *Breathe.* But it was more difficult than I deemed possible with my hips pinned to his. I wondered if he realized our position. My body tightened and I nearly fell over, but I kept my composure as he continued.

"She made sure she was at every practice, at every meet, and paid for it all on her own."

His mother sacrificed anything and everything to give the son, who was a product of rape, a life she never had, and Joy, my mom, the socialite who threw money at her problems, was the ice queen extraordinaire and more concerned about what I ate than what actually went on with me.

Kova's eyes grew distant, filling with longing and grief, his mouth a firm, grim line. "I did not need anything, though. I would give up everything, give it all back, to have her here." The warmth of his hands heated my hips. He breathed his pain into me through his touch. Sorrow coursed through his tone and I believed every word that left his mouth.

My heart ached, feeling so incredibly empty for Kova and the life his mother was dealt. Life wasn't fair sometimes.

"So after she died, I added an A to my last name for her. I did not want to ever forget her or what she gave up for me."

I couldn't take anymore, from both his words and this new skill. Tears brimmed the back of my eyes while I listened to him talk about his mother and her struggles. I placed my hands at the crook of his arms to comfort him, his hands still clutching my hips, tenderly now. Warmth spread throughout my body being face-to-face and just inches apart. Kova peered down at me through hooded eyes as I said in a cracked whisper, "That is the most incredible thing I have ever heard."

He continued softly. "She came to my first two Olympics with me. She was so happy, happier than I was I think. It meant so much to me she was there, too. However, when my third Games came around for me, she was too ill to travel. In fact, her doctors were highly against it, so I gave it up to be with her. She was upset I did, but I had no choice. She was always there for me. How could I not be there for her? The alternate gymnast on the team stepped in and ended up taking home some medals of his own, then went on to compete in the Games four years later." He grew quiet, seemingly lost in his thoughts. "I do not regret it at all. I got to be with my mom and take care of her as she did for me, and someone else got their chance at the Olympics. Is it not crazy how things happen?"

I knew what he meant. Being an alternate on the Olympic team pretty much meant you were a bench warmer—that was it.

I wanted to turn away from his anguished filled gaze, but I couldn't. He'd expose himself in ways I never anticipated. Raw emotion came from him in waves, and it was felt deep inside my gut. I didn't know what to do or what to say next. I had hardly experienced life the way Kova had, let alone death. I grew up with a silver spoon in my mouth and had everything I could ever want. Kova had not.

So all I stupidly said was, "Yeah, it is."

Kova leaned in and tightened his hold. One hand slid around to the small of my back as my hands moved to flatten on his firm chest. His fingers splayed out dangerously down my ass, one digit pressed between the center. I held my breath. The heat of his hands seared through my leo and I fought back a tremor. He was just an inch away from my lips when his eyes traveled down to my mouth.

"Thanks for listening to me, Ria."

Ria. I smiled, liking the nickname an awful lot.

Slowly, he inched closer, and my heart beat rapidly against my chest at his nearness. I had no idea what he was about to do, and I briefly wondered if he'd kiss me. He was my coach. No way would he do that.

Unease swept through me without an inkling of how to proceed. Never mind I knew what I was supposed to do, should've moved away, not silently wished he'd press his lips to mine.

The stillness between us was thicker than humidity, and it took all of me not to lean in to kiss him. I knew I should've been repulsed by him, but oddly enough, I wasn't. I was intrigued if anything. Every fiber in my body told me to lean in, not run in the other direction.

"A couple of weeks ago you said something in Russian… it started with an M. May-lash-a? What did it mean?"

A smiled curled his full lips. "Maa-lish. Malysh." My sight trained on his mouth, his tongue tapped his top teeth as he said again, "Malysh." The word washed over me in a wave of rapture.

"How do you spell it?"

"M-A-L-Y-S-H." His accent was stronger than ever.

Our breaths mingled, and one of Kova's hands carefully slid up my waist and rested on my ribs. His thumb ran in circles, his body creating heat between us as he caressed me. He slid his hand onto my back and up to my nape where he cupped my neck. My breathing deepened and I thought I was going to hyperventilate if I didn't calm my racing heart. His dark brows formed a deep V and his shrewd eyes didn't waver.

"What does it mean?" I asked softly, my back arching and my chest nearly pressed to his.

He shook his head as if he didn't want to say. "It was an accident. I did not mean to say it."

I frowned at him. "Please? I want to know."

His deep stare caused my stomach to flutter. One hand brazenly moved up to rest on his firm pectoral. My fingers spread out and he flexed under my touch, his fingers pressing deeper into me in response.

"Baby," he said gutturally. "It means baby."

Baby. He had accidently called me baby just weeks ago. I had to wonder why the word would have been on his mind to begin with if it was an accident like he declared.

My gaze traveled down his straight nose to his mouth, where it stayed. My head tilted to the side as my eyes traced his full, *kissable* lips, wondering what they'd feel like pressed to mine. His Adam's apple bobbed slowly, like he took a long, hard swallow.

This wasn't me. I didn't kiss my coach, teacher, or really anyone older than the legal age, or someone who was off limits. Not that I'd ever had the desire as I did now. I'd heard countless stories over the years of gymnast and coach relationships, some consensual, some not. Though, not nearly as many as the married moms having affairs with coaches.

With that being said, in this moment, I could fully understand why some of those forbidden relationships were acted upon. This was completely and utterly enthralling. Nothing was forced. It was a craving woven with lust, a newfound hunger clawing inside.

"You are done for the day," he abruptly said in a broken whisper. As Kova stood, something hard dragged up the inside of my thigh. He placed a hand out to help me up and I hissed as my skin made contact with his. I'd forgotten I had rips the entire time I was with him. He turned my hand over and inspected them, his thumb delicately running in circles on my palm.

"Sorry about these." Then he turned his back to me and left, leaving me speechless.

It was then I realized Kova had a thick and hard erection.

chapter 19

TWO THINGS I WAS SURE ABOUT.

One: Hayden was right about treating my hands properly.

Two: There was something mentally wrong with my coach.

I paced my condo, wearing out my carpet while I waited for Hayden to show up again. He'd be here any minute to help me out.

Today had been awful, the pain, unbearable at one point. So crippling, it nearly brought me to tears, but I sucked it up and refused to give them to him. I guess Kova thought I was in dire need of training because we spent hours together. Him screaming at all the little things I did wrong had me wanting to throw a block of chalk at his head. The tutoring between gym sessions that gave my hands a little break, but it wasn't enough. They needed days to heal.

After changing a few things up in my routine, Kova made me repeat it until I couldn't get it wrong. Every single skill, he had a conditioning technique for. Don't get me wrong, it was a good thing, but it can also become tedious, and quite frankly, fucking annoying at times. He was on top of everything I did, breathing down my neck, ready to attack. More so than usual. He reminded me of a gnat that just wouldn't go away. Always in my ear, always making sounds. I'd banged my shins, jammed my toes on the bars, and even lost my grip due to exhaustion and fell on my hips. The bar had caught me, not the floor. There was only so much one could handle after hours of relentless coaching.

It wasn't long after the change in my routine that my rips got caught and the skin tore back. Sometimes when the pain is so severe, you don't feel the injury, and that's exactly what happened to me. I was chalking up, too focused on Coach explaining something, when he paused and pointed it out. I looked down at my bloody hands covered in chalk and shrugged. There wasn't much else I could do at that point. I couldn't very well beg for mercy and ask to move to beam where my hands could get a little break. Although, I'm sure he would've loved that.

And as much as I hated to admit it, the outcome had been rewarding. I knew I had nailed my routine near the end, and the slight smile on his face confirmed it. He was proud of me, though he struggled with the words. Like every man in the world did.

My hands had gone through the stages of hell, from feeling like I had dipped them into a fiery red ant pile, to being completely numb. I had managed to block the pain and push through it and not complain, and I think that bought me some points in his book. At least I hoped it had.

I was sure Coach Kova thrived on the tears of young hopefuls, it was the only thing I could come up with at this point. He was a raging lunatic when he wanted to be.

But surprisingly, he could be rather tender too…

I could still feel his hands on me, the whisper of breath that rolled across my cheek, the way his erection glided up my thigh. I couldn't get the image out of my head. He'd been on my mind since our private session, and astonishingly for the first time, I actually looked forward to another one. Kova opened up and showed me a different side of him, one I was curious to learn more about. A side that made him human, one that had a heart.

A knock at the door shook me from my thoughts, and I ran toward it. Hayden stood on the threshold with another pharmacy bag.

"You know, I'm gonna have to start charging an in-house doctor fee."

I laughed, welcoming him in. "Bill me."

"So are you regretting not listening to me?"

"Do you think it would have made a difference in the end?" I held up my palms to him. Hayden grimaced, shaking his head.

"Honestly, I'm not so sure."

He placed the plastic bag on the counter and then walked over to me. Taking one of my hands into his, he used his thumb to feel around my palms. Aside from the actual blisters, my skin had rolled up and peeled in various places. Those weren't too bad, they were manageable. It was tender behind my knuckles, so that always tore first and caused the most pain.

"We should probably do this in the bathroom, or over the kitchen sink. It's going to get messy."

My heart dropped, fear exploded through me of what was soon going to take place. Before he began, Hayden pulled out a small steel container from his duffle bag.

"But first, you're going to need this."

"What is it?"

"A flask of vodka."

I frowned. "I can't drink all that. I'll get sick."

He was amused. "Not all of it, of course you'll get sick. Only a shot or two to help take the edge off. Have you ever had vodka before?"

A tremor worked through me at the memory. "Yeah, once with my best friend, Avery. Let's just say it didn't go over well."

Hayden walked through my kitchen and looked through my cabinets as if it was a completely natural thing for him to do.

"You look good," I admitted, slamming my mouth shut.

Hayden glanced over his shoulder with a saccharine smile I'd come to really like seeing. He wore a dark pair of distressed jeans, molded to his butt and thighs, and a solid white shirt that accentuated his biceps. He was jacked and looked better than any other guy his age.

"Not too bad yourself." I glanced down at my rolled up shorts and flannel, button-down shirt. My long auburn hair was braided loosely to the side with little pieces sticking out and I was makeup free. I looked ready for a hayride.

I walked over to Hayden and watched as he poured two small drinks. "This shouldn't really hit you hard, but it should help."

"Where did you get it from?"

"Snatched it before my mom packed up. She won't even notice it's missing".

"Why are you having it, too?"

"To help with what I'm going to do to you."

"Oh…" I frowned.

He handed me a glass and asked, "Ready?"

I took a deep breath. "Ready as I'll ever be." Then we clinked glasses and tipped them back quickly. I wasn't a fan of vodka, or any other liquor, so I swallowed fast and cringed, shivering hard.

"Gross." I made a disgusted face and Hayden laughed. "Do you drink often?"

He looked at me like I was dense. "No, Aid, how could I with training?"

I shrugged. "Well, I don't know! I'm just asking."

"No, hardly ever. Only when the time calls for it. Go ahead and wash your hands so we can get started." I did as Hayden requested while he rummaged through his stuff.

"You think Coach is going to go easy on you tomorrow?"

I turned my battered hands over and said, "I don't think he has a choice, you know? We worked on bars all day—"

"I know. He doesn't normally do that. You'd think he was purposely torturing you."

I paused. "What do you mean?"

Hayden turned around and leaned against the countertop right next to the sink, while I rinsed my hands. He crossed his arms in front of his chest. "I've been training there for years and I've never seen him work an entire day on one event, or push someone the way he does you. Don't get me wrong, he's a hard-ass coach and can be a real dick when he wants to be, but he grates on you. You'd think since your dad is friends with him he'd go a little easier, you know?"

I thought about what Hayden said and asked, "Do you think it's because I need a lot of work, more than what he's used to training?"

He shook his head, unsure. "You're really not that bad off, so I'm not certain what his issue is. Kova wants perfection, to be the best, better than anyone else. We can all appreciate it because it's what we want ourselves, but sometimes I think he pushes too much… I don't know. He can easily make people hate him, that's for sure. He only coaches the rings for my team, so I'm just analyzing from that, I don't spend as much time with him as you do."

I stood there, stunned. The only thing I could come up with was, "He must really hate me."

Hayden chuckled. "He doesn't hate you. Has he put you on a special diet yet?"

I eyed him wearily. "No? Do I need to be on one?"

"No, but his diets are ridiculous and we all swear when he reaches the diet level, it means he secretly despises you. Or so we all think. Don't reach that level. He's only been that way with a few and let me tell you, it wasn't pretty."

Hayden was giving me anxiety. "What do you mean?"

"He follows this insane paleo related diet that only lets you consume under a thousand calories a day. With our workouts and the calories and fat we burn, you know we need more than that, or else it isn't healthy."

No, it's not. "Well, it can't be much worse than the diet my mom has imposed on me, so I'm sure I'd be fine." I paused. "Who has he been like that with?"

"Reagan and a few others who aren't here anymore."

My jaw dropped. "You're kidding."

He shook his head. "I wish I was."

"But Reagan's so good."

"Now she's his golden gymnast. He only had to build her to his level of perfection." He looked at me with raised brows. "And so were the others. Some went on to compete at Division One colleges, some even went to the nationals training camp in Texas. I'm telling you, he's a mean bastard, but he gets results. Don't give up or take it to heart."

I exhaled, releasing an envious breath over this news of Reagan. He knew my mom had me on a diet where my meals were delivered, so maybe I was already at that level since there was nothing left for him to do.

Feeling the vodka course through my veins just a little bit, I said, "Let's get this over with."

Hayden and I walked to my bathroom. He flipped on the lights and placed everything on the counter, pulling out the pumice stone, needles, a lighter, and hydrogen peroxide. I groaned when he sterilized the needle and wanted to cry at the sight of the brown bottle.

He filled the sink up with warm water and I soaked my hands for a few minutes to soften them up. Aside from the rips, I also had calluses on the backs of my fingers and middle of my palms, which were now raised and white, easy to find due to soaking.

Hayden took one of my hands into his and looked into my eyes before snipping the dead skin away. Then he took a dull butter knife, placed it at a ninety degree angle, and very gently shaved off the calluses. Little white flakes pooled in my palms. This part hadn't hurt, but my heart began to throb and panic battered through me. I didn't want to do the next step. My knees trembled and I thought I'd be sick. With the fear so high, maybe another shot of vodka would've helped.

"I don't want to hurt you, Adrianna."

I nodded and stepped closer to him. With the pumice stone in one hand, he held it above my palm and gripped my wrist tight so I couldn't pull away.

"I'm just going to file down the calluses and scrub around the rips." Tight lipped, I nodded. "Close your eyes."

The moment the stone hit my hand, my fingers retracted and curled up. Hayden forcefully held my hand open. He scrubbed each finger, filing down the calluses and then feeling for smoothness. It didn't hurt, but it didn't feel good either. Moving on to my palm, he used the stone for the rough skin around my rips. He accidently nicked a corner, apologizing profusely. I gripped Hayden's arm with my other hand, my nails dug into him as I gasped loudly, and my eyes squeezed shut as he began to scrub.

The pain.

The throbbing, pulsing, pain.

Heat seared my palm and went straight through my skin, hitting muscles and nerves as it radiated out the back of my hand, only to repeat, continuing on an endless loop. He was cautious not to hit an open rip, he knew better, but he did a few times.

Hayden scrubbed back and forth, pressing down so roughly I thought he would hit my bones. I instantly became nauseous and worried I'd throw up. I tried to focus on the scent of Hayden's cologne. The beach. Avery. Nothing helped. It hurt so much!

"Oh, my God! Please stop for a minute!" I shouted and he jumped. Opening my eyes, my stark white bathroom sink had crimson water running toward the drain and blood splatter that speckled the sides. With Hayden pressing down, blood automatically pushed through my rips. I couldn't see my palm, blood completely coated my hand.

"I'm sorry, I didn't mean to scream in your ear," I panted.

"It's okay. I'm just sorry I have to do this to you."

I swallowed hard, shaking with a pain so unbearable I couldn't find words. This was agony. Teardrops rested on my eyelids, but I refused to let them fall. After this, I'd make damn sure to never grip the bar wrong again.

"Here," Hayden said, seeing my eyes. "Try this. Stand behind me, wrap your other arm around my waist and squeeze me when it gets bad."

I nodded and did as he suggested. If I wasn't so consumed by pain, I would've noticed how nice it was to be pressed against his backside, or how well our bodies fit together.

My arm went around his stomach and I held him lightly, leaning my head against his back. Taking a deep breath, I exhaled. Maybe if I focused on his body, it wouldn't be as bad.

Who was I kidding? When he picked back up, I pressed into Hayden so hard, I felt his feet shift from my weight. I squeezed, holding him to me while I dug my head between his shoulder blades. I used every ounce of strength I had and held on for dear life. I didn't care that my boobs smashed into his back, or how my hips rolled against his ass and molded to him in a bit of a sexual way. The shots of pain were so awful, I bit him. I rose up on my toes and sank my teeth into his bicep. In some odd way, it helped.

"Almost done with this hand," he said over the running water, ignoring my bite. I leaned into him when he placed my hand under the warm water, removing the blood and feeling for the dead skin. Unconsciously, I squeezed him tighter, ringing his shirt in my fist, using him for strength because I knew what came next.

Hydrogen peroxide.

When I heard the cap flip, I gripped Hayden's stomach so hard I felt him flinch under me. I didn't mean to hurt him, but I didn't think I'd make it much longer before I passed out.

"How's it going with your private sessions with Kova?"

"Wh… What?"

More scrubbing. "Think about the question, Aid, not the pain."

"The question… What was the question?"

His back vibrated with a chuckle. "How are your private sessions going?"

"Ah, going well I guess…" I struggled for breath. "Not as bad or as weird as I expected."

"I take it you found something to talk about?"

I gripped his shirt tighter as he rinsed my hand. "We did…" I didn't want to go into detail about the conversation I'd had with Kova. It was private and I had a notion he didn't tell very many people, so I said, "As much as I appreciate what you're trying to do, Hayden, I can't think straight right now."

"Take a deep breath."

The cool liquid poured over my hand and I inhaled loudly, throwing my head back. White-hot pain shot through me and I almost blacked out. Tears coated my eyelashes but they didn't stream down my cheeks, and I clenched my teeth so hard I was sure I was seconds away from chipping one.

"Hayden, please," I begged. My hand shook violently under his hold. My fingers tried to curl up again, but Hayden held them open as he rubbed around the rips.

"Shhh… It's all right. We're almost done," he said apologetically. Hayden rinsed my hand again and plucked off any dead skin he missed with the nail clippers.

"I think I need another shot… Or an entire bottle. Make that two bottles before you do the other hand."

He laughed, his back vibrating against my cheek. "I'm pretty sure you'd die if you drank two bottles of vodka."

"I'll take my chances. It can't be worse than this."

Shutting the water off, Hayden turned around and I stepped away from him. My jaw dropped when I looked at my trembling hand. It looked like raw meat.

"We need to let it air dry before we put anything over it for the night," Hayden instructed.

"Do you think that's a good idea? To put stuff over it? Shouldn't I cover it during the day and let it breathe at night?" He looked at me like I should know the answer. "I've never done this before, Hayden, so I have no idea what to do."

Hayden's eyes softened. Using the pad of his thumb, he wiped away one lone tear. "Don't cry," he said sympathetically. The gesture was sweet and for some reason made me tear up even more. My jaw quivered and my chin dropped to my chest. I hated this, this pain, these emotions, this sport. I hated it all and wished it would go away. There was no way I could go through something like this again. If Kova made me do any kind of bar work tomorrow or in the next few days, I would straight up murder him.

Hayden pulled me into a hug. Cradling my hand to my chest, I leaned into him and let the tears fall. Screw fighting it. This kind of torture would bring a grown man to his knees.

Exhaustion suddenly consumed me and I let out a loud sigh. "I'm sorry for crying."

He rubbed my back in circles and his hips dropped to the counter to sit. "Want to know a secret?"

"You seem to have a lot of secrets, Hayden."

He laughed. "The first time I had rips this bad, my mom had to take care of them the way I just did for you. I cried. Like a little baby I cried and sobbed into her hard and she had to hold me afterward. It was embarrassing and I never forgot it. Since then, I've made sure to do everything humanly possible to avoid rips to this capacity ever again. I know it's inevitable, but I do try and I know you will too from here on out. I'll help you and show you what to do to toughen your skin up a bit more. Once your palms heal and new skin grows over, you'll need to pumice them every day. I feel your pain, Adrianna. I do, babe. And I'm sorry I had to cause you more."

I let his words sink in and relaxed a little into his body. For someone who was built with as much muscle as he was, Hayden was unexpectedly soft.

He dropped a friendly kiss to the top of my head and then said, "Let's take care of your other hand. Lucky for you, it isn't that bad off, so it shouldn't be as painful."

Shouldn't, being the key word.

chapter 20

WHEN I FIRST MOVED TO CAPE CORAL IN MARCH, I WORRIED I'D BE A LITTLE lonely, even though I was ready for more freedom.

But with the training and long hours, and getting accustomed to my new life, I hadn't had time to actually feel alone. I guess it was a good thing. Weeks flew by, and before I knew it, summer training arrived. With no more school, it was train, train, train every minute of every day.

From what I'd heard, the members of World Cup and the coaches got together each year and had a Fourth of July barbecue. It was their way of bringing the team and coaches together and blow off a little steam. This year it was held at Kova's impressive two-story home that overlooked the intercoastal. Considering he was from Russia, I found it amusing he would host a holiday that celebrated America's Independence.

With the help of GPS, Alfred drove me to his house. Reagan arrived at the same time as me and we walked in together, without saying a word except to exchange pleasantries before going on our separate ways. They walked toward the grand windows that overlooked the river to where other people were outside, but I knew the first thing I needed to do was greet the host. Manners went a long way, and my mom always made sure we were courteous.

Kova's house was much bigger than I anticipated. He had a large, open floor plan and I wasn't sure which way to go first. From the amount of parties we had back home, it was a given the host would be in the kitchen prepping, so that's where I headed off to. I followed the sound of voices and water running and found the kitchen. As I drew closer, a pan clattered to the tile floor and I jumped. Faint, hushed voices filtered the air and I scrunched my brows trying to figure out who they belonged to. Rounding the corner, I knew for sure one was Kova, the other, I did not. My chest drew tight when I realized I walked in on Kova and a stunning brunette having an obvious argument. Kova's jaw dropped then snapped back together, his arms flexed at his sides. The woman's face faltered when the bitter bite of low words were exchanged from Kova. The tension was so thick between them it was suffocating. I couldn't make out what was said since it was in Russian, but whatever it was couldn't have been good because she looked on the verge of tears. Kova turned and forcefully threw something into the sink, and it rebounded around the stainless steel. He placed his hands on the ledge and leaned over, his eyes clenched shut. The woman placed a comforting hand to his shoulder only for him to shrug it off. Her face dropped and she threw her hands in the air, muttering under her breath and sauntered away.

I receded quickly before they saw me, but stood near the wall wondering what happened between them. I'd never seen Kova so worked up before. Sure, he was a dick at practice, but seeing it outside of the gym was not something I expected. I just figured he was that way because he was trying to bring out the victor in us. Maybe it really was just his personality.

I needed to find some friends to talk to quickly only to realize I didn't have many here.

I heaved a sigh. I still felt a bit like an outcast among the rest of the team. They were nice, but mostly reserved and kept to themselves. Very cliquey. I probably should've made more of an effort to be friends with someone other than Hayden and Holly, but it wasn't something I was pushing for. I came here to train, to be the absolute best I could be and gain the title of elite. Not to win Miss Congeniality.

Trying to befriend Reagan had been a challenge. I wasn't any competition to her, she was an amazing athlete and much better than me. She knew it, and I knew it. So I wasn't sure what the issue was. There was just no friendship with her, I was on my own. Sometimes I liked it, but most of the time it was frustrating when you wanted a friend to vent to who understood what you were going through. Maybe if I had pushed for it, I wouldn't have been standing by myself, staring at…I had no idea what the hell I was staring at. A shrine?

Before me hung medals upon medals, framed photos, trophies, articles galore. You name it, it was here. And it was all about Kova. This was something only a proud mother would do, so I found it oddly bizarre a man of his stature would have his own hall of fame in his home.

Then again, I hadn't accomplished what Kova had, not even remotely close, so I guess I shouldn't really say anything. I could only hope. I'd probably have the same thing in my house. Hell, I had medals from competitions displayed in my condo right now.

Moving closer, my fingers grazed one of the gold medals, my heart yearning for one. Just one. God, what I wouldn't do to have a beauty like this of my own one day. I'd probably never take it off. Well, maybe to sleep and shower, but that was it.

Kova had three gold medals and a handful of silver from two Olympics, the rings being his top event. I chuckled to myself. He probably hated the silver ones.

"What is so funny?"

I jumped, my hand flying to my racing heart. I looked behind me and saw Kova holding a glass of beer.

"Jesus!"

A sensual grin pulled his full lips to the side. His eyes softened and I swallowed. Totally different side of him from what I'd seen earlier when I walked in on the spat he was having. He seemed relaxed now, not tense. This man's beauty was in a league of its own. He was charismatic when he smiled, and I could feel his goodness. A rare occurrence, and it was times like these I forgot he was my coach.

Kova looked incredibly amazing in his navy blue dress pants and crisp white button-down shirt. His sleeves were rolled up to his elbows, a silver watch with a large face adorned his wrist. His hair, although messy, looked as though he ran his fingers through it so it matched the two-day dusting coating his jaw. This was the first time I'd seen Kova wear something other than shorts in a long time. Amber skin, perfectly straight nose, and emerald eyes complimented him. He could've passed as an Armani model with flying colors.

"I did not mean to frighten you."

"It's okay. But I'm going to need you to put a bell around your neck as much as you sneak up on me."

Kova looked down at his glass and swirled the amber liquid. He stepped up next to me and looked at his wall. He smelled like cinnamon and tobacco with a hint of citrus. I knew he wasn't a smoker, yet the scent on him was seductive and sophisticated. I drew a silent breath into my lungs and felt it all the way to my core.

"What did you find so amusing?"

"Ah…" I turned back to the wall, heat rising to my cheeks. I seemed to blush a lot when

Kova was around. I snuck a glance and he nodded his head, waiting for me. "I was just admiring your medals and wondered what you thought about your silver ones."

He squinted with discerning eyes and looked at his wall, pursing his lips together in thought. I zoned in and noticed he had a deep cupid's bow, where as I had full, ample lips.

Maybe Avery was right. He was Coach Kissable.

"I think I am very fortunate to have them, but also that I worked very hard and that I deserve them. Going to the Olympics is an accomplishment very few can achieve. Not even luck can get you there. It is pure determination, unwavering commitment to the sport, and a love that runs so deep for it that you would give up anything to achieve it. Sometimes even your life and childhood." Kova took a sip of his beer. "Though, the truly dedicated would say gymnastics is their life, it is the air they breathe, so you are not really giving up your life at all if you are living it through gymnastics, are you?"

I read the underlining meaning in his eyes and felt the tone in his voice. He gave up everything in his childhood to achieve his dream. His devotion was contagious. My heart soared and a lazy smile spread across my face.

I looked back at his wall of medals and agreed. He was right in every sense. Luck had very little to do with it, but he forgot something else.

"You forgot timing," I said, looking directly into his eyes. "Timing is everything, especially in gymnastics."

"You know what else I did not mention? Selfishness."

My brows cinched together, not fully agreeing with him. "Selfishness? I wouldn't necessarily say that."

"Sure it is," he countered, stepping closer to me.

"There is nothing wrong with being selfish," he continued. "Gymnastics, once you reach a certain level, becomes your entire life and everyone is just revolving around you. It is all about *you* meeting *your* goals, *you* competing, *you* spending hours upon hours in a gym fighting to be the best. It is climbing a rope and everyone is just sitting back watching *you*. You have to give one hundred and fifty percent with this sport. Gymnastics, in a sense, is all about you."

Rope. I smiled to myself at his gymnastics analogy. Most people said climb mountains, but he used rope since part of conditioning for many athletes was rope climbing.

"I hadn't really thought of it like that before. I mean, in a sense, you're right, but isn't everyone selfish in some form then? Why a gymnast more so than others?"

He shook his head, disagreeing. "It is not the same."

I knew what he meant, and he was right. It wasn't the same. Most people were selfish to an extent. This was a personal drive trapped inside no one could help with, except one thing. A coach who understood. Gymnastics was like a drug. No matter how many times we got knocked down, no matter how many injuries we sustained, no matter how many times we're told we're not good enough, not the best, we always came back for more. It was a need that ignored all those around until it was filled, no matter the length of time it took. A gymnast's drive outweighed everyone else's and it never died.

"You know, I would almost rather have a bronze medal than have a silver," he said, changing the subject.

"Why's that?"

Kova shrugged one shoulder, as if the answer was obvious. "Silver is the first place loser."

My eyes widened. I'd never thought of it like that when I'd won silver at meets.

"Coming in second place is the worst feeling after you just gave your all. There are winners and there are losers. You play a sport to win—that is it. Nothing else. You have one chance to prove yourself. One." He shook his head, his eyes distant as he reminisced about the past. "I remember feeling completely and utterly gutted, like I was just given a consolation prize for all my hard work. I was up on the podium, thinking about what I could have done differently. Did I wobble? Did I take a step on a dismount? Did I bend my legs? Did I not have enough control in flight? Did I not train enough? I knew I should have been happy I secured silver, but it was not enough to win gold, and that was heart wrenching." He looked at me as if trying to remember what he did wrong. "You can lose it all by a tenth of a deduction. So small, yet so powerful it can bring you to your knees in a mere second. It all happens so fast, you know? Once the flame is lit, the Games begin. You are there, in the moment, living it, breathing it, fighting for your dream. You are at each event for such a short period of time until you rotate to the next one. Once you get home and you finally have the chance to think about your experience, you have to ask yourself if it was real because it does not feel like it. It is like a blurry movie you want to tune and focus, but cannot…"

Kova's words trailed off. He gave me a questionable look, as if he wanted an answer I didn't have. His words stung my chest. I could hear the vulnerability in his voice, felt each word as he relived his past and tried to cope with it. The sincerity written on his face was full of meaning and emotion, and what he said packed a punch.

He spoke from his heart, and I felt every bit of it.

chapter 21

THIS WAS A PIVOTAL MOMENT BETWEEN US.

He stood so close his words trailed over my skin, igniting a flame under me. He'd exposed deeply personal parts of his life again and it unknowingly opened a connection between us. I felt it, saw it. His eyes bore into mine and his lips slightly parted, a little opening in the center of them. The silence in the air caused a stirring. Without saying another word and with his eyes trained on mine, he lifted a hand and moved a lock of hair from my shoulder, tucking it behind my ear. A shiver ran down my arms as the back of his hand delayed, his finger peppering my jaw with the lightest touch possible. He stepped closer to me and I held my breath as his eyes took in every inch of me. His knuckles danced down my neck to my clavicle, his callused index finger gliding over me like a soft breeze.

"I bet your mom was proud of your silver medals," I said softly.

Kova's face dropped, his smile vanishing along with his hand. His eyes took on a blank stare and I suddenly regretted my comment.

"She was. She was proud of everything I did. She was my biggest supporter."

I swallowed hard. "How long ago did she pass away?"

Kova took a deep breath and exhaled. "Eight years ago," he said delicately.

My heart sank even more at the sadness in his tone. Instinctively, my hand reached out to comfort him.

"I'm so sorry."

I rubbed his arm, my thumb going in circles. It wasn't a wise decision, but I think I did it mostly because I felt his loss so strongly I wanted to soothe him. He flexed under my touch and his eyes shot to mine. I dropped my hand and cleared my throat awkwardly.

Kova shook it off.

"Was it cancer?" I asked curiously.

"I wish it could have been that."

He wished it could have been that? "What do you mean?"

Him being vague wasn't working for me, but that was Kova. Always so elusive. I wasn't sure I should use the opening to ask more questions, so I stayed silent and waited for him to collect his thoughts.

"Since we have been upfront and truthful with each other…She was HIV positive," he whispered quietly.

My jaw dropped, along with my gut. HIV. I was glad we hadn't eaten yet, otherwise with all this tumbling between my heart and stomach, I'd probably vomit right now. That was extremely personal and not at all what I expected. Not one bit.

Wait a minute. If she was HIV positive, then that would mean…

My eyes popped, my head snapped to look at him. "I do not have HIV," he answered my questioning stare. "She contracted it many years after I was born." Kova sighed sadly, looking into his beer mug. "I would not be in this profession if that were the case."

I was about to ask how she contracted HIV when a woman walked in, looking radiant as ever with a perfect sway to her hips.

"I was looking for you."

I looked over at the singsong voice. It was the woman from earlier. Whoever she was, she was the definition of flawless. A perfect, glossy shine to her pin straight chestnut hair. Ivory skin, bright hazel eyes and a megawatt smile complemented her supermodel body. There wasn't a thing wrong with her on the outside. Truly perfect from her French manicured toes to the top of her deep brown head.

Kova cleared his throat. "I apologize, *malysh*, I was just explaining my medals to Adrianna and how it was not done by having luck." Kova looked at me, strained. "Adrianna, this is my girlfriend, Katja."

Malysh. He called her *malysh* like he'd once called me. Blood drained from my face, a knot formed in the pit of my stomach at the endearment he used on both of us. I knew he said it was by mistake when he said it to me, but it bothered me, and I wasn't sure why. Maybe because she was perfection and I was not. Maybe it was because I secretly liked that he used it on me more than I wanted to admit, and now knowing he used it on her made me slightly envious. My insecurities I worked so hard to overcome, thanks to my mom, were making an appearance and I didn't like it one bit.

She smiled and placed her hand out.

Katja looked back to Kova with a pointed brow. The tension was thick between them once again. "The grill is almost ready. Would you like me to get you another drink?"

"No, thank you."

"What is that?" she asked, brows angled together.

"Beer."

She pulled back like he spoke another language. "Beer? No vodka for you?"

His sheepish eyes shot back to me. "I was thinking it would not be such a good idea to put my Russian half on display tonight." He chuckled, his hand reaching out to cup Katja's cheek, his thumb circling her immaculate skin. Her face tilted to the side, a honey smile on her lips. I got the feeling they were putting on a show after what I'd seen.

"Ah, I see. Well, we need you on the grill soon and more guests just showed up." Katja placed a kiss to his lips, turned, and walked out.

Quietly, I admitted with a sliver amount of jealousy, "Katja is very pretty."

He flattened his lips, his face faltering and I was curious to know why. "Yes, she is a very beautiful woman."

Woman. Whereas I was a teenager.

Wanting to change the focus, I asked, "What other nationality are you?"

"I think I have spilled enough today… again. You heard Katja, I need to go." And there was the stone-faced Kova I knew.

Coach Kova was back, ignoring my question. All I did was ask about his heritage and he shut down. It was by far the least intrusive of everything he exposed.

Kova left and walked back in the direction of the dining room and I followed behind, but the vibrant colors of a Georgia sunset caught my eye and pulled me into a room just off from where the awards were.

Looking out the window, deep pinks and an array of blues swathed the darkening sky behind a body of water. I smiled to myself at the warmth filling my heart. I seriously loved living in Georgia.

Glancing around, I realized I'd stepped into an office. It was similar to my dad's but smaller. The desk was placed in front of the window and a bookshelf adorned one wall. My eyes locked on a framed picture of Katja on a shelf.

Walking over, I picked it up. She wore a white button-down men's shirt. The sleeves were rolled up, but the front was left opened so it showcased an outline of her plump breasts and toned stomach. She looked like she just woke up. Her messy hair was flipped to the side while giving a wide, playful smile as she sat upon an unmade bed. She appeared to be the happiest woman on the planet, and there was no doubt in my mind she wasn't. I could only hope to be as naturally stunning as her one day.

Placing it down, I looked around and noticed another framed photo, this time on his desk. Curious, I brazenly walked over and picked it up. Katja was sensually sliding off a rumpled sheet, wearing black stilettos and black thigh high lace trimmed stockings in a matching bra and panty set. Her dainty fingers just grazing her fair cleavage while her hair was curled loosely around her. She was every man's fantasy in this picture. Her back was partially against the side of the bed, her breasts perfectly round and plump as they pushed up. And the look she gave the camera screamed sex as she twirled a lock of hair around her finger.

The photo was breathtaking, striking.

I bet Kova took these photos of her. Why that stung, I had no idea. It shouldn't have. After all, he was my coach, but something in my belly tightened at the thought of Kova framing provocative images of her in his office. In that moment, I envied Katja. She oozed confidence and power. This was tasteful, artistic… and it made me realize this was something I'd want my future husband to do one day.

"Adrianna?"

Startled, I gasped, nearly dropping the frame.

"What the hell are you doing in here?" Kova spat each word, a hand propped on his hips.

"I, ah," I was rendered speechless. Completely speechless. My jaw bobbed and my eyes were huge as I tried to find words.

Kill me now.

Kova slowly stepped toward me, eyeing my fingers that gripped his frame. "I caught a view of the sunset as I was walking back and stopped to look at it."

He lifted a brow and waited for more. "And?"

"And… And I saw a picture of Katja." Fuck. I was scared.

"Keep going?" His voice was low. "Were you snooping around my office? This is a very private picture of her for my eyes only. Who said you could just waltz right in here?"

He was goading me, but with every right. I was in his personal space. "I wasn't snooping, I swear. I just happened to see the photo on the bookshelf. Then I saw this one on your desk and wanted to see it."

I glanced down at the frame clutched to my chest and pulled it back. Handing it to him, I apologized.

"I didn't mean to be nosey. I've just never seen photos like these before."

"They were a gift."

Confused, I asked, "What was?"

"The photos, they are boudoir photos taken by a local photographer. Katja gave them to me on our second anniversary. At first I fumed she would let someone photograph her in hardly anything, but once I cooled down, I found the photos alluring."

This was getting strange, and I wasn't sure how to respond. It was one thing to talk about his life and his mom, but not about Katja and how *alluring* her photos were. Kova stared lovingly at the frame while I stood awkwardly next to him. I felt like I was invading on his moment. "She really is beautiful," was all I could think of to say.

Hard eyes snapped to mine. Kova loomed over me and stared down. His eyes traveled down my face, pausing on my lips. His jaw flexed as he exhaled. The throbbing vein in his neck caught my attention, it was beating as fast as my heart.

Tension swirled and the air thickened as his gaze landed on my chest. Only the tension wasn't like it was with him and Katja. Sensuality was woven around us and it changed the whole dynamic. I wore a white, low scoop neck shirt with a push-up bra that gave me heavy, supple cleavage. It wasn't often I wore clothes other than a leotard, so I took extra time getting dressed, carefully picking out my outfit. I wanted to look better than all the other girls combined.

The room grew hot as the weight of his stare was felt on every inch of my skin. This wasn't the first time an older man had stared at me, I'd met some men who were acquaintances of my dad's, but this was different.

Everything a woman could want in a man, Kova had it in spades. The perfect body, the perfect face, a successful business, goal driven. And no matter what I did, I couldn't get him out of my mind. He was tall, dark, and handsome. And the more he stared at me, the more I found myself liking it… wanting more of his attention.

Kova took one small step toward me and my lips parted. I could hear my heart thumping loudly in my ears as my chest rose faster with each breath I took.

"Kova," I whispered. "What are you thinking about?"

He swallowed and said hoarsely, "Things I should not be."

My stomach tightened, my panties suddenly wet from the raspy sound of his voice, it rumbled in a deep baritone. Rolling my lip between my teeth, I tucked a lock of hair behind my ear. "What do you mean?"

He groaned low under his breath. "Do not do that."

"Do what?"

"Look at me the same way I am looking at you."

My heart was pounding so loud I wondered if he could hear it.

"You are blushing."

"You know, that only makes me blush more," I whispered.

One more step closer, and we were almost touching. "I like the way it tints your skin." The back of his hand grazed my flushed cheek. "You know, you are just as beautiful. If not, more. Gorgeous."

A little gasp escaped my lips. My heart raced a mile a minute, my fingers trembled. Kova called me gorgeous.

Dropping his hand, he looked down at the picture frame and then back to me with remorse in his eyes. "I am sorry I made you rip so badly on bars that day… I have felt terrible ever since." And then he turned, and walked out of his office, leaving me speechless.

What in the ever loving fuck just happened?

chapter 22

ONCE I CAUGHT MY BREATH, I LEFT KOVA'S OFFICE AND WALKED TOWARD THE formal dining room.

My head was spinning and I needed some fresh air.

Long, elegant crimson drapes held back by a gold sash gave a spectacular view of the intercoastal. I stopped to take in the breathtaking sight before meeting up with everyone outside. After what just happened only moments before, I needed to get my head on straight and taking in the view did the trick. There was something about the water that washed away any stress and helped me focus. Growing up, I'd had a stunning view of the Atlantic Ocean from my bedroom. Anytime I needed to get away, needed to think, the ocean was where I went. Nothing could compare, but this was just as spectacular. The sun was setting over the winding canal that was wrapped between heavy trees. A warm cascade of colors illuminated the sky, the most evanescent sunset worthy of being framed. It was all so grand, and not at all what I expected from the man I saw every day in the gym to have.

Freaking Coach Kova. Confusing. Contradicting. Exhausting… And maybe a little sinful. I expelled a heavy breath and decided I'd deal with that moment later.

Stepping outside, people were gathered around chatting with one another. It was late afternoon, and with all the foliage in the backyard, thankfully it wasn't too hot. Despite making the effort to avoid him, I glanced around and my traitorous eyes automatically found Kova. His back was to me as I watched through intrigued eyes. My head tilted to the side. I could hear the lilt in his voice drift through the air. He appeared deep in conversation, his hands moving fluidly as he spoke.

With my shoulders back, I took a deep breath and confidently made my way to a group of girls to make it appear like I wanted to be involved in their conversation. Though, if I was being honest, I didn't feel like talking to anyone here. My mind was everywhere at the moment and I needed Avery to talk to. I smiled politely, but I couldn't take my eyes off Kova as he turned and began grilling. His girlfriend was at his side, dutifully helping him. He did a quick flip of the meat and shut the grill lid. He placed the cooking utensil to the side and wrapped a loving arm around Katja's lower back. Kova pulled her in, their hips meeting and he dropped a kiss to her cheek. With all the one-on-one time I spent working with him, it was obvious to me his jaw was set tight, but she smiled timidly in response and my heart gave a little pang. After what I witnessed when I arrived earlier, coupled with what happened in his office, I was more baffled than ever. I began wondering if this meant I had deeper feelings for my coach. I knew it wasn't right, but this feeling inside, this feeling of being unsure, the way my stomach tightened, and my heart fluttered, the longing said more than I wanted to acknowledge.

Kova must've felt my confused stare. He looked over his shoulder and his emerald eyes traveled up to mine. Something in my gut said to hold his gaze. His hand tightened his hold on Katja's hip and he tugged her closer to him. I swallowed hard at the sight and realized how I stupidly wanted that to be me. With a small nod of his head, Kova gave me a tight lipped smile, clearly only meant for me, then turned around.

Thankfully, thirty minutes later the food was placed on the table and chairs were quickly filled. I looked around and saw an empty seat beside Reagan. I'd rather eat my mom's bark flavored, pre-packaged meals than sit next to her.

To my left, Holly took a seat next to someone I wasn't familiar with. I moved to walk toward her when Hayden called my name.

"Adrianna! Come sit here." I groaned through a faux smile. There were chairs opened on both sides of Kova's. One of them obviously reserved for Katja. From the corner of my eye, I caught a glimpse of Reagan's scowl. I ignored her and made my way over to Hayden. He pulled a chair out and whispered in my ear, "I know how much you'd rather sit next to Reagan, but sit with me."

"You know me so well," I chuckled. Hayden thankfully sat in the seat next to Kova's. There was no way I could sit that close to him. This was enough. "The view is stunning." He followed my gaze.

"Growing up here, the view doesn't do anything for me anymore." He shrugged carelessly. "It's just a bunch of canals and rivers on this side, but people love them and pay good money to live on the water. I bet you feel the same way about back home."

I thought about what he said. "Yeah, I guess so. People from all over come to our beaches, but it's nothing to me either. Now that I'm here, I do kind of miss waking up to the sound of the ocean, the smell of the salt water, sand between my toes. I never thought I would."

I drifted off thinking about Palm Bay and how I was a bit homesick and I didn't even realize it until now. With gymnastics constantly on my mind, I didn't have time to think about anything else. I hadn't spoken to Avery in over a week, except for a few texts here and there.

"So, aside from this fabulous view, people mainly come here to apple bob."

I looked at Hayden with an arched brow. "Apple bob?"

"Yeah, haven't you gone apple bobbing? We're famous for that. There's a fall festival every year and a big apple bobbing competition. People from all over come to watch and partake in the festivities. We're a very homey town."

I stared at Hayden's straight face, gaping at him. "Tell me you're joking." Surely no one would travel for apple bobbing. Finally, he burst out laughing, a contagious smile spreading across his face. I found myself giggling and I playfully backhanded his arm. The empty chairs rustled next to Hayden. I looked up as Kova and Katja pulled out their chairs and took their seats. Katja was all smiles, not a worry on her serene face, while Kova stared intensely at me. His eyes darkened and shifted over to Hayden. My smile faltered the way he was watching him.

"I'm joking with you," Hayden said, grabbing my attention. I looked at Kova once more before giving my full interest to Hayden, but he was no longer looking my way. "You should see your face right now! Priceless!"

"You jerk. I thought you were serious!" I punched his arm but felt the weight of someone's gaze on me. My skin prickled in awareness but I refused to look up. I knew who it was. And call me crazy, but I had a sinking suspicion he wasn't keen on the idea of Hayden being by my side.

"I know you did." He paused. "For real though, no one comes here to apple bob. I don't even know if that's a thing here. Cape Coral is a great place for an outdoor enthusiast. Boating, fishing, lots of water shit to do. Much like what you're used to, I'm sure. There's no apple bobbing competition. Not that I know of, at least," he finished with a grin.

Before I could respond, Katja exclaimed, "Let's eat!"

Dinner was served and it was probably the best I'd had in a long time. It felt good not to hold back for once and eat what I wanted. I could now, since I was on my own, but I was so used to my mother either watching me or making sure my meals were proportioned that it was an unconscious habit of mine to be careful.

Plus, I didn't want to be one of those "extra cardio" girls.

Dessert was being brought out when Katja asked, "Adrianna, so your parents allow you to be here alone? Kova mentioned to me that you are here by yourself."

I glanced at him before I answered. "Yes."

"I must be honest, I cannot imagine allowing my teen daughter to live on her own even though I know others do it and cohabit with each other. How do you get around since you do not live with the other girls?" She had asked each one of us a few questions, so I knew my time was coming.

I sipped my water then responded. "Well, my parents hired a driver for whenever I need to get around. Where I come from, it's not uncommon for teens to be on their own at my age, or with a chaperon other than the parents. Plus, it helps that Coach is friends with my dad."

"Coach is friends with your dad?" Reagan repeated, with a look of disgust.

"You have a driver? Like a personal one? How did I not know this?" Holly asked.

"I do. He's been with my family since I was a kid."

"Your family?" Reagan asked.

I swallowed back, trying to figure out how to answer her statement without giving away too much. Thankfully Kova jumped in.

"Her family…is an affluent one," was all he said. He used his hands when he said affluent, as if it described the word. Everyone's heads turned my way. Heat rushed up my chest, to my cheeks. My ears burned from the stares.

"My dad's a real estate developer. Think the Hiltons, only smaller," was my explanation.

"That's pretty damn cool. So he can build me a house one day?" Hayden asked.

I smiled, silently thanking him. "Possibly."

"So what's your driver's name?" asked Holly.

"His name is Thomas, but I call him Alfred."

She grinned. "Like Batman."

"Yeah," I smiled. That lightened the subject. "Once I start driving he won't be here. So I'm not really alone per se, since he's always around…somewhere."

"It must be really lonely to have no one," Reagan said, feigning sympathy. "That's the one plus of living in a shared apartment, nothing like having a mom around to lean on. It's really the best feeling."

I nodded slowly, pretending to take in her words like they meant something. If she only knew how happy I was to not have my mom around.

"My dad is a bit of a control freak. There's no way I'd be allowed to stay in an apartment with someone he doesn't know, so I live in the penthouse in one of his condos. It's really safe and private. I love it. The view is incredible and I have a ton of space. If I need anything, Thomas will get it for me, or he'll take me. And since my dad and Kova are friends, if there's some sort of emergency, he's always here for me too. I'm really very fortunate to have what I have and the people around me."

My eyes locked with Kova. He deepened the stare before agreeing with my statement. That shut her up.

chapter 23

FEAR WAS A BITCH, AND IN THIS SPORT, IT COULD CRIPPLE YOU.
Literally.

Fear challenged courage. It challenged the mind. Once we found courage, it meant never looking back. It persevered and defied. It gave strength to conquer the obstacles that rendered one weak.

Successful people fought for what they wanted, what they desired in life no matter what they were up against. Willpower was key, and maybe if I turned my fear into desire, it would override my anxiety. It was the only way to escape the emotion.

I knew I needed to practice what I preached, but it was easier said than done. As was everything. I'd rather train for a new tumbling sequence with front flips, or Level E release moves and bar changes before jumping on beam.

I hated beam. Dreaded it. It was the one event I needed the most work on. I feared the four-inch piece of wood like it had the ability to incapacitate me. But only I could do that.

When I was a child, my dad surprised me with a small, low balance beam for Christmas one year. My fear of the beam started early and I hardly used it. This fear I created in the front of my mind was hard to break. Balancing on a piece of wood that was four feet off the ground didn't sound like much, but when you factor in leaps or turns while balancing on the tips of your toes—let's not forget the back-flips and full-twists with blind landings on a four-inch width—yeah, good luck.

Then try sticking it without straddling the beam and slamming down on your crotch and getting beam burn. That's what I called it, beam burn. It was like rug burn, but from the balance beam. It looked and felt the same. Hurt like a bitch from my inner thighs to my crotch. I'd fallen so hard in the past I actually bled.

It was literally like getting smacked with a piece of wood between your legs. Talk about excruciating pain.

"Come on, Adrianna," Kova groaned, while I wobbled on the beam after landing a double switch leap.

He almost sounded defeated. Again, I jumped off one foot, split my legs as far apart as possible, then switched them quickly so that the leg that was in the front ended up in the back. Once I landed, I took one step, and did it again. After landing quickly—wobble free—it required a full twist.

"Your hips are leaning forward which is why you are taking the extra step at the end! Do it again but without the turn!" Kova ordered, and my heart started to race. "*Relevé* your foot so you are up on your toes and bring your shoulders back before you leap!" He slapped the back of his hand into his palm to get his point across.

It was my stupid fear, even after years of practicing, that I was going to fall.

Stepping into the jump, Kova yelled, "Square your hips so they are centered over the beam!" I dropped my arms and looked at him. He was livid, past the point of angry and ready to move into seething with fury. The team girls stared at me and I was embarrassed. I chewed my bottom lip as I watched his expression turn darker while the fire in his eyes seared my skin.

"I told you to *relevé* into it first! My accent may be strong, but I know you understand what I am saying. Or did you forget that in dance already? Slowly lift your back heel before stepping into the leap. Do it again. And with some damn grace. You look like you are jumping on a trampoline."

He may be hot as hell, and I may have wanted to lick and slap him at the same time, but he could be a complete asshole. Kova muttered something in Russian. He was in rare form today. I had no idea what his deal was. I wish I had some knowledge of the language so then I'd know what he was saying.

I leaped again, but was shaky on the landing. I think I bent my legs too. I was second guessing myself and could feel how off-kilter I was. Kova made me nervous, and his constant yelling was affecting my performance. I hated today. I hated beam. And damn it, this was one of those moments where I wanted to quit altogether.

If I didn't get my nerves under control, I could critically injure myself.

"Tuck in your hips and tighten your stomach. Your chest will stay up and therefore your split will be wider. What part of that do you not get?"

"I'm trying, Coach."

He cracked his neck, sharply twisting it from side to side. The sound made me cringe. "If you were trying, you would do it the correct way. You are not trying hard enough."

Gritting my teeth, I said, "Yes. I. Am," enunciating each word. "You think I like messing up and having you yell at me?" I said out loud. I *was* trying, I was just doing a shitty job.

Another gymnast paused on the beam next to me, her arms slowly fell to her sides as Kova stood stock still. His eyes were wild, huge, and the vein in his neck noticeably pulsed. Fear streamed through me, which was only felt tenfold because I could feel my teammates' as well. I was legitimately frightened of my coach.

And I was quite sure he was about to strangle me.

"I am going to pretend I did not just hear that," he said, his voice low and controlled.

Flexibility has never been my strong suit, or keeping my mouth shut apparently, which was why I had difficulty with jumps sometimes. My legs did not split like they should. Lots of gymnasts suffered from inflexibility—it didn't come with the nature of the sport. Gymnastics builds muscle, which in turn hinders flexibility. It was a vicious cycle to find a balance. Typically, gymnasts who are good on vault and floor, often times find beam isn't their strongest suit.

People automatically assumed being a gymnast meant being able to flip into a pretzel at any given moment. It was quite the opposite. Long hours of manipulating your body at odd angles did it. Bending, flipping, and twisting, I could do. But my legs and my back did not curve the way some of these girls did. It was unnatural, but still, I strived for it.

"Jump down," he sighed, running a hand through his unruly hair. "Adrianna, you have to lift that leg up higher. And stop shaking up there, you look like a leaf blowing on a tree," he spit angrily. "Here, do it on the low beam first."

A leaf blowing on a tree… I let that one pass. He's Russian after all.

I leaped again, splitting my legs wider, but this time when I looked back at him, he looked puzzled.

"I do not think you are squaring your hips." He placed his jaw in his hand. "No, that cannot be right…"

This had to be some sort of joke. I knew how to square my hips.

"It is either that, or you lack more flexibility than I thought, which would explain why your jumps look like shit," he muttered to himself. He went from veins-in-his-neck screaming to quiet and pondering. "But you are still not hitting that one hundred and eighty degree split." He stared at me intently, his brows angled deep toward each other while rubbing his jaw. "Go into the dance room and do split jumps in front of the mirror. I will be there shortly."

I swallowed back the lump in my throat and nodded, making my way into the dance room. There was a piece of long white tape perpendicular to the mirror. I stood on it and began doing split jumps, making sure to land on the make shift balance beam. I watched my body closely. My hips looked squared, but Kova was right. It didn't look like I was hitting the split all the way.

I wasn't sure how long I was in the dance room for or how many split jumps I completed by the time Kova walked in. He studied my jumps through critical eyes. I didn't ask questions and I didn't stop until my legs felt like rubber. Kova strutted over to me. He placed his hands on my shoulders and looked into my eyes, radiating confidence into me.

"Focus. Take a deep breath and exhale," he paused. "A quiet and controlled breath, Ria. Like I taught you." His palms warmed my shoulders as he massaged them to loosen me up.

"Shoulders back," he pushed my shoulders back which brought my chest forward. "Chest out," he dipped his chin in approval. "Like that." He grasped the sides of my jaw and said, "Chin up." I nodded. Before I could turn back to face the mirror, his knuckles slid beneath my jaw and danced across my throat seductively. A shiver broke out on my arms and his eyes darkened. "Perfect." He dropped his hands and I turned around to prepare for another jump. Kova came up behind me and repeated the movements, his eyes never leaving mine. He stood so close his clothes brushed against my tepid skin. Once I was standing how he wanted me, he placed his hands on my hips, the tips of his fingers searing my bikini line as he pressed deeper to make sure my hips were square. His nearness caused my heart to thump wildly against my chest. He'd never been this daring before, this forward, and truth be told, I welcomed it.

"You see how you are standing? This is how you prepare before you leap." His breath accelerated. The tips of his fingers curved down and brushed my ass, dangerously low. Goose bumps immediately broke out across my skin and I was sure he felt them as his hands lingered evocatively, causing a rush of wetness to surge through me. A low, deep groan reverberated in the back of his throat, but I'd heard it before he stepped back. Kova gave me a slight nod and I forced my racing heart to get under control. I executed a split jump, which ended up looking much better this time.

"Beautiful," he said quietly, looking into my eyes through the mirror. It was so hard for me not to smile over his approval. "Again." With a nod of his head, he ordered me to perform the skill multiple times. My legs split higher, more gracefully, but more importantly, correctly.

At this point I was out of breath from doing them repeatedly. I waited for his next order with burning thighs while balancing on the balls of my feet. His incredibly handsome poker face was hard to read.

"Back to the beam."

Once we were back, I chalked up my feet and headed to the beam. I gripped it between my hands and jumped, feeling my thighs rub against the suede before I stood tall. I performed about a dozen split jumps perfectly before I moved on. Kova seemed pleased with me. I tapped the beam with a pointed toe and then stepped into the leap. I landed, slightly shaky and saved it, but I knew Coach saw it. He never missed a beat. His eyes narrowed to slits and I felt them inching up my body until they met my eyes. I exhaled a low and steady breath and waited for what he had to say.

"Adrianna, you should be able to land your leap on the beam if you can do it on the white tape. Get it right."

I blinked my eyes, abruptly feeling light headed. It'd been hours since I'd eaten. My lunch had been light, not wanting to work out on a full belly. And since I was at the gym for hours, half the time I was starving. After I finished on beam though, I planned to eat my protein bar to hold me over until practice was over.

I wanted to impress my coach and show him I was worthy of being here, but with him riding my back over a stupid leap, along with my gnawing hunger, I was stressing out big time.

"While I am young, Adrianna." He clapped twice. We were back to Adrianna. "Get moving. Ten more."

I gulped, then completed the leap eleven more times instead of ten. My legs were rubbery and I began to feel nauseous. I was training on an empty stomach with a barking coach in my ear.

On one of the jumps, I came down with shaky legs. My arms and legs went out to the sides just a little to balance myself. I tried to make it flow into a pose to cover it up, but any coach with a sharp eye would spot it immediately.

I wasn't sure why I even tried to hide it from Kova.

"Lock your leg, Adrianna," he gritted, his eyes were drilling holes into my head.

Coach dropped his head. Running a hand through his hair, he pulled at his scalp. Snapping his head up, he turned to the bars and yelled, "Reagan! Over here! Now!"

Great. My biggest fan was coming over to show me up.

"Yes, Coach," she said with a syrupy voice. It made me want to dry heave.

"Get up there and show Adrianna how a switch leap is done."

She smiled and said, "No problem, Coach."

I hoped she fell.

On her face.

chapter 24

Turning toward me with her back to Kova, a conniving, small grin tugged at her knowing face. I couldn't help but want to smack her for it. I wasn't an aggressive kind of person, but she really knew how to get under my skin like no other.

Reagan jumped up on the beam and naturally landed a perfect leap. Of course she did. Balance beam was her favorite event, one she excelled at. Even though I couldn't stand to look at her at times, she really had skill.

Kova dipped his chin in approval before saying, "Do it again, but this time make sure you are watching, Adrianna."

Reagan landed a beautiful leap, as if she was born to do it. "Thank you, Reagan. You can go back to bars."

"Yes, sir." She hopped down and looked over her shoulder at me, grinning.

My patience was wearing thin. I was starving, tired, and I had a bitch on my team I shouldn't even care about who would love to see me fail.

"Don't fall, Ana," she whispered as she glided past, patting me on the shoulder.

The urge to stick my foot out and trip her, then kick her in her pinched face was stronger than ever.

Coach looked at me expectantly. I jumped on the beam and focused on the end of it, but I could feel someone's burning gaze on me. I refused to look up. I chewed the inside of my lip. I couldn't mess this one up, I just couldn't.

I got this, I got this, I got this, I chanted to myself. I *had* it.

Shaking out my fingers, I exhaled into the jump. Just as I was about to land, I could tell my body was off balance. I just knew—like a gut instinct, sixth sense sort of thing—I was off-kilter.

Peeking down to spot the beam, I froze mid-air, the worst thing a gymnast could do. I should've never looked down. I should've believed in myself more, trusted myself. Landing, my foot nicked the edge of the balance beam. I desperately tried to curl my toes around the edge, but I slipped and fell fast.

My stomach sunk with my body and I held my breath as I plummeted to the balance beam.

I quickly dropped my arms in an attempt to grab the beam to lessen the impact of my crotch slamming into the wood, but it was futile. My body tightened, slanting to the side; and my leg rubbed down the suede fabric, feeling the fiery burn immediately. My ribs crashed into the wooden slab and a gush of air left my lungs.

The sound of a gymnast straddling the beam was always a noticeable one. The impact was loud, and in my peripheral vision, I could see heads turning, but I didn't look. I couldn't. My eyes clenched shut and I was pretty sure a bone broke inside my crotch from the snapping sound the fall made. I reached blindly for the beam with my other hand, but my body rotated and I flipped over, falling onto the cushioned mat and into a fetal position.

Eighty-seventh time of straddling the beam. And moments like this made me hate gymnastics with every fiber in my body.

Fuck, I wanted to cry.

Oh, God, it hurt so bad. I was curled up into a ball on the floor, my feet cushioned under my ass with my arms wrapped around my waist. My forehead pressed into the mat as I took a deep breath preparing to stand. Tears formed in the back of my eyes, but I refused to cry and further my embarrassment.

As I knelt trying to summon the strength to get up, a large hand came to rest on my back. The weight of his body created a slight indentation on the mat. *Kova.* As if I wasn't in enough pain already.

Of course.

"Are you okay, Adrianna?"

I nodded silently.

"Let me help you up," he offered as his hand cupped my bicep and pulled me up.

"I'm fine." I choked out behind false bravado.

But I wasn't. My inner thighs were raw, my crotch was aching and on fire. It felt strange, like something moved inside and broke. I knew that wasn't possible, but something didn't feel right.

"Shake it off," Coach said. "Do you need a break?"

"No," I responded, then reached for the beam. I climbed up, feeling the heat race from inside my crotch area out and down through my thighs. Pushing back the tears, I bit my lip so hard I tasted blood. *I got this.* I knew I could do it. I just needed to refocus on the move and not what people were thinking—and staring at.

With my shoulders back and arms positioned, my knees trembled. The pain from the fall had my nerves all over the place. *Maybe this wasn't a good idea*, I thought as my heart beat frantically in my chest. I felt sick, and I knew I looked pale. I was truly scared.

Kova's deep voice eased into the next sentence, almost as if he was worried for me. "Lock your legs, Adrianna."

I exhaled, then stepped into the leap, but fear took hold of my heart before I could complete the sequence.

I slipped and fell. Again.

"Jesus Christ," Kova mumbled, his voice drawing closer to me.

Only this time it wasn't as bad because my ribs didn't hit the beam. However, my crotch suffered severely from the impact and I needed to check on it in the bathroom immediately.

My jaw trembled as tears burst from my eyes. I covered my face and cried silently into the blue mat that smelled like feet. I couldn't do this anymore. I was done, I wanted to go home. It hurt too much.

"Let me see," Coach said, squatting in front of me as I sat holding my stomach. The girls stared at me. Fresh tears dripped from my eyes and he used his thumb to wipe them away.

Kova's eyes met mine. He pushed my knee open to get a better look. From the tops of my knees to my inner thighs, they were both bright red and had scrape marks. Kova hissed. "Go get some ice and sit on it."

I kept my eyes trained on the floor as I made my way out, worried I'd see their gawking faces over my poor performance. I sighed inwardly. Today was the worst day of my life and I wanted to be done with it.

I looked like an amateur. No one fell the way I had today. Twice.

Before going to the cafe for some ice, I stopped in the bathroom and tore my leo off. Damn thing stuck to me. The stabbing pain inside my vagina was like a knife slowly slicing into me and I had to check. Something wasn't right.

Looking down, there were small, red droplets of blood. *Shit.* And I wore a violet leotard, so I'd need to change into another one before I went back out. Or just throw on some shorts.

With two fingers, I gently moved myself around and winced in pain. I was already the color of a cherry and swollen, and I knew by looking, it was going to take a good week to heal. And probably hurt to pee.

Redressing, I washed my hands then made my way into the kitchen. Thankfully no one was around to talk to or question me. I gathered two bags of ice and wrapped both loosely in a paper towel. Placing the bags on a chair, I carefully sat down so one bag hit my center and the other was on my inner thighs. As much as it burned from the chill, it actually felt good at the same time. I leaned over to find a comfortable position on the table and held my weight up with my elbows and dropped my head into my arms. I was trembling inside and sulking at how terrible I performed this afternoon.

As I sat alone icing myself, I visualized the switch leap over and over, landing it perfectly each time with elegance. How I could mess up something as simple as a leap but land a double back handspring back layout sequence perfectly made no sense. I pictured Kova nodding in approval, his striking face looking up proudly at me. Even when he was livid he was gorgeous. Anyone with eyes would agree with me.

Kova was attractively annoying. He put more pressure on me than anyone else and I couldn't decide if that was a good thing or not. I wondered if there was a motive behind pushing me the way he had aside from helping me achieve my dream of going to the Olympics one day. I wasn't that bad off, there had to be more. Couldn't he see I tried my hardest to prove to him I wanted to be here? My stomach was in knots and I clenched my eyes shut, fighting the climbing tears. I couldn't think of anything else to prove any of this to him.

Maybe he hated the ground I walked on. Maybe he saw potential. Maybe I got under his skin. Maybe in some obscure way he liked me. Maybe not... I thought of his stunning girlfriend and knew I was just making stuff up in my head. Katja was the complete opposite of me. Her eyes were a kaleidoscope of amber and peridot. She had a flawless ivory complexion. Not to mention a super model body girls would kill for. There wasn't a thing wrong with her. She was beautiful and smart, and to top it off, she was genuinely nice. The perfect package. Any man would die to be with her.

Since the Fourth of July barbecue, Katja had been to the gym a few times. Watching him embrace her made my heart throb. He'd lace his fingers through her perfectly styled waves, look deeply into her eyes, and pull her mouth to his with passion. As if he needed her to get through the rest of his day. When he pulled away, her mouth would be swollen and red, her eyes glazed over with bliss. But it wasn't just me who watched, the entire girls' team watched in awe, too. They were the perfect couple and we all wished we were her.

Then I remembered when Kova had said I was just as pretty. Gorgeous, even.

The vivid images of his hands roaming my body and not Katja's hit me with force. Wishing I was her was wickedly wrong. I groaned, both in pain from the fall and frustration over my deviant thoughts. There had to be something wrong with me to think of my coach this way, but I couldn't stop. I wanted him to look at me with the same intensity he did her.

His lips grazing my supple ones, his fingers digging into my backside, crushing me to him. His penis pushed against my stomach, not letting me move, hard and hot. His tongue sliding into my mouth and taking control, but with passion and heat like in the movies. He was much bigger than me. Brute strength and compelling eyes.

He ripped my clothes off, I yanked at his shirt and his buttons went flying. He couldn't take his wild eyes off of me.

"How are you doing, Ria?"

My head snapped up in surprise and my lips parted. Coach stood beside me and stared down with inquisitive eyes while he waited for a response. Shit, my breathing deepened while my cheeks flushed from the tainted thoughts I had. I was beginning to notice he only used that nickname when it was just us.

His eyes grew heavy, pupils dilating. As if he knew what I'd been thinking. I blushed again, remembering how he said he liked the pinkish color in my cheeks.

I swallowed and said nothing, averting my gaze to his crotch for some reason. Eyes widened, I looked back at his brooding face.

God, what was wrong with me to picture myself as Katja?

chapter 25

I KNEW TWO THINGS.
I was going straight to hell. And I was as red as a fire hydrant.
"Adrianna."

"I, ah… I'm okay," I responded, finding my voice.

He shoved his hands into his pockets. "How bad is it?"

I swallowed, wondering how much to tell him. I went for the truth.

"Pretty bad. I was bleeding a little from the fall. I'm not anymore though." After twenty minutes of icing it, the pain was numb.

Coach's jaw flexed. "Bleeding, huh. And your thighs," his voice was smoky.

Unsure at this point, I pushed the chair out and removed both ice bags. Looking down, I said, "They're pretty red. Scratched up. I'll have a nice burn for a few days."

Squatting, Kova got to my level. He placed a hand at the back of my chair to steady himself, the other on my thigh. I flinched, my legs automatically trying to close, but he stopped me.

"Let me see."

I gulped. While I was uncertain of what he wanted to see, I was positively certain the stain would show through. Talk about embarrassing.

My brows creased together as a shadow cast across his eyes. His thumb began rubbing small, slow circles on the inside of my knee. His touch was exhilarating and soothing, and I couldn't help but wonder if this was his way of apologizing for how he treated me earlier.

"Your thighs, where you hit the beam… let me see." With that, he placed his other hand on my opposite knee and slowly pushed my legs open.

The rise and fall of his chest matched mine. Our breathing grew heavy as the air thickened. Kova's large hands moved slowly toward my hips, pushing against me and opening my legs wider. My hips rolled up and my back arched, pushing my chest out.

He paused before he reached the apex of my thighs, and I mean *right* before. I held my breath and my heart froze. The room grew significantly smaller. He wouldn't dare go any further, would he? Desire coursed through my body and the thought of stopping him never once occurred. I actually wanted him to touch me where he never should go. The forbidden facet was possibly the calculating equation. His palms and fingers dug into my flesh, scooting me closer to him.

I began to tremble under his hold and he slowly licked his bottom lip. His eyes never left mine as I let him know it was okay. I arched my back, leaving only my shoulders to rest against the chair.

Gone was the cold shock of the bags of ice I had been sitting on moments earlier, and in its place was scorching, hot heat. Need. Want. Something, I just wasn't sure what. Kova paused, then resumed his glide up my thighs.

"It is a pretty bad burn." His eyelids lowered and he groaned in the back of his throat. "You are going to be sore for days, make sure to put some balm on it..." he trailed off, his focus at the center of my legs. His thumb soothed the burn that marred my tender skin. He was so close to my sex, I began to throb for his touch.

I nodded instinctively, and without thinking, I reached out. My nails digging into the curve of his bicep when his thumb stopped. He created an ache that needed to be released, a buildup was flowing inside of me.

He knew what he was doing. What he was creating within me.

If I breathed, he'd touch me in a place no one had ever touched me before.

And maybe I wanted that.

My hips undulated when the back of his knuckles swept over my thigh, the tips of his fingers brushing the side of my sex, close to the seam of my lips. A little gasp escaped my mouth, my chest burned from holding in my breath. The touch was so light, so faint, but I felt it, and I think he knew too.

Kova held stock still, frozen in place, as a throbbing pulse resonated from deep within me.

Oh God, it felt like I was ready to come apart and I wanted him to do it again. Imagine my shock when his eyes lowered and his thumb cautiously reached out and deliberately stroked the side of my pussy.

I didn't say stop. Or not to touch me. I'd always been taught to say no to bad touches, but this wasn't bad, it felt good. He made me feel good. It wasn't like he was a stranger. This was my coach, a friend of my dad's.

And deep down, I wanted it.

"Kova." His jaw flexed at the sound of my cracked voice. He fought to lift his head, his eyes trained in one spot. My legs widened further, signaling I wanted him to do it again, ready to feel whatever was brewing inside. I was so close, I could feel it. Seconds went by and the pleasure receded.

And then, just when I thought he was going to pull back, his thumb moved a fraction and slid between my lips, over my leo, from bottom to top in a swirling motion on my pussy.

Sweet Jesus!

Instinctively, my nails dug deep in his golden skin as I pushed my chest out. My nipples tightened, hardening to little points. I gave Kova full access as my hips unwound in the chair, reveling in his touch. He growled low as I moved myself against his hand. I needed more, I wanted it. A million tiny explosions were climbing inside me, building up higher and higher. I wanted to reach that pinnacle of bliss.

Kova pressed his thumb hard against my clit and pushed in circles, his fingertips seeking entrance, but my leo was too tight. A rush of wetness coated through the fabric, directly beneath his thumb. Kova rumbled deep in the back of his throat as he rubbed the wet stain. My legs shook and it took everything in me not to yell out from the intensity of the pleasure.

"Oh," I breathed ever so quietly. "Oh... God. It feels so good." I was right there. My entire body came apart, tingling with the euphoric bliss he brought me as I blew up. His thumb circled faster, my hips rolled in a wave as I exploded in front of him. I gripped the side of the chair, and released a heavy breath. My shoulders relaxed back.

Kova was breathing low and heavy when I finally found my voice. "What... what was that?"

His shocked gaze snapped to mine and held still. When he didn't say anything, I asked again, "What was that?"

Removing his hand from my sex, he squeezed my knee painfully hard. His hand shook and the skin on his knuckles tightened. The vein in his arm twirled down in a spiral as he stared at the ground, lost in thought.

"An orgasm, I presume," he choked out.

I shook my head vehemently. "No way. I've had orgasms before and they never once felt that incredible."

Kova's knees cracked as he stood, his pelvis directly in front of my face... along with an obvious erection. I swallowed back and looked up at him, his intoxicating eyes were already trained hard on me. He cupped himself, stroking his hard length. I glanced down, mesmerized as I watched him wrap his hand around his thickness, moving it around almost as if he was trying to push it down.

I licked my dry lips and glanced up. Kova had never taken his eyes off me. He dragged a hand through his hair and expelled a loud breath. His eyes finally left mine and scattered around the cafe.

"Do you think you will be able to go back out and train again?" he asked.

Wait—What? He wanted me to train after that mind-blowing orgasm I just had—he was certifiably insane.

I cleared my throat. "Yeah, I need to change my leo first."

That got his attention. "Actually go home, Ria." His face was void of any emotion and my stomach tightened. "You had enough for today." He coughed. "That, ah, fall was a bad one."

I frowned. I didn't want him to send me home.

"But I still have a half day of training left."

"I am giving you the rest of the day off."

I stood to get my point across. "But I need these extra hours, you know I need all the help I can get. I don't want to go home."

"Adrianna, at this point I do not care what you want. I said go home, so go. For once, can you not fucking argue with me and just go?"

I flinched and forced back my rising tears. He'd never used such a menacing tone with me since I began training, or cursed. At least not that I could remember. His sudden, hurtful glare got to me. "No, I won't."

Muttering in Russian, he glared at me.

"I'll suck it up and deal. It's my problem, not yours. It was only a little fall anyway."

Slowly, he looked in my direction, as if he was ready to body slam me to the floor. My heart pounded painfully against my ribs. I wasn't sure what I'd done that was so wrong.

"I do not want to see your face until tomorrow. Am I making myself clear?"

Breathing deeper and pulling from within, I pushed back. I was ready to blow, and not in a good way. The Sicilian in me was coming out.

"You can't make me go home for this. It was a stupid fall, and no one else has been sent home for falling!"

His eyes softened. "You misunderstand. If you do not go home and recover, tomorrow is going to be painful for you."

This man confused me. One minute he was growling and ready to strangle me, the next, like right this instance, he was concerned and caring.

I nodded. Actually, he was right. "I don't understand you."

"You are not supposed to."

Then he stalked off and left the room as if nothing happened.

chapter 26

SOMETIMES WHEN THE DAY ENDED AND EVERYONE WENT HOME, I LIKED TO COME into the gym late at night just to lie on the floor and stare up at the ceiling, visualizing my routines over and over.

My body would flinch and jerk as I pictured myself nail each skill and dismount, pleasing my coaches.

Every gymnast had access to the gym with just a swipe of their card, yet I'd never seen any here the few times I came.

In the hushed silence of the night, being surrounded by the equipment was freeing, and it brought a sense of security that filled my soul. No one to yell at me or stare down and tell me how wrong I was. No cold shoulders from my teammates. No side-looks or smirks to shake my confidence. It was just me and the gym as I breathed in the chalky air.

Switching on one light, it illuminated over the parallel bars, leaving the rest of the gym cased in darkness, which was just what I wanted. I liked the obscurity. It was serene and comforting.

A nice little bruise had formed on my pubic bone. I'd had falls on beam before, but this one was probably one of the worst since I'd fallen back-to-back. I iced myself religiously three times, soaked in a bath, and took four Motrin to alleviate the swelling. And nearly a week later, I was good to go.

Walking toward the blue-carpeted spring floor, I zipped up my sweater. The chill hit my bones, a tremble waked through me. Without the heated bodies to fill the gym, it was actually quite cold in here. Once I was in the dead center, I laid down and a shiver crept up my spine.

Meet season would soon be here and I needed to mentally prepare. I wasn't sure which meets Kova would put me in, but since this year was an Olympic year, elite season dates changed. I had roughly four months to go, then December to June would be nonstop. The competitions were much larger than what I was used to, competing outside the state, and competing against new athletes, mostly younger than me and with harder skills. The younger part worried me the most, though I would never in a million years admit it to anyone. The last few months had been pure hell, both emotionally and physically, and divulging it would make me appear like the weakling I felt I was at times. So I bottled it up and kept my mouth shut.

Just like I did back home.

Expelling a deep sigh, I had to find trust and belief from within to gain the confidence I needed. I had experience and maturity due to my age and upbringing. Hopefully that would work in my favor.

I slipped my ear buds in and began playing *The End* by Kings of Leon. His deep, baritone voice along with the beats drowned out the negative voices in my head and allowed me to think freely. I was able to forget the weight of my life for a little while without the added pressure of anyone. The music spoke to me and I listened.

I wasn't sure how long I'd been there when something caught the corner of my eye. Craning my neck to the side, I looked toward the light from the door and my stomach dropped.

Coach Kova.

I had no idea what he was doing here. Surely, he got enough of the gym being here all day.

He looked to be on a mission as he strode toward the now illuminated rings, determined and completely oblivious I was present.

Thank God. He probably figured he berated the gymnasts enough they wouldn't be here after hours.

Wait, I take that back. He only berated me to that extent. I was his punching bag on a bad day.

Reaching behind his neck, he fisted his gray shirt and pulled it over his head. It slid off his back smoothly, like a piece of silk, and dropped it to the ground. I sucked in a breath as he undressed under the muted light. I'd never seen him without a shirt before. Other than an occasional tumbling pass where his shirt would rise up and show a hint of his stomach, it was all the skin of his I'd ever seen.

He toed off his sneakers, leaving only a pair of black basketball shorts on, then cracked his neck, rolling it around in circles. He threw his arms out to the sides, swinging them around wildly to stretch them out. From behind, his golden back was lean, honed to absolute perfection, the muscles flexing as he stretched out his upper half. I couldn't help but lie still and stare at him in awe. His back was a work of art. Just like him.

He was fucking gorgeous.

I whimpered internally. Only I would see having a hot coach as a curse.

Kova jumped and grasped the rings. The corded muscles in his shoulders tightened and I watched as he began whipping his pointed toes back and forth while he held steady. Arching his back, then hollowing his chest, he had great form.

He went straight into full swings, handstands, and flips, warming up his body. My jaw went slack. He maneuvered the rings with precision, like a champ. I'd never seen him use any apparatus at practice before. He was focused, completely unaware anyone was watching. And I was happy he was oblivious. I was mesmerized by the sight before me. He had such grace and beauty coiled in his toned body that I think if he knew anyone was watching he'd stop. His control was remarkable at his age. Thirty-two wasn't old by any means, but for a gymnast it was ancient. Christ, eighteen was over the hill for a gymnast.

Most gymnasts retired around the age of eighteen, very few made it to their mid-twenties. Not by choice, but because their bodies could no longer handle the physical strain and demand of the sport. Almost always, there was an injury we sustained.

We defied gravity on the floor with insane jaw dropping tumbling passes, ran toward stationary objects to flip over, and balanced on a four-inch piece of wood with turns, tucks, and fulls. All the while killing our backs and feet from landings and dismounts. The impact shocked our ankles and zoomed up our spines, making us wince in pain. But we grinned and dealt with it and did what we were born to do, because we couldn't imagine life without it. Just as Kova was doing now. He couldn't let go.

Kova pulled up into a handstand then slowly extended his arms out to the sides so now he was in an upside down T, his back facing me. His body was pulled tight and locked solid. Roped muscles in his shoulders jutted out, and cut sharp as he began to slowly lower his body into a plank position. I held my breath as I watched. The skill was not an easy one to master.

I'd seen teammates shake from the brute strength it took to hold this form. But Kova didn't move, he didn't shake. His arms were as steady as the rest of his body. There was no blowing like a leaf, as he once said I had on beam. It was beyond remarkable my coach could still do a skill of this capacity.

With incredible accuracy and control, he rotated his arms just a fraction so they were turned out. From his sculpted shoulders to the veins that snaked around his arms, he didn't waver in his hold. It was utterly fascinating. His body exuded raw power and strength, and it was beautifully captivating. Remarkable. I've tried so hard not to associate Kova with anything other than him being my gymnastics coach. But seeing his determination and fight to make me a better gymnast on a daily basis compelled me to think of him in more ways than I should. And now, with how he was conveying control without anyone around, it was hard to see him as just my coach.

Once in a forward facing T, he pulled his legs up into a pike position. My gaze traveled down his solid chest, taking in his lean abdomen.

And my mouth gaped open, a gush of hot air rolling off my lips.

Mother of all hell.

There was a fairly large Olympic ring tattoo on the left side of his ribs. Unlike the colorful rings the symbol was known for, Kova's five ring tattoo was in solid black. And with each breath he took, the tattoo moved as if it were floating on his skin.

Sweet Jesus, Mary, and Joseph. I was gawking at his body, and it was hard to tear my gaze away. The tattoo and placement was unbelievably sexy. It upped his hot factor by ten million, not that he needed it.

Suddenly, he began swinging hard in circles and then landed a back tuck dismount. His feet pounded the ground, the chalk lifting in the air from impact. He rose to his full height, eyes closed and shoulders rolled back as his chest expanded from deep breaths. The tattoo grew then shrunk with each breath he took. It was almost impossible to tear my eyes from his ribs. My gaze traveled down his waist to where his shorts sat extremely low. He had those indents on his hips that formed a V, and my God, my mouth started to water.

For a split moment, I forgot he was my coach. I pictured myself running my hands slowly up his stomach, massaging his worn muscles, before tracing his tattoo and exploring his body. My fingers gliding over his arms, roaming over his shoulders in the dark where no one could see us.

Ten more minutes passed while I secretly watched Kova as just him, a man on the rings, and nothing more. I didn't move a muscle, just watched in awe… until my phone started ringing.

Fuck. Fuck. Fuck.

Grabbing my cell, I silenced my mom then looked back over to the rings to see him glaring at me from under the apparatus. Standing up, I had no choice but to walk over to him.

Kova let go of the rings, whipped his hands back and forth, and firmly crossed his arms in front of his bare chest, his stance intimidating as he stood under the rings. His biceps grabbed my attention and I could feel his searing, pissed gaze focused on my face.

"Adrianna," he stated more than called my name.

"Coach."

"What are you doing here?" he asked, dropping his arms to rub his wrists then crossed his hands behind him, his pecs flexing. I openly raked my eyes down the length of his gorgeous body. There was no way not to, and honestly, I didn't care that he saw me do it.

I shrugged, closing the distance between us. "I needed to think. Sometimes I like coming here when it's empty."

"So you come to the gym to just lie on the floor?"

He was skeptical. It was obvious, but I told him the truth. He could decide what to do with it.

"I do… I feel free in the dark, no one here to judge me," I said, pinning him with honest eyes.

"But you are lying on the floor?"

I let it all out. "Exactly. No one can say I'm doing anything wrong, that my form is incorrect, or how my legs aren't locked. Stupid things I already know. I'm not fearful I'll slip on the beam, or I'm not blocking hard enough on vault. No one to make me feel like I'm not good enough, that I'm not graceful enough. There's no one to hate the ground I walk on in here when I'm alone. No one can see me in the dark to point out my imperfections. It's just me and the gym, all by myself to do as I please."

He almost looked remorseful at my admission. "And you cannot do this at home?"

I looked away to conceal my emotions. "No, it's too quiet there. Usually the loneliness doesn't bother me and I embrace it. Some nights it gets to be too much, so I run away and come here," I finished quietly. "The oddness of it all, I feel more at home here than anywhere else. Tonight, the silence in my condo was deafening and I needed to get out. The gym speaks to me."

He took a step toward me so he was only inches away.

"It is okay. I understand why you are here alone."

His eyes locked with mine, and through the muted lights a shadow covered half his face as something stirred between us. My heart stammered, feeling it, and I knew he felt it too by the look of his dilating pupils that took up most of his bright eyes. His jaw locked, shifting back and forth.

Kova continued, as though talking to himself. "Why do you think I am here?"

chapter 27

TIME STOOD STILL.

"How do you do it," I whispered. He took a small step toward me and I held my breath. I watched as his eyes skated across my face, my eyes, nose, to my cheeks… where they locked on my mouth. We were balancing on a fine line and we both knew it.

My heart raced, the blood in my veins heating as his gaze struck me to the core. My lips parted, a soft breath expelling. I didn't know what to do, what to say. Kova was so close as we stood alone in the darkened gym. I thought about how he touched me the other day in the cafe and the way he looked at me. It was nothing compared to the way his eyes were boring into mine in this moment where no one could see us. It rendered me speechless. Anything could happen now—and that intrigued me.

Tension crackled and I knew he felt it. There was no denying the invisible pull or the gleaming look in his eyes. Lifting his hand, the back of his chalk covered knuckles brushed across the edge of my jaw. I knew he shouldn't be doing it, he sure as hell knew he shouldn't be, but I tilted my head into his hand, asking for more.

Leaning down, he whispered, "Do what?"

"How do you hold steady on the rings the way you do? I was in awe watching you. You move so quietly, I can't tear my eyes away."

"Control."

The heat of his body radiated on to mine and I felt his response on my lips. My heart pounded painfully against my ribs. Kova was as exhilarating as his touch. I wanted so badly to reach out and grab him.

"Control. Power. Muscle memory," he responded huskily, the look in his eyes piercing me. "You have to know your body inside and out. When to let go. When to hold on. You have to feel it, visualize it… want it."

"How do you know when to let go?"

"Your body will tell you. Listen to your body, Ria. Trust it. What is it telling you?" he asked in a smoky voice, sending goose bumps down my arms. I loved when he called me Ria when no one else was around.

Biting my bottom lip, my eyes slowly met his as I gripped his thick wrist that cupped my face. My other hand reached for his waist and latched on. I couldn't stop myself, I wanted to feel him… I *needed* to. If he was touching me, I could touch him. It was only fair. At least now I had an excuse—a justification. But what I really wanted to do was trace the tattoo on his ribs.

My fingers caressed his taut hips, the back of my knuckles dragged along the waistband of his shorts ever so delicately. Kova's eyes widened and he drew in a shaky breath as his stomach flexed. He wasn't expecting it, and truthfully, I didn't know where I got the courage to do it. I stepped closer to continue my exploration.

I couldn't keep my hands to myself, I didn't want to. I wanted to know what it was like to be pressed against him, my heart to his, beating at the same time.

Our chests nearly closed the distance, our gazes locked, and I could feel the heat of his skin under my hand. A million thoughts were running through my mind. Every second passed was like torture. His body was solid as stone but soft to the touch. I slid my hand up his ribs, my thumb finally circling the tattoo.

"I like your tattoo," I admitted. "A lot." A slow breath rolled off his lips and into my face. A faint hint of cranberry and vodka.

"I want to learn control like you," I whispered.

"All in good time."

"Teach me."

"Control?"

I nodded, taking in every inch of his chest.

"You ask for too much."

I stared up through my eyelashes, trying to conceal my emotions. He was right. I was asking for more than gymnastics and he knew it, but at the same time I didn't know exactly what I was asking for. I had no idea what I wanted and more importantly, I had no idea what the hell we were doing.

We'd been dancing around each other for weeks now. The lingering touches, the long stares. It was building, simmering between us.

With both trembling hands now resting on his firm chest, one of his hardened nipples grazed the bottom of my palm and he contracted. His head angled down, his eyes boring into mine. If only I was a little taller.

"Is this what control is?" My gaze traveled to his mouth as I slightly tilted my head and lifted up to the balls of my feet. I wanted to kiss him desperately, to feel his lips pressed to mine. "Wanting to try a new skill without preparing for it first? That I could be risking everything?"

I was purely infatuated with him.

Kova reached out and gripped my arm from my temptation laced words. His fingers dug into my bicep. I watched his control waver, and for a selfish moment, I hoped it snapped.

"That is exactly what it is," he said quietly. "Wanting to try something so badly but knowing it is not the right step. At least not yet. Knowing when to spring forward and knowing when not to. You perfect your craft to the best of your ability when you are ready. It is also about control and trust. Trust more than anything in yourself."

"When will I know?" I whispered.

"Practice. Practice. Practice. It is all about being able to execute a flawless routine. A feeling that streams through your body. You will know when the time is right."

"What if I don't?"

He paused, his cool breath hitting my face. "Gymnastics is very similar to everyday life. It is trial and error, Ria. It is about taking chances, is it not? It is about power. A mental war. It is about not being afraid to try something new even if it scares you. If you do not jump, you will never know how high you can soar. It is about controlling your leap once you let go, but not being afraid of switching your directions. It is a chance you are willing to take."

"And what if I take the leap and slip?"

My heart was racing. His hands cupped my jaw, tilting my head back. "Then you get back up and try again."

For a moment, time stood still. Everything was forgotten except the two of us standing in the empty gym. We were inches apart, an intake of breath away from doing something that would go against the rules, and the law. The code of ethics. Morals.

And for whatever reason, none of that mattered to me.

Kova's thumb circled my jaw so softly that it took everything in me not to shiver. It was as if he was touching me beneath my flesh, purposely heating my body and tugging on every fiber. His caress was powerful.

The look in his beautiful, deep green irises stripped me bare. I couldn't seem to tear my focus from his. And truthfully, I didn't want to. His eyes were hypnotic. Spellbinding. Alluringly tantalizing, and I felt him down to the bone.

My hold tightened on his bare skin. The palm of his hand grazed my cheek and slid down to my jaw, leaving a trail of heat in its wake where his warm hand cupped my nape. My heart pounded and my breathing grew shallow. I wanted him to lean in and kiss me, to press his lips to mine and kiss me hard. I just wanted to feel his flesh on me.

My body ached from standing on my tiptoes, but I didn't dare back down. Instead, I tilted my head, giving him access to my mouth, the same way I gave him access to my hips. His stare shifted down to my parted lips… then to my chest.

I waited to see if he would take it or not.

Kova inhaled deeply and I curled into him like I was the air he was breathing in. His fingers found the zipper to my jacket. Carefully, he pulled the zipper down. His gaze met mine again as he reached the bottom. Kova's callused fingers slid under the material and pushed it down my shoulders until it fell silently to the floor. He hissed, his eyes crinkled. Looking down, I wore a solid white cami, sans bra. And there was no mistaking the outline of my breasts or the hardening of my nipples. Attentively, his hand came up and his knuckles grazed the outside of my plump breast ever so slowly. Our breathing mingled together and my body reached for his touch.

His arm circled my lower back and tenderly pulled me to him. *Yes.* He was so big, so strong and dominating in the way he held me. A long, hard length lay angled against my pelvis and my body melted into him. His erection tapped my pussy and my eyes rolled shut. I placed my hand on the curve of his neck, feeling his raw power contract beneath my fingertips. The man was a walking sin. I kept telling myself I couldn't help it, that I needed to feel more of him, to make something happen. Sometimes a little self-convincing helped.

His stubble grazed my cheek, and his breath tingled my neck. I gasped, my stomach tightened.

He made his move, and I mimicked it.

Something shifted deep inside me, an awakening of an emotion heated my blood. A dark desire inside my belly was aching to come out. I tilted my jaw seeking his mouth. No words were needed, just a single touch and a sigh would be enough to get what I—we—wanted. We were so close to closing the gap fully, our lips pressed to one another, but neither one moved. Probably because whoever took the first step knew better than to.

I wanted to kiss my coach… And I was positively certain he wanted to kiss me.

It was that simple. Only it really wasn't. A gymnast and a coach? That was anything but simple.

What it was, was morally wrong.

But who was asking?

"What are you doing, *malysh?*" His breath tickled my neck. *Malysh.* He called me *malysh* again and I almost melted.

"Maybe I'm…" I paused to lick my lips. "I think… I don't know."

I had no idea what the hell I was doing. The only thing I knew was I was in way over my head and there was no going back. Nothing was going to stop me from moving forward. I wanted his mouth on mine. I wanted to taste his lips and feel his tongue tangled with mine. I was just too nervous to take the plunge.

"You should be practicing control," he whispered, angling only a breath away from my lips. His Russian accent was stronger than usual, and I liked it a lot. His erection grew harder and I loved it, loved that I caused it. The tension was stifling and my chest burned from the rapid beats of my heart. I wished he'd just kiss me already.

"But you are not practicing at all."

"I asked for your guidance. Show me control and I'll practice it."

"You should step away."

"I should? Or I need to."

"Both."

"And if I don't? You told me to use you, remember? So here I am, asking."

He paused, his lips curling in satisfaction.

"After a workout, my body is weak, and my control sucks, Ria. I have no control now," and then he slammed his mouth to mine.

chapter 28

A-FUCKING-MEN!

I whimpered into him. His lips were firm and bruising, much like his personality. My hands slid up his chest and I squeezed his shoulders, my nails scoring his skin. A flood of heat pulsed through my body, my hips rolled into his, feeling the hardness between them. Finally, we were touching the way we both secretly envisioned it.

At least how I have.

The tight grip on my arm moved to my waist, pulling me flush against him. His fingers threaded my hair, holding my loose ponytail in his hand. We didn't stop moving our mouths back and forth. His plump lips were soft, pliable, coercing me to bend to his will. They were exactly what I imagined they'd feel like.

I wanted more. My body craved more, to see how far we could take this.

With a flick of my chin, I reached up and grabbed the back of his head and pressed him further into me. His hair was damp with sweat from working on the rings. He groaned, biting my bottom lip and pressed his hardness into my stomach. It was sexy as hell to hear him moan and I was desperate for the sweet sound again.

Sweet Jesus. Yes… Screw the embarrassment over the sounds I was holding in. I moaned in the back of my throat, letting Kova know how much I liked this. I was hot, achy, and reached blindly for something I wasn't sure of.

With a tilt of my head, I opened my mouth and gently pulled his bottom lip with my teeth. He clutched me to him hard, his fingers dug into me and he exhaled into my mouth. Hesitantly, tracing the seam of his lips, I slipped my tongue inside. A soft whimper escaped me. The taste of him was as sweet as candy, and cool with the hint of vodka I'd smelled earlier.

Just as I was getting comfortable with him, Kova stiffened. Shockingly, he pushed me away and covered his mouth, uttering a string of Russian curse words hidden behind the back of his hand.

The hurt in my eyes could not be contained from the sudden ache he just caused in my heart. Glancing down, I eyed the mat.

"Shit," he muttered, followed by something in Russian again. "Adrianna, I am sorry."

I was confused. "It's okay."

"No, it is not okay. I should not have let this happen, let anything happen for that matter. Like the other day after you straddled the beam. It was wrong of me." His stomach hardened to granite with each hard breath he drew in. "Do you know how wrong this is?"

My head snapped to his. "Wrong? How is it wrong? I don't understand. It was just a kiss."

Appalled, he looked at me sharply and I flinched. "Do not look at me like that."

"Like what?"

"Like you are hurting, upset. It…" he stammered, "affects me more than I care to admit."

Rolling my lip between my teeth and releasing it, I said, "I am upset. It isn't like you're hurting me, or forcing me to do anything I don't want. I don't see how this could be so wrong when it feels so right." I sighed dejectedly. "I didn't want to stop."

"You are not making this any easier." Then he strode toward me and crushed his lips to mine.

Kova wrapped an arm around my back and hauled me to him, his fingers trembled beneath his touch. It was obvious he struggled with what he shouldn't be doing. But there was no denying the way he held me, the way his passion and emotion oozed into me. He wanted me. The hard length pressing against my stomach was evidence.

Our tongues collided, heat flared between us. They wrapped around each other, grabbing and fighting, twisting with desire. My God, the man was a skilled kisser and knew exactly how to tangle his tongue with mine and tug, stroking it simultaneously. My body tingled in his hold. This kiss was unlike any other I'd experience in the past. He was untamed and wild and it made me want to feel every inch of him.

"Adrianna…" He growled against my mouth before he kissed me again.

"Shhh, I'm practicing control."

"This is control?" He chuckled between kisses and I realized how much I loved his laugh.

I replied by searching for his tongue again and sucked on it. Kova's fingers dug into my back before skimming down to my ass. Cupping me, he hiked me up and my legs automatically locked behind his back. "You're so light," he said when I nearly slammed into him. I gripped his shoulders for support. His body shook as he held me, fighting to hold back, and I loved it. I loved how strong he was, how he could do anything to me, and I'd let him.

Slowly, Kova turned around with me in his arms. He walked a couple of feet and pressed me up against a tall spotting block that shielded us from the front window of the gym. Darkness surrounded us and gave way to the illicit act. He leaned against me and the softness of the block pressed into my back. His erection strained between us, long and hard, the back of it rubbing against my clit. I sighed, and his eyes lowered at the wispy sound that escaped me.

"Adrianna…" he said, his voice thick and husky. He placed his hands on my hips and gripped me with power. There was a real struggle to resist around his eyes that made me almost break contact with him. I wanted so badly to ask him what he was thinking as he searched my face, his breathing deepening by the second. But the fear of being rejected was high, so I didn't.

Instead, I pulled him closer. "It's okay, no one can see us."

My body was simmering with rapture, and he began to move my hips ridiculously slow, up and down. I skipped the panties, so the only barriers between us were my paper thin yoga capris and Kova's usual basketball shorts. The thought of too much clothing passed through my mind, but the friction was just perfect as he stroked his dick against me. I rotated my hips up to feel the pressure against my sex. As he glided against me even more, a breathless whimper escaped.

"Kova…" I whispered when his lips touched my neck, the dusty shadow of his beard scraped along my skin. His hips moved against mine.

"You are missing the point. I am your coach, and a man. You should be repulsed by me." The ache in his voice hurt my chest. "Girls your age do not look at men like me. You are supposed to like guys from boy bands or something."

A smile caressed my lips. I shrugged. "Quite the opposite actually."

Placing my hands on the back of his neck, my fingers threaded his hair and a rumble sounded in the back of his throat. I was getting hotter by the minute. Kova didn't break his stance and kept on rolling his hips into me. My orgasm was climbing higher and I wondered if he was close to having one too.

"God, that feels amazing," I cried out. Even in the dim lighting I could see every rigid plank of muscle from this angle. My fingers timidly trailed over his chest, skating down his arms. My back bowed and Kova hissed.

"Adrianna." His tone disagreed with himself and his body contradicted his words.

I could tell his conscience was weighing heavily on him as his nails dug into my skin and his breathing became ragged. As selfish as it was, I didn't care or really give it much thought to how he felt. I didn't even try to bring this to an end. Instead, I opened up the gates and gave him free access to do as he pleased.

Kova tilted his head down and slammed his mouth to mine. He kissed me hard and inhaled like he was trying to breathe me in. My arms wrapped around his back, my hands kneading him roughly. He continued like he was a starved man in need of vitality. My heart bloomed inside my chest and I loved it. I loved that he wanted me.

I broke the kiss. "I want to touch you."

He swallowed so hard his jaw flexed. "I guess we are both learning control tonight," he quipped, shaking his head. His tongue slipped out to lick his lips. I wanted to look and feel every inch of him, to watch him respond to my fingers, to see the rise and fall of his muscles.

"I cannot stop kissing you," he admitted. Kova leaned down and took my mouth with a growl, nipping and biting. This time though, much slower. Like he was savoring me.

I never dreamed a kiss could be so sensual.

Kova's tongue was dangerous. No, he was dangerous. I was shocked by how slow he could kiss. He was precise and seductive. And it was erotic—torture. He knew how to bring a girl to her knees with just the touch of his lips.

With a kiss like this, he could have anything he wanted.

He groaned into my mouth, much louder this time, a vibration rumbling against my chest and I scratched his back. It made me feel more like a woman knowing I could draw this sound from him. His length hit the spot between my thighs and I melted into him, rubbing myself on him. *Heaven help me now.* A million sparks went off inside of me, goose bumps coated my skin as an orgasm shimmered through my body.

Unlocking my legs, they slid down his hips so I could stand on tiptoe. He bit my lip and tugged it into his mouth when I stepped to close my legs, trapping his penis securely between my thighs. The waistband of his shorts angled down and my eyes fought to get a better look. There was no denying that Kova was hard and *really* big. His hands trailed up to my nape, my stomach clenched at how rough he fisted my hair and tilted my head back. I moaned loud enough for him to hear, letting him know how incredible the sensation was. The tight hold he had on me coupled with his thickness felt unbelievable. It was doing things to my head. My hips rolled into his, needing more. We were at the right height when he started rubbing my swollen flesh with his. I gasped, clutching him to me, pleading for him not to stop.

"Oh, fuck. You like that. Tell me you do not like it." He begged against my mouth.

"Yes, just like that." And I did. I loved it.

Another orgasm was brewing, soaring from the growing friction. My hands were everywhere on him, drowning in the sensations surrounding us. A fiery concoction of heat and craving swept through me. He kept hitting that one tender spot, and if I arched my pelvis into his, I'd get a better angle.

Sweet Jesus, I was ready to combust.

Inhaling his sultry blend of cinnamon and citrus scent, Kova's hand cupped the back of my head and guided me to his chest. I took note in how his hands stayed above my shoulders the whole time, like he was afraid to touch me anywhere else. I dropped little kisses to his heated flesh, tempted to run my tongue over his nipple.

Glancing down his stomach, the waistband of his shorts pulled forward even more and I was able to get a peek at his black curls.

I couldn't resist. I delicately traced his tattoo with my middle finger, circling the rings. He inhaled and watched my fingers. I pressed my hands to his abs, feeling every rigid abdominal muscle until I reached his hips. Kova held still as he allowed me to explore his body. My nails grazed the indentation toward his groin, dipping lower until a softness touched my knuckles. His stomach flexed in response.

Kova swiftly gripped my wrist and pulled my hand away.

"No, Ria."

chapter 29

I PURSED MY LIPS TOGETHER, UNHAPPY WITH HIS DECISION.

"Adrianna, we need to stop." I ignored him since I didn't agree, but he pressed on. "It is hard for me to control myself when your hands are on my body like this…" His eyes darkened and he licked his lips.

"Don't stop just yet. I want… I want to…" I trailed off.

"To what?"

My teeth dug into my bottom lip and I looked at him coyly. "To have an orgasm like this."

A low growl escaped him. "What I would give to feel the real thing, to feel you on my cock."

SWEET JESUS! MOTHER OF ALL GODS!

He just said that.

To me.

And I didn't know how to respond.

My heart pounded against my ribs, and despite how scorching hot I was, I shivered from the searing heat that zipped down my spine when he looked deep into my eyes.

Kova whispered in Russian and clenched his eyes shut. I loved when he did that. It was so sexy. "Imagine the pressure building between your hips, the tightness," he groaned. "Your small, wet little pussy wrapped around my cock. So tight… "

"Kova," I breathed, almost gasping for air. I was about to combust. Who knew dirty talking could be so hot. Never, had I ever, had anyone talk to me like that before.

"I… want… yes…" I couldn't find the words, so I let my actions do the talking. I dug my nails into him again, scoring his skin as I struggled with temptation. Poor guy was going to have nail marks all over him.

I was so close, and I think he knew. Kova began stroking me with himself, bringing me higher and higher. His hands clenched around my hips, pulling me forward and then back. I had a sudden image in my head of throwing him to the floor and jumping on him. I gripped the back of his biceps and shook with need. My head dropped to his chest and I released a heated breath against him.

"Look at me," he demanded. "Tell me how you feel, I need to know you want this."

I looked up and met his gaze. "Good. Too good," I panted.

"You want this? You like how you feel?"

I nodded rapidly.

"Do you want me?" he asked, pressing against my center so hard I whimpered.

I nodded again, reaching for his mouth with mine.

"Good. I like that you want me," he said with a wicked grin that matched his eyes.

Once again, my hands went everywhere when our mouths locked together. They moved to his backside where my fingertips dipped into the waistband of his shorts, feeling his warmed flesh. I wanted to push in more, but I was nervous. Another groan left his mouth, my thumb skimming his pelvis near his groin again.

"Do it," he ordered.

Do what, I wasn't sure. And I think he could read my mind when he grabbed one of my wrists and moved it to the front of his pants.

"Do it," he ordered again, his voice husky. "Touch me."

There was no way I could resist his command. I was high on Kova. I couldn't think straight, only that I would do anything he told me to do at that point. Swallowing hard, I teasingly traced my nails along his shorts.

"Inside. Put your hand inside my pants, *malysh*, and touch my cock. Feel what you do to me." He finished the last sentence with pride in his voice.

I slipped my hand inside and felt fine, little hairs thread through my fingers as I shyly reached for him.

"That is it, keep going," he said in a guttural voice. "A little farther. Do you want to come?"

I nodded eagerly, because, hello, there was no other possible response.

"Then put your little fingers around my cock. Stroke it hard. You know you want to."

Truthfully, I was kind of afraid to keep going. Not afraid of Kova, but because for the simple fact I had no idea what to do when I reached him. I mean, my friends talked about it, I knew, but I'd never done any of it myself.

"Go ahead," he encouraged.

Desire to please Kova took over. I didn't want to show my inexperience, so I did as he commanded and wrapped my hand around his erection. His skin was soft as silk yet his dick was as hard as granite, not at all what I expected. I kind of liked the velvety soft smoothness. My fingers curved around his meaty tip and a sticky moisture slipped through my fingers.

"Like that... just like that. Keep going," his voice cracked, hips moving. His hands reached above my head and gripped the edge of the spotting mat. "I am about to come in my pants," he openly admitted. Interestingly enough, so was I. "Right there," he whispered. Reaching down, he clutched my ass and hitched my knee around his hip.

I imagined what I thought would feel good for him; I stroked him from tip to base, twisting my wrist. Inaudible sounds laced with pleasure were coming from him. He was... thick. Heavy. Large. Kova devoured my mouth, kissing me so hard I was sure I tasted blood. His body was a rolling wave crashing into me and I couldn't help but wonder if it was how he had sex. Because if it was, well, fucking sign me up. He could have my virginity any day.

"Use your other hand," his hot breath tickled my neck. "Cup my balls and play with them."

Wanting to please him, I reached inside and the elastic of his shorts stretched open. His balls were heavy and firm, similar to his shaft. I couldn't stop staring at his body from this angle, the defined lines of his muscles, and the movement of my hand. The brute strength he yielded. The sensuality of it caught me off guard, a flush of ecstasy hitting me hard. My hands caused his shorts to push down and I became needy. I wanted to sneak a quick look at his dick, but the overwhelming desire to have an orgasm hit me hard. I moved to angle myself so I could rub up on his length, but his hand landed on my pussy, hitting the tiny bundle of nerves.

"Oh, my God," I cried out when he began rubbing me vigorously, my hand pausing for a second. "Yes..." I purred, my head rolling back.

He growled. "Christ. You are soaking wet. Fuck," he rubbed me in rough circles. My leg supporting me became weak as my orgasm climbed. I strained on my toes, thrusting my hips back and forth all while jacking him off.

"That is a good girl," he said when I used the moisture that seeped from his tip to coat his penis. He twitched in my fingers. I'd given myself plenty of orgasms in the past, so I figured he would like this. "Come on my hand."

I didn't think anyone could come on demand, but I was sure as hell going to try. He rubbed faster, harder, hitting my clit. My breathing labored and I felt a flame ignite within.

Just as I was about to reach that pinnacle of ecstasy and combust, a sound echoed in the distance and I froze. It was delicate and far away, but I'd heard it.

"Kova?" a honeyed voice called out.

Oh, my God. We both paused instantaneously. My heart dropped into my stomach, my throat closing up. Kova had gone ghostly white himself.

"Katja," he whispered, wide eyes looking down at me. Heels click-clacked against tile while Kova looked around, his eyes landing on the foam pit next to us.

"Jump in there and hide. Wait a bit and then sneak out." I nodded frantically. Kova looked disoriented. He kissed my forehead then pushed his dick down and quickly regained control. He thrust me toward the pit where I jumped in and hid. I shimmied myself lower to conceal every part of my body. I hated the pit. It was great for practicing new release skills or landings on a high bar, but it smelled terrible, probably due to all the sweaty bodies that fell in here daily. Plus, it wasn't so easy to pull yourself out of ten feet of blue foam squares.

Nestling down, I panicked when I heard Kova's voice. "Katja?"

"What are you doing here so late?"

"It is my job to be here, Kat," he snapped angrily, picking up his shirt from the ground. He looked to the left and our eyes connected. I shimmied down more. "Have you not figured that out yet? After all these years that I need to be here?"

I pulled back at the sound of his insensitive voice.

"You never spend time with me anymore," she whined. "I miss you."

Kova sighed and began walking away from me. "What do you want from me? I am doing the best I can."

"I want you to spend time with me, but you are always here. You know I have no family. I am lonely." She paused and said, "I thought we were going to talk about our future tonight? You said we were. I cooked dinner and waited for you, but you never showed. You did not even call."

His voice grew more distant and he scoffed. "I wish you would understand there are going to be days when I need to work late, days when I need to work out to relieve the stress and pressure of everyday life. I work so you do not have to, therefore no stress for you," his voice boomed furiously. "I have not heard you complain about your days lounging around by the pool or going shopping whenever you feel like it."

My heart hammered in my chest. I thought back to the argument they had at his house. I would've never guessed there was still any strain between them, and now I was more curious than ever to find out why.

"Why am I even here? I came to this country for you, but all you want to do is spend every second in the gym. This is not what we agreed to!" she yelled back. "My time is running out."

Kova began sounding off in Russian, his voice heated and muffled as they moved farther away. I couldn't make out the low rumbling between them before a door slammed shut and I flinched. Probably from Kova. It echoed throughout the gym and I was left alone.

Once again he left my mind confused, and now my body ached for the orgasm he failed to give me. I waited a good five minutes before I climbed out, found my hoodie, and left.

chapter 30

NEARLY AN HOUR AFTER MY FIRST KISS WITH KOVA, I WAS HOME.
And I was still aching, swollen, and aroused.

Between the material of my pants and throbbing wet lips, I was heightening by the second. The urge to finish myself off was strong. I'd been so close to release until Katja showed up, and judging by how heavy Kova was breathing, I'd say he'd been close too.

Once inside my condo, I couldn't get to my bedroom fast enough, stripping off what little I wore along the way. I climbed into the center of my bed and brought my knees up and spread my legs wide. My hand immediately went to my sex. I sighed as I slowly circled my clit. I couldn't remember a time when I'd been so desperate to come. As visions of Kova entered my mind, I knew it wouldn't be long.

My hand glided against my bare pussy, the same hand I touched him with. It had been a first for me. I thought of his soft skin beneath my touch. His hard cock. His dirty words. *"What I would give to feel the real thing, to feel you on my cock."* Little moans vibrated in my throat as the friction from my fingers took me higher. God, I needed to come. I shivered as I remembered the feel of his mouth devouring mine. Our tongues tangling and teeth nipping at lips. Beads of sweat broke out across my skin as my orgasm climbed, reaching that point of no return.

Rolling over, I pressed my stomach to the bed and began riding my hand. I thought about how he told me to fuck his hand as I was fucking mine right now. My hips lifted in the air and I rubbed faster, remembering the way his penis stroked me through my clothes. The comforter felt cool against my hardened nipples. The weight and pressure, divine on my clit, and I moaned into my sheets. Slipping a small finger inside my pussy, I went in just enough and rocked back and forth, creating a firestorm of pleasure that was just seconds from erupting from me. *"Your small, wet little pussy wrapped around my cock. So tight…"* Sweet Jesus, I wanted to come all night, as many times as I could, to the beat of Kova's hand and erotic words. I'd do anything for it to happen with him.

Shit. This was wrong on so many levels. I shouldn't be thinking of him in this manner. But I couldn't stop. An orgasm ripped through me so violently I shook from the gratification zipping down my body. My eyes squeezed shut and I felt Kova's touch in place of mine and pretended I was riding his hand instead, coming harder than ever. A loud rush of euphoria escaped me and I cried out, sighing breathlessly while the orgasm carried on.

Turning over, I swept my hair away from my face and caught my breath. My breathing evened out. I was completely sated and didn't want to move. I couldn't believe how something that felt so deliciously good could be so morally wrong.

Clearly, we both weren't thinking straight to let something like this happen. It was beyond dumb and careless, not to mention we could've gotten caught. My heart nearly stopped when I'd heard Katja's voice. I couldn't even begin to imagine what the repercussions would be.

I debated calling Avery. I wanted to tell her everything that happened but was hesitant, given the nature of the situation. It probably wasn't the wisest idea, even if she was my best friend and we told each other everything. This was a totally different scenario. Totally different. I needed to talk to someone though, and she was dating an older guy at the moment, which her parents had no idea about, so she really was perfect. I needed to get my thoughts together first and the lies I would need to tell her. Because let's be real, there was no way in hell I could admit it was my coach.

After I took a quick shower and got dressed, I grabbed my cell and dialed Avery's number, but after one ring it went straight to her voicemail.

Holy hell, she just hit the fuck you button on me.

I called her again. It was nearly eleven at night, so I knew she was home. Bringing the phone to my ear, it rang twice then went to voicemail. She did it again, and then I decided to text her.

Pick up your phone, b. I need to talk to you. I know you did not just hit the fuck you button on me.

The fuck you button was just the decline button on the phone. When I caught my boyfriend cheating on me last year with a mutual friend of ours, I dumped him immediately. He was devastated and regretted it, or so he said, and wouldn't stop calling me. One day, Avery grabbed my phone and yelled, "FUCK YOU!" and clicked decline. We laughed so hard and it stayed with us ever since.

BFF: I'm w/bf! Shhh… give me 5

Her older boyfriend, the one I knew nothing about. Finally, forty minutes of stewing later, my phone flashed with a picture of Avery and me.

"I hate you." I skipped the pleasantries.

"Fuck you, no you don't. You love me."

I grimaced. Avery was right. I could never really hate her.

"Now what's going on that you had to blow my phone up while I was blowing my man?"

"Ugh, Ave! I did not need to hear that!" She began laughing. "Wait, you stopped to text me in the middle of it?"

"You didn't get the hint when I sent you to voicemail—twice!"

"Ah, yeah. You're not allowed to hit the fuck you button on me, just like I never would with you. Next time you don't answer for me, I'll know why."

She chuckled. "All right, what's going on that you're making me call you at midnight?"

I had to be careful with my words. "Let me ask you something, this mystery guy of yours you refuse to tell me about, which I secretly hate you for by the way, is nineteen. Isn't that, like, illegal since he's over eighteen?"

Avery sighed into the phone as if she couldn't believe I asked her that. "You have so much to learn, bestie…"

Now it was my turn to laugh. "Seriously?"

"Of course I looked it up. Google is my second best friend and my father would murder me if he found out. I did my homework and it's not actually illegal. The law is different in each state. Regardless, my mom is the one who introduced us, so she only has herself to blame. Plus, we're just having some fun."

"She didn't introduce you for the sole purpose of having sex!" I laughed.

"Well…" She trailed off. "She didn't deliberately introduce us. We met at an event my family put on. Our family met his… you know how it goes."

"Yeah, I do. So he lives on the island?" The island was fairly small. I'd figure out who it was eventually.

"His family does. He goes to college but was in town to see me. Enough about my amazingly wonderful love life. So why do you wanna know about the ages and what's legal?"

I laughed at her sarcastic response. Avery was hardly ever serious. "Sooooooo, I have something to tell you. And before I do, you have to swear on our friendship that you won't tell a soul. No one, Avery. Not even if your life depended on it."

"Oh, this has to be juicy! Let me grab my cup so you can fill it right up."

I rolled my eyes and stifled a laugh. "I'm serious, Ave. You can't tell anyone."

Avery scoffed. "I can't believe you would ask me this. You know I'd never betray you," she said dejectedly. "You can trust me."

"I know, but this is a big deal. You know we say it to be sure."

"True. Now, spill."

I swallowed hard. "How would I know if I had an orgasm? I think I did… but I don't know."

"Whoa. Hold. The. Phone. I was not expecting that! With whom?"

I had a feeling she'd perk up. "Just answer my question."

"You answer my question," she retorted in a high pitch.

"Ave, I can't say," I said regrettably. "I can't."

"Really? You're not going to tell your best friend?" Avery was hurt, and I immediately felt bad. We told each other everything, we never held back. The fact that I was for the first time didn't sit well with me. But this was different.

So I lied. Again. "I didn't want to say, but have I told you about my library friend?"

She clucked her tongue. "It seems you're holding out on me."

"I'm not holding out on you. It's just, he's older and I don't want to get into any trouble."

"How old?"

I bit my lip nervously. "I don't know, I haven't asked."

"Can you at least gauge it? Ten, fifteen, twenty?"

I grimaced. "Years? Twenty years older? Ave, that's gross."

"That's why I said give me an idea."

"Okay… so he's about twenty-ish years old?"

"Keep going."

"So library guy… We kind of hooked up."

"Define kind of."

"I just need to know if it's legal."

"Define kind of," she repeated stubbornly.

I gave Avery all the details, but instead of Kova, I used the name Ethan, and instead of the gym, I said the library. I told her how he'd been there when I was studying, how our eyes locked and we couldn't stop looking at each other. Real mushy shit.

"But how did it happen?" she asked, perplexed.

"I needed help reaching for a book. There was no one at the desk and when I turned around, he was behind me. He saw the annoyed look on my face and asked me what was wrong. I told him I was studying and couldn't do my work without this book. He said he'd help me."

"Can you just speed up and get to the orgasm? This part is boring me to death."

I laughed. "No, I can't. You have to listen. When we got to the aisle, he pressed up against me and reached for the book. I looked over my shoulder and his face was right there."

She groaned, unimpressed. "Keep going…"

My eyes scattered around my room as I thought of how I could continue this lie. "He leaned down and kissed me. One thing led to another, and his hands were all over me and it happened quickly. It was completely unexpected. He touched me, I touched him… he said some really hot, dirty things to me… someone almost caught us…"

"He did not! Who? Where? You have to tell me everything!" Now Avery was too eager for her own good.

"That's all really irrelevant. I told you what you needed to know."

"Adrianna Francesca Rossi! I'm your best friend, practically your sister! You have to tell me! I demand that you do. How often do you see him?"

"You are such a pain in my ass." Quickly, I conjured a lie and kept my voice steady. "It's just on and off when we see each other, I guess a little while after I started tutoring."

"So this has been going on for a couple months and I hardly know a thing," she stated.

"I've been busy trying to be an elite gymnast, you know."

"A quick text would've been sufficient."

"I could say the same about this mystery beau of yours. You barely tell me anything."

She became quiet. "I'm just not ready yet… please don't be mad at me. I want to know more about what happened between you guys."

My voice softened. "He calls me Ria. No one has ever called me anything other than Adrianna or Ana. You know how much I hate Ana, so I kind of love this."

"Awe, that's nauseatingly sweet. Let me grab my detective cap while my computer is starting up. I need his real age, *Ria*." She mocked. "And don't guess. I know you know." I laughed and decided I needed to write all my lies down so I could keep track.

"He's in his late twenties. He took a long time off before going to law school."

"How old, Ria," she insisted. "You're hiding something, I know it."

"Ave, haven't you ever heard someone say, the less you know, the better?"

"Psh. That doesn't apply to your bestie. Like, ever."

I heaved a loud sigh at her response. She had a point. "Thirty-two."

"Thirty-two."

"Thirty-two."

"That is *not* late twenties. That's not ten, fifteen, or twenty. That's old! You sneaky thing, you. I'll be right back, I need to alert *Fox News* over this Breaking News before I can comprehend anything further."

"Avery, please do not tell a soul—I'm begging you." My heart was in my throat at my own admission, regret soaring through me. I was beginning to sweat. Maybe this was a mistake.

"I'm just playing with you. I swear on my trust fund I won't ever say a word."

Avery loved money, so I believed her. "Promise?"

"You can't see it, but I'm crossing my heart."

I smiled to myself. I knew she would never open her mouth, but I still had to ask it. It was a girl thing. She'd do the same to me.

"Okay, back to your original question," she said. "I'm not sure how to describe it other than you'll just know when it happens. Like, you'll know. An orgasm is an indescribable feeling, one that rocks through your whole being, and once it starts, it only builds higher and higher until an explosion goes off inside of you, and you see stars. It's the best feeling ever." She paused. "Wait. Was this your first time having one?"

"No, but it just never felt this good before. It was incredible."

"When were the other times it happened?"

"With my stupid ex… and myself."

I didn't want to tell her I just used my hand, and thankfully she didn't probe.

"Some orgasms just feel different. That's all. Your hand isn't going to feel as good as the hand of the guy you like. It's just how it is."

I felt bad for lying and like a total jackass for not realizing the difference. It was just so much more intense. If I was being honest with myself, I wanted it to happen again.

I could hear Avery typing away on her computer. "All right… It looks like the legal age of consent in Georgia is sixteen so long as it isn't with an old man and saggy balls—"

She was back to this. "Ave—he's not old and his balls are not saggy. Be serious for a second. I don't know why—" I paused. The line went silent. "Avery?"

"Wait. Wait. Wait. Back the fuck up. "Did you say his balls aren't saggy? How would you know that?"

I groaned inwardly and clenched my eyes shut. "Fuck."

chapter 31

"OH, MY GOD!" SHE YELLED, AND I HAD TO PULL THE PHONE AWAY FROM MY EAR. "You saw his balls! Did you touch them! What else happened, you lying sack of shit!"

I chuckled at her odd enthusiasm and said, "I didn't see or touch anything. I'm just saying they're not saggy because he's not old. They're firm, I assume."

"Lies, all lies!"

I couldn't stop laughing at her playful tone. "I'm not lying. Just get back to what you were saying."

"Yeah, okay. Whatever. If I find out you lied to me, there's going to be hell to pay." Avery cleared her throat. "So what you did is not illegal, and since he's in law school, I'm pretty sure he knew he was skating the line. Just don't have sex with him. Oh wait—"

"What is it?"

"Hang on. I'm still reading."

I sat still, biting my lip until she finally spoke.

"Oh, never mind. Good thing we're not in Florida. They got some fucked up laws, probably because people are on flakka there and do some crazy shit. I would just be really careful if I were you."

I frowned. "Why's that? If I didn't do anything wrong, what does it matter?"

I felt like I needed to write down what she was saying next to my list of lies.

"Call me crazy, but I just think there shouldn't be any penetration with the old man. I mean, if you consent, you're fine since you're of age. Consent is consent once you're deemed legal by the state. But that doesn't mean it won't bring a whole new shit show to the table if you bang him." She paused, then her voice rose. "Could be fun though."

"Did you just say penetration?" I couldn't help laugh. It sounded so comical coming from her.

"Yes, because that's what old people say when they're having sexual relations, *Ria*." Sarcasm laced her tone and it caused me to smile. Avery was hysterically funny tonight. She didn't judge, only teased me. "They don't say fuck."

"I didn't know you were an expert."

"Wait—you don't think your tutor is hot, do you? What about Alfred? Because that would be breaking the law since he's like eighty years old. Not to mention, really fucking gross, Ria. I would have to reconsider this friendship based on your horrid taste."

"Now those would be some saggy balls," I laughed into the phone. "No, I'm not attracted to any of them."

"Oh, good. And yes, penetration is sex and no sex is allowed," she stated.

I was pretty sure I was never going to have sex with my coach so I was good to go.

"Speaking of penetration, we should give the balance beam a name," Avery suggested flippantly.

Closing my eyes, I shook my head. "What do you mean a name, Ave?"

"Well, you know how my mom named her car, Bradley Cooper?"

I chuckled, thinking back to the day Avery's mom came waltzing through the front door, saying she fell madly in love with Bradley Cooper because he gave her a ride like no other. Her mom was a riot.

"And you know how she named her Kindle?"

"I do. Isn't it like Mikko or something?"

"Mikko? What the fuck kind of name is that? Not even close. His name is Cole, and Cole brings her more pleasure than any other man ever could. He's up all night with her and never talks back. She can cry ugly tears and he never makes fun of her."

I groaned. "Avery, your mom is crazy. I can't believe she tells you those things. Mine would never say something like that to me."

She laughed.

"So, I'm thinking we should name your beam, so every time you fall we can say..." She trailed off. "Johnny! Johnny Depp! We can say Johnny Depp fucked you again today."

I knew Avery was happy with herself from the other end by the high pitch of her voice. Her and her wicked sense of humor. "Because every time you fall it's like you're getting fucked."

This time we were both in full on belly laughs. She had a point.

"No way! You're insane!"

"Oh, come on," Avery said. "If you don't like the name Johnny, we can pick another. What are the names of the other guys on the team?"

"Well, Johnny's pretty hot, but there's a Hayden on the men's team I've become friends with. But Ave, I just can't call the beam, Johnny. I would die if anyone heard me say, Johnny fucked me good again today. No, just no," I snickered.

"Let's use Hayden. It would be more fun that way!"

"You're sick, you know that? You have an evil sense of humor."

"I'll take that as a compliment, thank you very much."

I paused, thinking about what she suggested. "The girls on my team would think I was talking about Hayden. I can't do it. They hate me as it is."

"Oh, my God. We have to use Hayden! Because fuck them."

I shook my head from the other side of the phone. Avery. She was my polar opposite, yet I loved her so much. She knew how to make me laugh when I needed it the most.

"Say it."

"Ave... I feel weird saying it."

"Don't be a little bitch."

I laughed again, shaking my head. "Fine! Johnny fucked me pretty hard today... I'm all red and sore. It even hurts to walk." I bit my lip, waiting for her response.

"OH MY GOD!" Avery shouted, laughing again. "Look at you! I wasn't thinking of adding to it!"

"Well, it's what happens when you straddle it." Looking between my thighs, I thought about the day I straddled the beam and what transpired after. I told Avery everything, minus the Kova touching me part.

"My thighs were all roughed up, too. God, Avery. I even bled from it."

"That bad?"

"Yeah. And it looked like a contusion was forming. I had to ice myself three times a day."

"A contusion? You mean a black and blue? Can't you just say bruise?"

I laughed and she heaved an exaggerated sigh. "Just think, by the time you're actually ready to have sex, the impact won't be as bad."

I paused. "Where do you come up with this stuff?" Shaking my head, I stifled another laugh. "There's no filter with you."

"Nope," she said proudly.

"Can I break a bone in there? Because that's what it felt like when I fell. I swear something shifted."

"Well, I'm no doctor, but I don't think there's a bone in your vagina."

I grinned. "You had a bone-r in yours tonight."

"Oh! She's got comebacks," Avery yelled sarcastically. "I sure did. But seriously, why don't you see an OB and find out. Or maybe head over to Planned Parenthood so you can get birth control while you're at it. Rather be safe than sorry."

"What do I need birth control for?"

"Do you plan to stay a virgin forever?"

"Well, no, but I only have time for one piece of wood in my life right now, and his name is Johnny."

Avery burst out laughing. I was pretty proud of myself for that one.

"That being said, it wouldn't be such a bad idea if I planned on having sex soon, not that I am. I'd have to withdraw money before I went. I can't imagine my dad would be happy seeing a visit to Planned Parenthood on his credit card statement."

"I doubt he even looks."

Avery had a point. "Still, I can't take the chance."

"How's practice going anyway?"

I huffed into the phone.

"That bad?" she responded to my sulk.

"Some days are harder than others, but I refuse to give up. I'm not where I should be so I took on extra training, but I feel like I'm progressing. I'm pushing my body to the brink of exhaustion. The team girls have like a *Mean Girls* type club, so the only friends I really have are Hayden and Holly. Some days I wonder if I would be here if it wasn't for my dad's money. And to top it off, my mom wants me to send her pictures of the scale while I'm on it."

"I really hate your mom."

I puckered my lips together. Some days I hated her too.

"Still, I won't quit. I love gymnastics too much to do that. It's my life, and with this sport, I only have so much time left. I really have to get my ass in gear. Meet season is coming up and I need to be in top shape."

"You know what else is coming up?"

I paused, scrunching my brows together. "What?"

"Your birthday!"

"Ave. It's not like I can plan anything, I have to train."

Her excitement vanished. "Can't you take one night off?"

"To do what? Sit by myself?" I laughed bitterly, thinking about how my mom forgot my birthday a few times in the past. What a joke. "Unless I'm on my death bed, there's no taking an extra day off. It's really not a big deal to skip my birthday, I'll have more."

"God. You're such a bore. I can always come up for your birthday, so you're not alone," Avery said, taking me away from my thoughts. "And if my parents don't want me to drive for some reason, maybe I can convince our brothers to ride with me." I paused, at a loss for words, as she continued. "You know, they're older, and our parents would trust them for some bizarre reason. Plus, if they know there are hot girls, I'm sure they'd be quick to come."

Her parents were pretty lenient. I couldn't imagine them saying no to her driving two hours away.

"I guess. While we hang out, they can go off, but you'll be bored during the day since I can't take off from practice."

"That's no biggie. I'll come for a weekend and watch."

That could be worked out.

I yawned and looked at the clock. "I'm gonna go. I'm so tired and luckily I don't have gym tomorrow. I plan to sleep in and catch up on my homework."

"Let me know if you need me to do any more research for you. If you need to talk about it, I'm here for you, Ria."

I smiled into the phone. "Thanks, girl. You're the best. Are you going to call me Ria from now on?"

"Every minute I can," she retorted. "And remember, no penetration, Ria." Then she hung up.

After grabbing a bottle of water, I jumped into bed, thanking my lucky stars I didn't have to face Kova tomorrow. I had the following day off to panic about what had happened. It was going to be awkward once I went back to practice, but I knew how to train my emotions and conceal my thoughts. Only thing I needed to do was not make it obvious and ignore Coach as much as possible. That wouldn't be a hard feat. He tended to be an asshole at the gym anyway. An angry Russian dick.

Just before I was about to doze off, my phone beeped.

Coach: Did you make it home okay?

My heart dropped. I responded with a quick yes, clutching my phone to see if he would say anything else. But after ten minutes of silence, I ended up passing out.

chapter 32

IGNORING COACH WAS AN ISSUE I EXPECTED TO HURDLE AFTER WHAT HAD HAPPENED between us, but fortunately I didn't have to work through it the next day.

Or the next.

He'd been absent from the gym for three days now and I wasn't sure whether I was happy about it or not. Madeline took over and I worked closely with her. While she was my vault coach, Kova was my main coach and he oversaw my schedule—which skills I'd learn and when. It was a completely different type of training with her. I wasn't stressed to the max, I didn't make mistakes, and I felt a bit more confident. I was actually able to eat something, too. I didn't feel the need to impress her the way I did with Kova. She didn't ridicule every little breath I took, she encouraged me and gave me hope. Hope was what gymnasts thrived on, and mine had gone down the drain. There were moments of the day when I wished she was my coach. She was a great instructor, but Kova's attention to detail was exceptional, and that mattered in the world of gymnastics.

Kova's absence only built the impending awkwardness of having to see him when he did return, which was apparently today. No coach or gymnast ever missed gym time unless it was absolutely life altering. No one knew why he was out, only that he had business he needed to attend to.

But I had a feeling I knew what it was.

Alfred dropped me off early to practice. None of my teammates had shown up yet, so I shoved my stuff into my locker and did my usual morning run. My calf started acting up again, a twinge of heat encompassed it, but I shook it off and finished. I noticed it flaring up a little more lately. Nothing a little Motrin couldn't fix.

After I came inside and wiped myself down, I got ready to head inside the gym to start stretching. I loved being the only one here, breathing in the air and mentally preparing myself for training. I smiled. A new day, a new goal, a new ambition. My love for the sport was embedded deep in my bones and something I couldn't quite explain.

Rounding the corner and walking down the quiet hallway, I wasn't paying attention as I separated the wristbands that had gotten stuck together by the Velcro, and I walked straight into someone.

A whoosh escaped my throat. "Oh, I'm so—" I froze.

Kova.

My jaw dropped, all logical thoughts escaped me. "Hey," I said delicately.

Kova stood tall in front of me, his broad shoulders back, and his face unreadable. I wasn't terribly short, but he was over six feet, so he towered over me.

"You were gone."

He said nothing.

"Are you okay?"

Again, nothing.

"We should probably talk?"

He just stared right through me.

"Ummm…" I proceeded but stopped when his hands locked on my upper arms. He shuffled me to the side, walked past me and ignored all questions.

Oh, good. So we skipped dick and went straight into asshole mode—awesome!

Anger bubbled in my veins. Arrogance was written all over his saunter as he made his way back to his office. I had to grind my jaw to keep from lashing out.

"So you're just going to overlook… everything?"

He said nothing, so I took a risk.

"What does Katja mean to you?"

Kova paused, his stance rigid. Interestingly, that must have struck a nerve. After witnessing two arguments between them, one he didn't even know I knew about, I wanted to know if she was more than just a girlfriend to him, if he saw a future with her. I rested my hand on my hip, waiting for him to turn around. I was so positive he would respond that a smirk crept along my face.

I was shocked when his head twitched to the side, and he continued walking away from me, slamming the door shut to his office.

A good part of my morning workout had been fairly demanding. I had my ballet classes, which kept me busy for nearly two hours, then I moved on to conditioning. The two things I despised doing were the most strenuous and challenging. Challenging in the sense that it was easy to cut corners and do it half-assed and not get caught. Which I didn't. I'd only hurt myself in the long run.

When I moved on to vault with Madeline, I made a conscious effort to avoid Kova. I purposely didn't look in his direction and I acted like he didn't exist, but it was a difficult feat. He was on my mind every few seconds and the fight to not look for him was a struggle. I got the feeling I was being watched, but didn't want to make it obvious I was aware of his gaze. I could feel his eyes on me, crawling over my body. But I didn't acknowledge it. The fear of seeing disgust sat heavy in my gut, and not something I wanted to face.

This morning I'd been working on my vault. I was trying to perfect the Amanar, a two and a half twisting Yurchenko. It was the hardest vault for women to master because of its level of difficulty, but also gave the most scoring points in difficulty too. If I didn't pull through and only completed two twists instead of two and a half, I'd be downgraded for difficulty and not execution, surprisingly. The key to execution was a huge block. I had to push with all my might off the vault table using my shoulders and keeping my arms straight. If I bent my arms, it absorbed my power and I'd really mess up. But no matter what I did, I just couldn't stick it. I'd step forward, land on my butt, land off to the side, bend my legs. I either under rotated or over rotated. I was an utter disaster. All of those landings would earn me deductions I couldn't afford. The last thing I wanted was to lower my vault to two twists, but I knew if I didn't start making progress soon, I would be forced to scale it back. I wanted the Amanar so bad I could taste it.

Vault was mine. I normally excelled at it, I just needed to stick my landing. But since I had come to World Cup, I'd been doing terribly. At least, it felt that way. I needed to be a little tighter, a little faster, a little higher, and I'd have it.

Easier said than done. Nerves and self-doubt got to me, I knew that was playing into my overall performance.

Madeline had mentioned we needed to start working on my alternate vault soon. Gymnasts always had two vaults, usually one that brought more points to the table. The new vault would be front flipping, I just wasn't sure which one yet. Doing a front vault showed diversity.

"Adrianna. Instead of starting at seventy-three feet, try seventy-five. Do a double and land it. You're getting there, but you may need more momentum."

I nodded.

Madeline pulled her arms up to her chest, her hands in fists, and jerked to the left—giving me an example of what she meant. "Pop off the table and pull up high, squaring your shoulders and then twist hard. Got it? You really need to block."

"Yes."

"Good. Go for it."

I walked back to the end of the runway, looking for seventy-five feet. Grabbing a piece of chalk, I drew a line where my toes needed to start and then chalked my hands up good. I raised an arm and then took off running. My arms stayed like sticks by my side until I gained speed, and they bent. I pumped my legs harder than ever about twelve feet away and did a round-off onto the spring board, then a back handspring onto the vault table to complete the Yurchenko, popping off with my shoulders with a loud huff and pulled my twist up and into a double. I had height, a tad more than usual, but ended up taking a huge step forward on the soft practice mat.

Looking over my shoulder with my arms still in the air, I raised a brow at Madeline. She chewed her lips, staring at me curiously.

"Try starting off a bit slower." I looked at her with a question in my eyes. I needed speed if anything. "Meaning, take a few larger, but slower steps at first, and then gun it around twenty-five feet away. And throw the Amanar instead. The double isn't helping."

I got to the end of the runway and chalked up again when Madeline yelled. "Practice a few slow starts first."

The slow starts had a funny look to them. The knees came up higher, slower, and the step was much wider. It looked like giant skips at first. I knew what she wanted me to do, I just had never done it, and honestly, I didn't think this was what I needed. But she was my coach so I listened.

I quickly practiced a few off to the side while Holly vaulted twice.

I took a handful of slower, wider steps and performed my vault, but I didn't stick my landing. When I stood straight, the back of my calf started to glow with heat again, but this time it traveled down to my ankle. Bending down, I rotated my ankle around and massaged the muscle to relieve the warmth.

Her brows angled toward each other. "Are you okay? What's wrong?"

I nodded. "It's nothing, I'm fine."

Her eyes narrowed. "Are you sure?" I nodded and she asked, "Okay, so how did that feel?"

"It makes sense to start off slower, I think, and I can feel the change in momentum. I have more power. Can I try it again?"

"Of course."

I got in line and waited for Holly to go. Once she finished a couple sets of vaults, it was my turn. I took off even slower by pulling my legs higher to the ceiling, but it wasn't easy. I could feel my stomach clench and the muscles I needed to build in order to run like this. My vault was better, and my height too, but it didn't feel perfect and I knew it.

"Okay—I know I'm throwing a lot at you right now, but what if we try to get your round-off closer to the ground, too."

"What do you mean?"

Madeline stood in front of the springboard. She raised her arms and demonstrated what she meant. "You see how my shoulders are up with my chest, but back? You're too open up here, there's too much space between you and the board. But if you lean toward the springboard, when you rebound out of your round-off, you'll get the power you need to get the perfect flight. Let's try it into the foam pit so you can see."

Madeline looked over at Holly. "Can you practice on your own for a bit? We'll be right back."

An innocent smiled splayed her lips. It amazed me she was friends with a bitch like Reagan. "No problem."

"Use a cushioned mat, okay? I don't want you getting hurt."

"Okay."

We walked over to the runway with the foam pit where Kova was with Reagan. It was the same foam pit I hid in days earlier. Our eyes locked for a split second and his jaw set tight before he looked the other way. My nerves climbed with each step that brought me closer to him. When he looked at me again, he visibly tensed. Reagan looked like she wanted to vomit at the sight of me.

"Mind if we share with you? I want Adrianna to try something new." Madeline asked.

Kova stepped aside and waved his hand in front of us. "By all means."

Madeline turned to me and went over what she wanted me to try while Kova watched intently. His presence was powerful, and standing this close, it was hard to ignore him like I had tried pitifully to do this morning. He made me extremely nervous and I started chewing on my bottom lip, a habit I needed to break.

"Remember, slow at first, and stay low near the end. Got it?"

I swallowed, my eyes sneaking a glance at Kova before I nodded at Madeline.

Standing at the end of the runway, I took a deep breath and exhaled. I focused solely on the vault and what she told me to try. One last breath and then I took off running. My heart raced, not from the coaches, but of my love for vault. Adrenaline pumped through me and my feet pounded into the floor as I neared the springboard. The pain in my calf was back and stronger than ever, but I pushed through it. My nerves were on edge, but with Kova and Reagan standing there, I knew my legs ended up looking sloppy in flight, and if it hadn't been for this pit, I would've eaten shit when I came down.

"What the hell was that?" Madeline asked with shock in her eyes. "Thank God you landed in that pit."

"Let me try again."

Kova reached down with an opened palm and without thinking twice, my hand slid into his strong, callused one. Heat shot up my arm and through my spine. Shit. This wasn't good. He gripped my palm and yanked me out. Before Madeline could say anything, Kova spoke up.

"May I?" he asked quietly, and she nodded.

"I see what Madeline is going for. Slower start and a deeper angle near the board, yeah?" he asked her but was staring directly at me.

I groaned inwardly. He should never use the word deeper in my presence. My mind traveled back to the night in the gym, and the things he said and did.

"Yes, more acute," Madeline responded. Acute sounded better than deeper. Kova and his stupid Russian accent.

Gripping my arm lightly, he guided me to the board. When he placed a flat hand to my stomach and one to my back, I tensed. His eyes narrowed at me knowingly, telling me to get my shit together.

He cleared his throat. "You need to use your core for what you are doing. Chest back." He patted my stomach, and continued. "We may need to focus on building more muscle here to help you carry though. Prepare for a cartwheel."

Using his hand on my lower back, he leaned me over so I was head first toward the board and my back leg was up.

"You want your hurdle long and low, but your chest and arms up tall. Push off your back leg hard." He tapped my leg, as if I didn't know which leg he meant. "It is quick and fast and it takes time to learn, but this is where you start, so when you rebound off the board, you will have the power you need to go back and off the table for a strong block. From there, you know what to do." He paused and then asked, "Does this make sense to you?"

"Yes."

"Good, now do it, but just do a layout." A layout was no problem. No twisting, just straight as a board, stretched out body, flipping back once.

I walked and stood behind the chalk line, mentally picturing myself doing it correctly. Looking at Kova, he gave me a small nod. Leaning forward, I lifted my knee and took a few of the longer running steps and then went full force and ran as fast as possible. There was that burning again in my calf that seemed to make an appearance when I ran. When it came time for my round-off, I got low, knees to chest like he said, and felt my pelvic muscles tighten. Kova was right. I could tell I was going to need more muscle there from the strain inside.

He was also right about the exploding power I'd have if I got lower. I eyed the foam pit for my landing and saw how much extra height I had.

I came up, wide eyed and looked at him. "I wasn't ready for that kind of power!" I yelled enthusiastically.

He nodded, tight lipped and turned to Reagan and Madeline. "Would it be okay if we swapped gymnasts for a bit? I have a few things I want to work with her on."

"Of course. Come, Reagan."

Reagan scowled. I picked my wedgie and asked, "Where're they going?"

"We switched."

My stomach churned, excitement falling from my face. "Oh, okay."

chapter 33

WE STARED AT EACH OTHER FOR A MOMENT, MY CHEEKS BEGINNING TO HEAT. Clearing his throat, Kova rubbed his jaw and said, "Instead of running slower in the beginning, I think you need to just take off at your normal speed. I do not think slowing down will help you. Let us get your round-off right and then we will work on squaring your shoulders and reaching for height."

I nodded. "I wasn't crazy about slowing in the beginning either, but I did it anyway."

"If you do not think it will work, you can always speak up."

I gave him a droll stare. "Really? You once told me not to question you." When he didn't respond to my dig, I said, "I wanted to try it at least, but I didn't like the feel."

"What is your starting point?"

"I'm at seventy-five feet."

Coach contemplated for a minute. "Try starting at seventy-nine feet. You need as much momentum as you can get. And just do the double again."

I nodded and walked to the seventy-nine feet mark. I did exactly what he said to do, and honestly, I couldn't tell if I did it right or not.

"Again," he said.

I did a handful more vaults before he finally said, "I see things I want to do to you—" Coach stopped himself when my eyebrows nearly reached my hairline. "What I meant was…" He trailed off anxiously. His voice cracked and he used his hands to talk. "I think I should be working with you more on this, not just Madeline. There are different techniques you would benefit from." He exhaled with an exhausted sigh, broken almost, and it made me feel bad. "Let us work on this vault and do some layout timers."

Coach took me to the other side of the gym where there were huge, thick mats stacked behind a vault. They towered high, just roughly under ten feet and they helped with gaining height. It's where layout timers came into play. It was a back flip, pin straight body and legs, and instead of landing on my feet, I'd land on my back, rotating with a hollow chest.

"Okay. I am going to spot you and give you a little pop. Just land on your back. Yes?"

"Yes."

I wasn't sure if I loved the idea Kova was ignoring our little indiscretion or not. I guess it was a good thing since I was here to train. But I couldn't help but wonder what was going through his head.

I did my vault with Kova's help and nearly panicked when my heart jumped from my chest and landed before I did. I had so much air my feet came up and I rotated into a back roll.

"That wasn't a little pop. You nearly threw me in the air. I could've hurt myself."

He gave me a blank stare. "See the height you got?" he retorted, his voice stern. He ignored my comment, because the truth was, I knew my coach wouldn't let anything happen to me and he knew it too.

"That is what you need in flight. Do it again and keep your legs tighter. This vault, more than others, must have straight, tight legs and body."

I was well aware how tight and straight my legs needed to be, not just in this vault, but in so many other skills in gym. Hearing it over and over was annoying. I wished he'd tell me something I didn't know.

I did the vault, feeling Kova's pop on my lower back. He wasn't as hard this time and I felt the difference, I barely landed on my back.

"Feel the difference?"

"Surprisingly, yes."

Kova paused, not expecting my response, then continued. "The key to the Amanar is height, drive, and power. That is where we start. We do this a thousand times if we have to, until I feel confident you can move on," Kova said enthusiastically.

A thousand times, like he did with me on bars. At least I wouldn't get rips on vault. But I could break an ankle if I landed wrong.

I vaulted again, ending with a layout timer. After at least an hour or so, I was worn out and in dire need of food. My calf throbbed fiercely, but there was no way I would speak up. Kova's help and push really made a difference, so I stored the pain away and focused on the conditioning.

Walking back over to the pit, he placed thick practice mats over the foam squares to practice my landing since I wasn't ready to land on the floor yet.

Standing at the end of the runway line, I looked for Coach.

"Do your double without my help. Let me see where you are at."

After I landed my vault, I looked at him. He wasn't pleased.

"Stronger hurdle. Power, we need power, Adrianna," he ordered, clapping his hands. Thing was, the bottom half of my leg was on fire.

I nodded and vaulted again with his help. Over the next hour, all I heard was:

"Adrianna, squeeze those legs and make them straight as a damn board. Do you want to tear your ACL?"

"Adrianna. Tighter body."

"Adrianna," he said slowly, with irritation. "Set higher. Do you really think you can pull a two and a half like that?"

"Adrianna, push harder!"

"Do you really want this?"

"Block, Adrianna!" He groaned. "Get that set higher."

"You got it… crank it tighter now!"

"Faster, higher, stronger. That is no good!"

"You are under rotating, that is why you are hopping back!"

Then he started in Russian. At that point, my body was sore and I'd reached the point of exhaustion. I had another hour or so before I had to break for class. And for the first time in my gymnastics career, I couldn't wait to be done with gym and for tutoring to start.

"You are a power tumbler, but we need more muscle, so for the next thirty minutes we will condition and then cool down. Okay? We need to do this after every workout."

Ugh. I groaned loudly, my head falling back. Every gymnast hated conditioning with a passion, but we also knew not to skimp on it. We'd only be holding ourselves back if we did.

Kova took me to a side of the gym meant only for stretching and weight training. We didn't lift weights like body builders, but we did use them for specific muscle building drills where we needed to target.

"Okay, get on your back and lie flat. Arms by your ears."

No problem.

Coach picked up one twenty pound dumbbell and walked over to me. Getting on his knees, he sat behind my head and instructed me to open my hands, placing the heavy weight in my palms. He was so close I could smell his citrusy, cinnamon scent, not that powdery chalk smell of the gym.

"You are going to keep your arms by your ears. Lift your legs and arms at the same time and come together, but only half way. This is going to build muscle here." Kova placed a flat hand to my pelvic region and my stupid body heated all over from it. I looked around to see if anyone could see us. Tingles broke out across my skin. His fingers were like a sparkler on the Fourth of July, and I wondered if Katja had the same reaction to him.

"Now, slowly lift," he said, his hand still on me.

I lifted, but too fast. "You are not in a race to finish, Adrianna. Take it slow."

Be still my heart. I loved how my name rolled off his tongue.

Kova continued to stare at my stomach like he was unable to make eye contact with me. "Lift slower," was all he said impassively.

"Tighten," he ordered when I began lifting slower, hollowing my body into a small boat look. He pressed his fingers into my stomach feeling for muscle. "This is what I want to feel. Right here… tighter." He nodded to himself in satisfaction. His hand burned my stomach.

I cleared my throat and our eyes locked. "Seriously? You couldn't think of any other word to use?"

The corner of his mouth lifted and his emerald eyes gleamed. I dropped to the floor. "English is not my first language. Forgive me."

I lifted again and this time he placed a hand under my calves and the other hand under my arms. I was shaking. Lifting a twenty pound dumbbell wasn't really all that heavy, but in the position I was in, and how I was doing it, wasn't so easy. Kova helped guide me slowly up and then down so many times my muscles were on fire.

"Remember to breathe."

After another set, my arms were trembling.

"Okay. Let us take a break," he reached for my arm and began massaging the muscle, shaking it out. His knuckles brushed against my ribs. His fingers kneaded the tissue deep and the sublime feeling took over.

With Kova still seated next to me, I was able to get a good look. I watched him, where his eyes were, the tick working in his jaw. I wanted so badly to ask about our kiss that night in the gym, and what it meant.

"Kova," I whispered just for him. I tried to get his attention, but he wouldn't look my way.

"Not now, Adrianna."

"When?" He continued to ignore me so I said, "I'm not going to tell anyone."

He shook his head incredulously. "There is more to it than that."

"Please, look at me." When he finally did, I said, "I swear."

He shook his head in disbelief again, and murmured, "Do you understand the rules I broke? The fact that I could go to jail?"

"You wouldn't go to jail, I looked it up. We only kissed," I whispered, and looked around. "We didn't do anything else. It was just a kiss."

He stared at me in horror. "You do not see the problem because you are too young." Then he stood, and by the look in his eyes, I instantly knew he regretted what happened.

"Grab my ankles and give me yours."

I looked at him, perplexed.

"Put your hands around my ankles," Kova said slowly, like I was hard of hearing. "And bring your legs up."

Well, well, well. From this view, there was a lot to see, meaning Kova's bulge. The outline from this angle made me picture what was inside his shorts and if he was wearing boxers or not. I could tell he wasn't fully erect, yet still pretty large. At least I assumed he wasn't erect and I knew he felt big, but I hadn't actually seen it. My grip tightened around his ankles as I thought about how he stroked my pussy with it, a river of sensations streamed through my center.

"I am going to push your legs down, but you are not to touch the floor," Coach said, breaking my forbidden thoughts. "I will push you side to side and straight out, but never let your legs hit the floor."

"Got it."

Kova threw my legs out and my back bent in desperation to keep my feet from touching the carpet. I gripped his ankles tighter, holding on in order to bring my legs back up.

"Snap them up," he ordered. "Faster. I am taking time out just for you here."

"I didn't ask you to help me," I gritted out.

"Adrianna, I am here to make sure each gymnast reaches their maximum potential, so if that means taking over for another coach, I do it. It is nothing personal."

Nothing personal.

Screw him. I didn't ask him for this. I could've stuck with Madeline but he wanted to step in.

When he pushed my legs to the side, my hips swiveled and I snapped them back, struggling a bit. It was harder than it sounded and my stomach flexed every time. And every time, I looked at his bulge and watched it bounce.

I was going to hell.

My stomach burned, like fire ants coating my flesh. My legs were beginning to bend as I pulled them up. I wanted so bad to ask for a break, but I knew better.

"I am tired of telling you to keep those legs together and locked straight." He threw my legs down so angrily and fast I struggled to bring them back up. But they didn't touch the ground and I was proud of myself for that. My nails dug into his flesh, I let out a gush of air when I pulled them up. He repeated the motion.

"It will only make me do this to you longer."

In that moment, I decided I was going to study witchcraft and put a spell on him for this kind of torture.

And have him use correct English words, and some fucking contractions.

Every time he pushed my legs down, I took a deep breath and held it, using it to throw my legs back to him. Sweat dripped down the sides of my temples, and I was pretty sure I was going to pop a blood vessel in my eye.

Who knew how much time had passed when I reached the point where I couldn't take anymore. My inner thighs trembled, they shook so hard that in conjunction with my burning stomach, I was queasy. He must have sensed it when he said, "One last time." And when he threw my legs again, I let them drop to the floor with a thud. One leg fell out to the side, the other coming up in an effort to bend, but I didn't have the strength to hold it up, so they both fell open. The position wasn't very ladylike, but I was too worn the hell out to care.

Panting heavily, I felt like I just ran a marathon. "I think I'm dying."

"Do not be so dramatic."

My grip loosened and my elbows flopped to the side. "I'm not. That was hard." But he ignored my comment and stood above me, his gaze between my opened legs.

I should've closed them, it would've been the logical thing to do, but I was rooted in place. Partly due to the fact that I just couldn't move, but I also liked the way his eyes licked across my body. His heady stare caused a throb between the crux of my thighs, and my pulse quickened.

God. What was wrong with me? I should've been repulsed. Hell, maybe I should've gotten up and walked away. Maybe I needed to speak to a therapist about my Kova addiction.

Actually, scratch that.

Opening up about having a crush on my much older coach could seriously backfire on me. Keeping my mouth shut was the only plan of action I had.

Mustering the strength, I brought my legs together slowly, adding pressure to my swollen center with my thighs. Coach cleared his throat and reached out his hand to help me up.

"I will see you later for floor."

"Coach?"

"Go."

"No, I feel like we should talk."

Stepping toward me, his eyes quickly scanned the gym. "There is nothing to talk about. It was a giant lapse in judgment. It should have never fucking happened," he sneered. "And now I have to live with the fact I took advantage of a minor, my gymnast no less. I am sick over it, I cannot sleep."

I reared back, feeling only a small dose of pity. "You didn't take advantage of me."

"It is even worse you think that way," he gritted out under his breath. "You should have been revolted with what I said and did."

"I'm not, I wasn't. I liked it, everything, and I didn't want it to stop. You felt better than when—"

"Adrianna," he said sharply, cutting me off. Running a hand through his hair, his eyes traveled to my chest and lingered for a moment.

"I do not have anything else to say to you. I am a man, you are a… teenager," he said with disgust, making me feel two inches tall. "Had Katja seen us, we could have lost everything. I am not willing to risk that for anything or anyone, no matter what."

I swallowed back the empathy I was suddenly feeling. His eyes softened, shame filling them. "You have worked too hard to just throw it away, and so have I. Keep your hands to yourself and I will do the same."

Then he turned and walked away, gutting me.

chapter 34

TWO HOURS OF ADVANCED CHEM, PLUS TEN HOURS OF GYM TIME, AND I WAS READY to crash.

It didn't matter that I turned another year older today, it felt like any other day to me. Avery was out of the country. She hadn't been able to visit me for my birthday like she wanted. Her parents scheduled a family vacation to Spain and dropped it on her and her brothers last minute, but she promised she'd come and see me when she got back. My dad was away on business, Xavier was off with his friends doing God knows what, and other than a text from my mom, I hadn't heard a single word from my family. The gym was the gym, same as any other day.

I'd learned to turn off emotions when the time called for it, so being alone on my birthday didn't affect me.

However, Alfred gave me a cupcake with a candle last night when he handed over the keys to the Escalade, my very own Tonka truck. I thanked him and actually called him Thomas.

Aside from being famished and probably capable of eating a cow right then, I just didn't have the strength after the long and draining day I had.

Stepping out of the private tutoring room housed in the back of the library, the lights were soft and the vacancy in the air left me feeling a little cold. My grades were good and I stayed on track, so I really didn't need to come, even though I skipped class that morning to take my driver's test. Where my mom peeved about my appearance, my dad focused on school and how important grades were. I knew he was right, because at the end of the day, I wasn't naive to think money could buy everything like it had in order for me to come to World Cup. One day this would all be over and I'd be living in the real world with real responsibilities.

We were a few weeks into August and the weather changed in Georgia. Although still stifling hot during the day, the humidity was thicker and stickier by nightfall. I began fidgeting with my zipper so I could remove my jacket before I walked outside, but it was stuck on the material. I placed my books on a nearby table to fix it.

I was oblivious to the world when a whisper of breath brushed across my skin. "Do you need help with that?"

My hand flew to my neck and I spun around at the voice in surprise.

Hayden.

"Shit! You scared the crap out of me!"

Hayden grinned, his dimples showing. My eyes shifted to his shoulders, and even through the light gray hoodie, I could see his well-defined muscles.

"Sorry, I just saw you were stuck and thought I'd help."

Simmer down, hormones.

"Aid, do you need help with that?" he asked, nodding toward my hands.

Shaking my head, I snapped out of it. "Ummm, yeah, thanks."

Hayden fiddled with my zipper and asked, "Are you okay?"

"I'm sorry… I'm just exhausted." He grinned and my stomach rumbled.

"And apparently hungry, too."

Heat crept up my neck and into my cheeks, embarrassed over how loudly my stomach grumbled.

"Yeah, that too, but I'm too tired to eat, and the last thing I want is one of the prepared meals I have waiting for me at home."

Hayden's brows angled toward each other, so I answered his perplexed look.

"My mom has fresh meals prepared and delivered to me weekly. The thought of putting that in my mouth right now doesn't sound as appealing as face planting into bed. Most of the time I can deal with them, but if I never had to look at another piece of fish or bark again, it would be too soon. So I'd rather not eat."

"Bark? Like from a tree?"

I chuckled, thinking how funny that sounded. "Not really bark, just food that has nothing in it, no spices, and tastes horrible. Not to mention, they're small servings."

He nodded, accepting my answer. "Why don't you just go food shopping?"

I shrugged. "Truthfully, my mom would have a conniption if I bought something she didn't approve of. Plus, I just don't have the energy."

"So you're just not going to eat?" He fumbled with my zipper and finally got it down my body.

"I have some fruit I can pick at."

"Adrianna, you have to eat," he said, grabbing hold of my hips. Since that kiss in my condo, Hayden hadn't been this forward with his touch. So naturally I noticed his hands on my body.

"Let's go. We're going to grab something to eat together."

"Where would we go?"

"There's a Gino's Pizza up the street. How about there?"

"My mother would kill me if I had pizza."

Squeezing me closer, Hayden looked around aimlessly. I followed his gaze, curious to see who he was looking for, but I didn't see anyone.

"Adrianna, do you see her anywhere? She won't find out about it and I promise not to tell her." The corner of his mouth perked up.

Hesitating, I bit my lip. I haven't had pizza in so long.

"Come on," he coaxed, and grabbed my books, then laced his fingers through mine. "My treat."

I must've stayed in the library longer than planned. A murky fog sat low in the parking lot as we walked hand-in-hand. I didn't typically hold hands with someone I wasn't dating, but Hayden was different. Much to my surprise, he'd become a really good friend. I expected to be close to my team girls more than anything, and I wasn't.

"Which car is yours?"

I pointed to the black SUV with the almost illegal tint and twenty-two inch rims. It was the SUV Alfred had driven when we first came to Cape Coral earlier this year.

"That's your ride?" His brows rose, skepticism in his tone.

God, I just wanted to crawl into a hole and hide. To say Hayden was flabbergasted over my top of the line Escalade was an understatement. It was the Platinum edition and aside from being slightly embarrassed, I really did love it. No one's first car was this nice unless the family had money. But back home, this kind of thing was normal, and the kids I grew up with had even nicer cars. Avery had a sleek BMW that I voiced to my dad wanting on numerous occasions.

"Yes."

"When did you get that car?"

"Umm, well, I've had this car for a while now actually. I just happened to get the keys to it last night."

"Last night?" he questioned me.

I bit my lip. "Today's my birthday."

Hayden stopped in his tracks, jaw dropped and his face lit up. "Today's your birthday and you didn't tell anyone?" He slammed into me and gave me the tightest bear hug possible. I laughed when he picked me up and spun me around, wishing me a happy birthday.

He put me down and said, "When did you get your license? I can't believe you didn't tell anyone."

"I skipped tutoring and Alfred took me this morning."

"Dude, your car is sick. I'm buying dinner, but you're driving."

Relieved over his opinion, my shoulders relaxed. "I'm okay with that."

Hopping into the car, I pushed the button to start the engine as Hayden looked over his shoulder at the two rows behind him.

"Why do you have such a big car? And how come I've never seen it at the gym?"

I sighed before diving into it.

"My dad insists a bigger car is safer to drive, but he's wrong. He just worries about a small car crushing me to death, so he got me a Tonka tank. He's not the type you argue with and usually what he says goes. End of story. Plus, Alfred used to drop me off, which is why you probably never saw it," my voice trailed off.

"Hey," Hayden said softly, pulling my chin up to meet his steady gaze. "Don't feel embarrassed or ashamed of anything you have. I think it's pretty cool. Gotta be honest, I'm a little shocked to see you drive something so big as small as you are. It's a badass truck, but I'd never make you feel uncomfortable over it. I swear."

His thumb gently grazed my jaw, and I felt his touch all the way to my stomach. I nodded, accepting his genuine words.

"So what does your dad do?"

"He's a real estate developer."

"Oh, that's right. You mentioned it at Kova's barbecue. I forgot." I turned onto a busy street and he asked, "Do you live in a gigantic house?"

"Well, it's average sized… for the island."

"What's averaged sized?"

I bit my lip. "It's a little over nine thousand square feet. There are seven bedrooms, all the boring formal rooms, two kitchens, a guesthouse, movie theater, wine cellar, gym, sauna room, and a game room. We have a three car garage and live off a private road, which I actually like."

His eyes grew wide. "And it's on the beach?"

"No, we live on a golf course. My dad is a big golfer."

"Wow," he was speechless.

"It's actually really beautiful and originally belonged to the Post cereal heiress. It's a Mediterranean style home with the original floors and same architecture from when it was first built. Nothing was touched. So for my dad, buying it was a no brainer. He appreciates that kind of stuff. My mom wanted to rip the floors up and redo everything, but he put a firm stop to that." Unexpectedly, a shot of homesickness hit me and I frowned.

"The beach isn't far, which was where I spent most of my free time. Nothing compares to a Georgia beach. Pale sand, crystal clear water, endless rays of sun, it was really beautiful. Especially when the sun sets and the sky turned orange and pink sometimes."

"Well, it's settled then."

"What's settled?"

"That I'm coming home with you over Thanksgiving break. You're going to take me to a beach and then show me around the island."

I couldn't stop the loud laugh that erupted from my throat. It felt good to relax and let go, and surprisingly I could with Hayden.

"You do realize you have the ocean over here, right? You can go any time you want?"

"I do, but after what you just told me, I want to see where you live."

"Well you're in for a surprise then. People are different over there." I flipped my blinker on and turned into the parking lot. "I'm not like them, I don't want you to get the wrong idea."

"What do you mean?"

I shrugged, unsure of what to say. "First, you have to understand I'm not trying to flaunt my family's money or anything. Okay? Because I don't typically talk about it. It's embarrassing how people do, honestly.

"People on the Island are snotty. Everyone has money, and lots of it. Like an obscene amount. It's all about what kind of car you drive, which designer you're wearing, where your money comes from and so forth. A who's who pretty much. The air is full of wealth and The Islanders turn their noses up quickly and talk so much shit. Their children are even worse because they're raised with that kind of mentality, so their egos are the size of a watermelon by the time they enter middle school. And don't get me started on the socialites."

Hayden grew silent while I looked for a parking spot and slowly tried to pull in.

"What?" I asked, glancing at him.

Brows cinched, he gave me a skeptical look. "Are you okay driving? You don't look so sure of yourself right now?"

I laughed. "I'm still not used to driving a real life Tonka truck, so I tend to pull into the parking spot the way eighty year olds typically drive—barely able to see over the steering wheel and slower than a damn turtle."

Hayden barked out a laugh and I continued.

"The elderly give me road rage."

I parked outside of Gino's, and Hayden hopped out, making his way around as I locked my car and dropped the keys into my purse. Stepping inside the pizzeria, Hayden wrapped an arm around my shoulders and drew me to him. He rested his chin on top of my head.

We stood together looking through the glass at the pizza we could order by the slice.

"She's staring at you," I whispered to him, hardly moving my mouth.

Hayden pretended we weren't talking about the counter girl. "She probably wants to see my abs," he said casually, near my ear.

"I see them every day. They're nothing special in my opinion," I said teasingly, turning away to hide my grin. I knew his golden stomach was flat and toned. And don't get me started on his obliques and that tightness. Damn gymnast. She'd be in for a surprise if she saw what was under his shirt.

He tugged me closer and leaned in to the side of my neck. His lips brushed the shell of my ear. "Adrianna. Remember, I know what your lips taste like."

My eyes widened as Hayden's mischievous ones flashed back at me. I was instantly red, my cheeks blazing hot. I glanced around and spotted a girl a little older than me behind the counter.

"Lucky girl," she said and smiled. "What can I get you guys?"

chapter 35

"**S**O DID YOU LIKE THE PIZZA LAST NIGHT?" HAYDEN ASKED WHILE I CHALKED up my hands.

"Yeah, it was really good. Who knew there were so many different kinds? We don't have that kind of selection back home."

"Where is back home again?" Reagan chimed in. I was pretty sure I already mentioned this to her.

Glancing down at the chalk bowl, I grabbed the block of chalk and cracked it. Kind of the way I wanted to crack Reagan's head sometimes.

"Outside of Savannah."

She scowled. "I know that. Where?"

Squatting down, I looked inside my bag for my grips, but I didn't spot them anywhere. Shit. The last thing I wanted to do was answer her while I was frantically searching for my gear.

Pushing things around, I pulled out my extra leos and dropped them to the floor. I found the wristbands, but my grips were gone. I couldn't do bars without them, not again, and if I ripped my hands open it would take forever to heal at the rate I trained.

Gritting my teeth together, I responded. "Palm Bay. It's outside of Savannah. Amelia Island, to be exact. It's in—"

"I know where it is. I just don't understand why you would leave there and come here," she stated. "Your dad couldn't build a gym for you?"

Was she serious? The urge to roll my eyes was strong at her condescending comment. "I wanted a better gym and my dad happened to be friends with Kova, so it worked out perfectly."

I didn't like confrontation, but I also didn't cower away from it when the time called. She had absolutely no reason to feel the way she did about me. Plus, the last thing I needed was for Coach to think I had drama with any of his team girls.

"Seriously, Reagan?" I asked, and waited for her to look at me. "What's your problem? You hardly speak to me, yet you clearly can't stand the sight of me. What did I do to you? Let's just clear the air now because your attitude is getting old."

She gnashed her teeth together and stepped to me. "You want to know what my problem is? My problem is Coach pays you more attention than anyone else and I just don't get it. It's like his sole focus is on you and it's not fair. You don't deserve it."

Cry me a fucking river. "What are you talking about? He trains with you and all the other girls everyday as usual."

She shook her head, huffing. "He took time away from working with us so he can work on you more. I mean, God knows you need the extra hours and all, but it's still not right. And believe me, we've all noticed how he looks at you."

I froze. No. No way could someone see anything at all between us. We were good at hiding the tension, at least I thought we were. Reagan's words hurt, but I needed to shield my emotions immediately. I pushed away her last comment and planned to deal with it later.

"So you want more attention, then? Is that what it is?"

"I don't need attention. I need a coach who puts in as much time with me as he does for every gymnast here. He used to be like that, but once you got here it's like he completely changed, which can only mean one reason. You." She lowered her voice and looked down at me. "I work harder than anyone here, and I refuse to have it all taken away. I have goals and dreams, too. Not just you, Adrianna."

As much as I tried not to let her words bother me, they did. The looks, the comments, they all grated on my nerves. I was tired of feeling like I wasn't good enough. I worked just as hard as any of these girls.

"You're wrong." Standing up, I decided to walk away. Tears were welling in my eyes and I didn't want her to see. I refused to listen to any more of her bitter bullshit. Rips were most likely happening, so I knew I needed to load up with as much chalk as I could now.

With my stomach in knots and tears burning the back of my eyes, I felt myself slipping. The toll my emotions were taking came close to the edge and I needed to get them under control before I broke.

Grabbing the honey, I squirted my hands, and patted on more chalk. Reagan's words replayed in my head as I repeated the process, over and over again.

Walking to the uneven bars, Hayden grabbed my arm midstride to stop me.

"Where are your grips?" he asked, glancing at my wrists then back to my eyes, knowing the kind of end result I could face.

I shrugged. "I have no idea, Hayden." I said, dejectedly. "I thought I had them—"

"Hey Reagan, let Adrianna borrow an extra pair of your grips, would ya?"

"What are you doing," I whispered at him, yanking my arm away. "You know she can't stand me and honestly, I don't want any favors from her."

I could swear I'd seen my grips in my bag this morning. The thought crossed my mind that maybe Reagan purposely took them out. I wouldn't put it past her. She seemed hell bent on wanting me to fall.

"If she's so rich, then why doesn't she have more?" Her squeaky voice was like nails on a chalkboard. I'd give anything to rub chalk on her vocal chords so she didn't sound like a mouse.

"Don't worry, Reagan. I like the bloody rips on my hands. It feels so good when the chalk hits my red, irritated skin, turning my hands raw. What doesn't kill you only makes you stronger, right?"

Tightening my ponytail, I gripped the low bar and swung into a glide kip. With my hips back, I extended my legs as far as they could go so I was in a perfect horizontal line, and felt the pull in my stomach. I brought my toes to the bar and piked to a kip, then cast to a handstand, holding it for three seconds, before doing a glide kip out so my arms were straight and my thighs rested very lightly on the bar.

I turned to Reagan. "Guess this means Coach will just be giving me more attention since I'm without my grips today."

Casting to a handstand on the low bar once again, I piked down and swung around in a straddle position and released the low bar. With my hips high in the air, I twisted my body completely around and reached for the high bar.

Chalk sprinkled down lightly when I grasped the bar, and I closed my eyes. Doing a few light release moves allowed me to warm up as I swung from bar to bar with ease, while it stretched out my sore muscles. It felt good, and I had to admit I loved the pull on my body. Everything just faded away. It was like a stress reliever and I embraced it every single time. Especially now.

I warmed up with a few handstands and pirouettes, making sure I hit them in vertical, then a Giant to a flyaway dismount. I warmed up once more and decided instead of doing a flyaway again, I would go for a double layout. It wasn't really common in a warm up, but it was something I mastered long ago and could do in my sleep.

Two Giants completed, I released. The bar ricocheted loudly, springs bouncing. I flew through the air, making sure I kept my body straight as a board and my hips opened while I flipped back two times before driving my heels into the ground. I landed with a slight wobble. A rolling flame of heat shot up my calf, but I forced it out of my head.

"Nice, Aid!" Hayden yelled excitedly as he walked over to the pommel horse.

All Reagan could manage was a glare. Before I could say anything, Coach Kova yelled across the gym, "Nice job, Adrianna. Tighten up a little more."

Naturally he saw my wobble, but nothing got past the man. "It was just a warm up, Coach." I responded back and he nodded in approval, his eyes gleaming with contentment.

That was the first real thing Kova had said to me in weeks. I needed it, I needed his backing after what Reagan said. I needed to know I was making progress in his eyes, that my hard work did not go unnoticed. Other than commands about gymnastics skills, we hardly spoke. I'd come to accept his stiff personality after what happened between us.

I turned and smiled brightly at a seething Reagan, who stepped around to mount the bar and begin her routine. But just before she did, she threw an extra set of grips at my feet.

"You know, Coach works with you the way he does because he feels bad. You're not good enough to be here, and it's obvious you never will be. Why do you think he puts in so much time with you? It's the same way with Hayden. Holly told me Hayden said you have no friends and you're alone all the time, so he's friends with you out of pity. I'm not surprised, though. Hayden's a good guy. It's in his nature to go out of his way to help those in need."

The satisfaction I felt moments earlier was gone. Tears pooled in my eyes again at her heartless words. Months of hard work and emotional avoidance bubbled at the surface. I didn't want to cry, but her words stung and I felt them ready to spill over.

"No one here likes you, and the one friend you have isn't a real one. Your coach and your only friend have no faith in you whatsoever." She laughed, mockingly. "You should just leave now. You'll never amount to being an Olympic gymnast, Adrianna Rossi. You don't have what it takes and you never will."

With that, she smiled and turned to mount the bar. I walked back over to the chalk bowl, my heart pounding against my chest. I was sick to my stomach. Her words rang in my ears, getting louder and heavier. They couldn't be true.

A fat tear slipped down my cheek at the reality of my life and I quickly wiped it away. Embarrassment over forgetting my grips clogged my throat, and my chest tightened from the humiliation Reagan just dealt me. I was suffocating in a bowl of fucking chalk. Somehow I had been completely oblivious to my surroundings. I'd been used to snotty girls back home, but Reagan was a true mean girl, and I didn't know how to deal with it. I've been taught to handle things with poise and control, not act like a loose cannon, but her words were cruel and they struck deep. All I wanted to do was retaliate.

But I didn't. Instead, I took the higher road and began powdering my hands as another tear fell into the bowl, her words repeating in my head.

Taking a deep breath, I exhaled and let all the bullshit out. I looked up at the gym around me and locked eyes with Kova, who was staring at me intently.

I didn't want to appear weak, but there was no way to stop another warm tear from rolling down my cheek. Kova's eyes darkened, his jaw set tight. He glanced at Reagan for a long moment before giving me one more look. This time it was filled with concern that caused my belly to clench. His gaze said more than I think he wanted to give away.

Before turning toward the bars, I wiped the tears away so Reagan wouldn't see she got to me. I refused to show her she'd won this battle.

But she wouldn't win the war.

chapter 36

THREE LONG WEEKS PASSED WHERE KOVA AND I SKATED AROUND EACH OTHER.
To be fair, I kept my focus primarily on gymnastics.

It wasn't as easy as I thought it would be. In fact, it was downright hard. Being in a gym and training for nearly fifty hours a week was a daunting task alone. I'd been taking extra dance classes and spending hours transforming my body just so I could reach Kova's standards. Sadly, I didn't know if I'd ever meet them, because he sure as hell wouldn't tell me.

Add in an illicit act between a coach and his athlete and see where that got you. Especially an athlete he has to personally train for a number of those hours.

I'd caught him sneaking glances, touching me more than needed during gym, practices lasting longer. In his defense, I'd been doing the same thing to him. The tension was mounting between us, but where was it going? There was no outlet for any of it. It was just brewing, the pressure building to an unhealthy level.

Worst of all, I started to worry if anyone else noticed. Especially after the comments Reagan made.

Things were getting to me. Not to mention, I was almost positive there was something wrong with my calf, which wasn't helping the situation—or my life. The pain would come and go in the beginning, so I tended not to focus on it. But now that it was starting to appear more often than not, I couldn't help but wonder if it was something serious. It was stressing me out more than ever. My mind was on edge with all the thoughts running through it, and the silence of my condo was eating at me.

Today was my one day off. I'd been restless, all alone and nothing to fill the void. I needed to get out. Avery was nowhere to be found, which was pissing me off. If I knew her, there was a good chance she was with her mystery guy. She'd given me the fuck you button a few times already. I cleaned every square inch I could and there was nothing on Netflix worth watching. I even tried to read a book in hopes it would help me escape the monotony of my life.

Nothing helped.

I was beginning to drive myself crazy over everything that had happened since arriving at World Cup. My head was pounding. I needed to zone out and forget about it all, and the one thing that would allow me any form of relief was gymnastics.

I wanted to train, I needed to. I needed the release it brought on.

Pulling open the door to the gym, I blew an unruly auburn strand of hair from my face. The gym was typically closed on Sunday, which meant I would be alone and without the constant observation from my team and coaches.

Just what I wanted.

Flipping on the lights in the dance room, I dropped my stuff on the wood floor and walked to the shelf that held the radio. Funny how Kova had radios in the actual gym, but he wouldn't put one in the therapy room. I needed music, otherwise the silence would ruin my train of thought.

I decided I'd work on the skills I learned in the stupid ballet classes I was forced to take. I wondered how much longer I'd have to take them. They weren't as bad as I thought they'd be, I just didn't care for them. Maybe this was what separated me from being a mediocre gymnast and an incredible gymnast in Kova's eyes. It was no secret I hated ballet, but I wasn't naive enough to think I didn't need it anymore. I hated admitting ballet played a large part in gymnastics. The components had not only increased my flexibility and balance, but the coordination and discipline required made a huge difference, especially on the floor.

Dance, primarily ballet, corrected my posture that was thrown off by the constant bending and twisting of gymnastics. Just like ballerinas, gymnasts needed to be tight with every movement—eliminating unwanted movement—control. Spotting a sloppy dancer was easy, even to an untrained eye. Gymnastics was the same way and it all started with building my core.

After pushing a few buttons, *Love Me Like You Do* by Ellie Goulding vibrated through the speakers, rejuvenating my spirit in its wake. I felt a hundred times better already and allowed her poetic voice to take me away.

"You are dropping your chest."

I jumped, snapping my back leg down and spinning around in fear, my heart racing. Kova's unsympathetic voice startled me out of my concentration and I stared straight at him like a deer in headlights.

"What?" I asked breathlessly.

"Your chest. You are dropping your chest," he stated for the second time.

He casually leaned against the doorframe, his arms crossed. He took in the length of my body with a long gaze. Instead of a leotard, I went with black mini workout shorts and a green sports bra. Moisture dampened my skin as sweat trickled down the small of my back. I'd removed my oversized T-shirt earlier, throwing it to the ground. My long hair was thrown into a messy bun at the top of my head. Little hairs had slipped out I hadn't cared to fix.

I thought about what Kova said and I nearly growled. This man. I swear, he did everything he could to get under my skin. I most definitely was *not* dropping my chest.

"No, I'm not."

The corner of his mouth tugged up, as if to say, *Are you really going to challenge me?*

Dropping his arms, Kova prowled forward with determination. Each step made my heart beat a little faster. My skin prickled as he neared me, vibrations coursed through my body. I was suddenly hyperaware of his presence and how secluded we were in the dance room.

"Yes, you are," he countered. "Do it again."

Taking a few paces back, I inhaled deeply and visualized the Jeté before I moved again. With my shoulders relaxed back and my chest arched forward, I sashayed in two steps with my arms gracefully out to the side. Kicking one long leg forward, followed by a flick of my hip twisting in the air to bring my other leg around, I scissor kicked my legs quickly by tapping at the toes before I landed.

I looked at Kova who wore a lovely, sardonic glimmer in his eyes.

"Are you still going to tell me you did not drop your chest?"

"I didn't. I know I didn't."

Kova tilted his head to the side. "You have too much power in your back swing, so you cannot balance it out. Do it again, but do not try and force open your legs as wide. Watch yourself in the mirror."

I did as he said, only this time it felt less than perfect.

"That was a half-assed turn," I admitted.

Kova's lips curved upward, his eyebrows lowered, and I felt his agreement in my stomach.

"It was. It was terrible. But I told you why and you seem to think I am lying."

I did it again. And again. Four more tries and I became increasingly frustrated with each step I took, all while he watched closely with scrutinizing eyes. I wanted to prove him wrong, because surely I would know if I was dropping my chest or not.

After I finished the fifth turn, I ran my fingers through my sweaty hair and clenched it, groaning in irritation over the fact I couldn't master a move as basic as this.

"Show me how to do it correctly."

He raised an eyebrow.

"Please?"

He nodded silently. "Come with me."

Following Kova, he led me to the center of the floor. He stood in front of me and grabbed my forearms so my palms would rest in the crest of his elbows. He tugged me forward until both our arms were tightly bent at our sides, holding each other in place.

Looking directly in my eyes, he explained. "You are going to jump once for power, then jump again and do the same move as before, only this time you are holding my arms. It will give you momentum, but will also allow you to condition your back kick and keep your chest up. It is the same as you would do on the barre, but I am holding you. Your chest will not drop in my arms the way it would on the barre."

I nodded, took a deep breath and jumped into the kick, only to lean into his chest with a grunt, getting a hint of his cinnamon and citrus scent but with a trace of something more. Whatever it was, he smelled divine, and it assaulted my senses.

"Again. But this time stretch your legs as wide open as a kick split will allow you. Do it ten times, but on the last one stop with your leg in the air. Got it?"

My brows scrunched together. "But you told me not to open them as wide just before."

"This is different. You will not be able to lean in my arms. Just trust me."

I jumped and then kicked back ten times, just as he had instructed me to, stretching my legs as wide as possible with each kick. Kova was right. I couldn't drop my chest here and I felt the slight pinch in my back at this angle. I didn't move. My palms were sweating and I wish I'd chalked up my hands before I gripped his forearms to steady my balance. Our eyes stayed locked the whole time, never wavering. His persistence to see me complete this kick correctly shifted something inside of me.

Out of breath and leaning toward Kova's chest, I waited with my leg elongated in the air behind me for him to speak. The air circulated around us from the exercise and I could smell him even better at this angle, not that I should want to, but I also couldn't stop myself from drawing in a small breath.

God, he smelled so good.

Something felt different tonight while I waited in his arms to critique my form. I became more aware of the strength he exuded, the power in his hold, the way he stared down through his thick eyelashes. The complete domination. My stomach clenched at the sudden thought of what his strength could do to me... and the fact that we were alone in the gym... again.

Craning my head as far as my neck would allow from this odd angle, I peered through damp bangs that fell in my face.

The look from Kova's eyes seared heat into my skin. His fingers tightened under my forearms as if he was angry. Surely, I hadn't done it wrong again. A move that was normally so easy for me was giving me such problems tonight. Him staring at me like he wanted to wring my neck wasn't doing wonders for me either.

"What did I do wrong?" I asked breathlessly.

Kova's jaw locked back and forth at my question.

"Point your toe. Bring your chest higher."

Really? That was it? Point my toe?

He released the shell of my elbows and slowly slid his hands over to my ribcage, *my bare ribcage,* to rest right under my breastbone where the bottom of my sports bra sat. His hands held firm as my heart beat roughly against my chest.

"Steady your breathing. Remember what I taught you. Breathe with your stomach," he said, voice low.

I couldn't move.

I couldn't think.

And I tried not to take deep breaths as if I was gasping for air.

chapter 37

H IS TOUCH IGNITED A CLUSTER OF SPARKS THROUGHOUT MY BODY THAT WENT off simultaneously.

Never having this reaction to another person before, I didn't know how to respond to his presence. Heat pooled in my belly as my breath caught, not to mention, my calf and ankle started burning while my leg was still held high behind me.

"Your chest is too low and your hips are not squared," he stated, annoyed.

This fucking guy. He really knew how to push my buttons. He was irritating me, insinuating I didn't know what I was doing. My chest might have been at a little low, but my hips were most definitely squared.

My nose flared and I dropped my leg and stood defiantly. His warm hands slid to my waist then down to my hips.

"My hips are squared," I said through gritted teeth. "I learned that in beginner's gymnastics." He challenged me.

"Either you had a shit for brains coach, or you just never comprehended the correct way to do it. Your hips are *out* and your chest is *low*. This is a very common mistake among gymnasts if they are not trained correctly from the beginning. I have seen you do this during practice many times and I thought we might have corrected it last time you were in here, but I guess I was wrong. Do not argue with me again over this, Ria. I have been doing this longer than you have been alive. I know what I am talking about, little girl. Now get over to the barre and I will show you how wrong you are."

"Little girl?" I mocked and pushed at him. "I didn't ask you to come in here to help me out. You just walked right in and interrupted my time. And if you did see me mess up during practice, I highly doubt that you'd keep your mouth shut. You love to pick at every little thing I do. *'Not enough. Faster. Higher. Why are you doing it this way? That is no good. Again,'* is all that seems to come out of your mouth. If it's not that, you mumble in Russian under your breath."

My gut dropped. Oh God. Maybe I shouldn't have added in a faux Russian accent.

He stepped forward, and my heart skipped because I refused to step back. In a deathly quiet voice, he said, "If your obnoxious music was not blaring and echoing throughout *my* gym, I would not have had to come in here. Get your ass to the barre. There are so many things I need to correct where you are concerned. If I do not correct you now, you will just make more work for me down the line. There are not enough hours in the day for that, or patience."

Dropping my arms, I stepped back. "This wasn't why I came to the gym. I purposely came when no one was around so I wouldn't have to be ridiculed for every damn thing I did. I needed to not think about a gymnastics routine for once and let go for a few moments alone. I needed to be free, not having to practice."

"Needed to be free? Your life is gymnastics!" He roared. "It is all you are allowed to think about. Eat. Sleep. Flip. Repeat. Nothing more! I am not here to waste my time for fun. You are here because I get results and can take you to the next level, which is what you wanted. You want the Olympics. *You.* Not me. I have already been. You need me, not the other way around. I do not need you, do you understand? I took you in as a favor, a bargain for a bargain. If you are only here for fun, then we are done. I have spent a ton of time working on you, perfecting you, more so than I have ever done with another gymnast, God knows you need it. At least you can show a little respect in the process."

I hated him and his arrogant attitude and his deep green eyes and pompous tone. My chest was tight, his words struck hard. He brought me down and I didn't like it.

But he was right. And I despised admitting it.

Gymnastics was my life. It was everything I've ever worked for. I needed to shut up and take it, or take a hike.

Standing on my toes, I spun around and headed to a ballet barre that mounted to the wall.

"Teach me the correct way, Oh Master," I said sarcastically. I couldn't resist. I knew I was being bold tonight, more than usual. He probably didn't know what to do with my impulsive attitude, seeing as the only thing I did these days was take orders during practice. I'd reached my breaking point.

"Grab the barre and kick your leg back. Hold it there."

I didn't hear him move, but Kova was suddenly standing next to my shoulder. One of his hands gripped my inner thigh while the other was flat between my breasts to hold me in place. His fingers were splayed out, one fingertip accidently touching the plump mound of my breast. I gasped, sucking in the dense air and wondered if he realized it.

His warm fingers scorched my flesh. Kova squeezed my thigh hard, moisture pooled between my legs. I bit down on the inside of my lip, having to hide my reaction to him. I needed to control it, but I didn't know how.

"Look in the mirror," he spat out.

I looked.

"See? Your chest is angled too low for the height of your leg. Push off the barre with your arms to bring your chest up."

I raised my chest and a slight burn resonated in my back.

"More."

I did, but the burn crept higher up my back at the uncomfortable angle. "I can't go any more."

Kova shot daggers through his eyes at the word can't. Taking matters in his own hands, he ignored my resistance and pushed my chest up himself, never letting go of my leg, and bent my body in an unnatural position. I grunted as a gush of air burst from my lungs. I tried to lower my leg, but he wouldn't give.

"Your weakness is your lack of flexibility."

"I know," I gushed out. I was in serious pain and he wanted to have a conversation?

"You know and yet you do not condition yourself the way I taught you? Why did I spend time in those private sessions if you are not going to use the drills? That is not proving yourself to me."

He let up an inch so I could speak. "I've been conditioning, apparently not enough. I'll do more."

"Look at your hip now."

Son of a bitch.

"This is where you need to be with your form."

Christ, he was right. My hip was pivoted out and not squared at all with my shoulders.

"Hold your leg still and do not move," Kova ordered. Beads of sweat trickled down my neck as I fought to hold position.

Using the hand that was still tightly wrapped around my inner thigh, and dangerously near my sex, he leisurely slid it to the outer edge of my thigh, almost as if he was feeling for my flexed muscle. My breathing labored, and I struggled not to respond to the sensations of his touch as his hand glided up my leg almost provocatively. It was electrifying. And though I knew it was wrong, in this very moment, I wanted his touch more than I wanted to learn the correct stance.

"Do not move, Ria," he whispered.

His other hand drifted willfully over my waist, leaving a trail of heat dancing across my bare skin. I gripped the barre tighter, my knuckles turning white.

God, it felt so good. A purr resonated in my throat. I tried not to think of his touch in a sensual way, but it was pointless. I wanted his hands on me, I wanted them all over my body. I wanted him to show me the correct way to do more. I wanted the heat of his skin pressed against mine, to whisper in Russian across my neck. His fingers sat on my lower abdomen, and if I moved my hips just an inch more they would hit the throbbing spot begging for release. I needed his touch, yearned for his skilled hand to slide lower.

Kova's hand skimmed around my upper thigh, grazing my sex. His closeness made me wonder if he knew what he was doing, what he'd touched. I tried not to focus on the sensuality of his hand, but it wasn't easy when he was continually sliding past and dipping lower.

Leaning closer to me, he asked, "See how firm you are here?" Tight lipped, I nodded. "See how your hips are flat and down?" His hand slowly circled my pelvis. I nodded again. "This is what we want all the time. I know you can do it, Ria."

His belief in me, even over something as simple as squaring my hips, made my chest bloom with confidence.

Taking a deep breath, my hips moved just a fraction. I told myself I couldn't help it as I worked to breathe at this uncomfortable position, but I also couldn't stop the gnawing hunger of wanting his hand to move lower either.

The pressure of his fingers digging into my thigh, signified he was fighting not to move. Then finally, one long and unsteady finger hit the slit of my mound and I nearly groaned.

Swiftly, his hand slid to my hip and his fingers wrapped around and gripped me. Leaning in with his hip, he used it as leverage to steady, gluing himself to me. His pelvic bone dug into my side, showing just how close he really was. As he gripped my hip, he rotated it forward to square it correctly.

With a grunt, my leg involuntarily snapped down and my arms gave out. My knees buckled and I lost balance, crumbling against the barre with Kova crashing into me.

"Fuck," I muttered under my breath. All that touching so he could square my hips.

We were both leaning on the barre in a heap of heavy breathing when Kova's arm secured my waist and tugged me to stand. "Come on, try it again."

I didn't want to stand, I couldn't move. My body ached and I was exhausted after holding that position.

"Get up, Adrianna," his warm breath sent shivers across my damp neck. With my back pressed against his chest and my ass nestled between his hips, the hardness of his body was making it difficult to function.

Kova's hold tightened. A flush of heat coursed through my worn out body at his closeness, his breath on my neck, his fingers digging into me. My heart raced, and I knew he was the reason for it, not exertion. Strangely enough, I was okay with this reaction to Kova, this feeling streaming through my veins. Curiosity got the best of me and I embraced this moment.

Still glued to my backside, much closer than he truly needed to be, I decided to be daring. My lower belly was throbbing, an ache pooling inside for something more, so I leaned against him, slowly standing to my full height with a seductive arch of my back, hitting him in all the right places. Even going as far as to add pressure to the clearly obvious erection pressing into me.

Kova hissed. I was probably tempting him in ways he'd never been tempted before.

Ask me if I cared.

I didn't.

And the part that frightened me most—I wished he wouldn't hold back.

"What are you doing?" he asked in a broken whisper.

I answered honestly. "I don't know."

"You are treading a fine line, Ria. You are testing me."

I answered by pressing into his groin again. His arm tightened around me, a rush of moisture coated my shorts as his fingers skated along my waist.

God, I wanted him to make me feel what I felt the night we were alone together.

"What is it about you that I cannot stay away from?" he whispered. His head dropped to my shoulder and his lips landed on my skin. My body melted in his hold. His breathing deepened against my back as he struggled. He didn't move, and I knew why.

I was his gymnast.

He was my coach.

There were many laws we would break if we took another step.

Not to mention, our careers would be in ruins if anyone saw the position we were in right now.

But in this moment, I forgot it all.

chapter 38

Kova's grip was strong. I turned in his hold, twisting to face his body where he hadn't moved one inch. My back was to the barre with my elbows resting on it. Looking into his eyes, they were swirling with desire just as I was sure mine were. I may be a teenager, but I wasn't stupid. I could tell when someone wanted me. Lust, passion, want, need, it was all there. His mouth was only inches from mine, and if I stretched up on my toes I think I could touch his lips.

With lust overpowering the slight tremor in my nerves, I decided to push the envelope. I may never get the chance to be in this position again. *Carpe diem!*

The muscles in my calves strained as I stood on the tips of my toes. Hovering in front of his mouth, I whispered breathlessly, "If my flexibility is so terrible, show me ways to stretch."

Kova's jaw locked, the look in his green eyes penetrated me, and his hips pressed into me as if we were becoming one. I inhaled a strangled breath and gripped the barre, needing some type of leverage in this moment of insanity. I wished I could read the thoughts I saw running through his eyes.

One of his hands traveled down my ribcage to my hip. He squeezed hard and I groaned, my hips surging into his from the pleasure.

"You want ways to stretch out your hips? I can show you a few," he said in a deep, raspy voice, his eyes gleaming with words he couldn't speak. My lips parted with a sigh.

His hand curved around to my backside, rubbing in circles and heating my already tepid skin. He slid down the center of my ass and gave a good, hard tug, cupping me. A rush of wetness coated my shorts from his forceful pull. Kova pressed a finger between my cheeks while his large hand kneaded my small ass. My shorts rode up, the cool air hitting the crease as he continued to massage me into oblivion. If he asked me to give myself to him in every conceivable way and act out any fantasy he'd ever had, I wouldn't hesitate. He could have me. The thumping of my heartbeat echoed in my ears. My legs were already jelly, my hips curled into him, feeling his dick against my aching sex. A hum escaped my throat and my stomach clenched in eagerness.

I wanted him to go farther. I *needed* him to go farther. God, what the hell was wrong with me?

He gave a rough squeeze to my ass once again, his eyes never leaving mine. "Want me to keep going," he stated more than asked.

My eyes were heavy from just his touch and it wasn't easy for me to respond.

"Say it."

"Yes." Rolled off my tongue.

One side of his mouth tugged up, giving me a sexy as hell half-grin. His knees bent, pushing his hips into me deeper to get a better hold. My eyes rolled into the back of my head, a breathless moan escaped my throat, this time loud enough for him to hear. His hand rotated on the curve of my ass, turning and gliding up my inner thigh. I gulped hard, knowing my shorts were soaked and all he had to do was run his hand along the seam of my sex to know just how wet I was. His touch was electrifying and I prayed he wouldn't stop.

"I don't see how this will help me, Coach," I said sweetly. "I don't feel anything stretching out."

His paused for a moment and then moved with cat like reflexes.

His hand quickly slid all the way up the backside of my thigh so my leg was straight in the air and he was holding the back of my knee. There was a slight sharpness, a pulling on my hamstring, but it was nothing new for me. I was in an upright split after all.

"Square your hips."

I grinded down. "I am."

"No, you are not, Ria," he spat back, tightness laced in his voice. "Are you really going to try me again?"

I shrugged. I honestly thought my hips were squared.

He glared at my blasé attitude. "I am not here to play games with you."

"Who said I'm playing games?" I fought back with fire in my eyes.

Kova's jaw ticked. Eyes said so much when words couldn't. This position left me extremely exposed—and it didn't take much to know he was thinking about sex.

I mean, I was. He had to be, too.

Kova was able to let go of my leg and because of his height it rested easily on his shoulder. He slid both hands to my hips, and this time he squared them off, shifting my foot at the same time so it was positioned correctly. Little things like this, incorrectly squaring my hips, were what held me back. My leg moved on his shoulder and I could feel his erection through his thin gym shorts… and I wanted it. God, I wanted to feel more of it. All of it. See it.

My mouth began to water, blood rushed through me like a tidal wave. We held still in a seriously compromising position with his dick pressed into me, hard. It felt so good that I wanted to rub myself against him.

"Feel it now?" he asked.

"No, it feels like any other stretch I've done before," I lied.

He challenged me. "Oh yeah?"

"Yes," I rotated my hips just a fraction, feeling the hard tip of him. "Oh, God," I murmured.

Kova flattened his hand against the underside of my thigh and pressed my leg up higher, off his shoulder, and I grunted.

Then, I felt it.

Oh boy, did I ever feel it.

Not only the pull in my leg, but his dick straining into my wetness. Letting out a loud breath, my eyes rolled shut in pleasure. He pressed my thigh back harder to meet my shoulder. His power over me was incredible. It took so little for him to hold me in this position.

I was at his mercy.

"Is it too hard for you to handle?"

When I didn't answer, his other hand moved from the barre to my ass, gripping it. He shifted, settling deeper, locking me in as much as our clothes would allow. Kova didn't hold back this time as his hips pressed into mine without a worry he'd hurt me. I moaned loudly, and my head fell back.

Jesus…

Kova answered my sigh by pressing my thigh back even farther, past my shoulder where it began to quake. I couldn't take any more—I could hardly breathe. I wasn't fucking Gumby here. My body was being stretched to an unnatural angle, yet this is what I needed. The pull was tight, almost painful as the muscles ripped, but I said nothing for multiple reasons.

My breath caught in my throat as his hand ran seductively down my leg and his lips landed on my clavicle. He peppered my shoulder and neck with little kisses. The barre was bruising my back from the weight of both of us pressing into it, but I didn't complain. It's what I wanted, so I took it all.

"Tell me to stop," he croaked, breathing heavily. His hand crept down my back, shocking me as it slid into my shorts and touched my bare skin.

My lips were sealed, but if he looked into my eyes, he'd have his answer.

"Tell me to stop," he repeated, almost begged, against my heated flesh.

"Don't stop."

Kova lifted his head. His eyes narrowed, his fingers moving deeper, sliding toward my core and grazing my swollen lips for the very first time, from the back. He groaned loud, not holding back and his dick twitched against my center. Because of the tightness of the spandex shorts, I had gone without underwear.

His fingers rubbed along my slit, and I almost had an orgasm on the spot. Kova's tongue slipped out and ran across his bottom lip.

"You are supposed to tell me to stop."

"I can't help it. You make me want something more. Something I only feel when I'm around you."

Kova hesitated, my words rooting him in place. His hand stopped moving and he pulled away. I almost begged for him to pick up where he left off.

"You are too young to know what you want," he said gravely.

"Says who? You?" My leg slid down his shoulder and touched the ground. He stepped into me to close the remaining gap. His palms landed on my ass and he began rubbing in leisurely circles, warming my skin. I sighed, and rotated my hips into him, showing Kova just how much I knew what I wanted. I had a notion he was terrified to express what he craved, so I went out on a limb and did it for him. My chest constricted as I tried to interpret his gaze. If I was here and willingly giving myself to him, I wanted him to have me.

He grabbed my jaw, pulling it up to him in a savage hold and my stomach tightened. I looked him dead in the eyes while one of his hands slipped into my shorts. His fingers started up again and traced the outside of my lips, teasing my entrance.

"Please," I begged. "You didn't finish last time. I had to take care of it myself when I got home."

Kova's eyes darkened. "There is no need to beg, Ria," his voice cracked. "You can take what you want. In fact, I wish you would take from me. It would be easier that way."

Oh God. Why his words seized my heart, I didn't know. But one thing was for sure, I was right. He wanted the same things I did, he just couldn't actually verbalize it and needed me to take it. I wanted to take it, I just wasn't sure how to put everything into motion. Where to start, what to say. What to do. I was a bundle of nerves. How to make it uncomplicated for Kova while giving and receiving at the same time was a challenge, one I would gladly act on.

My body was on the verge of a powerful explosion, something so new I'd yet to fully embrace.

I decided to start with a kiss.

Straining on my toes, I cupped his face and pulled it to mine. "I want you," I whispered. "So much," and planted my lips to his, shocking us both.

He grasped the back of my neck while his other hand sought entrance into my opening.

I moaned, rotating my hips into his palm while his fingers caressed me gently. He kissed me hard, bruising almost, letting me know just how much he wanted me despite his hesitation.

Rolling my hips into his again so I could feel pressure on my clit, I groaned and silently asked for more. A skilled finger glided down my slit and nudged its way in. I pulled his tongue into my mouth as my hands drifted off his face, down his neck where he swallowed hard, to his taut shoulders. I gave a little squeeze, letting him know everything was okay. My hands roamed over every inch of his chest, his rock hard muscles that led to his beautifully strong arms I couldn't get enough of. Such curvature and sharpness at every arc. When my hands encircled his waist, I reached for the hem of his shirt.

The hand around my neck loosened its grip and his other hand gave one last caress over my opening before smoothly leaving the warmth of my shorts. He stepped back, separating our passionate lips, and I got what I wanted. Kova reached behind his neck and pulled his shirt off over his head and discarded it to the floor.

With a glint in his eyes and his arms spread wide, telling me to come to him, I tracked his every move as he backed away. *Take what you want.* Our eyes never wavered as he walked backward to the other side of the dance room. We both knew he wouldn't make the first move. He was going to make sure I really wanted this—and I did.

Once I reached him, I gripped the back of his neck and climbed up his body, wrapping my legs around his waist. I've fantasized doing this since the first time we were together. He was big and I was small and I wanted to be held in his arms just like this.

Kova hugged me tight, one hand behind my neck, the other under my ass as he turned me around and pushed my back to the wall.

Heat blazed in his eyes as he closed the distance and pressed his chest to mine. He was a breath away from my lips when he asked, "What are we doing?"

chapter 39

"I DON'T KNOW." I LOCKED MY LEGS AROUND HIS BACK, ROLLING MY HIPS UP. HIS shaft was long and heavy against my center, pressing into me. Kova's jaw flexed. Pulling his face down to mine, I licked my lips but he pulled back.

"Ria, think about what you are about to start." He breathed slow heavy breaths.

I nodded frantically. I already knew because I've imagined it numerous times. "What *we* are going to start." My fingers threaded his hair and warmth spread through me.

He ignored my last comment and asked, "You want this?"

I didn't hesitate. "Yes."

His eyes roamed my face, searching for an uncertainty he wasn't going to find. "Are you sure?"

I nodded.

"You realize the chances we are taking, right? What could happen to us?"

"I do."

His brows pinched together, his voice grim. "The repercussions we face?"

"I'm aware. I'm tired of fighting this, dancing around each other. I want you." I pressed my core against his erection.

"I am a man who can only be pushed so far." A tick worked in Kova's jaw. "You should not have told me that."

I bit my lip. "Why not?"

"Because then I will not feel as bad for doing this." He planted his mouth to mine with a fervor he'd held back until now, and I surrendered to his kiss.

Kova rested his weight on me, groaning loudly. The feel of his body on mine, the hardness of this man was euphoric. It made my head spin with bliss. He held me lovingly, his fingers caressing my face as if he was making love to my mouth. This kiss was much slower, methodic, showing me what he was capable of. His warm, thick tongue circled mine. My fingers tugged his hair, my hips undulated against him when his stubble brushed my face. He was suffocating me with his skilled mouth and I couldn't get enough.

Kova pulled back, panting against my lips. "We really should stop."

I ignored him. Licking my lips, I angled his head to the side and pressed my mouth to his neck. My tongue swept out, tasting his salty skin and pulled him into my mouth with a little bite.

Pushing off the wall, Kova spun around and brought our joined bodies to the floor. His lips found mine again and he quickly deepened the kiss. His arms planted on the sides of my head, caging me in. He was a beast over me, so big and large to my small frame. His raging erection settled between my legs. I wanted to feel his length, skin on skin, and maybe more. Sex would be scary the first time, no matter who I was with, but it wasn't like I was saving myself for anyone.

Not that I planned to sleep around, either.

"Is anyone else in the gym," I asked against his mouth.

He shook his head. "Just us. I looked around before I came in here and found you."

I wanted to get a better hold on him. My hands left his hair and made their way to his magnificently toned back, feeling every ridge and muscle as I skimmed down and slipped my hands beneath his elastic waistband to grab his ass.

Bare.

He was going commando and I wondered if he was always like this.

"Do you normally skip the boxers?"

Kova tensed when my hands touched his flesh, then relaxed. His grin was my answer, and I melted.

"I do not own a pair of boxers," he freely admitted.

His skin was so silky smooth, I wanted to touch him everywhere. If he didn't own a pair, that meant he didn't wear any to practice either. Why that enticed me more, I had no idea, but I loved the fact he was bare underneath. My hips widened as far as possible to accommodate his body, a light moan escaped my chest, allowing him to settle more deeply into my heat.

"God," I breathed. "This feels so good."

"More than I imagined it would."

His needy lips met mine again, his kiss was frantic, and his rotating hips never stopped. He slowly rocked his erection back and forth against me, eliciting another moan from my mouth. He hit my clit every time, pushing me higher. My body was on fire, my skin damp. I imagined this was how he made love.

"You're so hard, so big," I said between kisses and he chuckled. My thighs tightened around him, the pleasure almost unbearable.

Taking a chance, my hands gingerly moved outward to his hips. I hesitated, wondering if he'd let me or tell me to stop.

As my hand slid between our bodies, a thumb raked across my nipple and my hips bucked. I wasn't expecting him to touch me there and I surprised myself when I realized I wanted him to do it again. With parted lips and heated breath, I looked into his green eyes that had darkened while he ran his thumb in circles over my hardening nipple. Overwhelmed with sensations running through my body, I couldn't form words and just arched into him instead.

I pushed my hand between us, gauging his reaction as I did, but he gave nothing away. Little hairs tickled my fingers, his thumb picked up the pace, and his hips stopped moving. I threaded my fingers through the softness of his curls, circling his shaft before moving lower.

I was pretty sure he didn't expect me to cup his sack, his body tightened everywhere and his breathing became labored.

"Adrianna," he gritted, a vein jutted from his neck. His Russian accent was stronger than ever. I loved when he said my name like that.

"Don't tell me to stop," I begged, caressing him in my hand. "Oh, God. I'm…" I trailed off when he rubbed against me faster and faster. I needed to reach that high point so desperately.

Slowly, Kova leaned down to my neck. Not meaning to, I grasped his balls and held on. Kova cringed.

"Adrianna, lighten up. They are not stress balls. They are sensitive."

I chuckled into his neck and apologized, rubbing them softly. A throaty moan escaped him and I smiled inwardly. Lips pressed to my neck, he laid open mouthed kisses along my jaw as he said, "I have to go, I should leave." But he never got up. "You have to know," he said between kisses, "I have never done this with another gymnast before. Never looked at them the way—" he hesitated.

"The way what?"

"Nothing. Never mind."

He squeezed his eyes shut and ignored me. "Kova—" I lost all train of thought when his mouth suckled my neck so seductively. I relaxed my hold on him and moaned loudly, giving him more access.

"Ahhh... feels so good."

When I finally moved my hand, Kova pulled back and peered down at me. The back of my fingers gently scaled his erection from base to tip. Slowly, my thumb reached out and followed the same pattern, then circled the tip. Kova shuddered, his eyes tightly rolling shut. I wasn't sure if I was doing it right judging by the painful look on his face.

Moving to the top of his penis, moisture coated my fingers.

"Remove your hand," he demanded. But I ignored him. He was wet like me, only not as much. I had to be doing something right.

Opening my hand, hard, hot flesh scorched me while I wrapped my fingers around to stroke him. He was *really* big and thick. I couldn't fathom how anyone had sex with him. As I applied pressure, he pulsed against my hand and then pinched my nipple, forcing me to squeeze my thighs shut. My back bowed. The pain associated with the pleasure just about threw me over the edge. Kova dropped his lips to my chest. His fingers danced along my sports bra seeking permission but not entering.

"Remove your hand," he repeated.

"I don't want to."

"Adrianna, I can only hold on for so long before I snap. There is no going back once that happens. I will not be able to control myself."

I wasn't sure what that meant, but I acted like I did.

"That's okay."

"No, it is not. The things I am thinking right now," he said, and swallowed hard, "I should be appalled at myself."

"Tell me."

"Fuck, no."

"Please... "

"No."

"What if... what if I tell you what I'm thinking?" I whispered, squeezing the tip of his penis.

"Agh... Hell no. Please do not, I do not want to know." He dropped his forehead to mine, his eyes cinching shut as I stroked him. His hands moved and became fists on the sides of my head as he fought to maintain composure.

"I want..." I began, my voice shaking, "I want to know what this would feel like sliding in my pussy... deep inside of me."

"No. No. No. Not now, not ever." He grunted and groaned at the same time. His voice sounded like gravel. "Do not say those things to me. I am struggling to hold on here."

I whimpered. I was throbbing. "I need to come and I want to feel this here." I angled his penis toward my entrance, which ended up being a bad idea. My eyes rolled shut and we both strained against each other.

"Christ," he thumbed my clit.

"That feels so good," I whispered, my voice foreign. Even between the clothes it felt incredible.

Kova moaned so loudly I shivered. "No… We cannot…"

"We can go back to my place."

"Are you fucking crazy?"

I answered him with a stare and a slight tip of my brows. Kova made me want to discover more about my body, and his. "I would never say anything, I'm good at keeping secrets."

"Exactly. All the more reason for nothing more to happen. Your father would ruin me if we fucked, because you know if we go back there that is what is happening. I am two seconds from ripping your clothes off as it is."

My jaw dropped. I was rendered speechless.

He shook his head frantically. "I cannot be alone with you anymore. It is not safe for a number of reasons."

"Then let's do it here," I blurted out.

"Not a chance."

"Please, Kova, I'm begging you. I want to do it. You make me feel so good, I want more of that feeling."

"I do not do *it*, in the sense you are thinking, Ria. I would hurt you. Sex is not always gentle and sweet like you assume it is."

"I know, I'm not naive to think that." I paused, then said, "Please I… let's go to my place. It's discrete and we don't have to worry about someone showing up."

His head snapped up. "You think you have this all figured out."

"Honestly, not really. I'm just going with feeling, and right now I know what I want and what I want to experience." I took a chance and swallowed. "And I think you do too."

Kova pulled away and sat back on his knees between my opened legs. I should've kept my mouth shut, then maybe we wouldn't have stopped. Immediately, I missed the heat of his body, the weight of him on me, his thumb caressing my nipple.

He ran a hand through his hair as I looked down between us. He was sticking straight up like there was a pole in his pants. He followed my gaze, palmed his big erection, and began stroking himself over his shorts. His chest was as red as a cherry and his tattoo caught my attention. I was enthralled by the pure sexiness before me. I'd never seen another guy do this and found it extremely mesmerizing.

"You are soaking wet," he said in a throaty whisper. "I can see it." He licked his lips. Heat rose up my chest and burned my cheeks.

Releasing his dick, he placed both of his hands on my thighs, pressing my legs down. His hands cinched upward, his thumbs digging roughly into my skin. I clenched my thighs when he neared my sex, wanting desperately for his hand to be there again.

In what felt like an eternity, he placed a thumb to my clit over my shorts. My back bowed and my head flew back, a loud sigh expelling from my throat

chapter 40

"**P**UT YOUR ARMS ABOVE YOUR HEAD AND DO NOT MOVE. STAY STILL, RIA."
I did as he ordered and kept my eyes trained on his. "I want to give you what you need. This is the only way we can do anything… I do not trust myself." I didn't question his sudden change of heart and allowed him to do what he pleased.

He began rubbing circles against my throbbing little bud, that exquisite feeling came back full force. My thighs flexed, and he stopped. "Still."

I nodded vehemently, then blurted out, "It's not easy to sit still when you're on the brink of an orgasm."

He paused and responded, "It will make it that much better for you if you listen. Trust me."

Kova continued his rubbing and as much as I loved it, I wished there wasn't a barrier between my pussy and his finger.

Another slow, but steady circle around me made me gasp. My heart climbed in my throat, sensations tingled throughout my body. My thighs quivered. A drop of wetness slipped out of me and I wondered if he could feel it. My chest rose and fell, my nipples were little pebbles as his breathing grew deeper with each stroke of his hand.

Kova applied pressure to his touch and I expelled a loud sigh, loving every minute of this intense feeling. Needing more, my hips started to roll but he stopped.

"What are you thinking about?" he asked.

"Nothing," I lied, and he pinched my clit though my thin shorts. My back arched, the pleasurable pain caused me to fade in and out. "Kova…" I whimpered.

"Tell me what you are thinking or I stop." He rubbed harder and faster. "Tell me," he demanded, and paused.

I whimpered, actually whimpered at the break, and then gave him the truth. "I was thinking about how I wish there was nothing between us, no clothes or anything, so I can feel your fingers…" I swallowed, "pushing into me."

He growled. "And?"

I eased into it, his thumbing sliding dangerously low to the opening of my shorts. "I… I wondered if you could feel me getting wetter… like, see it drip down my ass." Christ, my face was burning and I held in my breath.

"Ria, I do not know how to say this any other way, but take your shorts off. Now."

I froze, my chest burning from lack of oxygen.

"Take them off, or else I will," he said.

Insecurity clouded my head at the thought of him seeing me naked. "But you told me not to move."

Kova's deep rumble in his chest caused my fingers to tremble at the waistband. With two hands blurring in front of my face, he swiftly ripped my shorts off, leaving me exposed and my bottom half completely bare to him. And I let him, without faltering. Even though I was slightly apprehensive going this far with a guy, the need for his touch, to be closer to him, overpowered everything, and I succumbed to his demand.

"Fuck," he hissed when his fingers immediately danced across my soft, plump flesh. My first impulse was to close my legs, but I found the inquisitiveness in his eyes to be appealing, so I fought against my own instinct. He was in awe while he stared down as a shaky breath left his chest, rushing from between his lips.

"I did not realize how bare you really are," his voice cracked, muttering something in Russian. "Not a hair to be found. So smooth…"

I wasn't expecting the change in touch to be so drastic, but Kova gripped my inner thighs and yanked me to him. He leaned down to my center, his nose grazed my buttery soft skin and inhaled. He tilted his head to the side, feeling me with his face before his tongue slipped out.

I held my breath again. *He wouldn't.*

Peering up through his thick eyelashes, he purposely locked eyes with me. His mouth was just centimeters from my pussy when his breath rolled against my hairless sex. My hips twitched against him and I let out a loud content moan. This was pure torture.

"I do not know what has gotten into me, I feel like a crazed man." I could feel his words drift across my pussy. "You are so beautiful like this, the things I want to do, what I am thinking," he admitted, his stubble tickling me. "You are glistening, soaking wet and dripping on to the floor for me. I love that I do this to you."

On the floor?

My chest flamed hot, the blood pushing to the surface. My clit was throbbing in pain, longing for release.

The tip of his nose touched the top of my slit. "Spread your legs more," he ordered, his words brushing against my center. He paused, his eyes taking on a new shade of green. "May I?"

My eyes were heavy with lust and they rolled shut. He was asking me? He didn't need to ask, he could just take and I'd allow it. All I could manage to do was nod and wait for him.

He flattened his tongue and swiped up my sex from bottom to top, kissing it gently. My head flew back, my hands slammed onto the wood floor as a gush of air exploded from my lungs. Never in my life had I ever felt something so incredibly delectable, so easily addictive. It was like being high on drugs, not that I knew what that was, but I imagined this was better.

His tongue was soft and careful, and his eyes closed shut as if he was savoring me. My entire body was tingling, my head a hazy mess. I was growing wetter against his mouth when an orgasm began rising. I burned for release, desire pooling in my belly when his teeth scraped my clit.

"Oh, God, Kova," I whimpered. The pleasure was so intense I could cry from it.

Kova pulled back and I immediately felt the loss. I sat up on my elbows and asked, "What… what are you doing? Where are you…" I trailed off.

He didn't answer me. Instead, he got on his stomach and sealed his mouth back over my pussy. I fell back to the floor and clenched my inner walls when his finger unexpectedly delved in and out, exploring every inch of me, massaging over my swollen lips teasingly, down and back up, like he was memorizing me.

"So good." I rocked into his mouth. I couldn't help the little moans that escaped my throat. Just when I thought it couldn't get any better, he inserted another finger. I wondered if he knew I was a virgin, but my nipples tightened in response and my thighs trembled before I could think any more of it. I wasn't sure how much longer I would last. I was on the edge of paradise, ready to fly, when his mouth sucked my clit. I jumped.

Pushing a little deeper, he broke the suction and said, "You are so tight, I can barely get two fingers in. Relax for me, *malysh*. I promise I will not hurt you."

His words squeezed around my heart. For some inexplicable reason, I believed him.

I looked at his face and I saw something else. A vein throbbed in his damp neck and his eyes were wild green orbs. He was straining, besieged with disturbing thoughts. I didn't want him to regret this, to feel as though I pushed him, so I reached out and searched for his other hand. Finding it, our eyes locked and I put everything into my gaze. I laced my fingers through his and gave him a reassuring squeeze.

He was risking everything.

I'd never seen a man bite his lip from desire, but Kova did. He swallowed hard and entered me again. My thighs clamped around his head and his eyes rolled shut.

"Fuck, I am going to hell for this," he said, curling his fingers inside of me.

"Ahhh," I gasped, my hips bucked. "Oh, God." He pushed deeper, his thumb circled my clit and I cried out.

"Christ Almighty, you are so tight."

"Kova, please." He circled faster, licking his lips. I was so close to an orgasm I could taste it.

My hips rocked against his hand and I couldn't stop. I wanted him to push farther in, but he didn't, and I didn't want to ask for more. If I was being honest, I was kind of scared for more. Not scared of what he was capable of, not scared he would cause me pain, but scared of the unknown, the future, and what he could emit from me.

And make me want again.

On the brink of release, I paused. Kova placed his mouth back on me and sucked, and thank God he did. The dense air suffocated us, my heart beat frantically in my chest while so many thoughts jumped around my head until the rising peak took over and I forgot everything.

I cried out, moaning. My hips propelled back and forth, rocking slowly in pleasure as the waves ripped through me. Clutching Kova's wrist that was around my leg, I held on for dear life as I blew up from the pure rapture of his tongue, never wanting this moment to end. I groaned, and a deep sigh escaped my parted lips.

"That is it, *malysh*, give it to me," he said, circling his thumb and pulling the powerful tremors from me. Once the orgasm faded, my hand loosened and my knees collapsed to the sides. I stared up at the ceiling in bewilderment, wondering how I could get Kova between my legs again. That was quite possibly the best feeling I'd ever had in my entire life.

I was utterly sated. Kova sat back on his hunches. Looking at him, his mouth was covered in my juices. So much so that I was embarrassed. He grabbed my little shorts and began slipping them back onto me. Once they were on, I sat up and scooted closer to him, noticing the massive erection tenting his netted shorts. He had to have blue balls.

When our eyes locked, I expected to see anything other than despair through the black webs surrounding his eyes. My brows furrowed, my stomach dropped. He hadn't wiped his face yet but that didn't stop me from leaning in and kissing him.

Kova held the back of my head to him as our tongues danced erotically slow together. I tasted myself on him this time, and it quickly turned me on. Again. My body warming, yearning for another orgasm.

I scooted over his hips and settled between his legs. I worried Kova would push me away, but he did the opposite. He held me close to his chest, in a lovers caress like he hated the thought of leaving me. He was warmth and comfort and my heart embraced him. As he tightened his arms, his erection strained against us. My hips began moving in slow waves against the hardness. Kova's fingers dug into my head, desperation radiating from them. A growl tore from his throat and I whimpered, rocking harder, grinding until my clit hit him each time. I was almost there, so close again.

Kova leaned back and laid on the floor so I could straddle his hips. My hair caved around us, having come loose long ago. His erection was a different angle, and the tip slipped from his shorts and hit my belly button. He was hot and hard. I nearly melted into him, moaning in his mouth at the feel of his heated skin on mine, moving more frantically, feeling the orgasm burn below. His width hit every inch of my sensitive lips, sending me higher. He moved his hands from the back of my head to grip my hips and helped me rotate and grind into him, rolling my hips hard into his. He slipped a hand into my shorts and grasped my butt cheek, hard, hitching my leg up. The more I moved on him, the more his dick came out. I'd yet to see it and wanted to so desperately. I'd give anything to tear off our clothes and feel the real deal, feel my lubricated slit slide over him.

A whimper of pleasure escaped my lips. Kova growled, his length twitching between us. Little cries released as we feverishly kissed like untamed animals. Kova's hands tightened, squeezing me as my toes curled under his legs. I rode him as an orgasm tore through me again. He rocked into me as a cry of pleasure left both of our lips. Kova groaned deep in the back of his throat, shaking beneath me while I rubbed myself all over his dick greedily.

Perspiration coated my skin as I floated back down to earth.

"Adrianna," came out like he was struggling for air. Adrianna, not Ria. Kova loosened his hold. I responded by pulling back and meeting his pain filled eyes. My brows creased from the pinched looked on his face.

"Go, *please*," was all he said.

I swallowed hard, agreeing. Standing up, I quickly headed for the door. Just before I left, I paused when a draft of cool air brushed my torso.

Glancing down, I saw my sports bra had a damp circle on it. I noticed a drop of liquid the size of a pearl on me. Confused, I touched the sticky substance, and rubbed it between my thumb and index finger.

I looked over my shoulder at Kova. He was seated on his knees, but the position of his body struck a pang in my chest. He was bent over, his elbows on his knees with his face buried in his hands.

His raging erection was gone and I put two and two together. He came, and he was mortified by it.

In that moment, I truly felt the weight of our actions. Looking at him physically hurt me. Any normal person would've ran in the other direction, morally disgusted by his behavior. Probably even tell someone of authority. But I didn't, and I wouldn't. Especially since I didn't think it was disgusting.

After all, my dad was twenty-three years older than my mom. Age was just a number to me.

chapter 41

I COULDN'T MAKE EYE CONTACT WITH KOVA WHEN I WALKED IN THE NEXT MORNING. It was too awkward. Seeing the way I left him had been on my mind all night. Broken.

When I pulled up to the gym, cars were already lined in the parking lot. The sun was peeking behind the building, the gloomy gray sky being pushed up. Sunrises used to be my favorite thing to watch when I was feeling down, and it just dawned on me I hadn't seen one in months. A twinge in my chest resonated, a sudden homesick feeling streaming through me once again.

Normally, I was one of the first to arrive, but not today. I'd been a few minutes late, and typically that would've bothered me and earned some rather colorful choice of words from Kova, but I was panicking about facing him, so I sat in my car for a couple of minutes to avoid him. I highly doubted he'd say anything to me anyway.

When I stepped into World Cup, I quickly went to my locker and undressed. I had on a simple black leo today. My hair was already pulled back into a ponytail, but I decided to add a couple swipes of mascara and a thin, black line of eyeliner. Voices drifted down the hall and my heart sped up the closer the footsteps grew. I shoved everything inside the metal locker and waited for them to pass before I closed it. Once they did, I quietly expelled a breath and left the room, heading to the gym.

My feet hit the blue floor and I made a beeline to the warm up area to start my morning stretches, adding in the ones Kova had taught me during our private sessions. I specifically ignored meeting his gaze, but his presence could not be disregarded. It was impossible. The hair on my skin rose and the back of my neck prickled. I knew he was on the other side of the gym talking with another coach from the boys' team. From the corner of my eye, I could see Kova glaring at me, but I didn't look over.

"Hey Adrianna," Holly said, walking up to me. I plastered on a fake smiled.

"Since the coaches gave us tomorrow off, we were thinking about hitting the sand and having a beach day. Did you want to come?"

I paused. "What do you mean we have off?" I couldn't afford to take off time.

"Listen, we don't question our rare vacation days, we use them wisely. A bunch of us are hitting the beach tomorrow and some of our friends outside the gym are coming too. I'd love for you to join us."

I bit my lip. Reagan would be there. After the way she treated me, the last thing I wanted to do was spend any extra time with her. That being said, I missed the beach and normalcy.

"Sure. What time?"

"We're going early to get in as much time as we can. So about eleven?"

"I don't know where any beaches are here. Can I meet you guys so I can follow?"

"Of course. Want to come over to mine and Hayden's place and you can ride with us?"

I smiled big. "That sounds like a plan."

Holly turned to leave, but I stopped her. "Hey, Holly?"

"Yeah?"

"Thanks for inviting me."

Her smile reached her eyes. "Anytime."

I should've known better, read between the lines. Any time a coach gave time off, they pushed and worked you to the extreme first. I was talking boot camp drills made for Marines kind of extreme. At this point, rest sounded like a better option tomorrow instead of beaching it. Even death.

"Why are they doing this to us?" I asked Holly after doing standing tucks, back and forth across the floor. I climbed the rope in a pike position until my muscles ached, walked across the floor in a handstand multiple times, executed front walkover front tucks until I was dizzy, and performed so many press handstands on beam I'd lost count. And that was only the beginning. We did standing dismounts off the vault, body tension exercises and sprinted until we saw stars in our eyes. We still had bars to work. We'd been at it for hours. Conditioning to the eighty-seventh million power. My stomach muscles were hardened with soreness and I was on the verge of vomiting. There had been no time to think of anything else other than what my body was being put through.

Holly shrugged. "Your guess is as good as mine."

"I bet he's fighting with his girlfriend," Reagan chimed in and I turned to look at her.

"Who, Kova? What do you mean?"

Reagan gave me a droll stare. "Have you not noticed his behavior today? He's been mean and nasty all day, more so than usual. I overheard Madeline tell Kova to calm down and he fired back at her. I actually got scared when he did. I've never seen him speak so harshly to another gymnast, let alone a coach and it surprised me. That's how you know something isn't right."

I had a sinking suspicion I was the root of his issue.

"Yeah, but Madeline isn't any better," Holly added, giving her a sideways glance.

Reagan agreed. "Let's just hope this torture session will be over soon. I'm not sure how much longer I'll be able to stand."

Three hours later, we were allowed to leave. My entire body was in shambles and I couldn't remember a time when I just wanted to crawl into bed and die. My back, arms, and legs hurt. Everything ached so badly.

The worst part of today? My right calf blazed with a searing heat like it was on fire when I ran for miles on the track outside. The pain in my leg was intensifying by the day, but today it made its presence well known. I was close to complaining to the coaches but instead I popped some Motrin and dealt with it. Hopefully an ice bath would help.

Pulling into my complex, Hayden followed closely behind. After he saw me limping, he'd offered to come over and help. I told him it wasn't necessary, but he insisted and suggested an ice bath.

Dropping the bags of ice at my feet, I dug into my pocket for my keys and unlocked the door. I looked over my shoulder as I pushed the door open, "Thanks so much for helping me, Hayden."

"It's no problem," he smiled, holding two bags of ice in his hands.

We walked into my place and I flipped the lights on. He brought the ice into my kitchen and placed it in my sink in case it leaked.

"I suggest making some tea first."

I paused, pursing my lips together. "Tea?"

"Yeah, something hot to drink while you're sitting in the tub. It probably won't make a huge difference at first, but if you focus on the heat of the liquid, it may help a little bit."

I rummaged through my cabinets only to realize I didn't have any tea. It wasn't something I normally drank, so I never bought it. However, I had coffee. Lots and lots of coffee.

I spun around. "Would coffee do the trick? I don't have tea."

"Yeah."

Hayden walked into my bathroom and began filling the tub. As I pulled out a little coffee cup, I thought about how nice it was of him to offer assistance. I was used to being on my own and taking care of my needs, but fortunately Hayden wasn't afraid to speak up and be pushy. So when he firmly told me his plans, I easily agreed to them. Anything to ease the pending soreness.

Just as I finished brewing a cup of coffee, a clattering caught my attention. I glanced down the hall to the bathroom and spotted Hayden bent over, dumping the second bag of ice into the bathtub. I couldn't help notice how tight his sleeves were around his toned biceps or the way his back flexed under the material.

The sound of my cell ringing startled me. I grabbed it from my purse and shook my head at *The One & Only BFFFFFF* on my caller ID before picking up.

"How nice of you to finally grace me with a phone call."

"I could say the same of you. I don't hear from you for two weeks and then you get all pissy on me because I don't answer for a few days? I've been busy."

"Let me guess, you and your new beau," I stated mockingly. "A text would've sufficed, you know. Not the fuck you button eighty-seven times. I thought something happened to you. I was ready to put out an Amber Alert."

Avery chuckled at my exaggeration.

"Where have you been?" I asked, my voice malleable. "I miss talking to you."

"I know, I'm sorry." Avery paused and then said, "I got into a fight with my boyfriend. It's been pretty rough… I think we broke up, Aid."

I was surprised to hear sadness in Avery's voice. "So why didn't you call me and vent? You know I'm always here for you."

"I didn't want to talk about it, I guess. I'm really just upset over it."

"This is totally unlike you to be so down over a guy."

"You mean for me to be a sap?" she laughed sadly. "Yeah."

Then it dawned on me. "For you to be this put off could only mean one thing. You love him. You love him and I don't even know who *him* is." Avery's silence confirmed my deduction.

"Ave? Are you crying?"

"No," she lied. Her throaty voice gave her away.

My heart ached for her. "I can't believe how upset you are and I'm not there to comfort you. I feel like a shitty friend now."

"It's okay, I'll get over it soon… I hope."

An idea sprung to me. "You know, tomorrow I have the day off. I was going to go to the beach with some of the gymnasts here. Why don't you drive over, come to the beach, and stay the night? The next day would be boring since I have practice and all, but you can come and watch for a little."

"Aid, you're like a million miles away."

"Don't be ridic, three hours at most, and that's with traffic. You have to see the guys here and what they look like. Whoever you're pining after will be easily forgotten once you feast your eyes upon the eye candy at my gym. The boys' team." I knew what would entice her.

Avery perked up. "Boys' team? You mean Hayden?"

"Well, there are more boys other than Hayden, I just don't talk to them often. Doesn't mean I don't look though." I laughed, and so did Avery. "So you'll come?" She groaned and I pushed. "Please, Avery?"

"Oh, all right," she agreed, I could hear the smile in her voice. I jumped up and down, grinning from ear to ear.

Hayden appeared at my side, concern written on his face. "You okay?" he mouthed. I nodded frantically. "Yeah! I'm way more than okay!"

"Huh? What?" Avery's voice brought me back to our conversation.

"Oh, sorry. I was talking to Hayden."

Her voice heightened, surprised to hear his name. "Hayden's at your place right now?"

"Yes, he's going to help me soak in ice water."

"Ice water?"

"He's filling my bath tub with bags of ice and adding water. It helps relieve swelling and re-pair my muscles so I can train at the same rate I've been going at, or so I've been told. Today was brutal, quite possibly the worst day yet. I'll sit for ten to fifteen minutes or so and say a prayer."

"Interesting… and boring. So, I'll leave around seven tomorrow morning?"

"Perfect! I can't wait to see you!" I said excitedly.

"Later, girlfriend."

"I'm so excited! Be right back!" I yelled dramatically walking into my bedroom and shutting the door. I shuffled through my drawers for raggedy clothes. Quickly changing into ones I could wear in the tub, I opened my bedroom door to let Hayden know I was finished. I hadn't seen my best friend in many long months and tomorrow couldn't come fast enough.

"I can't wait for you to meet Avery. I've known her since we were in diapers." I was fixing my shorts and sports bra, waiting for Hayden to respond. When he didn't, I looked up and my cheeks reddened.

"Pick your jaw up, Hayden. You act like you've never seen me in such little clothing."

chapter 42

HIS MOUTH MOVED BUT NOTHING CAME OUT AT FIRST. "I HAVE, BUT…"
I chuckled, a rosy smile spreading across my face. "Just shut up," I said playfully. "Now come help me out."

"Aid…" I looked over my shoulder at Hayden scratching his head. "You've got a hot body. Seriously, it's rocking."

I knew my body had transformed over the past couple of months from the intensity of the workouts, but I hadn't realized just how much until he mentioned it. Standing in my bathroom, I stared down at the ice filled bathtub and bit the inside of my lip.

"So I just climb in?"

"Basically."

I took a deep breath, my chest rising high and put my hand out blindly behind me, searching for his. He wrapped his hand around my hand as my toe dipped into the frigid water and I squeezed his fingers.

"Shit."

"You just gotta take the plunge."

"I know," I replied, staring at the ice cubes. "It's just the initial step into the water that's going to shock me." I looked at Hayden and expelled a deep breath. "Okay. I'm doing it." I bit the bullet and dropped one foot into the icy waters.

My mouth dropped open. "Oh, my God!"

"Keep going."

So I did, and once I had both legs in the water, I looked at Hayden for strength. Goose bumps broke out across my skin and a shiver wracked my body. "I don't think I can feel my toes."

"Don't be dramatic."

I puckered my lips and crouched down. The worst part was going to be the water hitting my pelvis. Even when I would swim in the ocean, the cold was always so shocking to my hips and boobs. Once I got that out of the way, it wasn't so bad. But I had a feeling this wasn't going to be the same thing. Not even remotely close.

Holding my breath, I let go of Hayden's hand and slowly eased in. My hands gripped the side of the tub, my knuckles turning white as my butt hit the ice and I squeaked.

"Ahhhh… This is so cold!"

Hayden laughed. "Keep going."

Every muscle in my body constricted from the shock. I was immediately frozen and my teeth chattered. There was no way I'd last five minutes, much less fifteen.

The water hit my stomach and rose to my chest, slipping over my boobs. My stomach clenched. Thank goodness I had on a black sports bra, otherwise Hayden would see my pointed nipples. I drew in an audible breath and tried to lean back, but I didn't want to press my back to the cold ceramic. I was already cold enough and didn't need to add to it.

I swallowed. "Okay—I'm in."

"Now breathe."

"How do you handle this?"

He shrugged. "I don't really have a choice. When I have a hard workout, harder than normal, I'll do cold water therapy. Some say it doesn't work, some swear by it. I truly believe it helps with muscle soreness and inflammation. Today was brutal on all of us, and I saw you limping. You're going to be in bad shape. Maybe this will help you."

My lips were chattering, my jaw vibrating against my will. The goose bumps became part of me. "Yeah, Coach was a dick today."

"Which one?"

"Both." I paused. "Hayden? How come you're so nice to me?"

He tilted his head to the side. "What do you mean?"

"Well, for instance, you're here, helping me. You've gone above and beyond. Why?"

He shrugged. "I don't know… There's just something about you that makes me want to be around you. Girls can be catty. I have Holly, and being here with no one to lean on and training this many hours a day is a lot to handle for one person."

Hayden stunned me. Our eyes were locked while I soaked up the sincerity of his words. An appreciative smile curved my chattering lips. "Thanks," I said softly. "Your friendship means a lot to me." His smile faltered for a split moment and I felt bad. "So you swear this will help?"

"I'm not making any promises, but I have a good feeling it will."

"Hayden, if I tell you something do you promise not to say anything?"

"Of course."

Expelling a serious breath, I confessed. "Something is wrong with my calf. It's been hurting for weeks and today, I was close to asking to take a break."

"I noticed. Have you talked to the coaches about it?"

"No, because I can't afford to take time off to rest and I know it's what they'll have me do."

He tilted his head to the side. "Adrianna, you know you have to speak up now so whatever it is can be dealt with and doesn't turn into something more."

"But if I do, I'll be told to rest it. I can't do that, Hayden."

"Not necessarily. Maybe you just need some muscle therapy, ice and heat application. I don't know, but what I do know is that you have to say something. You're only hurting yourself."

He had a point. "Next time it hurts, I'll see a doctor."

After another three minutes, Hayden stood and held out an oversized white towel for me. "Drain the tub and step into me."

Nodding, I tried to stand, but my body was crunched tight. It hurt to move and it didn't help that it felt like there was a glacial breeze in my bathroom either. Gymnastics was not always sunshine and roses, I knew that. Pain was inevitable. Gathering the strength to stand up was one of those times when my passion and dedication was tested. I would rather be doing a million other things than dipping my body in subzero temperatures. I'd just have to cross my fingers that all of this would speed up my recovery and one day be worth it.

Glancing down to step over the ledge, my back was hunched over, afraid to take a step without assistance. My nipples were outlined through my sports bra and I had a feeling Hayden could see, but in this moment, I didn't care. I was freezing and wanted to get warm as fast as possible.

I nearly plowed into his arms. "Hold me tight," I begged.

Hayden wound the towel tightly around my body then ran his hands up and down my arms trying to warm me. "I've got you." I dropped my head to his chest, searching for body warmth.

"In about thirty minutes, you can take a warm shower. Until then, let's get you some of that coffee."

"Thirty minutes! I have to stay like this for thirty minutes?"

He was rubbing my back in circles when he said, "You can change clothes, but that's it."

Nodding, I ran into my room and pulled out the warmest clothes I could find—a fluffy pair of velour sweat pants and an oversized hoodie. I peeled off my shorts and sports bra and dropped them on the carpet. I didn't care they were soaking wet, I'd pick them up later. It was too cold to bother with panties and a bra, so I quickly slipped on the hoodie, fluffy socks, pants, and grabbed an extra blanket I had folded at the end of my bed and wrapped it around myself. Taking a deep breath, I was feeling a little warmer on the outside, but I was cold to the bone on the inside.

I was so thankful for the plush carpet as I made my way to the kitchen. Hayden's back was to me, and without thinking, I walked up to him and wrapped my arms around his waist, placing my head between his shoulder blades. He chuckled, turning around. His calming arms and charismatic laugh were honest and real.

There was a certain kind of comfort I found in Hayden I hadn't expected. I wanted to close my eyes and sigh. He made me feel protected and wanted, and I liked that. I wasn't just a concern. Hayden made me his priority. Our schedules were jam-packed and he had just as much going on as I did, but he went out of his way to make an effort to help me. There were no pretenses with him, at least I didn't think there were from what I'd seen so far.

He shook his head and gave me a genuine smile. "Do you want something warm to drink yet?"

"I do, but not yet. Can you just hold me for a bit first?" All I wanted to do was curl up to his side and feed off his warmth.

Without answering, Hayden bent down and scooped me up under my legs, cradling me to his chest. He walked over and sat us down at the end of the couch where I burrowed into his side. I needed this. Hayden tucked the blanket all around and under my feet and held me in his strong arms.

"Thanks, Hayden, for everything," I murmured.

"Anytime, baby," he said, slouching into the couch cushions.

I froze and his hands stopped moving. I had a feeling he slipped and hadn't meant to say what he did. Biting my bottom lip, I took a chance and looked up, propping my chin on his chest. Hayden's jaw flexed as he stared at me. Steel blue eyes were fanned between golden brown lashes. High cheek bones and honey skin. My heart sped up. Hayden dipped his chin down, his lips coming just centimeters away. His breath mingled with mine, hitting my parted lips as I waited to see what would happen.

"I want to kiss you, but I won't," he confessed. Instead, he just held me closer and continued to warm me up.

"Hayden? Where are you?"

My eyes flitted open at the muffled, frantic voice in the distance.

"Oh, shit. I must've fallen asleep at Adrianna's." Hayden spoke into his cell phone groggily. He rubbed his eyes with the heel of his hand. "Of course I am. What did you think happened?

My phone's been on vibrate." Hayden looked at me. "Nothing happened, Holls. Don't worry." He yawned. "The beach? I thought that was a girls' thing."

I tried not to listen to his conversation but failed miserably.

"Yeah, I'll go. See you then," Hayden said, and hung up.

"You know your volume is turned up so high I heard every word, right?"

He shrugged, his eyes half closed. "I didn't feel like lowering the volume, it's too much work right now."

I laughed and eyed him wearily. "To push a button?"

Hayden snuggled down into the couch and pulled me to him. Resting my head on his chest, he pulled the blanket over us and said, "Yes, it is. I'm beat and I need a little more sleep." He stroked my hair. "Sorry I woke you up."

"It's okay." I curled into his side and said, "I could get used to this."

I felt him smile against me. "So could I," he whispered.

We fell asleep for another hour and then begrudgingly decided he needed to head out if he didn't want to receive another testy phone call from his twin. Avery would be here soon and I wanted to be ready.

I quickly gathered my things, slipping on a bathing suit, putting on a little bit of lip gloss and throwing my hair in a messy bun.

chapter 43

WITHIN THE HOUR, AVERY WAS KNOCKING ON MY DOOR.

"Ave! I can't believe you're finally here!"

"Oh, my God, I've missed you so much!" she exclaimed.

We threw our arms around each other tightly before I hauled her inside.

Avery pulled back and looked at me. "You look really good. A little skinnier than the last time I saw you, but overall good. More muscle or something, like you hit a growth spurt." She paused, tilting her head to the side. "Can we still hit growth spurts? Because I don't think I've grown since I was thirteen."

I chuckled. "Thanks, Ave."

"Just don't get skinnier than me. Then we can't be friends."

I gave her a quick tour of my home away from home and placed her bag in the spare bedroom.

"So you ready to talk about the ex?"

Avery's face dropped as she ruffled through her bag. A knot formed in my stomach. She was hiding something and it bothered me.

Raising her anguish filled eyes at me, she shook her head and her voice cracked. "No."

I walked over to Avery and threw an arm around her shoulders. I pulled her to my side and gave her a good squeeze. She let out a heartbroken sigh. I hated not knowing what plagued my friend.

I noticed the time on the clock. "We better get going."

We jumped into Avery's sleek BMW and drove over to Hayden and Holly's apartment, exchanging small talk on the way.

"I didn't know you two were so...cozy," Holly said, eyeing Hayden and me after I pulled up with Avery.

My jaw dropped, and Hayden and I spoke at the same time.

"It's not like that—"

"It's not what you thin—"

We both paused and chuckled. "Really, it's not what you think, Holly. He's been really great, a shoulder to lean on. Nothing more."

A look of hurt crossed Hayden's face, but he quickly masked it. I'd caught it and felt awful at my choice of words.

Hayden's eyes shot to me before he stepped forward. "Holls, please don't make it more than what it is. You know how the gym is about relationships."

"Don't worry, I'd never say a word, even though you guys would make a cute couple," she finished with a smile.

My cheeks flamed and Hayden clapped his hands to change the mood. He slipped on a backwards hat and popped a piece of gum into his mouth. "Let's hit the surf and make the most of today, because tomorrow, it's back to hell."

❧

The sun was setting against an incandescent ocean while soothing shades of pinks and oranges streaked across the sky. I was wrapped in a towel, my feet buried beneath ivory grains of sand as I stared at the roaring waves.

This was my happy place, where I found solace. Where the weight of the world left my shoulders as I breathed in the salty air, exhaling the pressure I was plagued with on a daily basis.

I've missed this so much.

The beach was my serenity, and I was glad I'd asked Avery to come visit. Maybe it would help her sort out whatever was going on in her life. There was something peaceful and calming about the crashing waves and salty air. It was where I used to come to get away from my chaotic world living on the little private island. I'd sit and stare at the ocean for hours, kind of how I was now, and think about nothing.

A small fire had been lit when a few friends of Holly and Hayden's showed up. I'd learned Emily and Gavin were both gymnasts at another gym a few towns over. They met through Hayden in middle school and stayed friends ever since.

They sat with us and someone suggested a game of Truth or Dare. We started off with easy, mindless questions to get acquainted until it progressed into something more.

"Hayden, I dare you to go streaking," Gavin, Hayden's friend suggested with a devious grin.

"Ah, come on," Hayden responded, standing. Stepping away from the fire, he turned his back to us, stripped off his trunks, and took off running, his hands thrown in the air. "Yeah!" he shouted, running down to the ocean.

I laughed, covering my mouth when Avery yelled, "Turn around!"

I looked over at her, feeling her enjoyment. Gone was her sadness and in its place nothing but happiness. Her eyes were huge, and she had the biggest grin I'd ever seen. She smacked my arm and said, "Oh, my God. Look at Hayden!"

Sure enough, Hayden had turned around and was running back. He was too far away to actually see anything, but once he drew closer, he covered himself with his hands. Gavin threw him his board shorts and he caught them with one hand. He turned around and slipped them back on. We all grew silent while we stared at his perfectly rounded ass.

"It's Gavin's turn to go streaking!" Avery yelled jokingly.

Hayden looked at his sister. "Truth or Dare."

Holly rolled her eyes. "Truth."

"Have you ever skipped out on conditioning?"

She gave her brother a droll stare. "Of course I have. Who hasn't?"

"Emily," Holly said. "Truth or Dare."

"Truth."

"Would you rather have rips on both hands or straddle the beam three times?"

I cringed internally at her question. Been there, done that.

"That's a good one," Emily said.

Emily pursued her lips together in thought. She held her hands up, showing her palms, and waved her fingers. "I think I'd rather straddle the beam. That would heal much quicker than my hands."

"Ah, you guys are boring," Gavin said. "Someone do a dare."

Emily looked around at the group. Reagan leaned in and whispered something in her ear. My pulse thumped harder as both sets of eyes made their way to me. A sly smile slowly spread across Reagan's face and her eyes brightened. I knew it.

"Adrianna. Truth or Dare," Emily asked.

No way in hell was I picking dare. She'd dare me to do something that would completely humiliate me. So I went with truth.

"Are you a virgin?"

All eyes were suddenly on me. The only sound was the crackling of the fire and the waves breaking at the shore as she waited for my answer.

"Well?" Reagan pushed.

Picking up a handful of dry sand, I clenched it tightly, wishing I could chuck it at Reagan. She just took the game up a notch at my expense.

"Yes," I said, letting the sand shift through my fingers. She cracked a side grin and raised one brow.

"Is anyone else a virgin?" Reagan asked the group.

Everyone answered at the same time, so the only one to know who was still a virgin was myself.

"Are you a virgin?" I asked Reagan.

"No," she responded, and I was actually surprised by her answer.

"I guess there really is a person out there for everyone," I quipped. Avery sputtered her soda as she laughed and leaned her weight on me.

Reagan's brows lowered, infused with anger and spite. "Ava."

Avery snapped her head over to Reagan and glared at her. "It's Avery."

"Same thing. Truth or Dare."

I chuckled to myself. Avery wasn't afraid of much. "Dare."

A wicked smile spread across her face. "I dare you to make out with Hayden," she said, proud of her dare.

I looked over at Hayden and his eyebrows nearly popped off his head.

I knew what Reagan was doing. She was trying to hurt me. But what she didn't know was having Avery kiss Hayden wouldn't hurt me in the least. I considered Hayden a really great friend and nothing more. Though, it was clearly obvious she didn't see that.

Before anyone could say anything, Avery jumped to her feet and crossed over me to Hayden. She dropped her knees to the sand in front of him, whose blue eyes were filled with shock as he sat motionless. I knew from experience he wasn't a prude, or a virgin, yet he sat stone-faced still.

Avery didn't hesitate and grabbed Hayden's cheeks, pulling his face to hers. Just before she pressed her lips to his, he glanced my way for consent. I knew he was being nice so I smiled in return. Knowing Avery, she was going to put on a show just to piss Reagan off.

His eyes stayed on mine for another second or two longer until they closed shut and he kissed her back. I watched, along with the rest of the group, in silence as the dare went on a little longer than we all expected. Avery climbed onto Hayden's lap, his eyes stayed shut as his brows lifted high on his forehead again. He wrapped an arm around her lower back and threaded the other through her windblown hair and kissed her the way he once kissed me. With passion and intensity.

Someone cleared their throat and the kiss abruptly broke apart. Hayden's lips were flushed and swollen, his eyes wide as Avery climbed off him and resumed her seat next to me, like she didn't have a care in the world.

I shifted my eyes over to Reagan and took joy in her expression. She was seething over her dare backfiring on her.

I smiled from ear to ear.

"All right," Avery said, rubbing her hands together. "Who's my next victim?"

chapter 44

"**A**DRIANNA, COME HERE," KOVA SAID, GESTURING ME OVER WITH TWO FINGERS. I'd been at practice for three hours now working on bars. Only another hour or so before my lunch break and I couldn't wait. I was waterlogged from the beach yesterday, so any break I got was essential.

"Yes?"

He lifted my hand to his face and scowled. "I cannot stand the sight of your wrists. Go in my office and in my desk drawer, there are a pair of wristbands for you." He looked square in my eyes. "Wear them."

I flattened my lips and nodded. Kova had a way of making something so small feel like such a big issue. My wrists were fine.

"Hey, Ave," I said, smiling from ear to ear as I stepped into the cold lobby. She had slept over and came to watch my practice before she had to drive back to Palm Bay. Having her around for the past twenty-four hours had been really good and I was going to miss her dearly when she left.

"What are you doing?" she asked, sitting in a folded metal chair, her cell phone in one hand.

I shook my head and rolled my eyes, holding up my wrists. "Apparently this bothers my coach."

She looked at me, perplexed. "Your hands?"

"*The sight of your wrists offends me greatly,*" I said in my best manly Russian inflection. Avery sat motionless for a moment until she erupted with laughter.

"Are you serious?" she asked, grinning.

I raised my brows, nodding. "He doesn't like how I wrap my wrists and has new wristbands for me. I just need to grab them real quick."

Her brows scrunched together, her chocolate eyes zoning in. "Fish Lips has new gym gear for you? He bought them?"

I laughed, shushing her with a finger pressed to my lips. "Don't say that too loud," I whispered.

Avery looked around the bare lobby. "Stop being paranoid, no one else is here. Would you rather I say Coach Kissable instead?" She looked over her shoulder and through the glass at Kova, who was making his way across the gym. "In person, he really does have some nice lips, not to mention, a seriously rocking body. I could almost see his muscles. But does he always look like he's mad at life?"

I glanced in her direction, locking eyes with Kova. "For the most part. How long will you be here for?"

She looked at the time on her phone. "Not much long—"

"Come on, Ria. You are on a roll and I do not want to break it." Kova barged into the lobby, cutting off Avery. Surprisingly, he wasn't mean about it, and his unexpected compliment rendered me speechless. Kova rarely remarked positively on my practice, but I noticed he'd been doing it more and more lately.

The sound of a chair sliding across the floor broke my slacked jaw stare.

"Hi," Avery said, walking over to Kova with her hand outstretched. "I'm Avery, Adrianna's friend from back home."

Kova shook her hand. "A pleasure to meet you, Avery."

"Likewise," she responded. "I was just telling *Ria* here how impressive your gym is compared to the one back home she used to train at."

Ria. The voices faded away, leaving me falling into a black hole. She gave nothing away in her expression, but I knew what that one sentence meant. The beat of my heart thumped wildly in my ears as one word played on repeat in my head.

Ria.

All I could process was how I'd once told Avery my library "crush" was the only one who called me Ria.

Subconsciously, I knew Avery would never utter a word to anyone, but that wasn't the issue. There were so many problems at the moment I couldn't think straight on which one to tackle first.

I wasn't sure how much time passed when I heard Avery mention how she calls me Ria. Dear God. I was going to be sick.

"Nice to meet you, Coach," Avery ended with a megawatt smile.

"Same to you." Turning to me, Kova said, "I have to get something from my car. Grab the wristbands and meet me back in the gym quickly." I nodded blindly as he walked out the front door.

Lifting my apprehensive eyes to Avery's, I prepared for the worst, but I came face-to-face with a Cheshire grin instead.

"You got some 'splainin' to do," she said in her best Ricky Ricardo voice. It was terrible.

"Avery."

She placed a comforting hand on my shoulder. "Shh," she lowered her voice. "Say no more. Your secret is safe with me. But you can bet I'm going to wait until you break for lunch so we can talk."

I gave her a thankful smile.

"Just one question," she said.

My eyes widened. "Yeah?"

"You couldn't go for that cutie, Hayden? You had to go for *him*? Are you trying to get your ass kicked in?"

A low chuckled escaped me and Avery laughed too. "It just happened."

She hitched her thumb over her shoulder and gave me a blank stare. "*That* does not just happen. Hayden happens. Not Fish Lips."

I pursed my lips together, feigning a smile.

Avery's face fell. "Oh, God. What are you hiding?"

"Hayden may have kinda happened."

Her eyes grew wide and she playfully backhanded my arm. "You have some serious 'splainin' to do now!"

The sound of a deep voice caused us both to look over our shoulders at the window. Kova was outside pacing back and forth on his cell phone. He stared at the sky furiously, gripping the phone as a string of Russian left his kissable lips. The only thing I could make out was the name Katja. My heart kicked up a notch and I was starting to sweat.

"I better get back to work. He can be a real dick when he wants to."

Avery nodded and sat back down. "Go."

Walking toward Kova's office, I opened the door and made my way around his cherry wood desk.

Sliding out the center drawer, I fished around for the wristbands, moving pens and paperclips from side to side. I checked the drawer to the left and repeated my steps, but found nothing. Moving on, I opened another drawer, but something stopped it from opening completely. Bending down, I got eye level with the drawer and stuck my hand inside, trying to move whatever was in the way and pulled it open, shuffling things around the deep drawer looking for the wristbands. His drawer was a disaster and in dire need of organizing.

A lightly crumpled piece of paper caught my attention and I could see my name scribbled on it in thick, black marker. I debated whether I wanted to open it or not. I slowly stood with my back straight and the paper balled in my hand.

I mean, it wasn't my business, but curiosity got the best of me.

My Dearest Ria,

I find myself thinking of you more so than ever, knowing full well that it is beyond immoral.

Most days I am not sure what to do with myself. I am sick, angry, and most of all guilt ridden for wanting you in ways I should not. I hate myself for it. I am disgusted by it, and I know that it is wrong on so many levels. There should not be a fire that simmers within me every time my fingers grip your body in an effort to train you. Appalled over my thoughts does not even scratch the surface.

I have tried desperately to stay busy, to not look in your direction when you are working with another coach, but I have failed miserably. You are always there—on my mind, in my view.

But the worst part of all? Some days I do not give a shit that it is wrong. Some days I allow my thoughts to wander off and pretend you are not my gymnast. Because I have seen the way you look at me, I feel it in the touch of your hand on my body. I know deep down you want me just as badly as I want you. My body comes to life with a craving so unfathomable at the wishful thought of your innocent tongue caressing my skin, your timid hands roaming my body. You have created a profound ache I cannot seem to sate. Your iridescent, green eyes captivate me. Your drive to never give up, no matter how much I push you down, inspires me. You thrill me, Ria. You make me want so much, to take a chance and see what happens. Something as little as a conversation with you makes me forget our situation.

It would be the sweetest sin to have you just once. But a kiss would lead to another, and another, and then my hands will roam your perfect, youthful body.

Just like it has already. And I am afraid I will not be able to stop myself next time. I want to feel your lips pressed to mine, your naked flesh on me. Our heat infused sex saturating the air as I take your tight body. This does not even touch on the things I feel, and want, to do to you, all the while knowing it is so wrong. Morally wrong. Improper. Not to mention, forbiddingly against the rules. And law.

Jesus Christ, you mess with my head whenever you are near. You, my sweet Adrianna, are pure temptation. I know I should not want you. I should not even be thinking of you in this capacity, but I seem to have no self-control when it comes to you.

Oh, but the repercussions would be so worth it. I would even let you set the pace. At first.

See what I mean, malysh? I am all over the place, I cannot think straight. And if I do not release this need pulsing inside me, who knows what will happen.

I hate that I think of you in this way, that you do this to me. It is not ethical. I am a man who can only take so much and I hoped getting my thoughts out on paper would help deal with the situation.

I wish I could give you this letter so you could see the inner turmoil I am harassed with on a daily basis, but I cannot take the chance. I could lose everything if someone found out.

For now, Katja will have to do. But I am not sure how long I can suppress this need I have for you.

K

Oh.
My.
God.
What the hell did I just read?

Finding this letter was the last thing I expected in a million years. Bewilderment clouded my head as I stood in utter shock staring at the piece of paper between my trembling fingers. Coach Kova had these thoughts of me, and Katja had to curb his needs. The same thoughts I had of him nearly every single day.

Okay, not exactly the same, but similar ones.

Holy fuck.

Kova had deep seeded feelings for me and a state of want only he could fathom, because right now, it was blowing my mind trying to comprehend just how far it went. But the thought of Katja being the one to receive these deep desires didn't sit well with me. Jealously sprouted inside like a tree with roots growing in slow motion. It slithered around my nerves and squeezed my chest tight.

With shaking hands, I returned to searching through the rest of the drawer for the wristbands. I stood up and looked around, thinking maybe they were on the floor or a shelf, but again, I found nothing.

Expelling a thick breath, I walked back into the gym with my eyes trained on the floor and the letter folded tightly in my hand. I didn't want to make it obvious there was something wrong, but I couldn't make eye contact after his secret confession.

I clenched the paper tighter in my hand, frustrated by the fact that he couldn't say these words to my face. He had to write his feelings on paper where anyone could find it. We'd been open and honest and forthcoming with each other numerous times, it's what our connection built on from the start. At least I assumed it had.

Christ. The letter was profoundly personal. But why he left it in his desk at the risk of someone finding it puzzled me. The only logical reason for keeping it here would be due to him and Katja living together and he didn't want to get caught. Still, that wasn't enough in my eyes. The last thing I wanted was to be questioned about my inappropriate relationship with my coach. I wasn't sure how many people went into his office on a daily basis, but if anyone had found that letter, it would be the end of us. Gymnastics. My life. His life.

Opening the door to the sound of someone landing a tumbling pass on the spring floor, I chewed my lip raw as I headed for Kova. My heart was racing, my skin prickled from anxiety. This was going to be the most awkward conversation in the history of the world.

"Kova?" He looked over at me when I neared. "I couldn't find the wristbands."

"Well, then you did not look hard enough because they are there."

I flushed, feeling nauseous. "Um, I did look hard enough, but one of your drawers was stuck and I…um," I began to stammer. "I, um…"

"You, um, what, Adrianna? Spit it out." He mocked, running his hands in circles telling me to hurry up. Lowering my voice to a whisper, I said, "Something was keeping the drawer from opening. When I was finally able to open it and pull it out, I found this."

When I held my hand out, he looked down at the white crumpled paper. "I wouldn't suggest opening it here. You need to get rid of it, burn it, or something, anything." I watched a confused expression slowly form between his eyes. "Please," I begged quietly.

At first he didn't seem to know what it was, then the shock and revelation showed on his face. I looked around, making sure no one could hear our exchange. No one looked our way and if they had, it just appeared like Kova was instructing me on something. His cheeks flushed, but he quickly turned ghostly white and grabbed the paper from my hand, shoving it into his pocket.

"How dare you read this," he gritted through his teeth.

My jaw dropped. "How dare I? Maybe I shouldn't have read it, but I saw my name on it. How dare you leave it in your desk for anyone to find," I hissed. "You're lucky I found it and no one else did," I retorted. Kova looked down at me with an intensity I wasn't used to. "Please, get rid of it."

He took a deep breath and glared at me. "You are sure the wristbands were not in the drawer?"

I shook my head, perplexed once again. He was just going to ignore his little love note? "Positive. I couldn't find them. What are you going to do about this?"

Kova rubbed his jaw with his hand, his eyes distant. "I will take care of this tonight."

chapter 45

"**E**XCELLENT JOB TODAY, RIA. I AM VERY PLEASED WITH YOU," KOVA WHISPERED near my ear.

He placed his hand on my hip and gave me a tap before walking away. I fought not to look in the direction of his hand and I didn't pick up my head to acknowledge his comment. All I could do was nod. I wasn't exactly sure what that meant since the morning practice was just about over, but it was the first thing he'd said to me since finding the letter. Unless he was training me, he never openly touched me like this and it made me wonder if he even realized what he'd done.

"What did he say to you?" Avery asked when I strode into the lobby.

Lost in thought over Kova's praising words and how happy they made me, I stared at my best friend trying to decipher what she said. She was studying my face with a quizzical look then dropped her stare to my chalk covered hands.

"What?" I asked.

"Your coach. What did he say to you just now?"

I continued walking into the locker room and she followed me. "Nothing...that I needed to stick my landing if I want to add another skill to it." I dropped my bag at my feet and opened my locker door. As I went to pull on my pants, Avery placed a hand on my shoulder.

"I find it hard to believe that's all he said for you to have had that little smirk on your face."

My face dropped and my knees shook. Shit. She noticed the grin I thought I concealed. And here I thought I was being slick not looking up. Needing to come up with something quickly, I said the first thing that popped into my head.

"Wouldn't you be excited to hear you're allowed to add a half twist to your vault after working on it for so long?" I finished with a knowing smile. I was petrified someone would hear us.

Avery nodded slowly with an intent stare. She paused and said, "You're lying. I know you're lying."

I closed my eyes. "Not here, Ave. Wait until we get into the car. Okay?"

She agreed and backed off.

I thought about Kova's words and what they could mean as I put on my zip up jacket. "*Excellent job today, Ria. I am very pleased with you.*" He never complimented me to that degree.

We weren't in my SUV for more than ten seconds when Avery said, "Okay. You better start spilling now. I want to know every little thing that's happened and do not leave out any detail. If I find out you do," she paused and looked ahead, thinking about her next words. "Well, I don't know what I'll do, but I'll do something to you."

Stifling a laugh, I rolled my eyes. She tried to sound so intimidating and she wasn't in the least.

"You want all the juicy details?"

"Fill my cup right up!" she exclaimed, holding out her hand as if she was holding a cup. I shook my head with a faint grin. She pulled her knee up and turned to look at me.

"I don't know where to start," I said, pulling out of World Cup and driving onto the main road.

"How about at the beginning?"

Taking a deep breath, I exhaled. "Nothing really happened…We kissed. Big deal."

"Umm, that's a huge deal. Massive. So anytime you mentioned your library boy, it was really Kova. And considering the fact you withheld library boy for a few months until you caved, this has been going on a lot longer than I know."

I bit the inside of my lip. "Yeah."

"Okay, another lie. More than a kiss happened, then. The orgasms were from him?" I groaned and she smacked my arm. "Stop making me piece it together and do it for me. Did you guys have sex?"

I looked over at her. "No, we did not have sex. Honestly, Ave, I don't even know how it happened. Look how closely we work together, how many hours we spend one-on-one, six days a week. We just started talking one day during a private session and it carried on from there. He's actually a really decent guy when he's not in coach mode. Talking to him feels natural…I like it."

I told her everything that happened while I drove to our destination, not leaving out one detail or word, including the note I just found hours earlier. Deep down, Avery was trustworthy, but telling her was terrifying due to the nature of the situation, another reason why I kept it to myself. I couldn't skate over this slip though. And surprisingly it lifted a weight from my chest.

Pulling into a shopping center, I parked my truck and looked over. Avery sat stone-faced. She didn't move a muscle as she stared through the front windshield.

"Avery? Are you okay?"

She slowly turned my way, exorcist style, and said in a low voice, "You're going to hell for this."

My face dropped and I punched her arm. "No, I'm not. Stop acting like a fool. Let's go eat. I only have so much time."

We both hopped out and walked side by side toward a small outdoor restaurant. After such a grueling workout, I was famished, but my stomach was in knots so a salad was probably best.

"My cup is brimming, Ria, about to spill over. I didn't grab a tall enough glass. Then again, I don't think there's one tall enough for the juice you just poured me. I wasn't prepared for this onslaught of thoughts running a marathon in my head!" she exaggeratedly exclaimed.

"Don't be so dramatic."

"Please tell me you don't have serious feelings for him," she pleaded once we were seated. I looked around for listening ears and was thankful the outdoor tables were somewhat empty.

"Truthfully, I don't know. Do I like him? Yes, more so than I probably should. And before you say another word, believe me, I know how morally wrong it is. But I can't help it."

"You know it could never go anywhere, right? It just isn't possible."

I shrugged.

"You're smart, think about it." Distress etched her face. Avery took a sip of water. "Do you plan on having sex with him?"

I told her the truth. "I don't plan on it, but if it just happens, then I guess I will. Yes."

She gave me a comical stare. "It doesn't *just* happen, Adrianna. You can't just accidently fall and a dick slips into you. It doesn't work like that."

"Shh…" I said with a finger pressed to my smiling lips.

"Well, it doesn't!"

Before Avery could continue, a waitress appeared at our table. She took our lunch orders and then turned toward me.

"What kind of dressing would you like with your salad?" She rattled off a list of them when Avery spoke up for me.

"She'll have the Russian! She loves that slightly spicy, thick, creamy consistency in her mouth."

My jaw dropped and my cheeks were hotter than ever. I gave my best friend a murderous glare and wondered where the hell she came from. The waitress gave me a bewildered look and I confirmed it with a tight lipped smile. I asked for the dressing on the side and grilled chicken to be added.

"You're an asshole, you know that," I said when the waitress walked away.

Avery laughed loudly. "I had to! Okay, listen, I'm going to play devil's advocate for a minute."

"Oh, God."

"Even though I'm pretty pissed you didn't tell me, I completely understand why you didn't. I probably would've done the same. Thing is, whatever is going on between the both of you, I'd really consider stopping it now. This isn't just some older guy you randomly met in a giant skyscraper building you both work in. This is a coach who owns a reputable business and has a steady girlfriend. Not to mention, that pesky little age difference. Maybe if you were older, then I wouldn't say anything. But you're not. You need to really think about your actions and the ramifications you both will be faced with if you guys get caught. It could get ugly. It would be wise to stop while you're ahead instead of throwing it all away on some flavor of the month."

"Flavor of the month? Avery, where do you come up with these lines?"

She grinned, shrugging her shoulders. "My mom."

"I know, I know…I just don't know, though. I mean," taking a deep breath, I exhaled and looked at the parking lot. I had so much weighing on my shoulders and despite telling Avery, it was all coming back.

"I don't want to have these feelings for him, and call me crazy, but I don't think he wants them for me either. But after reading that letter, it's clear as day how he feels. It's like we're so aware of each other when we're in the same room, it's hard to ignore. He's my damn coach. A lot of people would be hurt, and regardless of right and wrong, these aren't flavor of the month feelings."

"Aid, you're only a teenager. Nothing serious would happen to you. He's risking his life doing this."

"I know, and I would lose gymnastics, he stands to lose much more." I paused. "Do you think it's all in my head?"

"No, but maybe there's a bit of infatuation that's driving it. Good looks, rocking body, Olympic gymnast…" she trailed off with a raised brow. "What's not to like about that? You'd have to be blind not to be drawn to him. Even in the pictures I looked up when you first met him, I was blown away. In person? There are no words. He's gorgeous."

"He has to know what he's doing and the chance he's taking, right?" I asked.

"That's the thing. You would think he knows…and maybe he does and maybe he just doesn't care. Men don't think with the right head. He knows how old you are, that's for sure. Common sense says red flag stay away, but his dick is like, young, hot girl, right ahead!" Her back straightened and she pointed over my shoulder.

I looked around to see if anyone heard Avery's fake British accent. "You should be a comedian with all the voices and reenactments you do. Was that from the *Titanic* movie?"

"Sure was," she said proudly.

The waitress brought out our lunches. I picked off the croutons and drizzled very little dressing on the salad. There was a lot of fat and shit in this dressing, something my thighs did not need.

Taking a bite, I chewed slowly as I thought about our conversation and my feelings toward Kova. "I'm just going to roll with the tide and see where it takes us. As long as we're discreet, we should be okay."

"Should, being the key word. Just be careful," she said and I nodded. "I don't want to see you get hurt…or him be taken away in handcuffs."

chapter 46

K NOCK, KNOCK, KNOCK.

Confusion etched my tired face as I tried to figure out who would be knocking on my door at nine at night. Throwing the duvet off me, I looked down at my outfit as my feet padded across the plush carpet. Black bikini panties and a cropped, pale pink, tank top wasn't proper attire to welcome visitors. It was rather thin and if I looked closely, I could see the outline of my breasts.

However, I wasn't planning on answering the door. That was, until I looked through the peephole and spotted Kova.

Dear God. What the hell was he doing here? My heart pounded fiercely against my ribs before it dropped into my gut. Taking a deep breath, I exhaled and unlocked both dead bolts and pulled the door open. The cool air caressed my skin.

Kova stood with one arm propped on the ledge of the door. His face was tilted down, despair written all over him and it hit me like a ton of bricks. My heart hurt for him. He dressed in dark distressed jeans and a jet black shirt. A firm body filled his outfit out and when he picked up his head, my lips parted.

"Kova," I whispered, staring into eyes as dark as the rainforest. "What are you doing here?"

A snarl erupted from his throat, the top of his lip lifting. He peered through his black lashes. "Is that how you always answer the door?" he asked before pushing inside.

"Yes, please do come in." Sarcasm dripped all over my words. "For your information, this is what I wear to bed. I wasn't expecting you, or anyone else." I paused, and gave him a droll stare. "And this really isn't much different than what I wear at the gym," I responded, shutting the door and locking it.

Turning around, Kova raked a heated glance down my body, his eyes landing on my chest. I followed his gaze and noticed my nipples were hard little pebbles from the cool air. I sighed inwardly. I hated when that happened.

Clearing my throat, I crossed my arms over my chest and stood confidently. "Is there a reason you're here?"

"We need to talk and I did not want to do it at the gym. I think you know about what."

I nodded and walked past him to the kitchen. Kova followed closely behind. Pulling open my stainless steel refrigerator, I grabbed a bottle of Aloe water.

"Would you like one?" I asked over my shoulder, but his eyes were on my ass. Seeing that I wielded a little power over him felt good, and I smiled. I knew I shouldn't like his eyes on me, but I secretly loved that they were, so I arched my back and naturally pushed my butt out to give him more of a view while I reached for a drink.

"No."

Turning around, I leaned against the fridge, my knee bending for my foot to rest flat on it. I stayed quiet and waited for him to explain his presence.

"Can you put some clothes on first?"

I sputtered on the water I was drinking, the back of my hand coming up to wipe my chin. "Are you serious?" I barked out a laugh. "Again, this really is no different than what I wear at the gym every day. Not to mention, you've seen other parts of my body no one else does."

He glared at me. "No, it's not. Not even close."

"Yes, it is. I'm not changing. I'm tired, and once you leave I'm going straight to bed. After wearing a suffocating leotard all day in the gym, this is much more comfortable, lightweight and feels like I have nothing on. My body needs to breathe."

Kova appeared to be struggling to breathe himself. "I'm asking you to please put something on."

Taking a deep breath, I rolled my eyes and walked to my bedroom and grabbed an oversized off the shoulder shirt I loved. I slipped it over my head, not bothering to remove the tank top first. When I walked back into the living room, Kova was seated in the middle of my couch. He was leaning back, his eyes clenched shut with his hands propped behind his head and his legs spread wide. He was tense, stressed to the max, and the air was thick with anxiety.

I made my way over to the couch and sat against the arm rest with my knee propped up. Kova glanced over with heavy eyes and sighed loudly, brushing a hand down his face. He reached for his back pocket, pulling out a plastic bag and handed it to me. The wristbands.

A gentle smile eased my face and my heart softened. "Thank you for these."

He nodded. "These should help your wrists much better than all that tape you wear. In fact, you should not need tape with these. They are bigger and longer, more durable with extra padding. Give them a try. If you like how they fit, I will order more for you."

"That was really sweet of you. Thank you…" I paused, swallowing. "Kova?" His eyes, goodness, they hit me hard when he looked at me. Anguish filled them. "Did you bring the letter?"

He shook his head, and for some reason, my heart ached for him. "I took care of it so you will not have to worry anymore. It is gone forever."

Quietly I asked what had been on my mind all afternoon. "Why'd you write it?"

He shrugged, looking at the ceiling.

"Why?" I pressed.

"Moment of weakness? I had been drinking…It was careless of me." Clearing his throat, he said, "After my mother passed away, I saw a therapist for a while. She suggested it may be therapeutic if I wrote my feelings out on paper. At first I thought it was the most ridiculous thing I had ever heard, until one day I gave it a shot and I felt a million times better. I have done it ever since. Habit, I guess."

I became even more conscious of his presence in my condo. I shifted to my knees and sat back, trying to ease the sudden throb between my legs. "Kova, your note could've gotten us caught."

"Believe me, Adrianna, I am well aware of that."

"You don't have any more copies, do you? Like maybe you rewrote it a few times and threw it in the trash can that's still sitting in your office?"

He gave me an amusing grin. I put up my hands. "Hey, I'm just trying to cover all my bases."

"No, that was the only one. Usually all I need to do is one and it helps."

"Did…did it help you to write about me?"

Looking directly in my eyes, he didn't hesitate. "No."

"Not even a little bit?"

"It just made it worse." He shook his head, baffled. His hands were fisted above his knees. "I see your drive day after day and it fuels me."

"But all the girls have the same drive."

"No, they have a love of the sport and that is what propels them. Not every gymnast wants to go professional. Some are content retiring after high school and not even continuing to compete in college. None of them wanted the Olympics like you do because they know how small the window of opportunity is. That is where we share the same goals, the same spirit. You remind me of myself. I see the determination in your eyes to keep moving despite the obstacles you are up against."

My stomach churned over his admission. Mainly for the fact that this whole time he's seen me in an entirely different light than I thought he did. I had assumed he looked down on me, detested the ground I walked on, when it was actually the complete opposite. It moved something deep inside me and for a moment, I felt guilty about everything.

"I'm sorry."

Kova's eyes narrowed, shock pouring out of them. "Do not ever be sorry for the passion that lives inside of you. It is a gift not everyone is given. It is refreshing to see."

Swallowing back the lump in my throat, I thought about his words in the letter, the sincerity behind them. He wrote his feelings out because he was unable to express them in a manner that allowed him to. It wasn't uncommon to pen one's emotions, but I couldn't get past the fact he hid them so well…or he felt such a way.

With shaky words I asked, "Do you…do you really feel that way about me?"

When Kova looked back at me he didn't conceal his emotions or feelings. "Every word."

My lips parted, a flush of heat hitting my body hard. His conviction rendered me speechless. "Why didn't you just tell me?"

"It is not so simple." Leaning forward with his elbows resting on his knees, he stared at the ground as if he was ashamed of his actions. "If you want to train with another coach, I would completely understand. Just say the word and I will change things around and make it happen."

"No," my voice cracked. "I don't want anyone but you." And I didn't. He was the best coach I'd ever had.

"You will do just as well with someone else at World Cup."

"No," I said, defiantly louder this time.

Kova blew out a remorseful breath and turned toward me. "Ria, I think it would be best. This thing," he shuffled his hands back and forth between us, "this thing has to stop. And with you being so close to me, me training you, I am afraid of what the future holds." The conviction was powerful in his eyes, I knew he meant it. "I need you to know I have never…" he ran his tongue along his bottom lip, "I have never done anything with another gymnast like this. I cheated on the woman I plan to marry someday. I could lose everything that means something to me. I could lose my reputation, my gym." I stayed silent and let him continue. Despite the ache and jealously spreading like wildfire in my chest, hearing he planned to marry Katja hurt more. "I never meant to take advantage of you."

I swallowed hard. "You didn't."

"It is fucking wrong and we both know it."

I got a little sassy because I didn't want him to hold all the weight. "You did way more than just touch if I remember correctly. You gave me two incredible orgasms." I bit my lip, heat tinted my cheeks thinking about how I rode him in the dance room. "It was the most—"

Fire blazed in his eyes as he cut me off. "I am fully aware of what I did," he snapped.

"So, why do we have to stop?"

"Are you serious right now?" Kova stood and began pacing my living room. "Can you not comprehend the magnitude of the situation?"

I stood and challenged him. "I do understand, but it's not wrong if I'm *consenting*. Do you not comprehend that?"

He shook his head and walked toward the door. My heart thumped wildly in my chest. I wasn't ready for him to leave yet, I didn't want him to go.

"Do not say those things to me. It is not the same thing, and it still does not make it right."

"I liked it, Kova, and I wanted it as much as you did. Don't blame yourself for anything."

He stopped dead in his tracks. "Do. Present tense."

I smiled softly at his correction as he turned and made his way toward me. Kova backed me against the wall in my living room. He placed his hand flat to the wall and angled his head down, pressing his forehead to mine. Tension radiated off him, the fight to walk away clear as day in his vacillating eyes.

"That is the problem. I still want you, Ria." He breathed into me and cupped my nape. "I should not, but I do, and it is so fucking wrong and sick. And I love it."

"I love when you say my name like that," I whispered honestly, staring at his lips. "Your accent is so sexy." I placed my hands on his firm chest and slid them up. He tensed, but I paid no attention to it. I wanted to kiss him again, to feel his lips pressed to mine, his tongue tangled with mine. The way he kissed me, so skilled and dominating, I loved the command he took. No one had ever kissed me the way he did. Confidence roared through me, so I grabbed a hold and took a leap.

My heart chased the anticipation as we closed the distance. Faces tilted, we touched lips lightly, and I whimpered into him. My hands tangled in his hair as he placed his hands on my hips and held me still. His thumb drew little circles on my pelvis, eliciting wetness between my thighs. I squeezed my legs together, trying to ease the sudden ache.

He didn't refuse me like I feared he might. Quite the contrary actually.

"Does it make me a pervert for wanting you so desperately?"

chapter 47

"**N**o," I RESPONDED IMMEDIATELY.

Because it didn't.

"Good, because if it did, well, I would not give a fuck. I want you."

Getting as close as I could so there was not an inch left between us, I leaned into his strong body. My breasts pressed against his chest and I kissed him passionately. He took the lead and set the pace, and I followed, which rewarded me with a squeeze of his hand. Our tongues swirled provocatively, mounting the desire between us. I knew this was wrong, but I didn't care. I didn't care that Kova could get in trouble, I didn't care he had a girlfriend he planned to marry one day. I didn't care about anything but this moment and seeing where it could take us.

Plus, I liked making him feel good.

One of Kova's hands trailed down my side and around to my back. He lifted the back of my shirt so he could cup my ass. He gave it a good, hard squeeze, biting my bottom lip at the same time. My eyes rolled shut as a light sigh escaped my throat. His touch was incredible, like a million little kisses coating my skin and I melted into him. His hips rose, legs spreading wider as the bulge in his jeans pushed against me.

My hands skimmed over his firm shoulders and chest. I was desperate to feel his skin under my touch. Giving him a slight grasp, my hips surged into his. I pressed hard and before I knew what was happening, Kova removed my oversized shirt and threw it to the floor.

As I went to lean back into him for more, he stopped me abruptly and pulled away by pushing my hands down. His fingers danced delicately over my collarbone to the thin strap of my tank top, slipping it off my shoulder. My breathing deepened, my shirt slowly rising and my nipples were hard little points, while his finger twirled across my chest but not dipping past the thin fabric. His hand slid around my neck, clutching me, his fingers brushing against my sensitive skin.

"Why do you do this to me, Adrianna," he said huskily. "Why do you make me want you so bad? You make me want you in ways that should make me ashamed."

"I don't make you do anything you don't want."

"No, you are right, but you do not make it any easier for me to stop either. You only push for me to take. My pleas backfired on me. You take and I want more, I want to give you more. I can see it, but I cannot stop my actions," he said honestly as the other strap fell off my shoulder with his help. The only thing holding up my shirt were my swollen breasts.

Biting my lip, I asked softly, "Would it be so bad?"

"More than you know."

I took a deep breath and arched my back, my breasts rising slightly into him with my hips. His finger trailed my skin so gently, clearly seeking permission to move lower. I watched the indecision in his eyes, the way a crease formed between them as he fought with himself. He knew right from wrong. A pang of guilt seized my heart for taunting him.

When he hit the plump part of my breast, he ran his tongue along his bottom lip again. The look in his eyes blazed a path of fiery heat across my heated flesh. Kova made me feel desired, wanted, like I was the only thing in the world that mattered.

"I want you." He shook his head, pushing my shirt down so most of my breast was showing except my rosy, pink nipple. His erection strained into my stomach and I found myself growing increasingly wet. There was something so deliciously forbidden about being alone with him in my condo where no one could find us, to do as we desired. My heart raged against my ribs, thumping so hard I wondered if he could see the pulse beating in my neck. My panties were sticking to me and his rough, calloused hand sliding up and down my waist wasn't helping. As my chest rose, my areola slipped past the rim of my shirt. Kova paused as I held my breath, and goose bumps pebbled my skin.

"The consequences could be damaging." He slowly pulled down the rest of my shirt, the back of his finger scraping my supple flesh. "But it is a chance I am willing to take," he growled, then sealed his mouth around my nipple. He sucked so hard my head flew back and hit the wall, I whimpered.

The neck of my shirt sat under my boobs, pushing them up and together, he palmed both and tried to suck my nipples at the same time. My tank top was loose, the straps around my biceps and I wrapped my arms around his waist. I stuck my hands under his shirt and raked my nails down his lower back and sides, bringing my hands around the front of him to his abs.

"Oh, my God," I breathed. "That feels amazing."

"I can tell by the way you are rubbing on my dick." I didn't even realize I was rubbing on him, but the delicious friction was building inside and I wanted more.

With his head tilted to the side, I leaned in and licked a wet trail up his neck. He made me wild with desire, and I couldn't stop the frenzy that tore through me. I attacked his mouth. My hands were everywhere, lifting up his shirt to feel his heated skin against my own as I kneaded and gripped him with everything in me.

Kova froze, swiftly stepping back until he was a foot away from me. "Fuck!" he yelled, making me flinch.

"What's wrong?" I yelled back. Talk about doing a one-eighty. I knew where this was going. Silence enveloped us as we stared at each other. Taking a chance, I acted purely on instinct, "I don't want you to stop. What don't you understand? I want this," I stated, adding emphasis to want. "If I didn't want this, I would be doing the complete opposite."

A tick worked in Kova's jaw. "You do not know what you want!"

"Oh, yeah? Says who?"

"It is nothing for me to make you want these things. I know where to touch you and how." Torture captured his eyes. "You are too young to know what you want. This is nothing more than lust for you."

I shook my head in disagreement. "You did this," I pointed to my bare chest, "to me." Walking up to him with my shoulders back, I reached out and boldly cupped his erection and stroked him through his jeans. His eyes rolled closed, a deep groan escaped him. His body hardened. "And I did this to you. If I didn't want this, if you didn't want this, we wouldn't have let it get this far." He opened his eyes, and I said, "Deny it all you want and go home to fuck your girlfriend, Kova." With a perfectly angled brow, I asked, "Isn't that what your note said anyway? That you have to fuck your girlfriend because you can't fuck me."

My pulse thrummed and I was struggling to keep my hands still and appear confident.

Never had I been so provoking when it came to us, but I was tired of being played and it was about time he knew it. All of his back and forth was giving me whiplash.

Kova's eyes were heavy, his lids dropping low. He took a step toward me, and I stepped back. He slapped my hand away.

"You know what? You are right. I want to be so deep inside you until you scream. I want to wrap those nimble, little legs around my hips and get as far in as I can." He stalked toward me until I couldn't back up any more.

"I want to watch your face as you orgasm with my cock buried inside you, your hands above your head so you cannot stop me from pushing all the way in." He gripped the base of my neck, his desperate words floating on my skin. "And the sickest part is that I want you to tell me no, I want you to fight me. But it would not matter, would it? I would take anyway. Because we both know it is what you want, is it not?" He picked me up and stormed to my bedroom, throwing me onto the bed and ripping my panties off with a fast tug before he could rest between my thighs.

"Wait." He didn't seem to process my request as a shadow slipped over his eyes. I tried to close my legs, but Kova had other plans. His thumb found my sex and all common sense left my head.

Kova's eyes were as dark as the night sky as he scanned my body.

"You are so fucking gorgeous it hurts." He shook his head in disbelief. "I have tried to fight it, this urge deep inside me to stay calm, but you are all I think about, all I want." He gripped my inner thigh and I bit my lip. "Your tenacity in the gym, the persistence to not give up no matter how much I wear you down, you are strong, Adrianna. You are a fighter, and that turns me on.

"I am going to show you just what your body needs." He paused, and softly added, "You are my greatest weakness. From the moment I set eyes on you, I have been fighting my attraction."

My heart swelled at his words.

Slowly, he removed his jeans and slipped his shirt off. He climbed onto the bed and settled between my thighs before I got a good look at his length. We groaned in unison at the flesh on flesh contact. My heart bloomed, loving the feel of his body on mine. The pressure, the weight, the heat of our bodies fusing together was a feeling I couldn't describe. Finally.

"Kiss me," I whispered, and he did. God, did he ever. He thrust his tongue into my mouth, taking me once again for all I had to give. His hands gripped my wrists, keeping them above my head where I was unable to touch him. Being restrained and wrestling against his hold was something I never thought I'd like, but it did things to my head that caused me to surrender to his every whim. Rolling my hips up in a wave, I moved so I could feel his hard length sliding against my inner thigh before it leisurely stroked my sex. I sighed breathlessly at the contact.

"Please, give me more."

"I am trying not to hurt you," he mumbled against my lips. His elbows were propped near my ears, caging me in. I felt safe and secure in his embrace and I couldn't imagine him actually causing me pain.

I whimpered, rolling a bit harder and slower again. I was rewarded with a sexy, deep groan and a thrust against my pussy. Fuck. Kova did this to me. He made my body want him in ways I never thought possible.

"If we are going to do this, we are going to do it my way. Got it?"

I nodded frantically. "Yes."

"Are you sure?"

My heart raged against my chest at the thought of losing my virginity tonight. He slid his bare length over the seam of my vagina and I inhaled with a gasp, nodding. I was soaking wet, and now he was covered in me.

A vibration rattled from Kova's chest against mine. The weight of his body and the muscle underneath his hard frame was exhilarating. To be dominated by such a man took over all rational thoughts.

He placed my hands on the headboard. "Hold on and do not let go. Understand?"

"Yes."

Kova sat back and fisted his cock in his hand. I finally got a real look and saw little trim hairs at his pelvis that lead to a long, thick shaft. He began stroking himself, slowly twisting his wrist up his length and squeezing the tip that was darker than the rest of him. Just when I thought he couldn't get any bigger, I watched his length grow. I could never get tired of looking at Kova's body, it was a work of art. He was sin, a man wild with lust, and I loved that I was the reason for it.

He leaned down and pressed his mouth to mine in a brutally hard kiss, tugging my tongue into his mouth. He slid his dick up and down my slit to coat himself and then pushed in.

I flinched. My legs automatically squeezed his waist in pain from the intrusion.

No preamble. No teasing. No foreplay.

I was ready, but it still burned.

And damn it all to hell, it hurt like a motherfucker.

But I didn't show it.

chapter 48

I COULDN'T.

He didn't need to know I was a virgin. Men didn't like taking someone's virginity because they assumed emotions were usually attached and that was something I couldn't let Kova think. The moan that vibrated against my chest from him made it all worth it.

This uncomfortable pressure inside me was foreign and not at all what I imagined it would feel like. My hands gripped the headboard tighter as I fought the searing pain of feeling like I'd been split in two, like a thick steel rod penetrated me. As much as I loved the fact we were finally doing this, I kind of wanted it to be over at the same time. The pain was intensifying.

I wanted to tell him to hang on, tell him to give me a minute so I could adjust to his width, but I didn't. The only thing I could think to do was start moving my hips to meet his. Even though I didn't know what I was doing or how, it didn't take a rocket scientist to figure out how to have sex.

Kova's hands were back on my wrists, gripping them so hard it actually hurt. "So. Fucking. Tight."

Believe me, I know.

Kova pulled out and thrusted back in, and I swear he hit my cervix at the same time he hit my clit. It was pain and pleasure combined, and for some odd reason it felt surprisingly good.

"Ria…You feel fucking amazing," he breathed against my neck, spiking my pulse. "Better than I imagined you would."

"So do you." I didn't know what else to say.

"I cannot stop." A vein throbbed from his neck.

"I don't want you to."

"You are so tight," he said, looking down at our joined bodies as his cock slid back in. "And I am not even in all the way."

Kova bent down on his elbows and licked a slow wet trail from my collarbone to my ear before taking my earlobe into his mouth.

"It is almost as if you are a virgin," he whispered before looking at me inquisitively. I froze and clenched around him. He bit my shoulder with a sigh as I tightened more. A hot breath escaped him and his head dropped to my shoulder. Kova growled, squeezing his eyes shut as his pleasure hit me in waves from the vibration in his chest. Our relationship was bound by honesty. I wasn't going to lie and say I wasn't a virgin. And if I had omitted something so important, I couldn't imagine the disappointment he'd feel. So I kissed him seductively hard, putting everything into it. He responded perfectly. There was no way he'd ever know.

Kova groaned when he pulled away. "Fuck, yes."

Instead of focusing on the searing, stretching and tearing pain, I focused on the bliss of the bite, the hold on my wrists, the way he kissed me, and the weight of his magnificent body pressed against mine. It was just enough pressure to make it feel good, like he knew exactly how much to apply. The painful strokes became welcomed ones and I started to soften. My chest rose into his, my hardened nipples grazed his heated skin.

Rising up on his elbows, he looked into my eyes before he cupped my face and leaned in for a kiss. Slanting his mouth over mine, his tongue dipped in as his dick pushed back inside me. The tightness I was struggling with was drifting away and I was finally beginning to enjoy it.

"There you go," he whispered. "You are loosening up."

"You could tell?"

He smirked, giving me a knowing look. Pushing deeper, Kova held it there. My breath caught in my throat and I rolled my bottom lip between my teeth.

"Like right now. I can tell it hurts for me to be this deep inside. You have a vice grip on my cock."

I swallowed. "Does it hurt you?"

He huffed, still wearing the smirk. "Hell no. It feels damn good."

"I've never been with anyone…like you. I'm not use to it." That was the truth, too.

Bringing his mouth to mine, he kissed me deeply. "Just relax and let me do it," he said against my lips, and I agreed. Maybe he sensed my inexperienced nature. I wasn't sure what it was. I was just happy he took control.

Reaching down, Kova hooked his hand under my knee and brought it up, placing it around his back as he reached a little deeper. A breath escaped my throat, somewhere between a sigh and a grunt. It was a different angle, but the smooth, even strokes made me enjoy it more than I thought possible as he hit my clit.

He slid in with ease, erasing the pain and replacing it with euphoria. Pleasure was completely taking me by storm and all I could think about was the fact Kova and I were having sex. My breath hitched in my throat, and I whimpered into his mouth. Quiet gasps escaped my chest. There was no way to stop it. I couldn't. The feeling of him pulling out and thrusting back in took my breath away. Long deep strokes with just the right amount of pressure. The way his fingers laced through mine, how he held my hands to the bed. The way his tongue slid down the column of my throat, tugging on my skin. And the way his hips picked up was a maelstrom of fire brewing inside of me. Every time he surged back in, he hit my clit…And God, it felt fucking amazing.

Pulling back to his knees, Kova gripped my hips. His hands nearly touched each other from the small width of my waist.

He kept the pace steady as his thumb slid over my clit and began rubbing in circles. My knees jumped from the unexpected touch and my hips rose off the bed. It was too much stimulation, too many sensations flying through my body, and I couldn't think straight.

Kova held still inside of me. With his eyes locked with mine, he brought each ankle to rest on each of his shoulders. Each position hit a different spot deep inside of me, so when he began moving again, I clenched my eyes shut and held my breath.

"Focus on the pleasure, Ria. Eyes on me."

I nodded, my body damp with moisture. His hand picked up speed and I felt an orgasm rising. Each time he thrust in, his thumb swirled faster and when he pulled out, he slowed down. Gone was the pain and in its place was sheer bliss. Nothing else. I felt high, like I was floating, feeling every inch, every sensation streaming through my body. My toes tingled, heat climbed up my spine…

"So, so good…" I moaned. "Right there…"

And before I could get another word out, an orgasm rippled through me and I yelled out.

My hips bucked roughly against his, quickly meeting Kova's as I rode out this high. A powerful surge hit me so hard, I swear I saw stars as a blissful wave of sex took over my body and I shuddered around him. I didn't want it to end. The incredible sensation flowing through my veins was an indescribable feeling one must experience to understand.

"I can feel you pulsating around me," he grunted, the veins in his neck straining. He had a rough hold on my hips as he held them to the bed, locking me down. He thrusted over and over, slowly riding me into a state of ecstasy, bringing my orgasm higher and higher.

My legs slipped off his shoulders, falling lifelessly to the bed. Kova collapsed on me, the weight of his body melding to mine was delicious, and I savored it. I gripped his neck and sealed my mouth to his in a brutal kiss. The gratification he brought me only moments ago was something I wanted to feel again.

And soon.

"Make me feel that again and again and again," I begged against his lips.

"Malysh, I am not done with you." Kova's hips thrusted against me, pulling his dick all the way out and slamming back in. My headboard rocked against the wall with each surge. With one arm, he lifted my hips off the bed so they were elevated while my shoulders were still flat on the mattress.

"Fuuuccckkk," a curse tore from Kova's mouth. His dick was twitching inside of me, and I was almost positive it became harder.

God, he was beautiful in the throes of heat.

Arching my back, I shuddered in his grip, feeling my wetness seep from my thighs.

Kova hissed then brought his mouth down to bite my nipple. Hard.

My body bowed and I screamed as he ran his tongue over the throbbing tip only to bite it again. My hands left the headboard and I gripped his strong biceps, my nails digging into his skin. I then pulled on the strands of his hair as pleasure once again ripped through me. I rocked hard against him, drowning in the exhilarated ecstasy that was taking complete control of my body.

"Ria," his Russian accent strong. "I need to come deep inside you."

Hearing his words, I moaned aloud. Before I could muster another thought, he pulled out and flipped me over so I was facing the bed. He pressed my head down and pulled my hips up with a yank.

"Arch your back, face to the bed. Now."

Then, he guided me to spread my legs open by tapping on the inside of my thighs. Gripping my pelvis, he jerked my hips up and angled them so I couldn't move. His dick was still erect and grazing my thigh, and just as I thought he was going to stick it back in, he shocked me to the core. I gasped loudly and tensed.

His warm tongue was flat on my vagina, where he circled my clit.

"Oh, my God," I sighed when he ran down the center and stuck his tongue farther inside me. All modesty out the window, I rocked against his mouth. Unexpectedly I clenched, feeling a heavy amount of fluid seep from me. He had to have me all over his mouth.

With his hand still holding me, I was at his mercy. But I didn't give a fuck so long as he made me blow up from pure rapture again.

Just when I thought I couldn't handle any more, Kova surprised me again by running his tongue all around, flicking my sensitive bud and then pinching my lips together and sucking them into his mouth. The pleasure hit me like a gust of wind and I rocked into his face.

With one last swipe, I thought this time he was done until he went past my sex…and to my ass.

I froze. As far as I was concerned, this was an exit only area. If he thought he was going to stick his massive dick in there when he was done licking me, well, he had another thing coming.

With one hand on each cheek, he spread them open. "Kova?" I asked with a shaky breath. "Shhh…"

"Kova," I was about to say stop, but when he pressed his tongue to my hole and began rubbing me with his mouth. I just about fucking died.

"What…what are you doing?" I asked breathlessly against my duvet.

I almost cried from the pressure that shook my body. I couldn't believe I was going to admit it, but what he was doing was highly stimulating. My hands gripped the blanket as he hit nerve endings that flickered through my body. Never in my wildest dreams would I have imagined the onslaught of feelings attacking me as he licked my ass.

Kova ignored me. Instead, he sat up and aligned himself with my sore sex.

chapter 49

"**A**DRIANNA?"

"Hmm…"

"Take a deep breath." My chest expanded. "Now, exhale. This is going to hurt but it will be so fucking worth it."

Kova pressed a hand to the swell of my back and surged into me in one long, swift glide. It hurt, he was right. God almighty, did it hurt. Tears sprung to my eyes and as I tried to sit up to relieve the pain, his hand held me down.

"Breathe."

Kova pulled out and a moan erupted from his throat as he slowly pushed back in.

"Are you okay?"

A long breath rolled off my lips. "I'm okay, it just hurts a little bit."

"As much as I love how tight you are, I need for you need to relax for me, *malysh*," he said.

Kova ran his hands up and down my ribs in an effort to soothe me. With him deep inside, he leaned down and dusted kisses to my spine, his hands coming around and cupping my breasts. His chest pressed to my back, he began to slowly rock into me without pulling out. There was something oddly calming with his body on mine the way it was, the buildup, the pressure of his weight. How large he was over me. Kova mounted me like he was trying to mark me. This position hurt so good and despite the pain, the pleasure was finally beginning to override it.

"You feel incredible. I want to stay buried in your pussy for hours." His nose dragged up the side of my neck. "But you know what I love?"

"What?" I whispered.

His hand slid between my breasts to wrap around my throat. He gripped it and I tensed.

"Licking your pussy. When my tongue moved over your clit, you leaked in my mouth." I whimpered, clenching around him. "It tasted better than I could imagine. So sweet and tender, soft and smooth. I could spend hours in your pussy."

I panted, a loud heated breath escaped me. I felt myself grow wet from his words. "Your pussy was made for me, Adrianna." The way he said my name, with so much passion, almost made me orgasm on the spot. "I am going to own it so you never forget what I feel like inside of you, after tonight, you will never forget me," he whispered harshly, grabbing my face and kissing me.

I was pretty sure I was never going to forget.

Sitting back, he quickened the pace and started moving his hands all over my body, squeezing my ass before he gave it a good smack.

I almost came undone.

Before I realized what I was doing, I was pushing back and meeting his hard strokes, silently begging for more. I spread my legs, needing a deeper angle. Kova's fingers wove through my hair, he twisted it around his fist and pulled hard, forcing me to stand on my knees. He pressed his mouth to my neck, his other hand pinching my nipple and holding me to him. My hips drove down on his, and I cried out at the new angle of him inside of me. I was so close to coming again, I wasn't above begging to do anything he'd ask if I could finish.

"Do you like it?" he whispered in my ear, the heat of his breath tingled my neck.

I nodded crazily, then he bit my neck and I shuddered in his arms. "Do you like my cock in your little pussy? Did you dream about it the way I did? Did you imagine me licking right here?" He asked, pressing a finger to my puckering butt.

Never had I felt the sensations pulsing through me as I did in that very moment, and it was then I realized I never wanted this feeling to go away.

"Did you imagine my hand sliding down your stomach and playing with your clit like this," he said, following the motion. When I didn't respond, struggling to clear the haze in my head, he asked, "Ria…" he gasped, "…you like it?"

I was moaning and groaning so much that I don't even know how I managed to get out, "I love it. All of it."

Then in all honesty, I said, "Kova? I want you to give me everything and anything you want to give me."

The moment the words left my lips, Kova unleashed everything he was holding back. Throwing me down to the bed, he grabbed hold of my hips from behind and began thrusting hard. There was no doubt I'd have bruises tomorrow from the way his fingers dug into my skin. I felt all of him, everywhere, and I fucking loved it. I was at his mercy.

Within minutes, I was coming again, rocking against him, feeling his balls slap my clit. My body was damp with sweat as a blast of pleasure shot through me. I was tingling with grat-ification, my body completely and utterly spent. There was no other feeling I could imagine that was better than this. Nothing could top it.

My vagina was tender and swollen, but Kova began pumping harder and faster. His fingers had to be cutting my skin, but I was too high on sex to notice. His hips smacked my ass so hard that I slid up the bed, and when he pulled out, I immediately felt the loss of him.

Kova's thighs quivered against mine and he made a strangled sound. Moving my hair from my face, I glanced over my shoulder as he came all over my back. His head was thrown back, his eyes were squeezed shut as white, warm fluid shot all over me, the vein in his neck straining. He had a vice grip on his dick, the tip of it purple as more exploded from him. His chest was scarlet as were the muscles in his arms from exertion.

Kova was singlehandedly the most erotic thing I'd ever seen. He leaned over and kissed my neck, his nose nuzzling me.

"*Malysh*, that was incredible, I could not ask for better. Do not move. Let me clean you up."

I was pretty sure I wouldn't be able to walk tomorrow—he didn't have to worry about me moving now.

Kova returned with a damp rag and wiped my back clean, and the inside of my legs. Having him clean me in the manner he was, was slightly awkward but intimate.

"Roll over."

I did as he ordered and he opened my legs and cleaned me there too. A look of relief eased across his face and I asked him, "What's wrong?"

He met my eyes. "I was worried I made you bleed with how rough I got, but there are only a few drops." Dropping the rag to the floor, he climbed into bed and turned me to face him. I curled up into him and stared into those bright green eyes. Kova's skillful fingers toyed with my hair, moving it around. Having someone play with my hair felt divine, but when it was after mind blowing sex, it was even better.

A few minutes of comfortable silence went by when he sat up on one elbow and leaned over me. Rolling onto my back as his hands massaged my scalp, I fell into the intensity his eyes held and submitted myself to him.

He whispered something in Russian as he leaned down, and just inches before my mouth, he spoke in English. "Adrianna, you are so beautiful."

Then he sealed his lips to mine and kissed me slow and deep. His thick tongue wrapped around mine, tugging as his hands never left my hair. He kissed me with passion, he kissed me with skill. Sliding a leg over mine, Kova climbed over my body and hitched my leg up around his hip. His growing length sat against my thigh, his knee pressed against my tender opening as all he did was kiss me senseless. With the weight of his body on mine, my heart was his in that moment. He consumed me, heart and soul.

Breaking the kiss, Kova pulled away and I looked into his grave eyes. Cupping my jaw, he confessed, "I do not know what it is about you, but I want you again and again. I want you all night, to take my time and explore every inch of you. Tell me no, *malysh*. Tell me no."

I didn't know how to tell him no because no was not a thought in my mind. I was guided by the hazy bliss of post sex and all I could do was stare into his eyes. And if this was it—if this was the only night I had with him, I was going to take everything he wanted to give. No was not part of my vocabulary when it came to resisting him, but as far as tonight went, it didn't exist.

I think he knew my answer. His thigh was wet from me rubbing on him. I'd lost count of how many orgasms I had, but I felt one more climbing. My hips gently swiveled on his flesh, my lips parted and my nipples were hardening. I couldn't refuse him, I didn't know how when my body was on the brink of pure rapture.

This time, I went in for a kiss, arching my back and finding his mouth. Kova pulled me to him and rolled to his back, placing me on top of him. With his leg propped up and wide, I panted and kissed his mouth as I rode his leg. I couldn't stop, it felt too good and I began clenching his heavily muscled thigh. I wanted to orgasm just like this, with his thigh pressing against my vagina. Kova's hands were all over me, on my back, in my hair, gripping my hips to him as my gasps became louder and more frequent.

"Come for me, just like this," he said against my mouth before biting my lip. Sex filtered the air and I was drowning in it. My hips bucked and I lost control, but despite being tender, I wanted him in me one last time.

Without asking, I lifted my hips and angled his shaft at my entrance and slid down, taking every inch I could. I was filled to capacity. Kova's fingers dug into my hips, the veins in his muscular arms appearing as he struggled. My back arched, pushing my breasts forward. Kova sat up and wrapped his lips around my nipple, sucking me and penetrating me at the same time. With one hand on the curve of my neck, the other wrapped around the back of my waist, Kova secured me to him. An orgasm quickly came, taking hold of us as we both fell into a state of bliss unlike no other while we rocked slow and steady against one another. It was subliminal. And the slow and steady was by far the best way. I moaned, whimpering in ecstasy. His penis twitched inside me, hitting the walls of my sex. Warmth seeped from between us, the heat of his orgasm coating my skin.

Pulling back, he pressed my forehead to his. My hair was everywhere, shielding the sides of our faces while we breathed in the hot air. We panted into each other, connecting at the seams as awareness coursed through us.

Pulling his soft dick out of me, Kova said gutturally, "Ria, you may be my undoing."

He cleaned me up once again and we lay in silence for a few minutes. My body was completely sated and my eyes were drifting closed when Kova spoke softly. "I could take you all night long and not get tired, but I need to get going."

My head was still a hazy field of desire consumed by lust. I didn't want him to leave, but I knew he couldn't stay.

Getting out of bed, I slipped some clothes on while Kova dressed. Once we were at the door, he turned to me. Gently taking my jaw in his hands, Kova pressed his lips to my forehead, lingering for a few moments. He angled my jaw up and slanted his mouth over mine, giving me his softest kiss yet. He pulled me in closer and I stood on my tiptoes as my hands wound around his back while he kissed me with everything he couldn't say. My heart soared through my chest, my emotions taking hold and grabbing onto him.

"Please, I hate to say this, but tell no one about us," his voice was a broken whisper against my lips.

I shook my head. "I would never," I promised.

Then, he was gone.

Bolting my door shut, my feet padded against the plush carpet until I was back in my room. Climbing between my sheets, I smelled Kova all around me. My mind played like a movie on rewind and fast-forward. Everything processed quickly, starting with how the day began and then ended. If someone would've told me I was going to lose my virginity to my gymnastics coach, never in a million years would I have believed them.

But it wasn't like it was planned. He came to me, waiting and watching for the right set to form. And when it did, I just rode it in with him. Just like the waves at the beach, once you start swimming at the curl, you have no choice but to take it all the way to shore.

Otherwise, you get pulled under and have to claw your way to the top to breathe.

Everyone who lives on the beach knows never to swim against the current.

chapter 50

I HADN'T BEEN INSIDE WORLD CUP FOR MORE THAN THREE MINUTES BEFORE I WAS surrounded by the sound of the apparatuses springing and the coaches yelling.

Anticipation bubbled in my belly as images passed through my mind of the things we'd done a couple of nights before. I was nervous. I hadn't seen him due to my schedule and his. I had no idea how he was going to act around me, and truthfully, I wish I could've called out just so I could avoid it.

After I switched out of my clothes and into my leo, I put my stuff in my locker. Paranoia flushed through me as I walked down the hall and toward the gym. I tried to act as if nothing was on my mind and keep a straight face. But everything changed. And it was all I thought about.

I lost my virginity to my coach. Though, I didn't actually see him as my coach. I saw him as Kova, a man with buried emotions and a bittersweet past.

A lump of trepidation sat heavy in my stomach. When my emotions and feelings got involved, everything melted away—his age, the fact he was my dad's friend, the consequences of our actions if we were caught. It was just two people connecting. But being back in the place that brought everything into context forced me to come face-to-face with our actions.

"Are you okay?" Holly asked, but I didn't hear her question. "Adrianna?"

I looked up. "Huh?"

"I asked you if you're okay. You look sick." Worry carved her face.

"Oh, I'm good. My lunch isn't meshing with me is all." The lie casually rolled off my tongue.

"Just a warning, Coach Kova is in rare form today."

My heart dropped. "What do you mean?"

"He's been walking around with a scowl on his face and barking orders nonstop. Even Madeline jumped at one point."

"That's not much different than any other day." I gave a nervous laugh. "But thanks for the heads up."

"Adrianna!" Coach Kova yelled, startling me with a loud clap of his hands and grabbing my attention. My eyes locked with his and my stomach tightened. "Two miles. Now."

Fuck. Two miles in this heat, he's insane.

I nodded hastily. I did a couple more stretches, the ones Kova had taught me, and then walked to my locker. I slipped on some shorts and sneakers then grabbed my headphones and iPhone so my run wouldn't be dull. Actually, running wouldn't be so terrible since I needed to get my thoughts under control before I started practice. And getting away from him and everyone noticing my strange behavior was probably best.

Not that anyone noticed. Paranoia at its finest.

Once my feet hit the pavement, I jogged across the street and turned on some music.

It wasn't long before I completed one mile and sweat was dripping off of me. A couple more laps and—

My thoughts stopped immediately when a searing blaze of fire traveled up my ankle and caused me to stop in my tracks. The air was robbed from my lungs. Jesus Christ, it hurt and I collapsed on the ground, clutching my calf. The sun was blinding and sweat poured down my temples as my fingers sought relief and massaged the muscle. Aside from practice, it seemed when I did any sort of running for long periods, my calf flared up. Maybe I needed to stretch out more, or maybe I was dealing with shin splints. I wasn't sure what caused it, but I needed to get it under control.

I did a couple of pointing and flexing stretches just on my left leg that hopefully would stretch out my muscle a bit more so I could finish running. Clearing my mind, I stood and wiped the pebbled dirt from my shorts. I started jogging again, ignoring the pain bursting from my ankle to my calf. I bit my lip, applying pressure to my other leg to relieve the impact on the injured side and fought it in spite of wanting to crumple to the floor. I pushed through the rest of the run and made my way back to the gym, limping in agony.

The moment I walked through the doors, the cool air hit my face and I sighed in relief. Georgia heat could be deadly. Between the pain and the humidity, I was lightheaded. I quickly grabbed a bottle of Aloe water my mom got me hooked on and drank half of it while sitting down.

I rummaged through my bag and grabbed a clean leo and went to change in the bathroom. I was sticky and hot. Stripping off my damp clothes, I slipped on a black leotard and then splashed water on my face. I patted the rest of my body with a towel and then applied deodorant. Looking at myself in the mirror, my cheeks were flushed and my green eyes brighter than ever. I fixed my ponytail, the scarlet undertones looked like perfectly placed highlights even though I never dyed my hair.

Luckily the pain at the back of my ankle had begun to subside. Just to be sure it wouldn't come back, or at the very least I didn't feel it, I popped some Motrin and then made my way onto the floor where I'd be practicing today.

Looking for Kova, my heart stammered in my chest when my gaze landed on his finely chiseled body. I chewed the inside of my mouth, taking in every inch of him when our eyes finally locked. He stood waiting for me on the floor, hands propped on his hips and shoulders tight.

"I am not getting any younger, so get moving," he clapped annoyingly.

I exhaled a sigh of relief. He was back to his normal Russian dick self. Maybe my anxiety was over nothing after all.

"Warm up. Sashays, handstand walks, front handspring passes, standing tucks across the floor. You know the drill. I should not have to remind you." He was right—he didn't have to remind me—so I wasn't sure why he was. Maybe if he gave me more than thirty seconds to be back in the gym, he'd see I was capable of doing it on my own like I'd done every other time.

"Then move on and do another pass of two back handsprings, ending in a full." He added, then stormed off. "Ten sets each."

My jaw dropped. Ten sets? We normally did three to five sets. Now he wanted one hundred—with fulls? After I just ran two miles, he was trying to kill me.

I shook my head and started up. The first thirty minutes I was good, then as I started my standing tucks across the floor, the ache was back in my lower leg, but so very light I worked through it. It wasn't until I progressed and began the double back handspring fulls that the pain blindsided me.

With both feet landing hard on the floor, I rebounded with a searing agony. Somehow

I knew if I didn't land easy it would end badly. So I tightened my body on the way down and landed as gently as I could on my toes to break the impact. I squatted to the floor and clutched my calf in distress, the air knocked from my lungs. I quickly massaged the muscle, kneading the ache, hoping to alleviate some of the burn, but it only aggravated it more. My stomach rolled in knots as I limped back so I could continue my warm up.

It was a stupid idea. The same thing happened after I did another tumbling pass, only this time I fell to the floor clutching my leg and gave out a little yelp.

Madeline rushed over. "What's wrong? What hurts?"

I flattened my lips and looked away. "It's nothing. I just landed wrong."

"It's not nothing when you look like you're about to cry."

I gritted my teeth and sucked it up. "I'm okay."

"Kova!" Madeline yelled across the gym, waving him over. "Take a look."

Kova jogged over, mumbling in Russian. He bent down to get a better look. "Let me see."

I pulled away and he tensed. His eyes darkened and nose flared, perturbed by my blasé attitude. "You seem to forget your place here. Give me your leg."

"I'm fine, I just landed wrong." I insisted.

With two hands, Coach Kova ignored me and began feeling around my ankle, twisting and turning, asking if it hurt. Then he grabbed the back of my ankle and pinched. I gasped in response, acting in reflex and yanked my ankle from his grip. He snapped his eyes to mine, and I panicked, falling back to my elbows because I knew what my reflex meant.

He knew I was lying. "Let us go."

"Where are we going?"

"Therapy room. I need a better look."

Tears sprung to my eyes at the realization I could have a serious injury. My heart pounded as I stared at the ceiling. I wanted to get this over with as fast as possible so I could get back to business. Every minute counted in my world, which meant I didn't have a second to spare.

Kova squatted down and scooped me up. This was the first time we'd touched since we'd had sex and I wondered if he realized it. He cradled me to his solid chest the way you would a baby. I wrapped an arm around his shoulder for support and dropped my head to his chest. He smelled really good and I tried to focus on his cologne over the pain. I was too distraught to make eye contact with anyone, so I kept my head down. His warmth calmed my emotions and brought me ease. An injury in gymnastics could go either of two ways: minor or catastrophic.

I didn't think mine was catastrophic, but I wasn't a doctor either. I knew there was no way in hell I could take a long period off to rest. I'd come too far since starting here for that to happen.

Kova carried me to the therapy room and set me on one of the exam tables with a deep blue, plastic cushion. As I went to scoot back, he stood in front of me and gripped my hips, shifting me gently. I had a hurt calf, I wasn't crippled for Christ's sake.

"Lie back." He stood on the side of the table, arms crossed in front of his chest grimly. "How long has your leg been bothering you?"

I bit my lip, deciding whether I should lie or not.

"And do not lie to me, Adrianna, because I will find out either way."

Shit. Kova lifted my leg. My knee bent as he propped it on the table. He began to examine me with his index finger and thumb. "A few months, I think. I can't remember exactly when it started, just have a roundabout idea."

"What kind of pain do you have?"

"My calf hurts. Certain activities cause it to flare up. It's like a burning sensation, but if I rub it out a little, I'm okay. Most of the time I just push through it."

"That was your first mistake. You never push through the pain, it will only prolong an injury. Keep going."

"Sometimes the pain goes into the back of my ankle. At times, when I point and flex, it hurts."

He began to massage the tender muscle and it took everything in me not to groan from relief. His fingers were magical. I clutched the edge of the exam table.

"Your ankle is swollen."

Looking down, I compared both and realized he was right.

"Did you ever at one time feel like the back of your ankle snapped, or did you hear a snapping?"

"No." He paused, looking at me for clarification. "I really haven't."

"I will call your parents and they will need to take you to the doctor to be further examined since you are underage and cannot be seen without a guardian present. Until then, we will massage it and ice it."

My stomach tightened and I sat up. "There's no need to call them. I can just wrap it up and I'm good to go. Really, I'm okay."

Letting go of my leg, Kova placed both of his hands flat on the table on the sides of my hips. Lowering his voice, he said, "Adrianna, I am not going to risk you being injured more than what you already are. This is my gym, and it is my responsibility to make sure everyone is safe and healthy to practice. From the looks of it, you might have a moderate Achilles injury. But without proper medical attention, I cannot tell exactly what it is or how to treat it, and until then, you will not practice."

My nails dug into my palms as I fought back the tears. Darkness surrounded me. My breathing became labored. There was no way this was happening. Swallowing back my frustration, I asked, "Can I at least ice it and finish today?"

He didn't answer me, just massaged the back of my calf. It felt heavenly, like he knew exactly how to work out my tight muscle with a touch of his fingers. Expelling a heavy sigh, I wiped the one tear that fell from my eye.

After a few minutes of attention to my leg, Kova quietly said, "You should wear shorts for now."

I eyed him, but before I could ask, his fingers grazed my skin. "People might ask what these are." Looking down, I noticed small circles of faint black and blue bruising on my upper thigh. They were close to my bikini line where Kova was feeling. I sucked in a breath and let him continue his gentle touch.

"I didn't notice them before," I said softly. "But I could easily say I bruised them on bars."

Concern carved his sharp jaw. He looked genuinely troubled from the bruises he left on me. "Do you have any more marks?"

I shook my head. "I don't think so."

"I hurt you," he stated more than questioned.

"You didn't hurt me, Kova," I whispered. "If you were hurting me, I would've told you to stop."

He paused, looking at me. "Would you have?"

chapter 51

I WANTED TO SAY SO MANY THINGS, BUT I COULDN'T FIND THE WORDS.

The air thickened as we stared into each other's eyes. Flashes of that night speared through my brain, flushing my cheeks and parting my lips. He knew my answer.

Kova's fingers trailed along my bikini line, dipping a little too far. My breathing slowed. We were in the gym in broad daylight where anyone could see what he was doing. Luckily his back was to the door of the therapy room, shielding his forbidden touch.

"It is hard for me to keep my hands to myself," he whispered so quietly it was almost hard to hear. "I cannot stop thinking about that night—how wrong it was, how good it felt to be inside you. How much I surprisingly did not care about the repercussions." His palm spread across my inner thigh, pushing it open. "Of all the years of coaching," He pulled me up to a sitting position to face him. "The persuasion from the mothers I fought off, the temptation of the gymnasts, then you come along and break it. I have been coaching for many years, had colleagues tell me about relationships with their athletes. I abhorred it."

My eyes widened, my heart stammered. The fiery heat of his touch only made my blood simmer more as I thought back to the night he took my virginity. My legs dangled off the table, his hands remained on my thighs.

The next words he uttered were ones I didn't expect. "It is not safe for me to be alone with you."

"Why not?"

"Adrianna, we cannot get into this here, but you know why."

He paused, then spoke the most devastating words possible.

"That night was a mistake," he confessed. My lips parted with my heart, a shallow breath bursting from my lungs. "On so many levels."

"Don't say that," I whispered, my jaw quivered.

He shrugged. "That is life. Do you realize I cheated on Katja, again? I have never once considered cheating on her, until you. Five years of a relationship down the drain, and I cannot even confess," he hissed softly, "because you are my fucking gymnast."

His fingers were digging into my legs, struggling to stay calm.

"If you regret it so much, then why are you here and not another coach?"

Kova didn't say anything, he just stood there glaring.

Smugly, I smiled and said, "That's what I thought."

I jumped off the table and limped toward the door. Before I could leave, Kova stepped ahead of me and slammed the door shut and locked it. He grabbed my elbow, turned me around and pushed me up against the door. With one hand braced above my head, his other held my thigh hitched around his hip. Thank goodness it was my bad leg, otherwise this straining would hurt.

Kova leaned down. Hovering above my mouth, I stopped him. "I thought you said relationships are banned," I panted.

"I make the rules, remember? I am the coach. You are the gymnast. And who said this was a relationship anyway? You have a lot to learn, Ria."

"This is much more than a relationship. You just don't want to accept the reality of it."

My leg hooked firmly around his hip as my toes struggled to remain on the ground. His hand slid over my thigh, rounding my ass to hold me to him. His erection strained against my center and my eyes flitted shut before I forced them open. His wild eyes looked into mine. Kova tilted his head and rolled his hips, a purr of pleasure escaped my throat.

"You confuse me," I said breathlessly.

"I confuse myself," he countered. "This is the one and only relationship you are allowed to have, if that is what you want to call it. Get rid of Hayden."

My eyes narrowed. "Hayden is just a friend, I really like him."

He gave me an amused stare. "I was not born yesterday. You guys are very close, too close for me."

"I'm not getting rid of him, he's the only true friend I've had since I've been here. I want him in my life."

"I do not like the way he looks at you. Or maybe you want him too?"

"He's just a friend." I reaffirmed.

"The looks you two share appear more than friendly."

Rolling my lip between my teeth, my eyes grew heavy. "We may or may not have kissed."

"You really know how to push my buttons." Kova flared, his lip curled. Revelation of his jealously coiled my belly. "What else happened? Did he touch you?" It was my turn to ignore him. He gripped my chin with his thumb and index finger. "There could be consequences for it, Adrianna. Do not test me."

"You mean test you more than I already have?" I quirked with a half-grin. Two could play at this game. "Hayden is staying in my life."

Kova leaned down and sensually nuzzled my neck, whispering, "When did this happen? Before or after I was deep inside your pussy and fucked you senseless? Did he touch you the way I did? Does he make you come like I can?"

A gush of air burst from my lungs. My entire body was about to combust. "It's none of your damn business."

With his eyes on my mouth, he pulled my face to his and crushed his mouth to mine. This was more than just a kiss. He kissed me with his entire being, surging into me. Kova's hips pressed forcefully into mine and marked his territory, claiming me.

I clutched his shirt in my fist, holding him tight, feeling his solid chest firmly pressed to mine as his mouth devoured me. I wanted Kova so badly, but I could tell he was holding back—and with reason. We were inside World Cup in broad daylight.

Reaching between us, I slid my hand down to his hardness, and grasped him through his shorts. He tensed. "I want this again," I admitted against his mouth, tugging on his length and bottom lip at the same time.

Kova pulled back and smirked, his emerald eyes gleaming with satisfaction. "Greedy little girl. I knew you would want it again."

Blood rose to my cheeks as wetness coated the fabric between my legs. What a cocky Russian he was and I fucking loved it.

"And what is this?" he asked coyly.

I paused, not understanding his question. He saw my confusion and reached down with his hand to cover mine over his growing erection. "What is this, Adrianna?" he repeated, and this time I understood when he squeezed my hand that was holding him.

Nervously, I bit my lip as my gaze wavered to his shoulder. My cheeks flamed in embarrassment once again at his question, unable to meet his gaze. I knew what it was, he knew I knew, but apparently he wanted me to say it.

"A penis," I said quietly.

"Wrong answer. Try again."

His deep, quiet voice had my heart pounding as my breathing intensified.

"Eyes on me, Ria." His commanding tone demanded my attention.

My eyes snapped back up, locking with his. "Dick. I want your dick."

He grinned, and God, was he gorgeous when he did. The kind of grin that soaked panties and made them drop—like mine. It made me wonder if he actually had stayed away from mothers and gymnasts like he said. He squeezed my hand in his again, and I could feel him growing harder.

Kova's head tilted to the side, his eyes flitted across my flesh. Leaning down, he placed his tongue on my collarbone and worked it up the curve of my neck. He pulled my skin into his mouth and continued until he hit my ear. God, what he was capable of making me feel.

"I want your tongue stroking me the way your hand is. Tell me, where is your hand, Ria?"

My lips parted. It was getting harder to breathe. There was no way to stop the shiver that racked my body from the feel of him on me, the way his words pulsated every vein in me.

He took a deep breath and exhaled slowly, the hot air trickling along my skin. "Try one more time." He whispered it ever so slowly right next to my ear and my legs almost gave out. I felt silly saying the word I knew he was waiting for. I hardly ever said it, and not many of my girlfriends back home had either, but then again none of them were in pursuit of an older man.

However, the reaction I drew from him topped it all.

Breathing in, I stood on my tiptoes and boldly whispered in his ear. "Cock. I want your cock, Coach."

He groaned hoarsely in my ear and it made my heart stammer. What was it about him that made me react the way I did to him? Kova's body tightened, his strength felt under the tips of my fingers as he internally struggled with the words I spoke.

A low growl rumbled in his chest, and I loved that I caused it. Being in the grips of a man compared to a teenage boy is something altogether different. It was an awakening.

"Exactly. It is *my* cock. And if you want it, you will have to learn to prove it to me. Do you want my cock?"

"Yes," I answered breathlessly.

Kova pushed into me with his *cock*. "Say it. And this time look me in the eyes."

I purred under my breath and it came out like a moan.

"Adrianna…" he groaned, and then straightened. "Do you really think you are ready for a relationship of this magnitude if you cannot use the word?"

I shook my head contradictorily and used the same line he used on me. "Tell me to stop."

He said nothing, but by the harsh look in his eyes, I knew exactly what his silence meant.

I stroked his cock, adding pressure to the head and said again, "Tell me to stop, Coach."
"Do not…"

My stomach tightened and I could hear my heart pounding in my ears. I didn't want him to end this after we only just started, but I also didn't want him to do anything he was opposed to either.

We stood inches apart, staring into each other's eyes, desiring so much more but not taking what we craved. I could read his internal battle knowing what he should do as my coach, as opposed to what he longed to do to me as a man. One glance at his hard body coiled with restraint and the greedy look in his eyes said everything.

I let go of his length and my shoulders sagged. Fearing I made a huge mistake, my eyes dropped to the ground unable to look at him any longer. I let out an exasperated sigh. I thought I'd read the craving cloaked in the indecision in his eyes correctly. Apparently, I hadn't, and it stung. This was my first real taste of rejection and I didn't know how to handle the onslaught of emotions it came with.

His decision was clear and I needed to get away so I could think straight, but before I could take another step from the invisible cage his presence held me in, Kova wrapped his fingers around my wrist, stilling me instantly.

Snapping my eyes to his face, I was confused when I saw his jaw grind down. He pulled my hand slowly back toward his body and placed it where it was before. On his cock.

"You did not let me finish before. Do not…stop is what I was going to say."

Leaning in, Kova was just inches from my mouth when a knock sounded at the door. We both jumped apart, equal parts of fear and shock matched both of our faces.

"Go to the table," he whispered ever so quietly. I ran, lied down, and crossed my arms over my chest staring at the ceiling. My heart was in my throat, the beat drumming in my ears so loud it was all I could hear. Nausea swirled the knots in my stomach and I fought shaking from panic. My mouth was as dry as the desert. There was no way I could make eye contact with whoever was on the other side of the door. Doing anything in the gym was careless and stupid.

Nervous sweat coated my body when the door opened.

"Madeline," he stated.

Fuck.

"Everything okay in here?" she asked, her eyes landing on me. "Why is the door locked?"

I froze.

"Forgive me. I did not realize it was locked. I have been meaning to replace the knob for that reason alone." The lie rolled swiftly off his delicious lips.

"Kova, Reagan's looking for you."

Kova rubbed his jaw before he spoke. "Ah, I will be out soon. I was just telling Adrianna she has to see a doctor before she can return to train. It seems she has been hiding an injury from us."

It wasn't far from the truth, but I needed to follow his lead so nothing looked out of the ordinary. I continued to stare at the ceiling as I spat, "I don't need to see a doctor. I just need some ice and a wrap."

Madeline turned to Kova and asked, "What's wrong with her?" He gave her a quick rundown.

She walked over to me. "You know, Adrianna, Coach Kova is right. If you don't seek medical attention now, you risk tearing your Achilles tendon completely and putting you out for weeks. I'd hate to see that after how far you've come."

I took in Madeline's heartfelt words and her concerned tone. For some odd reason, tears formed in my eyes. She was right, and in the back of my mind, I knew she had a valid point. I just didn't want to accept it.

Agreeing, I said, "I'll call my dad and let him know."

She brushed my hair back from my forehead. "If they don't want to come all the way over for just one appointment, I'll gladly go with you," Madeline offered.

I looked up at her and smiled gratefully. "Thank you."

"Of course. Just let me know and I'll be there," she returned the smile before she left the room. I may be stubborn, but I wasn't stupid enough to risk everything I've worked for. Being checked out by a doctor was the responsible thing to do, it just took a few moments to accept it. Downplaying an injury wasn't really the best idea. I was better than that.

Kova made sure the door was shut and then walked back over to me. He placed his hand on the table and peered down at me, looking almost nice and calm.

"Now, let me put some ice on you."

chapter 52

I T WAS NO SURPRISE MADELINE ACCOMPANIED ME TO THE DOCTOR.
Dad had been out of the state on business, and when I told my mom Madeline offered, she quickly agreed to let her. She said Madeline would be better off anyway because
she'd know what to do with the injury and treatment that would follow. She did, however, find
a reputable doctor for me, one well-known on this side of Georgia who could see me at the
drop of a hat.

Which was where Madeline and I were at the present moment. Dr. DeLang was a fairly
young looking Asian doctor only a little taller than me. Her petite frame contradicted her
stature and poise. After giving her a brief rundown of my injury, she ordered me to lie on my
stomach across the exam table with my legs hanging off. It was an odd position for sure, but
who was I to question her.

Holding my foot, she rotated and turned it gently around. I held my breath, nervous
about her diagnosis. "Your ankle is a little swollen. How does this feel?"

"Fine. It doesn't hurt too much." She pinched the spot above my heel. "Well, it doesn't
seem like you tore your Achilles tendon, I'd be able to feel it." Then she squeezed my calf muscle. "And you have good reflex. When does the pain start to set in? Any specific time?" She
patted me to sit up.

"Sometimes in the beginning when I start practice, but after a little while, the pain goes
away. I'll feel it come back once I'm home. Or sometimes when I'm running it will hurt."

"And your gymnastics training," she said, writing in the file, "is this a new schedule you
started, maybe where your body wasn't used to this type of pressure?"

"I started earlier this year…I went from twenty-five hours a week to nearly fifty hours a
week of training. What do you think caused it?"

She looked up. "Hmmm…I'm going to bring in the ultrasound tech to make sure the
tendon isn't ruptured. Medically speaking, I'd say your injury is due to overuse, doing things
too fast and too soon. However, it could be from landing wrong, the impact, or not warming
up enough first. It's a common injury among athletes."

"Is it treatable where I won't have to take time off?"

"Let's see what the scan shows first." Dr. DeLang smiled, and left the room.

Looking at Madeline, I said, "What do you think it is? I can't take time off, I just can't,"
I pleaded.

She rubbed my back. "Don't get upset. We don't even know what she'll say."

The ultrasound was performed, and another twenty agonizing minutes went by before
the doctor finally returned with the results.

"All right," she said, shutting the door behind her. "Good news. You didn't rupture your

Achilles." She smiled. "The bad news is that you have a pretty bad strain. There are a few options we have that can heal your injury."

I prayed to God she wouldn't suggest time off.

"Lots of good stretching before and after practice, icing your muscles every few hours, maybe an ice bath to reduce inflammation. Since you have to be on your feet a lot, taping it could help aid protection. Massage therapy is another one that helps. I'll get you in touch with a sports medicine therapist. You'll need to see her before you go back to training so you don't damage your injury any further. Until then, I can prescribe some medicine for inflammation."

Quickly, she scribbled something on a square piece of paper and handed it to me. "If you need anything or have any questions, just call and we'll get you in."

"Thank you," Madeline said.

"Do you think I'll be able to see the sports doctor soon?" I asked Dr. DeLang.

"I'm not sure what her schedule is, you'll have to call and find out." Flattening my lips, I nodded and thanked her.

Once we were in Madeline's car, I expelled a loud sigh and called my mom.

"Mom, it's me. I just left the doctor's."

"And how did it go?" she asked.

"I strained my Achilles tendon and need therapy. The doctor gave me a number for a therapist. Can I give you the number and you set it up for me?"

"No need. I'll find a doctor for you."

I paused, my forehead cinching together in puzzlement as to why my mom would find her own doctor. "Mom, I can't go back to training until I see the physical therapist. When do you think you'll call and make an appointment?"

"I'm pretty booked up today and—"

My heart dropped, my head flopped back. She'd make time when she could for me and not any sooner. Tears sprung to my eyes. "Mom, this is *really* important," I stressed.

"Not everything is about you, Adrianna. The world doesn't stop when you want it to. I said I will call, and I will when I get the chance."

Biting my tongue, I thanked her and hung up. Madeline drove toward World Cup. I stayed quiet while annoyance festered inside of me.

Madeline looked at me with sympathy in her eyes. "It'll all work out. Let's see what Coach Kova has to say."

"Thank you, Madeline, for coming with me."

She patted my leg. "Of course."

Pulling into World Cup, Madeline parked her car and we stepped inside. "Go sit in Kova's office and we'll be there soon."

Nodding, I made my way to the back, running into Holly.

"How'd it go," Holly asked as she shut her locker and faced me.

"Not good at all. I strained my Achilles tendon."

Her eyes widened. "Does that mean you're out?"

"No, luckily no. I have to do therapy though and just be careful not to tear it, I guess. That would put me out for sure."

Her mouth pulled up. "Be careful, with gymnastics that goes together like oil and water."

"Right? I gotta go to Kova's office and wait for him and Madeline. I'll see you later."

Brushing past me, Reagan flew in nudging my shoulder. "Going to the beach?" she asked, opening her locker. Her eyes scanned my attire with a scowl.

I looked down at my hunter-green, Victoria's Secret sundress and Tory Burch sandals.

Not wanting to give her the satisfaction, I rolled my eyes, ignored her, and walked away. After my doctor's appointment, I wasn't in the mood to deal with Reagan.

Stepping into Kova's office, I sat down and waited, thinking back on the conversation I had with my mom. Funny how in the span of a few minutes she could make me feel completely inconsequential. I'd asked her for help and she gave it to me. Asking her twice was a whole different story. Calling my dad would be a better alternative, and I decided I'd do it after I left here. I just hoped for once I took priority over whatever project he might have going on.

Within minutes, both coaches were in the office, Kova sat behind his desk. Madeline gave him a detailed update as I stared off, upset over the news. Devastation hit me. Angry tears formed in the back of my eyes. I couldn't believe this was happening after how hard I worked. Any injury, big or small, would hold back any athlete.

"Well, it could be worse," Kova said, gaining my attention after Madeline left, shutting the door behind her. His eyes stayed on my face as he spoke. "Good thing is you will not be out and it is treatable."

"You're not making me stay out until I see the other doctor?" Hope bloomed inside my chest.

"You cannot afford to be out, Adrianna. So you can do extra conditioning and light workouts for now. We will go from there. We may have to scale back some skills though." I knew it was a reach around comment, but I didn't care so long as he'd let me practice. "Since you are here, I should tell you that I signed you up for the Parkettes Invitational meet. We need to get you qualified as an elite, but first, you will compete as a level ten with your new elite skills and see how you do and go from there. This meet has some of the best level ten's and elites in the country competing, so this should be a good test for you."

The smile that spread across my face was ear to ear. Not exactly what I wanted to hear, I wanted to qualify as an elite, but I'd take it since this was a step in the right direction. "When is it?"

"A little less than three months from now—January. Which means we have a lot of work to do. Have you spoken to your parents yet about the injury?"

I groaned. There went my happy mood. Slouching back, I looked away and tucked a lock of hair behind my ear. "My mom, and she said she'll get in touch with a doctor when she has time." My voice softened. "I'd give anything for her to put me first, to show she really cares. She said she was busy, days could go by before she calls anyone. I was going to call my dad when I left here because who knows how busy—"

Kova picked up the phone and dialed away. "I will talk to him."

My eyes snapped back to Kova. We sat in silence, staring at each other with the phone pressed to his ear. I noticed he had a good day's worth of growth on his jaw and his hair was disheveled. Dark circles were prominent under his eyes, and before I could think better of it, I said, "You look exhausted."

His eyes weakened. Kova opened his mouth to speak, but I heard my dad's voice.

"Frank, it is Kova...Yes, she is okay." He told my dad about the doctor visit and treatment. "Adrianna said she spoke to your wife and she would call and make the appointment when she had time. Frank, time is not on our side, and I cannot stress enough how important it is that your daughter be seen soon. "

Kova stared at me, listening to my dad. "That is good, you will call me back and let me know? She cannot be out of the gym too long." He nodded. "Yes, she is right here." Kova held the phone out to me. I stood, reaching for it, but his desk was too wide, so I stepped around and stood next to Kova. Taking the phone from his hand, I leaned against the edge of the desk comfortably and lifted the phone to my ear.

"Hey, Dad."

"My sweet pea, it's good to hear your voice."

I smiled. "Yours too."

"How are you feeling?"

"I feel fine, the pain isn't so bad, and it's not a bad strain at all. I can push through it but no one will listen to me. I know what I'm doing," I said flippantly and he chuckled. "I talked to Mom… Do you think you can take care of everything for me please? I know she says she will, but this really can't wait. Coach said that he signed me up for my first elite meet, so I want to be ready for it."

"Don't worry your pretty little face. I've already got it under control. Kova will hear from me by the end of the day."

"Thanks, Dad." I paused. "I miss you."

"Miss you too, sweetie. I need to get back to work, but I'll talk to you soon. Put him back on."

I said my goodbye, and handed Kova the phone. I picked at my already chipped pale pink nail polish and stayed while he continued talking to my dad. I knew just as much as Kova did I couldn't afford to take time off. After all the long, rigorous hours I put in to get ahead only to take ten steps back? Not going to happen.

There weren't enough hours in the day, but come hell or high water, I planned to be at practice bright and early tomorrow morning.

Kova hung the phone up and angled his chair toward me, leaning back with his legs stretched open. He looked fucking sexy sitting back so casually with his head tilted to the side. His clandestine eyes were on my body. I wanted to know what he was thinking of for his lips to form a slow sexy twist and his eyes to sparkle when they met mine again. The air changed in the room. When we were alone, the intensity of his gaze always undid me, and I knew if I looked at him any longer I'd agree to anything he said.

The cell phone on his desk vibrated. Kova glanced at it only to reach over and silence it.

Staring straight at him, I said quietly, "You have to let me keep practicing."

"I do not have to let you do anything."

Kova was goading me. His phone vibrated again and this time I looked at it. I didn't get a chance to read the name on it before a grimace knotted his face and he sent it to voicemail.

"You and I both know I need to practice as much as possible. Especially if I want to reach my dream of the Olympics one day. I'll scale back on my floor routine if I have to, only practice on beam and bars to take the pressure off my ankle. I'm willing to do anything, just don't force me to take time off."

"Maybe it is not meant to be for you."

I saw red. "What does that even mean? Not meant to be for me? Why do you have to be a jerk all the time?"

He raised a brow. "I am going to let that one slide. Your body was not prepared for the kind of change you underwent and you became injured. Maybe going back to basics is a better idea."

Mumbling under my breath, I cursed him out in my head.

Kova tensed, leaning forward. "What did you say?"

"Nothing. I was talking to myself."

His office phone rang and I jumped not expecting it. When he leaned over his desk to look at the caller ID, his brows were pinched together and his shoulder brushed my thigh. I followed his gaze as he sent the caller to voicemail. It had to be important for whoever was calling and I almost suggested he pick it up.

Sitting back, he said, "Did you purposely wear that dress to taunt me?"

My head snapped in his direction, annoyed he'd think such a thing. His eyes were trained on my chest so I followed his heavy stare. My breasts were pressed together unknowingly by the pressure of my folded arms, giving me ample cleavage in my v neck dress. And by ample, I meant normal sized B cups on a good day. I hadn't given much thought when I slipped it on, but I guess subconsciously I wanted to attract his gaze.

Not surprisingly, the smug look Kova donned suited him. It wasn't often he smiled at gym, or even the few times I'd been alone with him. He was always so serious, so brooding, so…hot.

And let's not forget major asshole, either.

chapter 53

HIS EYES FLICKERED DEVIOUSLY AS HE ROCKED IN HIS CHAIR WITH HIS HANDS clasped casually in his lap.

His smile grew larger, and my heart began to melt. I realized in this moment I liked seeing Kova smile, liked seeing his cheek indent with a dimple and wished he did it more. He was carefree, and it dawned on me he was possibly flirting with me.

"Don't flatter yourself. I wasn't even thinking of you this morning when I got dressed."

His infectious smile only grew larger. I had to fight mine, and the shiver from the goose bumps on my skin. The phone rang again, and this time Kova reached for it.

"What," he snapped. A moment later he turned to his native tongue. He was short, clipped and angry. Quite the opposite just seconds earlier with me. "No, I do not want to do this," he bit back to the person on the other end. I was curious to know what the conversation was about and why he was abruptly so angry. When I heard the name Katja, I decided against it. Kova had opened up to me about his family life, but nothing about his girlfriend. I was curious to know about his relationship with her and how they'd come together, but decided today was not the day to ask with his sudden change of tone. "I refuse to—" he said, only to be cut off. I could hear her voice and she was just as heated. His eyes widened and a scowl formed on his striking face before he sputtered off in Russian again. His voice rose and his hand tightened on the receiver before he slammed it down with her still talking. He dropped his head to his hand and rubbed his eyes. Whatever happened couldn't be good. His body was rolled tight, fury radiating off him. A few moments of uncomfortable silence went by before I spoke up.

"If you think for one second I wore this dress for you, well, then, you're crazy."

Kova picked his head up and angled his body toward me, raking his eyes down my body. His shoulders relaxed and he leaned back in his chair, spreading his legs wider. This made me happy. I didn't like seeing him so bothered and upset. I couldn't help my eyes as they wandered over his broad shoulders down to the thick bulge in his shorts. There was no way to ignore the hard outline laying on his thigh. I tried to picture exactly how he looked under his clothes and my body warmed at the thought. He sat forward. His hand dropped to the side and his fingers danced up the back of my leg. His touch was as soft as a butterfly's fluttering wings and caused a rush of warmth to flow through my body. Expelling a slow breath, I fought it and didn't move, didn't show anything on my face.

"Oh, *malysh*, I am *definitely* crazy," he said in a low voice with a peaked brow.

I playfully slapped his hand away.

He only put it back.

"*Stop!*" I whispered with a smirk.

Kova chuckled, and God help me, I loved the sound of it, loved the big grin on his face.

"I don't know what you're up to, but stop it."

He shrugged as if he had no idea what I was talking about.

"What if someone walks in here?" His only answer was to skim higher up the back of my thigh. I slapped his hand away again and asked, "What has gotten into you?"

"Let us make a deal," he offered.

My head tilted to the side. "A deal?" I asked skeptically.

Kova clasped his hands together in front of his face like he was praying. He appeared deep in thought for a moment and then spoke, lifting his eyes to meet mine.

"I will let you come in tomorrow and train, do extra conditioning, even if I do not talk to your father or have an appointment set, if tonight I can see you. Of course your routines will have to be downgraded because I cannot risk you getting hurt, but I will not make you take time off. Taking time off really isn't needed. We just need to be cautious."

My jaw dropped. He had me thinking I'd have to take time off! And I think I stopped breathing for a second.

Kova stood up, forcing me to straighten my back as he stepped in front of me. His presence commanded attention and my heart gave it to him completely. This dominating, authoritative side of his is what lured me to him in the first place.

"I want to see you again," Kova admitted.

Dropping my hands, I gripped the edge of his desk as his leg brushed my thigh. He stepped even closer, so close there was hardly any space left to breathe, and I realized what I had felt hadn't been his leg.

The air crackled with tension, the chemistry between us was blatant. I could tell he was still on edge over his conversation with Katja, but I wasn't going to bring it up despite wanting to so badly. My heart raced, my skin prickled with the shiver I fought off. With my eyes cast downward, Kova trailed his hands up my arms, gently over my collarbone and around to cup my neck. He angled my jaw to look up at him where our eyes slowly locked. God, there were no ifs, ands, or butts about it. I was falling for Kova, and I was falling hard. His needy gaze captivated me completely. The swirling desire in his eyes, the way his eyelids lowered and his nose flared, the fullness of his lips. He stared at me like I was the only thing that mattered in the entire world. He was seducing me without saying a word, and I wondered if he felt the same way about me. Our ages forgotten in this moment of silence we shared, the obvious connection could not be denied. The intensity started to smother me. And my heart wrapped around a newfound emotion I couldn't name. I looked down, I had to. Kova had a way of making the world disappear when I was with him.

"Look at me," he said quietly. I shook my head. "Ria, I will not say it again." When I ignored him for the second time, his finger skimmed along my jaw and tilted my head up, but I closed my eyes.

With a breathless murmur, I asked, "What are you doing?"

He ignored my question. "Open your eyes." When I obeyed, his next words whispered across my tepid skin. "I have not finished tasting you." His thumb pressed down on my lip.

"It's not that easy."

"Oh, but it is." The back of his knuckles slid down my neck and over my clavicle. "Agree to my deal."

I hesitated, my mind going over what he offered.

His hand continued down, lightly brushing my breast. "Malysh…"

"What does tasting even mean? It sounds really odd." But hot, I thought.

He chuckled low under his breath. "Exactly why I need to show you."

"You don't need to do anything. You want to. There's a difference."

"If you had not come in here wearing that flimsy little dress and gold sandals, then maybe no deal would have been offered. But seeing you changed my outlook completely."

"But it's not even a real deal!" I retorted jokingly. He shrugged it off knowing I was right.

"So it's my fault you want to…*taste me?* Kova, your choice of words sometimes worry me."

The smirk that formed on his face almost made me smile. In fact, it did, and I laughed. Pressing a hand to his hard chest, I tried to push him back. He didn't budge. "No," I said again. "Go away," I chuckled.

Kova's hand dropped to my thigh, pushing up the seam of my dress. I half-heartedly slapped his hand away, worried someone could walk in at any given moment, but he quickly moved his hand under mine, going right back to his intended destination. He pushed my dress up higher on my silky smooth thigh, meeting the crease of my hip.

"What has gotten into you today? You're like a dog in heat." I clutched his shirt in an effort to push him away, but all I did was inch him closer. I was breathless, my heart raced as lust and adrenaline pumped through me.

A chuckle rumbled in his chest. "I think *your* choice of words worries me sometimes."

Rolling my eyes, I tried not to smile. "There is nothing wrong with my choice of words, thank you very much. Now, stop." I struggled with fighting his swift fingers as he tried to slip them into my panties. Heat coursed through me and I sighed into him. I really didn't want to stop, but after Madeline almost caught us, it would be wise if we stopped. I gripped his wrist and said, "Go…taste Katja and leave me alone."

"I already have. Many times."

"Getting tired of the same old…flavor?"

He shrugged with a smirk. "Quite the opposite, actually."

I growled, he laughed. His hand dipped past the lacy edge of my panties and I choked out, "Well, go do it again."

"I do not want her right now, I want you." His words caused a maelstrom of emotion and feelings to strum through me. "I bet if I touched you right now your pussy would be wet."

Shit. He was right, my panties were sticking to me, but I couldn't admit that. I tried to roll my hips back so he couldn't reach his destination, but I wasn't having any luck. He was fighting me, pushing me, and truth be told, I found myself smiling and laughing as he did. I tried to force him away again, but the man was built as solid as a boulder.

"Seriously, what does that even mean? Do we all have a specific taste?"

I nearly jumped out of my skin when his tongue licked a wet trail up my neck and his lips captured mine in a searing kiss.

"Do you like when I push you away?"

I shoved at him again and he stayed in place. I didn't want him to move and I was glad he didn't. I liked how he held steady, the strain and struggle between us. I clutched him closer to me and inhaled.

A low growl rumbled in his chest. "You could say that."

I thought about earlier and how he swiftly came back for more, how his hold became stronger. Acting on instinct, I leaned in and bit his bicep. Not too hard, but enough for him to pull back.

"I do not like it, I fucking love when you fight me," he admitted breathlessly, pulling back and nipping at my lips. "I like seeing the indecision in your eyes. It makes my dick hard."

His eyes darkened with desire and my heart flourished seeing his response. My belly fluttered. He looked like a starved animal and it intrigued me. It should have sent me screaming in the other direction, but there was no denying my body and how much I wanted to run to him. Knowing I could draw this reaction from him was exhilarating and empowering.

At the touch of his deft fingers reaching inside my panties, I grew wetter, and a frenzy of fire stormed through my veins, rocking me into him.

"Ah, I knew you would be wet." I tensed and fought a low moan in my throat. "Ah, so tight."

"Does Katja fight you?"

The slippery lubricant allowed him to slide a thick finger easily inside. I gasped and clenched around him. When his finger hit my clit, I trembled, gripping his biceps. My head dropped to his chest.

"Not how I want her to," he whispered against my neck.

For some bizarre reason, that pleased me. I loved how I was able to give him something she couldn't.

"Is she tight like me?"

He didn't answer my question and it burned my chest. Jealously flared through me because his silence was my answer. As much as I wanted to, as much as the heat made me want to agree to his every whim, I didn't think I should. Any time we were alone or intimate, I found myself wanting more from him. It was an emotion I wasn't used to or knew how to deal with just yet.

Now that I had his attention, I needed to bring him to his senses. A few more seconds and this was going to progress rapidly into something that couldn't be stopped, something that was very dangerous for both of us.

"What if someone walks in here?"

Gripping my jaw in his hand, he pulled me forward and held the back of my head to him as he kissed me hard and long, thrusting his tongue in my mouth aggressively enough for me to kiss him back. I wrapped my arms around his neck and held him close to me. He devoured my mouth with a vivacious tenacity I'd never experienced him do before. Full of zeal and hunger, and the tiny thread of control he was barely holding on to was palpable, tangible.

Kova pulled back. He removed his finger and brought it to his lips, licking his finger clean. He looked deeply into my eyes and panted, "Tonight, you are mine."

I slid out of his hold and sauntered away. When I got to the door, I stopped and looked over my shoulder when he called my name.

"Conserve your strength. You will need it for later."

"We'll see about that," I replied before exiting his office and shutting the door in his face.

chapter 54

SURE ENOUGH, KOVA HAD KEPT HIS WORD AND SHOWED UP AFTER DARK.
I didn't question how he got away from his girlfriend, and truthfully I didn't want to know. I was more than aware an actual relationship between us could never be, at least not any time soon, it still didn't change the fact that I didn't like him going home to Katja every night.

My nerves had been on edge while I waited for him. I wasn't sure he'd truly show at first, but I wanted to make sure I was ready just in case. When I showered after the gym, I carefully shaved every part until I was smooth and silky. I lathered every inch of my naked body in lavender scented lotion and air-dried my hair with a little mousse so the waves were fuller. Picking out clothes wasn't an easy task. I didn't want to appear like I was waiting for him, but I also wanted to wear more than pajamas. I went with a pair of simple rolled up, dark denim shorts and an off the shoulder oversized, ivory shirt. Wanting to be a bit audacious, I skipped the cami and bra I typically wore underneath.

It ended up doing the trick because when I opened the door to Kova, he had his hands threaded in my hair and his lips pressed to mine within seconds. He slammed the door shut with the back of his foot and devoured my mouth as he carried me down the hall to my bedroom.

"I cannot wait another second," he told me, and threw me to the bed. "You drive me crazy." My arms landed above my head and my shirt rose up my belly. My supple breasts tickled the sheer material and I knew my hardened nipples outlined perfect little circles. Heat strummed through my body as he peered at me with a craving so dark my stomach flipped. With a quick tug, he had my shorts off and on the floor, and he stood between my legs.

Kova dragged a hand down my stomach, twisting his wrist so he could cup me over my black panties, caressing my swollen lips begging to be touched.

His large hand slipped into the front and glided down the crease of my folds, one finger entering into me slowly. My hips undulated and Kova groaned. Looking between us, a thick vein was straining down his forearm. Why I found that to be so incredibly hot, I had no idea. He oozed muscular strength and sex appeal. His hips thrusted back and forth as if he was inside of me. He hadn't changed out of his basketball shorts, and his wide erection grew rapidly before me. I groaned, and became even wetter, gripping my bed sheets. It was almost embarrassing to be this wet.

Kova pushed his hips into my center which caused his hand to add pressure, making me moan. His thighs kept my legs open while his finger stroked every inch of me.

God, I could have an orgasm just like this.

I liked his strong touch, his powerful position over me. It was rough yet sensual. Skilled, like he knew exactly what he was doing, which was nice since I had no clue.

Pulling his finger out, my cheeks burned from the sounds accompanying the movement. Kova looked down and our heady gaze mimicked each other's. He slowly added another finger and the pressure was tight, but good. My hips bucked when his thumb landed on my clit and a moan vibrated in my chest. My hips began to move, gyrating on his fingers. More, I needed more, and I wanted it fast.

"Adrianna," he said huskily, pulling his fingers from my core. "I would love nothing more than to make you come like this, but I have other things in mind." He flattened his hand against me, hard, and I groaned again, his fingers resting past my pussy to my ass.

Fuck. He was teasing me.

The pressure and strength of his hand, his fingers resting low, felt so hot, I wanted him to touch me harder, grind his palm against my throbbing—

"Yes…" I sighed, loving what he was doing. It was like he read my mind. "That feels so good. Just like that."

Kova paused. "What does?"

Breathing heavily, I answered him honestly. "Your hand, how hard you're pushing on me. Soft touches are nice, but this feels a whole lot better. And I like when you hold my legs open." My hips rolled against his hand to show him and I spread my legs wider.

"Do you have any idea what you are saying?" Kova's eyes darkened. They were heavy from arousal, and his body tensed. He shook his head like he was fighting with himself to find the right words. "I like when you tell me what you want me to do. It is intoxicatingly powerful to know I make you feel so good."

I looked deep into his eyes so he'd know my words rang true. "You make me feel better than good, Kova."

"You are playing with fire."

"What do you mean?"

"Oh, *malysh*," he laughed throatily. Kova withdrew his hand, and reached behind his head and pulled off his shirt. "Let me show you."

The mattress dipped as Kova crawled over me on his knees. My fingers traced his granite-like abs, every indentation and every grove that carved his stomach was not missed. He drew an audible breath as my palms skimmed his firm chest and over his nipples. My fingers glided across the sharpness in his shoulders. Dropping his weight on me, Kova looked into my eyes before he kissed me senseless. My body circled around his, locking him in. His warmth spread across my body, our heat fused together. His tongue slowly delved in and out before moving to plant open-mouthed kisses down my neck, around my ear, and pull my lobe into his mouth. My back arched, pushing my chest into him. I was completely under his control and all it did was fan the fire even more.

My hands landed on his muscular back and I gripped him. Kova flexed under my touch and his hips began a slow and steady rock against my center. His erection pressed in and out, and I wondered if somehow he could feel just how damp I was.

Pulling back, he pressed his forehead to mine and squeezed his eyes shut. I was dizzy from his fervent kisses and clutched him tightly. Breaths of hot air blended together as we fought to steady ourselves.

Kova moved to sit back on his heels. His brow lifted, and he gave me the sexiest half-grin I'd ever seen as he pulled my panties off, then pushed my knees back out.

"Let me show you how I want to *taste you*."

Recognition hit and Kova smiled at my expression. *Taste you*…that's what he meant earlier. Fuck, this man was gorgeous and he wanted to do amazing things to me.

"First, I will get acquainted with your lips." He leaned down and ever so gently traced around and through the seam of my pussy with the tip of his tongue. A pleasure filled sigh rolled off my lips as I closed my eyes briefly.

"Does that feel good?"

"Yes," I moaned in agreement.

"After I warm you with my tongue," he looked up, and his eyes gleamed with devious thoughts. "I am going to stretch you out like this." He proceeded by pulling on my folds with force, suckling hard. His tongue speared inside and traced around my core.

I couldn't take it. This man. What he was doing to me.

I groaned, squeezing my eyes shut and thrust my hips into him. My legs wrapped around his strong shoulders. I wanted him.

No, I *needed* him.

All of him.

"Do not move. And keep your hands to yourself. Understand?" I nodded heatedly, not realizing my fingers were in his hair.

Fucking shit. I didn't want him to stop. He could have me any way he wanted when he was demanding like this. I'd do anything he commanded. The hunger for him bubbled, and the desire mounted like a volcano ready to erupt.

"Are you sure?"

"Positive."

"Good girl. Now where were we?" He leaned back down, and continued his wicked torment on my sex.

"After you are warmed up and stretched out, I will show you the steps it takes before you reach your dismount."

My mouth dropped and he grinned.

Dismount. Climax. Same thing.

Having Kova go down on me was both exhilarating and nerve wracking at the same time. While he had for a split second in the dance room that one night, it wasn't very long. I had no idea how much more I could handle this longer pace. The moisture dripping from me was slightly embarrassing and I worried he would find it unappealing.

"We will practice until you get it perfect."

His tongue swirled in and out, dancing all around, feeling every part of me. If he wanted power, I was going to give it to him. Reaching down, I threaded my fingers through his hair and pressed him into me, squeezing his shoulders with my thighs.

Abruptly, he pulled back. His green eyes now the color of a dark jungle. Wild. Untamed. Mysterious. Grabbing my wrists, he planted them by my hips, but I struggled against his hold. His fierce look told me I didn't listen to his no touching rule, and he was turned on by it. The power and strength he wielded was an aphrodisiac and I couldn't get enough.

"Do. Not. Move."

A gush of air rushed out of me as his tongue delved back inside, lapping and pulling at my lips so sensually I melted into the bed, and a moan left my throat. I rotated my hips in a wave against his mouth, completely unabashed by my actions. Each deep, luscious lick sent my head spinning.

Then he was frantic with need. His hands roamed around my body, everywhere. I knew he was holding back by how tense and tight his arms were, and I wished he wouldn't. I wished he'd let go and take me already, give me all of him, everything he had.

"Kova...Oh, my God. I'm so close."

He looked up and my heart stopped when our eyes locked. While we'd had sex, this felt so much more intimate.

The corner of his mouth tugged up with a dare, his eyes glittering with obsession.

"Go ahead and land your dismount."

chapter 55

HIS MOUTH RETURNED TO MY PUSSY AND A MOAN-FILLED SIGH GUSHED FROM ME as my eyes rolled back.

This feeling, his tongue on me, licking and sucking, was pure eroticism.

My back arched and I threw my head back as my hips rolled into his greedy mouth while he lapped at me. Kova's hands were firmly wrapped under my thighs, holding me to his mouth. The overwhelming sensations streaming through my veins had me panting loudly, gasping for air. Christ Almighty. I tried to fight Kova, but his tongue worked faster, hitting my clit. He locked me down and licked me with precision.

"Oh, God!" I cried out, my thighs tensing around his head. He slapped my outer thigh for me to loosen up and I quickly did.

"Kova, please, it's too much."

My body was a blaze of fire ready to erupt. My moans couldn't be contained and I cried out. My fingers threaded through his dark hair, clutching it in my fist, pushing my pussy into his mouth even more. Kova became ravenous. His grip on my thighs was powerful, and I wanted to give him everything in this moment. My legs scissored on his shoulders from the force of the pleasure slicing through me as he fought to keep his mouth in place.

Somehow when he came up for air, I managed to pull away and move higher on my bed. I panted, drunk on pleasure. My eyes, I'm sure, were just as glossy and matched Kova's. His mouth was covered in my essence completely, and I knew by the way he crouched low I should not have pulled away.

"Bad move, Adrianna."

He sprang forward and tugged on the hem of my shirt, pulling it off me in a blinding move. I was exposed, completely bare to him. Kneeling before me, he spread my legs open and grabbed them, hauling them over his shoulders. My hips lifted clear off the mattress, hovering in the air.

"No," I lied. What I really meant to say was yes, but telling him no did things to my head, and I couldn't stop.

Kova threw an arm over my waist and locked me in place, my boobs rolled up, and if I wasn't in such a state of crazed need, I would've been embarrassed by their placement. But I wasn't.

Leaning down, he said, "You taste incredible." Then he flattened his tongue and licked me from bottom to top. He flicked my clit and sucked on the swollen, little nub as I squirmed in his arms.

"I don't believe you," I whimpered. My body was flaming hot, my chest burning from pleasure.

"I could eat you every day and not get tired." He penetrated my pussy with his tongue, ignoring my statement. With my hips elevated, an orgasm was quickly rising. Different angle, different position, I wasn't sure why, and I didn't care. I began moaning, succumbing to him in a bliss-filled state unlike any I'd ever experienced before. My hips slowly rolled into his mouth as he suckled and devoured me with momentum and skill. One of his hands shifted and moved to rub my clit. The sensitive, little nerves in my body combusted into a million tiny, silver stars.

"Oh, yes, yes, yes," I moaned. I almost cried from the sheer impact of it all. His thumb rubbed harder and faster as the pleasure zoomed through me, my hips bucked against his mouth.

"Don't stop," I begged. The vibration from his mouth, paired with the tingly heat when his teeth nipped, caused me to blow up. An orgasm erupted, slamming into me hard and tearing through me with pleasure previously unknown.

But Kova didn't let up. He sucked harder, making slurping sounds as he took every last drop to the point where his tongue slid dangerously close to my ass to wipe me up. I couldn't stop making little noises, crying out from feeling such sweet rapture that rocked through my body.

My heart, as my body, was wholly his.

Once the orgasm subsided, Kova carefully lowered my hips to the bed. I was spent, a complete pile of mush with my legs wide open.

My heart, the same.

Coming down from the most incredible high of my life, heated eyes scanned the length of my body and my nipples hardened. A predatory hunger consumed his features while he kneeled between my legs. My eyes leisurely trailed down his torso. Rigid muscle from hours spent honing his physique coiled his stomach, but it was the vein protruding from his abdomen and disappearing beneath his waistband that drew all my attention. He gave me such a look that made me feel sexy when he cupped his shaft and stroked it over his shorts.

I placed my arms out. I wanted him to come to me. I needed him.

Kova gave me the most erotic come hither grin right before he said, "Now let *me* show *you* how *I* land a dismount."

Taunting me with his words and powerful body, his Russian accent blending with his hoarse tone made it almost unbearable. It was beyond physical at this point and had me on edge, nearly begging him to touch me more.

When his nose grazed my neck I whispered, "I like you, Kova." I finally placed my hands on his back only for him to tense.

"What? What's wrong?" When he didn't respond, I could only assume it was from my honesty, and I said, "This isn't fair. I'm getting tired of your hot and cold moods."

He pulled back and raised a brow, his eyes hard and silent.

"Yeah, I get it, but one minute you want me and the next minute a switch flips and you get all weird. You're giving me whiplash."

Kova mumbled in Russian under his breath. His playful, seductive mood was gone and in its place was Coach Kova. Serious. Meticulous. Perfectionist. *Dick.*

Running a hand over his jaw, he said, "Your candor catches me off guard and I do not know why it does since we have been nothing but honest with each other." He heaved a heavy sigh. Kova moved to get off of me, but I sat up quickly and grabbed his arm.

The urge to kick him in his balls, which I was sure were aching and blue, was stronger than ever. His eyes blazed. "You can't get mad when I'm honest with you. It's not fair to me or my emotions, or yours."

"Not fair?" he scoffed. "What is not fair is that I want you when I should not. I want you all to myself," he slapped his chest. "That is the truth. I want you to be mine in every sense of the word. I want to do dirty things to you I should not even be thinking about. The images…" he broke off, and shook his head. "I visualize myself bending you over and taking you as hard as I can, knowing you will bleed and loving it. I want to see your eyes water while you deep throat my cock. Tie your hands behind your back as I take you to new heights you have never even imagined. So you know what I have to do? I have to fuck my girlfriend the way I want to fuck you, I think about *you* while I am deep inside of *her* because I do not want to hurt you." He paused, and said, "And most importantly because it is wrong and yet for some obscene reason, I love that it is. I thrive on the risk of getting caught, thrive on thinking of you while I fuck her. This was a mistake and I should have never let it happen again, yet I am glad it did."

Commence ball kicking. He was purposely taunting me so I would fight him back.

"A mistake? Liar," I spat between clenched teeth, angry that he'd dare utter those words. "You're the one who put this into motion this morning at the gym, not me."

Kova paused, his eerie stare hitting me hard.

"I am a liar?" he breathe whispered.

"Yes, you are. I can see it in your blazing green eyes you're worked up, the illicit thoughts running through your head. It's obvious in this too." Kova sucked in a breath when I reached for his cock. "Tell me you don't want me," I said. His hand immediately gripped my bicep so hard it was possible I'd have a bruise in the morning.

"Worked up?" He bit back. "You do not know what worked up is. And that was only the cocktail hour. That was not even enough to whet my appetite."

Christ, that hurt. If he wanted to play games, fine. I'd fight back how he wanted, anything for him not to leave.

"Oh yeah? Then why can I feel you growing in my hand, huh? I feel your *cock* getting bigger. Harder." Leaning in closer, I lied and said, "Just like when Hayden's cock grew in my hand." Kova's eyes took on an unnatural shade of green. I began moving my hand to rub him. "Tell me you don't want it. That this was a mistake. That each time we were together was a mistake."

"Why do you want this so bad?" his voice cracked. "Why do you push me?"

Biting my lip, my eyes softened with my heart at the despair in his voice. I shrugged. This back and forth was really starting to get to me. I could tell it was getting to Kova just the same.

"I don't know, I just do. It's a feeling I can't explain. I like being around you, Kova. I like talking to you, I like your presence. Don't tell me you don't feel the same way, otherwise you wouldn't be here." I swallowed hard, praying my next words wouldn't be thrown back in my face. "You feel it, don't you? This connection? The chemistry? It's why you keep saying it was a mistake, isn't it?"

"You took the words out of my mouth." He shook his head in disbelief, clenching his eyes shut over his admission.

A gentle smile eased my face when he opened his eyes and looked at me.

"You need to let go of me." He groaned as I began working him through his shorts. His hips thrusting into my hand contradicted his words. "This is a dangerous game we are playing."

His chest began to move—slower, deeper breaths he thought he was hiding from me. His hand loosened on my arm and slowly, very slowly, began to slide down to my wrist that stroked his erection.

"Fuck it."

chapter 56

KOVA REACHED FOR MY CHEST AND PALMED MY BREASTS, PINCHING MY NIPPLES. Groaning from the sharp sting that radiated throughout my body, I soaked it up. Pain and pleasure combined. A hidden desire stirred deep in my belly for more.

Rolling my lip between my teeth, I tugged at the waistband of his shorts and slowly slid them down his tapered hips. His stomach flexed against the backs of my fingers. A light dusting of hair came into view, followed by a thick, heavy shaft.

"Christ," he groaned, fisting my duvet until his knuckles turned white.

I pulled his shorts completely off him and stared in bewilderment. Kova was rock solid, hard like his body, and standing tall. The sight of him splayed out caused a rush of excitement to coat my thighs. Goose bumps broke out over my skin, and it was then that it dawned on me just how much of a man Kova really was.

"How the hell does that thing fit in me?" I blurted out, and slammed a hand over my mouth. Kova chuckled, his shoulders relaxing, and he palmed his naked flesh.

"You would be surprised how easy I can work it in when you are wet."

Reaching out with my hand, my thumb moved on its own accord, rubbing the prominent vein on his dick over and over and watching as it flattened under my pressure then expanded up once I released. Kova sucked in a breath. The sudden image of my tongue doing this had me jutting out my breasts, longing for his touch once again.

While I played with his penis and got familiar with him, I realized my hand was damp. Glancing down, I noticed a droplet at the head and moved to touch it. I slid it through the tips of my fingers, and Kova placed his hand over mine. I looked at him and waited. He began to move my hand over his erection, signaling me to squeeze tighter.

I picked up the pace and stroked him harder and faster.

"Yes…" he mumbled unintelligibly, "like that."

Leaning forward, my lips sucked at his neck. Kova fisted my hair, tugging my head back, and cupped my jaw before leaning in to steal a kiss.

His greedy tongue took my breath away. He released my hair, and his hands traveled down to my breasts where he palmed them both in a rough grip, making me moan. His thumbs ran circles over my puckered nipples, and I continued to stroke him. But it wasn't enough for me—or him. I wanted to make him feel good, the same way he did me, but I'd never actually gone down on a guy before, let alone a man.

"Adrianna…" he panted, "do you have any idea how bad I want this? Want you? I want to slide into you again and fuck you senseless. God, I want you to ride me." His touch was everywhere, almost as if he couldn't get enough. I loved the attention he was giving me. I wanted more, as much as I could take from him.

"You undo me," he confessed. "You have played with yourself before, right?" he asked.

I nodded, unable to find my voice.

Kova jutted his chin up, but looked down through heavy lashes. "Touch yourself while I jack off."

Looking down at the thick erection in my hand, I asked, "Can I do it for you?"

"Do what, Adrianna?"

I bit my lip. "Make you come the way you make me."

His nose flared, and he paused. "No."

"Why not? I want to."

"I would rather you give yourself an orgasm while I watched."

I leaned back and placed my hand on my tender sex.

Kova's stomach flexed as he pumped into his hand. He was a thing of beauty and it wasn't long until I started to feel that newly familiar ache burning in my belly. But I wanted to be the one doing that to him, stroking him. Sitting up, I got to my knees just inches from him. I grabbed Kova's empty hand as he still towered above me and placed it in the V of my drenched thighs. He heaved a sigh. I peered into his lowering eyes and wrapped my hand around his cock, proving just how much I wanted to give him this pleasure. Needing more moisture, I spit into my hand the way I would if I were wearing grips, and returned my hand back to him. A low rumble escaped him and his chest expanded with a deep inhale.

Stroking him hard but slow, Kova's lips parted with an audible sigh. He cupped the back of my head and leaned down to kiss me, plunging his tongue into my mouth. He took control, and I liked it. A lot. More so than I probably should. He was wild, feral, and devoured my mouth with passion. The air was filled with sex and I swear I heard a growl.

"I'm close again…put it in me," I whispered against his lips. His thumb circled my clit and I was desperate to connect with him again, completely.

"God, I want to so badly. Anything to be deep inside your pussy again. To feel you clench around me."

I whimpered, and his dick twitched in my hand. "You can, I said you can."

"It does not work like that."

"Please."

"No…but keep doing that. Keep twisting the head a little tighter."

"I want it."

"With the way I feel right now, I will tear you up. No." Then he said, "Do not stop… fuck, just do not stop."

"Oh, yes," I moaned, riding his hand. My hips began rocking on their own. His palm kept hitting my clit and I couldn't get enough. I grabbed a hold of his bicep and he flexed under my arm. I was on the brink of tears from his taunting. Pure instinct took over and I climbed over his legs, positioning him at my entrance. Our eyes locked, and the moment he touched my opening I slid down. My lips parted as I felt myself stretch. Kova seized my hips to stop me from going down completely.

"This is not a good idea," he held on to me. Biting my bottom lip, I exhaled against his chest. Kova lifted my chin to look at him. He shook his head, his eyes filled with something I'd never seen before.

"You are something else, you know that?"

He kissed me deeply, fueling the fire, and lifted me up and down on him a handful of times before he pulled out and grabbed his shaft.

"Fuck!" he yelled, his penis throbbing. His body shook and it pleased me. White hot liquid hit my stomach. It stuck to me, slowly dripping down my flat tummy. It was the most erotic thing I'd ever seen.

I placed his hand between my thighs again. A gratified smile curved his sensual lips. I didn't know who I was in this moment, or who I had become, only that Kova had brought out a side of me I didn't know existed. I came just moments later.

"Baby," he said so quietly, but I heard it as he wrapped his arm around my lower back and held me against him. I relaxed and sighed into his body, inhaling his sultry scent that was now merged with our sex. My lips pressed to his neck, giving him little satisfied kisses. His dick throbbed against me as he continued to release himself all over me. And I mean, all over my stomach and thighs.

"This is why we cannot fuck again. You are too tight, it would hurt you more than it would feel good. I worried I hurt you last time."

I got serious with him and pushed back. "Way to kill the moment, Kova. How do you expect that to change unless you fuck me again? Your size would hurt anyone." I wasn't actually sure about that since I hadn't seen tons of penises before, I just assumed it, which I think he liked because his brows shot up and he grinned.

I smiled, happy I could draw such a reaction from him. Something shifted in the quiet air as we stared into each other's eyes. I wasn't sure what, but when Kova leaned in to kiss me, it was different this time. He was slower, more careful, and gentler. More methodic. It was a passionate kiss, one filled with more weight than meant to. I found myself falling into him, my heart opening up and holding on to him.

"I am enamored with you," he admitted honestly.

I was beginning to fall hard for this man. And that wasn't a good thing.

Breaking the kiss, Kova said, "Let us get you cleaned up."

My heart stopped. "You're not leaving yet, are you?"

He paused, looking to the side. "I have to leave soon, *malysh*."

"I know, but just stay for a little longer, please." I wasn't ready for him to leave just yet after what we shared.

Kova nodded, and we climbed off my bed and walked into the bathroom. I grabbed two wash cloths, wet them, and handed one to him. As I went to clean myself off, he pushed my hand away and cleaned me himself. For whatever reason, my heart melted as I let him do it. He was gentle and sweet, and the caring look in his eyes tightened something in my stomach. He pressed a kiss to my shoulder and used the same rag to quickly and efficiently clean himself, his eyes never leaving mine. We stood in silence and got dressed. This time I only wore boy short panties and a loose shirt. I pulled my hair into a ponytail when I was done.

Instead of sitting on my bed, Kova made his way to my living room and sat on my couch. I went to sit next to him, but he grabbed my hand and guided me to his front. I climbed up, straddling his thighs and lowered myself onto his lap. Placing my hands flat on his chest, he wrapped his arms around my back and snuggled me to him. Not once had Kova ever held me like this, so relaxed and so very intimate, but without any sexual motive. Almost like a lover's hold.

A few moments of silence passed when Kova spoke up.

"Adrianna, I need to ask you something," he said against me ear. "Are you on birth control?"

My heart stopped.

"No."

"Fuck," he muttered under his breath, but I'd heard the disappointment in his tone. His body coiled beneath mine and I felt bad I hadn't even considered it at the time. "I cannot believe how stupid I was."

Pulling back, I looked into his solemn eyes. His hands dropped to my hips. "It's not your fault, Kova. I should've been more responsible, too. I wasn't thinking clearly."

I looked down at his shoulder, lost in thought over the ramifications of our actions. I was smarter than that and yet I made a grave judgment call. It was beyond ignorant of me.

"Well, on the plus side, you didn't finish inside of me."

Kova gave me a sympathetic look, his hands slid to my hips. "I do not have to come inside of you for you to get pregnant, Adrianna. It is called pre-come."

I knew what it was called, I was just trying to give him some hope. "I know, but the possibility is really slim." That, I knew.

I bit my lip. *Come inside you...* My cheeks flushed at his sexy, baritone voice. My hips purposely snuggled into his lap, feeling his length under me. He was warm and comforting, and something about being in his arms was peaceful.

"And yes, I did. The first night we had sex, I came inside of you."

chapter 57

SHIT.

The blood drained from my face.

I'd completely forgotten, yet the thought of him coming in me sent a flush of heat down my spine. I'd never been overly interested in sex, but Kova was bringing out the inquisitive side in me, making me want to explore more.

"Anything is a possibility, Ria," he said softly. My fingers traced over his muscular shoulder as I thought about what I could do to lessen my chances of being pregnant. A thought popped in my head.

"What about the morning after pill?" I suggested, brightly. I didn't want to take something such as a morning after pill, who knew what the hell it was made of, but I also wasn't ready to raise a baby, either. I had goals, dreams, and aspirations.

Kova shifted uncomfortably under me and dragged a hand over his mouth. When he stayed silent, I said, "It prevents pregnancy when there is no protection used during sex."

He rolled his eyes back to mine. "I know what it does."

"Oh, well, you didn't say anything."

"I was just thinking about the idea." His distant eyes were staring at something behind me before they swung back to mine. "I cannot force you to take anything, Adrianna. It is your choice and your decision, but I think this would be the best thing for you to do. For us."

I nodded. "I think so—"

He cut me off. "I will tell you right now that if you get pregnant and it somehow comes back to me, I will deny it until the day I die," he said, brushing a fallen lock of hair from my face.

My stomach recoiled at his gentle tone but inconsiderate words. I was just as much at fault as he was, and that was the last thing I wanted. "I don't feel comfortable buying it though…Do you think you could get it for me?"

Kova didn't hesitate. "Yes."

"But what if someone sees you buying it?"

His brows bunched together and then eased apart. "I will go to a pharmacy in the next town over. Problem solved."

We both heaved a heavy sigh at the same time. A relieved look passed over both our faces. The last thing I wanted was to get caught, let alone have a damn baby. And I could guarantee Kova felt the same way.

"When will you go? I think there's an expiration date on how long you have before it's not effective."

He nodded. "I think it is a week or something…Katja—" He stopped, remorse plaguing his face heavily and it bothered me. When he regained himself, he quietly said, "Katja has taken it before. I will go when I leave here and get it. It will be in your locker tomorrow morning, so get to the gym early and take it. I will take it out of the package so no one sees it."

My chest burned. I wasn't crazy about the thought of Katja having to take the pill because Kova couldn't control himself around her. I wanted him like that only for me.

"What does it look like?"

"It is a little white pill. I will put it to the side with a bottle of Aloe water in front of it."

My heart shifted, that unknown feeling coming back. Kova's eyes were on mine as he tugged my hair loose, the thick waves falling down my back. He fluffed it up, pulling a few strands over my shoulder to rest on my chest.

"Your hair is always up. I liked seeing it down today," he admitted somberly. "You looked beautiful when I saw you in my office. I had no intention of doing anything more with you, or that ridiculous deal I had you make, but when I saw you, everything changed."

"I didn't purposely pick that dress out, you know that, right?"

Kova smirked, nodding. "We will agree to disagree on that."

I gave him a playful stern glare. His smile shifted, looking more serious, staring into my eyes with such depth I felt he could see right into my deepest thoughts. "You are different than the others."

I rolled my eyes. "Most clichéd line ever, Kova."

He gripped me a little tighter. "Think what you want, but no matter what I do and say, I find myself drawn to you explicitly. Like a moth to a flame."

My brows lifted.

His nose grazed my cheek sweetly. "It is true, think about it. I am the moth, you are the flame. It is an irresistible attraction that will end in total destruction."

How morbid. "Do you think the moth knows that it's being lured?"

Kova sat quietly, looking at my chest that was parallel to his face. Only he didn't stare with desire, he looked lost in thought, maybe wondering if the moth knew any better. I had on a razorback shirt three times too large that hung loosely on my arms, showing a little skin. The back of his finger came up and unhurriedly grazed the side of my round breast. My nipples puckered in return, showing through the shirt.

"Desire can be deadly. Temptation can be toxic. But do I think it knows it is being lured? No," he said quietly, running his finger in circles on my flesh.

"Like right now, I am tempted to push this thin material aside and press my lips to your tender skin. But I know if I get too close, get a taste of you again," he winked, and I smiled at the devious glint in his eyes, "then I will not be able to stop. I will want more until it is too late to stop. But if I do, do it," he pushed the arm hole over my breast, the back of his finger purposely dusting over my rosy nipple, "it does not mean I have to do anything, but the lust, the hunger, the want, it is all there, pulling with a force so powerful that an ending is not even a thought. It is pure desire."

My fingers continued to thread his hair as he became hard beneath me. His tongue slipped out and licked his bottom lip before he leaned in and delicately flattened it around my nipple. My heart raced, coming alive as he lapped and pulled on my sensitive skin. My back arched seductively as I pressed the back of his head to me. He was taking his time, flicking his tongue over the bud then running it in circles. A moan rolled off my lips and he pulled back with a pop. Looking down through my heavy lids, my nipple was hard and pointed as he stared at it like he wanted to devour me. He covered me back up, and met my gaze.

"You are the bright light that beckons me...And I am okay with it. Thing is, I realized I like talking to you, Adrianna. I like being around you. I have never told any other gymnast or friends about my mother and her secret, only Katja. It feels natural with you. You are a fighter, and no matter how much you get pushed down, no matter what you have against you, you do what you have to do and you do not complain. You are strong and resilient. You are relentless, and I find that fucking attractive as hell. It is a turn on, but it is also why I treat you the way I do."

"It's why you've been so hot and cold with me."

He nodded. "At first, it was the chase, the sneaking around that all builds it up. As a coach, I know better. There are classes we have to take to be aware of these things—at the end of the day, you are still a minor. But what they do not teach us is it is not always the coach who seduces the athlete. That sometimes, maybe sometimes, it is the other way around."

"You think I seduced you," I stated plainly. "Because I knew what I was doing with a man, so I set out to get you."

He shook his head, his forehead creased with lines. "I think a lot of it has to do with attraction more than anything. Attraction is the root of all evil, not money like some say. It can be everything you have ever imagined and destroy everything at the same time. All relationships begin with attraction that leads to some form of lust. It is a natural reaction that comes from the body. Do I think that you purposely seduced me?" He chuckled with a small smile. "Not exactly." Brushing a lock of hair behind my ear, he said, "The fire that burns inside of you to be better, to prove others wrong about you, is dangerous, and *that* is attraction in itself. It is a hell of an attraction. We will both be our ruin if we do not stop while we are ahead."

He paused and looked deeply in my eyes once again. The guilt woven through his face was strong and it froze me. The knot that formed in my stomach and matched with his features told me his next words would cause damage. A pang in my chest spread through my whole body. My face fell, my heart breaking. "Did I do something wrong?" The tears behind my eyes were steadily climbing.

"You did everything right, but you know as much as I do this has to come to an end. It cannot keep going on. No more skating around the edges. No more chasing. It is not worth losing everything over."

Biting my bottom lip, I studied my fingers as they glided across Kova's collarbone. His words weren't malicious, but they cut deep and I wanted to cry.

"You're right," I agreed with a shaky voice.

"We can never admit anything to anyone, you know this, right?"

Nodding, I said, "I'd never tell anyone."

"But even if anyone suspects it, says that they found out, do not fall for the trap." My brows angled toward each other and he continued. "I will never speak a word of this to anyone, no matter what anyone says. And you cannot either."

Kova's phone vibrated in his pocket. Pulling it out, I saw Katja's name flash across the screen. He scowled. It was close to midnight, and I wondered what he would tell her.

"I have to go." He lifted my hips and moved me off him to stand.

I fixed my shirt and crossed my arms under my chest. "What will you tell Katja the reason why you're so late?"

"She will not question me."

Perplexed, I asked, "Why not?"

"I will not give her the chance," he said, his eyes raking leisurely down my body. My nipples hardened and my cheeks flushed in response. Kova adjusted his shaft, causing me to look in that direction. The bulge in his shorts was blatantly obvious.

My chest tightened, my jaw slackened. He was hard, he wanted sex. And sex would be with Katja.

My heart crumpled at the thought of him having sex with her while thinking of me. I knew it was stupid to feel the way I did, but I couldn't help it.

I followed him to the door. He turned around with his hand on the knob. Kova looked down at me and brought a hand up to cup my cheek. My eyes closed shut as he leaned in and pressed a kiss to my forehead.

I bit my lip as he swiftly stepped out and left, a warm tear slipped down my cheek.

Turning around, I leaned against the door and hugged myself as I slid down and let the tears fall.

chapter 58

I T WAS PITCH BLACK WHEN I PULLED UP TO THE GYM A LITTLE EARLIER THAN I NORMALLY did.

My eyes were swollen, and I was mentally and physically exhausted as I put my truck into park. My face was devoid of its usual makeup and my hair wasn't even brushed today. Climbing out, I grabbed my gym bag from the backseat and shut the door. I slung it over my shoulder and walked into World Cup.

It was eerily quiet this morning. No gymnasts were on the floor, no music was playing, no springboards sounding. Just the scent of chalk and coffee coalesced in the air and the faint sound of papers shuffling as I walked to the locker room and opened my locker door.

I swallowed hard at what was staring me straight in the face on the little shelf. A four pack of coconut water with a Post-It note attached to it, a couple of new bottles of Aloe water, a new package of pre-wrap along with new wristbands, and a little white envelope. Without opening it, I knew it contained the morning after pill.

After Kova left, I climbed into bed and cried myself to sleep. My heart hurt, but the reality of the situation was clear.

There would be no more Kova and me.

Subconsciously, I knew it would never be more than what it was. It could never work in this lifetime. It was just too dangerous. This was for the best, but it didn't make it any easier to deal with the emotional fallout. I still had to see him on a daily basis. I decided I wouldn't engage in any small talk with him, I wouldn't look longingly in his direction, I wouldn't accept gifts from him, nothing. I'd keep it completely platonic. I had bigger things I needed to worry about and focus on, but my heart was broken.

I was falling for him.

Not love, I didn't believe in love. Not at my age at least. I was a realist with goals. Love didn't fit into the equation at this time in my life.

However, I had started to develop feelings for him that crossed the professional level and that worried me.

Yet, seeing his gifts in front of me, gifts I didn't want to accept, for some reason caused my jaw to tremble and my stomach to flutter. Reaching for the yellow sticky note, I read Kova's handwriting.

Thought you might want to try this out. Similar to your aloe water, but in my opinion, better for you.

K

Of course it was better. Kova knew everything.

I reached for the package, quickly tearing open the cardboard and pulling out a bottle. I uncapped it, brought it to my nose and inhaled. It smelled just like fresh coconuts and my mouth watered. I took a sip, actually liking it more than I expected, and drank nearly half the bottle before I picked up the little envelope and opened it.

Cupping my hand, a little white pill tumbled out into my palm. A pill that reminded me how foolish I had been. My heart began to pump viciously at the sight of it. One tiny pill had the power to irrevocably change a life. I didn't want to give it any more thought, so without hesitation, I threw the pill into my mouth and said a little prayer. I took a swig of the coconut water and swallowed. I may have been careless, but my future was at stake…as well as Kova's. No way was I going to jeopardize it in any way, shape, or form.

I crumpled the note in my hand and dropped it into my bag so I could throw it away when I got home. I wasn't going to be stupid like Kova and risk someone seeing it.

At the end of the day, I came to World Cup for one reason and one reason alone. To train with the best so I could achieve Olympic glory. I wouldn't allow my focus to deter again. I was going to dive into practice and work harder than ever. Gymnastics has an expiration date. And being that I was steadily getting closer to it, I had a lot to accomplish in a short amount of time. I was going to prove them all wrong, and throw every minute I had into the sport that was the first to steal my heart. Mind, body, and soul. I had everything I needed at the tips of my fingers. There was no reason not to have what I wanted.

Self-doubt kicked in while I undressed. It was like that pesky little gnat that just wouldn't go away. I questioned whether I had enough time or if it was even possible to make it to The Games like I once thought.

Unfortunately, I knew I had to downgrade some of my skills because of my stupid little injury. But it would be okay. It would only push me to fight harder.

After I shut my locker and locked it, I strode into the gym where Kova was waiting on the floor with a roll of tape in his hand. My heart jumped, reaching for him. My lips a firm, grim line as our eyes locked. He noticeably tensed, his shoulders bunching as a shadow cast over his eyes, shielding his emotions, giving nothing away.

I stayed quiet as I sat on the ground with my injured leg bent. Kova stood before me with a stoic face. While his eyes were unreadable and his movements professional, the facial hair casting a dark shadow on his jaw, and the puffy circles under his eyes gave him away. The smell of his cologne was faint, but enough to entice me to lean in and inhale the scent into my lungs. Spicy and daring, it made me think of what had happened only a handful of hours ago.

We were both quiet as he placed the white athletic tape in specific places on the back of my calf. This time his hands didn't linger and his fingers didn't stimulate. The sad part was, I desperately wanted them to.

Once he was finished, he stood and held out a hand to help me up. I couldn't look at his hand without thinking about where it'd been, what it'd done to me. Shaking the thoughts from my head, I pushed off the ground and stood.

"How does it feel?"

The aching organ in my chest? It hurt like hell.

I rolled my ankle around. "Fine, I guess."

"Look at me."

Snapping my eyes up to meet his, he pointed a finger and said, "If you have any kind of pain, anything at all, you need to speak up immediately. Do you understand me?"

"Yes."

"Anything, Adrianna. I am risking my neck for you right now." He gave me a knowing look, and I nodded.

Pulling my lip into my mouth, I chewed on it. I rolled my feet into the blue carpet, cracking my toes nervously. Kova's eyes followed the movement from my mouth to my feet and spat, "Spit it out, Adrianna. What is going on?"

Adrianna. Didn't that just sting. That was twice now.

"I took the pill," I whispered quietly, despite being the only ones in the gym. "And, thank you for the wristbands and coconut water. You didn't have to do that." I was still slightly perplexed at why he had, considering how we ended things.

Kova dipped his chin, then turned and walked away. His back was rigid and stiff and I could tell he was dealing with his own inner demons. It was a little rude for him to do so without so much as a you're welcome, but it was for the best. We really didn't need to speak unless it was gymnastics related.

I trained with my nemesis for a good three hours this morning—the balance beam. In between working with me and the other team girls, Kova helped me water down my routine. He was his typical Russian dick self the entire time, maybe more so to the other girls for once. When we would make eye contact, it was so he could give me an example of what to do. I kept a straight face and nodded when he barked out orders then would follow up and ask me if it hurt to land. This was the first time I didn't actually fear the beam, and that was cause for concern since I wasn't taking chances and risking my neck. A little fear was good.

Or maybe I was just lacking emotion for the day.

As I powdered my hands with chalk to prepare for bars, another event that would take the strain off my calf for now, I overheard Reagan talking to the other girls about a boyfriend she wasn't supposed to have. Not that I cared. It was the dumbest rule I'd ever heard, but I guess it made sense. We'd lose focus if that was the case, and it was. Just look how much time I spent thinking about Kova.

I thought back to the day she didn't want to let me borrow her extra set of grips, as if I had some deadly disease that was going to cost her a limb. I shook my head and huffed as I laced my fingers through my grips and wrapped the Velcro around the new wristbands Kova had given me.

The sound of classical music played in the background, pulling my attention to the floor. Holly was gracefully performing her routine, a routine that had skills I wasn't allowed to do for the time being. And unless my Achilles healed and was strong again, I wouldn't be doing them at all. I wasn't a jealous person, but I was the definition of envious at the moment.

I exhaled and shook my head, my thoughts were jumping everywhere. I didn't need anyone's approval. I wasn't the type to need a lot of friends. I learned living from on Amelia Island that it was better to have a few close friends and keep the rest at arm's length. Everyone was phony and only looked out for themselves. They were what I called *Wonder Bread* people. Fake, gluey, and tasteless.

The definition of Reagan.

God, I sounded like such a cynic.

Hayden strode by with a smile that made my shoulders relax. His charm was contagious and I couldn't help smiling back. Now, he had been a good friend, one I didn't think I could have gone without since coming here.

Rubbing some chalk on my thighs, I overheard Reagan say, "Hayden is so damn hot. Why Adrianna is a virgin is beyond me. Being that she's such good friends with him, it's honestly shocking she hasn't tapped that. Unless she's into girls."

I looked over my shoulder and the girls snickered. *Tapped that?*

"She doesn't know what she's missing."

"Or maybe it's because he wants an athlete at his level, not one who needs serious work and thinks she's better than what she really is," she said cockily. "Not one Daddy has to bribe either."

It got you your stupid café hall that you study in. That was what I considered a win-win situation, but Reagan was so narrow minded she couldn't see it benefitted her too.

Reagan continued. "Adrianna the prude. Miss Moneybags is saving herself for the perfect guy that I'm sure her parents need to pay off to be with her."

The girls laughed again. My blood simmered.

"You know, Reagan," I said sweetly, standing up and walking over to her. "I've about had enough of your shit. I never speak up or say anything about your constant belittling comments, but I am today. I'm sick of your condescending tone and glares. You think you're so much better than every other gymnast here, but I have news for you. You're not. So why don't you just shut the hell up and leave me alone."

My comment didn't seem to faze her. "Oh, you're tired of it?" She batted her eyelashes. I had the urge to punch her teeth out. I nodded, and she kept going. "Isn't that right, Adrianna," Reagan taunted, "You're saving yourself?"

I shook my head. "What are you talking about?"

"You being a virgin," she stated.

"Why does my personal life interest you so much? Unless you're the one into girls and you want me?" It wasn't in my nature to stoop so low, but today was not the day.

"How can you be friends with him," she looked at Hayden, "and not do anything? I would've given up my V card to him any day."

"Not that it's any of your information, but I don't have my V card," I said with air quotes. "There. Will that help you sleep better at night?"

"You don't? Since when?"

I was getting confused. How the hell would she know about my virgin status to begin with? "What do you mean, since when?"

"You don't remember our game of Truth or Dare where you admitted you were a virgin?"

Avery. But that was the least of my concerns right now. My chest heated, blood quickly rose to my cheeks and out to my ears as it dawned on me. Christ Almighty, I had said that! I couldn't remember what I ate for dinner five nights ago let alone what I said to the mean girl squad leader. However, with Reagan reminding me, I certainly had divulged my virginity status and now I just fucked myself admitting I was no longer a virgin.

"Well, I lied. It was none of your business back then and it sure isn't now. Shouldn't you be up on bars perfecting your routine?"

Reagan studied my face, my cheeks blushing even darker.

"You had sex since you've been here," she declared.

"I'm not having this conversation with you. If you're not going to get up on bars, I will." I stepped around her, but she stopped me by gripping my arm.

"You have, haven't you?"

"What does it matter to you?" I yanked my arm away, glaring.

Her mouth curved into a sly grin. "Well, well, well. Carrot top here has been deflowered."

"You know, Reagan, have you ever seen an actual carrot top? Because they're green, not red. So the term carrot top doesn't even make sense. And in case you're color blind, I'm clearly not a solid redhead."

Reagan's cheeks colored and I secretly took joy in it. She was pissed, and I could see the thoughts spinning in her head so fast that a slow smile spread across my face. I rendered her speechless, for once.

"I'm pretty sure I just heard you say you have a boyfriend. What, and who I do, in my spare time is none of your business." I had heard her correctly, right?

Palming the low bar, I swung and mounted it.

"I'll find out who you lost your V card to. Then I'll tell Coach since we're not allowed to have boyfriends," she said with spite. "Can't imagine Daddy can get you out of that one."

Ignoring her, I placed my feet on the bar and stood reaching for the high bar. She was pushing me to crack, but I refused to give in. There was no way she would rat me out, she was just as guilty if that was the case.

Casting to a handstand, I did a series of handstands to warm up and then began adding in connections. I had no pain in my calf yet, though everything I was doing was very light. My body flew seamlessly through the air from one bar to the other. I loved bars. I loved the feeling of shutting out the world and letting go, only relying on myself to catch the bar. It was an adrenaline rush, one I chased often with this sport. When I felt my arms and shoulders tightening, I slowed down to rest on the high bar by angling my hips against it and leaning forward. Up next were pirouettes and a light dismount, where I would start all over and do it again until I felt ready to move on from there.

After I tightened the Velcro on my wrists, I exhaled when my hands gripped the bar and visualized my next move. Awareness kicked through me. My back prickled with heat and I knew without a shadow of a doubt who was glaring at me from behind.

I looked over my shoulders. *Kova.*

He was staring at me furiously, like he wanted to strangle me. The blood drained from my face, my weight slowly descending further on to the bar as trepidation flooded my veins. Kova glared from the sideline, his impenetrable gaze knocking the air from lungs. He'd heard everything, the entire conversation with Reagan.

I was cold to the bone.

Numb.

chapter 59

"**H**OLLY WAS THERE WHEN YOU SAID YOU WERE A VIRGIN.**"
I cringed at her words.

"I'll get down to it." She chalked up, lost in her thoughts again as she mounted the set of uneven bars to the left, clearly unaware of Kova standing on the other side of me.

I didn't process what Reagan said. I couldn't. All I could focus on were the veins in Kova's forearms and the tick working in his jaw. His nose flared and I was sure I'd see smoke coming from his ears any minute.

I felt sick.

Nauseous.

He now knew I had been a virgin.

My heart raced so fast from his seething glare, it drummed in my ears. He heard everything. *Everything.*

And he was pissed. I can't imagine how I didn't see him standing there.

No, he was fucking fuming and looking at me with repulsion, and I detested it. His hands were fisted tightly at his sides, knowing he couldn't comment. So he just stood there, scowling, slicing me open with his loathing glare. The disgust on his face made my stomach churn. After everything we shared between us, the conversations and intimacy, I didn't want him to look that way toward me.

I needed to break the eye contact, so I fell forward and hung on the bar, pretending to fix my grips like they needed to be tighter. I clapped my hands to dust some of the chalk off. Anything I could think of to avoid seeing him when I looked up. My heart was racing so fast it hurt. I needed to get off this apparatus immediately. I needed to get out of here. I had too much on my mind to focus on what he heard, and how I was going to fix this.

No, I needed to tune out bitchy Reagan and pissy Kova and focus on gymnastics. That's what I needed to do.

Shit. Now my legs were quivering. Trying to ignore everything that just ruined my life in a matter of two minutes, I pulled up and continued with my warm up. I finished with a simple back tuck dismount. My mind was all over the place, my stomach was nauseous and I felt sick to the core. I quickly chalked up and tried to get back up on bars. Just before doing a kip, I paused with my hands wrapped around the bar. I couldn't do it. My gut told me not to take the risk. My hands trembled, my heart in my throat. I was off balance. Being around, and training with Kova, was fucking with my head.

Stepping back, my arms dropped lifelessly to my sides. I looked up and spotted Kova across the gym working with a gymnast on the floor. But he was still fiercely staring me down. His incredible eyes saying everything I needed to know.

Jesus, Mary, and Joseph. What the fuck did I do?

"Reagan, leave her alone."

My head snapped at the sound of Hayden's voice. Jesus. I wish he'd been here a few minutes earlier. The inquisitive look in his eyes said he knew there was more to the story than just Reagan being an asshole like she normally was, but luckily he brushed it off. I didn't know when he got here or how much he heard.

Reagan jutted her hip out. "Why? Are you two a thing? Because you know that's not allowed."

"I'm well aware of the rules, Rea. So is Aid. I'm asking you to back down and retract your claws. We're friends—nothing more."

"Aid?"

Hayden uncapped his water bottle and sipped it, never breaking eye contact with her. Replacing the cap, he said, "Yeah—Aid, just like when I call you Rea. It's a nickname, that's what friends do."

Hayden walked away, and I walked in the opposite direction. I couldn't breathe. I needed air. I needed *something*. I was starting to panic and I didn't know how to calm down because I had no one I could talk to. My nerves were lighting up and shaking me to the core. I began ripping my grips off as I exited to the lobby, the whole time I could feel my coach's eyes burning a hole into the side of my face. I didn't look though, because I already knew what they'd say.

Deceit.

Lies.

Trickery.

Loathing.

God, but it was so good. Amazing. And even though I omitted that fact, I still wanted him to want me. I still wanted him to desire me. I'd do it all over again if given the chance. Just thinking about it had my body warming and my heart pounding for all the right reasons. I may have been a virgin, but I knew no one would ever compare to him or the way his body felt against mine, or the pleasure he brought me. There was more to us than just sex and gymnastics, and we both were aware of it.

Shaking it off, I stepped into the bathroom and splashed cold water on my face. I couldn't go home, so I'd just have to act like nothing was wrong, and talk to Kova after practice when everyone left and we were alone.

Two hours later, I was screwing up my routine left and right.

I may have appeared to have nothing on my mind and only having a bad workout, but that was because I was taught to.

However, if anyone climbed inside my head, they'd see what a hot jumbled mess I was. I couldn't think straight. I couldn't swing neatly. My legs kept coming apart. I stumbled, my feet scraping the ground, and I couldn't land a clean dismount. I was all over the place. It was horrible. People had to see how terribly I was performing. I'm sure Reagan took note.

I wasn't even doing my release moves in fear of messing up and not catching the bar. Or worse, freaking out in mid-air and land on the bar with my hip. I stuck to basic bars and did easy skills, a few simple releases. Truthfully, I had no choice if I wanted to preserve what little sanity I had left.

Reagan and her friends whispered under their breath the whole time. I brushed it off, not caring what they thought. I already had an injury, I didn't need to add to it, so I played it safe for the day. And it didn't help that any time I glanced over my shoulder, I saw Kova looking at me. Not only was I performing like shit, he was watching me with his beautiful arms tightly crossed in front of his chest, critiquing my every move. He stared so keenly I decided to make an effort to avoid looking in his direction.

Only one more release before I did a copout dismount and would rotate to my last event for the day. I needed to be done with bars, done with practice so I could talk to Kova.

One Giant into a blind change, another Giant to gain momentum, I took a deep breath and released the bar to move into a Jaeger.

Only to fucking miss it.

I panicked, my heart sunk in mid-air, slamming to the ground before I did. A move so simple I'd been doing for years, and because my mind was in a million different places, I messed up royally. I either tapped too early or released too early…or I ducked my head…or I wasn't fully extended. It could be a number of things, and I had no idea which since my mind and body were not in sync with each other.

Falling face down on my stomach, I kept my arms out and in front of me so I wouldn't break any bones on the way down. The dumbest thing a gymnast can do is try to break their fall. *Hello broken bones and goodbye gymnastics career!* At least I had a little common sense left.

A gush of air burst from my lungs as I flopped to the thickly padded blue mat and bounced, chalk flying up around my face. My chest rose and fell heavily as I kissed the mat. My mind ran a million miles a minute trying to figure out how the hell I messed up so badly. While it was a common fall in practice, I was both embarrassed and shocked, and I didn't want to face all the gawking stares I knew I was getting.

Taking a deep breath, I exhaled and opened my eyes only to see Kova hovering above me. He reached down with an opened palm to help me and I grabbed it, not thinking twice.

"Girls," he said, looking directly at me, "rotate to the next event. I will be there in a bit."

A low snicker came from Reagan as she walked past us. I was seriously beginning to fucking hate the air she breathed.

"Get back up on the bar now."

Fuck. Fuck. Fuck. My heart raced, fear exploding through my veins over falling again. To fall so badly and then to get back up and do it again wasn't easy. Fear was suffocating me.

"I…I think I need a break," I stammered.

Coach ignored me as he dragged over a tall, solid mat for him to stand on. A spotting block. He dropped it near the metal post and climbed up, looking at me expectantly and waiting.

"Did I give you a choice? You just screwed up on a simple release move. In fact, I have been watching you screw up all afternoon, Adrianna. You are a sloppy mess and it is embarrassing. I guess we are going to have to take it back to basics since you cannot hit simple skills a twelve year old can master. So get up there now and do it again."

Shaking my head subtly, I slapped some chalk on to my grips and stood in front of the bars. Doing a kip to mount the low bar, I let go and jumped to the high bar.

"Cast to a handstand. Blind change. Jaeger."

I nodded, rotating my hands so they were considered backwards and my knuckles were against my thighs, a half pirouette. Blindly falling forward was not something I was in the mood to perform after the day I've been having, but I took a deep breath and prayed to God I would be able to pull off a Jaeger. Bouncing off the bar with my hips, I cast to a handstand. Coach positioned his hands on my stomach and back, holding me in place, leaving a touch of heat in each fingertip.

"Breathe," he whispered only for my ears. "Calm down, and focus. You got this." I nodded, then I was blindly falling forward into another handstand where he gripped me in the same place again. His hold was firm, secure, and overall, confident. It gave me a sense of comfort knowing he'd catch me if I fell.

"Tighten up." He slapped the back of my thigh lightly. "Squeeze your butt, straighten your legs."

I squeezed every muscle I could in my body and fell back again to hit another handstand.

"Better. Do it again."

I did it again.

"Tap harder," he demanded. "I believe your tap was not hard enough and the reason for your fall."

"Kova," I whispered once I was in a handstand. Coming down, I rested my hips on the bar with my arms locked straight. I turned to look at him.

"Do not," he mumbled.

"We need to talk."

"Adrianna, if you say another word to me, I will put your body through so much conditioning you will not be able to walk tomorrow."

My lips parted and his eyes traveled down to them. The five o'clock shadow paired with his emerald eyes was scorching, and when he looked at me with commanding authority, my body blazed. The bite in his tone was a clear warning to stop, so I listened. I didn't want to push him. It was obvious he wasn't playing around, clearly past the point of pissed off.

"Now is not the time or place to talk about anything. Be smart, Adrianna. Until then, you will land this skill until it is solid and then you are going home. I do not need you breaking bones on me."

I nodded. He was right.

"Now let us go. Do the Jaeger. I will spot you."

Before casting to another damn handstand, I looked at him and whispered, "I'm scared."

His eyes filled with empathy. "Fear is not a bad thing. It is what keeps you alive and trying. Visualize it and then go for it. Be confident. Push for it. I am right here spotting you, I will not let anything happen. I promise."

I believed him. I nodded frantically, picturing the skill in my head. Once in a handstand, I looked for his hands to spot me and when it came time to release again, I arched my back and tapped my feet hard. I released the bar and flipped forward into a pike position. Spotting the bar, I reached for it as if I was about to fall a hundred feet to the ground and gripped it tight. Coach kept his word and heavily spotted by flattening his hand right under my chest and on my back.

He had me.

I followed through with an easy kip and rested on the bar. My heart was racing, adrenaline pouring through my veins as I caught my breath. I looked at him and smiled brightly.

"Again." He tapped the back of my thigh.

He didn't even give me thirty seconds before I was back up. My nerves were shot and only by some miracle did I catch the bar thereafter. I lost count of the number of times I practiced the Jaeger after the initial one. Even with my grips, my palms were on fire, but I blocked out the agonizing pain. My shoulders felt like Jell-O. With each release, the fear dissolved a little more. But it never disappeared. Kova was right about fear, it kept me alive and motivated. Otherwise, I'd lose the thrill of the sport to keep going. He gave me self-belief with his firm touch, the courage to keep going. It was a coach wanting to see his athlete succeed and nothing more.

He ordered one more Jaeger where he said he would spot me, only he didn't. He only stood there to give me piece of mind. I should have expected this, but I was so lost in the moment I didn't.

Panting and out of breath, I bent over the high bar and breathed the chalky air heavily into my lungs.

"Get your stuff and go. Skip tomorrow's practice and do not question my authority." Flipping down, confidence roared through me. Normally I'd be upset over skipping practice, but ending it the way I did made me feel the complete opposite.

I smiled to myself, unwinding my grips and removing my wristbands. I felt good about the Jaegers, about how Kova pushed me to redo them. Had he not, there would be a chance I'd fear them the next time. This practice had started out good, moved to shit, and quickly into a disaster, and then actually ended on a good note for the most part.

I was bent down and shuffling through my bag when Kova strode back over. Standing up, I threw the duffle over my shoulder and looked at his hard face.

His voice was low, only for me to hear. "If you ever perform in the way you just did again, you will be kicked out of here so fast your head will spin. I do not give a shit who your father is. It was reckless and stupid and I never want to see it again."

And then he walked away.

chapter 60

I T'D BEEN A COUPLE OF DAYS SINCE THE JAEGER FIASCO.

I tried not to dwell on it since the past couldn't be changed and nothing good could come from constantly thinking about it. Instead, I blocked it out as much as possible and kept training in the forefront of my mind.

I busied myself and caught up on my homework. I even studied the material I'd be going over with my tutors the next couple of days. When I was done with the boring math I'd never use again in my life, I cleaned and did things around my condo so my mind didn't wander. I went to therapy for my Achilles, and then decided to get take out, something I never did.

The Penne a la Vodka was orgasmic. Too bad I couldn't eat it every day. However, considering it was Thanksgiving weekend and I wasn't with my family, I splurged. Not going home for this holiday wasn't a big deal for me. I'd go home for Christmas, though.

Yawning, I closed my chemistry book shut and dropped it on the couch. My eyes were puffy and swollen, and my hair was damp from the shower I took an hour ago. Relaxed with a full belly, I was ready to cuddle up in bed.

I didn't know what to do, and I had no one to talk to about it. I didn't want to tell Avery I had sex with Kova because I didn't want her to judge me. Not that she would, but after the talk I had with her and how she insisted Kova and I stop, I had a gut feeling she would be disappointed. When the time was right I'd tell her. Until then, it was better this way.

Looking through the sliding glass door, I gazed into the pitch-black sky thinking about what the future held, where I would be a year from now gymnastics wise. The moon hung high and I stared at it when I heard a light knock at my door.

Standing up, I walked across the plush carpet and stood on my tiptoes to peek through the peephole. Taking a deep breath, I unlocked the door and opened it.

All the air left my lungs. God, he was so fucking gorgeous.

He had one arm propped up against the wall as he leaned down and stared at me. His piercing green eyes peaked out from under his thick, black eyelashes, and he had more facial hair than I'd ever seen him with before. It worked in his favor and I wished he'd grow in more. He scanned the length of my body with his heady gaze until our eyes locked again. It seemed every time he stopped by my condo, my outfit was the same—panties and a shirt. In my defense, I wasn't planning on having company.

Kova dropped his arm and sauntered in past me. My heart leaped into my throat and I could feel my body simmering when I got a drift of his clean scent mixed with cologne. He smelled divine. I had a gut feeling he was here to yell at me, and luckily after a few days alone, I had everything planned I wanted to say.

Pushing back the hood of his jacket, I watched Kova unzip it and then remove it. He shook out his tight arms. Fury thickened the air, my heart catapulting in my chest. He was wearing distressed dark jeans and a tight black shirt. Dropping his jacket on the high back chair, Kova stalked toward me. A crease formed between my eyes at his harsh demeanor and I swallowed back the knot in my throat. He stepped toward me and followed me into the kitchen. My heart was wild with anxiety when I felt my back against the wall.

"Are you fucking crazy?" He gritted between clenched teeth. He got right to the point. "Is there something wrong with you?"

"You really had no idea?" I countered.

He snapped his neck to the side like he was cracking it, never leaving my gaze. "You were a *virgin*, a *fucking virgin*. And you let me fuck you the way I did? Let me touch you like that?"

My face scrunched up. He said virgin with a tone of repugnance and it hurt my stomach.

"I didn't let you do anything, you wanted it. We both wanted it, plain and simple. Okay— Maybe I did push you a little too far, but what's the difference, anyway?"

"The difference is you were a virgin, Adrianna. That is the difference. Are you not following the conversation?"

"Well, if it helps, I'm ninety-nine percent positive I broke my hymen on the balance beam, which means in a sense I wasn't a virgin." Kova paused, looking baffled, so I continued. "See, it's actually quite common for a gymnast to break her hymen from a bad fall on the balance beam, and Lord knows I've had plenty of falls. It's probably why I didn't bleed when we had sex."

Kova stepped closer. He placed his forearms on the wall near my head, boxing me in. His eyes narrowed and he was seething.

"Are you really going to school me on straddling the beam and hymens? I know all about that. I have been around the gym world longer than you have been alive. Breaking your hymen does not mean you are not a virgin anymore, Adrianna." Kova dipped his chin and looked deeper into my eyes, fury pouring out of them. "Penetration means you are not a virgin anymore. And while breaking your hymen on beam may be true, I was still your first form of real penetration, and that is fucked up beyond comprehension. I cannot believe you did not tell me."

My chest deflated.

"How is it fucked up?" I asked dejectedly.

"You should have been honest with me." He mirrored my tone and for the first time since he found out about my virginity, I actually felt remorseful.

Kova clenched his eyes shut and stepped away. He began pacing my kitchen frantically. The rage and fury he was casting out was thick and dense, hitting me hard and making me nervous. This was the first time I'd seen or felt real anger from him. It was completely different from the times he yelled at me in the gym, and honestly, I wasn't sure what to do with it.

"I cannot believe how stupid I was. I cannot believe I let myself fuck you, touch you, *drown* in you," he mumbled to himself. "I should have never done it."

I flinched, feeling the regret in his words. "What does it matter, anyway," I yelled, tired of his constant whiplash. "I wanted it. If you had known, would you have stopped?"

He stopped and looked at me, walking to stand close again. "Yes, I would have," he said between clenched teeth. "Because you never had a cock inside you before me no matter how you want to look at it, regardless if your hymen was already broken or not. I was still your first and while it never should have happened, it did. I took your innocence. I took your virginity. Why did you not speak up and say anything? I was always honest with you, Adrianna, always."

I shrugged feeling guilty. "I didn't know how to say it, and I was afraid you would have stopped."

He laughed low, manically. "This is so fucked up."

My heart crumbled. I loved being with Kova. He didn't push me. If anything, I pushed him.

There was no reason we couldn't talk about this situation civilly. He was being deliberately cruel and I didn't like it.

"Kova," I said softly, trying to calm him down. "You did nothing wrong."

His eyes locked on mine, forcing me not to move. "Nothing wrong? I sure as hell did not stop you. I hardly even tried. I saw an opening and took it. The moment I said take and you did, there was not a chance in hell I could hold back. I fucked a virgin. Over and over. Adrianna, I *licked* you, you had multiple orgasms," he said with horror. "An underage virgin at that. My fucking gymnast! There is a lot wrong with this picture. I could have gone to jail."

"You could've gone to jail before it," I muttered.

"What did you say?"

I stuttered when he glared at me. "Nothing…" This wasn't how I planned for this conversation to go.

"You know, this is *your* fault. I should have stopped your advances. I should have been stronger and turned you away like I did the others in the past. I have never," he fumed with rage, "been with a gymnast, let alone someone underage. What the fuck was wrong with me?" He questioned himself, pacing back and forth again. Running a hand through his hair, he repeated, "This could cost us everything."

That gave me an opening. "You've never with any other gymnast? I find that hard to believe with how long you've been coaching and how closely you work with them. That can't be possible."

He pulled back like I slapped him, disgust written all over his striking face. "Do you think I am some sort of freak, Adrianna? No, I have never been with any other gymnast, or underage girl in my life. I never desired to. What the hell makes you think that?"

He stalked toward me. "You actually believe I like young girls?" He revolted at his own question. I shrugged. "Answer me."

"I don't know. I guess I don't see how you couldn't have." I shook my head at his question, shrugging it off. "Kova," I said softly, and placed my hand on his shoulder. "It's not like anyone knows, or will ever know."

"Don't touch me."

My eyelids dropped, and I glared at him. Anger simmered inside me, mounting to the top and ready to explode. He acted as if we had gotten caught. The whole virgin thing really wasn't a big deal to me, so I didn't understand why he was so affected by the fact he was my first. I wish he'd just drop it.

"You're overreacting, and to put all the blame on me is absolute bullshit," I fought back. "It takes two to tango. I didn't force you to do anything you didn't want."

The look he pinned me with when he spun around should've scared me, but it didn't. His piercing green eyes were so vibrant and the veins in his neck strained. Deep down, I loved seeing him like this. He was rage and fury rolled into one beautiful package.

"You pursued me! And I let you!" He roared, his eyes racking a heated gaze down my body. His Russian accent was thicker when he was angry.

"I pursued you?" I repeated flatly. "Maybe I did, maybe I didn't. But in the end, it's all the same. You let me get close to you. You opened up to me and let me inside your world," I said, slowly stepping toward him. "You wanted me. And you knew you couldn't touch me, yet you did. You got off on it. Have you ever heard of reverse psychology?" He pulled back in horror but I kept going. "Why didn't you push me away? It's not like you can't overpower me, stop me."

"Adrianna. You are missing the point. It is not about overpowering. It is about removing myself from the situation."

And he was missing my point so I continued advancing on him. I wasn't sure where this courage was coming from, but I went with it.

"We both know you're way stronger than I am and could easily have put an end to anything before it started."

"Adrianna," he warned, a tick starting in his jaw.

"Acknowledge it wasn't just me."

"No," he growled.

"Do it," I whispered, staring up at him. Our chests were so close that if I took a deep breath my boobs would touch him. And I wanted to do it to tempt him and prove him wrong.

"Step back. Now."

"Make me."

chapter 61

GLOSSY, HEAVY LIDDED EYES STARED DOWN AT ME.

I was trying to stay strong, but the look he gave me sent a sensation throughout my entire body. Knowing he liked being told no, and knowing he liked when I fought him, only pushed my drive. It sent another thrill through me. His needs and wants turned me on and I embraced this side he was bringing out in me.

Gripping his wrist, I brought it around to cup my butt. I knew he was lying, he damn well knew he was, and I hated that. His fingers dug into my flesh for a split second before he moved in a blurring speed. He had me pinned to the wall with both of my wrists securely locked behind my back and him pressing into me. My heart skipped into my throat, my eyes went wide, staring into the depths of his.

"Stop fucking with me," he whispered thickly against my neck. "Why are you doing this?"

"To prove it wasn't all me...and I don't want to stop what's between us."

"You are fucking crazy, you know that? You are not right in the head."

"Maybe I am a little crazy in the head, but I think you like it," I whispered. His erection was a hard angle on my lower stomach as I stood on my tiptoes, pushing my hips into him. I couldn't help it, I needed to feel him lower. Wanted to feel him lower.

This was past just physical attraction.

This was animalistic.

And highly forbidden, which just made it that much better.

"See how easy it was for you to get my hand off you? You have such a tight grip on my wrists there's no way I could've forced anything on you. Now admit it wasn't just me."

His whole body was hard against mine, his breathing ragged. I was pushing him, teasing him...and I liked it. He was bubbling under my fingertips, and for some unknown reason, I wanted to see him snap.

Dragging my foot up the back of his leg, I hooked it around his hip and used my stomach and inner thigh to lift myself to his level, wrapping my other leg around his hip and climbed up his body. I put all that conditioning to good use. I needed to communicate my feelings with my eyes more so than my words since they weren't getting across. But the moment we were eye level with each other, I could feel his lust, his inner turmoil, his utter confusion with right and wrong, and his hunger for more.

"You can't, can you? Admitting it is immoral, and the immoral and wrongness of it makes it that much hotter. But that's not really why it feels so good, is it?" I breathed against his lips, our eyes locked in a gaze so strong neither one of us could break it. Our chests panted against each other, the air thick with tension. My wrists hurt from him squeezing so tightly, but I let him do it without complaint.

"We work well together, Kova," I whispered. "There's an attraction that's more than just chemistry between us."

I was breaking his resolve, I could feel it. This sensual prowess Kova unleashed inside me was untamed and new. My tongue slipped out and traced his lips. He began panting, his erection straining hard against me and the pressure caused my hips to undulate against his. Kova groaned, it was a deep and guttural sound that brought me chills.

"Let go," I pushed.

He didn't move.

He couldn't. Not because I was forcing him, but because he wanted to be here and knew he shouldn't.

Carefully, he maneuvered my wrists to one hand and used the other hand to grip my jaw. We were so close we breathed each other in.

"You are right. I do want you, even right now when you are literally doing everything in your power to seduce me, I want to fuck you senseless. But what you do not see is after this newfound knowledge, I never will again," he said deathly low.

Kova purposely rubbed against me, his cock rock hard and hitting my clit caused little moans to escape my throat. "Starting tomorrow there will be no physical contact unless it is during training. Try it and there will be repercussions. You do not look at me and I will not look at you unless it is gym related. We are through. In fact, I am removing myself as your coach."

He picked up his pace and I could feel an orgasm rising inside of me. The roles had been switched and he was tempting me and pushing me now. I tried to wiggle my arms free, but he smirked and didn't allow it. He had me locked tight and the glimmer in his eyes told me he loved it.

I fought his hold for the sheer purpose of proving my point. But I found being contained brought me higher and higher. I liked the power struggle...His touch seared my skin and I was as hot as an inferno ready to burst.

Locking my legs tighter, I said, "Starting tomorrow...then why are you touching me like this?" I reached for his mouth with mine, but he pulled back quickly, still gripping my jaw. "Why are you still here?" I paused, and then stated, "Unless you really want to fuck." I smiled wickedly. "Is Katja not available to you right now?"

He gave me a scalding glare. If looks could kill.

"Keep going," I sighed, my eyes rolling shut. I was going to have an orgasm any second, and I began thrusting my hips back and forth, grinding on him. He met my pace. My back arched, my nipples straining through my cami as his dick rubbed against my pussy faster and faster. "Right there..."

Kova let go of my jaw and punched the wall so hard with his fist that it startled me. My eyes shot open. His were fierce, pushed past the brink of sanity. Quickly, he let go of my wrists and disengaged my ankles from around his back, forcing me to stand. Keeping his eyes trained on mine, my lips parted when I heard his belt unbuckle and his zipper go down. I reached to help him, but he slapped my hand away. His jeans slid down his muscular thighs, pooling at his feet. With both hands, he ripped off my boy short panties, gripped my hips and lifted me up so my legs circled his waist once again. With one of his hands holding both of my wrists behind my back, he shoved me forcefully against the wall and reached between us to palm his cock, his hand grazing my swollen lips. My body became aware and anxious for his next move. Kova swallowed hard before he positioned himself at my entrance and thrusted in so fast and so hard my back bowed and I squeezed my eyes shut from the force. Fuck, that hurt. He stretched me wide and I squeezed around him, only intensifying the sting. He dropped his head to the curve of my neck and inhaled. "Baby," he murmured over and over and I melted. "Oh, fuck, yes." The groan that came from the back of his throat was filled with conflict, though incredibly sexy. My thighs squeezed his hips from the rough intrusion. Thank goodness I was soaking wet, otherwise this would've felt like I was being ripped apart.

"Is this what you want? To be fucked hard?" He pushed in and out, gripping my hips in a bruising manner and not giving me a second to breathe. I gasped loudly.

"Your body cannot handle me at this rate, Adrianna. I will break you. I am not even in all the way, I have never been in all the way."

"But your girlfriend can? Katja can take all of you like this?" I taunted, and moaned really loud from the intense pleasure he filled me with. I knew there were problems between them and I wanted to use them to my power. I wanted him to tell me no, that she couldn't.

Kova gnashed his teeth together. "Do not mention her right now."

I had to bring her up because she was the one he went home to every night. And deep down, hidden inside, I was jealous of her relationship with him. I wanted what she had.

"Do everything to me you would her. Don't hold back." The back of my head smacked the wall, but I was too lost in the moment to feel it.

"I am not going to think about Katja while I am inside of you."

Kova pushed in deeper at the mention of her name. I clenched around him, growing more aroused from it. Provoking him was surprisingly euphoric and I reveled in satisfaction. I jerked on my arms, trying to free my wrists, but his hold only grew stronger and his erection became harder inside of me.

Kova thrusted back in and held it. I squeezed my inner walls by reflex. "Breathe," he ordered huskily. "Just, breathe." His thumb dug into my hips, forcing me down and I pulsated around him, stretching to accommodate his width.

"This is me deep inside of you just like you begged for. Every inch. You have never had every inch until now." Kova ran his tongue along my neck, leaving a wet trail, nipping my heated flesh. I shivered in his possessive hold. "Can you handle it?"

I almost wanted to say no from being stretched so wide, but I didn't. So I said, "More."

"Such a bad girl. I love it." He countered teasingly, moving his hips harder. The glimmer in his eyes flitted across my skin. I felt a slight tightness but focused on the pleasure instead of the pain.

"You should not want this. I should not want this," he said roughly, and kissed me aggressively, showing me who's in charge. I moaned into his mouth, my body ready to let go. "But I do, God, do I ever," he said honestly.

"Oh, God, I'm gonna come." Three more pumps and I was having the most intense orgasm I'd ever had. I yelled out, but Kova stifled my screams with his tongue in my mouth, continuing to push in deep and then revert out, repeating the motion. I sucked on his tongue, fighting the hold on my wrists as the power of the orgasm swept through my body. I never wanted this high to end.

Breathing heavily, I could barely catch the rhythm of my heartbeat when Kova stood tall, hugging me to him. He stepped out of his jeans and then carried me out of the kitchen. I'd forgotten he still had them on. Kova let go of my arms and I wrapped them around his shoulders, resting my head on his chest and inhaling his dark scent. I shivered, my body stretched to the limit but loving the overly full feeling. Cool air kissed my bare skin and it was refreshing against Kova's heated body.

I assumed we were going to my bedroom, but he stopped at the couch and unwound my legs from around his waist. He carefully set me down next to the arm rest and I looked confusingly at his hips. His erection was glistening with my orgasm and I noticed he didn't finish. Glancing up, his deep green eyes peered down at me and his grin was so incredibly sexy it made my heart speed up.

With his hand in my hair, he pulled my head toward him.

"Suck it."

I paused.

"I don't know how," I said softly. It was true, I had no idea how to.

Kova lowered his eyelids, an impish smirk formed on his face.

"It is simple. Open your pretty little mouth, roll your lips over your teeth, and suck."

chapter 62

SOUNDED EASY ENOUGH.

If I could do a double layout on floor, I could do this.

Tentatively, I shifted to my knees, feeling the microfiber softness beneath me and leaned over. My lips parted as I stared at the tip of his penis. Kova moaned quietly. With his hand on the back of my head, he guided me toward him, but he didn't push. There was nothing forceful about it, which I appreciated. I was nervous, but I'd be lying to myself if I said I wasn't eager to see his reaction and what it would feel like.

My tongue slipped out and licked the tip. I wasn't expecting him to be salty and made an effort to hide the dislike on my face. Kova's stomach flexed, his abs hardening as I looked up at him for approval. I reached out and skimmed his pelvis, feeling the rigid muscles and the V on his hips as I took more into my mouth.

Kova groaned. "Wrap your tongue around me like you are sucking on a lollipop."

I stopped and laughed. "A blow pop?"

A deep chuckle came from him. "Yes." I pretended he was a lollipop and astonishingly it worked. His hips moved forward and he held the back of my head to him. "If you want to do what Katja does, you are going to have to suck harder. She loves sucking my cock."

My nose flared and I almost bit down on his *cock*. That just got my blood roaring. His dick twitched and I clenched my thighs shut. Kova was goading me, I knew he was, and I didn't care because somewhere hidden deep inside me I found joy and satisfaction in it. I picked up the speed and used my tongue, trying to take as much as I could into my mouth. It wasn't easy and my jaw began to ache. Kova moaned when his dick hit the back of my throat and I nearly gagged.

"You have to open the back of your throat."

I didn't even know what opening the back of my throat meant. I didn't want him to know I was clueless, so I nodded. Anytime he thrust his hips, he hit the back of my throat. To avoid him going any deeper, I wrapped my fingers around the base of his penis and held on as I did more of the guiding than him. His arm dropped from my head and I looked up. Kova's head was tipped back, pleasure rocking through him. I smiled to myself. Guess I was doing it right after all. I sucked harder, focusing on the tip.

"Fuck," he said huskily when my tongue wrapped around his length and tugged. My cheeks hollowed. Kova looked down, our eyes locked and something in my heart shifted. It was important to me he enjoy what I was doing to him, just as I had.

His gaze was lethal, protective almost, as if I was the only thing that mattered in his world. Forgotten were moments of uncertainty and inexperience. All I had to do was gauge his reaction and I knew I was doing it right.

He cupped my jaw, his fingers splaying on my neck and into my hair as we both held each other in place with just a look. Our eye contact never broke and his speed picked up. His hips pumped back and forth, the vein in his neck coiling into his shirt twitched. Abruptly, he pushed me away and I fell back onto the plush couch.

Wiping my mouth with the back of my hand, I asked, "Did I do something wrong?"

Kova grunted, holding himself. "No, quite the opposite actually."

A huge smile moved across my face, but then I realized he still didn't orgasm. "But you didn't finish."

"That is because I am not done with you." My eyes tracked him as he took two steps and moved to the end of the couch. He wrapped a strong arm around my waist and hoisted me up. Spinning me around, he bent me over as if I weighed no more than a feather. My knees landed on the armrest and my hands on the couch cushion. Without a second to catch my breath, he took me from behind. It was a different angle, and I wasn't expecting it when he thrusted in. A slight sharpness shot through me and I grunted in pain. I was still tender from the orgasm and I moved to sit up, but he pushed my back down.

"Stay."

I wasn't sure why, but hearing him demand I stayed down caused a flood of wetness between my thighs.

"You asked for it, you are going to get what she gets. Do not say her fucking name again."

Satisfied, I grinned. "Good."

Kova's fingers slipped under my cami, his nails grazed my skin and I shivered. He gave a good tug and ripped my cami off, throwing it to the ground in pieces. He aggressively palmed my breasts and squeezed before pinching my nipples. My back arched and my arms gave out, bending at the elbows. Kova's fingers tightened on my hips as he slid slowly back and forth into me, creating a maelstrom of pleasure. It wasn't hurried or rushed. It was slow and steady—sublime. The only sound was the suction of our conjoined bodies as he pulled out and slid in, holding it for a split second. Just enough time for my clit to throb and greedily beg for more.

"Ahhhh…"

"Tell me you like this, tell me how much you want me to fuck you."

"Yes, you know I do," rolled off my lips. I did, I liked it a lot. Somehow, I found my inner strength. My hips took over and started rocking back into him, meeting him for each thrust. This angle was deeper and slightly painful, but the pain turned to pleasure and the intense feeling streaming through my blood was like a soaring high I never wanted to come down from. A sensation so incredibly powerful I bet nothing could top it.

"Oh, my God." Another orgasm was quickly rising.

But then Kova pulled out before I could find that earth shattering release I knew he could give me. I looked over my shoulder ready to spout off what the hell he was doing when he tapped the inside of my thigh for me to spread my legs wider. He reached over and pushed my head down into the couch, then with a flick of his wrist, he rotated my hips up and back so they were angled high. Of the times Kova and I had been together, this was the most exposed I'd ever been to him. Under normal circumstances, I might have objected to this position due to my vulnerability, but I was in such a daze and lost in his touch, I willingly gave myself to him. No, was never a thought in my mind.

Kova knelt down between my legs and spread my pussy open and ran his tongue along my plump lips. I moaned, my hips arching back even more as my hands gripped as much fabric from the couch as possible. He focused on my clit, sucking and flicking it with his tongue while his finger pressed on my puckered little hole. Tears formed in my eyes from the sheer pleasure that took over my body. I was floating on another planet. I was so sensitive I nearly bucked into his face at the gentleness.

I tried to move but he just gripped me tighter, his fingers digging into me.

"Kova…I…I'm going to…" I couldn't get the thought out before an orgasm racked through me for the second time. Stars clouded my vision and I moaned so loud, rolling my eyes shut while he just kept sucking and sucking, his tongue flicked my sex like he was on a mission. Nothing in the world compared to this moment and his wicked tongue. Sweat dampened my skin, my entire body was on fire. Heat zipped down my spine, blood flushed my cheeks and I was free falling as pleasure tore through me.

I was done. Spent. Exhausted.

My hips melted, no longer able to hold my weight. My knees slipped along the arm of the couch. When the orgasm faded, Kova stood and without hesitation, he jacked my hips back up and drove all the way in.

"Fuck, that hurt."

My face pressed into the couch cushion. Tears prickled the back of my eyes but I wouldn't let them fall. My fingers dug into the cushion while Kova's hand flattened my lower back, arching my hips up. My legs quivered and struggled to hold still.

"I am not done with you. I do not think I could ever be done…" If it was even possible, the thrusts got deeper. At this point, I wasn't going to be able to walk tomorrow.

Kova drove in so hard and fast his balls hit my tender clit. I was sweating—my entire body was a blaze of heat. I almost wanted this to be over.

"You wanted it. You pushed me until my cock was so hard it ached. All I could think of was getting inside of your tight pussy. I am a man with only one focus when that happens."

Kova reached for me and pulled me up so my back was to his chest. My arms reached up and wound his neck from behind. Kova's soft spoken words nuzzled the curve of my neck as he whispered in Russian. I wished to God I knew what he was saying. My legs trembled and he used his strength to hold me upright.

Thankfully, Kova sensed how weak I'd become. I exhaled a sigh of relief when he supported me with his toned arms by wrapping one around my small hips. My head tilted back onto his shoulder when he rolled my nipple between his fingers, his thrusts becoming slower.

"How are you still going? I must not be good if I can't make you come."

His stubble nuzzled my jaw, adding pleasure to the sex, and I shuddered in his embrace. Whispering near my mouth, he said, "I am a man, Ria, not some little boy who cannot last more than a minute. Remember that. I fuck all night long, not three minutes."

I swallowed hard. After tonight, I had no doubt he could.

"Lean over the back of the couch."

I almost whimpered, but did as he demanded. I didn't want to leave the solace of his arms. His thrusts deepened. Long, hard, but slow strokes, like he was trying to feel every inch of me. Kova was close to reaching his pinnacle, I could tell by the frantic way he gripped me and the sexy sounds coming from his throat. I'd have to wear shorts in the gym tomorrow for sure, otherwise his fingerprints would show.

He reached under, and instead of rubbing my clit, he pressed my swollen lips together causing my head to fly back in bliss.

"Right there…that is what I want to feel," he groaned, hitting a new, deeper spot inside, like he had a special spot he wanted to reach.

"Keep that position, I know you can."

"I'll try."

"Not try," he rebutted. "You will do it."

A shiver rolled down my spine and my thighs quivered. Sweet Jesus Mother Mary.

He rubbed my lips faster, increasing the pressure and friction on my clit at the same time. The intense pressure shot straight through me, causing the walls of my sex to spasm, tightening around him.

"Yes, *malysh*, just like that," he mumbled in approval. His hand rubbed warm circles on my back, like he was enjoying this as much as I was, if not more. "I love it, do not stop." Just as my release made its way through my body, Kova removed his hand and slapped my ass cheek so hard that I came before I could even process what happened.

"Omigod." I almost choked. "Yes…More…"

"Ria…, just like that," he smacked my ass once more, the orgasm continued to sweep through me at breakneck speed. A burst of electricity exploded from within and I clenched around him. The slapping caught me by surprise and I was a bit confused by how much I enjoyed it. I almost wished he'd do it again.

One last thrust, and Kova squeezed my hips tight as he pulsed inside of me. I was sure I'd have bruises tomorrow. He pushed all the way in and grunted, his hips doing small, slow thrusts as he filled me. He came hard, the warm fluid leaking out and down my inner thigh. Kova's loud moan caused my body to shudder from the remnants of my release. I was coated with him and relished in this moment of unyielding bliss. I loved it. Every minute, every thrust, every touch.

I could easily become addicted to this kind of sex. The tension in the room settled down, and all that was left was heavy panting and the scent of sex lingering in the air.

Kova withdrew and walked to the bathroom, but not before I felt his palm smooth tenderly down my reddened cheek and a gentle kiss was pressed to my spine. I waited until he was out of sight to rollover onto the couch cushion. Reaching higher, I grabbed my ripped cami he threw earlier and covered my chest. I was too exhausted to actually find a new one to put back on just yet.

A few moments later, the bathroom door opened and Kova walked out. My brows furrowed and my lips formed a thin, tight line. Seeing as his release was still on my thigh, I thought he was coming out to clean me up like last time and then spend time with me before he left. Instead, he was completely dressed and he wore a scowl on his beautiful face as he stood before me. His eyes raked down my body, but unlike the heat they usually held, they were completely deflated and it crushed my heart.

A resigned sigh escaped him. Running a hand through his hair, he dropped a damp rag on my leg. I flinched.

"That is what you wanted, right? A good fuck?" When I didn't answer, he said, "Was it as good for you as it was for me?"

And then he stalked off and was out the door like nothing had ever happened.

chapter 63

MY ALARM BLARED ANNOYINGLY AT 5:30 AM AND I FELT LIKE I'D JUST FALLEN asleep.

The last thing I wanted was to leave the warmth of my cozy bed. I'd give anything to skip practice today, but I knew I couldn't.

With only three hours of sleep, I was tempted to feign a serious illness just to be admitted to the hospital so I could sleep some more.

Though, I was fairly certain getting a "good fuck" by a Russian dick wasn't a serious illness.

I was sleep deprived for a reason. Reality set in and my stomach flipped in anticipation, making me feel queasy. Kova had treated me like garbage last night. I knew seeing him would be awkward after the night's episode, but I was upset over how callous he'd been. I was still new to all of this and wasn't sure how to process everything. I liked it, I liked the bite of pain, but it hurt at times.

Maybe taunting him hadn't been such a good idea, and maybe withholding my virginity from him wasn't the brightest thing to do, because the more I thought about it, the more wrong it felt. Guilt ate at me. Kova felt lied to and that didn't sit well with me. He was upset because I had kept that little nugget of info to myself, but it really wasn't any of his business. Yet, in the end, I wouldn't change a thing.

Yawning, I stretched my arms above my head before rolling over into my pillow and snuggling up to it. My eyes were as dry as the Sahara Desert. The last time I looked at the clock, it was a little after one. I was beyond exhausted, my body ached all over. I wanted more than anything to go back to sleep, but that wasn't happening anytime soon.

My stupid alarm went off again, and this time I unenthusiastically got out of bed. Soreness resonated between my thighs and I winced. Fuck, it hurt. I wasn't expecting a sharp sting, like an enormous paper cut down there, but it's exactly what it felt like.

A shower was a must. I was too tired to just head to the gym like I normally did. I needed to wake up.

Grabbing a leo, a sports bra, and some sweat pants, I headed into the bathroom and turned on the shower. While I waited for the water to heat, my bladder made itself known like it was about to explode.

Sighing as if it was an inconvenience to pee, I sat down on the cold toilet to relieve myself only to stop and gasp in pain. Jesus Christ! I tried to pee again by only letting a little out, but my whole body tightened in agony from the sting. It hurt too much to go.

Kova must've torn me up pretty good last night.

Steam filled my bathroom and there I was, leaning over my legs with my arms wrapped around my stomach, holding my breath to the point where my lungs hurt. I could only take so much, so I only let half out.

I'd try again later. Even wiping hurt, so I only dabbed.

I took a fast shower, washing my hair and shaving my legs in record time, careful not to let soap slip to my sex. I once cut my lip down there while shaving. It was a small slice and when soap touched it, it burned like a bitch.

Turning the shower off, I grabbed a towel and stepped out. I wiped the foggy mirror down and then dried myself off quickly. As I did, my brows angled in confusion at the reflection. Standing up, I pivoted around and looked in the mirror so I could see my entire waist and backside. My jaw dropped at what stared back at me.

Kova's fingerprints covered my flesh in tiny little black and blue marks. From the tops of my thighs, to my hips, and the back of my legs. They were everywhere. I could connect the dots if I wanted to. It was hard not to notice them. Bringing my foot up and propping it on the ledge of the counter, I bent over and looked down at my pussy.

My skin was a rosy pink and swollen. I grimaced. I looked closely, moving my flesh around, but I couldn't see anything with the naked eye. Grabbing a small mirror, I placed it between my legs to get a better look. Examining as close as I could get, I noticed a tiny little red mark. I ran my index finger gently over it and I flinched. Kova tore me, which would explain why it hurt to pee. I guess he wasn't lying when he said he hadn't given me everything the first time. He sure had this time.

After I finished dressing, I grabbed an extra pair of gym shorts to cover up any marks and stuffed them into my bag. Typically, I didn't wear shorts unless it was that time of the month for me, though many gymnasts opted to.

I checked the clock and realized I was running behind. Coach was going to kill me. I grabbed a granola bar, approved by my lovely mother of course, and my schoolbooks before dashing out of my condo. It was Monday, which meant I had tutoring, lunch, and then more training later. Plus, therapy on my calf.

Luckily, World Cup was only about ten minutes away. I walked into the gym at five thirty, and all three coaches were already yelling.

It was going to be a long day.

Nearly four hours later, and practice hadn't been easy. Straight up—my vagina hurt. Any kind of split jump on the beam felt like I was ripping in two, and it wasn't like I could choose not to do them, I had to. Not to mention, I was mentally and physically exhausted—it was all the effort I could muster to keep my eyes open, let alone also have to do my routines.

Today, I realized just how many skills I had with my legs spread wide open.

Then came the Tsavdaridou, a round-off back handspring with a full twist to swing down. Those hadn't been pleasant either. As a matter of fact, nothing had been pleasant this morning. The skills terrified me today, and they never had before, but knowing I was going to come down with my legs opened and land with the beam braced between them, I hated it.

For once in my life, I wanted to perfect my turns so I wouldn't aggravate my Achilles.

I'd been extra careful to make sure I didn't straddle the beam as much as I could. I fell a few times, but I was able to catch myself. Dear God, I don't know if I could've handled that splitting pain too. Luckily, beam had passed quickly and now I was on vault.

The urge to pee hit like a ton of bricks. I hadn't gone since this morning because of the stinging pain and feared it would happen again, but now I couldn't hold it any longer. I had to go. If I did one more turn on vault, I was going to burst. And peeing on the vault was not a good look.

I wondered if I could slap some Vaseline on the tears. I figured it would help with peeing and my jumps, but then I also wondered what if I got Vaseline inside. I shuddered at the thought. Never mind. I couldn't take the chance. I'd just have to deal.

To top off my lovely morning, Kova hadn't looked my way once. Madeline had worked with me the entire time and it seemed like no matter where I was in the gym, he was on the opposite side of me. Almost as if he was intentionally keeping us as far apart as possible. Maybe he'd gone through and implemented Madeline as my coach now and not him. I prayed he didn't.

I knew I needed to stay focused on my training, but I couldn't help wonder what he was thinking about, if he was thinking about the night before at all. It was almost as if I wasn't even there. I hated the feeling, like I was invisible and I didn't matter.

I sighed inwardly.

Stepping into the bathroom, I locked the door and stripped out of my leo. This was the one part of gymnastics I detested—being sweaty and having to remove the one piece. It was like peeling off soaking wet, skinny jeans.

Taking a deep breath, I closed my eyes and prayed I could pee without it hurting. I bared down, tightened my insides and only let a trickle out…and paused. Releasing an audible sigh, I let go again only to feel the burning sensation come back full force. My hand slammed against the wall and I leaned against it for support. But I didn't let it all out. It just wasn't achievable. The urine burned the shit out of me!

That was it, all I could manage. I carefully wiped, pulled up my leo and washed my hands. I had one more hour until I broke for lunch and tutoring, then it was back to training for four more hours. After therapy when I got home, I'd soak in the bath.

I had this. I just needed to give myself a pep talk first.

Walking back into the gym, I immediately scanned for Kova. It was more out of habit and addiction than a conscious thought. I craved his glaring eyes and fierce words. They drove me to be better, stronger. To prove myself.

When we finally locked eyes, he didn't break my gaze. His posture was strict, his arms firmly crossed against his taut chest. I walked blindly, unable to focus on my surroundings. He tried to tell me something with his eyes, but I wasn't sure what. All I knew was he was staring like he couldn't stand the sight of me and it hurt.

"Watch out!"

I flinched and put my hands up, ducking.

"Jesus, Big Red. We all know Coach Kova is hot, but pay attention. Don't make it so obvious you're gawking at him. God…"

I closed my eyes and counted to five. Reagan and her stupid redhead comments. I would've corrected her, but I wasn't in the mood. I nearly walked into her dismount, which could've seriously hurt both of us. But she was right, I needed to pay attention.

I didn't apologize, I just ignored her and headed back to vault while she continued on beam.

"You okay?" Hayden asked, concerned. His observant eyes made me edgy.

Or maybe I was just being paranoid.

Nodding, I smiled sweetly and put on a happy face. "Yeah, I'm just exhausted."

Grabbing some chalk for the vault, I rubbed some on my feet, adding a little to my thighs when Hayden walked away. I clapped my hands to remove the excess powder and could taste it in my mouth.

I moved to stand behind the white line and took a deep breath when Kova turned to look at me. He nodded his head, gesturing for me to go. Madeline clapped her hands and yelled, "Get moving, Adrianna. I don't have all day!"

Rising up on my tiptoes, I leaned forward and took off running. I pumped my legs as fast as I could and only focused on the vault. My calf hurt just a bit, but I blocked it out. Everything else faded away and I forgot all the issues in my life as I zoomed in on the apparatus and felt the adrenaline hit me hard.

God, I loved this feeling. My racing heart, burning muscles. The anticipation.

Zoning in on only the springboard, I did a round-off onto it and arched into a back hand-spring. I popped my shoulders off the vault into a two and a half twist to complete an Amanar. I took a few steps back on my landing and fell.

Fuck my life.

Adding the half twist created a blind landing, so there was no spotting the floor. I had to wish on a prayer I would land it correctly. I could practice it a million and one times, land it at every practice, but it only took a split second where I didn't crank high enough, or my legs were bent, my chest was too low, anything to not land it at competition.

In gymnastics, anything was possible. And considering I was working on the hardest vault for women, that should say something.

Standing up, I heard Madeline sigh loudly. "I'm trying, I really am," I broke in before she could say anything.

She looked at me with pity. "I know you are. Let's do it again."

"Adrianna. Keep your legs straight in the flight, chest up," Kova chimed in, looking at me intently.

"He's right," Madeline acknowledged. "Your legs are sloppy and bent. I noticed your feet were crossed too, which is a big no, Adrianna. Try and set your twist just a tad higher. You need something that will give you points and move you up in the standings, not set you back."

I nodded.

"Is your calf bothering you?" she asked with concern.

"No." I could've lied and said yes, which would be the reason for my shitty landing, but I didn't.

Nothing was worse than being told you couldn't do something after trying so hard to achieve it. Swallowing back my frustration, I stared at the vault and pictured my landing perfectly. I could do this, I told myself. I'd done it before, I just needed to visualize it and be confident in my abilities.

"You got this, Aid," Hayden whispered, tightening his wrist brace with a nod. I smiled at him, my face softening.

Another deep breath, and I took off. Round-off, back handspring onto the vault, popped off and I reached to twist. I mentally noted my legs and straightened them, but it was too late at that point. I opened my arms to balance my landing, but I already knew I was leaning too far back and my hips were too low. It was a feeling inside that was unexplainable, but I knew my body and knew I wasn't going to stick it.

Trying to save it was pointless. I was literally in a seated position and hit the floor just like that, stumbling backwards and falling on the blue mat. Tears welled in my eyes as pain suddenly throbbed viciously through my back. Massaging my side, I felt like crying from being so frustrated and not hitting my marks. Self-doubt was beating me up today and I began to wonder if I was pushing too far.

Madeline sighed. "Go to tutoring and I'll see you later."

"Can I try one more time?"

Madeline nodded, then grabbed a mat to stand on. It was the shape of a box and high, leveled with the vault so she could spot me.

Dear God, please let me land this.

Swallowing, I began running, my feet pounded into the ground. I moved into the entry, and then sprang off the vault. Madeline's hands helped pop the back of my shoulders, lifting me higher in the air to help me set my element. I started rotating, cranking the twist as hard as I could muster to land properly. And by some miracle, I landed—only for another shot of pain to soar through my back, but I sucked it up. Albeit I landed sloppy, my feet hit the floor, not my butt, and that was all that mattered right now. A loud sigh burst from my lips and I closed my eyes in satisfaction, hiding my back pain.

"Again," Madeline said.

I did it again with her help and landed. Yes! Land was a word I used lightly, but the fact that I was standing upright was what motivated me and gave me that little push to keep going.

After three more tries, she pulled the mat away for me to do it on my own. Nerves wracked me hard and I was suddenly worried I wouldn't hit it again. It was an irrational fear that coursed through me, I knew it, but it came with the territory. My heart split between being in my throat and stomach. All eyes were on me. Fear and nerves were part of a gymnast's genetic makeup.

But so was winning.

I had this…I got this…visualize…

Adrenaline pumped through my veins fast as I ran toward the leather apparatus, but apprehension and nerves dominated when I hit the spring board. Fire shot through my back and I panicked in the middle of my rotation and only pulled a full. It was a clean landing, but Madeline glared at me.

Shit.

"You," she said between clenched teeth, and pointed at me, "get your butt back over there and do the Amanar. Now."

My stomach dropped. All I could do was nod and start walking. I didn't have much of a choice.

The urge to pee never really went away, and a wave of pain hit my screaming bladder. It was only ten in the morning, yet this day was going to shit fast. Very little sleep, a burning vagina, and now a raging coach.

And I only had myself to blame.

I did the vault once more and added the stupid twist, but without her push, I barely landed on the tips of my toes. My stomach clenched tight and I gave up and jumped to the side, my calf burning slightly.

Before I could speak, Madeline pointed toward the exit and said, "Go. Come back after tutoring. Maybe you'll be better after you've had a break."

"Can I try it once more?"

"No," she heaved a sigh. "Come back later and we'll work on it again."

My shoulders dropped in defeat. Turning around, I stared at the ground to avoid the gawking stares while I made my way to the locker room. I was beyond embarrassed with my workout and didn't want to see the judgmental look in my peers' eyes.

"Hey Aid," Hayden called out across the gym. I slowly raised my eyes, afraid to be greeted with a look of pity. Surprisingly, I saw encouragement in his eyes as he jogged over to me.

"Give me twenty and I'll be done. We'll ride to tutoring together."

I smiled kindly. After the shit storm morning I had, Hayden's bulldoze through life mentality was exactly what I needed.

Opening my locker, I pulled out my duffle bag and dropped it to the floor, shuffling around for my clothes. I was so upset with myself and wanted to cry. I was better than this, and I let things get in the way of training. I needed to be stronger and overcome my fears, but it was easier said than done. I was training in a sport that could literally paralyze me in one split second by not getting enough air in rotation or landing wrong. And I wasn't at one hundred percent because of my leg. My landings were shit today. If my timing wasn't absolutely perfect, the repercussions could be devastating. There was a reason gymnastics was considered one of the most dangerous sports. It was a risk to take, but my heart was all in. Even with days when I was at my worst, I would never give up.

Changing out of my leotard, I noticed little droplets of blood. Shit. It was a good thing I carried extra leos with me. I dressed quickly then shoved my bag back into the locker and slammed it shut as hard as I could muster. I should've done some stretching to cool my muscles, but I didn't even care to.

Walking into one of the physical therapy rooms, I laid on the blue, plastic table and waited for Hayden. I looked forward to hanging out with him. Throwing an arm over my face, I closed my eyes, thinking about my vault.

"Adrianna...Adrianna, wake up."

Opening my eyes, I was disoriented for a moment and confused at where I was. "H-Hayden?" My voice cracked. Jesus. It felt like I'd been asleep for hours.

He smiled down at me. "Come on, Sleeping Beauty. We've got tutoring."

I groaned. "Did you have to kiss me to wake me up because I feel like I could sleep forever."

His cheeks deepened in color. "I was about to."

"Can I just skip and go home and sleep?" Hayden reached his hand out to help me sit up. I yawned and took it.

"Rough night?"

"If you only knew."

"You look like shit."

A smile tipped my lips. "Be still my heart," I responded flippantly.

"Hey, I just call it like it is."

"I can obviously tell."

We stepped out of the locker room and made our way to the lobby. My brows cinched together when I heard Kova's voice in the distance. The closer we got, the louder it became, and my heart stopped at the soft tone in his voice.

"Hey, what are you doing here?"

I tried not to hold my breath as I listened to the response that met my ears.

"I came to surprise you for lunch." I knew that voice. Katja had one of the most singsong voices I'd ever heard, even with the thick Russian accent that accompanied it.

"You know I keep a schedule, Kat. You should have called me first."

As we rounded the corner, he had her pulled in for a kiss. His fingers were threaded through her chestnut hair in a sensual, possessive lip lock. My stomach dropped at the sight. He never kissed me like that. He never looked at me with love in his eyes. He never embraced me so tenderly.

"What was that for?" she asked breathlessly as they pulled apart.

He tensed and irritably bit out, "Why do I need a reason to kiss you? Can I not kiss you when I want?"

"You do not," she responded with flushed cheeks. "You know you can anytime." She looked at him with hearts in her eyes. "I love you."

I paled at her display of love, my stomach rolled in waves. Hayden was completely blasé to their affection, and luckily completely oblivious to my gut wrenching reaction, as he continued walking to the front door. It took all the strength I had to make my feet continue to move when all I really wanted to do was flop down on the floor and have a pity party.

I didn't want it to bother me, but it did. Watching them in their private moment told me everything I needed to know, and showed me everything I would never have.

With Hayden's keys jangling in his hand, they both turned their heads in our direction. Katja's chin dipped, embarrassment coloring her cheeks.

Hayden held the door open and I brushed against him walking outside. My eyes locked with Katja and then Kova, who held my gaze until I left.

"You okay?" Hayden asked at the sound of my expelled breath as the door shut behind us.

"What?" I glanced at his face distractedly, my mind totally not wanting to function today. I shook myself out of it. "Yeah, I'm just worn out is all. I'm ready for this day to be over."

"You realize it's not even noon yet, right?"

"Don't remind me."

We hopped into Hayden's car and he started the ignition, draping a strong arm over the top of my seat. As he peered over his shoulder to back out, he looked at me and smiled with his warm blue eyes.

"Don't sweat it. We all have off days."

"Off days? I sucked! Badly! I looked like an amateur!"

He chuckled over my exaggerated sigh. "You totally did."

I reached over and punched him. "You don't have to state the obvious!"

"Would you rather I lie?"

"No."

"Hey." He put a finger under my chin at the red light. "Keep your head up. It's just a bad morning practice, not a bad life. This afternoon will be better."

I smiled softly at him. "I hope so. I feel like I'm the only one having bad practices lately."

"It happens sometimes. You'll get through it."

"I know...it just sucks. Regina seems to thrive on my mistakes."

He gave me a perplexed look. "Regina?"

"Reagan, I mean. Have you ever seen *Mean Girls*? She's the Regina George of gymnastics. Loves to see people fail and shit. Like she gets off on it."

"Never heard of it, but why do I have a feeling you're right? Maybe one night we'll watch it together," he said, shifting into another gear.

I pursed my lips together. "You want to watch *Mean Girls*?"

He shrugged, pulling into the library. "Why not?"

"I don't know...because it's a chick flick?"

"So? We'll get some pizza and soda, pig out, and watch a movie one night."

I sighed happily. That sounded like such a great idea.

"I can't remember the last time I turned the television on. Our schedules are so intense and jam packed I fall into bed as soon as I get home. There's no time for fun."

The smirk that slid across Hayden's face told me I was wrong. "There's always time for fun."

I bit my lip. "I'd like that, but can we not tell anyone? Meaning your sister so she doesn't tell Reagan? I don't need any more shit."

"So you mean, I'm your dirty little secret?" He winked.

chapter 64

THREE HOURS LATER AND MY BRAIN WAS FRIED.

Math was not my strongest subject. When letters got mixed in with numbers, that was it. I was done. Luckily my tutor only made me do it for an hour then moved on to History. Which I loved.

"Want to grab a bite to eat before we head back?" Hayden asked.

I checked my watch and realized I hadn't eaten anything other than a granola bar.

"Eh. I have a salad at the gym, but I'm not really in the mood."

His face scrunched up. "A salad? Aid, you have to eat. You have four hours of practice ahead of you." He had a point, I was running on fumes, but my lack of appetite was due to reasons he was unaware of.

"Honestly, Hayden, I'm just too stressed out to eat right now."

Hayden pulled into a shopping plaza and parked in front. "Gotta eat to keep up that stamina." He winked, and jumped out of his car.

When we walked in, I was instantly reminded of Whole Foods. That place always has a strange odor. The smell assaulted me and I started giggling thinking of something Avery said once.

"What's so funny?"

"It's nothing."

Hayden paused, grinning. "Tell me."

"This place reminds me of Whole Foods. It has the same smell."

He looked confused. "And that's funny to you?"

"Avery swears Whole Foods uses natural cleaning products that are supposed to be orange scented but they actually smell like dirty jock straps. That's why when you walk into one it always has the same gross smell. I agree with her, not that I know what jock straps smell like, it's just a wild guess."

Hayden's eyes were gleaming with laughter.

"What? Don't look at me like that!"

"I didn't say anything," he laughed, putting his hands up.

"You have a look in your eyes. I'm going to punch you!" I raised my fist playfully and he didn't even flinch.

Before I could say anything else, the urge to pee sliced through me. "Can you order me a turkey lettuce wrap please? I need to use the restroom."

"No bread or cheese?"

"Are you insane? Of course not! Just turkey and lettuce. Nothing else."

He knew how strict our diets were. Carbs and dairy were out. I allowed myself carbs once a week, but it sure as hell wasn't from a wrap. Those little flat pieces of nothing were loaded with shit I couldn't afford to put in my body.

Finding the bathrooms, I reached to yank the door open only to find it locked. *Dammit!* I leaned against the opposite wall, counting the seconds and trying desperately not to do the pee dance. My mother would give me the evil eye all the way from Palm Bay if I did. From all the years of being obedient under my mother's watchful eye, I just stood with my legs crossed like a lady, and praying to God this person hurried the hell up.

After what felt like an eternity, a mother holding her son's hand exited the bathroom. As soon as their bodies cleared the doorframe, I dashed in. My bladder burned as I shifted from foot to foot trying to unbutton and unzip my jeans. I tightened my abdomen, feeling ready to explode while I hovered over the toilet.

Taking a deep breath, I closed my eyes and let it trickle out slowly like last time…and felt the burn. I stopped, my teeth biting into my bottom lip as tears threatened behind my eyes.

I hated this pain.

I tried again, but my urine was hot, so it stung even more this time. I expelled a gush of air from my lungs at the little bit I was capable of releasing and then zipped up my pants. I'd much rather straddle the beam than deal with this sort of pain right now.

I flushed, washed my hands, and was out of the bathroom to find Hayden paying for our lunch. I reached into my pocket, but he stopped me.

"Nah, don't worry about it."

I pushed the twenty at him. "Take it."

"No, no," he said, turning around and heading for a table. "I asked you to come to lunch, I can pay for it."

I stood there, dumbfounded with the money in my hand. "I'm not used to people paying for me. I almost don't know what to do."

Hayden whipped his head in my direction and stared at me. "You just stick it back in your pocket and say, 'Gee, Hayden, that was so sweet of you. Thanks,' and sit down and eat."

I tried to suppress the grin that formed across my lips, but it was useless. Hayden was adorable and charming. His dirty blonde hair had a perfect bed head look and he glowed with charisma. I couldn't help but want to be around him.

"You're such a dork. I know how to say thank you," I said, taking a bite of my boring lettuce wrap. "Thank you." Hayden smiled and pushed a small, peachy looking smoothie in front of me. My eyes met his.

"This was part of the special of the day. No carbs—relax. It's organic vegetables and fruit only. I watched her make it. You're allowed to have this."

"There's carbs in fruit and veggies." He just stared at me so I continued. "There was no fruit juice added to make it?" I worried about the amount of sugar in this drink. It looked incredibly good, but I had to be careful and not over indulge.

"She used coconut water. It's all natural so you're safe."

I smiled at Hayden, appreciating his thoughtfulness. He was making an effort by watching out for me.

Picking it up, I sipped the frothy concoction and swallowed. My eyes lit up as the icy drink hit my tongue and I took another sip, this time a larger one.

"Wow! This really is good. Here," I handed it to him. "Try it." Hayden swallowed and grinned, sipping the drink.

"I get the smoothies here a lot, but this was a new one they had today."

"It's really good. I can see why you get it."

After a couple of minutes of eating our lunch in silence, I drank about half of the smoothie and handed the rest to Hayden. "Take it. I'm full from my wrap and this, I can't finish the rest," I lied. I could finish it, and I wanted to, but watching my weight was more important.

Hayden finished with his giant sandwich and chips. He was lucky he could pretty much eat anything. I'd give anything to just eat whatever I wanted. Most of the guys' team could. Being full while at the gym was uncomfortable and I'd rather be a little hungry.

At least it's what I told myself.

Hayden squinted his eyes, and reluctantly took my drink and finished it. "You're lying."

"Fine! I'm lying!" I caved. "Truth is, I'm stressed about gym, so I don't really have an appetite." I bit my lip and then said, "Honestly, sometimes I question myself and why I ever came here. Maybe I'm not cut out for this."

Hayden tilted his head to the side, studying me. "We all have days like this, Aid. Tomorrow won't be as bad. You're still somewhat new so you're still transitioning into this lifestyle."

"I'm not new, I've been here for like, a million months now."

"I've been part of World Cup for *years*. I was overwhelmed and almost walked out a few times once I transitioned to elite. The training is way more rigorous, the hours are long. It's draining on so many levels that sometimes I wondered what I got myself into. But at the same time, I couldn't imagine not doing gymnastics. It's in my blood, just like it's in yours. Even when you have days where you hate it and want to walk out, you know you can't. Some days you compare yourself to your teammates and feel inadequate. You're not. You're just having an off day. Some days are really lonely too. It's the hardest when you go home and have no parents or friends to turn to. I have my sister and she understands this life, but that's different." Hayden paused and looked at his hands, thinking about what to say next. "You love the sport too much to give up. And you know you never will. It's just not possible, so you deal with the loneliness, you deal with the bad days, and you truck on."

I swallowed back the lump in my throat. "You're right. You're so right on everything you said." Tears were brimming the back of my eyes. I didn't want to cry, but I had so much on my plate and I felt them ready to spill over at any second. I was bottling it all up and I hadn't realized how lonely I was until that moment. Hayden noticed my change. He grabbed our trash, threw it out, and then took my hand and we walked out to his car.

I didn't say anything about the hand holding, because truthfully, it felt nice. I even leaned into his arm and held on to him. Even though he was only a little older than me, he gave me security in his touch and I soaked it up. He was my comfort, my shoulder to lean on. My heart softened a little for Hayden and I gave him a gentle squeeze.

Hayden pulled open the passenger side door, but before I could climb in, he pulled me into a bear hug. I automatically wrapped my arms around him and buried my head into the crook of his neck, closing my eyes.

"Don't stress about earlier. It's over with," he spoke against my cheek. "Focus on the future."

I nodded, unable to form words. "I'm not sure what I'd do without you, Hayden."

I was being emotional and I hated it. I didn't deal well with emotions, kudos to my mother. These feelings were foreign and unwelcomed and I wanted them gone. All they did was remind me just how human I really was.

Hayden held on to me, rubbing my arms and giving me strength. I hugged him a little tighter, taking everything he offered. "I'm always here for you."

"Thank you." Taking a chance, I asked with a shaky voice, "Do you think you'd want to come over tonight after gym? You know, just to hang out? I could use the company."

Pulling back, Hayden looked down at me. His face was soft and his eyes warm. "Sure. I'd love to." He smiled genuinely, then pressed a kiss to my forehead. "We can even watch *Mean Girls* if you want."

My stomach curled with anticipation. I needed to put my game face on and focus. I was here to train, not worry about what my coach thought about me or how bitchy the girls were.

I climbed into the car, my head flopping back against the leather headrest. I took a deep breath and turned to Hayden. "I got this."

chapter 65

I KNEW THERE WAS SOMETHING WRONG THE MOMENT I WOKE UP—TWO HOURS EARLY and in complete agony.

Pain tore through my lower belly as a fire ripped through me like an inferno that couldn't be doused. But it didn't just stop there. It went up my side and wrapped around. My back throbbed as if a heavy metal drummer was using my body as practice, the pounding was nonstop.

With my knees pressed to my chest bound by my arms, I curled into a tiny ball, wishing on a star this throbbing sting would go away. I'd never in my life had cramping quite like this before and I wasn't sure what to think of it. I squeezed my eyes tight and chewed my bottom lip raw in a matter of minutes. The only thing that shot through my mind was getting to the hospital immediately.

Thing was, I didn't think I was capable of driving. The pain was that intense. Nausea coiled my stomach and I fought to keep the contents I had for dinner with Hayden down.

Glancing at the clock, it was too early to call anyone, but I needed someone. Madeline was my first thought since she'd come with me to see Dr. DeLang, but something in my gut told me not to call her. The only other person I felt comfortable calling was Hayden. It was either him, or I drove myself.

I shot Hayden a quick text hoping he'd see it when he woke up. I told him I needed help and I was sick. In the meantime, I would take a heavy dose of Motrin—my go to drug—and soak in a hot bath. But trying to stand hurt and it caused me to hunch over and stop. Taking a deep breath, I slowly stood up again, a hand pressed to my stomach this time. As I walked, I could swear my muscles were being ripped to shreds. With this kind of pain, I knew there was no way I could train today. It just wasn't physically possible. That being said, I was terrified to call Kova and tell him, especially with how things left off between us. It was awkward, and I'd be surprised if he'd even answer me anyway.

I turned on the tub and waited for it to fill, I leaned down and pulled out a carton of Epsom Salt and a bottle of Motrin. I dumped a generous amount into the hot water and swirled my fingers around the filling tub. My mom always had this stuff in the house and swore it would heal internal ailments. Once I started training at World Cup, it became a staple in my condo.

Rising up from the tub, a sharp pain shot through my belly. I cringed, gushing out a loud breath. Even leaning over at this angle was agony. Whatever it was, I prayed a doctor could diagnose it and heal me by tonight.

I was a hot mess.

Stripping off my clothes, I looked in the mirror and my eyes widened. I was pale and looked like death. My eyes were hollow and the color weak. There were yellow tinted bruises all around my hips and I was skinnier than ever. Cruella de Vil, also known as my mother, would be proud of my weight loss.

I filled the glass cup I kept in my bathroom with water. The back of the ibuprofen bottle said two pills, but I was going to take four like I typically did. I quickly washed the orange pills down and drank another glass of water before stepping up to the side of the bathtub.

Lifting my knee, I dipped my foot into the water, hating the first steamy touch. I drew in a long, tired breath and exhaled before sinking into the water.

Once my entire body was in, I leaned back on a plastic pillow and propped my knees up, then closed my eyes. The water came up to my neck and I sighed in contentment. I sat completely motionless, trying to relax and allow whatever magic the Epsom Salt contained to do its job. Hopefully the pain relievers would kick in because not being able to move wasn't working for me.

A good five minutes into my bath, and I tightened my stomach as a blaze of fire erupted inside. The throbbing in my back still hadn't gone away. I panted and started a countdown for the pain to actually leave. When I reached one, I slowly stretched out my right leg, then my left. My hips were beginning to feel pinched and I knew I needed to release them to full position.

The hot water and pain relievers were finally loosening up my muscles. Being as tired as I had been lately, my eyes rolled shut and I dozed off in the tub, with the tenderness in my stomach floating away.

Somewhere in the back of my mind my phone was ringing, but it wasn't the right sound. It was faint, and a heavy pounding was waking me up.

"Adrianna!"

I rustled, feeling water splash around me. My eyes popped open and I jumped, realizing I had fallen asleep in the bath.

"Fuck."

Hayden was yelling my name, probably waking my neighbors up, probably petrified something happened to me.

I wrapped a towel around my body and yelled, "I'm coming!" as I headed to the door. A quick glance at the clock and I had my answer as to why Hayden was blowing up my phone and pounding on my door like a lunatic. It'd been over an hour since I sent him the text message. Apparently exhaustion took control whenever it wanted to.

Quickly, I unbolted the locks and opened the door.

"Adrianna, where have you been? I thought something was wrong with you! Are you okay?" He rubbed his forehead after throwing the questions at me. "What happened?"

Once he stepped inside, I locked the door. I wrapped the towel around me tighter and said, "I'm so sorry for worrying you, Hayden. I fell asleep in the tub."

"Do you have any idea how dangerous that is?"

I flinched. "I know. It was reckless of me."

"Everything okay?"

"Not really. My stomach hurts pretty badly. I don't know what's wrong with me, but I need to skip practice today and go to the doctor."

The look on Hayden's face mimicked mine. Distress. He knew missing gym was a huge no. He nodded his head and said, "Go get dressed and I'll call the gym and relay the message for you."

A tender smile eased my face. "Thanks. I appreciate it."

As quickly as possible, my feet padded across the carpet into my room. Before I shut the door, it dawned on me that Hayden himself was late for practice.

"Oh, my God, Hayden! You're going to get in trouble for missing practice!" I yelled. "I'm so sorry!"

"Don't worry about me, let's just get you to the doctor. My coaches aren't hard-asses like yours anyway, so it won't be as big of a deal for me."

Nodding, I closed my bedroom door and dropped my towel. I grabbed a pair of black yoga pants and a hoodie along with a sports bra and panties. I slipped on my clothes as swiftly as possible, the sudden onset of chills caused my teeth to chatter. The only thing I could think of was I had some sort of virus that caused the pain to zip line through my body. Maybe food poisoning. I had been on a carb free diet for weeks and last night when Hayden and I watched *Mean Girls* together, he brought pizza over. This could possibly be my stomach reacting to the junk food and grease. If this was my body's way of revolting against my one night of fun, then I was never touching pizza again.

Even with my door shut, Hayden's voice carried down the hall. Every time he went to speak, he barely got a few words in before he was abruptly cut off. This happened four or five times, the pattern repeating constantly, which was surprising to me. I felt like I was listening to an episode of Maury. No one spoke above the coaches, and when they did, they spoke louder and above people. Whoever was on the other line, they weren't happy with him.

In this moment, I would forever be thankful for Hayden Moore's friendship.

"Ready?" I asked.

His jaw dropped. "Your eyes are blood shot." He walked over and pressed a hand to my head. "You're hot."

I chuckled. "Thanks."

Grabbing my hand, he pulled me to the front door. "That coach of yours is a piece of work. Thank God I only work with him on rings."

The side of my mouth pulled up. "Tell me about it."

"Do you have a doctor or are we going to the emergency room?"

I paused in my tracks. "I don't have a doctor…and I really don't want to go to the ER. Let me do a Google search and find a local twenty-four hour urgent care center."

Hayden cleared his throat. "Ah, you don't have a guardian to sign off on anything should the occasion arise?"

My head snapped up and met his worried look. He was right. I didn't have a parent or a legal guardian while I was here. This could get tricky. Luckily for me, I'd gotten great at lying lately and had the ID Avery made me that made me legal.

"I highly doubt there's going to be an issue. They're most likely going to insist on payment up front, which I have cash I can pay with."

"Where's your insurance card?" he asked as we walked out of my condo. "Do you have it with you?"

"I do, but since I'm paying with cash I don't think I'll need it."

I rattled off the address to a local urgent care center and ten minutes later we pulled into a lit up facility with a big red cross on the front of the building. We were just in time as another wave of cramps hit my stomach. I prayed the wait wouldn't be long as I slowly walked up to the entrance, slightly hunched over with Hayden by my side. The doors slid open, and I looked around at the empty lobby.

Thank God.

A heavyset woman picked her head up and glanced at us as we made our way to the front desk. She sighed irritably and asked, "What can I do for you?" She clearly wasn't a morning person.

"I need to see a doctor, please."

The woman sneered. "What seems to be the problem?"

"My stomach and back are killing me."

She looked at the computer. "Are you pregnant?"

chapter 66

MY JAW DROPPED, AND HAYDEN FROZE.

"God, no!"

"You'd be surprised how many girls are pregnant by your age, if not younger," she mumbled under her breath, typing away, loud enough for me to hear.

"Ma'am, I'm not pregnant, I'm in serious pain though. I feel like someone is beating on my back and it hurts to stand."

"All right, let's get a few things squared away first." Ms. Attitude pulled out a folder with an impatient look. I handed her my fake ID and informed her I'd be paying with cash. An open chair was positioned next to the counter so I took the liberty of sitting down. I sighed in relief and closed my eyes, grateful Hayden took over filling in the blanks, asking me for the answers. He made a comment about how good the fake ID looked and I mumbled I'd have Avery get him one. That was as much effort as I could handle at the moment.

Thirty-nine agonizing minutes later, I was brought back to an exam room. She checked my vitals and noted a fever. Like every doctor's office, I was freezing and waiting impatiently on the paper-covered table. The pain was so intense in my back, I started rocking to find a way to ease it.

Knock. Knock.

A stout doctor waltzed in wearing bold, black-rimmed glasses pushed up high, resting on the bridge of his nose. He had a warm smile, something I desperately needed after Ms. Attitude in the waiting room and the way I was feeling.

No introduction, the doctor obtained some basic medical information and got down to business.

"All right Adrianna, lie back on the table please. Let's get a feel for what's going on. It says here you're a gymnast," he looked down, then back up at me, squinting his eyes. "And training around fifty hours a week?" He paused, a crease formed between his eyes. "Is that right?"

"Yes, sir." The doctor looked at Hayden like he was looking for confirmation.

He dropped the file onto the gray countertop, slapped on a pair of gloves and turned toward me. Instinctively, I moved my hands higher up on my stomach and the doctor pressed his fingers to my lower belly. I flinched when he gave a solid push, causing him to pause and look at me. I thought he was going to push through my stomach.

"That hurts?"

"A little bit."

"When was your last menstrual cycle?"

Pursing my lips together, I tilted my head to the side and looked at the corner of the ceiling. I had to think about that for a moment. "About three weeks ago? My cycle is usually off, so I don't keep track of it."

"Are you sexually active?"

"No!" I shouted it like a fool. Clearing my throat, I answered again. "No, I'm not."

Hayden threw his hands up. "And that's my cue to step out."

"And who are you, young man?"

"Her brother," he lied smoothly, walking toward the door. "I'll be right outside, Aid."

"Thanks, Hayden."

Once Hayden left, the doctor eyed me suspiciously.

His chin dipped to his chest and looked his specs. "I'll ask again since your brother isn't here. Are you sexually active?"

"Yes."

"Are you on birth control?"

"No."

"Is there any chance you are pregnant?"

"No. I recently took the morning after pill so I'm good."

"The morning after pill is not always effective. Have you considered going on birth control?"

My heart dropped into my gut at the mention of the pill not being effective. I stared, stone-faced at the doctor as a million thoughts ran through my head. This could not be happening.

"I…I only just became active," I stammered. My jaw quivered and I fought to regain control of my emotions.

His eyes narrowed. "It only takes one time to become pregnant. Unless you intend to become a mother, we have a female doctor you can follow up with once you are feeling better who can perform a Pap smear if you'd like and go from there."

"Thanks, I'll think about it."

The doctor applied more pressure this time, pressing down with both sets of fingers around my abdomen. My body tensed, my stomach flexing under his touch.

"That hurts really bad," I gritted out, crossing my legs as if that would help.

"Sit up." He listened to my heart, my back, and down my sides. As he pushed around near my spine, I grimaced in discomfort. When the doctor pushed on my side near my kidney, I went ramrod straight and sucked in an audible breath, wincing.

"Adrianna, I'm going to need a urine sample to rule out pregnancy and infection."

My stomach dropped. I froze. A pregnancy test? I'd only had sex with Kova twice. There was no way I could be pregnant…I hoped. Fear seized my heart and my breathing became labored as I realized I needed to get my hands on another morning after pill soon.

"I don't have to go, I went before I left," I lied.

He tilted his head to the side. "Luckily I only need a little." He handed me a small cup and gave me instructions before pointing me toward the bathroom.

I grimaced, knowing what was ahead of me.

Walking down the bland, gray hallway to the bathroom, I closed the door behind me and took in the small space. Just thinking about having to pee was causing me fear as the urge struck me. Spreading my legs and squatting over the toilet, making sure not to touch the rim, I positioned the cup under me.

Expelling a heavy breath, I looked down at the cup perplexed. My urine was a murky brown. Definitely not what it should've been. Maybe I was dehydrated and needed to drink more water. Lately, I'd been cutting back so I didn't have to use the bathroom as much. Guess that wasn't such a great idea.

After I put the plastic cup in the cabinet, I washed my hands and walked back to the room. The pressure in my belly had dwelled to a low glow. Despite not wanting to deal with it at all, I'd take this pain over anything else I'd been dealing with recently.

A few minutes later, the doctor came back. I was feeling better and realized I probably could've skipped coming to the doctor's if I had just gone to the bathroom and dealt with the pain instead of acting like a baby.

"Good news—the pregnancy test is negative, but your sample does show bacteria. I'm going to send it to the lab to be cultured. For now, I'd like to perform an abdominal ultrasound and draw some blood."

My brows pushed together. "Why do we need blood work?"

"Just a precautionary. Even though the urine pregnancy is negative, we still like to follow it up with a serum pregnancy test to rule out a false negative. The morning after pill is not always effective," he responded, head down and writing in his folder. My stomach churned at the thought. I knew no form of birth control was one hundred percent, but it never dawned on me until this moment just how big that tiny window could be.

Nearly thirty minutes later, I was stuck with a needle—four times might I add—since the nurse couldn't get it right, and then lathered with warm gel. I had to squeeze the sides of the table as the ultrasound technician pressed on my abdomen and bladder. I was thin, weighing in around one hundred pounds soaking wet, if that. She should've been able to see everything and not need to push as hard as she did. When I asked what she was doing, she said looking for cysts because they can cause major abdominal pain. When she asked me to turn over, she scanned my kidneys.

The doctor walked back in and shut the door. Looking at me, he took a pen out of the pocket of his lab coat and grabbed a prescription pad. "It appears you have a kidney infection. It's a pretty bad one, I might add. You could've had a reaction to the morning after pill that didn't help stop the infection, and the severe cramping in your abdomen is most likely caused by the pill. I suggest refraining from taking the pill in the future and be on a more consistent form of birth control." He paused and pushed his glasses up on the bridge of his nose. "Does it hurt to urinate?"

"It burns like you can't imagine."

"So you hold it in, then," he confirmed.

I nodded.

"That's the worst thing you could do—stop doing it. I'm going to prescribe you some antibiotics and a pain reliever. Take the antibiotics until they're gone and the pain pill as needed." He scribbled on his pad. "I'm also suggesting you take the rest of today and tomorrow off. A heating pad will help too."

"Doctor, there's no way I can take another day off. I just can't."

He ignored me. "If you're not feeling better by the end of the second day, call me."

"But I can't miss another day. I have to go back tomorrow." My heart thumped against my chest, anxiety taking over at the thought of missing another day.

He peered down his nose over his glasses at me. "I'll write you a doctor's note. If your coach has any problem with it, he can call me. Your body needs rest."

I nodded to pacify him, ready to go home.

"Like hell I'm going to take another day off. Coach would have my head on a stick if I did that," I said to Hayden once we were back in his car.

He chuckled. "Maybe it would be a good thing you did. That way you can rest up and not get set back even more. It will give you time off your foot too."

"My Achilles isn't going to heal in two days. It's going to take quitting gymnastics completely for that to happen."

"If that's the case, then why did your coach water down your routines?"

I sighed. "To help heal the strain as much as possible and work back up to that level, I guess. They don't want me making it worse where I have to actually take time off."

He looked over at me. "You must hate that."

"Like you can't even imagine. I've tried so hard, put everything into being here, and I get hurt. That's just my luck."

We pulled up to the drive-up pharmacy and Hayden dropped off my prescription for me. We parked and went inside while it got filled. I picked up a heating blanket, another big bottle of Motrin, then sat down and waited for my medication when Hayden walked off. He was back in minutes handing me a bottle of juice and a box of medicine.

Looking down, I asked, "What is it?"

"Cranberry pills. I read in *Cosmo* they should also help with UTIs and since it's kind of connected, I figured why not. It's all natural stuff so it won't counteract your medication."

My jaw hung open, my brows scrunched together. "Please don't tell anyone you read *Cosmo*, Hayden. That's so...not hot."

He grinned. "It pays to have a sister who reads them. You'd be surprised the stuff you can learn in there." He paused, pulling out his phone and did a quick Google search. "Most outrageous, psychotic tips *Cosmo* has suggested that will put you in the hospital."

Our eyes locked and we smiled. "Let's read it while we're waiting," I said.

chapter 67

THE DOCTOR HAD BEEN RIGHT—MY BODY DESPERATELY NEEDED THE REST.
All this training had finally caught up to me.

Overused, overworked, and not resting muscles properly probably added to my body shutting down and not being able to fight the infection. I had a fever all day long and well into the next morning until it finally broke. The painkillers were magical, and the agony I had been dealing with was finally starting to dissipate within twenty-four hours. Even if I had gone to gym, it probably wasn't the brightest idea to train while on them. They made me loopy, which Avery got to enjoy when I face-timed her and filled her in on all that happened, sans the sex.

None of my coaches or teammates had called, except Hayden. Not that they would anyway. And truthfully, I didn't know whether that made me happy or not.

Loneliness struck. Looking around, I liked my space and I was used to my privacy, but for some odd reason the solitude was hitting hard and beginning to upset me. My emotions were scattered about and frayed at the edges. I was going to break if I added one more thing to my fucked up lifestyle. Between training, school, keeping track of all the lies I told, I'd never had this much time to myself to reflect on my current state. Tears welled in my eyes as realization dawned on me at the person I'd become. A habitual liar.

My phone rang, distracting my thoughts. Picking it up, I glanced at the caller ID and a smile broke out across my face.

"Hi, Dad!"

"Hey, baby girl, how are you doing?"

"I'm okay. How are you?"

"Oh, you know, no rest for the wicked."

I grinned. That was his favorite line. "Yeah."

"So, Mom called me…" He trailed off, waiting for me to finish for him.

"I have a little infection, but I'm doing much better now. No need to worry." I really didn't want to go into detail about the kidney infection.

He released a stressful sigh. "Honey, I always worry about you. You're my daughter, and with you not being home it makes me worry even more."

My shoulders relaxed. "I know, but really, I'm okay. My friend, Hayden, took me to the doctor and then we went to the pharmacy afterward to get what I needed."

"The doctor prescribed you some medicine?"

"Yeah, antibiotics and a painkiller. They're helping tremendously."

"Are you getting enough rest, sweetie? I know you're probably used to the schedule by now, but maybe you need a break." He paused. "You can come home any time."

My heart softened at his thoughtfulness. "No rest for the wicked, Dad," I replied quietly.

He chuckled. "Tough little thing. What did Konstantin say about you being home?"

"I actually haven't spoken to him, and I'm honestly surprised the gym isn't blowing up my phone. Hayden did take in my doctor's note so maybe that's why."

"Good. That's because I took care of it for you so you didn't have to worry. I stressed to him that it would be in his best interest to give you time to rest. I had to smooth out his ruffled feathers when he called me," he chuckled lightly. "That piece of paper doesn't hold much water for some people."

I pursed my lips together, puzzled. "You spoke to Kova?"

"I did. We actually talk about every other week. I know you can take care of yourself, but I do worry about you there all alone, so he gives me updates and lets me know how your training is going."

This was news to me. I had no idea he spoke to Kova so often. While I found his concern over my well-being genuine, unlike my mom's, I also was disheartened by the fact he could call Kova and not me. Then again, the phone worked both ways and I didn't call home very often either.

My heart softened. "Thanks, Dad, I appreciate it."

"Get some rest, go to bed early."

"Same with you."

"Your mother sends her love."

I laughed under my breath. "I'm just sure she does," I said sarcastically. "Tell her hi for me."

"Will do, sweetie, talk to you later."

Hanging up the phone, nostalgia struck me. The painkillers were making me emotional. I changed into some pajamas, climbed into bed and switched on Netflix, searching for some mindless teenage drama to watch. As I was dozing off, my phone vibrated and the screen lit up.

Coach: Open the door.

My heart stopped.

Climbing out of bed, I ran to my door and checked the peephole, but saw no one. I sent a text back saying I didn't see him.

Coach: Coming up now.

Turning the lock, I pulled the door open and Kova walked in.

"What are you doing here?" I asked as he dropped his keys and phone on the counter. Before he could open his mouth, I spat, "And if you have one thing to say about my attire, I will lose my shit."

Kova ran a hand through his hair, his eyes raking over my body. My loose top and boy shorts were all I could manage wearing after breaking a fever.

"This was the first minute alone I had to get away from Katja." He let out an exhausted sigh and his eyes traveled down my body. He took two steps and stood before me. Palming my jaw, he tipped my head back and examined me.

"Your eyes are all glossy and red, and you have circles under your eyes," he said quietly. His hands threaded my long hair and fluffed it up. I remembered how much he liked it when I wore it down. "I did not mean to hurt you."

I pulled away and looked at the floor, ashamed he knew my absence was partly due to him. I was a little peeved it took him two days to check on me.

"You didn't though...I really did it to myself."

"Adrianna, do not fool yourself. If it was not for me, you would not be sick."

I swallowed, shrugging. "Partially. But also because I wasn't taking care of myself properly."

"I feel terrible about it, I am very sorry, Adrianna. I was too rough, too careless, I said some mean things, and I put one of my gymnasts at risk. It is just another thing I cannot forgive myself for."

"I won't deny you were rough with me. You were. My body was running on fumes, so it didn't help to fight off any kind of infection either."

Exhaustion took over and I walked to sit on the couch. Leaning over, I placed my elbows on my knees and clasped my hands together.

"This was a big mistake," I admitted, my heart aching with each word. "Catastrophic mistake. I wish nothing had ever happened between us. I wish I could take it all back. I came here to be the best I could and I let myself down." Looking up, I met his eyes. "Maybe I'm not as strong as I think I am." Kova shook his head and came to sit next to me. "I should've told you I was a virgin, it was wrong of me and I'm sorry. We could've ruined so many lives, Kova." Tears welled in my eyes and I hated that I showed any kind of emotion. Damn pain pills!

Kova brushed a strand of hair away from my face, cupping it behind my ear. Our eyes locked and I saw the inner turmoil he was faced with. He hadn't shaved in days, and there were black circles under his eyes too. Gone were the vibrant green eyes I'd come to love, and in their place was a dull shade of olive.

"You look like you haven't slept."

"I have not," he admitted dismally. "You have been on my mind day in and day out. You think you are not strong, but you are. You have taken everything I have thrown at you and ran with it. You are a fighter, Adrianna. Few can handle what you have at the rate you have, and that caused the lines to blur for me. You make me question so many things in my life right now. I wish I could tell you what they were, but I cannot. Just know you are not weak, not even close to it. You are strong, do not ever doubt yourself."

My heart sputtered in my chest. This was one of the nicest things he'd ever said to me. A tear slipped from my eye and he wiped it away with the pad of his thumb.

"But you are right about something."

I tilted my head to the side. "About what?"

"That this was a mammoth mistake. I was unfaithful and I hurt you in the process. I failed both you and Katja. For that, I could not be sorry enough."

I averted my eyes so he couldn't see the pain he caused. "There's a question I want to ask you, and I hope you will answer it." His forehead cinched together. I wasn't sure where this question came from or why I was asking it, but I had to know. Maybe it was the pain relievers talking again.

"I'm asking you one more time. Was I really the only gymnast you've ever been with? Or were there others? Please be honest with me."

My heart thumped wildly against my chest waiting for his answer.

"Ria, I am a lot of things, but I do not desire young girls," he spat with disgust. "I find it repulsive. There has never been another before you, though not for lack of trying on their part. There were some aggressive ones, but I never took it past the professional level."

"So you were never with Reagan?"

He pulled back in horror. "Reagan? Never. Where would you get that idea?"

I shook my head, feeling like an idiot for even asking now. "Just some things she said to me."

"Reagan, while she is an incredible gymnast, lacks the drive and willpower you have. There has never been more than a coach/athlete relationship with her, or anyone else. I can promise you that."

Reaching a hand into his pocket, he pulled out a little box. Flipping it over, my heart sank as I read the front of it. I shook my head, a sad laugh escaped me.

Kova and his stupid little, white fucking pill.

"We've been pretty stupid, haven't we?"

He huffed at my understatement and handed the box to me. "Me more so than you. I knew better."

Opening it up, I popped out the morning after tablet. I stared at the pill and hesitated. I had to decide whether I should just ignore what the doctor recommended and deal with the repercussions later, or hand the box to Kova and explain why I can't take it and how I'd had a pregnancy test already.

I glanced Kova's way. The last thing I needed was a baby or for him to go to jail. I reached for the bottle of water I left on the coffee table earlier. Popping the tablet into my mouth, I swallowed it without dwelling on the situation further. His shoulders relaxed visibly but then something dawned on me. He was more worried about me being pregnant than my well-being. Luckily for him, I didn't have the energy to confront him.

"Problem solved," I said dejectedly.

Standing up, I went to step past Kova, but he placed a hand on my thigh and stopped me. With him sitting on the couch and his height, we were eye level with each other. Turning toward him, I looked into his tempestuous gaze. His hand was high on the back of my leg, cupping the crease of my thigh and butt. His fingers moved in little circles, causing a warmth of heat to course through me. My nipples hardened. I didn't move, I couldn't, as his hand skimmed over my ass and up my back ever so slowly. Goose bumps coated my skin. He placed his other hand on my body and my breath caught in my throat as he pulled me closer. After what he said, I was confused by his actions.

"Kova?" I whispered.

He sat up higher. "I do not know what it is about you, but I have the hardest time keeping my hands to myself when it is just you and me. You understand me as I understand you. We have the same drive."

A pained look resonated on his face. He muttered in Russian as his hands roamed my body. Despite the pain he caused me a few days ago, my body came alive when he touched me.

"What are you doing?"

"Memorizing you with my touch." Kova shuffled me closer between his legs, and I could smell the faint scent of vodka on his lips.

My heart hammered against my chest. This man was so confusing. His words contradicted his actions on a daily basis. But one thing I knew for sure, there was no denying what he felt for me. The look in his eyes as his hands caressed my back, pulling me closer, solidified his feelings. My shirt lifted, baring my back and stomach. His palms grazed my nipples and my back bowed in response. His head dipped to the side, and a breath caught in my throat.

The way he looked at me broke my heart. He was struggling, and what he said earlier was in fact true. After everything, was Kova going to kiss me? I swallowed hard. I wouldn't refuse him if he did. I didn't think there would ever come a time I could refuse anything he offered.

"*Malysh*, I need one last kiss."

He was saying goodbye.

With a small nod, I licked my lips and wound my arms around his neck. Leaning in, my chest pressed to his, my nipples hard. Kova's strong arms wrapped around my lower back, crushing me to him. I loved how strong he was, how he held me and made me feel safe. Our lips grazed each other's, different than any other time. He was gentle and slow, and took his time as he nibbled on my lips.

I took this moment for what it was—he was using his actions to display the things he couldn't say.

When our tongues touched, it wasn't rushed or wild for once. It was deliberate and provocative. My body was a blaze of heat, desire hitting me hard. Our tongues caressed one another's, tangling around and holding on, in the most intense kiss we'd had yet. Wet, warm, and passionate.

My fingers weaved through his hair as I put everything into the kiss, just as he did. I knew after tonight, it was over completely and my heart ached. I had let myself fall completely for someone I could never have.

Kova's hands skimmed up my ribs, his fingers splaying out wide and palming my breasts. I moaned into his mouth, pressing harder into him and devouring him. My body ached even more, but this time for release and nothing more. His kiss made me forget every ounce of pain and replaced it with pleasure.

"I love how responsive you are to my touch," he whispered against my lips, shifting to the edge of the couch. His erection grazed my thigh and I leaned into him as his tongue collided with mine, the same time his forefinger and thumb found my nipple and pinched. A little purr escaped my lips.

Kova's strong hands landed on my hips. His fingers trembled against me as his tongue found my heated skin. My head fell back, I wanted to be the one who eased the pain for him, to give him what he wanted.

The sad reality of the story was I would never be that girl.

And he would never be that man.

His thumbs dug into the crease between my hips and thighs while his long fingers scooped under my ass. He stood and hoisted me up, one arm wound securely around my back, his other hand tangled in my long hair, holding me to him, like he feared I would pull away. I wouldn't. I couldn't. There was no possible way I'd be able to now. I was his for the taking.

I wrapped my nimble legs around his waist. My emotions were climbing and for some reason, tears prickled my eyes. I didn't want this to be over between us, the fire was too wild to contain.

"You can't do this to me and then leave, Kova," I whispered against his lips. "Either stop altogether, or don't stop at all. It's not fair."

I pressed my lips to his, pouring my heart out through my kiss. This fucked up relationship between us was against all morals. He knew it, I knew it, and we didn't care.

Kova pulled back and pressed his forehead to mine. "I need to go." I nodded, agreeing with him. Kova held me as if it was second nature for me to be in his arms. I never wanted him to let me go, but deep down I knew it was time. We'd carried on this affair long enough, because in the end, I knew that everyone gets caught.

Sliding out of his arms, I stood in front of Kova. He cupped my jaw and angled my head back.

"You are so beautiful it hurts. You hold yourself together even during the toughest times. You are a force to be reckoned with, something no one will see coming."

"Kova, why are you telling me this?"

He lifted one shoulder and shrugged like he wasn't sure. "It is just a few of the things I love about you." He placed a kiss to my forehead and held it for a minute. We inhaled at the same time, and I grabbed his wrists, savoring the last intimate contact we would share.

Kova stepped back and walked to the counter, grabbing his keys and phone. Without another glance, he opened the front door and left, leaving my heart shattered in a million tiny pieces.

chapter 68

UNWRAPPING MY WRISTBANDS AND TAPE, I DROPPED MY GEAR INTO MY BAG. I was covered in chalk, tired, and hungry. Just the thought of my bed lulling me to sleep in my quiet condo caused me to move faster. I'd reached past the point of fatigue, I could feel it in my body. Some days I hated being alone, but today I was looking forward to it.

It had taken me a little time to get back in the right mind frame, and I had, but I wasn't sure I fully let go. Working closely with Kova day in day out, I was constantly reminded of what we shared, the things we did in secret. He'd look at me with heat in his eyes, and my body would flush, but not before he quickly masked it. It was still there for him and the lingering of his touch always gave him away. He was struggling just as much as I was.

Today's practice had been an awkward one, but awkward doesn't even begin to describe the past month between Kova and me. I was certain no one noticed the strain between us. We'd been good at keeping things completely platonic. No more late night visits, no indiscretion, nothing reckless. We were never alone together and probably shouldn't have been from the beginning. I was just a gymnast, and he was just a coach, like it should've been. Nothing more.

"All right, team. Once you guys are done, come see me on the floor. We have a few things to go over before the weekend." Kova addressed us all and then left.

Pulling out my hair tie, I fluffed up my thick, auburn locks that were covered with white streaks of chalk before putting it back into a messy bun. I sat down and removed the sports tape from my toes and feet, my calf, freeing my body from all the adhesive. Therapy proved to make a huge difference. I was stronger, more confident. My new routines were solid and I had Kova and Madeline to thank. They both worked with me and got me where I needed to be. Well, mostly Madeline. Kova had kept his word and hardly coached me.

The qualifying meet was just a couple of short weeks away and every day I was growing more anxious for it. I put everything into gymnastics. I gave it my all. I trained harder, pushed harder, and I never complained. I did what Kova had told me to do—prove myself, make it count.

Taking a seat next to Holly, we all stared up at the coaches and waited. It wasn't uncommon for him to meet with us, but something wasn't right. I could feel it in the air. Kova's eyes dashed around at the group of team girls and boys, but he never made eye contact with me. My stomach knotted, unease swept through me. Something big was coming.

Kova rubbed his hands together, licked his lips and then spoke. "So, we have the holidays coming up, the New Year, and then the Parkettes Invitational. Reagan, Holly, and Adrianna are attending. However, after careful deliberation with the other coaches, we have decided to make a few changes."

An audible gasp surrounded the small group. My heart sank, and my fingers trembled. Somehow, I knew what was coming, but I gave him the benefit of the doubt. I looked around and knew my facial expression matched the others. We were not expecting this sort of news. Changing the lineup had never happened in my last gym, it was whoever was best for the team would compete, and I had a notion it was the same way here.

Kova cleared his throat, and I noticed he refused to make eye contact with me once again.

"This was not an easy decision, but here at World Cup, we feel that your injury is not something we should test just yet." Kova finally glanced my way and locked eyes with me, "I am sorry, Adrianna, but we are pulling you out of the meet."

Silence so thick, it permeated the air. My heartbeat drummed in my ears and my breathing deepened as I stared ahead, astounded at the devastating words I'd just heard. This couldn't be. Not after how hard I worked for this meet.

"I know this is a shock to you, and you should know this was not an easy decision, but it has been made and it is done."

No words, I had no words. My heart was in my throat, all the noise faded away. I was rendered speechless over this shocking decision. How could he do this to me? I was ready. There was no doubt about it that I was ready. I practiced harder and longer than the other girls. I worked my ass off, only for him to take me out of the meet. My heart started to crack, tears formed behind my eyes. But I refused to cry.

"Wha…" I paused, swallowing past my dry throat, "why?"

"Where you may be tighter with jumps and sequences, your dismounts are not solid and your releases are not clean. That is not enough, you need more time. It would only be setting you up for failure."

"I don't know why you're surprised. Your skills are not that difficult or steady," Reagan chimed in. I glared at her, my face conveying every emotion strumming through me

"That's enough, Reagan," Kova snapped.

"That's because I have an injury, you idiot." Turning to Kova, I said angrily, "You made me scale back my skills so I could continue training. Of course my skills are not that complex. This isn't fair."

"It is what is done when anyone is hurt, Adrianna. We did not single you out purposely. We did what we did to avoid any more injury, as we do with any gymnast."

Kova clapped his hands and addressed the group. "All right, girls. That is all. Practice early tomorrow as usual. The next week will be long and grueling before you break for the holidays. We want to get in as much practice time as we can."

Everyone stood up and went on their way as I sat stunned for another minute. I didn't see this coming a mile away, and I couldn't believe he would do this to me after everything. A tear slipped from the corner of my eye as my chest tightened. Not because I was upset, I definitely was, but because I was livid over the change.

"Aid," Hayden said, rubbing my back. "You okay?"

I nodded, not meeting his eyes and stood to walk away. Hayden wasn't the one who I wanted to talk to right now. It was Kova. I was going to rip him a new one.

Walking out of the gym, I made my way down the hall and toward his office. Each step pumped adrenaline through me at a high velocity. I was seeing red, and my blood was boiling. My routines were solid, there were other gymnasts doing skills as I was, I'd seen it on television. So there had to be more to his asinine decision than he alluded to.

I strode into his office and slammed his door shut with as much force as I could muster. Screw the repercussions. I didn't care if anyone heard me, saw me, whatever. I was so stark raving mad I couldn't see straight. My entire body, down to my fingers and toes, were trembling. How dare he do this to me!

Kova's head snapped up, glaring at me with fire in his eyes. I didn't give a fuck. He just told me I wasn't competing in the meet that I worked my ass off for, a meet already paid for by my parents. He had no choice but to hear it from me.

"Adrianna."

"How dare you not allow me to compete, I worked my fucking ass off for that position. You have no right!"

I was so angry I couldn't stop the bite dripping from each word. My hair stuck to my face, my cheeks were beet red. I was already starting to sweat.

Kova stood slowly, flattening his hands on his cherry wood desk and leaned toward me. "I have every right," he spoke slowly. "I am the coach, you are my gymnast. I make the decisions in the end, you do not." He paused, swallowing. "And do not ever come into my office the way you just did ever again, or I will kick you off the team. Now, goodbye."

Goodbye? Fuck that!

"You're jeopardizing my future!"

Kova resumed his seat, picked up his pen, and continued with whatever bullshit he was working on before I stormed in.

"I have already made my choice. End of discussion. And try to refrain from slamming the door on your way out."

I ignored him. "My parents paid for that meet."

"And I already called your mother and explained you are not ready just yet, that you need a little more time. She did not sound surprised at all and said to put someone in your place who has what it takes. Very nice and understanding lady she is." He calmly replied without giving me a glance.

A knot formed in my throat. I was beginning to despise my mother. How could she say that?

"You're lying. You wouldn't do that to me. You know how I feel about her."

He shrugged indifferently. "Call your mom. Though, I would wait a bit. She was not too happy about losing the money."

She'd gloat if I called her. "That money means nothing to her."

"Not my problem, Adrianna."

"Oh, so now I'm Adrianna to you?"

He peered up through his full black lashes, his head barely tipping up. I had gotten better at reading him and could tell I was starting to irritate him by defying his orders. Good.

"You have always been Adrianna to me."

I cocked my head to the side, arching a brow. "That's such a fucking lie and you know it."

"That is beside the point and has nothing to do with right now or my choice. As you can see, I am working here," he waved a hand over his desk, then pointed silently to the door, dismissing me.

Heart pounding, blood roaring through my veins, I walked over to his desk and threw everything off with a swipe of my hand. Kova went rigid, his knuckles a pasty white. His cold demeanor rocked me to the core and I fed off of it.

His jaw flexed and his nose flared. "Very childish, Adrianna. Stop acting immature, it does not suit you."

"Fuck you, *Coach*," I said with sarcasm, walking around to the side of his desk. The last thing I should've been doing was cursing at my coach, but I couldn't control myself. Kova was more than a coach and he knew it. Tears were burning behind my eyes and I was devastated over this change.

"You have no reason to hold me back."

In a blur, Kova stood, hooked a hand around my neck and yanked me to him. He was breathing heavily, his eyes piercing me with a mixture of rage and something I couldn't put my finger on. I shimmied up closer to him and he hadn't loosened his grip on me. Guiding me backward, he pressed me against the wall, his beige filing cabinet cutting into my arm.

Hovering over me he said, "Fine. You want answers, you will get them. Want to know the real reason why you are not going to compete?"

A sugary smile tipped my lips. "I knew it had to be something else with you. There's no way it had to do with my routines."

He fisted my hair, his mouth a mere centimeters from mine. I could feel the heat radiating off him as I stared into untamed eyes, waiting for the truth to spill from his lying lips.

"You broke the rules," he whispered.

I pulled my head back and it hit the wall. Glaring at him, I retorted, "I broke no rules."

Kova tilted his head to the side. "Oh, but you did. In fact, you signed the agreement when you first came here."

I wracked my brain trying to figure out what rule he was talking about as I stared deep into his eyes, but nothing came to mind. He huffed, a sardonic smirk spread across his handsome face.

"No boyfriends. I said there were to be no boyfriends, yet you defied my orders. Therefore, I have more power over you than ever. Your punishment is not to compete at the meet. Maybe next time you will listen."

My mouth dropped with my heart into my gut. I was going to be sick.

"Boyfriend?" I whispered, perplexed. "What boyfriend?" I was so confused. I hadn't been with anyone but him. "But you told my mom I wasn't ready to compete."

"Of course I had to lie to your mom." Coach loosened his hand on my nape, dragging it to my jaw where he slowly caressed my face. "You and Hayden. I told you," his gaze dropped to my mouth, "No boyfriends. I recall telling you to get rid of him."

"But…I…" Caught off guard, I stammered, unable to form words. I gripped his wrist that was still on my face. "He's not my boyfriend."

"Do you think I was born yesterday? I saw him come out of your building. I saw the smile on your face when he pulled away in his car, the way you looked at him. I knew there was more going on when he had to call in for you when you were sick."

"You were spying on me?"

He shrugged.

"He came over to watch a movie and that was it. You can't prove anything."

Hayden helped keep me focused. My friendship with him was really important and any time I was feeling too lonely, he was always there for me. He was the male version of Avery and nothing more, and I didn't know how to get Kova to understand that.

"That is the beauty of it, I do not have to. I am the coach. No one will question my word."

I shoved at his chest, tears filled my eyes and I could barely see clearly. "He's not my boyfriend. I haven't been with anyone other than you. I swear on my life, I haven't. Don't do this to me, please."

"It is done."

"No, it's not." I was going to be sick. "I hate you."

"I would rather you hate me than want me."

"I don't want you." *Lie.*

He shook his head. "You do not get it, do you?"

Confusion set in my face and he answered my question. "I want *you*, that is what you do not seem to understand. But you *never* refuse me. So you hating me will make this easier for you, for both of us. I want you to hate me, so when I do try to come after you, you tell me no."

My jaw dropped, a tear finally slid down my cheek. "So this is about you?" My voice low and crackling. How could he do this to me?

"Oh, *malysh*," he said, his voice softening. His eyes glazed over and I saw the real truth. "You have what it takes. Your body is in perfect condition," he groaned, his hand skimmed up my thigh and cupping my ass.

chapter 69

ON THE VERGE OF A BREAKDOWN, I DUG MY NAILS INTO HIM.

"Then let me compete, please. I'm begging."

"No."

"How could you do this to me? Please," I cracked. "I'll do anything. This isn't fair, you're sabotaging my career for the sake of yourself!" Kova ignored me, so I went in for the kill. "Let me compete in the meet or I'll come forward with our relationship." He didn't even flinch.

"No, you will not." His nose skimmed my neck and I shivered. I didn't want to want him, but my body gave me away.

"If you do, it will look bad for you too. You will ruin your career." His breath tickled my neck and I tried desperately not to react to it. I clenched his shirt in my hand, holding him and fighting him at the same time.

"You're ruining it for me by holding me back. What's the difference? Might as well go down in flames and take you with me."

"You will be pulled out of gymnastics and your father's name will be tarnished. Is that what you want after everything he has done for you?"

Guilt struck me. I swallowed hard. I didn't want to shame my parents. Then something dawned on me.

"You forget something huge."

"What is that?" he asked, his lips dusting mine.

I looked directly in his eyes and said, "People don't take lightly to rape. And everyone believes a girl who cries rape."

Kova didn't move, only his eyes widened a smidgen. "That is where you are wrong, *malysh*. It is consensual between us."

I bit at his lip, taunting him.

"Your fingers penetrated me the way your tongue did. I could easily lie and say you took advantage of me. I could even say it wasn't consensual, and no one would ever know the truth."

Kova said nothing, so I kept going. I knew I should've stopped, but I hurt and I was going for his throat. I was running on adrenaline from his expressions alone.

"We had sexual relations in *your* gym…in the dance room…in front of the rings…the therapy room…" My mother trained me well to smile with my eyes to get my point across. "I'm sure your security camera picked me up. Add me to the list or I'll come forward with our relationship. I will cry rape," I cemented.

Kova's eyes dropped, darkening. "You think you can threaten me?" He gripped my jaw in his hand, his fingers digging into my cheeks. "I am not so easily swayed. Go ahead and try it though, watch how fast you fall. I have never been anything but strictly platonic with every other gymnast I have ever trained. I am sure they will vouch for me. You, on the other hand, I doubt seeing as you do not have many friends here. In fact, I would not be surprised if some of your teammates concoct lies to have you thrown off the team."

"What do I have to lose since you won't let me compete? Nothing." I paused, letting that soak in. "I'm not afraid of you or what could happen. I mean, you took advantage of an innocent minor. A virgin no less. What was I to do?" I asked caustically, batting my eyelashes. "Let's not forget about the morning after pill I'm sure was bought on camera."

Kova ground his teeth, his jaw gnashing together, and I smiled sweetly at him with soft puppy eyes.

"Lies," he whispered harshly. "You pursued me every chance you had and you know it. A man can only take so much before he loses his fucking mind and caves."

"*No one* will believe you," I bit back. "You know I'm right. After all, I'm just an innocent teenager with a dream and you took advantage of my vulnerability," I said, purposely lying about my age with a pout.

"You made all the first moves—"

"That's a bullshit lie and you know it." I stared hard into his eyes. "If you think I did, then why didn't you stop me, *Coach?*"

He huffed, a half mocking smile displayed across his handsome face. "Not even a priest could have stopped you, or would want to at that, and you know it. You are not as innocent as you come across."

"Excuses, excuses. You should've tried harder." Testing him, I placed a flat hand to his chest, feeling his toned pecs clinging to his torso. My hips shifted into his, his hard length pressed into me as I cupped the back of his neck and angled my mouth in front of his. Taking a deep breath, I released it into his mouth. My tongue slipped out, dancing across his lips, but he didn't move. This was how we worked—the more I fought back and aggravated him, the more he got off on it. The push and pull. It was our foreplay, the tension and indiscretion that brewed between us. Kova stayed stock-still. His fingers strained, desperately trying to stay where they were as they dug deeper into my body. This was way more than just sex between us and he knew it. It was a chemical reaction that couldn't be stopped.

"I can take what I want, right? Isn't that what you once said?" I asked quietly. His eyes narrowed to slits.

Hooking his top lip with the tip of my tongue, I pulled it between my teeth and sucked on it. As I did, my other arm came around his neck as I pressed against him. I nibbled on his luscious lips, slipping my tongue into his mouth.

Four weeks. Four weeks of no touching, no kissing, and now we were at it again. I've dreamed about this, fantasized often. Kova hooked my leg higher, smashing me into the wall as he kissed me like a starved animal. He was rough and raw, taking everything I offered. Momentarily, I forgot why I started this kiss when his hand slid to my throat and applied pressure.

I became instantly aroused from the weight on my neck and moaned in pleasure.

His eyes glazed over. "You like that, Ria?"

I nodded and said, "You're supposed to resist." But he ignored me and hiked up my other leg. My hips pressed into his and I sighed. "What do you want? I'll do it. Anything to compete. Please, just let me compete."

His tongue left a hot, wet trail around my neck and up to my ear. Panting, he said, "Funny thing is, I do not have to ask for anything at this point. I know you will just give it to me. I win either way."

My back bowed, pressing my chest into his. I kissed his hungry, manipulative mouth.

His callused hand slid down between us and cupped my pussy hard, painfully hard, but I didn't stop him.

The sad part was that I wanted him to want me, so I took it.

Tongues lapped furiously, delving wildly into each other's mouths. I tightened my thighs around him to hold myself up, he snickered. I needed him. I needed the release I came to crave from him.

"You're the one person who's supposed to be pushing me, and now you're standing in my way." He huffed, and I became desperate. "If I let you have me, will you let me compete?" I asked huskily against his lips, praying he'd change his mind. I was willing to do anything to reach my goal at this point.

Kova fumbled with his shorts between us, his knuckles tapping my sex as he worked feverously to remove them. He pulled at the waistband and pushed it down just enough to pull his cock out, hitting my inner thigh. My legs trembled as a shiver sped down my spine. Hooking his fingers under my leo, he gave a good, hard tug and pulled it to the side. The elastic dug into my skin and I flinched.

"You will let me fuck you either way, and you know it."

He was right, and I hated it.

"Now take a deep breath," he said ever so quietly.

I did as he said. He palmed his length and slid right into me without a second thought to pass. My head whipped back from the rough intrusion and he covered my mouth with his to stifle my loud moan. I almost cried from the pleasure of the pain inflicted on me.

He pulled out and thrust in hard. He groaned, a vein pulsing in his neck. "Once again, you asked for it."

"So what? Maybe I did. And you should've told me no," I panted into him.

Kova pulled out and slid in slower, deeper, hitting the back of me. My lips parted from the ecstasy flowing through me.

"Be honest. Did you want me to refuse you, *malysh?*"

I shook my head, not that I needed to. He knew the answer.

"You want to get fucked, Adrianna, you will. And I have no problem doing it." His hands gripped my hips hard, pushing me down on him. Kova thrust in deep and held it, stretching me wide. My jaw fell open and my eyes squeezed shut. Leaning in next to my ear he whispered, "I know where to touch you, how to make you come, how to make you come back for more."

He was one hundred and fifty percent right. He knew my body, and knew I would come back for more.

Kova yanked down one side of my leotard and pulled my nipple into his mouth. By doing so, it locked my arm to my side. As if it were even possible, I felt myself becoming wetter, his cock sliding so easily into me that it worked me higher and higher, I could barely catch my breath.

"Are you going to try and threaten me again?"

I think he knew in the back of his mind I would never go through with my threat. Not yet at least. Instead of answering him, I said, "I'm close."

"Good, so am I."

"Let me compete, please."

"No."

"I fucking hate you."

"You may hate me, but your pussy doesn't."

"Anyone with a *pussy* would react to you the same way I do."

The climax I so dearly needed with Kova was about to come to a head. We kept going at it like caged animals. A shiver zipped down my spine, heating my body everywhere. Kova sucked on my neck, his tongue lapping and I whimpered, "You feel so good. Don't stop."

Kova seized my lips, nearly sucking the life from me as he fucked me with every ounce of strength he had. Our tongues collided with each other just as fast. I loved the taste of him, the feel of his body on mine, and I wondered if he felt the same about me.

"Feel it, *malysh*, feel it deep inside you." He pulled out and thrust back in. His cock twitched inside me and I squeezed him with my pussy. "Right there," he groaned into my mouth and I nodded. I felt what he said, and I loved it. His hands came up and tangled in my hair, his breathing became heavy and I knew he was close to losing it. "God, I fucking love being inside of you. Love everything about being with you," he admitted with a moan. His words seized my heart. "I love the pressure around my cock, the way your pussy squeezes me. You make me crazy. All I can think about is fucking you and watching you come. You are gorgeous when you come for me." Chills flitted across my skin, because I loved it too. I loved his touch, his mouth, his arrogant, pushy attitude. I loved so much about him.

"I won't orgasm if you won't let me compete."

"Like I care," he said, then swiveled his pelvis into my clit, proving what a liar I was. "Funny thing is, I can make you come."

"You're nothing but a fucking asshole, you know that?" I panted into his neck as I held on for dear life.

"You are just now figuring that out?"

He knew exactly what my body needed, where to touch me and how to take me. Kova held my hips down on him just how I liked it, and we began to orgasm together when someone knocked on the door twice before barging in.

"Hey, Coach—" Hayden said, then froze, his mouth gaping wide open.

The orgasm ripped through me as I locked eyes with Hayden. I couldn't stop it from happening—and I didn't want to. Kova tried to pull away, but I locked my ankles and squeezed him hard. I needed this orgasm and so did he. "Keep going," I demanded, only for his ears while my eyes were glued to Hayden's. I could only imagine what he saw, what he was thinking. Glossy eyes, rosy cheeks, and a man clearly thrusting into his friend. At least his pants weren't down and it just looked like he was holding me here.

Kova's hand gripped my waist so tight that I knew I'd have a bruise tomorrow. Again. His orgasm flew into me and I took all of it.

Kova looked over his shoulder and gave Hayden a murderous glare, and yelled, "Get out!"

"Ah, oh…my…" Hayden stammered before slamming the door shut and leaving.

My head dropped to Kova's neck. We were breathing so deeply when he asked, "What've we done?"

Kova pulled out and my legs slid weakly down his hips. Thick, warm semen dripped down my inner thigh. I wanted to wipe it away, but I quickly fixed my clothes so I was covered.

"I have to go. I need to find Hayden and make this right."

I didn't have time for anything else.

Kova flattened his hand against the wall, caging me in. I looked up and locked gazes with his steely green eyes.

"You better fix this, Adrianna, this is your goddamn fault. I swear to God, if he utters a word of this to anyone, you will regret it." He was seething with anger but with every right. "Do you understand? I will personally make sure your career is over."

I nodded in understanding.

Quickly, I fled from his office. Luckily no one was in the hallway as I dashed to my locker. I threw on my sweats, jumping into the pant legs and then raced to the parking lot to find Hayden.

"Hayden! Hayden!" He was pulling open the driver's side door when he looked over his shoulder. Disappointment. I saw nothing but disappointment laced in his eyes.

"Hayden," I repeated breathlessly in front of him. "Wait."

"What the fuck are you doing, Aid? Are you seriously sleeping with the coach?" My shoulders dropped. I wanted nothing more than to lie, but I refused. Hayden knew the answer. It was written on his crest fallen face.

He shook his head in disbelief. "Why, Aid? How could you?"

I didn't respond—I couldn't. There were no words for what he saw other than pure abandonment.

"Is he forcing you?" When I didn't answer, he exclaimed, "Jesus, say something!"

I pulled my bottom lip between my teeth and contemplated what to say. Hayden just kept staring at me, waiting for an answer, but I was rendered speechless. I averted my gaze, ashamed of the truth. How did I explain I wanted everything without looking desperate?

Hayden placed both hands on my shoulders. "Answer me."

I shrugged helplessly. "What do you want me to say?"

"You need to come forward and go to the police. This is rape, Aid."

I shook my head frantically, my heart drumming against my ribs. "I can't. It's not rape, Hayden. It's not."

"Yes, it is. You're underage."

"He didn't force me though."

"Regardless if you consented or not, he still took advantage of you. You're under his training, he preyed upon you like a disgusting sick fuck." He ran a hand threw his hair. "I can only imagine who else he's treated this way."

"No, he didn't. It's not what you think. Please, you don't know what you're talking about."

Hayden furiously yanked the car door open. "If you won't do it, then I will."

"No! Please!" I begged, on the verge of tears. "Please don't. I'll deny it if you do."

He looked at me, stunned. "I think you need mental help. He brainwashed you, didn't he? Threatened you if you told anyone?"

"No," I lied. "I'll deny it."

Hayden slammed his door shut and stepped up to me. He cupped my jaw and I stared into his sincere blue eyes, my fingers laced over his.

"Did you do it to get ahead? Because you didn't need to. You have what it takes, babe. You've improved greatly," he said with such sorrow that my heart ached. "You're a different gymnast, you're not what you used to be. You're so much better. Don't be one of those girls who sleeps her way to the top. That's not who you are."

A fat tear slipped from my eye. Hayden saw it and pulled me to his chest, his lips pressed against the top of my head. I sobbed quietly on him, holding him. I needed him to understand the repercussions if he opened his mouth, but fear was taking over.

"Please, Hayden. Don't tell anyone. You can't."

"You're putting me in a tough spot. What he did is wrong. How long has this been going on?"

I swallowed. "Months."

"How many months?"

I went with the truth. "I'm not positive, but about six months or so after I came here."

Hayden cursed under his breath, hissing with anger.

"You don't understand and it's not what you think, I swear. There's so much more to it than you know." A heavy sigh burst from my throat and I said quietly, "He took me out of the meet for his own personal reasons."

His brows bunched together. "What are you talking about?"

"He's taking me out of my first meet, that's what you walked in on. I went in there to yell at him and one thing led to another. He even called my parents and told them I wasn't ready, even though he told me I was. He purposely took me out for his own personal reasons." Tears began falling while I cried into Hayden's chest. He wrapped his arms around me, comforting me and protecting me at the same time.

"He can't do that."

"He can, and he did," I said between hiccups. "There's nothing I can do about it now. At the end of the day, he has the right to take me out of a meet."

Hayden cursed under his breath agreeing with me. "This is a big deal, Adrianna. We need to notify someone."

I sucked in a breath and clutched his shirt in my hands. My heart was broken for two different reasons and I didn't know how to deal with it.

"Please don't get involved, Hayden. I'm begging you. This is my mess, not yours. I'll explain everything to you if you promise not to speak a word of it to anyone."

He groaned, torn between standing by his friend's side and doing the right thing.

"You're killing me here. Don't sleep with him again. Okay? It's not right. You'll get caught eventually," he paused. "We'll figure something out together. Until then, be smart, focus on your love of the sport, nothing else. Fuck him—not literally."

A sad laugh escaped my throat. Easier said than done.

Truth was, I couldn't stop.

I didn't want to…and I wouldn't.

To be continued…

execution

BOOK 2 IN THE OFF BALANCE SERIES

To the patient and loyal readers who've waited for this book…

I'm sorry about the cliffhanger in Balance.

Just kidding.

"Listen, human nature is fucked up. It's more honest, and more humane, to just lie."
—Anonymous

chapter 1

KOVA WAS A HEARTLESS, CUNNING MAN.

Hate swelled through me at an alarming rate. Rage unlike I'd ever felt before slithered through my veins, consuming me. I detested the ground he walked on, the air he breathed. I loathed every fiber of his being. After everything we shared, after all we knew about each other—our goals and desires in life, our dreams and aspirations—this was the dirtiest move of all, and I wasn't sure how we would come back from it.

There was no one else other than Kova who knew how important each gymnastics meet was on my journey to the Olympics, yet he had the audacity to rip it from me for his own selfish reasons.

His job was to catch me if I fell. Not sweep the rug out from under my feet and watch me hit the ground.

I had played him dirty too, though. I'd threatened rape. A low blow, and I felt terrible for playing that card, but he deserved it. I wanted to ruin him, but ruining him meant ruining myself, and that was something I couldn't chance.

Overcome with exhaustion, I stood at Hayden's car and released an anguish-filled breath. I'd run out to the parking lot to stop him after he caught Kova and me having sex.

The image of Hayden's expression when he barged into Kova's office played like a broken record in my head and slowly seared my brain. Stunned, mortified, shocked, and the absolute worst of all, disappointment had flitted across his face. He'd been rendered speechless and left Kova's office. I had to beg him not to open his mouth and report us to the authorities. And by doing so, I promised to come clean with him. Not something I wanted to do, but I would in return for his word.

I cried into his shoulder, not caring I got my tears and snot all over him. He only hugged me harder to him. My heart ached. My head hurt. I was drowning inside, sinking. The more I thought about the whole thing, the more my heart shattered into a million little pieces. Tears continued to trickle down my cheeks as I cried harder.

I let out a desperate sob, and he kissed the top of my head.

"I can't believe he did this." My voice was muffled in his shirt. "He's heartless, Hayden. He knew how much testing elite meant to me. He knew the Olympics was my endgame since I'd come to World Cup."

"Shhh…" He held me tighter. "Let me take you home."

I swallowed a sigh and stepped out of his embrace. "Okay, but I have to take care of something first. Meet me at my place in twenty?"

Hayden grabbed my forearm, confusion written all over his face. "Where are you going?"

I eyed the ground, reluctant to answer. "I need to tell Kova something."

"No!"

I looked up. "Hayden, I'll explain when I see you later, but you have to let me go talk to him."

Hayden's nostrils flared, not pleased with my response but he agreed anyway. The very last thing on earth I wanted right now was to look at Kova after we were caught, but the truth of the matter was I needed something from him. I needed that stupid little white pill he loved to feed me like candy.

With my shoulders back and chin up, I marched back toward the entrance of World Cup. Each step filled with a little more determination. By the time I reached the front door my emotions had cooled and my tears had dried up. I pulled the door open and stepped inside. The smell of powdery chalk permeated the air and the sound of parallel bars ricocheted in the background. Making my way to Kova's office, I turned left and walked down the narrow hallway. Once I reached his door, I grasped the handle and flung the door open, then slammed it shut behind me.

Kova sat motionless, his eyes unmoving. His eerie silence and calculating stare riled up my nerves. I sucked in a small gasp, my heart pounded as his eyes lowered to thin slits, and an unspoken warning filled the air.

Barely concealing his feelings, I could feel his anger simmering below the surface. My skin prickled with awareness. He quietly laid his pen down and leaned back in his leather chair.

"Did you fix things with Hayden? He is going to keep his mouth shut, yes?" It was a statement, not a question.

"Yes…for the most part."

He growled, his top lip curling under. "For the most part is not enough for me. Fix it, Adrianna. Now."

I lowered my eyes. "I trust him not to say anything."

"And I do not."

"Seems like a personal problem." Deep creases formed between his brows and I let out an aggravated sigh. I shook my head. "I made an agreement with him to cover your indiscretions."

One brow lifted to a high peak. His eyes hadn't moved from mine. "Surely you must mean to cover *our* indiscretions. You are as much to blame as I am, and very willing if I remember correctly." He smirked. "The way you tightened around me as you came… How you breathed hard in my ear and locked your legs around my back. Do not pretend that you did not enjoy what you got or that this is somehow all my fault." He paused, and his eyes darkened. "You loved every second of it. Admit it."

I looked away, my cheeks blushing. I was embarrassed. "Listen, you need to get me the pill again."

"What makes you think I will get it for you this time?" he asked, his voice low and controlled.

My lips parted, astonished by his indifferent attitude and lack of caring if I got pregnant. "Why wouldn't you? You've gotten it every other time."

He gave me a blasé shrug. "You are a big girl, more than capable of getting it yourself."

I clenched my jaw, my anger growing from his unmoving gaze. He got under my skin in one sentence and monotone voice. "God! Why do you have to be such an asshole? Do you wake up every day with a goal of people to piss off? Do you get off on hurting people? What is your issue?" I shook my hand back and forth, dismissing him. "You know what, don't answer that. I don't give a shit. You're a disgusting person."

He frowned, but didn't say a word. Unbelievable. Seething, I marched to the door and grabbed the knob.

"Adrianna." He called my name and I ignored him.

"*Adrianna.*" I stiffened, my back rigid from the way Kova stressed the pronunciation of my name a second time. I peered over my shoulder and watched as he grabbed a set of keys off his desk. Leaning down, he opened a drawer and pulled something out. He slammed it shut, relocking the drawer, and waved the offending box in my direction.

My eyes narrowed, fury igniting in my veins once again.

"You kept that hidden in your office?" I said in a high-pitched whisper. "Where anyone could find it? What were you thinking?"

I stalked toward him and reached out. Before I could pluck it from his hand, he shot forward and grasped my forearm.

"Why would anyone assume it is yours? Ria, have you forgotten I am in a long-term relationship with Katja and have been for many years?" I couldn't help focusing on his lips as he drew out every word. The heavy inflection in his accent sent chills up my spine, while warmth pooled in my belly. Stupid Russian.

"Of course I haven't."

"People would assume it is for her, not you."

I tried to wrench away, but Kova tightened his grip and ran his thumb in soft circles under my wrist. I lowered my gaze in shock, hating that my stomach fluttered in response.

"Say please."

My eyes shot up, and I saw red. "Fuck you."

I yanked my arm out of his grasp, box in hand, and stared at him, trying to fathom how he could be so harsh and callous yet blessed with the face of a god.

He'd fed me lie after lie until I pushed him hard enough to finally confess the truth—he had pulled me from my first gymnastics meet of the season for selfish reasons. He wanted me to hate him enough so I would refuse his sexual advances because he couldn't control himself around me.

What a dirt bag. A deceitfully charming dirt bag who lied through his teeth because it was easier for him to deal with his urges. Asshole.

A low chuckle dripped from Kova's lips. I took a tentative step back, then another, and another. He was heartless. Cruel. My stomach fluttered again but for a different reason. The hair on my arms lifted as he peered up through thick, inky black lashes. The remnants of his anger gone, replaced by eager desire.

Tears stung the back of my eyes at the realization of how truly sick the situation was. My emotions were rising, my heart pounded viciously against my ribs. I wouldn't cry in front of him. I had to leave before I broke down.

Turning on the balls of my feet, I slammed out of his office, uncertain what would come of this heartbreaking, disastrous situation we'd both caused. The echo of his malicious laughter chasing me as I fled.

chapter 2

RELEASING A LOUD SIGH, I THREW MY CELL ON THE PASSENGER SEAT AND TURNED up the music loud enough to block out the thoughts in my head. My hands trembled and my palms burned as I gripped the steering wheel hard.

I picked up my cell and tried calling Avery numerous times, but once again, she had disappeared. Her absence was starting to bother me. I had fire flowing through my veins and my emotions were on a rampage over what had happened with Kova. I needed my best friend. I needed her guidance. And she wasn't answering her calls.

I could lean on Hayden, but I wanted Avery.

I turned into the parking lot and pulled into my designated space a little too fast. I hit the curb with a jolt, propelling forward until my chest hit the steering wheel. I blew out a gasp and quickly shifted into park. Looking down, I realized I'd forgotten to wear my seat belt. Nerves and Tonka trucks didn't mesh well together. Climbing out, I walked around to the other side and opened the door. I slung my gym bag over my shoulder, then grabbed my cell phone from the cup holder. Glancing at the screen, I noticed a text from Avery.

BFF: Sorry! I promise to call you soon. I have a lot going on right now and can't talk. <3

I clenched my jaw. *She* had a lot going on? I just got caught having sex with my coach and was about to take the morning after pill, *again*, and *she* had a lot going on. I slammed the door shut in disbelief with as much force as I could muster and made my way through the lot to the lobby of my condo. Guilt filled me and I immediately regretted the hostility I felt toward her. This was Avery. She would never blow me off if it wasn't a serious matter. I just wish I knew what it was.

Ocean air blew against my heated cheeks as I headed toward the entrance. Considering how worked up I was, the cool breeze felt incredible against my skin.

I spotted Hayden as soon as the doors slid open. He sat bent over in a black leather chair with his hands twisted together. Head angled down, he appeared deep in thought as he cracked his knuckles. I fisted my duffle bag and took a deep breath. This was going to be interesting.

"I'm sorry it took more than twenty minutes," I said, striding up to him. Hayden stood, alarm crossing his face. "Dealing with Kova took a little longer than I anticipated."

Hayden shook it off and grasped my arms in his hands. He gave me a tender squeeze.

"It's fine. I would've waited until you got here because I was worried about you. Are you okay?"

My brows shot up. "Okay? No, Hayden, I'm far from being okay right now."

Hayden let out a sympathetic sigh. He wrapped his arms around my shoulders and drew me in. His worry for my well-being was as strong as the hug he gave me. I laid my head on his firm chest and took a deep breath, surrendering to his warm embrace. I closed my eyes for a moment and breathed him in. Hayden was my solace, my comfort zone.

"Yeah, that probably wasn't the best question to ask you. Sorry about that, I'm just worried."

My face softened. I appreciated his compassion more than he knew.

"Thanks," I said, pulling back. I laced my arm through his and placed my hand on his bicep, loving the arc of curvature in his muscle. "Come on." I nodded toward the elevator.

A roar of thunder cracked behind us as we walked side by side. I stopped to glance over my shoulder through the tall, tinted, glass windows and listened as another round of thunder boomed outside. Lightning lit up the darkening sky and rain began to fall fast and hard. Hayden withdrew from me and draped his arm across my shoulders.

It was about to pour, and not only outside.

Once inside my condo, I placed my bag on the breakfast bar, then reached inside for my wallet. I rummaged through my extra leotards and gymnastics gear until I found it. Hayden took off his jacket and draped it on the cushioned seat of one of the barstools. Holding on to the high back chair, he twisted and turned his body while keeping his feet in place, and cracked about every bone in his spine. The sound ricocheted through my silent condo. I glanced up.

"Feel better?" I asked.

"Not in the slightest."

I held out my credit card to him. "Here, order us some dinner. I don't care what it is, I'm not picky, just get us something good. I need to take a quick shower." *And wash Kova off me.*

Hayden took the card in his hand. "Is this one of those black cards?" He flipped it over and tried to bend it.

"Yup. Do your worst to it—you won't break it. It's made of titanium."

His head popped up, his jaw slack. "You know you can buy, like, a Bentley on this card, right? I once read someone bought a thirty-million-dollar teacup with their black card." He paused, brows angled toward each other. "Who buys a teacup for thirty million? Teacups are so delicate and fragile. Could you imagine if it broke?" He snapped his fingers. "Thirty million down the drain, just like that."

I shrugged and shook my head. A light laugh escaped me.

"How did you get one?"

"My parents each have one and you can add one person to the account. So, my brother, Xavier, and I were added. I'm on my dad's, he's on my mom's."

"That's awesome."

"I'm going to jump in the shower, but I'll be quick," I said, heading for my bedroom.

"Need a hand?" Hayden shouted in jest and I laughed.

I grabbed some clothes and made my way into the bathroom. Once I cranked up the water and waited for it to heat, I removed my leotard and sweat pants. I looked at my reflection in the mirror. All the work I'd put in since coming to World Cup was beginning to pay off.

There wasn't an inch of fat on my body—not that there had been before—but where I used to just be thin, I was now toned, my muscles sculpted but with soft definition. Upper arms curved with new strength, my stomach had obvious abs, and my hips were profound with obliques. Turning around, I tilted my head to the side to get a better view. My ass was round and firm and high, with an arc that could rival a supermodel's. Steam fogged the mirror as my gaze fell to my legs. Thighs were noticeably larger, firmer, solid. Pliable, yet tender.

Pulling my hair tie out, my hair fell around me. The wine undertones laced perfectly with the rich brown waves. The curled ends tickled my breasts causing my nipples to pucker in response. I looked down. I was almost positive my breasts had grown too, but not by much. Maybe it was the muscle growth behind the fatty tissue that caused them to look bigger. Maybe it was my wishful thinking and my eyes playing tricks on me. Because what girl didn't want bigger boobs?

I checked the water temperature with my fingers, then stepped under the shower. I sighed, the sound vibrated in the back of my throat. I closed my eyes as the piping hot water cascaded down my overworked body. I loved a scalding shower, even though Mom insisted it would wrinkle my skin.

As I washed myself, I imagined how the night would play out. I wondered how Hayden would react and if he'd come to understand. To the outside world, it was a hard pill to swallow. Inappropriate. Corrupt. Vile. Appalling. People would say Kova was a disgusting excuse of a man, that he stripped me of my innocence, possibly even tainted me. And while I wanted to agree with those things out of spite because I was furious, I also knew they weren't true. There was more between Kova and me than just sex. He didn't strip me of anything I didn't willingly give to him.

Our connection altogether was extremely difficult to defend. He understood me, my dreams and ambitions; but more importantly, Kova understood what gymnastics gave me—individuality and freedom. A singular way to express my true character and show my resilience in the world. I was my own person.

We connected on a different level, I just needed to make Hayden see that.

Turning off the water, I stepped out of the shower and wiped the mirror with my palm before quickly drying off. I dropped the towel and slipped on clothes, then I blow-dried my long, thick hair.

Anything to stall time.

Opening the bathroom door, my stomach twisted into knots. I took a hesitant step, steeling myself, before padding across the plush carpet to the living room. The closer I got to Hayden, the closer I was to revealing the truth.

"Chinese," I breathed out, stepping into the kitchen.

He smiled, trying to cover the agitation around his eyes. The past few hours had weighed heavily on him and that upset me. He didn't deserve to be dragged into this shit.

"I ordered you the sweet and sour chicken."

"Thanks," I said, then hurried to the refrigerator to avoid eye contact. I grabbed a bottle of water and handed it to Hayden, then grabbed one for myself. I uncapped it and took a sip, watching him. The silence between us was dense, I didn't know how to broach the subject.

"If you think I'm using chopsticks to pick up rice, you have another thing coming. I can't understand, out of everything that could be used to eat rice with, someone thought two sticks would be best," I blurted.

"You mean, *zhu?*"

I finally looked up at him. "Zoo? Like where animals are caged and put on display?"

Hayden barked out a laugh and I felt myself easing into a smile. "No, *zhu* means chopsticks."

I paused. "How the hell do you know this? It isn't common knowledge."

He regarded me with a gaze that said he was fully aware I was dodging the real conversation.

"My parents went through an adventurous phase where they wanted to try food from different cultures. I know that it's *hashi* in Japanese and in Korean it's something else."

I feigned disappointment, placing a hand over my chest. "I'm a little let down that you don't know what it is in Korean."

"Stop being a wiseass. Want to eat at the coffee table?"

We moved to the living room and sat down next to each other. We opened the lids and a puff of steam appeared before my eyes. I inhaled in delight. It'd been a long time since I had Chinese and I couldn't wait to dig in. Hayden plucked a few packets of sauce from the bag and tore them open.

Before I could take a bite, I needed to address the topic at hand. A lump formed in my throat as I turned toward him and rested my knee against his thigh. "Okay, Hayden, what do you want to know first?"

He shook his head. "Eat first, then we'll talk." He reached inside his pocket and pulled out a small flask. He held it up between us and shook it. "Vodka."

I stared at the stainless-steel container. Liquid courage was everything I needed and didn't need. "Vodka? I hate vodka. You couldn't pick something else?"

"Hey, it gets the job done, and you have a lot of explaining to do, so it'll help. I thought we could make a game of it."

A game. That's what my life came down to. A fucking drinking game.

Shame veiled my pounding heart. Averting my gaze to my crisscrossed legs, I chewed my lip. I wondered if Hayden would look down on me or see me any differently. Tightness seized my chest and I tried to rub the ache away. Tears prickled the back of my eyes. This mess was my problem and I had only myself to blame. Crying wouldn't solve this.

"Hey," Hayden said. "I know what you're thinking."

"You can't possibly," I mumbled.

"I'm not going to judge you. I promise. I just want to know what happened, Adrianna. Help me understand."

I looked at him. "Okay, maybe you did read my mind," I said through a sad chuckle. "If I must do this, you better drink with me."

A friendly smile lit up his face. "I can't get sloshed, I have to drive home."

"Stay the night," I suggested, not giving it a second thought. "But let your sister know first so she doesn't call in a panic tomorrow morning like she did last time."

His brows angled toward each other. "You want me to stay the night?"

"I think I *need* you to stay," I said. He accepted, and gratitude in the form of tears filled my eyes. I glanced up at the ceiling to hold them in. My jaw trembled. Once I got my emotions under control, I said, "I don't know if I have any clothes that will fit you to sleep in though."

Hayden leaned forward and pressed a tender kiss to my forehead. He pulled back and looked down. "Don't worry. I sleep in my boxers."

Wrapping my arms around his neck, I climbed onto his lap and buried my face into his shoulder. I squeezed him with all my might and let out a weighty breath. A few tears slipped from the corners of my eyes. Hayden held me tight, comforting me. I needed him to hold me, to tell me everything was going to be all right. I needed him to make promises, ones I knew he'd hate to keep. The kind that would cause him to struggle between morally right and wrong.

"Shhh…" he said when I sniffled. "It'll be okay. We'll figure something out, but it will be okay. I promise."

I nodded, sniffling. Something in my gut had me on edge. His words comforted me, but I was certain this was a changing point. My life would never be the same. Snuggling into him, he rubbed circles on the small of my back. I was grateful for Hayden and his friendship. His head dipped and his cheek met mine. We sat in silence, save for my soft weeping, as he let me unload my tears on his shoulder.

I needed to come clean, and soon I would, but in this moment, Hayden was exactly what I needed.

chapter 3

"USUALLY PEOPLE TAKE A WHOLE SHOT WHEN THEY'RE SPILLING SECRETS," Hayden began as I watched the clear liquid fall into one of the shot glasses he'd grabbed from the kitchen. "But since we're both not heavy drinkers, let's start with a half shot so we don't fall on our faces."

Hayden handed me the glass and I agreed. "Good idea." I paused. "So, if I take a shot when the truth gets too hard, you take one too?"

He nodded. "Or when I have a question and the answer you give me is not what I was expecting. But first, we take one just to get things going."

I watched as he poured another half shot for himself. After I had climbed onto his lap, he didn't say a word, didn't push me to speak, he just held me in his warm embrace and wiped the tears from my eyes. His faded blue shirt still had a wet spot from where I cried.

He capped the silver flask and nestled it between his thighs that were the size of tree trunks. Looking up, his crystal blue eyes glimmered with mischief. A timid smile curved the corners of his lips and I felt mine do the same. He was trying to ease me. His sandy blond hair was disheveled, like he'd run his hand through it.

"Ready?" he asked.

I exhaled. "Nope. Let's do this." We clinked our glasses. I brought the glass to my lips and our eyes locked as the cool liquid went down the back of my throat. I cringed. How anyone drank this crap was beyond me. Alcohol was not my thing.

"It feels like fire in my throat," I rasped through the burn.

"Sounds like a symptom of an STD." Hayden laughed.

"You should know, before you ask me anything, that Kova never pushed me," I stressed to him. "Not once."

His lips formed a flat line and he nodded. "You know it's hard for me to believe anything considering his age and status, right? He wields a lot of power, Aid. Maybe you don't realize it."

"I can see where you're coming from and why you would think that, but it's not the case. I promise on my life, it's not."

I could tell by the look in Hayden's eyes that he wasn't convinced.

"When did it start? Who else knows?" he asked.

"A couple of months after I moved here. The only other person who knows anything is Avery, but she doesn't know everything yet."

"Are you going to tell her?"

"Eventually, yes. She's my best friend, but I'm worried she'll judge me."

"Would you have told me had I not caught you?"

I contemplated my answer for a long moment. Hayden knew the answer before I told him. "Probably not."

"You gave him your virginity," he stated more than asked.

I thrust my glass toward him for a refill. "Wow. No foreplay." We both threw back another half shot. The memory of losing my virginity filled my mind. Just like anyone's first time, it was uncomfortable and painful; but Kova had gone slow and allowed me to adjust to his size, then brought me more pleasure than I could've ever imagined.

"I did," I finally said, heat rushing to my cheeks.

He blinked. "So Kova knew you were a virgin and he didn't care?"

I shook my head in protest. "I didn't tell him. He didn't know."

He scoffed. "That's impossible."

"It's not. How would he have known if I didn't tell him?"

"I don't know, a hymen being there for one."

I ignored that. "He found out afterward and went ballistic."

A dark shadow cast over Hayden's blue eyes. They reminded me of the deep ocean. "What do you mean *ballistic?*" he growled.

"We had an argument over it. Things got a little tense."

"A little tense," he repeated under his breath. "Where were you when it happened?"

"Here."

Hayden went ramrod straight. "You mean to tell me he came to have sex with you here? In your condo, where you couldn't escape him? Did you do it so he'd pay more attention to you?"

That upset me.

"There was no need to escape him because I didn't want to." My voice rose as I accentuated each word with a sharp bite. "I wanted it, I liked it." The thought of having sex with Kova caused a stir of sensations to stream through my body. My cheeks flushed again. Even though I was devastated over the fact that he took me out of the meet, I couldn't stop my body from reacting to him. Everything we shared was everything I wanted, and trying to get Hayden to comprehend that was deeming to be a challenge.

"You're blushing." Hayden's head tilted to the side and his jaw dropped. "You're thinking about it, aren't you? You're thinking about fucking him." Shaking his head in disbelief, Hayden poured himself a whole shot and quickly threw it back, then he filled mine but I didn't move to drink it. "I can't believe it," he muttered under his breath with disgust.

My brows shot up. I looked over his shoulder. "No, I'm not."

"You're lying. I can see it in your eyes."

"Fine. I am. What do you want from me, Hayden? I'm telling you the truth—it's what you asked for. I liked having sex with Kova, I liked everything about it. I can't help if thinking about it gets me all hot and bothered." Hayden went to speak but I cut him off. "And he didn't come here to fuck, he came to talk to me. One thing led to another and it kind of just happened."

He gave me a droll stare. "Things like that don't just happen, Aid—"

"I can't just fall onto a dick, I know," I mocked. "Avery said the same thing."

Hayden let out a laugh, lightening the tension in the room. My shoulders relaxed. "Well, Avery's right. It's not possible."

"Yeah, I know, but Hayden…you don't understand. It's honestly not what you think. We connected on a purely psychological level. We understand each other and want the same things. Never in a million years did I expect this to happen."

He shook his head, disagreeing. "He's your coach, though. He, more than anyone, knew better than to get involved with his gymnast. Let alone, your age. I place the blame solely on him for what's happened, he's the catalyst in all of this. I don't understand how he could take advantage, Aid. It's disgusting."

I flinched.

Hayden sighed. "I'm trying to understand this, but I don't think I ever will. He should've put a stop to it before it could even start. How can you not see what he did to you is wrong?"

I was tired of it all. "Maybe it's not something that needs to be understood."

"It doesn't work like that in the eyes of the law." He paused, his forehead creasing. "Were you at least using protection? Please tell me you're on birth control."

I gave a subtle shake of my head in answer.

"Bareback," he bit out. "Please don't tell me he fucked you without a condom." I averted my gaze. He continued. "Unbelievable. He's a dumb fuck if I ever saw one. What guy doesn't carry a condom?"

My brows furrowed. "You mean, you always have one on you?"

"Yes!"

"Oh." I paused. "Like right now, you have one on you?"

"Yes!" he exclaimed, like it was an obvious thing. "Don't be so naive, Aid."

I took offense to that. "I'm not naive. I just didn't think all men carried a condom around, it's so cliché."

"Getting an STD is not on my to-do list, and girls don't typically carry them in their purses."

A sad chuckle escaped me. "That's true." My eyes popped. "Fuck!" I took the shot and hastily handed Hayden the little glass. I didn't even have time to cringe from the bitter, disgusting taste.

Jumping up from the couch, I ran to the bar where I left my duffle bag, and shuffled through it. I wasn't a drinker in the slightest, so the vodka had started to flush my blood with warmth and loosen me.

"What are you doing?" he asked, following me. Sighing in relief, my shoulders sagged when I found what I was looking for. I turned around and held the box up next to my face. Hayden glanced at what I held in my hand. His face slowly transformed into a fusion of puzzlement, wrath, and revulsion. His jaw hardened and I bit my lip. The air changed around us.

"He makes you take the morning after pill? Are you fucking kidding me? Do you know how bad that is for your body?" he roared. Hayden yanked it out of my hand and flipped it over to read the back.

"He doesn't make me take it, it was my suggestion since I'm not on birth control. I never needed it before."

"Let me guess, he just happens to keep a stash of these babies laying around." When I didn't say anything, his blue eyes lit up. "I'm right, aren't I?"

I shook my head in denial. "No, not really. He's had to go buy them in the past. Today he just happened to have some on hand."

Hayden shifted from foot to foot. He let out a heavy huff. "So he was prepared for the next quick bang is basically what you're telling me." He paused. "Wait. How many times have you taken this garbage?"

"A few."

"A few," he retorted. "How could you put this in your body after how hard you work?"

"I don't know, Hayden. I wasn't thinking."

"Damn straight you weren't thinking. Do you even know—" he stopped himself, and slowly lowered his arm. Hayden's face paled, twisting into a nauseating clarity. His eyes widened. "When you got sick, this was the cause of it? When I took you to the doctor?"

I clenched my eyes shut. I hadn't planned on telling him that little tidbit.

"I think we need another shot," I suggested, deflecting. I tried to step away, but he reached out and clamped a hand over my wrist. His grip wasn't painful, but ferocity pulsed through his hand and his eyes were dark with fury.

"It was, wasn't it?"

"Yes and no. We had an argument that led to some rough...ish sex. It hurt to pee the next day so I held it in, which was stupid because it's what caused the infection. The doctor said it could've been a combo of the pill on top of the kidney infection that caused the severe cramping."

"Un-fucking-real. How many times have you taken this shit, Aid?"

I winced at the bite in his tone. "This would be my third time."

His jaw slackened, and so did the hand holding my wrist. His shoulders dropped, like he'd been defeated for not protecting me sooner. I had no intention of hurting Hayden, but he wanted the truth, and honestly, I needed to get it out.

Dragging a hand through his hair, he tugged at his scalp. He paced the living room, shaking his head, and muttering under his breath. Anxiety clenched my stomach as I watched. His grip crinkled the box, and I sent up a silent prayer in hopes he wouldn't crush the pill. His other hand was a tight fist at his side, the veins in his arm twirling down his forearm. He was so mad, so pissed off I thought he was going to punch my wall, but his next move blindsided me.

Hayden strode up to me, and before I could blink, he tugged me into a hug. He aligned his body with mine and placed his big muscled arms around my shoulders, caging me to him. His entire body trembled with rage. I dropped my fight against him to accept what happened and wound my arms around his lower back. Somehow, I think he needed this more than I did.

"I'm going to fucking kill him," he said with his lips to the top of my head. "He should've never allowed himself to be in a situation where he would be tempted."

"It wasn't all him, you know. I'm to blame too."

Hayden ran a hand down my hair and kissed the top of my head. He nestled me closer to him and gave me a comforting embrace. The vodka was pulsing through my veins and I relaxed into him with a warm sigh. Despite confessing parts of my torrid affair to him, it was a relief to talk about it.

"Do *not* have sex with him again. Please," he begged, his voice cracking along with my heart. Hayden was my closest friend here. The last thing I wanted to do was hurt him, and while he demanded the whole truth, the truth affected him.

"If you want it...if you want sex, use me. We don't have to be in a relationship, and we don't have to tell anyone."

"He thinks we're in a relationship," I said, staring at his honey-colored arms.

Hayden pulled back and looked down at me. One of his hands rested on the small of my back, the other at the base of my neck. His gentle fingers massaged my nape and my body flushed from his touch. I looked up at him and realized the vodka was hitting me faster than I thought...as well as him. We both had the same glossy-eyed look.

"What do you mean?"

"Well, it was one of the reasons why he pulled me, but also really because he wants me to hate him to the point where I won't let him come near me since he can't seem to stay away from me, if you catch my drift..."

His lip curled up. "Unreal. He's a real piece of work. So, he took you out of the meet because he thinks you two are in a relationship, all the while he's screwing his girlfriend at home on a regular basis, and because he can't control himself? Can we say double standard?"

"He said he wants me to hate him."

"And do you?"

I thought about his question before I responded. "Yes and no. It's complicated."

Hayden released his hold and stepped back, staring at the wall behind me. I'd blindsided him with my bible-sized list of confessions.

He ran a hand through his hair again and said, "Let's get another drink, and then maybe that will be it for the night. We don't want to wake up with a wicked hangover."

Before I could respond, there was an insistent tap at my door. My heart dropped. Blood drained from my face and Hayden observed me with a confused look.

I knew who it was. It could only be one person.

chapter 4

T HE RAP ON THE DOOR SOUNDED AGAIN, FOLLOWED BY KOVA'S MUFFLED VOICE.
"Adrianna, open the door."

"Oh hell fucking no," Hayden bit out, and casually tossed the small box of morning after pills onto the coffee table.

He stomped toward the door, and by some miracle, I got there before him and stood in front of him.

"Hayden, please, stand back," I begged, my hands flat to his chest trying to push him away. His pecs flexed against my palms, but he didn't budge. "Don't say a word to him. He obviously already knows that you know and I'm sure he's worried."

"Why are you sticking up for him?"

"I'm not." Maybe I was just a little. "Just let me talk to him and see what he wants."

He cracked his neck to the side and gritted out, "Fine."

"Thank you."

Hayden took a small, small step back. Taking a deep breath and praying for the best, I unbolted the door with trembling fingers and pulled it open.

My lungs burned at the sight of Kova. I hated him. I hated the ground he walked on, the air he breathed.

At least, I wanted to. That's what I told myself.

The unexpected presence of him caused a stirring inside my belly and a drumming in my heart. For a split second, I forgot all the turmoil he's caused, the havoc he's wrecked. One look into his green eyes and his raw emotion was on display for all to see.

He was overcome with despair. Distraught.

There was something downright magnetic about Kova that drew me to him. An allure, a fascination.

And something as powerful and as captivating as him could only ever end in utter destruction.

I stepped back to let Kova inside and bumped into Hayden. His chest was flush against my back, his arm stretched around my abdomen and rested possessively on my hip. It was then that Kova lifted his stare and looked behind me. His jaw tightened and his eyes darkened at the sight of Hayden. Something flickered in his gaze, a shadow of knowledge, but it was gone as quickly as it came. Kova pushed his way into my condo like it was a natural thing for him.

Hayden released me, and before I could stop him, his fist flew toward Kova in a blur of motion. "Hayden, no!" I gasped at the sound of his knuckles connecting with Kova's sharp jaw, the crack splintering the tension in the room.

"Oh my God!" I barely had enough time to move when the back of Kova's larger than life body fell toward me like a building about to collapse. Luckily for my sake, he quickly regained his footing and stood upright. I walked to stand between them and put my hands out. I wasn't sure I had the ability to stop them, but I was sure as hell going to try.

Kova brought the back of his hand to his mouth, his eyes gleamed, a wicked grin spread across his face. He *would* smile.

"Are you crazy, Hayden?" I cried out, shoving him back with a huff. He didn't stumble. I shoved again, this time pushing with everything in me. "Get back!" Trying to move a giant boulder while tipsy proved to be harder than I anticipated.

"You're really going to ask me if I'm crazy right now?" he asked, his eyes like poisoned daggers trained solely on Kova. The air was combustible between the three of us and the dense silence made it even more volatile. Hayden resembled an untamed animal. I'd never seen this side of him before. So protective and defensive. If he could spit bullets, I had no doubt he would.

Hayden moved fast and stepped around me. I knew I didn't have it in me to hold him back, so I positioned myself in front of Kova. I plastered myself to him and wrapped my arms behind me and grabbed on to Kova's legs. My heart beat wild and frantic against my ribs. I held my breath and watched as Hayden raised his fist in the air.

"Hayden! Stop!" I screamed, but he didn't hear me.

Kova draped one arm over my chest and cuffed my shoulder as he blocked the punch from Hayden with his forearm. I gasped in horror as he ducked, shielding my body with his as Hayden's fists tried to strike again. Kova flung me to the side and out of the way.

I braced my fall with my arms outstretched and turned my head as my knees scraped across the carpet. I sucked in a breath, wincing from the rug burn and listening to the grunting of curse words between the two men. I glanced up and brushed the loose strands of hair from my face that blocked my view, tucking them behind my ear. Eyes wide, my knees trembled as I slowly stood, mortified at the sight before me.

"What the fuck are you doing, Hayden!" Kova raged, ducking from another blow. He stood to his full height and shoved Hayden back with a push to his chest. "You almost hit her!"

Kova maneuvered himself behind Hayden, putting him in a chokehold. He looked up, eyes gleaming. Blood trickled from the corner of his mouth where his lip was cracked. Hayden had surprisingly gotten in a good punch.

"Nice to see you answering the door in actual clothing this time, Ria." His mouth twitched. The hint of something more in his words didn't go unnoticed. Hayden wrestled in his arms, but Kova had a firm lock on him. He wasn't going anywhere.

I glared at him. Of all things to start a conversation with, he picks that.

Hayden twisted in Kova's arms. "Are you trying to get hit again?"

"That was a sucker punch, Hayden. It will not happen again. It is obvious you are no match for me. Now stop trying to fight me so I can—"

"You're fucking scum!"

Kova paused. "I have been called worse."

"Hayden!" I screamed. Vodka, and about twenty different feelings and emotions, ran through my system, making me hotter by the moment. My fingers tingled with adrenaline. "Fucking stop it!"

"If you promise to act civilly, I will release you," Kova said to the top of Hayden's head.

Hayden mumbled under his breath and Kova freed him. He ran both hands through his dirty blond hair and adjusted his now wrinkled shirt. He shot Kova a scathing glare, then looked at me. I recoiled at the look on his face. He hardly held back how he felt.

"How can you defend this piece of shit after what he did to you?" Hayden asked, gesturing toward Kova.

I squinted at Kova. He'd lifted the hem of his shirt to wipe the blood from his mouth.

My jaw trembled, upset he still believed I was forced against my will. "I told you, he didn't do anything I didn't want. You're never going to believe me, are you?" My voice sounded as fragile as my emotions felt. "I don't know what I can do to make you believe me."

He squared his shoulders back. "Knowing the position he's in, there's nothing you can do or say that will change how I feel. Nothing. It's *wrong* and he should've been the one to know better."

Tears blurred my vision. "It's not wrong if I wanted it. It's really not."

"I feel like I'm talking to a wall right now," he responded.

"You have some nerve saying anything, Hayden," Kova cut in. "Especially after everything I have done for you and your sister." He gave Hayden a cutting look that sent him into a frenzy.

Hayden's face went stark white. "That has absolutely nothing to do with this!" he roared. "Nothing! So, what, because of *that* you can do whatever it is you want and I should be okay with it? Like I'm indebted to you for the rest of my life? Where do you get off with your line of thinking?"

I looked back and forth between the two, lost. They were having a conversation over something I had no clue about.

"What's going on?" I asked.

"Why do you think there were rules implemented, Adrianna?" Kova asked me while staring at Hayden. "Why do you think there is a dating policy that I enforce? Ask your beloved friend right here. Holly is the reason for it."

I glanced at Hayden, but he was focused on Kova.

"Kova," Hayden growled. He took one step toward him. "Don't."

"Don't what?" I asked, looking back and forth between them again.

Kova lifted an elegant shoulder like he didn't have a worry in the world. He was secure in his stance, confident.

"I am just reminding you what I did for *you*, Hayden. Now you will do the same for me and grant me with the same discretion I did you." He finished with a raised brow.

I was more lost than ever. "Do what for you?" I shouted. "What the fuck is going on?"

Both men turned to me, the whites of their eyes more visible than the color. I inhaled a lungful of air. Pressure mounted in my chest as I tried to take deeper, bigger breaths. My lungs burned from the restriction. Horrified by their reactions, my heart shattered into a million pieces and I burst into tears. I wept over a battle I never had the chance to win—making Hayden a believer, and losing out on the gymnastics meet. Both were irrevocably unattainable and the gravity of that realization produced an effect so severe, my throat closed and hot tears clouded my vision. No matter what I said, Hayden would never understand, and no matter what I did, Kova wasn't going to let me compete at the meet.

Heart pounding, I dropped my head into my hands and turned around, but a hand with a vice grip stopped me.

I shrugged Kova off like his touch contained a disease. He tried again. "Go away. I don't know why you're here anyway," I said, eyes trained on the floor. I was too embarrassed to look up.

"Adri—"

"Leave me alone," I gritted out, slapping Kova's hand away. Just as I took another step, his hand clamped down on my bicep.

Something in me snapped and I whipped my arm back. My eyes lifted as heat rose to my tear stained cheeks. I stared at nothing but the space between both men and felt everything roaring to a head inside me. I couldn't look at either one. Wrath flowed through from the tips of my toes to the top of my head at an alarming rate. I stiffened.

"Get away from me." He stepped toward me as I stepped back. "Are you deaf? Get away. I don't want you here."

"I just want to talk to you," Kova pleaded.

"I have nothing to say to you. You've made it perfectly clear what your motives are."

"*Coach*, I think it's best if you leave," Hayden suggested.

Kova glanced over at Hayden and gave him an exasperating once over from head to toe. "I do not take orders from pony boys." Then he looked back at me.

"I. Hate. You." I looked into his eyes as I let the words slip from my lips in disgust.

Kova didn't blink, his expression blank. He acted like the words didn't faze him and stepped closer until he invaded my personal space and I was forced to shove at his rock-hard chest. He didn't budge. His hands clamped down on both my arms to confine me to him and I began thrashing in his arms.

Between the vodka and my out-of-whack-emotions, I broke down. "Get out!" I bawled. "Get. Out." His fingers tightened around my arms and I thrust my palms under his chin to push him away. Hand rearing back, I tried to slap him a few times across the face, but he moved too fast and dodged my attack each time. Kova began speaking in his native tongue, his Russian growing louder and louder with each spasm of attack and assault I rained down on him. "I hate you! I hate you!"

An arm wound around my narrow waist from behind. "Adrianna. Stop," Hayden ordered, trying to grapple me. I wrenched and yanked and twisted my arms in circles in an effort to loosen Kova's iron grip. Just when I thought I'd won, Kova let go, but I was too slow. He dropped both arms over my shoulders and pulled me to him. Still, I fought, arching my chest back, making it difficult on him. I thrashed in his hold, and raised my knee to kick him as both he and Hayden tried to control me.

"Last chance," Kova said, but I didn't listen. He tightened his arms and squeezed until he restrained me, like he had me in a damn straitjacket. Sandwiched between Kova and Hayden, I couldn't move, my entire body was locked between the two. I could only wiggle my fingers. Emotions soared. I wasn't strong enough to win, and for a split moment, I wondered if I ever would be strong enough for anything. Anger fled and deep dejection filled me.

Surrendering every ounce of myself, I dropped my forehead to Kova's chest and sagged against him, depleted.

Hayden hadn't moved. He left a protective hand on my hip as he stroked my hair while I whimpered quietly.

Stupid alcohol. Stupid Kova. Stupid Hayden.

chapter 5

I DON'T KNOW HOW LONG WE STOOD THERE BEFORE I HEARD KOVA SPEAK.
"I am not going to hurt her, Hayden," Kova said in a tender tone I didn't expect.
"Step back."

Hayden listened and created a small amount of distance between us. "Don't you understand, you dumb fuck. You already have."

He was right and more tears seeped from my eyes. Kova had hurt me more than anyone I thought physically possible.

"I hate myself for that more than you can ever know," Kova admitted, and the conviction in his voice broke my heart. He did hate himself, that I knew. One of his hands drifted to my lower back and ran in soothing circles. I let out an exhausted breath.

"And what about Katja?" Hayden demanded. "Do you hate yourself for hurting *her*?"
Kova tensed.

"She does not know anything…and it is going to stay that way."

Hayden drew in a breath. "You're a real piece of work, you know that?"

"You think I am happy for what I have done? You do not know anything, Hayden. Not even the half of it."

Pulling back, Kova looked down at me but I was too mortified to meet his gaze. My nose was running, my eyes couldn't stop leaking, and my hair was matted to my face.

"Come."

Taking my hand, he guided me into the kitchen. I gripped the counter behind me and jumped up, sitting on the edge as Kova's eyes skittered around before he went looking for something.

With my hands on my thighs, I stared at my palms. While I hadn't had rips in a while—thankfully—I still had calluses. I began picking at the dead skin and pulling little pieces off at a time. Kova's feet appeared in my line of vision and another silent tear slipped from the corner of my eye.

Without thought, I widened my legs to accommodate him and hooked a foot around the back of his leg and pulled him closer. He leaned in so his cheek touched mine.

"*Malysh*," he whispered only for me to hear. "Take this."

For whatever dumb reason, that made me cry harder. I nodded and reached for the tissues that appeared between us.

"Kova, I think you need to leave," Hayden said. "I'm serious. Go."

"I am not going anywhere right now," Kova bit out, not bothering to look at him.

I wiped under my eyes with the tissue and Kova smoothed my hair back. My stomach was in knots. I was nauseous to the core over everything that had transpired tonight and I fought to push it down. The vodka wasn't helping.

Kova placed a finger under my chin and tilted my head back. He took the tissue from my hand and dabbed around my face.

"Open your eyes. Look up."

I did as he said and let out a long breath. He sniffed. "Vodka? You have been drinking."

I pursed my lips together before I asked, "How can you tell?"

"I can smell it."

"Liquid courage. Isn't that what they call it?"

The corner of Kova's mouth twitched and his eyes softened. "I suppose so."

"That stuff tastes gross. I don't know how you drink it."

"It is an acquired taste."

"So is rape," Hayden chimed in, his voice tinged with bitter resentment.

I looked over my shoulder at Hayden and gasped, ready to deny that Kova did such a despicable thing.

Kova went ramrod straight and angled his body defensively toward Hayden.

My gaze shifted between them. I panicked, my heart pounding viciously against my chest. I knew what was coming.

"I did no such thing!" Kova bellowed. "I am not what you think I am, Hayden, and I am not going to try and make you understand when you refuse to open your mind."

"You're right, I can't understand it. In fact, I think you liked what happened. I think you're a sick individual who took satisfaction in the power of authority you have. Things don't happen unless you want them to." He paused and sent a fleeting glance in my direction before he was back on Kova. "I think you belong in jail."

Jail. Dear God. Fear set in. The friction in the room intensified as the temperature dropped. The vicious pounding of my heart echoed in my ears. I wasn't sure how much more I could take. Jail was the last thing I wanted.

"Hayden," I begged, hiccupping for air. "You promised me you wouldn't say anything to anyone, including the police, if I told you the truth. You promised."

He stared at me, pity evident in his eyes. "That was before I knew everything. This is so much more. He needs to be held accountable for his actions."

"This is how you repay me after what I have done for you?" Kova sneered at Hayden.

"I'm not entertaining that topic, so drop it."

Terrified he would call the cops, I gasped for air. I couldn't think straight and feared the worse.

Gripping the edge of the countertop, I pleaded with him. "You think we're the first people to ever have an affair? Because we're not."

Kova cupped my cheek to turn my attention back to him. "Breathe," he ordered, his eyes soft as he regarded me. With Kova, that was all I needed. One deep look to know his thoughts, and right now, guilt prevailed to be the strongest emotion. "Are you okay?"

"No, she's not okay, you asshole," Hayden snarled.

"What can I do for you to see it from my perspective?"

Hayden shook his head, and my stomach dropped like a ten pound weight had settled in my gut. "We're running in circles here. I don't even know how to respond to that." He put his hands up. "You know what? Fuck this. I'm out." He grabbed his keys and made his way to the door. "I can't sit here and watch this *fucking disgusting prick* manipulate you," he spat in unreserved disgust and I recoiled. "I'm going for a run. When I get back later, he better be gone."

"Get back later? Why would he come back?" Kova probed, his heated glare scorched my cheek. I looked at him.

"He's sleeping over."

"He is *sleeping* over?" he growled.

"Yeah, since we're dating and all," Hayden antagonized. The gleam in his eyes overshadowed the revulsion he exhibited moments before.

"Oh, my God. Seriously?" I asked in annoyance.

He shrugged. "It's the truth." His gaze moved to Kova. "Right, *Coach?* It's why you took Adrianna out of the meet, isn't it? Because you thought we were fucking, meanwhile you were the one screwing her all along." A sardonic snicker escaped Hayden. As he grabbed the door knob, he paused to get in one last word. "It's pretty fucking sad how he brainwashed you, you know."

My lips parted as he pulled the door open, letting it bang against the wall, then slammed it shut on his way out. In the time that I'd known Hayden, I'd never seen such aggressive emotion or heard him curse in the way I just had, and it was all my fault.

My shoulders slumped as I glanced at Kova. A tick worked in his jaw. If looks could kill, Hayden would be a pile of ashes right now.

Kova looked back at me and our eyes locked. Inches from my face, I inhaled his cologne that I'd come to love. Dark notes of tobacco with a sensual blend of light citrus and warm cinnamon enveloped me. My gaze travelled to his mouth. The light dusting of jet black facial hair was becoming his signature, lazy look. My heart thundered in my chest, beating against my ribs, as I reached out tentatively to feel him. His eyes followed my hand as he held still, and the tips of my fingers gently grazed his cheek, brushing the stubble of hair. "I like this," I whispered. My thumb glided along his sharp jaw toward his ear where my fingers threaded in his hair. The man was gorgeous on the outside, but I had to question the color of his soul.

Kova didn't move a muscle. My eyes focused on his inflamed lip where Hayden sucker punched him and I wondered what he'd tell Katja. I had a good idea why he was here, but then again, this was Kova. Always enigmatic.

"Why did you come here?" I asked.

Kova grasped my fingers in his hand and brought them to his lips. Closing his eyes, he gently kissed each finger like he was savoring the touch of my skin.

"To talk."

"Talk about what?"

He opened his eyes to reveal a startling emerald color. "How I treated you earlier, what I said to you, it was wrong."

A burst of hope bloomed in my chest and I sat up higher. A little smile tipped my lips. "You mean you're apologizing for taking me out of the meet." He stayed silent as I stared at him for a long moment, waiting. "That's what you're apologizing for, right, Kova?" I asked again, almost demanding that was what he came here for. I waited… and waited… and waited. When he didn't answer, I jerked my hand back as the smile fell from my face.

"You're not sorry at all, are you?" I asked, my voice barely audible.

Kova exhaled a breath and glanced away. He wasn't sorry. Not in the least. He may be ragged with shame, but my heart could only take so much. It wasn't fair what he did, and I wasn't going to allow his guilt to make me forgive him. It wasn't okay.

While the vodka had allowed me to momentarily forget the mess I was in, his nonexistent words brought everything back full circle and slammed into my gut.

"I think we're through here." I tried to jump off the counter, but Kova placed a hand on my thigh to stop me.

"Wait."

His nostrils flared while his eyes darted around every surface, besieged, I'm sure, to find the right words. Wouldn't be the first time.

Scratching the back of his head, he finally spoke. "I am incredibly sorry for what happened between us in my office. It was not what I expected, nor what I would have wanted to happen. I am disgusted. The words I said to you, what I threatened you with, it was heartless and cruel and I hope one day you can forgive me. I should have told you sooner that I planned to pull you from the meet instead of catching you off guard and embarrassing you in front of the team." He shook his head and looked around my condo again, unable to meet my gaze. He let out a long sigh, his voice dropping to a whisper. "I do not know who I have become... I hate myself for the pain and agony I have caused you."

Kova left me utterly speechless.

I didn't expect an apology from him, let alone one to carry so much weight. This man surprised me every day. One minute he made my blood boil, the next he was the most encouraging person in my life. It physically hurt to see such anguish fill the depths of his beautiful eyes, but I knew in that moment I needed to stay strong. Otherwise, if I caved, then I'd be tolerating his heinous actions, and I couldn't allow that. It would only give way for it to happen again in the future.

"Ria, please, say something." His voice cracked.

"Thank you for your apology, but it doesn't take away how you sabotaged me. I thought that's why you were here, to apologize for that, but you're not even close to feeling bad about that." I scoffed. "I thought you would understand more than anyone how important each competition is, what I need to do to achieve my dream. But you stripped it from me. You hardened me in mere seconds with your words and your actions, and I don't know if I could truly ever forgive you for what you did."

"I am not seeking forgiveness when it comes to the matter of the meet. There is motive behind it, and soon I hope you will understand why."

A disdainful huff rolled off my lips. The audacity of this man. My heart plummeted to the floor but I inhaled strength deep into my lungs and prayed for my next set of words to come out fierce.

"You've accomplished what you set out to do."

He stared straight at me.

"And what is that?"

I repeated the words he first said to me soon after I arrived at World Cup, though he used them in a different manner.

"I can't stand the sight of you."

chapter 6

SORROW SAT HEAVY IN EVERY FEATURE OF KOVA'S FACE.

I'd say he was completely heartbroken and devastated—as he should be. His hand gave my thigh a little squeeze and his lips formed a thin, flat line. I shoved his touch off me and his face completely fell.

"I deserve your hate."

"You deserve my hate and all that comes with it. It's what you set out to do, isn't it? Make me hate you? So you got what you wanted."

He scrubbed his hands down his face. "No, not at first it was not. I do not know what I was thinking, what came over me, but it was not right and I am so, so sorry."

"You make no sense," I said, trying to keep my voice from cracking. I had a notion he still wasn't talking about the meet and that set fire to my blood.

"This has never happened to me before and I do not understand what to make of it, *ma-lysh*," he stressed. "I was ready—"

I held up my hand. "I do not want to ever hear you call me that name again."

He paled. "Adrianna." My name was a pained whisper on his tongue.

"I don't understand anything either because you never express yourself. You're a very difficult man to follow."

"Do you not see how I cannot say what I want? *I cannot*," he urged, pointing to his chest. "It is too much of a risk."

I scoffed. "Bullshit. What risk? You mean speaking your thoughts honestly for once? So you can fuck me, but you can't talk to me? How does that make sense? How is talking a risk? Who am I going to tell?"

He pursed his lips and glanced to his right, dropping his head onto his arm. I tried desperately not to break my resolve, but it was difficult when it came to Kova. While my words were outlined in truth, his were contradicting or deceptive, but I knew what I needed to do to get him to open up.

I needed to touch him. He needed human contact.

Slipping my hands under his shirt, Kova jolted when my fingers glided along his tapered waist. I loved the indentations on his hips and ran my knuckles over them. The thought of my tongue mimicking the motion crossed my mind.

"You are blushing," he said in a rasped voice. "I would love to know what you are thinking about right now."

This fucking man and the way he stared at me. My heart raced a million miles a minute, and in this moment, I could forgive everything he did just from the way he looked at me.

But I wouldn't. I was on a mission to get him to express himself, to help me understand why he did what he did if I was truly ready like he claimed I was.

I continued my roaming until I'd touched the small of his back, and moved upward toward the center where his muscles flexed beneath my palms. I sat up and brought my chest to his, pressing myself to him. Kova angled his face down as his breath mingled with mine, our lips mere inches from touching. My stomach fluttered and I dragged my legs up the back of his thighs and wrapped them around his hips. Kova straightened and I removed my arms from beneath his shirt, coiling them instead around his broad shoulders. I scooted closer and my fingers threaded in his hair. All the while he hadn't laid a finger on me.

"I hate you and want you at the same time." The confession rolled off my tongue before I could stop it.

"I know you do," he breathed into me. "Listen, I cannot make you any promises, but I will try to be better. I am only human, and I wrongfully acted out. And contrary to what it may seem, I never want to see you hurting like today. Your first meet to test elite is a big one and I want you prepared."

I stole a quick glance at his lips, a fraction away now, and mine trembled with the urge to close the distance. Heart racing, blood on fire, I was desperate for the next move. His hands found my waist and settled there, giving me a squeeze. A spark of energy passed through us and zipped up my spine. He exhaled as I inhaled, and I drew in a lungful of his breath. Kova ran his tongue along his bottom lip and a smile curved at the corner. I melted into him. Goose bumps peppered my arms as he angled his mouth toward mine.

He was going to kiss me. And damn it all to hell, I wanted him to.

But I wouldn't let him.

Just as he was about to press his lips to mine, I moved my hand over his heart and stopped him. He looked at me. In another place, in another time, things would be different. I'd let him kiss me, let him have me however he wanted. But right now, I couldn't, and I wasn't sure when I'd let him ever again.

"Your heart is beating so fast," I whispered.

His pulse thumped beneath my fingertips. His eyes were the darkest green color I'd ever seen. They captivated me, hypnotized me. He leaned in closer.

"No," I begged, my voice ragged and tortured as I pressed on his chest to push him back. "Please don't kiss me."

Kova cupped the side of my neck, pressing his thumb under the edge of my jaw, and with a gentle ease, he tilted my head back to grant him control. He dominated the air between us…and me.

"Do not deny me."

"You told me to deny you."

"I lied," he growled.

His thumb stroked my throat while I swallowed. There was something intimate about it and I found myself arching into him. I couldn't tear my eyes from his hooded ones.

"Give me what I want." His lips brushed against mine.

"No." My voice cracked.

"Yes," he demanded against my mouth. Kova's warm tongue slipped ever so slowly along the seam of my lips, coaxing me. He held the back of my neck firmly until I surrendered to him, allowing him access. He licked the roof of my mouth, dragging his tongue seductively along the top, then pulled my lip between his teeth. A throbbing in my sex shot through me and I gasped.

"This is what you do to me." He licked me again. I had no control over my body when he was like this. "Every time I am near you, every time I think about you, I feel this way, *malysh*. You have awakened a beast inside me."

I returned his kiss, plunging my tongue into his mouth, and hating myself for caving in. He sucked it, stroked it. I wrapped both my arms around his neck and he pulled me closer. I whimpered, craving more. My inner thighs squeezed around his hips as I surged up, angling myself right where I needed him. My clit throbbed as I rubbed against his erection. Kova placed a hand on my knee, and then dragged it up the side of my thigh and clutched me at my hip.

He broke our kiss. The dark of his pupils overshadowed the green of his eyes. "Every fucking time. Never in my life has this happened to me. It drives me crazy that I cannot get enough of you." He kissed me again, his lips hard and demanding. Kova devoured me with a ferocity unlike ever before.

I pulled back and attempted to regain some semblance of control. "Kova?"

"Hmm?" He nuzzled my neck, his facial hair scraping my tender flesh.

"Do you think you could refrain from calling Katja *malysh*? At least in front of me?"

His head popped up and he looked me square in the eyes. For a moment, I thought he was going to lash out and reject my request.

"Only if you promise to never bring her up again when we're alone."

I smiled, but it didn't reach my eyes. The situation was a disaster—depraved and immoral and everything right at the wrong time.

"How will I know if you keep your promise?"

He looked at me. "You just have to trust me." Kova swallowed, his Adam's apple bobbing slowly. "Adrianna?"

My head tilted to the side. "Yes?"

Kova's nostrils flared and his chest rose faster and higher. Just as he opened his mouth, he was cut off.

"Hey."

Both of our heads snapped toward the sound of Hayden's voice. We were so lost in each other neither of us heard him walk through the door. Kova cleared his throat and stepped away, putting distance between us. I jumped down from the counter.

"Hayden," I welcomed. Coming to stand next to us, he eyed Kova with a sickening stare.

Drenched in sweat, Hayden's clothes stuck to him. He must've ran hard. Reaching behind his head, he pulled off his shirt, eyes still trained on Kova. I watched in fascination as a drop of sweat slid over a pointed nipple, down each ridge of his rock-hard abs, and come to a stop at the waistband of his shorts. I tilted my head to the side. Funny, I hadn't noticed the narrow strip of sandy colored hair that disappeared into his shorts until now. My mind began to wander, and I was curious to see how far down it led.

A low growl caught my attention, and I looked over. Kova glared at me, his astute eyes not pleased with me assessing Hayden.

"I think it's time for you to go," Hayden said, stepping closer. Kova glared at him for a long minute before dipping his chin in agreement. "And you might want to take some ice with you," Hayden suggested. Then he turned to me and said, "I'm going to take a shower." I nodded.

I glanced at Kova's swollen lip. Hayden had gotten him good. It would leave a mark for a few days. As I pulled opened the freezer door, Kova placed a hand on me.

"No need. I will see you tomorrow," he said.

"How will you explain it to Katja?"

He gave me a look, one that said I already negated my promise not to mention her. Embarrassed, I looked away, trying to hide my timid smile and followed him through my living room.

Kova turned to look at me when we reached the front door. His intoxicating eyes trained on my mouth. He bent down and pulled me flush against him. I stood on my tiptoes and closed my eyes as his delicious scent invaded my senses. His lips brushed my cheek while he brokenly whispered, *"Lyubov' ne to, chto vy mozhete ponyat', eto to, chto vy chuvstvuyete v svoyem serdtse. Net slov, eto prosto tak."*

I opened my eyes and looked at him, wanting so desperately to know what he'd just said but afraid to ask. I knew whatever he spoke in Russian he couldn't risk in English.

And the look in his gaze said he meant every word. Whatever that was.

Placing a gentle kiss to my cheek, Kova pulled the door open and took part of me with him when he left.

I locked the door and walked into my living room. I was going to take another shot but then I noticed the box on my table, and my stomach sank. The longer I waited, the more chances I took.

"Fuck," I complained under my breath and picked it up.

"Everything okay?" Hayden asked. I fumbled with the foil sheet, trying to poke the little pill through. Tears brimmed my eyelids, and my focus became blurry. Hayden walked over and took the package from my hands. I swallowed hard and sent up a silent prayer. With all the petitions and wishes I've been requesting from God lately—begging, really—one would think I'd have a fresh red carpet waiting for me as I waltzed into Heaven.

Yeah. Fucking. Right.

Not after the year I've lived.

I didn't want Hayden to see me cry. Truthfully, I wasn't sure why I was about to cry, other than the fact that a hundred different emotions streamed through me at a rapid pace and I didn't know how to get a handle on them. I was on overdrive.

Hayden reached out with an opened palm. I threw the pill into the back of my mouth and grabbed the flask from the table to wash it down. The smell burned my nose and it reminded me of rubbing alcohol. Disgusting. I handed it off to Hayden.

"I can't believe he makes you take that shit." He took a swig but didn't wince like I did.

"*He* doesn't make me take anything. It was my choice."

Much to my surprise, Hayden wrapped an arm around my shoulders and pulled me close to him. My nerves steadied and I melted into his body as if it was a natural thing. Exhaustion hit me hard. I reciprocated the hug and dropped my chin to his firm chest, then tilted my head back with a faint smile. My eyes were heavy. With his biceps like two firm pillows on each side of my head, Hayden peered down at me, his sandy colored eyelashes encased crystal blue eyes.

"Come on," he said. "Let's go to bed."

Hayden leaned down and pressed a kiss to my forehead before taking my hand and guiding me into my bedroom. I followed easily. Our disagreement and differences forgotten for now, left behind us and kept out of my room.

There was something comforting I found in him I couldn't explain. An aura of peace, soothing, and I fed off it.

chapter 7

IOPENED MY EYES A CRACK AND WINCED AT THE HAMMERING PRESSURE IN MY HEAD. I wasn't a drinker. I knew any kind of alcohol, even the smallest amount, would affect me, I just didn't think it'd be this much. I clenched my eyes shut and let out a yawn, praying the spinning would stop.

Judging by the darkness of my room, I knew it was the middle of the night, but it felt like I'd only fallen asleep a few minutes ago. I hated when that happened. I blindly reached for my cell phone to check the time, and opened my eyes enough to take a quick glance at the screen.

3:42 a.m.

I placed my phone back down and turned over as a ball of fire steamrolled through my abdomen. My muscles cramped and I gritted my teeth as I groaned and curled into a fetal position. Naturally, the side effects of the morning after pill would strike while hungover. I let out a painful whimper, wishing away the ache. The cramping intensified and I held my breath, hoping it would quickly pass. I really hated this and made a promise to myself right then to never ingest that stupid pill again.

"Aid?" Hayden's sleepy voice came from behind me.

"I didn't mean to wake you." I pulled the blanket to my chin, not wanting him to see me like this.

"Are you okay?"

"I'm fine, my stomach just hurts a little."

Without another word, Hayden rolled over and wrapped an arm around my waist. He scooted behind me and pressed his front to my back, curling into me to fit perfectly. I closed my eyes and sighed. The heat from his bare chest against my back was a comforting balm in my ice-cold bedroom. The security of his arms felt like heaven.

"Go back to sleep, I've got you," he said, and laid a kiss to the back of my head.

I closed my eyes and relaxed in his arms, letting the world fade away...

"How long do you think you'll be gone for?" Hayden asked as I zipped up my suitcase.

He sat on my bed and watched as I gathered items to take home. A small spasm tore through my belly, stopping me in my tracks. Hayden stood, but I held up a hand to stop him. I hunched over and held on to my stomach while I squinted around the room for the bottle with the orange cap. Spotting it on the floor, I huffed in frustration that I had to deal with the aftereffects again. Thankfully the cramp wasn't as bad as last night, but I knew the worst wasn't over yet.

"I think when the Parkettes meet is over is when I'll be back," I answered him, ignoring the shame in his eyes as I swallowed four pills.

Hayden's brows shot to his hairline. He ran his fingers through his messy bed hair. I loved this look on him.

"You're going to be gone that long?" he asked. "I assumed you'd be back shortly after the new year."

"That was the original plan, but after what happened, I don't want to be the only one left here when everyone is at a meet I should be at too. I think it'll be a good time to clear my head and regain my focus, remember what I came here to do in the first place. You know?"

My heart squeezed at the thought of missing the gymnastics meet, but this time I wouldn't allow any more tears to fall.

I drew in a deep, clean breath and exhaled the bullshit.

This morning when I woke, I decided I wouldn't dwell on the past, or my sticky relationship with Kova. Nothing good could come of it. What's done is done, and nothing could be changed at this point. My plan was to move on and work harder than ever before, no matter how much pain he caused me.

"Think Coach will have a fit?"

I gave him a droll stare and drew an imaginary circle around my face with my index finger. "Does this look like the face of someone who gives a shit?"

Hayden let out a laugh and I shrugged.

"What can he do that he hasn't already done? I'm pretty sure he can't—and won't—do shit if I take my time to come back. I have too much on him." I paused with a pair of yoga pants in my hand. "Speaking of having something on him, what were you guys talking about yesterday?"

"Uh, it was nothing." He looked away for a guilty second and cracked his knuckles. "It was just something he helped me out with in the past. Nothing important."

"Whatever it was, it has to do with the dumb dating rules he enforced."

A dim shadow appeared in his eyes and he looked away. Hayden shifted from foot to foot and tried to crack his knuckles again. Whatever Kova had helped him with was serious, and that made me more curious than ever.

"It's really nothing, Aid. Nothing I want to talk about anyway. A secret I swore I wouldn't tell anyone."

"A secret?" I giggled. I couldn't picture Hayden exchanging secrets with anyone. "Who do you tell secrets with?"

"My sister."

"Oh." I paused, my smile fading. I hadn't expected that. "But you know about my secret, and it can't be worse than that. Please," I begged sweetly, batting my eyes. "Tell me what it is. Tell me why your sister is the reason we have dumb dating rules."

"Aid. Let it go."

Of course, I couldn't let it go.

"If it weren't for your rules, I wouldn't be in this mess."

His eyes flared. It was the wrong thing to say.

"I know you can't be fucking serious right now. You're in this mess because you had sex with your dickhead, possessive coach who has mental issues. This had nothing to do with me."

"Jeez." I pulled back, not expecting the severity of his voice. "I was only half-kidding."

Hayden sighed. "I'm sorry for snapping, but I'm not going to talk about it. Okay? So just drop it."

"Fine." I'd just ask Kova anyway.

"Want to get brunch before you leave?"

My stomach grumbled and Hayden lifted a brow. "I wish, but I'm going to see my mom soon. I need to be as thin as possible for her."

His forehead creased with lines of confusion and his eyes narrowed. "Thin? Have you looked at yourself lately, Aid?"

Hayden stood up and guided me to stand in front of my closet mirror. Standing behind me, he placed his hands on my waist. I wore faded denim shorts that sat extremely low on my hips and a simple buttercup yellow tank top. Few colors matched with my dark auburn hair, but this was one of them. Mom hated these shorts. She called them Daisy Dukes and said I looked like white trash wearing them. Naturally, I loved them.

Lifting my shirt, his callused palm roamed over my toned stomach. Hayden tried to pinch the skin around my abs and hips, but he couldn't grab it.

"See what I mean? No fat."

I shook my head. "I know, Hayden, I know, but I can't eat. I want to, but I can't. My stomach is in knots as it is. I'm sorry."

Hayden wrapped his arms around my shoulders and tugged me to his chest. I leaned back, relaxing into him. He was a foot taller than me and a good hundred pounds heavier, yet we fit together like two interlocking pieces of a puzzle.

"I think you're perfect the way you are. I'm sorry you have to deal with a mom like that," he said apologetically, then dropped a kissed to the top of my head. If he only knew how nasty she could be. "What about physical therapy while you're away?"

I held on to his forearms as a smile tipped my lips. I stared at our reflection. After I strained my Achilles heel a couple of months ago, I had to alter my training schedule to fit in treatment three times a week, and water down my routines so I didn't add excess pressure and tear the tendon completely. The pain in my calf and ankle was mostly nonexistent now, but I wasn't naive to think it was healed. I knew my boundaries...for the most part, anyway.

"You're so thoughtful and caring. I don't have an appointment set up, but I will when I get there. I already know who I'm going to call. It won't be an issue for me to get in."

And it wouldn't. My dad would make the call for me.

I patted Hayden's arm. "I need to get going. I have about a three-hour drive ahead of me."

He gave me one last squeeze and said, "I'll miss you." Releasing me, he bent down and grabbed the small suitcase I was bringing home. We turned off all the lights and left my condo.

As I was locking the door, Hayden shifted from one foot to the other.

"What is it?" I asked, pulling the key out.

"Is this considered the walk of shame?" He looked down at his clothes, then met my gaze. "I mean, I am wearing the clothes I came in, and I slept with you."

A smile spread across my face and a laugh escaped from me as I shook my head.

"I'm pretty sure the walk of shame is supposed to include more than just sleeping next to me."

We walked side by side to the elevator. "True, but I had a boner when I woke up," he said so casually, pressing the button to take us to the lobby.

I burst out laughing, not expecting that. "Did you just say boner? Who says that anymore?"

Hayden shrugged. "Woody. Hard-on. Erection. A stiffy. Full salute. Morning glory. Pitch a tent. Throbbing member. Which would you prefer?"

My eyes widened and I laughed harder as he rattled off more nicknames. "I guess if I had to pick, boner would be the best choice. Do people really say morning glory?"

"I don't know, Aid. I don't talk about boner names with my friends," he said, flashing me a wry smile.

"Yeah, I guess that would be weird."

Stepping outside, there wasn't a cloud in the sky considering it poured yesterday. For a December morning in Georgia, it was surprisingly breezy with a slight bite in the air. Goose bumps broke out over my skin as we made our way to my truck.

I opened my door and Hayden dropped my luggage into the back seat. He turned toward me and pulled me into a bear hug. His head dropped to the curve of my neck and I leaned into him and wrapped my arms around him. He lifted me up and hugged me tightly, and without thinking, I wound my legs around his waist and locked my ankles together.

"You're so light," he mumbled against my neck. I squeezed my eyes shut at the familiarity of those words. Kova had once said that when he held me.

Lowering me to the ground, Hayden kept me close as he looked down at me. His eyes crinkled around the corners and the intensity of his troubled gaze locked on to mine. He was worried.

"Are you okay?" I asked. "I did dump a pile of shit onto your lap last night that would take years of psychotherapy to sort and process." Even then, I wasn't sure if he'd ever see it through my eyes.

Hayden pressed his lips together and stared at me. He took hold of my side ponytail and curled it gently around his knuckles before letting it fall to my chest.

"Shouldn't I be asking you that question?"

"I think you've asked me enough."

I repeated my question. He sighed and looked above my head.

"Not really."

My heart dropped. I had a gut feeling it was too much to take in. No human with morals and dignity would be able to swallow something the size of a horse pill and act like it was nothing. Not even the vodka had helped.

The guilt began to eat at me. I knew I shouldn't have told him everything. He wasn't Avery.

"I'm so sorry you're involved in this mess."

"It's done. I'll learn to deal with it, even though I don't like it, so long as you promise me not to sleep with him again."

"I'm fairly certain that won't ever happen."

He looked down and his eyes narrowed. "Not *fairly certain*, Aid. I need you to be one hundred and fifty percent certain."

I gulped down the lump in my throat. "I'll be okay." It was all I could muster. I couldn't promise anything. The side of his mouth tugged up and he glanced away.

"Be careful. Text me when you get home?"

I nodded. Hayden gave me one more bear hug, then pressed a gentle kiss to my cheek before he released me.

"Thanks for everything. I'm not sure how I would've made it this far without you."

"I'll always be here for you." I smiled in appreciation. "See ya later. Drive safe."

My stomach twisted into a giant slipknot as I watched him walk away. I didn't need to ask the question I was about to because I had a feeling I already knew the answer, but I still did to be sure. It was a girl thing.

"Hayden?" I chewed my lip. He stopped walking and glanced over his shoulder.

I'd shed a layer of skin when I came clean last night. I had divulged my deepest, darkest secrets to him in a risky move. I'd kept nothing from Hayden, I had told him everything. No one knew exactly what I'd been through since moving to Cape Coral, and I planned to keep it that way. While I trusted Hayden, I had to be sure.

"Don't worry," he said, easing my fear. He'd read the look on my face. "Your secret is safe with me. I won't tell a soul. I promise."

My eyes searched his. I found nothing but genuine sincerity. I released a ragged breath, the panic subsiding. He nodded and turned around and continued to his car.

I couldn't find it in me to smile. To find relief. Not when he walked away carrying the weight of my secret on his shoulders.

chapter 8

I DROVE FOR OVER TWO HOURS LISTENING TO DEPRESSING SONGS AS I MADE MY WAY UP the coast of Georgia.

I'd called Avery numerous times to let her know I would be home early, but she never answered. She was my absolute best friend in the entire world and I wanted to spill every little detail. But after Hayden's reaction, I'd be lying if I said I wasn't petrified to tell her.

Exiting the highway, I headed east and drove for a few minutes until I reached one of two long and narrow bridges that sat parallel to each other. Growing up, I'd been terrible with directions. My dad always said, "The beach is east, Ana," which made it easy for me to learn navigation.

I crossed on to the island and rolled down my window to breathe in the salty air. Lavish cars lined the streets. Porches, Mercedes, BMWs, and Ferraris were the choice of cars driven here along with Lamborghinis. People of all ages strutted the sidewalks, their arms heavy with posh named bags. Every single person dressed to the nines, scarves donned their necks to protect them from the chilly weather. Noses held high in the air, an aura of money surrounded the uppity, entitled people of Amelia Island that was known as the South Beach of the South.

My smile faded. That was the one thing about being a little farther south that I really enjoyed. I never got the sense of privilege over there as I did here.

Thick garland swooped from store to store, red and gold fat bulbs arranged on wreaths topped with giant red bows. Trees expertly wrapped with white lights—never the gaudy colored ones—and leafy palms garbed with green lights. Christmas decorations were everywhere and the holiday spirit was all around. I had to give it to the town, it was a winter wonderland and looked stunning at night.

Veering on to North Ocean Blvd, Amelia Island was small, and it was only a matter of minutes as I drew closer to Avery's house, a large Mediterranean villa home like mine. Her car was vacant from the pebbled driveway where she always parked. I knew school was out for the winter break, but seeing as it was the weekend, I had no idea where she could be since she still hadn't answered her cell phone.

I continued past her house and flipped on my blinker and turned left, pulling into the long winding driveway of my home. The lush lawn, a manicured vibrant green, with two inclined palm trees lined the sides of the purposely weathered front door. I smiled as I parked my Escalade and glanced around, appreciating my home.

Walking toward the side door I'd used since childhood, I caught a glimpse of a BMW. It wasn't abnormal to see this kind of luxury car in my parents' driveway, but what caused me to stop were the jet black twenty-two inch rims that looked awfully familiar.

I strained my neck to see if there were necklaces hanging from the rearview mirror. The windows were pitch black, I couldn't see in unless I peered through the windshield. If there were—

There were, which left me even more stumped. Orange and blue beaded necklaces hung from the rearview mirror, the colors of the college she dreamed of attending.

I wracked my brain trying to figure out why Avery was here when she refused all my calls in the first place. She couldn't have known I was coming home.

The scent of the black currant and vanilla fusion candles Mom was obsessed with crashed into me as I pulled open the door. My eyes popped from the aromatherapy that promised relaxation. Designed in mind to soothe, all it did was give me an instant headache. I'd forgotten how strong this aroma was. This time she'd gone a little overboard.

"Dad? Mom? I'm home!"

Noise from every corner of the house caught my attention, but it was the familiar click-clacking of Louboutin heels that turned my head in the other direction.

Mom walked under the arched foyer looking as radiant as ever. She had her face painted on and not a hair out of place. Dressed to impress. Our eyes met, and the corner of my lips hesitated to pull up.

"Ana!" she exclaimed with her arms open. With Mom wearing heels, it put her just under six feet, so she had to bend down to hug me. Despite the many differences between us—and not just in looks, but also our views on life—she was still my mom and I loved seeing her.

"It's so good to see you, honey!" Her Chanel perfume engulfed me and I wrinkled my nose, too many smells going on. She placed her hands on my upper arms and my stomach tightened. I prepared myself for what would come next, yet I couldn't stop the hammering of my heart.

Mom's shrewd eyes moved down the length of my body. I held my breath. "Aside from your arms and shoulders starting to resemble your brother's, you look absolutely amazing. So skinny!" A backhanded compliment. I'd take it. "But those clothes…" She clicked her tongue in disapproval. "Oh, Adrianna. You know how much I hate that style, but you look like you're positively glowing."

I bounced on the balls of my feet. "Thanks, Mom. I missed you."

Her sparkling blue eyes softened. "I missed you too. It's so good to have you home."

"Is that my daughter I hear?"

I turned around at the sound of Dad's baritone voice rebounding down the foyer. He strolled toward us at a leisurely rate. A crystal tumbler filled with an amber color liquid clutched in one hand, and a delighted smile across his seasoned face.

"Dad!"

Dad placed his glass down on the counter and Mom hissed behind me. The table was Purple Heart and considered one of the most expensive woods in the world. Found in the tropical rainforests of South Africa, when cut, it swiftly went from dark brown to a deep, rich purple. It was my mom's favorite piece of furniture in the house and she made sure to keep it in the welcoming room for all to see. She adorned it with a monstrous vase of pure white exotic flowers.

"Sweetheart."

I met my dad halfway and threw my arms around his shoulders, jumping into his hug. He lifted me up and my knees bent behind me. He squeezed me tight and I feigned lack of air.

"Dad… Dad." I tapped his shoulder. "I can't breathe."

"You can breathe just fine, don't exaggerate. Let me hug my only daughter another minute or so."

I smiled into his neck, but he really was starting to suffocate me.

Placing me back on my feet, he beamed down at me. "I wasn't expecting you home so soon. Last I spoke to Konstantin, I figured another few days before you came back."

I bit the inside of my cheek. "Well, some things changed at the last minute, so I was able to come home early."

"Speaking of Konstantin…" Mom said, picking up the glass and handing it to Dad. She eyed the table for a wet ring. "He called a few days ago about the meet you're no longer competing in. We lost a few hundred dollars on that. He said something about you not being ready. After all that time away to train, Ana, you're still not in tip-top shape?"

Dad slanted his head to the side. His inquisitive eyes caused deep creases to form between his brows. "Konstantin didn't mention anything like that to me when we last spoke. In fact, he seemed very pleased with your progress. Now that I think about it, he was raving about you."

Pleased with my progress? Raving about me? No way. Kova had to be lying, or Dad was trying to protect me. In the past year that I'd been at World Cup, not once did he wear a smile around me, let alone show that he was pleased during practice. Either it was his way of giving me constructive criticism, or he was lying to my parents.

I twisted my fingers together, hot heat spread to my ears. "Well, Coach and I spoke about it, and he felt that I should wait just a little longer. Given my Achilles strain, and changing up my routines, he wants to be one hundred and ten percent sure I'm solid. That way I start off competition season with a bang and make a name for myself. I really need to make it count." I put a lot of weight into my words, hoping they picked up the importance of them. "Let's just say Coach is a little obsessive compulsive. He doesn't like to lose. He wants to make sure that when I go in, not a finger is out of place and I come out on top. While I can appreciate his attention to detail, sometimes it gets annoying."

Dad nodded his head as if he knew what I was talking about. "He still has that trait about him? Not surprised." He laughed under his breath and my shoulders loosened. "The couple of times we did house flipping, or when he bought property, he was particular about every little thing. He'd walked around and slowly inspected every square inch of the property. As a businessman"—he placed his hand over his heart—"his keen eye was welcoming. He picked out things I hadn't noticed. I once tried to bring him on to my company, but he refused."

"You did? I don't recall that."

I looked at Mom, bemused by her constipated looking face and narrowed eyes, she didn't like being kept out of the loop.

"This was many years ago, darling. Ana was just a young child."

She plastered on what I knew was a fake smile—her social event smile. The one she taught me. "Well, things worked out how they're supposed to, right, Frank?"

"Yes, darling."

Mom clapped her hands together. "I have a meeting I need to get to. This year we're doing a silent auction to help benefit the people of Zimbabwe. We're trying to raise enough money so everyone can have mosquito repellent tents to sleep under. Next week we have a gala at the Four Seasons. All donations will go to the Children's Hospital in Boston. I trust that you will be there, Ana?" She dragged her critical eyes down my body for the second time today. "Appropriately dressed? Yes?" She nodded with her statement and walked away. "Oh, Avery is here somewhere," Mom said, before exiting the room.

"Avery's here?" I asked my dad.

He shrugged his shoulders. "She comes and goes from time to time."

I stared, thoroughly stumped. "You mean she comes and goes with her brothers?"

"Couldn't tell you. I don't pay much attention." He swirled his glass and then took a sip. "It's good to see you, but I have to get back to work. See you for dinner, sweetie. I have a business call, then I'm flying out late tonight on a red-eye."

My face fell. I should've expected this, but I'd been gone for so many months that I assumed he'd take time off to see me.

"You're leaving? But I just got home."

"I'm off to Colorado for a few days. It won't be a long trip."

"With Michael?"

Michael Heron was his business partner and Avery's dad. They usually traveled together.

"Not this time. I'm meeting a potential new client." His eyes lit up as he raised his half-empty glass of alcohol, like he had tricks up his sleeve to win this client over. I sighed. He either traveled for a potential client, or to close a deal, which meant he was always gone. Money was his biggest motivator.

Dad dropped a kiss to the top of my head, then turned and made his way back to his office.

Pulling my cell phone from my back pocket, I checked my notifications. Still nothing from Avery yet her car was outside. She and Xavier fought like siblings. I couldn't imagine she'd be at my brother's pool house...unless her twin brothers were there and she was with them.

Curious, I walked through the kitchen to look out a window. Overgrown tropical plants edged the backyard, blocking the view of the pool house my brother had moved into after he graduated high school. It was like his own little hidden bungalow. Sliding open the glass door, I stepped outside and walked past the pool and under the archway that lead to one of two impressive guest houses on our property.

A string of high-pitched, fiery profanity carried through the air. I stopped walking and crouched behind the nearest pillar. Peeking through an abundance of plants, I caught a flash of blonde hair that dashed behind the leafy palms.

Avery?

A door opened and then slammed shut. Multiple footsteps pounded on the pavers. I stood up to get a better view and spotted Xavier.

"Get back here," he growled, storming after her. He was shirtless and in a pair of jeans that sat low on his waist. I was close enough I could hear what they were saying and luckily small enough to hide behind a stone column to watch.

I hadn't seen my brother in months, but there was a noticeable difference in his appearance. He had to be hitting the gym. He was much more muscular and way leaner than I remembered. He'd filled out and was in the best shape I'd ever seen him in.

"Avery!" Xavier roared. He had a black eye and a dried up cut on his lip. "I'm calling your name. I know you can hear me!"

"The dead can hear you," she snapped over her shoulder. "Go fuck yourself, you conceited bastard."

His eyes flared to life. Xavier reached out and yanked Avery by her elbow. He spun her around and she fell into him with a huff. He had her pinned against his bare chest, one hand on the back of her neck, the other on the small of her back. Xavier took after both my parents and got the tall genes of the family. He towered over Avery, she had to crane her neck to look up at him.

What the fuck?

Avery sagged against him, her shoulders loosened. I frowned, confused beyond hell to see them so cozy. My stomach revolted, mainly because she was my best friend, and because this was uncomfortable to watch. Chicks before dicks.

Their voices dropped and I had no idea what they were saying. With their bodies pressed together intimately, faces separated by mere inches, I strained to listen, but all I was granted with were whispers through clenched teeth. Avery moved to slap him, but Xavier grabbed her wrist before she could finish. He glared at her as she resisted his hold. She shoved and pushed against him, but judging by the smirk on Xavier's face, he knew he had control over her.

I couldn't take it. I was at the point of suffocating from covering my mouth so hard. A million and one questions floated through my head so fast I couldn't process them. I also couldn't be a sitting duck any longer.

"Avery?" I called out, walking toward them.

"Adrianna?"

Surprise laced her tone. She and Xavier jumped apart.

"Oh, my God. Is that you?" she squealed, then ran toward me with a huge smile on her face. We threw our arms around each other in a tight hug, rocking from side to side with happiness. I was curious to see if she was going to bring up that little scene I just witnessed.

"I've missed you!" I said.

"I can't believe you're home!"

I pulled back when Xavier walked over. "Hey, sis." He smiled and pulled me into a hug. He reeked of weed and I could smell the faint scent of day-old booze on his breath. "It's good to see you."

"I wish I could say the same for you. You smell like shit," I said.

He chuckled, unashamed.

"I wasn't expecting you until closer to Christmas."

"I finished my final exams a couple of days ago, so I came home early." Xavier's eyes lifted toward Avery for a split second before returning to mine.

I glanced at Avery. She had her bottom lip rolled between her teeth.

"I called you while I was on the road a million times to tell you I was coming home early, but you never answered. What are you doing here? Where've you been?"

Avery let out a loud and annoying huff. She reached into her back pocket and pulled out her cell phone. She held it up to my face. My brows shot up.

"This is why I didn't get your calls. My phone won't turn on. My dumb, fucking brothers thought it would be hilarious to paint my iPhone 'Bama colors while I was sleeping last night. My *brand new* iPhone, Aid. Not only that, with the help of your brother"—she shot him a murderous glare—"they doused my car in cake flour and eggs. I swear to God, I'm gonna murder them."

She handed me her phone and I looked down. I tried to scratch and flick at the streaks of white and gray paint, but it wouldn't scrape off. There was an 'A' painted in crimson on one side, and 'Roll Tide' written on the other in what looked like black permanent marker. At seventeen, Avery was a massive Gators fan. She wasn't a huge Bulldogs fan, but she detested Alabama. Georgia and Alabama were rivals of Florida. At least it wasn't Miami colors. *No one* liked Miami.

I glanced up at my brother, puzzled why he and her brothers would do this. "Really, Xavier? What are you? Ten?" A vein throbbed in the center of his forehead. He tried to stifle his laughter, but he was bursting at the seams like a one-year-old smashing blueberries in his hand as if it was the funniest thing in the world.

"It rained early this morning, Aid," she stated, her feet shifting from one to the other. "Flour was stuck to my car."

When she said stuck, it hit. My jaw dropped, and my eyes popped wide. I tried not to laugh but I couldn't help it. I swung back and slapped my brother in his midsection with the back of my hand. This was a typical senior prank at our high school. Only she wasn't a senior yet and they were just assholes.

"I spent all morning having my baby detailed, inside and out. I got enough off the windows so I could see where I was going, but when I got inside my car and turned the air on, I was shot with a massive puff of flour. There was flour everywhere, Aid, everywhere. I tried hosing off the flour on the outside, and it only made it worse. There's still flour and eggshells all over my driveway."

I couldn't contain myself and busted out laughing as I pictured Avery sprayed with flour. "Oh, my God. But why would they do that?" I turned toward my brother and asked him the same question.

"Why not?" Xavier said, shrugging.

"Because they're fucking assholes, that's why. Need any more explanation?"

I chuckled at her annoyed tone, and so did my brother. It was impossible not to.

"So, you came over here to yell at them?" I paused, thinking about what my dad said and the scene I just saw. "My dad said you come here from time to time while I've been gone."

She shot Xavier a fleeting glance before setting her eyes back on me. "I think your dad is drinking too much bourbon. Why would I come here without you? To see who?"

"That's what I said. But then I...I thought maybe..." My heart pounded. I had to get it out. "I thought...I thought maybe you guys might be seeing each other or something."

"What! Are you fucking kidding me?" Xavier exclaimed. His face turned a deep shade of red. He wasn't laughing anymore. "I'm not a fetus humper. Young bitchy Barbies aren't my type."

Avery stared straight into my eyes as if she was calculating his demise in her mind.

"A fetus humper," she stated, putting heavy emphasis into the words. "A fetus humper. Where do you come up with this shit?"

"I don't screw girls, especially ones much younger than me. Not worth the jail time, and I'm not a fucking sex ed teacher. I like them experienced and untamed."

I scoffed, pretending to dry-heave. "You're so gross." The last thing I wanted to picture was my brother having sex.

Avery chimed in. "Tell me, do you happen to have another brother I don't know about that I'd come visit instead of this fuckwad standing next to me?"

I feigned a smile. "You know I don't."

"I will admit that I've been here more lately since they came home for winter break two weeks ago, but that's it. Girl, I missed you, but I don't miss you that much where I need to sleep in your bed and shit and be close to your brother to feel close to you. What the fuck?" I relaxed, laughing at the expression on her face. "That's some psycho shit right there."

"As much as I'm loving this cozy little reunion, I gotta dip."

Before Xavier could leave, I called out his name. "What's with the bruise and cut?"

He tilted his head and gave me a side glance. At this angle, I could see he had dark circles under his eyes. He put up his fists and crouched down, pretending to box the air, throwing jabs and undercuts.

"Just fuckin' around with some friends."

Xavier walked away. I watched as he opened the door and a huge cloud of smoke slipped out. We couldn't be more different if we tried.

I pulled Avery into a side hug. "So, how do you plan to get them back?" She chuckled. Avery was already scheming.

We walked back into my house, making plans for the day to look for a gala dress. I was beyond excited to hang out with my best friend. My stomach flittered with butterflies and happiness radiated from her just as it did me. This time at home was going to be exactly what I needed. It had been many months since we got to hang out, being so far from Avery was way harder than I had expected.

I changed my clothes while Avery caught me up on all the drama at her school and how she worked her way up to cheer captain. I knew she'd make the team. When Avery set her mind to something, it was extremely rare she didn't achieve it. As she rambled on, I put on a little makeup and curled the ends of my hair. Despite praising myself on not being like one of the Gucci squad kids, I still had to keep up my appearance. I was fortunate, my parents gave me a lot, and doing something as simple as playing the part for them was something I could suck up and do.

Stepping back, I assessed myself in the mirror. I had gotten used to rolling out of bed and not having to get dolled up for anything that I'd forgotten how much I missed it. It was amazing how far a little mascara and nice clothes could go.

Just as we were about to leave, Mom walked out of Dad's home office and took in my appearance.

"Ana, *much* better," she said proudly, her eyes glittering. "Please make an appointment with Sasha to have your hair and makeup done for both the gala and New Year's Eve party. You two can go together," she said, waving her fingers between me and Avery. "I don't know if you've made any friends back in Cape Coral, but if you'd like to invite them, you're more than welcome to. They can stay in our guest house if it's okay with their parents."

"I have a few friends I could invite and I'm sure their parents wouldn't mind if they come here, seeing as they live alone." She gave me a perplexed look and I answered her question. "It's Holly and Hayden, they're twins. I think I'll invite them since we've all became pretty good friends. Thanks, Mom." I smiled cheerfully, thinking back to the time Hayden said he wanted to come visit.

"Why don't you invite your coach too," Avery suggested brightly.

This bitch. I glared at her, counting all the ways I could rip out each strand of hair on her head. I cleared my throat and said, "I don't think—"

Dad appeared in the threshold, leaning casually against the door frame. "I've actually spoken to Konstantin already and invited them. He said he had to speak to Katja and check their schedules. I'll follow up with him today." He took a sip of his amber liquid.

"I'm sure he and Katja already have plans," Mom said.

"Mom's probably right," I quickly added. Anxiety crowded my stomach. *Please, dear God, let them have plans.* The last thing I wanted was Kova and Katja here.

Dad shook his head. "I'll give him a call now. They can stay in our other guest house, and if anything, Ana's friends can stay in a guest room."

Mom sucked in a breath the same time I did. This was a terrible idea and I needed to have this plan overthrown.

"I'll need a final head count for the caterers by the end of the week, Frank," Mom said tightly. "You know, so we can prepare for any extra *friends* you might want to invite."

Dad dipped his chin in agreement. For whatever reason, Mom wasn't happy about this. She was downright seething and I had no idea why.

"Well, we'll see you later. We're going shopping," I nearly choked out to my parents, then turned to leave. They lowered their voices to just above a whisper as we walked away, a sharpness to each word Mom spit out stung, and I knew they were about to argue. I ignored it, I'd grown used to it by now.

Grabbing Avery's arm as we walked out the front door, I leaned into her ear and said, "I'm going to fucking murder you, Avery."

She laughed…and so did I.

chapter 9

I<small>T MAY HAVE BEEN THE SPIRIT OF THE HOLIDAYS, BUT I FOUND MYSELF GRINNING FROM</small> ear to ear when I picked out the perfect evening dress for the gala.

Thankfully I found a gown so Mom wouldn't have to make a call to have an assortment delivered. That would require her to critically assess my body, which was never fun. I typically hated shopping for these kinds of events for that reason alone, but I knew I couldn't go wrong with an Elie Saab floor length chiffon dress with a high slit up one thigh. The strapless gown's pleated black top showed off my sharp collarbone—which would please my mom immensely—and the vivacious array of purple, gold, and pink ombre colors on the skirt bled into each other. I paired it with nude, strappy heels.

"Ya know, I'm patiently waiting for new deets here," Avery said with a little singsong tone to her drawl. She looked through a rack of dresses, eyeing each one as if she was talking to the clothes and not me.

"Deets?"

"Yeah, Ria, deets."

I tensed, flattening my lips. I knew it was coming. "I was kind of hoping you'd forgotten about all that."

She held a black dress against her body and looked down. "About Fish Lips? Never." She shoved it back on the rack.

"What makes you think I'd want to tell you anything after suggesting my coach and his girlfriend come to my house? I almost strangled you!"

Avery burst out laughing. As much as I wanted to tell her every blissful—and despicable—detail that had occurred since the last time, I was nervous about it after the way Hayden reacted. I didn't want her to look at me the way he did, especially since she practically insisted I not have sex with Kova. The situation was sticky, and even though I could trust her explicitly, I was still uneasy about the whole thing. She didn't know about the sex, about the morning after pill, or that we hadn't used condoms. She knew nothing.

Instead, I deflected by ignoring her and continued shopping to buy time, piling a variety of items in my hands I didn't truly need.

I picked up an adorable onyx Chanel flap bag purse and flipped it over to look at the price. Avery eyed the high-end accessories as she strolled closer and I got a little nervous, so I pretended to need jewelry to go with my dress. I quickly made my way over to the glass counter and asked to see a bangle styled bracelet.

"What are you hiding? Whatever it is, it must be juicy," Avery said as I studied the rose gold band designed of ivy leaves.

My heart was racing, and if I kept evading Avery's question, I was going to rack up a hefty bill.

I eyed a pair of black stiletto heels I'd probably break my neck in and asked the jewelry clerk to have someone get me a size six. They would go fantastic with any gown.

"Okay. You have about twenty thousand dollars' worth of shit in your hands. What aren't you telling me? You're hiding something."

My eyes fell to my hands. She was right. I did have about twenty grand worth of merchandise, and coupled with the cost of the dress that was on route to my home, along with the bags of clothes I'd already purchased, I was close to forty at this point.

"Good thing I have the Black Card," I said with a blasé smile and made my way to the second floor used for private shows.

"You can't run from me."

A light giggle rolled off my lips. I didn't make it very far, maybe a few strides, when she figured out my secret. She whistled behind me. I peeked over my shoulder, biting the inside of my cheek. Shit. Her eyes were enormous with vivid certainty and a shocked smile spread across her face.

"You fucked him!" she hissed, walking toward me.

My stomach sank to the floor in a wave of nausea. Rattled with anxiety, I glanced around for listening ears and placed a finger in front of my lips, begging for her silence. Amelia Island was small. Everyone knew everything about everyone. A whisper of indecency was all it took to get the ball rolling. I felt like she was on a loud speaker announcing the loss of my virginity to the entire island.

"Avery. Please keep your voice down."

She ignored me and continued. "I knew it! I freaking knew it would happen! You little hoe bag."

Avery was hot on my tail and grabbed my elbow, turning me to face her. She eyed me strangely. "Why are you hiding this from me? Why can't you tell me?"

I shook my head and let out a defeated breath. "I'm not hiding anything from you, but remember the talk we had when you came to visit me? You were insistent about me not having sex with him."

"So."

"So?" I copied, my voice raised.

"Yeah, so what? I worried about the ramifications you two morons would face if caught. That doesn't mean I still don't want you to fill my cup up." Avery began playfully backhanding my arm while she pretended to hold up a cup with her other hand. It was an ongoing joke between us. *Fill my cup right up with all the juicy and dirty details.*

"Stop," I laughed and shooed her away. "Fine! I'll tell you everything. God." I rolled my eyes and heaved a sigh worthy of an Oscar.

"Does he have a big dick?" Her eyes were huge and humorous. I wasn't surprised in the least that was her first question. Avery was strictly dickey.

I lowered my voice to a tight whisper. "Considering he's the only guy I've ever been with, I'd say yes."

She squealed. Avery literally squealed, and I felt embarrassed for her over the sound that she just made.

"If we're going to have this conversation, it's not going to be inside Chanel where anyone can overhear us."

"Done!" she agreed. "I have the perfect place."

With a one-track mind, Avery tugged me down the stairs. I pulled her to a stop right before we reached the glass doors.

"Let me check out first. I highly doubt my dad wants to get a call from the manager saying we walked out with an arm full of high-end shit."

"Oh, right," Avery said, backtracking. "Orange was never your color. Then again, it might go with the six-six-six you have newly tattooed on the back of your neck."

Avery, always cracking redhead jokes and how evil they were. Jokingly, of course.

Two hours later, Avery was nursing what I'm sure was one hell of a mental hangover after I unloaded every little dirty detail on her, from the multiple doses of the morning after pill to the confrontation between Kova and Hayden the night before. We were sitting on a lounge chair facing each other on the small section of the private beach Avery's family owned. Each home on the water came with its own oceanfront walkway. While I lived on a golf course, her family lived on the water.

"You know, you should've told me to strap on a seatbelt for this crazy fucking story you just told me. I was not prepared for any of that."

"How do you think I felt when it was all happening and I had no one to talk to? I was a hot mess, Ave. So many times I wanted to call you, but I was scared." I didn't add in that the times I had called, she didn't answer.

She smiled apologetically. "I completely understand, I really do, but if you ever hold out on me like that again, I will fuck you up." A burst of laughter rolled off my lips and I fell back against the beach chair, amused at her harmless humor. "For the record, I hate Kova. Like, really hate him. Why couldn't you have gone for Hayden?"

"I don't know. It wasn't like I made a plan to pounce or anything. It just sort of happened."

"Oh, and you need birth control ASAP or you're never going to be able to have kids. That shit is bad for you, it probably fucks up your body more than the warnings listed on TV say. I can't believe you were so dumb. You made everything so much more—" Avery slammed a hand over her mouth. Her eyes were huge blue globes. "Ohmygod," she muttered behind her palm and dropped it. "I suggested Kova and Katja come for New Year's. What was I thinking?"

I shot upright. "Why did you think I wanted to murder you when you said that? I couldn't believe it."

"This is all your fault. If you had confided in your bestie, I would've kept my mouth shut."

Oh no she didn't. "Really? You knew something was going on between us. Don't act so clueless and innocent."

"True, and you're right, but this is a totally different ball game, girlfriend. You should just go hang yourself, because you're fucked. You. Are. Fucked." She paused. "Ohmygod! Hayden will be here too." She jumped up from the chair and began pacing. "And after he punched Kova! Jesus H Christ. I have a feeling this is going to be a New Year's party we'll never forget. That is, if you live to see it." She stifled a laugh. "Oh, this just got so fucking juicy. By the way, Hayden punching Kova upped his hotness factor by a lot. He may be a fuck boy, but you should really consider keeping him as a side piece."

Fuck boy? With Avery, you never knew what was going to come out of that motor mouth of hers.

"You know what this means, right?"

"Avery."

"Yes!"

"Stop squealing. I'm embarrassed for you again." She was too excited for her own good. She rolled her eyes. "You do know what this means, right?

"What?"

"You have to be dressed to kill for the party now. We need you turning heads and dropping jaws." She puckered her lips and stared up toward the sky. She gasped like the answer hit her in the face. "I have just the dress for you! A *killer* dress," she added with a huge grin.

My brows crumpled together. "Why would I do that?"

She looked at me like I was an imbecile. "Because both Fish Lips and fuck boy will be there."

"And?"

"And! What do you mean *and?* We want their attention on you."

I stared straight at her. "Are you mental? After the way he just treated me? I can't even stand to look at him."

She gave me a droll stare and I tried not to laugh. "Okay. I can stand to look at him, but…" I trailed off. "What good could come from this? You do realize Katja will be there, right?"

"And?" she asked like it was a nonissue when it was a massive fucking issue. "You're acting like an old maid."

"I'm not going to put on a show while she's here on top of everything."

Avery shook her head and put a hand up. "Just stop. You don't have to go parading around. You just need to look absolutely amazing. That will piss Kova off because Hayden will be there."

"Ave?"

She perked up like I had an awesome suggestion for her. "Yes?"

"Shut. Up. This is starting to sound like a soap opera. Drama for the sake of drama, and I don't do that."

Her shoulders sagged. "You're no fun."

I flipped her off and she smiled. "Why the hell would Kova care that Hayden is there anyway?"

"From everything you've told me, he sounds like a jealous ex and can't stand to see you around another guy. Taunting him with what he can't have would be fun after what he did. You should want to make him want you."

I mused over her words. I didn't have the drive to do that, not after how much he hurt me. Not to mention, it really wasn't me.

"I hadn't thought of it like that, but Kova is a man, Hayden is a teenager. That would be stupid if he really did get mad."

"God. Do I have to teach you everything?" She was overdramatic. "Guys always want what they can't have." Avery sat down next to me. "All jokes aside, how are you handling all this?"

I shrugged, shaking my head. My eyes focused on the long strip of white caps curling into crashing waves. I loved the sound of the roaring ocean kissing the shore. The beach usually helped me clear my head, but this time…this time was different. I was a mess. I didn't know how to answer Avery's question without throwing out a handful of adjectives.

"Honestly, I don't know. I'm usually pretty good with blocking things out so I don't allow myself to hurt, but this is different. I told myself I wouldn't let it bother me, but the truth is I feel *everything*, Ave. Every word, every action, every touch. I feel like I was sliced and diced into pieces without a single care. I'm so close to breaking down and I don't want to." I exhaled a heavy breath. "There are moments when my sanity is close to the surface and it's mocking me. I hate this jittery feeling, this feeling of unease."

"If it helps, by the looks of it, no one would ever guess you have too much chaos raging inside of you. I'd say you're doing a pretty good job."

"I wish I could be more like you and say fuck it all and not give a damn. So careless and free. That's what I admire most about you, you know. The ability to brush things off and go with the flow and not let it affect you."

Avery's face slipped as she pulled away, but I'd caught it. She reached between us and scooped up a pile of sand into her palm, then let the little grains fall through her fingers. "It's tough acting the part, you know?" Her voice softened. "Some days I feel like I'm fading inside while wearing a flawless smile. I have no motivation... I don't even know who I am sometimes or if anything matters anymore."

The hair on the back of my neck rose. Her voice was thin and raw, so unlike her, and it concerned me. I had a gut feeling when I couldn't get ahold of her that something was going on. It wasn't like Avery to completely ignore me.

"Ave, what's going on?"

She was quiet for a long minute. "Just thinking of past shit, you know?"

Something dawned on me. "How are you and your boyfriend doing? Am I ever going to learn his name? I think I've earned it after everything I've told you." I nudged her arm.

She popped up and gave me a megawatt smile, like what she said didn't even happen.

"Well, you still need to be dressed to kill, your mother wouldn't have it any other way."

I agreed. A brow lifted to a point the same time one corner of her mouth tugged up. Her eyes glittered with mischief. I knew that look.

"How about we go the extra mile?"

BETWEEN THE GALA AND CHRISTMAS, TIME FLEW AND BEFORE I KNEW IT, NEW YEAR'S Eve was here.

I'd managed to make time for therapy on my Achilles and a quick run here and there, but not much for anything else. The winter holidays were usually a hectic ordeal in my family, so I savored the last few minutes of peace in my bed before I had to get moving.

Mom had been more than pleased with the Eli Saab dress I'd picked out and couldn't stop showing me off at the gala the other night.

Isn't Ana turning into a stunning young lady? She's so beautiful and training in gymnastics at a top gym here in Georgia. Turn around so we can see you. Look how gorgeous my daughter is, while fluffing up my hair.

I hated when she did that. Like she was offering me up for marriage. A rare diamond. Look but don't touch.

Aside from a quick text I sent Kova wishing him a Merry Christmas, I hadn't spoken with him since I left Cape Coral. He'd gracefully responded with, *Merry Christmas to you as well, Ria.*

Ria. That nickname sent my heart into a dizzy spiral every damn time. I could hear the lilt of his accent, feel it stroking my skin as I read it. And I'd read it numerous times, anticipating the bubble would pop up with more text. But it hadn't. It was an irrational hope, considering everything that had occurred. For someone who'd been my constant morning, noon, and night, I'd grown used to Kova's presence. It was unusual not having him around and I missed it.

Hayden and Holly arrived late last night. They'd been home in Ohio when I'd sent the text about spending New Year's with me. Dad spoke with their parents, then made a few calls to have their plane tickets rerouted. They flew in on the red-eye and were currently sleeping in the guest house.

Two light taps sounded on my door before it was pushed open.

"Mornin'," Xavier said, his voice sounded like he'd smoked a pack of cigarettes in an hour. He looked like he hadn't gone to bed yet.

I yawned, then smiled at him. "Hey."

Xavier and I have always gotten along smoothly. There'd never been any sibling rivalry or where we went to war every second of the day. He'd looked out for me more than anyone and had been protective. A typical big brother.

"Dad said you have some friends flying in. Some guy and his sister. Does he need to borrow some of my clothes?" Xavier asked, leaning against my doorjamb. He sniffled, his black eye had faded to a brownish-yellow.

I smiled at his consideration. "Thanks. I'll check with Hayden and see." My eyes raked the length of his body. His jet-black hair was disheveled, eyes bloodshot, and his once pressed lavender dress shirt was half-tucked in and wrinkled.

"Long night?"

Xavier rubbed his eye with the heel of his hand and walked into my room. He plopped down onto my bed that I was still snuggled in.

"Something like that."

"I've barely seen you since I've been home. I was hoping we could spend a day together before life takes over and we part ways again."

He stared at the ceiling like he was deep in thought. "Sorry about that. I've been…busy."

"Yeah, so busy with Michael and Connor, right? Don't you guys spend enough time together at college?"

Michael and Connor were Avery's twin brothers. Around the island they were known as the Band of Brothers because they were inseparable and constantly causing trouble.

"It's not like that. We've been chillin' together, but I fucked up big time and I've been trying to make it right." My heart clenched from the anguish in his words. I'd never heard him sound so helpless. "But the more I do, the more I fuck myself."

"What happened?"

He blew out a long and hard breath. "Can't let it get out."

"Anything I can help you with?"

He shook his head. "Can't talk about it."

Hmm. That sounded awfully familiar. "You can't, or you won't?"

"Both."

"Then how can I help you?"

"You can't."

"Jesus Christ, you're starting to annoy the crap out of me. I feel like I'm going in circles here. Throw me something to run with."

The corner of Xavier's mouth half-heartedly tugged up. I didn't like how dejected he sounded.

"You sound like her."

And now it all made sense. "Oh, chick problems. Got it."

"Something like that."

I shrugged, not wanting to get into relationship problems with my brother. As if I was in any position to give advice.

"I'm sure you'll figure it out. Just move on to your next chase. You seem to have a list of harems you check off once you've conquered them. Cross her off in your little black book."

Xavier stared at the celling in a melancholy daze. "If only it was that easy. She's that girl who gets under your skin. Just digs and digs, until she's buried herself deep in your bones and you don't want her to leave…until she does and takes everything with her."

A soft knock sounded on my opened door, distracting me from my brother, just in time too. I looked over to see Theo, our butler, standing in the opening.

"Miss Rossi, your two guests were found roaming the back looking a little lost." He pushed the door open further and Hayden and Holly walked in, their eyes bounced around my bedroom, taking it in. "I took it upon myself to show them to your room."

"Hey guys! I didn't think you'd be up yet." I glanced at Theo and gave him an appreciative smile.

"Would you like me to bring you anything? Your rocket fuel, perhaps?" he asked.

I sighed. My coffee. The elixir of life. "Thank you, Theo, but you know I'll get it myself." He nodded once and then left.

Before I could utter another word to my friends, I watched a smile creep across Xavier's face when he eyed Holly. Oh *hell* no. I gave him a swift kick in the hip and glared at him. Just like that, his girl woes were a thing of the past.

Holly stood next to Hayden wearing navy blue shorts, a button-down denim shirt with sleeves rolled to her elbows, and a white cami underneath her shirt. Her light blond hair was braided loosely at the side of her head and pulled to rest on her chest. I loved that hairstyle, but I could never pull it off. She looked like she'd just walked out of a small town. So adorable.

"Your list is long enough," I said under my breath.

Xavier continued to smile, so I kicked him again, this time harder. "Get out." I glared at him.

"Did we interrupt something?" Hayden asked.

Xavier stood and walked toward them. He held out his hand. "I'm Xavier, Ana's older brother. I see she's lost the manners our parents heavily instilled in her."

I butted in. "I did not! I just don't want you talking to my friends."

"Hayden. It's nice to meet you." Hayden introduced himself with a smile. They exchanged a firm handshake, then he gestured to Holly. "This is my sister, Holly."

"Holly, a pleasure," Xavier said. Her chestnut eyes were all over him. I swear on all that is sacred, if my dumbass brother even thought about going after her for even a split second, I'd junk punch him myself. Holly didn't need her own line and a score in his little black book.

"Okay, goodbye, Xavier!" I yelled, making it clear it was time for him to go, but he ignored me.

He shot a scrutinizing gaze down Hayden's body. "I was told you may need to borrow some clothes for tonight, but now I'm thinking you might not be able to fit in them. You on 'roids, bro?"

I groaned and squeezed my eyes shut in humiliation, then opened them. Hayden and Holly didn't have the proper dress attire for a party like we hosted, so we offered to let them borrow clothes. "Xavier! You're such an asshole. What is wrong with you?"

"Ah, no. Never." Hayden laughed nervously and shot me a startled look. A rosy hue glowed on his cheeks. Hayden was stacked. He crossed his arms in front of his chest, and my dumb brother reached out to grab one of his biceps.

Xavier's eyebrows shot up. "So that's from doing gymnastics? Well, shit. Sign me up." He gave Hayden a friendly slap on the shoulder. "When you're done with my sis, come down to the pool house and I'll see what clothes I can hook you up with."

"What's rocket fuel?" Holly asked, shifting the conversation. It took me a moment to figure out what she was talking about. I chuckled. Saying I drank rocket fuel wasn't the best way to describe java.

"Ana's coffee," Xavier answered. "I've never met someone who drinks it the way she does—or the amount."

"Why did that man call it that?" Holly asked.

Just then, Avery waltzed into my room carrying a paper tray and a heavy armful of dresses in clear zippered bags. She was a blooming flower bouncing into the room.

"Because her coffee can stimulate the dead," Avery volunteered with a huge grin, then quickly said hi to Hayden and Holly. "She likes her coffee like she likes her men—dark, bitter, and bold."

"Yeah, the opposite of you," Xavier said, looking at Avery. "Light, weak, and boring."

Avery placed the tray that contained four cups of coffee on my nightstand, then swiftly backhanded Xavier in the ribs. He faked a grunt and held his stomach, pretending he hurt.

"Shut the fuck up, Xavier, and get out."

Avery glanced at me and I giggled. Her eyes lit up. "Hey, girl." Turning around, she walked over to the free-standing clothes rack and began to hang the dresses.

Long strides took Xavier to Avery. I watched them as he slid the clothes already hanging to the side to make room on the steel bar. He then took the heavy load from her arm and hung the items for her. His lips moved as he murmured something next to hear ear, but he spoke low, and I couldn't make out what he said. She shook her head, and he threw a hand up in the air and sighed before storming out of the room.

"He's *so* annoying!" Avery declared dramatically once my brother left. She handed out the Styrofoam cups. "It's like having a third brother."

I took a sip from my coffee. "That's how I feel about your brothers." Holly and Avery plopped down on my bed, while Hayden took a seat on the chair in the corner of my room. One more sip and I asked Avery, "What did Xavier say to you?"

She stared at me like a deer caught in the headlights. "Oh! For a second I didn't know what you meant. He asked me if I had any more clothes in my car to bring up." She shook her head and rolled her eyes. "As if I would give him the keys to my car after what they did. Mama didn't raise no fool."

"Good thinking." I turned toward my friends. "You guys slept well?"

"I did. That mattress is like sleeping on a cloud."

"Probably the best sleep I've gotten in a while."

"Oh good. I didn't want to wake you guys. Figured you needed it since you flew in so late."

Alfred had been the one to scoop up Hayden and Holly at the airport late last night and bring them back here.

"Your house is massive, Aid. You weren't kidding when you told us about the size of it or the amount of rooms. It's like what you would see in a magazine. If we hadn't run into your butler, we'd probably still be out there wandering around."

I smiled sheepishly. "Sorry about that. I should've told you where to go when you guys got in last night, but I didn't even think about it. Just figured you guys wanted to rest."

"You figured right," Holly said with a yawn. "What time is the party?"

"Party starts at eight, but guests sometimes arrive early." I glanced over at my nightstand and read the time. It was getting close to noon. "We should probably grab lunch and then start getting ready."

A crease formed between Hayden's eyes. He pulled at his shorts for more give at the knees and adjusted himself in the chair. "You need that much time?"

"No, but probably a good three hours. Hayden, I feel like this is something you should know."

His brows shot to his hairline. "How long it takes chicks to get ready? No."

"But you read Cosmo," I retorted, and took another sip of my coffee, eyeing him playfully.

Both Holly and Avery snapped their heads toward him in shock. "You read my magazines?" Holly asked, extremely embarrassed. "Real cool, bro."

"What!" Hayden threw his hands up. "Sometimes they look intriguing."

"That brings your hotness meter way down, dude. Don't ever admit that to anyone." Avery paused. "Well, maybe it doesn't. I take that back. I bet you know more about what women want than grown men do."

Hayden's response was a smile from ear to ear.

I gave them a rundown of what to expect. How the night would play out; how the house would be filled with millionaires and their snobby, entitled offspring; and how these parties typically ran until the early morning hours. Avery and I had appointments for hair and makeup after lunch, so I invited Holly to have hers done as well. Mom expected everyone—including us young adults—to be in tip-top shape. Like they're ready for their close-up at any given second.

My time home would be cut short due to the Parkettes meet Holly was competing in. She needed to train, and as much as I wanted to stay home for a little while longer to avoid Kova, I made a compromise to drive back early tomorrow so we could all ring in the new year together.

"We'll leave tomorrow afternoon, which gives you time to unpack and rest before practice the following day."

I took a big sip of coffee to swallow back the ball of anxiety in my throat. I'd been doing great with ignoring the fact that Kova was coming to my home, but thinking about Holly having to be back to train for the gymnastics meet made my chest tight with angst. My fingers started trembling, and it wasn't due to the caffeine.

"Speaking of practice, my dad took it upon himself to invite Kova and Katja." I took another sip of coffee.

My stomach flipped as Hayden's stark gaze landed on me. His jaw flexed, and I had to look away because I couldn't handle the weight of his stare.

"That should be fun to see them outside of the gym." Holly mused and gave a light shrug.

"Are they staying at your house?" Hayden asked through clenched teeth. My emotions teetered on a thin line between pure panic and nervousness. Not just from Hayden's response, but from Kova coming over, and the sudden extreme bout of anxiety steamrolling through me. I was edgy. Anything could happen.

"They're staying at the Four Seasons Hotel."

Hayden's shoulders eased just a bit. Guilt ate at me for the stress I had caused him, but more so for the new lie that flew off my lips like nothing. I didn't know what Kova and Katja were doing because I didn't ask any questions after I found out they'd be coming. Inquiring too much would raise brows.

Avery clapped her hands and rubbed them together. "Before we get pampered, how about we go get some lunch? A *light* lunch." She eyeballed me. "We can't be looking fat in our dresses."

chapter 11

WITH JUST A HALF HOUR TO SPARE BEFORE GUESTS ARRIVED, I SAT WITH AVERY, Holly, and Hayden in one of the spare rooms my mom had converted into a dressing room.

Tall mirrors with bright white lights lined the walls. There were clothing racks everywhere. All we needed to do was put on our dresses.

Hayden stood off to the side scrolling through his phone, looking as striking as ever. From the charcoal colored pants that hugged his thighs like a second skin, to the rich onyx shirt with the top two buttons left undone that gave way to a glimpse of his firm chest, he wore an impish grin that shouldn't have gotten me tangled inside. He was cool and breezy chatting with Avery about the Florida Gators, the school he'd hoped to earn a gymnastics scholarship from.

"Damn, girl, don't you look hot," Avery said when Holly stepped out of the bathroom.

To me, she looked a little unsure. Wide eyes scanned the room for her brother. The dress she wore was made for her body. A silver sequin spaghetti strap top with waves of bubblegum satin sat high on her lean legs. Pin-straight hair and natural makeup completed the look.

She bit her lip. "Do I look okay, Hayden?" she asked her brother, anxiety spiking her voice. "It's not too much?"

Hayden nodded with gentle eyes. "You look great, sis. Beautiful."

"Not too much skin?"

Avery expressed amusement and said, "You can't be serious. You walk around in a onesie all day, so what's the difference?"

An airy laugh escaped Holly. "I guess you have a point, but I'm just not used to this kind of dressing up. I feel like my boobs are on display, and if the wind blows my dress, my butt will show."

"Your boobs look fantastic," Avery offered. "Not too much, not too little. I'd ask Hayden to back me up, but that's just a little weird."

He put up his hands. "That's where I draw the line."

Two knocks sounded on the door, and Mom waltzed in looking as flawless as ever, while I was still in my robe. At least I had my hair and makeup complete.

"Holly, darling"—her eyes scanned the length of her body—"that dress fits you perfectly. Spin around for me."

Holly's cheeks flamed, and she shot me a fleeting look before spinning around with her arms out. I knew what my mom was doing, she'd done it to me numerous times, and I hated it.

Mom clicked her tongue. "Magnificent. That cocktail dress was designed for you, it doesn't fit Ana that way. Keep it. It looks much better on you than it ever did her."

My lips parted as the room grew silent. I sat stone-still, staggered by her comment. I wasn't upset my mom gave the dress to Holly—she could have it—it was the fact she had the gall to insult me in front of my friends without concern for my feelings.

I glanced at Holly and suppressed the pain *Mommie Dearest* dealt me. Holly's eyes were wide, and her jaw bobbed like she lost her voice. Her gaze shifted back and forth from me to my mom. Not everyone could handle Joy Rossi.

Nodding, with an artificial smile in place, I cleared my throat. "She's right. It looks amazing on you, I was going to tell you to keep it anyway."

She shook her head frantically. "Oh, no. I couldn't do that. Really."

"Nonsense," Mom butted in. "It's yours. End of discussion."

She shifted in her four-inch heels until her dissecting eyes landed on me. She glared, and my shoulders wilted like a deflating balloon. I guess her kindness toward me when I arrived was short lived.

"When do you plan to dress, Ana? After guests have arrived? Or do you plan to greet our visitors in a…a housecoat?" She snapped her gaze toward Avery. "And what about you?"

I straightened my back and answered for the both of us. No Victoria's Secret silk robe could ever be defined as a housecoat.

"Holly just stepped out of the bathroom, Mom, I was going in next, and then Avery."

She blinked. "Make sure to pat your face with finishing powder so you don't look oily. I don't want to see my reflection on your forehead. I expect to see you downstairs soon." She walked out, closing the door behind her.

Avery snapped a murderous gaze at me. Two seconds ago she was America's next top southern belle. "Can I put eye drops in her vodka so she can shit everywhere tonight?" Her face contorted with fury. She knew how my mom was, yet every time something happened, she was more appalled than the last. "I honestly don't know how you deal with her?"

I shook my head, shrugging it off. "What am I going to do, Ave? You know how she is."

"I know, I just…I don't know. She really gets under my skin."

Holly walked over to me looking like a sad puppy. "Aid—"

"Don't worry about it. Seriously. That's my mom for you. I'm used to it. I'm just sorry you had to experience it."

Her lips flattened into a thin line. "For what it's worth, I'm sorry."

Avery stomped over to the rack of clothes and pulled out the hanger that held her glittery dress. She ripped off the clear bag and thrusted it at me. Her blue eyes were lethal. Like someone dared to serve her unsweet tea.

"Here. Wear this."

My brows snapped together. "But that's what you're wearing tonight."

"Not anymore I'm not. I'll wear the Hervé Léger one I was debating on. This will piss your mom off."

My shoulders drooped a little. I wasn't the revenge type, especially when it came to my mother.

"Ave."

Her arm dropped to the side. "You can't let her constantly get away with how she treats you. It's not right."

Hayden walked toward me and placed his hand out. I took it and stood.

"Not that I'd ever encourage you to be defiant toward your parents, but I'm going to have to agree with Avery on this one. Even from Cape Coral I saw how she treated you over the phone. But in person…" He shook his head and scoffed in disgust. "I say wear it."

"Me too," Holly said, though her voice shook.

Impulsively, I swiped the hanger out of Avery's hand and walked into the bathroom. My heart pounded against my ribs. I *never* defied Mom. Ever. I couldn't believe I was going to wear this scrap of material Avery called a dress in front of my parents and their friends.

Dropping the robe, I stepped into the dress and carefully slipped it on. The straps were thin and nude while the rest was a surprisingly heavy material that fit snuggly against me. Avery's clothes were always a little too small. She liked them tight-fitting, which meant this dress hugged every curve. Not that I had noticeable ones, but tonight, in this Badgley Mischka gold sequined dress, I did.

I looked in the mirror and was rendered speechless. Good thing I was leaving tomorrow. While my boobs were average, they appeared supple and soft in the deep V cut. I had cleavage! The mini dress had ruching at my hips and pinched up, showing off my lean legs with a slight indentation at the crux of my thighs. I was glamour and sex fused together, and I loved it.

No need for eye drops in Mom's drink tonight, this dress was going to give her a coronary.

"Let's go, Aid. We want to see." Avery shouted, her excitement seeping through the door. I laughed. "Hold your horses!"

Fluffing my sultry waves, I flipped my mahogany hair to the side and exhaled. "What shoes am I wearing?" I asked, touching up my smoky eyes and pale pink lipstick.

"Open." Avery knocked on the door a minute later.

I cracked the door open enough to grab the shoes, then shut it. I smiled and shook my head. She handed me the shoes I bought at Chanel when I avoided her questions about Kova. The ones I thought I'd break my neck in.

I stepped into them and took one last glance in the mirror. Then I sent up a prayer that I'd live to see tomorrow.

"Ready?" I yelled through the door.

"We were ready yesterday." Avery said full of sarcasm.

Turning the light off, I opened the bathroom door and stepped out to three sets of eyes gawking at me.

"Holy fuck." Came from Hayden. I rolled my bottom lip between my teeth as I watched him. He couldn't tear his wild eyes from me. "Jesus." His guttural voice the only sound in the room. "Aid…"

I tried to pull the hem down. "Is it too small?"

"No."

"It's perfect," Avery said, a Cheshire grin slid across her face. She was proud.

"Wow," was all Holly could add. I chuckled. I guess I looked good.

"Excuse me, but there's something I absolutely must do."

All heads turned toward Hayden as he strode toward me. His blue eyes focused solely on me as he closed the distance and pressed his body to mine. My heart pounded viciously against my ribs and I held my breath. Threading his fingers through the hair at my nape, he angled my head back and looked deep into my eyes.

"You're so fucking gorgeous," he whispered. A little gasp escaped my lips right before he planted his mouth on mine and kissed me.

He kissed me good too, not caring that his sister and Avery were watching behind him. Hayden took charge and slipped his tongue into my mouth, a sensual stroke down the side as he curled his tongue along mine. My heart fluttered, my breath caught. A hot chill broke out over me. He stepped closer and cupped my jaw as he deepened the kiss, wrapping one arm around my lower back and holding me to him. His subtle cologne added to the moment as I fell into his kiss.

Forgetting that anyone else was in the room, I placed my hands on his chest and slid them around his neck. His muscles flexed under my touch and I felt the power of his strength.

A provocative whistle came from the other side of the room, and Hayden broke the kiss. He looked down, one side of his mouth tugged up into a flirtatious grin. His pupils were dilated, and cheeks flushed with a tint of pink. He ran the pad of his thumb along the bottom of my lip, wiping away the lipstick he just smeared.

"Don't be mad."

"I'm not," I said breathlessly. And I wasn't. I was more surprised than anything.

"I had to. You deserved to be kissed, especially when you look this stunning," he said, whispering for only me to hear.

My cheeks bloomed with heat, and I looked away.

"Well," Avery said dramatically. "Someone get me a cigarette. That was hot as fuck. Guess we all know who Adrianna is kissing at midnight."

chapter 12

"**Y**OU KNOW MOM IS GOING TO SLAUGHTER YOU FOR WEARING THAT DRESS, right?" Xavier stated, giving me a passing look as he sauntered into the makeshift dressing room, followed by Michael and Connor.

Their hands were occupied with bottles of champagne they must've swiped from the kitchen and glass flutes held upside down at the base between their fingers. The glasses clinked together as they walked. I winced inside. Mom would rip them a new one if they ruined any more of her crystal.

Xavier looked back at me again, examining my dress as he peeled the foil from the top of the bottle and threw it to the side.

When he turned away to pour the bubbly, I tugged the hem of my dress down a little.

"Will she be that mad?" Holly asked, walking up next to me. She looked worried.

"Fuming," Xavier answered as he handed me a glass. He still looked like he hadn't slept in days. "Normally I sure as shit wouldn't let my sister walk into the viper pits with her tits and ass out for all to see, but I'll let it slide this time to see her reaction. It's going to be priceless."

"Gee, thanks, asshole."

"Even I know she's going to blow her lid," Connor added, passing out the rest of the champagne flutes. "Your mother needs to loosen the buttons of her cardigan. She's so fucking uptight."

"I can work that right out of her," Michael said with a massive, sleazy grin on his face. His eyes gleamed as he wiggled his brows, and I cringed.

Xavier slapped him on the side of his head, then dropped his hips to the counter, leaning casually next to him. Michael didn't flinch. Instead, his grin reached his eyes.

"That's my mother, you sick fuck. Stop talking about her like that."

It was a known fact that Michael had a serious attraction to women who were older than him and already in relationships. It was like a prerequisite. The way he saw it, if he could make them sway even for a second, it wasn't solid. They were fair game.

"What? Can't stand the thought of calling me Daddy one day?" He chuckled.

"I guess you wouldn't mind if I fucked your sister, then, would you?"

Oh, shit. Xavier was out of line. Then again, he always knew which buttons to push.

"That's not even funny, bro," Michael growled, his gaze deadly.

I revolted at the thought of both scenarios and faked a loud gag. I didn't like the direction of this conversation.

"Michael, the last thing I want to think about is my mom, and your sister for that matter, having sex. Just stop."

"I think about it all the time," he instigated.

"Ew, you're fucking gross, Mike. You think about me having sex?" Avery shouted from the bathroom.

He didn't miss a beat. "No, you weird fuck! Not about you."

"Don't worry about anything Mom says to you, I'll take care of it," Xavier said, bringing the topic back to the center.

I glanced at my glass and swirled the contents. Little spurts of anxiety fizzed and popped inside me the way they did in the glass.

I looked up. "She shouldn't have embarrassed me in front of my friends."

I had no idea where my balls came from.

A little smirk tugged at one corner of Xavier's mouth. "A little freedom has made you a bit rebellious, I see."

I smiled, a little nervous, a little confident. I wouldn't admit it out loud, but I was worried to see her response.

"Defiant looks good on you," he added.

"I think she looks amazing."

Xavier whipped his head toward Avery and I swear his eyes dilated. "Ave." He dipped his chin, his intense gaze deliberately scanned the length of her body. "You look beautiful." He shot a quick look at Holly. "You too, Holly." But his eyes were already back on Avery while he loosened his tie.

"I look fucking amazing," Michael added, his arrogant tone made us laugh. He ran his hands down the front of his chest and smoothed out his shirt.

"Let's get this show on the road. People to meet, girls to do," Connor said, his voice a deep southern drawl.

I rolled my eyes. That dialect meant Michael would use the same one tonight. They once confessed they only used that voice when they wanted to pick up chicks. He thought girls loved a fine, southern gentleman.

Such pigs. What was funny was that southern girls could spot a fake a mile away. They just didn't know that.

We all raised our glasses, said a quick toast, and emptied the bottles of the remaining bubbly before heading down to the party.

The party was in full swing. There were guests everywhere dressed to the nines, music playing in the background, white gloved servers carrying trays of food and champagne. A proud smile slid across my face. I was enthusiastic about the night, especially since I got to spend it with all my friends I'd grown so close to.

A newfound attitude swept through me. It may have been the two glasses of champagne, but I felt free. I decided everything that had happened in the past was going to stay in the past. I wasn't going to dwell about how I could've changed things, or how I should've kept to myself and not engaged in a relationship with my coach.

What's done is done. New year, new me. New outlook, new goals.

Conner and Michael went in the opposite direction to do God knows what. Before they left, they told us if we wanted any alcohol to hit up the pool house, but I wasn't planning on drinking more, and neither were my friends. Possibly another glass of champagne when the ball dropped, but that was it.

Oh, God. Midnight. I could kill Avery. I had a sinking feeling Hayden was going to try and kiss me when the ball dropped.

Locking lips with him again wasn't on the list for the night—or year. An alligator walking on to my lawn was a higher possibility than that. My lips tingled at the memory and I brought my fingers to my mouth, curious as to what was on his mind. Hayden was a good kisser, but then again, I didn't have many kisses to compare it to.

I lifted my eyes toward Hayden and found him taking in the scene in awe. My home looked like something fresh out of a movie, and the more I studied him, more questions crowded my head. We'd kissed once before when I first moved to Cape Coral, a memory long forgotten, and nothing I'd thought would ever, in a million years, happen again.

But it did tonight. I didn't resist. I didn't pull away. I didn't question it. The slow caress of his lips said way more than what I was prepared for. Even though he'd been there for me at the drop of a hat when I needed him the most, I assumed he was disgusted after everything that went down with Kova.

I'd been wrong. So, so wrong. Friends don't kiss friends for the fun of it.

Stopping just before the steps to the deck and against my better judgment, I skimmed the crowd of Wonder Breads looking for one person. *Wonder Breads.* I laughed to myself at the use of Avery's phrase to describe fake, full of shit kind of people.

"Stop," Avery whispered in my ear, and clutched my forearm. I dragged my attention away from the crowd and frowned at her. "Don't make it obvious."

Recognition dawned on me and I gave a subtle, appreciative nod.

"Ana? Ana!"

Glancing over my shoulder, our eyes locked long enough between the flurry of people for Mom to get a glimpse of me. My heart froze when her eyes widened. Despite the rosy blush she'd dusted onto her cheeks, she looked like her oxygen had been cut off.

"I'm sorry your mom is such an asshole," Avery said, only for me to hear. I nodded, chewing my bottom lip, careful not to smear lipstick on my teeth. Inhaling, I drew in confidence and plastered on my social event face she'd taught me so well to wear.

"Hey, Mom," I said cheerily. Her freshly dyed blonde hair was perfectly coiffed, her appearance on point. I had to give it to her, she knew how to play the socialite part well.

"Mrs. Rossi, thank you again for allowing me and my sister to attend your party and stay in your home. It's very generous of you and we appreciate it."

"Hayden, what a gentleman." With a tilt of her head, she looked pleased. That was a plus. "You're more than welcome here anytime." Her voice was a perfect lilt of culture and wealth. "There's plenty of food and drinks, so make sure you help yourself to whatever you like. I know you guys are leaving early tomorrow, so if I don't see you, have a safe trip back and I hope to see you again." Just when I thought I was off the hook, she gave me the look. It was all I needed. "Excuse us, I need a word with my daughter."

"I'll see you guys in a few. Ave, keep them company for me, please?" She nodded.

Placing her hand on my lower back, Mom guided us until we were out of view of the wandering eyes and gossiping ears of Amelia Island, then she grabbed my arm and lead me straight toward Dad's office. Just steps from the door, Xavier turned the corner. Our eyes locked and his face grew grim when he saw the grip she had on my arm. He knew. I tried to smile but my nerves got the best of me. I felt downright ready to vomit.

Two dainty, light taps, and Mom pushed open the door. In a saccharin tone, she asked, "Frank, may I have a minute with you, please?"

Dad nodded. A man I'd never seen before excused himself from the room as Xavier walked in and went straight for Dad's private stash of liquor. They said nothing as he poured a glass of bourbon and dropped an ice cube into it, but I felt a hundred times lighter with him in there. I knew what was coming, as did he.

"Frank," she huffed, not bothering to disguise her displeasure.

"Joy."

"Tell your daughter to go change her outfit right now. I refuse to allow her to parade around in that scrap of material she calls a dress."

He squinted at me, a crease formed between his eyes. He looked at Mom. "What's wrong with her outfit?"

The white ring around Mom's eyes glowed, her sharp cheekbones turned beet red. "What's wrong with it? What's wrong is that she looks like a slut!" Her eyes settled on Dad with determination.

Just as he'd brought the drink to his lips to take a sip, Dad paused. "Watch what you say, Joy." He tilted his head to the side and gave her a dark, scathing glare that made the hair on the back of my neck rise.

"Mom," Xavier growled, his tone deep and protective. He took a step toward her, his eyes a glossy shade of red. Fury like I'd never seen before exuded off him. I didn't move—I couldn't breathe. "That's your daughter you're talking about," he spat.

Mom stayed silent, a contemptuous look on her face meant just for Xavier. He didn't back down, neither did she, she didn't care that her comment hurt me.

Taking a sip from his glass, Xavier shook his head. "If you think I'm going to stand here and allow you to degrade and humiliate my sister, then you got another fuckin' thing coming." Xavier snapped his fingers at me. I thought he was going to crush the glass in his other hand. "Adrianna, let's fuckin' go."

I sucked in a breath and regretted my existence. I'd never heard that tone from him before and it frightened me.

"Adrianna," Xavier demanded my attention, but I didn't move. He walked over, his eyes trained on Mom as he passed her, like a jaguar ready to pounce. He grabbed my hand.

"Xavier, wait," Dad ordered, then he looked at Mom. He stood up and prowled toward her, stopping less than a foot away, and pointed a finger straight down at her nose.

"If you ever call my daughter a slut again, *I will ruin you*. Do you understand me? *Ruin you*. You'll never be able to show your face in this town again." Dad's voice was deadly calm. Xavier nodded next to me and I almost fainted. He squeezed my hand. He had so much more bravado than I ever did.

Naturally, it didn't tame Mom in the least.

"Ruin me? Not a chance. Not the way I could ruin you." She fought back with a sneer.

Dad glared at her with fire in his eyes. "Don't fuck with me, Joy."

She hesitated for a moment. "But I didn't mean—"

"Yes, you did. In so many words, you did. Don't try and retract your statement now. Did you forget who you're talking to?" Defiantly, she pursed her lips together and propped her hands on her hips. She should've been an attorney. "If I ever hear you call her such a derogatory name again, you will regret it for the rest of your life."

"Is that a threat?"

Dad didn't hesitate. "Yes."

Mom lifted an arrogant brow and shifted her fiery gaze toward me. The tension between them was fierce. "Tell her to change her outfit…please."

"No."

"No?" she squeaked. Any minute now she was going to combust.

"I said, *no*. I don't see anything wrong with her outfit. A little revealing, maybe, but if she can live on her own, she can pick out her own clothes and live with her choices. Do I think she looks like a slut? Not at all, not even close. I'd never allow my daughter to walk around looking like trash. I think she looks like a young, beautiful woman."

Staring at the floor, I smiled on the inside.

"What will our guests think of us with her walking around like that?"

"I'll go change," I said, my voice barely audible.

"No, you will not," Dad snapped at me. I flinched at the bark in his tone. He looked back at Mom. "If I remember correctly, you used to dress very similar."

"It's not the same. I wasn't a child."

Dad swirled his glass. "Joy, I'm not going to entertain you. This discussion is finished."

Mom's nostrils flared. She pushed her shoulders back and lifted her chin. If looks could kill, he'd be a pile of ash.

Hell, I'd have been one first.

"Ana?"

"Yes, Dad?"

"You're excused."

I hesitated, swallowing hard. I glanced back and forth between my parents. I didn't want to leave. More than anything, I was afraid of leaving because I had a sinking feeling she wasn't through with me yet.

"Go," he ordered. Xavier tugged me toward the door.

Turning the knob, I left my dad's office, and shut the door behind me with a soft click. I flipped my hair to the side, fighting back the tears that blurred my vision. Under normal circumstances, standing up for myself wouldn't faze me, I'd brush off their indifferences. But when it came to my mom, I couldn't do it. I couldn't brush it off because she was my mother and I loved her and I wanted to make her happy.

"Hey," Xavier said softly. I couldn't look at him. I was too embarrassed. I wasn't as strong as I perceived myself to be. He crouched down to get in my line of view, and I chuckled sadly. "We may live miles and miles apart, but I'll always have your back. Don't ever let anyone speak to you like that, not even Mom. Stand up for yourself."

I nodded. Easier said than done.

"I'm almost sorry for encouraging you to wear that dress now," Xavier continued. "I didn't expect Mom to act that way. I mean, I knew she would flip a lid, but it never occurred to me she'd call you names and take it as far as she did. For that, I'm so sorry."

I looked away.

"Hey." He pushed, his voice full of concern. "She doesn't usually talk to you like that, does she?"

"She's never called me a slut, but you've seen how she treats me, how she's picked on my weight, what I wear, how gymnastics is a joke to her and I should be doing what she does. I never do anything right in her eyes. I guess it was a matter of time before she took it a step further."

Xavier's gaze fell deadly. He stood and pulled me into a hug. He pressed a brotherly kiss to the top of my head.

"From now on, you better tell me when something happens, and I'll take care of it. Watching her insult you like that really has my blood boiling. It's wrong and I don't fucking like it."

I half-smiled against his chest. My big brother being protective was adorable.

"I can take care of myself, you know."

"I know you can, but you're my little sister, and that's what I'm here for."

I nodded and pulled back, drawing in a comforted sigh, and stiffened when that all too familiar scent drifted past me.

I knew that smell. I knew it well. Too well, in fact.

My stomach quivered, anticipation rose inside me. Kova was nearby, and as much as I wanted to find him, I knew deep down I couldn't. Avery's words echoed like a blow horn in my head. *Don't make it obvious.* My chest tightened, but I heeded her advice. I had to. He'd be with Katja.

chapter 13

Aftter making sure I was okay, Xavier left me to make a quick run to the pool house.

I straightened my back and turned to scan the sea of faces when that recognizable smell hit me again. My skin prickled with awareness. I knew he was nearby, I didn't know where, but I could feel him watching me. Before I could take another step, I recoiled at the sound of my name being called out.

Drawing in a confident breath, I turned around.

"Yes, Mom?"

"Ana," she said in a honeyed voice that churned my stomach. She gave me a condescending smile as she tilted her head. Cupping my arm, she stepped close to my face. "Make me look like a fool in front of your father again, wear something like that scrap of white trash fabric you call a dress, and you will regret it. You are a Rossi. You come from money and class. Act like it." Her nails bit into the underside of my arm and I flinched. "If you don't, I'll take away the one thing you love most." Blood drained from my face and her nails dug deeper into the back of my arm. I tried not to make it obvious, but it hurt and my face contorted into a pinch of pain. Mom glared. Any harder and she would break the skin.

"Mom," I whispered a plea. My heart was pounding a mile a minute. She gave me a toothy grin and stepped closer to pat my cheek with a tenderness aimed for a baby.

"Do you like the life I give you? Being able to do gymnastics and live on your own with a credit card you don't pay for?" Her eyes hardened. "Then you'll do as I say."

She let go and walked away without a care in the world. I held my arm where she dug her fingers into my flesh and felt the half-moon imprints she left behind. Steadying my breathing, I needed a moment to myself, but I'd already left my friends alone longer than I anticipated and needed to find them.

As I made my way toward the backyard, my steps slowed, and I cupped the back of my neck. I skimmed the guests, faces of entitlement and wealth, surrounded in that citrus and cinnamon fusion I associated Kova with. I didn't see him, but I had a notion he saw me.

Shaking it off, a black-tie waiter wearing white gloves ambled toward me carrying a tray of champagne flutes. I plucked one off and kept walking, adding a little sway to my hips. I downed the bubbly and placed it on a counter before I stepped outside, allowing the crisp air to cool my cheeks.

Scanning the crowd, I found my friends and watched them from the veranda. They were laughing and smiling, having a good time. My heart was lighter as I took in the moment.

I walked across the pool deck filled with twinkling holiday lights, passing friends of my parents until I reached the circle. All eyes were on me.

"Everything okay?" Hayden asked.

"Are you all right?" Avery asked at the same time.

I gave a careless shrug. "Oh, you know. Typical Joy having a coronary."

Avery frowned. "She flipped out over the dress, didn't she?"

"Flipped out is an understatement. She was a raging lunatic. Luckily my dad and brother both sided with me and backed me up." I glanced at Holly and Hayden and smiled. "Sorry about that, guys. I don't want to talk about it anymore, it's finished. Let's just have fun and enjoy the night."

"We're here for you," Holly offered with a gentle smile, and then added, "Let's make this the best New Year's ever!"

"Yes! Let's!"

The band began playing a light tune in the background. They were calling up my family one by one to the stage. I groaned inwardly. I didn't want to go up there and pretend to be the perfect family, especially after what just happened.

"You best get moving. We'll be here."

I rolled my eyes at my best friend. "Do I have to? Can you step in for me?"

"And stand next to Dragon Lady and not kill her? No way, Jose."

I turned to Holly and Hayden with an apologetic expression. "Sorry, guys. Duty calls. I'll be right back...again. This should be it for the night, after that, I'm all yours!"

Carefully, I made my way to the stage on four-inch toothpicks with three glasses of champagne streaming through my blood and loosening me up. I smiled, feeling good. Now that was a drink I could get on board with, unlike that disgusting vodka. I shuddered at the thought. Not that I had time to drink or anything, but it was delicious and went down easy, which wasn't a good thing.

Xavier held out a hand and guided me up the steps. One would never guess he'd been drinking and smoking from the way he held himself, but stand two inches from his face and look into his eyes and the evidence was plain as day. He must've filled up in the guest house after he left Dad's office.

I stood between him and Dad, with Mom on the other side, thankfully. With the microphone in hand, Dad spoke to the crowd like a well-versed politician. He thanked everyone and meandered on about something so boring in the real estate world that I lost interest. Xavier became fidgety next to me. I stood poised and graceful, exhaling as I browsed the crowd of regulars. Roughly a hundred people were dressed in dark attire or glittery colors, except one person who caught my attention.

Katja.

She was wearing a virginal white cocktail dress that accented her curves. She was all wide hips, narrow waist, and heavy breasts, which were about to spill over. The dress stuck to her like glue and I was instantly filled with envy when I noticed a flat hand sitting low on her pelvis from behind.

I tried to balance my nerves as I studied her. Huge, full lips, the kind women in Hollywood paid for. A straight and sharp nose, high cheek bones, sparkling eyes, and tousled waves—Katja looked fresh off a runway.

It wasn't long before my gaze shifted upward. Locking eyes with Kova, all air left my lungs. Sound faded, twinkling lights disappeared. Faces dissolved into thin air and all that was left was us. I couldn't stop staring at him. His eyes were on me, though uninterested, like he was looking through me. I swallowed back hard. I hated that look. It was one I knew all too well, given to me by my mom. It conveyed that I was as insignificant as a fly on a wall. It was a *you don't matter* look.

Kova was devastatingly handsome, and I despised that he had the ability to make me feel two inches tall while my heart pounded for him. I was enthralled with this man and I had no idea why. A man who purposely set out to hurt me knowing full well I couldn't fight back. An underhanded move that was meant to hurt me. When I let myself think about the intention behind Kova's decisions, it hurt me, but what killed me the most was that even after all he's done to me, I was still spellbound by him in an obscene way I couldn't comprehend. An equation that didn't make sense. I couldn't connect the dots the way I could a sequence on the balance beam. It confused me more than anything because my feelings exceeded an emotional level so high I wasn't experienced enough to grasp the severity of them.

Another few minutes on the microphone, and Dad had finally finished speaking. As Xavier helped me down the stairs, my friends headed my way.

"Incoming, ten o'clock," Avery said from the side of her mouth. Hayden scowled under his breath when he spotted Kova and Katja as they made their way over to our small group. He walked to stand near me and placed his hand at the small of my back.

"Konstantin, glad to see you could make it," Dad said with a handshake. He moved to kiss Katja's cheek. "Katja, stunning as always."

My mother stiffened and dragged her sharp eyes down Katja's body. If I hadn't known any better, I'd have said Mom was envious of her, or intimidated, but that was ridiculous. Joy Rossi envied no one.

"Frank, forever a pleasure," Katja said with a husky lilt of her Russian accent.

"Yes, as always," Mom purred and plastered on a phony smile, her deceptive tone didn't slip past me. "Lovely dress. You and my daughter have the same taste."

Katja turned my way and I scowled at the wrong time. Confusion filled her eyes. No, my mom wasn't jealous, she was just a bitch. She thought we both looked like sluts, meanwhile she looked like a suffocating uppity housewife. I wasn't sure which was worse.

Ignoring the backhanded compliment, Katja said, "Thank you for the invite."

"Please, make yourself at home. If you need anything let me know. Excuse me, but I need to speak with the caterer." Mom quickly left.

Kova turned his attention toward me, Hayden, and Holly, though not really looking at me. "I expect to see all three of you the day after tomorrow? Yes?"

We nodded in unison.

"Fantastic," he said, not daring to look in my eyes. He acted as if I wasn't even here.

"Will you be staying in our guest house?" Dad asked. He took a sip of his bourbon. Like father, like son, I thought.

"No, we need to be on the road early to be back at the gym, so we have occupied a hotel for the night. But thank you for the offer," Kova said.

"You know my house is your house anytime, Konstantin. Anything you need, let me know."

"Ah, your gratitude knows no bounds. Thank you."

"Which hotel will you be staying at?" Dad asked, taking another sip. I figured it was a good time for us to leave, but I wasn't sure how to make that happen. We all stood there so awkwardly since we weren't involved in the conversation. I shot a glance at Avery hoping she'd catch my drift, but she was staring off into space. I glanced in her direction and frowned, wondering what she was thinking about, or who she was looking at, but nothing caught my eye.

"It was one your wife suggested." Kova looked at Katja and he tugged her closer to him. His fingers pressed into her hips and I glanced away. "Which one was it, *malysh*?"

Malysh.

My eyes slowly closed, the organ caged behind my ribs pricked by his choice of endearment.

Hearing Kova use the one and only word for Katja I begged him not to was a direct punch to the gut. He promised me he wouldn't call her that anymore. He looked me right in the eye and promised. Then he turned around and did it in front of me, knowing full well I couldn't say a word.

Something inside me died a little. I wanted to sink to my knees and hug myself. His apology, his words, they were nothing but hollow letters that held no weight. I was starting to think it was impossible for him to be faithful to anyone. The only thing he seemed loyal to was gymnastics, and himself.

"The Four Seasons," Katja answered. Kova's widespread hand glided affectionately to her lower stomach as she spoke to Dad. He tugged her closer, her heavy breasts pressed into his chest. Kova looked at them. His eyes trained on the rise and fall of her chest with each word and breath she took. She was about to spill over her scoop neck dress.

"My wife?" Dad said.

"Yes. When I spoke to your wife she suggested the hotel," Katja said, her Russian accent just as strong as Kova's.

He sipped his bourbon. "Huh."

I cleared my throat, this was getting boring. "Dad, we're going to walk around. See you later."

Dad dipped his chin, then reached out to kiss my forehead. "No more champagne," he said, loud enough for the group to hear. I pulled back with wide, guilty eyes. My ears hot with embarrassment. "I can smell it on your breath. That's the last thing I want your mother to find out." I nodded, unable to find the right words. Dad wasn't disturbed I consumed alcohol, but I was surprised he could smell it.

"You look beautiful, now go have fun."

I turned around on my toes. Katja was staring at me but I avoided her gaze. "If you'll excuse us…"

"Was that not the most awkward exchange you've ever witnessed?" Avery leaned in my ear, looking around at the large crowd. It seemed her focus was elsewhere.

"It was, that's why I butted in."

Holly and Hayden stayed quiet. They wouldn't know any better.

"You guys want to get something to eat?" I asked, changing the subject. They nodded. "I hope you guys like tea sandwiches and caviar."

chapter 14

HOURS INTO THE PARTY AND FORTY-FIVE MINUTES TO SPARE BEFORE THE BALL dropped, Hayden left to escort Holly to the bathroom.

I'd been antsy all night and couldn't shake the feeling of unease. Another minute longer and I'd be suffocating. I needed to get away.

Maybe it was the champagne. I did have another glass after Dad told me not to.

Maybe it wasn't.

Maybe it was because Kova and Katja were a stone's throw away at another table. He'd been enamored with her all night and hardly glanced in my direction.

Maybe it wasn't.

Maybe it was what happened with Mom.

Maybe it was the anxiety of Hayden possibly kissing me when the ball dropped.

Maybe it was knowing Kova would be kissing Katja that really twisted me inside and I didn't want to acknowledge it.

Too many thoughts were flying through my head. I just knew I couldn't sit at the excessively decorated table any longer, which was why I offered to take Holly with the need to stretch my legs and get some air. I had a feeling they'd get lost, but Hayden insisted I relax and he'd find his way.

Avery obviously had other things on her mind because she seemed absent every time I looked at her. I itched to pull her aside and demand to know what was going on, but there were too many people around, and with my friends in town, it just wasn't the right time.

"Ave?" I said, turning to her. "I'm going to run upstairs and freshen up. I'll see you in a few?"

When she didn't answer me, I nudged her and repeated what I said.

She eyed me. "You better not be changing your outfit."

I laughed. "No, I just need a couple of minutes."

I took in Kova one more time before I left. He only had eyes for Katja. Seated a few tables over, he had his hand deep in her wavy hair like he was massaging her while she spoke to him, probably in their native tongue. He twirled a lock of hair around his finger as she laughed. He returned the laugh. They looked perfect together.

With my heart in my throat, I walked around the pool deck toward one of the back doors. I stopped to turn around under a cluster of palm trees. Concealed by darkness, I stared from the shadows. Everything was seemingly perfect from this view. No one could see me, but I could see them.

Strings of lights swooped from the edges of the tent and met in the center where an eye-capturing Swarovski chandelier hung. Entwined with ivory fabric tulle, it was almost matrimonial looking. A giant flat screen television was erected behind the band with the channel switched to Times Square, the countdown at the bottom. Though muted, I didn't need to hear the anchors to feel their excitement and know it was almost time to ring in the new year.

This was the first time all evening I've had a second alone to breathe. Not that my friends were smothering me, but with Kova and Katja here, Mom degrading me like I was scum beneath her seven hundred dollar shoes, and how important the coming gymnastics season was, it was impossible not to stress. Everything was riding on the new year. Every little detail, and every little moment had to be calculated, as if the stars needed to align for my dream to be a reality.

The truth was, it was hard to move past what happened with Kova because I would be back training with him.

It was also why I was standing alone in the dark. I needed a moment of reprieve before I lost what little of my sanity I had left. I had way too much on my mind. My cheeks throbbed from plastering on a fake smile and my head was pounding. It was all a façade. Every second of my personal life was a front. It's why I loved gymnastics so much. I didn't have to be anyone but myself.

A faint hint of cinnamon floated through the air. My back straightened at the rustling plants and I glanced over my shoulder.

Kova emerged from the corner, our eyes locked. I'd once thought his green eyes reminded me of a tiger in the jungle when we first met, and in this moment, they truly did. He sauntered toward me in a lazy sway, his gait powerful and commanding, and it stole my breath.

"I have been watching you all night," he said quietly. Thanks to my ridiculously high heels, we were now shoulder to shoulder.

"That's a lie. You've been acting like I didn't exist."

A low chuckle escaped him. It sent goose bumps down my arms.

"You think I would do it in plain sight so everyone could see? Never. Believe me, I have watched you all night. How do you think I knew where to find you just now?"

I clenched my eyes shut at his cavalier tone. I knew he wouldn't be lackadaisical about his roaming gaze. He hadn't been in the past.

"Where's Katja?" I asked, even though I didn't want to. I was too curious how he could be here with me and not be questioned by her.

Kova lifted his shoulder. "I do not know. She said she was going to use the restroom and make a phone call to her mother in Russia."

I finally looked at him, confusion creased the center of my brows and he answered the question on my face.

"Time change. She is wishing her a Happy New Year. She only calls her during specific times of the day."

"Ah," was all I could say. I really didn't care to hear more.

A moment of thick silence passed between us. "I need to go," I said, stepping away. But Kova stopped me with his hand on my wrist.

"Is there somewhere we can talk?"

"No." I tried to pull away, but he pulled harder on my wrist.

A plead. He was begging through touch, much like how he expressed himself on a regular basis.

I sighed. "Talk about what, Kova? There's nothing to talk about. We already cleared everything up at my condo."

Kova didn't let up. His heady stare bore into me until he broke my resolve. For some godforsaken reason I loved when he looked at me with such desperation. I caved every time. His emerald green eyes framed between black-as-midnight lashes put me in a hypnotic state of mind.

"Follow me," I said, and he dropped my wrist. "Just don't follow too close. When we get to the staircase, wait three minutes. Go up to the second room on the right."

He nodded and I guided Kova through my home toward the stairs. I knew there would be eyes and ears everywhere, and even though there would be no earthly reason to suspect anything between us, I still took caution. One could never be too safe.

I made my way up the staircase and decided I would never wear these high heels again. Each step caused my dress to tug up higher on my thighs and my hips to sway as I struggled to keep my balance.

Or, maybe it was just my false bravado that caused my ankles to shake. Growing up with a mother like mine, high heels were of the norm.

Walking into my room, I exhaled a nervous breath and quietly closed the door behind me. I kept the lights off and headed straight for the balcony. I pushed the sheer white curtains aside and opened the sliding glass door, breathing in the salty air that helped steady my racing heart. My room overlooked the Atlantic Ocean across the road, and it was on the complete opposite end of the party.

I leaned on the railing, staring as far as my gaze could reach at the dark sea when I heard a soft click. I didn't move, and I didn't look over my shoulder, but I felt his presence as soon as he stood in the doorway.

Adrenaline kicked up a notch. Goose bumps broke out over my arms as a gust of wind blew across my skin while I waited in anticipation for him. I hoped he locked the door.

"You look breathtaking tonight," he said, his voice strangled. The way he said those words caused my heart to stammer. "I cannot believe your father let you wear that."

I finally glanced over my shoulder and pushed myself up.

"Why not?"

His piercing eyes looked at me in disbelief. Kova stepped forward until we were face-to-face with just a handful of inches separating us. I leaned my hip against the railing as he stared down at me.

In complete bluntness he said, "Because it screams sex, Ria. I want to rip that dress off you and spend hours inside you."

My nipples hardened, and my lips parted with a soft breath. He shook his head in blatant desire, his heated eyes openly trailed down my body. His gaze did not deny his words. His eyes lit up like he was imagining all the dirty and perverted things he wanted to do to me. Kova made sure I felt every inch of his stare.

"Hot, sweaty, rough sex in ways you have never even dreamed of, until you cannot walk. I had no idea you could look so... so..." He scratched his jaw. "I have no words."

His voice, deep and raspy, heavy with his Russian inflection, glided over me in waves of euphoria I didn't know how to handle. His tongue licked slowly across his bottom lip, and damn was it hot as hell when his eyes met mine again. The warmth of standing so close to his body hit me with a force so strong I wanted to lean into him.

Instead, I swallowed and glanced away. "You can't say those things to me. Not anymore."

"You cannot wear these...these kinds of clothes and not expect me to react."

I ignored his comment. I wasn't sure how to respond without reacting stupidly.

"I'm surprised you came tonight."

He was still looking at me as I stared at the waves. "Why is that?"

I shrugged. "So many reasons why, Kova."

Placing his elbows on the ledge, he leaned in. "I will be honest, when I mentioned it to Kat, she expressed interest and suggested we come. Had she not, we would not be here."

My brows pinched together, and I finally looked at him. My eyes shifted rapidly back and forth at him. Not because he stated he's only here for Katja, but that she wanted to come.

"That's odd. You don't…" My heart began to stammer thinking about all the reasons why she would want to be here. "You don't think she suspects anything, do you?"

"No," he responded quickly. His tender eyes offered me reassurance and I took it. I think I'd always be paranoid about the situation. "Not at all. I truly do not believe she does."

I sighed. "Well, that's a relief. Not that I wouldn't deny it or anything, but God, just the thought scares me half to death."

"And Hayden?"

"He won't utter a word." I knew in my gut he wouldn't.

His eyelids dropped low. "I do not like that he knows."

"You and I both, but I trust him. He won't say a word because he actually respects me and doesn't make promises he can't keep…unlike you." I looked away so I didn't have to see his reaction. "You know, kind of how you promised you wouldn't call Katja *malysh*, and you still did."

"I guess you are right. Hayden would not utter a word. Even I know that."

He ignored my *malysh* comment, which annoyed me, but his statement sparked something. I turned toward him and placed a hand on my hip.

"What do you have on Hayden that assures you he won't speak to anyone?"

The corner of his mouth tugged up into a sensual smirk. His eyes grew heavy and a shiver ran up my spine.

"Nothing he did not ask of me…first."

That both confused me and filled me with curiosity.

"What is it?"

He shook his head. "I will never tell. You must ask him if you want to know."

I pursed my lips together. I'd already asked Hayden and was shot down. "Really, Kova? I think we both know I'm capable of keeping secrets."

"But this is not my secret to tell." His lips flattened into a thin, straight line. There was something else he wasn't telling me, a piece missing to this story only Hayden and Kova knew.

I shook my head, annoyed. Gripping the railing, I balanced on the sticks of my heels. "Why are we even here? Please tell me it wasn't because you needed to tell me how amazing I looked tonight."

Without saying a word, Kova stepped close to me, grabbed my arm, and lifted it up.

"Wha—" I stopped mid-sentence and followed his gaze to the nail marks still present on my inner arm.

"Stay out of it," I gritted through my teeth and yanked my arm back.

"I heard your brother explode inside your father's office, then I saw your mother talk to you once you both left. Does she hurt you often?"

That lit a fire under my ass. "It's none of your business."

"What is going on?"

"Why should I tell you anything when you never open up to me? You never do, Kova." My mouth tugged down and I put a hand up. "You know what? Never mind. I've been gone too long and need to get back before someone comes looking for me."

"Wait." Kova stepped in front of me and placed a hand on my hip.

It took everything in me to utter another word when he gently squeezed my hip, his fingers pressing into me with tenderness.

I sighed in defeat. "Move, Kova. The ball is going to drop soon. We both need to leave."

"Stay… please." His fingers squeezed again, a silent plea.

I blinked. "Tell me something, anything, I don't already know, and I'll stay."

Kova glanced away, squinting his eyes. His chest rose as he inhaled, and he slowly released a breath. Flexing his jaw, Kova was unmistakably at odds with himself, whether he wanted to give me what I asked for or not. Always tangled with right and wrong and what move to make next. I didn't feel bad though. I'd given him so much of myself already when he gave me nothing in return.

"Tell me something, please," I whispered, pleading with him to just let me in.

A breeze of salty ocean air blew past us and I shivered. Kova removed his jacket and draped it over my shoulders. I was engulfed in his cologne and drew the scent deep into my lungs. I sighed, a small smile spreading across my face. I loved the masculine scent that followed him everywhere. Not even the gym chalk could mask it.

Pulling the lapels together, Kova's hands lingered over my chest before he dropped them to his sides. He tried to close the distance, but I placed a hand on his chest.

"I just… I just don't know if it's a good idea to be so…you know." I swallowed. God. I could hardly speak the words.

"If you want me to give something to you, I will, but I need to do it my way." I regarded him with a jaded look. "*Pozhaluysta…*"

It was all I needed. I wasn't sure what Kova spoke in his natural tongue, but it was enough to win me over. Something told me to take what I could get from this elusive man.

chapter 15

KOVA PLACED HIS HANDS ON MY HIPS AND SLID THEM AROUND TO THE SMALL OF my back.

His fingers were a gentle touch that contradicted his brusque personality. He pulled me close, pressing our chests together and held me to him. The beating of my heart sped up and butterflies swirled in my belly while I waited, trying desperately to steady my breathing.

Giving in, I wrapped my arms around his back the same way he held me, letting myself melt into his warm embrace with a soft sigh I hoped he hadn't heard. I waited patiently for him to speak. I couldn't look at him though, I didn't trust myself being this close, so I rested my cheek on his chest. Kova turned to the side and shifted me with him with a natural finesse, as if he'd done it so many times. Dropping his hips back against the railing, he stretched one leg out and kept the other bent, giving me just enough space to nestle between his hips. Lacing his fingers behind me, he rested them just above my butt.

It shouldn't have been right how naturally comfortable we were together.

"You are not going to like what I have to say," he murmured.

My stomach tightened. "I can handle it," I whispered.

"You know, that is something I admire immensely about you. You are always so ready to take on anything thrown your way without fear. It is an admirable trait."

I smiled. "I hope that wasn't the piece you were willing to share."

He huffed out a laugh. "No, it was not."

I stared into the sky, listening to the crowd around the corner and the fireworks booming prematurely in the distance. We were hidden, obscured, and in our own world.

"I am so stressed out," he started. "And I have no outlet, so everything is building inside me."

"What do you mean no outlet?"

"I have no one to talk to about it."

I frowned. "Have you been writing? I thought that helped."

He shook his head. "The more I write, the more I convince myself of the truth. I feel like it is backfiring on me. My thoughts go deeper and darker and I find myself more lost than ever."

"The truth about what?" I prepared myself for his answer.

He waited a long moment before he responded.

"About Katja. She is standoffish. She does not speak to me like she used to. I find her up at all hours of the night on her phone or lying there awake in silence. She has pulled away from me and it is messing with my head. Things are tense between us. I thought coming here would help since she wanted to, but something is off with her and I cannot put my finger on it. I feel like when two people are in love with one another, they should be completely consumed with each other."

I froze. Everything in me turned ice cold. My first instinct was to pull away, I didn't want to hear how he *wanted* to be obsessed with Katja. It was appalling and it shocked me to the core. It reminded me of where I stood and what I was to him.

But I couldn't show that. I knew I couldn't, not after I practically begged him to share with me.

"Are you saying you want to be consumed with her?" I hesitated. "Or that you are, and she isn't reciprocating the feeling?" I cringed on the inside, not liking the direction of our conversation.

I chewed the inside of my lip and held my breath waiting for his response.

"You don't have to answer," I said softly, letting him off the hook.

Kova sighed deeply, shaking his head against mine and tightening his arms around me. "I honestly do not know," he whispered.

"Would it be a bad thing if she wasn't?"

"Yes, it would be terrible. I cannot fathom it."

My heart broke at the dejection in his voice, and for myself. Here we were, wrapped in one another, and his big reveal was that his girlfriend wasn't consumed with him...the way I am.

A thought occurred to me then. I wondered if he yearned for affection more than wanting infatuation with someone. It made me extremely curious, and as much as I wanted to know more, I didn't push.

"Maybe you're projecting." I swallowed down my hurt and tried to ease his mind. "After everything that's happened between us, Kova, it's natural to be paranoid when you're guilty of the ultimate sin."

Kova shifted his legs, then briefly pressed his lips to the top of my head. "I had not thought of it like that, but it definitely makes a lot of sense. I was feeling guilty...because I *am* guilty. I am so guilty it sickens me. My mind replays everything and my anxiety builds. It is like taking steps up an endless staircase. I have been paranoid as fuck and I did not realize it until you said that word. My gut says she knows, but my head says she does not because there has been no trace of anything. It is just my own betrayal thinking she is unfaithful when she probably is not."

"Have you ever cheated on Katja before?" I asked, but I already knew the answer.

"No, never," he said immediately.

"Have you ever suspected her to be unfaithful?"

"No."

I swallowed and burrowed into him. His body was so warm. There were so many other emotions I should have felt other than the one consuming my heart and smothering me like a black cloud.

I should've been outraged, insulted by his admission. But oddly enough, I wasn't. He wasn't being dramatic or exaggerating, he wasn't looking for pity. Kova spoke from his heart, so I put myself in his shoes and thought about the burden he carried on his shoulders.

It was my fault. Not entirely, but I was a huge reason why he was stressed. He'd never cheated until me, and if I hadn't come around, he might not have.

Empathy was not something I expected to feel for Kova after everything, and it was running rampant through me. Sometimes I forgot he was human too.

"For what it's worth, I'm sorry she's been distancing herself from you. I think your mind is playing tricks on you due to our affair. Katja has no reason not to be committed." It hurt to defend her in a way. My head spun from the dizzying emotions flowing through me. I wanted him, but he wanted her.

"She has no one else here, though," he said, his voice full of regret. "So I feel like I am the reason for a lot of things that do not go as planned."

I lifted my head and looked up at Kova. "Stop thinking like that, she has friends. If she didn't want to be in the States and she wanted to return to Russia, would you let her go?"

He hesitated for a bit, and my hands roamed his strong chest as he brushed the blowing strands of hair behind my ear.

"I would never force anyone to be with me. That is not who I am or would ever be." His words penetrated my soul and the memory of something he once said flashed through my head. "I made her a promise long ago, and now I do not know if I can keep it, even though it would be the right thing to do. I am continually stuck between right and wrong."

"No, you would never make anyone do anything against their will, not after it was done to your mother."

Kova's lips formed a thin, flat line. He nodded subtly, his face softened like he appreciated someone understood him. He was the result of a rape, and his poor mother had been molested on countless occasions.

"It was a cousin, right?" I asked. I thought about my cousins and shuddered with repulsion. I couldn't imagine such a thing.

A shadow appeared in his eyes, and he looked away. "I lied to you that day." Oh, God. My stomach dropped and I waited. Another lie. "It was not her cousin. It had been her uncle, her father's brother."

That was somehow worse, but it all made sense why her parents hadn't believed her and had kicked her out once she was pregnant.

Kova might lack morals, and his ethics were downright questionable at times, but he was undoubtedly a man with a good—yet slightly twisted—heart.

The tips of my fingers slid along the dark hair around his neck and up his jaw. "I'm sorry I've made things difficult for you since I came to World Cup. I've made your life so much harder." I pulled my hand back and looked away, unable to hold his gaze.

Kova tugged me to him, gripping me with a little shake. "Look at me." When I didn't, he guided my face toward him. "Ria, *pozhaluysta*, look at me."

He knew that would get my attention, and a tiny smile pulled at his mouth.

"*Pozhaluysta*," I repeated the best I could, then whispered the sentence under my breath. "Please?" I asked.

"It can mean please, or you are welcome. Though, I did not place the word in the correct structure, I said it in a way you would understand." He paused and reached for my wrists. Bringing my hands to his mouth, he placed a gentle kiss to the center of each of my palms. My skin tingled where he pressed his lips, little flickers of desire trickled down my arms. With our bodies pressed together and the friction mounting between us, my emotions were on overdrive.

"You have not made my life harder—if anything, you have made it brighter. *Pozhaluysta*, do not doubt that for one minute."

"What else is on your mind?" I asked, trying to change the subject, and hopefully dousing the glow between us before it turned into something more.

"Has your mother always been so… What is the right word? Abrasive toward you?"

I looked far away over his shoulder. Kova gently tapped my temple with his index finger.

"What is going on inside that head of yours?"

Quietly, I said, "I thought I sensed you in the room." He dipped his head to the side to meet my gaze and regarded me with a look like he thought it was a strange thing to say. I chuckled, fingering the buttons on his shirt. "Haven't you ever gotten the feeling someone was watching you? Or you sensed a presence but didn't know where it was coming from?"

"Yes."

"Well, that's what happened. I sensed you were there, I just didn't know where you were." Kova wrapped his arms around me again. I loved the warmth he exuded.

"That is a scary thought, you know, to feel another person like that, to know who it is, but not see them."

My stomach flipped. "Yeah, it is. Has it ever happened to you?"

His eyes bore into mine. "Yes."

I took a deep breath, my chest expanded against his.

"I saw your mom with you. Though she smiled, I could tell she was hurting you, and it killed me that I could not do anything to stop her."

I shook it off. "It's nothing I'm not used to from her. My brother is pretty protective and laid into her right before that happened."

Kova lifted my arm and inspected the half-moon marks. His fingers brushed over the indentations. He looked downright ready to murder someone.

"I was looking for your father when I heard another voice raise from his study. I realized it was Xavier. Tell me, what did she say to you that had him so riled up?"

My brows furrowed as voices from the party guests picked up and carried around the corner. I strained to listen. The band in the background announced the ball would be dropping and it was time to tune into the television. A roar of excitement erupted. It was then that I realized how long we'd been gone. At least forty minutes, give or take. A torrent of unease rushed through me. My knees shook and I pulled away, dropping Kova's coat onto a cushioned chair on the balcony. I wondered if my friends were looking for me.

"We have to go."

I wasn't sure how much time was left, but we needed to leave immediately. The guests and band grew louder. I figured we had less than five minutes. As I moved to walk away, Kova placed a hand on my arm.

"Wait… Stay," he whispered.

My eyes widened. "Don't you need to find Katja? The ball is going to drop, and you need to be with her when it happens." I was supposed to be Hayden's midnight kiss, so said Avery.

Kova stood still as he looked deep into my eyes. With a subtle shake of his head, my stomach flipped.

"I am right where I want to be," he murmured.

chapter 16

KOVA LEFT ME BREATHLESS.

As much as I wanted to stay here and ring in the new year with him, celebrate the start of new beginnings, I knew we couldn't. The meaning didn't apply to us.

"Kova… Go. Please. This is wrong. Don't do this."

"I know," he whispered. Cupping my elbows, he pulled me close until I fell into him. I pushed against his arms yet gripped his biceps. My sense of right and wrong at war. His fingers glided up my arms and my breathing became strenuous. It was always in his touch how I knew what he felt, in his eyes what he was trying to say.

"We need to leave," I said, my throat dry.

He shook his head. "Not yet."

My heart dropped. If we stayed any longer, we'd risk being caught. "You're certifiable."

He smirked and pulled my hips to his. "Depends on who you ask."

"You're intolerable. What about everything you said about Katja? Your guilt and stress?"

His eyes darkened but he didn't release my hips. "My guilt does not compare to my need for you, Ria."

"I'm going to slap you," I deadpanned.

His eyes twinkled. I should've suggested castration instead.

"I want you."

I shook my head, my eyes pleading with him. "You can't. Please, you can't. I thought the whole reason you pulled me from the meet was so you wouldn't want me. That if I said no, in turn, you would say no." My voice shook. My emotions were climbing and I was on the verge of panicking. We were taking a big gamble being together when the ball dropped. "So all that…" I looked away, my eyes searching into the darkness as if I could see someone, but I couldn't. I swallowed hard. "That was for nothing?"

Kova sighed deeply and didn't say a word. His lack of dispute said it all. Everything he did was in vain. Everything. Pulling me from the meet. Feeling bad about Katja. All of it. Tears burned my eyes and I swallowed hard. I couldn't do this with him, the constant up and down. It wasn't fair.

"All you've done is treat me like shit. I need to go."

Kova's face contorted. A shadow cast over his eyes for a split second and I thought I had offended him. Tightening his grip on my hip, he pulled me flush against him. God, he smelled amazing. His knuckles trailed my temple and down my cheek. He brushed a lock of hair behind my ear and twirled the strand down his finger.

"*Krasavitsa*," he said, and his tone made my belly curl. I couldn't figure out the meaning of the word, but my nipples hardened in response.

The countdown began in the distance and people started shouting the numbers. My eyes widened and alarm set in. My brain said to leave, but my body wouldn't move.

I couldn't. I didn't want to.

I made the mistake of looking at Kova. The urge to trace his full lips with mine, then draw them into my mouth was strong. Our mouths were inches apart. I loved his lips, they were his best feature, but I didn't want him to know he still affected me after how harshly he treated me and think he could get away with it. But then he pressed his chest flush against mine and I gulped. The moment I felt his heart thumping against my breastbone, my worry became a passing thought.

I'd once read if you listened to someone's heartbeat that your heartbeat would mimic theirs. It was the connection and makeup of two people who were complete when joined together.

I wondered if the same could be said for us.

My gaze fell to the thumping pulse in the vein near his collarbone. My eyes grew heavy. Reaching out, I glided my fingers over his bobbing Adam's apple as he slowly swallowed under my touch. My nails gently and softly scraped his olive skin. His jaw flexed, his hands trembled on my hips. Behind his steel exterior, Kova was struggling. It was the same song and dance between us.

He started whispering, counting down each number as he drew closer to my mouth. "Five."

I shook my head. "No."

"Four."

His hand slid to the small of my back as he pulled me into him. "Kova, please…"

"Three."

He threaded his fingers through my hair and leaned down. He licked his lips.

"We can't…" My grip tightened, holding him to me.

He froze for a beat, then his lips tipped up in a sultry smirk. "One. Happy New Year."

His nose grazed mine, hesitating for a mere second before he closed the distance. His lips were soft and supple and gentle, unlike the man he was. The voices quickly forgotten at the stroke of his tongue along the seam of my lips. Surprisingly, he didn't push. He asked for permission, and without second thought, I granted it.

Heat surged through me and my eyes rolled shut the moment our tongues collided together in an obsessive bruising, yet slow kiss. Kova took control and kissed me hard. My breath hitched in the back of my throat, taking everything he gave, and nearly hating myself for it. I was weak when it came to him. Only him.

It was the slowest yet hardest kiss he'd ever given me that I found myself meeting his demands. I uncurled my hands and wrapped my arms around his broad shoulders and fell into the man who caused my emotions to run wild. Kova groaned in the back of his throat. A man succumbing to his unfathomable desires. He pressed and pulled, as if he was making love to me through his kiss. His hand held the back of my head so I couldn't move, not that I wanted to.

Kova's hand moved down my lower back, then roamed my butt. He gave me a good, hard squeeze and tugged me to him before his fingers wandered past the hem of my mini dress and trailed the crease at the back of my thighs and butt cheeks.

Kova abruptly broke the kiss and it left me dizzy. "Are you not wearing anything?" he asked, his voice guttural and raspy.

I lowered my eyes and gave him a flirtatious smile. Reaching down, I pulled his hand higher up my bare skin until he felt the lace of my thong along my pelvis. His eyes glazed over and he fisted the material.

"You know how easy it would be for me to rip these off?"

Growling deep in his throat, he went back to consuming my mouth as his fingers glided along my pebbled skin, playing with the delicate fabric. The cool ocean breeze coasted along my flesh and I quivered in his hold. Desire struck between my legs and my hips moved in a slow rhythm, rolling into his pelvis and the hard length that lay against his muscled thigh. I moaned into his mouth, wanting more.

Damn man knew how to kiss and how to kiss well.

The back of his fingers trailed around my outer thigh to the front. He slipped his hand between us and his knuckles raised the hem of my dress. His thumb pressed on my bikini line and I attacked his mouth with mine. A deep growl vibrated in his chest. Shifting my legs just enough, my panties were instantly wet. The throbbing pulse between my thighs intensified and I leaned into his touch. "Yes," I murmured. His nails teased the elastic. I gasped into his mouth, clenching the back of his neck as his middle finger trailed down the front of my panties, and along the seam of my lips. His touch ignited a blazing fire inside me.

Breaking the kiss, Kova pulled back but kept his nose close to mine. Asking but seeking without permission. I panted into his mouth, not caring how hard I was breathing, and wondered how the hell someone could turn another person into a state of euphoric bliss so easily.

With his compelling eyes trained on me, the back of Kova's finger was deliberately slow. His knuckle hit just the right spot as he explored the lace that made me feel incredibly sexy. I leaned into him with an audible sigh while he slid over my wetness, then back up to press against the top of my clit. My knees trembled.

He slid higher, eyes still on me, and pushed aside my thong. I dragged the pad of my thumb across his bottom lip as two of his fingers slipped inside and gently rubbed my freshly shaven skin.

"Ahhh," Kova moaned huskily, his head tilting back. "I like this," he said, looking back down at me.

His fingers stayed on my little patch of bare skin, rubbing back and forth over my flesh, and building a craving between my legs. He didn't go further, even though I wanted him to. There was a pounding in my ears that increased with each stroke of his finger. My hips pushed forward, tilting up. Our gazes didn't waver, and I was falling into an abyss I never wanted to crawl out of. He had a powerful hold on me. I begged in silence for him to give me what I wanted. He knew I wouldn't utter the words.

Snarling, Kova bit down on my bottom lip and tugged it into his mouth like the savage that he was. He kissed me roughly, then pulled back, taking my lip with him before he let go with a pop. "This right here is lethal." His fingers became aggressive as he rubbed harder, pinching the skin together until I'd almost reached that pinnacle high. His fingers slid over my throbbing clit, just enough to tease me, then he was gone. I moaned, and he stifled the sound with his mouth again.

We could be so good together, and so bad.

"Kova," I whispered against his lips. I tugged the back of his head.

"I want to get on my knees and devour you right now like this." He kissed the fuck out of my mouth like I imagined he wanted to do between my thighs.

"Please…" My head hazy, body filling with pure bliss from the stroke of his expert fingers. My hips undulated while my tongue licked across his lips and the roof of his mouth.

"Fuck," Kova growled, breaking the kiss abruptly. He pushed me away and stepped back. I panted, catching myself against the wall. I looked between his hips and caught sight of the raging erection he sported. I grinned. The depraved part of me loving that I could undo him like that. Adjusting my dress, I pulled the hem down and squeezed my thighs together to quell the ache he caused.

I looked around, momentarily forgetting where I was. "Just go," rolled off my lips nervously. "I'll follow in a few minutes. That way it doesn't look like we were together."

Always. It would always be like this with Kova.

We both stepped inside my room. Kova walked toward the door and I made my way to the bathroom to freshen up. When I came out only a few minutes later, he was standing by my dresser. I stalked over to him.

"What are you doing?" My eyes were huge. "You need to—"

He cut me off by swiftly maneuvering himself behind me with his hand over my mouth and his other hand on my stomach securing me to him. My heart flew into my throat. I instantly reached to pull his hand away, but he gave me a little shake and jerked his head in the direction of my bedroom door.

"Listen," he breathed into my ear. His chest rose and fell with rapid breaths. I nodded. He slipped his hand from my mouth and ducked his head into my neck.

Male voices carried in the hallway that I immediately identified as Michael and Conner, followed by Xavier. I couldn't make out exactly what they were saying, but I picked up some words. Pussy. Gator. Blue and black. I didn't know what any of it meant and I didn't care to. I swear those guys had their own language. All I cared about was the fact that we could've been caught.

When the voices drifted further down the hall, my head relaxed against Kova's chest and I exhaled a sigh of relief. His hand on my stomach loosened.

"Thank you," I said quietly.

Kova stepped out from behind me, his hand trailing along my lower back to rest on my hip. He faced me. Without saying a word, he leaned down and pressed a light kiss to my cheek, his lips lingering for a few seconds. My eyes rolled shut. I didn't like the feeling of this kiss. It felt too much like goodbye.

He lowered his head and jammed his hands into his pockets. "Another time, another life... You look absolutely breathtaking tonight, *malysh*."

He turned and left without another word, softly closing the door behind him, and rendering me speechless.

Once outside, I made my way back to the tent. I spotted my parents with Kova and Katja, each with freshly filled tumblers and their laughter filling the air. Dad saw me and lifted his crystal, and smiled. Both Mom and Kova turned my way. My stomach contracted with anxiety but I kept my face neutral. Mom turned her head the other way while Kova looked at me for a split second before returning his attention to Katja.

His entire demeanor changed and my stomach revolted against it. His vibrant emerald eyes flashed with excitement and lust. I swallowed hard and looked to find my friends, who stood an arm length away.

Hayden saw me first and met me halfway, followed by Avery and Holly.

"Where did you go? I looked for you," he said, his voice low but concerned. He placed his hand on the small of my back and drew me closer to him.

Naturally, I lied. I relaxed my face and slid on a peachy smile, though shame ate away at my insides. I knew without a doubt, he'd been waiting on me when the ball dropped.

"Oh, ah, I heard one of the servers saying they couldn't locate the champagne glasses."

"And did you pour all of them and serve them too?" Avery asked jokingly. She looked tipsy.

I laughed. "They needed help, so I offered." I eyed Avery, hoping she'd get the hint to shut the hell up and cover my lie. Eighty-seven years later, understanding finally dawned in her glossy eyes. She knew I was lying.

"I was looking for you when the countdown started," Hayden said, staring into my eyes, but there was another pair of eyes I could feel even stronger on me.

"I'm sorry I wasn't back in time," I said, feigning remorse.

Hayden's eyes softened. "If I'd known we would've missed our kiss, I would've found you sooner." I blushed, and averted my gaze to the grass. "Or at least made our earlier kiss more worth it."

"Adrianna," Kova called my name firmly. I looked over at him. His eyes were as hard as the grip he had on his glass of clear liquid. "I was just telling Frank, even though you are not competing in the meet that you should still come and watch. You can see what you are up against." He took a drink, his eyes hard. Telling.

He heard what Hayden had said about our kiss.

The last thing I wanted was to go to the meet as a spectator, not to mention, it was an asinine thing to suggest. Typical Kova.

"I don't think it's necessary to tag along. I've been to plenty of meets and know what to expect. I'd rather stay back and train."

Kova eyed me, downing the contents of his glass in one gulp.

"Would you like another vodka?" Katja asked him.

He looked at her. "Yes. Get one for yourself as well."

"I actually think it's a fabulous idea that Ana tags along," Dad agreed. He sipped from the tumbler plastered to his hand.

"You might learn and a thing or two," Mom added in a snide tone. "Everything is already paid for anyway, so why not?"

With my chin up, I said, "I'd rather train."

"You can room with me!" Holly said, her innocent blue eyes huge with excitement. If she wasn't in the dark about everything, I would be furious with her for suggesting that.

"Then it's settled. Ana will still go and support her teammates," Mom said, then excused herself. She always had to get the last word in.

I glared at Kova, pretending I had the power to drill holes into his head for proposing the idea. But he wasn't looking at me, he was staring affectionately at Katja.

He leaned in and whispered something in her ear. Her giggle was soft and feminine, her iridescent blue eyes glittered with delight. The way they were looking at one another didn't allude to infidelity. Not even close. They looked at each other as if no other soul in the world mattered. Like they were deeply in love and connected by an imaginary string that forever bound them together. It nauseated me. I turned my head, unable to take any more. Kova's concern over Katja pulling away was just his guilty complex rearing its ugly, deceitful little head and nothing more.

I couldn't comprehend how he could go from being with me, touching me, kissing me, and saying what he did, to acting this way with Katja. I had to wonder what lies he told himself to make it all okay in his head…and what lies he fed her.

"ALL RIGHT, LADIES, THE PARKETTES MEET IS IN FIVE DAYS, WHICH MEANS WE have four days to make sure your routines are solid and tight and there is no room for error. Yes?"

I nodded to myself, staring at my chalk covered fingers as I tightened my wristbands.

"Prepare to be pushed this week. Prepare to be disciplined and meet the demands your coaches ask of you. Suffer now and tomorrow you will reap what others cannot. It puts you one step closer to your goal, and goals should never be easy to obtain."

As much as I didn't want to agree with him, Kova was right. He was always right. He had a sixth sense about gymnastics that made me forget every strife in my life that could set me back. It's what made him a better coach above the rest. His words hit right where I needed them—in my gut—and lit a fire in my veins. They gave me hope and inspiration and changed my entire outlook. I glanced at each one of my teammates. Eyes glued to him as they soaked in his motivational speech. They felt it like I did.

"If you cannot feel your muscles screaming in pain, then you are not working hard enough. Your mind will tell you to stop, that you had enough. Only then should you push harder and give it more than you thought possible. Trust me. You will surprise yourself."

This practice was the first one since returning from the holidays, and I knew it was going to be grueling. Any practice before and after any break was usually the hardest, yet I was eager for the workout today. I needed the release, the conditioning only an asshole of a coach could give my body. While I'd exercised back home, a regular workout at the gym didn't cut it.

"Your only limit is yourself."

I took a deep breath and inhaled the dusty powder into my lungs. It revived me. It gave me life. God, I loved being at practice and I couldn't wait to start. His words were an elixir. They smoothly poured through my veins as I flexed and pointed my toes, rolling my ankles around.

"Okay, let us break." Just as I turned to walk way, Kova said, "Adrianna?"

I glanced over my shoulder. "Yes?"

"You have tutoring today and then therapy on your Achilles, correct?"

"Yes," I confirmed. "I have a full schedule today."

"Tonight, after practice is over, we will continue with your stretching therapy for an hour before you leave."

I groaned in the back of my throat and walked over to floor with the rest of the girls. *That* I was not looking forward to.

"Not sure why you're practicing with us today since you're not going to the meet, Ana," Reagan said with her nose stuck up in the air as classical floor music began to play in the background.

"I still have to practice regardless, Reagan. And, I *am* going to the meet."

Her brows shot up. "Since when?"

I grinned from ear to ear, happy the news threw her off. "Since Kova suggested it at my dad's New Year's Eve party. Ask Holly, she was there. Even Hayden. I'll be there cheering you on."

Reagan's nose scrunched up. She scowled and rolled her toes to crack them, then snapped her neck from side to side, all while glaring at me.

"Ladies, get moving!" Kova yelled.

We formed a straight line and walked along the edge of the floor. I stood behind Holly, swinging my arms up and around and front to back to loosen my joints. I lightly jogged with my knees high to my chest before transitioning into sashays. I shot a quick glance at Kova, I was curious to see the mood he was in, but he paid me no attention.

With enough space between each gymnast and my arms out to my sides, I stepped into a front kick—leg straight in the forward kick—until my leg came down and I shifted into back kicks—this time with my knee bent and head thrown back. We completed a variation of different warm-up skills, numerous ballet inspired ones, which went on for thirty minutes. Static stretching was important and helped prevent pulled muscles. And in my case, sprained Achilles.

"Ladies, drag the folded mats out. One on each. Jump on, jump off, legs straight and toes *pointed*. Kick up to a handstand on the mat, then snap back down into a back tuck."

Sounded easy enough, but executing it was another story.

"Whip those toes down!"

"Faster!"

"Tighter. Lock those knees and set!"

My abs were tight, blazing with burning heat. I knew my body—I needed more spring in my jump and for my knees not to wobble. I had to be tight, so I worked on all three at the same time. I took steady, measured breaths, and tried to be fast, but I knew if I wasn't breathing correctly that I'd wear myself out a lot faster than I should. Everything had to be timed and properly executed—even when conditioning and warming up. Otherwise I'd only be working against myself. Luckily, I made the change quickly. Gymnastics wasn't just physical, it was mental too.

After a set of twenty, Kova said, "Now start on to the mat. Punch down to a front tuck, then turn around and punch to another front tuck to land back on the mat."

This drill was difficult. It required me to keep my body in a tight form and steady my balance, hips raised and not dropped low. If not, the mat would slide, and I'd slip and fall.

"Adrianna, do not drop those hips. Any lower and they will be kissing the floor."

I often wondered if his choice of words were due to English not being his native language. Maybe he could teach me Russian and I could teach him how to use correct words… and contractions.

"Same for you, Reagan."

Laying on my back with my arms extended above my head, it was ab time. Breathing in through my rib cage, I lifted my chest and raised my straightened legs so they met halfway and were flat to my body. I tapped my toes, then lowered my legs to a straddle position and balanced on my butt. Then back to tap my toes again, never once touching the floor. If I wasn't firm, I'd fall over. It sounded easier than it was. Ten of these drills were completed in a row before I laid back and rolled onto my stomach, then back to my back to complete another set of ten.

No one spoke during this time—not that we could. It was focus, focus, focus.

"Do not stop until I say," Kova ordered, standing off to the side with his arms crossed in front of his chest speaking with Madeline. They spoke behind their hands as they took turns looking in our direction. Madeline nodded her head, agreeing to whatever Kova suggested, then they split up.

"Keep going," he ordered. I shot a glance in his direction. His sleeves were three sizes too small compared to the rest of his shirt, but they hugged his biceps nicely.

Kova walked toward us. He looked at every one of my teammates, purposely skimming over me.

"Line up along the edge of the floor. Front aerials, back handsprings, pirouettes. Five minutes. Go."

When it came to conditioning, five minutes never felt like five minutes. It felt like fifteen minutes, even twenty minutes, like it was never actually timed and ran longer. Once finished and warmed up well, I tightened my ponytail and got in line behind Reagan. It was tumbling time, my absolute favorite.

"Why was Kova at your house?" Reagan asked right as Holly took off tumbling.

"My dad and Kova are friends, you already know this. He invited Kova and Katja to our New Year's Eve party."

"And Holly and Hayden were there too," she stated more than questioned. The resentment in her voice evident. I should've felt bad about not inviting her, but she'd treated me like garbage this past year, so it was only fair I felt nothing for her.

"Yes, I invited them."

Reagan huffed under her breath before it was her turn. Within seconds, she finished her pass and I was going. Taking only a few steps, because it was a deduction if I ran too far, I hurdled long and low to build speed into a round-off back handspring, whip back, right into a double back tuck.

"A little lower on that whip back, Adrianna," Kova said. I glanced at him, but he was already looking in another direction.

"I bet you guys had loads of fun," Reagan said sarcastically once we were back in line.

"You know, if you weren't such a bitch, maybe I would've invited you too." Her back straightened and I kept going. "Maybe not."

I completed one more tumbling pass before it was time to begin the next phase—seven hours of back-breaking practice.

"Why are you making me go to the meet with you?" I asked, lying down on a therapy table in the back room. Today kicked my ass. I was past the brink of exhaustion. "I know what happens at them, I've been to plenty."

"You kissed Hayden." He seethed. Kova's mood took a drastic turn. We hadn't spoken about what happened at the New Year's Eve party.

Kova walked over and lifted my ankle. Pressing my knee down to my chest with his hand on my upper thigh, he got close to my face. Déjà vu hit, and I catapulted back to when we first started private lessons and how our relationship began. I grunted, feeling a pull in my hip. Only his touch could push my body to the extreme.

"First you pull me from the meet because of Hayden, then you tell me it's actually because of you and the ravenous desire you have for me, now you're making me go because of him? You make no sense, Kova. None at all. You're more frustrating to figure out than a female."

Kova pulled back, a smirk tipping his lips. "*Ravenous desire?* No."

"Then what is it?"

He shrugged. "I want you to see it through my eyes. What you are up against. I thought it would be a good idea, truthfully."

"But I know what I'm up against," I retorted. It seemed pointless to go to the meet.

"Have you ever been just a spectator and not a competitor?"

I shook my head. "No, I actually haven't."

He dipped his chin and pressed deeper into me. His fingers gripped me with strength and professionalism.

"I want you to sit with me and listen to what I have to say. Listen to my critique." His inflection caused certain words to have more emphasis. "Watch the other athletes around you, focus on them. Remember, Ria, they are going to have the advantage of being much younger than you and with a lot more vigor. You are talented, and while I have faith in you, you need to see firsthand what you are up against."

Kova switched legs and my heart crumpled a little. I didn't like this idea. It felt a little like torment and taunting at what I should've had but had viciously been ripped from me. I should've been competing at this meet, but thanks to Kova and his asinine decision, I was forced to withdraw.

"Breathe deep from in here," he placed a flat hand on my stomach and I jumped. Kova took a long, deep breath, his chest barely rising, and inhaled through his nose. I mimicked him, my eyes locked with his.

"Good. Now up," he ordered and gestured to the floor mat. "On your back. Hands by your side."

"Words I'm sure you love saying."

I slapped my mouth. The sarcasm flew from my lips without thought. I squeezed my eyes shut. Controlling my mouth around this man was my greatest challenge.

The corners of his mouth curled in an amusing smile. "Just because you and I have had a… liaison, I will let that one slide. But no more. Focus, Ria. Focus."

My jaw slackened, I gave him a droll stare. "A liaison? Good God, Kova, you need to take an English class and expand your vocabulary."

"When would you expect me to do that?" he asked. "Hmm? At midnight once I finish my office work? My free hours are spent working on your weaknesses and I am not even being compensated for it."

"You make me sound like a charity case."

"You are," he clipped, looking deep in my eyes. Talk about a punch to the gut. "That is exactly what you are. I am going out of my way to help and improve you, but only because I believe in you."

I glanced away. "That was cruel, Kova," I said quietly, laying on my back.

He was completely unaware of how hurtful his words could be. They crushed my heart, and while I knew it was his way of giving constructive criticism, they still caused damage in the end.

"You eat up my extra time. There is no room for anything else right now, especially since it is meet season."

I ignored that little jab and tried not to grind my teeth. "See, 'eat up' doesn't sound right."

"It does not matter to me, it is not relevant right now." Kova shook his head and dropped to his knees.

"If you took classes, you could learn contractions so you don't sound like a robot."

Kova squinted his eyes in my direction. "That is the last thing on my mind. If that is what you are thinking about right now, then I am not doing my job correctly." His eyes flared with new ideas.

I flattened my lips.

He huffed. "Okay. I will accompany you when you go to tutoring. Happy now?"

"No."

Sitting back on his knees, Kova huffed out a breath and pointed a finger at me. "Do not break, do you hear me? You will lose it all at the slightest fracture."

"What?"

"Do not break," he repeated slowly, like I should've understood what he meant the first time. "I can see it in your face. Focus on the big picture. Let the words roll off your back and forget them." Kova lowered his voice and his eyes softened as he said, "Remember, when we are inside these walls, I am not here to be your friend, I am not here to be nice. I am here for one reason, and one reason only. Eventually, you will thank me, but only if you just listen to what I say."

"With how mean you can be, I really can't see that ever happening." I truly couldn't see myself thanking him. "What? Thank you for being an egotistical, hard-ass dickhead? Highly doubtful."

His eyes twinkled with mirth and I felt the corners of my mouth tugging up.

"You will see," he retorted, smirking. "Just remember what I said."

Slipping a hand under my lower back, his palm was warm. "Lift," he ordered. "Feet flat on the floor, shoulders flat, chin up."

Once I elevated my hips, he placed a hand on my pelvis again and signaled for me to breathe. His palm spread across my abdomen the way a wildfire spread over grassland. Each finger grazed my skin with heat, igniting a scorching trail in its wake. Intensity blazed inside of me and I released a soft breath. I kept my eyes focused on the ceiling. They didn't deter in his direction like they had in the past that had only led to terribly wonderful things.

"Bring your hips down for three seconds, then raise them again."

We did this at least eighty more times in silence, maybe more. I stopped counting, and by the time we finished, I was surprisingly out of breath. My pelvis was tight. I finally looked at him, but Kova was already staring at me hard, unabashed, leaving a path of hunger as his eyes danced down my body. Small droplets of sweat trickled down my temples. He could look if he wanted to. In fact, I hoped he did.

Kova picked up an ankle and extended my leg. Then he took my bent knee and crossed it over my stretched leg and leaned down. I grunted while he applied pressure, flattening my lips as I grimaced.

"Why, after all this time, does it still hurt to stretch out?"

Kova studied my face. He was so close I could see the thin black webs against his lime green irises. Hypnotic. I thought his lips were his best feature, but his eyes captivated me on a whole other level.

"Muscles go through constant stress during exercise. At the rate you are going, yours will bear much more stress than normal. The beauty behind stretching out is"—he stood up and used his hands to talk—"yes, you are lengthening the muscle, and yes, you are manipulating it, but you are also helping it relieve the pressure by gently warming it down and breaking down the buildup. Since you have been off for holiday, once the soreness hits, you will be in more pain than usual. Keep Motrin on hand. Cooling down like we are now after a workout will help but will not alleviate it completely. If you want, come see me every night before you go home this week and I will stretch you out," Kova offered, then added, "Remember what I told you about training your brain to think a certain way?"

"Yes, and it was the most ridiculous thing I'd ever heard at the time." An airy laugh left my lungs. "It made sense though."

Kova slowly brought his hands down to his sides and closed his mouth. Lowering his voice, he spoke each word like he wanted to sink his teeth into my skin and rip it off. "Do not mock me, Adrianna. Nothing I teach is ridiculous, it all has a purpose. You know, my patience is running thin. Everything I do for you, to your body, has a reason. Sometimes I think you are too naive to see it right now."

I sat up. I tried not to take offense to that because he didn't take me in jest when I meant it that way. "No, I'm not. You misund—"

"Just shut up, take what I give you." His voice was angry and brash. "And fucking say thank you when I am done."

My jaw dropped. "I do take it," I bit out. "When do I not?"

The energy in the room shifted, and the aggravated energy emitting off him could be felt within a five-mile radius.

"Have you *ever* once said thank you to me? After all the times *you* have demanded from *me*, have you ever once said thank you?"

I pulled back and mused over his words. My forehead creased as I struggled to think. Moments flashed through my head like a camera taking pictures. Conversations, practices, moments when we were alone. Realization dawned on me. I swallowed, ashamed I'd never thanked him.

"That is what I thought. Instead you mock my training methods." He let out a harsh laugh. "Guess what, sweetheart? I got my medals already. I have traveled to international meets. I have been World Champion, and I have been to the Olympics. I have accomplished everything I wanted to—with the help from a coach ten times worse than me. You, however, have none of that. And the road you keep traveling down, you never will."

Kova looked down at his hands and brushed off the excess chalk. His head bobbed with an arrogant, puckered mouth.

Giving me his back, he coolly walked toward the door.

"Where are you going?" I asked in an elevated tone.

"We are done here," he said flatly.

"No, we're not. We have thirty minutes left."

Kova spun around. A gut-wrenching smile slid across his face. "If you will excuse me, I am going to devote my time to someone who truly wants it. My girlfriend."

"You're an asshole."

"Tell me something I do not know," he retorted, leaving the therapy room.

"See! Contractions would be useful there!" I yelled. I heard him grunt, but he never came back.

That night while sitting in the bathtub—a steaming hot bathtub I might add—I reflected over my conversation with Kova and how we left the gym. Truthfully, it was all I could think about since I got home. I was sick to my stomach because he was completely right. I came across as unappreciative and that was the last thing I'd ever want him to think. I wasn't. Aside from all the bullshit outside the gym, I was more than grateful for all the effort he put in. I demanded so much and he gave it to me when he didn't have to.

I felt awful for never once saying thank you. I felt the right thing to do was shoot Kova a text message.

I'm so sorry I upset you earlier. You were right. I've never thanked you for all that you've done for me. Thank you. I really do appreciate it more than words could ever express.

Surprisingly, he responded.

Coach: XX

chapter 18

WALKING FROM ROOM TO ROOM, I DOUBLE CHECKED EVERYTHING BEFORE I LEFT my condo for the weekend.

I wouldn't be gone long—the meet was in Pennsylvania and we'd be back early Sunday afternoon.

I switched the light off and shut the door behind me and locked it. I glanced at my watch as I made my way downstairs to the parking lot. The girls' team was meeting up at Kova's house, and from there, Katja would drive us to the airport where we'd meet the boys' team before we boarded the flight.

Throwing my carry-on bag into the backseat, I climbed in my truck and started the ignition. Within seconds, I hit the main road.

The closer I got to Kova's house, the more my stomach swirled nervously into tight little knots. Things between us were tense this past week. I tried to show my gratitude often, but Kova was strictly business and told me that if I wanted to show my thanks that I needed to practice like I meant it. I figured he thought I was trying too hard and it was showing. I was, and I wasn't. I just wanted to make sure he knew I was thankful, but instead it made him distant. With the way he'd acted, I had to wonder if Katja, or anyone, ever showed him gratitude. We were good in public, but I also felt like he was going out of his way to ignore me. I stressed over how he'd act the next two days at the meet.

I still didn't know why I was going with the team. It was stupid.

I pulled into the driveway and parked my car near Hayden's. I took a minute to gather my wits and wipe my face clean of any emotion before I got out.

Katja opened the front door seconds later like she was waiting near it. My stomach plummeted. Kova's guilt was rubbing off on me. I was insanely paranoid just looking at her face.

"Adrianna," she greeted, annoyingly drawing out the N's in my name. She appeared utterly clueless with her megawatt smile on full blast, and while that was great and all, I couldn't help feeling like a horrible human being.

There was a black throne in hell with my name on it.

"You can put your bag here and go into the kitchen." She pointed to a cluster of bags near the door as I stepped inside. "You remember where it is, yes?"

"Yes."

She shut the door behind me. "Would you like some coffee?"

"I never say no to coffee."

Her face lit up and she clasped her hands in front of her stomach. "I offered the other girls coffee but they do not like it. I did not know what to say to that."

I laughed and the knot in my stomach eased a bit. "My mom got me hooked on it to help curb my appetite. I hated it at first sip, but once I found the right flavor, there was no going back."

Katja's perfectly tweezed eyebrows angled toward each other. "To help curb your appetite?" Her eyes roamed down my body, then back up to meet mine. "So what Kova tells me is truth?"

Paranoia struck again, but I maintained my composure and kept my face neutral.

"I'm not sure. It depends on what he told you about me." I allowed a hint of uncertainty to layer each word.

"No, he did not tell me about *you*, but how gymnasts in general must keep an extremely strict diet. I knew some coaches enforced it, but I have always been curious about how the parents handled things behind closed doors, if they are strict or not."

We walked side by side toward the kitchen. "Oh, well, I can't speak for others, but my mom is extreme. She'll test any diet fad out to lose a few pounds. And if it works for her, she assumes it will work for me, and usually has me on it too. The only difference is that I'll eat when she's not looking so she thinks the diet isn't working."

We stepped into the kitchen together. I glanced at the group and said hi. My eyes softened when I spotted Hayden and I smiled at him.

"But why would you ever do that?" Katja continued.

I shrugged as if it was obvious and leaned against the marble countertop. "I wanted her to stop using me as her guinea pig and get off my back."

"Is she really all that bad?"

"Sometimes." I gave her an honest answer.

"Is who that bad?" Kova asked as he strolled into the kitchen. Good God, my blood pressure skyrocketed being this close to him and Katja at the same time. How does he stay cool and collected?

"My lovely mother and her obnoxious diet fads."

"Ahh. Joy. Does she still have those special meals ordered and delivered to you? I remember that being mentioned when you first arrived at World Cup," Kova asked. There was a distinct glimmer in his gaze that gave me such a rush. I tried not to smile like an imbecile, obnoxious teen but failed miserably. I liked that he remembered.

"Yes, but I do my own food shopping now," I answered. Kova's gaze shifted from me to his girlfriend. Katja handed me a cup of coffee, then leaned her elbows on the counter. We were shoulder to shoulder when a strong fragrance assailed me. I closed my eyes and inhaled, trying to sort out the scents. Jasmine and hydrangeas mixed with vanilla coffee. It was the most intoxicating aroma I'd ever smelled, and it seeped from Katja's skin.

I frowned and opened my eyes just in time to see Kova step to Katja. He wrapped his arms around her from behind and dropped his chin onto the curve of her shoulder as he gave her the warmest hug. My stomach flipped when he looked at me, a reserved smile tugged at the edges of his mouth. I'd love to know what he was thinking. If he took satisfaction in me and his girlfriend being in the same room together. The urge to turn away was strong, but I knew I had to fight it, otherwise it would look odd.

"I am sure you can afford to eat whatever you want," Katja said, and took a sip of her coffee. "You are young and athletic. You have a great shape to your body."

"Yes, she is in terrific shape," Kova added, too pleased with himself. "Perfect for the sport. She is much better now than when she first came to me."

My cheeks flushed and I gave them a timid smile. "I guess."

"Ah, that is because you have a gifted touch and a sight unparalleled to others when it comes to the gym, *statnyy*."

Kova chuckled under his breath. I wish I knew what that word meant. "You flatter me."

His voice was low and rough, and it tugged at something deep inside me. He kissed the corner of her mouth and she gave him a sultry smile in return.

"Katja, what kind of perfume do you use? I love the smell," I asked to distract my thoughts.

She turned and smiled sweetly. "Oh, I do not use perfume."

Kova snuggled her closer. I didn't understand.

"It is her body wash. I have it shipped in from Russia for her," he offered up.

Ah, okay. "That's cool." I wasn't sure how else to respond to that.

They probably took a shower together this morning and he washed her body with her special smelly shit. I kept my grimace to myself.

"Why are you wearing that?" Reagan walked over to us with her nose pointed high in the air. I'd never been so relieved to see her until now.

I glanced down at my attire, then at hers. She wore the custom team uniform typical when traveling for gymnastics competitions, where I was in boots with knitted socks, dark jeans, long-sleeved shirt, and a chunky scarf. I didn't like to be cold.

"What's wrong with what I'm wearing?" I asked, confused. "You realize we're going to Pennsylvania in February, right? It's going to be freezing."

"Yeah, but not *that* cold. We're supposed to dress up, you should know this." Her voice grated on my nerves, like nails on a chalkboard. "We're not going to Siberia, jeez."

I barked out a laugh. "I would need many more layers than this to go to Russia," I said. Katja chuckled softly next to me. "I'd need an Eskimo suit."

"I said Siberia," Reagan responded in her snobby tone. I covered my mouth and laughed. She looked around in confusion. "What?"

"Siberia is in Russia. I figured you mentioned it because of Kova and Katja. It's supposedly like the coldest town there."

Reagan looked down and fidgeted with her nails. "Oh."

"What do you care what I'm wearing? I'm not competing anyway. And the meet isn't until tomorrow night, no one will see us coming off the plane."

"I don't know… I figured you'd act like you're part of the team."

I saw red. "I am—"

"Ah, Reagan," Kova interrupted. He always said her name a little differently than the rest of us, like when people said tomato two different ways. "I told Adrianna she did not have to dress up." The austerity in his voice caused her to stand taller and close her mouth. He let go of Katja and stepped aside to face all of us.

He never told me that.

I smiled inwardly at his defense.

"All right, ladies," he said, and rubbed his hands together, "we need to leave in three minutes. Katja will be driving us to the airport where Madeline will be meeting us. Once we are there, you will not leave my side or Madeline's unless you ask. You all are old enough to know not to wander off, so this is the only reminder you get. When we arrive in Pennsylvania, we are going straight to the hotel. You are not to leave your room unless you phone me, or I come to you. Do you understand?" The three of us nodded in unison. "Once I get the itinerary from the gym, I will let you know. Since none of your parents will be present until later, Madeline and I will be your chaperones for now."

It wasn't uncommon for parents to arrive separately from their children. Gymnasts always traveled together with their coaches. We'd sleep together, eat together, get ready before the competition. We needed our heads in the game and our focus on the sport. No outsiders influencing us negatively, like pushy parents who lived vicariously through their children.

"Yes?" Kova continued, looking at all the girls, except me. My stomach clenched, I felt a little left out. "Sound good? Okay, let us go."

It was much colder in Pennsylvania than I expected. I was freezing, and I could tell Reagan was too by how hard her teeth chattered and the way she held herself. Even though we didn't see eye to eye on many things, okay, *everything*, I felt bad. I reached into my bag and wordlessly handed her an extra scarf I had. She accepted it with a tightlipped smile and wrapped it around her neck. Scarves made all the difference, and I knew she was thankful, even though she didn't say it.

The rest of the day was quiet and simple. After we checked into the hotel, we got settled in our room. There were two queen beds and one bath to be shared by Holly, Reagan and myself.

We all kept to ourselves and didn't speak much. I knew the girls focused on their routines and replayed them in their heads over and over and over. They set their sights on the meet. The steel determination on their faces said enough. They knew what to expect, and held their composure impeccably, like little toy soldiers. I took satisfaction in seeing this from a different perspective.

Later the girls went over their schedule with Madeline and Kova, followed up by a light dinner, where we ate next to nothing. Typical before a meet. No water weight, no bloating, no carbs, ribs protruding, and airy on your feet.

Once I dozed off to sleep early that night, a nudging startled me.

"Adrianna," someone whispered. I stirred, shifted in the bed, but not fully waking up. "Adrianna." The voice was sharper this time and so was the elbow to my side. I opened my eyes to find Reagan hovering over me. She had a pinched face to begin with, but now it scrunched up as she held a cell phone to my face.

I pulled back. "What the fuck are you doing, Reagan?"

"Your phone won't stop beeping."

"What?" My voice sounded rough from sleep. I felt like I'd just gone to bed. My eyes burned with fatigue.

Reagan held the phone closer to my face. She scowled. "You keep getting text messages and it's keeping me awake," she whispered harshly in my face.

I sat up on my elbow and looked to my right. Holly was asleep. I grabbed my phone and read the front of the screen.

My stomach sank. I had four missed messages from Kova. All within a few minutes apart, but luckily the text itself didn't show up on the screen. I had that feature turned off long ago.

"Why is Coach Kova texting you and no one else?"

I glowered. "How the hell should I know?"

We both laid back down and I placed my thumb on the home button to unlock my phone. Reagan's hot breath hit my neck.

"Back the fuck off, Regina." I cupped the phone to my chest and read the messages. I had a privacy screen on it, so she wouldn't be able to read much, but still.

Coach: Are you awake?

Coach: Tomorrow you will see why you are here and why I did what I did.

Coach: Just trust me on this. I only want the best for you.

Coach: I am sorry for being an egotistical dickhead and ignoring you. XX

I smiled to myself. *Egotistical dickhead* were words I used on him last week. I exited my messages and powered my phone off. Rolling over, I slid it under my pillow and curled up under the covers.

"What did he want?"

"Just to go over tomorrow since I'm not competing." She ate the lie right up.

She paused for a second. "He shouldn't be texting you, you know."

"And you shouldn't be snooping."

"It doesn't look right."

I was quick. "The only reason it doesn't look right is because *you're* making it not look right. What are you getting at?"

"I want to know what he said."

I sighed in annoyance. "He texted to tell me that my parents still have the hotel room booked, so I can stay in there tomorrow instead of here if I wanted to."

"And that couldn't wait until the morning?" she argued.

"Regina?"

"What?" she snapped, hating the nickname.

"Go the fuck to sleep."

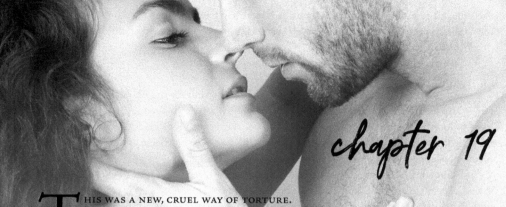

chapter 19

THIS WAS A NEW, CRUEL WAY OF TORTURE.

I sat on the bed and watched the girls prepare for the meet, desperately wishing I was competing too. My heart ached to be one of them, fixing each other's hair, doing each other's makeup, and applying hairspray to our butt cheeks to keep the leotard from riding up.

I glanced away at the same time a ping sounded from my phone. I picked it up from the nightstand and swiped to read the text message.

Coach: Please make sure you wear your leo and sweats. You will be sitting with me.

I let out a dramatic sigh.

"What's wrong?" Reagan asked as she shuffled through her bag.

I looked up from my phone. "Kova wants me to dress up with you guys."

"Oh, *another* text from Kova?"

I glared at her, silently begging for her to say something else.

"Yeah, I figured he'd want you dressed right," she said.

"How so?"

Reagan looked up from her bag and gave me a blank stare. "Because you're on the team, Adrianna. It's common sense. I wasn't sure why you dressed in regular clothes, to be honest."

I ignored her condescending tone and got off the bed.

"I guess I didn't think I needed to dress. I've never gone to a meet and not competed, you know?"

Reagan continued to stare at me in silence until she finally resumed shuffling through her bag. Her movements turned frantic and a look of dread filled her face. Clothes tore out of her bag, gym gear landed on the floor, some hanging over the zipper. She muttered curses under her breath as she grabbed the clothes and shook them in the air. The sound of a rattle filled the space, then a little white bottle rolled out from her clothing.

Reagan dropped the clothes and eyed the container. I frowned and we both froze. There was no prescription sticker on the bottle. Her wide eyes zoomed in on it, and I knew in my heart that it was not something she wanted anyone to see.

I shot a fleeting look toward the bathroom where Holly was standing. Reagan caught my drift and she glanced over her shoulder. I lunged for the bottle.

"Give it back," she demanded through clenched teeth. She rounded the bed toward me.

A sense of dread washed over me. "Diet pills… These are diet pills, aren't they?" She snatched the bottle from my hand, her nails broke my skin. "Are you insane?"

"Mind your own damn business, right?" She threw my words back in my face, popped the top, and poured two pills into her palm. She threw them into her mouth and scowled at me as she swallowed them without water. I never understood how anyone did that.

"Does anyone else know?"

She stared at me. "Of course not, and no one else *will* know."

"How long have you been doing this?"

"Adrianna." My name was said with so much venom I shut my mouth. She leaned in close, and whispered, "Are you that naive? Did you forget what we're judged on? How our bodies need to look? We can't have an ounce of fat on us. We need to look graceful and elegant and be as light as a damn feather on our feet. Besides, it's just a little caffeine and weight loss supplement. Some performance enhancers. Nothing that's banned."

I shook my head in both disgust and sadness by her revelation. I didn't believe Reagan. If it was just caffeine it would state it on the bottle. This was dangerous. Gymnasts were plagued with the constant pressure to be picture-perfect. I knew firsthand how unnerving it could be, but I never once would have considered this.

"I know damn well what it's like, but the image others have of me will not define me. I'm stronger than that, and so are you. Reagan, you're putting your health at risk. That shit could be bad for your heart."

She stepped even closer. Her eyes were leveled with mine as she spoke low. "I'm a better gymnast than you—we both know it—but I can't afford to train and compete for the Olympics like you. It's just not in the cards for me. My parents barely have enough money to keep me here as it is. What I do know is that I have a fighting chance to compete in college. So, I'm going to do everything I can to make that happen. I need a full ride, and only Division One schools offer that."

"But you're already good, you don't need them." I pointed to the bottle clutched in her hand. "Let me help you."

She laughed like my offer was stupid. "Help me? I don't need—or want—your charity. I can do it on my own. As my mom used to say, 'No pressure, no diamond. The greater the pressure, the higher the reward.' I want to be that diamond, Adrianna, I want it more than anything."

She didn't move and neither did I. We were at a standstill. I watched the flames in her eyes when it hit me—we weren't that much different.

In fact, we were identical.

Reagan was headstrong. She had a vision. A drive at a young age people couldn't comprehend. She would go to great lengths to reach her goal. I understood it because I was the same. As much as I wanted to tell our coaches, I would never. We all had our secrets, and I sure as shit had no room to talk. I didn't want to get Reagan into trouble, but I worried what the diet pills contained and how it could affect her body.

"What's a little hunger anyway?" She lifted one shoulder in a careless shrug. "Nothing we're not used to."

I shook my head. "I wish you'd stop. You're going to get caught eventually."

"You mean get caught, like you?"

I pulled back. "What are you talking about?"

Reagan lifted the corner of her mouth, her eyes thinned to slits. She smirked. "Like I don't see the way our coach looks at you." She snickered under her breath. "I see how his hands linger, how he insists on doing privates with you, the way he talks to you. He's *always* looking at you. He's hot. You'd have to be dead to not see how fine he is."

I shook my head. My heart raced so fast it rang in my ears. "Like I told you last night, it's all in your head, Regina. You're making shit up."

She hid her bottle away. "Tell me, why are you really here? A little rendezvous with the coach, perhaps?"

I gave her a deadly stare. "You're fucking sick."

She angled her face toward mine, and I could smell the peppermint mouthwash she had used earlier. She lowered her voice to an audible whisper. "You tell anyone about my diet pills, and I'll tell people you're sleeping with Kova."

My eyes widened. "Are you insane? I'm not sleeping with him." The denial burned the back of my throat. "Do you have any idea what kind of problems that would cause?"

"Then keep your mouth shut about me."

"Kova could get in serious trouble based on your lie."

Her eyes narrowed. My stomach churned at the deceitful cards she dealt. There was no doubt in my mind she would use them to her advantage. She was the type to throw her mother under the bus to get what she wanted.

"Who said it's a lie?"

"It is a lie." I drew out each word. "You can't be serious."

"As a heart attack."

"You have no proof," I whispered. My heart raced a mile a minute.

"Oh, *Aid*, you have so much to learn." Reagan turned away and zipped her suitcase shut with a pleased smile on her face. "Not a lot of evidence is necessary when it comes to sexual allegations in this sport, you should know that by now. You have an extremely good-looking, fairly young male coach, and a pretty girl who he spends more time with than anyone else, and when no one's around, I might add. You're so stupid you can't see that he's using his power to get what he wants. He's had the same girlfriend since he was born."

"You're so far off track you can't even see straight. Nothing is happening. Do you see what you're doing? You're believing shit you made up in your head."

"I may have a wild imagination, but it's all the authorities would need, that is, if you don't keep your mouth shut."

I lifted one brow and curled my lips. She forgot one important factor, one horrid side to this beautiful sport.

"And you seem to forget how an accusation such as this is cleaned up and swept under the rug faster than you can blink your eyes. Especially when it's a beloved, decorated coach. They *always* side with him and you know it. They protect the coach and the sport first, everything else comes second." It was heartbreakingly true, and I was disgusted with myself to use it to my advantage.

Reagan's jaw gnashed together. She knew I was right.

I hadn't elaborated one bit about how such claims were thrown out. It was one of those things that came with the sport that no one ever spoke about. It was rare a coach was actually arrested, let alone banned from coaching thereafter. Gymnastics officials did everything in their power to keep their image squeaky clean. There were many coaches and trainers accused of heinous crimes and still owned gyms and coached every day. But when there was a coach such as Kova, a legend in the gymnastics world, extremely important to the succession and achievement of the gymnast, it was all about protecting the integrity of the sport first. Touching, ass slapping, and lingering fingers were not out of the ordinary. It was common and never questioned because it came with positivity and attention and praise, something all gymnasts craved. No one gave it a second thought.

"Are you going to get up and get ready?" Her tone was always so patronizing when she spoke to me. My eyes reached hers in a daze, my forehead creased so hard I could feel indentations forming deep lines. I'd been lost in thought over the darker side of this sport. "We don't have all day to wait." Reagan scowled. "The world doesn't revolve around you."

I began to wonder if I had fallen for the same kind of manipulation countless others have. The same kind of abuse they were secretly victims of yet had no idea.

No, I couldn't have. I knew right from wrong.

My skin didn't crawl in revulsion when Kova looked at me. I wasn't repulsed when he touched me in the gym, or when we'd been intimate together. He made my heart race with desire. When it came to Kova, I never felt forced to do anything against my will. Reagan was messing with my head.

Holly emerged from the bathroom and I whispered in Reagan's ear, "I'm pretty sure if you had blood work done, your punishment would be much more severe than mine and Kova's." I smirked. "Just sayin'. So don't try me. I can make up believable lies too."

The worst part of what I'd just said, was that it was one hundred and fifty percent true.

I sidestepped Reagan and quickly entered the bathroom and locked the door. I stripped out of my street clothes and stared at the reflection of my naked body. I was thin, too thin, but I loved the way I looked. My skin had a healthy glow, the work of a dedicated coach and gymnast. I placed my hand on my stomach, where Kova's had once been, and imagined his fingers slowly caressing me as I worked toward my breasts. I fingered my nipples, pinching and tugging on the raspberry buds, visualizing Kova doing it. A shiver of need ran up my spine and my eyes rolled shut. My other hand slid to the apex of my thighs and cupped my bare sex. Kova said he liked that I was smooth. There was no use of power then, just need and expression. I shifted my legs open a little and glided my fingers along the plump, swollen lips. It had been months since I felt release. I pictured Kova delicately stroking me with his expert fingers, increasing that euphoric pleasure, taking me higher and higher. I swallowed hard at the dampness that coated my fingers as a soft, quiet sigh escaped my parted lips.

There was no way I didn't want him on me, in me, caressing me. Kova didn't repulse me in the least. In fact, it was the complete opposite…and I almost wished it wasn't.

I wanted—and craved—Kova's touch. I knew in my heart he wasn't like other coaches. An enigmatic essence with a touch of darkness and exceptionally gorgeous, Kova had a commanding aura that made me want to succumb to every word that rolled off his Russian lips. Another rush of wetness coated my fingers at the thought of him, and I slid one inside, imagining it was him pushing into me.

I gravitated toward him, we gravitated toward each other.

I knew the difference between abuse and manipulation, and want and desire. Everything that happened was because I wanted it to, not because he forced me.

I refused to let Reagan's words invade my head with shit that wasn't true.

I braced myself against the sink with my other hand and inserted another finger, visualizing it was Kova's hard cock thrusting into me with pure dominance. Pressure rose as I reached that desired peak. My knees buckled, and I fell into a small state of bliss, rubbing the little bud in circles as I came hard.

"Let's go, princess!" Reagan pounded on the door, and my eyes popped open. "I don't have all day!" she yelled.

I really hated her.

chapter 20

COACHES ALWAYS STAYED ON THE SAME HOTEL FLOOR AS THE GYMNASTS TO MAKE
sure focus stayed strictly on the competition.

There was no playing around, no staying up late. No sneaking into friends' rooms.
No laughing. We were perfect little soldiers ready for war.

The team huddled around Kova and Madeline in the hallway near our room. I snuck
a look at Kova, who stood across from me. He was busy writing something on the clipboard
in his hands. As if he could sense me staring, his eyes shot up and connected with mine. My
cheeks heated and I quickly glanced away in embarrassment. I was afraid he'd know what I'd
just done in the bathroom.

"All right, ladies." Madeline was cheerful this morning, it was the start of meet season.
She took a sip of her coffee, then flipped over one of the stapled papers she had in her arm
and read out loud.

"Since you guys aren't competing until about six-ish this evening, we're going to warm
up in the back in the warm-up gym. It's large and we'll share it with the other competitors. We
just want you guys to run through the motions and get you familiar with everything. For now,
we'll have a *light* breakfast"—she raised her eyes above her glasses without tipping her head
up—"and then head over. Kova rented an SUV so we'll drive together. I suggest texting your
parents now and letting them know what time the meet starts and what the plans are, then si-
lencing your phones and putting them away. We don't want any distractions. If they have any
questions, tell them to contact me or Kova."

Within the hour, we were pulling into the gymnastics center. We parked and I took in
the size of the building. It was massive. World Cup was large, but it had nothing on Parkettes.
I released a sigh of longing. I couldn't wait to see how the inside faired. Teams of all levels,
both male and female, made their way inside. Uniformly dressed, and ready to compete, they
were picturesque mannequins.

The Parkettes Invitational was one of the oldest and most prestigious meets. They had
one of the top elite programs in the world, the best elites would be competing here today. I
was curious to see who I would be up against in the next few months.

"Pay close attention to those around you. Listen and watch," Kova said only for my ears.
I looked toward him, but he picked up the pace and walked ahead of me. My eyes traveled
the length of his backside. His tailored black dress pants fit like a glove. Too perfect, really.
The slate gray polo shirt with World Cup's emblem on the front lapel was a nice contrast to
his dark hair and features. He topped it off with an expensive sports coat, and I bit the side of
my lip. While I loved the athletic look he typically sported at the gym, seeing him dressed up
caused a thrill inside my belly.

I had a serious love-hate relationship with this guy.

I walked inside and stuffed my hands into my pockets as I observed everything around me. At first the sights and sounds overwhelmed my senses. The overabundance of colorful scrunchies holding back snug, gelled buns; giggles; praises and criticisms from coaches; applause in the distance; and classical floor music were too much. My eyes and ears were on overload. But then I focused on every sound, every detail, and it was an exhilarating rush. I smiled to myself. I couldn't get enough. Gymnasts were everywhere.

"Hey, Madeline?" She turned and looked at me. "Should I go and sit in the stands since I'm not warming up?"

"I'm not really sure, you'd have to ask Kova."

I nodded and looked for him. It didn't take long to find him—he was already looking at me. I walked toward him, around a cluster of people. He didn't take his eyes off me until I reached him.

I rocked back and forth on my toes, a stupid grin displayed on my face. "Where do you want me?"

Kova looked at me like the answer was obvious and I should know it. "With me, of course."

I was confused. "Just standing here? Doing nothing?"

He gave me a firm nod. "Yes." An impatient breath blew from his lips. "Did I not tell you what to do? Listen and watch. You are at an elite meet, Adrianna. You have a ton of knowledge of the sport, use it to your advantage. These are the girls you will be competing against soon."

"What should I be looking for?"

Kova stepped closer and invaded my space. His gaze bore into my eyes and he lowered his voice. "Pick apart the routines. Watch the scores. Watch the skills. Watch every event. Pay close attention to detail, be their biggest critic. Be a heartless judge. Be callous. Be cruel. Find places for improvement. Being nice will get you nowhere. Remember everything, so when you are at practice you avoid making the same mistakes. You will see a lot of the same errors, but if you look closely, you will see even worse ones. These athletes are the best of the best, but even the best make mistakes. It is easier to pick out someone else's faults than your own. Use everything you see today to your advantage. Be greedy." He lowered his voice to just above a whisper, and his eyes turned tender. "Ria, you have a dream. I am trying to make it a reality. Go with it. Please, just trust me on this."

I jerked back and gaped at Kova. He was staring down at me, looking too deeply into my eyes, trying to convey something.

It was in that moment that realization dawned on me. Everything leading up to now, to today, struck me hard, and I wasn't sure how to handle it. I felt Kova's words, his passion, his fire, his desire to give me what I wanted more than anything. He understood it because his own dream became a plan that became a reality. He had someone behind him championing him to the finish line, just like he championed me.

Sometimes the moments in life that caused the most damage to the heart put us on the path of reward and gratification. To the greatest glory. And in that moment, when Kova explained what I needed to do, I felt like everything that happened up until this point, was meant to happen. Where there was perfection, there was pain hidden in darkness. Most days were brutal, and I often questioned my sanity. Others filled with regret, but then something magical happens and everything falls into place. All the heartache and pain once dealt washes away and forgotten when that one moment you've been chasing your whole life is caught and becomes reality.

I didn't give Kova enough credit, and that bothered me. I took him for face value and didn't look beyond the words. I hated to judge a book by its cover, yet here I was constantly judging him. I was ashamed of myself. He may have a cold heart and a black soul, a cruel demeanor as a front, but beyond that was a man who cared what happened to me. He cared about my future and what mattered to me.

"What did that one author say?"

"Huh?" I tilted my head to the side, puzzled by his question. "Which author?"

"The one who invented the Harry Potter? I do not know her name, but in one of her books she wrote, 'Anything is possible if you have got enough nerve.' It is true, and I have never forgotten those words. This—gymnastics—takes courage. It takes heart. And it takes nerve. You got this."

"You read Harry Potter?" I gaped at him.

He cracked a very small smile, one he'd only given me a few times when we were alone, and it seized my heart. His eyes glimmered. A laugh escaped his lips and I felt it down to my bones. "Possibly. Do you understand what I am asking of you now? Why you are here?"

I nodded. "I do now. Thank you." My eyes softened.

"I want only the best for you. You come out on top, we both come out on top."

"Sometimes you can be so nice, you know."

He chuckled. "Do not tell anyone. You will ruin my cover."

I swallowed back the knot in my throat and tried not to smile from ear to ear. My heart was so full I thought it was going to combust. When he removed some of his layers and gave me a real glimpse of the man he was, I had an overwhelming urge to be closer to him. He was more laid back, casual, confident. Even flirtatious. He was rarely like that with me. If hundreds of people did not surround us, I would've thrown my arms around his shoulders and hugged the shit out of him.

"I don't want to distract you. Do you want me to wait outside until practice is over?" I felt like I had asked this five times already.

"I want you with me." His voice was raspy, barely above a whisper.

I knew better than to allow those words to hold more water than how he used them, but I couldn't help but hear the double meaning. When he said things like that, I think he meant it.

"Okay Kova, I'll stay." *I'll do whatever you want.*

For the next few hours I stayed by Kova's side. I found it difficult to walk away. When I did, he'd look for me. The thing was, I liked being near him. Not because I was insanely attracted to him, but because he knew what he was talking about when it came to gymnastics and I loved that so, so much. I wanted to see from his point of view. I became enraptured with being on the other side of the fence, watching him coach instead of taking instructions from him. I pictured myself on the greener grass wondering if I could be like him one day.

I liked watching him coach my teammates on what they needed to do at the last minute. I could hear it in his voice how much he believed in them, the way he bent at the hip and clapped his hands when a skill was executed perfectly, or when he made a fist and whispered joyous words to himself. I got a thrill out of it because he got in the zone and his true passion and colors came to life. This was his reason. His eyes lit up, and it in turn made me happy. I watched closely and I listened to everything. I'd followed his gaze and started noticing little things, things I may not have noticed before, and wondered if I made the same mistakes myself. And not just the small wobbles either. The little jerks or bends in the knees of the perfect body line required in elite gymnastics. The hips out, shoulders too low. I thought I executed it right, like I was sure they did. Now I was curious if I looked like them.

Observing *them* made me more aware of *myself*.

I started paying attention to other gymnasts warming up and picked at their routines. Every little thing mattered. Something as stupid as an undergarment showing could cause a slight deduction. I saw split leaps not reaching exactly one hundred and eighty degrees. Legs separating when transitioning to the high bar. Knees separating in a double back tuck. And sometimes there were deductions for the legs not parted enough. Missed connections on the beam where the gymnast is required to complete a series of skills without breaking between them, no step or stopping or balance check. And another mistake I noticed was taking a long pause before attempting another skill.

An over-the-top, angry voice jolted me from my observation. I leaned over and glanced down the runway, spotting a coach bent over with his hands on his knees as he yelled at a gymnast just inches from her face. Spit flew from his mouth when he spoke and she flinched. Her eyes dropped to the floor, color filled her pasty white cheeks. I was embarrassed for her. I'd been yelled at in the gym countless times, but never at a meet. She nodded her head and walked past the coach.

The young girl, who looked no more than twelve at most, mounted the low bar. I scrutinized her routine while her coach shouted from the side of the bars. Her shoulders were closed when they should have been opened, her posture was horrible, and she struggled to extend her handstands. Her amplitude was low, easily a deduction, and it made my stomach drop because I freaked she was going to hit the bar on her way down. This was not the kind of emotion one looked for while watching gymnastics. This terrified me. She cast to a handstand and completed two giants before tapping so hard on the second swing that she used her hips to gain power for the dismount. It's not something easy to spot by the untrained eye, but it was obvious to me when she dragged her toes coming down and whipped her hips hard.

The bar ricocheted as she released, echoing throughout the gym. She completed her dismount but took a huge step, her knees dropped to the floor. I sucked in a breath at how awful her landing was and the fact that her coach was no doubt about to lay into her. But those knees hitting the mat was a massive deduction, and all because she didn't get enough power and height when she released the bar.

That was her coach's fault. The way he berated her struck so much fear in her she couldn't concentrate enough to focus on the task at hand. A little fear was good, but she wasn't calm and collected as she performed. She was frightened and unsure of herself. The kind of mentality not meant for gymnastics. His coaching skills sucked. He started once more. Her chin trembled, and my heart ached for her and the tears she fought to hold in.

I sensed a pair of eyes on me. Kova stood off to the side observing me with his hands propped on his hips. He tilted his head and waited. His gaze bore into mine. I knew what he was expecting, but it wasn't as easy as I thought it would be. I felt bad for the girl. He wanted my criticism, to take out the emotion so I could learn to recognize flaws without an ounce of compassion, something he would no doubt do. But the way the girl's shoulders hunched over…it was a sucker punch to the gut. Kova may work us to the bone, but he'd never humiliate us in public.

Kova walked toward me and followed my gaze. He did a double take, almost stumbling over his feet. He sneered and mumbled something under his breath.

"Her routine was atrocious. She did not do well under pressure. Then again, that coach is a piece of shit, so I cannot blame her."

I shook my head in sympathy. I had this overwhelming urge to go to her and give her some positive reinforcement.

"I kind of want to talk to her."

His head snapped down, and his eyes glared so bright I winced. "Adrianna, you better not go to her. Do you understand me?" Kova said through a tight jaw. His voice was so low I could barely hear him. "Do not interfere with what is going on between her and her coach. That is none of your business. Stay out of it. The last thing I need is for him to say something disrespectful to you. That guy is a dick and thinks everyone is below him."

I looked up at Kova. "Do you know him?"

He dipped his chin. "Yes. He used to coach with me. Guess it did not take him long to find another gym."

My brows shot to my hairline. "He did? When? What happened?"

"I fired him the moment I bought World Cup. I made him pack all his shit the day I signed the papers, then I kicked him to the street. All he did was degrade the girls. I have seen him physically throw and push them into things, bruise them, scream until they cried. I refused to put up with that shit," he spat.

I'd never seen that sort of thing happen, but I couldn't say it surprised me either. The rumors that floated in the gymnastics world were horrific.

Kova stepped closer to me and glanced above my head. He was quiet as he said, "Believe me, I know I have no room to talk when it comes to you, but I did not like the way he looked at the girls…it made my skin crawl. He is not right in the head—I do not trust him. He is a pig. Mark my words, someone will come forward one day and accuse him of something awful."

My heart went out to the girl. "That's terrible. I can't help but feel bad for her."

"Do not feel bad for her. Your feelings will only hinder your performance. Block out the emotion and watch how far you go in this sport. Think only about yourself and how you can better yourself."

That upset me. "I feel bad for her because I've been there, Kova. So have you. Working so hard to be the perfect gymnast and then failing. What she's doing matters so much to her. Making those mistakes hurts, especially when your coach sucks. I feel her pain."

"Yes, we all know what it feels like, but use her mistakes to improve yours. Leave your feelings at the door. You have one job to do, one chance to get it right. Adrianna, you will never get a second chance at a first impression. One chance, Adrianna. Make it count. Emotions will just screw you if you let them take over. Regret forms. It drives you in a direction you are not meant to go in. Block it out. Do not let that happen. Harden yourself and keep your eye on the prize. Ruthless, yes. Cruel, yes. You need to shut down inside and only allow your love for gymnastics to shine through. Only feel the sport and the motions and use all of it to express yourself in the best way you can. That is what you need to get ahead. Trust me. It will be worth it in the end. I give you my word."

His words were a hard pill to swallow. I needed to sacrifice my emotions to win and I wasn't sure how to make that happen. Keeping myself calculated and controlled would be a hard task to achieve, but it made sense because no one thrived in the business world with emotions riding on their sleeve. In some backwards way, he had a point. It would only improve my odds of reaching the podium.

"Okay. I can try."

The coach finally stopped yelling at the girl and stood up. She picked at her nails and kept her head slanted toward the floor. He glanced in our direction and locked eyes with Kova. He pushed his chest out, and his stare was lethal.

They glared at each other until his eyes traveled down to mine and he covered my whole body with his seedy gaze. Kova stiffened next to me, his hands fisted into tight balls, turning his knuckles white. I could see what he meant now. I shivered, my stomach churning with unease. I didn't like the way he looked at me. I wanted to get as far as I could from that man.

"Go take a seat. I will be there soon," Kova said under his breath, not taking his eyes off the coach. I nodded and he walked toward the man, intent heavy in his stride. His body moved like a caged tiger. His thick legs were strong and powerful, and his shoulders swayed with persuasiveness that demanded attention. As he stopped to speak to the coach, Reagan appeared in my line of view.

My stomach pitched at her icy glare and the apple I had for breakfast suddenly felt lodged in my throat. She was malicious, and the calculating look in her eyes tangled with me. Then I remembered her little secret, and like sap dripping from a tree, the anxiety over Reagan's accusations faded away and a smile slowly pulled at my lips.

Her eyes flashed as I winked and gave her a little wave, then I gave her my back.

A LL DAY I WATCHED EVERY MOVE KOVA MADE, THE WAY HE SPOKE TO THE GIRLS, and how he gave them last minute pointers.

I picked up on enough to absorb and reflect on it.

I hated being near him and I loved it at the same time. I found I craved his words, his instructions, his guidance. He'd whisper his thoughts to me while we watched routine after routine where he—and the judges—would find errors. I had spotted most of them, but then he'd surprise me with something I didn't catch or really put much thought into.

"Oh shit, she's screwed," I said under my breath when a competitor fell off the balance beam. A fall held an entire point deduction, which was huge and utterly devastating.

Kova slightly looked at me but kept his focus on the routine. "Not necessarily. Her routine is flawless so far."

I frowned. "A fall is never good though."

"True, but just watch and wait."

Once she finished, her score went up and it shocked me. Kova smirked like it was exactly what he expected.

"Other than the fall, she executed an absolutely perfect routine. She only lost, at most, a point and a half."

I pulled back. "Where did the other half come from if you said she had a perfect routine?"

He held his thumb and forefinger a centimeter apart. "She had a very, very slight balance check when she got back up."

Huh. I hadn't even noticed that one. "It is all about what is going on up here." Kova gently tapped the side of his temple and lowered his voice. "Gymnastics is just as much mental as it is physical, and the balance beam is the only event that requires the most mental focus. She knew her fall would cost her and that she had to get her head back in the game to come out on top."

The next girl who competed didn't fall, but was currently behind in the standings to the one who had fallen. I looked at Kova for clarification.

"I caught four errors just from the five major skills alone. Did you?"

I'd spotted some. "I saw she bent her knees in two of them."

"Good. Those are point two each time. So now we are at point eight in deductions in just that alone. While she stuck her dismount, she had a heavy balance check. The bigger the wobble, the bigger the deduction. With those two mistakes alone, she now has more deducted than the girl with the fall. Her body posture was terrible, and her toes turned in badly. I would say at least another point three, point four for just that. Now imagine you are sitting as close as the judges." He gave me a knowing look.

It was easy to forget how quickly deductions added up. And unless you had a trained eye for the sport, those mistakes were not easy to spot.

"Some judges curve the scores." He paused. "By the way, the girl with the fall, that is Sloane Maxwell. She is one of the top elites in the country right now. Everyone is after her. Did you watch her eyes when she was competing? She is a fighter that one. Falls happen to everyone. I do not care how incredible you are, it is almost impossible to correct your center of mass when flipping over a piece of wood that is only ten centimeters wide. In the end, it is your difficulty, but more so execution, that makes the difference. That is why when she got back on, she rocked it. That is why you practice until you cannot get it wrong. You forget what is happening around you and you only focus on what you are doing at that moment and nothing else. You leave everything else at the door."

I saw Kova in a completely different light. I was at odds with myself for wanting more of him. I hungered for his knowledge. His uncanny ability to see what I needed to succeed and to bring out the elite gymnast in me without a second thought. No one got me the way he did. His training was harsh at times, and he rode me hard in the gym, but it was because he had a bird's eye for precision. I knew it from the beginning, but to see this approach made me feel different toward him. It made me admire him more than I allowed my heart to, and that worried me.

I promised myself I would try my hardest to not look at him in that light anymore. Promised myself I would stay away, but when Kova took the time to look me in the eyes and break it down and feed me what I needed to thrive, I found him sexy as hell. Addicting. Kova had a potent hold over me and I wondered if he even knew his power.

A lot could be said about the man standing next to me, probably more negative than positive, but there was one thing I knew for certain—today showed he cared about my success in the sport. He did have my best interests at heart. Kova wasn't a man who divulged much about himself, but today said more about him than he knew.

Once the meet ended, I stood awkwardly off to the side as gymnasts were congratulated on their hard work and effort. Reagan was knocked down to bronze, a tenth of a deduction separated her from placing fourth. Holly held silver. The men's team would compete after us.

The team, parents, and coaches all had dinner together—and thankfully a fast one. Now I was back in my room alone while the girls had gone to stay in a hotel near the airport with their parents. Holly offered to stay with me, but I politely declined and reminded her that I lived alone and liked it.

Today had been overwhelming and I needed the solitude more than anything to relax.

I'd been so angry with Kova for forcing me to attend the meet he so ruthlessly pulled me from. I thought it was a cruel game he was playing and didn't want any part of it.

Turns out, I was naive. Kova wasn't as despicable as I thought he was.

My heart still burned with vengeance because of what he did, but now I realized I misjudged his intentions and the fire raging inside me slowly dimmed.

I had everything packed for the early flight home tomorrow and now I had a bath running. My goal was to clear my mind. I was insanely eager to get back in the gym with the newfound information I had. The strange thing was, I'd already had the knowledge, but I'd seen it through a different perspective today and that changed things for me big time.

As I undressed, a light knock sounded at my door. I groaned inwardly, hoping Holly hadn't decided to come back.

Grabbing the robe hanging on the back of the door, I quickly pulled it on and tied a knot around my waist. I wasn't tall enough to look through the peep hole, so I carefully opened the door.

"Kova?" I whispered. "What are you doing here?"

"May I come in?"

My eyes narrowed at the ridiculousness of his question. I swallowed hard and clutched the robe tight to my neck.

He wants to come into my hotel room with other coaches and gymnasts around!

"I really don't think that's a good idea."

With a tilt of his head, he gave me a pleading look. "It will not take long. I promise. Just a few minutes, *pozhaluysta.*"

I flattened my lips and amusement lit in his eyes. He got me. I resigned and stepped aside, letting him in.

The sound of running water had Kova glancing toward the bathroom. "Do you need to turn that off?"

I ran to the bathroom and quickly turned off the water and redressed. Stepping back into the room, I found Kova seated in one of two chairs at the round table near the window. Lounged back like he was the king of a fortune five hundred empire, he casually spread his legs wider as he scrolled through his phone. His dark wash jeans fit him to perfection. The way the denim molded his thighs screamed for me to climb him like a tree. My eyes trailed up his long-sleeved black shirt and paused on his biceps. One flex and the seams would give.

Then I noticed the ball cap…and I was done.

So simple. So easygoing. So fucking hot.

Damn this man and his sexual appeal.

A startling need to go to him and sit on his lap and just talk pulled at me. We could talk about anything, meaningless things. The weather. The future of the sport. I could teach him contractions or listen to him speak Russian. This need had absolutely nothing to do with sex and everything to do with a deep connection to someone.

I didn't know why, but the urge to capture this moment hit me like a ton of bricks. It wasn't the best idea, it was downright stupid, but I didn't care. I had to have him like this— natural, easy, relaxed. Like it was normal for us.

Quickly and quietly, I pulled my cell phone from my back pocket and snapped a photo of him.

Kova lifted his eyes from his phone and leisurely dragged them up and down my body without moving his head. I felt the heat from his avid gaze roam every inch of my body. One side of his mouth tugged up ever so slightly, and I snapped another photo as he watched. The man looked divine in a ball cap; I could stare at him all day. A smirk tipped the corners of his mouth as I captured another shot. Then he bit down on his bottom lip and dragged his teeth up. I swallowed hard and a soft exhale escaped my lips.

I managed to take one more picture before he motioned me to the chair opposite him. That stupid imaginary string pulling me toward him as I took a seat. Kova placed his phone facedown and sat up straighter, turning toward me.

"You know you probably shouldn't be here, right?"

Kova shrugged carelessly. "I am not concerned. No one will question me."

I raised a brow in skepticism. "That kind of arrogance will backfire on you one day."

"Ria, *pozhaluysta,*" he said suggestively under his breath. "When will you learn that I make the rules?"

I feigned a groan and smiled. "What's so important that couldn't wait until Monday?"

Kova chuckled and I felt it deep in my belly. "I want to know what you thought about today," he said in a low tone. "If you learned anything new."

"Of course I did."

"Like?" He motioned his hand for me to elaborate. He was too comfortable in that chair and it made my heart hammer.

"Like I need to tighten and clean my routines." I leaned forward. "Get any noise out that will distract the judges. I need to be innately mindful of everything I do. If I can feel it, they can see it. The girls made simple, careless mistakes. The kind I'm sure I make too." I looked him directly in the eye. "I need to break down my routines and perfect each skill, nail each one to sheer precision, even if it takes all day to break down a thirty-second bar routine. I have to have a firm understanding of the sport and what I'm doing. Focus and listen to my coaches, really pay attention, visualize it; and do it all with my mouth shut."

I leaned back and expelled a breath. I stared hard at Kova, like I was mad, but I wasn't. I felt every word and I couldn't wait to show him I meant it. To prove it, like he's always saying.

He slowly bobbed his head, and his sharp jaw held my focus. The man could cut steel with it.

He tapped his finger on the table. "You are eager to get back in the gym," Kova stated more than asked.

I nodded and a stupid grin pulled at my lips. It's what gymnastics did to me. "You can't even imagine."

Kova cracked a smile. "Believe me, I know the feeling very well. I can hear it in your voice. You want it bad."

I didn't want it, I ached for it. I burned with longing to do what I loved for both me and him. I felt everything. The clawing need in my stomach to get back into the gym. The desire to prove I had what it took.

"I like where your head is at. It is where you need to be—focused on not just shit inside the circle, but outside of it too. Become a coach. Be a judge. What would you critique about yourself? You must be aware of your surroundings, what you are up against. The more you work, the more strength you have, the stronger you become. Not just in your bones and muscles, but up here too." Kova tapped the side of his head. "Bloom under pressure and show them what you are made of. I want you to shine out there. I know you can do it. Find your weakness and improve it. Everyone has a weakness somewhere, Adrianna, you just have to be the bigger person to recognize it."

"What's your weakness?"

"You," he said without hesitation.

"Me?" I pulled back.

Kova nodded and repeated himself. "You. Now tell me, what is your strength? What keeps you going besides your love for the sport?"

You, I wanted to say. It was my first instinct.

Kova was my strength, but I was his weakness.

A weakness he worked on to improve and make resilient. A strength that I drew from.

God, the complexity of that tore at my center. We were going to sleep in different beds with the same appetite, wake up with the same drive and same focus, work together to come out as one. We were a team.

"Say it," he pushed on in a whisper. I didn't need to, he could read the answer in my eyes. "I want to hear you say the words, Ria. I need to hear them."

I swallowed, shying away. "You." My voice cracked. "You are my strength, Kova." God, it was so true, and it nearly knocked the wind from my lungs. He really was what I relied on to give me what I needed, and I didn't realize it until recently.

He didn't gloat. "What inspires you?"

"You," I said softly.

"Ask me what inspires me."

I asked him.

"You," he said. My stomach fluttered. "What drives you to push harder?"

"You," I said.

"We are a team—I exhale, you inhale. We fight together. We work together. It is an amazing feeling when you find someone who shares the same passion as you. The possibilities are endless. I am the beast beneath your beauty, pushing you. From here on out, we do it together. You come to me for anything and I will do everything in my power to make it happen."

We stared into each other's eyes without saying another word. We had it all yet didn't have anything.

I'd been incredibly wrong about him. He cared so profoundly it was suffocating. He was untrusting and put on a façade, and I could see why. When he gave, really gave himself, he invaded your personal space to the extreme and took control.

"I know I do not say this often, but you are a great gymnast. You have come a long way this past year, you just need some polishing."

"There is no gymnast who is absolutely perfect, Kova."

Cocking his head, he lifted one side of his mouth ready for a challenge. "I beg to differ. Nadia Comaneci was the first to be deemed perfect. Why? Because she had a coach who was relentless, who fought with her, not against her. He saw her potential, her drive, and pushed. That is how I feel about you. Do not mistake arrogance for confidence. It is not like that. Some days it is not pretty, but nothing is pretty that you do not work for." Kova shifted in his chair and leaned forward, tapping the countertop with his middle finger. "You are an athlete, a business that needs to be promoted, in a sense. You compete with others to get ahead. Use their flaws for your advancement and I promise you it will all fall into place."

I nodded my head, finally understanding his view. "I guess I always had the mentality that I didn't need to compete with others, only with myself to be better than what I was yesterday."

"Today you saw that is not the case." He looked me deep in the eye, and it unnerved me. "Ria, everything I do has a reason. Pulling you from the meet was not such a bad idea because you got a behind the scenes look. Am I right? It will make you better overall."

My jaw dropped. Way to kill the moment. "Kova, I realize now that your intentions were not bad when you took me out of the meet, but it was your delivery that was ultimately harsh and embarrassing. It was wrong and so cruel. You could have gone about it in a different way."

"I am not the asshole you think me to be."

"It was an asshole move, Kova. Therefore, you're an asshole."

He smiled and chuckled, and it pierced my heart. He sat back and strummed his fingers on the table. "You know, I would not let anyone else talk to me like that."

I blushed, trying not to smile. "But you let me."

He shook his head. "And I have no idea why," he said with a deep sigh. Standing up, he took two steps and stood in front of me. Glancing down, he motioned for me to get up. Confused, I did as he requested.

Kova immediately took my seat, then wrapped a strong arm around my waist and pulled me onto his lap. My heart rushed into my throat as he held me so warm and securely to him. Turning to face him, I grabbed the bill of his hat and flipped it around so his cap was now backwards. His grin hit my core and I squirmed in his lap.

Grabbing my cell phone, he opened the camera app and angled the lens toward us. I watched his thumb press down repeatedly.

"What are you doing," I whispered.

He snapped more.

"I realized earlier when you took a photo that we do not have a picture together."

My heart gave a little patter. "We shouldn't."

He eyed me. "There have been a lot of things we *shouldn't* have done, Ria."

My face lit up and I started to laugh. "Hey! You used a contraction."

"I know…it felt weird on my tongue." He grinned.

I adjusted in his lap and he helped me get situated. It was cozy and I didn't want to move. We had a way about each other that was so utterly confusing. In this moment it wasn't black and white, right or wrong. There were no colors, no ages, no blurred lines. I wasn't *that* girl, and he wasn't *that* guy. We were just two people who shared the same ambitions and a connection that couldn't be explained, only felt.

"There is one more thing I want to talk to you about."

The playfulness dropped from my face. "What is it?"

Kova placed my phone facedown the way he always placed his, then gently rubbed my thigh in soothing circles. He was staring tenderly into my eyes for a beat longer than usual and it left me apprehensive.

"Today at the meet when you saw the coach yelling? Please promise me you will never intervene if you see it happen again, not with just him, but anyone. I can see why you would want to, but it is not your place."

I looked down. He was completely right. "I know. I'm sorry."

Kova placed his knuckles under my chin and lifted it until we were eye to eye again. This time we were much closer together.

"The way he was talking to the girl, there was no doubt in my mind he would have stepped up to you and given you the same kind of treatment. Adrianna, I already cannot stand him, but I would have fucking lost it on the piece of shit if he said anything even remotely negative to you. I know I am an asshole, and I can be overbearing and bossy, among other things, but one thing you must not have realized about me is that I am fiercely protective over the ones I care about. All he had to do is say one wrong thing to you and I would have ended up in handcuffs. I am serious, Adrianna. I do not play games like that. Hurt what is mine and there will be consequences."

A reserved smile pulled at my mouth. Kova followed it with his gaze and pulled me closer to him. "You know you just unveiled another piece of yourself, right?" His forehead bunched together. "You care about me."

I didn't think it was possible for him to ever look bashful, but Kova self-consciously shifted in his seat. I caught him. He knew it and he tried to brush it off.

"Of course I care about you." He bristled.

"You said mine, though. You said, 'hurt what is mine.' I think you care about me way more than you let on. Am I yours, Kova?"

His Adam's apple bobbed, and his face contorted into a mixture of revelation and perplexity. I waited with baited breath. This was the first time Kova didn't know how to answer a question.

I watched as he ran his tongue over his lips. Clearing his throat, his voice cracked as he said, "Some things are better left unsaid."

I nodded solemnly.

Leaning in, Kova dropped a hasty kiss to my cheek. "Send me your favorite photo." He double tapped my leg, then he was up and walking toward the door.

"Kova?"

He looked over his shoulder. "I'm going to prove it to you. I'm going to show you that I want it, that you're not wasting your time with me. I'm going to show you that I'm worth it."

His eyes glossed over and he nodded with his chin toward my phone. "I already know you are worth it."

Then he was gone.

chapter 22

I PROVED IT ALL RIGHT.

    All month long I used the knowledge I obtained from Kova and the meet and worked my ass off. If I wasn't with my private tutor, or at physical therapy for my calf, I was in the gym. I kept my mouth shut and took everything Madeline and Kova dished out. I didn't complain or question them. Each of my routines were broken down and I was ripped apart. The coaches videotaped me so I could watch my progress. I consumed more Motrin in one week than I had in a month and I hardly slept. I was mentally and physically exhausted. But I didn't give in or give up.

I wanted this.

Tomorrow is Sunday, which meant the gym would be closed, but I was going to ask if I could start coming in to do extra conditioning. I'd need to beg and plead though since it was also Madeline's and Kova's day off and no one would be here. I had a few weeks until my first official meet and that wasn't a lot of time to become perfect.

I shoved my wristbands into my duffle bag and my stomach growled. I pulled out a bottle of coconut water, something Kova had introduced me to months ago, and drank half the container. That would hold me over for a bit.

Standing up, I didn't bother to dust the chalk from my thighs or fix my hair. I didn't slip on any pants, I wore only my leotard. The cold tile shocked my bare feet and I felt a zip up my spine as goose bumps broke out on my arms. The lobby was so much colder after practice. Rounding the corner, I headed down the hall to Kova's office, strutting past the locker room with determination in each step.

Taking a deep breath, I exhaled and knocked on his door.

"Yes."

I slipped my hand over the brass knob and opened the door. I hadn't been in his office since the day he pulled me from the meet. I glanced around. Memories assaulted me, both pleasant and horrible as I stood there waiting for his attention.

"What is it, Ria?" he said without even looking up. The lip of his ball cap shielded his view of me.

I stepped inside and shut the door behind me. "How did you know it was me?"

He huffed out a low laugh as he continued writing. "I always know when you are around. I can smell you." I pursed my lips together, bewildered by his response. I know I put deodorant on this morning. "It is not what you think, so relax." He placed his pen down, then folded his arms behind his head and stretched back. The leather chair creaked as his shirt pulled up and his legs widened. I stifled the groan in the back of my throat. I fought hard not to glance down at his rock-solid abs and patch of thin dark hair I knew was there. All month long we were behaving—he was the coach and I was the gymnast, nothing more.

But of course, I just had to look down. I couldn't not. The blue vein driving toward his groin taunted me to look. My gaze lingered for a second and I wondered just how far it went and if it was the vein that wrapped around—

I snapped my eyes up, stopping myself. Blood rushed to my cheeks before I could stop it. Kova grinned. I hated that knowing look that glimmered in his eyes. This was new territory for us. Friendship. At least that's what I thought it was, how I'd viewed it.

"Why are you looking at me like that?" I asked playfully and shifted from foot to foot.

"I have no idea what you are talking about, Adrianna."

I gave him a droll stare and tried not to smile. He knew. I was embarrassingly giddy. "You are such a liar." I laughed a little, and his grin widened. "Stop looking at me like that."

"You have a very subtle hint of the ocean that lingers on you. I can always detect it."

"That's not creepy at all," I said, looking away, trying to push back my flyaways from the day's practice.

Kova had a scent to me too, but I thought it was his cologne. I wasn't wearing anything scented. I never wore lotion to practice because the sweat would make me slippery. I wasn't big on body sprays or perfumes anyway. It had to be my shampoo, but he wasn't even that close to get a drift of it.

He shook his head. "Take a seat. What is it that you need?"

My nerves sparked at the ends. I was edgy and I didn't know why. I sat down, then blurted out what I came for.

"Even though I hate them with a passion, I want to add another dance class to my schedule. I'm not stupid, I know what ballet can offer a gymnast, so I'll suck it up if I must. I also want to keep up with the private classes with you to help with my flexibility. I don't want to revert to old habits or lose what I've already accomplished. I can stay longer into the evenings to make this work, and Sundays I want to come in and do extra conditioning, if that's okay with you, of course. I don't need you or Madeline here with me for that, I just thought you should know when someone is coming and going in your gym." Then, I got raw and honest with him. "I'm less than a month away from testing elite, and I'm nervous as hell that I'm not primed and ready enough. I want to know that I did everything I could to get at least the minimum points required to become elite. I want both floor routines to wow the judges and draw their attention but keep them elegant and artistic at the same time. I don't want to wobble on beam or jerk in my turns. I want to hit every handstand on bars and stick my landing on vault while getting the flight I need. I want to practice every waking moment so there's no room for error when the time comes. Please, Kova. I want this so bad. I won't complain or ask for a day off. I will do anything so that when my time comes, I will make it count. I want the challenge. I want to make the goals I set. I want it all."

"Breathe, Ria. I do not think you took a breath in between all that."

I blushed. Kova did what he did best and stared at me. He ran a hand down his face, and I noticed the dark circles under his eyes and the stubble around his jaw. He hadn't shaved in days. I loosely wondered if today wasn't the day to push for this.

"You ask for so much. You are here nearly fifty hours a week as it is. Adrianna, I think you are on track as you should be. I do not think you need to push any more than what you are. If I thought for one minute you were lacking anywhere, I think you should know by now that I would not hesitate to hold back. As of right now, you are still recovering from an injury that we do not need to reinjure or flare up. Every athlete needs a rest day for their muscles to recover. At the rate you want to go, you are going to need your own physical therapist to help you recover quickly. You are going to be soaking in ice baths every night, hot tubs, massage therapy, cupping therapy. There are so many things you may require to keep going, to keep you healthy. Eventually it will all catch up to you."

My Achilles had hardly been a bother. In all honestly, I'd forgotten about it. And the work was already catching up to me, but he didn't need to know that.

"You know money is not an issue. I can get the best of everything."

"Money cannot buy you everything, Ria," he said like it was common sense. "If you have that kind of mindset, you are not who I thought you were. After a while, your strength will deteriorate, and your mental aptitude will weigh you down. Not because you are weakening, but because you push too hard and do not recover properly. I will always be by your side pushing you, but I know when not to overdo it too. I was where you are at one time. It is not just about recovering your muscles, it is about your mind too. Your body can only handle so much."

I wanted to work more, work harder, to be the best, just like he wanted me to be. It's what he implied and suddenly he didn't want to give it to me. That lit a fire under my ass.

"Didn't you once tell me the body can endure anything, but it's my mind I have to convince?"

"Probably. It sounds like something I would say."

"Well, you did. And I'm trying to do just that."

Kova sat up, his face twisted. "Do not throw my words back in my face, Adrianna." His voice hardened, his accent strong. I loved when it came out like this.

"I'm offering myself to you to do whatever you want. You tell me to do five beam routines, I'm going to do eight. You tell me to come in at seven, I'll be here at six. You wanted me to prove it. Here I am, proving myself. I don't understand why you aren't agreeing to this. The whole reason I came here is for a coach who will push me hard and not give up. I want someone to coach me the way Nadia was coached. Someone who will back me. You're supposed to work me to the bone. I don't feel like I'm at that point, I don't feel like I'm doing enough, Kova. I want more."

Kova's emerald eyes flared to life. I'd hit a nerve.

He stood up and stalked his way around his desk in three steps. My stomach dropped when he neared me. I wasn't sure whether I should stay seated or stand, so I stood. If he wanted to argue, I'd go toe to toe with him.

"I back you," he spat low and angry, like I insulted him. "I push you. I work you harder than anyone. I spend more time with you than anyone else. I blow off my girlfriend for you, to give you more time, and look how you show your respect. You come into *my* office, shove *my* words in *my* face, demand I do what *you* want, in hopes of what? That I will bend to *your* will? That is not how it works here, Adrianna. And it never will. You need to remember your ground. Every athlete is different. Not everyone can handle more. I do not want to push too much. Yes, you are resilient, much stronger than what I have seen in years come through these doors, but you are nursing an injury that I do not want to appear again. Everything that you have worked on this past year will go down the drain all because you had to be stubborn and hardheaded when something did not go your way. I have things set up for your future I want for you. Things you do not know about yet. But you injure yourself again, and you are done." He paused. I crossed my arms in front of my chest and looked at the floor, ashamed he just put me in my place when I should've been humble. "Why can you not just trust me?" he asked with disgust in his voice.

His breathing deepened like he exerted himself, but when he clenched his eyes shut, I knew he hurt more than anything. I would never be done with gymnastics. Just like he wasn't, seeing as he coached. It was never going to happen. It wasn't possible.

I began pacing. He had a point, and while I understood his trepidation, I couldn't think past him saying he had plans for my future. Throwing my arms out to the sides, I dropped them with a plop and asked, "What things?"

His head angled to the side and he watched me. "Hmm?"

"You said you have things planned for me. What things, Kova? Why haven't you spoken to me about them?"

Kova leaned his hips back on his desk and crossed his arms over his chest. My eyes drifted to his pectorals straining against his shirt. The man was built solid under clothes. Suntanned and strong. I swallowed hard, my gaze dropping lower to take in the rest of his delicious body.

"Ria?" he shouted my name.

My eyes snapped up. "What?"

"I asked you a question."

He had? "What question?"

"When was the last time you had an orgasm?"

I gaped at the boldness of his invasive question. Full on jaw hanging to the floor, eyes as big as a full moon, heat so hot it flushed my cheeks, and my ears burned like they were on fire.

"I know you didn't just ask me that question." He grinned. "God! You are so abrasive. What is wrong with you?"

"I just call it like I see it. You are wound tight and overworked, have been for weeks now. Then you come in here like you took a hit of crack. You look like you could use the release."

My brows shot to my forehead. I had no idea what that even looked like.

"And so that gives you the right to ask when was the last time I came?" My voice rose, baffled he would ask me such a personal question. "I have a lot on my mind. Not everything can be resolved through sex, you know."

His eyes gleamed.

"I'm not answering you."

Kova's mouth twitched and the lopsided grin he awarded me with hit deep inside. "You did not have to."

"A while. Okay?" I caved. "It's not like I have a slew of boyfriends at my door waiting for me to call on them." Not that I would ever do something like that.

His entire face shifted from playful and flirty to brooding and dark. "You better not."

I rolled my eyes.

"How long?" he pushed.

I swallowed and felt my cheeks flush once more. No way would I admit to getting myself off to the thought of him last month. "Since the last time we were in here... When Hayden caught us."

The smirk that pulled at his whole face warmed my body. I knew every inch of my coach in ways I shouldn't. I knew how low his shorts sat on his tapered hips, how deep the V indented and how low it dipped toward his impressive cock. My eyes lingered on the outline of his shorts, the wideness of his hips. He didn't own boxers; he always went commando. A sensual stir lit inside me. His thighs were like boulders, the dark blue cloth contoured each muscle like a second skin. I dragged my gaze upward to where the fabric hugged his thick and long length. I could see how his shaft laid against his heavy sack, the way his thighs propped it up on display. The material was so thin it left nothing to the imagination. At least, not to my imagination. I remembered what it felt like in my hand, inside me, how I stretched to fit his size. I knew what he was capable of with that thing and my body heated all over wanting it.

"Subtlety is clearly not your specialty. Are you done? Or do you need more time?" he asked in a low, husky tone that only fueled my desire.

Fuck. My. Life. This just proved his question.

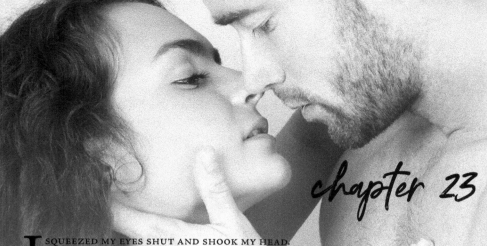

chapter 23

I SQUEEZED MY EYES SHUT AND SHOOK MY HEAD.

When the haze cleared and my heart rate steadied again, I tried to change the subject. "Why don't you ever tell me that you think I'm strong?"

He shrugged. "It is not my job to reassure you. If you have confidence in yourself, you would not need reassurance from anyone, especially a man, Adrianna."

"I am confident in myself. You don't know what you're talking about," I said defensively. "It would be nice to hear from my coach though. Praising your gymnasts every once in a blue moon wouldn't kill you."

He got serious. "Come here." His expression cleared of any playfulness.

I shook my head.

"Come," he ordered, and beckoned me toward him.

I shook my head again. When I didn't move, he reached out and grabbed my wrist, pulling me to him.

Spreading his legs, he guided my hips so I nestled between the warmth of his thighs and pressed my pelvis to his with determination. Moisture seeped onto my leotard and I blushed, hoping he couldn't feel it. Kova was right. I did need the release. I leaned my head against his chest, too embarrassed to look up at him. His body was so warm against mine.

Wrapping his arms around my lower back, Kova crossed his wrists and pressed on my butt cheeks until his dick pressed against my sex. A quiet gasp lodged in my throat. The tight pressure to my clit caused a deep, intense ache. I was at just the right angle and I tried not to make any sudden movements, tried not to inhale too deep in fear a moan would escape. My hands came up to his chest, and I clutched his shirt, fighting and begging for things I wanted yet wouldn't admit. I wish I knew how to handle myself better around this man, but like clockwork, all thoughts and morals went out the window when it was just me and him.

Kova's head dropped to my neck, his breath a hot trail across my collarbone as his hands sensually massaged my butt. His fingers ran in circles, pushing down and through the seam of my ass, then back out to form another circle. My head rolled to the side, granting him full access to leave a wet trail on my neck. His teeth grazed my skin like little knives, each sharp bite heightened my arousal. My breathing deepened and I couldn't hold back from grinding my pussy against him. His cock twitched and a sigh fell from my lips. He was right. I was wound up and tense.

"Kova…" I whispered, and closed my eyes.

"Tell me what you need."

My mouth was parched, and I was dizzy from his hands roaming my body. He pressed me harder to him, making me feel what he was blessed with. I bit down on my bottom lip to stifle the moan. "People...there are people still here. I need to leave. I told myself I wouldn't go down this road with you again."

Kova's hips rolled up so desperately and painfully slow while he pushed me down on him that I almost came. I imagined he was some sort of sex god in a past life with the way he moved.

"Oh, God." My back bent forward and I gripped his arm, trying to hold back the pleasure that sped through me. "We have to stop. Someone will catch us."

"Adrianna, you are the only lunatic who trains the hours that you do. You are a workhorse. There is no one else here. Trust me. I checked my cameras right before you walked in when I noticed the time."

I could swear I saw cars parked outside before I walked in here.

"Still, this isn't a good idea, Kova."

He chuckled low and deep and it sent a rush of euphoria down my spine. My hips moved over his length thickening beneath me.

Tipping my chin up to look at him, he whispered, "This has *never* been a good idea, Ria. Never."

"So we need to stop before it goes any further. I thought that was the plan, us never to be like this again."

"Stop thinking and tell me what you feel, what you want, Ria. Tell me what you need."

I shook my head, and swallowed hard and stayed quiet. I didn't trust myself.

Kova reached up and pulled down one strap of my leotard. Chills broke out on my skin as he dragged his tongue from my shoulder to my ear. I arched into him. "It is okay... your body tells me what you want, and I plan to give it to you," he said, and tugged my lobe into his mouth.

I groaned and squeezed my eyes shut. A part of me wanted to say no, but I couldn't form the word. My nipples strained against my leotard. I curled my fingers around the collar of his shirt, I was so close to ripping it. I needed to feel his skin, to see if he was as hot as I was. He had to feel how wet I was, there was no way he didn't.

"You *know* I think you are strong," he whispered.

"Ohh, ah...it would just be nice to hear it occasionally. Tell me that you're proud of me, tell me you notice how hard I work."

I didn't know how I managed to get all that out.

"Believe me, *malysh*, I notice *everything* about you." Kova chuckled.

Pulling back, he forced me to look at him. His eyes blazed as hot as a roaring fire. His lips were plump and delectable, and I wanted to bite down on them when he drew closer.

"We have a very complicated relationship." His voice was hoarse against my lips as he pulled down my other strap, stopping just before my breasts fell out. "If I applaud you for your hard work, hard work the other elites are putting in as well, then you might slack hearing you did well. People succeed when they do not hear it because they push harder hoping for it. I hardly praise anyone. I need you focused and solid, just like I need all my gymnasts. There is a method to my madness, Ria." Kova paused and tilted his head to the side. "Do you trust me?"

I hesitated. Such a loaded question when it came to him. Nevertheless, I answered honestly.

"Yes."

He yanked down the top of my leotard and my breasts fell free. Cool air teased my nipples, causing them to bunch and pucker. Kova didn't look down though, he kept his eyes trained on mine.

"Do I give you what you need?" he asked.

In the gym? Yes. Right now? No. Like hell I was going to tell him he had me so worked up I wanted to have sex with him. I hadn't been this intimate with him since New Year's Eve, not even in my hotel room last month where no one could see or hear a thing. Yet, here we were, in his office, where anyone could just walk in whenever they wanted. If I didn't know any better, I'd say Kova had a thing for living on the wild side and thrived on getting caught. Maybe an exhibitionist was hiding in there.

Maybe I did too.

I swallowed hard and met his dark gaze under his hat. His nostrils flared. His hand reached out and palmed my breast. I sucked in an audible breath and stretched up on my tippy-toes at the pressure he applied, and almost came. But when his fingers danced across my nipple, tugging on the rosy bud, I lost all common sense.

Spinning his hat around so it was backwards, I pulled his face to mine and attacked his mouth.

"Good girl." He grinned against my lips. I tried to wiggle my legs out from between his thighs so I could climb him, but he wouldn't let me. My attempt turned into me riding his length over his shorts, panting as I did. The pressure and force were too much to bear. Moisture coated my skin. I was about to combust.

"You are so wet I can feel it through our clothes," Kova growled into my mouth. I bit and pulled and sucked on his tongue like a starved animal. Grabbing the hem of his shirt, I tore it up his body and ripped it off him. His hands were back on my breasts, massaging and kneading them. My eyes rolled shut, and my hands roamed his firm chest, down his abs, over each sharp muscle until I reached his hard pecs. Kova was so strong and virile. It'd been too long since I had sex, and I needed it desperately. I didn't realize how badly until now.

I whimpered, wiggling again, but he didn't move. "Kova, please, let go."

"No, you are going to come like this, riding my dick. Then I am going to fuck you."

"Fuck..." I tested the word on my tongue and shook my head. "Fucking is definitely a bad idea."

"I am getting back inside your pussy, *malysh*. It has been too long."

Well. Shit.

My lips parted and my eyes glazed over when he spoke like that. Reaching forward with my mouth, I bit down on his nipple. Hard. His cock twitched and Kova flinched. His hand flew to the back of my head and tugged on my hair. He tried to pull me away, but I bit down harder and ran my tongue in circles over the bite mark.

Kova moaned. I couldn't believe he moaned from nipple play. Another thing he shared with me without realizing it. My hands scratched and pulled at his flesh without a care in the world from the orgasm rising inside me. I wanted to break his skin, score it with my nails and teeth, mark my territory. The power he had on me, restricting my movement, heightened everything. I throbbed with need.

I bit down hard and a metallic taste filled my mouth. There was something about Kova that turned me into a savage.

"Ohhhhh, *malysh*," he moaned, "bite harder." Kova thrust his hips up and I cried out, my teeth locking down. A growl vibrated in his chest. "I can feel your wetness, your pussy pulsating... I cannot wait to be deep inside you, to blow all over you."

"Kova, please." I didn't even know what I was begging for, but I was panting harder and harder as the pleasure rose and rose, and then I saw stars. My head whipped back and I tried to rub myself into him as I orgasmed so hard I couldn't see straight. His cock was swollen and wide and it felt divine like this. I'd never come in this position before, but between the width of his dick and the extremely little space I had between my hips, I cried out in absolute bliss.

"That is it," he gritted. "Let me hear you."

Just as I finished, Kova loosened his hold and spread his legs. He ripped the leo completely off me as I tugged his shorts down and his cock sprang free. It was magnificent and beautiful and already dripping…and bare. I knew I should've told him to wear a condom, especially after everything that went down between us, but I couldn't, not when I was this far gone in the heat of the moment.

I didn't give him any time. I climbed his body and he gripped my hips, guiding me over him. He slid his hands down to my ass and impaled me hard and fast. Our lips collided and I screamed into his mouth. Despite the orgasm I just had, I was tender and it hurt. He freed a hand and held the back of my neck, holding me to him as he swallowed my scream. It'd been months since I had Kova inside me and it felt like I was a damn virgin all over again.

"You are so tight, baby." He breathed against my mouth. "Do not fucking move or I will tear you up."

I didn't move. He shoved my hips down and I went willingly, melting over him and tearing a little bit. I clenched, and he twitched in response. He rolled his pelvis into mine, hard and hot, barely moving his hips, so I got both his cock inside hitting the back of my pussy and the pleasure on my clit at the same time. I bit his shoulder and lapped at him with my tongue. I'd never bitten anyone before and I couldn't stop myself from doing it. He brought it out in me.

I rubbed myself on him. Kova tilted his head back just a bit. Our eyes locked. He lowered his eyelashes halfway and the brilliant green of his eyes glowed with sensuality and forbidden thoughts.

"I know what it is you want," he whispered as he slowly thrusted in and out of me. I was so damn tight, I could feel every inch of him, every groove, every vein. A hot breath escaped me. "I always know, Ria. Let me give you what you need. I just need you to trust me."

I pulled up, then slammed down, and panted against his lips. "Trusting you terrifies me. You broke that trust once." I had to figure out a way to keep my emotions out of this. I couldn't trust him not to hurt me again.

His pupils dilated, hurt flashed in his eyes but it was gone as quickly as it appeared.

Kova's callused hand skimmed up my side. My body heated and I tried desperately not to show how much his touch affected me. Without pulling out of me, he carried me to his couch and sat down. He tilted my head up until I looked straight into his eyes. "Ride me hard and fuck me good, Ria. The way I fuck you. Let me inside."

All air left my lungs. I'd never heard a guy say that before and for some ungodly reason, I wanted to give him what he asked for. Between his Russian accent and flushed cheeks, he could have anything he wanted.

Except… I bit my bottom lip and chewed on it. I didn't exactly know how to ride anyone. I assumed it was a specific position or a speed or something. Kova noticed the lost look on my face and took the initiative. He grabbed my wrists and placed my hands on his chest, then the back of his knuckles dragged along my bikini line before he gripped my hips roughly and guided me up, then rolled my hips under to get that delicious friction when I came down. God, it felt so good, I moaned. He could just keep doing this. It was too good.

My stomach dipped and I held my breath. I loved his hands on me. Like he wanted them there as much as I did, like he couldn't get enough of touching me. He showed me the pace he wanted and when he let go, I continued, but I didn't go all the way down, it hurt a little for that.

His hands palmed my breasts. Then he pinched my nipples so hard my mouth fell open and a breathy moan escaped me again, somewhere lost between pain and ecstasy. Fire zipped through my body. I almost asked him to stop, but he let up, somehow knowing just how far to go. I clenched his cock with my inner muscles, both from the pain and mind-blowing pleasure only he could give me. His head arched back. His eyes were dark and hooded. I glanced away and smiled, liking the satisfied look on him and knowing I gave it to him.

"Just like that… You feel so fucking incredible."

Another husky sigh rolled off my lips. "I've never done it like this before… Where I'm on top. It feels different…better than being on the bottom."

His eyes flared. "I would sure hope not, Adrianna. You better have not had anyone else's cock but mine."

A devious surge sparked in me, my opening to play with him. To give him what only I knew he wanted. A sly smile graced my face. I didn't know why I got off on taunting him, especially while he was inside me, but I did. I loved it. I fed off it, and I know he did too. It just heightened the pleasure for both of us.

A deceitful honeyed giggle fell from my lips. I smirked and my eyes grew heavy, alluding there was more going on than he knew.

I hadn't been with anyone else but him, but he didn't need to know that.

Kova sat up and roughly gripped the back of my neck while his other arm circled me. He held me down on his cock until he was balls deep—I could feel them between my ass. My breathing deepened as I felt him jerk inside me.

"Do not taunt me. You know how much I like it." He slowly thrusted his cock into me, inch by inch.

I panted into his mouth. "It's not taunting when it's the truth."

"Adrianna," he warned, thrusting hard. I gasped, my eyes closing. I never wanted this feeling to end.

"You can't possibly think I'll only ever have one dick for the rest of my life," I said, rising up and coming all the way down, and holding it. My pussy clenched again, trying to adjust to his width. "Not when it can feel like this…" I moaned again, rocking back and forth, feeling my orgasm climbing higher and higher. With his hold on me, I leaned back and palmed his knees behind me. I grinded my hips so hard, my clit could feel it. Kova was a poison, a drug. He made me wanton and untamed. I became someone I didn't know, but most of all, he made me feel desired and sexy, and I was realizing that I craved that feeling.

"I guess that is fair." He bit my breast, then soothed it with his tongue. "You might be the tightest pussy I will ever have, but we both know you are not the only pussy I will ever have, not tonight at least," he growled and thrusted so deep I was certain he hit the back of my cervix.

"You're such a fuck, you know that?" I tried to get up and slapped his hand away. He snickered and dropped his face to my neck, his stubble grazing my skin.

"What, *malysh*, only you can play the game? You asked for it, I gave it to you. Do not act like you are hurt."

He was right, I did ask for it, and the truth stung. I may not be the only pussy he'd ever have, but it was my pussy currently wrapped around his cock. My body he was beneath. My teeth and nail marks that reddened his skin—*have fun explaining those to your girlfriend.*

"Why are we having sex?"

"Why the fuck not," he retorted, pushing hard into me. "You want me, I want you. End of story. Now shut up."

I shook my head in disbelief. He was such an arrogant asshole, and I realized he'd never change.

"News flash, I still don't trust you. Truth is, I can't. What the fuck was I thinking? You have a girlfriend," I spat.

Fire ignited so bright inside me I was ready to shatter. My heart pounded, as well as a throb on the side of my head. I wasn't sure where that came from or why, maybe pent up resentment I had toward him I hadn't realized I was harboring. It wasn't often I exploded like that, I was usually good at curbing my emotions. But it took a six foot plus Russian with hella good looks and a dick attitude to set me off.

"You're an asshole."

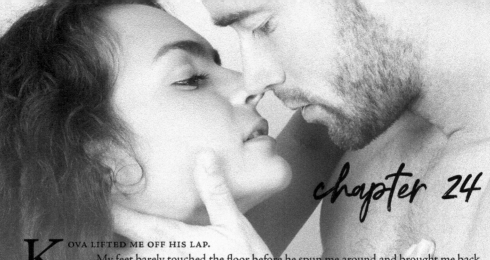

chapter 24

KOVA LIFTED ME OFF HIS LAP.

My feet barely touched the floor before he spun me around and brought me back down on him. My back landed against his chest and I lashed out, trying to free myself.

"You and that mouth of yours." He dropped his forearm across my front and pinned my arms to my sides. Slamming our legs together, his long, thick penis pushed against my sex.

"Let go of me!"

"Not everything is what it seems, Ria. Just because I am with Katja, do not presume you know what goes on behind closed doors, even if I insinuate there is more. Everyone's life is nothing but a façade. We all lie."

I thrashed again, only this time it backfired, and I whimpered from the feel of his cock against my clit.

"I don't lie to you, Kova."

"I can recall a time or two when you have lied."

The past year flashed through my mind. He was right—I had lied a few times. The thing was, I wasn't really upset at him. I was mad at myself for not being strong enough to refuse him, because the reality was that I wanted him. Needed him on a primal level it scared me.

"Stop fighting me or I will hold you down and fuck you senseless."

The thought of him doing that sent me into a tizzy. Wetness seeped from me on to his warm shaft. My head fell back, my eyes rolled shut, and I clenched my thighs together, squeezing his dick between my tender lips. A sensual wave started in my hips and I rubbed myself on him.

"You like that idea. Do not try to deny it, your body tells me you do."

"Kova." His name was a faint whimper on my lips. I squeezed his cock again out of pure animalistic need.

Kova inhaled a large breath of air. I opened my eyes just a crack and spotted the crown of his penis, purple and swollen, peeking out between us. His thighs were massive pushed up against my slender ones and it reminded me of something he said earlier—I was the beauty and he was the beast.

Kova's fingers trembled as he struggled to fight his feral appetite for sex. Fingers dug into my flesh, his palms were slick with sweat as he raised my hips and rolled his back. My feet couldn't reach the floor, so he pretty much had me suspended above him. I didn't move, and he didn't push inside.

"What are you waiting for?" I whispered. I reached out and gripped the armrest of the couch to steady myself.

Without another word, he pulled my body close to his and pushed the tip inside. I sighed, and he pushed in a little more.

"Oh hell," I said, melting on him, and my legs fell open over his knees. His large hand gently squeezed my breast and I almost sank all the way down.

"I think my girl likes the idea of me holding her down and surrendering to me," he said, his words surrounded me like a tightening rope. I did. I really did. "I could take away your power, your control, and make you forget your name." Then he slid all the way in. I tensed. It hurt in this angle. It was different and not all that comfortable.

"It feels like you're going to pop through my pelvis." I gritted my teeth together and tried to stand.

"Just relax," Kova whispered. He sat up, leaned forward, and wrapped an arm around my waist. The warmth of his body against mine pacified me and brought me an odd sense of comfort. I reveled in his embrace. He shifted deeper into me until we molded together too perfectly. "Give it a minute."

After what felt like an eternity, Kova's hands began a sensual roam of my torso. My nipples puckered and his hips shifted in the most erotic way. He slid in and out, slow and delicious. Legs spread wide, I was exposed and didn't care as long as he didn't stop. The blood in my veins ignited and I let out a blissful sigh as I laid my head back against his chest.

"That is what I want to hear." Kova grabbed my hand and placed it over our joined bodies, making sure my fingers touched his velvety skin where it glided in and out of me. "Feel that between us? That chemistry, that fire. The harmony of two people who are so wrong for each other but somehow come together, throwing everything off balance to the point that nothing makes sense but it feels right. That is us. That is trust. You do not let someone into your body you do not trust. Look how wet you get when my cock is inside you, how wild you get when our lips collide, how hard I am every single time I am around you. I do stupid things, I know I do, but when it is just us, it all makes sense."

Guiding my hand down, Kova placed my hand over his heavy sack. He squeezed hard and tight, too tight in my opinion, then he loosened his grip as he pulled out, only to squeeze again as he thrust in.

"Kova…please…" My mouth was dry, and I couldn't open my eyes. I squirmed on him, the pressure was the most powerfully intense eroticism yet. Spreading his legs wider, my hips opened more. One of his hands found my clit and ran in circles over the tight bundle of nerves, the other reached up and wrapped around the front of my neck.

"Trust me," he said near my ear.

My heart sped up, panic tore through my body, frightened that Kova was going to choke me to death. "Trust me," he said again. Applying pressure to my throat as he thrust in, he seized hard. A sharp ache shot through my pussy and I tried to cry out but I had no voice. The air in my throat constricted and I waited until I couldn't take it any longer. I gripped his balls hard and dug my nails in, twisting slightly. He twitched and let go, so did I.

I swallowed hard, and licked my lips, shocked that I almost came.

"Holy. Fucking. Shit. Kova. Do it again. Please, do it again."

Obsession filled me over this newfound pleasure. My body started moving of its own accord as I became ravenous for more. I twisted my feet around his calves and held on. I wanted him to do it again, and again, and again.

Kova turned my face toward his and our eyes locked. He grasped my neck again, this time a little harder. "I wish you could see yourself through my eyes, only then would you realize how much you mean to me."

His voice shook with candid raw honesty. It was almost unbearable. We were beyond lust, beyond infatuation. This was way more, a crazed obsession with deeply seated emotions we didn't want to acknowledge because everything in society told us it was wrong.

I leaned forward and captured his lips with mine, and gave him the deepest, slowest, sexiest kiss I could. I made love to his mouth. His hand came up and threaded in my hair at my nape, holding me to him, but I took his wrist and moved it back to my clit.

Chuckling, Kova resumed his ministrations. I was close, so close to the peak of forbidden desires I was ready to tip over it with him.

"Oh… Oh…" My voice grew louder. I didn't know who I was anymore.

The pleasure was so powerful it propelled me forward and I sat up and tucked my knees under me. I saw stars from this angle and I realized I wanted Kova to show me more. More ways to get off. More ways to find pleasure. More. Everything. I couldn't think straight.

Placing my hands on his knees, I gasped, and cried out. Kova was quick and had one hand around my throat, the other around my hips. My back arched, and his hips plunged into me at the same time I shoved down on him so hard I didn't even recognize my voice.

"Don't stop." I trembled violently.

"That is it, *malysh*, fuck me." I slammed down again. He squeezed my throat. "Keep going. Fuck me. Fuck me. Fuck me harder, Adrianna."

Jesus Christ. Moisture dripped from between us and I saw it hit the floor. It was tinged pink but I didn't care.

"My girl likes that? When I tell her to fuck me?" I nodded. When Kova demanded that I fuck him, and he drove in deep and rough and held on to me, it was a high no drug could ever bring. They were magical words infused with a secret elixir by the damn devil.

"Do I have your trust? Say it."

"Yes, Kova. You have my trust."

Kova placed a kiss to my shoulder blade. He bit down, lapped at my skin, and then pumped his cock harder into my pussy. Heavy breathing and the sounds of raw, passionate sex slapping together echoed in my ears. We both were making sounds, both on the edge of something so extreme that I had a feeling he'd never orgasmed this hard before.

"Your pussy is squeezing me, you are close. I bet all I have to do is say the word and you will come all over my cock."

He rubbed my clit faster with four fingers and leaned close to my ear. The stubble from his jaw grazed my skin. "Fuck. Me. *Malysh*," he whispered, then he bit my neck.

I went off like a rocket. I cried out and clawed the shit out of his legs, then reached behind me and grabbed his hair.

"Kova… Oh my God, don't stop!" He shoved my hips down on him and continued rubbing my swollen clit as I came so hard my thighs quivered and my body shook.

"That is it. Give it to me. I love feeling you come on my cock." When my orgasm subsided, Kova said, "Now, my turn."

"Take it." I managed to respond.

It didn't take but three hard as hell pumps and his penis was pulsating. Pulling out, he hauled me back to his chest and blew his load all over my stomach and breasts. His groan turned into a growl and vibrated against my back as his body flexed and constricted while he orgasmed all over me. His hold on my waist was tighter than ever.

As he came down, his body softened beneath me and his fingers loosened. He looked over my shoulder and we both looked down at his fluid all over me. I'd never seen it like this before—there was so much. He lifted his hand and rubbed it into me, all over my tender breasts, down my stomach to my pussy. He pressed on my clit, then cupped me before pushing his fingers inside. He kissed the side of my neck, lapping at the curve of my shoulder. He cupped my jaw and turned my head to his and kissed my mouth.

We sighed together in ecstasy. This was the most intense sex I'd ever experienced in my life, with a man who should've never given it to me.

Pulling me down to the couch, Kova cradled me to his body, keeping his fingers tucked into my sex. He expelled a restful breath and threw his leg over mine.

The room was hushed, peaceful, and infused with the smell of sex. I burrowed into his body and Kova murmured a string of words in Russian, words I'd never heard him speak. I didn't stop him to ask what they meant, I just waited until he was done. His breathing slowed, deepened, and I knew he'd fallen asleep.

Sated. Kova was completely sated. And surprisingly enough, so was I.

chapter 25

A BUZZING SOUND RESONATED IN THE BACKGROUND.

I nestled deeper into sleep, swathed in warmth, and feeling so incredibly good I didn't want to wake up; but the sound grew closer and closer and music played until I had no choice but to open my eyes.

I was confused by my surroundings. My mind fuzzy, eyes shadowy. I looked down at the weight pressed upon me…and everything came roaring back.

What time was it? When did we fall asleep? Was it the next day? Where were my clothes?

Then I remembered I'd only had a leo on, and it was now on the floor. Heart racing in my throat, I tried to sit up, but Kova locked his arm around me. He pressed tighter, his erection straining against my butt. Warmth surged through me for a moment but I was able to block it out.

"Hmmm…" He nuzzled against my neck, licking me and wrapping his lips around my fevered flesh. Pushing his thigh between mine, he said, "*Malysh*," and I had to wonder if he knew it was me and not Katja. His fingers were still inside my wet pussy, his other hand cupping my breast, and the head of his penis pressed into my ass.

I elbowed him. That was a one-way street.

His phone rang again, but he didn't hear it. My heart pounded in my ears, it had to be Katja calling him, but Kova was in a bottomless slumber; I had to think quick how to wake him up.

"Kova," I whispered, nudging him again. Either this man could sleep like the dead or he was seriously exhausted. I looked over my shoulder and saw his eyes were closed and not moving.

His fingers pinched my nipple too hard and I reared back, my ass pressing into him, which caused his head to press at my puckered hole. His phone rang again.

"Kova," I said, swallowing hard. I could hardly find my voice, my nerves were sky high. If Kova didn't answer, I could bet she'd drive over here looking for him. I would if I were her.

A guttural moan escaped Kova's parted lips. Low and deep, the sound came from his chest, and it was sexy as hell. But then he uttered a name I never expected to hear while he was sleeping, and I almost died. *Died*.

"Adrianna." He pushed his cock harder at my ass. I froze in shock. There was no way in hell I was allowing him to stick his dick there, but more importantly, he said *my* name. Not Katja's.

I had to wonder if he'd said my name in the past while sleeping next to her.

Lapping the curve of my neck, Kova breathed hot air across my skin before he bit down and latched on.

I shivered, my back bowed, and I moved just enough so his cock wasn't in my ass.

His phone rang again.

Sharp teeth bit down and broke my skin as he rocked against me so seductively I couldn't stop the moan from falling from my lips. He held me with his mouth as his dick pressed against my entrance, right where his fingers were. He removed his fingers then pushed the tip in and my body surged with lazy warmth. I lifted my leg and placed it on top of his, driving my hips back. Another new angle for me that brought me more ecstasy than the last. Chills danced through my entire body from the smooth glide. No pain, just pleasure, and a perfect fit. My eyes rolled shut and I sank into him.

Kova held still, his body tensed, and for a split second I thought he was going to unleash on me.

"Kova," I murmured. He reared his hips back and then slammed into me with a grunt. I was using his arm as a pillow and turned my head to bite down.

His phone rang yet again and anxiety shot down my spine. My stomach knotted with fear that something bad was about to happen.

"Kova," I said louder, but it came out as a moan. How the hell he fucked this good in his sleep was beyond me. His mouth loosened on my neck and his hand that cupped my breast slid to my throat. His fingers wrapped around and applied pressure. I swallowed and steadied myself for what I knew was coming.

My heart raced with excitement. I couldn't fucking wait.

His grip around my neck grew tighter, and he pumped harder. He pulled on my knee, yanking my leg back to my chest to settle deeper in me.

I almost orgasmed from this new angle.

"*Malysh…*" he said, his hips an unadulterated wave of giving and taking. He surged in, my legs trembled, and my toes curled under. Nails clawing and elbows connecting with his ribs, I bit down harder than ever and yelled his name over his ringing phone.

Kova stiffened. "There is no better way to wake up than with you in my arms. I wish I could wake up like this every day." His voice was rough from sleep.

I blinked in surprise at his admission. "Your phone has been ringing nonstop."

He grunted and continued to pump into me. "Fuck the phone."

I tried not to laugh but I couldn't stop the giggle that escaped me. "Kova, I'm serious. I think something is wrong. It hasn't stopped ringing. I think you should get it."

Extending my leg in a straight line near our bodies, he leaned up on one elbow and loomed over me so he was on top. He grabbed my jaw and pushed all the way in. I inhaled.

"Think again. If you would rather I stop what I am doing right now to answer a fucking phone call, then you are not being fucked properly. The only thing I give a fuck about right now is your tight pussy and how I am going to fuck you senseless."

Kova leaned down and kissed me. His kisses got me every time. One touch of his tongue on mine and I was drunk on him, imagining filthy thoughts of things he could do to me that I would never speak out loud.

"I want to fuck until we both cannot walk. Why, why, why…only with you do I ever act like a goddamned savage." His face was a field of ruined emotions. "Only you…"

Holy. Shit. I blushed so hard my cheeks burned. Grabbing his jaw in both hands, I yanked his face down to mine and delved into his mouth. He moaned in response, I loved when he did that. It got me so hot. His phone rang and I pulled back, wide-eyed and worried. He narrowed his eyes and gave me a warning look. Kova sat back and put my leg on his shoulder, my other leg hung helplessly off the side of the couch. I was open to him. He reached between us with his free hand and I thought he was going to play with my tender clit, but he shocked me.

He placed his thumb to my ass and applied pressure as he rubbed the puckered little hole. I tried to pull my leg away to move, but he had a firm grip on it. My body convulsed and I shuddered around his cock, squeezing tighter. My hips flew up and my head whipped back, eyes rolling into the back of my head. I clawed for his chest but I couldn't reach. I yelled out. Wetness dripped from me. This was a different kind of pleasure that sent me into oblivion. I couldn't think straight, not liking his fingers where they were, but unexpectedly wanting it even more.

"Still thinking about my fucking phone, Ria?" he asked, pushing on my little hole as he withdrew his dick, then slowly reentered me. He kept doing this, his cock sliding in and out, his finger teasing my hole, timing it perfectly. Whimpers and moans sounded from me. I didn't hold back. My clit throbbed. It was like two different kinds of pleasure, and I wanted it all, and more.

My teeth dug into my bottom lip, then I opened my mouth, but the only word that came out was his name in a breathless sigh.

I couldn't even open my eyes.

He snickered. "That is what I thought. Now reach back and grab the armrest. I want to see your tits bounce."

"Ko…Kova…" I couldn't even muster his name.

"Look at these beautiful tits and the way they move as I fuck you. I bet I can fit my whole mouth over one. Your nipples are so red and hard…" A throaty laugh escaped him. His thumb massaged my back entrance and I let out a soft moan, liking the feeling way more than I should have. It was euphoric and erotic and forbidden, and everything I should not want. But I did. "I see you like when I play with your ass."

"No… Yes… No, oh fuck." I made no sense. Truth was, I did like it, but I was too embarrassed to admit that. All I knew was that I was about to come hard.

He leaned over me, his lips above my mine. "Remember the night I took your virginity?" I nodded at his wild eyes, the desire climbing inside me. It was a night I'd never forget. "Then you must remember when I played with this… How I used my tongue here." His thumb rubbed harder and faster. My hips surged into his. I nodded subtly, and he smiled ever so slowly as a groan slipped from his lips.

I'd loved it, I'd just never told him.

"Maybe I should push harder, to see how much you can take. Every time I push"—he applied more pressure to my sensitive hole—"your pussy squeezes my cock. Ah, it makes me want to do filthy things to you."

I was panting so hard, my chest rising and falling. I was close to the brink of insanity.

"No. Too much. Please."

His hips undulated into me with precision, thrusting slow and hard. His body rolled in the most delicious way. His abs contracted. He made little sounds himself and I never wanted him to stop. The pleasure was too divine, to the extreme, and damn good. He pulled his hand back, licked his finger, and placed it back at my hole.

Our eyes locked and I let him see what I desired, what I craved, hoping he could read my thoughts and give me what I couldn't say aloud.

Kova slowly pulled out of me and I started to protest, when he reached under my waist and flipped me around. I grabbed onto the armrest to steady myself and he hiked my hips up so I was on my knees. I glanced over my shoulder. Kova stood like a Greek god behind me with one foot on the floor next to the couch and his other leg bent right behind me.

"Turn around," he ordered, his voice thick and husky. With his palms spread out on my lower back, he slid them higher with pressure along my spine, pushing my chest to the couch. "Arch your back. Yes, like that." He leaned in, his long erection grazing my inner thigh while his hands skimmed around to cup my breasts. His chest was pressed to my back and I gripped the armrest as he played with my nipples.

Kova slid one hand lower to my sex. I pushed my hips back into him when he found my clit and drew little circles around the tender bud. I drew in a breath and angled my face toward his, searching for his mouth. He kissed me, nibbling my lip, then broke the kiss and pressed his mouth to my back, nipping my skin as he made his way down. Tiny little sparks of passion pulsed in my clit with each bite.

I was breathless for this man.

Using his hand, Kova tapped my hip. Hot with need, warmth seeped down my inner thigh when I spread my legs apart. My cheeks flamed from embarrassment. Kova gripped my hips and rotated them back, then his tongue was flat on the inside of my leg, licking up the wetness dripping from me.

I gasped in surprise. I would have died of mortification if I wasn't so curious as to what he would do next.

His warm tongue trailed upward to my pussy, where he licked me from top to bottom. I moaned, which in turn made Kova growl.

"Oh…do that again, please," I asked. He did, and released another growl. I felt the vibration on my sex. My legs quivered with desire. A heavy amount of fluid dripped from me and Kova made sure to lick every bit up. My ass pressed into his face, and I didn't care one bit. His palms covered each butt cheek and spread them apart. I froze for a moment, equally anxious and excited.

I had a feeling I knew where he was going, and the thought made my knees shake with desire.

With his tongue flat to my center, he swiped up and slid it into my pussy. I let out a cry, pushing even more into his face as his tongue stroked me on the inside, curling and sliding. Kova's mouth closed around my sensitive lips and his teeth grazed my tender flesh, and bit down. Instinctively, I swung back with my hand, but he caught my wrist and wrenched my arm behind me and held it down to my lower back, just as his tongue made contact with my ass. My eyes rolled shut and my body turned to putty as his magic tongue rubbed against the little hole. I moaned, not hiding how I felt about this, and opened my body to him, eagerly pushing my ass into his face.

"Please," was all I said. He didn't stop. Not when he slipped two fingers into my pussy and stroked me the way he kissed my ass. He went to town, pleasing me and showing me just how much he enjoyed what he was doing.

Kova was a giver.

He pulled his mouth away but left his fingers inside me. I whimpered and wiggled my ass in the air. Kova chuckled, and gently rubbed my butt cheek. Before I realized what he was doing, he lifted his palm and brought it back down and smacked my ass. Not once, not twice, but three times, his thumb and fingers stroking my pussy as he did.

"Again," I asked and gripped the couch. My hips surged back. He smacked me again, and this time I almost came.

"How do you do it?" I asked breathlessly. I could feel myself pulsating and on the verge of letting go. "How do you bring me so high and make me feel so good?"

He slipped his fingers out and flipped me back around. Our eyes met and something snapped into place. My body opened to him immediately and his fingers were back on my clit, pinching the pink bud, his other hand stroking his heavy cock. He positioned himself at my entrance and I raised my hips to him.

The room stood still as we stared at each other. "I know what my girl likes. I always know what she likes, even when she cannot admit it to me."

He pushed the tip of his cock into my pussy and my eyes widened thinking about what he said. He did know me, sometimes better than I knew myself.

"Tell me, Ria," he said, thrusting all the way in, then he pulled out and slowly pushed back in. His hips rocked back and forth and I clenched around his thickness and sighed. "I know how much you love my tongue on your tight ass, but what would you do if I put my cock there?"

My back arched, and my body shivered with need. The thought sent me over the edge. "Oh my God, Kova. I'm gonna come. I'm gonna come. I'm gonna come. Don't stop."

"Tell me when you finish completely so I can pull out. I am going to come all over your sweet pussy while you think about all the filthy things you want me to do to you that you cannot admit to."

I clenched my thighs and shook my head. "Don't you dare pull out."

"Fuck!" His dick jerked. "Do not say that to me. I have to pull out."

My pussy pulsated as the orgasm climbed higher. A faint sound echoed in the distance but I couldn't focus on it, not while his fingers were playing with my ass. I didn't want him to stop, I wanted us to come together, and I wanted us to come hard. I wanted to feel him shoot his load inside me, feel it seep out, feel him throb, and watch his face as he experienced sheer bliss with me.

I locked eyes with Kova, his face was flushed, like I knew mine was. His lips were swollen and his eyes were lost in a dark cave of desire. I licked my fingers, and he watched as I brought them to my clit and rubbed. I widened my hips and wiggled my ass on his fingers, whispering for more as his eyes stayed fixated on my hand. He pushed just enough for the tip of his finger to enter my ass.

It was all too much and I wasn't prepared for the euphoria that shot through me.

I cried out. Tears fell from my eyes. I'd never had an orgasm like this before. Kova grabbed my hip. "I… I am…" I couldn't find words. I was lost to sensation. My pussy throbbed, quivered, and I was two seconds from coming hard.

"Give it to me," Kova demanded, leaning over me. His finger pushing in more, but not too much. "Oh shit, Ria, you are squeezing so tight… I need to pull out."

I couldn't let him do that. It was irrational but I was too far gone to think. Too addicted to what he was giving me. Too obsessed. I needed to feel this moment with him, in me, touching both entrances.

Reaching up so quickly, I pulled his face to mine and bit down on his lip. He fell onto my chest and I locked my ankles around his back and dug my heels in. I loved his weight on me. There was so much fluid between us. My inner thighs were slippery with it and I knew his were too.

"Finish with me. I need to feel it," I said against his mouth.

He clenched his eyes shut, fighting it. "No."

"Yes," I countered. "Come inside me."

"No…" he said, so full of pleasure and desire.

I scored his back with my nails and bit his chest and pulled his hair. He was going to need to be covered up by the time I was done with him. I sucked his neck and pulled away with a pop. I didn't know who I was anymore.

He groaned. "Oh God, why are you doing this to me?"

"I gave you a hickey." I bit where I sucked.

Kova surged forward and I met his thrusts with mine. We grunted with each drive. I yanked his hair and twirled my tongue with his, just barely, making him work for it, as I pulled his hair even more. He was like a starving animal. His pace sped up and his hand wrapped around my throat. I huffed, pushing my breasts to his chest as he hit the right spot when I lifted my hips off the couch.

"Right there," I said, nearly choking myself. "It feels so good right there."

"Fuck… I feel it. I am so deep. Holy shit, I cannot stop."

Our hips slammed together. I tightened my ankles around his back, and I licked the shell of his ear and moaned.

He didn't hesitate. I didn't expect the force. Or the pleasure that followed either. "Fuck!" His voice thundered.

I gasped, throbbing, and coming so hard. My eyes rolled shut as Kova applied pressure to my neck. He roared and pulled his hand away from my ass, and gripped the armrest next to my head, using it to push off and drive into me as he pumped his hips hard against mine, and released inside me.

"I can feel you coming in me," I said, rubbing myself all over him.

"I…cannot…stop… You are mine and only mine." He wrapped his arms around my back and grasped my neck and lower back as he pushed off the couch and drove into me like a fucking pro.

"Only you, Ria," he groaned, "only you. I cannot live without you or this feeling you bring me. I want to be in you every day, all day, for the rest of my life. I want to wake up next to you, make you only mine, and do this every fucking day. This is heaven. You are my everything."

His voice broke and my heart shattered at the conviction and desire he shouldn't feel but did. Kova's head reared back, a vein protruded from his neck as we exploded together, crashing into oblivion.

Kova fell on top of me and gave me all his weight. I pulled his body close to mine and wrapped my arms around his back, and lazily dragged my nails over him. His cock twitched, still inside me.

"Is this normal?" My voice cracked.

"What?" he asked, not moving. My heart was racing, I could feel his heart beating against my chest.

"When two people connect so deeply when they have sex, is this normal? I feel like I'm on another dimension when I'm with you."

Kova looked at me. "No, it is not. It is not normal at all," he said with such genuine sincerity I knew he wasn't lying.

"Have you…" I glanced away for a second and licked my parched lips. "Have you ever felt like that with anyone else?"

I swallowed, not sure I should've asked that. He used his finger to trace over my lips. "No, never. Only you."

My eyes shot to his. "Really?"

He nodded. "Only you, Ria. Why do you think I cannot get enough? I have never felt like this with anyone else. All I know is that I am hooked on all of you. Hooked on your body, hooked on your smile, hooked on your personality, hooked on your ambition, *hooked on you*. I can only hope you feel the same way."

"Yes," I said softly.

Leaning forward, Kova licked his lips before he pressed them to mine and kissed me. But this wasn't any regular kiss. It was a kiss that wrapped around my soul and embraced the worst and best parts of me.

He kissed me like he loved me.

Pulling back, Kova stared at me with nothing but raw affection. The ache in his gaze rendered me speechless and I found myself staring back. In the stillness of his office with our naked bodies pressed together, he studied me for a long moment. He reached forward and brushed back the strands of hair that stuck to my mouth.

His jaw was propped on his fist as his eyes lovingly roamed my face. A lyrical melody of Russian filled the space between us, like he was singing me a song. With my heart in my throat, I didn't do anything other than blink and listen. He spoke softly, intimately, grazing my cheek with the back of his finger. I watched his mouth move, his tongue tapped his teeth between words. His brows furrowed and thin lines creased the corners of his eyes as he spoke. A dozen emotions crossed his face. This was his vulnerable side, a side of him I was not often privy to. Only when the layers peeled back, and I got to the core of him, was I rewarded with juicy little seeds I coveted for myself.

Our small moment of closeness broke at the sound of Kova's cell phone ringing again. He droned on about not wanting to answer the phone, but he rolled off me with a content smile. As he stood, I took in his magnificent back and round ass until I saw all the marks I left on him.

I hissed. There was no way he was going to be able to hide them from Katja, or the hickey that I stupidly gave him.

Shit. Shit. Shit.

He turned around on his heels with his phone cradled in his hand, distress spanning his face. He looked up. His Adam's apple bobbed and he sputtered, "Get your stuff now, Adrianna."

I froze. Immobile. The unnerving tone of his voice sent chills down my spine.

"Adrianna. Now. Get your stuff, now!" he yelled as a flash of light traveled across the windows.

"What's going on?" I asked as I shot up.

His wide eyes scanned the floor. Kova threw his shirt on, and said, "Katja is on her way."

"What!" I panicked and picked up my leotard. "I told you to answer the phone before!"

"Let us not discuss that again. Hurry up and get your stuff."

There was no way I was going to be able to get the leotard on right now, so I held it to my chest and walked to the door. I turned the knob and the door creaked open a sliver.

"Konstantin!" I froze at the sound of Katja's shrieking voice echoing down the hall. Her shoes slapped against the tiled floor.

My blood turned ice cold.

The world faded around me and the walls closed in. This was it.

Call me naive, but I truly never thought we'd get caught. I thought we'd been careful. I thought we had put up the perfect pretense and disguised our attraction to each other well.

Maybe we had, and nothing could've prepared us for someone catching us. Just like when Hayden had caught us.

I backed up and turned to face Kova, who was fully dressed. *She's here*, I mouthed, terrified and on the verge of vomiting. His eyes widened and he grabbed my shoulders to scan the office for a place for me to hide. He didn't have a closet, or a personal bathroom.

There was nowhere for me to go.

Katja's fearful voice echoed in the distance, but much closer this time.

I was trapped. We were trapped… Until my eyes fell on his desk that was enclosed all the way around.

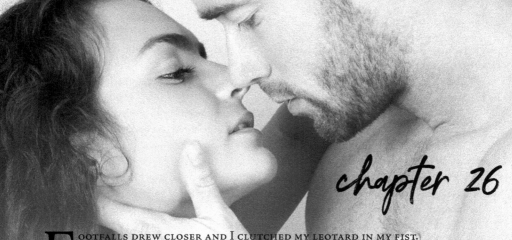

chapter 26

FOOTFALLS DREW CLOSER AND I CLUTCHED MY LEOTARD IN MY FIST.
      I huddled in a corner under the desk and covered my mouth just as the door flew open and banged against the wall.

"Konstantin?" Katja bawled. My breath caught in my throat. "Konstantin?" she said again. I wished I could see what was happening.

"Hmmm..." Kova sounded groggy.

"Wake up. *Wake up.* What are you doing?" she questioned, a shuffling noise followed.

He yawned, faking sleep. "Katja? What is going on?" I rest assured a little, not completely, that he pulled off the act. I was still naked under his desk and afraid to move my hand in fear of a sound accidentally escaping me. That'd be my luck.

"What time is it?" he asked sleepily.

"I have been calling you, texting you. I did not know where you were. I worried for you."

"Where else would I be but here?"

She continued to whine and it started to grate on my nerves. "Why did you not come home? I waited hours—"

"I had work to do, Katja," he said, his voice abrasive as steel wool. "How many times have I told you that I cannot just leave when everyone else leaves. I cannot leave when you want me to. I own a company, I have an overhead. Money does not grow on trees, you know. Someone has to do the books."

"I know that but—" She paused. "What is that mark on your neck? Is that... Is that a *hickey?*" A stiff tone replaced her saccharine one.

My eyes widened and I cupped my mouth harder.

"I missed the high bar during my workout. I fell, just barely catching myself," Kova growled. "I had a shitty night, Kat. I decided it was best I finish early and came in here to do paperwork, but I fell asleep."

Katja transitioned to her native tongue. Words like velvet fell from her lips that I assumed were terms of endearment.

"Whose car is outside?"

Fuck! I'd completely forgotten my SUV was parked out front. I really hoped this conversation would end soon so I could get out from under here and go home. The problem was, I was afraid to leave the building knowing Katja could be nearby, but I also didn't want to leave alone in the middle of the night either. In fact, I didn't even know what time it was.

"What?" he questioned.

"A car is outside. Is there someone else here with you?"

"At this hour? No, I did not know there was a car there. What does it look like?" he asked, playing dumb. Katja described it, and Kova said, "Ah, that is Adrianna's. She had a late practice, then went home with one of the other girls."

"You worked her too hard," Katja said sympathetically. I almost laughed. Damn right he fucking did.

"Then I did my job." Kova said each word with gratification, and I smiled.

"Have you ever considered that maybe she is not as talented as you think?" Katja hesitated. "Just because she wants to go to the Olympics does not mean she is qualified to. She seems… I do not know the right word…mediocre."

My heart ached at her question. A thousand different kinds of insecurities slammed into me at once and I questioned whether I was good enough. I wanted to leave. I felt like an intruder listening in on their conversation and I didn't want to hear any more.

"I would never put my time and effort into someone who was *mediocre*. I know God given talent when I see it, and Adrianna has it." Kova turned defensive. "She is brilliant, artistic, and imaginative. There is nothing even remotely *mediocre* about her. Mark my words, she is a rare pearl that is about to shine in the gymnastics world."

I was flabbergasted he spoke about me in such a way to his girlfriend.

"But how much more extra time is she going to steal from me with you? How much more time are you going to devote to this gym over me?" Katja whined. She'd never understand what gymnastics meant to people like me and Kova. "I should be your number one priority, but as always, I am last on the totem pole."

"A lot more actually," Kova bit back. "A bunch of the teammates have extra sessions coming up, it is competition season, as you know. I have told you this a hundred times."

"It is late. I did not mean to upset you." Katja's voice gentled. "How about we go home now?"

Yes! Go home. What a grand idea.

"I will go home when I am ready."

I scoffed at his stubbornness.

"What was that?"

Oh God. I bit down on my knuckles.

"What was what?" Kova acted clueless.

"I just heard a noise…" Katja's words lingered in the air.

"Oh that? It was me. I, ah, was adjusting myself and kicked my phone by accident."

"You are aroused." Her voice took on a seductive tone that made my stomach curl with nausea.

"You know it is hard when I wake."

"Let me take care of that for you."

I closed my eyes and prayed for them to leave already.

"Not necessary. Let us go home now."

"No, I insist," she said. My heartbeat thundered in my ears; no way would Kova allow anything sexual to happen, not with me in the room, or with my remnants on him.

"Katja," he growled.

"Konstantin. Baby, you know all you have to do is call me and I would run over."

"Katja," he warned over a rustling sound. "Now is not the time."

"Since when?" she teased.

"I am serious," he barked. "Go home and I will meet you there. I just need to lock up; I will be right behind you."

She was quiet for a moment. "What is going on with you?" This was the first time I truly ever heard Katja angry. "You have not let me touch you in weeks like this. Do you not want me anymore?"

I perked up. Kova remained abstinent for weeks? Why?

"It has nothing to do with you. I have been under an enormous amount of stress. I am really feeling the pressure right now. That is all."

Each word was clipped and short. If he was telling the truth, I wished he'd open to me the way he opened up to her so easily. It was like pulling teeth to get him to communicate with me.

"You act like you do not want me anymore," she said with a note of dejection in her voice. I almost felt bad for her. Almost.

He sighed deeply. "You know that is not the case. I just have a lot going on."

"It has been a while for us and I need you," she whined again. I wished she'd stop doing that.

"No, now is not the time."

"Did you just push my hand away?" she said, enraged. My jaw dropped. Pushed her hand away from what exactly?

"Yes, I did. Now go home, Katja, I will be there soon."

"I do not understand why now is not the time. You say it is not me, yet you will not let me touch you or give you the release you so clearly need. You ignore me for hours on end, you stay at work late, you come home when I am sleeping, and leave before I wake. To a woman, the signs are all there, Konstantin."

"Nothing is there, I promise, sweetheart," he said, softening his voice. "You are reading into it too much."

Nothing is there. The nothing being me. I was nothing. I wasn't naive, I knew he couldn't say anything else, but the way he spoke it stung my heart in a hundred different places.

"You work so hard... I just want to help you," she offered, and the rustling sound I heard moments ago returned. "I love you, you know."

"I know you do, and I love you. Just please, go. Let me lock up and I will follow right after."

Katja switched over to Russian. Just when I thought he convinced her to leave, I heard the unmistakable sounds of clothes shuffling, a faint moan, and a sound I wasn't prepared for.

Slurping. Wet, sloppy, slurping. My stomach flipped and I swallowed down the bile in my throat.

This couldn't be happening.

"You taste different," she said. I paled at the repugnance in her voice. This time I actually felt bad for her. She was licking me off him and didn't know it.

"I sweat a lot while I work out. How about we wait until I get home to shower and then we can pick up where we left off, yeah?"

"I do not mind," she said sweetly. "This is just a little of what is to come."

"Katja, please," he begged.

After a moment's silence I heard a long slurp and a pop, followed by an incoherent moan that had to have come from her.

"Katja..." he growled, his voice was deep and guttural.

I had to see for myself what she did to him. If she was on her knees like I assumed she was, then her back would be to me.

I peeked around the corner of the desk, careful not to make a sound.

Kova was on the couch with his legs spread wide and Katja between his thighs. As if he sensed me watching, he looked up and locked eyes with mine.

A deep sigh expelled from his lips and he sank further into the couch. His mouth parted in bliss. "Yes," he drawled out, and pushed her head down on him. He pumped his hips harder into her face, not breaking eye contact with me. Her gulping moans filled the room, and her nails dug into his thighs in almost the exact places where my marks could be seen.

Kova fisted her hair and gritted his teeth. His facial expression was stuck somewhere in between remorse, pleasure, and guilt. The only thing that kept me from breaking down was the fact that he wasn't carnal in the way he was with me, and I found solace in that. Still, there was no way to mask the hurt written all over my face, and I let him see it.

Three more rough thrusts, then Kova pulled Katja's head back.

"I cannot fucking do this!" he bellowed and quickly put his dick back in his pants. Katja wiped her mouth and they both stood.

I backed up and returned to my dark hole and waited.

"For as long as it has been, I am surprised you are able to hold it right now," Katja mused, and I could hear the coy smile in her voice.

"Please. That should not be a surprise to you."

"Hmm…" she said, like she was recalling something in her mind.

Kova came twice earlier, his semen was still inside me after I begged for us to finish together. God… I don't know what I was thinking. I lost my common sense when we were alone.

Their footsteps drew closer. My heart raced and I held my breath.

Something dragged across the desk over my head, and I heard the clanking of keys. "Get your shit and let us go," Kova mumbled under his breath. "Hurry the fuck up, Katja. You got what you wanted, as always," he spat. Then they both left his office.

I burrowed into the floor, holding my stomach, and fighting back the tears. My jaw trembled and I rolled my lips between my teeth, sniffling. I stayed in a tight ball trying to pretend this never happened. That the words Kova spoke earlier, with his passionate touch and persuasive words, to what we shared, and what I just witnessed, was nothing but a figment of my imagination. Otherwise, I was that stupid girl who never learned and always went back to the boy who wrecked her heart time and time again. And I didn't like that. Seeing Katja on her knees in front of Kova was upsetting, but seeing him take pleasure in me while I watched them was something I couldn't process. It hurt, that I knew, but this was a more profound kind of hurt that was deep seeded. I didn't know what to call it or how to explain it.

I remained hidden under his desk long enough to wallow in self-pity before I had the courage to poke my head out. I quickly pulled my leotard on and waited a bit longer before heading to the door. I stood and strained my ears, listening for any little sound. The phone on Kova's desk rang loud, the jarring sound made me jump.

There was no reason for anyone to call this late at night, so I figured it was Kova giving me a signal to leave. I fled from his office and ran to the gym where I'd left my bag. Then I threw on my sweats and stormed out to my Escalade.

I dug my cell phone from my bag and noticed I had two text messages from Kova.

Coach: You are clear to leave.

Coach: Please forgive me.

It was two in the morning by the time I got home. Distraught and queasy, I took the hottest shower my skin would withstand while I cried under the streaming water.

The night had been so high at one point but then took a drastic turn. Deep down, I didn't believe Kova would purposely inflict pain on me, not after the way we had been together. But he sure as hell didn't try hard enough to stop her either, especially when he saw me.

I got out of the shower and dried off. Not bothering with clothes, I climbed between the bedsheets naked. Tears continued to run down my face as I pulled the comforter to my chin. Tonight had shattered parts of me I didn't know were so fragile. My mind kept replaying the image of Katja on her knees, Kova's hands fisted in her hair, and his eyes on me. My emotions were a disaster of a mess, and I knew I'd never be able to talk to Kova about this, because talking about it would mean I'd have to relive it. Truth was, I didn't even know if I wanted to talk to him. There was nothing he could say or do to make the hurt go away.

chapter 27

DAD HAD ALWAYS SAID IF YOU WANTED SOMETHING DONE RIGHT, YOU MUST DO IT yourself.

And that's exactly what I was about to do.

I was in rare form after last night.

After being intimate with Kova, more than once, and listening to him open up a part of his heart and confess how he felt about me, then watching Katja go down on him while I hid, I was a mess. My thoughts were everywhere. I couldn't tell if I wanted to laugh or cry. I think the best thing to do was to let what happened go, and move on.

I popped four Motrin, then made a cup of coffee. Running on only a couple hours of sleep was a stupid idea. I was exhausted and mentally drained, but I pushed the thoughts away. Dressed and out of my condo within thirty minutes, I headed to the gym to condition alone. That was another thing—we hadn't finished talking about the extra classes before things went from zero to sixty in the blink of an eye. I still wasn't sure if he was okay with me going in or not, but I planned to go in regardless.

Reaching over to the passenger seat, I shifted around inside my bag and felt for my phone while keeping my eyes on the road. I grasped it in my hand, and after a quick glance, I went to my favorites and clicked on Avery. I wanted my best friend.

Pick up…pick up…pick up… I chanted to myself. When she didn't answer the first time, I tried a second time to no avail.

I pulled up to a red light and sent her a string of text messages, bitching at her for not being there and venting at the same time.

BFF: WTF! It's 5 a.m. That coach of yours brings more trouble than he's worth. Think of him as a crawfish—bite his head off and suck him down, then get rid of him.

That was all I got back from her. A fucking crawfish reference. Granted it was extremely early, but I had always been there for her no matter what.

With a scowl, I dropped my phone into the cup holder, hitched up my knee and drove to World Cup.

It was still pitch black when I pulled into the parking lot. Not surprising, there were no other cars here but mine. What lunatic went in to practice like they were training for the Olympics on their day off—and before dawn?

Me.

I quickly got out and punched my code into the keypad and walked inside, making sure the door shut behind me, even though it had an automatic locking mechanism.

Since there was no one else here, I brought my cell phone into the gym and started up my playlist. I always started off stretching the way Kova taught me. The man knew his shit, even if he was an asshole at times.

Okay. *Most* times.

"*Bozhe moi.* You and that horrible music of yours."

I jumped, my heart nearly exploding from me. "Jesus, Kova!" I shouted and grabbed my chest, then turned my music off. "Why can't you ever make some noise before you enter a room?"

He stopped walking and looked down at me as if I'd just asked him the dumbest question in the history of questions.

"It is my gym. I do not need to do no such thing."

"Yes, you do. One day you're going to give someone a heart attack." I stood up and fixed my shorts that had ridden up. Since I figured I'd be alone in the gym, I opted to wear a sports bra and mini shorts. Scratching my nose, I asked, "What are you doing here?"

He threaded a hand through his hair. "I am here to help you."

"But you seemed so against any extra work. Why would you even come?"

"Because you need me."

"I'm not doing my routines, so I don't need you for conditioning. I can do it myself. It's not hard."

He tilted his head toward me and his voice softened, playful even. "Yes, you do. You need me. Just admit it."

I wasn't going to be diverted. I was tired of the back and forth of our relationship, and still seething from how the previous night had ended.

"The only time I need you is during practice, you know I'm right. Plus, I'm sure Katja isn't happy about you being here after what I heard last night." I undid my ponytail and shook out my hair, then put it back up.

Kova lowered his head and stroked the dark scruff on his jaw. His eyes searched the floor. "Adrianna, I think we should—"

I put my hand up, bracing myself for what would come. "I know what you're going to say, and I don't want to talk about it. Let's just forget it ever happened, okay? It is what it is."

The muscles in his face tightened.

"What could you possibly say anyway? Sorry for allowing Katja to suck your...your... dick in front of me? Yeah. No thanks." I let out a harsh laugh and walked away.

"Ria."

"Drop it. You should just go home, Kova. Spend time with Katja. We both know you'll just be wasting your time here when it can be better spent with your girlfriend."

He followed closely behind me. "Not likely. I want to make sure you are working the right muscles accurately. I do not want all the work I put into you to unravel because you had to go and be stubborn."

He knew all the right buttons to push. "I'm not stubborn. I'm driven. Stubborn sounds like you're referring to a child, and I don't like that."

"Then do not act like one and I will not have to," he retorted, then grabbed my elbow and spun me around. "Just like when you bring up Kat. You sound like a jealous obsessed ex. It is not very becoming of you."

My jaw dropped. He did not just say that.

"You know, you're such a dickhead sometimes." I gave him my back.

"Where are you going?" he asked, ignoring my comment. He was probably used to it by now.

"To work."

"You are going in the wrong direction. The balance beam is the other way."

I kept walking and he repeated himself, then added, "Beam is your weakness and where we need to focus first." His voice was firm and full of authority; I couldn't ignore him.

Turning around on my heels, I walked toward him. He held his hand out with a jump rope in front of the balance beams. I looked down in confusion, then back up at him.

"What do you want me to do with that?"

"Get up on the beam and jump rope one hundred times. You wobble once, you start over."

My brows met my hairline. "You're so strange." I grabbed the jump rope and then hopped up on the beam. At four inches wide, I could easily do standing tucks and connect a series of skills both forward and backward. And he wanted me to jump rope? This would be a piece of cake.

I took a deep breath and swung the rope around, jumping lightly the first few times to get a feel for this.

"Lock your knees," he ordered.

I began counting.

"Eyes up. Shoulders back. Keep your posture straight. Do you know why I am having you do this?"

"Nnn—"

"Start over."

I stopped and looked down at him with one foot on the beam. "What? Why?"

"You wobbled and bent your knees. Start over."

Knees. I growled low in the back of my throat then began jumping again. I focused my gaze ahead of me. My mind immediately went to Kajta on her knees. I was still upset over last night but I tried to not let that effect my practice. Kova was quiet for a few moments before he said, "This will work the core of your body and help you punch the beam with straight legs. It also keeps your focus." He paused and added, "Do not turn your feet in, keep them forward."

It was a natural reaction for me to turn them in. I felt safer, like I had a better hold on the beam, but I also knew it could cost me.

I finished the first set the correct way with a slight burn in my thighs. Nothing bad though and I wasn't out of breath.

"Now jump rope traveling forward and backward. This will keep your body aligned and your concentration centered on what you are doing."

"How many times?" I asked between jumps, my words short and tight.

"Fifty each way."

This was a lot trickier than I expected. Just like Kova said, I had to keep my focus strictly on the beam and how I jumped—legs straight, body tight, hips squared. I wobbled a few times going backward and cursed Johnny under my breath.

Johnny was what Avery named the beam after I fell two times in one day. She said if I was getting fucked by the wood, then we needed to name it. The balance beam was now known as Johnny Depp to Avery.

"Tighten up, Adrianna. Squeeze your thighs and butt. Everything needs to be firm so you do not sway. The tighter you hold yourself, the less you fall. You cannot loosen for one second. I do not want to see anything jiggle on you. Keep your focus." He paused. "By the way, your mother gave me a ring yesterday. Such a lovely woman she is. So caring of her daughter."

I stopped and looked down at him, letting out a gush of air I hadn't realized I was holding.

"Uh huh. Start over."

I ignored him. I couldn't believe Mom called him. "What did she say?"

"Start over."

"What did she say, Kova?" I pushed, snapping at him. I probably looked like a psycho to him, but he held firm and wouldn't speak until I started up again. I huffed under my breath and jumped. Typical Kova. He always had to get his way. My coach was an exasperating man.

"Just that she wanted to know how her precious daughter was doing. I told her you were getting there but still had a long way to go."

I lowered my eyelids. "Of course you did. What else?"

"She said she was concerned about your diet and wanted to make sure you were eating nutritious meals. She mentioned when you went home for the holidays you let go and ate everything in sight. She wanted to make sure you are not still on that same path. Something about you had to buy new clothes because your old ones did not fit."

My heartbeat sped up, and my lips parted. The animosity in her words rang like a siren in my head of things she'd said to me that I did wrong in her eyes. Moisture beaded above my top lip. I gripped the jump rope handles tighter, my skin burning against the plastic. I jumped faster and harder.

Kova was still speaking but I only caught the tail end of a few words. I wasn't processing any of it. All I could focus on was the fact that my mom had called him and fabricated lies, and he listened like a good little sheep. She took vindictive to a whole new level and I had to wonder why she was trying in vain to sabotage my gymnastics career. She wanted to ruin me for the sake of ruining me. It was the only plausible reason I could come up with and a side of her I hadn't yet seen. I was her daughter, she was my mother. I didn't understand her attitude toward me.

A prickling sting deflated my chest and my breathing grew strenuous. I slowed down until I stopped completely. My arms dropped to my sides, and I stood with one foot positioned slightly in front of the other, staring in a blank trance at nothing but feeling everything.

A muffled cry burst from my lips and I threw the rope to the floor. Kova jerked back. Tears filled my eyes and my heart ached, not because I was sad, I was, but more so because I was so irate and filled with resentment that my own mother would purposely set out to hurt me. I hopped down, formed a fist, and dropped it down on the balance beam as hard as I could. I shoved at the side of it, trying to push it over, shoving my weight against it, which could never happen. It was too heavy, but it felt good fighting against something.

"God! I hate her! Hate her with a passion!"

"Hey," Kova said softly, coming up behind me, but I couldn't stop.

"I can't stand her! No matter what I do, it's never enough. I never over ate anything, and I bought new clothes because I lost weight. Because we had stupid parties she forced me to attend. She is such a liar." I kept my back to Kova so he wouldn't see the tears in my eyes. "And you played right into it, making me sound like I'm hopeless, like an amateur who still needs years of work, and even that might not be enough. You gave her exactly what she wanted and she fed off that, I know she did. She has it out for me, always has, always will. Nothing I do will be right for her."

A fat tear slipped from the corner of my eye, and I walked away. I didn't take more than a few steps when Kova clutched my arm in his hand.

"Stop," he said gently. "Ria, I told her you still had a way to go because the truth is I am not ready to let you go yet."

I didn't know how to respond to that.

"Just give me a few minutes, Kova." I yanked my arm away and pushed at his chest. "I'll be right back."

Kova grabbed my wrist. "Stop. Listen to me."

I shook my head. "Please, just let me be for a sec and I'll be fine."

"Adrianna."

"Kova! Just leave me alone!" I screamed.

But he didn't. Kova pulled me to his chest and I immediately fought against him.

"Get it out," he said. I shoved at him and cried harder, giving him everything I could. I hated that he was doing this to me and appreciated it at the same time. "Fight harder, hit me if you have to, just get it out." I struggled between crying and shoving, but Kova didn't let go, and something in me cracked.

My efforts slowed, and I covered my face and let the tears flow. I poured everything out against his chest. Everything I held in over the past year. From my mom and her backhanded compliments, to the rigorous training I demanded of my body, to the illicit affair I had with my coach. I cried over everything, and he let me.

"Shhh…just let it out," Kova said, rubbing soothing circles on my back. "It is okay."

When my cries and hiccups subsided, I sniffled and expelled a huge breath. I felt like a burden had been lifted from my shoulders and I could breathe again.

Stepping back, Kova tried to lift my chin, but I kept my gaze cemented to the floor. I was too embarrassed. I didn't like crying to begin with, and I sure as shit didn't want to show him my tears. Tears showed weakness, and I wasn't weak.

He tried to lift my chin again, and when I didn't budge, he sighed and got down on one knee so he was eye level with me.

"Jerk." A sad chuckle escaped my lips. "You always find a way to get what you want."

He cupped the side of my face and wiped away a few tears. He was sweet, but concerned, and I appreciated it.

"Stop crying. She is not worth your tears."

"I'm not crying because I'm sad, Kova."

"I know you are not."

I swallowed. "How do you know?"

"I spend more time with you than she does. You think I do not know you by now?" he asked and stared at me. "I know more about you than you think." One corner of his mouth pulled up. "I watch the way you walk, the way you talk, how hard you work, your dedication with anything you set out to do." His eyes softened as he continued. "I know the intonation of your voice lifts during certain topics you are passionate about. Your eyes lighten or darken depending on your mood. You do not even need to speak for me to feel your emotions. You have so much compassion inside. I see it. I see you, Adrianna."

The honesty in his green eyes suffocated me. I took in everything he said and clung to his words. I held on to them as they breathed life into me.

He saw me.

Not just as a coach looking to polish the flaws of his athlete, or in a carnal way full of sexual desire. He saw me on an entirely different personal level. He cared about me and wanted to see me flourish. He paid attention to me and my needs, both on the mat and off. He didn't look over me.

"I was going to ask how things were with your mother since New Year's, but I guess I do not need to now."

"You know what my mom used to say if I cried?" I asked. He shook his head. "Crying gives you wrinkles. I wasn't allowed to cry, at least not in her presence."

Kova brushed back a few strands of hair that had fallen from my ponytail. "While I am unsure about that theory, I would rather you not cry at all simply because I cannot do anything to help you. No man knows what to do when a woman is crying. We are useless creatures when that happens." I sniffled, and clenched my eyes shut to hold back the tears. "Use your anger and frustration to fuel you, Ria. Make it your energy. Do not let her bring you down, you are better than that. Make her eat her words." He paused, and then quietly said, "Prove it. Prove her wrong and do not let her win."

I desperately wanted to hug him. I needed it.

"You love saying that, don't you?"

He shrugged, his face softening along with his eyes. "It packs a punch, yes?"

I sighed. "I suppose so."

"Good."

Kova stood and looked down at me. Stepping close enough so his body was pressed to mine, he cupped the back of my neck with both hands and his thumbs grazed my jaw. My arms automatically wound around his back and I held him tight, getting the hug I so badly needed.

"For the record, I would never give anyone ammunition to use against you. Ever. Remember that." He dipped his head. "Now get back up on that beam and show me what you are made of. Do it with determination, do it with intent. Use your body and show everyone you want it without having to utter a word." Kova played with my ponytail a few times, twirling my thick locks around his fist, and then letting it go. "Your silence will be your success."

I nodded. Before I could react, Kova dropped a kiss to my forehead then stepped back.

He was right. I needed to be silent but strong if I wanted to come out on top. He regarded me with hope and confidence, then he walked away.

Strength didn't come from what you could do, it came from the power within one's heart, a determination unlike no other to thrive.

Sometimes I needed someone to remind me of that.

M Y THIGH MUSCLES WERE TIGHT, BURNING FROM JUMPING ROPE SO LONG. Like tiny fire ants creeping up my calves and into my legs. I wanted to stop and take a small break, but I knew if I did I'd only regret it. Instead, I focused my eyes ahead on the wall and endured it. I took long, calm breaths and I kept going until I hit three hundred jumps. I stopped on the last one and exhaled loudly, my back slouching over. That was way harder than I expected.

"Nope. No way. Do another set."

"What? Why?" I shrieked, glaring down at him. Coach Kova was back and he was insane. No, he was certifiable. I already knew this. Gone was sentimental Kova, and in his place was Coach Dick. I just completed two hundred more jumps than he asked for and he wanted another set.

"You do not finish with showing exhaustion," he yelled at me with fire in his eyes. "You finish as if it cost you nothing. Like it was a walk on the beach. Not like you are a dying cat. Suck it up and do it again."

A dying cat. Kova could kick rocks. I swallowed back my words, it wasn't easy, but I managed and did as he ordered like it was no sweat off my back. After all, I promised not to talk back.

"Toes!"

He muttered in Russian under his breath. "Remember to breathe properly."

A cramp resonated in the arch of my foot. I chewed the inside of my lip and held my breath, blinded by the discomfort. It throbbed wildly, and I wanted to stop for a second to flex my foot. The spasm rippled, tightening and contracting into a hard ball. I gritted my teeth to ignore the pain and made a mental note to drink more water. By the end of another set, a fiery burn vibrated in every indentation of my abs. Gymnastics was all core strength, so no matter which drill I completed, I had to use my stomach to balance my center and keep my body tight.

"See? Was that so difficult?" Kova asked. "Jump down."

"I had a cramp in my foot."

He looked down at me, baffled. "And? What would you like me to do for a cramp? Baby you? Drink more water and watch your diet. Toughen up." Before I could bite back, he said, "Turn around and face the beam. Curl your toes under and bend your knees."

Nothing but orders from this man. It wouldn't kill him to be polite every once in a while.

I did as he requested and held the beam to steady myself. Kova came up behind me and placed his hands on my shoulders and pushed down against my body. My thighs hardened and flexed to hold myself up, just bouncing slightly. He used the ball of his foot to press on my heel and push it forward to extend the arch and stretch it out. He did this repeatedly on both feet. Surprisingly, it didn't hurt at all. The pull felt good. I was one of those weird athletes who liked stretching and conditioning.

"Good. Stand up and turn sideways. I want you to place your hands around your foot and extend it up. Hold it there." Once my knee was flat to my chest, he stepped closer. "Eventually we will do this on beam, but for now we will work it on the floor. Lock your knee then relevé. We want your hips squared but relaxed. We do not want any tightness. You would be surprised to hear how many gymnasts have weak hips, how their leaps and jumps are not one eighty. As you know, points are deducted for anything less than one eighty. This will help with that."

Holding this position was much harder than I thought. Unless he was up on the beam with me, I wasn't sure I'd be able to do this. It took complete control. I swayed to the side but Kova caught me. He slapped my thigh, silently advising me to tighten up, and pressed his fingers into my skin to hold me steady. Leaning into me so his body was flush against mine, he reached around to press on my glute to open my hip, then he angled me forward, still holding on.

He counted to five before we switched legs. Then we completed the drills again, this time in an arabesque with my leg extended behind me and my chest forward, and then with my leg to my side nearly meeting my ear. Once I did all three positions, Kova had me work them in order with him directing me the entire time. He made sure my hips were in and my legs locked. Each pull and stretch improved my range of motion and flexibility. By the time we finished those, I felt fantastic.

"Good. Now get on the low beam and raise your arms." Kova moved behind me and kept one foot on each side of the beam. The low beam was the perfect apparatus to test new skills as it was only raised off the floor by a few inches.

"You are going to do a stretch jump. The key to the jump is to stay firm and straight because I am going to twist your body around fast. If you are loose, you will swing out and hit me, and seeing as I am going out of my way to help you today, I would really like to avoid that. I am not going to tell you which way I am turning you, just stay tight and try to land on the beam."

I nodded.

Kova's hands found my bare waist and gave a little squeeze. His fingers gently pressed into my skin and his breath danced across the back of my neck. Memories from the last time I'd worn only shorts and a sports bra to the gym flashed in my mind. It had been a Sunday then too and no one was here; I had the place to myself. I was in the dance room lost to the music when he had showed up. My body temperature rose as I continued to think back on that night. What started out as Kova insisting everything I did was wrong, as was typical then, led to one of the most unexpected and erotic nights of my life that opened the forbidden door.

He had kissed me in places I'd never been kissed. He had touched me with skill and brought me pleasure so intense I had to question if it was normal. Wetness formed between my thighs as my thoughts scattered. It would be easy for him to slide his hands toward my pelvis and slip his fingers into my shorts. I'd lean back into him where he'd nuzzle my neck and dust my jaw with wet kisses. Then I'd reach behind me and stroke his cock until he was rock hard. I exhaled a silent sigh as the throb continued to grow while I pictured him bending me over the balance beam. I loved his hands on me. The way he was precise with every touch, every graze, meticulous about where his hands went.

A slap on my ass made me jump. I dropped my arms and turned around to face Kova.

"What the hell was that for?" I said.

He snapped his fingers repeatedly in front of my face. "I have been calling your name, but you were ignoring me. You were in la-la land and that was the only way to get your attention."

I flattened my lips and tried not to laugh. "La-la land, Kova? You did not just say that."

"Okay, fine. You were daydreaming."

"So you thought the only way to get my attention was to hit me?"

Kova gave me a droll stare. "Do not exaggerate. I did not hit you, I merely tapped you. Your attention was elsewhere when it should be focused on me, what I am telling you to do. Nothing else. Why must I constantly remind you? Am I wasting my time?"

I was certain my face turned ten shades of red by how hot I was. Little did he know he had my full attention, just not in the way he expected.

"My attention was on you, I swear. It won't happen again."

The silence between us thickened while Kova watched me. He was an intuitive man and sometimes that worried me. He saw *too* much.

"You are a terrible liar."

I moved to stand in front of him again, giving him my back. "I'm not lying, but whatever you say."

"I am sure that muttering of yours came with a classic eye roll."

He replaced his hands on my waist, and I raised my arms again so they were close to my ears. Just before I sprung up, I said, "Kind of like when you speak in Russian. I guess you'll never know what I was thinking, just like I won't ever know what you're saying." The moment the words left my lips, he spun me around so fast and stopped me right in front of him to complete a half-turn. His hand landed on my stomach to balance me. I exhaled a huff of air into Kova's face. My toes curled around the four-inch beam tightly so I wouldn't wobble.

I flattened my lips. The back of his hand tapped my stomach and I flexed. His attention shifted to my arms and he slapped my bicep. I hadn't realized I let go when he spun me. I straightened my loose arm and hardened my stomach. He was in the zone, and I loved when he was like this. He wasn't thinking of illicit thoughts like I was. He was doing his job and doing it well.

chapter 29

I DID MANY MORE HALF-TWISTS BEFORE WE MOVED ON TO FULL-TWISTS.

The first few half-twists surprised me, and my leg flew out to the side a time or two. I was loose. Kova steadied me and a second later we were moving again. We both stayed silent except for Kova's counting. When I jumped, he jerked me both left and right since the requirements for balance beam called for elements turning in both directions. Naturally, I favored one side more than the other, all my tumbling started with my left leg, but with gymnastics, we had to work both sides for it to count. Once he was satisfied, he had me climb back up on the high beam and complete the drill without him. A few times I shook, but I stuck it and thankfully didn't fall. Back flips and front flips were a piece of cake on the balance beam, but any turns, leaps, or jumps, and there wasn't one gymnast who hasn't wobbled. It was always the damn turns that inevitably got us.

"Okay, let us break for some water, use the restroom if you need. Come back here in two minutes."

I nodded and took off for the ladies' room to quickly relieve myself. Then I grabbed a bottle of water from my duffle bag and took a hefty swig and recapped it. Hearing and feeling any liquid move and swish around in my stomach bothered me. I just needed enough to hold me over until I got home.

I made my way back to the balance beam and spotted Kova pacing the floor with his cell phone pressed to his ear. He was speaking in his native tongue. Even though I had not one iota of what he was saying, the rise and fall of his clipped words, the bite in his tone, the hardened look on his face, along with his whitened knuckles told me he was arguing with his girlfriend again. Probably because he was here with me.

Kova's voice rose one last time before he pulled the phone away and hung up on her. I could hear her high-pitched voice until the last second. He took a deep breath and released a ragged sigh when his phone started ringing again. He silenced it, then dropped it to the floor facedown.

I stood next to the balance beam, casually swinging one leg forward and backward as I waited uncomfortably. There was nothing I could say to make his situation better, mainly because I had no idea what the hell they had talked about, but also because it was just an awkward situation all around.

Clearing his throat, he strode up next to me and stared off to the side, lost in thought.

"Trouble in paradise?"

Kova scowled.

"Want to talk about it?"

"No."

"If you need to go home, you can. I don't plan to stay all day anyway."

"It is not up for discussion," he snapped.

I looked at him and felt the tension radiating from his body. "I'm serious, Kova. You should go home to keep the peace. I feel bad."

He scoffed. "Please. You do not feel bad."

I shrugged. I really didn't.

"Place one hand on the beam and the other out to the side." Kova moved to stand on the opposite side of me, behind my shoulders. "You are going to swing your leg forward, back, and then forward."

I sighed and did the motions as he spoke. I knew by familiarity with how slowly he enunciated the words that he wanted me to complete them. So I did. I just wished there wasn't this awkward tension between us now.

"No, do not bend it. Here, give me your leg." I lifted my leg behind me. Using one hand, he held my calf and raised my leg, his other hand gripped my shoulder closest to the beam, and draped his forearm across my clavicle to press my chest back toward my leg behind me.

"The key is to lay your shoulders back, relax them"—he shook me a bit to loosen me up—"because we want your shoulders to meet your hamstring. No, do not bend it. Just lift it for now." He glanced down. "Relevé. Yes, perfect. Gymnasts have a bad habit of dropping the knee to the side. It is ugly and looks like a dog peeing. We do not ever want that. We want grace and beauty. Effortless, elegant gymnastics. Now, bend." I bent my knee and spotted my toes. My foot was so close it could touch my forehead. "This. Feel your body? Feel the position you are in? How it is like a ring? This is where we want you. It will make a world of difference points wise with your ring leap and sheep jump. If your head is up and not relaxed, you will get a tenth of a deduction. We want your head almost touching your foot. In order to get to this, we will work on your swing, then bending of the knee. Once we get your ring kick mastered, it will help tremendously."

Kova slowly let go of my leg and I dropped it to the side. I glanced at him. "We are doing both sides, correct?"

"Of course."

I nodded and then started up, just kicking front to back without bending my knee. I knew this was to prep for my jumps and leaps. If I could stick the skills beautifully, any balance check I made could counteract it.

Because let's face it, I knew a balance check or two would happen.

With every kick, Kova guided me. He sped me up and slowed me down. He made sure I was precise and performed to the best of my ability. He corrected my arms and hands, making sure they were back and inverted, not out. He took time out to stretch my shoulders too, made them a little more elastic and said he'd do it before each practice as well. He had me practice the jumps on the floor using a piece of white tape as my balance beam.

And the entire time his brows stayed pinched together and his forehead creased with lines. I knew he was trying not to think of his phone call.

"Move on to sheep jumps."

I nodded. A sheep jump required me to keep my bent knees glued together as I jumped and arched my back, making sure my toes just about tapped my forehead. And of course, a relaxed head. I needed to create a circle with my body.

After I completed ten, Kova scowled in disgust, and said, "Your knees are coming apart. Put some chalk between your thighs."

He picked up a bright yellow stretchy tension band while I powdered the inside of my legs to keep them dry. He had me step into the thick elastic and pulled it up to my knees. The band was used to help retain position for numerous skills and drills. Right now it served to keep my legs together.

Kova looked at me and nodded, then dropped his eyes to watch my legs.

"Jump," he ordered.

In mid-flight, I could tell I tried to separate my knees by the pull in my outer thighs. It was unintentional and I had no idea I was even doing it.

"You felt that, did you not?" Kova demanded, his eyes hard.

"I did."

"Now you know. Your head is relaxed nicely, but we want your legs tight and closed. Let us do another ten."

After ten, he said, "Ten more."

When I finished, I was breathing heavily, but I made sure not to show any kind of sluggishness.

"Up on beam and do them."

Since I had the band around my knees still, Kova stepped behind me to help me mount the apparatus. He placed his hands on my hips to hoist me up. Swiveling to the front, I moved into the jump. In air, my heart dropped into my stomach. I was nervous that if I shook I wouldn't be able to catch myself because of the tension band around my legs.

"Again. And relax your head."

Steadying my nerves, I focused on something to spot. Then I jumped and placed my arms out to brace myself.

"What is wrong with you?" he asked in displeasure.

"What do you mean?"

"You are shaking up there. You look like an amateur."

My jaw dropped. "Forgive me, but I'm not used to tape around my knees. I need to get used to it."

Kova tilted his head to the side and raised a pointed brow. He was annoyed with my response. "Get used to it, *now*," he said, low and controlled, using his index finger to point at the floor. "Get used to it, *now*."

Flattening my lips, I nodded hastily. Swinging my arms down to gain power, I put everything into the jump. With my hips squared with my shoulders, I let go and relaxed my head, arching my back as much as I could humanly manage, and tried to spot my toes. Coming down, I landed with both feet and squeezed every muscle I could in an effort to not wobble.

"Excellent. Only do not come down sounding like a goddamned elephant. You cannot weigh more than one hundred pounds soaking wet, if that. Act like a feather delicately floating down. We want elegance."

I ground my jaw. "Yes, sir." I didn't look his way, but I saw a smirk dazzle his face for a split second from the corner of my eye. It was the first hint of something other than brooding since he spoke to Katja and that made me happy.

"What was that?" he bit out after I jumped.

I glanced down. "What?"

"That noise?"

I dropped my arms to my sides. "What noise?"

He squinted his eyes. "Did you grunt up there?" he asked calmly.

I bit down on the inside of my lip. "No."

Kova stepped closer to the balance beam and leaned in like he was listening for a pin to drop.

"Do it again."

Looking for a spot on the wall to focus on, I swung my arms down and moved into the sheep jump. Coming down, I took note in how I landed and tried to appear as graceful as possible.

"There it is. You did it again!" he yelled in shock. But he looked mostly disgusted and that made me flinch.

"What am I doing?" I responded, exasperated by his attitude.

His eyes were huge orbs. "You are grunting when you jump, as if you are exerting yourself to the max. Like you are out of shape and cannot run twenty feet in front of you. It sounds horrible, not to mention embarrassing."

"I honestly had no idea I was."

His brows lifted in disbelief. "You mean to tell me that you cannot feel or hear that god awful sound come out of you?"

I shook my head. "No, I can't."

"I do not believe you. Do it again. Come on. Get moving." He rushed me with his hand movements.

Taking a deep breath, I exhaled nervously and sent up a silent prayer before I jumped.

And heard it.

Fuck. Fuck. Fuck!

I snuck a glance at Kova, which was a huge mistake. He looked like he was ready to climb up on the beam and kill me.

"Do you have Tourette's?"

"What? No. You know I don't."

"You sound like a pig. Is that what you want the judges to hear?"

"Of course not."

"Then control it. If you must put so much into the jump that you have to grunt, then you are doing it wrong. You are exerting yourself way too much."

I nodded and tried to figure out how the hell I would control a sound coming out of me I hadn't realized I was making until now.

"Think about the breathing techniques and go from there. Do not hold your breath when you jump. This is all basic shit you should already know," he mumbled, running a hand down his face. His eyes were bloodshot and I felt bad.

Two hours later I had finally stopped making the sound, and we moved on to handstands for another hour before he called it a day.

I. Was. Drained.

I was beyond sore and tired, and my muscles ached.

When I planned to come in today, I had it all mapped out. I was going to designate a specific amount of time to each event, work on skills I knew needed attention, follow up with intense conditioning and drills, and then end with a run.

Then Kova had showed up and blew my plans to shit.

chapter 30

THERE WAS NOT ENOUGH MOTRIN IN THE WORLD THAT COULD HELP ME RIGHT NOW. I could barely walk. My thighs quivered relentlessly, and my stomach was so tender to the touch that I hunched over like an old lady.

If I had to guess, I'd say Kova ran me ragged because of his phone call with Katja. This was by far the hardest workout to date.

"You okay?" Kova asked, eyeing me with concern. I was on the floor, knee bent as I unwrapped the ACE bandage from my ankle. My Achilles had flared up earlier from Kova's merciless conditioning. I'd pushed past the pain. It was nothing I couldn't handle, but he had sensed it and told me to wrap it up, then handed me an anti-inflammatory. My eyes had lit up at the sight of the little orange pills in his palm. I didn't argue. Within an hour, it helped dull the pain.

"I'm fine," I responded on autopilot. And I was.

Kova crouched down and got on his knees. He tapped the side of my thigh for me to roll onto my stomach. He began to massage my calves, working his way up to my thighs to work out the lactic acid. God it felt good when he dug deep with his knuckles and pushed in a circle.

"I want you to eat something full of high protein when you get home. Add some whole grains into the mix and green vegetables. Make sure to ice that leg of yours. Actually, I would like you to take an ice bath. That would benefit you more."

I groaned under my breath. An ice bath was the last thing on earth I wanted after the workout I just had. Talk about suffering even more.

"I'll just ice it. Thanks for the suggestion though."

"Adrianna, I do not speak just to hear the sound of my voice. I am trying to inform you how much you are going to ache tomorrow and little things, like an ice bath, will help immensely. It will help your Achilles as well and bring down the intense trauma your body endured today."

I barely had the strength to drive home, let alone buy ice.

Kova moved on to my other leg and repeated the motions. An ice bath would be the best solution, but there was no way I could do it again. I didn't want to. Memories assaulted me like it happened yesterday and I squeezed my eyes shut. It was horrific, like thousands and thousands of tiny needles repeatedly stabbing my entire body for what seemed like an eternity. All I could focus on was the chunks of ice and the slow ticking of the timer counting down until I could get out.

I moaned as Kova made his way to my shoulder blades and groaned in the back of my throat as his hands worked magic on my sore back and neck. I could fall asleep to this. It was getting late and I needed to get moving, but the mere thought of standing exhausted me even more.

"I know how well ice baths work, Hayden helped me last time. And for the record, I detest them."

"Nobody likes them."

"I don't want to sit in an ice bath ever again."

Kova's hands stopped and I turned over to look at him and sat up. He scowled at me. "Then do not come in and train like a beast if you cannot handle the aftermath. That is being negligent, not to mention, plain old stupid on your part. Now, get up."

My eyes lowered as Kova stood. I said nothing. I didn't move.

I didn't like his tone.

He shifted on his feet, clearly annoyed with me. "Those little tears happening in your muscles right now that you cannot see, they need the cold water therapy. If not, you are going to be swollen and useless tomorrow." He paused. "And you will be here tomorrow regardless."

I rolled my eyes. I had a headache. "I know that. I wouldn't dream of skipping."

With swift speed, Kova leaned down and slipped his hand under my arm and pulled me up. The world spun around me, I was instantly dizzy from being forced to stand.

Gripping my arm tight, Kova leaned down in my face. "I am not putting up with this defiant, childish behavior. You said you would do anything I said and would hire all the best people to help you recover. Remember? You continue like this and I will lock you out from coming in on your days off. I am trying to help you. Stop fighting me on every little thing, Adrianna. It is like you wake up and write up a checklist of things to do and say to get under my skin to infuriate me. Remember your place."

Kova was way off base, that wasn't what I intended at all. I yanked my arm back, but he had a firm grip on me. I had my reasons as to why I didn't want to soak in a stupid bath, reasons I didn't want to share because I knew in my gut they'd backfire on me.

"I'm not trying to defy you."

"Then what are you trying to do?" he asked, his eyes filled with concern as they searched mine. "You worked extremely hard today, you need to recover properly, or you will be useless and no good for your first meet. Is that what you want? Because it is not what I want for you. I want *more* for you."

I puckered my lips, determined not to answer honestly.

"Please, what are you thinking? Tell me?" he begged. He seemed truly bothered, and that didn't sit well with me for some asinine reason. The pleading in his voice broke my resolve and before I could stop myself, I gave him what he wanted.

"Kova," I said, in an uncomfortable sigh, "I don't have the strength to carry bags of ice up to my condo, okay? Or to prepare a bath. There. I said it. Hayden helped me the last time, and I have no doubt that he'd help me now if I asked. But seeing as he already knows so much about what happened between us, I really do not want to call him for anything."

He looked at me completely flabbergasted, and I almost laughed. I continued, "Truthfully, I'm in worse shape right now than when he helped the first time. I didn't expect this today, and something in my gut says you didn't either." He tilted his head down and scratched the back of his neck. "The thought of driving to the store, buying ice, walking to my car, driving to my condo, bringing it upstairs, and filling my tub is just tiring to think about. *I don't want to do it.* I'm one hundred percent depleted, I've never felt like this. I swear you made me work muscles I didn't even know I had. All I want to do is face plant on my bed and go to sleep." I took a deep breath. "Happy? Now you know. And don't give me that look. I can handle the work you dish out."

The silence between us brewed into palpable tension. I knew Kova by now. At least, I'd like to think I did. I knew when I pushed his buttons. I knew when he was frustrated with me in the gym. I knew when he was pleased with me, even though he'd never admit it. I could even tell when he was fighting with Katja.

But this Kova...the one standing eerily still in front of me, was a new side of Kova I'd yet to see. One I'd have to add to my list of Kovas I'd met. Frustrated was an understatement. More along the lines of he wanted to rip my head off with his bare hands and feed my limbs to the gators along the freeway right outside.

"You know, for someone who is so determined to be the best, who wants to go all the way to the Olympics that so few have the ability to actually do, someone who has the *gall* to stride into my office and demand what she wants and will not take no for an answer, you can be so incredibly stubborn and dumb. Blatant stupidity standing in front of me." He spat the words out like little daggers. The vein in his neck protruded and pulsed with each passing second. "This is when I question if you truly want it, because if you did, you would show me, not just in the gym, but outside of it as well. You would show me that you are responsible. You would ask for help and not care about your pride." He clenched his jaw and sighed deeply, exhaling through his nose. "I do not understand you, Adrianna. You tell me what you want, you get it; but when you need assistance with something outside of the gym, you do not ask." He shook his head. Hurt filled his eyes, warring with the profound anger written all over his face, and it pierced my heart. "I told you I am here for you. Take what you need from me, Ria."

The wrath radiating off Kova was impossible to ignore, but so was the troubled look in his eyes. He was worried. I stood a little taller, speechless, resenting him for the truth in his words. He worked me like I demanded and I retreated on my promise when I said I wouldn't. He had every right to be angry with me.

"Are you just going to stand there and say nothing?" Kova asked, crestfallen.

I shrugged helplessly. "What do you want me to say? That you're right and I'm wrong? Fine, Kova. You're right. You're *always* right. My ego stood in the way today. I didn't want to show weakness because I got exactly what I asked for and then some. I was afraid if I did then you would think I couldn't handle it. I wasn't expecting not to be able to walk. Push came to shove, and I acted on impulse and bit off more than I could chew."

Without hesitation, Kova reached down and scooped me up into his arms.

"What… What are you doing?" I slapped his shoulder as he bent down to grab my bag before heading toward the front door. "Put me down."

"You were right—I worked you too hard. I was cross earlier and took it out on you. Believe me, I know you can handle what I dish out, but no one would be able to do what you did today and walk out skipping. I was being a dick."

I threw my hands up dramatically. "There is a god! I'm so glad you recognized your dickness for the first time in your life. I feel like we should have a moment of silence."

"Dickness?" he repeated like it was a bad taste. "Sometimes I do not understand you Americans and your choice of words. You make sayings up as you go."

I laughed. "Yes, your default personality is a dick. It means you can be an angry Russian asshole sometimes."

He side-eyed me. He knew I was right based on that look alone. "I swear, your goal since coming here is to aggravate me as much as you can. Why are all women the same? Every one of you females are born with a brazen tongue us men want to cut out."

"Oh, so you expect us to just allow you to speak any which way you want and we take it? Typical man." I patted his chest. "Put me down."

He ignored me and kept walking.

"You know, this is why I sometimes call you Captain Dickhead in my head."

He feigned a grimace, and I smiled from ear to ear. He wouldn't stay mad at me for long. "Put me down. I'm capable of walking to my car."

"We are not going to your car, we are going to mine. I will pick up your slack today," he mumbled under his breath.

"Pick up my slack today? This is *your* fault, Kova. You just admitted it. Jesus Christ. Just put me down."

Kova pushed the door open with his back and carried me to his car. He opened the passenger door and carefully deposited me onto the seat. Within minutes, we were on the road.

"No more talking. Your voice is giving me a headache."

I glared at him. "It's Sunday. Surely you have plans with your girlfriend."

He didn't answer me.

"Why are you doing this?"

Kova's cell phone rang. It was hooked up to his Bluetooth so the ringing echoed loudly in the small space. The caller ID popped up on his dash. *Katja*. He declined it immediately.

"How am I going to get to practice tomorrow since my truck is at World Cup?"

Again, he ignored me and that fired me up.

"What is your damn problem?" I yelled, but he continued to ignore me and pulled into a gas station. He picked up two bags of ice and placed them in his trunk, then drove in the direction of my condo.

"See, this is the exact scenario where I call you Captain Dickhead in my head."

He stayed quiet. His cell rang again, and again he declined it.

I huffed under my breath with a shake of my head. "You know, I should've just lied and yes'd you to death. Then we wouldn't be in this situation together." I glanced over at him. "From now on, I'll just respond with yes to every question."

"I would prefer that, but we both know you will never hold true to it."

"Ah, so he speaks again. And here I thought you forgot your English. You're not coming in."

"Too bad. I am doing my job. I got you into this…condition." He waved his hand toward me. "I will help you get out of it."

Lowering my voice, I said, "I don't want you coming up to my condo." Didn't he know by now that nothing good could come from us being alone?

Kova parked his car and turned off the ignition. "I am."

My jaw slackened. "You can't just barge into my home whenever you feel like it."

Kova sighed and ran a hand down his face. He stared ahead at the wall of trees. "Adrianna, I do not want to come inside, I have better things I could be doing with my time, but you leave me no choice. If you have a problem with it, I will call your father and let him speak with you. I am certain he will be on my side."

"You would call my dad, wouldn't you," I stated more than questioned.

"Whatever it takes. Now, can you make it out of the car?"

It wasn't long until we were upstairs and in my unit. Kova had to carry me from the car to the lobby, as I walked slower than an eighty-seven-year-old.

I sat in a daze on the toilet and watched Kova bring in the ice bags and fill the tub. He ran the cold water and I dreaded what was to come next. There was so, so much ice. He had bought the twenty pound bags instead of the smaller five pound ones. Asshole. He rambled on and on about the importance of quick and efficient muscle recovery, but I wasn't listening. It was nothing I didn't already know. Combined with his thick accent, I could barely hear him over the roar of water and ice anyway.

Kova sat back on the ledge of the tub and glanced over his shoulder. He gazed down my body like he was waiting on an answer. Fatigued, I just nodded. I had no idea what he said.

"Ready?"

I sat up taller at his edgy tone. I just wanted to go to sleep. "Ready as I'll ever be."

Reaching into the convenience store bag, he pulled out a few medicine bottles. I looked away and eyed the freezing ice water I was about to sink into, trying desperately to mentally prepare for the dreadful temperatures that were about to shock my body. But I knew no amount of manipulating myself would work for this. It just sucked big time all around.

"Here. Take these." I glanced back at Kova who had his arm stretched out and palm open with a handful of colorful pills and capsules. They looked like multivitamins and a few more of the standard amount of Motrin that I usually took. His other hand held a water bottle.

I folded my palm up and the pills tumbled into my hand. He uncapped the water and handed it to me.

"What's this one?" I pointed to one of the pills.

"Melatonin. It will help you relax and get some rest. It is an all-natural sleep aid. There is also a few naturally extracted fruit supplements and a multivitamin to help with recovery."

I swallowed them all in one shot.

"I can take it from here, Kova. Thank you, though."

"I do not trust you to get in and stay for the correct amount of time. Come on." He reached out to take my hand, but I didn't move. I just stared at his hand. "What is wrong with you?"

"I… I can… I can do it on my own. I appreciate that you're here, I really do, but I got it." I didn't want him to see my hard nipples when I got out, or for him to wrap me with warmth. I knew myself, and I knew I would sink into him and beg him to hold me.

Kova's Adam's apple bobbed as he frowned down at me. "Do not make me pick you up and drop you in there."

"I will fucking kill you if you do that."

He challenged me. "Do not tempt me, Ria. I will do it."

"Can you just go? This… This is too much." He tilted his head to the side and propped his hands on his hips. "It just feels too intimate to me."

His jaw dropped, and his eyes widened in shock. This was the first time I had ever made him do that. "I know," I said, giving him a halfhearted laugh, "but we should really try to not put ourselves in such situations anymore, Kova."

"You have got to be kidding me. After everything that has happened between us, sitting in an ice bath is too intimate for you? Are you serious right now?"

A faint heat crept into my cheeks. I was embarrassed.

I looked down. "I know it sounds stupid—"

"It *is* stupid."

"It's just you are being nice and helping me like this… I don't know, Kova, it's too much for me, too much for us. It shows you care, and honestly, I don't want that."

His brows furrowed. "Why do you not want it?"

"Because it's not something I'm ever given."

"Ria." His voice rose. "Of course I care about you. I care about all of my gymnasts. I would not be here if I did not."

"Right, but you're not supposed to care this much," I stated.

"Why is it wrong that I do?"

I pulled back. "You don't see the real issue, do you?"

"No, please enlighten me."

"Because then you have officially crossed the line. It's one thing to have sex with some-one when you're not supposed to, sex doesn't have to come with strings attached. It's another thing entirely to care for them emotionally. Whether you want to admit it or not, we're crossing that line. You care for me far more than you're obligated to; you would not do the same for the other girls. You know I'm right."

Kova flattened his lips and looked away. If I was being honest, I'd admit I cared far more than I should too. I knew in my heart I did. That's why I was trying to create some distance between us.

When we were together—intimate or just having a conversation—it was explosive, the chemistry combustible. Only we mattered. I got him, he got me. We complimented each other in the most unusual way, and it just worked…when it shouldn't have.

Kova glanced back at me. The onyx that flickered against the brilliant emerald of his eyes captured my attention. I stared back at him for a moment before he nodded, but just barely.

I knew him well enough to know that would be all the acknowledgment I would get, but now he knew too.

chapter 31

KOVA SQUATTED DOWN IN FRONT OF ME AND PUT HIS HANDS ON MY KNEES. "I am trying here, Ria, I really am. Let me be here for you as your coach right now, and nothing more."

"You don't see that this is more than what a coach does, Kova," I whispered. "I'm trying to keep more from happening. We were almost caught by Katja for Christ's sake. I think we should take that as a warning, don't you?"

"I see your point, but with coaching you in the nature that I am, it brings more responsibility on both our parts. For you not to properly take care of yourself afterward physically hurts me. You will cause more damage to your body in the end. Let me help."

When I didn't immediately answer, he dropped his head and rubbed the scruff on his jaw.

I released a sigh of frustration, then tapped the underside of his bicep. I put my hand out when he looked up. He didn't hesitate, he took my hand and stood, helping me up in the process.

"Would you like for me to turn around as you get in?"

I stared at the ice cubes sloshing back and forth. "I'm not taking my clothes off, so no, you don't have to."

I sat on the side of the tub and dipped my toes into the frigid water. A chill zipped up my spine. I pulled them out and huffed out a breath. I couldn't go slow, so I took a deep breath and braced myself. Squeezing Kova's hands, I counted to three, then I placed both feet in and sank down. I yelled out, gasping as the water came up to my neck and slipped over the ledge. A shiver tore through me and my teeth began chattering instantly. The urge to pee hit hard.

"Christ on a stick! I hate this!"

Kova sat on the toilet lid and placed his elbows on his knees. He swiveled my way. "It is a little price we have to pay that will go a long way. Trust me."

I scowled at him. "Easy for you to say. You're not sitting in negative temperatures right now."

"Do not exaggerate. That is roughly ten degrees."

"Same shit, Kova," I spat. "How long do I need to be in here for?"

He glanced down at his watch. "I would say fifteen minutes will do just fine."

My eyes popped wide. I made it to eight minutes with Hayden. There was no way I would last that long. Fuck my life.

"While you are in there," he said, clasping his hands together, "I think now is a good time to talk to you about your future in gymnastics outside of the Olympics."

My eyebrows bunched together. "My future outside the Olympics?"

"Have you considered college yet?"

I pursed my lips together and pulled up my knees. My nipples were aching. I felt like they were going to fall off.

"Well, no. I mean, I have, but I just really only ever had one goal."

"Not necessarily. It is important you know your options. Have your parents not discussed this with you? You can continue your education as well as gymnastics."

"No." My lips were turning numb. "My mom thinks this is just a hobby to pass time. And my dad is wrapped up in his business. Neither of them have brought up college."

He observed me quietly for a moment. "Your brother is in college, yes? How did that happen?"

"Yes, but no one talked to him about it, not that I can remember anyway. In my family, we don't even discuss college. It's just a given that you go. He's at the University of Florida. It's only like a three-hour drive from here. He basically went where his friends went."

Kova's forehead puckered and his mouth set in a hard line. "This is important for your career and something you should be aware of. Say you make a splash in the gym world and people start to recognize you. You make it to the World Championships or another international event and you place on the podium. From time to time, you will have the option to accept award money or endorsements. It is not a whole lot, but if you accept either one, you forfeit your eligibility to compete in college." He angled his body toward me. "It means you are going pro. But what happens if you go pro, and then, God forbid, you are injured before or after the Olympics? Your career as an Olympian is pretty much over. If you do not go pro, your career as a collegiate gymnast is not. I want you to be aware of that."

"But I want to go pro, Kova. I want to reach the highest level of this sport. I thought you understood that."

He shook his head. "You are misunderstanding me. I know what you want completely. I know it is to go to the Olympics, I just want you to think about college gymnastics too. You can still compete in college and go to the Olympics at the same time. It is accepting the prizes and endorsements that will change everything. Taking money means no collegiate gymnastics. Ever."

"So you are saying not to take prize money," I confirmed.

"I would never tell you what to do or what direction to take. I just want you to be informed. Some have regrets going pro while others say it changed their lives."

Kova's cell phone rang and he slipped it out of his pocket. A slight sneer pulled at his mouth before he declined the call and put it back. It had to be Katja.

I looked at the chunks of ice in front of me and mused over what Kova said, thankful he was taking the time to explain this. I'd forgotten I was in the tub while having this discussion, and the moment I looked down at the water a shiver ripped through me. I squeezed my toes. I wasn't aware of this caveat in the sport. My head was as misty as the frosty air elevating around me. If I accepted a prize, I couldn't compete in college…

But the real question was, did I want to compete in college?

I'd never given it a thought until now.

"Well, I clearly don't need the money, so I feel like it's an obvious choice."

He raised his index finger, indicating he wasn't finished. "You would think that, but what if an agent comes along and wants to sign you? Says she will put you in commercials and billboard ads with other top gymnasts around the country?" he challenged. "What if she promises she can make you an abundant amount of money, where you will be able to support yourself within a year and even pay for college should you not be awarded a scholarship? Because surely you will want to support yourself eventually, yes?"

I chewed my lip. Okay. He had a point. And I was upset with myself for being so in the dark about it.

"Of course I want to support myself one day."

I stared at him, not knowing what I should do. Not relying on my parents would be a dream come true, and if I could build that from doing what I loved, the choice was obvious.

Kova threaded his fingers together. "You have a small period until the awards start coming in. I want you to use this time wisely to look past the Olympics. Think about universities. Now is when you want to get noticed by a Division One school. Where do you see yourself in ten years? Surely not competing in your late twenties. Give it some thought."

I chuckled. "Well, no. I don't think my body will make it that far. I thought maybe I'd coach. I don't know…obviously something in gymnastics."

I frowned and studied the sea glass tiled wall in front of me. Beautiful shades of pale greens and ocean blue swooped in between hues of creamy whites. I had been so focused on going all the way that I lost sight of my future. Panic simmered under my skin for being so obtuse. I was mature, I had a stable head on my shoulders, but when it came to the real world, I was as blank as a sheet of paper. I suddenly felt like a two-inch-tall fool. Of course I'd want to compete in school if I could. Why wouldn't I?

"Did you plan to compete in college? Or no?"

"I… I never gave it any thought." My voice quieted. The corners of my mouth tugged further down, embarrassed it never crossed my mind. I glanced at him, my eyes squinting. "I was so fixated on making it to the Olympics that I never considered anything else."

"That happens more than you think. It is not uncommon. If for some reason you do not make it within the year, come the next Games, you will be over twenty."

"Yeah…" I mumbled. I already knew that.

"Did you plan to skip school altogether?" he asked gently, no hint or rise in his voice to make me feel any less.

"No," I said, my voice low, dejected.

I looked away and shifted my legs to a more comfortable position. Cubes of ice nudged my shoulders and neck and I drew in a gasp. The conversation with Kova made me completely forget I was sitting in ice. My sole focus had been on something else entirely to help pass the minutes in the bathtub. Yet it brought an overwhelming burden to my shoulders and a moment of reality slamming into me at the same time.

"My two cents?" he offered.

"Go ahead."

"Forget about the endorsements and prize money. Do not turn pro. You can go all the way without it. You do not need it. Instead, look into colleges, mainly schools with a Division One top-ranking gymnastics team. You are that good and it's where you should be. Just be in the know. It cannot hurt you. If you play your cards right, you can have the best of both worlds. The coaches will be attending competitions soon to start scouting. They make inquiries if they feel you would benefit their school."

I nodded, feeling an abundance of emotions for Kova, but more grateful than anything for this talk. I sat staring into his eyes and wondered if this topic would've ever crossed my mind. I think it would have, just not as soon, and probably too late.

I had no idea schools made inquiries. That was just another reason to give my all when I competed.

Kova studied me, then rolled his broad shoulders and dropped his head. He rubbed the back of his neck and kept his gaze engrossed on my tile floor. Hopefully there weren't a million strands of hair everywhere.

Against my better judgment, I reached out and placed my hand over his and squeezed. He jumped and his head popped up. My frozen fingers shocked him.

I smiled softly, appreciative. It was all I could manage between the shivers that wracked my body. Just when I thought he was going to pull away or say something for showing affection, he stunned me and gave me a squeeze back. My stomach twisted. I didn't want to feel anything for him, but I couldn't help it when he pierced me with those emerald eyes of his. I'd let my guard down…and so had he.

Kova turned his wrist over and glanced at his watch. He hadn't let go of my hand in the process.

He cleared his throat. "Look at that… Time is up."

I pulled the stopper on the drain while Kova went to find a towel. I shivered violently as I stood there listening to the water slurp down. Stepping out of the tub, I hugged myself, certain I would develop hypothermia if Kova didn't hurry up. Every muscle in my body squeezed and my teeth chattered nonstop. Talk about tightening up. Kova walked in with a towel and shook it out, then halted when he looked up. His jaw locked, his eyes slowly roamed my wet body.

I glanced down and gaped.

Shit.

My white sports bra was practically transparent. I might as well have been naked. My breasts were firm and round, plump from the artic temperature. My nipples were embarrassing hard little mauve pebbles enclosed by rings the color of raspberries.

I was throwing all my white undergarments out after this.

"Ah, Kova?" I reached out for the towel. When he didn't respond, I yelled his name. "Kova!" His eyes snapped up to meet mine. "I'm going to die of hypothermia. Give me the goddamn towel!"

Kova grumbled in Russian. "I apologize." He held the towel open and looked away. Without a second thought, I gripped the hem of my sports bra and ripped it up and over my head, then yanked down my shorts and stepped out, leaving them in a messy wet ball on the floor. Goose bumps trailed across my frigid flesh. I hugged myself and stepped into Kova's outstretched arms.

"Hold me tight, please," I whispered into the warmth of his neck.

Kova wrapped his strong arms around my back and pressed me to the length of his body as I rested my head on his chest. He moaned under his breath and I felt the vibration in his chest. I reveled in the warmth of his body. "I like when you need me like this," he whispered, low and warm, and I felt it. His arms tightened, fingers pressing into me as he stepped closer to close the distance. My teeth continued to chatter, my entire body wouldn't stop shaking, and I nearly groaned in misery when the air conditioner flicked on above my head. Chilly air floated across my shoulders and I winced, hunching closer to him.

"Shhh…" he said against my head. "It will pass."

"The…air…" My voice was muffled. Kova glanced up and spotted the air vent.

"Let me get you out of here," he said, then scooped me up and cradled me to his chest. He was so broad and wide that if I curled my body tight enough I could fit from shoulder to shoulder. I eyed the pulsing vein in his neck that was glazed in a sheen of perspiration as he carried me out of the bathroom. I snuggled closer to his warmth and sighed in content.

Kova kept his focus straight ahead while he carried me to my room. He flipped the light switch, and in two steps, he was at the side of my bed. With one hand, he pulled back the comforter and carefully deposited me. He brought the comforter to my neck, all while looking at my headboard. Not me.

"Turn off the fan, please," I begged, already missing his body heat. Kova did as I asked then left the room without making any sort of eye contact with me. I frowned as I listened to the water trickling in the next room and realized he was wringing out my sopping wet clothes. I heard some more shuffling that sounded like he was in my living room. I wasn't sure what he was doing. All I knew was that I felt like he was avoiding me.

Note to self: Strip naked in front of Kova if you want him to ignore you.

I shook my head and curled up in a ball on my side. My only concern now was to get warm, not Kova's precious cracking resolve.

chapter 32

Popping my chin up on my hand, I listened for Kova, but it was oddly quiet. I shuddered under the covers and pulled them tighter to me. Maybe he left without telling me, which would be a blessing in disguise, but at the same time I hoped not. God, I was so indecisive. The way we were with each other, both too drawn to each other, it made us equally awkward and stupid.

Expelling a heavy breath, I climbed out of bed and gripped the towel to me. I tiptoed to the living room, questioning how people lived in places cooler than eighty-five degrees. I'd give anything to sit in a sauna right now.

I hated this.

Crouching down with my knees pressed to my chest, I shivered as I tried to unzip my duffle bag with shaking fingers. The towel loosened around me and draped low down my back. Cool air struck my bare skin.

"What the hell are you doing?" Kova's raucous voice stopped me in my tracks. I didn't need to look over my shoulder to know he was on my couch. He must've been lying down because I hadn't seen him when I walked in. I clutched my cell phone in my shaky hand.

"I got it from here. Th-Thanks for everything, but I-I think you should leave now."

"Get back in bed."

I scowled. Of course he ignored my request.

"Kova, I appreciate everything you-you've done, I-I do, but please leave."

"I will not say it again… Get back in bed." The inflection in his tone caused my heart to skip. His deep, rough lilt sent a new wave of goose bumps over my arms. Releasing a quiet sigh of agitation, I told him my plans.

"I'm having Hayden come over. I need him to h-help me right now. You ca-ca-can't be here when he gets here."

The loud cracking in Kova's knees told me he stood. I risked a glance over my shoulder just in time to catch him scowling at me.

"Like hell you are. Tell me what you need and I will get it. Hot tea? Coffee? Something to eat? Another blanket? What is it that you need?"

You. I needed body heat.

I shook my head and pouted. As if that was possible. I stood, the brisk air wafted across my uncovered flesh. A hard tremor shot down my exposed spine.

"None of those right now."

He threw his hands out in front of him, his brows shot up. "Then what?"

"Just go," I said, scrolling through my phone for Hayden's name. When I found it, I began texting him with jittery fingers. Kova stalked over and ripped my phone from my hands before I could press send.

"Wh-what are you doing?" I reached for my phone. He stepped back when I stepped forward.

"Adrianna."

"What?" I snapped.

"Put your towel back on," he said in a guttural voice. A crease formed between my brows and I glanced down.

Shit. I hadn't even noticed.

If being naked in front of Kova bothered him so much, then this would help get him out of my house faster. Placing my hands on my hips, I pulled my shoulders back and stood bare as the day I was born…and shook. I was frozen to the core.

"If it bothers you s-s-so much, then get out. Because what I need, you ca-can't give me."

Kova's nostrils flared, his eyes burned bright green. "And Hayden can," he stated.

I lifted one shoulder and gave him a blasé expression. "None of your business."

He stepped closer to me, then squatted down slowly and grabbed the towel in his hands without taking his eyes off mine. He raised it along the back of my thighs, my ass, my back. All the while I felt his heated breath dance across my skin. I almost sighed.

"Why must you make this so complicated?" he questioned with a shake of his head and wrapped the towel around my shoulders.

"Everyone knows th-th-the one way to get warm is through b-b-body heat." I shuddered. "Common sense, Kova. Hay-Hayden did it the first time and it helped."

"And that is what you want. My body with yours."

"I don't *w-want* it," I said, dragging my teeth along my bottom lip. "I *need* it. There's a d-d-difference. Right now, I don't f-f-feel right. This is a million times worse than before."

Kova rubbed the ebony stubble on his jaw and glanced away. "What you make me do…" he said hoarsely, then reached behind his head and pulled his shirt off. He dropped it in a soft heap to the floor. My eyes immediately found the Olympic rings tattoo on his ribs I loved so much. His body flexed and contracted, sizzling with energy. I swallowed hard. I didn't think he had the balls—

Never mind. This was Kova I was talking about. Of course he did. He had balls of steel that hung from a body made of stone. A delectable body that had to be derived from cocaine because all it took was one hit and I was addicted.

Kova snatched me up in one swift scoop and carried me back to my room, huffing under his breath in Russian. That's how I knew when he was truly mad—he spoke in his natural tongue. Anger in his steps, he marched as he bound me close to his chest. I wrapped my arms around his shoulders and sank into his heat, sighing. His body was as warm as an inferno and I loved it.

Once in my room, he stopped in front of my dresser and pulled open drawers until he found an oversized T-shirt and sleep pants.

He took two long strides and stood in front of my bed. Carefully releasing my legs down his body, I stood less than an arm length away. I peered up at Kova, breath tight in my throat as my eyes took in his muscular chest.

I loved this man's brutal strength.

With his eyes locked on mine, he reached out and loosened my towel, gently tugging it off. The cloth slid down my breasts and fell to the floor, his darkened gaze following. I stood naked before him without a worry in the world, innocent and young doe eyes looking up at him. His nostrils flared, his blazing eyes sashayed across my nude body. Tentatively, he reached out and glided the back of his fingers over the side of my plump breast. His thumb ran over my hard nipple, and then down the soft curve of my waist. I swallowed hard, trying with effort not to shiver.

"So beautiful it hurts," he whispered. I raised my arms for him to dress me. He put the shirt over my head then slowly pulled it down, the back of his knuckles purposely grazed my raised breasts and pointed nipples. I leaned into his touch and drew in a silent breath.

Dropping to his knees, he nodded to my foot and ordered me to lift. Both feet in, he pulled the elastic waistband up my slender legs. As he slid the material higher up my thighs, his fingers lingered to a standstill when he reached the center of my body. I held my breath as the sinewy muscle coiled around his shoulders flexed. He was a heartbeat away. The beautiful golden honey color of his skin blushed with raw, unabated emotion. My hands formed into fists. I dug my nails into my palms so I wouldn't reach out and touch him.

Carefully, and ever so slowly, I steadied my breathing as his palms slid around the thickest parts of my thighs. Kova grasped my small waist once the pants were securely in place. His head hung sluggishly bowed between us. It tugged at my heart. Yet, I remained still and didn't touch him, even though my fingers itched to.

Kova struggled to stay in control. He trembled, his fingers dug into me. Not hurtful, but more like a man who was on the brink of losing it. I felt his veiled emotion, his vulnerability through his touch. It was how I knew what he was feeling without speaking a word. It was why I hadn't wanted him here, why I had wanted him to leave. Why I knew this was a terrible idea from the beginning, because I knew without a shadow of a doubt what it would lead to. Us being alone had always been a bad idea because no matter what, we always, always, surrendered to our darkest, most forbidden desires.

I relaxed my fist and reached for him with timid fingers.

"Please," he whispered in a strangled voice. "Do not touch me. I am trying to give you what you need and nothing else."

My icy heart splintered. Placing my hand on the nape of his neck, I caressed him. My fingers threaded in his inky black hair in a passionate swoop. Kova trembled below me, his head falling against my hand.

"Ria, please, take your hands off me." His jaw rubbed into my palm.

Ria. I loved when he called me Ria, a nickname only he used. A fire stirred within me as I ignored his plea. The jagged sound of his voice woke the devil on my shoulder. The temperature between us escalated as I continued to play with his hair while he kneeled before me.

"I said, take your hands off me."

I wanted him to make a move. To snap.

I wound my other hand into his hair and began tugging near his scalp. My hips rolled in a gentle wave. I wanted to kneel onto him.

"Ria… You are doing this on purpose and testing my self-control. Stop."

I blinked. I was…and I hadn't even meant to.

My heart pounded viciously against my ribs. I secretly loved pushing his buttons for the sole purpose of his reaction and how passionate he became. A predator with one motive—to attack and devour.

God. What the hell was wrong with me to provoke a man of Kova's stature? And even worse, to want this.

I was disgusting. I was literally the reason why he acted the way he did.

Kova lifted his head and blew out a hot, tortured breath. His hands trembled.

"Why is it so hard for me to be faithful when it comes to you?" His lips were ridiculously close to my naval. "It is like my resistance breaks and you are all that I see, everything I want."

"I don't know. I don't do it on purpose," I confessed. "It's wrong, and I hate myself for wanting you, for putting you in this situation."

"The feeling is entirely mutual."

I should've been hurt by his response, but I wasn't. I understood where he was coming from. An energy between two people so powerful it couldn't be contained, no matter how much they tried. No matter how wrong, how illicit, how morally sinful.

Some things were meant to be without reason.

Kova scooped me up and carried me to the bed in two long strides. He climbed under the covers and aligned his body to mine. He was so damn hot, and I snuggled closer, relishing his body heat. Tipping his head forward, he pressed his sensual lips to my forehead, then sandwiched one thick leg between mine and locked together. I drew in a slow and deep lungful of air, and tried to steady my breathing. Kova held his lips to my skin, as if he was afraid to move. We were that in tune. Wrapping his arms around my slim waist, he inhaled through his nose and applied another gentle kiss.

He glanced down.

I held my breath.

He held his.

I stared into his troubled eyes. He was in agony, on the cusp of doing wrong. My mind was tangled with warnings, while my heart was entwined with his.

I couldn't explain why, but I liked that I could tempt him, seduce him. It was a powerful feeling. There was too much we could do in my condo without being caught.

With my hands cupping his sharp jaw, I leaned in to close the distance, and hesitated. My mouth itched for his, the electricity thick as fog. I hovered in front of him, wanting this and terrified of the domino effect it could cause, just like the other day in his office. We breathed each other in, our eyes frantically shifting back and forth. I contemplated for a moment—

"Do not do it," he whispered.

But I did. I pressed my mouth to his. Kova's hands slid up my back and rested on my shoulders where he pulled me to him. His greedy touch contradicted his words, just like they always did, and I melted into him.

chapter 33

KOVA'S SIZZLING HEAT PRESSED TO MY ICY ONE.

He inhaled deeply and angled his mouth against mine, tugging with little nips of his teeth. His tongue danced seductively along the seam of my lips. I sighed as he slipped his tongue inside and caressed me, stroking with a gentle passion that was full of fire. His nimble fingers laced my hair and I wrapped my arms around his shoulders. He rolled onto his back, taking me with him. I straddled his hips with ease. A small moan escaped me when his hardness pressed against my center. I lifted my shirt over my head and tossed it aside. Pressure throbbed between my thighs, building as my hips slowly moved against his rigid shaft, like a languid wave reaching for the shore.

"Why can you never listen?" he said between kisses.

An airy laugh flowed from me. "You pulled me with you."

Kova wrapped a strong arm around my lower back and one across the top, seizing my neck in his grasp. God, I loved his hold over me. How dominant he was. I liked being on top of him, it showed how small I was in comparison to him. There was nowhere for me to move other than how he was coercing my body by the power of his touch. I succumbed to him.

"Why?" he pressed on, pulling me back just enough to look into my eyes. A shallow moan escaped him, abandoned pleasure intensified in his watchful gaze. My body moved of its own accord, my hips swiveled on his until he put a firm stop to the motion, securing me in place. His cock twitched and he groaned.

"Why? Answer me, please."

"I don't have a real answer for you other than we both want this and you know it."

He shook his head, vehemently denying it. "I am trying to do the right thing."

"Lies. Your body lies."

"You do not heed my pleas. I tell you to stop, but you do the complete opposite. Why must you do this to me?" He clenched his teeth, pushing my hips hard to his. I let out a gasp, wetness seeped from me. I tried to rub myself on him, but he stopped me again. I whimpered. "Does the fact that I have a girlfriend mean anything to you?"

"No," I said in all honesty. I really didn't care.

"You are fucked up in the head, you know that? What if she was my wife? Would that make a difference to you then?"

I ignored the little dig. "Would it make a difference to you?"

"It would not, would it?" he asked in complete shock when I ignored his question.

"No. If it doesn't matter now, why would it matter then?"

He scoffed, yet he was still holding me to him. "Unreal."

"You fucking like it, Kova, so stop pretending that you don't. We both want this."

"You are a big contradiction, you know that?"

I tried to kiss him, but his fingers threaded in my hair and he pulled on it, close to the roots to keep me back.

"Any man with a cock would like it, Ria," he mocked, cupping my breast. He twisted my nipple between two fingers until it blazed with heat and I gasped, my back going erect. "It is science. Chemistry. Anatomy. A tight pussy to fuck."

"Any tight pussy will do, then?" I whispered, staring into his eyes, finally grasping his cock. I gripped him tight in my little fist and used my thighs to slide up and down, rotating my hips against his like I was giving him a lap dance, even though I'd never done one in my life. Arousal heightened my blood and my body flushed with need. A husky sound vibrated in Kova's chest. His jaw tightened. If he could play, so could I.

He shook his head. His fingers dug into me. "You will regret this tomorrow."

I didn't answer, instead, I asked him a question. "Will you regret it?"

"Yes."

He didn't hesitate. The look in his frenzied eyes exposed the truth, and it bothered me.

Another pinch to my already sensitive heart. I was completely off. Maybe he really didn't want this. Perhaps he was trying to behave himself.

Perhaps I didn't care.

I faltered for a moment, his gaze focused solely on me. His hard, unyielding body nestled beneath mine as he breathed across my cheek. "I like watching you fall apart in my arms. It is the most beautiful thing I have ever seen…but I have regretted it every time more than you can imagine. Especially the other night. I do not want to live with this regret anymore, *malysh*. It is killing me," he admitted, and I felt the pain in his words. He was honest, and while honesty was important to me, it also hurt. "Have mercy on me," he begged, his eyes pleading with me.

I was too far gone with desire for this man to heed his plea.

Leaning forward, I looked straight into his glossy eyes and whispered, "Why do I crave you so bad? Why do I have this desire to be with you whenever you're around? For you to make me orgasm the way you do? I want you inside me, and I know you want to be there." I licked a wet trail along his bottom lip and delved my tongue between his warm lips. Widening my hips, I rubbed myself on him and pleasure shot through me. His erection stroked my sensitive clit and I panted. Kova responded immediately and I grinned against his delicious mouth. "Please."

Using my hand, he guided it to my sex. "Touch yourself."

I shook my head and pinched his chest with my free hand. Kova stared back at me with huge eyes.

"I want *you* to touch me."

He dragged his teeth along his bottom lip. God that was so sexy.

I needed more. I needed skin-on-skin contact.

I pulled his wrist away to slip it into my pants. He went willingly. My back arched, my head fell to his shoulder as his fingers found my clit. He rubbed in circles, using my wetness as a lubricant.

"Oh God," I said breathlessly. I ground against his fingers. My lips found Kova's neck and I sucked hard, lapping my tongue around his salty skin as I pulled him into my mouth. He moaned with a shutter of pleasure, and breathed heavily against my skin. His chest heaved against mine. My teeth trailed his muscular shoulder as his palm slipped further toward my entrance. He played with me. I bit down, a dark desire swirled inside me to break his skin. A deep and husky moan lifted from his lips when he felt my wet pussy. My fingers wound to the back of his head. I seized his hair in my hand and tugged. Kova grunted, his arm tightening around my lower back. Squeezing my eyes shut, I battled the release I craved so desperately, but my hips picked up speed, rocking in a slow and delicious motion.

"That is it… Come for me, *malysh*. Come just like this."

I moaned, shaking my head against his neck. "Come with me… I need to feel you," I mumbled, drunk on Kova. This was a sure fire way to rid my body of the effects of an ice bath.

He murmured in Russian, his breath hot as it caressed down my neck. It sounded like he spoke a series of sentences, none of the words sounding similar, but all coming out deeper and guttural than the next. His finger pressed against the tight bundle of nerves that was embarrassingly wet. I could feel myself seeping with desire and that only fueled the grinding of my hips even more. I rose and placed my hands flat to his chest.

"Eyes on me," he demanded. "I want you to take your pants off and get back on me the way you are now."

I nodded hastily and did as he asked…and so did he. Kova tugged his shorts down and his erection sprang free—tall, and thick and hard. Waving me toward him, I climbed back onto his hips and straddled him, his penis between us. He grabbed my wrists and put my hands on his stomach, then took my hips in his hold and lifted me. Just when I thought he was going to push into me, he didn't. Instead, he pulled me higher up on him so my pussy was pressed to his penis and nearly flat to his stomach. Guiding my hips, I watched as he rubbed me up and down his length. The pleasure that tore through my body was mind blowing and my arms buckled. I fell on top of him.

He slapped my thigh. "Hold yourself up and watch," he said. I nodded and looked down, my orgasm beginning to take hold, starting at my toes. His shaft glistened from me and my lips were spread wide to hug his thickness.

A breathy moan rolled off my lips and I sat back so I could pleasure myself on him. My hips picked up speed and I couldn't tear my eyes from watching my pussy glide up and down his cock. It was erotic and a huge turn on.

"No, no. Pay attention. Softly and slowly move on me, that way you can feel every inch of my dick. Caress me with your pussy, slow and sweet." My pace slowed, and he guided me to do what he wanted, rotating my hips up with a flick of his wrist. "Yes, like that."

Heavy breathing, panting.

Kova moved his hips with a deliberate seductiveness that enthralled me. Damn. This. Man. My eyes were glued to the bare, toned flesh of his stomach that contracted and flexed with each shift of his body. He used his thighs and rolled his hips ever so slowly up and down. My mouth watered, my chest burned for the real deal. I wanted him to make love to me just like that. A slow thrust in, a slow pull out.

"Watch us."

Like I could watch anything else. His hips moved up and down, just enough to create a maelstrom of insane desire between us. I started following the motion, mimicking his hips.

"Yeah, baby. Just like that." I slowly moved over him, grinding as I did. I rose, and he curled his fingers forward and pushed on my tender flesh. The stroke of his fingers felt fucking divine. Then as I lowered myself, he straightened them. "You are dripping all over me."

I knew I was. My inner thighs were drenched and I could smell it in the air.

"Kova," I said breathlessly. "This is incredible. The best."

He lifted one side of his mouth. A hint of arrogance showed. "Of course it is. Do you not know by now that I am always right?"

"More, I want more. I want to know how to do more, feel more." So close. I was so close to exploding. "Oh God! I'm almost there." My hips picked up speed. "Stay just like that," I cried and stroked his length, feeling the ridges as I moved, just like he said I would. I hit just the right spot and yelled out, throwing my head back. My nails dug into his skin, striking solid muscle. Seconds later, and with a hold so strong around my back, I was coming on Kova with a vengeance.

He groaned, riding the swell of ecstasy with me. "God what I would give to feel that around my cock right now. To be so deep inside you. *Krasivaya*, to feel you squeezing and pulsating…"

"What does that mean?" I asked, trying to catch my breath.

"Beautiful."

Kova slid a finger over my sensitive clit and gently rubbed it. I shuddered, goose bumps coated my flesh. Just that touch alone made me want to do it all over again.

My eyes narrowed in awe as he tilted his head slightly and brought his fingers to his mouth. I watched him slide them, glossy with wetness, between his lips and suck them clean.

I felt something twitch against me. I looked down and my brows furrowed together.

"You're still hard," I stated. "Why didn't you finish?"

Kova flattened his mouth and grimaced. He looked away and I climbed off him to sit next to him. His raging erection still standing straight up. It had to hurt.

"Are you going to ignore me?"

"I do not have to answer to you." Each word packed a punch. I reeled back at his harsh tone. The air in the room changed completely and I was confused. He looked down at me with shrewd eyes.

"How do you feel?" he asked.

"Oh, so we're back to this?"

"Yes, we are."

I pursed my lips together. "I feel just peachy," I said sarcastically.

"Do not get cute with me. You got what you wanted."

"I did, but why didn't you?"

He shook his head and kept his mouth closed. As if the answer was obvious, but it wasn't. Kova got out of my bed and walked into the living room to collect his shirt. I followed behind.

"Kova. What's your problem? Why the sudden change?" I pushed.

"Because it is not what I wanted!" he roared, spinning to face me. "I told you, I did not want this, but you push, and push, and push until I break. I do everything I can to keep you away. I take you out of a meet, I am purposely mean to you, and yet you keep coming back. But then I see you need help and I cannot stop myself. Anything you want, I want to give you. I cannot not bend to your will. I wish I could, but I cannot. I do not understand what else I can do anymore. You are breaking a man. Do you not get that? You are breaking me," he bellowed with his hand to his chest, his eyes pleading with me to understand him.

My jaw dropped. "What about what happened in your office? That was all you." I retorted.

"Just let it go," Kova said dejectedly, staring at the floor, hands propped on his hips. "Go. Come on." He looked up and stalked toward me.

"Where are we going?" I asked.

"*We* are not going anywhere. You are going to rest in bed while I get you something to eat."

"Just stop. I feel like you're babying me."

Kova replied in Russian and that set me off. "You know damn well I don't understand what you said. You did that on purpose to talk shit."

Kova stared right through me. I felt two inches tall.

"Words hurt, and I am trying not to hurt you right now."

"We just had sex not even twenty-four hours ago, so that hurts even more than you can imagine," I said quietly.

Filled with more remorse and regret than I thought possible, I turned around and walked to my room.

chapter 34

"**T**HANK GOD YOU DIDN'T HIT THE FUCK YOU BUTTON ON ME…AGAIN," I SAID quietly into the phone while sitting on my bed.

Kova was still in the other room and I didn't want him to hear. I needed some time alone. He had hurt me; but it appeared I had hurt him more, and that caused a massive amount of guilt to weigh down on my shoulders.

I didn't want to hurt him.

"Where have you been?"

"Around," Avery said casually. "Sometimes you get busy and I can't get ahold of you," she added in a snippy tone.

I frowned. "That's not true. I don't have any missed calls or texts from you."

"Whatever. Things have been hectic. What's going on?"

I didn't like the perturbed sound in her voice, but I also didn't push. "I just miss talking to you, I miss hanging out with you. I wish you were here."

"You're getting mushy. Wait. Why do you sound so fucking sad?" she scoffed. We didn't do mush. "We haven't talked in a cool minute and when we finally do, you sound like you're ready to drive off a bridge. Please don't tell me you're listening to cutter music now."

Something between a huff and a laugh escaped me. "Cutter music?"

"Yeah, cutter music. You know, music so depressing you want to slit your wrists? Cutter music. Like Lana Del Rey for instance. She sounds fucking miserable in every song, I can't take it. As if she hates her life and wants to end it for no good reason, not that there should ever be a reason, but still. Stunning beauty with the classic Hollywood look, but then she opens her mouth and she just sounds *so* damn sad and I cringe. I don't know, I just can't stand it. Same with Sia. Don't get me started on her. Another beauty, but her voice and lyrics drip with misery. She's worse than Lana."

I laughed. She had a point. "No, not my style."

"Thank God," she exaggerated. "Are you getting excited for your meet? Wish I could be there with you."

I smiled into the phone. "Yeah, but I'm nervous more than anything." And I was. No matter how much I prepared myself, no matter how much Kova whipped me into gear, stress-filled thoughts consumed me every minute of the day. "I upped my training, so now I practice every day for the next three weeks. I want to be ready when I test for elite."

"With Mr. Kissable, I presume."

I was silent for a minute.

"Oh hell. What aren't you telling me?" Avery asked.

"Nothing."

"Don't nothing me," she quipped. "You're lying. Spill!"

I looked over my shoulder at the door, as if I could see through it to what Kova was doing. "He's here," I said quietly.

"Who's there? Why are we whispering?" Avery lowered her voice to match mine.

I chuckled. "Why are *you* whispering?"

She paused, then with a laugh resumed her normal tone. "I have no idea. Who is at your place?"

"I'll give you three tries, but I have a feeling you're only going to need one."

It didn't take long for my best friend to catch on. "Oh fuck me. What is wrong with you? It's like you have Lucifer on both of your shoulders cheering you on. The louder he gets, the dumber you get."

I laughed. "It just happened."

"Ria, it doesn't just happen." She scolded me as if I were a small child. "We've gone over this, you can't just fall onto a dick."

"That's not what happened at all. Not this time at least."

"So, you mean to tell me there was no touching or orgasms?"

"I didn't say that…"

"Of course you didn't." I pictured her rolling her eyes. "An orgasm is just expected when you're alone with the perv. I need to break you of this habit. It won't end well for anyone." Avery stopped and then shouted, "Oh my God! He really is Lucifer! That's what I'm going to call him from now on. It's very fitting, wouldn't you agree?"

"Ave—"

"Lucifer needs to change the title of his gym. How about…World Cup Academy of Orgasms. Or, World Cup Academy of Gymnastics—where everyone walks away with a happy ending, you just have to hand over your virginity first."

A loud laugh erupted from me. Avery had wit and once she started, I didn't want her to stop. In a strange way, I was addicted to her personality. She had a fearless and cavalier attitude I wished I had.

"Seriously," Avery said, her tone switching to serious. "What's going on? Why is *he* there? Tell me everything and don't leave even a smirk out."

One side of my mouth lifted. I debated what to tell my best friend. I was used to lying when it came to anything me and Kova related, but I didn't feel like I needed to lie to Avery anymore.

"I had conditioning today, and it broke me. It was just me and Kova, nonstop, all day. No breaks, no lunch, just some water. Then full-on physical and verbal contact. Ave, I could barely stand when it ended. Never in my life have I been so depleted of energy. I was so out of it that when Kova asked me a question, I told him exactly what I was thinking instead of giving him what he wanted to hear. Long story short, we spat a bit and he left me with no choice but to allow him to drive me home."

"How long were you there?"

"About eight hours."

"Eight hours! You guys had sex for eight hours?" she yelled. "Who does that! And with someone fresh off the newly broken hymen express!"

I pulled the phone away from my ear at the sound of her high-pitched voice and looked at it. *The newly broken hymen express?* What in the ever-loving hell was she talking about? Just as I was about to ask her, it dawned on me what she meant.

"Oh, my God. We were working on gymnastics skills all day. You're a moron, you know that? A full-fledged moron."

"Jesus fuck. Thank you. There is a God sometimes." Relief flooded her voice.

"I can't believe you thought we were having sex for eight hours," I whispered, cupping my hand around the receiver. I pulled my knees to my chest. "You're demented," I added for extra guilt, then told her the rest of the story. I even went as far as to confess my darkest, most enigmatic thoughts. I told her how I liked persuading him to do things he didn't want to, that it created a swirling, climbing power inside me to see him bend at the knee. How I nearly made it my goal to push him to the brink of madness, only to watch him surrender and give us both what we wanted, how we wanted it. How I made him talk to me about things on his mind.

Avery was extra quiet by the time I finished.

"Ave?"

"Yeah." She cleared her throat. "I'm here. Honestly, I never know with you anymore. I don't know what to say because I'm concerned it could be the opposite of what you need. When it comes to that man, you're reckless and wild and risky. It worries me." Quietly, she added, "You're a stranger when it comes to him. The things you tell me, I never expect to come from you. I wouldn't even recognize you if I passed you on the street."

I mused over her words, not liking how they hit home. But she was right. I sensed a change in myself and how irresponsible I'd become with him around. It was another reason why I hadn't wanted him to come over, why I hadn't wanted to be alone with him any longer. I knew myself and how I would react. He was a temptation I couldn't resist. I was a desire he craved. We were the worst and best kind of combination.

I sighed inwardly and looked up at the ceiling.

"I think I know. The only reason anyone ever changes is because there's more going on. Deeper feelings. Ones not obviously addressed or acknowledged. I think that's what's going on with me and I didn't realize it until you said it. It worries me because when that happens, people become reckless when they're trying to hide something. Eventually, they slip up and every liar gets caught. I have feelings for him, Avery, both good and bad. I don't know how to shut them off either. I thought I did, but I really don't. There are moments when I need to breathe in the air he expels, but then I want to turn around and suffocate the life out of him at the same time. I don't know what to do," I said softly. "Maybe I'm just not strong enough to combat them."

I shook my head. I was hollow inside. My eyes watered from staring so hard and not blinking. I hated to think for a moment I'd been defeated without a worthy fight, but it's exactly how I felt. Hopeless.

"It really isn't your fault, though. It makes me angry to think that you think it is. The *coach* knows better. He is a grown adult," she said, enunciating each word. "He didn't have to do anything today, not even bring you home, but he forced himself. He's taking advantage of your naive innocence."

I shook my head vehemently, surprised she would talk with such animosity. It completely caught me off guard.

"He isn't taking anything; I'm giving it to him, Avery. That's the problem. I'm physically and emotionally attracted to this man. I want to be around him all the time. I like learning from him. He teaches me and listens to me. And as much as I try to hate him, I just can't. I mean I do, but I don't. God. I don't know what I'm saying other than there's no taking anything. I swear to you," I whispered, my voice almost taking on a falsetto range. "If anything, it's me trying to take."

"It's too hard for you to see it through my perspective. He didn't *have* to come over. He didn't *have to* stick his hand in your vagina and teach you how to fuck his fingers like a porn star. He's literally teaching you how to fuck and getting you off to encourage more. I feel like there's a motive to everything he does. It's a choice he makes, and you dangling yourself in front of him to play with doesn't help the cause. It's just weird, especially given his age."

I reeled back at her disgusted tone, momentarily speechless. A headache formed at the center of my forehead.

"Pot calling the kettle black?" I became defensive. "What about your *older* mystery boyfriend? The one I've never met, or even know his name. I have never given you crap about him like you are to me. I gave you my shoulder and supported your decisions. Shelve that attitude for another time. It's not warranted."

"Mine is just under five years older," she retorted, raising her voice. "Not sixteen years or whatever it is. I can't do math. It's completely different."

"It's not."

"Oh, but it is. It was all fun and games at first. I figured since Hayden found out it'd knocked some sense into you. Or when the bastard took you out of a competition, or when he fucks you bare then throws some Tic Tacs your way. How the hell do you know he doesn't have an STD? You don't. Nothing has gotten through your thick skull and it's only a matter of time until you're really screwed. You're lucky Hayden won't speak a word of it…yet. Mark my words, the next time you're caught will be worse. That's how it always happens, Aid. All the lies will catch up to you one day. The thorns will grow longer, and the vines will get so twisted you won't be able to walk out unscathed."

"What if *you* get caught," I countered.

"No one would care," she scoffed.

"Oh, really? Then why is it such a secret? Who is he?" Avery was silent. I smiled and repeated my earlier words. "See, pot calling the kettle black."

She sighed deeply. "I don't want to argue with someone who believes white lies, and I never want to fight with my best friend. It hurts too much to, but I can't talk to you right now." Her voice sounded as tight as my chest felt. "I have too much going on to add this to my growing pile of shit. Too many people upset with me for the things I've said out of emotion, and I don't want you to be one of them now. I'm trying to fix things before I jump off a fucking cliff. Just trust me that your secret affair is a million times worse than mine. I'm only trying to look out for you, but I can't deal with this level of stupidity anymore."

Avery hung up, shocking me to the core.

I stared down at my phone, dazed and confused, staggered into silence. I wasn't mad. I didn't have it in me to be upset. Not when I could tell deep down Avery was dealing with something on a grander scale. Something I had no real clue about. She was hurting inside, and that in turn hurt me because she didn't confide in me the way I had her.

A tear slid down my cheek. I relied on her too much. It was selfish of me, and I didn't realize she needed me the way I did her. I was too consumed with my life to recognize anyone else's.

A light tap sounded on my door. I quickly wiped away my tears as Kova stepped inside. Our eyes locked and his face crumbled when he took in the site of me. He wasn't angry with my antics anymore—his face showed nothing but sympathy for me.

Everything came roaring back. How conniving I'd been toward him, how self-centered I was toward Avery, how I forced Hayden to carry a burden of lies for me. Tears fell like a waterfall and Kova rushed over and gathered me into his arms.

"Come, *malysh*. Come here," he said, pulling me close to him. "I take it that was your mother?"

I shook my head. "Avery," I said through the tears.

"I imagine that is worse for you."

More tears fell and I nodded. My heart hurt so bad. Kova climbed into my bed and got under the covers with me. He aligned his body with mine and I cried silently into his chest. He kept me warm and comforted.

"I'm sorry for ruining your life," I said, my voice muffled. It felt like I left a tarnished imprint in everyone's life lately.

He kissed my forehead and snuggled me to him. "You have not ruined my life. If anything, you have made it better."

My jaw trembled. "Kova?"

"Yes," he said, rubbing the back of my head. Fatigue hit me hard, I could barely keep my eyes open much longer.

"You should probably go home. It's getting late." *And I'm sure Katja is wondering where you are*, I wanted to add.

"I am right where I want to be. Now go to sleep."

chapter 35

EXHAUSTION HAD CAUGHT UP TO ME.

"Adrianna, have you lost weight? You look awfully thin today."

I picked my head up and met Kova's concerned gaze. He stood before me, his face scrunched together while his eyes scanned the length of my body. He gawked unhappily while I dug through my gym bag searching for my wristbands. I had vault with Madeline soon.

"Um, no? Not that I know of, but even if I had, wouldn't that be a good thing?" I mocked with annoyance, rolling my eyes.

"Excuse me?" he retorted, placing his hands on his hips.

It's been over three weeks straight of this self-induced madness I had asked for. Over three weeks of long and grueling, hardcore extra conditioning. Fifteen-hour-day practices, muscles so overworked it hurt to walk or even lift a fork, sports tape covering various parts of my body, so much Motrin I should be committed for abusing it. Biting words crammed with harsh disagreements hurled back and forth. And of all things to say, my coach asked me if I had lost weight.

He should be fucking beaming if I had.

Okay…I was a little cranky lately.

I dropped my bag and stood taller, digging my heels into the floor. I winced. Today was not my day. I had an awful headache and my Achilles was throbbing terribly. It started out as a dull twinge here and there over a week ago and had progressed into a fiery pulse since then. But I had hidden it well, no one would suspect I'd been dealing with this new pain.

Not to mention, I peed blood again, only this time it wasn't as much.

Lowering my voice, my heart sped up as I said, "You repeatedly tell me I sound like an elephant when I land. Obviously, I'm too fat for your taste. My mom is *still* harping on me. It wasn't like I was trying to lose weight, but if it happened, then I'd called that a blessing in disguise. Wouldn't you?"

Kova stepped closer, a cruel darkness swirling about him. I swallowed hard.

"I am getting sick of your attitude, little girl. I have done nothing but give you what you begged me for every day, and every day you reward me with a sharp tongue I want to cut out. I do not know who you think you are talking to me like that, but it is getting old. You better get rid of that attitude fast."

"Or what?" I snapped, putting emphasis on the T. I licked my dry lips and Kova watched, his forehead creasing together.

Just when I thought he was going to come back with another ultimatum, he caught me off guard.

Kova titled his head to the side to scan my body again. Now he seemed alarmed more than anything, like he actually looked at me.

"Are you sleeping enough?"

"What?"

"Answer the question. Are you sleeping? You have bags under your eyes, you are haggard looking. I guarantee if I put you on a scale it would show weight loss. And you are moody."

"I sleep like a baby," I lied. I hadn't slept in weeks, not since the night Kova stayed over. I was running on fumes, past the brink of exhaustion, and yet, somehow, I was still here giving it my all. I think it was sheer will and determination that drove me, because my body was ready to collapse at any minute. Maybe a dash of hardheadedness. Who needed sleep when their future was a ticking time bomb? I had one week until my first meet. There was no time to sleep when I had so much to do.

He squinted his eyes. "Is there something you want to talk to me about, maybe? Did I do something? Am I pushing you too hard?"

I scoffed. "I'm dealing with PMS. My cramps are terrible and I'm about to get my period. Not everything is about you, Kova." Partially true. Mostly a lie.

All I ever did now was lie.

Kova closed his mouth, but I knew by the look in his eyes he didn't believe me. I *was* overworked, and I was fucking *tired*. I had no time to sleep.

I could sleep when I'm dead.

His arms dropped to his sides and pity filled his face. Kova's entire mood shifted. "Go home, Ria," he said softly.

Fire fueled me, my eyes widened. "What? No!" I rebutted, stepping back. "You have no reason to send me home."

He took a step toward me and cupped my shoulder with empathy. "I can see it in your face that you are drained. You look like shit. I worried practicing at this magnitude would set you back."

"Oh, please. I've only gotten better, and you know it. But Coach Kova has a bug up his ass. When he gets mad, gymnasts must leave," I mocked, rolling my eyes, and regretted the words the moment they left my lips. I sounded like a damn child.

He was still soft with me. "Yes, you give me lip, and yes, I take it, but this is not like you, Adrianna. It worries me. Go home and sleep. Your body obviously needs it. Take tomorrow off and go to the doctor. Get your vitals checked. You have not been yourself lately. If you do not, and you keep up this behavior, the closer the competition gets, the weaker you get. It will not end well for you."

I stood my ground, grinding my teeth together. "I'm not weak."

"I would never take you for a weak person."

"I'm not leaving. I have two hours of vault practice left. *Then* I will go home."

Kova shook his head in incredulity. "What is it with you? When are you going to learn I have your best interest at heart and to trust me? I am genuinely worried about you. You clearly need rest."

"The last time I put all my trust in your hands, you hurled it away. I can't afford to let that happen again."

"I thought we were past that. You just cannot let it go, can you." Kova looked away, his jaw tightened. I loved when it flexed like that. Such a masculine thing to me.

"Nope, and I won't. So, now, if you'll excuse me, I see Madeline growing more and more impatient with me by the second. I need to get to vault. I'm sure she'd love to know what this little spectacle was about. She doesn't like it when I waste her time."

Kova stared at me with disdain written plain as day on his handsome face.

I lowered my voice. "I'm going to do what I need to in order to get what I want."

"I understand that, Adrianna, but you are going about it all wrong. This is going to back-fire on you, trust me."

I shook my head and turned around.

"You are walking on thin ice with me," Kova said under his breath before I was two steps away.

Looking over my shoulder, I said, "What could you do that could possibly hurt me even more?" When he said nothing, I smirked and turned back around, walking away.

"Your legs separated off the spring board, and in flight."

I landed with the sound of Kova's voice to my right. I glanced at him and grimaced. I wasn't sure why he was here when he wasn't my vault coach, but one thing I was sure about was that he had other girls to coach and mentally break down aside from me.

"I know. Madeline already told me," I said dryly, fixing my leotard. It had pulled up on one side, giving me a wedgie. Hated when that happened. I walked past him as if he was a stranger.

It had been an hour since he tried to send me home, and I was still fuming.

"So lock your ankles together instead of trying to glue your thighs," he suggested behind me as I readjusted my ponytail and tucked in the flyaways. "Sometimes stronger quads make it hard for the legs to stay closed."

I gave him a thumbs up and kept walking.

I stopped in front of Madeline who looked at Kova behind me in question. My stom-ach churned. I prayed to the heavens above that I kept my face neutral as she glanced back and forth between us. I didn't need to look over my shoulder to know that Kova was cool as a cucumber himself.

"So the good thing about your leg separation"—Madeline returned her attention to me—"is that I know you're squeezing your butt really hard to keep everything tight. That shows you're trying, but now let's get those legs glued together. Try your vault again and focus on trying to glue your ankles together, like Coach Kova suggested."

I nodded with a firm mouth and walked back to the end of the vault runway and stood behind the line. Taking a deep breath, I mentally prepared myself by visualizing the Amanar, a two-and-a-half twisting Yurchenko, with closed ankles. The hardest vault for women to execute.

I breathed out a strenuous breath and whispered to myself, "I got this." I visualized what I needed to do.

Looking directly at the vault, I sprinted toward it, gaining speed with every pump of my legs. Just a few feet away, I hurdled into a round off, punched the springboard with both my feet and arched into a back-handspring. I made sure my block was strong with a pop of my shoulders off the vault to gain as much height as I could, an absolute must for this skill. Sometimes in flight, or really with any skill, it was difficult to tell if a gymnast made a mistake.

As I landed, exhaustion struck me with the weight of fifty bricks. A massive huff escaped my chest. My eyes rolled shut and everything turned dark for a split moment.

I glanced at Madeline for approval, completely ignoring Kova's searing gaze. I pretended like I didn't notice him.

"Better, but you had a slight leg bend. If we can just tighten it up and control it, I have a gut feeling you are going to turn heads with your vault, Adrianna. The height you get is unbelievable."

A massive smile spread across my face. Coach Madeline's words gave me hope, some-thing Kova loved to crush.

As if my smile could get any bigger, my cheeks burned when she said, "I love the improvement I'm seeing with you. Really great work." Madeline's enthusiasm was contagious. My belly fluttered with excitement and hope, erasing the tiredness.

After another hour of working on vault, I was feeling the effects of Madeline's coaching. My shoulders ached from arching back and popping off the table, and my stomach was tighter than a fishing knot. I had done so many practice vaults I'd lost count, but strange enough, I wasn't ready to go home. I was more pumped than ever.

Madeline was strict and tough, but with a feminine touch. She knew how to push without breaking down a gymnast. Many coaches trained with an iron fist. I had no issue with that mentality. I got it, and I understood why they did it, it worked in my advantage. It took a strong mind to ignore the harsh comments and push past them. But some days it was a nice change to have someone like Madeline coach you.

Most of the time I welcomed the change with Madeline, but I preferred Kova's training any day. Not because of what occurred between us, it had absolutely nothing to do with that. Kova could crush me in seconds, but he pushed me harder than anyone else ever had. And I loved it more than words could ever express.

A hard practice produced confidence.

Confidence could move mountains.

Adrianna Rossi. An emotional sadist at its finest.

"Come. I have some drills I think will benefit you I want to work on before you leave." Madeline's voice broke into my thoughts.

I followed her to the tumble tramp, climbed up, and stood feet together in the middle. There was a landing mat at the end with a massively tall rectangular blue mat made up of vinyl and nylon mesh fabric.

I loved this trampoline for the simple fact that I could practice tumbling passes until I was blue in the face without putting stress on my body. It reduced injury from multiple repetitions. At the elite level, that's all we did—repetitions.

"Let's do some handstand hops. I want you to be aware of your wrist extensions so when you push through, you don't put all the weight on your shoulders. You need to extend your wrist as much as possible when you pop up."

I nodded and moved into position. I'd never done this drill on a trampoline, only on floor, so I knew exactly what she meant. My palms touched the black spring mesh bound together by bungee cords on each side. I popped off my hands into another handstand without touching the floor, and came loose. My hips dropped to the right and my knees bent, pulling into my stomach. I caught myself and stood up.

Madeline looked up at me. "You weren't tight, but you got the power. Keep your chest in." She hollowed her chest to form a curve with her upper body and tapped it. "I don't want to see your ass, roll them hips under and open, girl. Hip flexors flat, so you're constantly working on keeping them flat and open. Closed hips show you're a frightened amateur, opened hips show you're in control and fearless."

My coach was one hundred percent correct. This time when I did the handstand hop, I did it correctly.

"Good. Now let's do a few passes of those up and down, say about"—she squinted her eyes like she was thinking about it—"thirty?"

Thirty was not a few passes, but I wasn't going to argue with her. If I could do them on the floor, then sixty rows total up and down thirty feet of narrow trampoline would be a piece of cake.

By the time I finished, my wrists were a bit tender. They cracked a few times mid-hop that produced a wince from me, but overall, I felt great.

Standing at the edge, Madeline reached up and handed me a blue square. I knew where she was going with this before she said anything. I did similar drills on bars with these foam squares.

"Put the block between your knees and squeeze. Back handsprings up and down the track. This will give you cleaner and tighter back handsprings. Use those inner thighs."

Not only would this drill really benefit four events, but it would also rectify legs separating when moving from low bar to high bar. Any time I saw legs split just even a hair open during a Shaposh, I would grimace. It annoyed me to no end and all I could see was sloppiness from there on out. That being said, it was a lot harder to keep them closed than together. I completely understood the issue.

"Now back tucks," Madeline ordered before I reached the end of the track. Once I'd gotten a little more than halfway down the mat, she yelled, "Look how when your legs are tightly squeezed together how your hips rotate faster. It's beautiful and clean. This is what I want all the time, Adrianna. Great job!" Just when I thought I was going to get a second to catch my breath and not jump, Madeline added, "Now full twists with the foam."

Shit. My stomach was a flaming ball of heat from squeezing my abs. At least this was a little easier in a way. All I had to do was complete four back handsprings and a full-twist, not pull up my knees and punch out tucks every time.

On my last pass, my arms buckled. Bent at the elbow, my back gave out and yet somehow I dug deep and still managed to keep the square between my legs. I gasped quietly, catching myself so it appeared I'd just finished the pass and nothing more. Landing, my heart pounded so loud I could hear it thumping in my ears, and my skin tingled with little pricks from the tightening of my muscles.

"Great, now move to the floor and grab a folded panel mat. Set it down at your feet." Madeline stood off to the side and called out instructions. My joints cried out from the inside but I kept my face neutral.

"Once again, handstand hops. This time up to the mat and remember to extend your wrists. Start with one knee bent so it's facing forward." I brought my toes toward the opposite knee. "Right. This is going to make it so you have to wind up and kick with the bent leg. Handstand snap down from the mat and rebound. Remember to keep your hips flat and press the hip flexors open. Go."

I wasn't sure how many I had to complete, I guessed I'd go until she said stop, or until I couldn't take anymore.

I wasn't sure which was worse.

Only a handful in and Madeline said, "We want a quicker rebound. Push it, Adrianna." She clapped her hands loud, rushing for me to speed up. "Chest in, hips under! You need to use your lower back and stomach so you don't pike down."

I grew more exhausted each time I punched the floor with my feet and snapped my hips down. My entire body was ready to cave in. And the truth was, I couldn't tell if it was because I was physically or mentally worn out.

"Head and arms stand parallel, I don't want to see your ears. Your head and shoulders are not to come out first. When you bend your body down, your arms and head go at the same pace and direction. Do not pop that head up like a turtle."

I grimaced. Coach Madeline was starting to sound like Kova.

I didn't give up though. Not once. I fought through the tiredness and pain. If I didn't sacrifice myself in those moments and push, then what I wanted would become the sacrifice. I was too close to the victory tape to give up now.

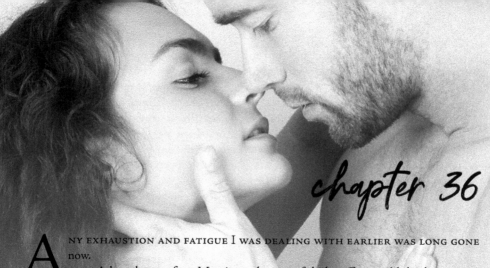

chapter 36

ANY EXHAUSTION AND FATIGUE I WAS DEALING WITH EARLIER WAS LONG GONE now.

A hot shower, four Motrin, and a cup of dark coffee would do that to you. Throw in some lemon garlic chicken and a detox salad, and I was ready to ride.

Too bad it was nine at night and I had nowhere to go. I hated this. The after effect following a long and demanding day made it difficult for me to wind down once I was home. I was restless, antsy, and anxious. I wanted to sleep, but there was no going to sleep until at least midnight. I was lucky if I got five hours of sleep, but it was never solid or straight through.

I had no homework. No one to talk to. And I didn't care to watch television. My body needed the rest, so it was a good thing, but I was jittery.

Alone, I sat on my bed with my knee bouncing, trying to read a book. My mind drifted every few paragraphs, I couldn't focus. I thought about the meet coming up, my routines, how I was faring. A sharp pain shot through my chest. I was confident I had a good shot at testing elite the first time, but I frowned when I thought back to Kova's comment earlier today about my weight.

He insisted I had lost weight.

Standing up, I considered the floor length mirror. I ripped off my pajama shorts and loose shirt and dropped them to the floor. I took three steps and stood in front of the mirror in only a pair of panties. With wide, startled eyes, I stared at my reflecting image as I studied myself from head to toe.

My heart sank. Kova was on the money.

I had lost weight. *A lot* of weight—at least a good ten pounds, maybe more—which was depressing since I didn't have much to lose to begin with. And ten pounds on a gymnast of my stature was a substantial amount. I hadn't even noticed. My leotards were made to be snug, so were all my workout clothes. And I didn't take pictures of my scale and send them to my mom anymore. Though if I did tonight, she'd be happier than a pig in shit.

While I hadn't skipped every meal, thinking back, I'd skipped at least one a day. I wasn't starving myself, I just wasn't hungry.

As I pulled my hair up into a messy bun, my collarbone protruded and caused ghastly indents. Thank goodness for my Italian roots that blessed me with olive skin, otherwise I'd look sickly. My ribs strained against my skin when I inhaled deeply, displaying the length of the bones. While I could count each rib, there was no denying I still had elegant muscle definition. Toned and lean. Even my breasts seemed perkier. I turned around and looked over my shoulder, my gaze wandering down each visible vertebrate, and over my high, firm butt that highlighted gorgeous glutes.

In my eyes, I was perfect. When I really studied myself, I loved the way I looked and that's what mattered most. This was the best shape I'd ever been in to date. A smile spread across my face when I spotted the distinct thigh gap so many woman envied. My hand slipped between my legs, my fingers roaming the soft skin on my inner thighs. Arching my ass a little higher, I could see my supple sex through my tiny, white panties. My lips parted.

I loved the way I looked from this angle. A little sexy, a little innocent.

Walking over to the bed, I reached for my phone beneath the rumpled sheets and quickly shot Kova a text message. I'd been a bitch for no reason earlier and needed to make amends.

I'm sorry.

His response was immediate.

Coach: For...?

You were right, I lost a good amount of weight. I'm staring at myself...

I chewed my lip, debating whether I should tell him I wasn't wearing anything, then thought screw it.

...naked in front of a mirror.

The corner of my lips curved as I stared at my phone, waiting. I felt like being promiscuous. Let him imagine me naked. I *wanted* him to.

Coach: How much weight?

He didn't make me wait long.

I didn't weigh myself. I can just tell by looking.

Coach: Please go weigh yourself for me or I will weigh you tomorrow when you come in.

I stepped onto the scale and sent him a photo, making sure my lean legs were in it.

I lost twelve pounds.

Coach: This does not please me. It leaves me very concerned. You should not be dropping weight this fast, Ria. I want you to see a physician.

I pursed my lips together. I could hear the devil whispering in my ear as I typed out my reply.

Nothing pleases you.

Coach: You know very well that is not true.

My brows shot up in part disbelief, part glee. I was a little more surprised he took the bait, though I wasn't sure why since I knowingly triggered him.

It is.

I waited a heartbeat.

You're never happy or satisfied.

Anticipation flowed through me, butterflies swirled in my stomach as I stood in front of the mirror clutching my cell phone eagerly to see where this conversation would lead. Turning around, I took a photo of the stance I was in earlier, and my phone chimed with his reply.

Coach: You know I have been satisfied plenty before...

I blinked, then blinked again.

My heart was fucking racing a mile a minute. He was going there. Kova was totally going there, and I didn't know what to say or how to act because I didn't actually think it would happen.

Taking a gamble, I sent him the photo I just took.

Then he shocked me even more. He replied with a picture of me...sleeping.

Coach: Ria, your weight does not displease me when you look like this.

My breath hitched in my throat. I stared in awe before tapping on the image to zoom in. I lay curled on my side with my loose shirt hanging low to reveal a sinuous curve of my breasts, just enough to hide my nipples. Crescent moon eyelashes lay thick against my make-up-free cheeks, my supple lips slightly parted. I looked flawless, and dare I say, sensual, rousing, even...erotic.

My fingers twitched to send a reply, but I was rendered speechless. I didn't know how to respond. So many thoughts crossed my mind. I wasn't bothered Kova had taken photos of me, I had photos of him, but I worried what kind of complications it could create if his phone ended up in the wrong hands with these kinds of images. They weren't pictures of two friends smiling from ear to ear. It was bad enough we've had sex, but this crossed another line completely. One neither of us could dodge.

Before I could respond, another photo came in. My eyes widened and my breath caught in my throat. This time I was on my back, arms relaxed above my head, crossing over each other. My nipples prodded the thin layer of my shirt that rested extremely low on my chest. Low enough that when I zoomed in, I could see the raspberry outline of my areola. My heart pounded against my ribs so hard I could feel the pulse in my neck.

Kova...

Coach: You say I have never been satisfied. This is proof that I have.

Of me sleeping?

Coach: Yes.

This was insane! I prayed to God he didn't have them in plain sight.

Where do you keep them? Please tell me not in your photo stream.

Coach: No, of course not. I have secret apps hidden inside other apps. They require passwords. No one will find them.

Okay, that's not creepy at all. I had no idea that was even possible.

Coach: Anything is possible if you want it bad enough.

How many do you have of me?

Coach: Plenty more. Does it bother you?

I paused and weighed his question before answering honestly.

It should bother me, but no, not really. I like them. They remind me of Katja's boudoir ones.

Coach: Trust me, these are far better than a boudoir picture. It is you in your natural environment. Beautiful.

Beautiful. A word suddenly laced with want and desire. I'd never forget it.

Kova sent another photo. The room was draped in darkness, save a shadow of light coming from the hallway. My knees were pulled up and bent, one ankle draped over the other. The hem of my shirt rested on my flat belly and my pale pink bikini panties showed. I looked alluring. I had no idea I could incite such a response while I slept. Another came in, the same position, only my leg had fallen onto the bed, exposing the center of my body. The dark hairs I hadn't shaved that day showed in a triangle at my center. I realized it was the night of the ice bath, when he stayed over.

Why do you have images of me like this in your phone?

Coach: They remind me to look and not touch.

Lol it's not possible for you to look and not touch.

Coach: You make me crazy when I am around you. All I can think about is touching you.

All the air left my lungs. I saw him seven days a week, a good ten to fifteen hours on days when I didn't have tutoring. He always had his hands on me during practice and our private classes. And yet that wasn't enough. He needed pictures of me.

This man confused me to no end. Just when I think I've figured him out, he hits me with something new, and it's as if I'd never known him at all.

You make me look beautiful.

Coach: I do not do anything. It is all you, malyshka.

Malyshka? I thought it was malysh.

Coach: My phone will autocorrect to the correct spelling. It is actually malyshka, but I shortened it to malysh. It is like equivalent to babe.

Seconds turned to minutes turned to silence. Figuring this was a good place to end the conversation, I placed my phone down and went to pick up my clothes I had dropped on the floor earlier. We'd never texted like this, and while I found myself liking it much more than I should, it struck a worry of fear through me. There had been no evidence of our relationship before, and now there was.

Coach: What would you title this photo? I want your first thought.

My stomach tightened as I sat rock steady waiting for the image to come through. Something in my gut told me it would be more suggestive.
Sure enough, I was right on the money.
It matched the last photo, except this time Kova's hand was gripping my inner thigh. His fingers were so close to the lining of my panties.
And it was hot as fuck. I replied, giving the picture a title.

The corruption of an honorable man.

Coach: Okay. And what about this one?

The camera was angled differently this time. Instead of it being at my side, it was taken further down the length of my body without the view of my face. Like he moved to sit next to me.
My lips parted, desire igniting within me as I stared in revelation. His hand was curled against the center of my sex, cupping me, his thumb pressed into my mound.
I was instantly wet from the image.
Shit. This was bad. This was very bad.
But it felt so fucking good that I couldn't contain the smirk that slid across my mouth. I wasn't that young. There were girls having sex at thirteen and babies by fourteen.
At least, that's what I told myself.

Lust and hunger. Sin. Wicked. Prey.

Before he could respond, I shot him another text.

I thought the sole purpose of these photos was to not touch.

Coach: Morals were never my strong suit.

Why can't you ever just be open and honest about how you feel? How you act confuses the hell out of me. It hurts.

Coach: I never said I was perfect. Being misleading is easier because I cannot explain the shit that goes on in my head. Both sound recklessly accurate in that moment.

I mused over his text. From his point of view, it made complete sense because I felt the exact way.

You're right, I'll give you that. I guess from now on, whatever you say and do, I'm going to have to assume you mean the opposite. Talk about a mind fuck.

Coach: Trust me, I confuse myself.

Show me more. I know you have more.

He just admitted he lacked morals, I presumed he had more photos of me hidden away.

Coach: You want more? You are not upset? Disgusted?

Not even close.

And I wasn't.

Kova sent another photo. He was seated between my legs, my knees spread out, and his hands gripped the top of my pale pink underwear, like he was ready to rip them off. They were teasingly pulled down half way, and the embarrassing dark little hairs peaked out. I was going to have my shit waxed religiously after this. I hated the way that looked. But then again, it also showed I wasn't as young as it originally appeared either.

God. I was just as bad as Kova.

The next image showed his hand underneath the thin material of my panties, his thumb pressing on my vagina. His covered penis was hard and in view. I noted a damp circle just below his hand. My body hummed with desperate hunger. I was just as wet in person as I visibly was in the photo.

Carnal. Everything about this photo is purely erotic.

No amount of words could describe the next picture that came in. Just feelings. And what I was feeling was *not* a normal response.

My panties were gone and so were his shorts. The hard tip of his shaft pressed against my glistening lips, hugging the swollen head of his penis while I slept.

Holy. Fuck.

A soft sigh escaped my lips. I became feverish and an aching throb resonated between my legs. My body tingled everywhere with feelings I didn't know how to put into words.

That was it. I was destined to go to hell for wanting more, for being soaking wet at the illicit image before me.

In the next photo, my entire body looked soft and inviting while Kova was partially in. Jesus Christ, a fucking moan vibrated in the back of my throat as I zoomed in on the length of his cock and our joined bodies. I was surprised he had such lewd photos of me, but thankful none showed my face.

But then he texted three little words that caused my stomach to plummet in what would undoubtedly change everything. My heart raced so hard my pulse thrashed in every spot on my body. I could hear it in my ears. My chest ached as I struggled for air. My panties were soaking wet and sticking to me.

Coach: It is live.

chapter 37

I HADN'T NOTICED THE LITTLE DOTTED CIRCLE IN THE TOP CORNER.
I'd been too focused on the content, I completely skimmed over it.
Turning up the volume, I held the image down with my thumb…and fucking died.
Erotic sounds of a drag and a pull that could only be recognized as sex teased faintly in the background. And to my absolute shock, my hips shifted of their own accord as Kova slid in halfway. I was as drenched in this live photo as I was while I watched.

Then it stopped.

No! I watched it again and again, secretly wishing for more, but there wasn't any more to it. Until he sent an actual video.

Heart in my throat, I pressed play and watched with parted lips and zealous eyes as fiery blood rushed through my veins. Kova had a hand clamped around my hip as he slowly pulled his bare cock out and inched back in halfway. My hips rose in need—or he lifted them—I wasn't sure, and a long mew echoed in the background. He pulled out and gripped his cock at the crown, using it to trace circles around my pink clit a handful of times before plunging back into my slumbering body, this time all the way. The view of the camera showed Kova's sexy toned pelvis contracting and flexing as he pushed his hips forward until he was flush against me. He was panting hard and a growl intertwined with a sensual moan. My pussy ached with desire as I watched his free thumb circle my clit, a loud sigh of pure abandon sounded in the background, and the faint flicker of a memory teased my mind.

His thumb picked up the pace and my hips stirred faster from his illicit touch. My breathing deepened, and I whimpered in noticeable pleasure in the video. There was no way to confuse the sounds fleeing me. Bits and pieces were coming back to me. I'd thought it was a deep sleep sex kind of dream I'd had that night. I remember waking up with a sweet, throbbing ache between my legs and wishing it were true. I undoubtedly loved every second, just like I did now. My hips moved and moved until I orgasmed over his cock in a slow, hard wave. A long dreamy moan played in the background that could never be confused for anything other than pure bliss.

The camera dropped from his hand and fell into the sheets. I couldn't see anything now save for a black screen, but I could hear the grunting and groaning and sounds of euphoria that came from Kova. My panties were soaking wet as I listened in fascination, my fingers itching to touch myself.

There was some shuffling and shifting and the camera view was back. The top of my sex was exposed and flushed with a cherry hue, his penis seated deep inside. My breathing labored, and in this moment, I wished this exact thing was happening.

As Kova slowly pulled out his glistening cock, a thin line of white dripping fluid followed. Cursing in Russian, he gripped himself and the rest of his orgasm unloaded all over my pussy.

He pressed his throbbing head against my center as he did. Fluid so thick and creamy seeped everywhere, like he was coming for hours.

The video stopped, and I was out of breath, and in dire need of an orgasm. Maybe five.

Fuck. That was the hottest thing I'd ever seen in my life and I knew nothing would compare. I quickly saved the video to my photos and chewed my lip. That was raw and uncut and hot as sin.

Come over

I needed him in me.

Coach: Make sure you delete all these photos.

Only if you come over. Otherwise, I'm keeping them, especially the video.

I should've deleted them. I didn't have sneaky apps like he had, but it was hot as hell and I wanted to be able to watch it again whenever I felt like it.

But then something dawned on me and I had to call him. I for sure thought he was going to click the fuck you button on me until the phone stopped ringing, followed by a rustling sound, low grunts, a door shutting, and then finally his rich voice. "Allo?"

"Can you talk?"

The silence on the other end told me he was not alone.

"Yes, but not for very long. Katja is in the other room."

"How did I not wake up?"

"Wake up?" he asked, his voice sounded perplexed.

"How did I not wake up from you touching me? From you having sex with me? How did I sleep through that?"

Kova sighed deeply on the other end. My pussy throbbed and my stomach clenched tighter than a slipknot as I waited for his answer.

Low and quiet, but with complete control, Kova said, "Remember the melatonin I gave you before your ice bath? It was a strong dose to help you sleep. I knew from earlier in the day you needed rest. It is all-natural, so you are okay, no need to worry."

No need to worry. My jaw dropped, a throb behind my eye began to thump harder with every passing second. I stared at the wall in complete shock.

"But…but how?" I stammered. Another memory stirred in my mind. It was faint but I couldn't quite grasp it. I'd been drained that night, exhaustion had settled in, both mentally and physically.

"Ria," he stressed my name.

"Did you plan that?"

"No. *Malysh.* Trust me, I did not."

Trust me. Those two words never did me any good when it came to Kova. They must've been equivalent to fuck you in Russian. I wish he'd remove those two words from his vocabulary.

"Then how did it come to that?"

He didn't answer me. My blood began to simmer but I rationalized with myself. My first thought upon seeing the video wasn't anger…it was the complete opposite, and it baffled me. I was turned on.

"You shouldn't have done that."

"You are upset," he stated, remorse heavy in his voice.

"I feel like I should be upset, but I'm not."

"Then how is it that you feel?"

I chewed my lip, trying to come up with how I felt, until I decided to show him. "Hold on a sec…"

I pulled my phone away from my face and opened the camera app. With him still on the phone, I flipped the camera to front-facing and held my cell phone up high, angling the lens to take a selfie, only it didn't capture my face. It captured me from the shoulders down. My breasts free and bare, I pinched my nipples to harden them even more, then pulled my knees up. I dropped my legs to the sides just a little to give him a clear view of my hand under my panties while I touched myself. My fingers coated the slippery wetness and my back arched in pleasure. I snapped a few photos then debated if I should show him how wet I really was.

What the hell. He had a video of us having sex.

Quickly, I slipped my panties down just enough and spread my knees wider. I placed the camera between my legs and the desire turned to a hard throb as I took a photo to show how I truly felt. Wetness seeped from me, dripping down my swollen lips with the knowledge of what I was doing, so I took another photo to show him. I was so worked up my breathing deepened, and my fingers ached to finish myself off. A little moan escaped me, but I resisted.

"Ria, what are you doing?"

I took a deep breath and texted the photos. "I shouldn't feel this way," I whispered.

Kova was quiet for a long moment before he said, "We know each other, Ria. I am not just some one-night stand or a guy you met three weeks ago. That is why you feel differently." He was right. Kova was completely right on why I wasn't furious with him. Had it been any-one else, I don't think I would've reacted that way.

"Fuck," he growled into the phone. He got the photos. "Holy shit… Fuck."

"That's how I feel." Then, I hung up.

Kova called back, but I didn't answer.

I scoffed, shaking my head as my trembling fingers flew over the keyboard. Everything I read for the next ten minutes said nothing but how melatonin was an all-natural remedy used to help treat insomnia. High doses could cause a solid six hours of sleep, which is what he must've given me.

I was torn. I remembered him telling me what he was giving me, along with the Motrin and other vitamins, I just hadn't known then what melatonin was exactly or how potent it could be.

I dropped my forehead into my palm, utterly and completely confused. I stared at my crossed legs in a daze trying to figure out what I should do. A thousand questions flew at me all at once, but the most important question I had to ask myself was did I feel violated.

The answer struck my gut, drove up, and pierced my heart so fast.

The truth was, no, I did not.

I couldn't find it in my heart to feel any other way. Not because I feared the repercussions, or what anyone would think, or I was worried about my future, but because it was Kova, and I cared deeply for him. And no matter how fucked up this relationship was and what we were doing, deep down, I knew he cared about me too.

And to be honest, I liked it. A lot.

My phone rang again, but I ignored it.

I was too fixated on my thoughts, my emotions, my feelings.

A knock resonated at my door minutes later, breaking me free of my thoughts. I quickly slipped on the shirt I had on earlier, then ran to answer it, and found a completely disheveled and wide-eyed Kova gripping the doorframe.

Before he could utter a word, I grabbed his wrist and pulled him inside. Kova shifted on his feet. His usually heavy shielded emotions were bare to me.

"Why did you not answer my calls? Are you upset with me? Because fifteen minutes ago you asked me to come over, then you send me a very erotic photo of your pussy. Then you ignore me. You are sending me mixed signals."

My cheeks reddened. I flattened my lips. He was right, and it took me a minute to answer. Kova stepped toward me and looked down at my chest, then back up. My stupid nipples were still hard.

"I did not video or photograph your face. We both know the truth and that is what matters." Kova's eyes sharpened in my direction but his voice was gentle, apologetic. "Do not try and twist it for what it is not. I thought you would find the absolute forbidden beauty in it, but I am very sorry I upset you."

I glanced away. I stupidly did find beauty in it. He knew that because I asked for more.

"Listen, I thought the videos were really sexy, but next time I'd like to be awake."

I chuckled softly. What the fuck was wrong with me?

His eyes softened and he looked at the floor. He was embarrassed, ashamed. Two emotions last on my list I'd expect from him. He stared long before he surrendered and dipped his chin in agreement.

"I truly am sorry," he said quietly, unable to meet my forgiving gaze.

Kova dug his hand into his pocket and pulled out a white, folded piece of paper. He flipped it over between his hands as if he was buying time. Lifting the paper, he looked at me and exhaled a tortuous sigh. His shoulders sagged, and I felt the weight he carried on them for a hundred men.

"Like everything that involves you, I probably should not do this, but I want you to read this." I glanced at him suspiciously. "I convey my thoughts better on paper," he stated. Which I already knew.

Rooted in my position, I stalled. I looked at the note, then I looked up at him. This was originally how I found out about his contradicting emotions and how everything really began between us.

He lifted the paper higher toward me. "Take it, please. Read it when I leave."

A light bulb went off in my head. "I have an idea." I reached for his forearm and turned, pulling him behind me to follow me to the spare bedroom. Once in the room, I backed him up to a decorative chair and pushed him to sit next to the desk.

He looked up in confusion.

Unless I had homework and wanted a change of scenery, I barely came into this room. It was like a store-all. I began rummaging through the shelves in my unorganized closet. One day I'd clean it up, just not today.

"Do you need some help?" Kova offered. I twisted over with my backside to him and glanced over my shoulder, his penetrating eyes took in every inch of my skin like he was concentrating hard. He dragged his teeth along the bottom of his plump lip, lewd thoughts danced in his animalistic eyes. We were forbidden chemistry. A lethal attraction.

With Kova, I had this dark desire to always want to be his little vixen and attract all his attention. I'd do anything for it.

Pretending I had an itch, I dragged my fingers across the back of my thigh. I could feel his searing gaze follow my hand across my bare skin, still only in panties and a shirt that rode up my back. At this angle, I knew if I leaned any lower that he'd be able to see my breasts. The possibility of events that could occur after floated through my mind.

"What did you say?" I pretended to not hear him the first time.

Kova cleared his throat and ran a hand over his mouth. "Do you need help finding something?"

"Nope. I got it." I feigned innocence and smiled.

A few seconds later, I pulled out a small spiral-bound notebook. It was a gift Avery had given me when she came to visit last year for my birthday.

I walked back to the desk and pulled the top drawer open to search for a pen. Kova's eyes hadn't left my body. A modest smile curved my lips. I leaned down and penned a few salacious thoughts to paper.

It was genius *and* inconspicuous, and the perfect solution to get him to open up.

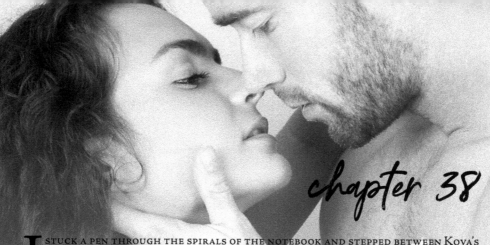

chapter 38

I STUCK A PEN THROUGH THE SPIRALS OF THE NOTEBOOK AND STEPPED BETWEEN KOVA'S spread thighs.

He immediately invited me to his lap and I handed him the notebook with a lazy smile. God, I loved how natural we were when no one was around. My heart was so full and content.

With a deep sigh, I inhaled his subtle scent that followed him everywhere. A sophisticated yet highly seductive fragrance that was cozy, warm, and *all* man. Kova's hand immediately palmed the curve of my hip, his fingers rested on my pelvis. They slid back and forth across my sensitive skin until the tips were under my lacy elastic. I basked in it.

"Any time you have something on your mind, something you want to say but can't, write it down. We'll both write stuff down and swap the notebook back and forth."

Kova glanced down. "This is probably *the worst* idea you have ever had," he said in a heavy lilt.

I turned toward him, bringing my knee up and resting my ankle on his inner thigh. Kova shifted me closer to him, his fingers pressing into my hips and staying there like it was the most normal thing in the world for us. Our gazes met, he wasn't backing down.

"You can't seem to communicate like a normal person and when you do, you hurt people. Writing it down is the only option for you."

Kova leaned forward. "And what do you think will happen when someone reads it? What if it got into the wrong hands?"

I shrugged and placed a hand on his firm chest. It was obvious how this would work.

"We never mention names. Never write my name and I'll never write yours. Don't use the words coach and gymnast. No one would know whose it is if lost and found. It's a perfect idea."

"No," he whispered, then transitioned to Russian. Kova shook his head and peeped down at the notebook before giving me an unimpressed look. "I do not like this idea one bit. It is too risky."

"Oh, but your porn videos were a brilliant idea," I said sarcastically, slightly hurt he didn't like my idea. Kova just stared right through me. "Why not?" I scoffed. "You do it with your therapist. Why can't you do it with me?"

This was no different and he knew it. My gut told me he was being difficult because I had cornered him with having to face his feelings for once.

Leaning forward, I rested my arms on his pectorals and shifted until I was straddling his wide thighs. His hands wound up on both my hips, his fingers splaying over the curve of my ass as I lowered myself. I smiled at the easy laid back look in his eyes. I wished he always had that look. Kova arched his neck back onto the cushion and swallowed as he looked down at me. A soft breath rolled off my lips. He was so fucking sexy.

"Please," I asked with huge doe eyes. "For me?"

"It is not the same, and you know it." His voice struggled with consistency. "This is a ludicrous idea, Adrianna."

My smile faltered, but I covered it. Using my index finger, I traced his collarbone with a feather light touch while his open palms dragged up my back. His sensual touch made me feel sexy and I loved that feeling.

Kova budged forward to sit up straighter and I chewed my lip, contemplating another alternative. He whispered under his breath in Russian, then adjusted himself so we were chest to chest. My arms automatically wound around his broad shoulders and I drew him in.

Leaning next to my ear, he said, "I caught the slip in your smile. What is wrong? Tell me what you are thinking about." He cupped my shoulders from behind, his callused hands kneaded my skin in a sensual massage.

"I would love to get inside your head. It would be insanely sexy to know your deepest, darkest thoughts."

I could only imagine what he daydreamed about. I was entirely too naive about sex still to think of anything wild the way I was sure he did.

His two-day old stubble rubbed along my cheek as he whispered, "You are already in my head, baby. More than you know." The seductive pull on each word caused goose bumps to trickle down my arms.

I pulled back. "You said baby and not *malysh*."

Kova gave me a one-sided smirk. His eyes a blaze of fire piercing every inch of my body. It was sexy as hell. I wondered if he had any idea of the power he wielded.

"You like when I speak Russian?" he asked.

I nodded. "I do. I wish you'd speak more to me."

A smile pulled at his face. "Even when you have no idea what I am saying?"

I nodded again. "But why did you switch to baby? See, that's something you could write in the notebook."

"And then what? Am I supposed to pass it to you in the hall after practice?"

Shit. I puckered my lips and gave him the truth with a smile. "I actually hadn't gotten that far yet."

Kova's head rolled back, a light laugh escaped him. "Of course you have not. No, this is definitely not happening." He went to move but I begged him not to get up.

"Please, don't leave yet."

Kova settled and looked directly into my eyes. "I have to get home. Katja was awake when I left. I am sure she is wondering where I am by now. Fuck…" His voice lowered to a whisper as he spoke to himself. A deep sigh groaned in the back of his throat and his hands tightened on me like he didn't want to let go. "I was not expecting to stay so long." Kova stared at my mouth as I licked my lips. I'd give anything to know what he was thinking. Pressing forward, I arched into him until I was an inch away from his mouth. Heart racing, my arms locked behind his neck.

"What did you tell her?"

"That the alarm was triggered at the gym and I had to go."

My brows shot to my hairline. I shook my head, smirking. I wish I knew why I didn't feel bad that he lied to his girlfriend again, but I just didn't care.

"You're so sly."

"The things I do for you."

In the silence that passed between us, Kova switched to his native tongue. His eyes found my mouth once again and never left. I watched while he spoke, his tongue tapping his teeth, his desirable lips closing and opening as words flowed off them suggestively.

"*V tihom omute cherty vodyatsya.*" Our eyes met. "Still waters run deep," he said quietly. His voice was deeper, huskier. "It is a saying in Russia that pretty much translates to the same in English. 'Under calm waters, the devil waits patiently.'" He paused and swallowed hard. He shot a fleeting glance at my mouth then looked into my eyes and said, "I fear nothing good can come from you."

"You want to kiss me. I can feel it," I whispered.

"*Beda nikogda ne prihodit odna.*" I waited, my breath heightening. He was so sexy like this. "Trouble never comes alone. This notebook, kissing you, constantly finding ways where we are isolated from judging eyes, would bring nothing but trouble from the devil." Kova wrapped his arms around my lower back, then moved so his lips were touching mine, and whispered, "*YA takoy ublyudkare'. Proklyatyy, yesli ya proklyat, yesli ne budu.*"

Then, he smashed his lips to mine.

"What did you say?" I asked between our pressed lips.

"I am a bastard."

I chuckled lightly, melting on him. "You are." I loved hearing his accent. It was incredibly erotic when he had a raspy intonation woven in the words.

"*Proklyat, yesli ya delayu, ya proklat, yesli ne… Damned if I do, damned if I do not.*"

I moaned softly as he continued to speak between frenzied kisses. That saying fit both of us perfectly. Kova growled and attacked my mouth like he'd been dying for this moment. I could barely keep up. He nipped at my lips, sucked my tongue, and dug his fingers into me. Like he wanted to climb inside me and live there. The pressure between us was destructive, and the power he elicited caused my hips to undulate on his. I ached for him. He lounged back and pulled me with him, his legs spreading wider so his hips thrust up. The only barrier between us were my thin panties and his mesh shorts. His hardness surged against my sex, I could barely think under his hold.

"I have to go," he said, crushing my pelvis in his grasp. Contradicting himself as always. He pressed my hips into his and groaned. I chuckled. His hands slid lower toward my opening. A carnal sigh rolled off his lips. I almost bit him from the sound of it. My body ignited within and I let go. The way I desired this man was something I couldn't comprehend. It went against everything and nothing I believed in. It would be considered wrong in everyone's eyes, but none of them mattered. I couldn't make sense of it, only that it felt right.

"No, stay a little longer," I pleaded. "Please." I squirmed over him, my body anxious. I needed more, just a little more. Especially after the photos and videos, and the way he rubbed me on him. Just a little longer…

But I also needed *him*. Deep in my heart, I knew I needed him just to be here. His presence soothed me more than ruffled my feathers.

"I thought you hated me." Kova ground into me at the word hate. *Fuck.*

My eyes became heavy with desire. "I do hate you. With every bone in my body."

God, I was a mess.

Kova chuckled. "You have a weird way of showing it."

I reached between us and cupped his thick erection. Kova's nostrils flared and he gripped my wrist. "When you show me basically a porno of us, you get me so worked up I can't think straight, it's hard to remember why I hate you. I should be angry over what you did, any sensible person would be, but I can't feel the emotion."

"I knew you would not be mad," he said smugly. "I knew you would like it."

A mischievous grin tugged at the corners of my mouth. I arched a high brow and he loosened his hold on my wrist. We were on the same page, more than one could fathom. We had nothing and everything in common. It made no sense.

The only thing I was positively certain about was that we were inexplicably wild about each other.

"Calm down, you cocky, arrogant man. I'm sure tomorrow when I can think straight I'll be mad."

Kova shook his head, his eyes were full of happy laughter. He didn't believe my words as much as I didn't.

"What would it take for you not to be mad with me?"

I was sure he expected me to stroke him, but instead, I rubbed myself along his swollen length. With each rush of my hips, I applied pressure to him and he indulged by thrusting forward. His eyes darkened to a suggestive hue that tingled in my belly.

Damn, his eyes. They made me want to unravel every layer of him.

"For something just like that to happen, but while I am coherent," I moaned. The pleasure bloomed inside my veins, a high was on the horizon.

Kova nipped the tender flesh under my lobe. His hands skimmed my lower back and his fingers slid into my panties. His palm covered one cheek and he gripped it tight in his hand and yanked me roughly against him. A little yelp escaped me.

"But it is so much better when you are sleeping… I can do whatever I want to you. The best part? Your body reacts and still wants it even when you are incoherent."

A shiver ran down my spine at the thought. I shook my head, surging faster and faster. "You're incorrigible."

His fingers danced illicitly close to my sex. I clenched the fabric of his shirt in my hand and waited anxiously, continuing to rub myself on him.

"Impressive." He drove up with his hips and I sucked in a breath. "A big word for such a *young girl.*" He groaned so deep and guttural that I think he liked the definition of the word and what he was doing to me.

"I am *young,* and you love it. Admit it," I said breathlessly. Kova growled, but didn't answer. He was a fusion of brooding and passive, someone who was indisputably crossed.

"How can someone like you always seem to know what I like?"

I smiled against his mouth. "I'm attentive."

Two fingers dipped further into my wetness. He caressed me softly, slowly, sliding all around. I arched my back and my hips came up, hoping he'd push inside. I moaned, wanting more.

"This girl wants you to make her come."

Another stroke over my swollen pussy and Kova was pulling his fingers out and sliding them between his lips. I let out a frustrated gasp and reeled back. Kova pulled his fingers out with a pop and smiled from ear to ear. I wish he'd smile more. His whole face changed.

He tapped the side of my outer thigh like he was proud. "Time for me to go, sweet girl."

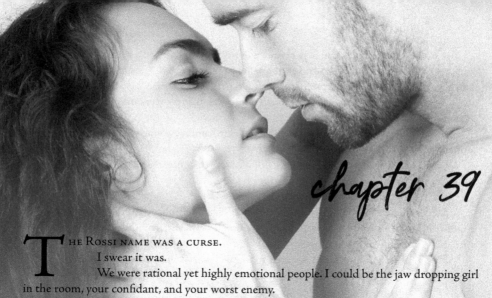

chapter 39

THE ROSSI NAME WAS A CURSE.

I swear it was.

We were rational yet highly emotional people. I could be the jaw dropping girl in the room, your confidant, and your worst enemy.

All at once if I had to.

And in those rare times when I was on the receiving end—because karma—I loathed it. I prided myself on being practical and levelheaded, but when my emotions slithered under and took root, spreading their vines when I least expected it, I acted just plain old stupid.

It was early Friday morning, twelve hours before our flight departed for the elite qualifier meet where I would test both Optional and Compulsory routines, when I woke up feeling downright weak. It was horrible. I didn't even have the strength to panic. I was lethargic and unable to process my thoughts and so physically drained that I called my mom. Holding up the phone was a job in itself.

Desperate times called for desperate measures.

Much to my surprise, she had gotten on the phone and within minutes had a private doctor on the way to my condo. It was one of those luxuries of the American Express black card. She heard the brittle tone of my voice and seemed legitimately concerned for my well-being, but then I replayed the conversation in my head and caught her last words.

I anticipate your youthful appearance, my darling daughter. I scowled.

Diagnosis: Severe exhaustion and fatigue.

The doctor had to administer an injection of a high dose of vitamin B12. The next two times I'd have to do it myself since he'd prescribed an extreme dose until I got home and scheduled an appointment to see him.

It didn't take long for the dose to kick in. I had a burst of energy and positive attitude. I felt confident, eager about competing in my first meet with World Cup since I started. I wanted to test elite, and I wanted to make my team proud. If that meant I had to stick a needle fifty times over in my leg, I would.

We had a five-hour flight to the Las Vegas meet, where we'd go eat dinner and then straight to the hotel to check in and head to bed. I wouldn't see my parents until after the meet. The coaches were adamant and enforced a rule that we not have any kind of contact with them, but I knew they were there. I sat by Madeline the entire time and read a book. I didn't want my focus to deter sitting next to Kova, and I wasn't in the mood for Reagan's shenanigans.

I was nervous and jittery.

At dinner, I barely looked in Kova's direction, despite sitting right to next to him, which he orchestrated to happen. It took every fiber in my body not to lean in and inhale his scent deeply into my lungs. He smelled divine while sipping on vodka. I couldn't think of oranges and cigars without thinking of him.

It wasn't like I was upset with him, I just lost all sense of self-control when I was around him and I couldn't afford to do that right now. I *really* wanted to win. So I put myself in the zone and blocked out all distractions.

Once back at the hotel, the teams split up and went to their rooms. Since the elite were such a small team, we all roomed together. None of us uttered a word, just went on with our normal routines and went to sleep.

Gymnasts were well-groomed and disciplined little soldiers.

And it's where I found peace the most.

My thigh was sore the next morning where I had to give myself an injection. There was a slight discoloration around the sight, but nothing that a little makeup couldn't fix. I hoped it wouldn't bruise until after the meet.

Other than that, I was feeling fan-fucking-tastic. My energy was through the roof. Like I'd had a bunch of energy drinks.

After a quick pep talk from the coaches, we had podium training at the site. We marched in dressed in our matching leos and sweats. Hair pulled back in slick ponytails with globs of gel combed through so not one single strand would fall out of place. My nerves started to kick in once we arrived, though I was oddly calm. Podium training was very structured and organized with limited time to warm up and get used to the equipment.

I had one chance to swiftly readjust all my routines so the timing was correct and find my mark to focus on.

Stone quiet and determined, I prepared for something I had never done.

Not every meet had podium training because not every meet is on podium. In regular gyms like World Cup, there was no podium, and every apparatus was anchored to cement.

On podium, nothing was cemented. The events would be raised three feet off the floor so spectators had easier viewing. It's why on television some judges were level with the apparatuses and some were not.

While it was safe and regulated and wouldn't be visible to the untrained eye, competing on podium wasn't the same. The texture may be different on beam or vault, the bars may give more, and the floor could be softer or rougher and have more spring. Usually a set routine was in place to only warm up specific skills set by the coaches. That's why podium training was so vital.

Just another way to fuck with a gymnast's head, really.

Lifting my eyes, I tightened my grips and glanced around. I dipped my hands into the chalk bowl and visualized my routine.

The level of tension that radiated throughout the gym was thicker than a block of fresh chalk. Never did I expect to see the coaches so overwrought with nerves. All you had to do was watch the movement of their eyes and you'd know. It was always the eyes that said everything. If not, just about all their shoulders were stiff and tight, and they sauntered around with their hands on their hips, speaking assertively to their gymnasts. While this was about the competitor and their talent, it also reflected on the coach. It was always about the coach. They wanted to look as amazing as their golden ticket.

Reagan had just completed her dismount when she came over to the chalk bowl. This was my first meet with her and surprisingly, she was calm and silent toward me. I gathered she remembered her first time testing for elite and how stressful it was. I for sure thought she'd try to get under my skin and mess with my head, but she didn't. Thankfully.

My warm-up for bars came next. I stood in front of the low bar and lifted my arms toward it. Just as I was about to mount, Kova put a hand up. Stepping onto the mat, he walked around the cable cords in my direction.

"Listen, I want you to do your full routine first so you get a feel for these bars. The equipment is different from ours, but if you keep your mind and body sharp, it will not be as bad as it seems. Do not stop when your heart drops, because it will, just keep going. After you complete your routine, I want you to get back in line and think about what you need to adjust and only warm up those skills. Small changes will add up to huge results. Do you understand?"

I nodded. "Which should I do first?"

"Compulsory."

I should've guessed he'd say that. Since compulsory had mandatory skills that every gymnast had to master, I'd have to prove myself capable before I could test Optional.

After I completed my warm-up, my nerves were a little jittery. I stood in line retightening my grips for no good reason with a racing heart. Kova had been right, every skill I did had felt different and I absolutely had to make some changes. My swing gave more, and my heart splattered to the ground a few times when I released. I knew it wasn't the best warm-up and that Kova would not be pleased, but I couldn't think about that right now. I didn't look in his direction, even though he was probably waiting for me to look for him. I just stared at the floor and visualized what I'd just done. I had to get in tune with my body and think about where I would make minor adjustments.

I needed to calm my stressed nerves.

The biggest issue would be timing. Timing was everything and I needed to adjust it just right for the routine to be executed properly.

Just as I was about to go my last time, Kova pulled me aside.

"What are you doing?" I shrieked in a whisper. "I'm going to miss my turn!"

It'd been drilled into our heads that everything was on a strict schedule and there would be no exceptions made. I seriously couldn't afford to lose my spot.

Kova placed his hands on my shoulders and calmed me with his touch. Looking directly into my eyes, he said determinedly but with a touch of tenderness, "Do not crack. You got that? Do. Not. Crack." I bit my lip.

After a full year of working so closely together, he knew when the weight of the moment got to me.

"I can see it in your eyes—you got nervous and that is okay, it is normal, but do not let that affect what you came here to do. Look into my eyes and see what I see. A warrior, a fighter, someone who gets kicked out but finds another way in. You are braver and stronger than you know. You are a fire that burns. Do not feed your doubts, Ria, feed your dream. Do not lose your focus." I nodded feverously, annoyed I'd shown emotion. "Now, do you want me to stand and spot you?"

I expelled a strenuous breath and nodded again.

"Look at me," he ordered. "Look in my eyes." He placed a hand on my shoulder and an eerie calmness seemed to wash over me. "Take a deep breath and release. Again." Then he smiled proudly at me and my stomach settled.

Words might have been lost on me, but Kova's thoughtfulness to ease my worries *and* spot me spread throughout my chest. Coaches were allowed to spot during the actual meets without receiving any kind of deduction. The spot was more for peace of mind. I'd never needed one in the past, but this was a whole new page in my storybook for me.

"I just want you to stand there."

Kova walked over and stood near the high bar. He got in position and waited for me. I was confident I could make the changes successfully but having him there quieted my fears. A comforting safety measure.

After I adjusted my routine, I also made the necessary changes to my optional routine. Kova was there the entire time. He didn't push me or ridicule me, he just let me do my thing. It was like a second chance to get used to the feel of bars.

My teammates and I moved onto vault. Just like with bars, I had two vaults I had to do—a front handspring double front tuck, and an Amanar. The only difference with vault was that I had two turns for each vault during competition as opposed to one. Both were extremely difficult, and both required minor changes that didn't frighten me in the way bars did.

"What the hell was that?" Kova questioned, striding up next to me. His eyes were huge and his hands were out waiting for an explanation. I reeled back, nervous with anxiety. I hadn't pulled the Amanar like I should have, which was why he wasn't happy. I freaked out in the middle of the twist and did a Yurchenko double instead. It wasn't uncommon for a gymnast to make the change midflight with this vault, but it would earn me a deduction in difficulty. The extra half-twist was hard as fuck to crank out.

"We need more flight."

I loved when Kova said we, because we were a team and that was important to me. He described with his body how I should be tucking and locking by making sporadic movements.

"Take one foot back in your start. Otherwise your block will suck again and you will not get the flight you need."

I glared at him when we got to the end of the runway. As if I didn't feel my shitty block. "Okay," was all I said.

Taking a deep breath, I exhaled and stomped my feet in chalk. I got into position a foot back and visualized what I was about to do. The changes felt great and I knew both vaults would be just like they were back at World Cup. Vault was my specialty. I excelled at it.

Floor was exactly what I had expected—super bouncy. I warmed up with a few passes to get a feel. Luckily, I hadn't gone out of bounds, but the height I reached made my heart plummet to the ground. I already flew pretty high as it was, so I reduced the steps in my tumbling passes to bring it down just a notch. I didn't need too much momentum.

Beam was same as any other day, but now it came with a slight wobble since it wasn't secured to the floor. I jumped, flipped, leaped, and it all came with a shake of the beam. I had to be extremely tight otherwise I'd be having balance checks every other second. In the press to handstand mount that went straight into my first combination sequence of a double back handspring into a full twist, I fell off the beam. My jittery nerves got the best of me and I shook more than I anticipated. Kova grunted under his breath loud enough to let me know how displeased he was with me, but I jumped back up, took a deep breath, and exhaled. Glancing ahead, I found my spot and began my routine, chanting to myself, *I got this.*

And I did. I fucking had this.

I concentrated on sticking every skill. I went deep and dark with my thoughts, into a different dimension, and only saw one word at the end of the tunnel. Success. The quickest way to overcome fear was hit it directly head on. I had to breach my comfort zone if I wanted to make any kind of advancement in this sport. I was my only limit—I decided my path. I was committed to this journey and I would succeed. I. Would. Make. It. Happen.

Once I landed my dismount without so much as a small step—I stuck it—I looked for my coach who was already making his way toward me.

As we walked side by side back to the resting area where my duffle bag was, Kova placed his hand on my lower back.

"I do not know what you did up there, but you caught me by complete surprise. Excellent work, Adrianna. You let go of your fear and allowed yourself to shine. You trusted yourself. I thought you may need a bit more work with this beam, but you shocked me and proved me wrong."

I sat on the floor and pulled up my knees in a butterfly position. "Gymnastics is so tricky," I said, unwrapping the ace bandages from my ankle. It alleviated some tenderness with my Achilles but not as well as the sports tape. "It's risky and messes with your head more than any other sport out there," I said as if it just dawned on me. "As much as I like to think I can control everything, I know I can't. So, if I stop thinking about all the things that could go wrong and think about all the things that could go right, and I try my absolute best, it should work in my favor. Should being the keyword." I chuckled to myself as I crumpled the bandage and dropped it in my bag. "Otherwise I'm always going to find errors."

Kova listened while I rambled on. His attention never left mine, as if every word I said mattered. It was the best feeling to see him already staring at me. I felt high on life, ready to tackle my next obstacle with Kova by my side.

"I'm not sure what came over me, but I was driven by power and determination. Maybe it was because I have you behind me, I'm not sure, but I do know that I have nothing to lose and everything to gain, so I just kind of let go and believed in myself."

I smiled brightly at him. The way Kova looked at me made my heart flutter. I couldn't stop it from happening. I felt great. Confident. Like I could take on the world. He was happy and proud, and I loved that I exceeded his expectations.

"Adrianna, I wish I could finish this conversation with you, but I have to go. Just know, that what you did up there is because you stopped doubting yourself. You proved it just like I knew you would. I cannot wait to see you perform tomorrow."

He turned away before I could say anything. I knew he wasn't leaving to purposely avoid me, my teammates needed his attention as well.

I tried not to smile from ear to ear. I tried not to stare at him with admiration. But I did and I didn't give a shit who saw. He was proud, and that filled my chest with so many emotions I couldn't put into words. Appraisal was not something I needed all the time, but in flashes of self-doubt, it changed everything. He gave me the courage I needed to move forward. He was my life boat.

Make it count. It's what he'd said since the moment I started with World Cup. And I would. For myself. For my coaches.

Kova moved to stand near the uneven bars again, this time to help Holly. I watched as he instructed her, giving her the same reassurance he instilled in me. He believed in us. Despite his flaws—and he had plenty—he cared about his gymnasts and the sport. He wanted us to succeed.

But what stole my attention wasn't Holly's impressive routine. It was the burning glare coming from my right, searing a hole into my head. It was impossible not to feel the intensity of those spiteful eyes.

Reagan.

My smile faltered as she stared at me with a scowl so profound it caused a shiver to run down my spine. She lifted one brow and angled her head to the side, then shifted her gaze over to our coach.

She'd seen everything she needed to. And I'd let her.

chapter 40

MY PARENTS HADN'T SHOWN UP UNTIL THIS MORNING.
Naturally.

My stomach fluttered at the thought of my mom coming to my first big qualifier meet. Not my dad, even though he'd been to less meets than Mom. I knew she was waiting for me to fail. My gut said she did because she never saw my dream as anything more than an expensive hobby, and that said more than anything else. Maybe Dad felt the same way, but he never openly stated it. He encouraged me and supported my hard work and dedication. Each slip up was an open door for my mom to criticize me, to insist I do something else with my spare time. I pictured her in the stands, glaring down at me, somewhere between uninterested and annoyed.

Anxiety seized my chest as a sharp pain tore through it. I closed my eyes and counted to ten, breathing deeply and slowly, just as Kova had shown me. Gymnastics was my life. It was my passion. My outlet. All you had to do was open your eyes and watch my heart speak for me.

I was going to show her that with my performance. Today was my day.

Swallowing away the worry, I opened my eyes and glanced around the gym. Chalk permeated the air. A springboard rebounded and feet slammed onto a dismount mat. Classical music blared on the speakers and the sound of the bars ricocheting echoed in the distance. The meet was in full swing.

There were three judges at every event. They sat at a long table, dressed in navy blue business attire with notepads and clipboards at their fingertips. Their beady eyes criticizing every little thing. With so much against me, I trained hard for this day. Blood and sweat. I pushed my body. My coaches pushed harder. Now I just had to allow my love for the sport to shine.

My team walked in a perfectly straight line toward vault. Chin up, shoulders back. World Cup was second on rotation. Which meant I had less than an hour until I competed.

We were dressed in matching black sweat suits with a leotard underneath. Of course, Kova would've picked black. It was the only color he ever saw and wore. Our leos were even black, but with swirls of peridot Swarovski crystals curving and swooping like ocean waves. Hair was pulled back into a tight ponytail, not a flyaway in site. Jewelry was removed and sports bras hidden away.

Stepping up to the row of chairs that lined the gym wall, we spread out and took a seat. I began shuffling through my duffle bag for my gear when my wrist caught a sharp corner. I pulled back.

Brows scrunched together, I slid aside the extra leotard I carried with me and I drew in a breath as a hard surface appeared before me.

It was the notebook I'd given Kova. I'd forgotten he'd taken it that night.

My eyes widened and I hastily tried to block the view of my bag by flipping down the top and concealing the contents. My eyes skipped around the small group to see if anyone saw or heard anything, but they were oblivious. My heartbeat thundered in my ears. When I felt confident no one saw anything, I looked back at the little notebook. I wondered when Kova had the opportunity to sneak it in my bag, and why he'd changed his mind after adamantly telling me it was a stupid idea.

Instantly I became paranoid. Again, my eyes shifted from side to side without turning my head to see if anyone caught anything. My adrenaline spiked, my heart rate jumped.

He played this game better than me. I never even saw him slip it in.

My fingers stroked the thin, hard edge. I contemplated opening the notebook now instead of later. I wasn't worried someone would see me reading, I didn't think anyone would care, I worried there would be something that could mentally mess with me before the meet. That's what I feared the most.

I chewed my bottom lip, unsure how to fight the curiosity that bubbled inside me. Maybe I could just peek...

But instead I glanced away, fighting the urge, and caught Kova's pointed stare. Our eyes locked and all the air left my lungs. He openly watched me with a prudent gaze that simmered with thirst. The chain linking us tightened around my heart and drew me closer.

He gave me a subtle nod.

Kova wanted me to read what he wrote.

Shit.

My anxiety was flying high. This time when I glanced around at those surrounding me, I took note of their actions. When I believed no one would question me, I pretended to stretch out and leaned down. I made sure my bag shielded what I was about to do and flipped open the hardcover to the first page.

I took a risk for you. Now take a risk for me and drop every fear you have ever had. Go out there and be defiant. Refuse to lose.

He didn't sign it. Didn't give himself away. He kept it discreet.

A silent sigh of relief rolled off my lips and my mouth curved into a fainthearted smile. This man. My chest was lighter and so was my fear. I closed the book shut. Then I grabbed the small bag I used to store pads and tampons in and quickly stuffed it in there. I zipped it up, then topped it with my clothes and closed my gym bag shut.

I sat on my knees and pulled on my wristbands. I recalled the words in my head, hearing his voice each time. He had taken a risk for me. Many risks. Way too many risks to count. My goal had been the same since the start and now it just took a little deviation.

I was going to do as he asked. I would take a risk for him and drop every fear I've ever had. I would be defiant. I would refuse to lose.

After my grips were on, I realized I hadn't taped my ankle to alleviate the pain. I should've done that step first since my grip was now limited, but my mind had been elsewhere. A disgruntled huff escaped me as I ripped back the Velcro with a scowl and dropped the wristbands to the floor. Just as I was about to wrap the sports tape around my foot to relieve the strain on my Achilles, Kova walked over and crouched down. He placed his palm out and waved his fingers for the tape without speaking a word. I slapped the roll of tape in his hand and gave him my foot, putting my weight on my arms behind me. I glanced away. Kova was better at wrapping up my Achilles anyway.

"You ready for today?"

"Ready as I'll ever be."

"You do not think you could be better?"

I huffed, shaking my head. I knew he wasn't goading me. "There's always room for improvement, Coach. You know this, but as of right now, I'm ready." I paused, then took a chance and debated quickly whether I wanted his answer or not. "Do you think I'm ready?"

He didn't lift his head, but the corner of his mouth curved up at my question. He took a moment to respond as he expertly wrapped up my injury.

Lowering his voice, he tipped his head up just enough for me to see his eyes. Damn those fucking eyes of his. They always got me.

"If I did not think you were ready, you would not be here. Trust me. You are more than ready."

Kova placed my foot on the floor, giving my ankle a gentle squeeze before he let go. His knees cracked as he stood to his full height, our gazes still connected. Reaching out with his hand, he helped me up. There was a stillness inside me amid the chaos surrounding us as we stared into one another's eyes. With Kova's support, confidence roared through me. He changed my whole mind frame. I was a cub, and he was the lion who breathed strength into me.

A bashfulness came over me. I turned away, trying to hide the happiness I knew rushed from within. My cheeks burned, which didn't help the plum blush I applied earlier. His raspy chuckle caught my ears and when I turned back around, Kova had a full grin spread across his charismatic face. My heart nearly stopped. This wasn't just any old smile. This was a full-on, I'm so proud to call you mine, type smile.

And he did it in a place filled with cameras.

Be still my wild heart.

Kova cupped my shoulder and squeezed. "Everyone will be watching. Show them what you're made of, Adrianna."

chapter 41

I STOMPED MY FEET IN CHALK TO ABSORB THE DAMPNESS AND WATCHED AS THE POWDERY white smoke formed a cloud around my shins.

I was next to perform.

My palms were clammy, and my body was jittery. I had an abundance of adrenaline pumping through me and shaky nerves to combat against it. I was worked up and excited, eager yet wired, but I also felt like I had eighty-seven shots of caffeine streaming through my veins.

Kova had walked with me to the end of the vault runway. I tightened my wristbands and shook out my legs as I listened to him speak only to me, giving me last-minute tips and reminders. Holly had already gone, so had Reagan. Holly took a giant step to the right, while Reagan stuck her landing. Naturally.

Now, it was my turn.

"Remember, you start a foot back. Long and low into the board. Get your body over and hands on the table fast so you get a good block. As soon as you hit the flight peak—re-member to glue your ankles together—crank as hard and as fast as you can."

I nodded hastily at Kova's directions and tightened the Velcro across my wrists. I'd started using wristbands for vault not too long ago, similar to the ones I had for bars, only these were padded and used to support my wrist from the huge block I needed to gain height. It also helped with the pinching and tenderness I had in my wrists after working tumbling passes on the floor for hours on end, but Kova didn't know about that.

"Breathe through your stomach," Kova suggested, a soothing tone meant to ease my worries. I looked at him with gratitude and my nerves immediately calmed down.

Kova placed his hands on my shoulders, bent down, and looked squarely into my eyes. "Focus. Do not crack. You got this."

I nodded again, eyes alert but words escaped me. Kova walked away, back to where the team and coaches were, while I stood at the end of the runway. I shot a glance at the judges' table. Three women of various ages in blue dress suits and stiff posture communicated over a table of papers and pencils as they decided on Holly's score. My stomach tightened. My heart was racing a mile a minute, pounding fervently against my chest while I waited for them to give me the green light.

Here we go.

Expelling a deep breath, I got behind the white line I'd drawn with chalk earlier and fixated my gaze explicitly on the vault. I shook my hands out.

Be defiant, echoed in my head. *Drop the fear.*

A wall came down and I envisioned my outcome. Lifting my arms, I saluted the judges and swallowed away everything except for what I was about to do. Within seconds, I was speeding down the runway, heading toward the large stationary object I was about to flip over. I tightened every muscle in my body as I pumped my legs, running as fast as I could. Within ten feet or so, I stretched my hurdle to prepare for the round-off, and everything Kova and Madeline had taught me came roaring at me. It hit me like a ton of bricks and everything locked into place. Muscle memory took over and both feet punched the springboard hard. I sprung back onto the vault where I blocked the hardest I'd ever blocked in my life and reached for the ceiling, preparing to twist into an Amanar. My block was like a rocket taking off. I got the flight Kova said I always needed, and I knew right then and there this was going to be a good vault. Squeezing tight, ankles glued together, I pulled hard and completed the two and a half twists required of this skill and spotted for the floor. I opened up and landed with both feet together on the blue mat, my arms raised above my head, and stuck my dismount. I nailed it. *I fucking nailed it.* Every muscle in my body was firm and solid as I saluted without a wobble or hop. I tried to veil the smile that slowly spread across my face, but executing *and sticking* the Amanar wasn't easy.

And I knew in my gut I had done extremely well.

Cheering erupted almost immediately, I could hear my teammates shouting their praise. Turning, I saluted unimpressed judges once more before stepping off the landing mat to look for my coach.

Kova wore a contagious grin with his hand in the air to high five me.

"Quite possibly the best vault I have seen you do to date." My eyes turned to wide saucers. His words shot through me. "I could not find even one thing to pick at."

"Really?" I was stunned. He nodded, brows raised high with a huge smile on his face.

"It was fantastic. It should put you in the top three, maybe two."

My heart leaped as I considered his words while I walked back to the end of the runway again. I repeated the motions in my head, visualizing myself as I waited for the okay to go. I applied more chalk, a nervous habit. It was crazy how fast feet could sweat in a such a short amount of time.

My score flashed, and I looked at the screen. I knew to keep my face neutral, but my heart wavered for a split second. The displeased crowd put their feelings on display, alerting the judges they were not happy. Chills shot down my arms. My empty stomach tossed around.

It wasn't what I had hoped for, I was pleased with it, but I wanted better.

Kova threw his hands in the air, grimacing at the numbers. His eyes hardened as he glared at the judges and yelled, wanting to know where they found an error.

Typical coach behavior. They all did it.

Once the judges were ready, I didn't waste any time. I swiped the excess chalk from my hands and moved straight into the second vault. Putting everything I could muster into it, I executed another Amanar and stuck the landing. It felt incredible, like I did it just as well as the first one. I saluted the judges and turned toward my team and coaches, stepping down the three steps to where they were. This time I didn't smile. I didn't show emotion. And I certainly didn't get my hopes up.

I spotted Kova first. The dark specks in his irises looked like black diamonds glistening against the energetic green.

It was clear. Kova was proud. And that made me so happy.

I slapped his hand and he pulled me into a quick hug.

"Excellent work, Adrianna." I drew in the scent of his cologne and felt his words deep inside.

Madeline strode over with her hands out and eyes wide, silently questioning me. There was a slight glimmer there. She pulled me into a hug. "Where did that come from?" she asked, sounding extremely satisfied and astonished. "You exploded off that table like you invented the skill. Well done, girly."

"Thank you," was all I could say through a toothy grin. My score went up and it couldn't have been better. Both coaches yelled their enthusiasm, and a massive smile split my cheeks. It pushed Reagan out of first place and down to second, third place held by another team's gymnast. I wasn't ahead by much, but it was enough to secure first place, for now.

"Not bad, Rossi," Reagan said without looking at me. "But I'd be careful with how you and Kova look at each other the rest of the meet. He has hunger in his eyes."

I deadpanned. "Hunger, Reagan? Who says that? And if I saw correctly, he looked at you just the same. And Holly. Stop trying to read into something that isn't there just because you're pissed that I knocked you out of the standings."

I didn't give her a chance to respond. And I didn't wait for her. I stood and grabbed my bag, placing it over my shoulder and walked to the next rotation.

Up next were the uneven bars. Once I secured my grips, I began pacing up and down the athlete area to keep my body warm and loose. My arms swung from side to side, and I hiked up my knees, jumping around. I didn't watch other competitors, and I didn't look in the stands for familiar faces. I kept my focus on my team and my routines and what my coaches instructed. That's it.

Like vault, I excelled at bars, but the ricketiness of them on podium rocked me a bit. I could see a subtle give and take while Holly connected skills, flowing from one bar to the other, releasing it with force only to grab it again.

It was mind over matter. Always mind over matter when it came to gymnastics. I knew this. But it was never that easy.

Holly's dismount was seconds away, which meant I had a handful of minutes until it was my turn.

"You are your only limit," Kova said quietly behind me. I glanced over my shoulder and turned around.

A small smile tipped my lips and I tightened my ponytail. "Are you going to say inspirational quotes before each event?"

He shrugged. "They are not inspirational when I mean them." He hesitated for a moment, then said, "I like seeing you smile."

I glanced away, trying not to let his words affect me. "You know, Reagan said something to me about how you look at me."

Kova muttered under his breath in Russian. There was a sting to his words, a bite, and after witnessing him and Katja argue a few times, I knew whatever he said wasn't pleasant. Though, he was just as good as I was at concealing his facial expressions. No one would've suspected anything.

"What was that?"

"Nothing you need to hear. What did you say to her?"

"That she was acting like a sore loser since I knocked her out of the vault standings." I wasn't going to mention her diet pill issue, even though I'd love nothing more than to rat her out.

He nodded. "Let us go. Your turn is next."

Without hesitation, Kova walked up onto the platform with me like he belonged there. We parted ways. He stood off to the side while I took a stance in front of the low bar. I'd told him earlier I didn't need him to spot, and I didn't, but I knew he was just trying to help calm my nerves since I wasn't used to everything being so unsteady. Which I appreciated.

Saluting the judges, I glided into a kip then cast to a handstand, smoothly swinging under the bar, a free hip circle to another handstand, then released and flowed to the high bar. Once on the high bar in a handstand, I saw Kova move in for my big release. Being there and doing nothing, for whatever reason, seemed to ease a gymnast's mind. A coach would never allow the gymnast to perform a skill they hadn't mastered a thousand times, but it also didn't mean that they weren't scared as shit at the same time.

It meant they were human.

Inhaling through my nose while in a handstand on the high bar, my chest hollowed out and I swung down. From the corner of my eye I saw Kova step in. My toes tapped hard to gain momentum at the bottom of the swing where I pushed my chest and hips forward to create an arch with my body. Right when I was parallel with the bar with an extended body, I let go and flipped through the air over the bar. The bar snapped back to give me a bit more of a thrust and I spotted for it as I came over and down, grasping it. Chalk dusted the air, specks hit my eyes as I breathed it in, and soared back up to a handstand seconds later.

Kova didn't step away as two more release moves were coming up back-to-back. He knew everyone's routines by heart. Once those were done, he backed off and crouched down, critiquing my form from a different angle. Everything flowed so effortlessly after that.

With two giants left and a dismount, I gave it my all and landed my dismount with a very small, slight hop. I saluted the judges and turned.

"Not bad, but not as great as vault," Kova said simply as I stepped to him, his hand cupping the small of my back. "There will be a few deductions, but not enough to keep you out of the standings."

I removed my grips. "Sometimes I wish you would just lie to me. You know how stressed I've been over this meet."

"We have never lied to each other before, I am not going to make things more complicated by giving you false hope now. Do not mistake me, it was good, maybe even great, just not fantastic."

I sighed. He had a point. I never wanted lies.

"Where did I mess up?"

Before he could respond, my score flashed on the high screen.

I stood there, motionless and stunned, stone-faced with my jaw hanging open. Kova said it wasn't bad, but it was better than good because I was now in first place, *again*, not only helping me, but helping my team's overall score as well. Happiness spread through my chest. I grinned from ear to ear and looked at Kova. He gave me a satisfied nod with a deep dip of his chin.

Madeline made a beeline for me. She wrapped her arms around my shoulders and pulled me into a bear hug, praising me on my form and score.

My heart was about near ready to burst. This was going better than I had expected. I needed a minimum score to test elite, and so far, I was on the right track. And through it all, I stayed relatively calm thanks to Kova. Deep down I knew he had more to do with my composed attitude than I was giving him credit for.

Looking up toward the spectators, I finally caved and searched for my parents but soon stopped. The meet was packed, not an empty seat, and finding them would be like looking for a needle in a haystack.

Floor was next.

Kova placed a hand on my shoulder as we walked side by side. "I know you want to take less steps in your tumbling passes, but you need to make sure that you use the length of the floor."

"I know."

It was true—if I didn't extend my body and use up the floor, not only would it throw off my routine, but it would earn me a deduction. The thing was, I got so much height as it was that I didn't want to step out of bounds either.

"Your perception will be off since we are on podium. Everything is going to be bouncier and harder to absorb the landing."

I nodded quickly, then walked onto floor. I jumped a few times, feeling the spring beneath my feet. It was much spongier, but I was confident I had it under control.

Once the judges gave me the okay, I stepped onto the royal blue carpeted floor and took my stance.

chapter 42

I HELD MY POSITION WHILE I LISTENED FOR THE FAINT QUE OF MUSIC TO BEGIN.

While I excelled in two other events, I loved floor. It was my absolute favorite. A classical melody reverberated around the room. I began counting in my head, flowing freely and softly as a feather into each skill that took me into the corner for my first tumbling pass. Bringing my arms down gently, I took a deep breath and exhaled as I eyed the corner at the opposite end of the floor.

Gearing up for the first of four tumbling passes, I took fewer steps and hurdled into a round-off, extending my back handspring, and threw a double layout…and controlled the landing without taking a step back.

I smiled from ear to ear, knowing I executed my first pass well and spun around, leaping through the air into a switch ring plus tour jeté full with all my heart. I put on a display, my love for the sport emerging wider and broader as adrenaline pumped through my blood. I couldn't stop smiling, feeling every bit of my choreographed routine I spent countless hours perfecting. Floor could be so technical at times, losing the softness and grace that once went hand in hand with the event. Kova and Madeline were adamant about exhibiting fluidity and elegance, keeping that aspect front and center. They pressed about exhibiting a sophisticated, well-oiled gymnast. And that's what they got from us. From me.

Spotting the corner, I stepped into the half circle drawn with chalk and brought my arms down. I panted, inhaling a deep breath into my lungs and remained calm. This tumbling pass required more steps to gain the momentum I needed. Starting off with small steps, I ran halfway across the space into stronger, longer ones, and punched the floor with both my feet, knees locked straight. Arms raised above my head, I flipped heel-over-head forward into a front layout—my body straight as a board—punching the floor again into a front-handspring, exhausting my shoulders to pop off the floor with all the muscle I could to flip forward into a full-twist. I punched the floor again and finished with a front tuck.

No extra hop or step in my landing. I stuck the tumbling pass. *Yes!*

A modest smile displayed on my composed face. I had squeezed and tightened every muscle in my core during the tumbling pass, and then even more so at the end to prevent myself from shifting. I wanted to keep the rhythm going but first prove I could settle into clean landings.

With frontward facing passes, a gymnast could rebound so far forward and out of bounds from the power generated if they didn't practice control. Or sometimes end with a leap to cover up the mistake, which never passed the judges keen eyes. They always knew. It was easier to tumble head first than backwards in general, and adding a front tuck to the end of my pass helped control it a bit more for me.

I'd rather tumble backwards. But that was just me.

I spun around on my toes, leg extended high above my head, clutching my ankle. I pulled it firm to my chest and turned in two full circles. For whatever reason, a turn on floor or beam were always harder than any neck breaking tumbling pass out there. It was bizarre. You'd think it would be the other way around.

With tasteful poise and agile paces, I lowered my leg and pivoted a few paces until I was tight to the corner to execute my last tumbling pass, a double back tuck.

Like a colorful ribbon standing out and floating through the chalky air, I concluded with a brilliant smile. A floor routine no more than ninety seconds long, and I was on fire, full of zeal and energy and heavy breaths. God, I loved floor.

Quickly, I saluted the judges and skipped my way toward my team. I did well out there and they knew it, judging by their ecstatic faces. Madeline gave me five and so did Kova, whose arms I jumped into for a hug. My knees bent and my feet came up behind me. It wasn't uncommon for gymnasts to hug their coaches so closely. It was just how things happened and no one questioned it. So much trust and faith went into the dynamics of the coach/gymnast bond. They're the ones who enabled the talent to be freed in the first place.

"Perfection," Kova said with his arms wrapped firmly around my back. He put me down. Laughter caught my attention and applause from Madeline before I made my way to the girls. All of them, even Reagan, gave me an approving smile, high fives, and good jobs.

I was floating on cloud nine. My heart beat faster and faster against my ribs, hardly a second to slow down. I still had one event left to compete, and my score was high enough to qualify Compulsory, even if I made a few mistakes on beam. I glanced into the stands again hoping to see my parents, but it was too tedious squinting at all the heads. Grabbing my items, my team rotated to the last event.

Within a handful of minutes, everything took a drastic turn. I remained rooted in my chair in sheer disbelief. One knee bounced rapidly and I chewed the inside of my lip. This was how much of a rollercoaster gymnastics could be on the psyche. One minute I was up, the next, I was severely down.

Reagan had fallen off beam.

Reagan. Had. Fallen. Off. Beam.

And yet, for some unusual reason I couldn't justify, I felt like *I* had fallen. Like our team had fallen. Balance beam was her event, the one she outshined everyone in the way I did with vault. It was her specialty. Gymnasts with specialty events rarely ever made a mistake. So when it happened, it was shocking.

"Don't let it bother you."

I glanced up at Madeline, unsure of when she appeared next to me. I was in a daze.

"It doesn't bother me… I'm just surprised is all." *Did it bother me?*

She gave me a knowing look. "Don't let her mistake affect you up here." She tapped her temple. "You got this."

I pursed my lips together and nodded. "I wasn't expecting it." Reagan was good. She was incredible actually, which was why when I saw her make a mistake I was shocked.

Madeline's brows nearly reached her forehead. "You don't give yourself enough credit. You're just as good, Adrianna. You've come a long way, you got this. I have complete faith in you."

"Thanks," I said quietly. Madeline patted my shoulder then walked away as Kova strode up. He looked down at me and opened his mouth. Just before he spoke, I put up a hand.

"Are you going to say some inspirational shit again?"

He gave me a spicy grin and my stomach fluttered. Those green eyes of his, they left me breathless. I knew this look. The look that could influence me to do anything he demanded.

Of all the times to remain tactful and thick with discreet, Kova was on full display. A memory flashed through my mind. Kova had once told me that he liked the thrill our strictly off-limits relationship gave him. It made him feel alive.

He shook his head, his smile remained plastered across his handsome face. "I am just going to remind you to take a risk. I know how you feel about this event, but if you let go of all the negatives, all the positives will surprise you. Trust me. It is there."

I was beginning to think Kova had more faith in me than anyone alive, myself and my parents included. It was a startling feeling.

He glanced over his shoulder, my turn was fast approaching. "Tape on good?" he asked. I hitched up my leg and turned to show him the back of my calf.

"Good. *Da-vai.*"

When he didn't disclose the meaning of the word he spoke in Russian, I asked him.

"It means, come on, let us go," he said, using his hands to speak.

"Let us go, or let's go? Since you don't use contractions I'm going to assume it's let's go." He smirked. "Let's go."

One day, I would teach Kova how to use contractions. Just not today.

Exhaling a deep breath, I stepped onto the podium and walked with pointed toes toward beam. I cleared my mind and swallowed back. Once I was given the go, I saluted the judges and zoned in on the apparatus. My mind strictly on my routine.

I got this.

Mounting the four-inch piece of wood, I remained cool and poised as I confidently flowed into every skill. The beam wobbled slightly beneath me, but since I kept my control intact, I was more than good.

Standing at the very end of the balance beam, I raised my arms up and flattened them to my ears. One benefit of being short with this sport was that I could fit a lot on the balance beam combination wise, meaning I could add a jump or leap at the end of the combo for bonus points. With my focus on my toes, I sat back and executed the sequence required for this level—a back handspring, back layout, back step-out.

I stuck the landing without so much as a balance check and effortlessly glided into mandatory dance skills while remaining lithe and free-flowing. Nimble. Calm and confident. I made sure to hit the one hundred and eighty degree mark in my split to receive the maximum points. I'd done countless over split jumps as conditioning, and thankfully the flexibility Kova was able to create in my hips this past year helped tremendously.

Elongating my arms out to my sides, I controlled my breathing to prepare for my dismount. A balance beam routine was quick—no more than ninety seconds at most.

I sashayed then lifted one leg forward immediately turning into a switch leap, a gainer pike then a pivot turn in under a couple of seconds. Arms raised in the air, I eyed the end of the balance beam and took a deep breath and exhaled. Stepping into a round-off back handspring, I completed my dismount with a double back tuck, both feet together and sticking my landing.

Anxiously, I waited on the judges. I knew I qualified based on the previous events, but seeing the numbers is what made it valid. Seconds turned to minutes to what felt like hours.

I removed the sports tape while I waited and pulled on my sweats. I drank water, fixed my ponytail, tried to find anything to keep me busy to calm my nerves.

I heard the elation from my coaches and teammates before I saw the score. I looked up at the board and a massive grin spread across my face.

I had qualified for Compulsory with flying colors, even earning a few medals for myself and for the team.

I. Qualified. For. Compulsory.

Holy. Shit.

The feeling inside, the joy, the pure excitement and satisfaction of seeing I'd done it, was all too much to explain. I was rushed by my team and coaches congratulating me. The hard work, the grueling and demanding hours, had paid off and I couldn't be happier.

With one half of the meet behind me, all I needed to do now was do it all over again, but with different routines. Then, I would officially be elite.

I could do it. I just had to make sure I held back the tears of excitement until it was all over.

chapter 43

WHEN SOMETHING IS TOO GOOD TO BE TRUE, IT USUALLY IS.

It was much later in the evening when I began to test for Optionals. Three events down, I had one to go. I couldn't stop checking the scoreboard this time around for some reason, the nagging feeling in my gut persisted with each passing minute.

Damn nerves. My hands trembled, and I had a raging headache, all caused by myself. My anxiety was through the roof.

My scores had been good, they were where I needed them to be, just not incredible like I had hoped for. I strived to be better, the best, but I was too close to teetering the line between qualifying and not qualifying. A balance check away from everything slipping.

I realized my best wasn't good enough for me. And the fear of that, never being enough, was as strong as ever. It took control of my emotions and I began replaying the events I already completed, wondering if I had given my all like I thought I did.

I released a deep sigh of criticism. "I could've done more."

"Could you have? Truly have done more?"

I stared at the floor, my next and last event, contemplating his words. "I think so. Everyone could always do more."

"You are not giving yourself credit. Your routines are much harder this time around, which means more deductions," Kova said when he saw the worried look on my face. "It is not easy."

All I could do was glare at him with flat lips.

His voice grew stern. "You are letting fear mock you, Adrianna. Do not let it win." He paused. "Where is this coming from, anyway?"

I said nothing. I wasn't sure where my feelings were coming from.

Kova shook his head. "If you still feel that way when this is all over, then when you walk into practice Monday morning you make up for it. Give me all you got, and I will take it and more. I promise you, I will take you for everything you are worth, but do not let your emotions soar so high that you lose it all in a ninety second routine. That fear will make you fail. Do not fail."

I gave him a long blink.

"*I believe in you*," he whispered low, only for my ears.

The corner of his eyes crinkled, and the candidness shook me. He meant it. Hand to his chest, he said again, "*I believe in you*." His cheeks turned a slight scarlet and his mouth twitched.

His declaration, the faith padding each word, his undying devotion to me and the sport. It was all there. It gave me chills to have someone in my corner rallying behind me the way he was.

I wasn't sure what happened, but something deep inside me shifted. The fear that had consumed my attention like a foggy, misty cloud that threatened to smother me lifted into thin air and dissolved. It scurried at the sound of conviction, the confidence too strong to be held down. I swallowed back my emotions and nodded, nodding at what, I wasn't sure, but agreeing with whatever he was putting off.

I relied on him more than I knew.

"Shake it out," he said gently. Kova clutched my shoulders and massaged them, coaxing me to loosen up. I released an extremely long, tension filled breath.

"Good. Now get out there and show me what you got. I did not spend all that time molding you into the perfect gymnast for nothing."

I gave him a droll stare. "Way to ruin the moment, Kova."

He chuckled lightly and I smiled.

I showed him everything. And I made sure to give my all, more than I felt I did with my last three routines, so I couldn't have any regrets. My calf throbbed painfully to the point that I feared I tore something, but I shook it off and ignored it. I pushed and pushed, and when the big screen flashed with my final score, the combined score of both sets of routines I needed to test as elite, a tiny gasp fell from my parted lips.

Frozen. Dazed. Stunned.

I was rendered speechless as I stared at the numbers, quickly doing the math in my head to make sure they were correct. Cheerful laughter erupted around me, but I couldn't hear any of it. Madeline pulled me into a tight hug, rubbing my back. She was speaking to me, but I still couldn't hear her words despite how close she was, I could only see her lips move. A friendly smile tugged at my mouth from the contagiousness of her excitement. She turned at the call of her name and walked away.

Frantic but silent, I stood there until I was lifted into someone else's arms.

Kova.

"See what happens when you let go of fear?"

I didn't say anything. I just inhaled his scent that reminded me of cinnamon and warmth, and wrapped my arms around his shoulders. I dropped my head into the curve of his neck and smiled against him.

"You win, *malysh*. You win." His lips brushed against my neck and I panicked slightly since we were in public. "You persevered with a purpose and you let your passion shine. This is only the beginning of small victories that will lead to big dreams. Triumph above all."

Kova lowered me to the floor. I stood before him, gazing into his eyes, studying his face. Appreciating all he did for me. My heart softened around his words. My hands came up and covered my mouth as it started to sink in. Tears burned my frantic eyes. *I qualified elite!*

"We did it." My voice cracked. Chills broke out on my skin and I bent my head down. I almost cried.

"No. *You* did it. You."

"But I couldn't have done it without you."

If he hadn't given me the courage I needed so desperately right before I went out on floor, I had a feeling we wouldn't be having the same conversation right now.

It was in that moment that I realized how much I relied—and trusted—in him.

He shrugged into me with his arms. "Semantics."

He pointed to the scoreboard above my head and smiled. Kova was ecstatic, and it tickled me.

"Want to take a picture of it?" he asked jokingly. I still couldn't believe it.

A year of challenging practices, days filled with frustration and tears, sweat and blood, and I'd *finally* done it.

I'd been so close to stepping out of bounds. I almost lost it all because I had a moment of uncertainty and doubted myself.

But Kova brought me back. He centered me and helped make my dream a reality, because he believed in me.

I owed him so much.

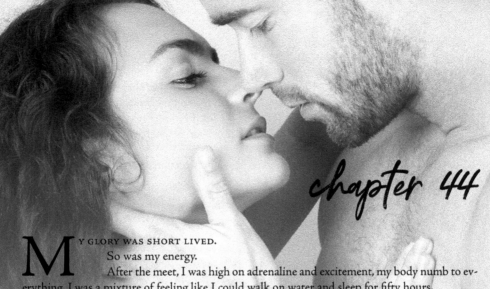

chapter 44

MY GLORY WAS SHORT LIVED.

So was my energy.

After the meet, I was high on adrenaline and excitement, my body numb to everything. I was a mixture of feeling like I could walk on water and sleep for fifty hours.

The rest of the night was a blur. After dinner with my parents, we retired to their enormous suite on the top floor fit for royalty. Dad and Kova spoke over glasses of bourbon and vodka, while I was left to the scrutiny of my mom in the living room that overlooked the city. Hoarse chuckles and clandestine wisdom sifted innately around the suite. Two friends deep in conversation, catching up. For more than half the time, I gazed out the window, absorbed by the twinkling colors that illuminated the skyline. Break lights glowed like burning embers, and I wondered where the people were in a rush to go.

I could stare all night. It was so much more beautiful in the dark.

Surprisingly, it wasn't as bad as I expected. Mom was…elated for me. And I wasn't sure how to respond to that. I wanted to make her happy, to be proud of me and my accomplishments, but every time I opened myself up to her warmth it always seemed to backfire on me.

I sighed silently. All I could do was try.

"I know it's months away, but do you have any time off during meet season? I'm trying to plan an Easter brunch and would very much like if you could be there. If not, no worries."

"I'm sure I could make it happen, even if it's for the day."

I pulled out my cell phone and opened my calendar. I knew I had many meets lined up, but I didn't know the exact dates.

I stared at my phone, confused. "It seems I don't have any in…" My voice trailed off. I glanced up at Kova, who sensed me almost immediately. Our eyes met.

"What is it?" he asked, cutting my dad off.

I held my phone up as if he could see the screen. "Do we not have any meets around Easter?"

"Your phone is synced with the calendar. It is up to date."

I glanced back at the screen. I saw nothing. Kova placed his empty crystal tumbler down, stood, and walked over to me. Leaning over my shoulder, he rested his forearms behind me on the headrest. With a wave of his hand, he silently asked for the phone and viewed the dates with me.

His thumb slid the screen up and down, his breath cool and smooth rasped softly against my cheek. "It looks like you have time off, which is a good thing since we have Worlds and the Championships the following two months."

Me and Kova eased into a light exchange about gymnastics. He shifted closer to me and I angled toward him, our bodies casually open and welcoming to one another. We spoke quietly among ourselves for a few short moments about my training that month, my parents long forgotten until I heard a glass clank on the counter.

We both glanced up from the sound and found my mother looking at us. Her eyes filled with disdain as they shifted to Kova, then to me, where they stayed.

A knot lodged in my throat. We'd let our guards down for a split second. There was no way she'd missed the natural harmony that occurred between us.

We eased back into the conversation. My heart hammered and I held stiff as a statue while Kova spoke. I'd been under my mom's examination too many times in the past to ignore her inquisitive eyes. Her stare seared my flawless skin with incomprehensible questions. While Dad was fixated on his phone, my mom continued to glare at us. I swallowed hard and glanced at Kova, trying my best to give him a look of cognizance, a look I'd given him in the past that would hint discreetly for him to pull back and slow down. He picked up on it immediately.

Kova scratched the back of his head and stood, clearing his throat.

"Are you always so intimate with all your gymnasts?" Mom asked as if she were inquiring about the weather.

All color drained from my face. "Mom!"

"Joy." Dad scowled low and deep. A warning.

She ignored us both, her eyes glued on Kova with a vengeance. "Refresh my memory, Konstantin, how many hours a week do you both train together?"

He tucked his hands into the pockets of his pressed slacks. Shoulders relaxed, not a worry on his face.

"Close to fifty hours. Give or take."

"Uh huh." She tilted her head ever so slightly. "That's a lot of time to be alone together, wouldn't you agree, Frank?"

My heart raced so hard and fast I felt every pulse in my body thrashing against my veins, the rapid beating in my ears so loud it was all I could hear.

"If you paid more attention to your daughter than your charity cases, then you'd see that's been going on for a year now. Clearly, it's paid off. Adrianna did excellent. She exceeded our expectations."

If only I could muster a smile.

Kova added, "I am not the only one who trains with Adrianna. Coach Madeline does as well. We rotate the gymnasts among each other all week."

"How convenient," Mom replied, sipping her wine. Her eyes hadn't left Kova's and she completely ignored the sneer Dad made.

I almost died, but thankfully, Kova was quick. "Yes, we rotate the girls so they do not get too used to our training methods, otherwise it would be useless for everyone involved. They all train the same number of hours, *together*."

A lie.

"Ana is a stunning *girl*, isn't she?" Mom stated, no question asked. Kova refused to answer. "You know, after the New Year's Eve party, my housekeeper found a sports coat on the balcony of her bedroom. It didn't look like Xavier's…"

There was no way to stop my reaction. My eyes shot wide and blood drained from my face. My memory went back to that night and I tried to remember anything about a coat…and it hit me. Kova had shrugged his coat off that night to put over my shoulders to keep me warm. I didn't recall him leaving it behind until now.

"It was Hayden's," I said quickly. "He said he misplaced it. He'll be happy to know it's been found."

"That's interesting." She sipped her wine with knowing eyes and a smirk so cunning that I shifted in my chair. She was hiding something. I knew she was.

"What are you getting at, Joy?" Dad crossed his leg in front of the other. His curiosity piqued, but annoyance prevalent more than anything.

"Nothing. Merely observing how gorgeous your daughter is." Her honeyed voice dripped with suspicion. Mom's eyes dropped to mine. I knew better than to look away—it would scream guilt and I made it a point not to waver as she put me under the spotlight.

Maybe I was too good because I caught a glitter of something in her eyes before she quickly blinked it away.

I swallowed hard and feigned exhaustion with a yawn. I stood, but I stood too fast and flinched with a hobble, gasping in pain. I closed my eyes and squeezed them shut. A twitch of heat jerked in my leg. *Shit.* I grimaced, grabbing onto the chair.

"Everything all right?" Kova asked. He gingerly held my bicep to steady my balance.

"Yes," I gritted through the pain that was no doubt connected to my Achilles. I stood with a bent knee. "My muscles are just a little tight right now. That's all."

Kova's eyes narrowed. "Hmmm. When we get back to town, make sure you see your doctor." Creases formed between my bows. "Why? I'm fine."

"I do not like the way you are standing. You are clearly in discomfort."

"You should listen to your coach," Dad added. "He knows what he's talking about."

"Yes." Mom dragged out the S sound. "Listen to your coach." She finished in a syrupy, sarcastic voice.

I scoffed. "Kova, I'm fine. I'm just sore."

Dropping to his knees, he ordered me to sit. He took my foot into his hand and massaged his way around my previous injury while Mom watched. My stomach contracted with discomfort but I held still, my lips in a firm line and face neutral as Kova glanced up when he pinched the back of my ankle.

I gave him my best see there's nothing wrong look while biting the inside of my lip and dying inside.

His touch was light, tender, and I still drew blood. He pinched again, and it was the same sting I felt zip up my spine when I ended my first tumbling pass on floor. I swallowed hard and stared into his eyes, hoping to prove to him there was nothing wrong. I couldn't afford another setback, especially after testing elite. I thought something snapped in the back of my ankle, but I needed to awe the judges with my floor routine, so I persevered and pushed harder than ever before. Eventually, I forgot about it.

It was the same event Kova talked me through. The one where I discovered that I was fierce and strong and that I needed to let my passion burn bright for everyone to see.

"I have been doing this a long time, Ri—Adrianna. I know an injury when I see it."

My heart sank and I didn't dare glance in my mom's direction. He almost slipped up.

"There's nothing there," I insisted.

"You have to see your doctor soon?" Dad asked, his eyes barely leaving his phone.

I nodded. "Yes."

"Good. Make sure you have them recheck your foot when you're there," he said. Your foot. I grimaced. It was actually the back of my ankle and calf, but who cares.

Kova placed my foot down and I let out a silent breath of pain. He glanced at me, but I masked the terror in my eyes and smiled. He sat back down and went into some mundane conversation with Dad, all the while my mom's eyes were trained on me like a cat in heat as she sipped her wine.

A stone boulder sat heavy in my stomach. There was something seriously wrong with my leg that left me panic stricken. But worse, the look in my mom's eyes shook me to the core. I knew in my gut she was scheming. If only I could see what she had up her Chanel sleeve.

chapter 45

I'D WOKEN UP IN A FOUL MOOD.

    Tired and in pain, I crawled out of bed like a ninety-year-old woman who needed a walker. Swollen eyes to match my swollen ankle. I was a broken record on replay every damn day and I was getting sick of my own thoughts.

Between trying to set two different appointments for two different doctors—one specialist, one physician—getting lost driving, almost running over a turtle from spotting a damn alligator on the side of the road, waiting for hours to see the doctors, and test after test, I was ready to call it a day.

The only thing that saved me from losing it was a bottle of Motrin and the strongest coffee Starbucks offered plus two extra shots of espresso.

A bowl of penne a la vodka would've been nice too. But I didn't dare.

The outcome from both doctors had been craptasic. Another day, another hurdle.

Pulling up to World Cup, I carefully stepped out of my truck and applied pressure to my good leg, which the doctor had advised against. Added pressure and added weight could eventually cause a tear on that side too.

With my keys and cell phone in one hand, I pulled open the glass door and limped inside the gym with a puckered face and fresh out of fucks to give. I was beyond aggravated I had reinjured myself. The frustration slowly dissipated as I inhaled the chalky, powdery scent that permeated the air. I treasured that scent and this place. It was home, where I was supposed to be, but once again it felt like it was being ripped from my grip, and I'd do anything to hold on to it.

The last time I'd come to see Kova after a doctor's appointment, I'd worn a green dress chosen with him in mind. This time, I wore navy blue shorts, a basic graphic shirt from Target, and a pair of stone-gray Converse. My auburn locks were tied up in a disaster of a messy bun. I wasn't in the mood for any shenanigans.

I spotted Kova through the glass window of the lobby where he was training the men's team. I caught Hayden high up in the middle of holding a skill on the rings. His triceps quivered, his face as red as a fire hydrant, but that didn't prevent him from smiling at me. A little more of my irritation melted away.

Kova looked over his shoulder and held up an index finger. I could see dark circles under his eyes from where I stood. He looked tired. The thought of how my injury would affect not only me but also him flooded my mind. He's put so much time and work into me, I didn't want to let either one of us down. Nodding, I turned and made my way to his office. The pain in my ankle was reduced to a low dull and I plopped down in one of his chairs with an exasperated sigh. I was thinking about it too much and needed to stop. My head lulled back and I closed my eyes, fatigue coming down on me once again. I laced my fingers together on my stomach and waited.

Within a few short minutes, I heard footsteps approaching down the hall.

"Ria."

I opened my eyes and my heart did an obnoxious little jump. I should've told him to stop calling me the nickname he had given me, but I couldn't find it in my heart. I liked the sound of it only on his lips.

My eyes immediately zoomed in on his toned arms. His muscles flexed as he walked around the desk, twirling in a downward spiral like powerful golden ropes. I wanted to reach out and trace them with my fingers from the curves of his shoulders to his wrists. Covered in white dust, he wore a sleeveless shirt with his predictable basketball shorts. Even his backwards hat had chalk on it. Air seized my lungs, a little knot clamped the back of my throat. I was so drawn to him, like a magnet ready to collide with its counterpart.

Kova ran a tired hand down his face. "I pray you have good news for me?"

I sat up straight and cleared my throat. "Good news is I have micro tears in my Achilles a little bigger than the last time," I said sarcastically. He sat stone-faced, unimpressed with what I considered good news, but I needed something to help me pass this hurdle I was suddenly faced with. "The MRI didn't show a complete rupture, which actually surprised the doctor. He was sure I tore it completely. Strangely enough, he concluded that I have an abnormal ankle joint. Apparently, I've been compensating on one side. Who knew? My foot has less than ten-degree flexion due to my ankle bones, so my Achilles takes the brunt of the landings. The area around my Achilles, the bursa, blows up and squeezes the Achilles, which is where the pain is coming from. So, they're going to do platelets-rich plasma injections," I said slowly, trying to make sure I got it right, "to promote fast healing and then do the Grayson Technique. He insisted I rest for several weeks, but I told him that wasn't an option." I paused to glare at Kova, dipping my head a little to reinforce my next words. "*Because it's not an option, Kova.* I know I should go easy when I condition and train, but we'll see. He told me with the PRP I should start to see signs of increased function within four to six weeks, as long as I don't do any extra aggressive physical activity, but physical therapy that's set up through my doctor." I added the extra in there.

"Graston Technique."

Damn it. I knew I got the name wrong. "Tomato, tomahto."

"Did your doctor say how many injections?"

"Four. At the most, six. But he said only time will tell."

"And how—"

"Oh! And he said no anti-inflammatory medicine, no matter what. That's a bummer considering Motrin is part of my food group."

Kova gave me a droll stare. "I am well aware of that. And how often is the blading to occur?"

My brows furrowed. "Blading?"

"Yes," he sighed. "Blading is a nickname for the Graston Technique, Adrianna." I stayed silent as he continued. "They run a steel bar over your Achilles to smooth it out." His brows lifted and he moved his hands back and forth like he was rolling out dough, exhibiting how it would happen. "It is usually done to help prevent swelling and immobility." He stared at my blank face. "It is a more extreme form of massage, if you will."

I didn't move a muscle. And barely moving my lips, I blandly said, "He didn't explain that part to me. I'll have to find out when I go back for the PRP." Blading did not sound like fun. It sounded like torture.

"Who is your doctor?"

I rambled off the name of the office as he leaned over and unlocked one of his desk drawers. He pulled out a manila folder and opened it, flipping through the pages inside.

"What are you doing?"

"Ah, so I was right," he said, reading the paper in his hand. "They have trainers at this office who go around to the sports clubs in the area and work on athletes with injuries so they don't have to leave the gym. The blading only takes about ten minutes or so, this is perfect if you need it a few times a week."

I grimaced, fighting an eye roll. "Great. Sounds like loads of fun."

Kova looked up at me. "This is not your first rodeo, remember? You can do this."

A chuckle escaped my lips, I couldn't help it. Hearing Kova use my line was amusing since it came out of his Russian mouth so stiffly. Like he was testing out the word.

"What?" A soft smile tugged at his lips and I hated that it affected me. "Did I say it wrong?"

"No, it just sounds funny coming from you."

Kova stood and placed the paper down before making his way around the desk to stand in front of me. He dropped his hips to the top and leaned over. He clasped his hands in front of him and his voice dropped as he said, "We will get through this, I promise. It is bad, but it could have been worse. The only good thing you have working in your favor right now is that you do not have to train for anything new, we will just go a tad lighter."

"I don't want that," I shot back quickly. I knew he was going to say that by the look in his eyes. Kova cocked his head to the side and took me in. My heart raced as my emotions jumped all around like fraying sparks. I stood up and stepped to him so we were eye to eye.

"I'm not doing this song and dance with you again, Kova. I'm so close to getting what I want. I can taste it. I need to go hard and I'm going to do whatever it takes, so don't expect me to go light on myself. The moment is *now*." I swallowed hard, fighting the tears threatening to climb. "I only have right now," I said softly. "The time is now."

Kova's face remained neutral. "I am trying to do the right thing for you. I want to push and make you work through the injury and pain and swelling and act like it is not even there, make you get up and brush it off any time I see you limp." He lifted his hand and brushed back a strand of hair and cupped it behind my ear. His voice lowered to a cracked whisper. "But I do not want to do that because I care about you, and if you injure yourself further, it would be catastrophic, for both of us." His eyes dropped to my mouth. "It is hard to fight you on wanting something so bad. I feel what you are feeling, that hunger inside of you that is never satisfied." His eyes were soft when they met mine again. "I get it. You are so close yet so far that if you let go, even for a split second, you will feel like it is gone forever."

I nodded hastily, taking joy in the fact that he truly understood where I was coming from. I tried not to smile from ear to ear. This is why we clicked so well. He more than anyone understood my drive and determination. The need to succeed in the sport, not just because I wanted to be on top, but because I hungered for it, craved it.

"I was in your spot once," Kova continued. "I understand what you are dealing with. What we will do is hone in on tightening up a few things and some conditioning. No tumbling passes for now, or vault. Let us get you started on the treatment first so your Achilles can begin to heal as much as possible. You are there, Ria, your routines are solid." Kova paused. "You are there." Kova grabbed my biceps and gave me a little shake. My legs trembled, nearly giving out at finally hearing the words I'd prayed to hear since coming to World Cup. "Coming in first place at the meet was huge. All eyes are on you right now. And you know how I know that? Because I have already gotten call after call wondering about who you are and where you came from. Make no mistake, those little tears are extremely dangerous. We will be smart about it, but we are not stopping."

"You got calls about me?"

He nodded his head, hiding a grin.

"What did they say?" I asked excitedly.

"Nothing you need to concern yourself with right now."

"Kova! Tell me!" I teetered on my toes anxiously. "Just give me something!"

"Just some colleagues asking about which meets you will be at. They were impressed with you and said they hoped to see you at nationals."

My eyes went wide. Nationals were meets I had to qualify for, and the most important ones. I had to be one of the top eight in my age division. No easy feat by any measure, but it still made me happy and gave me a ton of hope. A stupid grin split across my face. Nationals? I couldn't even imagine. I mean, I could, but for his friends to call about me and make that comment was exhilarating.

"Remember nationals is where the college coaches go to recruit," he stated.

I nodded hesitantly. It may have slipped my mind.

"Not to worry. We have a little time before that." He put a hand up before I could say another word. "I know college isn't on your mind, but I still want you to be well-informed of all your opportunities as much as you can."

Without thinking, I threw my arms around his shoulders and dropped my face into the curve of his neck. His words filled my heart as I leaned in between his hips. Kova wrapped his arms around my lower back and held me snuggly to him. He sighed into my neck. His confidence in me filled me to epic proportions. I needed that, needed to feel like I could do anything, and that he had my back.

Tears poured from my eyes as I cried and thanked him repeatedly. His words were music to my ears. I was petrified and angry when I walked in here today, ready to go toe-to-toe. I feared this meeting would be déjà vu all over again and he'd tell me we'd have to downgrade my skills. But he surprised me in many ways. I had no idea anyone had taken interest in me since the competition.

Kova's hand ran in soothing circles on my back. He leaned his face against the side of my head and murmured, "You got this, Ria. Focus but be smart. I will be right there with you every step of the way." He gave me a little squeeze and dropped a soft peck to my temple. My body warmed and I began to catch my breath when I heard the door creak.

I froze, my heart stopped, and I sucked in a breath as Kova's hand stopped moving. His body hardened against mine and before we could move, the door flew open.

"What…what is going on here?"

I looked over my shoulder and met Katja's vivid golden and peridot eyes. Fuck.

Kova pulled back. One of his hands slid to my hip and his thumb ran in small circles on my pelvis, only for me to feel and no one to see.

Katja's eyes shifted rapidly from me to Kova, the accusation in her gaze strong enough to render me speechless. Oh, God.

"Katja, what are you doing here?" Kova asked as he stood and put a little distance between us.

"Why were you two…embraced like that?" She stared at me like I was a roach she wanted to step on. "What is going on here, Kova?" Katja glanced at him, then looked back at me. "She is a child," she spat, and I paled.

"I am aware, Kat, but it is not what you think."

"Not what I think? Then what the hell is going on? Why were you two holding each other like…like lovers," she bit out.

Kova's eyes darkened and he moved lightning fast to stand in front of her. He began mouthing off in Russian, short and clipped words, but it didn't take a fool to realize he was furious. The tension in the room was stifling, so much hostility it was hard to breathe. I suddenly felt like a leper. Each time Katja tried to get a word in, he cut her off. Her eyes shifted to me, but Kova snapped his fingers and his voice rose every time. She jumped, and I rolled my bottom lip between my teeth as she looked back at him with shame in her eyes. The conversation tampered off, then an uncomfortable silence filled the room for a moment.

"As you see, Adrianna has an injury."

Katja's eyes dropped to my foot that had been wrapped in tape. Her jaw bobbed. Her cheeks blushed. I'd never been so thankful to have this injury until now. The chair had blocked my leg from her view when she had walked in.

Her tune changed immediately, but there was something in her eyes that didn't quite sell me. I wish I knew what he said to her.

"I…I did not know. I apologize greatly."

"It's okay. I got a little emotional thinking my gymnastics career would have to change once again, and I couldn't handle that after coming so far." My voice shook a little.

"Kova has mentioned what a great deal of improvement you have made in the past year. In fact, he says you are his best gymnast and sees big things for you."

My lips parted and I glanced at Kova. Blood pumped faster through my heart as our eyes connected. His body was stiff, his mouth a firm, thin line.

"Now, if you will excuse me, I will see you for dinner tonight, *malysh*."

Malysh. My eyes lowered.

Katja smiled and leaned in for a kiss, and I decided it was my cue to leave.

Grabbing my keys and cell phone, I mumbled my gratitude to Kova and that I'd see him tomorrow for practice. Hayden tried to get my attention once I was in the lobby, but I limped my ass out of there as fast as I could. The last thing I wanted to see was Kova kissing Katja. Or worse, hear her mouth slurping over his body.

chapter 46

O NE WEEK LATER, WE WERE IN CHARLOTTE, NORTH CAROLINA, AND AT ANOTHER
competition.

This one was a little smaller, but just as important as the last. Every meet for
the next three months was crucial. Not just for my journey to the Olympics, but placing in
the top at each one.

My stomach swirled with anxiety and impatience. I was so excited yet so apprehensive,
full of unease for my future. I had so much on the line with one shot to get there. I wanted it
all right now, but I didn't.

Things were going very well, better than I could've expected. I'd been sleeping better,
headaches were gone, and I had way more stamina than usual. All thanks to the vitamin shots
I was giving myself a few times a day. The doctor had ordered one injection once a week, but
I figured it was a vitamin and it couldn't hurt to take more. I think the stress of testing elite
had really taken a toll on my body because once I had that past me, it was smooth sailing…
for the most part.

I hadn't had the blading on my Achilles, thank goodness since it sounded awful, but I'd
had a steroid injection right into the tendon a day later, and it helped tremendously. Most of
the pain and aching went away, but I knew it wouldn't last forever.

The problem was finding someone who could provide me with the Graston Technique
without a waitlist. There were very few people skilled in my area who could do it when I needed.
Meaning immediately.

Kova and Madeline were both certified athletic trainers. They both could do therapy on
my Achilles, but both would require proper training first. It was a special course that entailed
four full days of training, two weekends, plus a certification test.

Kova told me he was considering it, but finding the time to fit it in his schedule was
another task altogether. Any spare time had been devoted to me at my request. But then I
thought of something.

"Kova?"

Kova turned and gave me a once over. I was up soon for my first event of the competition.

"Everything okay?" he asked, his voice full of concern.

I nodded. "I'm fine. I was just thinking that since we have another meet in two weeks,
why don't we skip next weekend's practice so you can take the first half of that class?"

Kova's eyes dropped to my taped ankle then back up to mine.

"Why? Are you in pain now? What do you need me to do?" he quickly shot off as if I'd
been in agony and crying out. He stalked toward me. I smiled, my eyes softened at his distress.

"I'm okay. I was just thinking about the future is all."

His features shifted back into place. Back into Coach Kova. "Adrianna, let me handle my schedule. You just focus on you, yes?"

I blinked. "I am focused, but I was thinking about these little tears and how I don't want to make it worse. I've been doing a lot of online reading and that blading is supposed to do wonders."

Kova studied me. I made no sense. I know I didn't. I pushed and pushed, and argued with Kova over not slowing down, despite his suggestions. I knew any worse and it would be a full-blown rupture, and then I could kiss my gymnastics career goodbye. I wanted to be bold and courageous, but I was a little lamb picking on an animal bigger than me. I was going to give it my all and then some, but I still had to be careful.

"Use your brain. Think about what you are doing, what you need to do, and do it. Your body will know. Focus on right now and yourself and nothing more."

"But, Kova, you take time out to help me, so I want to help you if I can." I paused and looked away, slightly embarrassed. "You do a lot for me."

"I appreciate that. And after this weekend, we will work it out. But for now, you are not to think of anything else but yourself and your routines. Let me take care of the rest." Kova glanced up and over my head, someone had called his name. "You are next on rotation. Get ready."

I nodded and took three steps before he stopped me. I looked up and over my shoulder, then turned around, puzzled. "Yes?"

"I do a lot because I *enjoy* doing it for you, not because I *have* to." He held up a pointer finger, a brow raised high. "Remember that. Also, stay off the internet. It is garbage."

An appreciative smile tipped my lips just a fraction, enough for him to see. The tension in my shoulders eased and I turned away to prepare for vault, beyond thankful I had someone like him in my corner.

Another meet in the books and I was flying high, until Kova announced he wouldn't be at the following one. My stomach knotted for a split moment. I needed him there with me, we were a team, but I figured he had taken my advice and planned to sign up for the class to get certified.

I placed second. Point zero zero one was the difference between first and second. One one-thousandth of a fraction was all it took to move me down one step on the podium.

Was that fraction even something visible to the eye? I wish I knew where my deductions were.

It sucked. God, it sucked big time.

"Hey," Madeline said when she saw my face just as we were about to board the plane. Both my parents had skipped the meet, common in the gymnastics world for parents to do, so I flew with my coaches and team. "Don't be so hard on yourself. You tried and that's what matters. You did fantastic, Adrianna. This is your second elite meet and you blew me away by your strength to thrive under pressure. So many girls let nerves get to them. You don't and that's what sets you apart."

I pulled my duffle strap closer to my neck, gripping it hard. I shook my head, still upset with myself for losing the top spot.

"But I didn't try hard enough or else I'd be coming home with a different color medal."

"You're new to this kind of competition. It's gymnastics on steroids. What you've done so far has been nothing less than impressive." She paused. "How's your leg?"

"It's fine." She tilted her head down and gave me the look, the kind your parents give when they think you're lying to them. I tried not to smile, but I couldn't help it. "It's fine, really.

I had that blood injection thing, or whatever it's called, and I've been taking the vitamins and it's been great since then. Honestly."

"All right. Let me know if you need anything, ever."

I nodded, and she walked ahead of me, leaving me alone with my thoughts. Kova had been right that time he said silver is first place loser.

"Coming in second place is the worst feeling after you just gave your all. There are winners and there are losers. You play a sport to win—that is it. Nothing else. You have one chance to prove yourself. One."

I made a vow to myself to never come in anything but first. It was already my goal to be number one, but now that I've had a taste of it, I wanted the whole damn plate. No low-fat, fat-free for me. Give me all, or give me nothing. Anything less than first was pointless and it made me question what else I could've done. I replayed my routines in my head, trying to figure out where I slipped up.

I questioned what my teammate had done better than me.

Reagan had placed first. I glanced over at her. Fucking Reagan had gotten first place by a fraction so small it could only have been due to an extremely small wobble, or slightly bent legs. Hell, my bra strap could have shown, and not knowing what it was, was eating away at me. Surprisingly, Reagan hadn't been smug about it. I think she knew in the back of her mind she wasn't far from dropping to second place, and that rocked her.

Or, I was finally just as good as she was…and she couldn't handle it.

I smiled to myself, letting the frustration roll off my shoulders. This meet was a lesson learned.

Goals were never easy. Practice. It was all about how much effort I put into practice, how I learned from my mistakes.

I was a winner. And I was going to focus on winning.

"Let it go, you did well," Kova said, then boarded the plane. "There is always next time."

But he wouldn't be there the next time.

I followed behind him and took my seat, thankful I had the row to myself. It was a mid-day flight on a Monday, and not very crowded. Once the seatbelt light turned off, I grabbed my duffle bag from the overhead. I needed a distraction. I sat back down and dug through my bag for the paperback I had tossed in there earlier, and froze. I took a quick glance around at my team. Reagan was two rows ahead of me. Across the aisle from me, Holly had nodded off. Everyone else seemed busy with their own thing, including Madeline and Kova. I turned back to my bag and took out the spiral-bound notebook.

My stomach filled with butterflies as I flipped through the pages. We'd managed to pass it back and forth a few times over the last couple weeks. We kept it short and sweet, and while we had fun with it, we got to know each other a little better. I got to experience a different side of Kova. He was light and carefree. I smiled at his responses to my mundane questions.

I love cotton candy. I have a bad sweet tooth and have bags hidden in my house.

I questioned if he was a five year old.

I turned to the next the page and reread the entry. He'd asked if I liked top or bottom. Top or bottom of what? He made no sense. A bagel? A bunk bed? A cupcake? I shook my head, I still didn't know what he meant. I had responded…

I guess it would be the top for all. I like the top.

Too bad. I do not bottom for anyone. You have a lot to learn. One day. Timing is everything.

He could be so frustrating, but anticipation filled me at the thought of what more he could teach me. I turned the page to write him a response but was surprised to find another entry from him.

I will always be by your side, that is, if you will have me.

My stomach dropped as the tone turned serious. I didn't know what this meant. Lifting my eyes, I found Kova staring right at me. The hungry look in his emerald eyes struck me deep to my core. It wasn't just sex though. There was more to his stare. More he was trying to say.

If only I could decipher it.

chapter 47

"ADRIANNA, WHAT'S THAT?" HAYDEN ASKED, POINTING DOWN TO MY LEG. I glanced down at the small bruise that marred my lean thigh and dusted the chalk away, the back of my knuckles smoothing over the hard lump. My vitamin injection site had turned into an ugly shadow of black and blue a few days ago, and now there was that brownish-yellow shade surrounding it. I usually applied concealer to the area, but I slept in a little today and completely forgot.

"The bruise? It's from the B12 shots," I said like it was obvious.

His blue eyes filled with concern. "What are you talking about?"

I shifted on my feet and looked over at Madeline to make sure she wasn't waiting for me. Holly was next, then me.

"Remember the meet where I was dealing with exhaustion?" He nodded, eyes leveled on me. "I have to take B12 shots now because my energy is so low."

His brows furrowed. "How often are you taking them?"

I glanced at Madeline. I was next. "Right now, I take them often, but once my levels are higher, then I can lower it to twice a month."

"And Coach Kova knows?"

I pursed my lips together. "You know, I can't remember. But I gotta go—don't want to keep her waiting."

After I executed a handful of vaults with suggestions from Madeline, Hayden found me again.

"What's up," I asked breathlessly, fixing my ponytail.

His forehead was deeply creased. "Who gives you the shots?"

I sighed. "Christ on a stick, get off my back. You act like someone is beating me. Why are you so concerned anyway?"

"I just am. If you need shots because you're tired, that's an obvious sign you need to slow down." He glanced over his shoulder toward Kova and glowered at him. "Or he's pushing you too hard and overworking you, which wouldn't surprise me if that was the case."

I stiffened. "He's not." I enunciated the T. "Do not tell me what I need and don't need, okay? A B12 deficiency can be from many things other than exhaustion. Look it up on the internet."

"Who gives them to you?"

I looked at him like it was obvious. "I do."

"So you've been giving yourself shots for, what, a month now," he stated in disbelief. "Because you're *tired*." Another statement, unimpressed this time.

"Ah, yes?"

"You know the reason why I worry about you," he said, lowering his voice to barely above a whisper. I looked around to see if anyone heard him. Reagan eyed us and I gave her a dirty look. I swear I couldn't escape her no matter where I went. She was always there, lurking, waiting, and watching. "But now I'm even more worried. This isn't good."

My brows wrinkled. I didn't need to explain myself to anyone, and I sure as hell didn't need to explain a goddamn vitamin the doctor prescribed me. If I could give myself a shot in the other suggested areas, I would. But I couldn't reach my arm without angling the needle, and my hip… I shuddered at the thought. It would be like going right into the bone and I couldn't handle that. The thigh was the most logical spot for me. It was the most active too.

All I could do was shake my head and walk away from this utterly ridiculous conversation. I gathered up my gear and proceeded to the next station—the balance beam—when I heard my name called.

Looking over my shoulder, my face fell. Both Hayden and Kova were stalking toward me, their faces grim and brooding. I released an aggravated sigh and forced myself not to roll my eyes. I was just plain old annoyed today and I didn't know why.

Kova's eyes immediately dropped to the center of my thigh. His nostrils flared and a tick started in his jaw.

"Why did you not tell me about these…injections?"

My eyes popped wide at the scowl in his voice, and I turned to Hayden. "What? Did you tattle on me? Are you seven?"

Real mature.

Stone-faced, he said nothing, so I turned back to Kova. "I'm not shooting myself up with heroine!" I retorted. "It's a *vitamin.*"

He blinked. I went on. "You knew I had a shot at the first meet."

"But I was not aware you were still doing them. This is news to me."

"So?"

"So?" He pulled back, his taut voice and glaring eyes only for me. "Do I need to remind you that you are under my authority? That means I need to be notified of every single change in your lifestyle, most importantly, medical changes, such as doctor visits and medication and so on? I need to be aware of *everything*, Adrianna."

I felt like my privacy, real privacy, had been invaded.

"You've been notified over everything that warrants reporting. Do you need to know that I also have my period, *Coach*? Because that's a significant change in my life I must make adjustments for every month. I took some Pamprin this morning. The cramps are crushing my soul this time around, and my boobs"—I palmed both of them—"are heavy and aching and so tender I want to cry. I can barely run they hurt so bad. Not to mention, my flow is stupid heavy this time. I have to change my tampon every two hours."

Kova didn't flinch, but Hayden blushed seven shades of red.

"Pamprin is not allowed," Kova stated blandly. "It is an anti-inflammatory."

This asshole.

I hated that he was right. I wasn't supposed to have any kind of anti-inflammatory because of my Achilles treatment; but more importantly, I hated that he knew what was in the drug at first mention, and I didn't. My face showed it and he gave me that knowing look.

Worked up and angry over something so minuscule that did not deserve this attitude or attention, I lowered my voice and stepped closer.

"I'm glad you're up to date on medications designed for menstrual cycles, I'm sure you and Hayden could exchange Cosmo magazines and experiment on homemade face masks together since you're so into girl shit, but this is ridiculous. *You both* are acting ridiculous over a fucking vitamin."

Kova's entire body tensed. He froze. A wall went up like I offended him. Hayden just stood there like he was used to the same treatment from his sister.

"There is clearly an underlying issue that you cannot see. I told you weeks ago I was worried. You should not need this many doses, Adrianna. I am extremely concerned."

"Save it."

"Adrianna," Hayden said gently. I glared at him like I wanted to strangle his neck until his head popped off. He recoiled, and both Hayden and Kova looked at each other, staring for a long moment as if they could read each other's minds. "We're just worried about you," he said.

"You two are like the husbands I never wanted—brooding and overbearing. I'm done with this conversation."

After an exhausting day at the gym, I was finally home and showered. My stomach rumbled, but I didn't feel like eating because my headache was so intense that it made me nauseous. I'd give anything to go to bed, but I had a few things I needed to do first, like catch up on school work and clean out my gym bag. Once I completed my school work, I found my duffle bag and began cleaning it out. I hadn't done this in weeks and desperately needed too since it was becoming full and difficult to find anything. Smashed protein bars I never ate, and multiple bottles of Motrin and opened coconut water that I never finished lined the bottom of my bag. I threw it all out save for the Motrin. Extra clean leos covered in chalk, and hair ties and tampons were scattered everywhere when I came across the notebook I shared with Kova buried under everything.

I'd completely forgotten it was in there.

Taking it out of my bag, I sat on my couch and stared at the front of it. Between Kova and Hayden today, my emotions were flying wild. I was already stressed about gymnastics in general. I didn't appreciate them bombarding me about my health on top of it. I was fine, just overworked. A little B12 was nothing to phone home about.

My fingers slid down the front of the hardcover. Flipping it open to the newest entry, my brows pulled together wondering when he had time to sneak this in.

Please. I am worried about you. Talk to me. You did not act like yourself today. What can I do to help?

I ground my teeth together. There was nothing to talk about except my aching boobs and heavy period. I was a little hormonal at the moment, but Christ on a stick, was I not allowed to have an off day?

I HAVE MY PERIOD. GET OVER IT. IF YOU WANT TO HELP, GO GET ME SUPER-SIZED TAMPONS AND DARK CHOCOLATE. AND NOT THE CHEAP SHIT EITHER.

I slammed the notebook shut and threw it to the side with an irritable sigh. Standing up, I marched into my bathroom and took out the B12 shot. I shoved my shorts down, took a deep breath, and jabbed the needle into my hip…and cried.

I hit my fucking hip bone.

AS LONG AND AS TIRING AS MY PRACTICE DAYS WERE, THEY FLEW BY IN A BLUR. I blinked my eyes and another competition was in sight.

Before we left, I had another round of the platelet rich plasma injected into my Achilles, though, I didn't mention it to Kova. I also gave myself an extra shot of vitamin B12 because my energy was low to the point I could hardly keep my eyes open at practice. I never thought the day would come where I would leave early, but I think Madeline saw how bad off I was. She didn't hesitate or give me a hard time when I asked to go home. She just said she'd see me tomorrow.

I crashed the moment my face hit my bed. I slept for a solid thirteen hours straight and woke up completely disoriented and in the same position I'd fallen asleep in. I did some reading online and found that my iron levels could be down, so I ran to the pharmacy and picked up a bottle of iron. I took two then, and another two later in the night. I figured it couldn't hurt.

I wondered if Kova would've let me leave early the way Madeline had. I missed half a practice plus tutoring and then another half the following day. But he wasn't there, and he wasn't going to be at the meet, so I didn't see the need to tell him. Madeline had just as much authority as Kova.

Kova hadn't been at practice all week, which I found extremely strange. Madeline was tightlipped and all she told us was that he was home and extremely ill. I didn't inquire too much because that would raise suspicion, and neither did any of my teammates, but I found it difficult to believe Kova would miss practice if he was sick.

With Kova absent from this meet, I felt naked and empty. Like my other half was missing. We'd been glued at the hip since I came to World Cup, so not having him with me was foreign.

Codependency and all that jazz was a real thing. I missed the arrogant Russian and his encouraging words of wisdom. I needed him with me.

I glanced down and my eyes caught the fading yellow circle on my leg as I slipped on my wrist guards. Injecting the B12 into my hip had been more painful than I expected, especially the following days when I worked bars and my grip slipped, causing me to slam my hips down. The pain took my breath away. The injection site on my hip was still tender, but it hid the bruising well, so I forced myself to grin and bear it.

This meet was a little bigger and on podium again. I had more competition this time around, but nothing I couldn't handle.

"Ready to roll?" Madeline asked. I nodded with a straight face and she waved me toward her. I pushed any pain my body was going through out of my mind. I relied on Madeline a lot and I think she noticed it because she kept checking on me. I stuck to her side as much as I could and absorbed every little thing she said.

I'd been to hundreds of meets since I started gymnastics over ten years ago, and every time I got butterflies in my stomach. Every time my nerves went haywire and it put me on edge. I shook it out, but the truth was I loved the adrenaline rush because I loved to perform.

"Remember, what we discussed. You've got the handspring and block down pat, just drive those heels and stay tight. Chin down and crank it hard." I nodded again and remained tight-lipped. She patted my shoulder. "Show them who owns the vault."

I smiled. Vault was my specialty, but one of my biggest fears was that I would trip while I was running.

Chalking up, I eyed the vault, visualizing my skill. When the judges gave me the okay to go, I only had a few seconds to salute them then step behind the white line. From the corner of my eye, I could see Madeline nearby, hands on hips, ready to study every detail when I took off running.

Within seconds, my feet punched the springboard and I was flying in the air, executing my skill, one that put me ahead of the other competitor's due to the difficulty of it. I stayed as tight as I could, legs together and straight, as I quickly thought about my coach's suggestions. Just like me, judges had one chance to take it all in. There were no instant replays in gymnastics like other sports. Judging is done in real time and it happens real fast.

When I landed, I *knew*. I knew I stuck my dismount. Not because I didn't move my feet, or take a step, but because my form was perfect in flight along with my dismount. I could feel it in my heart that there was no possible way it could have been any better. A stuck landing in gymnastics was monumental and always exciting because it was so challenging to achieve due to the complexity of the skill—and physics.

My teammates, my coach, the crowd, they all cheered and clapped. A massive smile shaped my face as I saluted three times before I leaped down the steps to greet Madeline.

I received high fives and smiles from all the girls.

"Gotta give it to you, Red, that was pretty incredible," Reagan said. My heart raced as I caught my breath. The amount of adrenaline pumping through my veins gave me a high like I could take on anything. I couldn't stop smiling. I felt like I was six-foot-three in a five foot, ninety pound body.

Madeline rushed me, pulling me into a hug so tight I could barely breathe. She pulled back and gripped my shoulders and shook me with excitement. "Well done! It couldn't have been any better! Girl, you keep on impressing me. What a way to start the competition. You're a true performer," she said. "How are you—" She started but my score flashed. We both glanced up at the same time and read the numbers.

My heart dropped.

Chills broke out on my arms.

Silence surrounded me.

I stared at the numbers, not believing what I saw. Madeline mumbled as we gawked side by side. She was just as stunned as I was. There was no way I had received *that* score. There was just no way. A perfect score was rare and incredibly difficult to accomplish. My score was too good to be true because that meant my vault had been nearly flawless, nearly perfect, nearly the best. I knew in my gut I had done well, I just didn't know how well.

My smile grew until my cheeks throbbed. I was only a tenth of a point from getting the perfect score. That meant I got all the points for difficulty.

Madeline glanced at me, her eyes gleaming with pride. I threw myself into her, jumping into her arms, something countless gymnasts have done when they're overcome with excitement. She squeezed me so tight and I smiled against her.

"Excellent, Adrianna. Unbelievable job and score. I knew you had it in you, but you continue to surprise me every day," she said.

Madeline released me, and I stood before her, so ecstatic I could barely see straight. That score put me in the lead on the first rotation.

"Keep that up and you'll be unstoppable."

"*We* will be unstoppable," I corrected her. She was just as much part of the team as Kova was, and I wanted to make sure she knew that.

"Get your mind focused on bars. Execute another flawless routine like you just did on vault and no one will be able to beat you today." I nodded. "I'm telling you, girly, you're one of those gymnasts who come out when they perform. I didn't expect it." Madeline turned away with a smile.

Bars was also my jam. My heart fluttered just thinking about it, anticipation flowing through me. I wasn't worried in the least when it came to bars, not anymore. I moved between the high and low bar effortlessly and smooth as silk. Vault and bars were my specialty events, the ones I did extremely well on and could perform more difficult skills the majority could not. Whereas beam was Reagan's specialty.

Once I had bars behind me, another almost perfect score, the rest of the competition flew by. I was on cloud nine and dominating the meet. My scores continued to blindside me—and my coach—and when more than one gold medal was draped around my neck, the only eyes I sought in the sea of coaches and gymnasts were a pair of bright green eyes that had made this all possible.

If only Kova was here to celebrate with me.

Later that evening, I couldn't sleep. My body was depleted of all energy, but my mind was running wild with thoughts of Kova and how I placed at the meet. I wanted to tell him how I did, but I needed privacy. I glanced around the dimly lit hotel room. Grabbing my cell phone from the night stand, I quietly got out of bed and achingly made my way into the bathroom so I wouldn't disturb the girls. The last thing I needed was Reagan to see me on my phone in the middle of the night. I decided if she or Holly woke that it wouldn't seem strange if I was soaking in the tub, so I quickly filled it and got in.

Reaching for my cell, I leaned back and texted Kova.

Hey…I just wanted to tell you that I placed first in three events today, and second in one. By far the best meet for me to date.

Much to my surprise, three little dots popped up and he responded immediately.

Coach: Madeline informed me how wellll you did. I am so proud of you. I kneew you could do it.

I had no idea she had messaged him, but I was happy she had. A small smile slid across my face and my fingers started moving.

She thinks if I keep going the way I have been that I'll be unstoppable.

Coach: I have no doubt about hat.

My smile grew bigger and I tried not to laugh at all of his typos.

I hope you're feeling better.

Coach: I fine Nnothing vodka cannot help

My brows furrowed at my phone.

Why are you drinking? I thought you were sick.

Coach: I am sorry I was there today

I giggled to myself and shook my head at his mistake.

Are you drunk right now?

Coach: Ria, I am a Russian man I do not get drunk

I laughed. Typical of Kova to get dickish with me.

You're drunk lol

Coach: I not

You are

Coach: Ria

I was full on grinning now.

Prove it

Moments later, Kova texted me a photo with the caption *You make me happy*. My heart fluttered in my chest. He was slumped against a couch looking comfortable and cozy, a slight smirk curved the corners of his lips. His eyes were heavy and glossy, almost lazy, with slightly flushed cheeks. He wasn't looking at the camera though, it was like he had stared at himself while he attempted to take a picture. He clearly had no experience doing this. I tried not to laugh. My eyes traveled down past his face. I noticed a thick roped silver necklace, and a crisp white dress shirt that was unbuttoned and hanging open to reveal his fine chest. Damn man looked sexy as hell.

I'm trying really hard not to laugh too loud right now. I didn't take you for the selfie kind of guy.

Coach: What did you take for?

A dick pic kind of guy lol

Coach: Riaa

Yeah, he was drunk. I covered my mouth to hold back the laughter. I felt like I could hear him saying my name.

You're definitely drunk and I'm being honest lol

Coach: You want a picture of my dic Ria

I chewed my lip and butterflies swirled in my stomach. I hadn't expected for the conversation to go this way, but I wasn't objecting to it either.

I mean, I wouldn't say no to a dick pic

Coach: Too bad I am not one of thoe guys

You're no fun

Just when I least expected it, Kova texted me a photo. It wasn't a real dick pic, but it was close enough. With his legs spread wide and his black dress pants unbuckled with the zipper down, his hand was deep inside, gripping himself. Kova never wore boxers so I could see the fine black hairs that led down to his thick length. A strong vein swirled around. I wished he'd move his hand. My mouth watered at the sight of how erotic it was to see a man like this.

Go lower

Surprisingly, he did, but he teased me. My brows raised at the vein I loved so much on his pelvis that swirled down his length. His penis was out of his pants, hard and erect like it was ready to explode, and his hand was fisting the head.

Thank God I'm sitting in the tub or else I'd have to change my panties. You give good dick pics
Coach: You seen a dick pic before you bette not

Lol I haven't until now, just imagined what they would look like

Another image came through and my jaw dropped. All the air left my lungs. I struggled to breathe at how incredibly hot the photo was of Kova squeezing the head of his cock as his thick and creamy cum dripped down his shaft and leaked between his fingers.

Holy. Fuck. There's so much.

It was all I could say. No way would I tell him what I was actually thinking. I couldn't even admit it out loud to myself, I was too embarrassed.

I was going to need to get a sneaky app like Kova's because this photo was one I sure as hell wasn't deleting.

I don't care what you say, I'm keeping that forever. What's the name of your app so I can hide it?

He told me, and I immediately downloaded it. Later I would save our photos and videos to it.

The water was getting cold and I was suddenly overcome with fatigue. As the water drained, I typed.

I miss you

And I did. The ache in my heart was proof. I didn't like that he wasn't at the meet with me. I felt like I was missing a part of myself.

Coach: I misse you way more. Trust me

It feels strange without you by my side. I kept looking over my shoulder thinking you were going to appear. P.S. You look wasted

Coach: I have drank myself into a stupor this week. Every time I take a sip of vodka I pretend it is your lips I am kissing. I am drunk on you

That's actually pretty sexy, I like the visual. But what if you lick the vodka off my lips instead...and off other places?

Quickly, I stepped out of the bathtub and got dressed. I found I was much more liberated when it came to texting Kova. I'd never say this in person or even suggest it. I glanced down at my phone, but he didn't respond.

Will I see you soon?

The three dots appeared, and I waited for his message before I left the bathroom to read it. I stood there waiting until my legs couldn't handle my weight any longer and my eyes were falling shut. The message never came. I left the bathroom and headed to bed, confused, wondering why he was drunk on me...all week.

chapter 49

I think I have a better chance of being struck by lightning than getting you to answer your phone.

Within seconds my phone was ringing.

"Jesus Christ, Avery."

"Hey," she said, her voice soft and barely audible.

Alarm gripped my chest at her tone and I sat up a little higher in my truck. I was on my way back to practice after a long tutoring session that involved final exams.

"What's wrong? Are you okay?"

"Yeah," she croaked. There was some shuffling in the background.

"Where are you? Are you sick?"

"I'm in bed. I just woke up."

I glanced at the clock on my dash. My brows furrowed. "Avery, it's midafternoon, and a school day. What's going on?"

"I skipped."

I frowned. It wasn't like Avery to skip school. In fact, I couldn't remember a time when she did cut class. Attendance was important to her. Being active in as many school functions was important to her. And so was getting into the college of her choice. She loved the social atmosphere, her teachers, she was class president and on track to be valedictorian.

She cleared her throat. Her voice still low and achy as she said, "I haven't been feeling well."

"But you never skip," I stated in shock. If anything, she would've gone to the doctor after class like she had in the past.

"It's just…my cramps are really bad right now and I've been nauseous." She paused. "I think I have the flu."

"You skipped over period cramps?" I asked, my voice raised in surprise.

"Not everyone can be as perfect as you, *Ria*," she bit out, insulting me at the same time. I flinched.

"I…I'm" I stammered, pulling into World Cup. I shifted into park and stared at the glass windows of the vast gym. "I'm just concerned because it's so unlike you. I'm sorry."

"It's okay. I didn't mean to snap at you, I've just been grouchy lately from lack of sleep. What's up that you had to disturb me from my beauty sleep?"

I laughed. "I wanted to tell you that I'll be there in a couple of weeks."

"Really," she squeaked. "I get to see my BFFFFFF?"

I laughed again. "Yes. My mom asked if I could be there for Easter dinner, so I'll be home for a few days."

"I can't wait! It's been *so* long!"

I smiled. As excited as I was about seeing her, I was still very worried about her behavior lately. "Really, though, are you okay? You're harder to get ahold of than the president, and now you're sick and missing school. This doesn't sound like you."

"I'm fine," she insisted. "Don't exaggerate, I just have a lot going on right now. How are you calling me in the middle of the day anyway? Shouldn't you be at practice?"

"I just pulled into the gym, actually. I have to start therapy on my Achilles today and Kova is doing it."

"Your Achilles? Kova? Please tell me you've used your brain and stayed away from that fine piece of meat. I know he's got those banging fish lips and Greek god body going on, but nothing good can come from that."

I gave Avery a rundown of all the things that had happened the past couple of months. From my injury to my meets to my parents. I had her caught up within a handful of minutes. My life was basically wash, rinse, and repeat. It didn't take long.

She ignored everything I said and focused on Kova. "Are you staying away from him?"

I sighed dramatically. "Yes. Nothing has happened. I promise I've been a good little girl."

"That's not what your broth—I mean, your mom said."

My brows furrowed, paranoia swirled in my chest. "When did you talk to my mom?"

"Ah, I mean"—she cleared her throat—"I overheard your mom talking to my mom and she made a couple of comments about how close you and Kova seemed at a competition. I thought I heard her say he put his arm around you in his jacket? I can't remember for sure."

In his jacket? I didn't understand that comment.

Nausea stirred my stomach. My first big meet in Las Vegas was the only one my parents had attended yet.

"When did they talk? What did she say?"

"It was a couple of weeks ago, I think? Shoot, I'm not sure exactly when. Things have been kind of hectic here."

"Focus, Avery. When?"

Her calmness rolled into annoyance in mere seconds. "I don't know. Two months ago?"

"You just said a couple of weeks. Now it's two months?"

"I didn't think it was that important, so I didn't log it in my diary," she snipped. Avery didn't have a diary.

"You didn't think it was important to tell me the moment you heard something about my coach being too cozy with me and my mom seeing it? That's huge," I screeched, shocked she'd not mentioned this sooner. "I can't believe this."

"I meant to text you but I forgot. I figured if it was at a meet and your parents were there that you wouldn't be that stupid to try anything."

"You forgot," I retorted in a flat tone, shaking my head. Unbelievable. "You forgot."

"What difference does it make if you're being a good little girl anyway?"

"It just does!" I yelled. "This is huge, Ave. I can't believe you *forgot!*" I was legitimately shocked to the core my best friend didn't notify me of this revelation sooner. A text would've taken ten seconds.

"Well, believe this."

Click.

I pulled my phone away and stared down at the blank screen. She hung up on me. Avery hung up.

I didn't think I was being unjust, and I also didn't think I deserved her blasé attitude either. If the roles were reversed, I would've had her back and got in touch with her as soon as I could. She let months slide by, months I could've prepared a believable lie.

Fury ignited my blood and I chucked my phone into the passenger seat. Tears burned the back of my eyes. My jaw trembled. I covered my face and threw my head back. Stars danced in front of my vision and my hands trembled from the anger bubbling inside of me. Avery should have messaged me immediately when she overheard.

I got out of my truck and marched around the front to the passenger side and opened the door. I bent down, searching for my phone, my hand skimming under the bucket seat until I found it. Sonofabitch. The screen was shattered and it wouldn't turn on. I would need to call Mom and have her order me a new one quickly.

I strode inside World Cup and went straight for the therapy rooms in the back, where I found Kova speaking to a man near one of the blue tables, both had their backs to me.

"Hey," I said softly, announcing myself. When they turned around, I stopped short.

Whoever this man was, he was drop dead gorgeous. I raked a stare down his sun kissed body. Khaki shorts and a fitted polo shirt clung to his tall frame. He had long, dirty blond hair that held a thick wave. It folded at his neck and cupped his tanned face. The lengthy stubble on his jaw was the same dirty blond shade, and he had no mustache. And his eyes, while not as spellbinding as Kova's, his blue eyes could rival the clearest ocean.

This man was a quintessential surfer. I bet he smelled like sun and salt water. I couldn't stop gawking. Have mercy on his rugged handsomeness.

Kova cleared his throat.

I shifted my wide eyes to him. His brows furrowed and he stared right at me, not fond of my blatant assessment of the man next to him.

He cleared his throat again and I stepped forward until I was in front of them. I was right…the man reminded me of the beach.

"Adrianna, this is an old friend of mine, Dr. Ethan Hart."

I held up my hand and waved. Waved, like a freaking moron. "Hi."

"Dr. Hart—"

"Kova." His voice was hoarse, like he could cut glass. "Cut the shit with the formalities. We've been friends for too long."

Kova laughed under his breath. "*Ethan* is an orthopedic surgeon. He drove up from the Keys to observe me perform the Graston Technique on you today."

That was an awful long drive for a favor. "You came all the way here for that?" I looked at Mr. Rugged Handsome.

"I wanted to make sure I was performing it correctly," Kova answered for him.

"Not confident in your capabilities?" I smirked. "Performance anxiety?"

Kova's eyes glimmered, his nostrils flared. I could tell by the twist of his lips he wanted to say something.

His friend barked out a laugh and glanced at Kova. "I don't know how you do it, man."

Kova side-eyed him, his twisted lips curving even more. "A lot of vodka, that is how."

His friend chuckled again, then looked at me. "Even though Kova is now licensed, and I have no doubt he could do whatever he puts his mind to, the first few times are nerve wracking. Having a trained professional by your side helps. I've been doing this therapy for many years and I'm constantly traveling to do this on pro athletes down in Miami. So when Kova called me, I got here as soon as I could."

My eyes shifted to Kova and I nodded. He was a perfectionist through and through. He aimed to be the best. I guess I shouldn't be surprised he called in a professional like Dr. Hart.

"Why don't you hop up on the table. Lay on your stomach and let your feet dangle off."

I climbed up and got situated, and watched as Dr. Hart rolled out a thick cloth on the table adjacent to me. It reminded me of something artists used to hold their drawing pencils and such. He began removing the tools and placing them in a uniform line, six shiny instruments with rounded edges. I frowned as apprehension surged inside me.

"How long is this going to take," I asked wearily.

He shot me a glance then went back to what he was doing. "It should take no more than ten minutes, depending on the size of the injury."

I looked back at the different instruments in worry. "All that for ten minutes, huh?"

"It's not as bad as it looks. You'll be sore the first time or two, but after that you should be good."

He looked over my head to Kova. "Ready?"

"Yes."

A minute or so later, Kova was rubbing some cream onto my calf and the back of my ankle.

"What your coach is doing is applying an emollient. He's going to rub it in from the top of your knee down to your foot. It's a lotion that will soften the skin and keep it from drying out, but more importantly, it helps with the friction."

Kova began running a dull-edged tool down the length of my calf. It was cool to the touch, but quickly warmed up after he repetitively moved in the same motion.

"Apply pressure and run the blade smoothly down her calf like you're doing now. Can you feel the sandy, gravel feel under it?"

"Yes," Kova said. "It is smooth in some areas, and others it feels like pebbles of dirt."

"Right. So, if you're feeling that grit, that's an area that's seen a lot of stress or has been injured before. Mind if I feel it?"

They switched places and the doctor ran a hand down my calf first before he started. "There's nice muscle definition here, but I can tell by touch it's tight and there are knots." He stroked the back of my leg with the tool, pressing much harder than Kova. I grunted and tensed up.

"Does that hurt, Adrianna?" he asked.

"A little bit," I grunted.

"More so than Kova?"

This time I pushed my butt in the air out of reflex. "Yes," I grunted.

"Relax." His voice was firm and demanding. I lowered my hips and he continued the raking as he spoke to Kova. "A lot of newbies are afraid to apply pressure. Don't be. You won't hurt her. The more you do this, the more you'll get a good feel for her and how much she can take."

"Hmm…" He hummed under his breath, like it was worse off than he expected. He ran the blade harder, trying to smooth out the bumps. It reminded me of when I was a kid and my mom wanted my hair in the perfect ponytail. She'd brush in the same spot over and over until it was smooth and perfectly leveled, not caring that my head was on fire from the impact of the bristles or that I had probably lost hair.

"That restriction you feel under the blade tells me this is an area that's seen a tremendous amount of stress, possibly an injury that has healed itself and has been reinjured." He applied more pressure. "There's some tissue buildup as well. Since this is the first time for both of you, I suggest gradually increasing pressure with each session." He switched spots with Kova again and turned to me. "Adrianna, you'll notice red blotches on your calf, they're nothing to be alarmed about. It's just blood flowing to the Achilles. It's great for stimulating circulation and healing."

"Okay," was all I said as I watched over my shoulder.

"How often do you suggest treatment," Kova asked. He was now working the blade midway down to my ankle, where there was more heat and an intense fiery burn but nothing I couldn't handle…yet.

"Treatments can be done regularly, or twice a week. I would suggest every other day for now, that way you give the inflammation time to heal before you start again."

Great. I'll just pencil *blading* into my schedule.

Kova hit the back of my ankle and I gasped, sucking in an audible breath as he held the back of my ankle steady. He paused, then resumed, and I gripped the blue table pad. My toes curled in response to the pain. *Fucking hell!*

"You feel more grit down by her ankle, don't you?" His friend asked and Kova nodded. "That's where you need to focus on more now."

The blade was shaped like a concaved butter knife, and he used the tip to swipe up and down around the hollows of the back of my ankle, hitting between the little grooves as he held my heel in his hand.

"If you're feeling a lot of gravel or sand, I suggest switching blades to really get in deep and fine tune that spot."

I no longer liked the handsome doctor.

He handed Kova another stainless-steel tool similar to the first one, only this one didn't have a concaved edge. It looked like a butter knife with no handle.

"She's going to feel it a little more intense now as you start up from the top and work your way down again."

For a novice, Kova's strokes felt precise and experienced. He was confident in his ability. I tried to focus on him and his assertive nature to block out the intensifying pain, but as I watched him maneuver lower to my heel, my brain went into overdrive.

"Oh my God, that hurts," I said through clenched teeth. He repeatedly scraped over the heel bone like he was spreading frozen butter on toast. It was the spot right where I'd had the most pain lately, and this pain felt like burning flesh just peeling off the bone. "It hurts," I choked out. Tears blurred my eyes and I grinded my jaw. I wanted to kick out with my other foot to get them away.

"You'll be sore tomorrow, but the following day you should see a noticeable difference, it will be well worth the pain. The first visit is always the most uncomfortable one." He turned toward Kova. "Go easy on her tomorrow."

"I make no promises," Kova said, chuckling.

"Always were a sadist," his friend joked.

"No pain, no gain. There is no satisfaction in easy."

"How do you two know each other?" I bit out, dying inside.

"College," Dr. Hart volunteered.

Kova focused on the back of my foot, scraping over where the tendon met the heel. He drew the instrument smoothly up the center of my calf, then back down and around my boney heel like he was sculpting clay and chiseling down stone. He repeated the motions, focusing at the heart of the Achilles tendon and injury. I tensed, flexing my foot, and Ethan tapped the back of my thigh.

"Loosen up. It's almost over."

"How much longer?" I was on the verge of crying. Kova didn't ease up either, he continued like I hadn't even spoke.

"Another few minutes then we should be good to go," Kova's friend answered.

"Another few minutes!" I shrieked. "I don't know if I can withstand any more of this ag-onizing pain."

I wasn't sure I'd be able to walk after this.

"Toughen up. Do not be so dramatic, Adrianna," Kova ordered.

My hands balled into little fists. I was seriously contemplating back kicking his face and walking right out. I wasn't sure if there was anything worse than this sort of pain on the planet. Not even my kidney infection was this bad.

"You see that bright red line? How it lights right up?" the wonderful doctor asked my dickhead coach. He motioned up my calf muscle. "That's the Achilles tendon. You can see she has got some issues going on there. You'll want to focus right over the line and pull in a down-ward motion toward her heel to promote healing and circulation, like you just were, and then upward and out to scan again. Make sure you score around the bone, get deep in the cavities and around the foot. Don't be afraid to hurt her."

I knew I wasn't supposed to take Motrin now, but something, any kind of pain killer, would be imperative after this.

As Kova pulled down the center of my calf with the convex side of the blade, I wanted to cry out and beg for him to stop. It felt like he was under my skin scraping the actual ten-don. I tried not to squirm on the table, but the rubbing hurt like hell and I wasn't sure I could withstand any more. It was pure agony.

"If she's having any kind of straining in her calf, then I'd suggest treatment into her foot."

"I believe she does," Kova said, up close and personal with my leg. I prayed to God they'd save that for another day.

"So let's work there as well."

Fuck. My. Life.

chapter 50

ALOUD BANGING REVERBERATED IN MY SLEEPY MIND.

Heavy eyes and immense fatigue prevented me from moving and the banging I thought I heard drifted away. I could hardly move and nestled further into my sofa.

After Kova and the evil doctor leisurely took their time working on my foot together, I was taped up and sent home to ice my leg. There was no way I could have practiced today. Dr. Hart had said the first few treatments would be the worst, and he was right.

Just as I was about to fall back into a deep slumber, the banging started up again, this time much louder. Someone was at my door.

With a groan, I sat up and leaned forward. I planted my elbows on my knees and rubbed my swollen eyes with the heel of my palms. Damn, I was exhausted.

"Coming!" I shouted and stood, and walked toward the door. I didn't bother looking through the peep hole, it could only be one of two people who ever stopped by.

Unbolting the lock, I opened the door to Hayden standing there, a concerned look crossed his face.

"Hey," I said softly. My face scrunched up. "What time is it?"

He titled his head to the side. "It's close to nine. Are you okay?"

My brows pinched together. Nine at night? Where had the time gone? I'd slept for roughly five hours but it felt more like a handful of minutes. I waved my friend inside.

"Of course I'm fine. I'm just tired. What are you doing here?"

"I wanted to see how you were doing after your first blading session, but I couldn't get ahold of you."

"I broke my phone earlier, but I should have a new one in a day or so."

"Oh." Hayden scratched the back of his head. "I was worried about you. I brought dinner," he said in a hopeful tone and lifted his other hand. I hadn't even noticed the bag in his hand.

A thankful smile formed on my face and I ushered him into the kitchen. "That was sweet of you, Hayden. What did you bring?"

He lifted the plastic containers from the brown paper bag. "I brought a few different dinners, I wasn't sure what you wanted and figured we could split it all." My stomach growled embarrassingly loud at the scents that wafted into the air. He paused and looked at me. "When was the last time you ate?"

I puckered my lips. "You know…I don't know?" I glanced up at the ceiling trying to remember what I ate today and when I had my last meal. "I think I ate lunch around noon. Then I picked up one of those cold pressed juices from that Hurricane Café before the session with Kova and Ethan, and that was it." I was suddenly ravished with hunger.

"Aid, you need to eat more." He slid a container toward me.

I lifted one shoulder and opened the lid. It wasn't a big deal to me. It wasn't the first meal I had ever skipped and it sure as hell wouldn't be the last.

"I lost track of time."

"But your body is burning way more than what you're taking in. It's probably why you're so tired and why you need those vitamin injections. You need to be fueling your body properly."

"Okay, Dad… Mom… Kova," I said sarcastically.

"I'm serious. Have you done blood work to make sure there's nothing else wrong? Maybe you're anemic."

I ignored him. I did have blood work done, but I was still waiting on the results. There was nothing wrong with me except for my drive to succeed.

Laid out before the two of us was a smorgasbord of food, quinoa, jasmine rice, fish, chicken, green veggies. So many items, enough to feed a family of six…at least.

"Jeez, Hayden. Have enough food here?" He shrugged like he had no other answer.

"So, how'd you break your phone?"

I told him about my conversation with Avery while we spooned food onto our plates. We sat on the barstools and dug in. Hayden, of course, had double the amount than me.

"I mean, I feel like I would've told you, but you did imply that nothing was going on, so I see her point too."

I grimaced. I wanted him to only see my point.

"But don't you feel that's her duty? That she still should have anyway?"

He looked at me, perplexed. "Her duty? I'm sorry, but I don't understand girl code."

"What would you have done?"

"Not thrown my phone, that's for sure."

I laughed. "I'm serious, Hayden."

He slowly chewed his food and looked straight ahead. I stared at the way his jaw shifted back and forth, contracting and loosening, as he thought about my question.

"Given the nature of the situation, I probably would have told you regardless, because even though you insist there's nothing going on, there's always something going on."

I stared at him, my jaw dropping and all.

"When it comes to Kova, I don't trust you." He angled the tip of his fork toward me as he continued to stare straight ahead. "Well, I don't trust him, really, but I don't trust you either. It's like you guys thrive on the excitement of getting caught or something, I don't know. The whole thing is just weird, but either way, I would've told you."

I threw my fork down. "Thank you!"

"Calm down," he laughed. "Yes, she should have told you, but there's also no reason to flip the way you did. Maybe you were *hangry*."

"Hangry?"

"Hungry and angry."

"I'm seeing her in two weeks."

"Who? Avery?"

"Yes. And I bet we don't speak until then. She's been so difficult to get ahold of as it is. I just hope when we do see each other that it's not awkward."

"I doubt it will be."

I nodded my head and polished off the rest of my dish over a light conversation with Hayden until he delved into the injection topic again.

"I'm trying out different injection sites. Okay?"

"What do you mean," he asked, helping me clean up. I had one plate of food. Hayden had three. Lucky bastard.

"I tried my hip, but I either did it in the wrong place or I stabbed myself too hard, because I'm fairly positive I hit my hip bone and now I have a massive bruise. I haven't done it as much because it hurts, which is why I've been so tired. My levels are low."

"So did you plan on just never taking it again because of me and Kova?"

"No. I mean, I would've eventually, but the bruise on my leg was pretty bad, so…"

"Show me."

I lifted my shirt and pushed down my shorts just enough to show Hayden the ugly bruise on my left side. The needle was small, but it left behind hideous shades of deep blues and brownish-yellows.

He bent down so he was level with my waist, his fingers gently stroked my skin. "Damn, that looks pretty painful."

"Yeah, especially when you slam your hips on bars on top of it."

He glanced up. "I imagine so." His words were full of sympathy. He continued to run his finger over the little lump that had formed under my skin. "I don't think the needle is supposed to go there…that could be the reason for the bruise. Want me to call my mom and ask her, and then I can do it for you?"

My brows furrowed. "How would she know?"

"She's a nurse, remember?" Then he held up his palms, both callused and over dry and peeling, and I noticed the rips.

My face lit up. "I totally forgot about the nipple cream!"

His face dropped, all expression voided. He tilted his head toward me and pointed his finger, his steel blue eyes narrowed. "Hey, don't knock the nipple cream. That shit is magical."

Laughing, I barely got out my next set of words. "Okay. Give your miracle worker a call and see what she has to say."

Ten minutes later, Hayden was poised with a needle and the area of injection rubbed down with alcohol.

"What are you waiting for?" I asked Hayden. When he didn't reply, I glanced over my shoulder and took in his gawking eyes. "What's wrong with you?" When he didn't reply, I said, "You've never injected anyone, have you," I stated more than asked. He shook his head.

"Of course not. When would I have? I don't want to hurt you."

"The first time I had to do it on my own, I was petrified. It took me over an hour to do it and a pep talk from my dad. Your mom's a nurse and gave you a step-by-step, something I didn't have. I have complete faith in you. I know you'll do it right and you won't hurt me." His eyes scanned the small area of skin. He aimed closer. "The first time is always the worst, so stick it in and let's go."

Hayden's flirtatious eyes snapped to mine, and I covered my mouth in realization of what I had said. I laughed behind my hand.

"I've been trying to stick it in," he retorted, grinning from ear to ear, and it only made me laugh harder. Hayden moved to stand behind me. Gripping my opposite hip, he inserted the needle with the utmost care and professionalism.

I screamed obnoxiously loud and jumped.

Hayden stepped in front of me, all worried and guilty. Needle poised in the air. "I'm so sorry!"

"I was just kidding. You didn't hurt me." I grinned.

His face dropped, unimpressed. "You know, you're a real jerk. I honestly thought I hurt you."

I couldn't help but laugh. "You didn't hurt me, I promise. I always gasp and jump because I hate needles, but you didn't hurt me."

Hayden stepped behind me and placed a Band-Aid over the injection site. I purposely wheezed in a loud breath of air.

"That wasn't so bad now, was it?" I asked.

I turned around as Hayden shook his head. He capped the needle and placed it on the countertop.

"No, it wasn't actually."

"I'm not sure what I would do without you, Hayden." I smiled at him, appreciative of his kindness and consideration. He always had my best interest in mind. "Just make sure you're free the next time I need you."

"Anytime you want me to stick something in you, I'm your guy."

chapter 51

"How do you feel?" Kova asked early the next morning as I shoved my duffle bag into my locker.

I had too much shit in there and had to squeeze it in. Maybe tomorrow I would clean it out. Probably not.

I glanced over my shoulder. Kova was leaning against the doorway, arms crossed in front of his chest, assessing me, and looking fresh as ever. Damn the man and his good looks.

Turning around, I shrugged casually, as if his presence didn't fluster me, but the truth was, it always did.

"Fine. Why?"

He tipped his chin toward my leg. Even that was sexy. Jesus Christ. I needed to get ahold of myself.

When I realized what he was referring to, my eyebrows shot up and my eyes snapped to his.

"Oh! You mean my Achilles?" I raised up on my toes and lightly bounced. I frowned. I didn't have a lick of pain. It wasn't even tender. In fact, when I woke up this morning, the injury hadn't crossed my mind like it usually did when I applied weight to my leg. I hadn't felt a thing.

"How could that have worked so quickly? I don't have any soreness. It feels…normal." And it did. I wasn't sure how that was possible, but it was, and I felt great. I hadn't not had discomfort in the past year, and right now I felt like a million bucks.

The smallest smile tipped his mouth. He was proud of himself. Cocky bastard. I shouldn't be surprised. Kova was a perfectionist and strived to be the best at everything he touched.

"Today, after practice, I will do a light massage and then tomorrow we will do another round of blading."

Great. "Will your friend be there?"

"Yes. I will have him with me for today and tomorrow to supervise. Just because you do not have any pain right now does not mean you should push hard and do more."

"I won't."

Kova hesitated, then said, "You look refreshed."

I mused over his words. "I had another dose of vitamin B12. It's been a handful of days, but Hayden helped me do it right this time. It usually kicks in pretty quick."

A muscle in his jaw twitched. His expression dulled. He didn't say anything for a long minute before he gestured behind him. "Come. Let me tape up your ankle."

I followed Kova into the gym where I sat on the floor and lifted my foot into the air.

"I take it you're feeling better?"

"Better?" he asked, his voice piqued.

"Yeah, remember when you were at home sick last week?" I tried not to blush as I thought back to the night we texted. When he continued with his blank stare, I said, "We texted after the competition…" His brows pulled together. "You had to have been deathly ill to be gone for so long. Did you eventually get on medication? What did the doctor say?"

Kova was quiet for a long moment. I studied his somber face, trying to get a beat on what he was thinking. He was void of any expression, his focus solely on the task at hand.

"Vodka cures what medication cannot," he said, avoiding eye contact. He expertly taped up my foot and calf, then helped me stand. I adjusted my leotard, pulling at the elastic edges to stretch and fit better, waiting for instructions. He looked everywhere but my face.

"Apparently so. You must've had so much vodka that you forgot about our conversation."

"Get to vault," he said stiffly. "Do not keep Madeline waiting."

I nodded. Leaning in, I said under my breath, "By the way, I still have your dick pic saved to my phone. I look at it every night." His eyes widened and I grinned, then sprinted my way toward Madeline, grateful I didn't have to do the two-mile morning run.

Thankfully the bug that had crawled up Kova's ass this morning at the mention of Hayden's name was long gone. For a man so sure of himself and his work, he couldn't seem to handle another man's name on my lips. That seemed to be a turning point for him.

After a long and demanding ten-hour practice with a small lunch break in between, I was ready for the day to be over. Covered in chalk and damp with sweat, my palms were red and tender as I picked at the dead skin while I waited on Kova and Dr. Hart in the therapy room. Luckily my rips weren't bad at all, but any time I had dried skin that had rolled up, I couldn't not pick at it. In truth, I liked picking it.

Gymnast problems.

A deep, raspy voice twisted with a heavy Russian accent echoed down the hall. My heart sped up the closer their voices grew, and moments later, both Kova and his friend strode into the room.

They were polar opposites and yet I didn't know who to look at first. Both were devastatingly handsome. Both were off limits. Both were capable of bringing me pain.

Okay. I was a little nervous and my thoughts were everywhere other than where they should be. I made no sense. I had a feeling this massage was going to hurt more than be relaxing, even though I knew the outcome would be worth it… I hoped.

"Worried?" Dr. Hart asked.

I sat up straight and looked him directly in the eye. "What would I be worried about?"

His eyes quickly drifted down to my mouth, then back up. "You're gnawing on your bottom lip."

I stopped immediately and he smirked. He was as astute as Kova.

Both guys walked over and stood in front of me and I held my breath. I was anxious for some reason.

"Even though you only have an injury on one leg, we're going to massage both today so Kova can mimic my technique. That way you can tell me who is pressing harder and so forth. Sound good?" Before I could respond, he said, "Good. Now turn over on your stomach and leave your feet to hang off."

I didn't say a word, just got on my stomach and then tugged at my leotard so my butt was covered as much as possible. I wanted this to be over as quick as possible.

"Ah excuse me." I looked over my shoulder at Kova's friend. His eyes were darting around the room and he was rubbing his hands together. "I just realized I left my bag in my truck. I'll be right back."

As soon as he left the room, Kova didn't waste a second and walked over to me, intent thick in his gait. I pushed up on my elbows and clasped my hands together.

Lowering his voice to barely above a whisper, he bent at the hips and said, "I see the way you look at him. He is married, Adrianna."

Adrianna. My first reaction was to flinch, but I held firm and remained emotionless. "And you have a longtime girlfriend but that never stops you."

He blinked.

"Who said I was going to do anything?" I never intended to, that was the last thing I needed, but I couldn't deny how attractive the man was.

"I am not kidding. Do not get any ideas."

This time I was unable to control myself and I gawked. Openly gawked at my moronic coach.

"You can't be serious."

"Deadly."

A slow, an extremely slow, smile spread across my face, like the cat that ate the canary. I lowered my eyes and tipped my head forward so I had to gaze through my long lashes. As much as Kova got under my skin for things that were so trivial it made me want to punch trees, I loved sparring with him. I loved garnering a reaction when he was fired up and couldn't do anything more.

"I'm beginning to wonder if I only have a thing for older, very attached *men*." I purposely stared at his kissable lips so he knew I was thinking about him. "Much like gymnastics, they're a challenge. And we both know how much I love a good challenge."

His eyes widened. I grinned, pleased with myself. And as if I couldn't have timed it better myself, Dr. Ruggedly Handsome strode back in with his bag in hand. I made a point to rake my eyes hungrily down his friend's body while Kova watched crouched next to me and seething in silence. I would never make a play for him, but Kova didn't need to know. That's what he got for being a jealous dickhead.

I turned back over, making sure to ignore Kova as I did, and dropped my head in my arms. Dr. Hart instructed Kova and guided him, then both of their hands were on my legs, starting near the back of my ankle and pushing up toward my knee to warm me up. My eyes rolled shut as their hands moved in circular motions. It felt so good.

"Do you ever get deep tissue massages, Adrianna?" the doctor asked.

"No. Never." Something told me deep tissue massages were in a cozy, relaxing room with lavender scented tea lights and rainforest music playing in the background. Not so clinical like this.

"You should. They're quite important for you considering what you're training for. The toxins need to break down, and muscles need to align with the connective tissue. It helps tremendously with faster recovery."

"She is already dealing with enough, and her schedule could hardly fit in an hour massage."

"Kova." His friend drew out his name as if he was scolding him. Then he asked me, "Do you have any issues with flexibility or mobility?"

I popped my head up and looked at the wall so my voice didn't sound muffled. "I had issues with my hip flexors, but Kova helped me with that. I'm in much better shape than when I first arrived."

"The massage could have helped speed up that process too."

That was when I decided to glare at Kova over my shoulder. I kicked my leg to get his attention and his head popped up.

"You know, I could've slept an hour less if I needed to. I'm sure we could've fitted it in somewhere."

He paused his movements, as his friend continued his. "Are you seriously going to question me? After everything?"

"Yes, I am. I would've managed if I had to. You know I would have."

"No"—he shook his head—"there was no way. You run on fumes as it is, Adrianna."

His friend chuckled. "You two spar like an old married couple. It's getting late. Not sure what you both have planned after practice, but we could do one after we work your Achilles."

"Yes," I said automatically. Anything would help. Kova didn't reply. He just stared at me like he wanted to strangle me to death.

"You'll be sore," Dr. Hart warned.

"Story of my damn life."

He laughed again. "Kova? What say you, man?"

Only someone intimate with Kova would recognize the glint in his eyes or the slight twist of his lips. It was a dirty and devious look that spoke of debauchery.

His hands commenced and this time they pushed into the muscles harder. My stomach clenched, and I tried not to react to the pain. Both men applied the same pressure. Their thumbs worked together, kneading the muscle and tendon.

"I need to call my love and see if Kat planned anything for us tonight."

My eyes dropped to a blaring glare.

That. Fucker. He would go there.

"Ah, the stunning Katja. When the hell are you going to marry her already?"

My heart stopped. I held my breath as Kova watched me with a look of indecision. He didn't know what to do, at least that's how I wanted to read him. But marry Katja? After everything? He'd never. Not after he'd cheated on her so badly with me. No way.

Right? How could he?

"You are going to marry her, aren't you?" he stirred. "I mean, you've been with her since you were kids. What are you waiting for?"

I watched his Adam's apple bob stupidly slow. With my eyes fastened on his mouth, I thought I misheard his answer despite reading his lips.

"Eventually, yes."

My lips parted, surprised, and I was struck with fear that he was telling the truth. Everything around me faded to black. I couldn't hear. I couldn't see. I couldn't do anything. There was no way to hide the hurt that spread throughout my entire being like a wildfire. My chest burned, and my face fell when I caught the fleeting look of remorse in Kova's eyes. He regretted it, but the damage was already done. Again. I wasn't sure if he truly meant what he said or not, but the truth was, I didn't want to know. He said the words he knew would devastate me the most and that's what mattered.

"Jesus. Your Achilles is brutally tight," Dr. Hart said, taking me away from my sorrowing thoughts. I never wanted to imagine Kova marrying Katja. The thought made my stomach churn. I was queasy. Maybe he'd marry someone else after he and I were one hundred and eighty-seven percent finished, and it was due to both of us agreeing it would never work.

But not Katja, because after all we shared between us, that meant I had never been enough for him from the start, that I was just a doll for him to play with, and she wasn't.

I glanced at the doctor, repeating his words in my head. I was too astounded to communicate.

"It blows my mind you haven't ruptured it completely," he said.

Dazed, I turned back over and dropped my face into my crossed arms, not caring if my voice was muffled now. "Yeah… I'm pretty conscious of it and try to be careful on that side."

I wasn't sure I made sense, but I didn't care.

An hour later, Dr. Handsome was gone and I was bent over in pain from the deep tissue massage, afraid to stand. I did and carefully hobbled across the hall to the lockers. I would be exceptionally sore tomorrow, but the doctor had insisted I'd feel like a new person with more bounce in my step come this weekend for the last meet before I went home.

I should've said no to the massage. I should've asked them to stop and feigned sickness or something. But I didn't. Instead, I took the sweet pain and considered it my consequence for provoking Kova earlier. I didn't utter a word, I didn't gasp or hold my breath, or shed a tear or ask for them to go lighter. I laid stone-still, facedown and dying inside from their crafted hands that knew how to manipulate and ease my muscles, and relinquish toxins and Kova's words.

If only I could relinquish Kova from me.

Karma. That's what I got for playing with the big boys.

Pulling out my duffle bag, I considered cleaning out my locker when Kova strode in. I looked over my shoulder, but I didn't say a word.

He leaned his side against the locker and stared at me.

"What is it?"

"Adrianna, if this is about Kat—"

"I really don't want to talk about it, Kova." I sighed, unable to hide the hurt I was feeling. "Maybe I needed to hear it to get out of this fantasyland I've been living in about us, I don't know." I swallowed back the tears and stared at the contents in my locker. I couldn't look at him just yet. My voice cracked with emotion. "I guess I didn't expect you to actually marry her after everything. Like how could you live with yourself after so much lying and cheating? I can't believe I'm going to say this, but it's not fair to Katja. Even though we're not in an actual labeled relationship, you can't be completely oblivious to the fact that there's more here between us. Am I saying let's explore that right now? God, no." I paused for a moment. "I don't know what I'm saying, maybe it's just one-sided, maybe I'm too optimistic and hopeful. Either way, it was something I needed to hear. It put things into perspective, that's for sure. I can always leave it to you to really cut me deep."

He wasn't angry when he responded. Instead, he was gentle. "There is a lot that you do not know."

"Because you don't tell me."

"Adrianna—"

"I'm just stupid and naive, I guess. I don't want to talk about it anymore," I said, softly shutting my locker. I finally looked at him and let him see the tears that threatened to fall from my eyes. "I have to go."

Much to my surprise, I'd never seen him look so upset and so guilty and full of shame all at once. His eyes scanned my face, my mouth, my eyes, they were everywhere.

Shaking my head, I stepped around him and walked toward the door. Right before I stepped out of the room, Kova's broken whispers in Russian caught my ears. I glanced over my shoulder and watched as his fist flew into a locker, twice. I quickly stepped out but peaked through the small doorjamb opening and watched.

Kova turned around and leaned against the lockers. His head fell back and he stared at the ceiling. His face was rigid, his jaw grated together. A sharp pain shot through my chest. I felt everything he exposed when he thought no one was watching. Everything. It took strength not to walk back in there and talk to him.

I shot a quick glance at his reddened knuckles. The skin had broken and blood dripped onto the floor as he clenched his fist.

I could be a lot of things when I needed to, but I refused to console him about his impending marriage.

I HADN'T SLEPT MORE THAN TEN HOURS ALL WEEKEND DUE TO THE HECTIC SCHEDULE of the competition and flying back and forth.

In truth, I couldn't afford to rest. Or to think about what Kova had said to Ethan, and how I'd left him in the locker room. I hadn't let myself. I had a one-track mind all weekend and it stayed that way. Even driving back to Palm Bay, I refused to let myself think about it. It hurt too much.

The clock was ticking. Each meet that I placed in the top three brought me one step closer to the Olympics. First place was always the goal. Despite second place being the first-place loser, I was still happy with it. Silver still put me on the grid. I was competing against gymnasts with no injuries, and much younger. The odds were unquestionably against me, but my drive and determination exceeded theirs and it showed in my performance.

This past meet, the Secret U.S. Classic, I had placed first in vault and bars, and second in floor. I had walked away with two gold medals and one silver. It was a tight squeeze for beam and I was close to getting bronze, but I didn't. Still, I was golden and feeling confident.

Monday came fast and hard. Crawling out of bed these mornings had been a task in itself. Even now I was dead tired and it was midafternoon. Three days of straight practice, two blading sessions—one late Sunday night when we got home, one before I left—and then I was free for an entire week. That had been my goal and focus and what helped me stay motivated.

The blading... Man. What a difference it'd made. Even more, the deep tissue massage. I couldn't believe it, but Dr. Hart had been right. I felt like a new person with a little pep in my step and when competition time came, I had a whole new body. It was remarkable to be pain free while defying gravity. I insisted Kova fit them in my schedule. I told him if *my coach* couldn't help me and make it work, I'd go to a physical therapist.

He gave me that infamous glare upon my demand.

I got what I wanted.

I couldn't help but wonder how I would've fared if I'd had them sooner.

"*Bez truda, ne vitashish i rubku iz pruda.*" Kova had said to me in Russian at the meet. "No pain, no gain."

I hated that saying, and when I had told him so, as well as reminded him I was not in pain, he had just shrugged his shoulders, indifferent. "Not physically, but your pride is," he had replied.

I hated that he was right. He'd asked me how I was doing, and I gave him a generic answer. It was how we maintained our relationship the entire weekend—a question with a basic response. Though, when I stuck a landing or received the most points allowed in my routine, we both grinned from ear to ear and threw around hugs like they were free.

But nothing was free. Everything came with a price.

Over two hours of driving, I pulled into my family's estate, ready to spend the Easter holiday with them. We may reside on a swanky island, but our opulent home was a secret oasis of peace and quiet, and my body was craving that. I needed the rest badly, especially since this month would be extremely chaotic with upcoming championships. And championships were very important. If I didn't place then, I was basically screwed.

My stomach churned, and a sense of dread clouded me as I passed through the iron gates. Without the B12 injections and sheer force of willpower to keep going, I could collapse any minute, but there was an unsettling feeling in my gut and it kept me alert as I parked my truck.

Glancing around the lush, tropical paradise my parents built before I was born, nothing seemed out of place. I disengaged the keys and sat back in the silence of my tinted car and stared. Maybe I'd worked myself up for nothing. I did have a lot on my mind as it was. But the driveway was empty, void of both my parents' cars.

It wasn't long until I was in my childhood home and unpacked and back downstairs looking for my mom and dad. I sent Avery a quick text to let her know I was here and to stop by, but she didn't respond. I sent texts to both my parents, and they didn't respond either. With nothing to do but wait, I decided to lay down and rest my eyes.

"My, my, my, don't you look incredible." Mom's honeyed voice rang from behind me. I turned around and my eyes met her proud ones that gleamed in delight. It left me a little sickened. I'd always been thin, and right now I knew I was extremely skinny. Waiflike. She was too happy over my appearance, and it made me question how she had felt about me a year or so ago when I was only twelve pounds heavier. I almost wondered if she wanted me to look, or be, anorexic.

Brushing it off, I gave her a hug. "Hi, Mom."

"I'm so glad you could come home for a little while. Easter wouldn't be the same without you."

"Glad to be home."

Mom hugged me a little tighter before letting go. She glanced down and frowned. "You look a little tired."

"I just woke from a nap."

"Ah, okay. Just be sure you're using under eye cream. It's never too early to start. A little concealer for the dark circles too. Yes?"

I nodded, a faint smile on my lips. "Of course."

She patted my shoulder, pleased with my response. Like I was going to worry about under eye cream at my age. I had enough things to carry on my shoulders as it was.

"Your father and I have something we'd like to speak to you about. Do you have a minute?"

I nodded and followed behind. Stepping into my dad's office, I was met with the most gorgeous sunset that bloomed through the large window that overlooked the rich, green lawn. Warm rays of blood orange and rosy hues filled the room. I inhaled as if I could breathe in the colors. I wished I was outside. I missed the beach. It smelled like old leather and comfort in here, just as I remembered. As a kid, I used to just sit on the floor and play with my Barbies for hours while he worked. Mom used to try and shoo me out. Even though I never uttered a word and didn't dare bother him, she'd said I was a hassle and that he needed silence to concentrate, but he'd always told her to leave me be. One day when I walked in, I found my Barbie dollhouse in his office. Dad had moved it in there along with a trunk of dolls and their dress up clothes. That was the last time she tried to pry me away.

Dad glanced up and a huge smile spread across his face the moment he spotted me. I ran and gave him a hug.

"Dad!"

"My little princess," he said, pulling back. "I'm so happy to see your beautiful face!"

I'd been a daddy's girl from the moment I was born. And he loved it.

Before I could speak a word, Mom cut in. "Frank, do you have a moment to go over what we spoke about?"

Dad glanced back at me, this time gravity weighed on his features. He nodded and gestured toward his cherry colored leather chairs. I took a seat and Mom took one next to me. She was poised with a Stepford Wife face that could cut glass. A nagging, worrying feeling settled in my belly. Silence cloaked us. I shot a look at Dad, who had reached into his desk drawer and pulled out a folded newspaper. He opened it, gave it a firm shake so it would flatten, then stood tall. His face contorted, and my stomach sank.

Lowering the newspaper, he flattened his lips and glanced away, sliding the paper toward me with a heavy exhale to follow.

Before I peered down at the paper, I glanced at my mom, thinking it might have been for her, but it wasn't. She gestured elegantly with her hand out and palm up for me to take it. Hesitantly, I reached forward and viewed what had made my parents' tune change so quickly.

I paled. My jaw dropped. My eyes widened. My stomach, and heart, plummeted to the floor. I blinked long. And I blinked long again, not believing the words written in bold black, purposely printed to catch everyone's attention. A deafening sound filled the room as I sat stone-still in my dad's office rereading the front page over and over, a newspaper strictly printed for the residents of Amelia Island.

'POSH PALM BAY PRINCESS GETTING AWFULLY COZY WITH HER COACH.'

Beneath the headline in italics, it read…

'Caught in the act; teen socialite Adrianna Rossi seduces renowned gymnastics coach.'

Next to the headline were pictures of me at my meets. Me hugging Kova with his back to the camera. Another photo zoomed in on my face as I gave Kova a megawatt smile, again his back was to the camera. The next showed him squatted in front of me, his hands on my hips and fingertips pressed to my butt over my leotard. His ball cap was pulled low over his face, only the stubble on his chin was visible.

None of them were offensive or distasteful in my eyes. All gymnasts and coaches were close and very hands on. It came with the sport. But the one photo that held my attention the most, the one that took up the most space and center stage, was the one taken somewhere outside of my complex.

Someone had hidden in the bushes.

Kova had me cradled to his chest, my face buried in his neck with one arm draped over his shoulder, as he entered my building.

Now this looked like the definition of intimate. The sun had set, and I wore very little, next to nothing clothing. *My* duffle bag was on *his* shoulder and it looked like I had fallen asleep. The angle of the photo hid his face and made it seem like Kova was pressing a kiss to my cheek.

Fuck. I swallowed hard, trying to figure out how the hell I would get out of this. Kova hadn't kissed me outside, we'd always been careful in public. I knew at once I had to play it off as nothing unusual, when in truth, this particular photo wasn't good. It looked bad, really bad, especially next to the others where I basically had throbbing hearts in my eyes while I gazed upon him like a lovesick teenager.

The other photos from the meets were common but completely taken out of context, and that's what I was going to go with. If this paparazzi had done their homework, then they would've seen that it was nothing out of the ordinary. But of course, why do that when they can spin it to make money. Especially when the family was well-known and lived on the prestigious Amelia Island. Fame. Money. Privilege.

I sighed inwardly and schooled my features. Placing the newspaper down, I looked up at Dad, then to Mom.

I feigned confusion, my voice piqued. "What? What's wrong?"

"What's wrong?" Mom retorted, her voice much higher than mine. She leaned forward and grabbed the paper and held it up for me to see again. She shook it, the sound of the papers thrashed together. "You don't see what the issue is?"

Straight-faced, I shot another quick look at the newspaper and then back to her. Of course I did, but I had to play dumb.

I shrugged blandly and thought she was going to pop a blood vessel in her eye. "They're pictures of me and my coach. What's the big deal? You can find the same kind of photos of any other coach and gymnast on the internet."

"So you're telling me every coach carries his gymnast to her home and kisses her cheek? You seriously don't see the issue?"

"He didn't kiss me." I glanced at Dad. He tilted his head to the side. I felt like he could see right through me.

Definitely not the welcome home I was expecting.

An exasperated, yet ladylike huff expelled from Mom. "Is this not exactly what I suspected when we were at the competition, Frank? That I said they looked a little too friendly at the meet, and then in our hotel room?"

He dipped his chin. I looked into my dad's optimistic eyes; I knew he was trying to figure out what was real and what wasn't.

"See?" She threw the paper dramatically onto the desk and sat back. "Even your father saw it."

He held up a finger. "Joy."

She stopped immediately.

"I *did not* think they were too friendly," he scoffed as if the thought disgusted him. "You're the one who assumed there was more. But this article…" He paused and looked at me. "You see how bad this looks, don't you, Ana? Especially on you."

I glanced down at the photos, then looked back up. I chewed my bottom lip to be a little extra. "I guess I do?" My voice was soft and quiet, and I pointed to the meet photos. "I mean, that's all normal. You guys were there. You saw the other girls, they were the same way with him, and other gymnasts and their coaches did the exact same thing. This isn't unusual."

Mom chimed in. "Those may not be unusual, but it draws unwanted attention to us. It makes it look like you…you…like you're mooning over your coach."

Dad ignored her. "And what about this one?"

I swallowed and stayed neutral. "I had a really rough practice that day. It was bad. I hadn't eaten, I could barely walk, my ankle was throbbing. I'd worked too hard and had exhausted all my energy. So I asked him to drive me home, and he did. That's my bag he's carrying." A partial lie. Kova insisted he take me home.

"They took the photos out of context and ran with it, Dad. You know they did."

Dad sat down and leaned back in his chair. We stared at each other, but not in a glaring, menacing way. He looked at me like he was trying to read me, to see the truth and hoped that it could never be like what Mom insinuated. His eyes flickered. I hated to lie to my dad about anything, but this wasn't anything, and I couldn't let them think more. I needed to put on my best social event face.

"You made this family look like trash. I don't believe a word you say, not one word. Something isn't right, and I know it. This little fantasy of yours ends now. You need to pack your belongings and come home."

"What!" I screamed, jumping from my chair. I saw red, my heart was racing. "Dad! Tell Mom that cannot happen! That it won't happen!"

"Joy."

"If anything, I help our image." I turned back to my mom. "You have a daughter who's an elite gymnast with the possibility of going to the Olympics. I've placed in the top three at every meet so far. Very few make it to this level. Do you have any idea what that means?"

She rolled her eyes. My mother rolled her eyes, and out of everything she could've done or said, that was the least of what I'd expected. Her blatant disrespect for me chiseled away something inside and dropped like boulders into my stomach. It hurt terribly, and if I wasn't already angry over her suggestion to leave my dream behind me, I would've felt my heart crack down the center.

My mother truly didn't give a shit.

"You're lucky I'm not one of those socialites getting drunk in clubs and photographed with my underwear showing. I have a brain and talent and I'm using it, unlike those losers."

"Adrianna."

No one listened to Dad.

"I'd rather that than you caught in a man's arms wearing what looks like a crop top and underwear. A man of good standing, no less, a friend of the family, and, not to mention, ten plus years your senior. *You're an embarrassment*. It makes us all look bad. At least getting drunk is expected of this lifestyle and could be written off. This is going to follow us. How are we going to cover it up?"

I stood there, slack-jawed, aghast. I wasn't sure how I'd been cut from her cloth. We couldn't be more different if we tried.

"Do you hear yourself?" I asked barely above a whisper. I was shocked beyond words. "You *want* a drunk teenager?"

She lifted an elegant shoulder and crossed her legs. "It's easier to deal with. At least you won't look like a slut."

"*Joy!*" Dad bellowed.

I reeled in my astonishment and stood taller, straightening my back. A wall came down over me as we stared at each other. She was despicable. The malice in her eyes shifted into resentment. I wasn't going to win this conversation. I'd never win with her. Not when she looked at me like this.

"There's nothing to deal with. I'm not coming home. I train in Cape Coral and that's where I'm staying. Dad, tell her I'm staying there."

I held my breath, praying to God he'd agree.

"Adrianna will stay in Cape Coral."

Mom's nostrils flared. I'd never seen her so enraged. She jumped up in her signature Louboutins without so much as a wobble and glared down at me.

"You will not run to your father for everything. I am your mother and you are going to do as *I* say! You're going to stop with this little hobby of yours and come home immediately."

My hands balled into fists, nails digging into my palms creating half-moons. I thought my heart was going to pop out of my chest. Through gritted teeth, I said, "I will do no such thing. No. Such. Thing. I'm not your puppet."

I wouldn't back down. She needed to see that.

I blinked, and Mom had her hand at the back of my head, her fingers clenched my long hair. A chair scraped across the floor and Dad was up, but he wasn't fast enough. Mom pulled back her other hand and landed a shocking blow. A faint gasp escaped me as my head whipped to the side in a sharp arc of my neck.

The sound of the smack echoed across the room.

"Let go of me!"

I tried to push her away, but she wound her wrist around my hair to get a good grip, and yanked painfully hard. I yelped and stumbled into my dad's desk. I wanted to pull back, but I knew if I did she'd pull my hair even harder. She tugged again so tight, tears brimmed my eyes and I lost my footing.

"Stop!" I begged. My scalp screamed in pain. She had to have ripped out my hair.

My vision blurred. Everything in me turned cold and quiet and I surrendered. Before she let go, she gripped my hair one last time, getting in one good pull.

With my eyes squeezed shut, I held my breath and covered my face as Dad whisked her away, throwing her out of his office.

I didn't scream.

I didn't yell.

I didn't fight back.

Ever still, I stood in disbelief at the red-hot pain that laced my face from my mom's opened palm. My heart was empty. I was hollow inside. Mom had struck me. And she hadn't stopped with her abusive words either. Hot tears began pouring from my eyes, my chest heaved up and down, and my hair covered my face. The sound of her voice was right in my ear, even though my dad had all but dragged her from his office.

I needed to get away.

"Adrianna."

Spinning on my toes, my throat was tight as I dashed from my dad's office. I held my chest as I sprinted in the opposite direction. My knees wobbled and all the muscle in my thighs turned to mush. It was all too much to withstand on top of everything else. I needed to escape, but I could barely hold myself up.

I ran through the foyer, through the formal living room and toward the formal dining area, when I trampled over my feet and caught myself on the arm of a couch, and crumbled to the floor.

"Why do you insist on torturing me?"

A small, depressed voice caught my attention. I stood up and rounded the corner and stood stock-still at the entrance to the dining room. The lights were turned down low, blinds drawn closed in a room we never used, but even through my tears I could make out the outline of their bodies at the opposite end.

"Why not?" His hand cupped her jaw. "I like to get a rise out of you. You're so fucking adorable when you're mad," Xavier joked.

I covered my mouth with my hand and blinked rapidly. My lips still burned from the slap.

No… This wasn't what I thought it is. My best friend and my brother would never go behind my back.

His hands slowly roamed down the sides of her body. I was so lightheaded I thought I was going to faint. I squinted, trying to see if my eyes were fooling me.

Dad's worried footsteps drew closer, my heart ached in tune with my head, trying to put it all together. Avery wouldn't do this to me. She was the only real person I had left in my life. She'd never go behind my back like this.

Her forehead dropped to Xavier's chest and I stared in shock, not really processing it. She wrapped her arms around his back. "You make my blood boil," she said softly. "I want to junk punch you."

"And you make mine burn for you; even after everything you did, I still ache for you." He dropped a kiss to the top of her head.

I blinked long and quietly stepped away. It was too much to fathom and I really couldn't even process the scene in front of me. My mind was playing a cruel joke on me. This was a bombshell of a secret that couldn't be true. It just couldn't be...

"Adrianna," Dad said tenderly as he came up behind me. I turned around. Something inside me broke at the sound of his voice. He opened his arms to me, his eyes softened with sympathy, guilt written all over his face that it physically hurt me to look at him like this. I'd never been hit in my life, and it shocked me down to the marrow in my bones.

"Don't worry, you're not going anywhere. I promise."

I fell into his arms and cried until I couldn't open my eyes or think any longer, blocking out everything that had happened and praying it was all a terrible dream.

chapter 53

I STEERED CLEAR OF MY MOM, AND EVERYONE, FOR THE NEXT FEW DAYS.

She hadn't made an effort to apologize, and neither had I.

And I wouldn't. I refused. Not after she had hit me and left me with a swollen, fat lip not even the best concealer in the world could hide. Even with all that my brother has done to shed a negative light on this family, not once did she ever put her hands on him. Yet, for the first time in my life I stood my ground, and her world went up in flames. It made no sense.

And she wondered why I loved gymnastics so much. With gymnastics, I could be who I wanted to be, not what she wanted me to be.

The tension between my parents since that awful day had been tangible. I wasn't stupid. I knew it was because of me. At night when I couldn't sleep, I could hear them arguing downstairs. Doors slammed, curse words were thrown around, and I could hear the crystal of Dad's decanter opening and closing. Mom wanted me punished, but my dad objected, saying they'd never disciplined Xavier for the far worse offenses he'd committed. Like when he was part of the lawsuit filed against his fraternity that took the life of a student. A deadly hazing that he'd been part of yet miraculously got out of.

In public, they put on a good show, but the skeletons in their personal closets were mounting.

But today, I wouldn't be able to avoid her. Today was Easter Sunday, and we always had a very intimate, very extravagant family dinner for the four of us in a dining room that typically collected dust three hundred and sixty-four days out of the year. The same dining room where I discovered my brother's and my best friend's little secret.

My stomach was in knots, and the thought of being forced to sit across from the same woman who scrutinized everything I put on my plate and into my mouth made me nauseous. I was stressing out big time having to be in the same room with her. Especially since I knew she was still reeling with resentment.

As much as I was originally excited to be home, now I couldn't wait to go back to Cape Coral.

Since my parents hired help to handle the prep work and serve the food, I wasn't needed until right before. Thankfully.

Even though I knew she was keeping things from me, I decided to spend my free hours with Avery, who'd only gotten out of school yesterday for the holiday break. We hadn't spoke about the day she hung up on me or why she'd had such an attitude. I let it go because I missed her and wanted to spend as much time as I could with her before I had to leave.

We were in her massive walk-in closet, where she was trying on different outfits as I sat on her custom floral love seat. Rows and rows of clothes, drawers filled with accessories and fine jewelry, purses and designer shoes, all perfectly placed with a dramatic chandelier in the center.

"Ria," she said in a horribly fake Russian accent, distracting me from my thoughts. Every so often she used Kova's nickname for me to get my attention. I laughed. "I have a rash on the back of my head. It is really bad and I do not know what to do about it."

My brows pinched together as I studied her, trying not to laugh at her terrible imitation and lack of contractions.

"Is this you being serious? Or are you being an asshole?"

Avery was staring at herself in the mirror, head slanted while she debated if she liked the tenth outfit she'd tried on. "I am being serious."

"Okay…so go to the doctor."

She turned around and walked toward me. Before I knew it, she was sitting next to me with her bleach blonde hair held up and a view of the back of her head just centimeters from my face. I pulled back.

"Will you look at it for me?" She leaned into me, and I put a hand on her back to stop her.

"Do I have a choice?"

"No."

We both laughed.

"First of all, you need to dye your roots. They're almost black and resemble the color of shit."

She groaned like she was tired of my existence. "Just shut the fuck up and focus on the issue at hand—my bumps, please."

"Only because you said please," I countered and leaned closer to get a better look. There was a trail of pale bumps with a rosy undertone that formed around her ear and down the back of her neck. "It's not bad, just a light allergic reaction if anything. Maybe some prickly heat?"

She whined her complaint. "It itches and won't go away! I've had it for weeks now. How's someone ever going to want to have sex with me again with this?"

"Right…because when you have sex he stares at the back of your ear. Is this a secret spot where you like to be licked or something? If so, then I could see the issue."

Avery started laughing and turned around to face me. "No, but it's on my neck and everything."

"I can't believe you even have sex considering what a Jesus freak you are."

Avery came from an extremely religious family. They attended mass every Wednesday and Sunday and all the holidays, whereas my family never did. We didn't even attend the important ones.

She laughed again. "Of course I have sex. Although, if the next guy I meet is a strong Christian and wants to wait until marriage, I would do that."

"But if he finds out you're not a virgin, are you going to lie and insist that you are? Because lying is a sin, and you've already sinned in the Lord's eyes by fornicating before marriage. A double sin. And if he's a strong Christian and wants to wait to have sex, chances are he's a virgin. But I guess if you lied about your virginity, he would never know, because I'm sure he wouldn't know what a broken hymen feels like." I paused, then said, "Basically, you're doomed either way."

Avery was silent as she mused over my words. Her crystal blue eyes twinkled. A slight smirk tipped her lips, and then a full-blown smile followed.

"Oh my God. You're so right! And with all my issues, I'm sure I'd bleed in the middle of it anyway!"

I busted out laughing. "With your luck, that would happen, but that's also what I call winning. The virgin husband would never know and probably think he got lucky with a wife who knows how to have sex the first time."

Avery's head rolled back onto the cushion. She clutched her chest. "Ugh. My life is a mess."

"I think you're overstressed about the possible STD you have spreading on your neck." Avery punched my arm. "Ow! I'm just kidding. Maybe you need to read a book to decompress. And turn up the air at night so you don't sweat. I honestly just think that's prickly heat."

Avery rambled on about books she didn't like and the ones she loved. She was impossible to please, and commented negatively on everything, so I never suggested books to her anymore.

"Hell no," I said when she suggested I read a book she loved. "You have the worst taste in books. Cheesy, clichéd lines that are embarrassing to read. It amazes me you've had a secret boyfriend for so long considering how picky you are. I'm surprised you haven't found something so trivial to pick at to break it off with him." Avery gave me a droll stare. "What? You know I'm right."

"Read one of my books, and I'll read one of yours at the same time."

"I don't even have time to breathe right now, and you want me to read one of your books?" I laughed sarcastically.

"Just give it a try! At least read the sample. I know you'll love it. You just can't give me the satisfaction."

I chuckled. "No, thanks."

"But I always read what you want!"

I gasped jokingly. "No, you don't. You read three pages and tell me you can't read my book because you don't like the hero's name."

"Well, if his name is Garth, I'm not reading it. There is nothing sexy about a Garth, Adrianna! Nothing. And I know you agree with me."

I started laughing uncontrollably at her tone and reasoning. She had a point, but I also never read about a Garth before.

"If his hair is red, that's a deal breaker for you," I added. "If he's a doctor, a lawyer, a firefighter, hell, if he's the fucking CEO of a billion-dollar company, you would tell me no."

"Excuse me for knowing what I like. A fiery, flaming bright orange head of hair and eyebrows is not hot to me. His pube hairs will be the same color, and I cannot deal with that. Just fucking stop right now, bestie."

A loud laugh burst from my throat as tears blurred my eyes from laughing. Avery joined in, chuckling over her own comments like she usually did. I missed my friend so much and wished in moments like this that we lived closer together again. Between her wicked sense of humor and array of timbre in her voice, this was more than what any book could give me.

"You'd rather read about smelly hobos. I bet that's what you love."

She nodded, agreeing with me.

"I knew it."

"You're missing out. My book is forbiddenish."

I gave thought to it for a moment. That piqued my interest, but I knew her better.

"*Ish*. You lie. That probably means a boss can't date his employee. Lame. And, Ave, have you forgotten I'm living the forbidden life? The book can't possibly be better than real life."

"Have you spoken to Konstantin since coming home," Mom inquired after her third glass of vodka. She was putting them back faster than Dad.

This was the first thing she'd said to me in days and it left me momentarily speechless. A feeling of doom settled on me the moment I walked into the dining room. It was the same feeling that struck me when I pulled through the iron gates only a handful of days ago. I stared into my mom's eyes trying to muster an answer. She was goading me.

The two of us were seated at the grand table, across from each other, little appetizers placed sporadically around us. Dad and Xavier were in the other room refilling their glasses. I hadn't touched one morsel of food. I was too on edge.

Steadying my heartbeat so the lie would sound authentic, I said, "No, I haven't."

It wasn't entirely a lie. I had tried to contact him after my mother ambushed me with the newspaper article. He wouldn't return my texts or phone calls. But there was no way she could've known that.

"No?" she repeated, soft and patronizing. Delicately, she twirled the glass on the table, staring me down with nothing but animosity for reasons I could never fathom. "No," she said again, so regal. "I know you're lying."

I ground my teeth and looked her straight in the eye. "I'm not."

"I should be proud with how well you've managed to live a lie. It sure isn't for the faint of heart."

It was so easy for Mom to get under my skin with her refined manners and the confident yet clipped tone she loved to use. My stomach churned viciously. I didn't like the way this conversation was going.

I subtly shook my head. "My life isn't a lie. I don't know what you're talking about."

"Want to try that again?" she asked. Her eyes were too knowing, and it made me queasy. There was no way she could've known I tried to contact Kova.

"I don't know what this is about, but I haven't spoken to him, Mom," I said confidently.

She took a long sip from her crystal tumbler and licked her lips. "You can't fool me... I know you're fucking your gymnastics coach."

I inhaled with an audible gasp, my heart nearly stopping. She said it so soft, in such a gentle tone it terrified me. Pure evil. My world tilted, my face fell. I was starting to feel light-headed. The room was at a standstill. Our eyes bounced back and forth, she was spewing fire in my direction.

"That's not true," rolled off my breath, but no one heard me. I shook my head, I could hardly breathe. "It's not true." My heart was racing so fast and hard it hurt. I clutched my chest, trying to ease the pain. The walls started to close in, everything was shifting.

This was it. She knew.

I shook my head vehemently. "No," I whispered.

A glimmer of malevolence sparkled in her eyes, one that scared me. One I'd never seen before.

"You're a little whore."

"No, I'm not," I gritted out. I'd never been called such a vile word in my life, and it didn't take long to realize it hurt being called that when I was anything but.

I thought back to my time here so far. The times I'd left my phone unattended. I didn't think I had to worry when I was home. But I always made sure to lock it before I put it down. And my phone had a passcode on it.

My forehead creased together, my mind running a mile a minute.

The beating of my heart was so loud I could hear it in my ears, pounding away louder than a marching band as my mom's eyes blazed with fire.

She took a sip from her glass and watched me as I hopelessly tried putting two and two together. The air in the room dropped and I grew cold. My stomach rolled with anxiety and I actually thought I might get sick all over the table.

"I found your phone late the other night, you were in the shower and it was sitting on your bed. I felt bad for what I had said…that is, until I read the text messages." An evil smirk slid across her face. "Tsk, tsk, Adrianna. Going after an older man like that. Who knew you had such a promiscuous, trashy way about you. The photos were one thing, but the video? That was icing on the cake." She sipped her vodka. "I planned to apologize, you know." Her eyes hardened. "But I don't apologize to whores."

Planned to apologize.

My lips parted and I fought to keep my face neutral. I swallowed a knot the size of a golf ball and wanted to choke. The back of my neck prickled with heat, and it was in that moment I understood why I had that gut feeling of dread when I arrived home, like it was some sort of intuition this visit would end badly.

"Always were a daddy's girl," Mom said with a slight curve of her lips. She lifted her crystal tumbler near her head. The whites of her eyes were glossy. "I guessed it on the first try."

My face fell. Dread consumed me.

My passcode was my dad's birthday.

The pulse in my neck thumped rapidly. I began to sweat. I took low and controlled breaths like I would if I was doing my floor routine. This was bad. This was very bad.

"Imagine your dad finds out? What do you think he'd do? To you? To his dear old friend?" She pouted and lowered her voice. "He'd take a baseball bat to his face, that's what he'd do."

My lungs constricted. I could hardly breathe. A sinister chuckle rolled off her lips as she finally looked me straight in the eye. She was a polished woman with a heart full of hate.

"He'd probably pull you from your precious gymnastics and send you to an all-girl finishing school." She tapped her chin and looked up at the ceiling. "You know, that doesn't sound like a bad idea, now that I think about it. I could have you out of my hair for good."

I couldn't do anything but sit there and stare. I was up against a woman with a vendetta larger than life and no way to fight it. There was no way I could talk myself out of this, not with the evidence she had.

"What? Cat got your tongue? Don't have anything to say now, *Ria?*"

"Mom." Holy shit she knew his nickname for me. "Please…"

"I think your dad needs another look at the photos from the newspaper again, sweetheart," she said, the endearment meant to mock me. "The way he holds you, how you look at him… It's as clear as day now. I'm sure I could request a transcript of your cell phone records for your dad as well." She paused, then said, "I was right to use the word slut the other day."

"Why… Why are you doing this?" I asked.

She ignored me.

"Why haven't you asked me for Hayden's sports coat?"

"What?" I asked, confused.

"The jacket Hayden left on your balcony. You said he was looking for it, so why haven't you asked me for it so you could bring it to him?"

My body was cold to the bone, yet my cheeks felt flushed. I chewed my lip for a split second. "Oh, I forgot all about that." It was the best I could come up with but something flashed in her eyes.

"Don't worry, I shipped it to Katja. You know, his fiancée."

My lips parted and blood drained from my face. Katja wasn't Kova's fiancée. There was no way he had proposed to her. He would've told me first. I know he would have. Mom was just saying that to get a rise out of me, but thankfully I played it well.

"She was so thankful to have it back since it was a gift from Russia she had custom tailored for him."

The room was thick with a mixture of hostility and bewilderment. The silence was deafening. I didn't know how to respond to the chilling tone she used. I didn't know how to do anything but sit there. All I could do was stare at the woman who birthed me and question why she hated me so much.

"What did you ship to Katja," Dad asked curiously as he waltzed into the room with Xavier. The kitchen doors flew open behind them and servers came out carrying the first entrée. Everyone stayed silent as trays of food were removed and new ones were placed down. The food looked divine, but there was no way I could eat even a crumb with the way my nerves were on edge.

Mom looked me dead in the eye. "Just Konstantin's coat he left behind at our New Year's Eve party."

Please, God. I will do anything if you could stop her right now. Anything at all.

"That was nice of you," Dad responded, sitting down.

"Your precious daughter is turning out to be just like you, Frank." Her eyes glistened with devious intentions that had my pulse sky rocketing.

Dad took a long pull of his amber liquid before he responded. He smiled at me and winked. "I would say that's a good thing.

"Or maybe she takes after her mother."

Her mother? Goose bumps trailed down my arms. Mom was so inebriated she was speaking in third person and not making sense.

Dad's silverware crashed to the plate. I flinched. He used the corner of his cloth napkin to wipe his mouth, then tossed it onto his plate with disgust. His chair slid back and an aura of anger surrounded him. I sat watching in shock.

"This is not the time or the place." He leveled his gaze on her and his look shook me to the core. Dad was done playing whatever game Mom had in mind. And quite frankly, I was too. "The issue you have with me has nothing to do with her. Leave Adrianna out of it."

But she wasn't looking at Dad. She was glaring at me.

chapter 54

Mom's hard eyes were fixated on me as she took another long sip of vodka.

I don't think she heard one word Dad said.

"Put the glass down, Joy. I think you've had enough for one day." Dad sneered. He was still on his first tumbler of whiskey and much more coherent than her. "We talked about this."

Xavier was in his own world, texting feverishly on his cell.

"Actually, she's identical to her slutty mother."

"That's enough," Dad hissed. He was livid and had his eyes exclusively on Mom. "Joy, you are going to regret this if you don't stop right now. This is your last chance." He pounded his fist onto the table. The plates, glasses, and silverware all wobbled from the sheer force of his hand.

He didn't faze her. She gave him a scathing glare that would make anyone tremble in fear. "I think it's time we put the truth on the table. Wouldn't you agree, Frank?" she said his name like it was coated in venom.

Xavier finally looked up. One of his eyes was swollen, but not discolored or bruised. He placed his phone face down on the table as his brown eyes jumped back and forth between me and Mom. "What's going on?" he asked.

"If she's such an adult like you claim your princess is," Mom said, looking at Dad from the other side of the table, "I think it's time she knows the truth."

"What truth?" Xavier asked. He sounded just like Dad. "What are you talking about?"

"Nothing that concerns you, son. You have enough going on as it is, what with that little predicament you were in a few weeks ago," she said.

"Mom," Xavier growled in a warning tone. "Stop."

"Joy," Dad spoke at the same time as Xavier.

"What?" Mom said as if it wasn't a big deal.

Dad was up and out of his chair in seconds, hands balled into fists as he marched toward her. She was up and walking away from him, surprisingly fast for someone who was sloshed.

"Can someone please tell me what the fuck is going on," Xavier exclaimed. His eyes were so wide all I could see were his pupils. I was just in the dark as he was.

Mom continued. "It doesn't take a rocket scientist to figure it out."

Dad's eyes narrowed to dark little slits. "Joy," he warned. "That is enough!"

"Did it ever occur to you where your red hair and freckles come from?" she asked me, ignoring my dad. She took a long pull of her clear liquid.

"What?" I said, my voice shaky. "What does that have to do with anything?"

Dad shoved one of the heavy dinner table chairs to the side. It fell hard with a clank. "Stop it, right now!" He glanced at Xavier and said, "Grab your mother." The table was so long that he couldn't catch her. He'd take one step, and she'd take one in the other direction.

"Where, Adrianna!" Mom yelled.

I started to shake and a crease formed between my eyes. I had wondered where it came from, but figured it came from another family member. It happened all the time.

"I assumed it came from Dad's side of the family, just like Xavier's hair and eyes came from yours."

She snickered. "Your father is a womanizing whore, just like your mother was. A slut. Just. Like. You."

Chills zipped down my spine.

I was frozen to the core.

My jaw bobbed up and down. I tried to say ten different sentences at once but all I could muster was huge eyes and a tied tongue.

"My...my mother? But..." I stammered, my head was spinning, and I reached behind me to grab the arm of the chair and sat down. Bile rose in my throat. I looked to my dad, begging for help, then back at my mom as her words echoed in my head in that sickening, slimy tone she used. I searched her eyes for the truth.

Xavier's eyes hardened, and they scared me more than Dad's. "Did you just call my sister a slut?" he asked, leaning forward with his head tilted to the side, demanding to know if he'd heard right.

"You will not speak of my daughter in that manner!" Dad's boisterous voice boomed across the room. His white-knuckled fist slammed onto the table.

Mom snickered again and took a long sip, swallowing half the contents in one gulp, then held the glass near her face. She traced her bottom lip with the pad of her ring finger, her eyes trained solely on me.

"I know you're not talking about Adrianna like that," Xavier said.

"I'm warning you, Joy, do not do this because you're angry with me. Go take a nap or something."

Xavier grabbed Mom's boney upper arms. She tried to yank herself away, but her vodka went flying and splashed onto the floor.

"Mom, you're drunk. Just stop," my brother pleaded as Dad reached them. Mom wasn't going anywhere. A scuffle started between the three. Words were thrown around and it was a clear effort to reel her in and stop her before it was too late.

I dazed off and stared at the marble floor. A slide show of moments flashed through my head, all scenes of my life when I questioned her actions, her comments, her coldness toward me. How I was nothing like her, how I could never be what she wanted, no matter how much I tried. I never did right. I was never enough. How my dad always had my back, how he gave me whatever I wanted and often disagreed with her.

I was beginning to pant at the realization. I couldn't breathe.

No...it couldn't be true.

She didn't mean it. She was just upset.

I looked up and scanned her bleach blonde hair. She had naturally dark roots, so I never questioned the hair, or the color of her eyes, or how our opinions were never on the same page. I never thought to. Many families were like mine with visible differences. Many mothers and daughters didn't get along.

"I'm done trying to keep this family together," she spat at Dad. "Done trying to make us look good when all you want is to ruin this name! I'm done covering up your lies and years of infidelity and making me out to be a fool. *It's over! Over!* The truth is coming out. You're nothing but a fake bastard!" she screamed like a woman scorned. Never in my life had I seen her behave like this before. But the more I heard Dad yell, and the more I heard my brother beg her to stop, the more it became painfully real. Through blurry eyes, I watched them struggle.

"Ah, I see you put two and two together." She looked directly at me. "You're a little whore, just like your real mother was, trying to seduce men who aren't yours, take what's not yours. It's bad enough this family is a lie, a mockery, but I refuse to be shamed and disgraced in front of the world any longer. I went to the ends of the earth to cover up your father's accident seventeen years ago because I loved him, but I refuse to do it for you."

His accident...meaning me. My accident...meaning my affair with my coach.

She did it because she loved him, but she wouldn't lie any longer.

She wouldn't go to ends of the earth for me because she didn't love me.

She had never loved me.

And the worst part of all, after all these years, deep down I had never felt like I had a mother's love either.

"Mom…" Xavier said softly, heartbroken. He let go of her arms and stood as shocked as I was.

My heart dropped into my gut. Air seized my lungs. I wasn't sure how much more I could handle. Her cruelness knew no bounds. The woman I knew only as my mother was a monster clothed in Chanel and draped in diamonds.

I was going to be sick. I gripped the arm of the chair and held my stomach with my other hand. Nausea spun like a tornado through me, the vomit climbing up my throat. Any second I was going to lose it.

"How dare you hurt her like that," Dad said, danger coating his every word. "She's our daughter."

"She's not my daughter and she never will be. I never wanted her. *I can't stand her!* She was your assistant's daughter! Your assistant who was a fucking loser, worthless, and no good. All she had to do was spread her little virgin legs and you went running." She sneered and continued. "A loser who you paid off to keep her mouth shut and disappear. But I'm the loser, too, because you paid me to play house and pretend that Adrianna was mine, didn't you?"

I couldn't take anymore, I needed to get away.

"Mom…" Xavier's voice cracked, but his eyes were a fury of rage. My gaze dropped to his hands. They were balled into fists, the whites of his cracked knuckles showing. "This isn't Adrianna's fault. Why are you doing this to her?"

"Adrianna," she chewed out, disgust laced in the four syllables of my name. "Adrianna is a prostitute's name. I wanted to change it, but your dear old father wouldn't let me change his precious daughter's name. His whore of an assistant picked it out. That southern country bumpkin teenage trash that she was and her bible thumping parents."

It happened so fast. I didn't see it, but I heard it. The loud, cracking sound that couldn't be mistaken for anything other than a backhanded blow. There was not one ounce of guilt or remorse that came with it.

I wasn't sure what stunned me more—Dad hitting mom right across the face, or when Xavier grabbed him by the collar of his Robert Cavalli shirt and shoved him hard and fast up against the wall.

"Dad," Xavier said low and quiet. Anger poured off him in waves. "You should *never* hit a woman. Ever." I shot a glance at Mom. She cupped her cheek, her jaw aghast, tears floating in her eyes. "You taught me from a young age to always protect my sister," he said. My heart soared for my brother. I was thankful I had him in my corner. "I don't give a shit if what Mom claims is true. Adrianna is my sister, and she always will be my sister. She's good and doesn't deserve to be called vile names and attacked, but hitting Mom because of that? What does that make you? I will not stand to see a woman hit, especially my mother."

Dad's eyes narrowed at my brother. "Xavier, stay out of it," he ordered, grabbing my brother's wrists. "You don't know the half of it." Xavier pulled Dad and shoved him against the wall again. The fury radiating off him scared me. He could unravel at any given moment and I didn't have the power in me to stop either of them.

"Mom, you knew Adrianna would never fight back and disrespect you, that's not who she is, and you know that. You went for her jugular knowing she had no defense," Xavier gritted out.

"You want to talk about respect?" Mom said hoarsely. Standing tall, she dropped her hand. A lick of fire still blazed in her eyes, and a deep red mark marred her cheek.

She fixed her stare on Xavier.

"You want to talk about respect," Mom said again, her brows raised high. She pulled her shoulders back. She wasn't finished with us.

"Why don't you tell your *sister*," she spat, "how you respected her friend so much that you got her pregnant. Why don't you tell *Adrianna* about you and Avery? About how I had to cover up your mess for this family and the Herons." She sneered, shaking her head. She pointed to her chest, sloppily stabbing herself with her index finger. "About the abortion I paid for?" she spat with a bite. She still had fight in her. "And you want to talk about respect?" Mom scoffed. "What a joke." She pointed at all of us. "You all are a joke with not an ounce of respect in any of you. You should be bowing down and kissing the ground I walk on for all I've done for you."

She strode from the formal dining room without so much as a falter in her step, leaving us all speechless.

C HILLS TRICKLED DOWN MY ARMS.
         I was stone cold and in shock.
         "Is it true?" I asked, not recognizing my voice.
   Both my dad and brother looked at each other, their eyes shifted back and forth at one
another, searching for an answer. They looked confused as to who I was talking to, and truth
be told, I wasn't sure which one of them I questioned. I just knew I needed answers. They both
had lied to me so bad that I didn't know where to begin.
   I stood and took a few steps until we were all standing face-to-face. My stomach was
heavy and twisting with cramps, like my intestines were wrapped around stones with gritty
edges. I pressed a hand to my belly. God, I felt so small staring up at them, wishing on a prayer
it wasn't true. Hoping that what Mom said was all a drunk lie to hurt me because of something
Dad did to her, or Xavier getting on her bad side.
   But deep down, I knew the answer. I wasn't a fool.
   "It's true, isn't it?" I asked again, looking my father in the eye. I started with him. I'd never
seen him so torn with guilt. He'd always been so strong and sure of everything. Now he looked
shattered, too devastated to speak. Not the father I knew. He couldn't give me the satisfaction
of an answer either, even if it was a bittersweet one.
   I turned toward Xavier. "Did you know?"
   He shook his head frantically, innocent in the shocking reveal. "No. I had no idea until
just now."
   "He didn't know. No one knew except for me and your mother."
   "But she's not my mom."
   His eyes hardened. "She *is* your mother."
   "Were you ever planning on telling me?"
   "No."
   My mouth parted, a faint gasp rolled off my lips. My heart began to speed up at the
thought of being lied to my entire life by the one person who I thought I could trust and
would support me.
   "Why? Why wouldn't you tell me."
   "To protect you," he stated like it was obvious.
   I tilted my head to the side. "Protect me from what exactly?"
   "To protect you from the backlash you would receive. You must understand something,
Rossi Enterprises was on the rise at the time; our name was everywhere. Investors were com-
ing out of the woods. Everyone wanted a piece of what I was building because anything I
touched turned to gold. I'm a phenomenal businessman, but one slip up, one mistake that shed

a negative light on our family, and we could've lost it all. It was a different time. What happened in the dark never saw the light. It was a game of politics and it had to be played a certain way."

"So you did it for yourself, not me."

"I did it for us."

"No." I shook my head. "You did it because you love power, but you love money more. If your *slip up*"—I almost choked saying the word—"got out, you'd lose everything. I was a risk you couldn't chance. You needed the picture-perfect family to keep everything intact, and Mom was willing to give it to you."

Something dawned on me and my chest hollowed out.

"Even though she hated me for what you did, she covered up your mistakes because she loved you and believed in you. But what did you do this time that she refuses to play along? Why is she taking her resentment out on me?"

Dad's mouth pulled down. "I tried, Adrianna. I really did. I tried to make up for it by giving you everything you ever asked for."

"You wanted to buy me."

"No, it isn't like that."

"Then what's it like!" I yelled. "Everything I've known is a lie. I deserve to know the damn truth. If anything, it would've all made sense had I known."

My blood was boiling faster than it ever had. My fingers tingled, and my heart was about to beat through my ribs. I was a fusion of hurt and rage, fire and ice.

"Mom's hatred toward me. The way she's never supported me or my dreams. How she would incessantly nag me over my weight. I was never good enough, and the worst part of all, you watched it happen. You knew the reasoning behind her behavior and never did anything to stop it."

I stepped back and turned in a circle, giving them my back, thinking about all the ways she'd treated me over the years. Tears burned the back of my eyes and I didn't want them to see that. I tipped my head up to stare at the ceiling, I refused to let them fall.

"She's hated me since the day I was born…and you know she has, and yet you never did anything to protect me from her wrath."

I wasn't sure how much more I could take before I broke. I was supposed to remain a lie until I died, and long after. I tried to speak again but the knot in my throat prevented me. I placed my hand on my hips and bit the inside of my lip to fight the emotions clawing inside me, begging to spill out.

I was strong, but this…this was a sucker punch that nearly knocked me out.

"Aid," Xavier said gently. "Dad loves you more than anything in the world. He'd never purposely hurt you. You know that."

I put my arm up and gave him the back of my hand. "I have *nothing* to say to you," I spat. "Of all people, you just had to have my best friend too." God, I was sick to my stomach. I couldn't handle that confession too or else I'd surely break.

By some miracle compelling me, I strode from the dining room, found my car keys, and left.

It took less than a handful of minutes before I was sitting on the ivory sand, staring at the roaring teal waves and white caps crashing on the shore.

The beach was my savior, my serenity. The smell of sand and salt was my tonic. It was the one and only place I felt could remedy anything I was going through.

Salt water cures everything were words I lived by. Anytime I was dealing with something—grave or minor—I found myself sitting at the beach and staring at the rippling ocean. Every burden, every grain of anxiety washed away with each kiss and retreat from the waves on the powdery shoreline. The sand over my toes and the wind in my hair revitalized me. It was a place where I could find myself when I felt like I was at a fork in the road, a place that would help guide the way at the sound of crashing waves.

I sat with my elbows perched on my pulled-up knees, gazing at the beauty of the sea, trying to process what just happened. Goose bumps covered my arms. The wind was chilly today, but I didn't feel it. I was too numb, overwhelmed with thoughts and emotions to handle them.

My mom wasn't my real mom, and Avery and Xavier were together. So together they made a baby…then aborted it.

I was embarrassed to admit that I didn't know which one hurt more.

Joy not being my real mother should cause more of an impact than Avery lying to me, but it didn't. And what kind of person did that make me? I loved my mom, but I was never close with her. I had never confided in her. She was never the first person I ran to with a dilemma or looked to for advice. There was always some sort of disconnection between us despite being related. I'd made the effort for years, but we never had that mother-daughter bond. I always figured I was too much of a daddy's girl for anything else, but after today…

And I was oddly okay with that, which made me feel even more like shit. It should affect me, yet it didn't.

Or maybe I was blocking it out.

What she had said to me, the harsh way she delivered it, I'd never forget it. She was deliberately cruel. Revenge was a piping hot, bitter coffee served in a foam cup, and that's what she had planned for me. She wanted to burn me and watch me dissolve through a flimsy barrier.

But Avery was a different story altogether. Her lies and deceit hurt more than anything.

A gust of wind blew past me and I inhaled the salt air deep into my lungs. I would rebuild myself from here. It was just going to take a minute or two.

As much as I wanted to talk to Avery, I needed to speak with Kova first. What happened between my best friend and my brother wouldn't bear an impact on my life the way the secret of Kova and me would.

Exhaling a heavy breath, I picked up my cell phone and dusted off the tiny grains of sand. I was about to delete the text messages but decided against it. I needed to reread them to see what she saw through her eyes.

I also needed to change my passcode.

I dialed Kova's number and pressed the phone to my ear. After two rings, it went straight to voice mail.

I sulked. Maybe his phone had died, or the call didn't go through, or the signal was lost. I dialed again, this time it rang three times before being abruptly cut off. I tried once more and got one ring.

Pulling the phone away, I glanced down at the blank screen…

Kova had hit the fuck you button on me.

A somberness settled quietly over me. Tears prickled my eyes. The feeling of being unwanted and alone struck me and I retreated a little bit, nestling myself further into the sand, into myself. My emotions climbed as fast as my rising chest, further and further until tears blurred my vision and the waves rolled into a mirage before me.

I didn't know what to do. I was breaking inside, the pain in my chest squeezing until I could barely breathe.

I tried Kova one last time.

And once again, he rejected the call, which both puzzled me and angered me all the same. If he saw me calling more than once, and repeatedly like I was, then he had to know there was a serious matter at hand, right?

I pulled the phone away and swallowed back my tears. I would not cry. Against my better judgment, I sent him a three-worded text that would sure catch his attention this time.

My mom knows.

He called immediately. And immediately, I hit the fuck you button.

I smiled to myself and wiped away the lone tear that fell. It felt good to reject him. He called a few more times and each time I shut him down. I bet he was regretting his actions now.

You get what you give. Asshole.

As I sat staring at the ocean clearing my thoughts and seeking guidance, I didn't turn around when I felt the presence of someone behind me. There were only a handful of people who knew about this spot on the beach that I liked to visit. I figured it was my brother...

But it was Avery.

I pulled my knees tighter to my chest, my mouth a firm, thin line. She didn't sit down, and I didn't look up. Her milky legs were in my view, visibly shaking and unusually skinny.

"Adrianna," she said, her voice sounded cracked and so brokenhearted that I almost caved. She was my best friend after all. But I didn't concede. It was the biggest struggle of my life not to turn to her. I just swallowed and continued to stare straight ahead.

"Please, Adrianna, let me explain." When I didn't acknowledge her, she said, "I'm so sorry."

She purposely left me in the dark when I'd entrusted my secrets to her, ones so grave they could send people to jail and ruin lives. Avery didn't return the same courtesy, and that's what hurt so profoundly that I wasn't sure how to talk to her without lashing out first. She had to assume I'd object to the relationship to never come to me. She was right. I would have. Even still, she should've come to me. I shouldn't have had to find out through my drunk mother. She didn't deserve the pain I knew full well Xavier probably dished out to her. I would have done everything in my power to keep her from experiencing it. We were closer than that and I wanted to shield her from his playboy ways. I loved her.

"Please..." she said, shaking as she crossed her legs and sat down to face me. I had to wonder if she still would've gone through with the relationship knowing I'd be against it. My gut said yes.

I sighed inwardly and glanced around. On top of everything, she'd had an abortion, and it made me wonder if Joy had wanted my real mom to abort me too. I shook my head in disbelief. She probably did given how much animosity she's had toward me since day one.

The knot in my throat grew and became painfully hard to swallow when Avery's cold hand rested on my forearm. Her fingers looked small and dainty. A sharp pain shot through my chest. With the amount of times my heart rate picked up in the past few months, I was going to need to see a cardiologist soon. I felt bad for Avery, but I was so hurt and angry that I didn't know how to open up and let her in.

"I can explain everything if you just give me the chance."

God. I wanted to give her the chance, but I couldn't see past the pain. Not even when she scooted forward and wrapped her boney arms around my shoulders, and dropped her head onto my arms and cried. Her knees were smooshed alongside mine and her entire body trembled with each intake of air she took.

She didn't say anything. She just cried silently. Her soft little whimpers severed something inside me, and before I could stop myself, the tears came pouring out.

Avery cried harder at the sound of my despair. We fell into each other and let out our own heartbreak together, both of us going through traumatic events and desperately needing one another.

But I couldn't do it. I couldn't give her what she needed and be there for her. I felt so broken, damaged, both for myself and for my best friend.

"I'm so sorry," she said. "I never meant to hurt you, or lie to you… I didn't expect for any of this to happen," she sobbed. "But I had no choice. I did what I had to do because of your brother and what he did… If you'd let me explain everything, I know you'd understand."

I cleared my throat and shrugged her hold off me. With a haste, I stood and wiped the sand off my butt and the tears from my eyes.

Looking down, I said, "We always have a choice, Avery. After everything we've been through together, the things I've told you…you purposely left me in the dark." I shook my head. "You know what, I have to go."

Between the news about my fake mom and lying best friend, I decided in that moment I was returning to World Cup early. Bad news traveled in threes and there was no way I'd be able to withstand another blow. My world had crumbled in a matter of minutes and I needed to be alone and escape it all.

"Wait," she yelled, reaching for me with massive worry in her eyes. Avery stood. She looked so frail that it concerned me. It was on the tip of my tongue to ask but then something dawned on me.

"Did Xavier tell you what I found out about my mom?" She tilted her head to the side. Her eyes crinkled, and the center of her brows creased. He hadn't told her. "I didn't think so."

"What happened with your mom?"

I looked at the ground and stepped away. "Nothing."

"Aid, tell me, please."

Tell me. An ironic chuckle escaped me. She flinched.

"Bye, Avery."

"Wait. Does…are you ever going to talk to me about this?"

"I don't know."

She paused, her eyes searched the sand as she stammered over her next set of words. "Does…does this mean we're not friends anymore?" Her chest rose and fell so quickly I knew she was on the brink of hysteria and yet I couldn't find it in me to be gentle with her. I just couldn't.

"We'll always have our friendship, but I don't know if we'll ever be friends again."

She hiccupped and her face fell. "You can't mean that."

I rolled my lip between my teeth and bit down to stop myself from saying something I'd only regret.

"I'll talk to you later, Avery."

chapter 56

"**I** THINK YOU SHOULD TALK TO HER, XAVIER. SHE LOOKS REALLY BAD," I said stiffly, stuffing my clothes into my bag.

Thankfully I hadn't brought too many things home. I wanted to leave as fast as possible.

When he was silent for too long, I looked up and our eyes locked. I let him see the full fury of hurt I felt from the knife they stabbed into my back. He shook his head, the hard stare in his eyes said he was standing his ground. "No. She did it to herself. She brought this upon us."

I scoffed in disbelief. I could hardly look at him, I wasn't sure I even wanted to talk to him.

"Us... I can't believe you two. Honestly, Xavier, I have nothing to say to you right now, that's how angry I am."

"And yet you are because I'm your brother."

Brother. I turned away. The word blurred my vision and my jaw trembled. I inhaled and swallowed back my stupid emotions. "And Avery is like my sister. What's your point?" I hastily grabbed a shirt and slammed it into my bag. "All the lies. So many lies. I'm so sick of being lied to."

"Aid," Xavier said gently as he walked over to me. He placed his hand on my forearm and I quickly yanked it back. We stood next to each other in silence for a long moment. I could tell he was waiting for me to look at him before he spoke, but I didn't. I was so furious with him, I was worried I'd say something I would later regret.

Angling his head down near mine, he asked, "If you're so concerned about her, you talk to her."

I squeezed my eyes shut and tried to block out the image of how I left her. So broken and distraught. I should have spoken to her, and for a second, I wished I had, but I just couldn't. My heart hurt because of that.

I shook my head. "I can't. You don't understand. There are things you don't know between me and Ave. I confided in her. She should've done the same with me. Especially since it was you." I paused and clenched my teeth, then said, "God, Xavier. Why did you have to go after her? Of all girls, you pick my *best friend?*" My emotions were climbing again and this time my sadness swirled into a simmering rage.

Xavier stepped back until he was leaning against my dresser. "Did she tell you what happened?"

"No," I said softly as I stared at my rumpled clothes. I was trying to calm myself down and not lash out, but the weight of their deceitful lies was getting to me. "She tried to, but I wouldn't let her. I'm too hurt over everything to talk to her, because no matter what she says, it wouldn't make a difference right now. Same goes for you."

"I understand. You did get blasted with a bunch of dirty secrets. It's a lot to take in."

"You could say that again."

"Let me ask you something."

I growled under my breath. "I really wish you would just leave me alone. In case you didn't notice, I'm as mad at you as I am Avery."

Naturally, Xavier ignored my plea. "If Avery had told you, had the courage to say that she was in a relationship with your brother, what would you have said?" His voice turned hard, almost defensive. "Would you have been okay with it? Truly be okay?"

I stared at my scattered belongings I had thrown across my bed in my haste to leave, and contemplated his question. "Honesty, Aid," he pushed, his voice deepening with anger. "Look at me and tell me that you'd be straight with me banging your best friend." The hairs on my arms stood up. My fingers tightened around the shorts I had clutched in my hand until my knuckles turned white. His words got under my skin and were meant to provoke me, but I forced myself to stay silent. "That's what I thought."

I swallowed and finished up packing.

"For what it's worth, I really did love her."

Love! My head finally snapped toward him. "Love who?"

Xavier gave me a lopsided grin. "Avery. I cared about her a lot, way more than I ever thought I would, but after what happened"—he dropped his sad gaze to the floor and shook his head—"there's no going back. She completely dissolved anything we had. She ruined it."

"Funny. She said it was your fault."

"It kills me to say this, but I can barely look at her without wanting to strangle her fucking neck and kiss her face." Xavier's voice cracked, and I almost felt bad for him and whatever happened with Avery.

"So you're not going to talk to her?" I asked against my better judgment.

"No, quite the opposite. I'm going to get as far away as possible from her."

My shoulders sagged. Our families would forever be joined. Xavier couldn't ignore Avery for the rest of his life. That would be impossible.

"We've known Avery long enough to know she's a blunt bitch with a big heart. I'm sure she didn't mean whatever she said." His face softened, and I paused, swallowing back the dejection that settled over me thinking about what else had been revealed today. "Did you really not know? About Mom not being my mom?"

His eyes widened with innocence. I didn't need to hear his answer to know it. "No, I had no idea, Aid. None at all. I swear it."

All I could do was shake my head again. My life was a mess, and everyone was a liar. The one thing I had in my life I could count on to bring me happiness and stability was gymnastics, and that's what I needed to be doing.

Gymnastics had always been my outlet.

I zipped up my bag, ready to hit the road, when my cell phone started ringing. I glanced over my shoulder. My phone was on the dresser Xavier was leaning against. He followed my gaze and picked it up. Lowering his brows, he stared at the screen before glancing up at me with inquisitive eyes.

"Coach?" he asked, snooping. "Is that Konstantin calling you?"

My heart dropped.

His eyes hardened. "Why is he calling you?"

My jaw bobbed up and down. I tried to find the right words to say without appearing guilty. I reached for the phone the same time it stopped ringing. Xavier placed it in my hand and I released a breath, staring at the device like it was layered with poison. Thank goodness he didn't answer it.

"Yeah," was all I could muster, avoiding eye contact. *Smooth, Adrianna. Real smooth.*

"Why is he calling you, Adrianna?" His tone went from tender and understanding to brisk and demanding.

"Probably to make sure I'm keeping up with my cardio. Yesterday Madeline called to make sure I'm seeing my physical therapist. They're always on me for something, especially since it's meet season."

I didn't do cardio. I didn't do therapy. Not while I was home, anyway.

"You're lying."

"I'm not."

His head angled toward me but I refused to make eye contact. "Yes, you are. I can see it in your face."

"Drop it, Xavier."

"If I find out he put more than a friendly coach whatever-the-fuck you want to call it hand on you, he won't live to see the next day. I'm not kidding, Adrianna. I will fucking kill him."

I was a liar just like them. Possibly the dirtiest with the most shameful secrets. The sight of Xavier's balled-up fists and strained forearms spoke louder than his labored breathing. His appearance had changed drastically in the course of a year. He shifted from healthy and charismatic to lean but gaunt. His eyes were sunken in, bruises—both new and old—peppered his body, and there were often scabbed up cuts on his lip. His attitude was dismal at times. And while I hadn't been around him much aside from holidays, my brother was obsessed with social media. He uploaded and posted about every waking minute of his life for the world to see. Tracking his change had been too easy. I didn't know what caused it, and I never inquired. Not while I was presently swimming in a black sea of depravity with something that could taint the family. That would be a dead giveaway. Playing naive was a better alternative.

With my eyes still cast on the floor, I walked back over to my bed and slung my duffle bag over my shoulder.

"So, you're leaving early," Xavier stated, breaking the silence.

I nodded, then turned around. The truth in our eyes collided in a flash—we both knew there was more going on behind the scenes than either of us were willing to let on.

"I need to be back at World Cup…it's my home now. I need to center my focus again."

He bobbed his head and rolled his lips between his teeth, unsatisfied with my response.

"I'm always here if you need me, *sis*," he said as I stepped past him.

Sis.

The word lodged in my throat and I had to squeeze my eyes shut to stop the tears from climbing. I wanted to shout at him he wasn't really my brother, that he was actually my half-brother. But I didn't. There was too much confusion and chaos in my life now to react unjust toward someone who truly didn't deserve it. Not after he put his emotions and feelings into the one word that held so much weight for me about how he truly felt.

chapter 57

I DIDN'T BOTHER SAYING GOODBYE TO MY PARENTS, NOT WHILE THEY WERE HAVING A screaming match in their bedroom that was based on the foundation around my birth.

Instead, I left a note on the table in the foyer, and made sure Xavier told them I was gone. I didn't think they'd have a problem, it was a blessing in disguise, really.

I hit the highway with my phone face down and on silent, headed down to Cape Coral. I turned up the music, lowered the windows, and for the next few hours, I drove in peace with nothing but miles of black asphalt in front of me as the wind carried my worries away.

It was sheer bliss until I pulled into my complex and parked my Escalade.

I'd missed fourteen calls from my dad, and a slew of text messages from Kova and Avery that I didn't bother opening. A stream of anxiety rushed through my veins with thoughts of a death. I was instantly overwhelmed with dread.

No one called that many times unless it was an emergency.

Before I got out of my truck, I called my father back. Kova could wait. Fourteen missed calls was extremely nerve-racking.

The phone rang for a split second before he picked it up.

"Hey, Dad," I said.

"Ana? Are you okay? Where are you?" He was frantic.

"Yeah… I'm totally fine. Why? Is everything okay with you? Why did you call so many times?"

"You left without saying goodbye, before I could explain things to you."

I sulked. Another person who needed to explain things and eventually apologize to me.

"Yeah, sorry about that. I hope Xavier told you I left?"

"Yes, but sweetheart," he said, his tone coming down a notch, "you shouldn't have left the way you did. You were not in the right frame of mind. What if you had an accident or something? You could've been hurt, and Adrianna, if anything ever happened to you, my life would be over."

My heart softened for him. He truly felt bad. "I just felt like things would be better if I was gone, so I hit the road. I have a meet coming up anyway, so I could use the extra conditioning. It's not a big deal."

"It's a big deal to me."

A small smile tipped my lips and I climbed out of my truck. Grabbing my bag, I made my way up to my condo while Dad went on to apologize profusely until I had to cut him off.

"Dad, it's okay. It's fine, I'll deal. It all makes sense, really. I just wish I'd known the truth from the beginning."

"That's the other thing…" He trailed off. I had the key in the deadbolt and halted, grabbing my stomach from the sound of those four words, wondering what else he could say that would cause worse damage. "I know I said I never planned on telling you, but that wasn't the whole truth either. I just hadn't planned until you were at least eighteen, maybe twenty-one, and not with so much on your plate."

My shoulders dropped in relief. I quickly unlocked the door and went inside.

"Well, that honestly makes me feel better. I hated the thought of going through my whole life not knowing I'm someone's dirty little secret *and* constantly questioning why my mother detests me so much. Seriously, Dad, it all makes sense now." I bit my lip. I tried hard not to be sarcastic, but I knew it came out that way.

"Sweetie, you're not a dirty little secret. It breaks my heart to hear you say that. Things were done to protect this family. I hope one day you'll come to understand that."

A tremble racked my body at the reality of my life and what their utmost concerns were. It was a grand spectacle of wealth and power. A who's who and whatnot. Emotions did not mingle with the formula and were left to be dealt with after, if they ever were.

It was in that moment that I realized I would never treat my children in the same manner. I'd put them first. I'd do everything I could to not be like my parents.

"As usual, appearance is first and foremost for the Rossi family. Everything else comes after." I hesitated, debating whether to ask my next question. "How many people know?"

"Know what?"

"Dad."

He sighed deeply. "Very, very few. We went to great lengths to remain discreet."

And didn't that make me feel grimier than ever.

"Please, I want to know who. I deserve at least that much."

Dad paused long enough that I pulled the phone away to see if we'd been disconnected.

"Just the Herons. No one else. Not even your biological mother's family knew anything."

My lips parted, and I reached for the counter to steady myself. How did they manage to hide it from her family? How old was she? Was she not close to her parents? Did they never see each other?

My stomach churned at all the endless possibilities flying through my mind. I was instantly nauseous and prayed to God that Avery didn't know and purposely kept it from me this whole time. That would seriously be the icing on the cake.

"Which of the Herons know?"

I held my breath.

And waited.

And waited.

And waited.

"If you're asking me if the Heron's children know, they do not. Just Michael and Lily." I exhaled a heavy breath and moved to sit on the couch. Thankfully just the parents knew. Leaning forward, I propped my elbows on my knees and dropped my head into my palm. "No one else will ever know."

"Where is she now?"

"Upstairs," Dad replied with annoyance. "I'm sorry—"

I cleared my throat. "No, my biological mom. Where is she now?"

His silence unnerved me. "It doesn't matter where she is."

"Yes, it does. It matters to me, Dad. I want to know."

He idled into his next string of words while I sat in a daze and stared at the ivory carpet. "I'm not sure where she is now. Probably long gone. I haven't spoken to her in some time."

I wasn't sure why that affected me so much when I had no real tie to her, but it did. I couldn't fathom how a woman could carry a baby in her belly for nine months and then give it up without batting an eye. I didn't think I would be able to. But then again, when a stressful situation arose, emotions ran amok, and people did things in haste because they thought they had no other option, only for it to end with regret later. I was so curious about her and I'd only just found out. I had to wonder if she had thought about me for the last seventeen years.

Dad cleared his throat. "Much to Joy's dismay, your biological mother stayed in contact for a little while after you were born. I allowed it."

"Why?"

"It was difficult for her and I felt bad. She was young, and had no one to turn to, so I gave her updates and sent photos so she could see you." He paused. "It was hard to let her go."

Tears lodged in my throat. My chest ached with heavy sadness for everyone involved. "And how did she manage to stay away for good?"

"What do you think, Ana? You're a smart girl."

I knew instantly. "Money." I shook my head. The love of money was the root of all evil and I hated it.

"How much was I worth to her?" I gripped the phone tight in my hand, waiting for his response.

"That's not something you need to know—or will ever know."

"Dad, I want to know."

"Ana, just know that I would've paid any amount for you. She couldn't give you a future on her own, not even if I gave her child support every month. She wasn't equipped mentally or financially to handle a newborn at that time, let alone emotionally."

"How do you know she wasn't able to handle a newborn? You didn't even give her the chance."

"Adrianna, what's done is done. You are priceless to me. I would do anything for you. Anything. I would've gone to the ends of the earth to protect and shelter you the way you deserved to be. She was a mess and I wasn't going to risk it."

"She was probably a mess because you took her baby from her. I bet her hormones were all out of whack."

"Adrianna, please…"

"I'm sure *Joy* didn't make it any better on her either. She probably saw her as competition."

His groan turned into a deep sigh. "She definitely didn't help the situation, aside from playing the role she begged for. She could've won an Academy Award."

Salty tears slipped from the corners of my eyes. I held my breath and covered my mouth so Dad wouldn't hear my silent cry. I asked for the reasoning and he gave me what I wanted. He loved me, I knew he did, but it still hurt so terribly bad to hear the truth.

"Thanks for telling me, Dad," I said, my voice was throaty and small. There was no denying how upset I was. "What's her name?"

He softly groaned, and I knew he regretted telling me anything. "Don't cry, sweetheart," he said with so much sympathy it hurt to hear his pain.

"It's just a lot to take in." I was still unsure why Mom…Joy—*I didn't even know what the hell I was supposed to call her now*—turned on me the way she had, but after today, I wasn't ready to breach that topic just yet.

"That it is, and exactly why I wanted to wait until you were older. You have a lot on your plate right now."

I swallowed. "I can handle it."

"I know you can, you're a strong girl, but I'd rather try and shield you from as much as I can for as long as possible."

A small smile tipped my lips. "I appreciate that, but eventually I'm going to have to grow up. You have to let go one day."

"I've let go a lot already, considering where you are currently living, wouldn't you say?" He didn't speak with malice or to remind me how privileged my life has been, but to show that he's been compassionate with my dreams and desires and tried to give me the life I've wanted.

"Yeah, I guess you have."

"One day you'll see, Ana," he said, his voice was a mixture of poise and regret.

I sighed, exhausted over so much that happened in one day. "I'm going to go now, Dad. I'll talk to you later."

"I'm here anytime you need me, and I'm truly so sorry for what happened today. I love you, Adrianna. Don't ever forget that."

chapter 58

JUST BEFORE I WAS ABOUT TO DOZE OFF, THERE WAS A POUNDING AT MY DOOR.

I grunted under my breath and cursed Kova to seven shades of hell. I knew it could only be him at this time of night.

Climbing out of bed, I flipped on the hallway light and rubbed my eye with the heel of my hand, and begrudgingly made my way to the door. Quickly unlocking it, I immediately scowled at the sight of him.

"I'm gonna move so you can't show up like this anymore."

"Where have you been? Why are you not answering your phone?"

I pulled back, my eyes widened at the bark in his tone. "Go home, Kova. I've had a rough day, probably the worst day of my life and I'm not even exaggerating. I'm tired, let's just talk tomorrow." I went to shut the door but he pushed it aside and stepped in.

"Sure, make yourself at home. I wasn't trying to sleep or anything," I said sarcastically.

He spun around and narrowed his eyes at me. Hands on hips, he spat, "You think you can just text me what you did and ignore me?"

I glared at him with a hint of a satisfaction on my face. "It sucks being ignored, doesn't it?"

We stared at each other, both of us refusing to back down. He was wrong, and I was going to make sure he knew that, but then something dawned on me. I shifted on my feet and angled my head.

"How did you know I was home?"

"Your father, of course."

"You spoke to him?"

"He called me."

"He called you," I reaffirmed in suspicion. Now I was worried what Dad told Kova and if he, too, knew the truth.

"Yes," he said, like I had asked him what color the grass was.

Crossing my arms in front of my chest, I asked, "Why would he call you?"

"He was worried and suspected you were headed back this way. Apparently, you like to ignore everyone when you are in a mood."

"Okay, so why are you here?"

"So we could talk about what happened and how your mother knows." He began pacing. "This is not good, Adrianna. Not good at all."

I waved it off, taking a seat on my couch and laid back. I was so tired. "There's nothing to talk about. My mom didn't even tell my dad, she came to me, and seeing as he called you, she obviously hasn't told him anything…yet."

He stalked over and took a seat next to me. Angling his body, he pulled his knee up to rest on the couch and opened himself toward me. He threw an arm over the back of top of the couch and leaned into me. My gaze trailed over his dressy attire—crisp white shirt and na-vy-blue slacks. A silver watch adorned his wrist. His vascular forearms were thick with veins snaking down that caught my attention.

I loved when he wore clothes like this. Kova could play both parts so well—athletic and professional—and get away with it.

He looked incredibly delicious, but I frowned.

"Why are you so dressed up? It's midnight. Where were you coming from?"

There were only a few times that I could recall when color had drained from Kova's face. It took a lot to unnerve this man into silence and cause his eyes to dilate in surprise. He was typically cool, calm, and collected, but in that moment, something was off with him. He glanced away, and a tick started in his jaw. His nostrils flared, and my eyes narrowed.

Looking anywhere but at me, he said, "I had a dinner party I had to attend. This was the earliest I could get to you."

Kova shook his head, more to himself than to me. He seemed distracted. Whatever he was thinking about bothered him. There was a distinct change in his attitude, so I tried not to jump down his throat.

"A dinner party? And you couldn't leave until midnight? I called you early in the after-noon and you ignored me."

He swallowed, still unable to make eye contact with me. My stomach tightened. "It was an all-day affair," he said.

"So let me get this straight, you couldn't find the time to verbally speak to me, not even during a bathroom break, but you could send text after text while you were at a dinner party? That makes no sense."

Something wasn't adding up. My stomach was a mess, my eyes hurt from crying so much earlier, and now Kova was hesitating after we had made so much progress. I couldn't tell if my mind was messing with me after everything that happened today, or if Kova was in fact hold-ing something back from me.

Everyone was a liar to me now. Me being the biggest liar of all.

"Adrianna, stop changing the subject. I am not here to talk about my dinner party, I am here because we have a big situation on our hands and I need to know what happened so I can be prepared." He rubbed his temples. Finally looking at me, he lowered his voice and said to himself, "Grebanyye yamy," in Russian, then said it again, shaking his head like things couldn't get any worse.

"Kova, I'm not worried about it," I tried to reassure him. "If my mom was going to do anything, she would have already." I didn't like the agony that was slowly taking shape on Kova's handsome face.

"No, it will not be okay. Everything is fucked up right now, beyond repairable, Ria."

I glanced away, not liking the brashness in his voice, but I gave him what he wanted be-cause he deserved to know.

Painfully, I told him all that happened, down to the conversation before my dad and brother walked in, to the name calling and the smack that had happened a few days earlier. He sat and listened while I explained everything and answered any question he had, his stoic expression void of any emotion. My eyes filled with tears while I delivered all the gritty details. At one point, he pulled my feet into his lap and began massaging them. I relaxed further into the couch, fatigue taking over. I didn't care that I had so few clothes on, and neither did he.

Gripping my thighs, he pulled my body down so my butt pushed up against his thighs. He situated my legs, then his hands took on a steady movement and moved up my calves. My body was so sore, and the way his fingers kneaded my muscles was sublime. It felt so good, I was close to falling asleep.

He angled his head. "What else are you not telling me?"

I could ask him the same question.

"Nothing."

Kova was anything but obtuse.

"It is not nothing. I can see it in your eyes."

"Kova." I swallowed. "Please. Just let it go."

I didn't tell him about Avery and Xavier. Or about having another mother somewhere else in the world whose name I didn't even know. My jaw trembled but I fought it. There was no way I could open up about that, I wasn't ready.

All I knew, without a shadow of a doubt, was that Kova was the only one who brought a sense of normalcy to my life that I craved right now.

"So all those tears are from your mom?" he asked, not believing a word I said.

"What tears?"

"Ria," he said with a soft smile, "your eyes are puffy from crying. I know the difference from being tired and from being upset. Now, tell me what happened."

I swallowed. My chest felt empty. Exhaling a heavy breath, I said, "Nothing. I told you everything."

"Ria," he smirked. "You make me open up to you, now it is your turn."

"I'm just tired, Kova. I'm so, so tired…tired of it all. Of everything," I glanced away, eyeing the sliding glass door. We sat in a comfortable silence until Kova spoke.

"Tell me something," he said gently.

My eyes shifted to his.

His fingers continued moving higher up my legs, massaging the tight muscles. If he kept this up, I was really going to fall asleep.

"Where do you see yourself in ten years?"

I mused over his question. "I don't know… A lot can happen in ten years. I guess if I had the power to make it happen as I wanted, I hope to be doing something that involves gymnastics, maybe coaching. I would hope to have done some traveling, I'd love to see the world. I hope ten years from now that I'm close to starting a family…somewhere far from here." I paused.

Maybe meet my real mom, but I didn't say that.

Kova regarded me with cautious eyes then said, "If you were backed up against a wall with a decision that could change your life, what would you do?"

"Well, that depends on the situation."

"What would you do?"

"Would this decision make me happy or sad in the end?"

His eyes left mine for a second then came back. He hesitated before saying, "It is hard to say."

I exhaled and looked into his eyes, trying to figure out why he would ask such a serious question and how I could answer it the right way.

"I guess I'd have to ask myself who would be benefiting from my decision, who I would be hurting or making happy, and how I would feel waking up every day with the choices I've made. Sometimes we do things for others, even if it hurts us. Some of us are stronger and can handle the burden, while others cannot." I paused, something else coming to me. "To make the impossible possible, you have to twist the situation around so you're not the only one left with your back against a wall. Everyone needs a hero, but you have to save yourself first before you can save everyone else."

I reflected on myself, and wondered if what I was saying was actually what I was feeling. I lost a little of myself while I was home. It left a hole in me that I wasn't sure would ever heal. It damaged me and left me in a corner hurting and crying and feeling so alone. I needed a friend, I needed someone's guidance, someone to show me how to make everything right when it felt so, so wrong.

It was exactly what Kova was asking, and what I was feeling. And I had to wonder if he was feeling the same way too.

I swallowed back my emotions and tried to smile, but it was forced, and he saw it. We were holding back, and we both knew it.

Kova waved his hand, his eyes tight around the corners. "Come, let us go." Before I could protest, Kova scooped me up and I melted into the security of his arms, loving how strong and powerful he was. "Come, *malysh*. You are going to bed. You need rest."

I wrapped my arms around his neck and nestled my face into his shoulder. He gripped my knees to his chest. "I was resting until you barged into my condo, you know," I said, jokingly.

"Ria, you are far too light. It worries me."

I didn't respond as Kova walked toward my room. Closing my eyes, I inhaled his cologne.

"Did you just sniff me?" he asked, like he had a mouthful of sour lemons.

I chuckled. "You always smell so good. Even at the gym, you smell amazing."

"*Spasibo.*" Kova paused. "Thank you."

Leaving the light off in my bedroom, Kova gently laid me on my bed. The hallway light was on, leaving a pale light to shine in my room and a shadow to cast over his face. Kova removed his hands from under my legs, but I didn't let go.

"Don't leave yet," I whispered. I wasn't ready to let go.

"Ria, I have to go."

"Please?" My voice broke. "Just for another minute, stay with me."

"Ria," he urged, "I really must leave."

My throat tightened, and I nodded without saying anything. I couldn't. My jaw trembled, hurting as I fought back my emotions. If I spoke, I'd cry.

Pulling back just enough, Kova looked down at me. He sat on the edge of my bed and brushed back my hair. His knuckles stroked my cheek and wiped away the lone tear that fell. His other hand found my hip and he pressed his fingers into my skin. I pulled my knee up and leaned into him. He took in my glossy eyes as I did his pensive ones. I knew he had to lie to Katja to come to me, and I wished he had a reason to stay the night. I really did, and if that made me a heartless person, then so be it. After the week I had, I needed him. I didn't care how selfish it sounded, I needed Kova to feel safe, to forget the world. He was all I needed to make the ache go away, because I knew deep down he cared about me, like I did for him.

Pressing a kiss to my forehead, he held it there for a long moment. I gripped his shirt in my fist, my hands shaking as I fought with him to stay with me. My breathing deepened, and I exhaled a shallow breath. My heart ached so bad, as if it were ready to break at any given moment. He pulled back and I cupped the side of his face, hoping he'd feel the plea in my touch.

"I will see you tomorrow, yes?" he asked.

I stared at his mouth and nodded. "Tomorrow," I said, just above a whisper.

Kova hovered above me, a few short inches from my mouth. He was so close I could feel his breath.

The beating of my heart picked up and I helped guide him closer until his lips were so close to touching mine.

"I need you Kova, I've never needed something so much in my life."

My hand skimmed the side of his jaw, down to his neck, and over his shoulder to rest on his firm, warm chest. Another tear fell, and he kissed it away, then dipped delicately enough to brush his lips over mine.

"I lost a little of myself this past week," I admitted so quietly. My heart was racing so fast.

"So did I, Ria… So did I."

My eyes shot to his and my heart broke hearing the truth in his whispered words. In those three little words, Kova said more than he'd ever had, and it concerned me deeply. Not once has he ever opened like he just did. Whatever was raging inside this beautiful man, he needed to get it out, and I wanted to help him.

chapter 59

I DON'T KNOW WHO MOVED FIRST BUT NEXT THING I KNEW WE WERE ENTANGLED IN A passionate kiss.

I drew in a small breath and he surprised me by dipping a little further and softly pulling on my top lip with both of his. I angled my jaw up, giving him what he wanted, but what he so desperately needed too. His fingers pressed deeper into my hip and my hand threaded the hair at his nape. Our mouths held steady, I could sense he was holding back. His lips trembled on mine, the beating of his heart pounded viciously against the palm of my hand.

This time, I opened my mouth a little bit and searched his, curious to see what he'd do. It didn't take more than two milliseconds for his tongue to seek mine.

My hand slid to the back of his neck so both my arms circled his shoulders, and I guided him to me while I took in his slow, sensual kiss. Kova's tongue swept around mine like a cozy fire stirring deep inside my stomach. He let out a soft, almost heartbreaking whimper, tugging the strings of my heart as he kissed me deep. This was a man who knew how to express his emotions through a kiss.

Leaning into him, our bodies pressed together. Kova's hand skimmed the side of my body, over my hip and up my ribs. His thumb moved around my bare breast beneath my shirt, then under my arm and behind my back. I moved to fit him on the bed, but he surprised me by nudging my knees open to rest between my thighs.

I swallowed, taking his lips with mine. We fit seamlessly together. We'd never just kissed like this before, carnal yet slow, as if we were exploring each other's mouths, and I loved it. It was different. The most sensual yet emotional kiss, as if he was trying to tell me something through his kiss that his words could not express. I couldn't help but feel it in the pit of my stomach that something wasn't right, but I pushed the negative thoughts aside and gave him what he clearly was in need of…

Me.

He kissed me slow and deep, and so damn good.

But he needed more. I could sense the resolve in his lips.

Our bodies acted on their own harmony and wrapped around each other until there was no breathable space between us. The friction heated and soon we were both engulfed in the most passionate kiss we'd ever had. Our hands were everywhere, we couldn't get enough of touching each other. Kova carefully rested his weight on me, pinning me to the bed. He was heavy, but for whatever reason, I loved feeling his body hold me down. It was sexy and so very primal the way he covered his body over mine.

My hips widened, allowing him to nestle further into me as our mouths continued their assault on each other. He rolled his hips up and into mine, his knee slid under my thigh to get closer to me, and he pressed his erection into my sex. I was already wet and aching for this man. The man who had been there for me in more ways than anyone else this past year. A man who I owed so much more than just my gratitude.

Kova's fingers dug into the skin at my hips. He tugged on my panties and I lifted my hips for him to pull them off. I moved my palms to his waist and pulled on the material of his shirt to untuck it. Kova let out a low breath as I unbuttoned his shirt, my hands instantly going for his skin like they ached to touch just him. I could never grow tired of him and feeling his strength.

Breaking the kiss, he kept his lips to mine as he breathed into me. Our eyes locked onto each other's and my chest sank at the emotion shining in his.

Regret clouded Kova's entire face and I felt it in my gut he needed so much more than I could give him right now. I would try though, because he deserved no less from me.

My fingers immediately found his lips and I traced them, my eyes frantically scanned all around his face, trying to figure out why he was hurting so bad, what he was fighting inside his chest.

"*Prosti*," he said. "*Prosti…*"

"Kova…what's going on… Talk to me," I asked softly, worry etched in my words.

He shook his head and kissed me, then pulled back and sat on his knees and stared down. He removed his shirt as his gaze moved down my body. I sat up and placed my hands flat to his chest.

Kova didn't say a word. He just stared into my eyes, pleading, begging, but for what, I didn't know.

"*Prosti*," he said again, this time a little more broken.

Whatever he needed was his to take.

He placed his palms on my hips and skimmed higher, taking my shirt with him. Slowly, he pulled it over my head and my thick hair tumbled around my shoulders. He watched it fall, then cupped my neck, his fingers threading in my wavy locks as he slanted my face and kissed me like he did before.

There was no denying Kova was speaking to me through his kiss, through his body, through the hurt that he was going through. In this moment, I knew he needed me as much as I needed him.

I knew it. My heart knew it.

Tentatively, I reached for the buckle of his belt, then the button, and then I slowly unzipped his pants. Kova leaned into me and guided me gently onto my pillow. He drew back and stood, removing his pants and dropping them to the floor. Our eyes never leaving each other's, the connection too strong between us to break our gazes, as he climbed back into bed and crawled toward me.

"*Pozhalyusta prosti, menya,*" he said that prosti word again and I started to wonder why he repeated it over and over with such suffering. Settling himself between my legs, he looked deep into my eyes while he positioned himself at my entrance.

"You deserve so much better," he said, then slowly but firmly pushed inside. Reaching behind him, Kova pulled the blanket over us and pushed in a little deeper. The look in his gaze made me want to cry. My heart was breaking because I knew with every fiber of my being that something wasn't okay. The finality of his words, the way he spoke them, it was like he was saying goodbye.

"Go slow, it's been a long time," I said so soft and so gentle. I didn't want him to pull away, but it'd been a while, months, since we'd been so intimate. He could be a savage when he wanted to, but I got the impression it wasn't like that this time for him.

I got the feeling Kova needed someone to breathe air into him.

Nodding, he dipped his chin down and kissed me. I savored the feel of his body. I wrapped my arms around him and pressed my heels into the back of his thighs, holding him tighter to me.

"*Prosti*," he repeated, and my heart started to split down the center.

Kova pulled out and pushed slowly back in all the way. I sighed into his mouth, trying to adjust to his width. It was tight for me at first, but I blocked out the discomfort and took all of him. He did it again, kissing me deep and hard as he thrust in. My back arched, my chest rose, meeting his, and I gasped into his mouth. Strong arms enveloped me. Kova trembled as he held me tightly to him, as if he were holding on for dear life.

"Take what you need," I said, panting against his lips. I looked into his distressed eyes. "Take all of me… I'm yours."

And he did. Kova didn't hesitate. His hips pulled back and slammed into me, a wave of euphoria rushed through me. My eyes rolled shut from the pleasure as he pulled out so devastatingly slow I could feel every inch of his hardness, even the vein I was familiar with that twirled down the front of his shaft. I felt every inch of his bare length. Kova pulled out just enough so I could feel the crown of his head teasing my entrance.

"Look at me," he demanded in a whisper.

I did…and I blew out a breath.

Kova said a string of words in Russian, trying desperately to keep his emotions together. Just as I thought he would surge back in and ravage me, he pressed in so slow I almost begged him to go faster. His eyes never left mine and a gasp rolled off my lips as he took me all the way. I moaned and so did he. I reached up, but he pressed both my hands to the bed next to my head and laced his fingers with mine. He was breathing so hard.

"No, let me, please. I need this control right now," he begged, breaking. "I need you."

"Anything," I said softly.

He shook his head. Bending down, he pulled my bottom lip into his mouth while his hips rolled in and out into mine, hitting the little bundle of nerves every time. I couldn't stop the sounds escaping my parted lips when he dipped his mouth to my neck and kissed me everywhere. My hips met his thrusts, over and over, and the groaning sounds Kova made, made me feel sublime. His fingers held mine so tight, I felt his struggle, and when he let out a low and long moan, I almost came. It was the sexiest sound in the world.

"Oh, my God," I said breathlessly. "Kova…" I needed to touch him, he somehow managed to release his hold on me, and I grabbed the back of his head, clutching him.

"*Mne ochen zhal*," he responded on another moan. He twitched inside me and I didn't have it in me to ask him to pull out.

Fuck the consequences.

I tried to hold still, but he made me feel too good. I just hoped I made him feel as good. I grabbed the skin over his ribs, pulling on him. My hands dragged down his back and I pulled on him everywhere I could touch, allowing my nails to score him. My back arched, and my chest pushed into his. Kova held me as he drew back so he was sitting upright and I was straddling his hips. The covers fell, and I gasped against his mouth as he cupped my jaw and the back of my head while he drove into me much deeper. He rose up on his knees and held me with his powerful strength. Wrapping my arms around his broad shoulders, I pressed my breasts to his chest and kissed him with everything I had. Kova encouraged it by meeting my kiss with the same ferociousness. We were frantic, neither one of us wanting to let go.

This was Kova. He either gave all, or he gave nothing.

And he was all in.

If I hadn't known any better, I'd say he was making love to me. Heartbreaking, soul-crushing lovemaking. The sheer desire and pain he emitted was devastating. If he could crawl inside me, I'd let him, just to take away his pain.

The pleasure was mounting. His groaning got closer and closer together and the vibration inside me was close to exploding. His thick length twitched, and I gasped, my head falling back while I let out a dreamy moan. My thighs quivered, and his hips drove in long and hard, the head of his erection as far as it could go. I shook, trembling hard and Kova slowly licked my neck before gently biting it. I was so close to finishing and I could tell he was too. Wrapping one arm around my lower back and the other just below my shoulders, Kova palmed the back of my head and brought my gaze to his.

I knew my look mimicked his. Glossy eyes, flushed cheeks, swollen lips.

My breathing grew heavier and he thrust in at the same pace, drawing out the ecstasy until I couldn't take it anymore. I tried to kiss him, but he pulled the hair at the back of my neck and held my face inches from his as he watched while I breathed into him, my pleasure rising to the top. My nails dug into his neck, lips parted as I felt myself exploding. I let out a passionate sigh and squeezed my inner walls, trying to wait for him, but I didn't need to.

Kova was coming with me.

His hands gripped my heated skin as he released his orgasm inside me, moaning in Russian. The pleasure was too much and I was shaking so bad from the sheer complexity of this moment. This was more than just sex for us. I knew it was.

Kova wrapped his arms around me tighter as our mouths collided and we lost ourselves in pure abandon together.

As the pinnacle of our release slowed down, Kova broke the kiss and looked into my eyes. He brushed back the hair that was matted to my cheek from the heat we had created, then carefully laid me back down while he was still inside me.

He wasn't ready to let go, and neither was I.

He pushed in one last time, and I gasped. Kova kissed me again before pulling out, and I felt the warmth of his orgasm seep from me. I immediately missed him, and I let it show.

Much to my surprise, he didn't get up just yet. He rolled to the side and took me with him. I rested my head on his bicep and looked up at him, one of his thighs pressed between mine. Kova fingered my auburn hair, playing with it.

"I wish you could stay," I said honestly. I knew he'd have to leave soon.

"I do too."

His eyes penetrated my composure and I shifted closer to him. Kova wrapped an arm around me and pressed a kiss to my forehead, holding me for a long moment until I was close to falling asleep from the way his fingers grazed my back so gently.

Eventually he withdrew, and I watched as he picked up his clothes and put them on. His face was tight and I could tell he still had so much on his mind.

Soft and quiet, he buckled his belt and said, "I do not like that she put her hands on you again. It sounds like she is out for vengeance, Ria, but I do not know why and that worries me."

But I did. I knew it had something to do with my dad, I just didn't know the details surrounding it.

"I'll be okay."

"I know you will, you are strong, but I still worry for you."

A soft smile pulled at my lips. Kova walked over to me and I went to sit up, but he stopped me. "Do not get up, I will lock the bottom lock when I leave." I nodded, and he pulled the blanket up to my chest and quietly took me in. There was longing in his eyes, like once he left he'd never see me again. My brows pulled together and my heart dropped.

Leaning down, he gently kissed my forehead, then pressed his lips to mine. My hand cupped the back of his head as he kissed me like he was saying goodbye forever, a thought that terrified me.

Kova pulled back and I licked my lips.

"By the way, I would find you anywhere." I tilted my head to the side in confusion. "You said you are going to move so I cannot show up whenever I wanted. Ria, I will always find you. You have a part of me that no one has ever had, as I do with you."

Then he was gone.

chapter 60

DESPITE THE ODDS, I WALKED INTO WORLD CUP THE FOLLOWING MORNING FEELING a little recharged.

I fell asleep shortly after Kova left with a lot still on my mind, though I slept soundlessly, even if it was only for a couple of hours. That's what exhaustion did to me. On days when my body just couldn't take another minute, it fell into a deep slumber and I slept like the dead. Everything was put on hold and that's it. I wish sleep always happened like that. Most days I tossed and turned in bed no matter how tired I was.

I sighed. I still needed to call and get the results of my blood work. I'd missed the doctor's office call three times now due to training, and because I had forgotten to call back. It slipped my mind and I assumed them calling meant they found the reason behind my low vitamin levels. I prayed they had a better alternative to the damn shots they had prescribed. I wasn't sure how much more I could take of those.

Speaking of shots, I'd have to ask Hayden to give me another injection soon.

I'd gotten to practice early to see how Kova was doing. With the way he was last night, I was worried about him. Something wasn't sitting well with me and I had this gut feeling he was trying to tell me something more. We never had sex like that. Kova never showed his emotions, because it made him vulnerable, and he never allowed himself to be exposed. But last night he had, and I wanted to understand why. More than that, I wanted him to tell me what was on his mind yesterday. I planned to leave our notebook in his desk at some point, so he could write down his thoughts.

Though we both expressed ourselves through touch last night and kissed our pain away, I knew Kova did better with writing it.

But he still wasn't here, which I found strange.

I quickly checked my cell phone to see if I had a text from him, but I didn't. I did have one from my dad checking on how I was doing, which I responded to, and one from Avery, which I ignored. I couldn't deal with her right now. I wasn't ready for that.

Stuffing my bag into my locker, I snuck the notebook into Kova's desk, then I made my way to the gym and started my morning conditioning for the next hour before practice began.

I couldn't stop checking the front door to see if he was about to walk in. Unease settling into my stomach, I was so anxious. Two hours passed and Kova still wasn't here. I was beginning to fear something had happened to him.

"What are you looking for?" Reagan asked, fixing her ponytail. She stomped her feet in chalk.

"What do you mean?"

"You keep looking at the front door. Are your parents coming to town since we have qualifications soon? Mine always come when there's a huge meet the week before. I hate it. It stresses me out big time, but they want to be there for me."

I regarded her, wondering why she was actually going out of her way to talk to me. "Yeah, my dad said he was going to try and come earlier. Apparently he has business in the next town over." The lie rolled off my tongue much too easily.

"That's cool. Are they going to dinner after?"

Creases formed between my eyes. I really wanted to ask her why she was talking to me. "Dinner?"

"Yeah, there's a big parent-coach dinner planned, but I think they're celebrating too."

I shrugged, applying chalk to my feet too. "Maybe, I have no idea."

"Well, I figured since they recently—"

"Girls! Line up on the floor!" Madeline yelled, cutting off Reagan.

Saved by the coach.

I smiled at Reagan.

We began with light tumbling passes crossed with dances skills before we started practicing our routines over and over. The week before a meet was always so hectic but exciting. At least it was for me. Lots of work and stress. Lots of energy draining workouts. Some would say it's too much training, but it was necessary.

Ten vaults including timers.

Ten beam routines.

Two full floor routines.

Five bar routines.

This was my life for the next three days and most of it fueled by adrenaline, muscle memory, and a dream. A dream that could be ripped from me if I made one mistake and hurt myself.

I performed a round-off back handspring layout when something caught my eye.

Rebounding off the floor, I glanced toward the lobby and caught sight of Kova's back just in time as he strode inside marching toward the back, presumably to his office.

I smiled inwardly. I hoped he'd read what I wrote before coming out here. Then maybe we could talk when he did another blading on my Achilles later tonight when no one was around. I also needed to ask if he had picked up Plan B for me. I really didn't want to take it, but after last night, I couldn't chance it. I made a mental note to ask my doctor for birth control when I spoke to him later. My cramping had been terrible lately, my cycles were off, and my last period was much thicker than usual, so I could always use that excuse to get on birth control.

Ten minutes later, Kova walked into the gym. Anticipation curled my belly at the sight of him. I shot a quick glance at him. He looked at me then quickly averted his gaze to the floor.

Kova pointed to one of the corners. "Get in line. You know what the week ahead looks like, ladies. I expect nothing less than perfection from you all. Winners train. I do not want to hear any complaints this week. Let us get started."

Walking briskly to the opposite corner, he dragged over a landing mat and stood a little in front of it. Clapping his hands, he signaled for us to start. Holly went first. She started running toward him, Kova bent his knees and eyed her steps, then stepped closer to her running form, gauging when she would take flight and flip. He stepped in to spot her and raised his arms in the air to help her twist. His shirt rose, showing a hint of his toned stomach as he grabbed her waist with his forearm then guided her to stop with his other arm once she executed a double twist.

He gave her instructions and nodded, then waved for Reagan. He repeated his stance and eyed her as she took off running. As she went to perform a double back tuck, he popped her lower back up with his hand on the first rotation to give her a little more height, then raised his arms in the air to spot her landing, moving with her as she rotated.

Then, he nodded for me and it was strictly coach mode. Taking off, I performed a full-in, a double twisting double back tuck with the first twist performed on the first back tuck. His arms came up, helping me spin my twist a little faster, popping my lower back for more height and then putting his hand behind my back to stop the power.

"Good," was all he said when I landed. I looked at him, but he was already looking for Holly, waving at her to go.

I frowned. Good? That was all? He'd given my teammates suggestions and all I got was good? I didn't want to hear I did good, I mean, of course I did, but I wanted to hear where I needed improvement more. There was always room for improvement and I knew Kova lived by that.

I paid attention to Holly and Reagan. Kova gave them both detailed suggestions.

When it was my turn again, I looked into his eyes, but he wasn't looking at me, he was watching my feet to prepare to spot me.

I performed another full-in. I had so much momentum that I rebounded and kicked back with one leg. My heart dropped and Kova placed a hand on my stomach to stop me, then quickly removed it like touching me burned his skin.

I knew my mistake was because my chest was too low to the floor, a typical landing during warm ups.

And he said nothing. Absolutely nothing. This was a man who didn't like the way I breathed on the balance beam and yelled at me for it. But I take a huge step out on floor and he's tight lipped.

Something wasn't right.

I looked at Kova, but he was looking over my head for Holly, purposely avoiding my gaze. A sharp pain shot through my chest and I rubbed the ache.

I waited for Kova to give me instructions.

But nothing ever came. He just continued to look over my head. My stomach knotted and my face fell when I felt the springs of the floor recoiling from Holly taking off. With no option but to get out of the way, I got back in line.

The same thing happened the next ten, maybe twenty times I went. I lost count. He said nothing to me, hardly physically spotting me, not that I needed it, and he wouldn't look me in the eye. Detached and distant, after last night, this was the last thing I ever expected from him. Kova was a cold stranger on edge.

His lack of attentiveness was messing with my head big time. Kova thrived on barking orders, yet he gave me none. Not even a sigh. He demanded precision and perfection and dedication. My dedication was there, but the way he was behaving, pretending like nothing I did mattered, when I knew in my gut everything I did mattered to him, threw off my perfection and precision. I knew he knew that, he had to. There was no way he didn't notice I was off. The man had an eagle eye, yet he was holding back from me, and it was making the cramping in my stomach much worse because I couldn't stop dwelling on it.

I chewed my lip, trying to figure out what to say when he finally spoke.

"Please, get back in line, Adrianna," he said above a whisper, still not looking at me. "Please." The tightness in his voice rendered me speechless. All I could do was nod silently and turn around.

As I walked to the opposite end of the floor, the front door to World Cup opened and in stepped Katja.

God, she was the perfect Russian Barbie. Pulling her sunglasses up to rest on her head, something sparkled in the light as she moved her hair. Her gaze immediately shot to the gym. She looked around like she was looking specifically for something…and her eyes stopped on me. I gave her a friendly smile, but she didn't return it.

Instead, her hostile gaze raked down my body and I stiffened, despite my heart pounding against my ribs. A chill exploded down my spine and my stomach churned.

All the noise in the background faded away and I immediately looked over my shoulder at Kova. He stood with his hands on his hips, intently watching Katja, but he wasn't looking at her with hearts in his eyes.

No, he was staring at her like he was terrified he was about to lose everything, despite his confrontational stance.

I glanced back toward Katja and her eyes were still on me. I shook it off and walked to step in line as Kova made his way toward her. He opened the door and stepped up to her, placing a kiss on her cheek. I looked around the gym to see if anyone had noticed anything, but it appeared they hadn't. Holly and Reagan were having their own conversation, and Madeline was watching Kova and Katja with a big grin on her face. The rest of the gym was in their own world.

Confused, I looked around again. I was missing something, I just didn't know what.

Trying not to let the awkwardness of the situation bother me, I shook it off and took off running and completed another tumbling pass, landing it nicely this time.

A cramp formed in my stomach and I looked around, trying to make a point not to stop on Kova and Katja and make it seem like I was aloof. My skin prickled with awareness, but nothing seemed out of the ordinary.

Maybe it was just me. My nerves were jittery, and I was guilty of sleeping with her man.

I got back in line and watched Holly tumble. Reagan stepped up behind me and my gut told me not to take a turn.

But I did. I had a meet coming up and I had to practice. I took off running again and heard Reagan say something to Holly about celebration right as I started my tumbling pass halfway across the floor, but I accidently undercut, making it difficult to perform the next sequence of skills because of my poor hand placement. I didn't do the double back twist, instead, I did a simple back layout mid-flight.

I tried not to look toward the lobby, but I did. All I could see were lips moving and Katja's startling peridot eyes fixated on Kova. Her eyes shifted toward me and I quickly averted my gaze, pretending I was looking somewhere else.

She definitely caught me looking at her. Guilt consumed me, and I kept my eyes focused on the floor as I got back in line.

I was too ashamed, yet I wasn't. He needed something she couldn't give him, and he found it with me.

"Yeah, I'm so happy for them," Reagan said cheerfully to Holly. I applied some chalk to my hands to absorb the moisture then stretched my wrists, flexing them back and forth, pushing on my palms. They'd been aching lately from the hard impact they often took. I'd have to get my wristbands from my bag just to be safe.

"Me, too," Holly responded. "It's about time. I mean, I knew they would eventually tie the knot after how long it's been. They seem so in love."

My head snapped up and I glared at Holly, but Madeline called my name to go. Reagan eyed me too curiously and I struggled to look away.

But I didn't. Our eyes locked onto each other and something tender shifted in her eyes that said everything, *everything* I needed to know.

I blinked. There was no way.

Lips parting, my chest rose and fell faster with each intake of air.

"*Adrianna! Today!*" Madeline shouted, clapping her hands, but I couldn't tear my eyes from Reagan's or allow my mind to drift from replaying what I'd just heard over and over.

It couldn't be. There's no way Kova would do that to me. Not after he made love to me last night.

"Adrianna," Reagan said gently, "let me go first." My vacant eyes shifted to hers, but I ignored her and took my position.

My mind thought back to the sparkle I'd seen when she walked in. I felt like I would be able to spot an engagement ring.

The knot in my stomach tightened. Had I and not realized it?

"Keep going and I'll be right back," Madeline said, then jogged away toward the lobby.

Inhaling then exhaling a huge breath of air, I tried desperately to focus as I rose up on my toes and leaned forward. I started running, eyeing the corner, and angled into a round off, my mind replaying their conversation.

"*It's about time.*"

"*They would eventually tie the knot.*"

"*They seem so in love.*"

There was no way Kova wouldn't tell me if he got married, especially after last night. My mind had to be playing tricks on me, it had to be.

No, I thought to myself as my feet punched the floor and I leaned backwards into my back handspring. *Eventually* meant they had gotten married, I thought as I rebounded and reached for the sky, turning into a full twist, and rotating my hips so I could pull a double back tuck.

But I didn't.

I only executed one twist and landed with both feet, a sharp pain shooting up my leg. I feigned a rebound and grabbed my leg, then hobbled away, pretending like it never happened and I was stretching it out. This time, I kept my gaze strictly on the floor as I made my way back to the corner, even though I could sense eyes were on me.

Holly was in front of me when I uttered the words to Reagan, though my focus was anywhere but on her.

"Are they married?" I asked, barely moving my lips. I knew I shouldn't ask her, my tone giving a lot away, but I couldn't not. I had to know. I had to.

My eyes lifted to the scene in the lobby. I watched as Madeline leaned in and kissed Katja's cheek. I assumed they exchanged joyous words, judging by their happy expressions and how Madeline lifted Katja's left hand, but she blocked the view.

My heart dropped. *No… It couldn't be. It just couldn't.*

"I found out two days ago from my mom. I thought you knew too," Reagan said quietly under her breath. I shook my head, staring straight ahead. "It's why there's a big celebration dinner for both parents and coaches tonight."

She found out two days ago.

All air left my lungs.

My chest caved in and I struggled for oxygen as my eyes locked onto Kova's grief-stricken eyes that were begging, literally begging me for forgiveness.

Kova was married. No. There was no way in hell he would marry, let alone leave me in the dark for everyone to know but me. He wasn't that cruel.

Tears tickled my eyes, my jaw ached with a pain so severe I fought to conceal my emotions. Kova subtly shook his head but I ignored it.

I didn't understand why he was shaking his head no, but I refused to allow this bombshell to mess with my focus. I refused. Not after how far I'd come.

Feet together in the corner, I made an effort to complete another tumbling pass...but I couldn't. My foggy mind wouldn't let me. I ended up executing a skill, something so simple and almost mundane for my level, then got back in line, totally empty inside.

I couldn't help myself and I shot a brief glance over my shoulder toward Kova. His eyes were already looking for me and all I could think was, *you married her.*

His burning green eyes held my gaze for a long moment and the stone-cold conviction in them made me look away.

It told me everything I needed to know. Everything.

Kova, was in fact, married.

I FORCED MYSELF TO LOOK IN THE OPPOSITE DIRECTION TO HIDE THE ANGUISH IN MY eyes.

Kova was married and I was the last to know.

"So they got married two days ago?" I asked Reagan, mumbling out the question.

"No, I only found out two days ago." I looked at her with curious eyes to see if she knew when. "Apparently, they married a few months ago," she whispered.

I gasped. A knot the size of a tennis ball lodged in my throat, my hand flew to my pounding chest.

A few months ago? That couldn't be right. Because if it were, then Kova had ample amount of time to tell me he was in fact married to Katja, and he hadn't. I didn't even know they were engaged.

Not only that, he'd had sex with me just last night. I still had his semen in me.

I tried so hard not to cry. Why would I? He hadn't promise me anything, and I shouldn't have expected anything other than truth and honesty because we weren't anything anyway, so it shouldn't hurt me, but it did. Never in a million years did I see this coming. Kova should've been the one to look me in the eye and break my heart. I shouldn't have had to find out through the grapevine, he should've told me he was going to ask Katja to marry him.

But he hadn't, and I didn't know what to think about that.

I looked at the lobby again and stepped aside to let Reagan go so I could see for myself. I had to see the ring, that would make it official.

It just so happened that Madeline moved to the side to come back into the gym…

And I saw the massive multi-diamond engagement ring and blaring gold wedding band that could not be mistaken for anything else other than a woman who's very much married.

My blurry eyes shot to Kova's. He looked utterly heartbroken, devastated, it was obvious he felt horrible, but I didn't feel bad for him. I wouldn't let myself, even though it was hard not to when I was tied to him in ways that I wasn't sure could ever be severed, no matter how hard I tried.

Kova had betrayed me.

In this moment, I knew there was no way I could feel bad for him with how desolate I felt inside. There was no way, when he didn't give a shit about me.

I wanted to crawl inside a hole, light myself on fire, and die a painful death.

I didn't have any emotion left to give; my entire being had been sucked dry. I just couldn't. Kova should've been man enough to tell me the truth. I mean, he's had months to at least try and tell me, and yet he never did. I was breaking inside. Just when I thought I couldn't possibly feel any more pain than I did when I learned the truth about my mother, this topped it all. Kova destroyed me, and I was the stupid girl who let him.

My mind went back to last night when he was deep inside me and repeating the words in Russian.

Oh God. Was he telling me way more at the time and I didn't realize it? I'd been too lost with trying to help him ease his pain that I hadn't thought about anything else. I was going to be sick. I'd meant to look up the words but I'd forgotten.

I should've known. I really should have known. I knew Kova expressed himself through touch, through his kiss, through sex. I just never would've thought this was what he was trying to tell me.

Ignorance at its finest when someone else is trying to heal another's pain.

I looked away and tried to focus on the tumbling pass I needed to complete. I tried to think about each skill, the physics of it, then visualized it.

In the corner of my eye I could sense someone shaking their head no. I saw someone move. But it didn't register.

Leaning into the tumbling pass, I attempted to concentrate on the skill at hand, but it all happened in the blink of an eye.

I took a few steps, power hurdling into a round off, into the back handspring that I made sure to extend and not undercut—and my mind flashed to last night when Kova spoke in Russian—my feet punched the floor and I raised my arms as high as I could reach and began rotating into the twist—hearing the words in Russian that I thought he was asking for help, the way he looked at me—turning into the first twist, rotating my hips back again into the second flip, but something happened, and I panicked in the air before I could complete the skill.

I freaked out mid-flight.

I didn't execute the second twist and my body moved of its own accord. I shifted and turned however my body wanted to with little to no control to stop it. Every once in a blue moon this happened, and when it did, I couldn't control it. It was impossible. The only thing my brain could process was folding myself into a ball so I didn't break a bone on the way down.

And so, that's what I did. I hugged myself tight as my back made impact with the floor. I hit so hard, my arms shook and loosened, my knees hit my cheekbones. My head flopped back, the back of my head hitting the carpeted spring floor, and I choked out a breath of air. My body ricocheted, and I came loose until I flipped over again, landing haphazardly on the floor, this time trying miserably to catch myself.

Panting hard, I clutched my injured ankle, pain shot through me. Somewhere in between I hurt myself trying to land, but I couldn't figure out where. It didn't feel like my Achilles, more like a twist, but I couldn't think straight to focus on it.

I rolled onto my back and held my ankle until I rolled onto my knees and tried to force myself to stand quickly to roll it off my back, like nothing happened. I held my breath. No tears fell. I wouldn't let them, because I knew if I did, I would lose everything, and I wouldn't be able to stop.

Kova came running onto the floor and I eyed him with disgust and disappointment. He tried to help me stand, but I brushed him away. He tried again.

"Ria," he said low, trying to help, gathering me into his arms.

"Get the hell away from me," I nearly cried and pushed his hands away. "I'm fine."

"Please," he begged, trying to lift me. "Let me help you."

"Help me?" I said, scoffing sarcastically. I stood up, unable to make eye contact with him. Pushing back the tears, I choked out, "You've done plenty."

I limped off the floor toward the exit, but the only way to leave was to pass Katja. I exhaled a sigh and put on a façade of happiness and made my way into the lobby.

I'd never been so terrified in my life to meet someone face-to-face. I knew, deep down in my gut, I knew Katja knew the truth. There was no denying it.

"Congrats, Katja," I bit out with a cheerful smile while balancing on one foot.

"*Spasibo*," she responded, her eyes twinkling.

Thank you. I deciphered that one. I smiled again and went to walk past her.

"You know, Konstantin wanted to keep it between us for the past couple of months, but I could not wait any longer," she said exuberantly. "I just wanted to shout it from the top of my lungs."

"The past couple of months?" I asked against my better judgment. I had to hear it from the horse's mouth.

"Yes, did you not know?" she said, one brow raised, eyes boring into mine. "Konstantin asked me to be his wife forever. When I said yes, he couldn't wait, and made me his wife the very next day."

I tilted my head to the side…waiting…dying…until it slammed into me. Kova was married the week he was supposedly sick.

Vodka cures what medication cannot, he had said. I figured he was one of those people, like my dad, who didn't believe in medicine and drank his sickness away.

But he wasn't sick. He was getting married and drinking his way through it. No wonder he was so dressed up in the pictures he texted me. I firmly believed that now.

"We married two months ago," she stated. I didn't like the way she looked at me. The gaze in her eyes was too vindictive, like she knew something I didn't know.

Two months.

Two. Months. Ago. Kova married Katja.

I closed my eyes. God, I could barely breathe. The pain slicing me wide open hurt so bad.

Kova and Katja were married two months ago. I couldn't get that number out of my head. Two months ago he slipped a ring on her finger and promised to be faithful to her for the rest of his life, then last night he made love to me and came inside me.

I balanced on one foot, the tips of my toes on the other. I was going to be sick. There were too many opportunities in the last couple months for him to tell me he was fucking married.

Swallowing back my emotions, I quickly glanced at Kova then back at Katja with a straight face. I had to act like it wasn't a big deal. So I put on a sunny smile while my heart was breaking. I had to pretend it wasn't killing me inside, when in reality it was destroying me.

"I had no idea, neither did my other teammates, but things have been hectic since meet season started."

"Ah, typical Konstantin. He is such an honorable man. He puts everyone before him. I told him when we go on our honeymoon that I plan to make sure he gets all the relaxation he needs," she purred.

Fuck.

"Yes," I bit out. "That he does. I'm sure he could use the break." I paused, giving a very empty yet fulfilled smile to throw her off. Despite my fake mom, I learned from the best. She wouldn't know the difference anyway. "If you'll excuse me, I have an appointment I have to be at," I lied through my teeth.

My appointment wasn't today. I didn't even have one. All I knew was that I had to get out of there because if I didn't, any minute now the dams were going to break, and I didn't want to fall apart inside World Cup when they did.

"Of course," she said.

I turned and made my way toward the locker area, where I opened my locker and tried to pull out my duffle bag. It got stuck between the metal walls, so I began pulling and yanking and shoving hard, grunting and on the verge of tears when someone leaned over me and helped me yank my bag out.

I glanced over my shoulder and found a remorseful Reagan.

Why the hell… Why was she being nice and helping me? I shook my head, not having the time to care to think. She handed me my bag and I rummaged for my keys and cellphone. When I couldn't find them, she dug them out and handed them to me.

I almost broke down from that.

"Just go," she said quietly.

So I did.

Throwing my duffle bag over my shoulder, I swallowed back every emotion I was feeling and walked out of World Cup with my head up.

"Congrats, guys! I'll be back later! Off to tutoring," I said, then pushed open the door. I sucked in a huge breath of air and stalked toward my truck as my cell phone rang. I didn't recognize the number, so I didn't answer it.

Once I reached my truck, I glanced down at my phone and saw whoever had called had left a voice message.

Expelling heavy breath after heavy breath, I listened to the voicemail.

"Hello, Ms. Rossi, this is your physician's office. We've been trying to reach you regarding your test results. It is imperative that you contact us immediately to schedule an appointment to come in and go over them."

Tears coated my eyelashes. Clicking out of the message, I gripped the door handle and fell against the side of the truck. I squeezed my eyes shut, they could wait. I'd call the doctors tomorrow for sure. Just not today. There was no way I could do anything else today other than sulk in a dark corner and cry.

Sucking in a lungful of air, I scrolled through my contacts and called the only real friend I had left. My chest rose and fell so fast, tightening, I thought I was on the verge of a panic attack. I could hardly catch my breath.

"Hello?"

I gasped, my chin quivered. "Hayden?"

"Aid," he muttered under his breath. Hayden wasn't stupid, he knew Kova was involved by the sound of my voice. "What's wrong? Are you hurt?"

"I'm not hurt, but…I…" I didn't bother to hide the breathless crackle in my voice.

Kova was married.

Kova was married.

Kova was married.

My chest caved in and my knees shook. I was dizzy, and close to fainting. God, the pain was so bad. I trusted him. I gave him everything and all he ever did was deceive me. Everything that came out of his beautiful mouth was a lie my heart held close.

Lies were equivalent to breathing air for Kova. It was amazingly terrifying how much destruction one person could cause with the slip of a tongue.

My head was a mess and I couldn't think straight. Fat tears started falling so fast I couldn't stop them. I started crying, the hiccup in my voice couldn't be hidden. "I…I need you," I choked out.

"Where are you?" I could hear the urgency in his voice.

"World Cup…by my truck."

"On my way. Stay there. Don't move."

I hung up my phone and stared at my reflection in the dark tinted window, frozen in place. Whether Kova knew it or not, he had destroyed me. I grabbed onto the door handle tighter, but I couldn't move. The world was spinning around me as I spun in the opposite direction, the walls closing in with each spin. My breathing deepened until my ribs crushed my broken heart and I struggled for air.

I was a fool. A young, naive fool who ate lies for breakfast and spouted them just as fast as Kova did. We were the same, yet we were not, because I'd never, ever hurt someone the way he hurt me.

I blinked, and something dawned on me. Last night when Kova was deep inside me and I was trying to ease his pain, he spoke many things in Russian, but there was one word he said over and over that I had meant to look up.

Prosti.

Pulling open my truck door, I dragged myself inside and googled what *prosti* meant.

It took two seconds to figure it out. Chills ran down my arms as I stared in absolute shock.

"I'm sorry," I whispered aloud.

Kova was sorry, because he knew, and he didn't tell me. He knew, and the worst part was that he took what I so freely gave...because I loved him.

I loved Konstantin Kournakova.

I fell for this beautiful, Russian man, who slowly destroyed me, and I had no one to blame but myself.

It was startling. My hand flew to my chest as I struggled to breathe. My eyes scanned around my car, over the rich black dashboard, the leather seats, the wood grain. I inhaled the fresh new car scent and wanted to throw up. The car was getting smaller, the seats were shifting closer. I squeezed my eyes shut and tried to block it out. I needed to get out.

"*Prosti.*"

Oh God. The reality that I loved him and what love caused me to do, shattered me completely. I believed everything he had said, I'd misread his touch, his kiss. While I thought he was expressing his love, he was actually breaking my heart. I lost myself to him and he took it. He didn't care about me. There was no way Kova cared about me, or he would've done something, anything, to prevent the agony tearing through me. He didn't want me, just like my mom didn't want me. I would never be enough for anyone.

I wasn't sure how I would come back from the damage he'd caused. I was strong, but I could only handle so much.

My heart was reaching out for help. I needed Hayden. He was my only friend. The only one who didn't cause me pain and exhaustion and devastation. The one constant who I could lean on when things got rough.

It was only a handful of minutes and a lot of tears and gasping for breath until he was there opening my truck door and pulling me into his embrace. I sagged into Hayden's chest, feeling his warmth, even though I was so cold inside. I shivered, goose bumps ran down my arms and my knees buckled. I fisted his shirt and cried silent tears while his hand rubbed slow circles against my back, holding me tight as I lost myself.

"It will be okay, Aid, I promise," Hayden said softly, then he kissed the top of my head. "I promise to take your pain away. Let me take you away from here."

I nodded and exhaled.

We were a team, he had said. *I exhale, and you inhale.*

A lot of time passed when my eyes couldn't produce any more tears. I felt myself completely shut down inside. Exhaustion taking over, I was void of any emotion.

Everyone had a breaking point, and I'd just reached mine.

I was so tired. Tired of thinking. Of feeling. Of hurting. Of giving.

I just wanted to *release* it all, and so I did...with Hayden.

To be continued...

release

BOOK 3 IN THE OFF BALANCE SERIES

To my faithful readers,
I'm so sorry again for the cliffhanger I left you with in Execution.
If you thought that was bad, I suggest grabbing a pack of smokes and a bottle of vodka.
Buckle up.
You haven't seen anything yet.

I am slowly destroying myself and nobody is able to stop me.
—Anonymous

I WAS STUCK IN A NIGHTMARE I COULDN'T WAKE UP FROM.

Locked inside a dark box, I sucked up my oxygen. My lungs burned for fresh air and my heart beat faster and harder. That harrowing moment cruelly replayed in my head over and over, mocking me for my gullibility. I begged for someone to pull me from the darkness suffocating me, but no one could hear my fists hammering on the wall.

Kova was married.

He'd deceived me, and continued to, after I'd given him every fiber of myself. He'd married Katja three months earlier in secret.

My mind flashed with innocent moments we'd stolen over the course of a year. I tried to recall every instance we were together and what I could have possibly missed or mistaken for something else, but I drew up blank every time.

He was Konstantin Kournakova and I was Adrianna Rossi. He was my coach, and I was his gymnast. Nothing more.

I'd made the frantic call to Hayden, knowing he wouldn't waste any time. He was at World Cup in less than five minutes, pulling me into his arms and holding me tight. I fisted his shirt, fitting so perfectly into him, as if our bodies were made for each other. In a way, we were, but not in the way that mattered.

"Why do I have a strong sense of déjà vu?" he asked, compassion filling his voice. There was no judgment coming from him. "God, you're shivering."

Hayden was there for me when no one else was. Not my mom, my dad, Kova, or even Avery. They all had deliberately lied to me without a second thought. Yes, we all told little white lies, every one of us, but there comes a point in time when we make the conscious decision to bleed those lines red.

"I'm so stupid." Tears streamed from the corners of my eyes and my temples pounded viciously. "I knew better."

I'd been so naïve to think what we had actually meant something to a man like Kova. For him to go and marry Katja was soul-destroying. And even worse, he'd kept it a secret for months and made love to me while he had a wife. How he lived with himself after the way he treated someone he supposedly cared about was astonishing. I truly had no words.

I felt used, dirty…disgusting.

We are a team—I exhale, you inhale. He was the air I breathed, and ultimately what suffocated me.

The heartbreaking truth was, when it came to Kova, I'd always been an afterthought for him, second to his precious Katja. He didn't want me, had never wanted me. He'd picked her. He'd married her.

"You can't keep putting yourself through this," Hayden said softly.

"I know." My head spun faster than a rollercoaster, unprepared for the onslaught of emotions. I was too cold and numb, and breaking inside. "You're right."

"What happened this time?" Hayden brushed back the hair stuck to the side of my damp face. The thought of telling him left a sour taste in my mouth.

"Just take me home, please."

I couldn't keep allowing that man to wreak havoc in my world. My heart ached in ways I didn't even know was possible. Actions spoke louder than words, and while Kova was a clusterfuck of contradictions, his last action spoke loud and clear.

A secret marriage was the ultimate betrayal.

I wasn't sure when or how—everything was a blur—but Hayden put me in his car and drove us back to my condo. I'd changed out of my leo, and we went to my room. He hadn't pushed me for answers, but he wasn't oblivious either. He knew why I was so distraught. We'd been down this road before.

"Aid, say something. You're scaring me. You haven't spoken since we left the gym."

"I don't know what to say."

Hayden shook his head, disbelief crossing his face. Deep creases lined his forehead and his nostrils flared, proof that he knew the underlying cause of my pain. Still, he said nothing while I stood there in a daze. I knew he was disappointed, and he should be. I let this happen again when I'd promised I wouldn't.

My jaw ached from grinding my teeth. I was sure if my mom saw me now, she'd tell me I was worthless, and ask me why a man of wealth and stature like Kova would want a teenage whore over a beautiful bombshell he could proudly show off on his arm.

My mom. I couldn't even let out a sarcastic huff. That was a whole other story. Joy. I would call the woman who raised me Joy from now on.

Hayden brushed a few strands of loose hair behind my ear and wiped the fresh tears from my cheek before placing a kiss to my forehead. My eyes rolled shut, heavy with exhaustion and the weight of the day. I sighed, pressing my body closer to his, and he responded immediately. I needed to feel. I didn't like this emptiness, this hole, this huge void in my chest that Kova had created.

"It kills me to see you like this." Hayden pressed his hand to my lower back and held me closer. He groaned in the back of his throat, and I felt the deep, gravely vibration in his chest on the side of my face. "Tell me what I can do to make it better for you. I'll do anything you need, just tell me."

He was hurting for me. Where Hayden warmed my soul with his presence, Kova darkened it with his passion. Light versus dark. Good versus evil. The contrast always existed between them. Hayden was selfless, soft-hearted, an all-around good guy. Kova, however, took, and took, and took, leaving me shattered and broken. Vacant.

An agonized tear slipped from my eye as I remained silent. Hayden took matters into his own hands and carried me out of my bedroom to sit us down on the couch. He may not be as big as Kova, but he wasn't average in the least. I felt small but safe in his arms, and I needed that.

Adjusting my legs to the sides of his hips, I dropped my head into the curve of his neck and sat there until I was ready to speak. I breathed him in, absorbing everything he had to offer. He moved my hair to lay over my shoulder and his hands stroked my back soothingly. I molded myself into his heated body and finally took my first deep breath since coming home from the gym.

"Did you know?" I asked.

"Know what?"

"That Kova is married."

Hayden froze long enough for me to pull back to look at him.

"Hayden?" My heart raced as I stared at him, waiting for an answer that wouldn't blindside me.

Oh, God. He'd known?

I tried to stand, but his hold on my hips prevented me from moving.

"What the hell are you talking about?" The heat from his fingers passed through the layers of our clothes. "Kova isn't married."

"Yes, he is. He's been married for months."

Hayden's blue eyes turned glacial. Thick tension filled the space between us until my nerves rattled.

"Let me guess, the bastard never told you."

I didn't say anything. I didn't need to.

Hayden's lips curled in disgust. "And he let you find out at practice?"

Embarrassment flooded me. My entire body started to tremble and breathing became difficult.

"I'm gonna kill that motherfucker."

"I'm sorry." It was all I could think to say.

I'm sorry.

My stomach churned.

Prosti.

I squeezed my eyes shut, trying to push back the tears as the night before filled my mind. It was unlike any other time we'd been together. Kova had acted like he loved me. He had worshipped me in the most loving, heart-wrenching way.

And it turns out, he'd been apologizing to me the whole time he was making love to me.

"When was the last time you were with him?" Hayden questioned. His eyes narrowed, like he was waiting for me to confirm his worst thoughts.

I opened my eyes and drew in a deep breath. I couldn't tell him it was only last night.

"I don't want to talk about it."

"But he was fucking you and his wife at the same time?" Hayden paused. "Aid, I think you should get tested."

"Tested for what?"

He didn't bother to mask the look of incredulity on his face. "STDs."

My jaw dropped. I hadn't even thought of that until now.

"He uses protection when he's with Katja." The lie flew from my lips. I didn't need him to make me feel even shittier than I already did.

Hayden tilted his head to the side and narrowed his eyes. "And how do you know that?"

"I asked him once." Another lie.

"This is beyond fucked up. So he uses a condom when he has sex with his wife, but not you? Aid, stop lying to me and yourself."

"I don't want to talk about it anymore," I said before nestling into his warmth.

"Adrianna," he said softly, and I snuggled further into him in a silent plea for him to drop the conversation.

I shook my head and sniffled. "I don't know what to say. I fucked up."

Another tear slipped down my cheek and I closed my eyes again. I needed to stop crying but I didn't know how.

Hayden palmed my jaw, lifting my face up to his. Our eyes met. I'd only known him for a short amount of time, but he was proving to be a better friend than even Avery.

Avery. Another situation I didn't want to think about.

My jaw trembled. I'd been so hurt by the few people I truly cared about. I had no one left but Hayden, and luckily, I knew he'd never let me down.

"Come on, Aid. This isn't you. This isn't the girl I know. You fought to qualify for elite. Sweat, blood, tears, and maybe a little too much Motrin has gone into you achieving your goal. Everything you've worked so hard for will be gone in the blink of an eye because you let this dickhead ruin you. Don't let him strip you of your dream. You're better than this."

He was right.

"Talk to me. Let me in." Desperation tinged his voice. "What is it you need from me? Whatever it is, it's yours. Let me help you get past this."

I stared over Hayden's shoulder. The thing was, I didn't want to talk, didn't want to utter a word. I didn't want him to know the real truth behind why I was so upset.

That would require admitting that I loved Kova, and I'd never admit that out loud. Ever.

I HAD ALWAYS BEEN UNDER THE ASSUMPTION THAT LOVE WASN'T SUPPOSED TO HURT, that it was supposed to be like walking through a butterfly garden high on the vibrant colors of life.

Love was easy, natural, and all-encompassing.

A *butterfly*. Further proof that I'd been so naïve. I should've known it wouldn't be like that. Love was a vicious cycle and as delicate as butterfly wings. I've even heard someone say that a flutter of a wing could cause a typhoon halfway around the world. It's ironic really—one tiny flutter, like a signed marriage certificate—that two delicate and common things held the power to wreak a lifetime of despair.

"Your eyes change color when you cry." Hayden distracted me from my thoughts.

"Do they?"

His brows lowered. "Hasn't anyone ever told you?"

"No."

Understanding filled Hayden's tender gaze. "You don't let anyone see you cry, do you?"

I'd let my guard down and he saw right through me.

A sad smile tugged at my lips, and he returned it immediately. There was no judgment in his startling blue eyes, only acceptance. The budding feeling that had been cultivating in my heart for the past few months slowly formed into recognition.

I loved Hayden. But I loved him in an entirely different way than how I loved Kova. Hayden was the definition of a good friend. Despite everything, he never wanted to ruin my happiness, only heighten it.

"I was so blinded and stupid. I seriously don't know what I was thinking, but I just can't let go of the fact that he's married. It bothers me so much," I said.

"Yeah, it's a lot to take in and a total mind fuck. He never should have been with you in the first place."

This was too much emotion for my seventeen-year-old self to deal with. But then again, what seventeen-year-old got involved with a man in his thirties?

My calloused fingertips wandered over his strong shoulder, curving around the back of his neck, and I played with the little hairs at the base of his neck. I curled them around my index finger and gave a little tug. Normally, I'd be embarrassed by the roughness of my hands, but since Hayden was a gymnast and he had the same touch, it didn't bother me.

Expressing a heavy, mentally exhausted sigh, I prepared to tell Hayden at least the partial truth. At this point in my life, it was all I was good for—incomplete facts.

"You're not going to like what I have to say."

Hayden eyed my bare shoulder. His knuckles delicately grazed my collarbone, drifting to where my shirt had fallen. Goosebumps pebbled my skin and my nipples turned into hard little peaks from the intense stare in his eyes.

Licking his lips, he placed my shirt back onto my shoulder, then slid his hand alongside my ribs, his thumb shifting soothingly back and forth close to my breast.

"Lay it on me. That's what friends are for."

A sad smile splayed my face. *Friends.*

Hayden's head dipped toward mine. There was a small dimple I'd never noticed before. "What are you thinking about?" he asked.

I studied him, catching the hint of playfulness that flirted with me in his eyes. My head spun with questions I'd never have real answers to, and things I didn't want to think about any longer. I wanted to forget, even if it was just for a little while; I wanted this raging headache of grief to disappear.

Hayden shifted in his seat, my hips sinking deeper into his lap. I blushed at the feel of his length under me and kept my focus on the corded muscles in his neck, the curve of his shoulder, his strong jawline. Everything but his eyes.

"I'm sorry," I said, a hair above a whisper. "You must be so annoyed with me and this drama by now. You must think it's ridiculous how I feel."

"What you feel is not ridiculous. He made you feel this way and I hate that for you. I wish I could make it better."

He nestled me further into his lap and I felt a growing thickness I wasn't expecting. Our gazes met and he clearly wasn't ashamed over the fact he was hard.

"I care about you, Aid, more than you probably know…more than I should allow myself to. Seeing you hurt, hurts me."

"You're the only one who cares about me," I said so quietly, and that was the sad truth.

"Don't say that. You know it's not true."

"Oh, it is, trust me. I don't know what I did to deserve this trifecta of shit dumped on me."

We looked into each other's eyes and I knew he could see the melancholy written all over my face.

My heart ached with this unending need to be desired, wanted, loved by one specific man, and the boy in front of me was open and honest and wanted to give me everything the one man I wanted couldn't.

Hayden placed his hands around my hips and shifted me closer to him, pushing me against his hardened length. The smoldering look in his eyes made my stomach flutter.

"I see so much good in you," he said. "I just wish you could see it too."

My teeth dug into my lip and his gaze dropped to my mouth, where it stayed a little too long. He was too good to me—too good in general—and I didn't deserve that. His head angled to the side, his eyes growing heavy with hunger. I felt my own telltale sign of desire stirring and briefly wondered if I should act on it. Could I use Hayden to my own advantage? Use my friend to help me escape the thoughts running through my head, even for a little while? What kind of person did that make me, and did I care?

"Hayden…" He lifted his gaze and I decided to take a chance. "I just want to forget. Make me forget Kova."

Eyes wide, he shook his head. The struggle was written all over his face and the wound in my heart widened upon seeing that. He knew what I was asking for, and I knew his answer before he'd even opened his mouth.

"You're vulnerable right now, and I'm not a monster."

I disagreed. "I'm *asking*, though. There's a difference. It doesn't make you a monster if I'm asking, right?"

"It wouldn't be right," he said, regret heavy in his voice.

My jaw trembled and a sigh rushed past my lips. I shouldn't have asked, because I *was* an emotionally charged mess gasping for air. Asking him to go that extra mile was wrong, especially when he was the one person who'd always had my best interest at heart, who'd dropped everything any time I've ever needed him. And for what? Sex wouldn't accomplish anything. It wouldn't change my current situation. It wouldn't magically erase the past...

But it would make me forget for a little while. It would make me feel wanted. It would ease the pain in my heart and the nauseous feeling in my gut.

Hayden tilted his head to the side and took me in. I bet he would be gentle and caring between the sheets, someone who showed me respect both inside and outside of the bedroom.

"God." The word came out sounding more like defeat. "You must think I'm the worst kind of human alive."

I lifted my knee to move off Hayden, but he stopped me, raising a hand to my cheek and turning me to face him.

"Hey," he said, his voice low and raspy. His fingers laced through my chalky hair and he pulled me close to whisper against my lips. "I could never think that about you. I think Kova is the worst kind of human alive, but not you. I think you're amazing. I think you're strong. I think you're ambitious. And, I think you're beautiful." The corner of his mouth quirked up. "But I would feel wrong having you like this. I want you to come to me willingly, not because you're hurt and trying to forget someone else."

"I pushed you away because of Kova, because I foolishly held on and hoped that there would be more. But I'm done. I'm done with him. I promise. Even if we don't do anything, I'm still done with him."

"So you only want me now that he's out of the picture?" He pulled back. Hurt masked his features and that made me feel even worse.

"No. No, it's not like that. You know that's not true." I sighed, regretting what I'd said. I wasn't making any sense and wished even more that I hadn't asked what I did. "I just wanted to forget him, forget the pain...just for a little while."

"Tell me the truth, Aid. What was really going on between you two? It was more than just fucking around, wasn't it?"

I sat there in stunned silence. Hayden was asking too much from me. I couldn't answer him, not honestly.

"Jesus Christ, you fell for him. You fell for that fucking piece of shit."

Oh fuck.

chapter 3

WIPED AWAY THE WARM TEARS FROM MY CHEEKS WITH THE BACK OF MY HAND.
I was such a mess. I rarely cried before Kova came into my life, and now I cried all
the time. Today I was a blubbering Sensitive Suzie with a river of tears.

"Aid. Come on. Talk to me," Hayden begged. He'd followed me into the kitchen after I'd
gotten up, unable to sit still while he picked apart my biggest secret.

"Just go," I said with my back to him. Hayden placed a hand on my shoulder and encouraged me to turn around. I fell into him without looking, my chest splintering down the center.
I swallowed hard and hiccupped. "I'm so embarrassed, I can't even look at you."

"I'm here, Aid. Tell me what's going on."

"He was… I never thought I would fall for him the way I did. I never thought any of
this would happen."

Hayden listened in silence while I poured my soul out.

"Don't get mad at me," he said when I finally caught my breath. "But what did you expect
would come from your relationship with him? Did you think you guys would end up together?"

"I have no idea, not him marrying someone else, that's for sure. He doesn't love *her*, I
know he doesn't."

Hayden hesitated for a moment. "He has to love her, even a little bit to marry her. I'm
not saying this to hurt you, but there's no way he can't not love her after being with her for so
many years."

Another tear slipped down my cheek. I nodded, chewing my lip raw. He was right. I was
lying to myself. Of course, Kova had to love Katja.

"God, how can I be so stupid?" I expelled a heavy breath.

"You're not stupid." Hayden pressed a kiss to the top of my head.

"I never saw it coming. Shouldn't I have seen it?"

"No, because he wanted it that way."

My chest burned with the reality of how right he was. "How am I supposed to forget him?"

Hayden lifted my blotchy face to his. Our eyes locked. The startling diamond-like crystal blue pierced my gut. His eyes held a passionate look I'd seen very few times. His hands
cupped my jaw and I held my breath as his gaze drifted down to my mouth, his lids becoming
heavier the longer he stared at my lips. He stepped closer until I was forced to step back and
lean against the counter. I grabbed onto his arms, while his palms slid to the back of my neck,
then through the hair at my nape.

"I can't erase your memory, though I would if it were possible. I'd do anything to see you
smile and forget that piece of shit." His callused fingertips kneaded my sore shoulders and a
little sigh rolled off my lips.

"I know," I murmured. My head tilted to the side and my eyes closed from the touch of his fingers that felt too good. Hayden leaned against me, his body fitting to mine and igniting a feverish hunger between us.

Hayden drew in a deep, resigned sigh. "Be easy on me, Aid," he breathed against my mouth quietly before he descended. His lips were soft and supple like Kova's, yet the impression was entirely different. I clenched his shirt and kissed him back, pressing my lips into his, wondering if I would regret encouraging this come tomorrow.

Only Hayden surprised me, and I lost my train of thought. He took the initiative by slipping his tongue between my lips. I softened at the stroke of his sensual kiss and the way he caressed my mouth. We fell in sync and it reminded me of our moment together on New Year's Eve. He tightened his embrace, his hands quickly roaming my body like he couldn't get enough.

It didn't take long for the lust to thicken between us. Heart pounding against my ribs, my hands slipped beneath his shirt, and his abs dipped a little as my unsteady fingers found his taut skin. I was so nervous, and I didn't know why. Before I could move higher, Hayden broke the kiss and stepped back to look down at me.

"I've wanted you for what feels like forever. I'd rather it be under different circumstances, but I'll take what I can get."

Reaching behind his neck, he grasped his shirt and pulled it off in that sexy way all guys do and dropped it to the floor. My lips parted and butterflies swirled in my stomach at the attraction. His gorgeous pecs caught my attention and I placed my hands on his stomach and dragged them to his rock-solid abs, feeling the indents while I skimmed to his chest. I felt him take a few deep breaths before he attacked my mouth. He was assertive but gentle, his tongue twirling around mine, tugging and pulling, igniting a glow throughout my body. My arms coiled around his shoulders and I threaded my fingers through his hair and gave in to the sweetest passion rising in me, unlike the dominant need I was used to with Kova.

Hayden's erection nudged my hip while he devoured my mouth with a vengeance. A low ache resonated between my thighs. All logical thought left my mind as he hoisted me onto the counter and began rocking into me.

"I've wanted you too," I admitted, because I have wanted him. He was attractive in a different way than what I was used to, but I needed different right now.

"Don't just say it to say it. You got me already."

"I'm not," I said. "I mean it."

Wrapping my legs around his back, I locked my ankles together and tugged him closer. A soft moan sounded from the back of my throat. I pulled on his bottom lip with my teeth and he grinned. He broke the kiss and I instantly reached for him, but he pushed my hand away and quickly removed my shirt, dropping it to the floor where his was.

I watched his expression, his eyes widening while he took in the sight of me. It was almost as if he had never seen breasts before in his life. His heady gaze made me feel wanted. Kova had freed something inside me and made me feel comfortable in my skin, making it easy for me to let Hayden get his fill. My nipples hardened to tight little buds and I could see his erection straining against his shorts. He leaned in and I drew in a breath as he roughly cupped my breast and took a nipple into his mouth, sucking it hard.

A long moan escaped my parted lips and I leaned back on my elbows, not expecting the tingle between my thighs. Even though I'd asked for this, in the back of my mind I couldn't believe I was letting him. But as quickly as he'd started, he stopped.

"I can't do this up here, it's just not physically possible."

I thought back to when Kova fucked me up against the wall just a few feet from where we stood with no issue, but I didn't mention it. For obvious reasons, of course.

Within seconds, Hayden had lifted me into his arms and carried me to the living room. I had one of those oversized couches wide enough to sleep on comfortably. He laid me down, my legs spreading willingly for him. For a split second my stomach tightened, and I felt myself slipping.

Forehead creased, he hesitated. "What's wrong?"

I shook my head. "Nothing," I lied through a forced smile. I wanted this, but something felt off until he grinned, and his boyish face hit me smack in the chest. I softened beneath him, letting everything go.

I gripped the elastic of his shorts and pushed them down, and he pulled mine off in return. Hayden was rippling with muscle. Wide but lean, no narrow hips on him. I could hardly tear my gaze from his golden amber body that exuded a sensual side of him I hadn't been privy to. Confident and proud, with an erection that almost reached his belly button. I'd never seen a penis that wasn't circumcised before, but it was definitely interesting looking. Immediately I searched for that pulsing vein I loved only to not find it. I guess not all men had it, which was probably a good thing, otherwise I'd always be looking for Kova. Hayden was my flawless, all-American boy next door.

He was also vastly different compared to Kova.

"I want you," he said, then closed the distance with his mouth. His hips surged against mine and his hard, hot length lay pressed along my inner thigh. Normally I'd be embarrassed by how wet I was, but I wasn't. I wanted him to see how turned on he made me.

"You're a hot kisser. Slow, and just enough to make my body melt," I said, trying to bite his lip.

His groan prickled my skin and it was pretty sexy. Gripping the back of my thighs, he jerked my hips to him. I liked how assertive he was with me. His cock teased my pussy and I lifted my hips for more. My back arched and my breasts pressed against his chest. A desirable energy coursed through my veins. I grabbed his hair and tugged on it. My nails scored his back and he flexed under my draw. I needed to feel him, feel something other than sadness, and he was giving me just a taste when I needed something more.

Hayden peppered kisses down my neck, dragging his nose over my collarbone. His teeth scraped seductively across my sensitive skin. His fingers dug into me like he was struggling on the edge. He knew what he was doing, the storm he was creating within me, just like I knew what I was doing to him.

"I need to make sure you want to do this," he said, his voice gruff.

I nodded. There was a voice in the back of my head telling me not to do this, that Kova would be distraught if he found out, but I was too far gone to stop. Kova had married Katja, and now I needed to release the hold he had on me. He was like a tattoo on my skin, the blood that rushed through my veins, and the only way to be free of him was to replace how he made me feel with someone else.

If I was a better person, I'd tell Hayden to stop.

But I wasn't.

"Yes," I whispered. "I want this."

Hayden reached down for his shorts on the floor and swiftly pulled out a condom from his wallet.

"You always carry those around?"

He grinned as he tore the package open with his teeth. "Of course. What kind of animal would I be if I didn't? Plus, an STD wouldn't look good on me."

I flinched, but was completely deserving of his bluntness. I thought of Kova and how he never had condoms on him. I'd been careless, and Hayden unfortunately knew that.

"True," I answered in all honesty.

Hayden rolled the condom down his erection, then palmed his thickness, squeezing the head of his cock and rotating his wrist. My chest rose and fell as we were suspended in the height of anticipation. Watching Hayden touch himself was hot. I could hardly tear my gaze from him, from the way he gripped his thickness, how he stroked it and worked it even harder. Just like Kova would.

For one split moment I wavered in my decision. I wanted Hayden, but what scared me was that I didn't need him, not like I had needed Kova.

"Are you sure?" he asked.

The hunger in Hayden's eyes stirred my blood and caused heat to rush through my body the longer he stared. I wanted to tell him to go down on me so I could come on his tongue, but that nudging feeling was swirling in my stomach, like someone was holding my shoulders back and covering my mouth from allowing the words to spill from my lips. In the back of my mind I knew why, but I didn't want to acknowledge it, so I didn't.

Arching my back, I stretched my arms above my head to tease him, my nipples aching for his mouth again.

"Hayden, stop staring and fuck me already."

His brows shot up. That'd done the trick.

chapter 4

POSITIONING HIS TIP AT MY ENTRANCE, HAYDEN THRUST IN HARD AND FAST IN ONE single motion until he was as deep as he could go.

I swallowed, expecting it to hurt a little and thankful that it didn't. Our eyes locked, our lips parted a fraction away from each other's, and we groaned in harmony as he lowered himself against my flesh. His tongue traced the seam of my lips, then he kissed me like he was starving. I exhaled through my nose and relished in the little bit of gratification I tried to allow myself to have.

Reaching behind him, Hayden hitched up one of my legs and brought it to rest on his shoulder. An agonizing heat tore through my calf and I fisted my hands from the pain of the little tears I had in my Achilles. I exhaled through my nose again and blocked it out. His hips reared back and he drove in so deliciously slow again that my eyes rolled shut.

"Oh," I said when he pressed into my clit. I needed stimulation there in order to have an orgasm, and mercifully he hit it because I honestly wasn't sure I could let go with everything on my mind. My back arched from the pressure between my thighs I hadn't expected to feel. I focused on it, trying to build that feeling I desired. Hayden grabbed me, giving my hips a good yank to seat himself further inside. Warmth flowed through my body and a low, sexy groan flowed from his lips.

"You feel that?" he asked amid thrusts.

I nodded and captured his mouth with mine. I bit down on his bottom lip and tugged it into my mouth.

"You like to bite," he observed. I answered him with my teeth. The slight bite with pain always pushed me over the edge and I wanted him to feel that way too.

Perfectly smooth strokes brought our pleasure to a new level while my tongue caressed his. A guttural little moan vibrated in the back of my throat, encouraging Hayden to push in deeper, move faster. I gasped as he almost hit that one desirable spot that craved attention, and I thrusted my hips to meet his.

"Hayden," I whimpered. "I need more. Harder."

I hungered for something harder, darker, something to take the edge off and carry me to another level. I needed something like what I was used to with Kova. I knew it was wrong, but I couldn't stop my thoughts. I wanted what I got with Kova from Hayden. He had to make my pleasure his the way Kova did or this was never going to work.

Pulling back, Hayden sat on his knees and paused. He took a deep breath like he was winded, and the pleasure I had finally felt started to diminish.

"Hand me that pillow," he said. I did and he signaled for me to raise my hips. I exhaled a heavy pant and glanced at his face, unsure of where he was going with this.

"Trust me," he said with a smirk when he saw the look in my eyes.

Placing the pillow under my butt, he gripped my elevated hips then rose up on his knees. He pulled out ever so slowly, then slid back in and held still. I exhaled a breathless sigh. This is what I needed. My thighs quivered as a wave of pleasure finally tingled down my spine. At this angle, I felt everything Hayden was blessed with. His length, his width, the strength in his grip, how he pressed on my lower belly to hold me down. Everything.

"Again." I panted.

Hayden's hips began a rhythm of their own, taking the bliss higher than I could have hoped for. The way his body moved, like he was an erotic dancer, made it all that much better. He hit my clit and that hidden spot deep inside me. As if it were timed, little gasps and moans escaped my parted lips the more he increased his speed and power.

"Oh… This… Amazing," I managed to get out. Little stars appeared in my vision. His hand flattened on my stomach and moved until his thumb found my clit, then he pressed down on it. My neck arched back, and I clenched around him, my knees squeezing his waist, not caring how I sounded when I moaned his name. The aching pleasure building inside amplified at this angle. I reached for something to hold on to and gripped the edge of the couch. I tried thrusting my hips, but I had no leverage. Hayden was in complete control and, surprisingly, knew what he was doing.

His thumb circled my clit with every stroke of his shaft. I couldn't take much more and I squirmed, stretching my legs until my toes were pointed and I was squeezing him with my thighs.

"Oh, Hayden…"

"I want you to come like this…bared to me," he panted, his voice not his own. "If you could see what I see… Fuck, you're beautiful."

He watched our joined bodies meet, his greedy eyes solely on my sex, his chest flushed from exertion.

"Your clit… your lips are soaking wet. What I wouldn't give to feel you bare."

I gasped, my heartbeat soaring. Never in a million years would I have expected good ol' boy Hayden to talk like that. "Do it then, do what you want."

He shook his head and my heart dropped a little. I was hoping he'd become a savage and take me roughly.

Gritting his teeth, he said, "I've only done that with one person."

Pinching my clit did the trick, and I yelled out as I hit that desired peak of intense pleasure. My ankles locked behind his back and I squeezed. Maybe a little too hard, because he rewarded me with a slap to my thigh. The orgasm wracked through my body so violently I shook everywhere. I released a long sigh and squeezed him again in hopes he'd slap me once more. He didn't, but his thrusts were faster and rougher, and that helped. My body pulsed from head to toe and I reached out blindly, finding his wrist, and I latched on. My nails dug into his skin. I was sure he'd have little half-moon imprints tomorrow, not that I cared.

"That's it, baby, give it to me."

Hayden didn't stop. Between circling my clit and pinching it, he rung out every bit of pleasure he could.

Just as I came down from my enjoyable high, he came. The pulsing of his dick elicited little bursts of ecstasy from him. I felt him spasm, his body shaking from coming so hard. He breathed heavily, groaning from satisfaction as he slowed down.

"Oh, my…" I said through a light chuckle.

Hayden laughed. His fingers spread out as his hands sensually smoothed up my thighs, over my hips and to my ribs. He leaned over me and gripped my chin between his thumb and forefinger, forcing my face to turn toward him. He pulled the pillow out from under me, then leaned down and captured my mouth with a kiss that took my breath away. I wrapped my arms around his neck as he pulled out of me, never breaking the kiss until he was settled on top of me. My fingers found his hair and I caressed him. We kissed slowly and surely, making out like two teenagers with raging hormones, which we were. But I'd never made out like this before. And at the rate we were going, I wasn't going to want to stop.

A newfound ache resonated deep in my sex and it was rising again. I didn't understand where this craving came from, only that I wanted to keep feeding it.

I wanted more.

I needed more.

I wanted to take as much as I could get and not stop. Not until my body couldn't take anymore indulgence. That's how it always went down with Kova, and I wanted to replace that experience with Hayden. I wanted sex with the use of the pillow again. I wanted him to bend me over. And I wanted Hayden to give it to me the way Kova did but in his own style. There was nothing, and I mean *nothing*, better than the feeling of an orgasm. Nothing.

I rolled my hips against Hayden's and hitched my knee up, resting it along his ribs. I wasn't done. My body was humming high and I needed to feel him against my center again, I needed the pressure desperately.

Whimpering into his mouth, I tugged on the ends of his hair and became ravenous. I locked my arms and legs around him like a spider monkey. Hayden laughed and slipped his hand between us. His fingers stroked my swollen lips deliberately with a feather-soft touch and I sighed, my eyes rolling shut as he slipped a finger inside. I wasn't used to such soft touches like that.

"Fuck," he said with more shock than anything. "You're so wet."

"Mmmm…I want more," I begged, whimpering against his mouth. We were both damp with sweat, but I didn't care. I had a one-track mind right now. "Let's do it again." He laughed.

The sound of a phone vibrating broke my attention. "Ignore that," Hayden ordered, then pulled me up to stand with him. I hadn't let go, but was still wound around him. His hands palmed my ass and he carried us to the bathroom. Flipping on the switch, he strode to the shower and turned it on. Little pebbles of cold water speckled my back but did nothing to help cool me down. A couple of jerky movements later and I knew Hayden had removed the condom and dropped it into the trash. Stepping into the shower, he stood under the warm spray with me in his arms.

Hayden kissed me, then pulled back. Our eyes locked and a soft smile spread across my face. Even after what we'd just shared, I blushed.

"Your lips are red and really swollen. You look like you had injections."

He laughed, and said, "That's because someone has been attacking my mouth. She's a ferocious little cub. I could barely breathe."

My brows lifted and I shrugged uncaringly. I stared at his plump mouth and licked my lips. "I can't help it. You're a damn fine kisser, Hayden Moore, and I love kisses."

"I think you told me that once."

"I did?"

He nodded and leaned down, the spray of the shower streaming over us. With the tiles to my back, he said, "There's so much passion in you. I could kiss you all day, you know."

"So then do it." I suggested with a smile. And he did. Within minutes he was hard and hot against my pussy. "Do you have more condoms?"

"No. What about you?"

I shook my head, unable to find words. Now I wished I'd purchased a box. The tip of his dick was rubbing illicitly along my sensitive slit and I knew he loved it from the heavy look in his eyes. Arching my hips back, his erection slipped between us and stood tall.

"There," I said, and grinded against his bare length, hungry for more. Hayden's jaw flexed and his groan vibrated in his chest. He was falling into the eroticism of us being flesh to flesh.

"*Fuck me*," Hayden roared, dropping his head to my shoulder. His fist pounded the tile next to my head.

"I want more," I said.

"We don't have any condoms and I refuse to make you take Plan B like that asshole."

I whimpered, continuing to rub my pussy on him. A steady buzz built inside, a sigh rolled off my lips. "Please."

"We can't." He grunted, driving his hips up and down. His body contradicted his words—just like Kova—and I secretly loved it. "Fuck, you feel good."

Using my thigh muscles, I lifted so the crown was aligned with my opening, and I hovered above him. Our eyes locked as Hayden's chest expanded with each breath he took, and I knew he was fighting to do the right thing. It was not in his character to be cruel, but it would be so easy for me to slide down and not care, to take him how I wanted. I wouldn't do that to Hayden, though. Kova, yes, because he was a bastard and could take it. But Hayden wasn't and couldn't.

"Just the tip," I suggested, pressing my hard nipples to his chest.

Hayden chuckled. "Just the tip," he repeated my request in a sweet, yet mocking tone. I tried to sink down, but he was stronger than me and stopped it from happening.

"No." Hayden drew out his reply, but his actions defied his words. I hummed at the silky touch of his cock.

This was why I liked being with Kova. He was ruthless and obsessive and wicked. He wore devious as if it were a fashion statement. Without trying, he roused something deep within me that I gravitated toward. Neither one of us could comprehend it, but we complemented each other in the worst ways possible.

"I won't be able to stop once I'm in."

Leaning forward, I nuzzled his neck with my nose. His Adam's apple bobbed and I ran my tongue over it, twirling it across his neck and sucking the skin between my teeth. I bit down. His body tightened and trembled against mine.

"Fuck," Hayden muttered under his breath and I grinned. He was losing his battle and I realized I secretly thrived on breaking him down. The power of seduction was something I was finding intoxicating. I did it to Kova, and now I was doing it to Hayden.

"And stopping would be a bad thing?" I asked, trying to lower myself and clench around the tip to entice him. It worked, because he hissed, prodding forward even more. Pleasure wracked my body from the small victory.

"Very bad." His words were thick with need. "I can't take you raw."

"Why? It feels incredible, Hayden."

"Believe me, I know how it feels," he said. "Now I can see why Kova can't resist you. I'd never side with the bastard, but I have this feeling that everything that happened between you two was because of *you*. You make it fucking impossible. Fucking. Impossible. To. Say. No."

Then, gripping my hips fiercely, he shoved me down onto his length and selflessly gave me what I wanted.

I just hoped I wouldn't regret it.

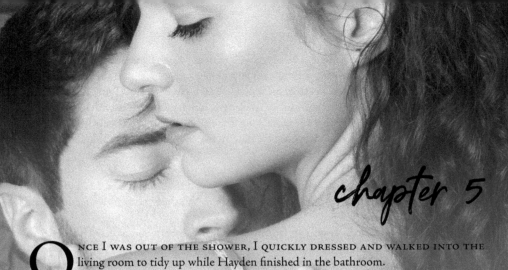

chapter 5

ONCE I WAS OUT OF THE SHOWER, I QUICKLY DRESSED AND WALKED INTO THE living room to tidy up while Hayden finished in the bathroom.

The weight on my chest was surprisingly a little lighter, though the sorrow still pulsed in my veins. I could breathe again, but only in short, tight breaths. A sting in the tail, but I'd take it.

Bending down, I picked up the throw pillows and placed them back on the couch. The back of my calf still felt a little sore and I knew I needed to take some Motrin soon. I folded the throw blanket, then picked up Hayden's shorts. A soft thud caught my attention. Hayden's cell phone lay on the floor near my feet. I picked it up and flipped it over, checking to make sure the screen hadn't cracked, when it began vibrating in my palm.

Reagan.

There was something about seeing Reagan's name flash on Hayden's cell phone that didn't quite sit well with me. Not that he was mine, or that other girls couldn't call him. I wasn't like that unless it came to Kova, but I was under the impression they were hardly friends and more along the lines of acquaintances. I'd never seen them talk in the gym, and considering we were there over forty hours a week, there was a lot to observe and note. You could learn a lot about someone without having to communicate.

Unless there was something wrong with his twin, Holly. That was probably the case. Holly and Reagan were good friends.

I walked toward my bedroom to let Hayden know his phone was ringing. As I reached the door, the ringing stopped, and so did I.

My stomach tightened. Four missed calls, all from Reagan. Not one from his sister. I stood there as the phone vibrated in my hand with an incoming text message, followed by another, then another.

Betrayal slammed into me like a semi-truck for the second time today. The air in my lungs dissipated and I clutched my chest, thinking the worst.

Reagan: What time are you coming?

Reagan: I need you.

Reagan: Hello? Is everything okay?

I'd been so blind. The thought of them together made me sick to my stomach. Reagan needed him, just like I had needed him earlier.

The phone buzzed in my hand again as a fourth message came in, totally confusing me.

Reagan: OMGGGG Where are you!? I need my pills.

Pills? What kind of pills? Why would Hayden have her pills?

I proceeded to my room and threw his phone onto my bed. It wasn't my business and I had no say in what anyone did, but this all made no sense. What pills did Reagan need? And why text Hayden about it?

I shook my head and a violent pounding ricocheted against my temples. I didn't know what to think about anyone anymore. A million thoughts passed through my head, a giant maze of inconspicuous lies used to pacify me were suddenly clustered together in one big conspiracy.

I was probably overthinking, as always, but I couldn't let this go. I just couldn't, especially if drugs were involved.

The day just kept getting better and better.

My stomach was a mess. I hated this unbalanced feeling brewing inside me. I was all over the place and not rock-steady like I typically considered myself.

Not since Kova dumped a pile of shit on me hours ago. Not since I found out about Avery and Xavier, and the truth about Joy.

Hayden emerged from the bathroom with a towel wrapped low around his waist. Steam filtered the cool air as droplets of water fell from his hair to his shoulders, trickling down his chest. He smiled, and for a moment I forgot why I was upset, until his gaze wandered to my bed. He stared down, his brows arched with uncertainty.

"Did you go through my phone?" His question was heavy with accusation.

I crossed my arms firmly in front of my chest. "Looks like Reagan is waiting for you."

Hayden gave me a pointed look. "What are you getting at?" he asked and picked the phone up from my bed. I glared at him, letting the fire in my eyes say everything I couldn't.

"What do you have going on with her?"

"Nothing."

"Nothing? Those text messages are definitely not nothing." Hayden didn't answer. Instead, he unlocked his phone and read the messages. "She mentions pills, Hayden. That's not nothing."

"Aid," he said my name in a casual tone, like we hadn't just been naked together moments before. "I've always been your friend and there when you need me, but this is really none of your business."

"None of my business?" My jaw dropped, my pulse thrashed in my ears. "After everything I've shared with you in confidence, how can you stand there and tell me it's none of my business when someone is messaging you about pills?"

Hayden shifted on his feet and gripped the towel firmly in one hand. "This isn't something you need to know, Aid. Stay out of it."

"Stay out of—" I paused as a memory jogged my mind. I recalled the moment with Reagan in the hotel room at the meet I was pulled from. I'd confronted her over a bottle of pills. She'd insisted they were diet pills, but I knew better. "Who are you?" I took a hard look at Hayden. Sweet, laid back, always there for me Hayden. Was he supplying her drugs? No. Hayden would never do that. He wasn't the kind of guy to sell drugs. Was he?

Hayden shook his head and flattened his lips. He almost looked a little hurt, which confused me. Either I was way off, or I had just found out his dirty little secret. "You're unreal, you know that? You're suddenly doubting me because you were snooping. You're being irrational."

"I'm not being irrational." I walked up to him. "It's clear you're not who I thought you were. Tell me the truth."

His chest contracted and he blew out a breath through clenched teeth. When he didn't respond, I pushed. "Are you dealing her drugs?"

Hayden scoffed. "Dealing her drugs? Really, Aid, this isn't an after-school special."

He hadn't denied it, and if he was supplying to her, who else on the team was he supplying to?

"What about others? Are you dealing to more than just her?"

"It's none of your fucking business, Adrianna. Just drop it."

"Who else? Tell me. I deserve to know."

There was ice in his blue eyes now. "You *deserve* to know? Are you kidding me right now? As if you're some innocent angel." He sneered. "Who do you think you are? You've been fucking our coach and you think you deserve to know what I'm doing in my private time?"

I sucked in a silent breath, taken aback by his hostility.

"Why don't you tell me when you were last with Kova?" he countered. "I bet you guys have been fucking like animals this whole time and you're too ashamed to admit it, because while he was defiling you, he was balls deep inside his wife."

Tears burned the back of my eyes. I'd never seen this side of Hayden before, a side where he became defensive and confrontational. A side where drugs were possibly involved. His tenor, his furious gaze, his body language, it all blew into me like a hurricane.

Hayden glanced over my head and looked around the room, presumably for his clothes. "You got what you wanted, right? So we're done here?" Hard eyes landed back on me.

I couldn't believe this. His response lit a fire under my ass and brought me back to reality. "We are nowhere near done here," I said quietly.

"What I do in my spare time really doesn't concern you. Like I said, it's none of your business. You already made your mind up before I could say anything anyway."

"Oh, but it's totally your business who I have sex with, right? I had to tell you everything about Kova, yet you can't tell me whether you're dealing drugs or not."

A huff rolled off Hayden's curled lips. "You're fucking delusional, you know that? It's no big deal."

Giving me his back, he walked toward the living room where his clothes were, his shoulders growing tenser with each step. He dropped the towel and glanced around the floor.

"No big deal? You prey on our teammates!" I needed some kind of answers.

He pulled his shorts up and let go of the elastic with a snap, his severe gaze piercing me. "I give them what they need, that's all!" he yelled.

I reared back. "But why would you do that? It's illegal. They could get hurt."

"That's all you need to know. I'm not talking about it anymore."

"Aren't you worried you're going to get caught?"

"Seriously, drop it."

Everyone around me was a liar, so why would he be any different? *You are who you associate with.* My dad's saying echoed across my mind. He used to tell me I needed to surround myself with people who were a reflection of me, a mirror of myself, otherwise I wouldn't be perceived as someone respectable and trustworthy. So what did this all say about me? This newfound understanding wasn't something I wanted to deal with right now.

"Hayden, help me understand this."

"There's nothing to understand. It's none of your fucking business, Adrianna. I don't do anything differently for them that I don't do for you."

"I don't use drugs."

"No, but you use me, don't you?"

An eerie, cold silence came over me. A wall immediately erected, and I shut down inside.

"Get out," I said, low and contained. "Just get out, now." I shoved at Hayden's chest until he stumbled back. "Get out!" I yelled, full of hurt.

He latched onto my wrist with a firm grip and yanked me to a stop. "Aid," he said softly, changing his tone, "I didn't mean—"

"Get out!" I screamed.

"Adrianna. Stop. Listen to me, please—I'm so sorry. I didn't mean it," Hayden said. His grip tightened, but I was able to pull away. "I didn't mean it like that. You have to know that. I was just angry because you wouldn't stop pushing." Hayden spoke gently but the words were already out and couldn't be taken back.

Shaking my head, I stared at the carpet and pointed toward the door. "Please, just go."

Hayden stepped toward me, but I quickly raised my hand for him to stop, and he did.

"I trusted you and for you to say that… Friends don't do that."

"Aid—"

"Just go."

But Hayden apparently wasn't going to stop until he got his point across. Raising his voice, he spoke over me, his chest flushed with irritation from straining. "You were giving me shit for what I do in my private time. You made assumptions. I got defensive. Anyone would."

"Not fair enough," I said low and quiet. "What I do in my private time has nothing to do with you and yet I still confided in you when I never had to. I'm always giving and you're always taking."

Hayden stood grounded in his spot for another moment. His nostrils flared and I could sense his frustration. "I knew this was a big fucking mistake. But here I am, trying to be the nice guy, as usual, and give you what you want because I care about you. And for the record, you take more than anyone I've ever seen. What have you given me or anyone else out of your own free will? Nothing."

My teeth gnashed together. "Don't make it seem like having sex with me was a chore. You've wanted it for months. I finally gave you the opportunity. Do you just screw anyone to be nice? Maybe throw in a couple of *pills* and call it a day? Is that what you call being a 'nice guy'?"

His face fell and I almost wished I could take it all back, but I was so tired of being lied to by the people I trusted most.

With my lips sealed, I dropped my gaze to the floor, and a moment later the door opened and then slammed shut. Hayden was gone.

I looked around my empty condo, feeling as hollow as my chest. All the material items gave the illusion of a dream world. Staged, perfect, and so far from the reality of my life. I rubbed my arms, trying to hold myself together.

For the first time in my life, the silence was unwelcome.

chapter 6

RAPID POUNDING ROUSED ME FROM MY SLEEPY STUPOR.

   I rolled onto my side, wiping my hair from my eyes, and yawned. I felt like I'd just fallen asleep two minutes ago, but a quick glance at the clock on my nightstand indicated I'd actually been asleep for hours.

Damn, I was tired.

I sat up and stretched, my lower back throbbing viciously with pain so intense that it took my breath away. I gasped, squeezing my eyes shut and wishing it away.

I needed Motrin. Stat.

Slowly I stood, my body aching from head to toe. I was too young for arthritis, but it felt like there was no cartilage between my joints and it was just bone on bone rubbing together. I wiped my face with my shirt and expelled a fatigued sigh as I walked to the bathroom. I turned on the lights and flinched at my reflection in the mirror. My eyes were swollen and red, just like my nose. When I cried, my lips swelled. It reminded me of Joy when she got Botox, only I looked like I had triple the amount in one shot.

Ugh. I was an ugly crier.

I grabbed the Motrin bottle and threw back five little orange pills before heading back to my room to face-plant on my bed. A loud pounding from the living room made me jump, and pain shot through my ankle. Shit. It felt like someone was holding a match to it. With everything going on, I'd forgotten I'd landed wrong earlier during my tumbling pass and I hadn't treated it properly. I had become good at overlooking my injury and pushing through, but now I felt every ounce of agony in my body. I was a mess.

The pounding started up again and I exhaled a heavy breath as I made my way to the door and threw it open in haste. My frustration swiftly morphed into rage at the site of Kova standing tall and dignified on the other side, and dressed too damn good for his own health.

"Oh, hell no! Get the out of here. How dare you show your face here!"

"Ria—"

"Fuck you, Kova."

"Ria," he drew my name out. "Everyone can hear our business."

"You wrecked me, and I don't want to talk to you. You let me find out about your marriage in the worst possible way. You're so pathetic that you couldn't even tell me yourself."

I tried to slam the door shut but he curled his fingers around the edge to stop me.

"Go the fuck away! I don't want to even look at you."

"I will not go away until you open up." He pushed at the door and I used my hip to push back.

"Then you'll be standing there all night!" I yelled through gritted teeth. "I don't want to see you!"

"I just need to explain." His voice cracked, and I almost slipped.

"It's a little too late for that, don't you think? Go home to your *wife*."

I gave the door a good shove, and this time managed to slam his fingers between it and the jamb. Kova hissed but held on tight. I took satisfaction in that little feat.

"You know I am not trying, right? I could easily come in, but I do not want to hurt you."

"Too late for that. All you know how to do is hurt me."

"*Prosti*," he sighed, and I fucking felt his sorrow in that stupid Russian word.

Something exploded in my chest and I detonated like a rocket.

If I didn't know the meaning of that word, I'd say his tone led me to believe he was genuine, but that wasn't the case.

"I never want to hear you say that again!" I yelled, pushing on the door with every ounce of force I could muster. I wanted to break his fingers so he could never use them on me again. "You are not *prosti*, you fucking liar! *Prosti, prosti, prosti*."

Oh, yes, I totally mocked him.

"I am going to count to three before I force my way inside." He sounded pissed. "*Raz. Dvah*." I got a little nervous, and right before he said *"tree,"* I jumped back.

Words evaded me as I stood two feet from Kova. He slammed the door shut so hard the painting on the wall rattled. He eyed me with contempt and I ground my teeth, feeling the blood rush through my veins. I was on edge and past the brink of sanity because of this crazy Russian.

"If you don't leave, I'm going to scream so loud people will think I'm being murdered."

He raised a brow at the same time one corner of his lips tugged up. "You know I love a good challenge, Ria."

My heart pounded viciously against my ribs. "Kova."

"Adrianna."

"I fucking hate you." The look in his eyes screamed guilt, but I didn't let it affect me. "I fucking hate everything about you."

"I could never hate you." He stepped toward me, and the tenor in his voice weakened my knees.

"You'd be surprised of the dark kind of emotions a person can evoke from another when they've been ruined by someone they care about."

He took another step. "Please…"

I shook my head, a cunning smirk slowly drawing at my lips. I wasn't planning on telling him about Hayden, but it was the only leverage I had that was somewhat comparable to the knife he'd put in my back. He wouldn't like it. In fact, he'd hate it. Kova was a real jealous, bitter man, and I wanted to hurt him. I bet he didn't even share his toys when he was a kid.

Taking a deep breath, I felt like I tugged on every uncertain nerve in my body and exhaled boldness in my next words.

"I fucked Hayden." I was purposely bold and gave him a moment to let the words to sink in. "More than once."

He didn't react as I'd expected him to. He just stood there like my words hadn't fazed him. I exploded then, lunging toward him and slapping him as hard as I could across the face. The sweet scent of alcohol burned my nostrils. He smelled like he had bathed in bottles of vodka. I was almost concerned over the fact that he drove here drunk.

"I wish I'd never met you."

I gasped as he clutched both of my wrists in one hand and wrapped his free arm around my lower back. He lifted me off the floor and carried me into the living room.

I ignored the pain in my ankle and kicked my legs around, fighting him tooth and nail, but he was much stronger than me. All I saw was red and the need to make Kova suffer. My foot connected with his shin, and he grunted, then yelled something in Russian. He moved his head to the side and I saw my opportunity. Throwing myself forward, I clamped my teeth down on his neck, biting down harder when he winced.

"Hurts, doesn't it, asshole?"

Kova flung me onto the couch, and a gasp of air flew from my lungs as my back connected with the sofa. I glared at him in shock. His eyes were glossy, and he didn't appear as drunk as I knew he was.

"Goddamn it, Adrianna," he said, then shot off another round of Russian when I kicked him in the stomach.

"I hate you. I hate you. I fucking hate you." I clenched my teeth as Kova grabbed both my ankles and roughly yanked me toward him, forcing me to slide halfway down the couch. He climbed over me and pressed his knees to the sides of my hips and dropped his weight on me. He locked me in place, using his tight grip to press my arms into the cushion over my head.

"I deserve all your hate, and more."

"How could you!" I seethed on the inside, my blood boiled to a destructive level. "How could you do this to me, after *everything*!" I screamed in his face and thrashed against his hold, trying anything I could to get this man, whom I both loved and hated with the same voracity, off me. "You didn't even have the decency to tell me, you fucking coward."

"It is not what you think."

"It never is. Get the fuck off me and leave me alone. I don't want you here. Go home to your wife, where you belong."

"How can I when all I think about is you? You live in my mind every miserable second of my life. I cannot escape you, no matter how hard I try." I heard him swallow. "When I saw you on the mat, the way your face paled and you nearly collapsed to your knees, it fucking *broke* me, Ria. You do not know what it did to me. I did not know the definition of pure, raw torture until I saw your face. I thought I was going to have a heart attack. I did not know what it felt like to hurt someone I care about until that moment. I would give everything to go back and erase what I did, to not see that look on your face again."

He had no idea what he meant to me. My heart raced so fast that I knew he could feel it.

"You're married now. Don't you care that you broke your vows?"

"For the first time in my pathetic life, my hands were tied." Kova's voice was a notch lower and filled with sorrow. "I could not go against her because it would not just destroy me, but it would ruin you too. I never wanted it, but I had no choice in the matter."

"You always have a choice." My voice splintered between trying to stay strong and fucking breaking inside. We were two halves of a whole that no longer fit. Our pieces had been torn apart, altered and destroyed, with no chance of ever being whole again. "Last night you had more than just sex with me. How could you do that when you're married?"

"Adrianna… There is a lot you do not know."

"I know we're done, Kova. This is it. We're through."

"That is where you are wrong. This is not over. *We* are not done."

My mouth fell open. "Did you actually think I would continue with you once I knew you were married? What kind of despicable person are you?" Cheating on a girlfriend, though shallow, was one thing, but cheating on a spouse was an entirely different situation.

"Those vows mean nothing to me."

My eyes widened. "You are seriously insane. Did you even wait long to break your vows?" He answered with a cavalier shrug.

This man had no heart and lacked even the simplest emotion. I was sure of it.

Kova squeezed his eyes shut and averted his gaze. I'd hit a sore spot. When he didn't respond, I kept going.

"Do you even love her?"

I wanted him to say yes. At least that way it would ease the pain and make a little sense. Instead, he shrugged again, as if I had asked him how he liked his mediocre house salad. "Katja and I have a history. It was always coming, you know."

I gawked. My lips parted on a heartbroken sigh. *It was always coming.*

"So, you sleep with me, knowing all along what your endgame was? Are you that narcissistic?"

Kova's gaze hardened. "I am not a narcissist. I am a man conflicted between wanting to do what I want, and needing to do what is expected of me. There is a difference. A big fucking difference and I hate it. One of us was going to lose and I had to make a choice I did not want to make."

"That's your reason for being a dick? You can't just own up to the fact that you took the easy way out?"

Kova tensed, his body trembling with defiance. Sitting back on his knees, he raised his voice. "What do you propose I do? Get a divorce and confess my love for you in front of everyone and act like it is no big deal, when it will in fact ruin everything? Use your brain, Adrianna. That could never happen. Never."

Seething over how heartless he could be, I sat up and shoved against his chest. Kova fell back and I stared down at his slumped body.

"I'm not asking you to declare anything. I'm asking you to be a decent human being. It's really not that difficult."

Kova flattened his lips. I got the impression that he was trying avoid saying something he would regret. "It is more difficult than you could ever know. I made a promise many years ago to Katja, and I always fulfill my promises. I made you no promise. Not in this relationship, and not in gymnastics."

My heart plummeted, and a cold shower of clarity washed over me. I'd been so utterly stupid. I didn't know what was worse, the fact that I'd allowed myself to fall so deep, or that he'd allowed it knowing his intentions.

"You're right. You never made any kind of promise to me. You used me instead. You flat out used me for your own benefit."

Kova vehemently shook his head. "Take those words back," he demanded.

"No," I said, hanging on to what little strength I had left. "You created this lie. We were never a team. You exhaled false promises and I inhaled your bullshit. You ran the show and I danced to your tune, trapped in this elite bubble of lies you created. I was never your weakness. That's the truth and you know it. You just don't want to hear it."

Sitting up, Kova reached out and grabbed my jaw. His glossy eyes glared at me, and I could see him struggling between losing it completely and trying to retain his sanity. "I never used you. Ever." His voice was a broken whisper. "If there is one thing you believe, believe that, Adrianna." Kova's breathing deepened, and for a split second, I wanted to believe him.

"Go ahead. Tell me another lie."

Kova expelled a heavy sigh and glanced at the ceiling.

My jaw trembled and I took a deep breath. Oh, God. I wished he didn't have the power to make me cry. I didn't want him to see how much I needed him, because I didn't want to show Konstantin Kournakova that I actually loved him. I couldn't begin to even fathom what he'd do to me if he knew the truth.

Kova smoothed the hair back from my face with a gentleness I wasn't expecting. His hands shook and I tried not to read into it. He was too close, and it was suffocating me.

"I never meant to hurt you."

His words caused a deep ache in my chest and my eyes narrowed to slits. I didn't want to hear it anymore. If he never meant to, then he wouldn't have hurt me. His words meant nothing.

"Please leave. Go home to your wife. You know, Katja? The woman who's wearing the diamond you put on her finger?"

Kova's jaw flexed and he tilted his face toward mine. He tried to graze his nose against mine, but I swiftly turned my head away.

"I do not ever want to hear those two words in the same sentence ever again." His nose drifted along my jaw down to my neck. "Especially from your beautiful lips. In another time, another world, that ring would be on your finger and you would not be fighting me. I would be making love to you all day, every day. I would not be with her."

My breath lodged in my throat. He knew no bounds. He said *her* with such malevolence and loathing that I almost questioned him. But I couldn't. I didn't want to engage.

"How much did you drink tonight?" Not that alcohol was an excuse, but I couldn't imagine that even for one second he actually meant what he said for once. I knew better now, and I refused to allow his words to affect me ever again.

"Not enough," he chuckled, and damn it all, it sent a shiver through my body. I wouldn't be deterred, though. I ground my teeth and put up a wall so big he'd never be able to scale it.

"It's been a long day. I need you to go. I want to be alone now."

Quietly, and very much to my surprise, he agreed with the slightest dip of his chin. I let out a silent sigh of relief and watched as he stood up and patted his pockets for his keys.

Kova glanced down and the look of devastation on his face broke my heart further into pieces. His eyes…his eyes always got to me. But I wouldn't be swayed. Not this time.

Swallowing back the lump in my throat, I said, "I'll see you early Monday for practice."

He didn't say anything. He just stood there, his eyes asking for so many things. Silently pleading for me to forgive him, for me to ask him to stay. And that wrecked me because he was reaching for me without doing anything, but that was us. We could feel without touch, could listen without words. All we needed was that one look, that intake of breath, and that was it. Kova didn't need to do anything but just be there.

"You have a blading session afterwards," he said, his voice resigned.

"I know."

I wish he hadn't shown that he was looking out for me. I wanted him to not care. I needed him to leave me alone. I needed to let go emotionally and detach myself, and I wondered how I was going to do that. Even though my body was an empty shell, my heart still beat for him. Beat for his seductive lies. Beat for who he was deep inside. Kova wasn't a bad man. He just made awful choices.

After another moment, Kova turned and gave me his back, his shoulders slumped. I counted each step he took toward my door as he walked away. It took everything in me not to yell out and stop him. My fingers itched to reach out and my chest continued to cave from the loss.

Six. Six heart-wrenching steps was all it took for him to reach the door and pull it open. But it was the next step that did me in.

Seven was supposed to be a lucky number, but it represented our demise. On the seventh step, he gave me what I wanted and walked out. Seven steps, and he was taking my heart with him, the only thing that had any feeling left in me.

Kova had consumed my mind, heart, and soul. I couldn't let him consume my life any longer. Falling in love with my gymnastics coach was the most excruciating form of self-destruction. From here on out, I would only love him in the dark.

chapter 7

I WALKED INTO WORLD CUP ON MONDAY A DIFFERENT PERSON.

Same goal. One destiny. And one less priority.

My soul was quiet. No obstruction, no disturbance, no complication. My emotions were stagnant, like I'd shut a door and they were no longer in my way. I didn't feel hollow anymore. I was at peace, but I wasn't. It was like I didn't exist. I was neither here nor there. I was indifferent.

I stuffed my bag into my locker and threw my hair into a messy bun, tucking the flyaways behind my ears. The last time I had stood here was when Reagan helped me after the shock of Kova's marriage. That felt like ages ago.

My mind still reeled over why she had been so nice to me, and had been there for me with sympathetic eyes I couldn't refuse. I hadn't spoken to her since then. My gut told me she wouldn't tell anyone, and if she did, well… I just didn't care. I'd deny it anyway, and frankly, between her pill addiction and Hayden supplying them to her, I now had something to hold over her head.

Taking a deep breath, I slammed the metal locker door shut. Today would be interesting. I was prepared for the off chance that Kova cornered me. No. He wouldn't do that. That was too personal. He would be just Coach from now on. I planned to tell *Coach* that unless it was gymnastics related, he wasn't allowed to talk to me.

A headache began to form near my temple and I pressed on the painful area with my hand. I felt warm, like I had a fever. Quickly, I reopened my locker and dug out some Motrin. After downing them like they were candy, I made my way into the gym on unsteady legs. The last thing I needed was to get sick.

Naturally, Coach and Madeline were already there, along with the rest of the team. His eyes met mine. There was no sorrow in his gaze or any impression that he had something on his mind. My heart fluttered when my eyes drifted to his left hand and caught sight of the flashing platinum band. That ring was going to be the death of me. My stomach roiled like crashing waves as the feelings I'd kept at bay tried to emerge.

"Ladies, you have a meet this weekend." Coach clapped his hands, regaining my attention. "A very important one. Let us start off with stretching and then running two miles. I want you to hop straight into warm-ups. We will work floor and beam for the first part, and bars and vault the second half of the day."

He and Madeline stayed off to the side where they chatted and jotted stuff down in her notebook while we stretched for thirty minutes. Once warm-ups were finished, the team walked back into the locker room and the coaches went their separate ways. We pulled on shorts and slipped on running shoes, took a few sips of water, then made sure our hair was tight in ponytails. As I shoved my duffle bag into my locker, I felt the sharp corner of something lodged inside. Leaning in, I slid my bag aside and saw a familiar silver spiral.

Rage instantly boiled inside of my veins at the sight of our notebook. My locker was a disaster and needed to be cleaned so I hadn't noticed it in there the first time, but now that I had, I wanted to shred it with my teeth. How *dare* he put this in here. If he thought I was going to write my feelings in this dumb book after what he'd done, he had another thing coming.

I slammed the door shut and turned around to lean against it. Folding my arms across my chest, I dug my nails into my skin. I was furious. He thought he could write down a few heartfelt apologies and all would be forgiven. He was delusional if he thought I would accept a few fake diary entries. We were through. There would be no more Kova and Ria. That ship had fucking sailed the Atlantic and sank next to the rotting *Titanic* when he decided to get married behind my back.

Reagan sidled up next to me. I watched Hayden's twin walked out of the room, wondering what she'd done that caused the no-dating rule to go into effect. Hayden wouldn't tell me, and neither would Kova, but I was going to make it my mission to find out.

"I'll meet you outside. Is that cool?"

Reagan studied me for a moment, then nodded her head before walking out of the locker room.

Once I was sure they had left the building, I reopened my locker and yanked the book out, then marched my way to Kova's office. When I got closer, I heard him speaking in Russian.

He was on the phone with his wife.

Without knocking, I threw open his office door. Kova sat behind his desk with the phone pressed to his ear. He didn't have time to react. With as much force as I could gather, I chucked the notebook at him, aiming for his fucking head. I was terrible at throwing a ball, so I didn't expect it to hit him. I closed the door quickly, hearing him curse a few times, then I jogged outside.

"Why is there a no dating rule?" I blurted to Reagan when I caught up to her, but not loud enough for anyone else to hear. She glanced at me, then looked straight ahead, her brows bunched together as we walked side by side until we reached the track. "What did Holly do, and why is it such a secret? Do you know?"

"I don't know," she said.

"Don't bullshit me, Reagan. I have a feeling you know since you've been spending extra time with Hayden." She didn't miss my double meaning as she tripped over her footing and shot me a crazed, aggravated look.

A small smirk tipped my lips, but it wasn't malicious. I wanted her to know that I knew about her little secret, but not that I would do anything with it. I'd never throw someone under the bus like that, but it was nice to have it in my pocket.

Before she could speak, I said, "Don't worry. Your secret's safe with me. I think we both know by now I'm like a vault anyway."

Reagan chewed her bottom lip and glanced away. She stayed quiet until we reached the track. Our feet picked up simultaneously and we jogged next to each other.

"Why do you care?" she asked.

"I'm curious."

We'd completed one lap when Reagan finally said, "I don't know. I've asked both Hayden and Holly and they're very tight-lipped about it. They refuse to tell me anything. Eventually I gave up because I honestly don't give a shit. I'm just nosy."

We completed another two laps. My head spun and the overthinking exhausted me. "What could it possibly be?"

"I don't know. It could be anything, really. You know how Kova gets. He can be a Nazi and his word is law, so who knows. It could be something big or something small. I mean, if you mess with his OCD schedule, and waste his time, he gets pissy. So who can tell with that guy. He's so hormonal, I swear."

This time I laughed. "Yeah, he totally is."

"I do remember Holly crying a lot and then missing practice for a few weeks. It was…" I glanced at her as she looked up toward the sky and squinted. "I would say no more than a year before you came to World Cup, but definitely over six months."

"She missed practice for a few weeks?" I was truly shocked she was allowed to miss so much time and still train afterward.

"It was also around the time another coach was fired unexpectedly. I was happy he was kicked to the curb. I couldn't stand him."

"Why?" I asked.

"Why what?"

"Why couldn't you stand him?"

"He made my fucking skin crawl. He had that look, you know, the rapey kind of look you can spot a mile away. The one your gut says stay the fuck away from. His smile was creepy and he always stared too long, like he was thinking nasty thoughts. I was glad Kova fired his ass. I almost quit because of him."

A memory flashed through my head as I stared ahead, trying to remember if I'd heard about that situation. I recalled Kova mentioning that he'd fired someone, but I couldn't place when or where he told me.

"Was he a mean coach?" I breathed heavily as a low, dull pain started in my lower back, but I brushed it off. I knew if I stopped even for five seconds that I'd be in trouble.

"Dude, he used to spit when he spoke. Every. Time. It was so gross. He was a nasty coach and so verbally abusive. He made Holly cry all the time. Kova and Madeline might ride us to the ground, they might push us to the brink until our bodies are ready to collapse, but they aren't like him. Not even close. Kova got into it quite a few times with him because Kova didn't agree with his method of training. He was the kind of coach you hear about in the news."

We had two more laps to go. I was so parched. Thighs tight, my lower back ached each time my feet hit the asphalt. I needed water soon.

"So are you really going to ignore the massive elephant in the room?" Reagan said.

I groaned inwardly. Fuck. My. Life. I knew this was coming.

"I mean, you couldn't have expected me not to question you. I told you I'm nosy."

"And what do you do with the dirt you have on people?"

She tapped her temple, her head twitched to the side. "I keep it in the vault."

"Until you need to use it," I shot back.

"You either ride or die, Adrianna."

Reagan was cunning. I couldn't fault her for that, but I still thought carefully before I spoke. A sharpness cut through my chest and I took a deep breath to expel the pain, hiding it as much as I could from her.

"What do you want me to say? That I like our coach? Okay. Fine. I do. He's gorgeous as hell and he's got the body of a Greek god. You can't tell me you don't think so."

"Oh, I think he's sex on a stick, but that doesn't mean I'm going to bone him."

She went for the jugular. "I'm not boning him, Reagan."

We'd finally reached the end of the eighth lap and slowed down. Using the back of my hand, I wiped the sweat dripping down my face. Reagan took a few moments to breathe before she spoke again.

"Everyone likes him, Adrianna. But people don't react the way you did the other day if they weren't invested. Don't bullshit me."

Panting, I asked, "Why did you do it? Why did you help me?"

She shook her head and shrugged, staring ahead like she was asking the question herself.

"I don't know. I guess I had a moment of compassion and felt bad, which I rarely do. If people have the cognizance to make the stupid decision in the first place, they can handle the outcome. You knew what you were doing, but for some dumb reason I can't explain, I felt bad."

"What happened to you?"

"What do you mean?" She looked at me, perplexed.

"You're so cynical. Unforgiving. Something had to happen to make you this way."

"I was born a bitch with a monstrous chip on my shoulder, Adrianna."

When I gave her a pointed look she continued. "Okay, fine. Let's just say when your ambition and means don't exactly align it can change a person. Harden them. I have the talent and drive to surpass this place"—she nodded toward the gym in general—"but my parents don't exactly have the funds for more than this. And I want more. I got my full ride. And I got it by letting nothing and no one stop me." She arched a brow, as if to point out that I'd been doing the opposite.

I understood her underlying message. She hadn't let anyone get in her way, especially me. She was a girl after her own dreams.

"By the way, we're not having a powwow here. I'm just telling you like it is this one and only time because of your sexcapades with our coach. Believe me, it won't happen again."

I laughed. "You can be such a bitch sometimes."

"I am what I am."

I knew we'd never be best friends, but I now viewed Reagan in a different light. She had to grow a thick skin to stay afloat so she wouldn't sink and drown. I knew that feeling. It didn't excuse her being a bitch, but at the same time I understood why she was the way she was.

MIDWAY THROUGH FLOOR PRACTICE, I COULDN'T HIDE THE THROBBING IN MY ankle anymore.

It was a low and dull heat, tingling with little sparks, but enough for me to suck in a quiet breath through my teeth at the end of a tumbling pass and limp back to the end of the line.

"Go get your tape, Adrianna," Kova ordered.

I turned around to respond but did a double take. There was a pinkish knot at the top of his forehead with a slight indentation where the corner of my notebook must've hit him. I hadn't noticed it when we'd come back in from running, but now that it'd been a few hours, I saw it as clear as day. He was going to have a bruise from it.

I pursed my lips together and fought a smile. *Victory.*

"Adrianna." His voice was firm this time. I looked at him and his eyes dropped to my feet. "Get your tape." I stared at him for a few seconds then subtly nodded. "And no Motrin," he shouted when I walked away.

I mumbled under my breath and ignored him. I applied the same mentality to him as he did to me—what he didn't know wouldn't hurt him.

Quickly, I reached for the side pocket of my bag and popped two little orange pills, then I reached above to the shelf and grabbed my coconut water. Swallowing, I recapped the container and then dug through my duffle bag for my tape when my hand caught the corner of something.

The notebook.

Again.

I was going to murder him.

Irritation filled my veins. He must've snuck it in while we ran laps. I had a fierce urge to open it and see what Kova wrote, but I knew if I did it would consume me. Enrage me.

Oh, who was I kidding? There was no way I could go all day and not read it. Flipping it open, I noticed there were two new entries. I went to the second to last one first.

I am eternally sorry. I know you do not want to speak to me, but you need to know this was not what I wanted.

For a split second I felt bad for throwing the notebook at him, until I remembered that he breathes lies. Lies. Lies. Lies. It was all that I processed. He was trying to fix his fuck-up and feed me lies he thought I'd eat up. Who did he think he was? Did he think I'd be so easy and fall for his bullshit again? Arrogant Russian.

I flipped the page to the next entry.

If gymnastics does not work out, you should look into shot put.

Shot put? What the hell was shot put? Probably some Russian game no one's heard of.

I shut the book with a grimace and threw it back into my locker. I slammed the door and made sure it was locked, then walked back into the gym with an icy expression on my face.

I sat down on the blue carpeted floor and brought my knee up. The tape was precut, so I tore off three pieces as Kova came over and kneeled in front of me. The jerk smelled delicious but I refused to look at him. I handed him the tape and leaned back, giving him my foot while I watched as my teammates practiced on floor.

Kova had one hand on my heel as he flexed my foot and pointed my toes with his other hand.

"Any pain?" he asked.

"Nope."

His hand slid up my calf and gently squeezed the sore muscle. "What about here?"

"Nope."

He squeezed a little harder. "Now?"

"Feels great." I bit out, still not looking at him.

Then, he went for my Achilles. Literally. Kova pinched the back of my injured ankle, not hard enough to hurt me, but enough to garner a reaction. My nostrils flared, and I ground my back teeth together.

"How is this?"

"Feels fine."

"I bet this feels great too," he shot at me, pinching a little tighter.

My toes curled in pain. "Perfect, *Coach*. Just like that knot on your big head."

Kova froze, and I smiled, feeling a little triumphant. The only things that moved were his piercing green eyes that shot straight through me. I looked at him, still grinning. I didn't move. I didn't blink. I didn't hint at any other feeling. Just stared right through him and showed him how things were going to be from now on.

Without saying anything, he taped my foot, stretching the elastic just enough to help alleviate the pain, then stood. He placed a hand out, but I got up on my own.

"Get back in line," he said.

"Yes, *Coach*."

I'd skipped tutoring, had a small lunch, and worked through the rest of the day until sundown. I didn't have an appetite, but I knew I needed to eat something, so I forced myself to eat a "healthy" fatty protein bar. Shit was not good for you, but keeping my mind off things was key, and if I had to forgo some school work and eat garbage, then so be it.

Even now as I waited for Kova to finish up so we could start the blading, I wasn't hungry, but I had a raging headache and my bones ached so bad they felt brittle. My cheeks were tinged pink and I felt hot. The Motrin didn't do shit for my fever, but I pushed myself and kept my focus on point.

I yawned. I was most likely dehydrated, tired, and in need of sleep.

As I sat there in an old leo with chalk covering my body, I stared blankly at the wall and thought about how none of us really had time to rest. Not even the coaches. We were all focused and determined. I took every one of their orders and critiques with tight lips. Anything they said to do, I did. They hadn't criticized me for mistakes today, which was a first.

I glanced at the clock, wondering how much longer I'd be waiting, when Kova strode out. Our gazes met, and he let me see the sorrow he'd hidden all day.

"Ready?" he asked. I nodded and stood, feeling each step shooting through my bones as I followed behind him down the hall to the therapy room. Kova flipped on the lights and I walked toward the table and climbed up, waiting, watching. Just going through the motions.

He moved so quietly, meticulously, as he unwrapped the tools. He too was covered in chalk, his hat backwards, his back so beautifully shaped and strong. There was something intriguing about just watching him. Kova moved a tool to the side and the gleam of his wedding band reflected under the bright lights.

Air constricted in my throat. Emotion threatened to pour from me. We were alone, and the devastating, glinting symbol reminding me that he was taken gutted me. I wanted to ask him not to wear it around me, but that would show that I cared, and I was trying to act like I was indifferent.

Don't cry. Don't cry. Don't cry.

"You looked pale today, Adrianna," he said with his back still to me.

I rolled my eyes and stayed quiet, inhaling my feelings. Either he was dense or plain ignorant if he couldn't see how his actions had affected me.

When I didn't respond, he glanced over his shoulder. I just stared at him with an unreadable look on my face and an empty pit in my chest.

My head was all sorts of fucked up.

"Did you hear me?" he asked over his shoulder.

"Yes," I said, keeping my voice low.

Kova turned around and leaned back against the counter. We stared at each other, so many unspoken words hung in the air between us. He was itching to talk, but I didn't care what he had to say.

"You worried me today."

I didn't respond, just stared. His knuckles turned white as he gripped the counter behind him.

"So this is how it is going to be?" he asked.

"What do you think, *Coach*?"

Kova's jaw flexed, and his chin dipped deep and slow like he was aggravated. "Turn over," he ordered.

Turning around, I got on my stomach and propped myself up on my elbows. I felt my entire body sink like a stone with fatigue. Luckily this would only last fifteen minutes and then I could leave. I had my night planned out. Eat, shower, sleep. That way I wouldn't have time to think about anything.

Kova stood at the end of the table and pulled the tape off my calf and heel. He applied salve and massaged it into the sore muscle.

"Do you hurt anywhere?"

"No."

"I need an honest answer from you, Adrianna."

I stared at the white wall. "I have no pain, *Coach*."

His hands paused. "Why are you calling me Coach?"

"Because that's what you are."

"I have never just been Coach to you."

I kept my voice neutral and steady. "Well, that's what you are to me now."

His hands slowly moved up my calf like he was deep in thought. "I know you are angry with me, but I do need to know if your Achilles is acting up."

"Okay."

"Adrianna, I did not go through training for you to give me one-word answers and lie to me." His accent was so much stronger when he was annoyed. "I spent time and money learning to do this for you. It is important that I know."

There was so much I could say, but I wasn't going to.

"Okay, *Coach*."

Kova clucked his tongue under his breath. His hands pulled away and I heard the steel of the tools clash together. I knew he was frustrated with me.

Welcome to my life.

The chill of the metal touched my skin and I took a deep breath. This was going to suck, but on the plus side, I'd be ready and healed from the treatment for the meet this weekend.

Kova ran the concaved blade up and down my skin, pressing and smoothing out the calf muscle. After a few minutes, he said, "You are all red and inflamed." I didn't say anything. He moved down to my ankle and scraped around the hollow spots. "You are all gritty here..."

Kova didn't hold back, not that I expected him to, as he dug and cut into my skin like he was carving stone with a butter knife. I chewed the inside of my lip as I replayed my routines over and over in my head to block out the searing fucking agony. I swear, God hated me.

"You will be sore when I am done. Tomorrow we will go a little lighter with practice."

No, I needed the practice, the focus to take my mind off all the shit around me. "I'll take extra Motrin. Problem solved."

Kova paused. "You know you cannot have that while you are doing the plasma injections. No anti-inflammatory medication at all."

Shit.

I'd forgotten I couldn't take it and I'd been eating it by the handful. When I didn't say anything, Kova tapped my leg with his instrument.

"You have not been taking it, right, Adrianna?"

"Nope," I lied.

He went back to treating me, this time pushing a little harder. I didn't flinch, but it hurt so fucking bad.

"You are lying to me."

"I'm not."

I glanced over my shoulder and watched him. Focused, Kova's perfectionist fingers peppered over the instruments. His thumb slid up and down the edge of one tool I remember his sexy doctor friend, Ethan, said is more defined to get deeper into the grooves to even out overworked spots. Basically, it was going to be agonizing.

His bright platinum wedding band clashed with the dull silver and I glanced away.

I wish I didn't spot it every time I looked at him now.

"If you take any kind of anti-inflammatory meds, you will hinder the growth and recovery of your Achilles."

I was going to throw out every bottle in my condo when I got home. I may have made some questionable choices when it came to my love life, but I wasn't that dumb when it came to my health. I didn't want to further worsen my injury, but I had forgotten not to take it. Taking Motrin was like drinking water to me.

"I know you have it in your bag, and probably a bottle in your truck. I want them before you leave."

"Okay."

"Stop taking them," he said.

"I said I wasn't taking them."

"You are a terrible liar."

"I'm sorry. I'm not as well versed in the field of playing with people's emotions and lying to them as you are."

"That was a low blow, Ria."

"Adrianna. Call me Adrianna."

He waited a long minute before responding. "You make me out to be a monster," he said, sounding distant, and I despised my traitorous heart for feeling bad.

"You're two-faced. You did this to yourself. Now let's just get this over with so I can go home."

"We need to make time to talk. There are things you do not know."

"No. There's really nothing to talk about at this point. You lost your chance when I found out the way I did. You should've had the decency to respect me, but then again, you're Kova, and only care about yourself. From here on out, unless it's during practice and about gymnastics and my future in gymnastics, I don't want to speak to you at all."

He continued scraping around my ankle. "You cannot ignore me forever."

"I can."

"You are my gymnast—"

"And we only have to talk here or at meets." I paused. "Don't push me on this, *Coach*."

I rose up higher on my elbows and looked over my shoulder, letting my unsympathetic glower show him I wasn't playing around. At least I got one look correct today.

When push comes to shove and you're thrown off a bridge into a dark and frigid world of hurt, you find out how dirty you'll fight to keep your head above water. I wasn't wild and free anymore. I was a slave to myself and I trusted no one.

I would recover, but I'd never forget.

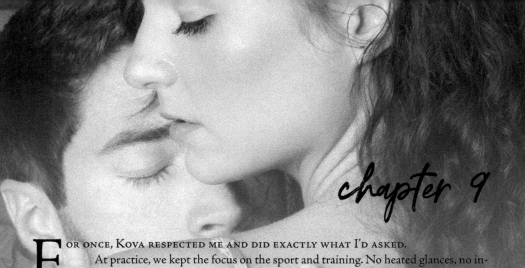

chapter 9

FOR ONCE, KOVA RESPECTED ME AND DID EXACTLY WHAT I'D ASKED.
At practice, we kept the focus on the sport and training. No heated glances, no in-side jokes, no lingering touches. He had listened, adhered to my wishes, and never once pressured me to talk to him. At night, he stayed home and didn't make midnight appearances at my condo like he had so many times in the past. I was secretly relieved because the moment I got home until I went to bed, I drowned myself in an endless pool of tears.

I could hardly sleep despite how fatigued I was. If it wasn't the exhaustion, it was the coughing that kept me up. Some nights I sat in a ball under a hot shower and sobbed, and in turn it would help ease the itch in my lungs. When I wasn't crying, I was in my head trying to figure out how naïve I was to miss that he'd gotten married. The only thing that came to mind was the night he'd been texting me when he was drunk and I'd thought it was cute. Now I didn't think that so much.

I didn't understand why I couldn't just move on, or why when I stepped over the thresh-old at my condo and the mask fell that the tears would come seconds later. Who knew some-one could be so empty inside and still cry their eyes out from holding everything in?

In the mornings I used an ice pack to bring down the swelling and all sorts of expensive creams to reduce the puffiness under my eyes. I even wore concealer to hide behind, something I'd never done. Wearing makeup to practices and workouts never made sense until this week. Makeup helped me hide the ugly truth.

About midway through the week I started to notice that Kova hadn't ridiculed me once during all the time we trained. And considering we spent close to ten hours a day together, it was noticeable. He didn't force me to do extra conditioning, he hadn't yelled at me, hadn't made me do my routines or skill over so many times to the point I lost count. He wasn't acting like his usual, dickhead self, and that concerned me.

Thing was, I might not have liked his dickish ways at first, but now I was used to it and I found that I thrived on it. So the fact that it stopped all of a sudden and I wasn't getting the same treatment I had been concerned me. It made me feel like he'd either gone soft on me, or just didn't give a shit about my career in this sport any longer.

He stayed focused and only spoke to me when we practiced, and when he trained someone else, he never looked in my direction. Usually I could feel his eyes on me, but not anymore. His eyes, though, had lacked the dazzling green I used to know and had come to love. He looked grim most of the week with dark circles under his eyes, but I chalked it up to him being wor-ried about the upcoming meets and how critical they were for all of us.

I wanted so badly to ask him what his deal was, but that would require actually speaking to him alone, and I didn't want to. I didn't want to show him concern or give him the chance for the conversation to go in a different direction. If I did, then I would weaken and cave. I didn't want to do that when I was struggling already to keep it together on the outside.

By late Thursday afternoon it was starting to bother me, especially since I had a meet coming up in less than two days. Madeline wasn't even riding me, and between both of them, my stomach was churning with self-doubt. I was past the point of being stressed out and was now dripping with insecurity. I felt like I wasn't doing enough, but I still refused to speak to him, so instead I pulled out the notebook and asked him one question.

Why are you being soft on me? I don't like it. Push me like you used to.

I slipped the notebook into his desk drawer, not expecting a response that night, but much to my surprise, he had replied before practice ended and left it in my bag. Thank goodness I'd read it at home and not before I got into my truck, because not only did I reread his previous note saying he was eternally sorry, the one he'd written before I'd thrown the book at his head, but his new, stupid response made me tear up.

You do not need it. You have been practicing better than ever before. I am in awe and cannot wait to see you compete this weekend.

As I sat on my bed fighting the urge to text him, my phone vibrated in my hand. I frowned, not recognizing the number and let it go. After listening to the voicemail, I realized it was my doctor calling from a different phone number. It sounded a little urgent so I called back immediately, only to get sent to their voicemail. I'd call her back again tomorrow.

I stared at my phone, debating whether to send Kova a text or not. He wasn't the type to lighten a workload when things were going well. Easy was not in his vocabulary. It was always go, go, go, especially during meet season. For him to write what he had did nothing to ease my worries. The last thing I needed was mind games before a competition, and Kova was king when it came to them. Taking the notebook, I shoved it into my nightstand and slammed the drawer shut.

Against my better judgment and my previous "No Contact" rule, I started to text Kova, but right before I hit send, a raging headache tore through my skull and the pressure in my eye sockets ached from the light in the room. It pierced right through me, and I gasped so hard I started coughing. I threw my phone down on my bed and immediately got up to turn out the lights.

Ten minutes later I was almost writhing in agony. The headache was so severe that my entire body felt heavy and sore. I could barely move. I couldn't focus on anything but the searing pain, which only intensified as the seconds passed.

I gave up and called Kova. Not texted. I needed help quickly and I knew he'd have an answer. He better, since I couldn't take Motrin like I wanted to.

He picked up on the second ring. "Adrianna?" His voice was groggy.

"I'm sorry to wake you, Coach, but I need your help."

"What is wrong? Are you okay?"

His tone turned to concern. I heard some shuffling in the background and Katja speaking in Russian.

"Yes, I'm okay, but I need to ask you a question."

"Okay. Hang on." Kova's voice was muffled for a second as he spoke off to the side, responding to his wife. "What is going on?" he asked.

"I didn't want to call, but I have an excruciating headache that came out of nowhere and my body is aching. Even my joints hurt so bad. I know you said I can't take any anti-inflammatory, but what can I do? I have a cold wet rag on my head but it's not helping. I think I have the flu."

"Why do your joints hurt?"

"I don't know, they just do."

"That is not normal, Adrianna. You have not done anything extra or out of the ordinary this week. Your body should not ache so badly."

I clenched my eyes shut. "I'm well aware of that. Thanks." I deadpanned. "Can I take Tylenol? What about Excedrin?"

"I would rather you not take any of that. Do you happen to have Epsom salt?"

"I don't know, let me go look."

"While you are looking, why are you up so late? You should be sleeping. Your body needs the rest."

I walked into my bathroom and squatted down to look under the sink for the bath salts without turning the light on. I shuffled some things around, but it was too dark to read labels.

"I'm tired, but I just can't sleep," I replied.

"But you have to try. You have practice in five hours."

"Yeah, I know."

When I couldn't find the salt, I flipped on the light and instantly felt sick. I groaned, holding my stomach, praying I didn't start vomiting. I almost dropped my cell phone.

"What was that?" he asked, worry in his voice.

"I had the lights off because of the headache, but I think I'm sensitive to the strong glare or something because this has been happening lately. When I turned the bathroom light on, it shot straight through me." I resumed looking and found it. "Got it. It says Epsom salt with soothing lavender…" My voice trailed off. I don't remember buying this.

"Perfect. I want you to take a lukewarm bath with the salt, nothing scalding hot that will burn your skin. Turn the lights off and light some candles. Lord knows you have plenty," he mumbled.

Sadness streaked through me at that. He did know me. I did have a lot of candles around my condo, almost on every surface.

"No medicine, though?" I asked, hopeful.

"No. You need to stop relying on that stuff anyway. You take far too much and are going to destroy your organs. I told you that you looked pale—"

Before Kova could continue, he was cut off by Katja. She was shooting off in Russian and speaking a mile a minute. Her voice rose, the pitch getting higher and higher. Kova cut her off and their voices became muffled.

They were arguing like they always seemed to. I could slightly sympathize with Katja. Slightly. It was late at night and another woman was calling her husband. If it were anyone else, I could understand her issue, but I was his gymnast, so I wasn't sure why she sounded so irate. I needed help, and he had to give it to me.

My stomach knotted and I tried to focus on something other than the cramps when I caught sight of a large clump of hair on the floor. My fingers pressed into the side of the tub. There were a lot, and I wondered how I hadn't noticed them before. I reached for my hair and tunneled my fingers through it, slowly pulling until I reached the end. Opening my hand, I saw that more strands had fallen out.

A door slammed through the phone and then Kova was back. It sounded like he was putting a few cubes of ice into a glass and for some strange reason I found something intimate about it.

"You know how you looked pale on Monday?"

"Yes. I know. You told me. What would you like me to do? Wear blush?"

He sighed into the phone. "Why do you get defensive?"

"I don't get defensive. I just don't care that I look pale. I'm not trying to impress anyone anyway, so what does it matter?"

"You are not sleeping, and your body aches when it should not. You do not look well. Do not blame me for being concerned."

I changed the subject. "How long do I soak for?" I didn't look well for a reason, and we'd done this song and dance before. I was not going back to it.

"Until it gets cold."

"Hang on," I said. I grabbed my candles, lit them, then stripped my clothes off and got into the tub. "I hate baths, by the way."

"I never understood why women take them, to be honest," he said. "You are soaking in your own filth."

A sad laugh unexpectedly rolled off my lips. "That's how I see it too. I would never take one if I didn't have to." I realized I was laughing with him and hardened my heart again.

"You put in what you have to now, even if you hate it, and you will be successful. Time, pain, your body. Your mind. It will all be worth it. One day you will wake up and ask yourself how you did it. *Kak vy popali iz tochki v tochku A v tochku Z*, got from point A to point Z. You will look back and question yourself over and over, and it will baffle you because you really will not know. You will feel good that you did not give in when shit got rough. I do that now. I have no idea how the hell I accomplished what I did. I cannot answer it, it is all a blur, but what matters is that I achieved my goals. You will feel the same way one day. I do not know of any pro athlete who regrets putting in the work. The result makes it all worth it."

I swallowed, thinking about what he said. I'd already spoken to him enough and gave him too much of my time.

Softly, I said, "I'm gonna go now. I'm sorry for waking you up, and I'm sorry for Katja getting mad. I'll see you tomorrow."

"Wait."

I paused, waiting, breathing hard but slow. I should hang up.

"Bye, Coa—"

"I did not go soft on you this week." He quickly got out. "You trained exceptionally well. Better than ever before. If I felt for a second that you needed more, you should know by now that I would never hold back, regardless of what happened between us. Inside World Cup, we are coach and athlete. Nothing more. Outside those doors, we are a big fucking mess that makes no sense. If that makes me an asshole, then so be it. I do not give a fuck. We already knew I was anyway. But I know what this, gymnastics, means to you. I would never take that from you. Ever. If anything, I would only push you harder."

I heard him take a sip of something and place his glass down. We were supposed to have nothing but honesty between us from the beginning, and now I questioned every word that left his sinful lips. He pacified me with fabricated words and feelings I craved from someone who I thought cared about me.

Lifting the stopper with my toes, I let the water drain and said, "I'll see you tomorrow afternoon. Bye, Coach."

I CHALKED UP MY HANDS THEN SPIT ON MY PALMS BEFORE SUBMERGING THEM BACK into the huge chalk bowl once more.

I moved them around under the mound of powdery chalk to build up a thick coat, clapped my hands together, and then pulled on my grips. Leaning my face into my shoulder, I coughed.

With vault under my belt, I had three rotations left for this competition: Bars, beam, then floor.

I was in first place after one rotation, which wasn't really a surprise. Vault was my specialty, and very few gymnasts could do what I could with a clean landing. I was only two-tenths away from a perfect score, but I'd take it. I had worked hard for that vault, no one was going to take it from me.

"Do you want me to spot you?" Kova asked when he walked up to the bowl.

I shook my head, flexing my fingers to make sure my grips were on just right. "Nope. I got this."

"Are you sure? I can be there if you need me, or if you would rather Madeline, she can as well."

It would be nice to fuck with Kova and have Madeline in his place, but I wouldn't go there. This was too important for both of us to play childish games.

"I'm good, Coach. Thanks," I replied as if I was talking about the weather.

Kova stared at me for a long moment, not blinking once. "Okay. If that is what you want."

"What I want never matters." With a saccharine smile, I walked away.

I was surprised by how much Kova had backed off. He hadn't so much as been flirty, or shown me a sarcastic side of him, and he hadn't given me any encouraging pep talks before each event. Even though I did sort of miss those little moments with him, I was relieved. It was helping me focus.

Between arriving at his house last night with the team, flying out of state, to now, we'd spoken maybe five words to each other. That showed me he had at least an ounce of respect for my boundaries.

Baby steps.

Reagan landed her dismount, her feet slamming into the mat. Chalk rebounded around her calves as she saluted the judges.

Taking a deep breath, I walked onto the mat and stared at the uneven bars, visualizing my routine. I let everything roll off my shoulders and exhaled what little nerves I had left.

My dismount was more difficult than Reagan's, but her routine had a slight edge over mine. It really came down to execution. Come next week, though, I had planned to add another element or two and a change to my dismount that would kick up my difficulty score by a lot. Once I mastered those skills, which shouldn't take more than a week, I'd outrank my teammates on vault and bars. I also had plans to add one more tweak to my floor routine that would put me in a league of my own.

Until then, now was the time to risk it all and do whatever it took to prove I had it in me to go the extra ten miles.

The judges gave me the green light and I raised my arms. Clearing my mind, I mounted the low bar. I had approximately forty seconds to complete seventeen skills effortlessly while floating from one bar to the next. With pirouettes and twists, and multiple release moves paired together for extra points, I pushed hard and moved freely and elegantly between the six-foot-width distance. My form was tight, with my body elongated in handstands, and toes pointed. I prepared for my dismount, tapping hard to gain momentum, and released on my second rotation. I soared through the air, flipping backwards and twisting, knowing in the back of my head I had to reach a height and distance acceptable for max points. Spotting the ground, I landed, sticking my dismount with both feet together. I swallowed, saluted the judges, and finally exhaled.

I felt good, really good.

Trying to catch my breath, I walked off the mat and peeled back the Velcro strips of my grips and replayed my routine, wondering if anything was off. I stepped down from the platform, shoving one grip and wristband under my arm when Kova rushed up to me with wide, wild eyes.

I glanced up and my movements slowed. Dread filled my stomach. Shit.

"How bad," I croaked.

His brows furrowed and he pulled back. "Bad? No." He almost laughed. "Not bad at all."

"Then why do you look so panicked?"

"I am speechless."

I pulled off my other grip and walked around him toward my duffle bag. "Your words are not matching your expression," I said sarcastically. "I hate when you get like this."

He brushed my comment off. "Between vault, and now bars, I just have never seen you perform so... incredibly."

I looked at him in confusion. "I've done well at previous meets, though."

"Yes, but not like this. This is perfection. This is not holding back. This is showing no fear. This is flawless and impossible to look away from."

His eyes were wide, luminous from excitement. I watched him pace as he spoke like he was in awe of my performance. A sliver of excitement curled in my veins. I felt his pull, the energy radiating off him. I looked at him and I knew I wore the same zealous look in his eyes. We were both bursting with triumph, though still reserved.

"Oh...thanks," I said, and went back to my duffle bag.

His eyes narrowed. Just as Kova opened his mouth to speak, the crowd exploded around us. My back straightened with his and we glanced around trying to figure out why they were roaring.

Kova's lips parted. I couldn't remember a time seeing his jaw slowly fall or his eyes enlarge like that. I followed his gaze and looked ahead.

Oh.

Oh.

Next to my name, and the event, was my score.

I almost didn't believe what I was seeing. I blinked again and looked.

I'd scored the maximum points allowed. For the first time, I'd gotten a perfect score, and I didn't know how to react, but Kova sure did.

He threw his arms in the air, his hands in fists like he'd just crossed a finish line. He spun around, looked down, and immediately caged me in a tight hug and hoisted me up.

"I told you. Flawless," he said, so damn happy in my ear. I had no choice but to go with it. His heart was pounding so hard against his chest I could feel it hitting mine. "You got a perfect score, and the first perfect score of the elite season. Do you have any idea how big this is?"

Jaw slacked, I shook my head in disbelief. A perfect score was a big deal, I just didn't know how to process such an achievement.

"Wow," I said under my breath.

He yanked me back, perplexed. "Wow? That is all you can say?" I glanced at the scoreboard again and felt the faintest smile tip the corner of my lips. "I am so damn proud of you," he said, pulling me back in for a hug so tight I grunted, then he put me down. My teammates and Madeline came over and high-fived me, congratulating me, and then we moved on to the next rotation.

I had to admit, it felt good to be the first elite of the season to obtain a perfect score, but I wasn't going to get my hopes up. Getting a score like that, where I maxed out on both the difficulty and execution categories, took a ton of effort and was not often seen twice from a gymnast at the same meet. It wasn't unheard of, just almost impossible to attain.

Floor came next, my favorite event. I decided I wasn't going to watch my team or anyone for that matter while I waited and warmed up.

"Do you need anything," Kova asked, walking up to me. Energy was radiating off him. "Feel confident?"

I shook my head and pursed my lips together. "I'm good."

Hands on hips, he squared his stance. "Perform like you have nothing to lose."

"I don't," I responded quickly. "I have nothing to lose. I'm going to do whatever it takes."

"Do not forget to smile."

I flashed a fake smile and his eyes twinkled. I wouldn't forget. Gymnastics was the whole reason why I smiled. Patting on a little chalk between my thighs and then some on my hands, I exhaled a tense breath and mentally prepared when I heard the warning sound.

Walking around Kova, I walked up the steps and onto the blue carpeted floor, toes pointed, I took my position and felt my soul come alive.

Floor was my absolute favorite. I'd done this routine hundreds of times and could perform it in my sleep. Now I was going to show the gymnastics world just how much I loved this sport, how much it meant to me, all with a healthy dose of cockiness. If I was going to win this event, I needed to prove it with a little sass and pride. I was going to move the world with my body.

The music chimed and I blocked out the background noise, letting my body take over. Through muscle memory, all those dreadful ballet classes, and hours upon hours of practice, I released every fiber in me. I danced light on my toes from corner to corner, allowing my passion to shine through. Balletic, effortless grace, whimsical body lines. With floor, it forced me to feel emotions whether I wanted to or not, and I needed that. I needed that release.

Leaping through the air, my heart flew higher than my body, and when I completed a neck-breaking tumbling pass, I didn't have to force myself to smile. My entire face lit up with happiness. I could feel it from the top of my head to the tips of my toes. If only I could share with the world how I felt inside when I performed. It was indescribable. It was a natural high and a rush like nothing else.

Ninety seconds later, I was ending my custom floor routine that left me more out of breath than usual but feeling incredible nonetheless.

I saluted the judges then walked off the floor. Madeline gave me two high fives and praise followed by my teammates. I took such a deep breath that a sharp pain shot through my chest, but I ignored it. Squatting down, I took out a carton of coconut water from my bag. My mouth was so dry I downed all of it.

I was still so thirsty and rummaged through my bag for another bottle when Kova's shoes appeared in my view.

"Everything okay?"

I glanced up. "Yes. Why?"

"You are frantically searching your bag."

"I'm just looking for my water…" My voice trailed off. "I thought I had another bottle of water in here." I stood up and looked around for the big cooler with paper cone cups that was kept at each event.

I turned around to tell Kova I'd be right back, but he was already walking away. He stopped in front of his belongings and reached down.

I gnawed on my bottom lip. He was going to give me his drink, I knew it, but I didn't want him to. I knew the thought was stupid, but I didn't want anything extra from him, even if it was something as simple as water.

Kova walked toward me with his arm stretched out. My mouth watered just looking at it and I took it. I didn't say thank you, though. All I could do was look him in the eye, uncap it, and chug half of it in one gulp.

He took two steps closer and my heart kicked up a notch. Lowering his voice, he said, "You are poetic when you perform. The way your body moves, your lines, the way you feel the music." He shook his head like he couldn't believe what he was thinking. He seemed so far away. "The way you let go and feel the sport, it was almost—"

Kova pressed his lips together. Whatever he was thinking caused his voice to shift and pause. I watched him, his gaze longing, as if he was savoring the memory. I almost wanted him to finish.

He swallowed, his Adam's apple bobbing. "Never mind. It is hard to tear my eyes from you. I could watch you for hours."

I scanned the large room of spectators, trying not to let my heart feel a thing when it came to his fake words anymore.

"Isn't that your job, Coach? To watch me?" I asked without looking at him.

He didn't say anything for a long while, and I finally looked at him.

"You just surprise me every day. Your performance was, once again, flawless."

I sucked on my lips so I wouldn't respond and squinted at the screen waiting on my score. In the past when the judges have taken long to release a score, it meant there were deductions, or they couldn't agree on something.

"What's taking so long?" I asked him, impatient. An ache began on the side of my waist, probably from anxiety, and I pressed on it in an attempt to ease it a little.

He looked over his shoulder at Holly. She still hadn't gone, but she knew better. Kova was adamant about the score being posted before the next gymnast competed. That way if he wanted an inquiry into the score, he could get one. If the next gymnast went, and a score came back for the previous gymnast after her rotation, he couldn't challenge it.

Finally, in what felt like an eternity, my score flashed above our heads just as I took a sip.

chapter 11

THE CROWD EXPLODED ALL AROUND US.

Slowly, I pulled the bottle from my lips as goose bumps ran down my arms. I recapped the water while I stared in absolute shock.

Underneath my name was a perfect score. By some miracle, I'd gotten the maximum points allowed for execution and difficulty for my routine again. I'd had a feeling I'd done well, but I didn't think I'd done *that* well.

I blinked a few times, hoping it wasn't a deception of my mind. Two perfect scores were almost too good to be true, and I was dealing with exhaustion. Hallucinations were possible.

Kova yelled, actually yelled in excitement, and pumped the air with his fist. I almost laughed. I'd never heard him make a sound like that before or seen him fist pump. He turned around, squatting until he was my height, and grabbed onto my shoulders, giving me a little shake. His entire face lit up and he started speaking in Russian.

I felt the slight pull at my lips again. Kova, like every other coach with their gymnast, yanked me up into his arms and squeezed me into a tight hug for my perfect score.

"Coach… Coach!" I said, tapping his shoulder to get his attention.

"Yes! What?!"

"You're speaking in Russian. I can't understand you."

Kova drew back. He hadn't realized he slipped into his native tongue and I found it comical. His eager green eyes sparkled under the arena lights and were full of adoration. There was a familiar stirring in my belly. I tried not to laugh, but it was impossible. I smiled and that produced an even bigger smile from him. In this room, Kova was happy, and for a brief moment, I was too.

Kova studied me. He threw his head back and a boisterous laugh roared from his chest.

"This is incredible! Two perfect scores! I am so proud of you!" he said, setting me down.

"Thanks," I replied, a little bashful. "I'm a little surprised."

"I am not."

He couldn't tear his eyes from me and his gaze lingered a little longer than usual.

"I gotta get ready for beam now," I said, and he nodded subtly. "I think Holly is waiting on you." Kova shot a glance over his shoulder, then back at me. "Okay. Your grin is starting to look creepy. Go see Holly." I joked.

"Wherever your head is at, keep it there. You are doing extraordinary."

"Easier said than done."

"I have complete confidence and belief in you. You may not see it, but you are far better than them. And I am not saying that just to bullshit you. When you let go and surrender yourself, you are absolutely magnificent."

Magnificent? Who said that anymore?

When I could feel the candid notes of his voice hit deep in my bones and wrap around me, it truly made me question who he was. It messed with my head. I wanted to believe Kova was a good person with a good heart, but in the back of my mind all I could see was his wedding band and the lies embedded into it.

An anxious feeling seeped into my blood stream and clung to me. I didn't like feeling his words in my heart, and that was what I needed to work on blocking out. His praise encouraged me to be the best version of myself. Inspiration increased the way energy brightened a room. Though, I knew this song all too well. Eventually the light would burn out, misery would set in, and the darkness would be the centerfold of my chest once again.

I sighed inwardly and regained my focus. My team rotated to the final event and I prepared mentally, releasing every anxious nerve and let go. Beam was all about controlling my thoughts and allowing muscle memory to step in. I needed to trust myself, but that was so much harder than it sounded.

Saluting the judges, I stepped onto the mat and placed both hands on the four-inch piece of wood that could make or break me. Grasping the apparatus, I steadied my soul and began.

Immediately, I moved into a series of required skills that took no more than ninety seconds. Agile leaps, smooth ballet steps that looked like I was dancing blindly, and combination skills that incorporated potentially paralyzing connecting flips. I remained focused despite the low pain throbbing under my ribs. Not one wobble or second of uncertainty. Not even when I completed triple turns on the tips of my toes. I was secure, without an ounce of trepidation, and it was liberating.

Standing at the end of the balance beam, all I had left was my dismount. I hurdled into a round-off back handspring, my feet pounding into the wood and my toes curling around the edge. I reached up to set up my dismount and pulled my knees to my chest, tucking tight to rotate backwards into a double back tuck. I spotted the ground and landed—both feet together, arms up—and squeezed every single muscle in my body.

But it wasn't enough, and my heart sank.

I could feel how compelled my body was from the weight of my landing to take a step out to regain my position. I held my breath and squeezed every muscle as tight as I possibly could and saluted the judges to show that I'd stuck my landing.

It only lasted a few seconds, but those few seconds felt like nine months. I lowered my arms and intended to release a quiet breath, only it flew out of me with a huge huff. Surprisingly, the smile stayed on my face as I walked off the floor. Even if I didn't place on this event, I was happy with my outcome. I didn't feel like beam owned me anymore and that was a feeling that was indescribable.

Kova was waiting for me the moment I stepped down the stairs. Before I could say a word, he pulled me into a bear hug and squeezed me until I could barely breathe.

"*Fantastika! Fantastika! Fantastika!*" Kova said. "*Ty sdelal neveroyatnoye!*"

"Thanks, Coach." I smiled as he put me down.

Kova's eyes flickered for a brief moment like I'd insulted him, but I needed to keep it that way, even though I was starting to feel bad.

"If those judges do not give you the max points, I will file an appeal."

My brows shot to my hairline. I coughed, covering my mouth with the back of my hand. Stupid chalk in the air.

"I did that well?"

He looked at me like I spoke a language he didn't understand. "Yes. By far the best."

I was speechless. Kova never applauded me the way he had today. Occasionally he would here and there like he did with the other girls, but not after every event or to this extent. Either he was being nice and trying to soften me, or he was telling the truth.

I wanted to believe he was telling the truth if he said he was going to appeal it. That required a large sum of money on the spot, a write-up of my entire routine where my coach felt I should have received the maximum amount of points, and a viewing of the video. And it had to be done in four minutes flat. I'd never had that happen before, but I didn't think it would come to that.

Madeline and the team walked over and congratulated me, just as we did with all the girls.

"Nice job, Big Red," Reagan said, and I smiled. "I hope you beat Sloan." Sloan Maxwell was one of the top three elites and currently in first on beam. While I outranked her on the other three events, beam was her specialty.

I waited anxiously next to Kova, wondering if my splits hit one hundred eighty degrees, if my pause in between was too long for bonus connecting points, or if I had enough connecting acrobatic and dance skills. His arm wrapped around my shoulder and he pulled me to his side. I thought nothing of this gesture, since it was another common thing among coaches.

Our heads were tilted up at the screen for the numbers. My hands were clasped in front of me, my fingers wrenched together and twisting with uncertainty while Kova stood stoically.

Finally, my score appeared on the screen overhead.

My heart dropped and I stepped back, stumbling on my toes. I stared in absolute shock, repeatedly blinking to see if I read the numbers correctly. I hadn't gotten the maximum points, but I didn't have many deductions and received the highest score due to the difficulty in my routine.

"You did it! Adrianna! You did it!" Kova said, shaking my shoulders excitedly. I'd never come in first in all four events at a meet, let alone at an elite meet.

He pulled me into a hug and kissed my cheek. My arms wrapped around his shoulders and I closed my eyes, dropping my face into the curve of his neck. We were the cliché coach and gymnast the way we cheered together. In this moment, I couldn't hate him. In this moment, what happened to me, happened to the both of us, and it was something we should share together.

With his lips next to my ear, he said, "See what happens when you trust in yourself and let go? You shined out there. You pushed and pulled and got what you wanted through all the chaos, because you are fierce and wild and strong and have what it takes to go far. I knew you could do it."

Kova released me and Madeline walked up, pulling me into a hug next, but our connection was too strong to sever. We couldn't tear our eyes from each other, even as Madeline hugged me. Kova stared a minute longer and then turned away, taking my heart with him.

"Tell me, what was going through your mind?" Madeline asked, her eyes sparkling.

I paused, contemplating an answer. I became fearless after I'd become foolish, emotional, and on the verge of losing everything. I found strength because I had no choice. I did it, not just for myself, but for the one thing that kept me going—and feeling worthy enough since I was a child—gymnastics. When I hit rock bottom, it handed me the courage I was unknowingly holding back and armed me with the confidence I needed to attempt such a daring endeavor.

I looked at her and went with what was in my heart. "It's not just myself that I'm doing this for. I'm doing it for you guys too. I remembered who I was, what I wanted, and I changed the game."

Madeline cupped my jaw and smiled again. "Well done, sweetie."

"Well, that was impressive," Holly said. She'd walked up next to me and we began pulling on our sweats together.

"Thanks," I said, zipping up my duffle bag. "It's surreal, you know?"

"Oh, yeah. I bet it is. I can't imagine."

"What do you mean?"

A dim smile shown on her face. "I've never medaled in all four events in one meet before."

"Oh." I hadn't known that.

"It's not easy." She paused, acting a little covetous. "Congrats, girl."

I wasn't sure what to think of it other than I knew I needed to remain humble. Being knocked from medal contention would be devastating, which is what happened to Holly today.

Throwing my bag over my shoulder, I zipped up my sweat jacket and wiped the excess chalk from my hands. I watched my coaches and teammates walking ahead of us, and thought about how the series of events played out today. It was medal time, then after dinner we'd be boarding a plane to fly back home.

Kova peeked over his shoulder and our gazes immediately found each other's. A flutter started in my heart. He had his bag slung over his back, gripping the strap tightly in his fist. A moment passed between us, his green eyes filled with so much adoration that I stumbled. Even though I resented him, he was a still huge part of my accomplishment. I knew the right thing to do was to express my gratitude, even though it hurt me to.

A timid smile tugged at one corner of my mouth. I didn't want to give him an inch because he'd take a mile, but I couldn't not. I didn't have that in me, not today. Kova caught it and his shoulders relaxed. Nodding subtly, he turned around.

I knew success could go one of two ways: drown in darkness and lose yourself, or swim in the light and bask in the glory. It came from a series of events that I did consistently to reach achievement, but also one moment that would test me to the point of breaking. And that's what had happened. I'd been backed up against a wall with the anxiety of losing everything because of someone else's actions. No one could win for me. I had to win for myself. I had to want it bad enough. I had to drop everything and listen to that voice in my head that told me to give it my all. I couldn't think about trying again tomorrow. I had to stay focused and worry about right now. So that's exactly what I did. I fought hard and gave it my all. I had what it took. I had the want, and I had the drive. I wouldn't let anything stand in my way.

It was going to take everything from me...

Just like Kova had.

chapter 12

I FELT HIM BEFORE I SAW HIM.

I glanced over my shoulder just in time to see Kova sauntering up to me. I raked my eyes down the length of his body, taking him in. Butterflies swirled in my stomach when he was around and that was not a good thing. It was downright tortuous. Talk about swagger. He was so fucking sexy and I hated that he had it in spades.

I looked away and fixed the rubber bands on my grips that held the straps back and played it cool. I didn't think I'd ever become immune to him, but we'd gotten better at keeping a platonic relationship with each other. Or at least I had thought so.

Kova stopped in front of me. He eyed me for a minute. Something was spinning in the back of his head.

"What do you say we change up your dismount on bars?" he suggested.

"What do you have in mind?"

"A blind full to a laid out full-out."

Eyes wide, my brows shot up. While a blind change was a popular combination right before the dismount to get a couple tenths bonus added—it was just changing the way I gripped the bar mid swing—the laid out full-out was what concerned me. I had been practicing it here and there, but I wasn't sure I was ready to incorporate it into my routine any time soon.

I was already doing a full-in—a double back tuck with a full twist. Now, he wanted me to do the same thing, except with a straight body. Both were difficult, but the laid out was much harder.

"You think I could do that? And change it midseason?"

His forehead creased as if I had asked him the dumbest question in the world. He didn't bother answering me.

"I also thought we could work on a layout Jaeger to an L-grip, then straddled Jaeger."

My jaw dropped. "As in one combination?" The L-grip was so awkward to use, not to mention difficult. And I wasn't sure I had the core strength for two Jaegers back-to-back.

He nodded, again giving me the same look like I was a raging moron. "I want to up the stakes and make you unbeatable on bars. Maybe throw in a hop full and stalder or two."

"So you want to completely change up my routine. Basically, you want to re-choreograph it."

I caught Reagan in the corner of my eye watching us, but I didn't pay her any attention.

Kova crossed his arms in front of his chest and glared at me. "Do you have a problem with that?" His voice was stern and authoritative.

My jaw bobbed. "No."

"Good." He clapped his hands together and walked away. Picking up a thick, mesh royal blue landing mat, he placed it in front of the high bar. The mat would absorb my landing and not create a shock from the impact. Perfect for the injury I was trying not to irritate even more.

"Let us get to work. I estimate, at most, a week for you to master this skill."

It was one thing to swap out a skill midseason. Most gymnasts will work skills during off-season and won't put them in until they build up their endurance. It was another thing completely to change my entire routine. If Kova wanted to do that, I would learn this dismount in three days flat.

"For this dismount, you need to stay completely hollow in the tap and not open up too soon. It will give the bar a bend, not a whole lot, so do not get too excited. But it will give your chest a nice pronounced arc position so when you kick, you will get the height you need in flight and be able to easily complete the rotation."

The women's bar hardly gave any bend or slack the way men's did, so it was harder to use the bar in the way we needed. We just had to work more for it.

"We will start with straight body double layouts. We need to get your timing right."

I nodded and headed over to the chalk bowl, where Reagan already was powdering up.

"Morning quickie?" she asked drily. Here we go. "I like morning quickies. In and out and you're good for the day." She kept her voice low for only us to hear. "Looks like Kova had a good one with that pep in his step and all. He actually seems happy for once."

I pursed my lips together. "You must not be getting the right dick if you need pills to get you through the day."

She sneered. Thankfully she left and walked to another a set of uneven bars. Spraying the palms of my grips with water, I placed them in the powder and envisioned what I was about to do, then I clapped my hands to dust off the excess, only to repeat the motions two more times for good friction. The chalk floated in the air, tickling my nose.

Standing in front of the low bar, I looked at Kova, who stood behind the high bar to watch my landing. He was close enough to also train Reagan on the other set of bars next to me. She glared at us, resentment dripping from her for Kova giving me attention. I had to tune her out.

"You need a fast giant. That is going to be key here. Fast turnover for proper layout."

I nodded. Kova wasn't giving me any wiggle room. He wanted fast giants, but he was only allowing me to do two. Drawing in a big breath, I had to dig deep.

Mounting the low bar with a standard glide kip—body extended forward, hips flat—I quickly moved my legs to a pike position and my toes to the bar until my hips swung back. I dragged the bar to my shins and thighs and pulled up so my arms braced snuggly at my sides where I swiftly stood. Looking up, I reached for the high bar and completed another kip, casted to handstand, and tightened my body before circling down to complete two full three hundred and sixty degree rotations. Just as my feet passed the low bar, I tapped my toes, kicking them up hard to gain as much momentum as I could and released, performing two back flips with a straight body onto the soft landing mat.

"That was shit. Your legs separated, your hips were closed, and you did not have enough amplitude in flight, which resulted in your chest being low. Again."

I mounted again, and when I reached the high bar, I took a deep breath and swung down.

"Chest… Chest… Hollow out."

He said each word with each swing. I landed and it was better, though nothing to phone home about.

"Again. We need more of a scoop in your back swing. Once you are vertical, you can hyperextend your chest in the forward swing." He explained, using his hand, then he looked at Reagan as I chalked up again. I watched his face as he watched her, proud and pleased at her level of skill and execution.

Back up on bar, I did exactly as he instructed.

"Pay attention to your form. Your flyaway will look more beautiful and, more importantly, it will prevent injury. I know the urge to arch your back is there but resist it."

The urge was there. Just like the urge was there to whip my hips too, to stick my head out, to add another giant. There were so many things I wanted to do that I felt would help me, but in reality they would only set me back or give me deductions. Form was everything, but so was listening to my coach. All I had to do was listen to him the first time and it would all work out.

I nodded, feeling a tad more confident. Doing a double layout was nothing new to me— I'd done it before, I just didn't practice it often enough to incorporate it into my routine just yet, let alone adding a full twist.

Using his hand, Kova bent his fingers to represent my body. "Tap at about forty-five degrees horizontal and release. Toes pointed toward the ceiling when you release." His hand represented a partially opened L as he looked into my eyes and gave me instructions.

I nodded.

"You are not releasing after your tap. Do you want me to spot you?"

Though he had an eagle eye, it still blew my mind he could see that because I couldn't even feel that I didn't tap hard enough. Of course, I didn't want him to spot me, I wanted to prove I could do it on my own, but I also didn't like the idea of releasing so soon.

"Yes."

"Do you want to do it in the foam pit?"

"No, I can do it here."

By the gleam in his eyes, it was the answer he wanted, and deep down that made me feel good.

Kova moved to stand closer to me and it made me jump. "Relax for me," he whispered, and he placed one palm on my chest and the other on my upper back between my shoulder blades so they were parallel to each other. My hand brushed his thigh and I quickly moved it out of the way, lacing my fingers in front of me.

"Raise your arms." I put them above my head next to my ears. Kova pushed my back forward just slightly so my chest stuck out. "You will hyperextend your body in the forward swing so you are open"—he pushed my chest in and snapped it back—"and you will hollow out like this when you tap and release. Got it? Legs glued together, toes pointed, and lock your knees."

"Got it."

"It is very important to do as I say, otherwise you could land too short and risk an injury to your ankle or knee. That is the last thing we need after coming so far."

I nodded. Guilt hovered over me like a black cloud. If he only knew the kind of pain in my ankle I dealt with at night when I was home.

"I know."

"Spot the ground and land with your knees slightly bent, straighten them out, raise your arms, then salute."

"Got it."

I dropped my arms and Kova walked back toward the high bar where he stood with his legs open and ready for quick measure.

I dusted my hands with more chalk and processed what he said. Right before I mounted the low bar, I glanced up from the heavy weight of Kova's stare and met his eyes while picturing the skill in my head.

It was like he knew what I was thinking, because he comforted me by saying, "I will be right here spotting you."

My bottom lip rolled between my teeth and I nodded. Within a few seconds, because that's all it really took to get to the high bar, I sucked in a breath and cast to a handstand, listening exactly to what my coach said no matter how scared it made me. If my grip slipped and Kova missed catching me, which I highly doubted he'd let happen, at least I'd hit the soft-landing mat and it wouldn't be bad. As long as I didn't land on my neck. Trying a new skill the first couple of times was always nerve-wracking. I feared I'd miss the bar, or I wouldn't get enough height and hit the bar coming down, or that I'd panic midway and do something crazy. But having Kova standing there placed a level of security and encouragement I needed.

Two giants and I released when he told me to, feeling for the right timing. I spotted the floor in rotation, Kova prepped, ready to catch me with his arms raised in the air. A little nervous, I kept calm so I wouldn't freak out mid-rotation. I had to have faith in my coach and myself, even when I was terrified.

But I landed. On my own.

On. My. Own.

Excitement hit me hard and I immediately looked at Kova with a beaming smile. My landing was a little messy, but at least I did it. The first time was always the hardest and scariest.

Of course Kova didn't smile. In the gym he was on autopilot and incapable of feeling.

"Not too bad considering you are an elite, but nothing we could take to a meet, that is for sure. We need to perfect your timing. Get back up there and let us do it again."

I was still smiling. I was happy that I was able to do it the first time. When you let go of everything to make a courageous decision, you saw the greatest reward in gymnastics and gained the confidence to do more.

Kova playfully slapped my shoulder and pushed me in the direction of the low bar. His eyes lightened, and he said, "Go."

After completing so many double layouts that I lost track of the number, Kova was ready to move on to the next step. I was getting a little tired again, and for once, I was hungry, but I wasn't going to tell him that. We were on a roll and I didn't want to stop.

"I'm just going to grab some water and go to the bathroom. Is that okay?"

"Yes, just do not take too long."

I nodded then skipped out of the gym to the locker room. Shuffling through my bag, I searched for my little orange friends, when it dawned on me... I'd gotten rid of all the Motrin because of the treatment I had to my Achilles.

I groaned inwardly, annoyed as hell. I wouldn't last all day, not with how intense the pain already was. Maybe Kova had something I could have.

I went searching for Kova and found him standing by the bars. He looked down at me when I approached his side.

"Good. You are back."

"Um, actually..." I twisted my fingers together, hoping he wouldn't shoot me down. "Do you have anything I could have that's at least similar to Motrin? I know I can't take it, but my ankle is killing me and I have a headache."

"Follow me."

Thank goodness he understood how important anti-inflammatory was in a gymnast's life and didn't ridicule me for it. Eagerly, I followed behind Kova out of the gym and to his office. He opened the door and flipped on the light, then walked behind his desk where he opened a few drawers as I stood off to the side.

"I am glad you came to me instead of just taking them."

I gave him a tight-lipped smile. Just as he found the bottle, a light knock sounded and I turned to see who was there.

Katja.

chapter 13

"**K**ONSTANTIN," KATJA SAID IN A WAY OF HELLO.

"Katja, what are you doing here?"

She tilted her head to the side, her eyes narrowing. "Did you forget we had a lunch date?"

Kova gave her a blank stare. He had clearly forgotten about their lunch date. Looking toward me, he threw the bottle in an underhanded throw and I caught it.

"Oh, Adrianna, I did not see you standing there." Her eyes raked down my body. I was in nothing but a leotard and covered in chalk. "Have you lost weight?"

I shifted on my feet and gave Kova a fleeting look of unease. "Uh, I've been working really hard and might have lost a few pounds, but I also put on some muscle mass," I lied. I mean, I was working myself to the bone, but I didn't think I had lost any weight.

She looked down at my hands, then toward Kova. "You give all the gymnasts medication?"

If she only knew the kind of pills he's given me.

"You do not know, and you will never understand, what a gymnast's body goes through. That"—he pointed toward me and I opened my palms, the bottle rolling in my hands—"is an athlete's elixir. They need it to survive in this world. Lord knows I still wake with pain every morning."

I had no idea Kova was dealing with the aftermath of being a professional athlete. He'd never once complained before or appeared to be in any sort of pain. More concerning, I also didn't understand the hostility in his voice toward her.

She looked toward the floor, her lips pursed tight in annoyance.

Kova glanced my way and gave me a look that said he needed to be alone with Katja. Kind of the way my dad would give me the look, the one every child never wanted to see from a parent.

"Ah, it was nice seeing you, Katja. I have to get back to practice."

She didn't respond.

I sent a silent thank you toward Kova and went back to the locker room. Once there, I read the label and grumbled. This was a natural remedy and probably not nearly as strong as the real stuff. Still, it was better than nothing. I popped a couple of pills and took a swig of coconut water, then shoved everything into my locker.

Hushed voices carried down the hall as I exited the locker room.

"But, Konstantin, you promised to have lunch with me," Katja complained.

"I am sorry, Katja, but I cannot leave now."

"Why not?"

"I am in the middle of training Adrianna on a new dismount. I cannot go."

Katja's voice hardened. "You have not spent any time with me in weeks, and whenever we do have plans, something always comes up. I am your wife. Why are you treating me this way? You treat me like I do not mean anything to you."

I tiptoed toward the door and hid behind the frame. I couldn't help the curiosity.

"You have the audacity to walk into my gym and demand why I am treating you this way? You know why, Katja. You are not my wife, not in the real sense of it anyway. You forced this lie upon us. You forced my ring on your finger. I will never forgive you for making me do this." Kova's voice was laced with malice, causing confusion to swirl through my head.

"You never put me first and it is getting tiring."

"You feel like I put you last? That is because I *am* putting you last." The brutal honesty was startling. I cupped my mouth. "It is where you belong."

"You say I have audacity? Look at what you have done. At least I am putting effort in and trying to make it work." She sighed. "It is what it is, Konstantin, why not make the best of it? I am here, and, after all, I love you. At least give us a chance. You promised me all those years ago. We have always been destined to be together."

"You are okay being married to a man who is not in love with you, Katja?" Kova said with a hint of disgust.

My eyes widened. Nothing but absolute shock registered inside of me. It took a lot of nerve to tell a person they'd been with for years and years that they weren't in love with them. While I didn't think Kova was *in love* with Katja, I did think he loved her. He had to, even if just a little. No one married for shits and giggles.

Nothing made sense.

"In time you will see that we are meant to be. I am here, Konstantin. Right here, every single day, trying to do what is right. I love you and I want you. I know what I did was wrong, but I know you can forgive me, just like I have forgiven you for what you did. Your sins are far worse than mine. It will take time, but I believe we will be fine. So, do what you have to do. Take out your frustrations on me. Use me."

I stared at the floor, waiting in silence, hoping he wouldn't actually use her.

"Fine. You want me to use you, Katja? Take off your clothes and get on your knees."

My stomach dropped. I should've known. Bile rose to my throat as I heard what I could only assume was the shuffling of clothes coming off. I needed to leave, but I couldn't stop listening.

"I will do whatever you want, Konstantin," she said, her voice brittle.

I couldn't help but wonder what had happened between them, and why Kova said that Katja forced his hand. It sounded like their whole marriage was a sham, and deep down I wasn't sure how I should feel about that.

"Do not talk."

His cold words were distant, and if I wasn't listening, or I didn't know the sound of his voice, I wouldn't have pegged that as Kova.

"Katja, we may have come to this country to build our life together, but things have changed. We both have changed, and nothing will ever be the same. Now, get me hard and open your mouth."

Thick gasps and Russian words whispered through the air. I had to get out of there, the sounds, their voices, their words, were making me ill. But what set me over the edge was the sound of grunting, followed by a soft yearn of a moan that reminded me of sex.

"*Ty moya lyubimyy.*" He spoke only for her ears, his tone instantly reminding me of when he said *prosti* to me, and it made my heart drop.

I kept my eyes trained on the linoleum as I made my way back to the gym. I wondered how often Kova and Katja had sex in his office at World Cup during training hours.

My head was foggy, like I was trying to feel my way through a cloudy maze with no more than a foot of visibility in front of me. I didn't know what to think anymore other than it was all a game to Kova. It had to be. What he made me feel, he made Katja feel the same too. What he told me, he told her too.

He made me admit to myself that I loved him. It wasn't fair. It was vindictive and unforgiving.

Stepping back into the gym, I looked up and spotted Hayden. He gave me a tentative smile, but I couldn't find it in me to return the gesture. I wasn't sure how long my coach's romp would be, so I decided to work on the double layouts on the high bar over the foam pit instead of on the uneven bars. I hated climbing out of that thing, but I didn't have my coach there to spot me.

I also wasn't in the right frame of mind to risk landing on the actual floor. So there was that.

Coming up from the pit, Hayden was there waiting with his hand out. He was covered in chalk and looking so cute. My heart dropped for the second time in less than an hour. I missed my friend.

"Thanks," I said.

"I see he's got you working on a new dismount."

"Yeah."

We stood there, studying each other. It shouldn't be this weird between us. Yes, I'd had sex with my best friend, but there was a whole other issue we had to deal with.

"Where's your coach?"

"He's on lunch break. Yours?"

"Banging his wife in his office." I rolled my eyes, trying not to show how hurt I was knowing what Kova was doing—that he *would* do that—right now.

Hayden's brows shot up and his eyes flickered with mischief. Stepping closer, his breath tickled the curve of my neck. "Meet me in the locker room?" he whispered.

I tilted my head just slightly. A deep blush filled my cheeks.

"Please, Aid. We should talk. Let me explain myself and then we can have a happy ending." He smirked and I got the hint loud and clear.

"Hayden," I whispered. "Anyone could walk in there."

"Come on, let's go."

I stopped him and got serious. "Only if you tell me the truth about you and Reagan. I tell you everything, so it's only fair you tell me about the pills."

He hesitated for a split second, then agreed. "It's not like I sell pills to tons of people." Hayden kept his voice low as we walked toward the lobby. "And I'm not a dealer by any means. I only sell to a handful of people, and one of them is Reagan. She gets Adderall to focus and painkillers I never use."

I looked around nervously. No one could hear us, but I was still paranoid. "Why can't she just go to the doctor to get it herself?"

"Because you can't just walk into a doctor's office and ask for specific medication, and from what she's told me, she's tried and has been refused. I get a small pharmacy of medication every month, so does Holly. I sell Reagan what I have."

We stepped into the lobby and Hayden took my hand in his, pulling me toward the locker room. Drawing closer to Kova's office door, I shot a glance in that direction, my heart instantly dropping into my stomach, twisting into a dozen knots when I heard something fall to the floor. I forced myself to look in the other direction. They weren't loud, but since we were right across the hall, and I knew what was happening, I couldn't stop myself from thinking about it.

Swallowing thickly, I asked, "Does Holly know?"

"No, and she never will."

I shook my head as we stepped into the locker room. "But why, Hayden? Aren't you worried about being caught?"

"I need the money. There's a whole story you don't know about, and I'm not about to go into detail right now." His face hardened, telling me not to push him on the matter. "There was a time when Holly and I had to live with Kova and Katja. They took care of us until my parents and Kova could come to an agreement. We needed money and gymnastics doesn't allow for a part-time job, so I decided to do what I could and started selling my prescriptions."

My brows shot to my hairline. What else in the ever-loving hell went on inside the walls of World Cup that I didn't know about? Hayden and Holly lived with Kova? That was a huge bomb to drop with no time to process it, let alone ask questions.

"I'm not a bad guy," Hayden said, quietly shutting the door and turning the lock I never even knew was there.

"I never took you for a bad guy."

Hayden pushed me up against a wall and his gaze lowered. I left everything outside the locker room in that moment and closed my thoughts off. I had to if I was going to do this. Pressing his body to mine, he said, "I'm not hurting anyone. We need money to live, and this helps out. Did I answer enough questions?"

"I don't agree with what you're doing, but I get it. I'd just rather not know about it."

"Deal," he said, then slanted his mouth over mine.

"Hayden," I whispered, breaking the kiss. "What if we get caught?"

"Don't worry. We won't. No one will know."

For a split second I got the feeling he'd done this before, but I dropped it because I didn't want to fight with him again.

Oddly enough, he was prepared, condoms and all. It didn't take us long, maybe five minutes tops from start to finish. I had Hayden take me from behind so he didn't have to see the anguish split across my face. He didn't argue and told me it was his favorite position anyway. It was the definition of a quickie, and it was my first.

"We should try to sneak in here more often," Hayden said, and I just nodded. I hadn't even been wet and he didn't notice.

We went our separate ways and I chalked up, feeling more tense than relieved and I wanted to scream. I didn't know what I was thinking, but I should've never agreed to go with Hayden. I'd yet to have an orgasm the way I did with Kova and it was starting to bother me. I could hardly get myself off the way he did, so I wasn't sure why this time would be any different.

Fixing my leotard, I climbed onto the tall blocking mats and gripped the high bar. I felt the pull in my shoulders and sighed, feeling good. I inched my way across, chalk dust sprinkled down my face, then I did a pullover so my thighs were resting on the bar.

Rebounding off with my hips, I swung down and performed giant after giant first. I needed that free-floating speed to feel like I was flying so fast that everything I was holding inside was banished from within me. Gymnastics was all about having the courage to hang on but the strength to let go. I wish I knew how to apply that to my personal life.

When I was alone and in my head, it only took me seconds to break down and weaken emotionally when I needed to be brave and strong. Swinging on the high bar gave me just that, and it was why I tried to spend as much time at World Cup as I could. An adrenaline high was rushing through me, making me stronger and bolder…and I loved this feeling. It was one I chased and inhaled into my lungs.

Letting go, I did a flyaway into the pit. I climbed out and got back up, this time getting right to business and completed a double layout. I lost count of the amount of practice dismounts I completed—a blessing, since the last thing I wanted was to keep track of how long Kova was having sex with Katja.

"Now, when you are on the second layout, you are going to clap."

Surprised, I looked up from the foam pit. The devil himself stood with his hands on his hips glaring down at me. My stomach was in knots and I could barely look at him.

"Look who decided to grace me with his presence," I deadpanned.

Kova continued to glare. "On the second layout—"

"Oh, we're going there. Got it." I couldn't believe he was going to act like nothing had happened. I had planned to do that since I was just as guilty for eavesdropping, and more, but the way he walked up and acted like he had done nothing more than grab a drink of water seriously got me revved up.

"Adrianna."

"What?" I snapped. Kova reached down with an opened hand, but I didn't take it. I hid my disgust with both him and myself and got out on my own. I stood in front of him and fixed my leotard. The foam pit always gave me a wedgie.

"On the second—"

"I heard you the first time." I cut him off again. "What do you mean, clap? Like an actual clap?" I'd never heard of that before. I literally pictured a clap.

"Yes, like an actual clap," he said. "When you are flipping, it is sometimes hard to get your hands together because of inertia, but it is a good drill to get your timing right so you know when to start twisting. Once you are in rotation, your body will want to keep going that way. It will take an external force for you to change the direction of that motion, and clapping at your center"—he looked at my torso and pointed to near my belly button—"say right there, will help you with that."

"Huh." You learn something new every day. "Did you learn this in Russia with your lunatic coaches?"

He lowered his eyes, unimpressed. "No, at the Olympic Training Center."

chapter 14

I PURSED MY LIPS TOGETHER AND WALKED TO THE CHALK BOWL, RUBBING SOME CHALK onto my hands before getting onto the bar.

I swung up and straightened my arms at my sides until the bar rested on my hips, and visualized a clap on the second layout. I stared down at the giant pit of square foams. It didn't seem too difficult. Usually my arms were glued to my sides in a double layout.

"Adrianna."

I glanced down my shoulder to where Kova was standing.

"Just do a double. I will call out when you should clap."

I nodded. "That's a good idea."

Casting to a handstand, I swung around the bar twice and let go, listening for his direction. Right at the beginning of my second back flip he yelled, "Now!"

Bringing my hands up to clap was much harder than I anticipated. My stomach tensed and the force of gravity worked against me. I wasn't expecting that.

Landing in the pit, I popped up and reached for his hand. He yanked me out and I nearly flew into him.

"Awkward, right?"

My eyes widened. "Yes. It was kind of a rush."

"But now you have an idea where you need to clap, yes?"

I nodded and turned around. It was going to take a ton of these drills to get the timing right. I could already tell.

"Ah, Adrianna?" I looked over my shoulder just before I added more chalk to my hands. "Let us practice these over there." He hooked a thumb over his shoulder toward the uneven bars. "I do not want you getting used to it on the high bar with so little time to practice."

I followed him and stopped, my back to the low bar. I didn't need to say what I required of him, he knew to hoist me up so I could reach the high bar. Kova stood behind me and placed his hands on my hips. Nothing unusual for a coach to be this close, but the heat coming from him right before he lifted me didn't go unnoticed.

"Are you okay?"

I nodded.

I knew what he meant and that was all the thought I was giving it right now.

Once I was mid-flight, I clapped on the second layout. It was a much different landing than I prepared for and I felt a little shock shoot up my ankle. My form wasn't so great, but that was expected the first time.

I grunted, grabbing my ankle. He picked up the mat and placed it under the bar without having to ask. "Are you in pain?" he asked, bent over adjusting the mat to the right place.

"No." I shook my head, looking past him to the girls on the balance beam.

I refused to look at him. I was too embarrassed. Reagan was over there with Holly and Madeline. I stood beneath the bar again, waiting. Coming up behind me, his hands found my hips again. This time they sat lower, his fingers splayed out, softly touching my bikini line, his thumbs just barely above my ass. I drew in a quiet breath and waited until his hands slid up to grasp me.

But they didn't. Kova stepped closer to my backside until I felt the front of his hard body against me. His hot breath rolled down my neck and I swallowed.

"Do not be upset with me. It is not what you think. Far from it," he whispered only for my ears. "I knew you were standing there listening," he added. My heart crashed like dead weight into my gut and I instinctively took a small step forward, but he stopped me by pressing his fingers into my skin. "One day you will understand."

"You are seriously the worst human alive," I said. "You make me regret ever meeting you."

"We do what is required to get through each day to survive. Some days are harder than others, and we may not be able to look at ourselves in the mirror, but we do what we have to do."

My nose flared. He was testing me. I glanced around nervously. We were too close, way too close, and it made my heart rush. Without saying a word, I raised my arms to see what he'd do. Much to my relief, Kova lifted me up, but not how he should have.

He purposely slid me slowly along the front of his body. I fit against his every curve and I held my breath in anticipation. "I did not come," he breathed into my ear.

He wasn't lying. I felt every hard inch of him. I closed my eyes, trying not to feel what he was doing. I wanted to let go of the bar and drop to the floor so I could push and shove and curse him out.

Of course, I didn't.

His hands slid down my thighs way too seductively, and his fingers grazed the bare skin near my ass. He wanted me to feel him, but I pretended like I didn't and kept my focus trained straight ahead. I bit down on the inside of my lip until I tasted blood and pulled myself up.

Up on the bar, I cleared my mind and visualized the clap to begin, putting my entire being into the skill, and landed without a balance check. It was like my way of saying fuck you, asshole.

"Clap sooner next time." I nodded and padded on more chalk. "You train better when you are angry," he said quietly, standing behind me again.

Anger. Hurt. Hostility. It all made me see things clearly. It also compelled me to focus more.

"You're a master manipulator. Let us go." I mocked him and raised my arms, waiting to be lifted. He wasn't impressed with my crappy attempt at a Russian accent. I sighed. I had no right to snap considering he was married, but he knew how to get under my skin like no other.

This time when I did the double layout clap, I set my timing sooner and felt a noticeable difference.

"Good. Do that again." Back up on bar and ready to go, I saw Kova crouch down from the corner of my eye. He was in the zone and it was seriously hot seeing him like that. Elbows on knees, he scrutinized me. The moment I landed, he jumped straight up. "Excellent! Just like that. Again."

I didn't want him to see me smile, so I quickly turned around. Seeing him happy that I was able to execute his directions made me insanely ecstatic inside.

We were so toxic yet so perfect together. I wish he hadn't gone and screwed it up.

This time I mounted the low bar and jumped to the high bar, where I immediately went into a kip, cast to handstand, and swung down. Kova was crouched down again and I felt him watching me, making sure I released at the right time. On my second layout, I clapped where it felt right and landed. I looked at him.

"Again."

He was proud.

Rinse, lather, repeat.

I did so many repetitions of this drill that I lost count. Easily hundreds, and the whole time I didn't utter a word to my coach, I just took his guidance. Hours had gone by and I didn't even notice. The entire time was a rush of endorphins for me. As crazy as it seemed, I loved what I was doing before I realized that most of the gymnasts had left for the day. My wrists were killing me, and my ankle was definitely inflamed, but it was nothing compared to the throbbing pain in my lower back. Probably from the force of the landings.

I sprayed some water onto my grips as Kova walked over to me. "Next time when you clap, I want you to complete a half twist. Only a half twist, though, yeah?"

"Yeah," I said, looking at the chunks of chalk in the giant bowl.

"Do you want me to spot you?"

I paused, thinking about his question and the new skill I was about to perform, one I'd never done in my life. It was probably best if he did.

"That'd be great, Coach."

I rubbed my grips together then clapped my hands. A veil of chalk puffed in front of my face and I turned away. Kova reached out to grab my wrist and pulled me to a stop. For the first real time this afternoon, I let him see how mad I truly was. There was no holding back my disdain, I wore it loud and proud and added resentment as an accessory. Recognition dawned on his face. He knew what he'd done. And the worst part? He didn't give two fucks.

Kova guided to me stand under the high bar. With his hands on my hips, too low again, he angled his head against mine and slowly, obviously, inhaled. Goose bumps broke out on my arms when he allowed a single finger to travel along my bikini line. It was, much to my disappointment, incredibly seductive and I reveled in the way it felt. It'd been so long since I had felt his touch.

"I like when you need me," he said, his voice smooth like vodka. "I also like when you despise me."

"You're delusional."

He chuckled under his breath, then lifted me. Ready to pull the half twist, Kova moved to the side. With one foot propped on the mat, he held his hands up. Anticipation steamrolled through me, but with my coach spotting me, I knew I was safe. Despite everything, there was a bond, a trust that was too thick to penetrate between us. I knew he'd catch me if I fell.

On the second flip, I clapped and cranked to the left. I had so much power that Kova reached out to guide me safely to a stop so I couldn't continue the rotation. Landing, I stumbled to the side and fell into his chest. His arms wrapped around and caught me.

"Jesus. I think I pulled too hard. Sorry about that." My eyes were wide and I was breathless.

"Do not ever be sorry. That is what I am here for. Let us do it again. I will stand here the whole time until you get it right. I knew it would be awkward at first."

Panting, I couldn't look at him after that one. Too much animosity and adrenaline sped through me to accept his candid sincerity. He was being nice, and I didn't like it. Perhaps that was because he was rarely nice to me unless he was inside me. This side of Kova was one I wasn't used to and I didn't know how to accept it without being a bitch to him.

After an endless amount of repetitions, literally over hundreds of the clap and half twist, the gym was now empty and the sun had set. Upon my request, we stayed an hour longer than scheduled so I could start with the full twist tomorrow. I was insanely tired and sore, and I couldn't wait to go home and crash.

Kova walked over to where I sat while I removed my grips and wristbands. He shifted on his feet.

"I'm completely depleted. I feel like I won't even be able to drive home at this rate," I said and dropped the gear into my bag.

"I will drive you."

"No, thanks. I'd rather have an Uber serial killer driver take me before I get into a car alone again with you."

"Suit yourself."

I walked out to the parking lot and climbed into my car. Slamming my truck door shut with more vigor than necessary, the light dimmed and I was encased in darkness, still parked in front of World Cup.

I pulled my cell phone out and did an Internet search of the Russian Kova spoke earlier to Katja. It had been bothering me and I wish I knew what he'd said to her.

I wish I had never looked.

He calls me *malysh*, but she was his *beloved*.

All it took was the weight of the word and the loneliness of the silence in the night surrounding me to break down two seconds later. Uncontrollable hot tears streamed down my cheeks while I cried my eyes out against my steering wheel, replaying Kova's last words. His tone said he was sorry, I could feel it in the pit of my stomach, but the "my beloved" part was crushing. I couldn't wrap my head around the words he'd said to me or why he even would speak them in the first place if he was calling his wife his beloved. I was missing a part of the story. I knew it from the pieces of their conversation I'd overheard. But he'd told me he was sorry and said he didn't come. People didn't act that way unless they were guilty, unless they were angry and couldn't communicate what they truly felt. I wasn't going to give him an excuse, but it was almost like he was mad and projecting.

I sank into my seat, my body diffusing at the already fragile seams. Bone-jarring sounds passed through my lips, ones I'd never heard myself make before. Nothing made sense. My chest hurt, tight with self-pity, and my fingers circled the leather of the steering wheel. If the light were on, the blood beneath the skin of my knuckles would show just how much I was restraining.

I had no one else to hold me. And I needed something to hold on to. I was too unsteady.

I wasn't sure how much more of this I could take. I didn't need this, but I couldn't get past the thought of Kova having sex with Katja while I was in the same building, or the things he'd said to her. Before this marriage, I'd felt closer to him than ever before and I'd thought he felt that way with me too, but maybe it was all an illusion that I wanted to see. Maybe that's what he wanted. Maybe I was just a pawn in his game. His callous words hurt, and I was sure I'd never forget them, but it was the bite and caress of his tongue that belted me harder than I could handle. Like a damn knife to my throat. He wanted to hurt me, but he was sorry too. I didn't get it and for some asinine reason, I didn't think he did either. I showed him what I was made of at the cost of my dignity today. A terrible combination that initiated a deeper strive in me.

Tomorrow I'd walk in with my head held high. I'd foolishly let down my guard. I had too much to lose, and I refused to allow some coach to take it from me.

In two days, I would be boarding a plane for another competition.

But tonight, tonight I'd cry myself to sleep.

chapter 15

"ADRIANNA?"

Coughing a few times, I glanced over my shoulder at Kova, who stood next to Madeline without so much of an ounce of emotion on either of their faces. I had my hand on the glass door about to walk out of World Cup when my name was called.

"Yes?"

"We would like to speak with you privately before you leave, if you have a moment."

"Of course."

It wasn't like I could say no, even though I was about to collapse from fatigue any second. The last two weeks were some of the most chaotic and exhausting weeks of my life. Between a meet last week, another one that had just passed, two-a-day practices in between, I was running on only four to five hours of sleep a night.

Kova tipped his head toward the hall. "In my office. It should not take long."

I shot a fleeting glance at Madeline, but her face was stoic. I hoped they made this quick.

Following close behind, I tried to wipe off some of the chalk from my thighs and arms, as if I needed to clean up for some stupid reason. I tightened my ponytail and pushed back the flyaways from my face, wracking my brain trying to figure out why both coaches would want to speak with me, and why they looked so serious. Practices had been going really well and I hadn't screwed up.

Kova held onto the doorknob as I walked past him to enter his office. I shook my fingers out, hoping to release the onset of nerves. I felt like I was in school and caught doing something I shouldn't have been and now I was in trouble.

Madeline sat in one of the empty seats and crossed her legs while I took the one next to her. I placed my bag by my chair and waited. Kova strode around his large desk that was covered in files and papers and sat down. He leaned forward, lacing his fingers together. My eyes caught the flash of metal from his wedding band. Fucking platinum. Instead of looking away like I had in the past, I forced myself to look at it as a reminder of what he'd done. He caught my gaze but didn't follow it.

"Madeline…" Kova gestured for her to speak.

Madeline turned toward me. "Coach Kova and I have had an in-depth conversation about your progress, the meets you have coming up that we feel are best for you, along with various opportunities that may present themselves based on your performances. Are you aware the National Qualifier meet is in a few weeks? The U.S. Classic?"

"Yes."

"After your scores this past weekend, we think you have a strong chance of making the national team. If you do, the meets you attend will change and so will your practice schedule, meaning we'd add in various camps for you to attend and so forth." I glanced at Kova with wide eyes. "You're aware that only twelve will make the national team, right?"

I nodded slowly and said, "And from that twelve, only four would make the Olympic team."

"If you continue to compete the way you have been…" Madeline left her statement open. A brow raised, she whistled through a grin. "Kova's been telling me that you're ready for more for quite some time now. I was a little skeptical, considering how much you had to train to reach this point. So few can take on what you have. Then your injury happened, and I worried that your gymnastics career was in jeopardy. An Achilles could snap at any minute." She paused, and looked into my eyes with amazement. "But you proved yourself, your strength, and your energy. I never should have doubted Kova."

"I am never wrong, Madeline." Kova joked, and they both laughed. I didn't.

"I see great things in your future," Madeline said.

This time I smiled. I knew from experience that before something great happened, everything tended to fall apart. And I had to wonder if I was already past the bad part and if this was my moment.

"You have another meet this weekend," Kova said. He had circles under his eyes and his face looked a little drawn. He looked as tired as I felt. "In between, for the next few weeks until the qualifier, you will do nothing but practice. From morning to night until the day before we leave, you will work your ass off. Kind of like a cram session before a test. I will call your father and have him put your tutoring on hold, that way you will have nothing to worry about. You will forget everything except the meet and the routines. That will have your undivided focus. Nothing else. Do not cloud your mind with things that can go wrong. You must remain focused on everything that will go right. Because it will. You will practice like you have never won a damn thing in your life and you will perform your heart out."

I wasn't an idiot. The look in his eyes and the way he twisted his thick wedding band said everything it needed to. Kova was the master at being discreet. The subtlety of his actions and the pointed stare was loud and clear—he needed me to forget about his marriage. And since he knew I wasn't going to speak to him privately outside of this room, he had to get it all out here while he could. He needed me to let it go, so I could focus on this new goal.

What he didn't know was that I'd already been working on that.

I sighed inwardly but kept a straight face. If it were only that easy. Deep down, I was still recovering from the head-on collision his secret nuptials caused me. It was playing with my mind. One minute I was as empty as a broken shell, the next minute I felt enraged and so full of emotion that I was ready to combust like fireworks on the fourth of July. Memories of our past conversations flipped through my head, along with the moments we'd shared outside these walls. There was nothing more I wanted than to forget them all and start over. Instead, I had to learn to deal with it the best I could, and by doing that, I shut down.

I studied him. I knew Kova. There wasn't a chance he would've suggested this, let alone been on board if he thought for a split second I didn't have what it took. That wasn't Kova's style. He took risks, yes, but his risks were measured and calculated. Planned. Well-thought-out and guaranteed success.

"We believe in you," Madeline said, her tone motherly. I looked at her and smiled. "We know you can do it. And after what you said to me at the meet a few weeks ago, I knew it too."

Tilting my head to the side, I asked, "What did I say?"

"You said that you remembered who you were, what you wanted, and it changed the game. For your age, that's powerful and inspiring."

Kova was eyeing me. His stare was heavy, willing me to look at him but I didn't pay him any attention. I didn't remember saying that, but I knew it's what I'd been feeling lately, so I probably did.

He was nervously tapping the tip of his pen on the desk, something I found odd for him to do. Steadying my breathing, I decided to go a different route and let him know I was still upset for what he'd done with Katja in this office and that I'd heard everything.

"There was a moment where I was slipping. I was letting go and I was unconsciously putting gymnastics second. This sport means everything to me. I built my life on it. What I do here is not just for me, but all of us. I got where I am because of both of you and the dedication you guys put in too. Sometimes I get stuck on one speed with one goal in mind, and I need to slow down. Thankfully a friend's been helping me do just that. Gymnastics is *my* most beloved, and this friend holds a dear place in my heart for reminding me of that. I owe them everything."

Kova was anything but stupid.

He stopped tapping his pen and I could feel him tense even though he was sitting across from me. Victory unfurled inside my stomach and I allowed the feeling to flow through me. It felt good. What I said was true, but I made sure to use the words he had said to his wife and he knew it.

"It's actually very common to have moments where you question everything and forget why you're here. Whoever this friend is, you're lucky," Madeline said. "Don't let them go."

My cheeks bloomed with heat and I smiled. "Thank you," was all I could muster. I was stuck in between emotion and numbness again when I turned to look at Kova and released my feelings for just a second.

I gave him the tiniest smirk. It was enough. He caught it loud and clear.

I exhaled a loud breath and feigned a smile from ear to ear for both of them this time. I needed to show them I was ecstatic on the outside and not dying on the inside like I was. Positivity brought optimism that carried confidence and self-assurance on its back. It was the key to victory, and that's what Madeline and Kova had both given me. I had to give it back, even if it was a fake one.

Silence stretched between us. When it became slightly uncomfortable, I reached down and grabbed my bag and stood up. "So… I guess I'll see you guys tomorrow?"

"Yes. I have a few things to discuss with Madeline first, then I will call your father. Expect two-a-days until Thursday. Friday we fly out for comp, then it is back to the grind."

I nodded. I could do it.

"Try and get some good rest tonight," Madeline said, her gaze studying my face. "Your eyes are a little swollen and it looks like you have a rash on your face. Have you eaten something new? Allergic to anything maybe?"

I thought about it for a moment. I'd barely eaten lately but that was because my back pain made me so nauseous I couldn't even stomach thinking about food.

"No, not that I know of."

Her head bobbed slowly up and down as she processed what I said, still taking in my face. "Get some rest tonight. These next few weeks are going to get chaotic."

"Goodnight," I said quietly.

Stepping out of Kova's office, I mechanically made my way to my truck and drove home. My condo was cold and lonely. Typically, I preferred the solitude, but lately it was eating away at me. When I was alone, I reflected. I overthought everything and then I regretted. I wanted to call Avery and tell her the good news, but I wasn't ready to talk to her yet. It was selfish of me, I knew that, but I needed to preserve what little of myself I had left. I could call Hayden. He'd come running, but I wasn't up for his company.

Everything I did was wrong except when it came to gymnastics.

Lighting a few scented candles, I ate dinner, as much as my stomach could handle, then took a shower and cried in a ball on the tile, counting the strands of hair and wondering how there could be so many on the floor.

chapter 16

THE WEEK PASSED THROUGH HAZY EYES.

I didn't know where it began or where it ended, and now we were landing in a new city.

I hadn't spoken to anyone save for my dad for a few short minutes so he could tell me he wouldn't be at this meet, but he'd make it to the next one. That was two meets he'd miss in a row. All I'd done was practice from sun up until well after sun down. Not a minute was wasted. Push came to shove and I'd been ready. Heart and soul, body and mind. I blocked everything out, kept to myself, and trained like a beast. I was on autopilot.

"It's going to be a hectic week," Madeline said. Talk about an understatement.

I pushed myself so hard I was certain I made myself sick. I felt more worn down than ever before, so unhappy and so weary. I'd secretly taken more Motrin to try and alleviate some of the pain and I'd had more ice baths this past week than I'd had my whole time at World Cup. I knew I shouldn't have taken the medication, but I had to. I couldn't handle how awful my body felt. Deep tissue massages, sports tape, blading... Kova even had me roll on some stupid foam log he insisted would release lactic acid and help me recover quicker. I never complained, though. Not once. It was grueling and exhausting and overwhelming, but I wanted it and I loved every taxing minute, even though I was falling deeper and deeper into my depression.

Before we boarded the plane, I took some Benadryl and slept until we landed. My bones ached horribly, my whole body inflamed, and I felt as stiff as an old woman when I walked off the plane. Shortly after we arrived at the hotel, I unpacked then passed out. I'd been woken up for dinner but begged to sleep, and stayed asleep, until the next morning. I was so physically drained that I woke up in the same position I'd fallen asleep in.

In truth, I felt weak and it scared me.

"Are you okay?" Madeline asked, concern filling her voice. She'd come to the hotel room I shared with my teammates. We were getting ready to leave for the meet but they stepped out at her request so she could speak with me privately.

"Yes, why?"

"You seem out of it and we need your head in the game right now."

I yawned. "Just a little tired, but I'm okay."

The space between her eyes creased together and she pressed the back of her hand to my head. "You're warm."

I pulled away. "A fever won't hold me back. Don't worry," I said and slapped on a smile. "I thought I felt a little warm last night and took some cold medicine with a few Emergen-C packets."

"Are you wearing blush?"

"Yes, of course." My lips pursed together. "Why?"

"You just look a little more flushed than usual."

Now it was my turn for my brows to bunch tight. I glanced in the mirror and shrieked.

"Oh, my God." I laughed. "I didn't blend it in enough," I lied. I did look a little more flushed for some reason. Looking back at my coach, I said, "My mom got me new blush. It was my first time trying it out and I went a little too heavy." I grabbed my makeup bag and brushed on some foundation to help tone down my cheeks. "Better?" I asked.

She didn't seem sold but nodded anyway. "Did you take Emergen-C this morning?"

"No."

"Open up two and take them now." I did what she said and forced them down. "Good. That stuff works miracles and you should be good soon. When we get back, make sure you schedule an appointment with your doctor. Let's not mention this to Kova, though. He hasn't been himself lately."

"Good idea."

I refused to be concerned with what I could do to help him anymore, but also because it would look a little odd delving into my coach's life and asking Madeline for more information. Staying out of his personal life was key to preserving my sanity.

"Ready to roll? You got this?"

"Ready? Psshh. I was made for this," I replied and produced the biggest, fakest smile I could from ear to ear. Madeline laughed, her eyes twinkled, and I followed her out of my hotel room with one thought.

Okay. Two.

Sometimes pretending to be something I wasn't took more energy than what it took to be real.

My second thought was that I was going to release everything in me and dominate this meet. I wasn't lying when I said I was made for this. I was.

It was unfortunate how aware I was that I was slowly killing myself. An insidious circle of self-destruction that I couldn't stop because I was obsessed with gymnastics.

Okay. That was three thoughts.

The next day I was on a plane headed back to Georgia with four medals again. All gold.

The following Monday I woke with the fear that I wasn't sure how I would make it through the week in one piece. I was feeling so rundown and bone tired. The pressure and stress to qualify for the national team was already weighing heavily on me, but now I wanted to remain at the top of the sport like I had been, and that brought a new burden of anxiety.

It was startling how weak I felt. Almost like I was anemic. Maybe I had the flu and I didn't know it. Pulling up to a red light, I called my doctor and made an appointment. Naturally they had to remind me they'd called numerous times and their messages went unanswered. I apologized, because they had been calling. I'd had too much on my mind and not enough time to spare, but after this past weekend, and waking up this morning, I knew something wasn't right. I could feel it. I wasn't even eighteen yet. I shouldn't feel this ragged.

On the way to World Cup, I got stuck at the draw bridge. I took a long sip of my Emergen-C concoction—two green tea bags, two Emergen-C packets, and honey. I'd read online this nasty tasting drink was a miracle cure. While waiting for the boats to go through, I put my truck in park and pulled up the Internet on my cell phone and typed in my symptoms.

Severe exhaustion. Bone pain. Body aches. Headaches. Fever. Hair loss. I wouldn't really consider hair loss, but I had noticed more and more on my floors lately.

I pressed enter, and immediately regretted it.

Anemia. Thyroid cancer. Tick bite. Lyme disease. Mono. Hay fever. Low blood sugar. Acute stress disorder. Depression. Dementia from a head injury.

The last three were way off. I wasn't depressed or stressed. Okay, a little stressed and slightly depressed, but who wasn't? The world survived on antidepressants. Maybe a little demented for putting my body through what I have, but the rest were out in left field. The only thing that was a possibility was mono, but that didn't even make sense. Kova would be just as bad off as me. So would Hayden, and they seemed fine.

Annoyed, I clicked out of my phone and dropped it into the cup holder. I watched the draw bridge slowly go down, thinking I might as well add elbow cancer to the list. Looking up symptoms was a terrible idea and got me nowhere. I mean, a tick bite? Really?

Shifting into drive, I turned up the music and made the short drive to the gym. I needed to block out my hypochondriac thoughts and focus on gymnastics, not self-diagnose myself and spiral into a dark hole worrying I had every single illness under the hot Georgia sun.

Once inside, I settled into warming up, reaching for my toes, feeling my muscles stretch and pull tight in my hamstrings. I shot a glance at Kova and studied him, his face, his eyes, his movements. While he did look a little pale and drawn, and his eyes weren't as bright as they usually were. He didn't appear to be stiff or worn down like I was. He lifted big safety mats up and moved them across the room as if he were carrying bags of groceries into the house. He spoke to Madeline. Jotted stuff down in his notebook. Took a call on his cell phone. There was clearly nothing wrong with him. He must've felt my eyes on him because he shot me a look and I foolishly averted my gaze just as fast as his eyes landed on me.

Shit. I'd been caught staring.

I cringed inwardly and moved into another position. Just as I was about to look up, I felt him behind me. His presence wrapped around my senses, and holy hell he smelled so good. His cologne was fresh and potent in the mornings.

"Lay back. Hands on the floor," he ordered, kneeling next to me. I did, and he brought both of my knees up then crossed one in front of the other. Grabbing my ankle, he pulled my foot toward me and pressed on my knee with his elbow. He was stretching out my hips.

"What is on your mind?" he asked, looking ahead. I followed his gaze and watched the boys' team. Hayden glanced at us.

"Nothing, why?"

"Because you were looking at me."

Damn it. I knew he'd caught me. "So. I can't look at you? You're my coach. I was wondering where you were and if I was going to get caught skimping on conditioning and warm-ups."

He ignored that and kept his gaze ahead. "You never look at me anymore, Adrianna. Never. And you were just watching me like a hawk. Do you have something you want to say to me? Something on your mind?"

"Nope. I'm good."

"You sure?"

"Yup."

Kova moved on to my other leg. I did want to ask him how he was feeling, to see if he felt sick the way I did, but I couldn't bring myself to. I didn't want to breach the wall I had put between us and allow him to walk into my life again. I also didn't want to let him know I wasn't feeling well.

"You are the worst liar I have ever met," he mumbled under his breath.

"You're the only one who tells me that."

"Because whether you like it or not, I know you better than anyone else."

His words struck my heart and I ground my jaw together. It was true. He did know me better than anyone else and I wish he didn't. I should've been grateful he was concerned, but instead tears of regret branded the resentment I felt for him. "Your eyes… You are so far away and it kills me because you will not come to me. I know you have a lot on your mind. I also know you are blocking everything out. I cannot say I fault you, though. You are protecting yourself. I just wish you would let me be there for you."

My breathing deepened, my chest rose and fell. I had a lot on my mind. Too much. And with no outlet, which he knew.

"See," he said quietly. Our eyes locked and my breath lodged in my throat. "*I know you, Adrianna.*" His warm, deep voice wrapped around my gutted heart. There wasn't an ounce of cockiness in his words, just genuine sincerity that shook me. "I hate that I can see everything you are feeling, because I feel it too." His sober gaze didn't waver from mine. I wanted to look away, but I was constricted by the rope his voice devised. A faint sharpness sliced through my breastbone. This was the first time I'd allowed him to look at me like this and he had me glued to him because I could hear what he was saying, what he was begging for. Kova wanted the one thing I couldn't give him. Forgiveness.

Kova didn't look sick. No, he looked gutted.

"I know you do not want to talk to me, but if you do not release that built-up emotion inside you, you will snap. Usually when you least expect it and on the wrong person. Trust me. I have been there. If you will not release it on me, at least write it down."

I looked to my side, watching the gymnasts practice. His voice was so sad.

Quietly, I swallowed, and said, "I don't need to write." *I just need to sit in the shower and cry.*

"You would be surprised how therapeutic it is."

My brows furrowed. I looked back at Kova. "Where is the notebook?"

He looked down at me. "You have it."

"No, I don't."

"You do."

"Ko—Coach, no I don't."

Kova sat back on his knees. "Adrianna, you never gave it back to me."

I stared up at Kova, slightly panicking inside. My brain ran through the motions since I last saw the notebook and where I had placed it.

"It must be in my condo somewhere," I answered softly.

His brows furrowed. Panic spanned his eyes. "You are sure you did not leave it somewhere?"

I studied him, thinking. "I probably shoved it in my nightstand so I wouldn't have to look at it. I know I didn't bring it anywhere, so it's somewhere in my condo."

Relief flooded him. "When you find it, use it."

Sitting up, I crossed my legs in front of me and kept my focus on the floor, picking at the carpet. "I'd rather not. Writing isn't for me."

Kova blew out a lengthy sigh. "You are so stubborn. This is going to backfire on you."

I flattened my lips but didn't acknowledge his comment. It wouldn't. I'd make sure of it.

"Does your Achilles hurt?"

I shook my head. I debated with what to tell him. "No, it's fine. I'm just really, really tired."

"It comes with the territory."

Standing up, I yawned. "I'll see you on bars." I was only a few steps away when Kova called my name. I glanced over my shoulder.

Scratching the back of his neck, his mouth pulled tight to one side and his nervous green eyes dropped to the floor then up to me. We stood no more than a few feet apart and he closed the distance.

"For the record, you would never skimp on conditioning. That is not who you are. You are not lazy. That kind of mentality would only hurt you in the long run and you know that. You always, always go the extra mile, even when you should not, but it is impossible for you not to. It is why you are you."

I rolled my bottom lip between my teeth and reflected over his words. He was right about everything he'd said, but I wasn't going to respond. I didn't need to. We both knew the answer.

Slowly turning back around, I lowered my gaze to the floor as I made my way to bars. That was the most he'd spoken to me since I'd put my foot down. I may have allowed it, but somehow, I think he knew that was all the rope I'd give him.

The rest of the week he kept to himself. I trained. I slept. I trained. I ached all over. I barely slept. I trained. I had pounding headaches. I sank deeper into myself. I was so tired that I almost missed practice.

But I didn't. I sucked it up and championed on. It's what I did.

THE ENERGY IN THE ROOM REVIVED ME, GIVING ME LIFE, WASHING AWAY ANY KIND of exhaustion I'd been dealing with over the past few weeks.

Like a contagious beat to a song. Shivers ran down my arms, like little needles tickling me. I looked all around, turning in a circle, taking in every moment, every person I could see, breathing it into my lungs. I smiled. My dad was somewhere in the stands.

This was life. Gymnastics was life.

Today was the American Classic, my last meet before the National Qualifier. Today would determine if I got to compete in the U.S. Classic.

Inhaling a deep breath, I let everything go. I was invigorated, excited, and for once, not tired. I was probably on overdrive and didn't know it.

Yesterday after we arrived, we ran through our routines, doing light warm-ups. We didn't push it or do our full routines, just ran through the motions and adjusted to the equipment. I kept my focus on myself and didn't watch anyone else, just like I was doing now. I blocked everything out and compartmentalized my thoughts.

"Breathe in through your stomach," Madeline said, taking a deep breath and exhaling through her nose. I nodded, staring at the vault as I hopped on my toes to keep my muscles warm. "As long as you block hard and stay tight, you got this, Adrianna. Vault is yours. Open up when you come out of the half."

I nodded again, and bit the inside of my lip. Madeline walked away to speak with Holly. I had one of the most difficult vaults—the Amanar. My body had to rotate nine hundred degrees, get at least six feet off the vault table, and finish with a blind landing.

I had this. I wasn't worried. I was confident, but I wasn't cocky. I could do this vault in my sleep. I just had to get the mechanics of it and rely on muscle memory.

There was only one other vault so dangerous that it paralyzed a gymnast many years ago. Vault may be my specialty, but I wasn't looking to never walk again. I knew my limits.

Patting my hands in the chalk bowl, the powder filled my nostrils as I grabbed little clumps and broke them. I applied some of the chalk between my inner thighs and on the bottom of my feet to absorb any moisture.

I exhaled.

Walking toward the end of the walkway, Kova met up with me and we walked side by side. I kept my gaze on the floor, imagining my vault over and over. My hands formed into tight balls and flexed, and my fingers were a little cold.

"Stay tight, start low. Your body will know what to do once you are in the air."

Once we reached the end of the runway, I stepped into the small chalk box on the floor and added a little more to my feet. My heart was starting to pick up speed. I wasn't nervous, just anxious.

"Did you hear me?" Kova asked. I nodded. "Hey. Look at me." My eyes shot up to his. "You got this. Just release everything and trust yourself." I nodded again, serious.

After giving me a friendly pat on my shoulder, Kova walked away and only stopped when he got to the opposite end where my dismount would be. Our eyes locked and his chin dipped.

It was go time.

Swallowing, I looked at the judges. I stepped onto the runway mat behind the white tape and cracked my toes, standing on the tips of them. I focused on the vault, noting Kova in my peripheral vision. Black dress pants, royal blue polo club shirt, hands on hips.

While I was confident in what I was about to perform, his presence still comforted me.

I glanced at the judges' table, waiting. They gave me the green light.

Quickly, I saluted them and a handful of seconds later I was running. My feet pounded into the floor, my heart filling with exhilaration as I neared the springboard. The adrenaline was a rush, speeding through me. It was addicting and I wanted to chase it.

This was another reason I loved gymnastics. I was free and wild. No one could slow me down.

Rounding off, feet locked together and slamming into the springboard, I reached back and flipped onto the vault, popping my shoulders hard and allowed my muscles to take over. Tight, I took flight as high as I possibly could reach and twisted two and a half times, then opened and landed.

Both feet together.

No hop.

Just a perfect stuck landing that made my heart drop and my stomach tighten.

It was the longest four seconds of my life.

I could hear Kova and Madeline shouting, feel the vitality of the room.

Arms up, I acknowledged the judges, then turned toward the other side…and smiled. Scratch that. I was fucking beaming on the inside and outside.

Madeline had both hands up for a high five as I reached the stairs. Stepping down, she said, "Unbelievable! The best you've ever done! I gotta run to prep Holly, but fantastic!"

My eyes lit up.

Automatically, I high-fived Kova and our eyes met. There was a moment my heart skipped a beat. To share something like this with him formed a deeper connection between us. I felt it and there was no doubt in my mind he did too.

"How did I do? How was it? I mean, I felt good, but you know how that goes," I asked him, but he looked at me like I was utterly insane. I laughed, actually laughed and said, "You look like I'm the one speaking Russian to you."

"Sometimes I wonder what is going through your head to ask me such questions. Adrianna, you perform best under pressure. By far…just…" He shook his head and ran a hand through his hair and looked away. "It was just incredible. Flawless."

I almost squealed. Thank God I didn't. "Thanks!"

Kova looked down at me. The way his enamored gaze took in my face as he studied me caused butterflies to erupt in my stomach. I wanted to pluck their beautiful wings off so I couldn't feel that connection with him, but at the same time, I wanted them to flutter harder.

"It is good to see you smiling again."

At that my smile faded a little.

"I have not seen your face light up like that in quite some time." He swallowed hard, then turned his head. I followed his gaze and watched my score pop up.

I stared at the bold, black numbers. My lips parted. Was this real life?

Kova looked back at me. Shaking his head, happiness bloomed in his eyes. "I told you," he said, shaking his head like he was awestruck. "Flawless."

Then, he was gone.

"You're going to be labeled as vault queen soon," Holly said sweetly as she came up to me and wrapped her arms around my shoulders.

I barked out a laugh. "That will be the day."

"Girl, you don't even know your greatness," she said, then stepped away.

With bars already under my belt, I'd only been deducted a few tenths, but I was still leading. Bars was like vault for me, another forte of mine.

Beam, my arch nemesis, though. I fought that bitch tooth and nail. She was being compliant for now, but I knew deep in my gut it wouldn't last. Everything good always came to an end.

Yeah, I was starting to wonder if I was demented since I was comparing the balance beam to an actual person who could bring me down. Only I had the power to bring myself down. No one else.

And that was the kind of mentality I went into the beam with. I knew I had what it took, I'd done it twice now. I was my only limit.

"What are you thinking about?" Kova asked right before I was about to go on.

"What's the worst thing that could happen? I straddle the beam? Fall off completely? My foot slips on the second back handspring of my connection, but I can't stop the next skill from happening because my body is already in motion and I'll land on my neck on the beam and break my collarbone?"

He looked into both of my eyes, his gaze shifting back and forth. A little scared. "Is that really what you were thinking?"

"Yes."

Kova shook his head, at a loss for words.

It really was what I'd been thinking about when I mounted the beam. I let go and trusted myself, trusted the faith my coaches had in me, and when I saw my score flash on the board shortly after my dismount, I was insanely proud. While I hadn't snagged first place, I was in the top three and I'd totally take it.

Letting go was hard, but fear was crippling. I refused to be a prisoner of my own fears and self-appointed limitations.

As I stood waiting to rotate to the last event, the back of my neck prickled with awareness. I felt the heavy stare of someone and turned around. I tilted my head to the side and took him in, trying to figure out where I'd seen him before. I saw a lot of forgettable faces at meets, but this one, he looked so familiar and it annoyed me I couldn't place him. I'd seen those beady eyes before that were now raking up and down my body.

I shivered. I didn't like the way he looked at me, or the sleazy smile that pulled at his weathered mouth to reveal yellow-stained teeth.

Kova stepped in front of my view and I pulled back, brows gathering up at him.

"Do not look at him." His eyes were hard as dried cement. "Do you hear me? Do not look at him again." His voice was deadly.

I hesitated with my question. "Why?"

If possible, his eyes darkened, and I swear I heard him growl. "Adrianna—"

"I'm not asking to aggravate you, Coach. I'm just curious."

Placing his hands on his hips, his chest expanded as he shot a fleeting glance over his shoulder, then back at me. I didn't follow because for once I didn't want to annoy him. And, because that guy creeped me out.

Looking down at me, Kova ran his teeth over his bottom lip like he was debating whether he wanted to tell me something or not. His indecisive eyes bore into mine, so I did what I always do. I pushed.

"What is it?" I asked. "Do you know him?"

"Do you remember the Parkettes meet, where we discussed what you learned from just watching the competition and the room as a whole? We got on the subject of that coach and how I warned you—"

"You mean threatened—"

"—to stay away from the coach who was demeaning his gymnast and how it disturbed you?"

My eyes widened. "That's him!" I muttered under my breath. "I thought he looked familiar. He's the coach you fired."

Kova's chin dipped long and slow. It was the same guy Reagan had told me about.

"For once, listen to me when I say do not engage him. Do not look his way. Pretend he does not exist."

"Okay."

"I am serious, Adrianna. There is more to him than I want to disclose, and I will not get in to it right now, so do not ask."

I nodded solemnly. I thought back to the day in my hotel room where I sat on his lap as we discussed his actions and my perception, and I remembered how Kova said he had a gut feeling one day someone was going to report him. Dread creased my forehead. I didn't want to go there, but I had to wonder if he was one of *those* coaches who were more than hands on and got away with it.

I frowned, my stomach churning with rancid thoughts. "Don't tell me he—"

My words were stopped short when *he* stepped up to us and intruded in on our conversation.

"Konstantin. Pleasure seeing you here." I recoiled while Kova appeared calm. A sour taste filled my mouth. But I knew him. I noticed the veins that twirled down his arms like snakes contracting with power, the way his hands contracted into fists. There was bad blood between them, and I wanted to know why.

"Too bad I cannot say the same for you," Kova responded with no tact at all. I choked back a laugh. His Russian accent ground out each word and I loved when it made a show.

"Why don't we let bygones be bygones already," he suggested. Kova stood stone still and silent. "I've been following you this year. You wouldn't have gotten as far as you have without me and we both know it." Blatant disgust bled from Kova for the man in front of him. "Except for this one." He pointed to me, his eyes glistening. He made my skin crawl. "Where did you find her?"

"Adrianna," he said without looking at me, "go get ready. I will be there soon."

I didn't move. I was too enthralled, and luckily Kova didn't notice because his rage took center stage.

Kova stepped up to his former partner so they were nose to nose. My heart stopped. The fury burning off him chilled me to the bone. I took a small step back. I'd seen him all shades of angry, but never like this.

"Let us get something straight, *sobaka*," he spat in Russian. I made a mental note to look that word up. "I got where I am today because of me, of the work I put in, and the work my girls put in. Not because of your piece of shit self. I taught you everything you know. Not the other way around. You got lucky because of me." He scoffed, jabbing a finger into the man's chest. "For more than one reason, might I add. This is your only warning—stay the fuck away from me and my girls. I let you off once, but I will not do it again. I do not want to see you, smell you, or hear your name mentioned. I do not want you within a fifty-mile radius of me and my gymnasts. If we are at the same meet, you will keep your distance."

"Or what?" the guy rebutted. "What do you think you're going to do acting so tough and macho?"

"I am not acting, just defending those who cannot defend themselves against dogs like you. Do not fucking test me."

He laughed. The guy actually laughed, but Kova was eerily calm and said, "I have enough evidence to easily have you placed in solitary confinement. Funny thing about prison mates, they eat pieces of shit like you for breakfast."

His laugh died down immediately. His eye lids grew heavy then quickly shot to me. Kova looked over his shoulder and I froze. I'd heard everything. He didn't like that, but he didn't show it.

Without another word, the former coach at World Cup turned around and walked away.

"Coach." My voice was high-pitched. "What did he do?"

Kova scrubbed a hand down his face then looked above my head. He seemed so guilty all of a sudden. "Nothing that we need to discuss now. You need to get ready. I want you focused on your routine."

"I am ready and focused. Tell me."

"Another time."

"Please?"

Kova sighed deep. Lowering his voice, he said, "I caught him." My brows furrowed, and he continued shifting on his feet. "I caught him in a position he should not have ever been in. The dating rule began because of his actions."

My eyes popped. "Oh, my God. This is scandalous."

Face drawn, he didn't share my excitement. "No, Adrianna, it is not. I almost killed him. I know what you and I did goes against everything I believe in, and the code of ethics set forth by the gymnastics committee. I knew it was wrong, but I never *preyed* upon you." I frowned. No, he never had. "But that bastard preyed upon one of my gymnasts and couldn't control himself."

Kova's eyes lifted over my head and I turned around to follow his gaze.

Holly.

I had tons of questions I wanted answers to, but now was not the time. I had to clear my head and get to my last event. Easier said than done after the bombshell Kova had just dropped on me.

I blocked out all the noise and focused on delivering a flawless floor routine. Ninety seconds later I stood next to Kova waiting for my score. We both turned toward each other, our faces mimicked each other's. Another medal to hang on my wall, all thanks to our teamwork.

On the plane ride home I couldn't stop thinking about Holly and that coach, coupled with the information Reagan had given me weeks ago on the track. I tried not to stare at Holly, but so many questions ran through my head. At the top was, what had Kova meant by that guy preying on her? I couldn't just ask her, so I was left with more thoughts filling my head.

I'D FORGOTTEN I HAD MY DOCTOR'S APPOINTMENT EARLY MONDAY MORNING AND would be late to practice.

Instead of texting, I called Kova as soon as I got on the road.

"Allo?"

"Hey, Coach, it's Adrianna."

"I know who it is. Why are you calling me? Is it to tell me you are missing practice?"

I chewed at my lip for a second, listening to a springboard rebound in the background.

"Um, I forgot I have a doctor's appointment this morning I need to go to, but I'll be at practice afterwards."

"What? What appointment? Are you sick? Why have you not told me about this?"

The noise faded behind him and a door shut. He must've walked to his office. I stayed on the right side of the road and looked for the highway.

"I guess I forgot."

"Adrianna, I need to be made aware of things like this when they are scheduled, not last minute."

"I know, and I'm sorry. I've just had a lot on my mind lately."

Kova was quiet for a moment. His voice dropped. "Okay. I will give you that. Is there anything I can do for you?"

"No, I just need a physical," I partially lied.

"I expect a full update when you come in. I would like to do another treatment for you soon. Either before we leave, or when we get back. This weekend is a big one for you, especially after the way you qualified on Saturday. You are doing exceptional, Ria. People know who you are. Timing is everything in gymnastics, and we need to utilize it properly. We leave for the U.S. Classic in four days, and the head coach of the national team will be there inviting those to her camp who are in the top of that meet."

I swallowed back hard. *Ria.* He slipped but I let it go. He only used that nickname when he was passionate about something.

About five exits away, I grew quiet thinking I should just turn around. "Maybe I should cancel my appointment and just go when we get back."

"No." His voice was firm. "Absolutely not. Your health is important. Go and do what you need to, just come straight here after."

I nodded, as if he could see it.

"See you soon, Coach."

Knock, knock, knock.

Finally. The door opened and Dr. DeLang walked in. She always seemed to catch me off guard with her height and youthful appearance. She was no taller than me with the same build, but about twenty years older. At least.

"I apologize for the wait, Adrianna, we got a little backed up."

A little backed up? I'd waited over an hour in the lobby, and almost another hour in the exam room.

"No worries. I'm not in a rush." I plastered on a fake smile.

She opened my patient file and leaned her hips against the counter as she began to scan page after page, her pen running down each one. I waited quietly, wondering what she was reading, trying to slow down my heart rate. Doctor appointments always made me a little anxious.

"Last time you were here we drew blood." She paused and flipped over another paper, taking her time to scan the page. "That was almost four months ago. And you haven't been back since to get the results?"

"No." She eyed me. "I've been a little busy with training."

"I understand life can get a bit hectic, but if you put your health aside and it deteriorates, how will you continue to train?"

I flattened my lips and one of her brows pulled up. She had a point.

"Are you on any medication right now?"

"Other than doing the plasma injections, no."

"All right, tell me about your symptoms and what brought you in."

"What were the results of my blood work?" I asked.

She closed the folder and set it on the counter. "We'll get to that. Tell me what's going on."

My mind went blank and I started to stammer for some stupid reason.

"Well, I'm-I'm really tired. Like unusually tired. To the point of exhaustion. Some days I don't know how I'll get through anything. I know I train a lot, and I probably overdo it, but I feel like I shouldn't feel like this."

"Describe to me what it is you're feeling."

"My body aches, but it's deep in my bones, like inside of them hurts, if that makes sense."

"Go on."

"I have terrible headaches. Like the blinding pain kind of headache that makes me turn off lights and have to lie down. Sometimes there's a sharpness in my chest that catches me off guard."

Dr. DeLang reopened my file and began taking notes. "What about your period? When was your last cycle?"

I glanced at the ceiling for a second, then back to her. "You know, I can't remember. It's been on and off. I figured the irregularity was due to the heavy training."

"For sure, it can be. You're still training about forty to fifty hours a week, correct?"

I nodded.

"Are you on birth control to regulate your period?"

"No."

"Having sex?"

"Sometimes."

"But you're using protection, correct?"

"Of course." Plan B was a sort of protection. The only other time I didn't use protection was in the shower with Hayden, and he'd pulled out.

Christ on a stick! Was I pregnant this whole time and didn't know it?

No. There's no way.

I may have thrown myself headfirst into gymnastics because I'd been so consumed with everything else going on that I wanted to forget, but I think I'd know if I was pregnant.

"Good. What about illnesses? Any that run in your family?"

"As far as I know everyone seems to be healthy." Not that I knew much of anything about my biological mom, and I was too embarrassed to broach that topic.

"No cancer? Any diseases?" she asked, jotting more stuff down.

"No." I shook my head. She probably thought I was a hypochondriac.

"How well are you sleeping?"

"Some days I pass out as soon as I walk in and don't wake up until my alarm goes off. Other days I'm so exhausted but I just can't seem to fall asleep no matter what I do. I'm all over the place."

"Any fevers?"

"I had a fever a few times."

She looked up at me. "How high was it?"

"I didn't take my temperature."

"Okay. Anything else I need to know about?"

I started to shake my head no, then stopped, recalling something Madeline had said. "One of my coaches said it looked like I had a rash a few weeks ago."

"Where was it?"

I shrugged, helpless. "My cheeks?"

Dr. DeLang made another note before setting the file down. She reached into a cabinet and pulled out a little clear cup with a lid. She wrote my last name on the affixed label before handing it to me. "I'll need a urine sample from you, and then I'll send you for a new set of labs. I'd rather not go on your last blood panel since it's been so long."

I perked up, the hair on my arms stood tall. "Were there things in it that concerned you?"

"Your vitamin levels were up and down, your iron was below normal, and so was your red blood cell count."

I froze. Her words caused instant anxiety to soar through me. I didn't know much about proper levels, but anything below normal scared me, especially red blood cells.

"Not to worry." She must have sensed my alarm. "A low red blood cell count can be attributed to a lot of things. Nothing to get your mind going until we get the new results."

I went to the bathroom and returned within three minutes. The doctor was busy noting stuff in my chart and looked up when I walked in. She put the folder down and pulled out a pair of latex gloves and snapped them on. She took the sample from me and stepped out of the room for a moment.

"What are you testing for?" I asked when she returned.

"Pregnancy, kidney levels, see if you have a UTI, your liver, blood in your urine, any bacteria. It's just a rapid test to see if I need to start you on antibiotics. The blood work will give us a more comprehensive look at what's going on."

I frowned, and jumped back up onto the table. I didn't think I had anything wrong with me in those areas, but I also wasn't a doctor either.

Leaning over the counter, she reached for a referral sheet for the blood work and checked off boxes for what I assumed would be the standard lab tests.

There was a light knock on the door before a nurse poked her head in. She handed a sheet of paper to the doctor and closed the door behind her.

"As of right now, there's some protein in your urine," Dr. DeLang said after scanning the sheet.

"What's it caused from?"

"Protein in urine could mean a number of things. Typically, it's a sign to test the kidneys, but given your age, and the pressure you put on your body to train, it easily could be due to dehydration, strenuous exercise, and even extreme emotional stress. Your high protein diet could also easily be the reason."

Emotional stress. Fuck. Of course, that was it. And coupled with my diet? A recipe for disaster. Only problem was, I couldn't tell her how stressed out emotionally I was without it raising flags for more questions.

"I'll see you back in a week or two." She peered at me over her glasses and gave me a look my dad would've given me to indicate he was serious.

"I have a couple meets back-to-back so it may be a month before I can get back here."

She eyed me, then handed me the lab sheet. I jumped off the table and stood up to face her. "No eating after midnight—you need to fast. Go first thing in the morning. Until then, go home and rest, Adrianna. Do not go to practice, go *home*. And don't make it more than a month till I see you again."

I nodded, ignoring the rest part. I could rest when I was dead.

"Could the protein be due to taking too much Motrin?"

She tilted her head to the side, observing me. "The medication itself wouldn't cause it. You'd have to ingest a great deal of Motrin over time for it to affect your kidneys."

"I have. I was going through a few big bottles a month at one point."

Her eyebrows shot up. "While I don't think that could have caused any kind of long-term side effects just yet, absolutely no more until we get the results in." She paused briefly to look in my chart. "If I recall, you can't have any kind of anti-inflammatory with the plasma injections."

I didn't answer. Just flattened my lips and told her I'd be at the lab bright and early.

Pulling out of the office building complex, I dialed up Kova to tell him I'd be at practice within the hour.

"Adrianna, go home and sleep. Lord knows you need it. I will see you tomorrow morning. And by the way, we are going to sit down and talk. I had no idea you had anything serious going on with you."

My jaw dropped and I missed the entrance to the highway. "What? What are you talking about? There's nothing serious going on."

"Do not take me for a fool. This conversation is over. I will see you tomorrow."

"What? I have to practice!" I screeched, instantly heated as I made a U-turn. I'd just qualified to compete at the U.S. Classic, where the national team would be picked. I had to practice this week more than ever. "How do you even know?"

"Your doctor phoned your father, and then he called me. Get your ass in bed."

I ground my teeth together. I'd forgotten everyone was connected.

"Did you just growl?" Kova asked.

Maybe. "I assume you know everything, too," I said.

"Of course," he answered flippantly. "Your father told me. I told you to stop with that fucking Motrin."

I didn't respond, just hung up on him and threw my phone to the floor. Damn Russian.

"**W**HAT IS WRONG?" KOVA ASKED BEHIND ME.
　　　　I didn't answer him, I didn't even look over my shoulder. After a ten-hour day, I got my items together and shoved them into my bag like I was punching someone.

I was still upset that he'd made me take a rest day from practice during such a critical time for me. Nationals were just days away, there was no time for rest. While I may have slept all day yesterday until my alarm went off this morning, I didn't need to. I'd been bored and stewing with annoyance that I'd tried watching television only for my eyes to roll shut before the first commercial.

"I asked you a question," he said. "Are you going to answer me?"

No.

Pulling out my hair tie, I fluffed my dry strands before tying it up in a messy bun. There was so much chalk in my hair that I didn't need to use dry shampoo.

I reached forward and pulled out my sweats and my keys fell to the floor. I ignored them while I slipped my shirt on over my sports bra. When I pushed my head through the neck hole, Kova was standing next to me, jingling my keys in his hand.

I stood and reached for them, but Kova lifted his arm and put them out of my reach. There was no smirk, no hint of laughter. He just stared at me, waiting on an answer. Something came over me, I'm not sure what, and I shoved his chest.

"Give them back," I demanded, seething.

"Why are you so mad?"

"Because you're breathing in front of me." I reached for my keys again, but he lifted his arm higher. "Why do you act like such a child?" My leg twitched as I considered kneeing him in his junk. That would make him drop my keys immediately.

His eyes looked back and forth between mine. "I am just getting on your level. Now, why are you so mad? I thought for sure you were going to throw a block of chalk at me a few times today."

"How observant of you," I said blandly. "Now give me back my keys. I want to go home."

"Talk to me, Adrianna."

My eyes flared. "You don't deserve my time."

"You are still upset about yesterday," he stated. I jumped, trying to reach, but I was too short. "I called you last night to come in for conditioning after hours because I knew how you were going to react, but you never answered."

He had called, but I never heard my phone ring. Of course, knowing now why he'd called only made me angrier, because I would've left my condo in under five minutes if I had known.

Unexplainable red hot rage surged through me and I shoved at his chest again until he fell into the wall. He wrapped his free arm around my lower back and pulled me to him. I drew in a breath, gasping at the closeness of him. A veil of cinnamon and citrus incased my senses, his natural aroma with a hint of tobacco that I hated to love. All the feelings I'd been locking away came roaring back, overpowering me. I fisted his shirt, my chest lifting and falling fast, my head a hazy mess. I needed to back away, but the feel of his body, the warmth, the hardness—I realized I'd missed it so much.

"I was only looking out for you," he said, breathing into me. I shivered. His gaze turned heavy, eyes glossy. "Be mad at me all you want, I do not care, but one day you will see that what I do is only to ever help you and never hurt you." He paused. "The thought of hurting you makes me sick, Adrianna."

"Stop," I murmured. "Don't say that." Staring at his chest, I shook my head vehemently. He wasn't looking out for me, he was looking out for himself, as always. "Please, just give me my keys and let me go," I whispered.

Kova dipped his head next to mine. My lips parted as he got closer. "You are the one holding on to me."

My heart stopped. I *was* holding onto him. I unclenched his shirt only for him to press his hand into my back. Tension thickened between us and the air grew hot. I swallowed, heart pounding, I fisted his shirt again and leaned my weight into him.

Kova softened a little. "I would never force you to do something against your will," he said near my cheek. "If you want to leave, leave, but I do not think you want to. I think you miss me as much as I miss you, and you hate yourself for it. And you know what? I hate myself every fucking day for wanting you the way I do."

I pulled back and watched his gaze drop to my mouth. I may have been surrendered in his hold, but I was just as dominant as he was. We both had a power over the other that was too lethal, too toxic, too suggestive for our own good.

"Coach."

"Every day is a battle raging within me to keep my distance. Some days all I want is to just be around you. It is that simple."

Oh God. I needed to leave, but I couldn't find it in me to move.

"Coach," I said again.

"Hmm…"

"I have to go."

"So leave."

But my body wouldn't move. I wanted to stay like this a little bit longer. I wanted to lean into him and unwind in the security of his embrace, but I was too afraid.

I looked into his eyes. "What are you thinking?"

His eyes remained focused on my mouth. He ran his tongue along his bottom lip and my heart skittered against my chest. I knew that look. I knew it too well, like he wanted to devour me and leave me breathless, just as he had many times before.

"So much. I do not know where to even start."

I got it. I felt the same way.

"You have no idea how it is killing me, Adrianna, the way you hate me, the way you look at me with such contempt. I deserve your hate and everything you feel inside, but I cannot stomach it."

He raised his head and our eyes connected. Being like this again brought it all back. The desire. The need. I still craved this stupid Russian man.

"Kiss me," I said, my voice an array of sinful tones. "Please."

He shook his head. "No." His chest rose and fell rapidly, the lines around his eyes deepened with anguish. "You will regret it and hate me even more."

He was right. I probably would hate him, but then I thought of something.

"What if I kiss you?"

"Why? Why would you want to do that?"

This time I shook my head and the words fell from my lips before I could stop them. "I don't know. I really don't. Maybe, just for a second, I want to forget everything and not feel so empty inside. Because when I'm with you, I don't have a worry in the world. Like I'm me and you're you, and nothing else matters."

I closed my eyes, instantly regretting what I'd said.

"You should not want to kiss me..." He left his response open, and I picked up on it.

"No, I shouldn't. You're no good for me," I said.

"I am terrible for you." He paused, his mouth turning down. "I wish I was not. I wish I was a better man for you."

We were both bad for each other. He was power, I was obsession. No matter how highly charged our connection was, the result would always be the same. Destruction. Obliteration. Ruin. But yet, we couldn't break apart completely. Like we were tied to each other with no chance of escaping.

My eyes drifted to his full lips and I felt his body tremble against mine. My fingers were numb from how tight I held him, but I knew if I let go I'd lose control. Kova was toeing the line and despite all the wrong, it still excited me. He was struggling for me.

"Would you refuse me?" I asked, my voice soft. My heart thundered against my ribs.

"If that is what you want to give me, then I will take it. I am yours."

I didn't hesitate, I moved like a viper.

Latching onto his top lip, I stroked it with my tongue, then bit down. His body yielded to mine and he exhaled a sigh of pleasure. A deep, animalistic groan vibrated from his chest pressed against mine. Kova dropped my keys and cupped the side of my head and held me tighter to him. He kissed me back hard, inhaling deeply through his nose like he was breathing me in.

His tongue delved into my mouth, and I sighed, letting go of everything like I always did with Kova. We couldn't get enough of each other. Our kisses were fueled with greed and longing, tangled with passion only we understood. His thumb drew circles over my hammering pulse, while his other hand warmed my body, trembling with uncontrolled need.

"No more," I said, breaking the kiss.

He was breathing heavily. "Okay."

His quick acceptance switched something inside me and I leaned into him, taking control, and kissed him again. Kova slid his palm down my hip and over my butt. He grabbed my thigh and hiked my leg up around his hip, his hands desperate as they roamed my skin. His erection nudged my waist, and the tips of his fingers dipped inside my elastic shorts.

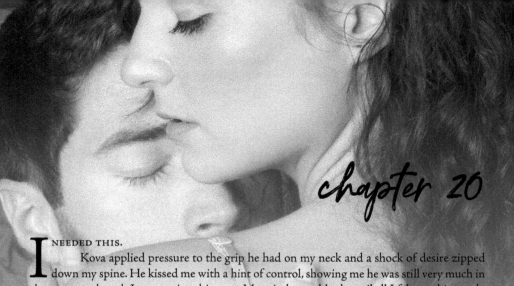

chapter 20

I NEEDED THIS.

Kova applied pressure to the grip he had on my neck and a shock of desire zipped down my spine. He kissed me with a hint of control, showing me he was still very much in charge, even though I was setting this pace. My mind went blank until all I felt was his touch, and I focused on the pleasure he ignited throughout my body. His hand slid further into my shorts, and I drew in a quiet breath as his fingers taunted me until I was rocking into him.

My teeth sank into his lip and he moaned, cupping me with a fierce grip. My back arched and I broke the kiss to breathe, dropping my head to his chest. I sighed against him and squeezed my eyes shut, trying to steady my breathing. I suddenly realized how much more I felt with Kova. Not just with my body, but in my heart too. He was my everything, what I needed now and always. He wasn't a quick hookup. Kova was a lover while Hayden had only been a distraction in that moment.

"We can stop," he said, much to my shock.

All I could do was shake my head no.

Flattening his tongue, Kova drew a wet trail slowly up my neck to my ear. I drew in a lustful gasp and clutched his shirt, trying not to shudder. He shifted until he had one thigh between mine, and then swept a finger over my wet slit. It'd been so long since I had felt the kind of pleasure only he could give me.

Kova scowled under his breath, a lilt of Russian danced decadently across my skin. "I can always tell when you want me. Your pussy drips with need, so swollen I can feel it throbbing." A purr released from my throat. "You love it." He breathed heatedly down the column of my neck. I tried to block out the sensations coursing through my body. My head rolled to the side as goose bumps broke out over my scorching flesh. "You love that I can make you forget your worries and let you just be you."

Kova ran his forehead along my nape, his facial hair grazing my jaw. His teeth nipped my sensitive skin. I inhaled deeply and his finger was in my panties, breaching the folds of my sex. My eyes rolled shut and I groaned in response as he teased my entrance, pressing on my opening before pulling away.

"Admit that no one will ever make you feel the way I do. Yes, I lied about some shit, but do not tell me that we do not belong together. This, right here, this is not normal, and that is why we cannot stay away from each other. I know I ruined you, but trust me when I say it has destroyed me just as much."

"Getting married is not *some shit*." I managed to chew out.

"You are completely right."

Oh hell, I couldn't take the tightness in my chest much longer. Tears filled my eyes because I hated that he was right and that he'd ruined it for us. Hated that he lied. Hated that he'd had sex with me while he was married. Hated that I was allowing him to touch me now, making me crave more of him, and that I wanted to come. I hated the whole situation and my traitorous body. I sighed, suddenly drained from this back and forth we were doing.

"I regret not telling you from the start. It is my biggest regret. I want to make things right between us."

My heart pounded. "How will it ever be right?"

"I do not know, but I will try to find a way," he said, leaning into me. A deep moan rolled off his lips onto my heated flesh when he placed his hand on my aching pussy. "I will do everything in my power to correct this between us. I hate myself for hurting you. I need you, more than you know."

I whimpered, trying not to let his comment affect me. I wanted to believe him, and there was a part of me that did, but a repeated mistake was a conscious decision. I thought I was strong, but when it came to Konstantin Kournakova, I was completely defenseless. My head knew better, but my heart didn't.

Kova lifted my chin and dropped a light kiss to my lips. His nose grazed mine. Heart racing, I looked deep into his eyes and felt a mixture of anguish and affection that I couldn't deny, no matter how much I hated him.

"Let me make you feel good. You need the release, I can feel it."

I swallowed and answered with a push of my hips as that divine rush of bliss started climbing. Our lips met and two fingers pushed into me deliberately slow. This wasn't just any kiss. He kissed me like he was begging me to believe everything he'd said.

It was hard not to.

His hardness prodded my side but he didn't make any attempt to do anything for himself. Knees weak, I wound my arms around his shoulders, and Kova held me tighter with his free hand. I released a lusty moan and my nipples tingled from the orgasm that was steadily climbing. I caught a sharp corner of something after each thrust, then the smooth glide of his hand against my skin.

Soft and hard, just like us.

He pushed into me, and I clenched, almost close to the edge when I felt the sharpness again. "Something is cutting into me," I said against his mouth.

I arched my hips and his mouth parted on a breath. "So soft and dripping."

We moved against each other, and I ignored that rigid material that was actually starting to feel good. Pleasure with pain, something Kova had taught me to crave and love. I wondered if he was imagining he was thrusting into me with the way his hips rolled, with how seductive his tongue entwined with mine, and the way his chest rose and fell. It was erotic and made me desire him even more.

"Let go," he said. "I can feel you holding back."

With his demand, Kova hit the right spot and it catapulted me over the edge. He deepened his kiss. He slid two fingers into my pussy and I ground harder against his hand, clenching as I came on his fingers, rubbing so hard I saw stars. There was a little pinch, but it was soon forgotten about. I needed this orgasm and I realized the times with Hayden had been a total waste. He didn't hold a candle to Kova.

I let out a satisfied moan as he caressed my tender pussy. This intense feeling was addicting, and I always wanted more afterwards.

A rush of breath left his lips. "I love seeing you like that," he said. "So beautiful."

"You're still hard." I found myself saying. He shook his head.

Sliding his hand from my shorts, his eyes bore into mine as he brought his fingers to his mouth. They were slick with my pleasure, evidence of how much I enjoyed what he did. His wrist tilted to the side and I caught the flicker of something as he slipped his fingers into his mouth.

My chest tightened and I grabbed his wrist, turning his hand to the side. A knife jammed right into my heart.

My lips parted. No. Please, no.

Regret thumped frantically against my ribs. A coldness washed over me. He was right, I would hate him even more and I wanted to, but this time it was my fault. Not his.

The orgasm I'd willingly given Kova saturated the platinum ring his wife had given him when they'd exchanged their vows.

Body trembling, I stepped back. My eyes skittered across the floor, confused, overwhelmed, lost. Kova reached for me, but I brushed his hand away and sat down on the bench, trying to catch my breath. Shame filled me to the point I was fighting the tears threatening to pour from my eyes.

Finally, I looked up at him.

"Did you do it on purpose?" My voice was quiet and low. "Did you purposely use your ring finger? No—I know you did. That's a total *you* move. I can't believe I was stupid enough to do this again with you. You're disgusting and I wish I'd never met you."

He looked horrified, but he'd hurt me so many times that I wanted to hurt him back.

"You think I would do that to you? I was not even thinking about which hand I was using. All I was thinking about was that I had you in my arms again."

I shook my head, my heart not able to handle another word. "I can't stomach this thing between us anymore. I can't do this back and forth."

Kova held up his left hand and I flinched. "You think I like wearing this fucking ring? The truth is I have to, as it is part of the agreement. Otherwise I would have had it fucking melted and dumped into the sea."

He shook his head, and dropped his arm to his side, but I just couldn't do it anymore. It wasn't fair to everyone involved, especially for the person who would ultimately lose in the end. Me.

"How do you do it?" I asked. An eerie calmness settled in me.

"Do what?"

"How can you be with me while you're married? How do you look at yourself? Don't you have any guilt?"

Kova swallowed hard, his Adam's apple moving up and down. His black brows furrowed, his green eyes danced across my heartbroken face. Tears blurred my vision. I wished I'd never allowed myself that moment of weakness.

Clearing his throat, he scratched the back of his neck and looked away. "No, I do not. Not when it is you who I am with."

My jaw dropped. "Oh, really? Then why do you call Katja 'my beloved' in your language when you're speaking to her?" I asked, crossing my arms. "I know what it means. You called Katja your beloved." He opened his mouth to speak but I kept talking. "Enough! Stop playing games with my mind. Can't you see what it's doing to me?" My chin quivered. "Can't you see that it's killing me? Can't you see that you're breaking my fucking heart?"

His eyes filled with guilt and I actually felt a sentiment of sadness for him. "What am I supposed to do? What do you want me to do? Help me out here because I am just as fucked as you."

I reared back, swiping a tear away. "No, you're not. Not even close. Pick one person and be done. I know today was my fault, and I don't blame you for this, but you can't be with both of us. I won't allow it."

"You want me to pick you? Is that it? And what if I did? Where would that get us?" He paused, his face a twist of emotions I didn't want to read into. "Nobody wins, Adrianna. There are consequences to every decision. Do you not get that? Someone will get hurt."

Typical man. He was so dumb. "Can't you see that I'm already hurt?"

His jaw flexed. "What do you want me to do?" he conceded. "You think I do not see how you are hurting every day? I see it, and my hands are tied right now. I have no choice in anything."

I stayed quiet as I stared. I didn't want to answer for him. I wanted to *be* his answer.

"That's the thing, you already chose."

"Just so you know, I did not pick her," Kova said, his shoulders wilting.

"How do you live with your lies?" Kova tilted his head, his gaze confused. "You know what? Just go. You have no respect for me or your damn wife." I took a few steps until I was in front of him. "We're done. We have to be done. I don't want you near me, I don't want you to talk to me. Not unless we're in practice or at a meet. Other than that, there's no reason for me to associate with you."

His face fell, and he took a step toward me. "Adrianna—" My name was a desperate whisper on his lips. "You wanted this, and I gave it to you. Please…"

I shook my head. "I know, and I take full responsibility, but no more. I'm done. Tell me no if there ever is a next time, which there won't be."

Kova propped his hands on his hips and angled his head toward the floor, staring like he was lost and didn't know his way.

"No more," I choked out and reached down to swipe my keys from the floor. "I just can't do it anymore. It's too much for me."

The pinch of his wedding band was a reminder of the emotional pain he'd created, and while I knew I loved him, I equally hated him. But after today I wouldn't be able to look at myself in the mirror without feeling disgusted with myself.

chapter 21

THE U.S. CLASSIC WAS THE BIGGEST COMPETITION OF MY CAREER THUS FAR. I'd be competing against the top elite gymnasts in the country for one of the coveted spots on the national team.

I'd be lying if I said I wasn't nervous. Getting to this point, to this day, wasn't just taxing on the body, but also on the mind. My nerves were shot, and I'd hardly slept the past couple of nights, but I was containing it. Cool, calm, and collected.

I blew out a shaky breath as Kova rubbed my shoulder.

"Do not be scared."

"I'm not."

I was terrified.

This was it. What I've always wanted. My Olympic dream was within reach, and there was no one here to share it with except Kova. None of my teammates had qualified to be here. Not even Madeline came. She'd stayed back with everyone else as they continued business as usual.

I scanned the growing crowd and briefly wondered if my dad had made it. He may not have been to every practice or meet, but he always showed up when it mattered. As for Joy, I wasn't sure if she'd come with him or not. I hadn't spoken to her since her drunken revelation. I thought maybe she'd reach out to me, considering she was the only mother I'd ever known and, oddly, I'd even held a sliver of hope that she would. But the more I thought about it, I knew she was the kind of negativity I couldn't afford right now.

I was next in line for vault and watched a gymnast take a huge double hop on her landing. She had the same vault as I did—the Amanar. While the Amanar was mostly muscle memory, not every gymnast could reach the height required for this skill.

"Opportunity only knocks once. This is your moment to let go of all the bullshit and show the world who you are." Kova stepped in front of me, his eyes lit with a contentment that soothed my flustered nerves. "You are going to come out a champion because this is what you were made for. That is what differentiates the gymnasts who are a dime a dozen. The ones who say they are going to do it, versus the ones who are resilient enough to get the job done." Kova paused, his gaze dropping to the floor before looking back up. "I know I do not say it often, but I am so proud of you. You are extraordinary. All those times when you hesitated, when fear simmered beneath your control, you were still courageous enough to try when others would have given up. You fought. You gave your all. Be proud of yourself, Adrianna. You have achieved massive accomplishments."

Acting on impulse, I jumped into Kova's arms and hugged him tight. It took him a moment to return the hug, but he did it, just a little stiff and unprepared. Not that I was surprised. This was the most contact, verbally and physically, I'd allowed us since the other night in the gym.

I rested my head on his shoulder and squeezed my eyes shut, absorbing his words I didn't know I needed to hear. They rolled off his lips in an inspiring tone and left me feeling self-assured.

An energy to thrive was brewing.

My wings were spreading, ready to coast.

Kova was feeding my soul, fighting off my demons, and he didn't even know it.

"Thank you," I said softly, squeezing him again. "I needed to hear that." He ran his palms in circles on my lower back before he pulled away.

"Go show them what you are made of."

I offered Kova a smile, then walked to the little box at the end of the runway that contained chalk. I slapped some on the bottom of my feet and inner thighs. I blocked out the noise of the crowd and kept my focus on each routine, rotation, and, of course, the scoreboard.

Inhaling a deep breath, I shifted on my feet and visualized the vault I was about to perform, like I'd done many times before. My eyes shifted to Kova for any last-minute directions, but all he did was smile. I exhaled, and stepped behind the white line.

It was go time.

Raising my arms so they were extended in front of me, I stood on my tiptoes and stepped into my run, swinging my arms back for momentum.

I got this… I got this…I got this… I chanted to myself as I neared the apparatus, running as fast as I could. Speed was absolutely crucial for this skill. Hurdling into a round-off, I rebounded off the springboard and arched back, my body a steep angle, remembering all the times Madeline and Kova had yelled at me to block as hard as I could. I exploded off the table. My stomach fluttered and my body snapped down to generate power. I started rotating while I continued to fly upward, squeezing every muscle to stay tight. It all happened so fast and yet it felt like slow motion. My body glided off muscle memory and I opened up for my landing.

Ankles glued together, my feet pounded into the mat. I let out a gush of air and raised my arms; chalk floated around me from the impact of my landing. I smiled and saluted, then turned to salute the judges.

No hop. No shift in my stance or step out.

I'd stuck my landing perfectly.

The huge grin was still on my face when I turned toward Kova, who enthusiastically clapped his hands and threw a fist in the air, yelling his excitement. He spotted me as I stepped off the podium and I flew into his arms.

"*Velikolepnyy!* Magnificent!" Kova shouted, and kissed the side of my cheek. "*Velikolepnyy!*"

Giving me one last squeeze, he released me and grabbed my shoulder. A little shake and he yanked me to him for another hug. I laughed, feeling his surge of happiness roll into me.

It didn't take long for my score to flash above our heads. Excitement bloomed inside my chest. Much to my surprise, I was currently in first place on the first rotation.

"*Put' k rabote!* Way to go!" he shouted in Russian. "Ah, *velikolepnyy*, Adrianna!"

My cheeks ached from grinning so big. No matter how hard I trained, seeing my name in first place was always a shock. "Thank you."

"Come. We must get ready for bars now."

I nodded and quickly grabbed my bag to follow Kova to the next rotation. I kept my focus only on my coach and didn't look around at the audience or the other events. I needed my head to stay in the game, and Kova was my center. Even when I was panicked and at my worst, Kova always kept me focused and balanced.

After I pulled on my grips, I chalked up. I'd be performing the new release skills Kova and I had worked on the last couple of weeks, along with my dismount.

"Remember, do not hold on too long when your dismount comes," he said as he stood next to me, then he gave me some other last-minute pointers. I nodded and nodded, and nodded some more. I stepped behind the mat and waited for the green light, while Kova moved to stand parallel to the apparatus.

Once I was given the okay from the judges, bars went as smoothly as vault, and my routine was over before I could take a breath. I landed my new dismount, smiling from ear to ear, and immediately searched for Kova. One look into his eyes and I knew he felt the same thing I did. Satisfaction. I thought he was going to fly onto the mat and sweep me off my feet. He was beaming, his green eyes large and evoking passion.

I felt good. Really damn good.

Kova engulfed me in a hug. "You took my breath away out there," he said near my ear. Goose bumps broke out over my arms. "I was in awe watching you."

I pulled back and lifted one side of my mouth into a shy grin. "Thanks, Coach."

There were two events down and two to go when that shadow of doubt crept into my mind as we moved on to beam. Had I practiced hard enough? Made all the necessary adjustments? Had I put enough heart into everything? I may finish in the top eight, even the top three at the rate I was going, but that still didn't mean I'd secure one of the twelve seats I dreamed of having.

Butterflies swirled in my stomach. I wanted to be in the All-Around, a gymnast used in all four events, but I could easily be a specialist and only compete in one event. While my performance today weighed heavily in their final decision, all my past meets played a part in it as well. There had been various times when a gymnast hadn't performed up to par at a nationals meet but had excelled in previous competitions and still picked for the team. It was all about who could perform under pressure and handle representing the country, and I had to wonder if I'd done enough.

Kova snapped his fingers and I immediately looked at him. "Focus. Do not go where you just were again." I nodded. "Now, you have the option here on beam. Do you want to push the difficulty, or perform your usual routine?" Kova asked.

Every gymnast had a list of backup skills with a myriad of difficulty they could add or remove to a routine depending on what happened at a meet and who they were competing against. That way, if a gymnast before me fell off the balance beam, or touched it with both hands after a large wobble, then I'd be able to lower my difficulty for a safer, cleaner routine if I wanted. The same went for all the other events. I had choices, though not many, and I'd only changed mine a select few times.

Chewing my bottom lip, I considered my options. I could keep it safe, or I could take a risk. I was quick to chance the difficulty with other events because I was more confident in them, but balance beam always fucked me sideways.

But not today, Satan. Not. Today.

I glanced at Kova. "Let's do it."

He studied me, the corners of his mouth twitching. I knew he was sizing me up, making sure I was mentally ready, and I appreciated that. Finally, his shoulders relaxed and he nodded his head, a grin spread across his face. Kova was excited and that made me feel good because I wanted to make him proud.

"Excellent."

We went over strategy and what I would change. It wasn't a lot, but it was enough to give me that extra edge.

Right before I saluted the judges, I patted my hands in the chalk bowl to absorb my feelings, and I wondered for a split second if I had made a grave mistake by pushing it.

Mental blocks. Anxiety. Overthinking. A gymnast's worst nightmare.

I exhaled a deep breath. I hated when I did this and reminded myself that I had one thing a lot of gymnasts didn't have—a supportive coach who would never put my well-being at risk if he thought I didn't have what it took.

Smiling to myself, I counted my blessings.

Too late to turn back now, I mounted the beam and surrendered myself to the sport.

STEPPING ONTO THE PODIUM FOR MY LAST ROUTINE OF THE MEET, I WAS UNSTOPPABLE and focused.

This was it.

After owning beam and making it my bitch, anxiety was no longer an issue. I turned vision into victory and conquered the obstacle of self-doubt. I had nothing to lose and everything to gain by tackling every fear plaguing me.

As soon as my feet touched the blue carpet, I was on a different level mentally—confident and passionate as I sashayed across the floor in graceful movements. I put as much passion as I could into this sport that had captivated my heart from a young age. The chalk became my shimmer and I floated effortlessly, hitting all my required skills, remaining fluid and light as a silky ribbon on floor as I had been on the balance beam.

Stepping down the stairs, I high-fived Kova and went in for a quick hug.

"There was one tumbling pass where you came dangerously close to stepping out of bounds and a double turn where you came out a little too early, but overall I am not concerned," he said.

Hot as hell and breathing heavily, I nodded in agreement. I propped my hands on my hips and waited. I could tell he felt good and that relieved me, but just knowing the smallest mistake could cost me everything was still always a thought in the front of my mind.

"I almost completely fell out of the turn. I don't know how I didn't, to be honest. My hips were so off-centered, I could feel it. Did I take too many pauses? Were they long? How were my leaps? Did I look like a stiff robot?" The corner of his mouth tugged up on one side and his eyes shone down on me. "I almost changed my last tumbling pass," I blurted out.

His brows bunched together. "Of course, I am glad you did not, but what happened?"

Panting, I shook my head. "I don't know. It was like this exhaustion took over me and it would've been easier to downgrade, but in those few seconds I had, I knew I'd regret it if I did."

"You are done and it is out of your hands. No more stressing. You were incredible today, Adrianna. You gave it your all. Regardless of what happens, this is possibly the best day of my life. You made coaching very rewarding."

My shoulders sagged and a smile of gratitude tipped my lips.

Turning around, I dug through my duffle bag for my sweats. My throat was taut with the emotion I'd blocked out and the adrenaline was feeding my blood. The months leading up to this day, the struggle, the climb, it all came down to this afternoon and the work I'd just put in, but also the dedication of my coaches. They were my backbone, especially Kova.

"Yeah!" Kova erupted behind me. "*Bud' ya proklyat. Vote to da!*"

I spun around and immediately looked up at the screen for my name. I stood in shock, unable to form words or even blink. My brain was a pile of mush. I couldn't think straight while I stared at the numbers like they were roman numerals and I was trying to remember which one meant what.

I didn't anticipate a maximum score after the few errors I knew I made, but I also didn't expect it to be that good either. I was in the lead, but only by a tenth of a point. The only event I wasn't first in was beam, but that didn't shock me.

Kova spun into me with a hug and pulled back just as quickly. My face lit up and I laughed through a smile. His tongue was rolling with Russian words I didn't understand and his entire face was bursting with joy.

"What do you have to say?" he asked.

"Ahh, ahh… I don't know. I'm just shocked right now. Is this real life?"

I covered my face with my hands and smiled, feeling so giddy over this moment. I glanced up at the standings again in disbelief. There were still a few rotations left for the gymnasts who'd started after I had, but I held my head high with hope.

Taking a seat, I leaned over and placed my elbows on my knees, and stared at the floor. I clasped my hands together and took in this accomplishment. I was a little deep in my emotions and wanted to remember this moment without the flashing of lights and cameras everywhere. Within the next hour I'd know if I had made the national team.

"Adrianna," Kova said, taking a seat next to me. He placed a hand on my back. "Have faith and trust me. What you did today was nothing less than extraordinary."

I looked at him. "I trust you as my coach, but you know I can't blindly trust you. Trusting you has gotten me nowhere."

A shadow crossed his eyes and remorse instantly filled me. I wasn't sure why I said that. It was cruel and just as soon as it left my lips, I regretted it. He'd given me everything I'd asked for in the gym, but the word trust and the name Kova didn't mesh well together and grated under my skin.

"I'm sorry."

"I know what is going through your head right now. You are an anxious ball of nerves and questioning everything. You are edgy. Your fingers are tingly. You have too much adrenaline pumping through you. It is normal to feel that way." I nodded, ashamed. It was like he was in my head. "And," he added, leaning in closer, "if you actually meant what you said, we would not be here right now."

I rolled my lips between my teeth and bit down, pushing the tears back. "You're right… I'm sorry. I shouldn't have said that."

"Do not apologize. In all fairness, I have given you reasons to doubt me, but never when we are coach and gymnast. I have given you my all and more because I believe in you. I hope you can see that."

I tilted my face to the side and listened to his voice. "I can."

Kova nodded and handed me my jacket.

"I can't wear that right now. I'm sweating." He laughed, and I laid it on top of my bag. "Do you really mean that, though? That I did excellent today?"

"You should know by now I do not sugarcoat. I would not say it if it were not true." He placed his hand on my knee and I turned to face him. "You are a performer and you blew me away today, but you have since the season started. If the judges and head coaches for the team do not see that, then I have lost faith in the sport. You deserve to be on the national team. You gave it everything, and if we were not in front of hundreds of people, I would show you exactly how I truly feel and pull you in and kiss you right now. You radiate with a glow that draws me in in ways I cannot explain."

"Coach…" I kept my voice low, fearful someone could hear.

He put a hand up and waved me off. "I am sorry. I know it is wrong of me, but it is what I feel inside right now. I am enamored with every part of you—mind, body, and soul. I am addicted to the way your body takes over when you are under pressure and perform. I cannot tear my eyes from you. You are going places, Adrianna Rossi, and I wish I could be there with you every step of the way."

I shook my head, not understanding. "What are you talking about? You will be there."

His lips turned down and it caused a twinge in my chest. "Not forever."

I closed my mouth as realization set in. Time passed painfully slow, my emotions a disastrous mess I couldn't make sense of. Tears burned the back of my eyes and I struggled to steady my breath. Kova was, once again, right. He wouldn't be there forever as my coach, and despite all our grievances, I didn't want to fathom that. There were no two people as in sync as us, and moving further apart. It wasn't fair.

We sat together in silence as the meet finished. The announcer's voice thundered across the gym with directions for the coaches and athletes.

Kova's throat bobbed as he swallowed. "Come on. Let us go and wait as the final scores are tallied."

I nodded, and picked up my gym bag and slung it over my shoulder. After sitting for the last hour, my body had time to decompress and the weight of the day set in. Everything was tight and the pain under my ribs was back. I drew in a quiet breath and applied pressure to my side. Clenching my eyes shut, I prayed the pain would go away and accidently stepped into Kova.

"Are you okay?" he asked.

"Oh, ah, yeah. I was just yawning and tripped," I lied.

I followed closely by his side, purposely not looking at the scoreboard. The last time I viewed it, I was still in the top eight, but I didn't want to get my hopes up.

We joined the other coaches and gymnasts. Kova patted my back, giving me words of encouragement and praise for my effort. The chatter grew louder, as did the pounding in my temples. Stars danced in my vision, either a sign of dehydration or stress. Reaching into my bag, I pulled out a bottle of water and took a large swallow.

Heavy clapping reverberated throughout the arena. I looked around in confusion, then I spotted the head of the women's USA team, Elena Lavrov, walking onto the gym floor in her usual red, white, and blue sweats. My heart stopped and I automatically grabbed Kova's hand. He gave me a reassuring squeeze without looking and then released it.

Elena was an iconic figure, a legend in the gymnastics world, renowned for her ability in training and keen eye. Born in Romania but now a citizen of the United States, she was known for taking drastic measures to be the absolute best.

The flat-screen televisions overhead were now blank in preparation to list all of the national team members. The noise in the room died down. This was the moment we'd all been waiting for.

I placed my bag and water by my feet and took a deep breath, trying to steady my emotions. I used the back of my hand to wipe the little beads of sweat from my top lip, then I tightened my ponytail. This woman, who was all of five-foot-five, wielded so much power. She was the scissors who cut dreams in half, and the super glue that bonded them forever.

Taking the mic, Elena spoke with a heavy Romanian accent almost too thick to understand. I leaned forward as if it would help me hear her better.

"Today, we had a tremendous outcome with many fine and extremely talented gymnasts. Your dedication to the sport, and yourselves, shows no bounds. You all are the best of the best and should be very proud of your accomplishments." Elena paused, her eyes bouncing over the gymnasts. "For some of you, today marks the end of the season. Do not be discouraged. Never give up on what you believe in or what you dream of, because then you are giving up on yourself, and that would be a tragedy." She smiled and I felt it in my chest. "Take a moment and look around this room. Four of you will go on to represent the United States at the next Olympic Games."

Applause broke out, then quickly dissipated.

"Everyone wants to come out on top, but remember, at the Games, gymnastics is a team sport. If you are chosen today, you are chosen for what is best for the team and your country. Whether that be an All-Around competitor or a Specialist, or an alternate, either way, consider it an honor. Gymnastics is based on a system where you amass points for difficulty, then execution. We want the highest level of gymnasts inspiring each other to do more, to gain that top spot on the podium." Elena held up her index finger. "You must remember, this is not just about winning. We all want to win. This is about how much more you are willing to sacrifice for the sake of the team and yourself. How much you are willing to give up, to reign supreme as a whole. It is not about what you do, but how you do it. This is only the beginning, my girls."

The arena was in complete silence as she unfolded a piece of paper in her hands. Pandemonium was about to break out, both tears of joy, and tears of downright soul-crushing defeat.

Everything I had worked for depended on this moment. Everything.

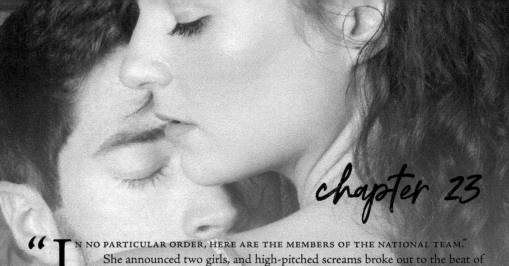

chapter 23

"I N NO PARTICULAR ORDER, HERE ARE THE MEMBERS OF THE NATIONAL TEAM."
She announced two girls, and high-pitched screams broke out to the beat of her broken English. She read off two more names, then another, and another. Her deep accent caused her to mispronounce a few. When she got to number seven, and my name still hadn't been called, dread formed in the pit of my stomach.

Gymnastics was a merciless sport.

If my name wasn't called, I'd walk away stoically and figure out my next step.

I. Would. Not. Cry. I had to be strong.

Elena announced girls eight and nine, leaving only three spots left.

The tenth gymnast was named and everything around me faded to a blur. My heart plummeted to the floor, taking my confidence with it. Another name was called that wasn't mine. The back of my eyes burned and my jaw trembled from intense emotions hitting me all at once. I thought I was going to faint when I got a small nudge in my side.

"Go! What are you waiting for?" Kova nudged me harder and yelled in my ear. I blinked, my brows drawn together and my gaze disoriented.

Kova shoved me forward and I almost cursed at him, but then he gave me the look. I straightened my shoulders and spotted Elena. She wore a huge grin on her face as she happily waved me forward. Tears immediately blurred my vision and chills broke out down my arms.

The pressure in my chest eased and I looked over my shoulder at Kova for guidance. He clapped and shouted my name, mouthing for me to go, to keep moving.

I looked back at Elena in complete and utter shock.

Elena had called my name. I was number eleven.

I couldn't control my emotions any longer and burst into tears. Gymnasts rubbed my shoulders and congratulated me through sobbing giggles as I walked past them. I observed my new teammates while I strode to the end of the line, each girl held the same reaction as me—blotchy faces, teary eyes, giant smiles stretched from ear to ear.

Oh. My. God.

My name had been called. I'd done it. I'd made the national team! I was one step closer to making the Olympic team.

My face fell into the palms of my calloused, chalky hands, and I bawled uncontrollably. My shoulders shook while I stood in line with the others. I'd made it. I'd thought this was the end of my career as a gymnast, that I hadn't been picked… But I'd made it.

"Here are the members of the United States National Women's Gymnastics Team," Elena said into the microphone, her voice rebounding off the walls of the arena. She waved her arm toward her new team. "Let us give a round of applause to those who made it, and to those who fought so diligently to be here. You all deserve to be rewarded for your hard work."

With the back of my hands, I wiped my eyes and looked up. I took a deep breath and exhaled. My heart broke for the girls who stood in front of me with tears of sorrow streaming down their cheeks. I knew what was going through their minds. They felt like failures, like their lives were over. They wondered if they would ever make it. Questioned what else they could've done to be standing on this side. They would torture themselves, questioning every moment and if it was worth it. Some would give up after this, and some would fight to come back. It was a vicious cycle.

"When I call your name, I would like you to step forward," Elena said. She called out a total of six names, mine being one of them.

Adrianna Rossi. Vault. Uneven bars. Floor. "Here are your specialists."

Chills wracked my body, then a smile tore across my face again. Even better than I'd hoped for.

Once we were released, I didn't have to look far to find Kova. I could feel his eyes on me, all over me, covering my body. I pivoted to face him, and without hesitation, I ran into his arms. Kova lifted me up and I buried my face in his neck as he wrapped his arms around my back and crushed me to him. I hugged him tightly, drew him into me, breathing in the only scent that instantly comforted me. In this moment I couldn't help but forget all the negative things we'd been through. He'd seen me at my worst, and I'd seen him at his worst. But this was something else entirely. A feeling that couldn't be explained or understood, just a connection with my other half.

There were no words spoken. None were needed. All the sacrifices, the injuries, the hurtful words, the grueling hours, were worth this moment. To be in his arms, to make it this far with him, and be on the team, was worth everything.

"I knew you had it in you," he whispered. His lips brushed my ear. My heart fluttered against my chest and I wondered if he could feel it.

I swallowed hard. "I couldn't have done it without you."

"Yes, you could have. You had it in you all along. You just needed a push."

"From the right person," I finished for him. "I needed it from the right person."

Kova lowered me down. I slid against his body and my feet met the floor, but we didn't release each other. We stood close, embracing with my hands in the curve of his elbows. It may have seemed strange to be so intimate and touchy with each other out in the open, but other coaches and gymnasts were doing the same thing, some having to console their athletes. I looked at him with gratitude and respect, and he acknowledged it with a small smile.

"Let us go find your father. I spotted him earlier."

I nodded. We didn't have to search long, being that my dad found us first. How he got onto the meet floor was beyond me because no parents were allowed, but I didn't question it. He strode toward us, grinning from ear to ear. He wore dark denim jeans and a white polo button-up shirt with a flashy colorful design on the fabric where the three buttons were left open. His casual attire was a stark contrast to the suits he usually donned.

"Adrianna!" he said with a proud smile, and then lifted me into his arms with a giant hug. He quickly released me and looked down. "I'm so proud of you. Congratulations."

"Thanks, Dad."

He was positively glowing and that made me so happy inside. Dad patted my shoulder. "You were incredible out there. I'm so glad I got to see you perform. I'll never forget it."

I beamed up at him.

"Frank," Kova said, putting his hand out. My dad greeted him.

"Konstantin, I can't thank you enough for getting my daughter one step closer to her dream."

"Ah, I am flattered, but it was not me. Your daughter had it in her all along. I just gave her the direction and means she needed to take it to the next step."

"What's next for her?"

Kova slipped his hands into his pockets and lifted his chin. "She will have camps she is required to attend, and international meets that will be added to her schedule. It is going to be a lot of stress to perform on demand and under pressure, but Adrianna has it in her. I need to meet with Elena, and then we can mull it over with dinner and drinks."

Dad agreed. "Whatever you need, let me know."

chapter 24

KOVA WASN'T EXAGGERATING.

My eyes widened as I peered down at my revised calendar in both hushed shock and eagerness. He'd devised a six-month itinerary for me that left my dad's forehead creased with apprehension. While I was impatient for it to begin, I could tell it was overwhelming for him. If I took a guess, he was probably wondering how I'd manage to do it all. My schedule would change drastically in the form of meets and camps. Seeing what I was about to take on caused a flutter in my heart. This was a challenge I was determined to win.

"I know I questioned this when my daughter first came to you, but I have to ask again because this is just…a lot." He picked up his copy and scanned over it for the tenth time. We sat at a table in the corner of the restaurant in one of the hotels Dad owned. "Will she be able to handle the traveling on top of everything else? The training and the camps? The time change is going to throw her off. I'm worried she's going to get burned out."

I raised my chin. "Of course I can." Kova and my dad looked in my direction. "I can manage, just like I did before."

"She only has so much time," Kova said, and leaned forward. "Adrianna is at her prime. We need to capitalize on it while we can. Not to say that she cannot go for a second Olympics, as it is always a possibility, but her time is now and we want to make the most of it. She has a valid passport, yes?"

"Of course," Dad replied, and scribbled down a few notes. "Surely the parents attend these meets in…" He squinted at his paper before his voice rose to a higher pitch. "Italy? And Scotland?"

Kova cleared his throat and folded his hands in front of him. "Some parents do. However, it is very costly, and the majority cannot afford it."

"So they travel alone to a country they've never been, where they have no jurisdiction? That's not going to happen."

All the air left my lungs.

"They travel with their teammates and coaches," Kova corrected him.

Dad's shoulders relaxed marginally. He was worried about the international meets, but with every right. I'd probably feel the same way if I were in his shoes. Any time I'd traveled out of the country, it had always been with my parents. Never alone.

"It's one thing to allow her to live on her own. I can get here in no time and I'm familiar with the area. It's another thing entirely to travel thousands of miles to a foreign country where she has no rights or protection. You mean to tell me parents just let their children go alone? Without a care in the world?" He shook his head and placed the papers down. "No way. Not going to happen. I'll have to check my work schedule and see what I can do."

There went the little bit of air I had left. My ribs throbbed from the pounding they were taking.

"What about Mom?" I couldn't call her Joy in front of Kova.

"Don't count her in on anything at this point," he said. He picked up his cell phone and moved his thumbs swiftly over the screen.

I pulled back, retreating into myself again. I closed down. *Don't count her in on anything at this point.* She isn't even my real mother.

My forehead pounded. I couldn't wrap my mind around how she could go from raising me as if I were her own to discarding me like yesterday's trash. True, Joy wasn't my real mom, but she was the only mom I'd ever known, and despite our differences, she was still my mom and I loved her. Maybe Dad was wrong. There was no way she would just write me off for something I had no hand in.

"What do you mean don't count her in?" I asked gently. "Can I talk to her about it in case you can't be there?" My voice sounded small and brittle. "I've never asked her for anything, but I'll ask her for this. She can't possibly say no."

He didn't respond, just continued to type away on his cell phone.

I swallowed the thick lump in my throat and glanced toward Kova, panic stricken and hoping he'd get the hint. *Do something*, I pleaded soundlessly. He gave me a subtle shake of his head, and I dropped my gaze. If I had to, I'd ask Kova to speak with him privately. There was no way I'd come this far and then not be able to travel to qualifying meets. I wasn't sure what I'd do if it came down to that, but I'd find a way to go.

"Dad—"

"Adrianna," he said my name. Just one word. And it was enough for me to understand the meaning behind his tone.

I sank into my chair, with my stomach churning bitterly and my heart in my throat. It seemed like every time I got one step closer to my dream I was shoved ten feet back. Dad shot out a series of texts and mumbled angrily under his breath while we sat in silence around the table. Finally, he exhaled a heavy sigh then turned his phone face down.

"Dad—"

"Not now." His head snapped in my direction and I recoiled at his leveled gaze. "We'll talk later." He turned toward Kova. "So, what's next?"

Kova cleared his throat. "Apart from the various meets that are overseas, Adrianna has two camps she must attend. The camp is in Texas and held at the U.S. Olympic Training Site. One is this coming weekend, and the other is next month. Both will last one full week and she will be surrounded by the best of the best in the sport, meaning coaches, doctors, and therapists. She will be well taken care of. She will not be permitted to leave the grounds, but she will have everything she needs. Her meals will be taken care of and she will room with other gymnasts."

"Will you be there with her?" Dad asked.

"I will not."

"Hmm…" I'd traveled alone to other states before, so this one should've been a shoe in, but judging by my dad's tone, I wasn't so sure now.

"I have many connections there, if that helps you," Kova added.

My dad and Kova continued to discuss what my future entailed in detail until dinner arrived.

"Excuse me." Kova stepped away to take a call midway through our meal. Dad waved him off and ate away at his rare steak like he didn't have a care in the world. We at quietly together.

"I do not mean to be rude," Kova said, returning a moment later, "but I need to continue this call with my wife in private."

I pretended not to care and cut a small sliver of flaky snapper. I took a bite and wondered what he and Katja were going to talk about, then just as quickly let the thought go. I had enough on my plate now, so to speak.

"Not to worry, I'll have the waiter pack up what's left and send it up to your room," Dad said.

"Thank you, Frank. Adrianna. I will see you both tomorrow." Kova left with his phone pressed to his ear.

Tomorrow we would fly back to Georgia. I'd practice like a beast for the next four days, then fly to Texas for a week. I wasn't sure what to expect at camp—I'd only heard rumors— but in between camp I'd be practicing my regular schedule, and critiquing every part of my routines just like I'd done thousands of times before.

"What's wrong?" Dad gestured toward my plate with his steak knife. "Is it not to your liking?"

I took another small bite and swallowed. "It's perfect. Probably the best yellowtail I've had in a while."

He smiled. "You know, if your mother was here, she wouldn't let you eat the potato soufflé."

"I know. She would've had it yanked from my plate and made the waiter take it back."

I glanced down at the little ramekin of puffed up potatoes and my mouth watered. Carbohydrates. How I missed them dearly. I'd only taken a small bite. I'd give anything to lose myself in the bowl of shitty carbs, but I knew better. One little taste wouldn't kill me, but there was not a chance in hell I'd be eating them now since I'd made the national team.

"Speaking of Mom…"

"There's nothing to talk about."

"Dad, please," I begged. "What's going on?"

"Nothing we haven't already dealt with in the past. Trust me, sweetheart, everything is going to be as it should've been in the end."

I lowered my eyes. He made no sense. His words certainly didn't match his cloying tone, but it was the last thing he said that troubled me. The urge to delve deeper into that statement nagged at my gut something fierce but something told me he'd wind up angry.

"Adrianna, the only thing I want you to worry about right now is gymnastics. That's your first and only focus. I will take care of the rest."

Take care of the rest, as if he could sweep it under the rug. We weren't talking about an old friend I hadn't seen in years, we were talking about the woman who begrudgingly raised me and then shut me out.

Dad gestured toward a small menu. "Do you want dessert?"

I shook my head. "Does she hate me?"

His eyes softened. "No, sweetheart, she could never hate you."

"Then why does she always act like it? Ever since I found out that I'm your dirty little secret—"

Dad's eyes popped and he pointed his finger toward me. "First of all, you're not my dirty little secret and don't you ever say that again."

Tomato, tomahto. "Then why hasn't she made any attempt to contact me or be part of my life?"

"How is that any different than before?" he said.

I snapped my mouth shut, sinking a little inside. I thought about his argument, and he was right. Dad was absolutely right on the mark. She had done so little to be part of my life, and only when it was convenient for her. She never went out of her way for me, and everything she did had a motive. The more I thought about it, the more it sickened me. Nothing had changed, and I was sure it never would now. I swallowed hard, the reality of the situation breaking my heart.

"I apologize," he said, regret filled his voice. "I shouldn't have said that."

"It's fine," I replied, shaking it off and cleared my face of any emotion. "You're right. There's no difference. I guess it's just wishful thinking is all."

I was sure there wasn't anything worse than being rejected by a parent for something you had no control over. It wasn't my fault I was born, or that I was the result of an affair. *Joy*—what a name for someone who was so miserable with her lavish life—took her hurt and anger out on the wrong person, and it was unjust. I needed to remember that, but pretending like the truth didn't faze me was a tough pill to swallow when it was killing me on the inside.

I had to wonder if I ever had a mother who cared. Joy certainly didn't. She made it blatantly obvious she was in the marriage for herself, and my biological mother had been paid off.

I was human. With emotions. Destroyed by the deceptions of my family. And Dad wanted me to forget it as if it were old news.

"Sometimes I forget you're not an adult."

"Dad, I'm not a baby anymore, but you're right," I said with an empty smile. "My only concern right now is gymnastics and nothing more."

If only it were so easy to believe the lies I told myself daily.

chapter 25

I HADN'T CRIED IN DAYS, BUT THIS MORNING I WOKE WITH A SORROWFUL EMPTINESS in my chest that nagged at me.

I'd hardly slept despite the crippling exhaustion. My eyes were swollen, and I used the best, most expensive under-eye serum to reduce the puffiness and hide any strain that I could find.

That was how I got through each day, pretending I didn't have a care in the world. I was a goddamned robot all the while dying inside.

Recklessly bound together by sports tape, eye cream, and lame all-natural anti-inflammatory medicine Kova had given me, I was on the verge of a breakdown. I could feel it. It was as if the impending doom was curling inside of me. I really didn't know how I got through each day, but today, I was deep in my feelings and hating it.

I'd been parked and sitting in front of World Cup for an hour in the rain now when I saw Holly and Hayden get out of their car. The plan was to come in early and train, but the moment I'd parked I was rendered motionless. Something about the weather and my emotions were working double time. All I could do was sit and stare. But now I was out of time and had to go in or Kova and Madeline were going to have my head. Especially since we'd revised my training schedule.

I watched Holly run inside, and then I popped my earbuds in and pulled my hood from my sweater over my head before opening my car door. I wanted to avoid talking to Hayden. With the way I was feeling, my new goal was to evade every other obstacle in my life that involved crushing a little more of my soul. It wasn't his fault, but having sex with Hayden had been a mistake I wished I could take back. I'd never tell him that, of course, but it was something that I should've never let happen.

Walking toward the front door of the gym, I was home free when a hand came down on my shoulder and stopped me. I spun around.

"Hey," Hayden said softly, his brows drawn together.

I pulled one ear bud out. "Hi."

"You didn't hear me calling your name?"

"I was listening to music," I lied. My phone started vibrating in my hand. I glanced down and my stomach dropped. It was the doctor's office calling me. They must've gotten the results of my blood test back.

"Do you need to get that?" Hayden asked, using his chin to point toward my cell phone.

I pressed the ignore button and sent them straight to voicemail. I didn't have time to go over the results now with practice about to start.

"No, it's fine. I can call them back during lunch."

"Congrats on making the national team. I'm not surprised though. I had a feeling you'd make it."

"Thanks," I replied. Not even the reminder of making the team could get me out of my dark mood.

"I've been trying to reach you for a while now," he said.

My gaze averted to the ground then back up. He had called a few times but I'd hit the fuck you button every time. "I know," I said quietly. "I'm sorry. I've just been really busy."

Hayden tilted his head to the side and gave me a knowing look. "I can see past your bullshit, you know, but it's cool, I get it." He shifted on his feet and offered me a small smile. He wasn't the type of guy to ever make someone feel bad. "Listen, there's something I want to talk to you about. Something I wanted to tell you that I haven't told anyone yet. I wanted you to be the first."

"You haven't told anyone? Not even your sister?"

"Of course I told her. I just meant no one else, not even Reagan," he added. The corners of his eyes crinkled as he gave me an impish smile, and that alleviated the pressure on my shoulders. Being the good guy that he was, Hayden pulled me into a hug and I melted into him. A few moments of silence passed. I found the reprieve that I needed, and one that our friendship needed as well.

"I'm sorry I was a dickhead and ignored your calls," I said, my face smashed against his chest.

Hayden tightened his arms around me. "Don't worry about it. We all have our moments. Think we could meet up later?"

I pulled back. "Is everything okay? I have a few moments now if you want to talk."

"It's all good. Very positive actually. I just want your opinion about something."

"Sure. Want to grab dinner later? I probably won't get out until seven-ish."

Hayden nodded. "I'll pick you up around eight."

I smiled. "Perfect."

I wracked my brain trying to figure out what Hayden wanted to talk to me about. Maybe he'd decided to quit dealing to our teammates. But did his sister even know about that side of him? I only had about an hour to really put any kind of effort into it since I'd been focused on practice, but while I got ready for dinner, I came up with nothing. Absolutely nothing, and it drove me crazy.

Taking the elevator down to the lobby, I stepped outside and spotted Hayden's car.

"Okay. Spill," I said the moment I sat in the passenger's seat, throwing a huge grin at him.

Hayden shifted into gear, and chuckled. "Calm down. I'll tell you soon enough."

I turned toward him. "Really? You're going to make me wait? Fine. But can you at least give me a hint?"

He gave me a fleeting look before turning his attention back to the road. "You look nice."

"You do too," I replied quickly. We were both dressed casually, my favorite style. My hair was damp and my face makeup free.

"Where do you want to eat?"

"Anywhere." Another quick response.

"Something fattening?"

I hesitated for a split second and it produced another chuckle from Hayden. "Sure."

"Wow. You'll agree to anything right now if I give you a hint, won't you?"

"Pretty much." I laughed. "You're killing me! Give me something." A giant, contagious smile spread across his face. "See!" I said, pointing at him. "You want to tell me."

"Fine," Hayden said, pulling onto the main road. "It involves my gymnastics career."

"And…"

"Is pizza okay? I'm starving and don't want to wait long."

I grimaced, my mood changing instantly. My mouth watered at the thought of eating a supreme slice of pizza. One day, I told myself. One day I'd order a whole pie just for me and scarf it down with a two-liter bottle of Coke. But not today.

"Remember what happened last time I had pizza? The horrible stomachache I had? I don't want to chance it. I'll order a salad, if that's okay."

Hayden eyed me. "Of course it's fine."

We pulled into the shopping center and parked. In less than five minutes, we were inside and seated with drinks.

"So, what kind of pizza should I get?" he asked, looking at the menu. My patience was running thin. I wasn't good with surprises, much less waiting for them. Not that this was a surprise, but it sure felt like one. I could never hold back when it came to birthdays or Christmas gifts and always caved beforehand.

Basically, I ruined surprises.

And friendships.

And relationships.

And marriages.

When I didn't answer, Hayden peeked over the menu at me. I leveled a stare at him and he busted out laughing. I tried to hold the flat line of my mouth and the heavy I-want-to-strangle-you-with-my-mind look, but I couldn't and started giggling. Picking up the straw wrapper, I formed it into a ball and threw it at him.

"Alright, alright, alright," he said.

"Get on with it, Matthew McConaughey."

"Since this is my last season with World Cup, I've been thinking a lot about my future and what I want to do. I debated whether I wanted to continue gymnastics in college or not. I kind of want to just experience college and the whole party and fraternity thing, but the thing is, you know as much as I do what this sport means. I don't want to give up gymnastics yet. Letting go would be extremely difficult, but given the hours we practice now, I wasn't sure I'd be able to get the full college experience and train at the same time. The more I considered collegiate gymnastics, the more I realized I could have both. Apparently, we only have to train like half of what we're training now."

"Half?" My eyebrows shot up. Half was a walk in the park.

"No more than twenty hours a week."

"Oh, my God! That's nothing. I practice twenty hours a week just in my sleep." I joked.

"Right? Once I figured that out, I applied to schools all over the country. Ones that offer degrees in something I'd possibly be interested in, and ones with a decent men's gymnastics program."

I stared wide-eyed. "When did you have time to apply?"

"Over the weekends when the girls team was away at meets. I didn't apply to all of them, some recruited me."

While Hayden worshipped and found misery in the sport in the same manner as I did, going to the Olympics was never his dream.

I smiled. "That's so good. Where did you apply?"

"University of Florida, though they don't have a men's team. I just like the school. Stanford and Berkley both have men's teams, as well as Oklahoma and Arizona. But it was a school I'd never considered that requested for me to apply. University of Michigan. I figured there was no way I was getting in there"—he shrugged—"but I thought, why not? It couldn't hurt. Not my ideal school, it's cold as fuck there, but I have nothing to lose."

"Michigan has a great men's team. Some of the guys even competed in the Olympics, I believe."

"Yeah, I know. I mean, I found out after I looked at the school. I was pretty shocked."

His pizza came out with my salad, and Hayden slid a slice onto my plate just to be nice, then slid one onto his. I took a bite and nearly sighed, but I pushed it aside and dug into my salad. I took two huge bites when a thought popped into my head.

"What is Holly going to do?"

"She applied to the University of Alabama, but she hasn't heard back. It's the only school she applied to and it's been her dream to go there since we were kids. I think she just likes the colors." He laughed. "I thought you knew?"

I shook my head and averted my gaze to my plate. I'd been so involved with myself that I hadn't spoken to my friends much lately. I'd become a bit of a loner, and man, did I feel like a shitty person because of it.

"Michigan is offering me a full ride and a spot on the men's team." I stopped mid-chew and gaped at him. "I could also get a degree in engineering there," he added, "which is something I've been thinking about."

I swallowed. "That's incredible, Hayden. Tell me you're going to take it." I shouted a little too loud and looked around to see if anyone had picked up on it.

Hayden wiped his mouth with a napkin, then crumpled it in his hand. He looked at me, the flat line of his mouth creased with indecision. "Honestly, Aid, I don't know what I want to do. I'm leaning toward Florida, but at the same time, I don't know if I'm ready to say goodbye to gymnastics either."

The tone in his voice surprised me and I took no effort to hide my reaction. To me, the choice was an obvious no-brainer. Being offered an academic scholarship *and* going after the career one wanted was a rare thing, and it seemed he'd been offered the best of both worlds.

"What's holding you back? Why wouldn't you want to go to Michigan?"

"I've always loved Georgia. Plus, I'll be closer to Holly if she needs anything."

"Your sister would only be a plane ride away. I feel like your choice is an obvious one."

Hayden took another slice of pizza.

"Have you considered your future?" he asked me.

"I've given it a little thought, but my main goal right now is focusing on the Olympics. I feel like everyone is probably sick of hearing it, but the way I feel about it…it's hard to explain. It's all I think about, day in and day out. I want it so bad I can taste it, and if that means deferring school for a little while, then maybe I will. I admire you for knowing what you want, though."

"Any idea where you may want to go?"

"Honestly, no. I haven't really looked into schools, but I should probably start."

"So you've never thought about it at all?"

"I mean, I have." I paused. "Kova was the one who brought it up to me and said I needed to think about universities with Division One gymnastics teams. Aside from that, I haven't given it much thought since I have a one-track mind right now." I paused. "Stupid of me, right? I should have been planning for that too."

"Kova brought it up to you?" he asked, ignoring everything but my mention of Kova.

I nodded, taking another bite and thinking back to that day in my condo when Kova had talked to me while I took an ice bath.

"Yeah, he wanted to prepare me for any monetary awards I might be offered, and said if I decided to go pro, I would be waiving my chances of competing in college. I'd never given it any thought until he said something. I remember thinking how naïve I'd been for not knowing what could have happened if I'd have accepted money without knowing the consequences. I'm glad he did because I didn't know about any of that. Being awarded cash would be cool, but I don't really need it, you know?"

"Wow. Kova thinking about someone other than himself for a change." I glared at Hayden and he threw his hands up. "I'm sorry, but I couldn't resist. I'm just surprised is all."

Needing to get the focus off me, I asked, "When do you have to make a decision?"

"The end of the week."

My brows shot up again. At this rate, I was going to have wrinkles by the time we were done with dinner.

"What did your parents say?"

"What do you think they said? Of course they want me to take the scholarship, but they said they'd support whatever decision I made."

A relaxed smile spread across my face. "You're lucky to have such a supportive family."

"I am."

"If you want my input, I'll give it to you, but I'm sure you already know what I'm going to say. You should take the scholarship. The answer's obvious. I know how you feel about gymnastics, so what if you give Michigan one year? If you aren't happy when that first year is over, transfer to Florida and retire from gymnastics. That way you can say you gave it a shot and you won't have any regrets."

Hayden stared at me quietly for a moment. "I hadn't thought of that. See, this is why I wanted to talk to you. Problem solved."

I chuckled. "Really? That fast?"

"Yeah, I was so torn. I'm not ready to put gymnastics behind me, but I didn't want to continue training like I do now *and* try to go to school. I've been all over the place. I want both, but I feel like this is a good choice. And who knows, maybe I'll end up loving Michigan and want to stay."

"I thought you hated cold weather."

"Hey, anything is possible." He laughed.

"I'm glad I could help. But this means I only have so much time left with you, doesn't it?"

"Yeah, unfortunately it does. I have until early summer, I think, before I have to go."

Hayden pulled out his cell phone and sent off a series of texts. I didn't bother asking to who but I figured it was to Holly and his parents. Summer wasn't too far off and my schedule was already mapped out for the most part. One way or another, I'd make plans to spend time with him.

"Thanks, Aid."

"For what?" I said, his comment pulling me away from my thoughts.

"For helping me decide. For being a good friend. For being you."

My smile faltered. Our eyes met. "I haven't always been a good friend."

"Neither have I. We're human, Adrianna. We all make mistakes." We chuckled together and Hayden asked for the check.

"A pass. I've gotten a lifetime of passes from you."

Hayden finished off his pizza and paid the check. Once I was home and about to fall asleep, I laid in bed feeling a little lighter and a bit relieved. Hayden had appeared while I'd been trying to avoid him, but he was exactly what I needed and I hadn't realized it until now. He was a friend who never asked for anything in return. Tonight he was just a friend who wanted to talk about his future. I was helping him, but he had no idea that he was helping me out too.

chapter 26

THERE ARE OVER SIX HUNDRED MUSCLES IN THE HUMAN BODY.
I would bet my future in gymnastics that I'd used every one of them this past week.

Every. Single. Muscle. Seven days a week, sixteen hours a day.

I was borderline crippled. My limbs were numb and I ached in parts of my body I didn't even know were possible to hurt. My lower back was on fire and my Achilles was killing me. I could barely put my hair into a ponytail and just breathing was a strenuous task. I wondered how long it would take to get over the soreness and worried it would be longer than usual. But the worst part? The worst part was the emotional state I was left in.

I didn't even know where to begin, but I wanted to cry for what I had just endured.

I'd gone to Texas with a solid mind and body. I'd looked forward to the training camp, eager, full of zest and persevering enthusiasm to learn from the absolute best in the sport.

I came back utterly broken and fearing the next camp. I almost didn't want to go. My body was in shambles, and my mind felt like an egg had been cracked open and over beat.

A full week of some of the most dangerous training I'd ever experienced for the ultimate goal of Olympic glory. It truly was survival of the fittest, and three days into it I'd started questioning whether it was worth it.

Konstantin Kournakova had nothing on those coaches. Nothing. His training was child's play compared to what I went through. Fucking child's play.

And I couldn't even have Motrin.

Cue the violins.

I was beyond thankful Kova had offered to drive me to and from the airport, because there wasn't a chance in hell I could have driven myself home. Yeah, I wasn't so keen when he'd first brought it up. I thought he was full of shit when he said the camps are quite arduous and I wouldn't be in tip-top shape afterward. At the time I couldn't imagine the training being any more rigorous than what I'd already done. Boy, was I wrong. So. Fucking. Wrong. I could hardly stand in an upright position without wanting to cry. The moment the plane touched down in Georgia, it was like my body said "you're free" and released a traumatized breath. I didn't need to hide how I felt anymore. I didn't need to wear a mask. I didn't care who saw how I really felt. Everything gushed from me like I'd been holding my breath the entire week I'd been gone. Instantly, I felt like I had aged fifty years. I was so exhausted.

Scouring the crowd, I wearily searched for a familiar pair of green eyes over the sea of heads. I needed a week's worth of sleep and an IV pumping me full of caffeine, painkillers, and vitamin B to bring me back to life, and I needed it all right this second. Not to recover, but because I had less than two days until I was back in the gym.

No rest for the wicked.

And as grateful as I was for Kova picking me up, I was reluctant for him to see how fragile I was. I didn't want him to see me weak and that I was ready to collapse at any given second. I didn't want him to see that someone else had the power to make me suffer more than he could. I didn't want him to see me broken and limping, and on the verge of losing my mind.

The truth was, I didn't want him to doubt me. That's what scared me more than anything.

My eyelids were heavy as I dropped my bag to the floor, fingering the strap and scanning the airport. I blinked long. I could fall asleep standing at this point, until I saw him.

The moment our eyes connected, my lips parted on a sigh and he rushed forward like a force was pulling him to me. Relief washed over me and I opened up, falling into him.

"*Malysh*," he said softly in Russian. "I had a feeling you would be like this."

Kova threw my duffle bag over his shoulder, then scooped me up and gently held me. I expelled a sigh, faltering in my gratitude. Despite everything and my need to keep our distance, I collapsed in his arms like thousand-pound weights were strapped to my body. I just couldn't move another step and I think he knew that. I nestled my forehead into his neck and closed my eyes. I should've cared that we were in the middle of an airport where anyone could see us, or that a photo could be taken and used out of context again, but I didn't. I needed him. I needed his strength. I needed to draw from it and build myself up. I needed Kova to make me strong.

It was like what he'd said that night after Parkettes—he was my strength. I needed Kova to exhale his strength because only he could give me what I needed right now.

Pretending to be strong took a toll on me, both mentally and physically. Maybe I wasn't the gymnast I thought I was. Or maybe I was, I didn't know. My mind was a hazy mess. All I knew was that I wasn't used to the physical abuse I'd been dealt for breakfast, lunch, and dinner this past week and I feared it would be more of the same with Olympic training. I guess it was the price we paid for success.

"Thank you," I said quietly, my eyes rolling shut. I was so damn tired. Kova carried me to his car in under a handful of minutes and carefully deposited me onto his bucket seat like I was an expensive piece of porcelain he was afraid would shatter into a million little pieces.

He reached over and buckled my seatbelt, his delicious cologne dusting the air, bringing a sense of comfort all around me. I breathed his scent deep into my lungs as he placed my bag at my feet.

"I don't know if I can do this again," I confessed quietly once we were on the highway. I had another camp three weeks from now.

He looked over at me, but I kept my eyes on the busy road. I was in a daze. I didn't want to see the disappointment that most likely tinted his features.

"Do not say that. You do not mean it."

I shook my head. "How do you get past this bone-aching, mentally-draining feeling and keep going? Right now I feel like I'm never going to recover. I want to roll over into a pile of crushed Motrin, then swim in a pool of alcohol and drown myself in it until I'm numb from the pain."

Kova chuckled lightly, and I felt it warm my belly. I laughed, holding my stomach, not knowing where my comment came from, but it was the truth.

"Anything I ate at the camp was monitored and limited. You know I'm already cautious of what I eat, and now I'll be even more aware from here on out after being verbally abused at the camp by the coaches."

Kova frowned and shot me a worried look. "What do you mean?"

"If we weren't being called fat slobs with pig faces and cellulite thighs, our waists were pinched so hard they left nail imprints. We were looked at with disgust and impatience, berated over our weight, and had fear shoved down our throats until we choked with tears. And yet, none of us requested to leave. I wasn't sure we could even if we wanted to. All we were given each day was a slice of gluten-free, dry bread that tasted like shit and a small apple for breakfast, a handful of nuts for lunch, and dinner was some nasty ass frozen meat and vegetable washed down with laxatives for dessert."

"Laxatives?" he questioned. "You took laxatives?"

My eyes closed shut as I recalled the horror of being forced to take them and the cramps that followed shortly after.

"Not by choice. The coaches told us that succeeding at an elite level required intense sacrifices. Judges wanted to see lines, not curves. Once all the national team members arrived at camp, we were weighed and measured before training began. Everything, *and I mean everything*, was noted. I can guarantee that we'll be weighed and measured again when we go back. Who knew that meant being deprived of food and forced to suck lemons? Sleep was almost nonexistent due to the amount of times we were in the bathroom because of the laxatives. Cramps worse than the period kind, and at one point, I only had water coming out of me. My stomach was on fire, like there were flames growing bigger by the second. Considering how little food we were given, I was baffled the coaches would think there's anything left to expel from our fragile bodies." I shuddered at the thought of the repercussions they'd face if that were the case. "God, I bet this is the last thing you probably wanted to hear. All I'm doing is complaining and telling you gross things. I'm so sorry," I said, and inwardly groaned at all the TMI I'd just shared.

"You know they are testing you, right? To see if you have the strength to handle the pressure and sacrifice it takes to train for the Olympics."

My eyes widened. "So you agree with everything they did and you're okay with it? It's borderline abuse."

"I did not say that, but I was already aware of most of it," Kova said, turning onto a street. He accelerated. "It is nothing new, Adrianna, and it comes with the territory. There is not one sport where athletes are treated any differently. It is just not spoken about."

My jaw dropped. "What didn't you know?"

"The laxative part."

I blushed a little bit. "Considering we're pretty well-acquainted with each other's bodies, I didn't see the need to hold back, especially on anything that happens inside the walls of the U.S. Olympic Training Site." I stopped when it dawned on me he had the chance to warn me ahead of time but hadn't. Anger shot through my veins and I turned toward him, leveling a stare. "If you knew what kind of conditions to expect, why didn't you warn me in advance?"

Kova glanced at me. "What would that have accomplished? Would you have changed your mind and given up the opportunity so few are granted?"

My eyes widened. "No, never, but at least I would've known what to expect. The lightheadedness was so bad one day that I started seeing spots in my vision. I was afraid to perform a tumbling pass because I was terrified I wouldn't land properly or black out midair. My gut said don't do it but I had no choice in the matter. Hunger made my heart pound violently in my chest like I was going to have a heart attack. Another day I straddled the beam and was nearly condemned for it. My fingers are raw, and my thighs are still shaking with soreness, and you didn't think to warn me, even a little bit?"

Kova was quiet for a moment. I don't think I'd even breathed while I'd berated him.

In a tedious tone that almost made me regret what I had said, he asked, "Would you have changed your mind if you knew how demanding it would be? Knowing this was your end result, would you have changed your mind? Answer me, Adrianna."

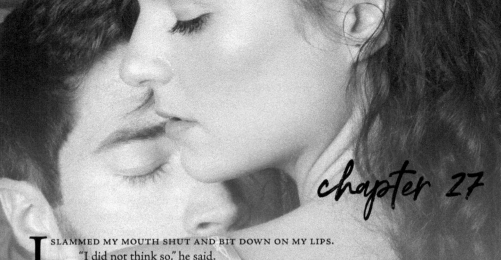

chapter 27

I SLAMMED MY MOUTH SHUT AND BIT DOWN ON MY LIPS.

"I did not think so," he said.

"How did you do it?" I asked miserably, sitting back. I didn't want to fight with him. "How did you push through?"

I hated myself for the way I felt. Like someone was able to finally break me down while I had no power to stop it.

"Mind over matter," Kova said.

"That's all you have for me? You participated in two Olympic Games, almost three, and went through the same treatment as me. If not worse because Russians are freaking lunatics. How did you keep on going?" Lowering my voice, I said a tad dejected, "This is the first time I feel like I can't convince my mind that my body can endure anything like this again."

Kova gently placed his hand on my thigh and gave me a sympathetic little squeeze. The urge to reach out and hold his hand was strong, but I didn't.

"You will find a way because there is no other option for you."

I looked over at him. His shoulders sagged just a bit and the corner of his mouth formed a frown. I noticed his hair was longer than usual, which I liked a lot. It was hair I could weave my fingers through. I wondered if he was growing it out.

"Tonight and tomorrow will be the hardest for you. You just endured ninety-nine per-cent more than most people have at your age. You are human. I am not judging you, I would never judge you for that. It is the vicious reality of the game and I get it. How much your body can take versus how much your mind can handle. Two days from now you will not feel that way. Two days you will wake up sore and bruised, and you will ask yourself how the hell you did it, but you will have the determination to go on because you will realize that you survived." He paused, then said, "There is not a shadow of a doubt, because it is what I went through and what I thought. We are cut from the same cloth, Adrianna."

I mused over his words and thought back to something he'd said when I'd first arrived at World Cup.

"Your body can endure just about anything, it is your mind you have to convince," I whispered.

"What?" he asked, pulling into my condo complex and parking his car.

I repeated what I said and he turned toward me. "It's something you said to me shortly after I got here for the first time. We were in your office going over my schedule after you had me evaluated." I laughed sadly. "You were not happy at all with my performance that day."

He scrubbed a hand down his face and laughed, then looked out the front windshield. "No, I was not."

"You were being such a dickhead that night, I couldn't believe it. But I'll never forget the words you said to me about digging deep, how to not expect anything in return, and to push even harder when no one is watching. Your speech awakened something in me and it's stuck with me ever since. I look back on it when I'm feeling lost and confused and use it as motivation."

"I remember going home that night and regretting the deal I made with your father," he says softly. "I reread all the paperwork I had signed for hours and hours, trying to find my way out of it. Frank is a brilliant businessman who covers every corner. No stone was left unturned. I was at my wits' end when Katja walked into my office and said to me that I always follow through on my deals and to not give up or else I would not be me. I was so aggravated with her when she said that, but she was right. Anything I say I am going to do, I do. So, I changed my view and looked at you like you were a challenge I needed to conquer." He grew quiet. "I just never, in my wildest dreams, expected it to go the way it has. You shocked me in ways I never saw coming. I do not know whether to embrace it or reject it."

We both sat quietly in the confinement of his car. Kova had shared a very personal side to him and I felt it in my core. It was so rare for him to let me in, but those moments I wasn't often privy to were ones I held close to me because I knew they were real. He looked straight ahead. He sat quietly, like we'd done this so many times. He was open and welcoming and his honesty was far from menacing.

"We both challenged each other without realizing it. I pushed you as a coach." He turned his head in my direction, and with a tight mouth, he nodded in agreement. "Thanks for not giving up on me."

We tested each other's limits, went at one another at a hundred miles an hour without stopping, and the only conclusion would be a beautiful destruction of sinful harmony. We were both aware of it, too, and I couldn't figure out what that said about us.

"I could not give up on you, even if I wanted to."

"Why? Because of my dad?"

He shook his head, his pupils dilated. "No, I could have easily handed you off to Madeline." His body mimicked mine. He leaned against his door, propping his elbow on the arm rest. "You countered me, you sparred with me. I pushed, you pulled harder. You made me regret my existence ninety percent of the time. You were the challenge I always wanted that no one could give me. I craved you before I even knew you, Ria. Why would I ever let go of that? Every day is a new day with you and something I look forward to. You are what keeps me going and the reason why I wake up each day." The whisper of his last words seemed to mystify him, but he just looked into my eyes to let me know he was being honest.

Breathing a little heavier, my voice a little throaty, I said, "A sane person would walk away."

He gave me an all-too-knowing look. I almost laughed. "We both know I am not sane."

Wasn't that the truth. "You're psychotic."

"True, but I got the greatest bonus of all."

"Which is?"

"You."

I shook my head and tried not to laugh. My abs were so sore. "I don't think bonus is the right word. Maybe you mean reward."

Kova smiled softly and I didn't like the way my stomach fluttered in response. Even if I wanted him to have me, if I gave myself to him again, I'd still never have him in the way that mattered most. I'd already learned that the hard way.

"You misunderstand. Because of where you are now, the national team, that is the reward. It is what we both wanted. The challenge was getting you there when the journey seemed so dark and daunting. Almost unattainable."

"It went horribly right."

He nodded. "It did. Were the sacrifices worth it?"

I didn't hesitate and looked into his green eyes that I loved. "You know they were." He smiled because he knew it was the truth. "Even if I only made it this far, it was all worth it. Every insult, every tear, every bruise would remain with me forever like a scar on my heart. They were and continue to be the stepping stones of my future."

Reaching his arm out, the back of Kova's fingers grazed my jaw, but it was his gaze that bore into me that got me. I leaned into his touch automatically, my heart yearning so badly for my coach. When we had these moments, I just wanted to forget all the negative and focus on the positive. His fingers spread out and cupped the side of my face, delving into my hair. His thumb lovingly caressed my cheek.

It wasn't supposed to be like this. It was never supposed to be like this. And yet, by some unfathomable phenomenon, it was, and I was allowing it despite everything. This wasn't the first time I'd drawn from his strength and words, and I knew in my gut that it wouldn't be the last.

The truth was, I needed Kova.

And something told me he needed me just as much.

Unbuckling my seatbelt, I reached down and grabbed the strap of my duffle bag, but Kova stopped me. I glanced over my shoulder at him.

"You know you can lean on me. I am always here for you."

I swallowed. "I know."

"Tonight will be rough. Probably the worst yet to come," Kova said, his voice low. "Let me help you."

I wanted so badly to say yes—my heart was screaming out for him—but I shook my head. Kova was a giver to those he cared deeply about, but I had to learn to not take what he offered.

"Please, Ria." His eyes begged, pleaded.

I diverted my gaze, unable to handle seeing the need inside him. I needed to do this without him, and I needed to show him that he couldn't control everything around him. He wasn't mine anymore. He never had been, and I had to remind myself of that too.

I knew it was killing him by not being able to help me. He was respecting my boundaries, my wants and needs, and I felt the wall I'd erected around my heart chipping away piece by piece. But I didn't *want* it to chip away. I wanted to keep it strong and tall and whole, but when he was finally seeing me and recognizing what I needed from him, it was hard to keep it upright.

"I need to do this myself. Let me do it." It was something so simple, but I had to do it on my own. "Mind over matter, right?"

I saw him nod from the corner of my eye, and he slowly retreated. Opening the car door, I placed one foot outside and even that was difficult. Exhaling, I reached for the roof of the car and the ledge of the door. My fingers curled as I attempted to rise from the seat. I held my breath, then stepped out of the car and threw my bag over my shoulder. I winced. My entire body was as stiff as steel and tight as a noose. This was going to be loads of fun.

I pulled deep from within and said, "I'll see you at practice." I slammed the door and took a step, then heard the window roll down.

"Adrianna." I turned around. "Take a day or two off. You do not know what you are in for."

I shook my head. Aching and slow, I walked toward the entrance, taking baby steps. I felt like I'd been beat to a pulp and just released from the hospital.

When I reached the sliding doors I looked over my shoulder. Kova had reversed and was waiting for me to safely step inside before he left. His tinted window was rolled halfway up and his gaze was fixated on me. Sadness clouded his features and it left me secretly craving for him to be his brutish self and come upstairs anyway

I often wondered what crossed his mind when our eyes met. What he was thinking. Today, I didn't question it. Today, I saw my reflection blink back at me…and it was startling. We were both hurting, both not able to console the other the way our hearts desired.

The only thing that stood between me and Kova was reality and society.

Oh, and a marriage.

Once I was inside my condo, I showered, cleaned, and dressed, then dug through my drawers and found some compression clothing I'd never used before. The theory behind the clothing seemed a little far-fetched to me, but I gave it a shot and hoped the increased blood flow would help speed up the recovering process to my calf. I didn't have anything to lose at this point as I pulled the sleeve up and around my lower leg.

The one good thing I could say about World Cup was that Kova and Madeline were cautious when it came to injuries. While I'd been scolded countless times to push through the pain by both, I had never been forced to train on a severe injury and pretend like it wasn't real. I wasn't starved or ridiculed over my body. Every one of us trained with injuries—it came with the territory—but at camp I saw something entirely different, and it made me realize just how good I had it at World Cup and I hadn't even known it. At camp, tears were a common occurrence, and some gymnasts walked with a limp, sports tape, or braces at every joint, all while being reprimanded for their insolent limitation of their bodies. It was the definition of mind games. Between the perilous coaching and lack of nourishment, I wouldn't be surprised if one of us ended up paralyzed or injured so severely we'd be forced to retire due to the way things were carried out there.

The coaches had so much power over us and all for the little slice of hope they provided when we were most vulnerable. I'd taken everything they dished out with open hands and a begging mouth. I'd take it ten times worse if that meant promising me my dreams. Kova was right. Even if I had known what to expect, or how crippled I'd be when I came home, I still would have gone.

Crawling into bed, I got under the covers and scrolled through my phone, reading the messages I'd missed while I was at camp. Some were from Hayden checking up on me, and my dad had called. My heart stopped when I got to a series of messages from Avery. I ached with the desire to call my best friend. I wanted to talk to her, to hear her voice, laugh at her jokes. I missed her big time, but I was still reeling from everything that had transpired between us. I couldn't say I was mad anymore. I wasn't mad. I was disappointed and sad more than anything that she'd felt the need to hide her relationship with my brother from me. I got it, I did, but I couldn't wrap my head around the secrecy or even fathom what they'd go through if they were to announce they were dating. I didn't believe either family would be against it—our fathers were business partners—so what were the repercussions they felt they would face?

If I'd had sex with her brother then aborted his baby, I would've been terrified to tell her too. But I'd have told her, just like I'd told her everything about Kova. That was the difference. She was my best friend and she'd lied to my face for many long months. She hid a massive secret and that was more devastating than anything. I'd thought we were close and could tell each other everything. It crushed my heart and made me feel like she didn't care enough about me to tell me. Did she really think I'd tell her to stop dating him? Well, probably, but I knew his playboy ways better than anyone and would only want to protect her.

I clicked out of her messages and listened to a voicemail from a number I didn't recognize. My heart sank when I heard the nurse from the doctor's office. They'd called over a week ago when I'd been with Hayden, and I'd forgotten to call them back. Then they called twice while I was in Texas. My results were in and I needed to schedule an appointment to go over them. I shot a quick glance at the clock to check the time. It was too late to call, and tomorrow was the start of the weekend. I made a plan to call on Monday during lunch to schedule an appointment.

Placing my phone face down on the night stand, I turned on my side and curled up with the blankets, praying that I wouldn't be in so much pain tomorrow.

chapter 28

TURNS OUT, KOVA HAD BEEN RIGHT.

    The night he dropped me off and the day after had been horrific. Brutal. I felt like I'd been hit by a freight train, and then ran over by a cement truck. A little dramatic, maybe, but it was the only way to describe the agony I was dealing with.

Call me crazy, but I typically loved the after-day suffering, just not to this extreme. Soreness was proof of an intense workout. It meant I'd pushed back just as hard as I was pulled, but this was something else entirely that I hadn't even known existed. This was pure torture and I honestly couldn't imagine going through it again. But then I told myself that others had walked on the same stepping stones and came out alive. If they could do it, then so could I. It would be worth it one day.

Then there was the deafening silence I'd tried to avoid whenever I had free time. I swear I could hear the blood flowing through my veins, it was that quiet.

I should've taken Kova up on his offer to rest a few more days. The two days I'd had off weren't enough. Not even close. I ached, I was worn out, and I all but crawled on my hands and knees out of my condo to my car to drive to practice.

The exhaustion, the weariness, the discomfort…it was nothing compared to the blow I got when I arrived at World Cup. I wasn't there for more than a minute when Kova pulled me into his office and shut the door. He started asking numerous questions back-to-back, but I only focused on one thing.

"What are you talking about, Coach? What do you mean you want me to go home?" My heart beat frantically. Of course I wanted to go home, I was tired as hell, but I knew that wasn't an option.

Kova's eyes narrowed and I could see the vulnerability in them. "I did not tell you when I picked you up because I did not want to worry you, but I received a call from your father. Your physician called him and I was told they have been trying to reach you, something about blood results were in and you needed to schedule an appointment."

Hands propped on hips, I was aggravated. "You have to be kidding me. Why would he tell you?"

"Why did you get blood work?" he countered.

I shrugged, keeping it cool. "Just a regular checkup is all."

"Your father added me as a guardian in case anything happens to you and he couldn't make it here in time."

Made sense, but I didn't like it. With my gaze still hard on his, I asked, "What else did he tell you?"

Kova shifted on his feet. He studied me, his gaze raking up and down my body. "What are you hiding?" he asked, deep and curious.

I reared back, cheeks hot. "Nothing. Not that it's any of your business anyway."

"It is very well my business and you know that."

My eyes flared.

My temper took off.

And there went my control.

"Like hell it is! You don't need to invade every damn aspect of my personal life, Kova. If I want you to know something, I'll tell you."

Kova strode toward me until we were an inch or two apart. He angled his head down, his eyes roaming over my face, taking in every feature. Using his index finger, he tipped my chin up. Green eyes fastened on my mouth and my gaze dropped to his full lips I loved so much. He dragged his teeth over his bottom lip, and I swallowed hard, feeling a stroke of heat pool in my stomach.

I hadn't felt that kind of stirring in a while.

He dragged the tips of his fingers along my jaw to the back of my head and palmed my neck. I stood immobile, at his mercy, while his thumb delicately rubbed the pulse in my neck. I leaned into his touch and got lost in his green eyes. Kova always knew how to calm me down. This wasn't the first time he'd touched me since I'd found out he was married. I struggled with what to do and went with fisting my hands. The caress of his fingers felt divine, so I dug my nails into my palms until I made little crescent moon imprints in my skin. It was the only way I could maintain my self-control, otherwise I'd have my hands on him.

"There you go," he whispered. His thumb slowed. "You were about to pop a blood vessel."

"You make me that way. I swear you bring out the worst in me."

The corner of his mouth tugged up. "You are so beautiful when you are fired up."

"See? Contractions would be useful there."

"You're beautiful when you're fired up," he said, the words so foreign to him I grinned.

My head fell forward onto his chest. I tried not to laugh, but when I replayed the words in my head I chuckled quietly. Kova's hand slid up my neck, his fingers threading through the hair at my nape as he took a small step toward me.

"Say it again," I asked, eyeing his other arm hanging at his side. Kova had this one prevalent vein I loved that wound around his forearm like a tattoo. It was so hot, and my fingers ached to touch it.

"You're beautiful when you're fired up."

I chuckled again. This time when he said it, there was a funny incline in his tone when he said you're. Like he was trying different variations of the word to see which fit the best. Without thinking, my hands came up to rest on his hips. I grabbed him, holding on as I laughed, and felt the ridges of his strong muscles.

"You sound like a robot."

"You called me Kova," he whispered, his lips pressed to the top of my head. His fingers stroked my scalp, soothing away the tension.

Fucking hell. I hadn't even realized I'd slipped.

"I don't think clearly when I'm around you," I admitted, feeling defeated. I looked up and our eyes met. "You make me so mad sometimes, but then other times I just want to let it all go and forget and just be us again." My words were a murmur, but I wanted him to know how he affected me.

"I know the feeling all too well," Kova replied, barely above a whisper. "You look sad."

"I am," I replied honestly. We were close enough that I could breathe in his words and allow them to wrap around the organ thumping in my rib cage if I wasn't careful enough.

"I do not like seeing you like that." I stayed silent. "I know you probably do not believe me, but it hurts me to see you this way. You have looked sad for weeks."

I had to wonder if he knew he was the root of my sadness.

"Does that feel good?" he asked, still massaging my head. I nodded, wishing he was massaging my entire body.

"Hmmm… I think I need to call a chiropractor and schedule a full body massage. Will your friend be back anytime soon?"

"Who?"

"The doctor… Ethan. He can do a full body, sports kind of massage. I could use it. He suggested it, remember?"

Kova peered down at me, face blank, but his eyes bore into mine with such intensity it left me breathless. Much to my astonishment, I stepped closer until there was no space left between us and wrapped my arms around his back. I let out a long breath and sagged against him.

"If you need a deep tissue massage"—he gave me a casual shrug—"I can do it for you."

He didn't hint at something more, and he wasn't his usual bossy, over-controlling self, but I was taken aback by my quick response.

"Okay," I replied so easily. "I should probably do another round of blading before I go back to Texas too."

He nodded, and I dropped my chin to his chest. His fingers mellowed me out, my eyes heavy with fatigue. Exhaling, I let out a long sleepy breath.

"I need you to do me a favor," he said, like he was begging for me not to argue with him. I looked up to see Kova's face shift into a handful of different emotions that made me want to ask what he was thinking about.

"I need you to stay home until you see your doctor. I am not asking for a doctor's note for you to come back. I am going to trust that you went. I just need to make sure you are okay and healthy. It is my main priority."

I wanted to fight him on this, because I needed to be in the gym, training as hard as I could, but I was so tired that all I did was nod my head in agreement.

"*Spasibo*," he said in Russian.

Leaning down, Kova pressed a kiss to my forehead. My eyes rolled shut and I took a deep breath. I was too weary to pull away.

"I planned to call on my lunch break, you know. I was going to go."

"Okay, well, now you can call from home. In your bed." I groaned. "What is wrong?"

"It's so quiet at home. I feel so alone there."

Kova pulled back and it forced me to look at him. "You do not like it?"

"Usually I don't mind, but lately it makes me a little depressed."

I hated to admit that I was depressed because I felt like it made me weak. My gaze dropped to his shoulder. I didn't like feeling this way, but I also didn't know how to pull out of it. The more I thought about it, the sadder I became, and the emptier my chest felt.

Cupping my face, Kova brought my attention back to him. "Come to my home. Katja is out of town and I can do the massage there. You will not feel alone. I will be there shortly. I will let Madeline know I am leaving early. I have the masseuse table and everything we need."

My heart clenched.

"You are certifiable." He grinned, and dammit to hell, it was sexy. "What if Katja comes home early?"

"Trust me, she will not show up early. I know how she operates." Kova's gaze lowered to my lips. I could tell he had more to say so I waited. "I think we could both use the company anyway."

"I don't have the energy to entertain this. I think it's best if I just go home."

"Exactly. You do not have the energy. Please…" he said, stepping closer and taking hold of my hands. Kova's eyes softened, yet flickered with anguish. My lips parted.

"Stay the night. Let me take care of you," he said.

I couldn't help it and immediately fell back on my familiar defenses. "I bet you used the table with your wife."

Kova's shoulders tightened. "Adrianna, enough. The table is still in the box, unopened. You can watch me put it together. I promise, you are the only one who will use it. In fact, I will give you the damn table if you want. Please, just stop being difficult and let me help you. You need me, and deep down, I think you want me to help you but you are too stubborn to ask," he said. His tone was too genuine for me to question his motives and I instantly felt bad for jumping down his throat.

My heart was already broken, my body in constant pain. I forced myself to stay emotionally distant from him to protect myself, or at least I tried to. I didn't want to give in. I was stronger than that, but he was right. I did want him to take care of me. I needed him, and no matter what I did or what I told myself, I didn't have the power in me to hate him, even though I tried. And the scariest part? It wasn't just a carnal need. I needed Kova in his entirety. I just wanted to be around him. I missed his arms, his body, the way he never used contractions, how he just let himself *be* when it was us. I just missed *him*. Like there was a Kova-sized hole in my life only he could fill. But I knew if I agreed to this that my heart would be irrevocably shattered even more.

Still, I was trying to fight it.

Kova spoke over my indecision. "If it makes you feel more comfortable, I will close the gym early and we can meet back here." My brows shot up. Kova never closed World Cup early for anything. "I will go home and get my table. I am trying to make it so you are not alone, but comfortable. Whatever you need, I will do. Sometimes when you are alone and feeling depressed, being inside your head is the worst thing. I do not want you to go down that road any more than you already have, it is not healthy." Kova paused and let out a long breath. "I just want to help you, but what is it that you want?"

Looking at him, I went with the truth, even if it hurt both of us. Tears sprung to my eyes.

"I just want to remember what it's like to not feel broken."

chapter 29

KOVA'S EYES FLASHED. HE SHOOK HIS HEAD LIKE HE HATED TO HEAR ME UTTER those words. I felt his breathing deepen, his chest expanding against mine. I felt the heat of his body warm me and I hadn't felt it in so long. His hands roamed over my back until his arms wrapped around me. He held me tight, his hands gently pouring his emotion into me.

"I hate that I am the one who broke you more than you will ever know." He dropped his head until his lips were just above mine. I gasped and drew his words into me as they rolled off his heart and onto mine. "You need me, and it is killing me because I want to fix what I did, but I am trying to respect your boundaries too. I have never struggled so much in my life to remain on the sidelines to give you your space. Every day I wake up hoping today will be the day. The day you will allow me to do what I need to get us there. Back to where we once were. I am so sorry. So, so sorry, Adrianna. I see you. I see everything about you, what you are feeling, what you are thinking, and I die a little more inside every day not being able to give us what we both need."

"And what is it we both need, Kova?" I whispered against his lips, yearning to press mine to his. He swallowed thickly, then grazed mine ever so softly.

"Each other, Adrianna. We need each other."

Each day Kova slowly cooled the fiery embers that fell from my heart. He was extinguishing my rage toward him and reigniting my passion for life. I felt his composure dissolve.

"Do you really just happen to have everything at your house?" I asked, my chest tight. He'd done so much for me yet he'd hurt me just the same.

He nodded, breathing hard. I clenched his shirt, my hands forming fists at his silent response.

"Yes. I got it shortly after I got my certification training for you. I just have not had time to bring it here. I got it for you. Everything, so many things I do, I do for you. You just do not see it yet," he said, pleading with his eyes for me to understand him.

Dear God. Too many emotions, too many truths. Swallowing hard, I blinked hard, pushing back the tears climbing at his selflessness and moved with what felt right in my heart.

I kissed him.

Kova froze. With my lips pressed to his and his body taut with surprise, I melted a little more when he didn't move. His body trembled against mine, his strength suspended between us. I leaned into him and he growled, finally kissing me back.

His arms were tight around my back as he devoured my mouth, pushing into me, forcing me to step back. The back of my knees hit his desk, and Kova hoisted me up to sit on it, stepping between my spread legs. His palms cupped my jaw as my hands slipped under his shirt, needing to feel his skin. A little moan escaped me, and he kissed me harder, bruising my mouth. I loved when he ravaged me like this, like a consuming need had taken over his body. My palms moved over the hard planes of his chest, grazing over his nipples, then to the sexy muscles that dipped around his hips. My hands slid around to his back and I grabbed him hard, needing to feel more. I couldn't stop touching him. I wanted to touch him everywhere. Kova reached behind his back and grabbed my wrists, shaking his head as he brought my hands to the front of his chest and over his shirt.

"I am trying to control myself here," he stressed, but kissed me again. His tongue swirled around mine, tugging on it obsessively. His hand cupped the back of my neck, holding me captive, not that I minded. A shiver ran down my spine and I moaned into his mouth. I loved when he did that, like he was possessed with power and could make me surrender to him.

"I love when you lose control," I confessed, breathless and in between kisses.

"I know you do."

Kova growled, and the sound caused a score of heat to trail down my spine. He tugged my bottom lip into his mouth, his teeth scraping over the sensitive skin enough to cause a shrill of pleasure to stream through me. Wetness seeped onto my leotard. My eyes rolled shut and a long groan escaped me when he let go.

"And I love when your eyes get that glassy look in them. Your body becomes pliant and soft and willing. It means you will allow me to do anything I want."

A purr vibrated in my throat. Opening my eyes, I looked up at him, letting him know he was right. My nipples were hard, my body flushed with desire, and my skin tingled. All from this man's kiss.

I wanted more.

Leaning forward with his hand still gripping my neck, Kova stared me down, his eyes blazing with need. He stood still as I ever so slowly traced his lips with my tongue before slipping it into his mouth. I kissed him slow, how I knew he liked. His fingers tightened around my neck, pressing into my skin the more I lapped at his mouth. His body trembled against mine. Feeding both our cravings, I undulated against him, triggering him to act.

In a blur of speed, Kova pushed me down on his desk and leaned over me. I grabbed ahold of his biceps, a gush of air expelling from my lungs. My legs automatically circled his waist, locking around his back.

"It has been months since I have fucked you, *malysh*." His voice was a cracked whisper against my lips.

I released a soft moan as Kova pressed a kiss to my mouth, then moved down my neck. His hands were in my hair, guiding me to turn my head to the side. His tongue trailed along my collarbone and the slope of my neck, his teeth scraping my skin at the same time. Fingers trembling in my hair, he nipped at my heated flesh, then tugged on my ear as he started rocking his hips forward. My back arched and I moaned at the pressure of his erection pushing against my sex. I could feel the outline of his cock through his shorts and I could clearly tell that he didn't have boxers on underneath. The thought made me wetter and I prayed he couldn't feel it through my leotard and little shorts.

"Fucked me, yes," I responded, rolling my hips against his, "but it hasn't been months since we had sex."

At that, Kova's teeth locked down on my jaw. He applied pressure, not enough to hurt me, but enough to make my pussy throb and beg for more. I let out a breathy sigh. Pulling back, he looked down at me, our noses touching. His cologne invaded my senses and I breathed it deep into my lungs, still loving the smell of him. Kova continued to stare at me, passive but sympathetic. We didn't need words in that moment. He knew I was talking about the night he kept apologizing in Russian while he made love to me. I didn't allow myself to think about that night often—it hurt too much—but he needed to see that I knew there was a difference in the way he was with me.

Kova swallowed, his eyes fixated on mine, looking back and forth. The back of his knuckles moved to my cheek and he gently grazed my skin. He nodded. It was the slightest of nods, and if I had blinked, I would've missed it.

Then, to my complete and utter surprise, he said something in a tone packed with sorrow and guilt that crushed the air in my lungs. I'd never forget it for as long as I lived.

"It was not just sex that night for me, Ria."

"I know," was all I could say.

He kissed me again, devouring my mouth and proving just how much he truly cared by the way he consumed me. And he knew I would know the different shades of sex with him. Kova's fucking was fantastic. He was animalistic and savage, usually angry about something. His sex was needy and controlling and demanding. But his lovemaking? It was intense and passionate and his way of conveying how he felt. It was like I got a glimpse inside his soul as it latched onto mine and became whole for a little while. It made me forget everything and put us on another dimension without the restraints of the world.

"What are you thinking about?"

I shook my head, not trusting my words not to spill the truth. It seemed every version of sex with Kova came with mind-blowing orgasms and a heavy dose of heartbreak. I wasn't sure why I thought kissing him was a good idea, or that I could handle it. Even just a kiss from this devastating man fucked with my head.

Pulling us up into a seated position, Kova reached into his pocket and took out his keys. My gaze followed his movement and I caught sight of the bulge at the center of his hips. I stared, tracing the outline of his cock with my eyes, imagining the vein I loved pulsating with desire. I thought about how he would feel inside of me and I realized how much I missed it.

He jingled his keys in front of my face and my eyes snapped up as he took two keys off the keyring. I held my palm out and he dropped them into my hand. I was slightly surprised at myself for not fighting him on this. I guess today was just one of those days that I had to pick and choose my battles.

"You can rest in my room or the guest—"

"I'll take the guest room. I can't lie in the bed you share with your wife."

"Adrianna." He paused, looking so deep into my eyes that I was afraid of what would come out of his mouth next. "She has not slept in my bed in over a month." My lips parted in absolute shock. Yeah, I definitely hadn't been expecting that admission. "She uses the guest room with the yellow blanket."

Christ on a fucking stick. That was the last thing I had expected, and honestly, I'd rather not know. But now I was curious. I wanted so badly to ask what happened, and the look in his eyes told me he wanted me to because it would be an opening for him to explain his actions. But I couldn't. Not yet at least. Not when I felt so fragile. His words were draining and they sucked so much energy from me half the time. I wasn't sure I had the power to stay strong and not break down right now. His truth and confessions needed to wait until I was ready.

Instead, all I could do was nod and take the keys.

"Make yourself comfortable. Eat whatever you want, but make sure you call your doctor first before you do anything."

"When will Katja be back?"

"Not until the end of the week. You have nothing to worry about. Just get some rest."

"Okay. Thank you for doing this. I really didn't want to be alone anymore."

Kova stepped back and I slid off his desk. I adjusted my shorts, then looked for my duffle bag. I smiled inside. I couldn't believe I was actually looking forward to getting rest.

"I should be home soon," he said. "I will bring you dinner."

I didn't plan to stay for dinner, just long enough to fill the loneliness in my chest. He was my lifeline, and it was frightening how much I needed him.

"Is there an alarm on your home?"

"No. Adrianna, promise me you will call your doctor as soon as you get to my house."

Nodding, I picked up my duffle bag. "I will."

He called my name when I got to the door of his office, and I glanced over my shoulder. "You know how I know you are not well?" I frowned. "There is no fight in you. Your fire is missing. Go home. I will see you soon."

It didn't escape me that he had said the word home, as if his home was one we shared.

chapter 30

MAYBE KOVA WAS RIGHT.

Maybe there was something wrong with me, I thought as I unlocked his front door and stepped over the threshold.

I was alone. In Kova's home. The one he shared with his wife.

I set the keys on the table in his foyer so I wouldn't lose them and walked down one of the halls, looking for the room with the yellow blanket. I wanted to see if he had been lying to me.

My heartbeat increased with each step I took that brought me farther into his personal space. The first door on the right was closed, so I opened it, and saw that it was a bathroom with a massive claw foot bathtub and lots of blurry and pixelated windows. The walls were pure white, as was the furniture. So sterile looking and not an ounce of color. Like a mental hospital.

I closed the door and walked to the next room. It was a spare bedroom, but not the one I was looking for. The last door in the hallway was on the left. Walking to it, I realized it was already cracked open.

My heart dropped at the sight of yellow. This was the room. I pushed it open slowly. Even though I knew Katja wasn't there, I was still nervous I'd get caught snooping.

I stepped inside and was immediately hit with a familiar scent that I recalled Kova saying was Katja's special body wash that she ordered from Russia. I needed to find the bottle. Not because I wanted to smell like her—that would be creepy—but I just really liked it and was curious what the hell was in it.

I glanced around. Everything was tidy and neat, but with no ounce of life. The curtains were drawn and there was a chill in the room. I'd been in other parts of Kova's home before, but they didn't feel like this. Like a bland and frigid museum. The bed was made with a hideous, buttercup yellow, overstuffed comforter, and too many pillows. The nightstands were empty except for a single white lamp on each one. There were even fresh vacuum marks on the white rug. God. What was with all the white? It didn't look like anyone lived in this room. My stomach knotted, and I was quick to call Kova a liar until I looked at the dresser and saw two picture frames that were turned face down. I frowned and walked over and picked them up. With everything so meticulous, I knew that wasn't an accident.

Turning one over, I saw that inside the frame was a photo of Kova and Katja. They were smiling and appeared to be so in love. Kova stood behind Katja with his arms wrapped around her shoulders while he kissed the side of her head through a grin. I felt bad as I stared at the image of the seemingly happy—and now married—couple and wondered what had happened between them.

Swallowing, I placed the frame back how I found it, face down, and picked up the other one. It was another image of Kova and Katja. They were walking hand in hand on a beach where the sand was a pale pink and the water a crystal-clear blue. There weren't many places in the world with pink sand, so this told me they had been on vacation somewhere, probably the Bahamas. Both of them trim and in shape, looking like the ideal couple everyone wanted to be. I glowered at Katja's flawless body and the bikini she wore that only a Victoria's Secret model could pull off. I wasn't a jealous person, but it annoyed me how perfect she was from head to toe. Perfectly sized boobs I didn't have, wide hips I didn't have that gave way to a sexy thigh gap, and long, lean legs. Of course Kova was looking at her, smirking with black sunglasses, a black backwards hat, and black board shorts that sat extremely low on his trim waist. Kova was too attractive for his own good, and he looked like he wanted to devour every inch of her body.

Scowling, I flipped the frame back down a little too hard and heard the glass splinter. I froze, sucked in a breath, and panicked. I carefully lifted the frame and looked at the glass, and saw I had cracked it in a few places. Fuck! I placed it back down and prayed no one found it, or that Katja would blame Kova for it.

Before I left, I pulled open the drawers and snooped. If Katja was staying in here, then there had to be something of hers…and there was.

Relief coursed through me and the pressure in my chest eased. I let out a long sigh. Each of the six drawers had woman's clothes in them. Lastly, I checked the closet and found tons of designer garments and shoes and purses. Making sure I left everything how I had found it, I left Katja's room and left the door cracked, just as it had been before I entered.

My phone pinged and I jumped at the sound. God, I felt so guilty for sneaking around. Glancing down, I saw a text from Kova.

Coach: Do not forget to call the doctor.

Pulling up my contacts, I found my doctor's office number and called. The receptionist picked up on the second ring.

"Hi, this is Adrianna Rossi. I'm calling to make an appointment to go over the results of my blood work? Is there any way I can come in today?"

"Okay… Let me see what I have available," she responded. I could hear her fingers flying over the keyboard.

"Are you able to tell me anything about my results?" I asked while I waited.

"Unfortunately, I can't. I'm not a doctor."

"What about if a nurse called me?"

"You'd have to come in regardless, and as of right now, it looks like the doctor is booked out until the end of the week."

"The end of the week," I repeated, freaking out.

I shook my head. This couldn't happen. I refused to miss that much practice. I walked over to Kova's couch and sat down. Bending over, I placed my forehead in my palm and stared at the marble floor.

"I need an emergency appointment, please. The doctor was adamant I come back as soon as possible based on the results of the first round of blood that was drawn. I was out of town and received multiple calls to the point my emergency contact was notified. Obviously, something is wrong. I need to come in sooner and if you don't believe me, you can ask the doctor herself."

I didn't want to be rude, but I had no other option.

"Please hold." Heart pounding, I waited for what felt like an eternity for the receptionist to come back. "The doctor can see you first thing in the morning. That's the best she can do."

I squeezed my eyes shut.

"I'll take it."

"Perfect. We'll see you at nine." She confirmed, then hung up before I could say another word.

Expelling a loud, unladylike sigh, I sat back and stared at the ceiling, wondering what I was going to do with my time until then.

My appointment is tomorrow morning.

Coach: Good. Thank you for letting me know. I should be out of here in two hours.

I stood up and walked toward the other end of the house, looking for the master bedroom. I wanted to change out of my leotard, but I didn't have extra clothes with me; Kova wouldn't mind if I borrowed one of his shirts.

I was walking past his office and the room where he kept all of his gymnastics memorabilia when the memories assaulted me. Chills broke out down my arms. It was where he'd told me about his time in the Olympics for the first time, about his mother, and where he'd told me I was beautiful, if not more so than Katja. Where he softly touched my face and looked at me in a way a coach should never look at his gymnast. It was in that moment that everything changed for us.

When I reached the end of the dark hallway, I took a deep breath and placed my hand on the cold knob. Turning it, I pushed the door open and anticipated another crisp, stiff bedroom. Instead, I walked into a room that didn't match the rest of the house. While there was a cold and sterile feel to Katja's side of the house, Kova's side was masculine, warm, and elegant. His side was so much more inviting.

I stepped inside and was immediately submerged in Kova. This room was undeniably his and where he let himself be free to express himself. I was immediately cloaked in Kova's scent and my skin tingled with awareness. The heavy curtains blocked out all light. In the center of the room, against a slate gray accent wall, was an inviting king-size bed made up with a thick, deep blood red and dark gray comforter. There were no decorative throw pillows that suggested a woman's touch, just four large black ones. In front of his bed was a black leather sitting bench. No matching carpet like the other bland guest rooms, but charcoal gray wood floors with a giant animal hide rug in the center. On one side of the wall was an enormous armoire that made my jaw drop. I walked over to it, in awe of the detailed craftsmanship and brought my hand up to touch it.

Scrolls of tropical leaves were scored into the wood, wicker accents giving off an island feel, flanked by two bamboo inspired columns. On the opposite side, parallel to the armoire, was a workout area fitted with a stand used to work the upper body, and some free weights on a shelf off to the side. There was nothing on the walls save for a television mounted to the wall closest to the door with a large dresser underneath that matched the armoire. The TV was larger than me.

I glanced around. Who the hell had decorated this room? It was seductive and dark and mysterious and lush and unlike anything else in the house.

I loved it.

This had to be Kova's touch. His essence filled the room the same way he made a statement with so few words. Less is more and all that.

Curious to see the bathroom now, I strode toward the en suite and stopped short, sucking in a breath.

Wide, slate gray tiles lined the walls from floor to ceiling. A grand shower with no doors and a massive rain showerhead was next to the black marble vanity. There was a rectangular bathtub carved from stone directly in the center. It was so big I could stretch out in it and still not fill it. The last thing I had on my list of things to never do anytime soon was to take a bath, but after seeing Kova's, I wanted to test it out. Much to my surprise, there was a window with no blinds or curtains. It wasn't blurred, nor did it have mosaic tiles to block curious eyes. It led to what I assumed was his backyard and had a view of rows and rows of bamboo trees bunched together.

I stood back in utter shock. Kova's house was impressive to begin with, but his room and bathroom were something else. His own oasis. It must have been the one room he'd demanded to design and decorate. Everything was elegant and lavish. I'd love to see what he'd do with an entire house. In truth, I was surprised he could afford something this opulent. I knew money when I saw it thanks to my upbringing, and Kova had way more than he let on.

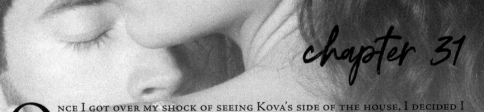

chapter 31

ONCE I GOT OVER MY SHOCK OF SEEING KOVA'S SIDE OF THE HOUSE, I DECIDED I had to test out his bathtub.

I searched through Kova's drawers until I found a shirt to wear, then I ran the water. I didn't even bother looking for a pair of shorts, since I knew there was no way they would fit.

With the bath filled, I looked for some soap for bubbles but found lots of Epsom salt instead. I should have known better—it was Kova's favorite. I dumped a bunch in and waited a minute or so before stripping down and climbing in.

A heavenly sigh rolled off my lips at the heat of the water and how good it felt on my aching body. Grabbing my cell phone, I placed my legs on the ledge of the tub and crossed them. I took a picture and texted it to Kova. Seconds later, he responded.

Coach: There better be bath salts in there.

LOL there are.

Coach: I like seeing you in my tub.

It's so big I could swim in it. The jets feel so good.

Coach: I am glad you are using it. It does not get any use at all.

I had to ignore that one.

I'm just glad it's not an ice bath for once.

I took a picture of the window and sent it to Kova.

Why does this not shock me?

Coach: What?

The fact that you have a window with no covering and anyone can see in.

Coach: What can I say? I am a bit of an exhibitionist.

I thought of Kova walking around naked and how he was not modest in the least. I got the notion that he liked when people looked at him. His body was to die for, especially naked, so I shouldn't have been surprised. My pussy tingled from the image of him in my head, of him under the cascading shower, stroking himself into oblivion. I looked at the window and realized it was angled perfectly toward the shower *and* the bathtub. I had to squeeze my legs shut from the sudden throbbing. Water sloshed from side to side.

Now THAT doesn't surprise me. LOL I'm gonna take a nap soon.

Coach: Only in my bed. See you soon.

After the water cooled, I got out and grabbed a towel hanging from the wall to dry myself. Chills coated my body from the cool air, but the towel was hot to my touch. Wrapping it around my body, I sighed at the warmth and thickness. His towel rack was heated. At this point, I didn't want to ever leave his room. This was heaven.

I dried off and glanced around. The only thing decorating the room was the fresh, white orchids in a huge square black vase on the vanity right in the center.

Reaching for his shirt so I could slip it on, I retracted, thinking the towel would be warmer and cozier under the blanket.

Clutching the material to my chest, I stepped into his bedroom and pulled back the covers to reveal soft, gray sheets, and climbed in. I loosened the towel to get situated and pulled the blankets over me. I took out my hair tie and fluffed my hair. For me, taking a hair tie out was the equivalent to taking a bra off after a long day.

This was a mistake. A big, fat mistake, because once my head hit the pillow, Kova's scent surrounded me, stimulating my blood with shameless ideas. This whole time I'd thought he wore cologne, but it was just his natural aroma. He didn't wear cologne to bed, no one would do that, and he'd told me Katja hadn't shared his bed in a month, so I knew this smell was all him.

Rolling over onto my side, I closed my eyes and tried to block out any illicit thoughts that flitted through my head. Sighing, I felt at ease and not lonely for the first time in a long time. I hugged the king-size down pillow to the length of my body and hiked a knee up, expelling a breath. I needed to sleep. I was exhausted.

But sleep wouldn't come. I shifted to my other side and faced Kova's workout equipment. I imagined him in the zone doing dips and pullups, in nothing but shorts, his muscles straining with sweat dripping down his flushed chest. The shorts would sit low, low enough for me to see the carved muscles around his hips that led to his plump ass, defined and incredibly delicious looking, and the dark hairs that led to his cock. Maybe he'd even be wearing that backwards hat I loved so much. Or, maybe, he would be naked except for the hat. I noticed a weightlifting belt for his waist and wondered if he strapped weights to it while he used the stationary machine. I wondered if I could plaster myself to him like a spider monkey while he did dips. That would be insanely hot.

Christ on a stick. I needed to stop. A throb resonated between my legs, my pussy becoming wet. God, this was humiliating. All I had to do was imagine Kova working out and I was getting turned on in a bed he had at one time shared with his wife.

I closed my eyes and sighed, pushing all thoughts from my head. I was relaxed and in a good place—even my mind was relaxed—which was so strange considering where I was. But I knew. I knew why I felt like this, and I didn't want to admit it.

It was Kova. It was always Kova, and though his presence could rile me up, it also had the ability to calm me down.

Shifting, I hiked my leg up even further and cuddled the pillow closer to me. The material of the towel and thickness of the pillow pushed against my clit in just the right spot. My body lit up with hunger in response. I groaned at the pressure and tried not to move, but it felt too good and my hips rolled against it. My clit dragged down the uneven material of the towel, my pussy aching with the need to be touched. I did it again, and again, and the heat coursing through my body intensified with every thrust, making me even wetter with desire.

I squeezed the pillow to me, knowing I needed to stop, but wanting to roll over and climb on it too. I wanted to rub my aching clit all over the place where he rested his head at night and caress myself on it until I came. I pretended it was Kova's face I was riding and froze. I was so close to coming. My eyes clenched shut. I had to stop. This wasn't right. I was in his bed, but my hips wouldn't stop and I ground myself against the towel as I squeezed the pillow harder with my thighs, loving the friction and feeling like I'd die if I didn't have more. My nipples puckered to hard points, the towel teasing the sensitive skin. Long, breathy sighs rolled off my lips, my moans echoing through the room. I wanted to come, and I desperately wanted to come in Kova's bed.

Oh God. My body was flushed with heat. I rolled onto my back and pushed the blanket off but kept the towel on. I needed to stop this, but my hand was already under the towel, sliding through the swollen lips of my pussy and rubbing my clit. Hips bucking, I cupped myself as hard as I could, almost painfully, and undulated on a wave of euphoria. The towel slid off, exposing my body to the cool air. I moaned, climbing higher, when a sound outside the room caught my attention. I froze, my heart hammering. I looked to the side and found Kova standing in the doorway.

I gasped, breathing heavily, and yet I couldn't stop touching myself, especially now, with him watching me. I closed my legs and ground myself into my hand.

Kova pushed the door open fully and sauntered in. Our eyes locked onto each other like an imaginary force was pulling us together until he reached the side of the bed and loomed over me. His gaze darkened with a look I knew all too well. I bit my lip, embarrassed that I'd been caught.

His eyes blazed with lust and his tongue rolled over his bottom lip. Kova picked up the towel and tossed it to the floor. My hand was still tucked between my legs. He dragged the back of his knuckles alongside my thigh, softly and gently stroking my creamy skin. He opened his palm and skimmed my hip. He gave my hip a squeeze, and my back arched. My gaze dropped to his shorts, his obvious erection straining against the material.

"Please do not let me stop you," he growled.

My cheeks flushed and I swallowed. "How long were you standing there?"

"Long enough to see you about to fuck my pillow." My eyes widened and my cheeks flushed again. I wanted to fucking die of embarrassment. "I would not have minded, you know. In fact, I wish you had. I was waiting for you to put the pillow between your thighs and climb on. You could have put your hands on the headboard so I would see your back flex and contract while you rode the same place I put my face every night. You could have rode it hard until you came." I continued to stare at him in silence, wanting to do just that. "Why did you stop?" he asked, still touching my leg.

"Stop what?" I all but panted.

"With my pillow. Why did you stop grinding your sweet little pussy all over it?"

I averted my gaze, trying to figure out how to handle this conversation. Kova wasn't mad, he was turned on and rock hard. His cock was even bigger now, my pussy instantly craving the outline of his thick length.

I whimpered and went with the truth, seeing as he liked hearing it. "Because I didn't want to leave a wet mark on it."

"You are not shy in front of me," he stated.

"No," I responded softly. "I think with anyone else I might be, but not with you."

Kova's jaw flexed, his nostrils flaring, his eyes hungering for more. Then, he shocked me. "Do it. Touch yourself."

Chills rolled down my spine, my body flushing so hot I felt like I was on fire at the thought of him watching me. I wanted it. My heart hammered in my chest, my pussy soaking wet at the thought of actually doing it. Kova climbed onto the bed and kneeled in front of me, his hands going to my knees to spread my legs…and I let him. His hungry gaze immediately went to my sex and I felt moisture seep out. His nostrils flared and he looked at me, his eyes heavy and dark. I pulled my knees up, showing him what he'd never have again, only for him to quickly lean down and give me one long, good swipe of his tongue.

"Oh God," I moaned, gasping as pleasure rocked through me. My back arched from the way he flattened his tongue.

"I have missed your taste on my tongue," he said, his voice guttural.

Kova shifted closer and placed a hand on each of my inner thighs. He glided them roughly up until he reached my bikini line, the anticipation that he'd go farther was so crazy I almost asked him to. Right before he reached my core, he squeezed my thighs hard. I let out a moan and when he did it again, I almost purred. His strength alone turned me on.

Reaching out with two fingers, I offered them to him. Kova hesitated to slip them into his mouth. His tongue wrapped around seductively, nibbling. I pulled back, but he tightened his grip and guided them to my sex. With our eyes locked, he pressed my two fingers to my clit, his index finger on top of mine, and circled it painfully slow. He stopped at the center of my clit and paused, then pushed into it. I dragged in a breath, lips parting as a shock of pleasure vibrated throughout my body. He circled, then pushed again, until I felt liquid run down my ass. Using the tip of his finger, Kova pushed mine aside and expertly caressed my aching clit.

And I let him. I couldn't stop him. His eyes were too hungry and my body craved his touch.

Kova circled a few more times, enough to leave me breathing heavily and my thighs quaking. Using my fingers again, Kova slid down with purpose until he reached my entrance. He stopped. I held my breath and waited.

Kova pressed on my entrance with all three of our fingers and I swallowed thickly. He inserted just the tips, caressing my walls, and then curled them. We both let out a strangled breath of hunger. He did it again, and again, pushing a little deeper each time.

"Kova," I whispered. Pulling our fingers out, a wet suction followed by a pop sounded in the silence of his room, and it was so damn hot to me. He yanked me up, and I flew into his chest and onto his lap, my knees straddling him. He had my wrist in a tight hold, our faces so close to each other. He wrapped his other arm around my back, cupping my ass.

Sucking my fingers into his mouth, I watched his tongue slip between the digits as he licked the clear liquid off. I purred, my cheeks tinged with warmth. Lips parting, chest rising and falling rapidly, I drew in a breath as I leaned toward his mouth.

His eyes flared with heat. "You have said my name three times now, which tells me your wall is finally fucking breaking down. I am not your coach. I have *never* been just your coach."

chapter 32

Entranced, I couldn't stop staring at his mouth.

He'd gotten some of me on his bottom lip and that was all I could focus on. His scent enveloped me, sending me into a tizzy. He was right—he'd never just been a coach to me.

"The least you can do is fuck yourself where I sleep every night so I can smell your pussy and see the mark you leave when you're gone."

My eyes shot to his and they widened. Chills slithered down my spine.

"You're so filthy," I said, my voice thick with need.

"Do it," he demanded.

I was embarrassed to admit out loud that I loved when he talked dirty to me.

Kova tilted his head to the side, his eyes roaming my face. "Unless, of course, you want me to be deep inside you," he whispered seductively against my lips. "The way I am feeling right now, I can split you in two." Kova pinched my chin between his fingers. He licked over my lips and I felt more pleasure seep from me. "That is not why I wanted you to come here though—I hope you know that—but I am happy to oblige." He smirked, and I felt it in my soul. "I think you want my cock deep inside your pussy. I think you miss coming on my cock but are scared to admit it. I know I sure as fuck do. The only time I ever come hard is when I am coming inside you. Only you."

I let out a rushed breath, my heart ablaze and body screaming for more. I loved when he spoke to me like that. I found it provocatively hot.

"Or do you want me to play with you here," he asked, his hands sliding to my ass toward my hole. He pressed on it and I drew in a breath as I got on my knees. My heart thumped fanatically in my chest as the anticipation rose. "Between your pussy and your ass, do you know the things I could do to you? The things I could make you feel? The things we could feel together?"

The words he said turned me on so high I felt like I was flying. I was mortified I liked it so much and that I could orgasm just from hearing his raspy voice alone.

Kova smirked again, his eyes knowing. He tickled my ass and my clit throbbed. I moaned out a strangled sigh.

"You like when I say things like that, do you not?"

I licked my lips and nodded subtly. Kova reached between our bodies and cupped my pussy, then dragged his fingers up to put them in his mouth. I whimpered, watching as he sucked every bit of it off.

That was all I could handle.

Wiggling out of his hold, I grasped the seam of his shirt and pulled it up and over his head. My mouth was on his seconds later and I could taste myself on him, which only ignited my passion even more. I held the back of his head so he couldn't move. I kissed him hard, bruising, the way he would kiss me, and rubbed myself along the length of his shaft. His hips thrust forward and I knew he wanted me just as bad. We groaned into each other's mouths, grinding against one another. His hand smoothed over my ass as he played with my entrance. I kissed him harder, biting his lip. My hands were everywhere—I couldn't stop touching every inch of his delectable body.

I needed to come and I would do anything to get there. If I had to rub my pussy all over him until I orgasmed, I would. Wouldn't be my first time. And I knew he'd let me.

Kova broke the kiss. Without another word, he leaned around me and positioned two thick, huge pillows on top of each other next to me, then grabbed my hips and jerked me around until I was straddling them, facing the wall. I placed my hand on the headboard to steady myself, nearly drunk from his kisses, touches, and filthy words.

Kova came up behind me. "Put both hands on the headboard." His deep voice caressed the column of my neck. His calloused hands massaged up the length of my back, sending little sparks and shivers the higher he moved, until he cupped my neck and forced me to look back at him. Kova leaned around and squeezed my throat, his tongue coming out to lick my mouth and kiss me good.

"Rub your clit on the pillow," he ordered against my lips. I wasn't shy in front of Kova for the most part, but masturbating on a pillow? I'd rather use his thigh. I wasn't sure what this would do for me and I was kind of embarrassed to try. Kova tightened his grip. "Do I need to spread those pussy lips for you, hmmm?"

The thought excited me so much that I felt myself turn seven shades of red and my heart threatened to beat right out of my chest.

Biting my lip, I nodded.

Kova's eyes flared and he grinned. "This is what I love about you, Adrianna. You get lost in the moment like I do and you simply feel. You let everything go and allow your body the pleasure you so secretly desire."

Kova situated himself behind me, his thighs cupping mine. Reaching around to my front, I watched his hands slide along the pillow until they were under me. Goose bumps pebbled my body at the visual I had in my head of what he was doing. I was already soaking wet. I could feel the slickness on my thighs.

Carefully, his fingers spread my swollen lips apart until I was wide open on his pillow. I sighed, sinking down. Surprisingly, it felt good. No, it felt fucking incredible. The creases of the pillowcase bunched together and hit different spots. I whimpered when one of his hands left to reach behind me, and I felt him shift around until I heard elastic snap. With his other hand, he used two fingers to push the tender skin back so my clit was exposed, then his warm erection touched my spine. I moaned loudly, not caring what I sounded like. My head rolled back and I lost myself to the feeling.

"Do not remove your hands," he ordered.

"No sex, Kova." I had no idea how I managed to get that out.

"That is number four. Four times you said my name."

With both hands, Kova showed me what he wanted me to do by slowly guiding my hips back, then rotating them forward, pressing me downward into the pillows as I moved. A shot of adrenaline sped through me.

"Oh, God," I gasped.

"Arch your back." I did. "More." This time I almost saw stars. "You feel it?"

"Yes," I gasped. "On my clit."

"Again."

For about a minute straight, and with the help of Kova's hands on my hips, he guided me so I was rubbing myself all over his pillow, bringing my pleasure higher and higher. It was the perfect angle to make me lose control.

"Now arch again and hold it." He paused. "Arch more. Yes, like that."

God, I couldn't think straight. I was starting to pant from the sheer ecstasy he brought me.

Using both hands, he gently spread my butt cheeks, then positioned the tip of his cock at my puckered hole.

Kova placed his hand in front of my face. "Spit on my hand," he ordered, and I did. Then he used my saliva to stroke my ass.

"Oh, oh, God," was all I could say.

"Imagine," he said hoarsely, his hands caressing my back, "my cock in your ass while your clit gets worked at the same time." He pressed on the hole, and I didn't stop him. "It is the perfect position and height." Kova kissed my neck, then said, "Now relax for me, *malysh*."

Much to my absolute shock, I heaved myself backward and moaned at the forbidden pressure. Kova froze. Leaning forward so that his chest was pressed to my back, he slowly and carefully pushed the tip of his dick into me. I gasped, feeling the fiery burn. My breathing labored. I couldn't believe I was letting this happen. My clit throbbed and I felt like I would cry if I didn't come soon.

"Or, I can reach around and do this while I take your ass." His teeth sank into my shoulder as his fingers pinched my clit so hard I yelled out. My head whipped back. "You want it, do you not?"

Squeezing my eyes shut, I chewed my bottom lip and nodded before answering. "I forget who I am with you. I forget what I'm supposed to feel—and not supposed to feel—when I'm with you," I said honestly. Then I bared down and pushed back more as wetness seeped from me onto the pillow. I gasped in delight, feeling the tip of his dick breach the little hole even more. It was all too much though and frustrated tears sprang to my eyes. My head fell back onto his chest. "I don't know who I am."

"Maybe this is who you are," he said, his hot breath taunting my neck. "Maybe this is what you want, but you resent that because you are not used to it and it shocks you. Maybe even humiliates you. Like right now, my cock is barely in and it is stretching your little ass. You think it is wrong, but it is not wrong. How can it be wrong when it feels so fucking right?" Kova rubbed my clit, my orgasm climbing and climbing, helping diffuse the pain and place my focus elsewhere.

"I lose control when I'm with you like this," I panted. "I want more and more and more, and I feel wrong for wanting the things I do, for the things I think about."

He kissed my shoulder. "Do not ever be ashamed to want something, Adrianna. Everyone takes pleasure in different ways. *We* just happen to enjoy the same carnal things. Look down and see what you did."

I did, and my cheeks flamed so hot even my ears burned. There was a huge wet spot on his gray pillowcase, completely saturated with me.

"That is your cum. And you know what?"

I shook my head. "What?" He was still rubbing my clit, and my thighs were shaking in response. He slid his dick a little further into my ass but I tensed, shaking my head. "Too much," I said, completely breathless, and he pulled out.

"I fucking love it. I love knowing I can make you feel good. I love knowing you release this little vixen side of you when you are worked up. It is fucking sexy and such a turn-on because you are giving me your pleasure. You push, I pull. You fight, I attack. Can you come like this?"

"I don't think so. It feels good, but the pillow is too soft."

"You need it hard."

I swallowed and nodded.

"Squeeze the pillow with your thighs and try to close your legs."

I did as he suggested and felt a sharpness zip up my spine. My back bowed until I was fully raised up on my knees.

His hands moved up and tweaked my nipples, tugging on the little buds. My hips moved of their own accord and I rode the pillow the same way I longed to ride Kova. I whimpered because all I could think about was how I wanted his cock inside me.

Kova's tongue lapped my neck, his teeth scoring my flesh. He reached down with one hand and adjusted himself so his erection slid against my opened pussy. I bared down so hard on him I thought I'd break him.

"Kova, oh god…"

He growled like the fucking animal he was. "That is five."

My eyes rolled shut. I was in a daze, high on pleasure, on the verge of the biggest climax of my life.

"This," he said, moving in unison with my body, "is not something you will find with anyone else. I hope you remember that."

"More. I want more."

He groaned in my ear and licked my neck. "That is my girl."

Kova threw me to the side, and I rolled over onto my back. I panted, breathing heavily, and stared at the ceiling. I was shaking all over, my body drained and worked up at the same time. I glanced at Kova. His dick and heavy sac were pulled out and standing thick and tall. He lifted my hips and placed the same pillow I was just on under my ass and then looked down.

"You are so fucking wet and swollen. Your pussy is pink." I clenched at the word and his eyes lit up, "And your clit… I want to bite the fuck out of it until it bleeds." The passion in his voice went right through me.

"See." The word rolled off my lips, my pussy tingling. "I shouldn't want that."

"But you do."

I nodded. "I want you to bite me and make me bleed. I want your teeth marks all over my body. It excites me, the unknown, but I know it's wrong."

Kova got on his stomach and positioned himself so his face was right between my thighs. "It is not wrong if *you* want it. Give me your hand."

I could barely see his head over my mound as I reached to give him my hand.

"Touch yourself, use your fingers, but go slow. I want to hear it, the sounds your pussy makes when you are turned on." My eyes rolled shut and I moaned. "Ah, your pussy just dripped even more, so you *do* like when I say filthy shit."

It didn't take long until I was shaking with desire and on edge. "Stick a finger in." I did. "Add another." I did and clenched up. I strained to look at him, but his eyes were fixated on my sex like he was a starved animal. "Do you hear that?" he asked, finally looking at me.

"Yes." I did. The sound of me fingering myself was the only sound in the room. The wet suction was beyond hot and enticing. "It's tight though," I said.

"Add another," he responded, his eyes flaring. "I want to watch your pussy stretch."

"It's too tight for another finger and it's a weird angle for me."

"Do it, Adrianna."

I swallowed, pulled my fingers out, and said, "You do it."

He didn't hesitate but grabbed my hand and licked my fingers clean. Then he was insert-ing two fingers, moving them around and then quickly adding a third.

I was breathing so hard and my hips sinking on the pillows.

"Do not hold back," he said. "Let me hear you."

He couldn't want to hear me because I was on the verge of screaming.

"Kova, I'm close."

"That is six."

"Oh, God, make me come, please. I can't take it anymore." My thighs quivered and my body shook with need. I was so close.

"I wish you could see how beautiful it is to watch your pussy stretch. I want to fuck it. Then I want to come all over you, inside you, on you. I want to watch my cum pour out of you. I want to mark you so you know who you belong to."

I brought my hand to my clit and started rubbing fast. I was ready to burst, but he swiped my hand away. I shot a scathing glance at him, totally frustrated now.

"Please, stop torturing me."

chapter 33

KOVA REMOVED HIS FINGERS.

Before I could protest, he lifted my ass and looked at my sex like it was a feast, then leaned in. Starting at my ass, he teased it for a moment before licking a long, hot, thick trail up and penetrating my entrance with his tongue. His breath was hot and I bucked against his face, not caring how rough I was. My thighs shook and he lowered me. Inserting his fingers again, he wrapped his lips around my clit and bit down, his tongue lapping until I was rolling my hips into his face and holding his head to my pussy, forcing him to suck me. His fingers curled inside me and my hips jerked as he bit my clit again, and that was it.

"I'm coming, I'm coming. Oh God…"

I pushed the back of his head down hard, grinding into his face. I could hear him swallowing, humming against my pussy, could see my thighs shaking around his face, my hips churning from the sheer force of pleasure shooting through my body. This was by far the most intense orgasm I'd ever had in my entire life and I never wanted it to end. His fingers and tongue never stopped moving, not until I pulled his hair to force him back. Kova looked at me, his face almost feral. He looked like he was ready to pounce and mount me like a tiger. Looking at his mouth covered in my wetness propelled me forward. I leaned up, throwing the pillow aside and I moved. He sat back on his knees as I kissed the fuck out of him.

Our hands threaded through each other's hair as our mouths moved together. "I can taste myself," I said, and kissed him again like I was sucking myself off him. My tender sex glided against the length of his erection pressed between us and he moaned.

"Your pussy tastes better than anything I have ever had. I could eat it every day for the rest of my life if you would let me."

"Don't tempt me," I responded.

Apparently, my body wasn't done because I started rubbing myself on him fast and hard. Kova's breathing picked up, his hands everywhere. He pulled my hair, grabbed my ass, slapping it hard, then took my hips and moved them back and forth against his dick until I thought he was going to fuck me. My pussy hit his balls every time, making sure my opening and clit slid up his length.

"More, harder," I whispered, and he did. We stared at each other, never breaking focus. "I'm gonna come again. Oh, my God!" I cried out, wrapping my arms around his broad shoulders, and locked onto him. There was no space between us. I ground my clit into his thick cock and started coming, and then so did he.

I tried to kiss him, but Kova pulled my hair, holding me back. Our eyes locked again as he unloaded between us. He moaned, his body contracting as he orgasmed. He thrust his hips and I gasped when I felt him blow his heavy, hot load between us. His cock twitched against my pussy and his cum hit my stomach.

"Don't stop."

"Never."

I couldn't get enough and was suddenly in a frenzy, searching for more. I wanted to have sex with him so bad. I tried to kiss him again but he still wouldn't let me. Kova sensed a change in me and reached between us. There was so much sticky cum on us that my jaw dropped and my body erupted.

I came alive.

"I want to lick it off you." I found myself telling him, trying to push him down to the bed. "I want you to fuck me."

He groaned deep in his throat and mumbled something in Russian. "No, *malysh*."

"Please," I begged. "I need you to take me, I need to feel you. Let me ride you."

"No," he said firmly. "Shut your mouth and focus on my touch."

Using two fingers, he swiped some of the remnants of his orgasm and then quickly rubbed my clit with enough force that I was coming, for the third time, just seconds later. He slipped the two fingers into my tender pussy and I rode them, imagining it was his cock.

Exhausted, I let out a long sigh and my head dropped to his shoulder, finally coming down. Kova held me in his arms, kissing my cheek, my neck, wherever he could, until the effects of the orgasm left my body completely.

I picked my head up and looked at him with sleepy eyes. As strange as it sounded, I was glad he hadn't agreed to sex.

"See, I don't know who I am when I'm with you. I almost feel dirty."

He palmed my cheeks and kissed my mouth. "You are no one other than Adrianna Rossi. You are who you always have been. You just release your uninhibited side with me, and I am the only man who knows what to do with it."

I touched his bottom lip, gently sliding my finger over it like I was applying lip balm. Quietly, I asked, "Why didn't you have sex with me?"

He smoothed back the loose strands of hair from my face, contemplating his answer. "Because I know it is not what you wanted."

I glanced up. "Even after I asked for it, you knew I wouldn't want it?"

Kova nodded. "Yes. I knew what you needed, and that I could give it to you, but I was not going to take advantage. I did not want you to regret anything."

He was right. I was breaking down and that scared me. I laid my head on his chest and he stroked my back, dragging his finger up and down my spine while I sat in his lap.

"Kova?"

"Yes?"

"Thank you."

"I am trying, Adrianna. I know you are not ready to hear what happened and how things came to be this way, but I do hope one day you allow me the opportunity. Until then, I am just going to keep trying." He paused. "Do you regret anything we just did?"

I thought about his question and was surprised by my answer. "No, I don't."

Kova let out a loud breath and I pulled back to look at him. "What?"

"I thought you would say yes."

"Were you worried?"

"Yes, I was. I did not want to ruin any progress we may have made."

I frowned. "What makes you think we made any?"

He shrugged. "A gut feeling. Little things here and there. You would not have let me touch you had we not. I know there is nothing I can make you do. You are one of the strongest people I know, and I know you will have to come to me on your own. I will just be here wait-ing for you when that happens."

"I'm still heartbroken by what you did. Don't confuse what we just did for something it's not. I needed a release, and you were convenient."

A shadow came over Kova's eyes. His face drawn, he cleared his throat and averted his gaze, lifting me off him.

He got up and stood stiffly at the side of his bed.

"Go get cleaned up. You can use my bathroom or the guest one, whichever you like. Take a hot shower to warm your muscles up, then meet me in the guest room. I will set the table up there."

Before I could respond, he turned and walked away. I frowned, watching his back flex, wondering if he was being cold toward me, or if it was just my imagination.

Once I rinsed off, I put Kova's shirt on and met him in the guest room. He was on his knees, dressed in only basketball shorts and his baseball hat, opening the massage table box. He'd been telling the truth when he said he hadn't used it for anyone else. I softened a little inside.

"I hope you don't mind that I'm wearing your shirt. I only have workout clothes with me."

He didn't bother looking up.

"That is fine."

I glanced around, a little excited about getting a massage. "Is there anything you need me to do?"

"No."

"Where do you want me?"

"Wherever you want to be."

I frowned and bunched the hem of his shirt in my fists. "Do you want me to get you water or anything?" I felt stupid asking if he wanted me to get him a drink in his own house, but he was acting strange and I wanted to break the awkwardness. "Tools?"

Tools? I rolled my eyes at myself. Could I be any more embarrassing?

Kova pulled the tape off one side of the box. He turned his head away and reached for a box cutter. The Olympic tattoo on the side of his ribs caught my attention. It contracted and flexed with each of his movements.

"Help yourself to anything you want."

I chewed my lip. My eyes skated nervously across the carpet. I didn't know where to look and decided I'd get some water, even though I wasn't thirsty. I saw a glass with clear liquid on the table next to where he was working, and I had a feeling it was vodka.

He was clearly upset.

"Uh, okay." I walked into his kitchen feeling uncomfortable and began opening random cabinets, looking for a glass. When I found one, I filled it with some tap water, then leaned against the counter and drank it.

I studied the tile floor, staring in a daze, wondering what I had done to cause the swift change in his mood. I didn't think I'd done anything wrong, and I certainly hadn't left him with blue balls. Maybe it was just my imagination.

I placed the glass down and walked back into the guest room. Kova already had all the pieces out and lined up, a few of them already put together. I walked to a white wicker chair next to the window and sat down. I glanced through the sheer white curtain at the bamboo trees outside, then looked back at Kova, who was reading an instruction sheet.

"What's with all the white in these two rooms?"

He didn't respond.

"They're so cold and sterile, like a museum. I was afraid to breathe in them. Same for the bathroom. Does anyone use it?"

He remained silent, not answering any of my questions, so I decided to screw with him.

"Do you need any help?"

"Why did you get the table delivered here instead of the gym?"

"Did you decorate your room?"

"What would you do if I slept with Hayden?"

"Is white Katja's favorite color? Maybe that's why the feel is so different. Hot verses cold. Frigid bitch," I mumbled under my breath.

He didn't respond or react. Instead, he put the paper down and took a big swig of his drink, then picked up two pieces of steel and started assembling. He ignored my questions, and for some reason that hurt my heart.

I figured the question about Hayden would at least get a reaction. He wasn't listening to a word I had said and that got my head spinning. Now I knew I'd done something to upset him, I just didn't know what. Or rather, I didn't want to admit it to myself. I suspected my words had hurt him, but I wasn't sure because Kova had never let my words affect him so much. He'd always been unbreakable. At least that's how it had always seemed.

Something clashed together and I jumped. Kova spat out a long slew of Russian words that caused me to flinch without even knowing what he said. He shot a fleeting look my way and scowled, then picked up two pieces of the table and screwed them together.

"I guess you used up all your English words for the day," I said softly to myself.

Blinking, I turned away and glanced longingly out the window again. That black hollowness I was so used to spread to my chest and throughout my soul once more, taking up residence. God, I hated it so much that it brought tears to my eyes. I took a deep breath and pulled my knees up to my chest and exhaled. The whole point of coming to his home was so I wouldn't feel alone. But sitting here with this man who always filled every room he walked into with so much energy and color was making me feel more isolated than I'd ever felt before.

chapter 34

"**I**'M NOT WEARING UNDERWEAR," I SAID, CLIMBING ONTO THE TABLE.

I pulled the hem of his shirt down and laid on my stomach. I looked at him over my shoulder.

He grabbed his glass and took a long sip of the clear liquid. I swear his eyes were on my feet.

"It is no matter. I know how to keep it professional when I need to."

My forehead creased so hard I was starting to give myself a headache. I looked away, totally and completely baffled. Coming from Kova, I had no idea what that meant. Professional wasn't a word in our joined vocabulary.

"I will do a blading session since it has been a long while, then I will do a massage."

"Okay," I responded quietly, then focused on the wall.

Kova unraveled his tools and quickly got to work. He applied so much pressure my body clenched as he dragged the tool up the back of my calf, then down. The pressure wasn't unusual, but he usually asked if I was okay. Today, he didn't.

I gripped the sides of the table and ground my teeth together. I rambled off a bunch of questions just to take my mind off the procedure.

"I am trying to focus, Adrianna," was all he said.

I knew he was, but he usually obliged and assisted me in any way he could. Now he wasn't. Kova switched tools and I decided that as soon as he was finished I'd leave. If I was going to feel this alone inside, I could do it at home where I at least could cry about it. I didn't want to be here with him anymore if he was going to act like a stranger. I didn't like this melancholic cloud hanging over my head. I chewed the inside of my cheek, knowing this session would be over soon. Blading didn't take very long, thankfully.

I exhaled a long breath once he was finished. I didn't move but glanced over my shoulder at Kova putting away the instruments. The blading, while it helped tremendously, took so much energy out of me when I had so little to begin with. My eyes were heavy, and I blinked long and hard.

"I'm really tired. I think I'm going to skip the massage and just go home," I said.

Kova applied a salve to my other calf and began kneading it. "I did not leave the gym early and put this table together for nothing. You will have the massage and then you can leave afterward."

"Uh, okay."

Kova lifted the hem of my shirt until it reached the bottom of my butt. His hands expertly kneaded my inner calf, working their way up the back of my thigh, then down to the arch of my foot, where he pointed and flexed it. With each stroke, his fingers manipulated the tight muscles and worked my injured Achilles tendon to get blood flowing. I gasped a few times. I hadn't realized I needed this so bad.

"That hurts a little bit," I grunted out.

"Deal with it."

"I don't think I'll be able to walk after this." Let alone drive. But I'd figure it out.

"You will sleep here."

"I don't want to."

"It is not up for discussion," Kova stated as if we were done with the conversation, which only angered me. Grabbing his cell phone, he put on music. Hinder played in the background, "Lips of an Angel," a song that I actually loved. In the quiet I listened to the lyrics clearly and understood why he liked it too. It could have been our anthem. Wanting to remain faithful to the one you chose versus yearning for the one you wanted. It was us wrapped up in a heart-breaking ballad.

"You can't make me, you know," I said, blocking out the rest of the lyrics, but he didn't answer. He was lost in the song and using the music to ignore any word that left my lips.

His hands actually felt good on the backs of my thighs and I softened inside. Now this was the kind of massage I could get used to. Much to my surprise, he never breached the professional line, but acted every bit the qualified specialist he was.

Kova stepped out of the room for a few seconds and came back with a white towel.

I was beginning to hate that color.

Our gazes locked as he took another sip from his glass. His green eyes bore into mine over the rim of the crystal, shooting through me with what felt like contempt. I didn't like it.

Putting the tumbler down, he walked over and draped the warm towel over my butt, then tugged the shirt up in a conservative manner so no skin would show. I shifted, knowing where he was going with this, and carefully pulled the shirt off before laying back down.

Before he started, the tips of Kova's fingers grazed the hairs at my neck. He stood right next to me but felt so far away as he gently brushed the loose strands to the side so they fell over my shoulder. He whispered to himself, lost in his own mind, but I heard every word.

"What is it about you that I cannot let go? I am a fool for you, as you are for me. There is nothing I would not do for you."

I closed my eyes, his words sinking through his fingertips to my skin, painting the truth. Lotion on his hands, he started on my shoulders, digging and pushing and pinching every muscle. I was so tender is some spots and Kova's hands were unforgiving. He slid down my spine, his thumbs running over each vertebrae to my lower back. His hands spread out and his fingers slipped under the towel and over my hips and around my pelvis. He repeated the motion so many times I lost track, then he went over my legs again, and then worked on my arms with calculated measure and strict control.

"This feels good," I all but moaned. The next song came on and I felt like it was a message. "I didn't know you liked Bruno Mars."

Kova remained quiet. With each bout of silence, I shut down a little more. I didn't like being ignored. The whole point of agreeing to come to Kova's house was to rid myself of the deafening hush hush and loneliness I received in my condo. He was giving me a dose of my own medicine and it hurt way more than I could have ever imagined. It made me think about how I'd treated him over the past couple of months. I refused to feel guilty for my actions, though, not after how everything went down, but this was a horrible feeling and I decided I was going to change my ways.

I sighed. Maybe he didn't hear me. He did seem to be in the zone.

"Okay. You are finished," he said.

I glanced around. "Do you know where my shirt is?" Kova walked behind the table and bent down. He picked it up and handed it to me, then he reached for his glass and finished the remaining contents. "Thank you," I said.

Sitting up, I covered my chest with my arm and quickly slipped it on, but I didn't need to. Kova had already given me his back.

I climbed off the table, a little wobbly and lightheaded, but I brushed it off. I hadn't eaten anything today and it was already late in the afternoon. My stomach growled embarrassingly loud, but a searing headache erupted behind my right eye and I gasped. Kova spun around and eyed me up and down. I leaned against the table and dug the heel of my palm into my eye socket and rubbed in circles.

"Let us get you food."

"No," I grunted in agony. Fuck! I hated when a headache like this happened. "I'm just gonna grab my keys and go home."

"You will not find them," he said like he was telling me he was going to water his lawn. I glanced up with one eye open. "I hid them."

I blew a heavy breath through my nose. Not this shit again.

"You have to be kidding me. Kova, I am *not* in the mood for your antics right now," I said, my voice low and lethal. "Give me my damn keys."

"What do you want for food? Borsch. Zharkoye. Stroganoff..."

I grimaced, and yawned. I was tired and just wanted my bed. Putting my hand out, I said, "None. I just want my keys."

"Borsch it is."

Kova walked out of the room and I followed close on his heels as he walked into the kitchen and pulled various containers out of the refrigerator.

"I'm going to look for my keys."

"Good luck. You will not find them," he responded, his voice so pleasant that it pissed me off.

"I'm not a violent person, but I'm ready to knock you out." He ignored me and turned the stove on. "I don't want booshie, or whatever it is. I'm not hungry, and you can't make me eat. You said you can't make me do anything, and yet here you are doing this."

Kova froze. He rested his hands on the marble countertop with his back to me. "I will never make you do anything you do not want, Adrianna."

I threw my hands up, not that he could see. "Oh, really? Then what do you call this?"

He didn't answer me. Aside from feeling absolute emotional devastation, him being angry with me and not telling me why was the second worst experience, and I needed to escape it before I exploded. I felt the heat rising inside me, my heart thawing from icy cool to a fierce burn in a matter of seconds. I squeezed my eyes tight until I saw a glowing light, and shook my head, not understanding what the hell was going on when I decided I'd pull a fast one on him.

Calmly, I said, "Fine." Then I turned around and skimmed over the countertops, looking for *his* keys. If I couldn't take my car, I'd take his.

A few moments later, something jingled behind me. "I am one step ahead of you. Nice try, though."

That was it. My breathing labored, I panted with fury. Before I could detonate, Kova strode over and stopped right in front of me. I reached behind me and gripped the countertop so hard my knuckles hurt. If he came any closer, I would kick him in the balls.

"When did you have time to steal my keys? Was this planned all along?"

He swallowed, his throat bobbing. "The people who need the most help are the ones who never look like it. I will not make you stay, but you need me right now and you know it. You are far from immature, so do not start acting like it. Go lie down while I cook. If you want to leave after you eat, you can. At least I will know you are stable enough to drive by then. I saw how you came off the table, how your eyes looked, the headache you are hiding from me right now." I ground my teeth. "Whether you like it or not, I see you."

Tears burned my eyes. God, I hated that he was always right. Kova expelled a heavy breath. He lifted a hand and tried to brush back a few strands of hair near my temple but I swatted it away. I was angry and upset at the world.

Pushing away from the counter, my shoulder bumped into his arm but I kept walking. He caught up to me and yanked on my arm, forcing me to turn around.

"What?" I snapped, glaring at him. Kova stared down at me, quiet, penetrating the barrier I'd put up once more and long enough for me to question what he was thinking about. "How do you deal with your temper? How do you remain indifferent like you do? Are you incapable of emotion? Because I'm beginning to think you are."

He shrugged like the answer was obvious. "I drink vodka like all good Russians do."

"Well, I don't like vodka so I guess I'll just go stew in a mental hospital while I stare at a wall contemplating your demise."

I caught the faintest hint of a smirk, but only because I knew him. "There is the fire I love so much."

I lowered my eyelids and almost growled at him. Yanking my arm away, I marched out of the kitchen toward the guest room we were just in and slammed the door once I was inside, not caring that it was his house or that it shook the frame. My dad would've had my ass if I'd done that in his house.

I climbed up on the bed and sat cross-legged, staring at the wall, annoyed when he came in moments later holding out a half-full glass of red wine. I hesitated for a moment before taking it.

I glared up at him and took two huge sips before I said, "First you screw me like the savage you are, then you feed me Plan B, now you're giving me alcohol. If I didn't know any better, I'd say you're trying to corrupt me."

He angled his head to the side, not buying it. "Do not be so dramatic. I was drinking vodka before you were a thought in your father's head. You will live, and hopefully, fucking relax a little."

Right before Kova left the room, he got in the last word.

"If I recall correctly, you asked me to fuck you today, and I said no."

He smiled and shut the door.

I almost crushed the glass in my hand.

Later that night after I'd fallen asleep on a full, warm belly of wine, I woke up in the bed and saw that I was covered by a blanket. I sat up and glanced around, tired and feeling alone. It was three in the morning and the room felt too quiet.

I climbed out of the spare bed, the oversize shirt exposing my bare shoulder as I walked out of the room into his dark house. Assuming Kova was in his bedroom, I went there and found him.

I glanced down. His room was dark, nearly pitch black, but I could make out his outline thanks to the dim light from his closet he had left on. He had one knee cocked up, the other extended, and the comforter draped over his hips. He wasn't wearing a shirt, and I got to look at his insanely sexy body. He was resting on the right side of the bed, leaving the left side empty, as if he were waiting for me. With an arm thrown above his head, his face was nestled into his bicep, free of stress and worry. It was then I noticed his head was resting on the pillow

I'd come on earlier. I blinked, a little surprised. He had said he wanted to smell my pussy and see the mark I left. He hadn't been kidding.

I wasn't angry anymore. Maybe the wine had helped, who knew. What I did know was that I was lonely and wanted him to hold me.

Lifting the comforter, I slid in next to him, pressing my back to his front. He moved toward me almost like it was the most natural thing for him to do, even in sleep. He wrapped an arm around my waist and sidled up to me. I exhaled, settling against his warmth like this was where I was supposed to be.

In the stillness of the night, he softly called my name. "Adrianna?"

I hesitated for a moment. "Yes?"

"Do not *ever* call me convenient again."

For a moment my mind was jumbled and I flipped through events of the night until my lips parted in realization. My words *had* hurt him. Well, one word specifically. Convenient. It was the reason why his demeanor had changed so much, why he'd been so cold and ignored anything I'd said. I hadn't actually meant it, but now I felt bad that I'd said it.

"I didn't mean it," I responded quietly. He hugged me tighter and let out a breath down my neck. "I'm sorry."

"How is your headache?" he asked.

"It's okay now. I think the wine and sleeping helped."

"Good. Now tell me why you got so angry before."

"I felt like what you said was true about us making progress and that scared me. If we are making progress, does that mean I forgive you? I don't know what to think other than I don't want to be that girl who gets walked on all over by the guy she likes. That's why I said you were convenient. Then in the spare room I felt so alone and empty inside. I've never felt alone when I was with you before, but you ignored me and shut me out and it hurt me."

Kova squeezed me tight and placed a kiss on my shoulder. "You cannot deny we have made progress, because we have, just not a whole lot. Even I can admit we have a long way to go." He paused. "And as long as I am around, you will never be alone."

Just as I was about to doze off, he said my name again.

"Adrianna?"

"Hmmm?"

"If I ever found out you slept with Hayden, I would kill you both."

I couldn't fall back to sleep so easily after that.

chapter 35

MY NERVES WERE SHOT.

I was stressed about the second training camp, stressed about just being in the doctor's office sitting and doing nothing when I could be training, stressed that I had offended Kova—which is so fucking stupid considering all the things he'd done—stressed about Joy, stressed about Avery… Just. Plain. Stressed. Out.

Now I understood why people took up habits like smoking and drinking.

Drinking. Drinking made me think of Kova.

This morning I'd woken wrapped in his warm arms, his chest to my back in the hushed serenity of his room. His body, though usually solid and firm, was the opposite when he slept. He was a giant teddy bear that demanded cuddling and I was perfect for that, because I did too. I didn't want to get up. We'd clung to each other, limbs entwined like we were holding on for dear life. Where he moved, I moved with him. If he wasn't holding me, I was wrapped up in him. We never let go all night. Even in our sleep we needed each other. With him in his bed, I felt an odd sense of peace when I should've felt anything but that.

And when his alarm went off too early for anyone—four o'clock in the morning—we both got up and had coffee together. He brewed a large pot and I just cozied up next to him on the couch, my legs thrown over his and my head nestled in the crook of his arm while he watched the news—Russian news to be exact. News all about his country. Of course I didn't understand a word they said, but that didn't bother me. Being with him like that, something as trivial as watching the morning news, gave me sanctuary and brought a sense of intimacy between us, and that was all that mattered. There was harmony. We were Kova and Adrianna, and nothing more, and I realized how much I wished it was always like that. I knew I was treading a fine line getting caught up in Kova again and I couldn't afford to, but in the moment it felt right.

My phone dinged and I quickly pulled it out of my purse while I waited for the doctor.

Coach: I like the idea of you in my bed while I am not there.

I shouldn't have smiled, but I did.

You're insane.

Coach: I am, and you make me that way, but everyone needs a little bit of insanity.

"Adrianna." My head snapped up. A nurse stood in the doorway near the receptionist's desk with a questioning look.

"Yes," I said, and stood.

I followed her down the hallway and around the corner to a patient room. She placed my file on the countertop, then reached into a cabinet and pulled out a specimen cup.

"The bathroom is across the hall," she directed.

Within a few minutes, I was back in the room with a cup of urine. The nurse put on a pair of gloves and took the sample from me. She uncapped it, stuck a paper strip in it for a few seconds, then took the strip out and placed it on a paper towel before removing her gloves. She checked my blood pressure and temperature, then said, "The doctor will be in with you shortly."

The rising anticipation while waiting for the doctor always sucked and filled me with trepidation, leaving me to overthink every negative outcome.

I must've heard the doctor walk past the exam room at least seventy times before she tapped on the door and walked in all bright-eyed and cheery-faced.

"Glad to see you, Adrianna, and at a reasonable time." Dr. DeLang smiled.

"I know, and I'm sorry about that. My schedule is hectic with training," I said apologetically, realizing that's no excuse.

"How have you been feeling since you were last here?"

"Fine, honestly. Nothing new to report, nothing less. I feel the same as I usually feel—tired, sore, drained—but that comes with the territory." I hesitated, then said, "I think I may have reinjured my Achilles at camp, or just tore it a little more, I'm not sure, but it's not that bad. Nothing I can't handle."

"You should definitely have it reevaluated, even if you aren't having any issues, just to be safe."

"I'm okay. I'm being careful."

She walked over and placed her stethoscope to my chest and listened to my heart and lungs for a minute. "Careful can only take you so far," she said when she stepped back. "Considering you're training like a pro athlete, you shouldn't be taking any chances. If you make it past this season without completely snapping your Achilles, I'd say you have a guardian angel watching over you."

I swallowed, and nodded to myself. She was absolutely right. I should have it checked just to be safe, but between all the blading and plasma injections I'd had, I didn't feel it was necessary. The sessions helped tremendously, and I always felt brand new. I figured I was just overworked and worn out from camp.

Dr. DeLang took a moment to look over the urine strip on the paper towel before discarding it and washing her hands. She sat on the stool in front of the counter and flipped my file open. "Let's go over your test results, shall we?" She made a note before continuing. "Your pregnancy hormones came back negative."

"Pregnancy?" Jesus Christ! What the hell? I hadn't had sex in ages.

"It's standard procedure to check the levels in most menstruating patients, even if the cycles are off."

I stared at the doctor with wide eyes. Pregnancy had never crossed my mind since I took Plan B.

"Tell me about that rash on your face." She flipped a few pages in my chart. "When did it start?"

I brought my fingers to my cheek and grazed over the redness I thought I'd concealed this morning. "I woke up with it actually. I thought maybe I had an allergic reaction to something."

Dr. DeLang ran her finger down the page and frowned. "The last time you were here you mentioned your coach pointed out a rash on your cheeks." She looked up at me. "Is this the first time the redness has reappeared since then?"

I chewed my lip and nodded. Truthfully, I'd thought it was the wine since I didn't even eat, but I couldn't tell her that.

She eyed me for a minute before returning her focus to my file. "Your iron level came back low, and your red blood cell count has dropped even more. Your urine tested positive for protein again, only higher this time."

"Is it all the Motrin?" Those little orange pills were my lifesavers, but now I wondered if they had done more bad than good.

"Highly doubtful. You're running a temperature today, and your blood pressure is elevated."

Huh. I didn't feel like I had a fever. Other than being tired from camp, I felt fine. Nothing out of the ordinary.

"I'd like to run a few more tests." She opened a drawer and pulled out a lab sheet.

I frowned. "More tests? Why? I feel fine." Oh, yeah. My blood pressure was spiking by the second now.

"It could all be attributed to overtraining. But I'd like to check a few things." Her hand skimmed over the paper, marking off boxes. She paused and angled her head to the side, her eyes staring at me above the rim of her black, bold glasses. "Do any diseases run in your family that you might have forgotten about the last time you were here?"

My heart was about to jump out of my chest. "D-diseases. N-n-not that I'm aware of. I don't know." I shook my head.

She turned back to the form. "I know your schedule is chaotic right now, so we'll kill two birds with one stone and have multiple blood tests done."

Multiple blood tests?

I cleared my throat before responding. "I have a training camp coming up. I'll be out of town for a week."

"Another camp? When is it?" Dr. DeLang looked back at me.

"My last camp. It's two weeks from now."

"We should be fine, but get this blood work done before you leave. If anything pertinent comes up, I'll have my office call you."

I blinked a few times and decided to just be out with it instead of allowing the obvious to hang in the air. "Dr. DeLang, why do you want more blood? You think it's more than just overtraining, don't you?"

She looked up at me and sighed, then removed her glasses. "I tested for Rheumatoid Arthritis because of the pain you mentioned in your joints, but your numbers look good there." She looked directly into my eyes as she continued. "But with the high protein, dropping red cell count, low iron, joint pain, fatigue... I'd be remiss if I didn't run more tests."

"What do you think is causing it?"

"I'm not prepared to give you a diagnosis at this time," she evaded.

I grimaced. I had a feeling she'd say something like that. "But you have something in mind. I have the right to know what you're testing for."

"Yes, Adrianna, I have a suspicion. But that's all it is at this point. I don't want to worry you."

When a doctor tells you they don't want to worry you, that's exactly what you'll do. I scrunched my forehead and angled my brows. I wasn't going to let up on her. If she wanted more tests, then she'd damn well tell me why.

"Dr. DeLang." I pushed. "Not telling me only worries me more, and considering what I do every day inside the gym, putting me at ease would really help so I don't break my neck from a tumbling pass. Please, what are you testing for?"

She looked at me for a long moment, and I stared right back, not backing down. She sighed, then said, "I'm testing for lupus."

My stomach dropped and I remained silent as she continued.

"The issue with lupus is it can be confused for Rheumatoid Arthritis, but those numbers came back fine. Lupus is great at mimicking other illnesses, and thus can often lead to months and months of testing, trying to narrow it down."

"Lupus?" I tried to swallow the lump in my throat. "You think I have lupus?"

"I have nothing concrete at this point. But that butterfly rash"—she pointed at my face—"coupled with your other symptoms raises a red flag. I'd like to run a few analyses on your organs as well."

"My organs?" Chills rolled down my arms. I didn't know how to react, what to say, what questions to ask. I knew I should've been asking something, anything, but I couldn't think straight. "Which organs?"

She hesitated. "Lungs, heart, kidneys. Sometimes lupus can affect them. I want to rule out everything I can."

My heart fluttered. Lungs, heart, and kidneys? "How? Is this a genetic thing?"

"If it is indeed lupus, typically someone in the family tree would most likely have an autoimmune. But you've indicated there is no family history of illness or disease. So this is all circumstantial and inconclusive without further testing, and why I didn't want to worry you."

I nodded my head, mentally flashing to every family member I could think of and if they were sick—Dad, Xavier, Joy... Joy. My lips parted and I averted my gaze.

"Adrianna?" I blinked a few times. "Is there someone on either your paternal or maternal side that is sick?" She softened her voice.

Looking at the bland ivory wall across from me, I licked my lips nervously, thinking about how I would phrase this.

"I...ah... I just found out my mom isn't my real mom," I admitted out loud for the first time since that awful day. "I don't know who my biological mother is." My voice shook, cracking from the unshed emotion I'd been holding in for months now. I didn't want to look at my doctor. I didn't want to see the pity.

Tears filled my eyes. I blinked a couple of times to hold them in. Dr. DeLang reached behind her and plucked a few tissues from a box and handed them to me. She gave me a gentle and understanding smile that only made me cry even harder.

"I'm sorry," I said, blotting my eyes.

"There's nothing to apologize for."

I sniffled, and she gave me a few minutes to get myself together.

"If this is lupus, if there's something severely wrong with me..." One thought kept floating through my mind. One fear. One worry. One concern. I didn't want to know but I had to ask. "What does this mean for my future in gymnastics?"

"Lupus is debilitating and sucks the energy and life force from you. It weakens you, hinders your physical, and sometimes mental, well-being. Most people with an autoimmune can't do what you do, yet you have been, which makes proper diagnosing a bit more complicated. As I said, this is all speculation until we do more testing."

"But you think it's lupus," I stated. "Or possibly something worse."

"I prefer facts and data over probabilities." She handed me the lab sheet. "Go to the lab first thing tomorrow. You'll have to fast again, nothing after midnight."

I looked down at the form. My mind a scattered mess. Nothing made sense and suddenly I was filled with all these worries and fears I couldn't stop myself from thinking about.

"In the meantime," she continued, "I want you to take iron supplements and increase your water intake. You can try an antihistamine to see if it clears up the rash."

I hopped off the exam table and she walked me to the door. "Oh, and please check in with your orthopedic doctor. The littlest tear can lead to the greatest injury."

Within thirty minutes, I was at home and sitting on my couch reading over everything I needed to know about lupus. My chest tightened with anxiety and I clicked out of the websites I'd been reading online. Every single thing I'd thought was a result of training too hard, was in fact a symptom of lupus. All of it. And the worst part was knowing what lupus could lead to if left untreated.

I sat back and dropped my cell phone on the couch, and let out a deep sigh. The silence was a roar in my ears. I had so many questions swirling around in my head.

Standing up, I walked into the bathroom and flipped the light on. I looked at my reflection and touched my cheek. There was a soft, petal-pink rash. I looked down at the counter and noticed all the stray hairs. There seemed to be more each day, and I wondered how the hell I wasn't bald by now. I looked back at the mirror and wondered about my real mom. Wondered if I would ever find out the truth about her, and if she was where this autoimmune shit came from.

How could I be sick and not know it? No! I let out a loud huff and shook my head. There was nothing wrong with me. I felt fine, just worn out because I was stubborn and pushed myself too hard.

I turned off the light and returned to the living room for my cell phone. I glanced at the time, seeing that it was still early in the day. I hesitated, torn between wanting to know more and not believing there was anything wrong with me. Either way I needed to talk to my dad. I needed real answers about my birth mom that only he could answer. I knew he had to know something. There was no way my dad, of all people, didn't have some type of information on her.

I looked at the time again and decided to skip practice. I was going to drive back to Palm Bay. My dad couldn't evade me if I was in his face.

I shot a quick text to Kova before grabbing my purse and keys.

Blood work came back normal. All good here. I'll see you tomorrow.

Coach: Do not think I will not call your father and ask him for the results.

My blood simmered in my chest. He may be my emergency contact, but he wasn't privy to any results.

I'm not like you, I don't lie. Plus I'm on my way to see him now.

It didn't take long until I was on the highway. My phone chimed and I picked it up from the cup holder to see who it was. *Kova.* I wasn't one to text and drive so I placed my phone back until I could stop and read it. Another three messages came in, but I ignored them. If he really wanted to talk to me, he could call.

I wasn't sure how I was going to get my blood work done if I planned to be at practice bright and early tomorrow, but I'd figure it out. I guess I could "accidentally" sleep in and Kova would never know I lied. Actually, attending the camp and going to the doctor at the same time was a blessing in disguise. I could ask for one more day to rest, and I had a feeling he'd give it to me.

D RIVING ON A LONG STRETCH OF THE HIGHWAY FOR A FEW HOURS CLEARED MY MIND. Typically I didn't love to drive, but this was freeing and released a lot of the anxiety that caused tension in my neck, something I needed to remember. Especially when it came to Kova.

I pulled into the driveway and immediately looked for Joy's car. My stomach was tossing and turning—it'd been months since I'd seen her—and I wondered how she would react to my presence.

Shifting into park, my gaze traveled over the rows of cars looking for her Jaguar, but it was gone. Maybe she was out shopping or doing her charity stuff she loved more than her family. It wouldn't surprise me. There were a few other cars I'd never seen before, but nothing out of the ordinary.

I pulled my cell phone from the cup holder and stepped out of the car, then walked up to the front door. As soon as I stepped inside, Thomas was there to greet me.

"Miss Rossi," he said excitedly and hugged me. "It's been too long."

I smiled and squeezed him back. He'd been like a father to me and seeing him brought me happiness the same way seeing my dad did.

"I've missed you," I said.

"We were not expecting you or else I would have had your room freshened up. I can do that for you now."

I pulled back and shook my head. "It's not necessary. I won't be staying long, I just wanted to surprise my dad and talk to him."

His white, bushy brows angled just slightly together. He frowned. "Mr. Rossi doesn't know you're here?"

"No, I didn't tell him. Why do you ask?"

He straightened and forced a smile. "No reason at all."

I observed him. "What are you hiding?" I joked a little.

"Nothing at all. Are you hungry? Thirsty? Let me get your favorite coffee for you."

"Ah, diversion." I winked. "It's all good. Is my mom here? I didn't see her car outside."

He swallowed thickly and peered down. "I haven't seen Mrs. Rossi in quite a few months. I'm not sure where she is, to be honest."

I paled. "A few months," I repeated. "What are you talking about?"

Thomas's eyes widened and he panicked. "Miss Rossi, I thought you knew she wasn't staying here. Forgive me, please. I wasn't aware you didn't know she moved out."

My jaw hit the floor. This day just got better and better. "No, I had no idea. Dad never told me."

Thomas looked terrified. He shifted on his feet, using his hands to speak. "Please, I truly—"

"Don't worry, I won't speak a word of it, and I'll pretend I didn't know. It's not your fault this family is bound by secrets and lies. Dad probably was just trying to protect me and help keep me focused on gymnastics."

He nodded, speechless. His eyes filled with guilt, and I felt bad about it. Wiping the astonishment from my face, I smiled and said, "I'm gonna go see him. I only have so much time before I have to hit the road again."

I turned to walk away, but Thomas stopped me. "Ah, Miss Rossi?" His voice shook. "How about I let him know you're here first? You know, in case he's on a phone call."

The hair on my arms rose. Something was up and I didn't like it. "It's okay, I won't say a word when I walk in if he is. Thanks, though."

"I think it's best if I let him know."

I flattened my lips, not liking the vibe Thomas was putting out. Leaning in, I said firmly, "I've never needed permission to see my father, and I don't now. Thank you, Thomas, but you're excused."

Turning around, I pulled my shoulders back and walked toward my dad's office. My keys jingled in my hand and I wondered why there was a strange air in the house. I hated to treat Thomas like he was hired help when he meant so much more to me than that, but in this case, I had to get my point across.

As I drew closer to the doors, voices carried down the hall that caused me to slow my steps. I recognized my father's immediately, but there was a woman's voice I'd never heard before.

I swallowed thickly and cupped my keys into my hand so they wouldn't make any more noise and I listened harder. I heard my name mentioned, but the voices were still too distant to make out anything else. Eavesdropping always caused false assumptions. Still, I couldn't not try to listen.

Standing in front of Dad's office door, my heart raced a mile a minute, and I felt that impending doom fill my chest. I was a little nervous to demand anything from him, it wasn't exactly my style, but I needed answers. The voices were clearer now, and as I lifted my hand to knock, I heard someone giggle and caught the hint of a southern accent.

"Dad?" I said cheerily, opening the door.

The giggling halted and my gaze immediately landed on a woman who looked awfully familiar. I studied her for a minute, trying to place where I knew her from. She returned the stare, only she looked shocked to death.

"Adrianna?"

I turned toward my dad, who was standing behind his cherry desk looking just as surprised. I smiled and walked slowly toward him, thinking about who this woman was but wondering where Joy went.

"Hi, Dad."

He rounded the desk and put his arms out. "I'm surprised to see you," he said, his voice tense, and pulled me into a bear hug. My heart softened and I felt at home. "Why didn't you call first?"

"I figured I'd surprise you. There's something I wanted to talk to you about that couldn't wait."

Dad pulled back and looked at me, his eyes traveling the length of my body like he was making sure I was okay. "Whatever you wanted to talk about could've been done on the phone, you know. That's a long day of driving for you."

I shrugged it off. "It was actually a peaceful drive and something I needed to clear my head."

The woman to my right shifted from the corner of my eye and I glanced at her. She was still staring at me. Sunlight filtered through the room from the large window behind Dad's desk and cast over the petite woman. God, she looked familiar and I wished I could place her. I noticed the color of her hair was a dark brown, but when she tilted her head just slightly and the sun hit it at the right angle, there was a red undertone to it.

The same undertone as mine.

Something in my chest immobilized me and my arms went numb, my fingers tingling with iciness.

Dad cleared his throat and I tried to look at him, but my gaze was locked firmly on her cobalt blue eyes. She had porcelain skin, a small but pointy nose, and I thought I caught sight of sun-kissed freckles sprinkled across the bridge of her nose the same way mine were.

She stood up and instinctively I took a step toward my dad. My knees shook and my heart pounded. She didn't move closer, and she looked scared. She was about a couple of inches taller than me but had the same exact body type as I did.

"Dad? Who is this?" I whispered, blindly reaching for him. My voice actually shook, but somehow, in the pit of my stomach, I already knew the answer.

She looked at my dad then back at me, fear showing on her face. Her gaze told a story, and it was one I had a feeling I wouldn't be prepared for.

"Adrianna?" she said, in the softest, gentlest voice I'd ever heard. She covered her mouth. And somehow, someway, I knew who she was in that moment.

I gasped, air lodged in my throat. My heart raced faster than it ever had. I couldn't deviate my gaze from hers, it was impossible when she looked at me like she'd been waiting her whole life for this moment. Breathing in, my chest rose and fell so fast it was starting to ache.

Her eyes watered and she lifted her arm and reached out like she couldn't believe I was standing in front of her, then she pulled it back. She clasped her hands in front of her like she was struggling to stand in place. A tear rolled down her cheek.

"Adrianna, sweetie," Dad said with a bit of a wavering voice. He moved to stand to the side so he was in my vision. "This is Sophia."

"Sophia?" I whispered, testing the name out and her eyes flickered. "Sophia?"

It was the strangest thing. It was like Sophia and I were in a daze and it was only us in the room. I could feel her reaching out for me, I could feel her need to be closer, but she was scared and didn't know what she should do. Truthfully, I didn't know what to do myself. In some unexplainable way, I knew in my heart who she was the moment I'd stepped into this office, and I didn't know how to feel about that.

"She's your…" Dad paused, and swallowed. "She is your biological mother."

Another tear rolled down her cheek and something inside me chipped away. I was sad. I suddenly felt bad she'd never gotten to see her child in the flesh for nearly seventeen years, and I put myself in her place. I'd want to run to my daughter, wrap my arms around her and never let her go. But she couldn't do that since I was virtually a stranger, even though I gathered that her heart was crying out to. She probably didn't know what the right thing was to do, or how I would react. *I* wasn't sure how to react. She was the mother I was supposed to have but instead I grew up with Cruella de Vil, for reasons I still didn't know. But something in my gut told me those reasons were not because she didn't want me, not with how she looked like she'd been looking for me my whole life, like I was the missing piece of her heart she'd finally found.

So I took it upon myself and walked over to her until I was standing just a few inches away. I had to look up, but not by much. I put my hand out to touch her hair, and saw the color was exactly like mine. The resemblance was staggering. When I walked in and felt like she looked familiar, it was because we were practically identical. The only difference was the color of her eyes, but everything down to the heart shape of her face, the way the freckles lightly decorated her creamy skin, her full lips that were trembling, and her wide, downturned eyes, was all me.

This was why Thomas wanted to make my dad aware I was home. He'd known Sophia was in here.

"You look just like my sister," she said in awe. She stared, her eyes unblinking. Sophia's voice broke like she was on the verge of a breakdown. I definitely detected a soft drawl. "It's startling." There was a slight accent to her words, but I couldn't place it. "There are so many things I want to say to you, but I don't know where to start."

Something inside me perked up. "I have an aunt?"

Her eyes watered again and this time her jaw trembled. "You *had* an aunt."

"Oh," was all I could say. My shoulders dropped a little.

"Her name was Francesca. She died a month before you were born."

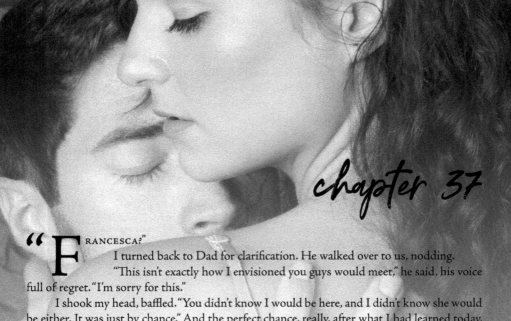

chapter 37

"**F**RANCESCA?"

I turned back to Dad for clarification. He walked over to us, nodding.

"This isn't exactly how I envisioned you guys would meet," he said, his voice full of regret. "I'm sorry for this."

I shook my head, baffled. "You didn't know I would be here, and I didn't know she would be either. It was just by chance." And the perfect chance, really, after what I had learned today. Only, I wasn't sure how I would broach the topic now that she was here. Was it acceptable to start digging around about her family history on the first day? Probably not.

I looked back to Sophia. "I'm named after your sister?"

She nodded, but the lingering silence worried me. When she finally spoke, her voice was as soft as a stroke of a feather.

"It's where your middle name comes from. We were extremely close."

"Where does Adrianna come from?"

"Francesca and I picked it together. She loved the name Adrianna Francesca and thought it sounded good with Rossi." Sophia paused. "I can't believe how much you look like her," she said again.

"That's funny because I feel like I look like you."

She covered her mouth and I noted that her hand was shaking. "I've seen pictures of you over the years, but in person…" She shook her head in disbelief and glanced at Dad. "I've watched you do gymnastics for years. Francesca was a gymnast too."

I wasn't sure how she'd seen pictures of me, but that wasn't important right now. Dad stepped closer to her and took her hand in his, helping her sit down. I frowned. It was like they were well-acquainted. In a sense they were, but I didn't expect them to be after all these years.

Just then, Thomas walked in carrying a tray of drinks, thankfully breaking the emotional reunion. Our eyes met and guilt shown in his. I didn't fault him. I just smiled and thanked him silently. He looked relieved.

"I know you said you didn't want your coffee, Miss Rossi, but I thought you could use it."

He handed my dad a crystal tumbler of amber liquid and Sophia a tall glass with fresh mint leaves and slices of cucumber in a clear liquid.

"Is there anything else I can get you?" he asked, almost like he was begging to wait on us. We all declined and he departed the room.

Dad sat near Sophia on the love seat, and I took a spot in the cushioned chair. He crossed his leg over his knee and relaxed casually. I wanted to be angry, I wanted to yell at him and demand answers, like why she was here, why he'd lied to me months ago and told me he had no idea where she was when he clearly did, where she'd been my whole life, but I couldn't find it in me. I wanted to ask why Sophia gave me up, how much money she got for me, and how her family didn't know about me. All things my dad once told me, and yet all of that didn't matter anymore.

"Well, this is weird," I said more to myself, and took a sip of my favorite java.

"Not that I'm not happy to see you, sweetheart, but why are you here? Don't you have practice? Does Konstantin know you're here?" Dad said. "It's not usual for you to show up like this, and it has me worried."

I swallowed. He was right. Reacting on my emotions wouldn't get me anywhere, and I needed to think straight and remember why I came. I shot a nervous glance at Sophia, wondering how this would go since it was about her.

Her lips quivered. "I can leave. You probably need to talk your dad privately."

She moved to stand, but I stopped her. "No, stay. It actually kind of involves you."

They looked in my direction, both bewildered. Couldn't say I blamed them.

"Are you sure?" Sophia asked. She glanced at Dad for guidance, but he was just watching me. I nodded and took a big sip of my coffee and decided to just be out with it.

"So I went to the doctor today, and found out some interesting things." My heart suddenly started jackhammering in my chest. I was more nervous than I thought I'd be. Looking at my dad, I said, "I came home to talk to you about my biological mom to hopefully get some explanation. Imagine my shock to find her here after everything you told me."

His face fell. "Adrianna, I know you're probably upset with me over that, but I can explain."

For some unknown reason, him withholding information from me didn't bother me as much as I thought it would. Maybe when I got home tonight it would, but right now, I needed a different explanation.

"It's okay, Dad. I won't lie and say I'm not upset, because I am. I'm pretty hurt by a lot of things, but there are more important things we have to talk about right now."

Deep creases formed between his eyes. "I'm listening."

Exhaling a huge sigh, I looked down at my mug and watched the steam rise into the air. I stared at it as I spoke. "I haven't been feeling well lately. More tired than usual, headaches, my chest hurts. I thought it was because I was training too hard, pushing too hard, too many competitions and not enough rest—"

"Fucking Konstantin." Dad sneered.

I glanced up, eyes hard and defensive. "It's not his fault. He has nothing to do with this. If anything, he's the reason I went to the doctor in the first place," I said quickly. "I'm going to sum this up. The doctor asked me about my family history and I could only give her one side. At first I was fine with that because I figured there was nothing wrong with me except for exhaustion, until she came back and told me she needed to run more labs." I looked up into my dad's fearful eyes. "She believes I have an autoimmune disease, lupus, and she said my markers aren't adding up, they're still too high. Something about my red blood cells being too low and there's protein in my urine. She's concerned about it affecting my organs." I paused, feeling my emotions rise. "She said lupus can affect my heart, lungs, and kidneys."

Sophia's glass slipped from her hands and shattered to the floor. Liquid spilled everywhere, the ice rolling over the wood floor, the mint leaves stuck on the sharp edges of the jagged pieces. She broke out in hysterical tears and in turn that made me get teary-eyed. I didn't know if it was because of what I'd just said or because she finally got to meet me and the first thing I said was that I'm sick.

"Soph," Dad said with a tenderness I didn't expect from someone he supposedly never spoke to. Dad pulled her into his arms like they were so familiar with each other and she burrowed into him, searching for comfort. He stroked her back, rocking her while she whimpered.

I watched them, lost somewhere between confusion and sorrow. It was like they yearned for each other and I while I didn't understand it, I felt it and it made me so sad. Dad glanced up at me, his eyes bloodshot.

"When is your next appointment?" he asked, his voice hoarse.

"I get blood drawn tomorrow, then when I get back from camp I'll see her. So three weeks."

Sophia sniffled and wiped her eyes with the back of her hand. "I'm sorry." She cried again.

"Francesca," Dad started gently, "when she passed, it was because she was sick."

Goose bumps trailed down my arms. Her soft cries were killing me. Dread formed in the pit of my stomach.

"Sick with what?"

Sophia looked at me. Her eyes were glossy, drowning in grief. She took a deep breath and looked at my dad. He dipped his chin like he was giving her the courage she needed to speak.

"Francesca had type 1 diabetes, but she also had another autoimmune disease on top of that." Her words shook and I felt myself on the verge of breaking down. "It was a terrible and rare one. Mixed Connective Tissue Disorder. But the diabetes is what ultimately took her life."

My lips parted in sadness. I may have only just met Sophia, but that didn't stop the tears from filling my eyes. I saw that autoimmune earlier on my phone when I was doing research, but I hadn't looked into it.

"How old was she?" I asked, nervous to hear the answer.

Her jaw quivered. "Francesca lived longer than expected," she said. "But her death was rough on me, and I think it's why I fell into such a deep depression after your birth."

"How old?" I asked again, almost afraid to learn the answer.

"Twenty."

"Twenty," I whispered. I wasn't too far from twenty, only a couple of years. Terror filled my veins and I thought back to how Sophia had just said her sister had lived longer than expected. I shifted my gaze. Swallowing thickly, I said, "Dad, you didn't think it would be important for me to know this at some point in my life?"

"I hadn't given it much thought, to be honest."

My jaw dropped, chin quivering. Tears threatened to spill over again, so I glanced up at the ceiling of his office, trying to hold them back. Learning life-altering news for the second time in one day was a lot to take in, especially when it involved death. The anxiety tightening the walls of my chest allowed this damp, dark loneliness to intrude and take up space. I didn't like the way it felt and I wanted it gone as quick as it appeared.

"But autoimmune is hereditary. How could you not—"

"I forgot she had an autoimmune, Adrianna. I just remember the diabetes and how bad it was for her. Have you had your blood sugar checked?"

"Ah, I think so? I know the doctor ran a bunch of tests. If not, when I see her, I'll let her know about the family history."

Family. It was a word I didn't know the meaning to anymore, or who my family even was.

"Are you sick too, Sophia?" I wasn't sure if I was supposed to call her Mom or not. It felt weird just thinking about saying it. Even though she gave birth to me, she was still a stranger.

"No, I'm checked often. I'm perfectly healthy."

"Guess I'm the lucky one," I said.

We spent the next hour or so talking about Sophia's family, where I learned more about Francesca and how close they were. They were twins, actually, which was surprising. I'd once read that when a twin died something inside the surviving twin died too, that there would forever be a piece missing. Like a void. I couldn't fathom that kind of loss and my heart ached for her. She had a few old photos on her cell phone she showed me of when they were young. Sophia had been right—I did look so much like Francesca that I could have been a triplet. It was surreal. I noticed her southern accent thickened and slowed when she was emotional. Joy had called her a southern country bumpkin, but she was just a small-town girl with big-city dreams.

When I left, I gave her a hug and she held on like she was afraid to let go. Her hands shook and she cried. She asked me if she could see me again, and I said yes. Dad stood to the side and watched us. He wasn't smiling or frowning, he just seemed like he was really far away, absent. I almost asked him what he was thinking about but I decided not to. I got the impression his feelings were private and he didn't want to share them.

I wasn't sure when I would see Sophia again based on my upcoming gym schedule, but something inside my heart told me it wouldn't be too long from now. It wasn't easy keeping it together. I felt bad for Sophia and the aunt I would never get to meet. But the truth was, I was terrified even more now for myself and what this could mean. It was like the universe was aligned for once in my life and some higher power knew I needed answers immediately.

The drive home was a blur. I didn't even remember it, and as tired as I was, my anxiety and thoughts kept me up all night. I laid in moments of emotionless silence shoving back the tears. I refused to cry, and I almost called Kova, but I didn't.

I couldn't stop reading about Mixed Connective Tissue Disorder, MCTD, and how it affected the human body, which only led me to read more about lupus. But more importantly, how dangerous MCTD could be. There were so many symptoms of both MCTD and lupus that it almost made them seem identical, and now I wondered if my doctor was on the wrong path. Both could result in kidney failure, complications with lungs, water around the heart, extreme fatigue, rash, fever, joint pain.

The list went on.

chapter 38

SOMETIMES YOU HAVE TO DISAPPEAR TO BE SUCCESSFUL, AND THAT'S EXACTLY WHAT I did for the next two weeks.

Mentally, of course.

Discovering I might have lupus and the chance meeting of my real mom was a lot to take in. I was filled with so many unanswered questions that kept me awake at night. Still, by some miracle, I stayed focused and driven, but I kept quiet.

The lab work had been quick and I was only an hour late for practice. The nurse hadn't been able to find a good vein and stuck me multiple times. Multiple vials had been drawn, all with different colored tops, some half full, some different sizes, some with whitish-yellow stuff at the bottom. From my vantage point, I'd counted ten glass tubes when it was over.

The first week had been the hardest. It took me a few days to get out of the slump I'd put myself in. I never should've done any internet searches about both illnesses—I'd known it was a bad idea from the start—but I couldn't stop myself. I needed to know more, but the more I read, the more anxious I became. I was insanely emotional and on the verge of tears a lot. After one night with only two hours of sleep, I woke up vomiting because my nerves were shot.

After that, I didn't allow myself to think about anything that could deter my thoughts from gymnastics, like Sophia and Francesca, or that I could be sicker than I thought. I promised myself I wouldn't look anything else up until I saw my doctor again. It wasn't good for my health, plus we didn't know anything concrete yet. I trained day in day out, tightening up my skills. I drank tons of water and took iron supplements. I ate healthy but light, lighter than usual. I wanted to be prepared for the starvation camp this time rather than going cold turkey, so I trained myself to eat very little.

Each day got easier and I was down to eating roughly eight hundred calories a day. The downfall was that I was in pain everywhere. I almost caved and took a pain pill, but I needed to cut out the Motrin. My ankles were covered in tape and I soaked in Epsom salt every night. I had constant headaches, I was drained past the point of exhaustion, and my back was killing me, but I turned off my feelings and kept my eyes open.

I was on autopilot.

Still, no amount of training could have prepared me mentally and physically for what I was about to endure for the second camp. I knew what to expect this time, yet for some unknown reason, I was blindsided.

Once I arrived back in Texas, I found out four girls hadn't come back. Between the training and injuries they sustained, three were forced to withdraw, and one decided it wasn't for her. I wasn't surprised in the least.

The first day was all about everyone arriving, settling in, and going over the schedules, then we were put on the scale and our bodies were measured. I'd lost six pounds since the last camp. To say the coaches were happy was an understatement. Six pounds on my height and frame was a lot to lose, not to mention they were foaming at the mouth with my training. I was in shambles, but they were happy and that's all that mattered.

Showered and ready to collapse into bed, I pulled out my cell phone and checked my text messages, debating whether I should send Kova an update, when I scrolled past a message from Avery.

BFF: Please talk to me. I miss you so much. What can I do to fix this? I'm so sorry. : (

Leaning my head back against the headboard, I thought about Avery and how much I missed her snarky personality, her carefree view, her laugh, the way she always called me out. So much time had passed, and my excuse was that my plate was full. It still was, more than ever now, but deep down I knew it was me. I'd shut her out and disappeared to protect myself. Avoiding situations was easier, but I couldn't do it forever.

I typed out a quick reply.

I miss you too. I'm in Texas and can't text right now but I promise to message you when I get home. XOXO.

Clicking out of my messages, I pulled up my contacts and scrolled to Coach.

I probably didn't need to give him an update, but something inside my bones compelled me to talk to him. I needed to hear his voice. I shouldn't miss Konstantin Kournakova—he wasn't mine to miss—but I missed him so much. I missed that effortless connection we never should've been allowed to have, that easy morning peace we secretly reveled in at his house, the little stares. I finally had to acknowledge to myself that we were making progress.

No matter how hard I tried not to, I still loved that stupid Russian. Once I dropped some of the anger I was holding on to, I started craving him again as fiercely as before.

I rubbed my dry eyes. It was because of him that I let go of the furling resentment, because he wouldn't have it any other way. With patience, he unknowingly forced me to love him more. He'd learned to respect my boundaries and even tell me no, but still remained the dominant Kova I loved. He'd invaded every part of my life he could. So I wanted to talk to him and tell him of my progress. I wanted him to know *our* work had paid off again and that *we* were one step closer to *our* dream. Because without him, I couldn't have made it to where I was today. Despite my best efforts to shut him out these past few months, Kova and I were a *we*, and I wanted to make him proud. Truth be told, I don't think we ever stopped being a *we*.

Exhaling a breath, I called him. Kova picked up after a couple rings. "Adrianna." His accent rolled strong over the *R*.

"Hi," I said shyly.

"Are you okay?" he asked.

"I'm fine for the most part. I just wanted to talk to you."

"Talk to me, then."

I didn't mistake the smile in his voice.

"The coaches seem pleased with my progress. I don't know… I wanted to share that with you."

"You know I already know, Ria. Tell me why you really wanted to talk to me."

I glanced up at the ceiling, my thoughts a muddled mess. Buried deep inside my heart were burning embers that gave me hope. I coveted them, blowing on them every so often to see if the light was still there for us. Like right now.

"I guess I just wanted to hear your voice." God, how fucking corny.

Kova chuckled, and said, "You mean you miss hearing my contraction-free words?"

I smiled to myself. "I guess I do."

"If you are being honest with me, I will be honest with you." I held my breath, waiting. "I miss walking into the gym every day and seeing your face. It is like a part of the structure is missing and I have to find a way to hold it up until you get back. I do not like it."

I glanced down at the faded comforter, my feelings rising to the surface. "I think I'm being emotional right now and I don't know why." I did know why, but he didn't need to know. "I'm fine, though. In fact, I've been doing really well. At least, I think I have. I feel very confident."

"I have been in close contact with the head coach and am extremely pleased with what they had to say about you and your progress. However, what I am not happy about is how much weight you have apparently lost." I chewed my lip. "You lost more than I expected," he added, and cleared his throat.

"It's not uncommon for a gymnast to lose weight, you know. It's like a rite of passage. If anything, it's preferred, sometimes even a requirement. I wouldn't be so worried."

"That is not healthy. You are going to lose your strength and that will lead to injury."

I contemplated my answer. His tone wasn't malicious, he was just being honest.

"I'll probably be smaller when I get back." I cupped my hand around the mouthpiece so no one would hear me since I shared a room with three other gymnasts. "They don't feed us. We're being starved. A slice of bread and a few scraps of deli meat, a handful of nuts. Sucking on lemons. Not to mention, worked to the bone. The working part I don't mind. I can handle that. It's the gnawing hunger that I'm forced to put my body through again that makes me mental."

I wanted to mention I had peed blood earlier, but I didn't. I kept that little tidbit to myself.

"They want us to be fucking sticks." Tears wove through my words.

Kova's voice was low but controlled, and filled with irritation. "They *commended* me for your weight loss," he said in disgust. "The last thing I want to be known as is someone who treats their gymnasts poorly. And now you sound like you are withering away."

"You're not treating your gymnasts poorly. Why would you think that?"

While Kova demanded more than any other coach I'd worked with, the one thing he always made sure of was that his gymnasts were healthy. Despite all his imperfections and weaknesses, he was a coach who cared. He molded our bodies, knowing how much we could endure without causing actual harm. He expected the best from us because he gave us the best of himself.

I swallowed back the tears blurring my eyes. "All I can say is I'm sorry I let you down. I'm sorry for bothering you. I just thought you'd be happy to hear about my progress."

Hanging up, I curled up into a ball and silently cried myself to sleep, something I hadn't done in a couple of weeks. I never should have called him.

THE NEXT DAY I WOKE TIRED, REGRETTING HAVING CALLED KOVA. My eyes were swollen when I rolled out of bed, and when I looked in the mirror, I had deep purple puffy bags underneath them. I applied under eye makeup hoping to conceal them, but it didn't do much good other than to hide the color. Just as I was ready to walk out of the dorm to the gym, a ping sounded from my phone and stopped me. Brows pinched together, I turned around and limped my way over to my phone.

Coach: Never once have you let me down. I worry about you.

I stood still, breathing deeply as I stared at the text message. I knew I should text him back, but I didn't need this. Not right now. He'd said what I wanted to hear, but just a little too late.

I had two full days of camp left before I'd be heading back home to Georgia, which meant I had one last chance to make a lasting impression on the national team coaches until the next competition, where they would be watching.

I could do it. Mind over matter.

And that's exactly what I did. I skipped breakfast—it wasn't much anyway—and got right to work. By lunch, I'd gotten so used to eating very little that I could barely finish the orange I was given. The back of my foot screamed in pain, the migraine caused silver spots to dance in my vision, and my back ached to the point I thought it was going to snap in half. And all the while, the coaches watched like hawks. I'd give anything for a handful of Motrin, but I ignored the pain, telling myself it would be worth it.

By late afternoon, my heart was pounding in rebellion and my hands were shaking. My head, light and dizzy. I felt delirious and in dire need of something, anything. I wasn't sure how much more of walking on a fiery wire I could take before I collapsed to the ground.

As we rotated events to the last one of the day, Coach Elena strode over and ordered me to sit on the floor. The perturbed purse of her lips and disappointment in her eyes worried me. She motioned for my leg with a wave of her hand and I extended it toward her. Stomach tight, I leaned back on my hands as she placed my foot on her thigh to inspect it.

"Stop limping," she commanded, then switched legs to check my other one. After a quick examination, she went back to my bad leg and clucked her tongue at how inflamed my one injured ankle was. It was bad, the worst I'd seen it yet.

"Oh, it's fine. Nothing to worry about," I said.

She paid me no attention. Looking up, she called for one of the assistant coaches and began speaking in what sounded like a mixture of Russian and Polish. I wanted to ask her, but I had a feeling she wouldn't be open to small talk the way Kova was.

"I'm fine, really," I said, but she was waving something over.

Sports tape.

As Coach Elena stretched the tape out, her gaze took note of how inflamed it actually was. She bent a little more, scrutinizing it, and without moving her head, she raised her hard eyes to mine. My stomach clenched in fear. For a small, petite woman, she frightened me.

"Coach Konstantin and I go way back. You understand?"

I nodded slowly, knowing what she was asking without actually saying it. She pinched the back of my ankle and I sucked in a deep breath, almost crying out. She noticed my reaction immediately.

"You limp, you show weakness," she said matter-of-factly, then stretched the tape up my calf muscle and pressed down. I winced and huffed in pain, but she showed no mercy.

"Weakness makes you doubt yourself." She placed another piece of tape down. "It makes me doubt you. Weakness is a choice. Stop limping. Eliminate pain from your world. Block it out. Pretend like it does not exist, or I will be forced to make modifications that will not serve you."

I nodded vehemently, keeping my mouth tight-lipped. She taped my ankle up and motioned for me to stand.

Two hours later and all the gymnasts were showing signs of slowing down. My calf throbbed wickedly, and I worried this week would reverse all the healing progress I'd made. Still, I tightened my ponytail and looked ahead. Even if I was given a choice to take a break or keep going, I would've continued, despite the excruciating pain working itself up my leg. In my gut, I'd never give up.

And then, it started...

"Mistakes. Show me you do not care!" Coach Elena yelled at no one and all of us. "I guess you do not want this."

"Performance takes bravery, you look like scared little kittens! Olympians are scared of nothing!"

She clucked her tongue, looking as us with shame. "You girls are a dime a dozen. A. Dime. A. Dozen."

"Flexed feet show lack of control and sloppiness."

"Smile. Show me you actually believe in what you are doing."

"Did you just roll your eyes at me?" My heart dropped. She wasn't speaking to me, but to another gymnast, and I feared for her. The girl shook her head nervously back and forth. "You are done. Get out!"

"You are not trying hard enough! If you do not complete the pass correctly, and clean, you are gone. I can have you replaced like this," Coach Elena said and snapped her fingers.

One girl over rotated and landed on her ass with a hard bounce, then rolled backwards and crushed her head into the floor. Her head snapped back and I gasped, covering my mouth at the harsh angle. It might have been a spring floor, but it still hurt.

"Get up. Do it again," Elena demanded.

"But my neck hurts," the gymnast said, clutching the back of her head. Her voice squeaked, and I wondered how old she was. She appeared to be much younger than me.

"That is your fault," Elena responded, not giving a single care as she pointed at her. "Now get back there and do it again. And do it right."

The girl shook her head. With that landing, I wouldn't want to tumble again either. "I think something is wrong with my neck," her voice squeaked again.

Coach Elena scowled at her like she wasn't worth the ground she walked on. "You are a disgrace. A mockery of those who would kill to be here. You must not want it bad enough."

The young gymnast boldly perked up. She pulled her shoulders back, pushed her chin up, and delicately walked over to the corner of the floor, the heels of her feet coming close to the white out-of-bounds tape. Much like everyone here, she wanted to prove herself, but there was no mistaking the unease and horror in her eyes as she exhaled a lungful of nervous air.

"This is something you have been doing for years, there should be no reason as to why you are making mistakes," Elena egged on, clapping her hands loudly enough to draw unwanted attention.

There truly were no reasons for her mistake, but shit happens in gymnastics that sometimes we can't control, and reflecting on how horribly we were treated here, I wasn't surprised in the least by her performance. My heart ached for her.

"You are wasting my time. Maybe you should not even be here." Elena reminded me of Kova with her lack of contractions.

All eyes were on this tiny, petite gymnast who could be no more than four-foot-seven and sixty pounds. She rubbed the back of her neck once again, and I silently prayed she didn't do the tumbling pass. I felt so bad. Even though I hardly knew her, I would've traded places with her if I could.

Bringing her rail thin arms down, she wiggled her fingers to shake out her nerves, and took a deep breath. Her eyes were full of fear and apprehension. I held my breath as she leaned forward on her toes for takeoff.

"Now!" Elena slapped her hands together. "Get moving, and you better pray to whatever God you believe in that you do not make any sort of mistake again or there will be hell to pay!"

Humiliation and guilt were the name of the game with a side serving of intimidation. There was a difference between encouraging an athlete with positive criticism, and being a bully. Coach Elena was a flat-out bully. And the worst part of all was that there had been rumors surrounding her means of coaching for many long years but no one could prove anything. What did anyone have to go on? Hearsay? A strict diet? Her facial expression and tone of voice? She'd acquired so many Olympic medals for the United States that no one ever dared question her. Everyone took what she dished out with a tied tongue.

Her methods created champions. It's what they wanted. It's all that mattered.

Balancing on the tips of her toes, the pixie girl hesitated. She shook her head and I released a strangled breath as I watched her step away. *Thank God*. With rigid shoulders, she walked off the floor and left the gym, not daring to look back as Coach Elena continued with her verbal abuse.

Her time at the camp and, possibly, the national team was through.

I was up next.

I had to perform a forward tumbling pass, which I always dreaded. Elena nodded and I took off—front handspring, front layout, double front twist. The goal was to add a leap at the end of the sequence for bonus points, but midway through my front layout, after punching my feet into the floor, I felt the fire of a thousand flames soar through my ankle up to my calf. Pain exploded inside my leg. I knew I only had milliseconds to decide if I would continue with my actual pass or water it down to play it safe.

I had to be a fool to water it down after what I'd just witnessed.

With my legs together and body as straight as a board, I punched the ground again and soared as high as I could. I brought down one arm and pulled tight, rotating as hard as I could to throw a double full twist.

The searing pain shooting up my leg cost me my breath. I thought I felt a snap, but I wasn't sure. My leg cramped up and bent, and my landing was nowhere near what it needed to be in order to add a leap at the end. Still, I persevered, knowing if I panicked mid-flight it would only make things worse for myself.

Landing, I rebounded high with my chest and shoulders relaxed and added the bonus leap as gracefully as possible. When I finished, I snapped my legs back together and landed lightly, when what I really wanted to do was drop to the floor in a ball from the inflamed heat that stole my breath. All I could do was bite down on the inside of my lip to conceal the pain exploding through my veins. I tasted blood, but it wasn't enough. My stomach with knots from the pain and I thought I was going to be sick.

"Your back has to be arched more through the layout to execute the double full with a straight back. It is more effective for twisting. Do it again," Coach Elena ordered. I nodded, but I didn't mistake the wandering gaze of her keen eyes to my legs. She was looking for the slightest imperfection, but she wasn't going to get it from me. I'd make sure of it, no matter what it cost me.

Her eyes were glued to me. "Now."

Fuck. Fuck. Fuck.

It took everything in me not to limp my way back. My fingers curled into my palms. The agony ricocheting through my body was unlike anything I'd ever experienced before, yet, by the grace of God, I managed to walk like I was striding on water with a straight face and not a care in the world. A quick glance down and everything I suspected told me I was right on the money.

I sighed deeply. On the inside of my foot, below my swollen ankle, a light bruise was forming. A telltale sign of a severely injured Achilles.

With my heels in the corner of the white tape, I took a deep breath and wished for the best. My plan was to land as softly as I possibly could on my toes and apply the weight to my good leg.

Swallowing back my trepidation, I shot her a fleeting look before I raised up on my toes and sprinted across the floor with one goal in mind, to show Coach Elena I had what it took. I might not be needed on beam since I was selected as a bars, floor, and vault specialist, but with gymnastics, anything was possible, so I still had to work my ass off to prove I was equipped to handle anything thrown my way. Most gymnasts typically added difficulty to their earlier tumbling passes to get it out of the way, but mine was at the end, which was incredibly challenging. Hopefully that would speak volumes to Coach Elena.

Focusing, I blocked out the pain and completed the tumbling pass with the bonus leap at the end. The pain shooting through my calf was horrific and I thought I was going to vomit. It took my breath away, but I clenched my stomach muscles and turned toward Coach Elena, making sure there was no emotion on my face.

"Again. We will do it twenty more times if we have to." She paused. "And, Adrianna?"

"Yes?"

She glared at me. Air lodged in my throat. "Remember what I said. Deal with it."

I nodded fervently and got back in line, breathing deeply as I tried not to hone in on the pain. I was on the verge of tears, but being handpicked to participate at this training camp was a huge deal and not something I would forfeit.

Countless passes later, and intense conditioning, I barely made it back to my room in one piece. I didn't limp, but the moment I shut the door, I crumbled on my bed and sobbed. Holding my bruised and severely swollen ankle, I prayed the physical and emotional destruction I was putting myself through would be worth it.

Gymnasts went to camp with hopes and dreams, and left broken and traumatized.

Some beyond repair.

"**I**S EVERYTHING OKAY, ADRIANNA? YOU LOOK TERRIBLE," KOVA SAID AS HE WALKED up to me.

"I just got off the airplane and that's the first thing you say to me? Really?"

I glanced down at what he saw. I wore white Converse sneakers, rolled-up jean shorts, and a loose, black shirt with the words THIS IS MY HANDSTAND SHIRT printed upside down. I didn't think I looked bad. All that was missing was a tan.

He frowned, his shoulders tight and jaw set firm. Glancing into his eyes, I couldn't get a bead on what he was thinking. There was no spark in them like usual. Kova was completely closed off and that raised questions.

"I told you they starve us. You don't listen."

His face scrunched up, but he wasn't being rude. He just looked completely puzzled. "You look…disgustingly thin, and kind of transparent. I almost believe it."

I brushed him off. "There went your attractiveness." He shrugged casually. "I know English isn't your first language, but where's your etiquette? My joints are as stiff as steel, and you have a stick up your ass. I don't need this after the week I just had, that's for sure."

Kova smirked and I felt a flutter in my stomach. "And you ask where my etiquette is?" he teased. "I say it like it is. Are you hungry?"

"Nice to see you too."

"Aside from the skin and bones, I see you are in better shape this time and do not need to be carried out."

"I didn't need it the first time either," I lied, looking into his eyes and fighting a smirk. I had needed it, and I desperately needed it now. I gathered he knew that much but was letting me be independent for once. "That was your barbaric, caveman side coming out."

The back of Kova's knuckles gently grazed my cheekbone, his eyes roaming my face. I stared up at him, catching a swirl of emotion in his eyes. "You have makeup on. You never wear that crap on your face. I do not like it." Lowering his voice, he said, "I like you natural. Wash it off."

Shaking my head, I walked around him toward the exit. He fell in stride next to me and I groaned under my breath. "Who pissed in your vodka?"

Kova looked over at me, the smallest grin tugging the corner of his mouth. "You Americans," he said. "No one touches my vodka."

I turned my head in the other direction so Kova wouldn't see me smile. He was a true Russian and loved his vodka.

We got to his car and I waited for him to unlock the doors. When I tugged on the handle and the door didn't budge, I stood on my toes and moved to look over the hood at him. Kova just stared back at me.

"Something feels off. What are you hiding?" he asked, his green eyes narrowing.

"What are *you* hiding?" I retorted sarcastically.

"There is something different about you," he stated.

"There is something different about *you*."

I'd missed a call from my doctor's office yesterday. They'd left a message asking me to come in as soon as possible. It had been on my mind all last night and the entire plane ride home today. Between that and my Achilles, I'd had better days. My calf was like a ball of heated sparks bursting with each step I took and I struggled to hide my limp from him.

I yanked on the door impatiently. "Please, just open the door. I'm tired and I want to go home." I was fighting to keep my eyes open, but he didn't budge. "Come on, *Coach*." I sighed dramatically and he finally unlocked the doors. Climbing in, I sat down and relished the softness of his leather seats, hiding the suffering pain that consumed my ragged body. I let out a long, drained sigh that made Kova look at me in concern.

"Thank you for picking me up," I said. He just gave me a subtle nod.

Kova pulled out of the parking lot with one hand on the steering wheel and one hand on the gearshift. Something was bothering him, and I could sense he was in a fickle mood. I gathered it didn't have anything to do with me, but every couple of stoplights he would look my way. I could feel the heat of his gaze on my face coming from under his baseball cap, and even though I didn't ask what was on his mind, I went on instinct. Reaching out, I placed my hand over his and he immediately turned his over to lace our fingers together. The tension coming from him dissipated and that made me feel better.

"I know today is your annual Fourth of July barbeque, but would it be okay if I skipped it? I really just want to go home and rest."

Kova flipped his blinker on, then made a right turn. "I decided not to host one this year. I was not in the mood."

"Oh, okay. That makes me feel a little better about missing it then."

He pulled into my condo complex, and I took off my seatbelt when I realized he'd parked his car.

"Come. Let us get you situated."

I closed my eyes, trying not to get all flustered. I had my afternoon all planned out. I'd take a long, scorching shower, eat something, and then binge a TV show on my phone until I fell asleep.

"It's okay. I got it from here, thanks, though. I know what to expect this time."

He blew it off. "It is no issue for me. Come."

"Don't you have a wife to get home to?"

"Katja is out of town with some friends again. I have all the time in the world."

"How convenient," I mumbled under my breath.

"I do not like this side of you."

"What side?" I snapped. I turned toward him, my hand on the door handle.

"This pale face full of makeup and black shit covering your eyes, clown cheeks, vulgar mouth, and rude ungrateful attitude of yours. You never wear makeup, and you never snap for no reason. I can look in your eyes and tell something is wrong."

Sometimes I wished he didn't know me so well.

My raccoon eyes flared as I stared at Kova. "My cheeks have been rosy for days. I figured I was allergic to the detergent used on the bed sheets, so I used blush to try and even out the tone." I gave him a sarcastic look. "Happy?"

He wasn't amused. "Not in the least."

I rolled my eyes and laughed. "For once, I don't care to please you. Thank heavens. Maybe I should run to Sephora and buy out the store so I can paint my face every day."

"Oh, I beg to differ on that one. You still please me very much, I just do not like how you are right now. Something feels off and I want you to talk about it."

"Jesus Christ. You're impossible!" I threw my hands up in mock annoyance. "Has anyone ever told you that?"

One side of his mouth pulled up into a smirk. "A time or two." I hated that I loved that look on him.

"When was the last time you had your period?"

Well, that escalated quickly.

Why did I even like this man again? Shaking my head, I pulled the door handle and stepped out of the car and walked to the driver's side.

I reached for my carry-on, but Kova was quick and pulled my bag out first. Dropping my arm, I glared. "Is there something wrong with you?"

"Not that I am aware of."

"That was a rhetorical question. You're demented and completely out of line. You have no right to ask me that and you know it. I'm beginning to think there's something going on with you but you're just not telling me. And for the record, I had my period like two weeks ago."

He stepped around me and walked toward the entrance. We walked side by side, me fuming with resentment, and Kova as cool as a cucumber. This was just like the time he asked me when my last orgasm was.

"I think we are well past that line you speak of. Has your hair started to fall out yet?"

My brows shot up. I couldn't believe he was asking me these questions. "Why would my hair fall out? What are you getting at?"

"I am extremely concerned with how you look. You are pale, and your cheeks are sunken in. You look like a bag of bones. Your father would be furious with me if he saw you now. Are you starving yourself? Making yourself vomit?"

An angry scoff flew from my lips. He thought I was purposely making myself sick. Many gymnasts had eating disorders, but I wasn't one of them.

"Since when have you ever cared about me in that sense? If I recall, you once told me I sound like an elephant."

We stopped in front of the elevator and Kova glanced at me, his face knotted, hurt. Good. Served him right.

"Just because I do not voice it, does not mean I do not care immensely for you."

Oh, yeah. I was getting good and heated.

"So *immensely* that you had to go and marry Katja, right?" I was still bitter about that. Obviously. "Are you asking me these questions as a concerned parent, or as an unhappy husband who's looking for a good time but wants to make sure everything is still in working order before he dips his dick into someone he shouldn't?"

He stared flatly at me. "Just answer the questions."

The elevator chimed and we stepped in. "No. I'm not answering them. It's none of your business." The doors closed and I stared at our reflections in the brassy mirror. I watched Kova's lips as he spoke, counting down the minutes until I could crash in my bed.

"Contrary to what you believe, it is my business. I bet your heart beats harder and faster than usual. Headaches?"

"The only headaches I have are the ones you cause," I quipped.

"Shortness of breath?"

"Only because I'm fighting the urge to punch you." Kova hesitated when the elevator opened up. Quietly we walked to my unit. "I'm not in the mood, and I'm really tired. Please, just go home."

"I want you to tell me what is wrong."

If this was his way of beating an admission out of me about the blood work I had done because my dad went behind my back, it wasn't going to work. Once Kova left, I'd have to call Dad to make sure he didn't utter a word.

"Why would you think anything is wrong?"

"Just a feeling."

I hated that he could sense something was off. Now it made me paranoid.

"Well, you're wrong. I'm just tired and want to go to sleep," I said again.

"You would tell me, yes?"

I hesitated, then let out a breath. "Yeah, the same way you tell me everything that's going on with you."

I unlocked my door and pushed it open without saying another word. As if I could tell him about the voicemail I had received, or the injury I was sure I'd reawakened at camp, or the results of the blood work I was scared to get.

"If you want me to leave, I will. Let me at least make sure you are settled in and then I will go. I remember how you were after the first camp and want to make sure you are taken care of." He dropped my bag to the floor and said, "But do not think for one second that I did not notice your limp."

I swallowed hard, my stomach tensing. I thought I'd done well with hiding it.

"Fine. But I don't know why you're pushing so hard. You were doing so good at respecting my boundaries and now it's like you're ruining everything with your controlling ways."

Kova released a deep sigh. His next set of words nearly broke my heart and I dialed back my attitude.

"I just want you to need me."

chapter 41

"**I** JUST WANT YOU TO NEED ME."

After he said that, I excused myself to use the bathroom. I was reaching for the toilet handle when I noticed there was blood in the water again. My heart dropped and I froze. I thought the first time was just a freak reaction to the training and stress, but now as I stared at the blood in the bowl, I noticed the color was darker, which told me there was more. I made a quick decision not to tell Kova but knew I would have to address it at my next doctor's appointment.

I'd taken a long bath in some sort of muscle relaxing salts Kova had brought with him, surrounded by my favorite candles. I soaked until the water turned cold, then I washed my face clean and clear. There was no blood in that water, so I made a mental note that it only seemed to happen when I peed. I wasn't really a makeup kind of girl, so it was no sweat off my back to remove it for him. I always felt like I had layers upon layers of paint clogging my pores and making me oily when I wore it anyway. I'd only worn it to hide what I was feeling, which turned out to be a total waste.

"You hardly have any food in this house," Kova said, seemingly frustrated once I emerged from the bathroom.

White clouds of steam filtered around me as I glanced toward where he was standing in my kitchen.

"I'm never home, and everything goes bad."

"You are home every night and morning. What do you eat?"

I shrugged. "Protein bars, coffee… Sometimes I pick something up on the way home. I usually have fruit and vegetables but I didn't buy them since I wasn't going to be here."

Kova stared at me for a long moment, and I realized I'd probably confirmed his suspicion about bulimia earlier.

"I'll go shopping tomorrow."

Grabbing his cell phone, he swiped the screen with his thumb and said, "What do you want to eat? I will order whatever you want."

I studied Kova and focused on the fact his simple question made my heart race. I didn't want to worry him, and I wasn't all that hungry, so I decided to take a different approach.

While I originally didn't want him here, I was secretly happy he'd pushed his way in and I felt I should show him that. I was a mess of contradictions as always when it came to Kova, but he was just as bad as me. He knew he should just go home, yet here he was. We were drawn to each other in the most inexplicable way. Our chemistry was so powerful that our bodies ached to be with each other. We fought our feelings only to fall deeper with each passing breath. We made no sense at all yet we made perfect sense to each other, because there was no such thing as immoral or wrong when you were with the right person.

I walked up to Kova, took his cell phone out of his hand and placed it on the counter, then I wrapped my arms around his back and hugged him. Stepping closer until our bodies were flush together, I laid my head upon his chest. He stood still, probably surprised because it took him a moment to return the hug.

"What are you doing?" he asked quietly.

"Just hugging you."

"I know. But why? You never just hug me."

I laughed as he tightened his arms around me. The warmth of his body made me sigh. I could feel his heart beating and how it sped up the longer I held on to him.

"Unless we're alone, I've never really had the opportunity to hug you when I wanted to." Kova stayed silent. I figured I'd caught him off guard with my answer. I nestled my face into his chest. "Thank you."

"For what?" he responded, his voice hoarse.

I looked up, my chin resting on his firm chest. I answered honestly, my voice soft. "For always taking care of me and being there, even when I don't want you to be. I know it might seem like I'm ungrateful, but I'm not. I've just been really hurt the last couple of months and I'm trying to deal with it and work through my emotions. I really do appreciate everything you do to help me. I'm lucky to have a coach like you."

There was a flash of emotion in Kova's eyes. He swallowed, his Adam's apple bobbing. "I would do anything for you, Adrianna. I hope you know that." He clenched his eyes shut like he couldn't believe it himself. "Anything."

I swallowed hard, nodding, as we stared into each other's eyes for a long moment. I believed him.

Even though it hurt the back of my calf, I applied pressure to my good leg and elevated on the tips of my toes to reach him. I brought one hand to the front of his chest as the other skimmed up the back of his neck. I slipped his hat around so the brim was facing backward. My heart raced as he loosened his hug and his hands roamed down my back to softly cup my hips. I drew in a little gasp, fighting how much I loved being in his arms and appreciating how hard he was trying to be good. I wanted to give him a little kiss, but I couldn't reach him. Even on my toes he still had quite a few inches on me.

But he knew what to do. Kova always knew what I wanted. Slowly and hesitantly, I pressed my chest to his and he leaned his head down to close the distance, giving me his lips. I didn't kiss him with tongue, though, I kissed him with my heart and let him feel my emotion, my lips sealed together. I kissed him softly.

I pulled back and kissed him the same way again, our tongues never touching but our lips separating a little. My mouth pressed harder into his and I felt a sizzle of electricity through my body. Kova's hands slid over my butt and just when I thought he was going to stop, his hands slid to the backs of my bare thighs. All I wore was a thin, jersey knit spaghetti strap pajama dress. Sometimes I liked to let my body breathe after all the hours I spent in a leotard, especially after the week I'd had with Coach Elena.

Wide hands spread out, his fingers all over me, Kova slipped his hands beneath my dress, but I pulled back. I didn't want him to know I wasn't wearing panties, or to get the wrong idea. I'd only wanted to show him I appreciated him with a little kiss.

I stared at his mouth, my index finger running over his full lips that I loved so much. Kova dropped a light kiss to my forehead, then stepped back. I took note of his facial expression. His green eyes were soft, and the warmth in his touch settled the rattling in my bones.

"What's wrong?" I asked.

Kova glanced away and ran a hand over his stubbled jaw. "No one has ever just hugged me like that."

My forehead bunched together. That couldn't be. He'd been with Katja for a long time. I was sure she had.

"Really? Not even your wife? She doesn't hug you just to hug you?"

"No."

"What about a kiss?"

"Not like that. Very rarely, and it is usually me who has to initiate it."

I stared at him for a bit.

"So," he said, "how about dinner…"

I sighed dramatically and rolled my eyes, a smile pulling at my lips. "I'm not that hungry."

"I have listened to your stomach growl nonstop since you got into my car."

I frowned and rubbed my belly. I'd gotten so used to disregarding my gnawing hunger that I hadn't noticed until he said something.

"Fine. I'm hungry, I just can't eat yet. My stomach is too upset. When I feel like this after a hard practice I drink bone broth."

His face screwed up. "Bone broth," he repeated. "You are kidding me."

I chuckled. "No. It really helps settle my stomach, and it's actually good for you."

Turning around, I walked into my kitchen and bent down to open one of the cabinets. I had twelve cartons of organic chicken bone broth. I looked at Kova.

"There is something wrong with you," he said, but in a way that made me bust out laughing.

"I can drink a whole carton."

Kova's mouth was lost somewhere between a frown and disgust, and I giggled.

"Please tell me you at least drink it hot."

I nodded, still smiling like a fool for some reason. "I heat it on the stove then sip it." I reached down and grabbed a box. "Would you like some?" He didn't answer, his face was still scrunched up. "Oh my God. You're a thirty-two-year-old man acting like a child. I didn't offer you frog legs and turtle soup. Just try it for me, please. If you eat mine, I'll eat yours. Whatever you want."

"Deal," he quickly responded.

Oh my God! Eyes wide, I slapped a hand over my mouth, realizing what I'd said and laughing in shocked surprise.

"That's not what I meant!" I yelled playfully. I really needed to think before I spoke.

He held up one finger, his eyes filling with vigor and life. It made me smile to see him like this. "Ah. And correction. I am thirty-four."

I pulled back. Confused. "Wait. What? Thirty-four? When was your birthday?"

He hesitated for a moment. "It is actually today."

"Today?" I responded, my voice a little high-pitched.

He nodded, his newly energetic eyes still focused on me as he shrugged like he couldn't care less that he was turning another year older. I should've known, but more importantly, Katja shouldn't have been away on vacation on her husband's birthday.

"I didn't know it was your birthday. I'm sorry. Happy Birthday, Kova."

He brushed it off. "Are you going to tell me what is wrong now since you know it is my birthday?" he pushed again, a brow raised in what I knew was hopefulness.

I pulled a pot out from underneath the counter and turned on the stove. "Honestly, there's nothing wrong with me other than the fact I'm grossly exhausted. I could probably sleep for the next two days."

He angled his head to the side, his eyes teasing and not malicious in the least. "Lies. I can always tell when you are lying."

I looked at him after I emptied the liquid into the pot, hoping my blush had disappeared. "Are you just going to repeatedly ask the same question until you get what you want?"

"Adrianna, I always get what I want."

A nervous chuckle rolled off my lips. The way he said my name, the roll of the R sent a shiver down my spine.

"Spoken like a true child. All you need is a foot stomp now to complete it."

He barked out a laugh, and I found myself smiling along with him. Kova didn't laugh very often, but when he did, I loved the sound and how it made my stomach flutter and tighten.

"I got my way. You washed that shit off your face, did you not?"

I looked over my shoulder as I stirred the pot. "I don't really like makeup, to be honest. I'm in the gym all day, every day sweating. It makes no sense to wear it."

"I am glad. I do not like it, and you do not need it. Contrary to what you believe, Adrianna, I do not prefer women to be perfect. I already have a Russian doll. I do not need, or want, another one. Please do not wear it again."

I flinched at the scowl in his tone. My stomach clenched. He was comparing me to his wife.

"I am sorry. I did not mean to bring her up."

"You're forgiven." I knew he hadn't meant anything by it.

Setting the spoon on the counter, I turned around and eyed Kova. "Why is Katja not here on your birthday? She should be here to celebrate with you."

I couldn't believe I was nonchalantly bringing up Katja. I never did. But I was exhausted and just too tired to fight, and truthfully, I felt bad for him.

Kova shrugged it off and his smile vanished. "It is just another day to me and not a big deal, Adrianna. One of her girlfriends is opening a new high-end boutique, so she flew to be with her at the grand opening."

"Who says boutique these days?"

"Is that not what they are called?"

I shrugged. "I guess. It just sounds funny coming from your Russian lips."

"Who says Russian lips?" he quickly countered, and I grinned at him.

I liked this, just being carefree and playful with Kova. Before things got complicated and heartbreak got in the way.

This was the reason his demeanor changed earlier when he picked me up. It's why he was standoffish, and why he was annoyed. It all made sense now. I couldn't blame him. I'd spent many birthdays alone and it was so depressing, no matter how hard I tried to pretend it wasn't.

"Couldn't she have said no and not gone?"

It disturbed me Katja skipped out on his birthday.

"Just drop it. I really do not care. It is just another day."

"No, I can't. You're her husband. You're more important than a dumb clothing store. It's too bad she can't see that."

Everyone should look forward to their one big day a year that was dedicated to them. My parents had never cared much about my birthday and it always saddened me. Avery would bring me a small cake and we'd eat the entire thing together.

Last year, I'd spent it in my condo by myself with a cupcake Thomas had bought me.

A birthday alone was a miserable one, and I didn't want that for Kova. He may be an asshole, but I'd learned it was all a façade. Underneath his tough exterior, it bothered him to be alone, even though he was trying to act blasé about it. It's why he wanted me to want him. I knew it was. He had a huge, tender heart he hid from the world.

"You know, if you don't have anything to do, I was going to sit out on my patio and catch some fireworks. You can stay and watch with me, if you want?" I suggested softly.

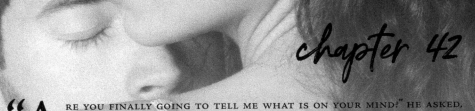

chapter 42

"**A**RE YOU FINALLY GOING TO TELL ME WHAT IS ON YOUR MIND?" HE ASKED, threading his fingers through mine.

I watched as he brought our joined hands to his mouth and pressed his lips to them. I swallowed, my heart leaping into my tight throat. Our hands stayed pressed to his lips, as if he was breathing us in and savoring the moment.

"As you can see, Kova, I actually love to eat. I was just worked to the bone and starved most of the time."

He eyed me. "I believe you."

"Do you?" I questioned, and he nodded.

I ended up drinking half the container of bone broth and Kova had the other half while admitting that he liked it. Then he ordered us dinner from a Mexican restaurant because he said we couldn't survive on a liquid diet and that I deserved to cheat and splurge after the week I had. And I did. I ate everything, surprising myself and Kova. I wasn't even sure what I ate. It had looked super unhealthy, but tasted and smelled amazing. I devoured the gooey, cheesy, meat-filled rolled tortillas with red rice and beans on the side. Apparently Mexican food was one of Kova's favorites. I never would have guessed.

Now we were sitting on the couch and my stomach coiled with emotions that defied each other. I glanced out the sliding glass door. The sun had dropped long ago and I could hear fireworks booming in the distance. I knew why I felt this way. I had two problematic concerns I thought about day in and day out.

One issue was that I liked how well we worked together, how, in this moment, we both just went with the flow like it was the most normal thing in the world for us. In my heart it felt right, and I knew he felt the same way. It reminded me of the day we'd spent at his house when Katja was away.

Letting my guard down and allowing trust to slither its way back in was my other issue, and what I feared the most. Simple moments like this made that happen. The trust thing was always at the front and center of my mind every damn day. If I welcomed him back in after everything, it would mean I was weak-minded. Yet holding up this wall I'd built took a lot more out of me than I wanted to admit.

Pulling my hand away, I moved so I was lying down and placed my feet in his lap. He leaned back and rested one arm along the back of the couch, the other grabbing onto my toes.

"There's nothing on my mind. I'm just worn out."

Kova gazed down at me, his emerald green eyes taking me in. The intensity of his gaze made me blush but I didn't look away. He looked too at peace for me to do that and something in my chest told me he needed this more than I did. Kova was a lot of things, but needy wasn't one of them. So the fact that I could feel his need told me I should let my wall down just a little and be there for him the same way he had been there for me.

"You have so much riding on this summer I want to make sure I have done everything in my power to help get you where you need to be."

"Thank you," I said.

Kova began to massage my feet. I sighed at the feel of his fingers pressing into my sore heels and sank deeper into the couch. "You're going to put me to sleep if you keep that up." I smiled lazily up at him, my eyes heavy and body laden with fatigue.

"So go to sleep."

"Will you stay?" I asked, but there was no way I could fall asleep.

"I will do whatever you want."

I felt the weight of his words and knew he meant what he said.

As his fingers moved to the arch of my foot, I drew in a silent breath and waited, praying to God he wouldn't touch the back of my ankle…but he did. I hissed, my back bowing as tears stung my eyes.

"Oh, God," I gushed, unable to hold it back. I saw stars.

"Adrianna." His voice held a note of worry and panic.

"It's okay. It's okay. I'm okay," I said, sitting up and reaching for my foot. The pain hadn't been so terrible since I got home, but this was also the first time I'd really taken a break to sit down, which meant I'd allowed it to tighten up again.

"Let me get you some ice," Kova said, and jumped from the couch. Within seconds he was back with a towel and a bag of ice to examine my foot. "I am terribly sorry, Adrianna. I saw how swollen it was, I just did not know the pain went that deep."

"It's okay. You didn't know, and to be honest, I was feeling fine and forgot about it."

"This happened at camp," he stated.

I nodded. "Yeah. I think I landed wrong on a tumbling pass, but it could've just been a combination of everything. I think Coach Elena caught on, but I couldn't stop to sit out, or ice it, or even tell her. One look in her eyes said all I needed to know. I couldn't do anything other than take orders, which is what I did. And before you go saying we always have a choice, you have to know I didn't."

I added a little more hardened emotion to my last sentence than I intended. We'd both used that *everyone has a choice bullshit* on each other before, but with each passing day it became clearer and clearer that not every option presented in life came with a choice. It's either you do, or you don't. That's it.

"I understand," was all he said.

"Do you? Really?"

He nodded, and that relieved me so much. "I do. You are too close to the finish line to complain now. You give everything you have to prove you want it, or you give nothing at all because anything less is not worth it. Sometimes that means breaking a little inside and sucking up whatever sanity is left and doing it with a smile. Sometimes that means loading up on painkillers and sports tape or extreme therapy to recover quicker so you are ready for the next day. Do I think it is a good idea to proceed? No. But I get it. Had you not made it to camp, and you were not upgrading your skills, or you plateaued in your training, we would be having a different conversation right now. But it is too close to the end and you do not have that option right now." He paused, still pinching around on my ankle. "But I knew… I knew something was off when you got off the plane. I could feel it. You did not want to tell me, did you?"

I glanced away, my heart thumping wildly against my ribs with the unknown. "No, I didn't. I figured you'd force me to take a day of rest. I honestly never planned to tell you."

He eyed me, all too knowing, and it made me paranoid. "Is there anything else you want to tell me? Now is your chance."

"No. I'll make an appointment with the doctor." Perfect opportunity to get my results too.

"Oh, you are without a doubt going to the doctor. I may be a gift from God, but even I need to know what I am working with here."

A chuckle rolled off my lips. Picking up a decorative pillow, I flung it at Kova. He smiled as he dodged it. I'd thought he would activate dick mode and go off on me, but he hadn't.

"You probably have some little tears in there, but I do not think you severed your Achilles completely or you would not be able to walk and you would definitely be screaming in pain. You would not have been able to finish camp, that is for sure." Kova looked at me, his eyes piercing mine. "You were scared to tell me."

I nodded, chewing my bottom lip. I averted my gaze to the carpet. "I have too much to lose. I didn't want to chance it."

Kova began wrapping up my ankle with the ice and the towel. "*Ya tak ponimayu, chto chuystyuyu sebya slishkom,*" he mumbled in Russian under his breath.

"What did you say?"

He shook his head and looked at my foot. "I understand that feeling all too well." Kova glanced away and leaned back, then rubbed his square jaw. He took off his hat, shook it out, and put it back on. He was anxious. I could feel it in his touch when he gently picked up my foot and placed it in his lap.

He repeated what he'd said in Russian, then looked straight into my eyes. My heart fluttered. I had a feeling I knew where this was going.

"Just that I know that feeling of being scared and having too much to lose. I understand you. *Proklyatyy, yesli vy sdelayete, proklyatyy, yesli vy etogo ne sdelayete.* Damned if you do, damned if you do not. What the heart wants does not matter, it all causes pain in the end. You are fucked either way, Adrianna, so you try to make the best decision you can knowing that neither choice was the one you wanted." He paused, and tilted his head to the side. "Do you have any Russian in you?"

"Not that I'm aware of. Why?"

"Because Russian women go hand in hand with love and pain."

There was so much more going on between the lines than just my Achilles that all I could do was stare back into his pensive eyes and agree. I knew he was trying to tell me more. I'd yet to give him the opportunity to explain himself, but that was because I felt like he'd made his choice and that was that. He could have spoken to me before he did anything, but he chose not to.

But now I wasn't so sure if the choice he'd made was the choice he'd wanted, or one he had been forced to make. I felt the same way with Coach Elena. I knew it was almost time for me to finally be ready to hear what he had to say. I could feel the door opening, and my biggest worry now was that I'd made the wrong choice and kept it closed for so long, sitting alone in the dark.

After my ankle was wrapped up in ice, we sat quietly on my couch for close to an hour. Kova used an app on his phone to watch the Russian news, and I debated whether I should call Avery like I'd told her I would. Knowing I'd need more time, I just scrolled through various social media apps and caught up on her life, along with my brother's and my dad's.

If Avery wasn't smiling in her photos, she was giving her best duck face I always made fun of. She had the most compelling, crystal-blue eyes that burst with energy. In one photo, she had a high, perfectly placed and super cute ponytail, Aviator sunglasses that actually fit her small face, frayed jean shorts that revealed supermodel legs, and a plain white shirt tied at the side. She was standing on the beach with two girls holding ice cream cones. It was one of those moving images. Waves reversed in the background as the girls moved their heads to the side while laughing and licking the ice cream. She looked happy, and I smiled, missing her, but my smile vanished and my brows bunched together when I viewed the next couple of photos.

Avery looked so far away, her gaze distant, and so damn sad that I actually felt bad for her. Her eyes were lifeless. No sparkle. No joy. Her vivacious personality was gone and that upset me. There was no sass and life surrounding her anymore.

That wasn't Avery. She needed me and I'd blown her off. I regretted my actions big time now.

The sound of fireworks going off in the distance caught my attention again. I sat up and looked through the sliding glass door.

"Okay. My toes are frozen solid and I can't feel a thing. Let's get this ice off my leg. I heard fireworks and I want to go outside to see if I can see them," I said, full of excitement. Kova laughed and sat up to unwrap my leg. Just as I was about to put my phone down, a new photo of Avery posted. I quickly viewed and read the caption.

When in doubt, add more sparkles.

I smiled, my heart a little lighter for her. It was another one of those moving images, only it was just a sparkler that flickered against the moonlight. Another hand slid in from the side holding a second sparkler. It tapped the top of hers.

I could tell instantly by the tattoo on the wrist that it was my brother's hand.

chapter 43

LOOKING AT KOVA'S OPEN PALM, I SAID, "IT'S OKAY. I GOT IT."

He ignored me and kept his hand out, waving his fingers, silently telling me to take his hand. "I know you do, but I want to help."

Being stuck in one position too long had wreaked havoc on my body after the training I'd endured. I didn't want his help—I wanted to be strong enough to do it on my own—but I was going to need it to stand up and possibly take a step or two to loosen up, especially because of my foot.

"Sometimes you can be a gentleman," I said, leaning on him.

"Chivalry is not yet dead."

A laughed erupted from me. "You would say that."

We stepped outside onto my patio and Kova glanced around. "I had no idea how big your terrace was."

"Oh, you know my dad. He spares no expense when it comes to building."

Kova was still surprised. "You could live out here." I followed his gaze. There was a double lounge on one side of the deck, and a bistro set on the other side. And at the far end where it wrapped around to my room was a swinging chair.

I chuckled. "That would require me to be home more often."

"Where do you want to sit?"

I looked around. "Can we just lay on that lounge? I'm a little tired and I think it would be fun to watch the fireworks like that. Kind of like underneath the stars. My dad texted me earlier and said I should be able to catch a good show from here." The lounge was the size of a full bed and had plenty of room for both of us.

"You spoke with your father?" Kova asked.

Once we laid back, I folded my hands over my stomach and looked up to the night sky, listening to the sounds of fireworks in the distance.

"I did…kind of. He texted to see how I was before I boarded the plane in Texas and asked me if I had plans tonight—oh, look!" I pointed excitedly, cutting off my train of thought. "There's one! And another!" Kova watched with me as the show began. "I told him I was just going to go home and crash. That's when he said the downtown area puts on a good show and if I wanted to catch it from home I should be able to see it. I didn't think I would because of the marina being so close, but I guess I was wrong. Dad said permits are granted to shoot fireworks off from barges on the water. Sounds dangerous, if you ask me."

I glanced around at the adjoining condos and the balconies filled with people drinking and laughing. Different genres of music wove together and it sounded like a nightclub. I thought about how I was here with Kova and what my dad would think. Scratch that. I knew what he would think. He'd murder Kova and then enroll me in an all-girl Catholic boarding school.

My forehead creased together and I lost myself to my thoughts and all the lies that had been told over the year. Joy claimed she knew about me and Kova, but she had no proof, because if she had any, she'd have told Dad by now. I had a feeling if she did tell my dad anything he wouldn't believe her after the way she treated me over Easter.

That being said, I shivered at the thought of the truth being revealed to anyone.

"Are you cold?" Kova asked.

"No, I was just thinking about what would happen if my dad found out about us. Even if I was legal, I don't think he would ever take the news lightly." I paused, and looked at him. "Do you ever feel guilty? My dad is your friend. Katja is your wife. We're hurting and lying to both of them."

Kova glanced away and stared into the night sky, watching the fireworks. He was bothered, but I think because of the guilt and lies he'd dished out.

"One thing my mother told me before she took her last breath was to never feel guilty for the things that make me happy. She said, 'Kova, I want you to live like it is your last day, because you will never get tomorrow back and the future is all you have.' I was holding her hand when she said that. She was frail and her skin was gray. The world is cruel, life is so short, and if two people out of seven billion in the world can find solace, no matter if it is right or wrong, then there is no reason to ever feel guilty. My mother always put my happiness before hers. She lived a lonely life so I could live a full one. She never married, never fell in love, never went out with girlfriends, never went on holiday, then she got sick. She did not want that for me. I made a promise to her that I would live for the both of us, and I am." Kova turned toward me. "So, no, Adrianna, I do not feel guilty for my actions, I know what I am doing. I made my choices. While they may not make sense to other people, I cannot worry about that. No one is truly selfless, and I cannot be responsible for everyone's happiness when no one cares about mine. I have tried that with Katja and look where it has gotten me. I am trapped in a loveless marriage I cannot fight my way out of. Do I love her? Sure. But I am not in love with her. I love her like a friend and it will never be any more than that." He paused to take a breath. "Do you feel guilty?"

I stared at him, unblinking, trying to contemplate an answer. I was momentarily rendered speechless. Kova was stuck in a loveless marriage and from what it sounded like, he was very much alone. I studied his gaze. His eyes never wavered from mine. There was no flicker of hidden emotion, no hesitation. He didn't lie. In fact, he was open and exposed. I could taste the honesty in his words and see that he was telling me the truth.

I licked my lips and his gaze followed the motion. "I only feel guilty because my dad is friends with you. He put his trust in me to be responsible while I'm here alone, and in you to watch over me and protect me. I can't imagine hearing his friend was having sex with his daughter behind his back would ever be seen as anything but deceitful." I hesitated, then said, "It would be really bad if he ever found out. The thought terrifies me. As for Katja, I honestly don't feel any sort of way. Every person, regardless if they're married or not, is fair game. A relationship can't be threatened if there isn't a bond to be broken. It's that simple. The connection has to be strong enough that nothing could sever it. Would I hate to be in Katja shoes? Yes, but I will never allow myself or my relationship to be in jeopardy, because I would make sure my partner knew my shoes were one of a kind and no one could compare." My voice dropped. "I should feel bad, but the truth is, I don't. Does that make me a bad person?" I sure thought it did.

One side of Kova's mouth pulled to the side. "I think you are asking the wrong person that question."

We chuckled and I rested my head back, thinking about how much had changed in the course of a year.

"I wish you were always like this."

"Like what?" he asked.

"No-holds-barred and completely yourself."

"Believe me, Adrianna, I do try." He was pensive and I believed he wasn't lying.

"So if today is your birthday, and last year you hosted a barbeque on the same day, why didn't you have a cake? Why didn't Katja make one for you? We could have all sang to you."

"The truth? She forgot it was my birthday."

My heart plummeted like a stone. She was grinding my gears and I was starting to really not like her.

"Is that what you guys were fighting about in your kitchen?" Kova turned toward me with confusion in his eyes. He brought one arm to fold behind his head, his bicep flexing in the moonlight. He stared straight ahead like he was thinking back to last year. "I remember you guys whispering in Russian, it looked like you guys were arguing, and you threw something into the sink."

"I do not recall what the exact argument was about, but it would not have been about my birthday. I was never big on celebrating it to begin with. I do not like to do anything extravagant."

"Singing 'Happy Birthday' is not extravagant. I can't believe she forgot last year, and now this year she isn't here. You'd think she'd stay in town because of that. I'm so sorry."

"It is no big deal."

"I can't believe that was around your birthday and this whole time I thought you were thirty-two."

He brushed it off, but I still felt bad. My mind flipped through what was in my cabinets and if I had anything I could give him. I never kept cookies or candy in my house for obvious reasons, but then I remembered I'd purchased a four-pack of big, double chocolate organic brownies and stuffed them in the back of my freezer for a rainy day. I hadn't even had one yet.

I had an idea. Sitting up, I said, "I'll be right back," then I limped inside my condo and went straight for the kitchen. I took out one of the frozen brownies and placed it on a plate, then popped it into the microwave. While it heated up, I grabbed a tea light candle since I didn't have actual birthday candles, and hobbled to get the lighter from my bathroom. The microwave beeped just as I got back. Gently, I pushed the tea light into the center of the brownie and lit it. Cupping my hand around the flame, I walked slowly back to the patio so the flame wouldn't burn out.

Kova's head turned at the sound of the sliding glass door. His gaze dropped to my hands and his entire face lit up as if it were Christmas morning. All I had to offer was a brownie and that was enough for him, and I loved that so much. Walking over, I carefully sat down next to him, making sure not to jostle my ankle. A gust of salty air flowed around us, and a few strands of my auburn hair gently whipped around my face. Kova brushed the loose hair behind my ear and I thanked him.

"Now, I'm not going to sing you 'Happy Birthday' because I'll make your ears bleed, but… Happy Birthday, Kova," I said softly as another flash of fireworks lit up over the ocean. I handed him the plate and Kova stared down at the brownie. "It was the only candle I could find that would work." When he didn't reply, and his brows drew closer together, I said, "Make a wish and make it a good one." Kova leaned in. Just as he was about to blow out the candle, he looked at me.

"What's wrong?" I asked.

He shook his head. The sadness in his eyes stung caused an ache in my chest. "Nothing," he said under his breath. "Thank you, Adrianna, for this." He waited a beat longer, then, with his eyes still glued to mine, he leaned in and blew out the candle.

"Do you want to know what I wished for?" he asked, still looking at me.

I laughed, a wide smile across my face. Taking the plate, I said, "No, Kova. You can't tell me! Then it won't come true." I carefully picked the candle out so I didn't spill the wax and placed it on the small table next to us. I handed him the plate back and the grin he gave me was felt down to my bones.

"Do you believe in that? That if you share your wish it will not come true?"

I shrugged, the thin strap of my dress falling off my shoulder. Goose bumps trailed down my arms.

"We all need something to believe in. I know it sounds a little naïve, but what's the point of making a wish of hope on your birthday? A wish is a secret, a dream, a goal. It's something we desperately want to happen more than anything else in the world, but we can't ever tell anyone because if it doesn't come true then we're left feeling full of despair. Kind of like when you throw a penny in a fountain. You're never supposed to tell anyone."

"But those pennies get scooped up each day, so where does your wish go then?"

I leveled a stare at him and his grin grew bigger. I couldn't help smiling in return. "Stop ruining it and take a bite of your brownie."

Kova barked out a laugh as he picked up the treat. Before he took a bite, he offered it to me.

"No way," I said, pulling away. "If you don't get the first piece and the first bite, your wish will definitely not come true."

"Ah, you make me feel so young." He huffed a laugh, then took a bite. "Are you a superstitious person?" The corners of his eyes crinkled with mirth.

"Only on birthdays."

Kova took another bite and I watched his mouth move. Not because I wanted a piece myself, but because there was something in the air that made everything about tonight feel like it was going to be okay. Like it wasn't weighted down with worry and anxiety. I smiled, a little sad, wishing it could always be like this with us.

Scooting closer to Kova until our arms touched, I rested my head on his shoulder and stared straight ahead, watching the fireworks. I could tell people were lighting them off and that the show hadn't started yet. There were too many pauses in between, and I was glad about that. Plus, they weren't that extravagant and show-stopping. The actual show and finale could be like a private birthday celebration just for Kova to top off this night.

Kova placed the half-eaten brownie under my nose. I shook my head and looked at him. "You eat it. It's your birthday."

"I want you to have some too."

"I don't want it."

"I want to share it with you. Please, for me?" Kova's bottom lip rolled out and his eyes became exaggeratingly sad.

Laughing, I said, "Oh, it's going to be like that? You're going to give me a puppy dog face that I just can't refuse?"

"If that is what it takes."

If it was even possible, he made his face even sadder and I rolled my eyes.

"You look like a lost puppy standing in the rain trying to find his way home. Fine. I'll try it." I tried to take the brownie, but Kova held it up to me. Leaning in, I took a bite and almost moaned. I hadn't had anything sweet in a long time. "Oh my God. That's amazing!"

He looked at me, confusion written all over his face. "You have not yet tried one?"

"No. I bought a pack of them and stuffed it into my freezer. I never tried them."

He offered me the plate. "Here. Eat the rest."

I swallowed. "No, I can't."

"Adrianna," he said, drawing out my name.

"I'll get fat, Kova."

"Not possible."

"I currently have a fat roll on my stomach you can't see right now." He stared at me like he didn't believe me. I grinned. "I do!"

"That is the most ridiculous thing you have ever said." He pushed the brownie toward me and raised a brow. "Finish this with me. It will not break you. Take two more bites and I will take two more, then we will be done. I cannot eat all of it, and I know you want it. It is my birthday. Do you not want it to be the best one of my thirties?"

I looked at him, smiling, but wondered if what he'd said was true. If it was the best birthday he'd had in a long time, I couldn't help but think about how many he'd spent alone.

I TOOK THE PLATE FROM HIS HAND, PLANNING TO EAT THE REST OF THE BROWNIE.
"Peer pressure, man. You make me do bad things."
His eyes sparked with dark humor. "And you love them all."
"Maybe."

I tried to hide the smirk tugging at my lips with a shrug that was neither here nor there, then took a huge bite. Then another bite, and another, until the it was gone. I handed him the empty plate, our grins matching.

Licking my lips, I joked, "You're over the hill now. You can't afford to indulge like this."

An energetic laugh erupted from Kova's chest. "Thirty-four is not over the hill."

"You're practically ancient." I purposely bumped into his shoulder. Kova laughed again. "I'm going to have to trade you in for someone who can keep up with me and all the bad things I apparently love to do."

Turning toward him, I poked his arm, his waist, his leg, his stomach. He flinched each time, then grabbed my wrist to stop me and I shook my head like it was unacceptable.

"Look at you. You're turning to mush already. That's it. I'm definitely trading you in for someone else. How are you going to take control of me when you've lost control of yourself? You probably can't even hold yourself up now."

In the blink of an eye, Kova spun us around until my back was flat on the lounge and he was laying on top of me. I giggled and poked him with my free hand. Seeing Kova laugh did funny things to me, and I wanted to see what else I could do to make him laugh again. Grabbing my wrists, he placed them on the sides of my head.

Our eyes met and a breath of submission softly rolled off my lips. Kova noticed immediately. My heart battered against my chest in anticipation and I could see his pulse thumping in his neck. The laughter died down and the teasing vanished. His eyes roamed over my face and inspired a different story. I realized I missed the weight of him on me and shifted so he was forced to give me more. Kova pushed one knee between my thighs until we were almost connected, my other leg on top of his. I drew in a shaky breath, and pulled him closer. His lips were a breath away and his body was so warm on mine.

He looked at me, his Adam's apple bobbed up and down, and fireworks danced around us. "Adrianna," he said quietly, intimately. "I wish I could make you understand how much I miss you. I miss being near you, being with you, being *inside* of you," he whispered in a sexy, raspy voice, moving his mouth to my ear. "I miss the way you smell, the way you taste. I miss every single thing about you. I try not to, and I fight it so hard, but you are always on my mind, and I do not ever see that changing."

Kova was healing my heart and breaking it all at once. These little moments were what locked me to him, because they were real, and they were what mattered. It was also these little moments that made me question so much, because knowing he was the one who threw away what we had was more devastating than anything. It didn't make sense that someone could do that.

"How can you say those things to me?" I asked softly. "You're the one who stripped it from us with two little words, Kova."

I do.

"I know," he said, his voice full of remorse. The intensity of his gaze moved me deeply. "Do you think we will ever have it back?"

I answered with the truth. "Honestly, I don't know. I don't see how it's possible to ever go back to *that*."

"But you are with me now," he said.

My face fell. "It's not the same. You're married, Kova. You went behind my back and got married. It's hard to forget that."

Kova agreed. "Sometimes I fear I will miss you for the rest of my life, to the point I ache with sickness just thinking about it."

"Like I'm that one person you can't walk away from, even though you know it will eventually come to that." He nodded subtly in agreement. "I feel the same way."

"I never realized how deeply entwined I was in you…how I still am."

Shifting my hands, I threaded my fingers through his. I wanted to tell him I missed him too, that I missed us, and that I felt the exact same way. My heart was racing, screaming with feelings I thought I'd closed the door on. Our connection was too strong and too rare to be denied. We both knew that. We were a sea of reckless abandon with endless possibilities. My attraction to him hadn't diminished, and being alone with him while his wife was away was an invitation on its own that laid out everything we should never be tempted to do.

I looked up at him and stared into his sorrowful eyes. While I didn't want to be susceptible again, Kova was making it impossible to stick to my guns.

"Why are you telling me this?" I asked softly, my heart was going to explode from his raw emotions. "Why now?"

He shrugged. "I do not know. I get this indescribable feeling, and once I feel it, I chase it. I crave it," Kova said, his eyes shifting back and forth. "And it never stops with you. It is like a high all the time. I do not know what to call it or how to make sense of it. Then, tonight, you did what you could to wish me a happy birthday. You are the only one who said it to me today. It was so simple and yet it made me happier than I have been in a long time." Kova paused, swallowing slowly. His brows bunched together like he was lost in an internal battle and needed help to fight his way out.

I frowned. "Katja didn't even call you? Text you?"

Kova rolled to the side, taking me with him. "No. It has been five days since she left. She has not called once, and the only time I have spoken to her was through a text, which I sent to her yesterday to check on her. That was it."

After days of silence from his wife, he still checked on her. My chest tightened. She hadn't even considered him. Talk about breaking my heart. I ached for Kova and what he was telling me. I couldn't believe no one wished him a happy birthday, not even his wife, who was a complete and utter bitch in my eyes now.

This was the real reason he was here, why he'd pushed himself inside and insisted he help. There was no doubt in my mind. I knew Kova cared about me in his own puzzling way and wanted to make sure I had a speedy and healthy recovery, but loneliness was a bitch and the worst feeling in the world. It was when the walls closed in and the silence became deafening, and the long moments allowed you to sulk inside your mind, where your thoughts ran haywire until they caused you to fall into a depression so deep it was hard to climb out of.

This wasn't the first time he'd pushed. I had to wonder how long he'd been stuck inside the darkness.

"Tell me how you guys met," I asked. I needed to figure out why this woman was so cold toward him. I was the only girl he ever cheated on her with, and from what Kova had said, she'd been this way toward him even before that. Despite that pretty and sweet demure look she had going on, Katja was a viper and would quietly go for the jugular when you least expected.

Now more than ever, I couldn't comprehend why he would marry someone who treated him so poorly. Maybe she blackmailed him. No. I quickly scratched that thought from my head. I didn't see Kova as the type to cower in a corner. He was a fighter, and someone who had no issue with confrontation.

Kova cleared his throat and shifted his legs closer to mine so they were entwined together. "Katja and I have a long history. We have known each other our whole lives. Our mothers were close friends. My mom and I lived with her mom for a short while after I was born." He hesitated for a moment. "Kat's mom is the one who got my mom a job at the gentlemen's club. They worked it out so that she would watch me on days my mom had to work, then when Kat came along a year later, my mom returned the favor. We were always at one another's homes, practically raised side by side. We became like brother and sister."

I couldn't fathom a friendship being forged between two women who were prostitutes with children around the same age. They both were saddled with baggage and stuck in a dark hole with no one to help them out of it except for each other.

Curious, I asked, "How did you go from a sibling type relationship to now?"

"Our roles shifted throughout the years. My mother made peace with what she did for a living. She was able to provide a somewhat good home for us, keep food on the table, put me through gymnastics, and never miss a competition. There was no other job she could have worked that would have allowed her that." He took a breath. "Kat's mom, however, grew discontented with the profession." His eyes were distant, a sadness filling them. "She began using drugs to numb herself and eventually became addicted to heroin, she still is. When we were in middle school, I went over to Katja's one day and found her mom passed out on the couch. I heard a commotion from Kat's room…" He stopped for a long heartbeat. I looked up and found Kova with his eyes squeezed shut.

I placed my hand on his chest. Quietly, I said, "You don't have to talk about it if it's too much."

Kova shook his head vehemently. "I ran to her room and found a sick scumbag leaning over her with his pants down to mid-thigh. Her nightgown had been ripped, and black, watery streaks ran down her cheeks. In seconds, I had him off her and on the floor. I snapped." Eyes wide like he was remembering every vivid detail, Kova continued. "I beat him until my knuckles bled, until pieces of skin were torn back from his face. I did not stop until Katja pulled me away."

I blinked rapidly, blindsided by this revelation. "What did you do?" My question came out hoarse.

Kova shook his head, pain thick in his eyes. "I dragged his bloody, beaten body out to the hallway and left him there. After that, I took her home with me. I went from her brother to her protector. Where I went, she went. Even when I had practice, she would sit out in the waiting area and wait for me. My mom pleaded with hers to stop using, but she would not. She was too far gone and that left me with no choice."

Tears burned my eyes, the fireworks long forgotten. I was nestled up to Kova, hanging on to his every word, too deep in the riveting conversation about his past to stop now. I wanted to know more. I wanted to know everything.

I yawned, exhaustion suddenly washing over me. I hadn't slept in eighteen hours and it was finally catching up.

"Is my story boring you?" He laughed lightly, the shadows fading from his eyes.

"No. It's quite the opposite actually. Keep going."

He laughed again. "Are you sure?"

"Yes."

"We can finish this conversation another night if you are tired."

"I'm happy right where I am."

Pulling back, Kova leaned down to kiss my forehead, his arms tightening around me. I was a glutton for punishment, wanting to know the gritty details of his life with Katja.

"Katja stayed with us on and off all through middle and high school. In high school our roles changed again…"

When he didn't continue, I glanced up at him and met his gaze. He tilted his head to the side and studied me. Whatever came next in his story, I knew I didn't want to hear it, but I needed to know. I needed to understand his relationship with Katja.

I rested my head back on his chest, willing him to continue.

Finally, he spoke.

"Katja had always been a beauty, but when she hit around sixteen she blossomed into something else entirely. Men and women looked at her everywhere she went. She turned heads, she still does. We were both teenagers with hormones. I would catch her staring, watching me, just like I did her. Not that I want to go into detail, and I am sure you do not want to hear, but we experimented a lot…until one day we eventually lost our virginity to each other."

An overwhelming burn of bitterness bubbled in my chest. I never gave much thought to Kova's first time, but if I had to guess, I would have thought it was with some random hookup at a party. A total clichéd assumption, but I should have known better. Nothing about Kova's life had ever been clichéd.

I should have prepared myself, but I hadn't.

chapter 45

"**Y**OU WENT STILL ON ME," KOVA SAID.

He pulled back and looked down at me, but I wouldn't meet his gaze. God, why did I have to be so irrational? I saw his lips curve up from the corner of my eye, but I couldn't look. "You are mad," he stated, amusement filling his voice.

"I'm not. I'm fine."

"You are." His voice rose, pleased with my anger.

"I'm not," I chewed out, causing Kova to laugh. He pinned me, his arms over mine, the weight of his body between my spread legs holding me down. I glared up at him and all he could do was smile like he'd won the damn lottery. "Get off me, Kova," I said, and used my hips to push him off, which only resulted in nudging him closer to me.

"You are jealous. Admit it." He chuckled, and I wanted to punch him in the throat.

"I'm not. I don't get jealous."

Obvious lie.

Kova grinned even more. "Then why do you look like you are ready to castrate me?"

My lips flattened, remaining silent. Kova leaned down with a smile on his face, his happiness striking me hard. It was totally irrational of me to behave like this and yet I couldn't help it. His mouth angled toward mine. Just as he was about to close the distance, I turned my head to the side. The tip of his nose grazed my cheek, the heat of his laugh tickling my skin. Sliding his hands, he laced his fingers with mine again as he peppered kisses along my jaw and down the length of my neck. My chest burned and my heart pounded. Just because he and Katja had a deep history didn't mean I had to like it.

"I think my Ria is jealous," Kova said, his voice almost singsong and proud. "I kind of like this look on you. Admit that you are and I will get off," he said, nipping my collarbone. My back arched, pushing my stupid hardened nipples into his chest.

"There's nothing to admit."

Kova pulled back and looked down at me, tightening his hands on mine. "Then kiss me. Prove to me you are not jealous."

"What? No."

"Why not? You gave me a birthday kiss earlier. This can be my good luck kiss."

"You don't believe in that crap."

"I had a change of heart."

A laugh burst from me. "Yeah, right!" I said, and Kova smiled. He nestled closer. We stared at each other, the warmth of our bodies pressed so close together it was difficult not to think about how perfectly our bodies aligned in all the right places.

It was too comfortable. Too natural. Too right.

Leaning down, Kova's lips softly met the corner of my mouth. Slowly, he took his time, kissing all around the edge of my lips with the same tenderness, until he was hovering above me. I looked at his mouth as he waited.

"Maybe I am a little jealous," I admitted in a whisper.

Kova's eyes softened. Tilting my chin up, I gave him the consent he sought to close the distance between us. Right before he kissed me, I said, "Okay. I'm a lot jealous and I don't like this feeling inside me."

He grinned and it electrified my blood. Kova's kisses were unlike any I'd ever had, erotic and as seductive as black lace.

"I would feel the same way you do if the roles were reversed," he said. "The thought of another man with you does more to me than make me jealous, Adrianna. It makes me down-right murderous, and it terrifies me. You are mine, and mine only."

A knot formed in my throat as the times I'd slept with Hayden flashed in my mind. I prayed to every god I could think of that Kova never found out.

"I'm not yours, Kova. Katja is yours."

"She was never mine," he responded immediately, and his words sank into my bones. "Not the way you are. It is...different."

"Yet she's the one with your last name."

Kova licked a wet trail up the column of my neck, and a sigh rolled off my lips. He let go of one hand and held my hips in place as he surged against me in a painfully slow motion. I moaned at the friction against my wet pussy, the desire to tear his clothes off strong.

"For now."

A soft breath rolled off my lips. I arched my neck and pulled his bottom lip into my mouth with my teeth, and kissed him. I was an addict for this man, and despite all the pain and suffering he had caused me, I still kept coming back for more.

It didn't take long for our passion to take over. Kova pressed into me. His lips moved, slow and steady, like he was both sad and in love, reminding me of the night he repeated *prosti* over and over.

I slammed that door shut and blocked it out. I couldn't go back to that night, so I kissed him back the way I thought he was kissing me—wholly, completely, and regrettably in love.

He gripped me hard and moaned into my mouth, a sound somewhere between pleasure and need. His fingers trembled against my skin as he moved his hand to my outer thigh.

Kova pushed against me slowly, and I squirmed as his cock hit just the right spot. Reaching around with my free hand, I slipped it under his shorts and grabbed his butt, pulling him into my center. I gasped into his mouth as he thrust against me again, the head of his cock straining against my opening. All I had to do was pull down the elastic of his shorts and he could slide right in...

"Kova..." I licked my lips. "I want you."

A deep growl sounded in the back of his throat. "Not yet."

Little flames licked my skin as his hand palmed my thigh. His touch, like his kiss, always drugged me and made me ache for more. His fingers dug into me, and I rolled my hips against his length, wanting more, secretly getting hotter knowing we were outside where people could see us. It was so daring and I loved it. I wanted everyone to see he was with me and not *her*. It gave me a sense of power.

"The thought of you telling me about your wife, while you're here with me, while your cock is pushing against my pussy, is intoxicating." The words dripped from my lips like venom. Kova's eyes flared and he let out a growl. "It's thrilling and wrong and I honestly love the feeling it gives me," I continued. "Like I'm high or something. I take pleasure in knowing you're here with me and not her. Somehow I get the sense that even if she were in town, you would still be between my legs."

"Why must you talk like that?"

"Because I know you love it, and it's the honest truth." I smirked.

"You have a corrupted, devious mind," he said. "And I love that you do. It is one of the things I love about you. We feed each other's cravings without guilt."

His hand skimmed higher up my thigh and reached the crease in my hip. His thumb gently stroked my bare flesh, then slid lower to my bikini line, where he groaned at the contact, realizing I wasn't wearing panties.

"I would be with you all the time if I could, and be in that tight little pussy all day long."

Slipping my other hand from his, I placed it in his shorts and rubbed circles on his perfectly round ass. Boldly but curiously, my palms slid along the seam of his cheeks, my fingers pushing in just slightly enough to spread him. Kova tensed then growled as he devoured my mouth. I did it again until the tips of my fingers touched his sack. We became fervent and passionate, breathing heavily, our chests pushing into one another's while fireworks continued to explode around us.

I reached for his wrist and placed his hand between my thighs, and bared down, grinding on his palm, guiding him to rub me how I liked it.

"Please," I begged, forcing his callused hand over my clit. I sighed in pleasure, the beginning of an orgasm climbing.

"Adrianna…" he groaned, looking over his shoulder at the next condo. He looked back at me. "People can see us."

"So." My hips moved of their own accord. The thought of being seen elated me and turned me on even more.

"Christ. You like it," he stated, his pupils dilating. "You like knowing people can see us." Speaking in Russian, Kova looked over his shoulder again then back down at me. "If I do this for you, you do it how I want you to."

I rolled my bottom lip between teeth and nodded in agreement.

Kova leaned over and said, "Do not touch me, and do not move your hands." I agreed. He then pulled the front of my dress up to my stomach. Grabbing my leg, he hiked it so it was over his hip. "Bend your other knee and spread your legs wide."

I shot a nervous glance at the nearby condos. I was way more exposed than I had been a minute ago. My legs were spread wide open like a butterfly.

"Adrianna," he warned. "This is what you asked for and now I am giving it to you. Do as I say."

"Okay."

"Now kiss me, and do not stop until you come. Do you hear me, *malysh?*"

I nodded, breathing heavily, primed to come any second. Taking two of his fingers, he placed them in his mouth to coat them, then he leaned down to kiss me at the same time they penetrated my pussy. I gasped as his fingers breached my entrance and his thumb circled my clit. My hips lifted, pumping onto his fingers brazenly. I kissed him deeply, hungrily, and my legs widened as that familiar, blissful pleasure flowed through me. Right as the desire peaked, Kova pulled his fingers away and delivered a hard slap to my pussy.

I yelped against his mouth at the shock reverberating through me. My hands fisted my dress, the sensations assaulting me confusing me because while I loved it, I worried someone would hear.

"Do not stop kissing me, Adrianna," he growled. I kissed him again and his fingers went back to work, pushing deep inside me and curling upward. His thumb tortured my clit and I panted into his mouth between kisses.

He pulled away and slapped my pussy again, loud enough to cause a stir. A rowdy group of guys next to us started to roar and whistle something, but Kova's voice brought me back to him. Grabbing my wrist, Kova placed my hand on his stiff cock and showed me how to stroke it.

"They cannot see our faces. Let them watch. Let them wish they were the ones touching your innocent little pussy. Focus on the pleasure and what I am doing to you. Trust me on this. It will be worth it. And Adrianna?"

"Yes?"

"Stroke me hard and fucking kiss me."

I nodded hastily and did just that, kissing him while twisting my wrist. The sound of the crowd and the touch of his fingers caused a frenzy within me unlike no other. My kisses became greedy, until I was leaning up on my elbows hungry for more. Hips undulating on their own, I couldn't take it anymore. Another slap to my clit and I whimpered hard, gripping his shaft to the point I knew I was probably painful. That rush of ecstasy hit me with a heavy force. Kova inserted his fingers and my pussy tightened around them as I came on his hand, his thumb never leaving my clit. The orgasm took over my body, my thighs quivering as I experienced another amazing release only Kova was able to give me.

Breaking the kiss, Kova placed his forehead against mine and clenched his eyes shut. I kept stroking him but he slowed my hand.

"You didn't finish."

"That is okay. This was not about me."

He rolled to his back, taking me with him. My head rested on his chest as his fingers dragged lazily up and down my thigh from my knee to my hip, my dress slipping higher and higher each time, until part of my rear was exposed. His fingers halted, and I looked up. He was already watching me.

"Leave it up… I like it."

Kova's eyes glimmered like he was about to say something but he remained silent. His hand drew lazy lines over my pelvis, dipping to the small of my back, and down the seam of my cheeks. Fisting his shirt, I lifted my knee higher and drew in a little gasp when the cool air tickled my wet sex.

Kova's hand slowed to a stop. "You should go rest now," he gently suggested.

"I'm okay. I like being here with you," I responded truthfully. Kova's chin dipped once and his hand started back up. I snuggled closer to him, breathing him in and basking in the feel of his arms wrapped around me. I was two seconds away from climbing on top of him.

It was too natural, too physical, too emotional.

Too perfect.

Kova was right… I missed us, too.

"I want to know the rest of the story."

I needed us to slow down, but I needed to know more. Kova sighed but obliged anyway.

"So Katja was your first?"

chapter 46

PLEASE SAY NO. PLEASE SAY NO. PLEASE SAY NO.

His mouth twitched. "Yes."

"Is that when you guys started dating?" I asked.

"No. We slept with each other often, but we were never official," he said. "It was more than that. I went from a brother to a protector to her lover. She supported my dreams, my goals, my addiction to the sport. When my mother passed away, she was there. Our positions changed yet again, and she became a provider, lifting me out of the darkness and looking out for me. We always just had each other."

My forehead creased and a headache pounded at the center of it. I squeezed my eyes shut and thought about what he'd just said, wondering how Kova didn't see it for what it was. He didn't understand the severity of the situation he'd just laid out for me.

"Do you not see how dependent you both became?" I said. "That's not healthy, Kova. That's convenience. You guys grew up like brother and sister, and now you're married. You guys didn't have to stay together."

Kova shook his head adamantly and that annoyed me. He sat up and turned toward me. Aside from his mother, it was apparent he'd never gotten close to anyone else other than Katja. They'd formed an attachment to each other under traumatic events in their lives and never severed the connection. It only grew as they got older, then they made it legally binding.

"When I suggested possibly moving to the States, she did not question me, she just started packing and asked when we were leaving. We were inseparable."

If that wasn't the definition of codependency, then I didn't know what was.

"Wait. How are you guys here? In the States?"

"Katja is here on a visa."

"And what about you?"

He shook his head. "I came here on a work visa and then became a citizen as quickly as I was able to. Because we married, she is now on a faster track to becoming one too. It will still take time, just not as long." He paused. "You do not understand, and you may never, but after everything we have been through, I felt like I owed it to her. I did not make it easy on her, not even when we moved here, and yet she was always there for me."

My brows shot to my hairline. All this drama was because he felt like he owed it to her? Because back when they were kids her mom became a drug addict and couldn't fucking parent, so he felt like it was his problem to deal with. Then their stupid teenage hormones led to them fucking for the first time, then his mom passed away, and he moved them here. To the land of opportunity. So he married her. Because he felt like he owed it to her.

I shook my head in disbelief and stared at the black sky with white clouds of smoke drawn through it. There was more to the story, there had to be. Like maybe he really did love her. A piece was missing, otherwise it was outrageous to think he'd married someone because he felt like he *owed* it to them. No one does that, and if he did, well, I didn't know where I'd go from here because then he'd have always known he was going to marry her, and still got together with me.

"Sounds like motivation to me. If she has a child, she's legally bound here, and to you."

"No, she knows I do not want kids. She would not do that to me."

"You're kidding me, right? What aren't you telling me?" I asked, turning toward him. "I feel like there's more."

Kova sighed deeply and ran a hand through his hair. He looked toward the dark ocean and watched the roaring waves crash into the shoreline. Tightness spread in my chest as his gaze traveled further away.

I was right. I had a feeling he was holding back, and it was obvious he was.

"It is complicated," he said, voice low.

I scoffed. "Do you even love her?"

He looked at me, his eyes lost, shifting back and forth. "I do not love her the way I am supposed to."

"What does that mean?"

Kova took my hand in his and kissed the top of my knuckles. "There was a period in my life when I thought I was in love with her. If I am being honest, until I met you, I did love her. But things changed and now I question if I ever truly was in love. Do not get me wrong, while I do love Katja and probably always will, I am not in love with her."

My heart pounded furiously against my ribs, my ears like little balls of flames on the sides of my head. Nothing made sense. Nothing added up. And it was driving me fucking crazy. He was giving me pieces to three different puzzles, and asking me to put them together to form a clear picture. It would never happen.

"Then why did you marry her? If you don't love her, why did you marry her?" My voice shook with emotion. I pushed his hand away and stood up, my stomach twisting in knots. Between the story of their upbringing and now this, I was ready to scream. "Why? And don't give me a bullshit reason like you made a stupid pact when you were kids, because I'm not buying it. And why didn't you tell me? Why did I have to find out the way I did? And why are you still married to her if you don't love her?"

I felt my blood rising, my blood pressure breaching the normal rate. My chest rose and fell, palms sweating. If he had told me he was in love with her, I would've believed it. I would've accepted it. Even that would be better than this. But he hadn't, because he didn't even love her.

"Adrianna." He shook his head sadly. Kova stepped toward me, but I stepped back. His forehead wrinkled and I wanted to fix the anguish in his eyes. "The truth." He sighed, and I frowned as his voice started to trail off. He sounded wrecked and it made my chest ache. "There is more to the truth, and it does not involve just me and Kat. It would destroy you more than I ever have, and I am not willing to risk that. When everything is said and done, and the Games are in the past, then I will tell you. There is a plausible reason, and it was never meant to hurt you. As ridiculous as it sounds, what I did was for you. You have to believe me."

I shook my head, my heart breaking all over again.

His gaze took in my face and scanned the length of my body. He rolled his lips over his teeth, then switched to his native tongue. I caught the hint of a smile and I wanted to smack it off him because now was not the time for it.

"*Ya lyublyu tebya. Ya lyublyu tebya, no eto nichego ne mozhet izmenit.*"

My head tilted to the side. I watched his mouth and stepped closer. "What did you say?"

He shook his head, the smile fading from his face. "It really does not matter what I said. It cannot change the past or the future."

I stepped closer and placed a hand on his arm. "It matters to me. Last time you said *prosti* while we had sex and the next day I found out you were married." I couldn't say making love because now I wasn't sure Kova was even capable of love.

"I should not have said it," he said, his voice low.

"You shouldn't have done a lot of things with me, yet you have."

"*Ya lyublyu tebya. Ya lyublyu tebya, no eto nichego ne mozhet izmenit.*"

I stared at his mouth. "Again."

I wished I didn't like hearing him speak in his native tongue. I wished I hated the dialect the way I did other languages. The times he'd spoken in Russian to me were times that ultimately decimated my heart. The way his tongue tapped his teeth, how his cheeks hollowed when he spoke, the way his lips moved, there was something to be said about a man who spoke a foreign language in a deep, robust voice.

"You've said that to me before. What did you say?"

"Things I cannot say to you." He swallowed, his Adam's apple bobbing. "I would love to teach you Russian one day."

One day. Closing my eyes, I shook my head and ignored his last comment. He was diverting the conversation.

"How… How could you marry someone you're not in love with? Explain it to me?" I pleaded again. I couldn't wrap my mind around it, and I didn't see myself letting it go anytime soon.

"Adrianna, how do you break it off with someone you have been connected to your whole life? Over thirty years. That is a long time to let go and never look back. It is not so simple when our history is muddled with secrets and lies and at one time, compassion and love. You want to believe the same person from long ago is still there."

I mused over his words, kind of agreeing, kind of not. I was stuck in between, and since I didn't know the whole story it was hard to form an opinion. Still, it didn't hurt any less.

Yawning, my eyes were suddenly heavy. I chewed my lip as I thought about my next set of words.

"This is not an ultimatum, but after what little you told me, and you stay—"

He cut me off, shaking his head vehemently. Worry circled his green eyes. "Do not do this, Adrianna, please, do not do this. I know what you are going to say, and please, just do not. Not yet."

"Then give me something, anything. You've been so fair to everyone but me. Please."

Kova waited a long minute, his indecisive gaze filled with trepidation. His piercing glare told me he was stuck between a rock and a hard place. He either couldn't tell me, didn't know where to start, or flat out didn't want to.

"You know what? Never mind." I brushed the topic away with a swipe of my hand, pretending I didn't care when it was actually destroying me. "I should've known better than to ask you for the truth. You know, you were right. We have made progress, but it seems every time we do, we end up taking ten steps back."

Turning, I headed for the sliding glass door when he called my name.

"You want to start with one of the whys, Adrianna? Start with your mother. She is the root of all evil."

chapter 47

START WITH YOUR MOTHER.

It was all I thought about after Kova left that night. We hadn't had time to talk in between practices, and now I was sitting in the doctor's office once again with time on my hands to overanalyze every aspect of my grand life.

It wasn't like I could call Joy and flat out ask her what she had to do with Kova and Katja marrying. Not after I'd learned she moved out. For Joy, my birth was a constant reminder of my dad's betrayal. Call me crazy, but I had a hunch that if she didn't talk to me for the rest of my life it would be no sweat off her back.

I definitely couldn't ask my dad about Kova's marriage. That was out of the question, so I was left with too many thoughts flashing through my head and the rapid rushing of paranoia filling my chest. I was drowning in a sea of sharks. The only person I could ask was the one person who didn't want to add anymore destruction to my life. I understood it, but I didn't like it.

The more I thought about it, the more I wished I could go back in time and not ask. I would've waited to demand anything from Kova at this point because all it did was lace me with uncertainty. I shouldn't have pushed but curiosity got the best of me. There were too many doors left open, too many options to choose from, and it seemed like they all led to one answer.

If I wasn't thinking about Joy's grimy hands, I was thinking about how Kova didn't love Katja yet he'd married her out of obligation. Kova not being in love with Katja was not something I ever once considered. It filled my head with so many questions that I didn't know where to start. Nothing added up. Kova wasn't the type to be cornered into anything he didn't want, especially a marriage, and especially not after he'd promised his mother he'd live for the both of them when she died.

Timing is everything, he'd said multiple times, and he was right, but I was hesitant to trust him. The last time I did I landed face-first in the worst heartbreak I'd ever felt.

I sighed inwardly and yawned, feeling a little tired. On top of everything, I'd started peeing blood and that fucked with my head even more.

For two days the toilet water had been a deep crimson color and I didn't know why. At first I thought I'd gotten my period early since it was so irregular, but using a few tampons confirmed that wasn't it. Naturally, I searched the internet, but most of what I'd found said it was related to my kidneys, which didn't help settle my mind. After learning about Francesca, and my doctor's concerns, plus my internet research, I was sure I had every autoimmune disease I'd read about. But I didn't feel sick, at least not worse than what I usually felt. Sure, I had some aches and pains, but I figured those were from the training camp.

My head was a tangled mess and I was being screwed from seven different directions.

"Hey, Adrianna," Dr. DeLang said politely as she knocked and walked in. A tall man with a weathered face followed behind her. He had to be at least ten years older than her.

"This is Dr. Kozol," my doctor introduced him as he reached over to shake my hand. "He's a colleague of mine I asked to come in and consult."

My brows bunched together and my heart instantly kicked up a notch. Why would my doctor need to bring in another doctor?

"Hi," I responded hesitantly, then immediately looked at my doctor.

Dr. DeLang took a seat behind her desk and placed a folder down, while the new doctor pulled out the chair next to me.

"I see the rash has subsided for you." My doctor smiled at me as her gentle eyes took in my face.

"Yeah, it's not bad anymore, thankfully."

I eyed the new doctor, not liking his presence. A team of doctors was never good and could only hint at something more serious.

I turned my attention back to Dr. DeLang. "So I found out some family history since the last time I was here." I offered.

"That's good news. Such as?"

"My mom was a twin, and her sister had a type of diabetes, I can't remember which one, plus another autoimmune disease." Dr. DeLang gave Dr. Kozol a quick glance. It was a signal, like a confirmation, and my stomach dropped.

"She has two autoimmune diseases? Do you happen to know the name of the other autoimmune?" Dr. Kozol asked, leaning forward in his chair.

The hair on my arms rose. I didn't like the peculiar tone in his voice. "Mixed Tissue she said."

Dr. Kozol pulled a small notepad from his coat pocket and scribbled something down, while Dr. DeLang flipped open the file folder on her desk. A lump formed in my throat. I didn't like either one of their reactions. I was ready to stand up and demand answers when Dr. Kozol cut off my train of thought.

"How old is she?" he asked, brows at a deep angle.

"She died…" He made a note in his little pad. "She was twenty. They said it was due to the diabetes."

"Hmmm. That helps." Helped what? What the hell was going on? He didn't give me any other information, just went straight into his next question. "And your mother?"

"She's healthy, nothing wrong with her." I looked at Dr. DeLang. "She said she's checked often."

"How are you doing overall?" my doctor asked softly.

I dug my teeth into my bottom lip and shot a nervous look at Dr. Kozol before looking back at her. "Well…the last couple of days I started to notice blood in my urine." My ears turned warm, embarrassment sloping down the bridge of my nose. It was the first time I'd voiced that out loud and it made my pulse thrum with actual fear.

Her face didn't move, didn't express a thing. "Every time?"

"The last two days it's been almost every time. I think there was a time before that it may have happened once, but I can't remember."

"Any other issues?" She flipped through a few pages in the folder and circled something.

I started to shake my head no, then paused. "My back is killing me."

"Where on your back?" I pointed to the place below my ribs and Dr. Kozol made another note, then sat back in his chair and studied me.

Dread formed in my stomach. I was sure I was pointing to an organ or three back there.

Combined with the blood, it didn't take a genius to know that wasn't good. I stared at my doctor, seeking answers.

She looked up from the file and adjusted the glasses on her nose. "Let's go over your lab results." She glanced down. "We ran an antinuclear antibody test to check for the possibility of an autoimmune disorder. I also requested the other labs since the ANA can be used to diagnose multiple autoimmune diseases if an autoimmune disorder is present." She paused, and I felt sick to my stomach. I didn't want to hear the rest of what she had to say, but I had to. "Adrianna, the ANA was positive. You have an autoimmune disorder."

I shook my head, feeling like the diagnosis was shoved down my throat. What did all this mean? That I had what Francesca had? I didn't understand. Or maybe the truth was that I didn't want to understand.

"So I have a disorder? Like what my aunt had?"

Dr. DeLang inhaled a deep breath before she continued. "You tested eighty-seven percent positive for lupus. That is way above the minimum. Your red blood cell count has been consistently low, too low." She went over a few other tests, but I was so clueless. All I understood was positive and below normal, and that I had lupus.

Fuck. My head was a mess.

"Remember when I mentioned lupus can affect other organs?" Dr. DeLang looked at me, and I nodded. "Based on your other symptoms and high marker levels, I had your kidney function tested. And now you're telling me you're urinating blood and that your maternal aunt passed away from an autoimmune disease."

"They said it was from the diabetes."

"Do you know what type diabetes she had?" Dr. Kozol asked. "Type 1 is an autoimmune, although, with the MTCD... That is one of the rarer AI's, and the survival rate is low, even if it's caught early. I'm willing to take an educated guess that it was a combination of everything. You probably don't know if it affected her organs, do you?" I shook my head. Why would I think to ask something like that?

"I think it was type 1?" I blinked rapidly and asked, "Are you saying I have what my aunt had?"

"I'm going to let Dr. Kozol take over." Dr. DeLang removed her glasses, her eyes shifting to the man next to me.

Dread consumed my veins. I could feel the weight of his words hanging in the air before he said them. I looked at the doctor but he was already watching me. Goose bumps coated my arms, and I hugged myself, hiding my fists. I wanted to scream out and say no, because if he was going to take over, I knew it wouldn't be good.

"The blood is coming from your kidneys, and quite frankly, that's extremely concerning. I'd like to have you admitted to the hospital immediately to start treatment and run additional tests."

"I don't understand. What tests, and what is the blood caused from? Treatment for what?"

"Adrianna," he sighed. "There is no other way to put it. Your kidneys are failing."

I paled. "Kidneys? As in both?"

He nodded.

"Both are failing?" My voice was low, cracking. I had to repeat it because I couldn't believe my ears.

And he nodded again.

A tremor racked my body. Chills tormented my arms and I stared, unblinking at the doctor, trying to process what he'd just said. My kidneys were failing? That wasn't possible and I was sure they were wrong. They felt fine. I felt fine. Hysteria flowed through my veins and I fought to keep calm. My brows furrowed tightly together, and I asked in a quiet voice, "What do… What does this all mean?"

"It means your kidneys are failing at a rapid rate and we need to be proactive now."

A chill washed over me, anchoring me to the chair. I was so cold, my bones aching with brittleness that the magnitude of the situation wasn't hitting me the way it should have. Dr. Kozol went into detail, telling me how much kidney function I had left, but it wasn't registering. I was stone-faced, unblinking, and emotionless. I could hear his voice, but I couldn't process his words into clear sentences. A heavy weight sat in the pit of my stomach, spreading throughout my body. While I wasn't well-versed on the human anatomy, I knew enough to know that if my kidneys were failing and he needed to act now, I was much sicker than I could have ever imagined possible.

My heart pounded against my chest and I started to panic. Now it made sense why he was here. He was a specialist, one who I would be handed over to.

"Adrianna?" Dr. DeLang sat forward. "Did you hear Dr. Kozol?"

I shook my head, and Dr. Kozol was kind enough to repeat what he'd said without making me feel bad that I hadn't listened the first time.

The numbers were alarming. Staggering. The house of cards I'd worked so hard to build were starting to fold, and all I could do was watch them drop to the floor. This was a *twist* I didn't see coming. It wasn't planned, it shouldn't have happened, and now I didn't know what to do because the reality was, it was happening no matter what.

"And you're sure?" I asked, my voice shaky.

He nodded gravely. "Without a doubt. Honestly, I'm not sure how you made it this far without visiting an emergency room."

I blinked. My mouth suddenly dry.

I'd been oblivious to the gravity of the symptoms and suddenly felt so naïve and stupid. Had they been so obvious? And, if they had been, would I have acknowledged them?

No.

I wanted my dad. I wanted Avery. I wanted Kova. I wanted to hold someone's hand and for them to tell me everything was going to be okay.

But it would never be okay now.

Instead, I had no one and nothing except an anxiety attack hurling me into a deep, dark spiral I couldn't stop.

I wish I had never found out.

"Well, what are my options? What kind of treatment can we start on? Some kind of medication?"

"You have a few options," Dr. Kozol said.

As he went through treatment after treatment, my stomach constricted with fear and the world around me faded away. Information circled my head, all revolving around my dreams. Side effects. The risk of growing sicker. Sitting out the rest of the season—possibly for good.

"What's next?" I interrupted him. Tears were threatening to climb but I wouldn't let them. I refused to have come this far, and be this close to my dream, just to have it yanked away. I wouldn't go down without a fight. "These won't work with my schedule. I can't afford to be out like that."

"Quite frankly, there is no next option."

My lungs struggled for air as anger infused my blood. That wasn't acceptable to me. "There can't only be two options."

"Unfortunately since this was detected so late, your options are limited. Until you find a match, you really only have one choice."

Unacceptable. I'd have to get a second opinion. Both treatments required too much from me, or they would make me extremely ill and I refused to deal with that. Medicine had come a long way. There was no way I would make time for either option if it put my gymnastics career in jeopardy. Surely a few more months wouldn't make that big of a difference. And, if I was forced to have the life sucked out of me, it would be from something that I loved, not sitting in a chilly hospital bed watching my dreams pass me by.

"You only get one life, Adrianna. Chose it wisely."

I rolled my lips between my teeth and considered what he said. "What if we hold off on treatment for a couple of months?" I asked, holding my ground. "That would be okay, right? Just a few months?"

Dr. Kozol and Dr. DeLang looked at each other for a long moment, their faces grim. I knew the answer before he even said it. Still, I wasn't ready for it. My chest tightened, fearing pushing its way in at the unknown. My lungs struggled for air, and I swallowed hard, waiting for a response.

"I don't recommend that. In fact, I'm highly against it." Dr. Kozol stared at me without judgment. "There is not one medical professional who would agree with that."

Breathing heavily, I swallowed past the lump in my throat. "I'm going to wait. I'll be fine."

I pulled my shoulders back. Dr. Kozol leaned forward and his voice dropped. "This is very serious. You're extremely ill and need to seek treatment. This isn't playing guinea pig to see which medication will help you. You don't have that luxury." He paused, his voice firm. "Your kidneys are failing." He stated it slowly, like I hadn't heard him the first time. He became a blurry vision as silent tears rolled down my cheeks. "It's not a matter of *if* you will die, but a matter of *when* you will die. This needs to be your first priority."

I shook my head, my lips a thin, flat line. Dr. Kozol sat back while Dr. DeLang wrote in my file. She reached for the phone next and started dialing, probably calling my dad. But so what, there wasn't a soul on earth who could change my mind. Not my dad. Not Kova. No one was going to take this away from me.

My love for gymnastics is what drove me, what gave me the out I needed to express who I was. I wasn't ready to say goodbye just yet, not when I'd only just gotten started.

Like the roaring thunder in the distance I could hear headed toward me, I felt the water level building, curling, the impending wave that would no doubt drown me. The pressure was already too great and it was growing by the second. Just thinking about what lay ahead for me sent an all-consuming wave of sadness over me. I'd come too far.

And the thing was, I wasn't going to try to stop it. Not yet at least, because the timing wasn't right, and timing was everything.

I would risk it all to achieve my dream.

Even if it killed me.

To be continued…

About the Author

Lucia Franco resides in sunny South Florida with her husband, two boys, and two adorable dogs who follow her everywhere. She was a competitive athlete for over ten years—a gymnast and cheerleader—which heavily inspired the Off Balance series.

Her novel Hush, Hush was a finalist in the 2019 Stiletto Contest hosted by Contemporary Romance Writers, a chapter of Romance Writers of America. Her novels are being translated into several languages.

When Lucia isn't writing, you can find her relaxing with her toes in the sand at a nearby beach. She runs on caffeine, scorching hot sunshine, and four hours of sleep.

She's written nine books and has many more planned for the years to come.

Find out more at authorluciafranco.com.

Lightning Source UK Ltd.
Milton Keynes UK
UKHW022015250722
406369UK00003B/132